Rowena Summers is a pseuer
career as a magazine writer   es
and some 80 novels. Ex   sts'
Association, she lectures at writers' groups in both the UK and USA,
appearing frequently on radio and TV. She lives in north Somerset
and is married with three grown-up children.

A BRIGHTER TOMORROW

Rowena Summers

PAN BOOKS

First published 2000 by Severn House Publishers Ltd

This edition published 2002 by Pan Books
an imprint of Pan Macmillan Ltd
Pan Macmillan, 20 New Wharf Road, London N1 9RR
Basingstoke and Oxford
Associated companies throughout the world
www.panmacmillan.com

ISBN 1 405 00282 4

1 3 5 7 9 8 6 4 2

A CIP catalogue record for this book is available from
the British Library.

Printed and bound in Great Britain by
Mackays of Chatham plc, Chatham, Kent

One

Celia Pengelly shivered as she stood on the chilly Cornish railway station, awaiting the arrival of the train from London. According to her sister, still determined to go on living in the capital despite the threat of being bombed at any time, the river Thames had frozen over for the first time in more than fifty years, and it was cold enough to freeze the proverbial brass monkeys.

Celia smiled faintly, recognising the kind of slangy terms Wenna had picked up. She was practically a Londoner by now, and far more worldly-wise than the family had ever expected her to be. But Celia conceded that it went with the job. Singing in a nightclub all these years, and being the star attraction, no less, was bound to have an effect on her.

It was only when she came home to Cornwall that she resumed her proper place in the family – her younger sister's place, Celia thought with a grin.

"Here it comes, Miss Pengelly," she heard the voice of the billeting officer saying. "Get ready for the onslaught."

Celia hitched the carrying strap of her gas mask more firmly onto her shoulder. She had faced this day with mixed feelings. Her mother was insisting that it would be marvellous to have children in the house again, and that the empty rooms of New World cried out for them. But these children would be strangers, coming from a different environment, and they would be frightened and bewildered.

"Not nervous, are you, Pengelly?" the more strident of the billeting officers asked her. "They're only children, and you must be sure to discipline them as instructed."

"Yes, ma'am," Celia muttered, resisting the wild desire to snap her heels together and give a Heil Hitler salute. It would be the most disastrous thing imaginable in the circumstances, when they were all here to welcome the latest wave of these little evacuees from London and take them into their Cornish hearts.

Though, to be honest, the names of the four they had been

1

allocated didn't fill her with enthusiasm. She glanced again at her list, even though she knew them by heart. Tommy and Mary Lunn, aged eight and four; Daphne Hollis, aged seven; and Butch Butcher, aged eleven.

It was this last name that had Celia wary of the whole thing. He sounded a real thug – even though she was well aware that it was wrong to judge him and expect the worst before he had even arrived.

But the train was snorting and steaming into the station now, and there was no more time to speculate. Nor had there been any chance of refusing the children. They had been allocated with the names and that was that. In wartime everybody had to do their bit and the Pengellys were no exception. They had plenty of room to take four, and four was what they would get.

"I'm not complaining," her mother had said cheerfully. "It will be just darling to hear the sound of children's laughter in the house again."

"I doubt that laughter's the first thing you're going to hear," the billeting officer had warned her, her eyebrows raised as usual at Skye Pengelly's quaint American way of speaking. "There may well be problems at first, but we all have to cope with them as best we can. The children will be far from home, and the younger ones will be tearful, while others will be resentful at what they see as their parents' betrayal in sending them away."

And that was what Celia fully expected from the eleven-year-old Butch Butcher . . .

As the train squealed to a halt and the carriage doors flew open, it seemed as though a great mass of chattering humanity was descending on to the small Cornish platform at once. The billeting officers and local teachers took charge, trying to form the children into some kind of order, shouting out names from their lists and inspecting the labels hung around the necks of those who were too frightened to respond at all.

Celia's heart went out to them. Poor little devils, she thought. They were clearly petrified by these bossy people with the strange accents ordering them about, even though it was the only way to organise the huge undertaking.

Moments later, she found herself looking into the faces of a brother and sister, the tiny girl clutching the boy's hand as if terrified of losing him. They each carried a brown paper parcel tied with string, which presumably contained their entire wardrobe, as well as the gas masks slung around their shoulders. These two, then, were Tommy and Mary Lunn.

Celia knelt down to their level, and looked into Mary's scared brown eyes.

"Hello, sweetie," she said, smiling encouragingly. "My name's Celia and you're going to come and live with me and my family for a while."

To Celia's horror, the girl immediately began wailing, and Tommy put his arms around her protectively.

"She don't want to come and live wiv you, missis. She wants to go home. She don't like the country. They say there's cows and fings and we don't like 'em."

"We don't have cows and fings – things," Celia repeated, parrot fashion. "We have a nice big house near the sea—"

"We don't like the sea. We ain't never seen it and we don't want to," Tommy Lunn said at once.

Celia recognised his determination not to like anything at all. She had expected trouble from Butch Butcher, not from these two. She had thought a small brother and sister would be tolerably happy to stay together, but she realised she had been wrong to anticipate anything.

As Mary continued snivelling, a dark patch crept down her spindly legs in their dark wool stockings. Celia turned with relief when the billeting officer called her.

"Here are your other two, Miss Pengelly. Someone will be calling on you in a week's time to check that all is well."

And with that, the woman moved away, leaving Celia to face an engaging little girl with the name Daphne Hollis pinned to her chest, and an overweight boy with ginger hair and freckles, whom she knew instantly had to be Butch Butcher.

She found herself full of anger at the inefficiency of the billeting people. Didn't they ever have the gumption to match the children? What the dickens did these four have in common, except having been brought to safety away from the dangers that London held for them now?

"She's wet herself," Tommy said, pointing at Mary's legs.

"Me sister used to do that all the time," Daphne piped up. "I'll see to 'er if you like, missis."

"Will you?" Celia said faintly, before mentally shaking herself, and steering the four of them out of the heaving station towards her waiting car. So far Butch had said nothing, but to her surprise Daphne caught hold of Mary's other hand and began pulling the small girl towards her, while Tommy tugged her the other way.

"I want to go wiv *her*," Mary suddenly screamed, kicking out

3

viciously at Tommy's shins. Her little boots were old and scuffed, but the kick was hard enough to make her brother howl with rage and give her a slap around the head, which made her scream still more.

"Good Lord, stop this at once, will you?" Celia said, appalled. "That's no way to behave. We all have to learn to get along together."

"I hate her," Tommy yelled, though minutes before he had been Mary's champion, "and she's welcome to her."

He pushed his sister towards the other girl, and before Celia knew what was happening, Butch had got hold of him by his collar. It was just as she had feared, she thought, her heart sinking. This one was a bully of the first order.

"You behave yourself, half-pint, and do what the lady tells yer, or I'll give you what for, see?"

Butch looked at Celia as Tommy subsided with a scowl. "Ain't that right, missis?"

"Yes. Well yes, I guess so. And you can call me Celia," she said, when nothing else came to mind.

This whole situation was getting very strange, she thought, and who was in charge here, anyway? But the minute she directed them all to her car and debated about where Mary was to sit, considering her wet knickers, she heard Tommy's awed voice.

"Cor, are we going to have a ride in that car?"

She resumed her composure at once.

"Yes, you are. Butch will sit in front with me, and you other three can sit in the back. There's an old newspaper in the back for Mary to sit on for the time being, until we get her tidied up."

"So how old is your sister, Daphne?" she went on, just to keep them occupied while they all piled into the car.

"Oh, she ain't nothing no more."

"What do you mean, nothing? A person can't be *nothing*," Celia said, abandoning any thought of grammar for the moment.

"They can when they're dead," Daphne said cheerfully.

Celia's heart jolted. The country had been at war for nearly five months now, and bombs had been falling, but she had never met anyone who had been personally affected by the German air raids. She felt emotionally drawn to this little girl with the perky face who looked as if she had already seen far too much in her seven years.

"What happened, Daphne?" she asked quietly, as she began to drive home. She knew it was a bad thing to question her with the other children in the car, but she had to know . . .

4

"She 'ad the diphtheria like me brothers. They was all sick and they all died one after the other, and me Ma said I was a bleedin' miracle, 'cos I never got it," she said, as proud as if she had won a trophy.

"Oh!" Celia said, too stunned by the enormity of such a tragedy to censure her for her language. In fact, apart from the way the child was revealing it so matter-of-factly, she couldn't help hearing the ghost of another voice from long ago, using the same words, in the same East End accent.

The very first time she and her sister Wenna had met her mother's acquaintance from the war that was supposed to end all wars, Fanny Webb had both shocked and charmed the Cornish children by her frequent use of the words 'bleedin' 'ell'.

"Blimey, is that the sea?" Butch said suddenly.

All the children craned their necks as Celia said that indeed it was.

"Don't it end nowhere?" Tommy said nervously.

"It goes from here all the way to America, where my mother was born," Celia told him, glad to give them something else to think about other than the deaths of Daphne's sister and brothers from diptheria. "In fact, I lived in America myself for about a year until last spring."

Daphne spoke up again. "Me Ma says all Yanks are film stars. Did you meet any of 'em, missis?"

"No, of course not," Celia said with a laugh. "Film stars all live in a place called Hollywood, but I worked for a family in New Jersey, picking apples—"

"You don't pick apples," Tommy said scornfully. "You buy 'em down the market."

Celia gave up. Clearly, they all had a lot to learn about one another, and life was never going to be the same again.

They had known that long before Mr Chamberlain's solemn announcement on the third of September last year, in the many months preceding the event, when everyone had been preparing not only for war, but for the heartaches and separations of friends and lovers.

She let the children chatter on for a moment or two, remembering Stefan, as she did every night when she gazed up the brightest star in the sky. It was *their* star, he had told her during their last idyllic time together, before she had to return to Cornwall and he to Germany. And as long as that star shone, his love for her would remain just as constant and everlasting, however long their two countries were at war.

It was a lovely and noble sentiment, but it did nothing to ease the anxiety she felt when there had been no further news of him since then. Correspondence had dwindled to nothing, and the needs of lovers were very far down the pecking order of what was important now and what was not.

"What are those things?" she heard Daphne ask now. "Are they mountains? I ain't never seen snow like that before."

Celia dragged her thoughts back to the present and followed the child's gaze away from the coast to where the soaring spoil heaps of china clay glinted on the skyline on the moors high above St Austell on that cold January day.

"I don't like them," Mary whimpered, starting to cry.

It was clear that Mary and Tommy were not prepared to like anything at all, and she spoke in a cheerful voice.

"It's not snow, Daphne. It's the waste material from something called china clay, which is a substance that helps to make plates and cups and saucers as well as other things like newspaper print, and even medicines."

From their faces, she realised that this was too complicated for them to take in, and she changed tactics.

"They're not real mountains, of course, and my mother always called them the sky tips, because it seemed as if they would reach the sky. It made my mother very happy to call them that. Can you guess why?"

When they didn't answer, she went on talking, starting to feel very foolish. She wasn't a teacher, and she didn't quite know how to handle this motley crowd of children. If they were all the same age, it might have been easier. As it was, she knew she was talking down to most of them, except for the infant Mary.

Tommy was older than his years, and Daphne already knew it all, Celia suspected. But she went on doggedly.

"My mother's name is Skye, and she liked to think the china clay heaps were called sky tips just for her."

She heard Tommy hoot with derisive laughter.

"Skye ain't a proper name! I ain't never heard of nothing so daft, and I ain't going to call nobody *Skye*!"

"I should think not," Celia said evenly. "You'll call her Mrs Pengelly."

Mary started to wail again. "I can't say that. I want to go home. I want me Ma—"

"Well, perhaps you could call her Mrs Pen. How about that? Would that be easier? Why don't you all think about it?" she said desperately, and was never more thankful to see New World come

6

into sight as the four of them debated and squabbled over whether or not this was an easy thing to do.

She only prayed that her mother would take to the four of them. Celia was becoming increasingly sure now that she could not.

Mary was only a baby, and maybe Daphne could be handled in time, but as for the boys . . . Tommy was obviously what they called a loose cannon, and she simply couldn't make up her mind about Butch at all. Either he was a thug waiting to burst out, or he was a big softie, hiding behind a nickname he'd simply been given because of his surname. She just didn't know, and she wasn't sure she wanted to find out.

She had committed herself to staying on at New World to help her mother with these evacuees for a time, but she was itching to do some war work, the same as her cousin Seb who had joined the army the minute he was called up, and her cousin Justin, giving up his medical training temporarily to go straight into an army medical unit for what he called practical experience.

She envied them both. And even Wenna, under her stage name of Penny Wood, was saying that she fully intended joining a concert party to entertain the troops if Fanny Rosenbloom, née Webb, decided to close the nightclub for the duration.

Personally, Celia didn't think Fanny would ever close the Flamingo Club, but in any case Wenna wouldn't be prepared to stay there for ever. Her young man had immediately joined up as a war correspondent, and was already at some unknown destination. Wenna declared she would feel closer to him by doing her bit, as they all called it now.

Wenna was the lucky one, Celia thought, with a burst of misery. There was no way in this world she could be close to Stefan except in spirit. She and her lover were on opposite sides of a conflict that had nothing to do with them . . .

"Is that your house, missis?" Daphne said in awe.

Celia said that it was, and gave up the idea of persuading them to call her by name for the present. Presumably it would come in time, and meanwhile it was a relief to get them all out of the car, where the smell of Mary's wet knickers was starting to become vinegary.

She gave herself a mental reminder to scrub the back seats the minute she got the chance, and immediately felt ashamed of her uncharitable thoughts as she saw the child's pinched white face.

"Come on, sweetheart, let's go inside and see your new room, shall we?"

She saw Daphne scratching herself, and felt an urge to do the same. To her horror she suddenly recalled the instructions they had all been given at the last billeting committee meeting.

"Many of the children come from the slums. They will have scabies or lice, and will need to be de-loused immediately with disinfectant. This must be diluted to prevent sores, of course, but remember that all the children will be regularly inspected on arrival at school, so attention to hygiene is vital if our own children are not to be infected."

Such a distinction had seemed mean and degrading at the time, but that feeling changed for Celia now, and with rising hysteria she suspected that the little beasts in her car had already infected her too.

And she didn't distinguish in her mind which little beasts she was thinking about.

"Wait here, all of you," she said sharply, and left the four of them standing forlornly outside the car.

As she did so, her mother came out of the house to usher them in out of the cold, and after Celia had spoken to her rapidly, Skye Pengelly took charge.

"Tell Liza to get the disinfectant baths ready for the children. The girls first, and then the boys. I have some suitable clothes for them to wear for now; all their own garments must be washed and boiled before they can be used again. Go to it, honey, while I see to them."

"But Mom, they'll infect the whole house."

"They're babies, Celia, and they're scared. *Go*, honey, and don't make them feel worse than they do already."

She walked towards the children, seeing how they huddled together. Skye had already been through a war, and fleas and lice held no fears for her. There were worse things. Any infestation obviously had to be dealt with quickly, but the most important thing was to reassure these infants that they were safe here.

"Let me guess your names," she began with a smile.

"You don't need to do that, missis," Tommy said rudely, jabbing a finger at his name label as if she was stupid.

"Oh, of course I don't," Skye said. "How silly of me to forget. Well, then, do you know who I am?"

They didn't answer, clearly silenced by the size of the lovely old house and grounds, so different from the crowded slum streets of London where they had all been born.

"It's Mrs Pen-something," Daphne said at last. "The lady said we was to call you Mrs Pen."

"Well done," Skye said. "So now that we all know one another, let's go inside the house and get you bathed, and than we'll have something nice and hot to eat, shall we?"

"I don't need no bath," Tommy yelled at her. "I 'ad one last week. I just want me tea."

"Mary needs a bath," Daphne said importantly. "She's gawn and wet 'erself again, but I can see to 'er."

Dear Lord, thought Skye, eyeing the smallest one properly for the first time. The child was practically dripping by now, and none of them smelled too sweet. A hot bath was definitely a priority, but from the look of Tommy Lunn's face he was going to run a mile if he didn't have something to eat first. She made up her mind.

"Right. We'll change Mary out of those wet things in the out-house, then go into the kitchen for some cake and lemonade, and *then* a bath, and then some proper dinner. All right?"

There was no way she could take Mary into the kitchen. She knew that Cook would throw a fit at the smell. The outhouse would have to do, and Mary could be wrapped in a large towel to eat her food while the offending knickers and woollen stockings remained well out of sight and smell.

A very long while later, four scrubbed, de-loused and well-fed children examined the rooms where they were to sleep.

"I ain't never slept in a room by meself," Daphne said uneasily, her bravado finally cracking as she surveyed Wenna's old bedroom. "There was five of us in one bed at home, top to tail, me Ma called it. Can't I sleep wiv the others?"

"I ain't sleeping wiv *girls*," Butch said at once.

"Then Butch can have this room, and the other three can have the old nursery," Skye said, revising all her plans.

"Nurseries are for babies," Tommy argued at once.

"Well, providing you don't behave like one, it won't matter, will it?" Skye said crisply, getting his measure far sooner that Celia had.

"You were wonderful, Mom," Celia told her when they finally had some time to themselves. "I must admit I panicked when I saw them, but you seemed to know just how to handle them."

"That's because I've had three of my own, honey."

And by now, if things hadn't gone so horribly wrong, there would have been another babe of my own in the nursery . . .

She pushed the thought aside as Celia went on, "Were we ever this bad? So *aggressive* and so ready to argue about everything?"

Skye's blue eyes sparkled as she looked at her daughter.

"Oh, honey, I assure you that you were – and you in particular! I'll never forget the little scenes at Lily's wedding, when you and Wenna were bridesmaids. You hated everything and everyone, especially your cousin Sebby, who you always referred to as a prize pig."

Celia laughed too. "My God, Mom, do you have to remember everything! I hope you're not including those kind of personal incidents in the history you're writing about the family. I'd be mortified if you did."

"Don't worry, darling. I'm keeping strictly to business matters and the background of the clayworks. Even so, a business doesn't exist without the people who worked so hard to make it a success. I still sometimes wonder if I'll ever write it, though," she added.

"Why ever not?"

Skye shrugged. "Things have a habit of happening to prevent my giving enough attention to it. Like a war, for instance. There are so many more important things to do than writing up the memoirs of a business that doesn't even belong in the family any more."

"But isn't that just why you should? It's what Daddy thinks, and what David Kingsley is always urging you to do."

"David's a newspaperman, and he's always wanted me to get back to work with him in some capacity or other. But in any case, I'll have my hands full with those four upstairs now."

As if to underline her words, the sound of wailing was heard again, and she gave a sigh. As Celia made to get up, Skye put a hand on her arm.

"Leave it to me, honey. You'll only lose your temper, and that will get us nowhere."

Celia knew it was true, but she watched her mother's still trim figure move towards the stairs with a small feeling of anxiety in her heart.

Actually, Skye could have refused to foster four children and taken only three, but she hadn't demurred at all, and Celia suspected she was doing it as a kind of substitute for losing her own late-stage baby last year. She had insisted on including a very young child, which many other families didn't want, so Celia concluded it could only be so.

Her stepfather found her staring into space when he came home that evening. By then she had carefully pulled the black-out curtains until she was sure that no chink of light could escape, before switching on the lamps in the drawing room.

Nick Pengelly peered around the door in mock fearfulness.

"Have they invaded us then? Is it safe to come in?"

Celia laughed. "They're here all right, and Mom's upstairs with them, trying to pacify the smallest one."

"And do I take it that all went well, apart from that?" he said cautiously.

She shrugged. "I guess so. I still think Mom's taking on far too much. She shouldn't have to be bothered with other people's children at her age—"

"She's not ancient yet, darling, and she won't thank you for doubting her abilities."

"I know. And I shouldn't begrudge the poor little devils a decent home. I did, though, when I began to itch," she added with a shudder. "They were practically alive with lice."

"Good God. I hope you've sorted that out," Nick said.

"We have. We're all bathed, and their clothes are either burned or boiled."

It was some time later when Skye came downstairs to join them, glad to find her husband home from his legal chambers in Bodmin, and already pouring her a glass of wine.

"They're settled," she said, in answer to his unspoken question. "It was Mary who was the noisy one, of course, but once she was asleep I realised Daphne was weeping into her pillow and needed the most comforting."

"What?" Celia said in amazement. "I thought she was the toughest little nut of all."

"Not deep down." She turned to Nick, not yet ready to tell them just how much agonised outpouring Daphne Hollis had revealed to her. "So now we have a houseful again, honey."

He raised his own glass to her. "And here's to all who sail in her," he said euphemistically. "Let's hope there aren't too many stormy waters ahead."

Celia groaned. "That's the feeblest thing I ever heard."

"And that reminds me," Nick went on, unperturbed, "have you seen the newspaper today? Food rationing's going to be stepped up, and it will soon apply to meat as well as butter, bacon and sugar. I hope your little darlings have brought their ration books with them."

"It's all taken care of, Nick," Skye assured him. "Cook's already ingeniously planning new dishes that will make the most of what we've got, and seeing it as her life's work."

"I wonder if this might be a good time to mention *my* life's work –

or at least, a little bit of it?" Celia said. "I said I'd help out here for a time, and so I will. But Mom, while everyone else is doing war work, I can't sit around twiddling my thumbs. The children will be in school all day except Mary, and I'll willingly take them and fetch them. But in between those times, I'm thinking of applying to be a tram conductress in Truro now that most of the men have joined up."

"Good God, Celia," Nick said angrily, just as she had anticipated, "you've been to a Swiss finishing school and become an expert linguist. We didn't send you there for you to become a tram conductress, for God's sake!"

"Then let me enlist properly if you're so snobbish about it. I daresay my qualifications will be useful in some capacity," she snapped.

"No," he said sharply. "Your mother needs you here."

"Does anyone mind if I speak for myself?" Skye said, just as angry as the two of them. "I'm perfectly capable of looking after children, and Celia must do what she feels is right."

"That's the trouble. I don't know *what* I feel is right," her daughter muttered. "I only know I feel useless."

"You're anything but that!"

"But it's how I *feel*, Dad," she said, rounding on him. "And people are starting to look at me as if I'm one of the privileged few—"

"Well, so you are, Celia," he said. "Your mother's family provided this house and the legacy of the clayworks, to say nothing of the successful pottery she founded. And I've always been able to give you children the best education."

She gave a heavy sigh. "I might have known you wouldn't understand. It takes more than an up-country accent to make someone acceptable today. In fact, I'm beginning to think it's the very thing that sets you apart in a community like ours."

Nick's eyes flashed. "Well, don't start talking like your Uncle Theo, or like that friend of your mother's in London, that's all, or I might just disown you."

He was teasing, and she knew it, but it was on the tip of her tongue to say that right here in his house he had four little Londoners who used far less than perfect diction, and probably knew more choice blasphemies than even Theo Tremayne did! But of course, he hadn't met the children yet, and that was a delight still to come, Celia thought mischievously.

She turned to her mother.

"So do I have your blessing to call at the tram company tomorrow and offer my services, Mom?"

"If it makes you happy, honey, then of course you do," Skye said at once.

But they both knew it would take far more than that to make Celia happy. It would take an end to the war that had barely begun, and a resumption of the heady life she had only just started to glimpse with Stefan von Gruber.

They both took the children to enrol at their new school the following day, knowing what an ordeal it would be for them. There were plenty of other evacuees there too, but they all stood out like sore thumbs from the local children and each faction stuck together warily at the sight of the others. To the Cornish children, it was clearly as great an invasion of aliens as if the Germans themselves had landed.

"You'd think children would all get along, wouldn't you?" Celia said to her mother. "Somehow you don't expect them to have the same reservations as adults have."

"Why not? They're as individual as we are, and they all have their own personalities."

"Some more than others," Celia added darkly, remembering how the self-assured Daphne Hollis had begun to assert herself as a leader among her own, even before she had been introduced to her class teacher.

"Well, we have some time to forget them, so since we're in town, let's call on Lily for half an hour," Skye suggested.

"Do you think Lily will approve of this one?" Celia asked, raising her eyebrows at the sulking Mary as they walked back to the car, having just managed to stop her wailing at having been left behind while all the others went to school. Celia was quite sure she hadn't wanted to go, anyway, but now the small girl was all alone with two strangers who she was perfectly prepared not to like, and was determined to show it in the most eloquent way she knew.

"Have you wet yourself again, Mary?" Celia asked her.

"Only a bit," she sulked.

"Never mind, honey," Skye said cheerfully. "We'll soon have you nice and dry again."

"Me Ma says it's only cricket's piss, anyway," Mary said, then without warning her eyes filled with tears while the other two were still gasping at this stunning statement.

"When can I see me Ma, missis? I want me Ma," she howled.

"Good grief, if the billeting committee hear all that noise they'll think we're beating her," Skye said uneasily. "Let's get to Lily's as fast as we can, Celia."

"And I'll leave you there while I go to the tram company, if that's all right."

The less she had to deal with the fractious Mary, the better, she decided, and in any case, her mother was so much more tolerant than she was. During the months Celia had lived in New Jersey on the fruit farm, she had been able to deal with the brash and noisy Stone siblings, but that was over a year ago, and she knew she had changed since then.

Just before war had been declared, she had been able to meet Stefan for one brief week in Gstaad, and their love had been as strong as ever despite having been so long apart. But there was no guarantee that they would ever meet again, and Celia was now more moody and impatient than she had ever been. The fact that she fully recognised it didn't help to conquer it.

An hour later she arrived back at her cousin Lily's riverside house and pottery shop in Truro, having signed on as a tram conductress for six days a week, with Thursday afternoons free. The pay was ludicrous, but it wasn't the pay she was after, just the need to be useful.

She entered the shop and paused in astonishment at the sound of laughter coming from the upper storey of the building where the family lived. The shop assistant told her they were all in Mrs Kingsley's living room, so Celia followed the sounds and went to find them.

"Am I in the right place?" she said, poking her head around the door.

"Celia, come in," Lily said with obvious pleasure. Lily was always happy with her company, seeing in Celia an echo of her own strong-willed character in the days when she had been a strident suffragette and proud of it.

"Where's Mary?" Celia said at once. "What have you done with her, Mom?"

She hardly needed to ask. Lily's twin boys were eight years old, and home from school on the pretext of having colds. From being such a stalwart in days past, Lily was far too indulgent a mother, Celia thought, but the boys were obviously making a pet of Mary, and she was revelling in it.

Peace at last, Celia thought, as she relayed the news of her new position within the tram company.

"Good for you," Lily said. "We all have to do something, and if I was twenty years younger I'd join up like a shot."

"We did our bit in the last war," Skye said quickly.

14

"But if they decided to conscript women as well as young men, there'd be no choice," Celia said, far too casually.

"I'm sure it won't come to that, honey. The war won't last for ever."

"I bet that's what you said last time, didn't you?"

In the small silence that followed, the three of them looked at one another, and then Robert and Frederick Kingsley came shrieking into the room, with Mary chasing them as fast as her little legs would go.

"Mind the ornaments," Lily yelled too late as a pottery vase shook and teetered on a side table and then went crashing to the carpet. It didn't break, but it stopped the children running around and brought a hunted look to Mary's eyes.

"Me Ma would've beat me for doin' that," she announced.

"Well, nobody gets beaten here," Lily said firmly. "Nothing's broken and you can carry on playing, but just do it more quietly."

Mary studied her for a moment. "I like you, missis," she said, and as an aside she added, "better'n anybody so far."

"Well, that's telling us," Skye breathed, trying not to laugh. "Anyway, never mind them. I haven't seen anything of Oliver for several weeks, Lily. Remind him he's got a home of his own now and then, will you?"

"I do, constantly, but you know what he and David are like once they get their heads together in the evenings. Sometimes I wonder why they bother to come home from the newspaper office at all, and why they don't take their beds there and be done with it."

"I know what you mean, but Nick would like to see his son occasionally," Skye said mildly, trying not to mind that Olly obviously preferred the company of this easy-going family to his own.

"I'll tell him," Lily promised.

For a moment she hesitated as if she would say more, and then decided it wouldn't do to worry Skye unduly.

Two

Betsy Tremayne wasn't one to fly off into a temper without good cause. She left that to her volatile husband, Theo. Between his bouts of gout and his natural bad humour, there was rarely a day when the house wasn't in some kind of an uproar. There were times when Betsy thought wistfully of the comparatively peaceful days when Sebby and Justin were small boys, with the innocent ability to smooth things over even better than she could herself. Not that such sentiments had applied in recent years, she conceded. Nothing pleased Theo these days. But this was the last straw.

"What's upsetting you, Betsy?" Skye asked cautiously when they met in a Truro tea-room on a late February afternoon. "It's not like you to get so ruffled."

"Can't you guess?" Betsy snapped, clearly having bottled up her resentment for too long. "He's gone too far this time. He just can't leave things alone, always poking his nose in where he's not wanted. And 'tis not as if 'tis any of his business no more. He should be taking things easy now, but he just can't stop his meddling and interfering—"

"Hold on a minute, Betsy," Skye said, putting a hand on her arm as she noticed the other tea-room clients glancing their way. "I presume you're talking about Theo. What's he done that's so terrible?"

She tried not to let the glimmer of a smile escape her lips, since this was obviously a serious matter to the normally mild-mannered and forgiving Betsy.

Whatever Theo did, Betsy could normally be relied upon to settle things, even to the extent of clearing up the unholy mess when Theo had hurled a vase through his precious television set. Not that it mattered a hoot now, thought Skye, since all transmission had been suspended after the outbreak of war, and their own set, that Olly had clamoured for so much, had been relegated to the attic of New World for the duration.

16

A good thing too, Nick had said, never happy about the thing sitting there like a blind, square grey eye in the middle of the drawing room.

Skye stopped her thoughts from meandering as Betsy's mouth became more pursed than usual in her tirade about Theo.

"You might not be so understanding when you hear where he's gone, and the rumpus because of it," she said darkly.

"Not to the clayworks?" Skye said, reacting at once. "We both made a bargain with the new owners not to go near the place. Theo fully agreed that it was for the best—"

"Theo will agree with anything for the moment. I know that better than anyone. I've lived with his lies and deceits for years, Skye, and I've overlooked it – most of it, anyway. But this could bring trouble on all our heads."

Skye felt her heart lurch. How could Theo possibly meddle to such an extent? Ever since Killigrew Clay had merged with Bourne and Yelland China Clay Holdings Ltd, to become the combined Bokilly Holdings, she had truly believed that like herself, Theo had refrained from all contact with the new way of things. It was no longer their business.

This obviously needed discussion and she spoke more urgently.

"Perhaps it would be better if we continue this conversation somewhere else before you tell me what he's done, Betsy. Is he at home today?"

"He is not," she retorted. "Nor any other day."

"Then why don't we go to the house?"

Betsy nodded, and Skye quickly paid the bill to the waitress. Even though she was becoming more alarmed than she allowed Betsy to guess, there was also a *frisson* of something else stirring in her veins. Until the arrival of the evacuees, there had been harmony in her own house since she and Theo had finally sold all their shares in Killigrew Clay and she had relinquished her interest in the White Rivers Pottery. Everyone had told her it was time she stopped being a businesswoman and took a more leisurely interest in life.

But in the secret heart of her, she had to admit that it wasn't a harmony she would have chosen. It wasn't her way to sit back and let the world revolve around her. It made her feel old and useless, which was why she had responded so readily to having the little evacuees at New World. At not yet fifty, being old wasn't how she wanted to feel.

The miscarriage she had suffered a year ago had undoubtedly made her assess her life, but not in the way everyone seemed to think. She had *wanted* that child, with a possessiveness that hadn't dawned on her until it was too late. It was a virtual certainty, now, that she wouldn't conceive again. And that made her feel old too . . .

Her thoughts became concentrated on the reason she was returning to the imposing Killigrew House with Betsy. Her cousin Theo was sixty-three years old, and clearly not ready to hang up his boots yet. And neither was she.

But she also began asking herself severely just what she was thinking about. She had been the one to push him into selling, following her husband's legal advice that a merger was the best way to keep both companies afloat. It seemed the best option for Killigrew Clay to cut the strings completely, but now it seemed that Theo couldn't let go so easily.

Once they were sitting in Betsy's comfortable parlour, she asked her bluntly to explain just what was going on.

"He's up there every day," Betsy exploded. "I swear to you I think he's going senile, Skye, and the clayworkers ain't going to play up to his shenanigans for much longer. He's up there lording it over them as if he's still one o' the clay bosses – far worse than old Charles Killigrew ever was in his day, by all accounts."

"But they all know Theo has no authority any more."

"Oh ah, they know it, and so far they'm all tickled pink by the way he goes on, and some of 'em are pretending to kowtow to him, funning with him, and then having a high old time aping his manner over jars of ale in the kiddleywinks, from what one o' the older clayers told me. Theo can't see that they're mocking him, o' course, but it can't last for ever, and I know they'll turn on him soon. He shames me, Skye, and that's a fact."

She paused for breath, and Skye sensed her humiliation. It was bad enough that the clayworkers had bitterly resented Theo Tremayne's caustic manner when he was in charge. They had no say then. But now, he didn't pay their wages and he amounted to nothing, and she could just imagine the way some of the younger ones enjoyed jeering and mocking him.

"He must know they're just baiting him," she said uneasily. "He's not stupid, Betsy."

"I told you. I think he's going senile," she repeated. "He rants and rambles on as if he's still a clay boss, and although he drives me to distraction, sometimes I fear for him. It's just like your Uncle Albie all over again."

"Please don't say that," Skye said quickly.

"Why not? The lapses happened to old Luke Tremayne as well before he passed on, and I ain't so sure the one who went to Ireland years ago didn't suffer the same kind of affliction too, so why shouldn't it be in the family?"

"Because I don't want it to be. Because I'm one of the family too, and both my parents were Tremaynes, and first cousins at that. If anybody's directly in line for any kind of abnormality, it's me."

Betsy recovered from her brooding fury over Theo's antics to realise that Skye's voice had become shriller and that she was deeply distressed.

"Oh my God, I didn't mean to upset 'ee, Skye," she said, acutely embarrassed now. "You know I wouldn't do that for the world, and anyway, there's none so bright as you, so you don't need to take no notice of my nonsense."

"But it's not nonsense, is it? It's just something I never thought about before."

"Well, you can stop thinking about it right now," Betsy said firmly. " 'Tis Theo who's the madman, and he's been one since he were knee-high to a grasshopper, so there's no cause to think 'tis something that's just caught on, is there?"

Skye knew that was true enough, but she also knew that something had to be done to stop Theo making a complete fool of himself over a business that no longer belonged to them. The family had been steeped in the fortunes of Killigrew Clay for almost a century, but when it was time to let go, you had to let it go completely. She thought he had understood that.

"I'll have to speak to him, won't I?" she said slowly, knowing Betsy didn't have a hope of making him understand.

"I reckon you're the only one who can."

She had intended going straight home to relax for an hour or so. Mary Lunn would be having an afternoon sleep in the old nursery, and their maid Liza always gave the child her afternoon tea now. Celia had managed to arrange her tram shifts so that she could fetch the others from school, and there wasn't much for Skye to do except to be the nominal matriarch of the family.

She shuddered at the word. A matriarch was an elderly woman, such as her Granny Morwen had been in her final years, and Skye wasn't ready for that yet. She instinctively turned her car away from the main road back to New World, and headed inland up to the huge, sprawling gash in the moorland that was Clay One, the remaining pit of the old Killigrew clayworks.

Life went on up here much as it had done for years, with the exception of the fine new electrical machinery that had been installed to make production faster and more efficient. The old days, that everyone referred to with such nostalgia, had been a time of hardship and poverty for the hundreds of clayworkers who had worked out in the open in all weathers, but this area had been reduced to a skeleton of those former times, and she doubted that any of her forebears would recognise it now.

The soaring white hills of the sky tips didn't change, though, she thought stoutly, and nor did the milky green clay pools that looked so serene and beautiful in the sunlight. No visitor to Cornwall could fail to be affected by the wild, futuristic, moonscape appearance of it all. The phrase surged into her mind at that moment, and she stored it away to use in her record of the family background.

"Come to help your cousin on his way, have 'ee, Mrs Pengelly?" she heard a voice jeer, as she gazed down unseeingly, trying to recapture the memory of this place alive with hundreds of clayworkers, instead of the comparative few who worked here now. Nostalgia wasn't only for the old . . .

She whirled around at the sound of the voice, and saw a group of clayers nearby, leaning on their long shovels, their thigh-high boots caked in wet clay, their clothes dusted grey-white with the substance. They were strangers to her, but they clearly knew who she was.

"Is he here?" she asked, knowing at once that they must mean Theo Tremayne, and sharing Betsy's shame.

"You'll 'ear him any minute now, missis," another one sniggered. "He's been at the scrumpy, and he ain't feelin' too clever. Pit Captain says he shouldn't drive 'is posh car and he should stay here and sleep it off, but now I reckon you can take 'im home."

"Where is he?" Skye snapped.

But she could already hear him, screeching his head off in the bawdiest song that was currently doing the rounds of the clayworks. Her face burned at the coarse words that weren't yet slurred enough to be mistaken.

"We'll fetch 'im for 'ee, missis," the men laughed, clearly enjoying the sight of the company lawyer's wife looking so mortified. And an ex-owner at that. It was one more black mark against Theo, she raged.

The men half-dragged him towards her car, and bundled him inside it. The stink of the rough cider was almost overpowering, and whatever else she had intended chastising him about today was forgotten in her need to get him home as quickly as possible, with all the car windows already flung open to rid it of the stench.

"What the bloody hell's going on?" he snarled, still befuddled, but finally realising he was on the move, and that his belly was starting to boil as the car lurched over the uneven moorland track towards Truro.

"I'm taking you home where you belong," Skye snapped.

After a startled moment he slurred on insultingly, "Well now, if it ain't my sweet, beautiful American cuz, whiter than snow and twice as bloody angelic."

"Shut *up*, Theo—"

"My sweet and lovely girl, who never let her knickers drop for her cuz, no matter how much he wanted her to," he moaned dramatically.

"For God's sake, will you shut *up*! The car windows are all open—"

The next second, she was more than thankful that they were, as Theo suddenly swung sideways towards the nearest one and spewed up the contents of his stomach onto the track. He disgusted her so much; how he could ever have thought she would fancy him in a million years was beyond her. She wondered how Betsy ever had.

Mercifully the urgent eruption of his stomach contents made him pass out completely, and he slid down on the back seat without another sound until she had returned him to Killigrew House.

She ran to the house, and Betsy came to the door with her lips tight, calling to the menservants to bring their master inside. The quaintness of the request didn't escape Skye, and she presumed it was the only way Betsy could preserve a little dignity at this disgraceful exhibition.

"I wasn't able to speak to him about the other matter," she said briefly. "He was too drunk, but I'll do it as soon as possible. And don't worry about his car, Betsy. I'll arrange for it to be brought back to the house."

"You can let it stay there and fall to pieces for all I care. He won't walk all that way with his gout."

"But you know how he dotes on that car—"

"Serves him right. No – leave it where it is, Skye. And if the clayers find it amusing to daub it with anything that takes their fancy, that'll serve him right too."

Skye drove away, sobered by the rage in Betsy's voice, and knowing that Theo had gone too far this time. But so had Betsy, in leaving his car to the wolves . . . and then, as the varying smells of

21

Theo's presence in her car almost made her vomit herself, she decided that if this was what Betsy wanted, it wasn't her place to argue.

"We can't leave the car there," Nick said angrily, when she had related all that had happened. "The clayworkers will never leave it alone. His bombastic interference is well known by now, and I know just how inflamed they are at his insults. I've no doubt it will result in slogans and scratches all over the car. No, two wrongs don't make a right, Skye. Common decency demands that we bring it back, much as I deplore having to do anything for him."

"Oh Nick, can't you forget your lawyer's conscience for once, and speak as a family member?" she said irritably.

"Not on this occasion. A lawyer is what I am, and you know it."

"I don't always have to like it," she muttered. At times she found his logical arguments for and against the smallest thing too much to take.

"Anyway, I can't do anything about it this evening," Nick went on. "I'm snowed under with paperwork, and I certainly don't want you and Celia going up there after dark."

"It wouldn't be the first time. My family knew the moors like the backs of their hands, and were never afraid of walking up there, night or day, let alone driving. In my grandmother's time, they never had cars anyway."

"Yes well, we don't live in miserable clayworkers' cottages, or have to scratch clay for a living."

His arrogance was too much. "Sometimes, Nick, you can be so *insufferable*," she said. She marched out of the room in time to meet Celia with the evacuees coming home from school, and had to switch her mind to listening to Daphne's moaning, and Tommy's yelling.

"Don't they ever stop?" she asked her daughter.

"You wanted them here, Mom," Celia said cheerfully. "But I gather they've had a bad day," she added in an aside. "Some of the older children have been telling them their houses are going to be bombed, and they'll have to stay here for ever."

"And that's a fate worse than death, is it?"

"Of course it is, poor little devils! What's wrong?"

"Nothing that can't wait for the telling," Skye said, shamefaced at her black mood, and forcing a smile on her face for the sake of the children.

* * *

It was Butch Butcher who reported the news much later that evening. He and Tommy had been squabbling in his bedroom over one of Wenna's old books, and in the end it had got ripped, and Tommy was yelling that there would be bleedin' hell to pay now, and that Mrs Pen would give his arse a good old tanning the way his Ma used to tan his.

Skye was on her way to find out what all the commotion was about, preparing to talk to Tommy in no uncertain manner about his language, when she saw Butch standing by the window, his head pushed inside the black-out curtain, so that only the rear of his large, ungainly body could be seen.

"Come away from there, Butch," Skye snapped. "You know the slightest bit of light shines for miles, and I don't want to have the Warden coming down on us."

He pulled his head back from the curtain, his eyes large and full of fear.

"I reckon we might as well go 'ome, missis, if the Germans have started dropping bombs on us here."

"What? Don't be ridiculous. Nobody's dropping bombs here, and you should know better than to frighten the younger ones, Butch. We're perfectly safe in Cornwall, and besides, there was no air raid warning, was there?"

"What's that, then?" he screeched, opening the curtains wider, uncaring now whether or not he showed a wide beam of light to a non-existent enemy.

Angry at his apparent scaremongering, Skye strode to the window to snatch the curtains across again, and then gasped. The ground rose towards the high spine of Cornwall from here, and by daylight or moonlight it was possible to see the moors and the ghostly white sky tips. It had always charmed her, but not now. Right now, all that could be seen was a huge fire burning brightly on the skyline, and at the same moment the sound of fire-engine bells as vehicles screamed towards it.

"My God," she whispered.

"I told you, missis," Butch was still babbling. " 'Tis them Jerries dropping bombs on us, and we'll all be killed."

"Are we going to be bombed, Mrs Pen?" Daphne Hollis said, dancing up and down, her eyes full of glee. "My uncle was nearly killed in France in the other war, and he's got a hole in his head and a wooden leg now," she added importantly.

"Don't talk such rot, Daphne," Skye said, regaining her senses quickly. "We are not being bombed, and it's merely a fire that's got out of hand on the moors. The firemen will deal with it. I daresay it was some foolish people playing with matches, as you children are always warned not to do."

But she knew exactly what it was, or thought she did. Just as, years ago, she had known exactly what it was when her pottery had burned to the ground, and who had been responsible. There was no similarity between those two events, except for the gut feeling that the irate clayers had got their revenge on the hated Theo Tremayne at last by setting fire to his expensive car.

By the time she and Celia had calmed all the children down and spent an hour assuring the snivelling Mary that they weren't all about to be burned in their beds, Nick had driven to the site, and come home to confirm what she suspected.

"It was Theo's car all right," he said grimly. "The bastards had poured petrol all over it, though God knows where they got it from. The car went up like a bomb and as it spread it set the moors alight. The authorities are questioning folk in the area, but they won't find out who did it. The clayers are like clams when it comes to betraying one of their own."

Although dumbstruck by what he was saying, Skye kept her eyes averted, afraid that he would see that she applauded this trait, no matter what the circumstances. And she shouldn't be approving of anything that resulted in an act of vandalism.

"We can thank God the night is so overcast," Nick went on savagely. "The German bombers won't be able to operate tonight, otherwise they might well have turned their attention westwards with such a beacon to guide them."

Skye realised the truth of his words. But if he hadn't stubbornly refused to collect Theo's car, this would never have happened at all. She couldn't forget that, either.

"Someone had better let Theo know," she said, full of a resentment she couldn't explain.

"My reaction to that is to let him rot until he sobers up," Nick retorted, still bursting with uncontrollable anger at the irresponsibility of the clayworkers, and utter contempt for his wife's cousin.

Skye looked at him coldly, wondering how such a tender and loving husband could sometimes revert into such a monster.

"I shall go and tell him myself," she declared.

"Mom, you shouldn't go out this late at night," Celia put in. Skye rounded on her at once.

"Why on earth not? What the hell is wrong with all of you? Do you think I'm a child, or too senile to drive into Truro after dark?"

24

she whipped out, immediately wishing she hadn't said the dreaded word.

But it was too late now, and she was damn well *going* to let Theo know what had happened. She had to be the one.

She realised the evacuee children were studying her silently now. Butch stood uneasily, while the other two, Tommy and Daphne, seemed oddly drawn together for once, with Mary burying her head in Celia's shoulder.

"Will you be all right, missis?" Butch said at last. "I could come wiv you, if you like."

"That's very sweet of you, Butch," she said, touched by his red-faced concern, "but this is something I have to do myself. It's family, you see," she added, shutting them and Nick out completely.

By the time she reached Killigrew House and approached the front door, she could hear the raucous sound of singing. Theo knew some ripe old songs, and she could only thank God that the house was well away from any others.

Betsy opened the door no more than a fraction, red-eyed and clearly alarmed to find Skye standing there. Late night callers traditionally meant bad news in a community that rarely left their homes after dark except by invitation, and Skye quickly reassured her.

"There's no family trouble, Betsy, but I have to speak to Theo," she said abruptly.

Betsy gave a shuddering laugh. "Whatever 'tis, you'll get no sense out of him, Skye. But you'd better come in and see the state he's in, if you can stand it. 'Tis good of you to bother, and more than he deserves."

The house smelled of vomit and disinfectant, and Skye had a job not to retch. She could only guess what kind of life Betsy had always had with her cousin in the past, with his philanderings and his evil temper. She followed the screeching sounds as Betsy led her to the parlour.

Theo was still bellowing out songs, of a sort. He was sprawled out on a sofa, a spilled glass of cider on the floor beside him. His face was puce, his shirt buttons stretched to breaking point as his beer gut protruded disgustingly through them. He was a disgrace to humanity, let alone his family, thought Skye.

But she tried not to let Betsy see just how much she despised him, knowing that the wife must still have some feelings for her husband, and truly amazed at her loyalty to him through all the years.

"Shall I leave you to him?" Betsy said.

"I think you had better stay and hear what I have to say, Betsy. He's not going to be too pleased," Skye said, with the under-statement of all time.

At her voice, Theo glared at her with narrowed eyes.

"What's this, then? Come to gloat, have 'ee, cuz? Like seeing your poor old feller in a poorly state, do 'ee?"

"I've got something to tell you, Theo, about your car."

It took a few seconds for him to comprehend. Then:

"The bastards had best leave it alone," he roared. "If they've scratched one bit o' paint on it, I'll whip the hides off 'em—"

Skye spoke brutally, without emotion. "They poured petrol on it – which I'm sure is against the law, considering the regulations," she couldn't resist adding, "and then they set fire to it and set the moors ablaze."

It was a revelation to watch his face, and see the varying, flickering emotions that passed over it. There was bellowing fury; blasphemies of the most profound invention; a kind of comic disbelief; a pathetic howling of tears; and then he became a shadow of the old, powerful Theo as he finally slid from the sofa into a shivering heap on the floor.

"My Lord, I could have been a bit more subtle," Skye said uneasily to Betsy.

She shrugged. "Don't see why you should, Skye. Theo were always blunt in the way he spoke to other folk, weren't he?"

"But his car was his pride and joy—"

"Oh ah. We all knew he thought more of it than he did of me," Betsy said matter-of-factly. "Look at him now, the dozy old fool. Such a fuss to make over a bit of burnt metal!"

Skye caught her breath at such a provocative statement as Betsy tipped the toe of her slipper beneath Theo's arm to make him move. He didn't react at all.

"He's passed out again," Skye said with relief. "Otherwise he'd have been roaring at you for saying such things about his car."

She paused, realising that Betsy was staring down at Theo strangely now. She knelt down beside him and pushed the great bulk of him over so that he sprawled on his back, completely inert. His face was grey and sweating, and his breathing was so shallow as to be almost non-existent.

Betsy's face was almost as ashen as her husband's when she looked back at Skye. "I think we should send for the doctor," she said quickly.

* * *

The official cause of death was a massive heart attack, but however incongruous it seemed, Skye thought privately that he died of a broken heart at the loss of his precious car.

"It was the most spooky thing imaginable to see the way Betsy sat there, stroking his face so tenderly, and crooning to him as if he was a baby, while we waited for the doctor to arrive," she told Nick later, still choked and shocked at the swiftness of it all.

"My poor darling, it must have been horrible for you both," he said gently, for once not condemning anyone at all.

"And I was the one to trigger it," she said, starting to weep in his arms. "If I hadn't rushed in and told him about the car so brutally—"

"Hush, my love, you know very well it wasn't just that. He was a prime case for a heart attack. The doctor said it was a miracle it hadn't happened long ago."

"I wanted to stay with Betsy, but she wouldn't have it. She wanted to be alone with him until Sebby and Justin could be contacted. After the miserable life he led her, and all those other women . . ."

Nick held her close. "But now he belongs to her alone, doesn't he? None of them can touch him now. He's totally hers, perhaps for the first time in her life. That's why she'll want to guard this last time with him so fiercely."

She leaned into him. "It's a long time since I had the feeling that you could be so perceptive, so *Cornish*," she whispered illogically, since that was exactly what he was.

"It was always there, sweetheart. We never lose it, but sometimes we have a hard time saying what we feel."

It comforted her to hear him say it now. She and Theo had been at daggers drawn for years, but now he was gone, she felt his loss more deeply than she could explain. She supposed it was because it was another one of the old Tremaynes gone, another link in the family chain broken.

But she hoped Betsy wouldn't have to keep up this silent vigil with him for too long before her boys came home. It wasn't healthy to sit over the dead, even though Skye knew it happened in many parts of the world and was thought perfectly natural. The body – the framework – was still there, and so was the soul, depending on your beliefs, but it still seemed creepy to Skye to watch over it, and talk to it, as if it could still comprehend. But maybe Betsy needed to do this, in order to make her own peace with her husband.

Skye shuddered, wishing time could move on, and they didn't have to go through the inevitable days of mourning and weeping . . . and as the thought slid into her head, she felt a huge shock at her own feelings. She realised she didn't *want* to mourn Theo, even though she knew she must. He had been a thorn in her flesh for so long, but he had chosen the way he lived his life, and to hell with the rest of them. And he was probably lording it over St Peter right this minute – if, indeed, his soul had winged its way upwards and not down.

She took a deep breath at the thought, and forced herself not to be too gloomy. Seb and Justin would soon be home on leave, and Wenna was coming back for a few days too. They still had a funeral to get through. The little evacuees were scared enough at knowing there was a death in the family, and had already clamoured not to have to go to it . . .

"Of course you won't have to go," Celia told them. "It's for people in the family to pay their respects and say goodbye, and he wasn't your uncle, was he?"

"Our Ma brings home lots of uncles," Tommy Lunn said importantly. "Sometimes we only see 'em once, and sometimes they stay all night too!"

"Is that so?" Celia murmured, guessing at the kind of men these uncles were, and not thinking too much of Mrs Lunn.

She was tempted to offer to stay at home with the children instead of attending the funeral, but that wouldn't be right, and the family needed everyone's support. Where there used to be so many of them, their numbers were dwindling, and unconsciously she echoed her mother's thought. The old order was changing, to use a boring euphemism.

Besides, Seb would need her. She didn't know why she thought of him particularly, but she knew he would take his father's death very hard. The two men had been so antagonistic towards one another, and yet she knew that love was there all the time. Some people just had a hard time showing it.

And right at that moment, Celia vowed that if she ever had children she would lavish all the love and care in the world on them, and never stop telling them she loved them.

It was a corker of a funeral, as an exuberant Betsy never stopped telling anyone who would listen. Theo would have heartily approved of the numbers of folk who turned out, bosses and clay-workers as well as family, all swelling the congregation in the little church and filling the churchyard where he was laid to rest next to his father's grave.

Back at Killigrew House for the bun-fight, which Betsy determinedly called it in Theo's own style, she flitted around as if she was the hostess at a society wedding.

"Is she all right?" Celia asked Seb uneasily.

Tall and dark in his infantryman's uniform, and clearly suffering with tight-lipped grief, he nodded.

"She'll do," he said. "This is her house now, and this is her way of stepping into Father's shoes."

"Don't you think that's odd, after the way they've been all these years?" Celia couldn't help asking. "I'm sorry, Seb, I don't mean to be crass—"

"You couldn't be crass if you tried," he said, with a small attempt to be jocular. "No, Mother's being the way she might always have been, if Father hadn't squashed her spirit years ago. He couldn't do it with Justin and me, and now it's her turn to be herself."

He said it without any malice, which surprised Celia, but she was encouraged to ask more.

"I wonder what she'll do now. This house is far too big for her now with you and Justin away for the duration."

She glanced across to where Justin was chatting to Wenna, just as if this was an ordinary family gathering, and realised at once how far away from them all the two of them had grown. Justin, the budding doctor, and Wenna, the nightclub star . . .

"She's already decided," Seb said abruptly. "She's going to offer the house for use as a servicemen's convalescent home. It won't be a hospital, and they'll have to be walking wounded, but I reckon she'll be needing helpers on a non-nursing basis, so if you're looking for a job in the area attending to a lot of helpless men, now's your chance."

"Good Lord!" said Celia, too stunned at the thought of Betsy having decided on her future so quickly to consider anything else.

Three

O liver Pengelly brooded over the fact that he hadn't been born a couple of years earlier. His cousins Seb and Justin had joined up, and the sight of them in their uniforms at their father's funeral had fired his blood anew. And the offices of the *Informer* newspaper were already depleted by several of the young men going off to war.

The very phrase had a dramatic and romantic ring to it, thought Olly. Not that he was stupid enough to underestimate what war meant. When you were in the newspaper business, you could hardly not know. But if only he had been born earlier there would have been no fuss about his wanting to join up at the earliest opportunity. It would simply have been accepted as the patriotic thing to do. As it was . . .

He gazed out of the office window on a late afternoon in July and scowled as he saw his sister approaching from the far side of the street, presumably at the end of her own working day on the trams, and knew he was in for a telling-off about not visiting home more often.

But New World wasn't home to him any more. He constantly argued with his stepfather, and he was far happier staying with David and Lily in Truro, where the Kingsley infants were his adoring slaves. He certainly didn't care for the influx of up-country brats his mother had taken in, either. He'd met them once, and once was enough.

Uncharitable was definitely becoming his middle name, he thought uneasily, but he couldn't help the way he felt, and he thought his mother was too damn soft-hearted for her own good.

He put that down to a peculiar kind of guilt, and he'd been rash enough to say as much to David Kingsley recently. And when he'd explained what he meant, big as he was, he'd got a cuffing around his ears for his trouble.

"Well, I reckon she sometimes still feels guilty for not being a proper Cornishwoman, and for being from 'over there'," he'd said belligerently. "And I know that years ago a distant American relative tried to make contact with her old grandmother and caused her to have a stroke. My mother still feels guilty on that account. Both Americans, see?" he added, knowing he wasn't making sense, his ego still smarting over his cuffing.

"You young oaf," David snapped, never mincing his words when he felt it was needed. "You don't know the half of it. The man was related to the Killigrews, and only distantly related to the Tremayne family. I hope you've got enough sense not to say such things in front of your mother, anyway. She has nothing to feel guilty about!"

Olly's frown got darker. "Well, she's American, isn't she? And you know what Mother's like. If anyone censures them, she takes a share in the guilt. Look how she fretted over the abdication crisis, as if she and the Simpson woman were practically blood relations!"

David looked at him thoughtfully. The boy was getting too hard for his years, and maybe it had been a mistake to bring him into the business so soon. But he knew as well as anyone that when Oliver Pengelly wanted something badly enough, Oliver Pengelly got it.

They both turned in some relief as Celia swept in, bringing the warmth of the July day with her.

"Mom wants to see you, Olly," she said flatly, once David had discreetly left them. "What the hell are you playing at by staying away so long?"

"I thought she had enough kids around her now without bothering about me," he said, defensive at once. "I don't see Wenna rushing home every five minutes, anyway."

"Don't be ridiculous. Wenna's three hundred miles away. She still telephones every week, though, and she came home for the funeral, didn't she?"

"Oh ah, and she and Justin were acting the townies all right, weren't they? Wenna was always a proper little angel, phoning home every five minutes, and you're playing Miss Goody Two Shoes with the vaccies now, I suppose—"

"The *vaccies*?" Celia snapped. "What kind of rubbish talk is that, for God's sake?"

Olly glared. He was too old for this, and he didn't need an older sister telling him what to do. He had always felt the underdog with her, and he felt it acutely now.

"Look, I'm doing a good job here, and I'll get over to see the parents when I can, all right? There's a war on, in case you haven't noticed, and somebody needs to report it."

He puffed up his own role in the office, and was incensed as he saw her hide a smile. She never had much time for him, he raged, forgetting that she had been instrumental in persuading Skye and Nick to let him take this job and move in with the Kingsleys in the first place.

Such things could always be conveniently forgotten as far as Olly was concerned. In journalist jargon, he considered it sorting out the wheat from the chaff.

One day, he told himself furiously when she had gone . . . one day they'll take me seriously. And soon.

At least the evacuees were settling in after the first hiccups, thought Celia, as she drove back to New World. The drive was slow due to the restrictions of the hooded car headlights everyone was now forced to adopt, even though she knew the road so well.

But she also knew the cliff edge was perilously near to the road in places, and she had no wish to go plunging over the side to the rocks below. Her great-uncle Walter had deliberately walked straight into the sea from somewhere along this stretch of coastline, breaking his mother's heart, and she had no wish to do the same.

In any case, it would be very bad form to have to have two funerals in such a short space of time, she told herself with mock cynicism.

Her thoughts reverted to the evacuees. Though Mary's sobbing bouts at home continued, the other three hadn't found school too much of a problem. Tommy had come home with a bloodied nose on numerous occasions, but had triumphantly proclaimed that they should see the other twerps.

Admittedly, a couple of irate mothers had telephoned Skye from time to time to complain about her charges. But apart from that, the children had dutifully written their laborious letters home – and sometimes the parents had written back. And all was well, Celia thought with supreme optimism.

She discovered the irony of that thought as soon as she arrived home. The sound of shouting came from the drawing room, and she was immediately enveloped in the smell of cheap scent as she went into the room. It was just as if a younger version of Fanny Rosenbloom had been reincarnated and appeared in their midst, as brash and blowsy as ever.

The only difference was that Mary Lunn, sobbing louder than ever, was clinging desperately to the woman's skirts.

Skye turned to her daughter with relief.

"Honcy, this is Tommy and Mary's mother—"

"Pleased, I'm sure," the woman said, without bothering to turn around. "So let's stop beating about the bush, missis. I've come for me kids and I ain't going back wivout 'em."

Celia intervened with a gasp as she realised what this was all about. "You can't do that. They're really settling down here, and Tommy's enjoying his new school."

Mrs Lunn looked at her through heavily made-up eyes. She was a tart, Celia thought brutally.

"He ain't enjoying nuthing. The kids want to come home where they belong and I should never have sent 'em away. My gentleman and me can give 'em a good home now, and no do-gooders are stopping us, see?"

"Your gentleman? You do mean their father, I presume?"

"That ain't your concern. He'll be back in a minute and if you're thinking of getting the rozzers on to us, we'll say you was taking our kids against our will, see?"

"Somebody's obviously schooled you well in what to say," Skye said, wishing desperately that Nick was here. Why was he always involved with other folks' affairs whenever she needed him? she thought furiously.

"We don't need no schooling. We just need the kids back."

"Why do you need them just now, Mrs Lunn?" Celia asked, knowing that letters from their mother had been sparse indeed.

The woman flushed under the heavy make-up.

"We gets a new flat if we've got the kids wiv us."

"That's the most terrible and selfish reason I've heard for taking the children away from here where they're safe," Skye snapped. "Don't you know the danger you'll be putting them in if they go back to London? It's a terrible time."

"They're my kids and I'll say where they live," she shouted. "You've missed me, ain't you, duckie?"

Mary snivelled that she had, and the next minute Tommy appeared from the nursery with their paper parcels of clothes. The other two children trailed behind him. Butch, never too bright, was uncertain of what was going on, and Daphne was clearly in admiring awe of the flashy Mrs Lunn.

"We're going home," Tommy announced to Celia. "Me Ma needs us and so does Uncle Bert."

"Yes, well never mind all that," his mother said hastily. "Have you got all Mary's things as well?"

But it was becoming clearer by the minute now why she wanted these children home. 'Uncle Bert' was obviously on the look-out for an easy place to lay his head, and if they presented a united family, the flat would be theirs.

"You can't do this," Skye said.

"I'm doing it," the woman said rudely, and at the toot of a motor horn, she bundled the children out of the house towards the waiting car where a large man in an astrakhan coat pushed them into the back seat and slammed the door shut.

It happened so quickly that the others were left reeling.

"I didn't even get the chance to give Mary a hug or to say goodbye," Skye said, her throat closing up.

"She 'ad to go wiv her Ma, though, didn't she?" Daphne said sensibly. "You only borrowed 'er, Mrs Pen."

Skye felt choked at the child's artless words. Oh yes, they were all on loan, all these children the country folk brought into their homes, and whose allegiance to them clearly meant nothing compared to what they felt for their parents.

That was absolutely right too, but she couldn't help feeling bad about not putting up more of a fight to keep the Lunn children here. She had wanted to care for them and keep them safe, and she had failed abysmally.

"We'll have to inform the billeting officer about what's happened, Mom," she heard Celia's crisp voice. "I'll telephone her now, and we can let the school know in the morning."

Skye looked at her vacantly. Her daughter was the practical one, the strong one, while she was beginning to feel as if she was falling apart, the way she had felt when she lost her baby. And there were still these other two to care for . . . As if to echo her thoughts, she felt the unlikely touch of Butch Butcher's hand clumsily squeezing her arm, his voice rough with embarrassment.

"You've still got us, missis, and I ain't going nowhere."

Skye gave him a watery smile, hoping the kindly meant remark wasn't a prophetic one. Hoping that at the end of this dreadful war, Butch Butcher would have a home and family to go back to . . .

She shook off the surreal feeling as Daphne tossed her head and resumed her usual toughness.

"They was cissies, anyway, and that stupid Mary was always stinkin' the place out wiv 'er widdle. We're better off wivout 'em if you ask me," she declared.

"And there speaks the voice of experience," Celia murmured, praying that her mother would see the funny side of it and not get too depressed at what she obviously saw as her own failure.

Celia knew very well that she was still grieving over her own miscarriage, no matter how she tried to hide it. It was one of the reasons Celia herself was still reluctant to think of enlisting, although she would dearly love to do so.

But if the London families wanted to withdraw their children from their country hosts, there was nothing to stop them, and everyone knew it. It was one of the things the billeting officers had impressed on the temporary foster homes before they took the children in.

And the worst thing any of them could do was to get too fond of the children.

Well, she would definitely never get too fond of Daphne, Celia thought now, seeing the way the little madam was noisily declaring now that she had never liked Tommy, anyway, and that Mary was a widdlin' weed.

Butch had turned out to be a gentle giant and not a thug, but what surprised Celia most of all was why her mother tolerated Daphne so patiently. She obviously saw something in her that Celia didn't. She gave up analysing and went to report the departure of the Lunn children to the billeting officer.

"Do we want to take in any more?" she asked Skye, careful to hold her hand over the mouthpiece at the officer's request.

Skye shook her head. "Not yet. We'll see how things go, honey," she said quickly.

She wasn't being cowardly, Skye told herself, but she just couldn't bear to have children coming and going and tearing her heart apart every time they did so. She knew she had babied Mary too much, and she dreaded what kind of life the child was going to have with that spiv of a 'gentleman friend' of her mother's.

No, Skye thought determinedly, if they had to open up their home to anyone in the future, it wouldn't be to any more evacuees – and she wasn't sure she could do what Betsy was proposing to do, either. She couldn't think any farther ahead than that for the moment.

One Sunday morning a few weeks later Lily and David Kingsley turned up at the house, and sent their boys out to play in the garden with the willing Butch and the reluctant Daphne.

"This is a surprise," Nick said with a smile. "To what do we owe the pleasure?"

"What is it?" Skye said, always more perceptive than he was when something was wrong.

Dear heaven, don't let anything be wrong with Lily, she thought, seeing her pallor. Lily had always been her strength when she needed it, but she looked positively ill as she put her hand on David's arm as if to caution him.

"Skye darling, we've got something to tell you, and I promise you we knew nothing of it ourselves until we found the letter this morning. There's one for you too, and we've brought it straight away. Don't be too hard on him."

Skye took the envelope mechanically, but she hardly needed to open it to know what it was going to say, or who it was from. Olly's large, scrawly handwriting was all over the envelope, addressing them as if he wrote to strangers.

"What's going on?" Nick said sharply.

"Can't you guess? He's enlisted," Skye said, choked, scanning the words that jazzed in front of her at speed.

"He can't enlist!" Nick exploded. "He's too young."

David spoke harshly. "They're all doing it, Nick, and the hell of it is they're getting away with it. I grant you some of them are brought back with their tails between their legs, but Olly's too canny for that. The army needs keen young men like him, and from the size of him and his self-assurance, nobody would guess he's not yet seventeen."

"And who gave him such self-assurance?" Nick said, rounding on him. "I always knew it was a mistake to let him work in your bloody office and to live with you. His place was here where he belongs—"

"Nick, please," Skye said, appalled at this outburst. "None of this is David's fault."

"It's all right, Skye, I don't blame Nick," David said soothingly. "It's the boy's own doing, and it's happened now."

"Well, I'll see to it that it bloody *un*-happens," Nick shouted. "And please don't patronise me, Kingsley. You can always soft-soap my wife, but it won't work with me."

"Nick," Skye said warningly.

With his paying clients, he was always the cool-headed lawyer, but once he lost his temper he never did things by halves. And she couldn't bear it if he became vicious and made some sarcastic remark about always having known that David was in love with Skye. Not in front of Lily . . .

It was Lily who spoke calmly then, unwittingly diffusing the situation by her logical thinking.

"What do you think you can do about it, Nick? He says in the letter he's going to enlist, but he doesn't say where. I doubt that he'll have done it locally. In any case, people would know his family connections here."

Nick's eyes narrowed. "You're quite right. He'll have gone elsewhere. Plymouth or Southampton or Bristol, maybe. I'll make some telephone calls tomorrow. He chose the right day to leave the letters, didn't he, knowing we'd be unlikely to get after him on a Sunday?" he added bitterly.

"He's a clever lad, your Olly," Lily said.

"Too clever and too proud to want to be hauled back here like a criminal or a naughty child," his mother said slowly.

Nick turned on her. "So what's your bright suggestion? Leave him to get on with it, knowing he's breaking the law? That's a fine way for a lawyer's son to behave, isn't it?"

"But he's not your son, is he?" Skye heard herself say.

She clapped her hands to her mouth as she saw Nick's stricken face and heard Lily's gasp. "Oh God, I'm sorry, honey! I didn't mean that the way it sounded."

"Was there any other way? We all know I'm not the boy's natural father but I seem to remember I adopted all three of your children after we were married, and I think I've always done the right thing by them," he said, stiff with anger.

"Of course you have," Skye almost wailed, wondering how this conversation had descended so rapidly into hurtful accusation and pain. And it wasn't helping things at all. It wasn't bringing Olly back. A small chill like a premonition fluttered over her heart then, and she willed it away.

She put her hand on her husband's arm. "Darling, please listen a minute. I think we have to let the army deal with it. They must have ways of checking up on these young men who think soldiering is all fun and games. I'm sure he'll be found out and sent back home without us humiliating him." She swallowed, imagining Olly's wounded pride. "If we do that, he'll never forgive us and we'll have lost him for ever."

She wasn't at all sure it was the right way, or if they too were breaking the law in not informing the authorities. Nick should know about such things . . . but this was a military matter and had no bearing on the domestic cases a country lawyer undertook in his everyday life.

She had to accept that her own instinctive need to hold the family around her like a kind of security blanket was of far less importance than the troubles in a changing world. The country needed their young men and women more than mere mothers did. All the government posters and propaganda told them as much, so it had to be true . . .

"I'm sorry, but I can't let it rest without making some enquiries,"

Nick said firmly. "He's still a child and we're responsible for him, Skye. If you can't see that then we're obviously on different sides."

In the brittle atmosphere that was quickly developing, the Kingsleys called their sons and wisely took their leave, sensing the erupting situation between the two.

Celia arrived home from an exhilarating walk along the sands to find her parents practically screaming at one another.

Discovering the reason for it filled her with anger and guilt, knowing how impatient she had been with her brother. But common sense told her she couldn't have pushed him into this. The idea for enlisting must have been simmering inside him for some time.

"What are you going to do about it?" she asked flatly.

"Find him and bring him home," Nick retorted at once.

"Nick, we *can't*," Skye repeated.

"Would you rather see him killed? War isn't a game, however much these gun-happy children think it is."

The words seemed to hang in the air between them all. Whatever else Olly was, he was still a child – *her* child. Skye was wretched, torn between the wish for her son to find his own feet and not be overshadowed by his successful stepfather, and her natural desire to keep him safe.

"Mom's right," she heard Celia say scratchily. "You can't humiliate him by bringing him back. The authorities will surely check all his personal details, and if they don't, then you should take it as a sign and let him go."

"And there speaks our so-called modern miss, apparently still ready to trust in signs and omens," Nick said coldly. "I still intend telephoning the three army recruiting offices I suspect he may have contacted. It's my duty as a lawyer and father," he added, without the slightest hesitation.

Skye knew then how much she had wounded him by her earlier remark, when in fact he had been all that a good father could be to her children.

"And if he hasn't reported to one of them you'll leave it alone?" Celia persisted.

She hardly knew why she was doing so, except that she felt bound to support Olly in this, having frequently been beastly to him in the past. And secretly envying him so much for his daring.

"For the time being," was all Nick would say.

*　　*　　*

But his telephone calls produced nothing at all. Eventually he even called his one-time business partner, now the owner of an antique shop in Bristol, in case Oliver should have found his way there as a kind of temporary refuge.

"Nick, by all that's holy," he heard his ex-partner's wife say delightedly. "It's so long since we've heard from you, we thought you must have died or something!"

"Thankfully no. But it's good to hear you're still bright and cheerful, Queenie. Is William available?"

"I'll call him. He'll be tickled pink to hear from you."

Even over the telephone line, Nick could hear her high heels clicking away, and her shrill voice calling for her husband. And then William was on the line, as hearty as ever, but instantly attentive when he heard why Nick was calling.

"I haven't seen him, Nick, but if he comes here I'll be sure to let you know."

"Don't warn him, though. He won't think kindly of us if he thinks we're about to haul him back, but I'm afraid the boy's as wild and passionate as the rest of his clan."

"I thought that was what attracted you to them – or one of them, anyway," William said, and then his voice sobered. "But don't worry, I'll be discreet if he does turn up here."

A few days after the hunt for Oliver James Pengelly had turned out to lead precisely nowhere, he was signing on the dotted line as Jimmy Oliver, at a military base in Wiltshire.

The first thing he'd had to do was get as far away from Cornwall as possible. And he wasn't going to waste his shrewd journalist's brain on rushing into what would be his family's obvious conclusion. They still considered him a boy, but Oliver always thought things through before he made a move.

They would naturally assume he wanted to be a soldier, since army talk was all that anyone ever discussed. His cousins Seb and Justin had enlisted in the army, and his own father and Nick had served in the last war. His mother and female cousins too, he remembered, as he carefully worked out his plan.

Joining the Navy was definitely not an option, he thought with a shudder. There had been drownings in his family and their connections in the past, and although it didn't follow that any ship he joined would be torpedoed, the very thought of being sucked under the waves into that infinite underwater hell was enough to chill his bones. He had the inheritance of his mother's vivid imagination to thank for that.

He had never felt any particular passion for flying until he had seen some of the small airplanes whizzing about the skies in practice manoeuvres as he took the train away from Cornwall. Through the train windows he had watched them soaring into the blue, the sun glinting like silver on their wings, and turning them into shimmering works of art.

In those moments he had felt a brief and poetic affinity with the flight of angels . . . and the heady certainty of what he wanted to do had become as inevitable as breathing.

But he had no intention of enlisting as Oliver Pengelly. Jimmy Oliver he now was, and he blessed his size and powerful physique, and the self-assurance that easily persuaded the recruitment officer that he had left his identity card at home, but it would be sent on as soon as possible. He felt a pang on his mother's account as he told the lies so glibly, but he was almost seventeen now. A few months more, and they couldn't touch him. He was simply anticipating the day.

The officer was jaded and anxious to get home to his wife and children at the end of the day, and Olly held his breath as his papers were finally stamped. He was now one of the lowest of the low in His Majesty's Royal Air Force.

The rank didn't matter. He was *in*, and that was enough to give him an adrenalin rush in his veins as he collected his kit and went to find his billet.

"It's just as if he's vanished from the face of the earth," Skye told Lily some weeks later, with a feeling of sheer desolation. "How could he do this to us?"

Lily looked at her thoughtfully, and decided it was time for shock tactics.

"Why don't you think about his needs for a minute, Skye, and not yours?"

"What? Well, thank you very much for that. I thought I'd have your support at least!"

"Darling, you have my support in anything you do, and you always have. But I think that as usual you've got blinkers on as far as Olly's concerned. Is Nick giving you a particularly hard time over it?"

"You could say that," Skye muttered after a few resentful moments. "He's taking it personally, thinking he's driven the boy away. But Olly left us a long time ago, and I don't mean to throw any blame on you or David for that. Olly was always frustrated by having a clever stepfather and three women in the house who either made a pet of him or laughed at him. Poor love. He really couldn't win either way."

Lily was silent, letting her work things out for herself. Privately, she admired Olly for doing what he felt was right. With the heavy bombing of London now, they needed every young man they could find to beat the Germans.

But, like Skye, she still remembered the trenches of France from the first war, and she shivered, not wishing for Olly or anyone to go through that hell again. She felt guiltily thankful that her own boys were far too young to be involved.

Skye saw her shiver, and tried to pull herself together. She had always known in her heart that Olly would enlist at the first opportunity. He was just jumping the age queue, like so many other young men, and all she and all those other mothers could do was to pray for his safe return.

God, she was being noble now, she thought in disgust . . . but she had to be, or go under. She drew a deep breath and tried to move her thoughts to other things.

"There's nothing we can do about it except what Nick's already doing, so let's talk about something else," she said with a huge effort. "How is the shop doing?"

"Poorly, since you ask. Few people have the money to spare on fancy goods these days." She hesitated. "In fact, I wanted to talk to you about that, Skye. So many of these evacuees are miserably dressed. What would you say to my starting a second-hand clothes section? People could bring in their unwanted children's clothing, things they have outgrown, for instance, and we could offer them at a small price for the evacuees, or even do an exchange arrangement. David could advertise the scheme in the newspaper . . ."

Her quick burst of enthusiasm faltered when Skye didn't answer. She knew it was a bad time to be discussing such things when Skye was so worried about Oliver. But then she saw that she had at least caught her cousin's interest.

"What a sensible woman you are, Lily. The clothes would need to be clean and pressed before we accepted them for sale or exchange, of course, and David would need to stipulate all that in the advertisement."

"Can I go ahead then? It's your premises, and I wouldn't do anything without your say-so."

"More than that. You have my blessing."

* * *

They heard from Olly just after his eighteenth birthday. He was now stationed 'somewhere in Wiltshire', he wrote grandly; he was in the Royal Air Force, and learning to fly a kite. They were not to worry about him. And he begged his mother to forgive him for running off the way he had, but life was good – oh, and he had some new pals who were simply spiffing.

"He sounds like a real toff, don't he?" Butch Butcher said when Skye read out the words to the family and the evacuees that afternoon.

"He sounds grown-up," Celia commented, with an unexpected rush of affection for her brother.

"It ain't grown-up to fly a kite. Anybody can do it," Daphne put in rudely. "I 'ad one once. Me Dad used to take me up on Clapham Common ev'ry Sunday morning when he come out of the Nag's Head. "Course, he was sometimes too tiddly to fly it proper," she added, with a giggle and a nostalgic tear in her knowing young eye.

"Yes, well this is a different sort of kite," Celia told her briskly. "It's how the airmen refer to their aeroplanes."

"Well, I think that's daft," Daphne said.

"She thinks everyfing's daft," Butch said. "But she's the daft one, ain't she?"

Any minute now, Skye could see, battle was about to be done. She told them instead to get washed for their tea, ignoring Daphne's grumblings that she hated margarine and she wanted proper shop-bought jam on her bread like they had at home, and not the home-made stuff.

"She's lucky enough to get any at all," Skye retorted after the children went upstairs, protesting all the way.

Now that everything was becoming rationed they all had to tighten their belts – though she had to admit it didn't do female figures any harm. She frequently longed for a good strong cup of tea, but now that tea was rationed to two ounces per person per week, even that resembled 'cricket's piss' – according to Daphne's colourful vocabulary.

But at any rate, now that they knew what Olly was doing she felt a little better. Ironically so, she thought wryly, since he was putting himself in the front line of danger. But not knowing was always the worst, and even Nick was showing a definite and belated pride in Olly's daring. She lulled herself into a false sense of optimism.

The Blitz began in September, with the heaviest bombardment that London had ever witnessed. As it continued unabated, through

Christmas and into another year, Skye constantly begged Wenna to come home where she would be safe, but Wenna stubbornly reiterated that the show must go on to keep up people's spirits.

Even so, the Flamingo Club had put up its shutters except for Saturday nights, and once the air raid sirens started wailing, few Londoners risked turning out of their homes for anything so fancy, even to hear Miss Penny Wood sing.

Like most of them, she and Fanny hurried to the nearest Underground station, where temporary sleeping quarters and coveted family corners were the order of the day now. It was the new community shelter, and although the sights and smells were sometimes indescribable, Wenna recognised the weird sense of belonging, of beating the Hun by the sheer defiance of not moving out of London. This was where they belonged; they were all together; and this was where they would stay. Even the King and Queen said the same thing.

But families, friends and lovers were being parted, and she hadn't seen Austin in months now, although he wrote as often as he could and she knew he was due for a few days' leave soon. She knew that her cousins Sebby and Justin were stationed 'somewhere in France' now, and that her brother Olly had enlisted. She was enormously proud of him.

But there was something else that drew Wenna to these people she now virtually thought of as her own. When the dull sounds of bombing grew louder and more frightening and rocked the Underground stations, no matter how deep they were, there were always those who started a sing-song to keep up the peckers of the rest, and to try to drown out what old Hitler was doing. She admired them all so much.

Even Miss Penny Wood wasn't averse to joining in the choruses, and eventually found herself leading the nightly singing. Most of the people who fled to the Underground were ordinary folk and not theatre-goers at all, and had no idea who she was. But they quickly realised they had a nightingale in their midst, and adopted her just as readily as she had adopted them.

"Gawd, I've forgotten me glasses. I'll have to go back for 'em, duck," Fanny Rosenbloom said as they rushed towards the Underground station one early spring night in 1941.

The ritual was routine now, and people took so much of their homes with them that it resembled a huge underground refugee camp. Many of the older women took their knitting, since making socks and scarves for soldiers was their contribution towards the war effort.

Fanny Rosenbloom always took her showbiz and women's magazines, but she had finally succumbed to the inevitable, admitting that she was as blind as a bat without glasses.

"You can't go back," Wenna said at once. "Just join in the singing tonight or try to have a sleep instead."

"I ain't sleeping while old Hitler's up there doin' his worst. I'll just be a few minutes, gel."

"Fanny, please don't—"

But there was no stopping her, and Wenna watched anxiously as she picked her way carefully over bodies preparing to settle down for another night of mole-like existence; young mothers trying to settle down their children; babies crying fretfully while the older men belched or farted or drank more bottles of ale than they should to try to forget why they were all here. She couldn't blame any of them.

"Come on then, gel, let's see your pearly whites! Give us a song from that pretty throat of yours," someone yelled, and others took up the call at once.

Wenna obliged at once, and the dimly-lit Underground immediately came alive with the sound of singing, so that the heavy bombardment didn't seem so bad. They could drown it out, and they bleedin' well would. Fanny always said so . . .

Fanny looked up at the maze of searchlights picking out the German bombers as they zoomed towards the London landmarks – like angry bleedin' dragonflies buzzing about, she thought irritably. The city was ablaze with light from the burning buildings by now, anyway, and they hardly needed the bleedin' searchlights at all. Fanny blasphemed cheerfully with the most inventive curses she could find, tripping and staggering through the rubble of a recently demolished row of houses on her way back to the Flamingo Club.

The buggers weren't going to stop her getting back to her own place, so sod 'em all. She gave the two-finger salute skywards as she reached the club, and stumbled in through the darkness and up to her bedroom to fetch her glasses.

She was deafened and consumed by noise now, as buildings all around her rocked on their foundations and the street was lit up with a blinding flash of light so intense that it was almost unearthly. But Fanny hardly saw it. Within seconds there was nothing left of her to see anything.

Four

The singing grew determinedly louder and more raucous as the noise of the bombardment from above penetrated the crowded Underground station. To those who were incarcerated below, it seemed to go on for hours, and voices were strained to their utmost as if to ward off the knowledge of what everyone knew was the destruction of their homes and businesses.

But one of them knew it was too long since her benefactor had gone. The sweetest voice of all had become silent, her vocal cords drying up with what her family would call a true Cornish premonition.

"Fanny," Wenna whispered brokenly. "Oh Fanny, no . . ."

Finally, she could remain there no longer. There was a frail hope that Fanny would have sheltered elsewhere, and she had to know. She clambered over the bodies of those who were either trying in vain to sleep, or ignoring Hitler's whole bloody onslaught, and tried to reach the exit.

"Where d'you think yer goin', gel?" one and then another shrieked. "The All Clear ain't gawn yet."

"Let me go," she gasped, as they tried to pull her back. "I have to find Fanny. I have to know what's happened."

As if to aid her determination, moments later they heard the long-drawn-out sound of the All Clear siren, and the sound of cheering replaced the hoarse singing.

Wenna clambered out of the Underground, swaying and blinking in horror at the carnage that assaulted her eyes.

Searchlights still criss-crossed the night sky in the moonlight for any stray German bombers, but there was little need for any natural or artificial light. It was a scene out of hell. The flames of the burning buildings lit the sky with a terrible red glow, and the acrid stench of burning flesh filled the air. Rubble and splintered glass lay everywhere, and the dust was choking and blinding. From several collapsed buildings where a bomb had struck a direct hit, rank sewage was pumping out with a stomach-turning stink.

People milled about in complete disarray. Among the rescue workers were half-clad folk peering out of home-made shelters in various stages of relief or fear or total disorientation. Others who had stubbornly remained inside their houses staggered outside the dangerously crumbling buildings, deafened and bewildered. But they were the lucky ones. They were still alive.

Wardens shouted angrily at Wenna to get off the streets as ambulances and fire engines screamed through them, seeking a passageway. Where they tried impotently to put out the worst of the fires, the firemen's hoses were instantly seared and scorched in the intense heat. It seemed as if the whole of London was on fire, lit up like a hideous red inferno.

Not knowing what to do or how to help, Wenna feverishly tried to ignore what the rescue workers were doing, willing away the anguished cries of the injured and dying. She closed her mind to the sight of blood and scattered limbs, screaming inside as she trod on a soft piece of flesh that had once been someone's arm, and at the sight of a bloodied and mutilated baby tossed into a pile of rubble as if it was a rag doll.

Weeping and almost demented, she ignored everything in her rush to reach the Flamingo Club and Fanny. She struggled through the winding streets and alleyways, and finally gaped in numbed shock and disbelief at what had once been Fanny and Georgie Rosenbloom's pride and joy.

There was nothing left of the entire street. Nothing but a heap of smouldering bricks and mortar. And somewhere beneath it all was the woman who had loved her like a daughter.

Galvanised at last into action, the sensations of pain and horror rushed through Wenna so fast that they made her gasp. Her chest was so tight with holding in the pain all this time that she was near to fainting. But she knew she had to do something, however futile the task.

She crawled over the broken stones and glass, ignoring the jagged edges that cut into her flesh, and began to tear frantically at the debris with her bare hands. They quickly began to bleed as the shingle ripped her tender skin, but she hardly noticed. Sobbing hysterically, she worked unceasingly until other hands pulled her away, and a man's voice she didn't know was shouting roughly in her ear.

"There's nothing you can do 'ere, duck. They're all long gawn, and you need 'elp yerself, by the looks of yer."

Wenna turned on the air raid warden angrily.

"I have to find her," she croaked wildly. "You don't understand. I live here," she finished, choking, and not noticing the compassion in his voice.

"Not any more you don't, gel. Come on now, into the ambulance wiv yer and get those cuts cleaned up—"

"I don't need a bloody ambulance! I'm not hurt. Go and see to those who need you."

Was the man completely stupid? Wenna glared at him as the cruising ambulance pulled up alongside them, and then saw the kindliness in his tired eyes. And instantly, she knew he had seen far more terrible sights than she had this night, and with a whimpering cry, she slid to the ground at his feet.

"My God," Skye said, white-faced, two weeks later.

She looked up from the letter that had been delivered that morning, her throat working and almost unable to speak.

"What is it?" Celia said sharply. "It's not Olly, is it?" *Dear God, don't let it be*, she prayed.

"This is from Wenna's agent. She's been in a London hospital for more than a week now after one of those dreadful air raids. She's in a state of shock and hasn't spoken since she arrived. Apparently one of the other patients recognised her as the singer in the Flamingo Club and the hospital almoner contacted her agent. He thought we should know."

She swallowed as she stared down at the letter, knowing how inane were her last words. Of *course* they should know.

"Go on, Mom," Celia said, going swiftly to her mother's side. "She's not seriously hurt or – or anything?"

Skye's eyes were flooded with tears now. "They found her scrabbling through the rubble at the Flamingo Club. Trying to find Fanny. She never did, though." She drew a shuddering breath, seeing from Celia's horrified eyes that she didn't need to explain any more.

"I have to go to Wenna," she went on distractedly. "She'll need me, and she'll have to come home now."

"Mom, you can't go to London! Dad will never let you!"

"He won't be able to stop me because I'll be gone before he gets home. You can hold the fort here, can't you, honey?"

Celia recognised the determination in her voice, but it was still her duty to try and stop her.

"You know I can. But I can't bear to think of you being in danger from these awful bombing raids—"

Skye was suddenly calm. "I've been in danger before, darling.

47

And now I'm going to pack a bag, as I don't know how long I'll need to stay. Explain to Daddy for me, won't you?"

"Well, at least telephone this agent person first, Mom," Celia said in alarm. "You can't just go off like that!"

Skye nodded. "You're right, of course," she said, thankful for her daughter's common sense. "I'll do that right away. And then I'll get ready to leave."

She asked the operator for the telephone number on the agent's headed notepaper with a trembling voice. She remembered Martin Russell from the last time she had gone to London to comfort Fanny after her beloved husband, Georgie, had killed himself, his mind tormented by the treatment his fellow Jews were receiving in Germany. God, this bloody, bloody war that ripped people and families apart . . .

The voice that answered was crisp and efficient, but it changed at once when she said who she was.

"My dear lady, I was so sorry to be the bearer of bad news about Penny."

In her agitated state Skye had to force herself to remember he was using Wenna's stage name, and that this man would naturally refer to her as such in the different world they both shared.

"Thank you for contacting me," she said huskily. "But how is my daughter, truly? Are there any physical injuries?"

"No more than a considerable number of cuts and bruises that will heal," he assured her carefully.

"And what about her voice?" Skye asked.

Her beautiful, beautiful voice . . .

"I saw her yesterday, and she can whisper now. They say the voice will return to normal now that it's started to come back," Martin Russell said, still cautious. "She had a terrible shock, discovering the Flamingo Club razed to the ground like that. Especially as Mrs Rosenbloom had returned to the place earlier. Penny left the Underground and went there to find her, but there was no hope for her, of course. No hope at all. I'm sorry. Very sorry."

His voice became jerky, and even though the words were short, Skye remembered that he had known Fanny Rosenbloom a long time. Probably longer than she had known her herself.

"Will you please tell Wenna that I'm leaving for London today and I'll be there to see her as soon as possible? And Mr Russell – I shall be bringing her home to Cornwall with me."

She hung up before he could argue about that. It was none of his business, and besides, where else would Wenna go? She had made her home with Fanny at the club for several years now, but this was where she belonged.

The peace and tranquillity of Cornwall would restore her spirits, the way it always did, and always had, for all of them. It was their own private sanctuary.

By the time she reached London and found a taxi to take her to the hospital it was evening and getting dusk, and for the first time Skye felt real fear in her heart as she saw the full devastation of the Blitz. She had never imagined it to be quite like this – so many buildings demolished, and whole streets looking as though an earthquake had struck them.

Dust lay over everything. A strong whiff of burning still lingered on the air, bitter, pungent, and unforgettable. Remnants of possessions could be glimpsed amongst the debris – a child's shoe, a toy, a torn jacket, the burnt pages of a book – bringing the whole scene into heartbreakingly human focus.

"You got somebody in the hospital, lady?" the taxi driver asked her chattily.

"My daughter," Skye said, her eyes as dark as midnight with fear and anxiety.

"In the Forces, is she?"

"No, she's not," Skye said, swallowing hard and trying to ignore the images of destruction all around her. "She's a – a singer in a nightclub."

And dear Lord, but how *useless* that sounded, when all around her now, she could see young men and women in uniform scurrying about their business as night drew on. She was proud of Wenna, but right now, it seemed the most ineffectual job in the world for a young woman to be doing in wartime.

Clearly the taxi driver didn't think so. "That so?" he said admiringly. "We need gels like her to keep up the lads' spirits. There's more ways of winnin' a war than sticking a gun up a Jerry's backside, if you'll pardon me French."

Skye swallowed again, blessing his generous heart, and thinking that he would never know how much he had done to restore *her* morale at that moment. People like him, in the midst of it all, could put things in their proper perspective.

When they reached the hospital she gave him a bigger tip than she had intended, and went to find Wenna's ward. Before she entered it, she was faced with the dragon of a Ward Sister and had to explain who she wanted to see.

"Is she all right? How soon can she come home?" Skye said all at once. "And what about her voice?"

"Her cuts are healing nicely, and she can speak fairly clearly now. The temporary loss of voice was due to shock and not from any physical injury," the Sister said efficiently. "As for going home, the sooner the better. I need all my beds for the wounded."

She swished away, leaving Skye feeling like a fly that had been squashed against a wall. Hateful woman. And then she tempered the ungracious thought, remembering that other war when she too, and all of them, had hidden their emotions beneath a wall of stoicism.

She strode down the ward until she reached the bed where Wenna lay, her lovely dark hair lank against the starched white pillow, her blue eyes looking listlessly the other way.

"Wenna, darling," her mother said in a choked voice.

She turned at once, her expression disbelieving, the tears spilling out of her eyes at once. And then she gave a huge cry as she reached out towards her mother, and was at once enveloped in her arms.

"Oh Mom, I don't know how you got here, but it's so good to see you. It's been so terrible. I couldn't speak, and I was so afraid – and Fanny – poor Fanny – oh, you don't know—" she sobbed almost incoherently.

"Darling, I do know," Skye said gently, overwhelmed with pity for her girl. "That nice Mr Russell wrote and told me everything. I know Fanny's dead, and I know you lost your precious voice for a time – but in case you haven't noticed, you've got it back now," she added, with a tease in her own at the sudden tirade.

"I have, haven't I?" Wenna said, unable to stop the sobbing all the same. "Just as if it mattered about my stupid voice. I'm never going to sing again now that Fanny's gone. I'll never have the heart for it."

Skye held her tight and let her cry it out. It was a long time before the paroxysm ceased, when when it did, Skye wiped both their eyes and spoke sternly.

"Now you just listen to me, honey. Do you think Fanny would want you to say such things on account of her? Don't you think Fanny would be the first one to tell you to stop feeling bleedin' sorry for yourself and to get on with things? She's probably somewhere up there right now, looking down at you and urging you not to let the buggers get you down. Can't you hear her saying it?"

She felt Wenna sniffling against her, and knew that several other patients were grinning their way, surprised to hear a well-dressed lady with an American accent speaking in such broad terms. But it wasn't *herself* speaking, thought Skye. It was Fanny, telling her what to say and how to say it. And forcing Wenna to give a wan smile at the end of it.

"She really is up there, isn't she, Mom? Or could she be somewhere much warmer? She was always a bit of a wicked lady, but in such a lovely, human way."

"I'm quite sure Fanny's up with the angels, honey," Skye said with a catch in her throat. "And once this war is over, she'll expect you to carry on doing what she groomed you for. You're not going to let her down, are you?"

After what seemed like an endless moment, Wenna shook her head slowly.

"I know you're right, but I'm not even thinking about any of that now. Fame and fortune seem such paltry things compared with just being alive, don't they?"

"You're absolutely right, darling, but you'll think differently about your career when you've had a good long rest. I've told Mr Russell you're coming home to Cornwall, and I won't take no for an answer. I'll find somewhere to stay for tonight, and we'll take the train home tomorrow."

She knew Wenna was about to argue, but before any more words left her lips the sound of the air raid siren wailed out, and the drone of many aircraft could be heard almost instantly. The heavily blacked-out windows blocked the sight of them, but they couldn't obliterate the noise of the bombs and the retaliating anti-aircraft guns as the hospital shook on its foundations.

Skye, still holding Wenna's hands, suddenly realised that it wasn't only the hospital that was shaking. With every burst of ear-shattering sound, her daughter was reliving the night when Fanny Rosenbloom had been killed, and she shook from head to foot.

"Take me home, Mom," she whispered. "Just as soon as you can arrange it."

Celia stood in the fragrant garden of New World, looking up at the stars and breathing in the accentuated night-time scent of roses. The children had gone to bed, and her father was busy in his study. She treasured this time alone, when her thoughts always winged towards Stefan.

She fixed her gaze on one particular star, and remembered how her lover had told her that as long as that star still shone, they would be together in spirit.

A sudden burst of resentment split the serenity of her thoughts. It had been such a sweet, wonderful sentiment at the time, but now . . .

"What use is being together in *spirit*?" she said passionately, knowing that no one was around to hear her. "When I want you close, to feel you and touch you, and feel you touching and holding me—"

She bit her trembling lips, wondering if it was wrong to want him so much. Wondering if they would truly ever meet again, or if it was a futile longing that could never be fulfilled, and full of bitterness at the cruel irony of fate that placed them on different sides in this awful war.

"Send me a sign, Stefan," she murmured inadequately to their star. "Anything, to let me know you're still alive, and still want me as much as I want you."

In the soft dark silence of the evening, she finally turned away with her shoulders drooping, and went back into the house. The telephone was ringing, and she guessed it would be her mother telling her what time to meet her and Wenna at the railway station.

"Is that you, Celia?" a man's voice said.

She stared at the instrument stupidly for a moment. The line was not good and the voice was crackly and broken up. She didn't recognise it immediately, but she knew very well that she hadn't somehow conjured up Stefan by wishful thinking.

"What's up? Don't you recognise your cuz-in-law?" the voice went on teasingly.

"Good Lord, *Ethan*," Celia spluttered into the telephone as the Cornish accent finally registered. "You're the last person I expected to hear. There's nothing wrong with Karina or Ryan, I hope."

God help her, she thought guiltily, but she had to think hard to remember the names of her mother's cousin Karina and her baby son. They had gone to Ireland to live right after Ethan and Karina's marriage, to escape from the disgrace of everyone knowing there was a baby was on the way. Too many terrible things had happened between then and now to make it of such great consequence, Celia reflected.

"There's nothing wrong," Ethan insisted. "But I'm glad you answered, Celia, because it's you I wanted to talk to. Not that I'd have minded a word with Nick, of course. How is my brother? Still sorting out everybody's problems, I daresay? And your mother – and Wenna. How's Wenna?"

Celia was suddenly choked, remembering how Ethan had always been Wenna's champion in the days when she had been a moon-

struck child, and the gangly fourteen-year-old Ethan had stood up
to their Tremayne boy cousins in her defence. How long ago it all
seemed now since they were children . . . She shivered, and made
herself answer his questions.

"Everyone's fine, though Wenna had a bad experience recently,
when her lady boss was killed in an air raid. Mom's gone to London
now to bring her home, and I thought you were her, telling me when
to meet them . . ."

Her voice dwindled away, not knowing what else to say. With the
intervention of time and distance and circumstances, they had
grown apart, the way people did, even families.

"Well, I've got some news that might be of interest to you, Celia,"
Ethan went on. "We've got a prisoner of war camp near here, and
the German soldiers are sent out to work on the farms. We've got a
few working for us. They're supervised, and some don't speak much
English, but they're sociable enough and one of them mentioned a
name that you might know."

"Go on," Celia mumbled.

"I believe he's a distant relative of your von Gruber fellow,"
Ethan said casually, never guessing how her heart was leaping now,
fit to burst in her chest.

"Stefan!" Celia breathed.

"That's the one. Wasn't he the owner of some big vineyard and
estate in Germany?"

"That's right—"

"Well, it seems that the house has been taken over by the
Gestapo, and because your man refused to co-operate, he's been
interned. The relative has no idea where he is now."

Celia spoke quickly without giving herself time to think.

"Ethan, as soon as Mom and Wenna get back, I'm coming over to
see this man. I have to talk to him."

His voice was dubious. "He won't be able to tell you anything
more, Celia. It'll just be a wasted journey—"

"He's a link with Stefan, and the first one I've had in months. I
have to talk to him," she repeated. "I'll let you know when I can
leave here."

"Well, all right," he said. "Karina will be pleased to see you,
anyway," he added as an afterthought.

She hung up the phone, her hands damp and trembling. But her
first sense of elation that she was going to speak with a relative of
Stefan's – someone who would have seen him since she had done –
was fast fading.

Instead, the word Ethan had used was seeping into her mind. Stefan had been interned. Locked up in his own country for refusing to co-operate with the Gestapo. She had no idea what that might mean, but her heart was breaking at the thought of him being tortured, or worse. And his lovely home that she had only heard about, being used by those evil men, must have broken his heart as well.

As the sobs welled up in her throat, she turned around to find her father watching her.

"Did you hear any of that?" she blurted out.

"Enough," he said, holding out his arms to her. She went straight into them, glad of their strength and comfort.

"I can't bear to think of Stefan being interned," she sobbed, when she had finally told him everything. "What will they do to him, do you think?"

"I don't know, darling," Nick said. "He probably hasn't done anything so terribly wrong, but presumably he has to be punished in some way. What I do know is that it's foolish to let your imagination give you nightmares. There's nothing you can do about it."

"I wish I could go to Ireland now, this minute," she said passionately. "This German soldier is the only link I have with Stefan."

"You can't go right now," Nick said more firmly. "There are people who need you here, Celia. Your mother and sister will be back soon, and Wenna has been through a traumatic experience. It's upset the evacuee children too, reminding them of what could be happening to their families. You have to be here to give them the stability they need, Celia."

"I know all that," she burst out in frustration. "But what about *my* needs? Don't they count for anything?"

As if to mock her, they both heard a sudden noise from the landing above, and Celia's head jerked up as she heard Daphne's voice, tinged with an unusually fearful note instead of her usual brashness.

"You ain't leavin' us as well, are yer, miss? Bleedin' 'ell, we might as well 'ave stayed at home."

Celia was choked, not knowing whether to laugh or cry or reprimand her at that moment. In the end she did none of it, and merely ran up the stairs and gathered the wriggling Daphne close and told her she wasn't going anywhere right now.

Her time would have to wait, even if it sometimes seemed as if she spent her whole life waiting for something that was as out of reach as her shimmering star.

* * *

Skye and Wenna returned home several days later, and it was obvious to anyone that Wenna was far from her usual self. The shock of Fanny's death had affected her deeply, and even though her voice had returned now, the scars of what she had heard and seen were imprinted too deeply in her heart to be dismissed easily or quickly.

She still grieved desperately for Fanny, especially at the thought that she couldn't even have a proper funeral, since there was nothing left of her to bury. That seemed the most horrible thing of all. A life was over, yet it was as unfinished as if it had never been. It was immeasurably sad, and Wenna had never felt so alone and insecure.

Knowing that her sister needed the security of having her family around her now, Celia still delayed going to Ireland, while briefly toying with the idea of suggesting that Wenna accompanied her. But Wenna had once dreamed of marriage to Ethan, so she didn't even dare mention it.

With the resilience of childhood and her usual macabre curiosity, Daphne Hollis quickly recovered from her temporary fear of losing all her Cornish contacts at once, and eagerly quizzed Wenna about the bombing.

"What was it like, miss? Did you see lots of blood and stuff?" she asked, her big eyes almost popping.

"Don't ask such horrid questions," Wenna snapped. "If you can't be sensible, then don't ask anything at all."

"I only wanter know," Daphne said resentfully. "Me Ma always says if I wanter know something, I should go ahead and ask. So what was it like?"

"If you really want to know, you can read the newspaper, and perhaps it will improve your education as well."

The last thing Wenna wanted to do was to relive it all over again for this little madam. She didn't have her mother's patience with Daphne – nor even Celia's, she thought in some annoyance. Her sister seemed, oddly, to be marking time about something, and as yet, Wenna had no idea what it was. The old sweet sharing of secrets had temporarily vanished like will-o'-the-wisp, she realised, and knew it was partly her fault for holding everyone at bay.

Each of them had secrets now, that neither was willing to share. Hers was the very real fear of death that had seemed so near on that night of carnage in the Blitz. What Celia's secret was, she didn't know, and couldn't guess, since she was closer than an oyster these days.

She became aware that Daphne was still glaring at her.

"I bet me Ma's dead and gawn by now," she said suddenly.

Wenna flinched, and stared angrily at the girl.

"That's a wicked thing to say, Daphne—"

"Why? Do you wanter get rid of me and send me back?"

"Of course not. Well, not while there's a war on, of course. When it's all over, you and Butch will want to go back where you belong, won't you?"

Daphne shrugged. "Dunno. Me Ma never liked me much, 'cept to fetch and carry for all the little 'uns. Now they're all gone, she won't want me back so I might as well stay 'ere if Mrs Pen'll have me," she said nonchalantly.

She stared Wenna out, and despite the arrogant too-old look in her young eyes, Wenna suddenly saw the pleading there. Good God, she thought. She actually means it. The little madam *wants* to stay here – unless her Mum wants her back, of course. Daphne was the type to keep all her options open.

"We're not so bad after all, then," Wenna said casually.

Daphne suddenly grinned. "I dunno about you yet. I'll show yer where me and Butch found some blackberry bushes if yer like, and I'll let yer know later."

She switched her thoughts with her usual mercurial speed, and reached for Wenna's hand. Without thinking, Wenna's fingers curled around the girl's. It was a gesture of a kind.

Celia had confided in her cousin Lily about the phone call from Ireland. She had to tell someone, since she and her father had agreed not to worry Skye or Wenna with Ethan's information. Lily was as practical as ever, sorting out the As-New clothes in her now thriving second-hand clothes department of the White Rivers Pottery shop in Truro.

"If you feel you need to see this man, then you should go, though I can't see why you should want to. Ethan said he wouldn't be able to tell you anything more – and he's a German, after all." She almost spat out the word.

"So is Stefan," Celia reminded her.

"But that's different. He's part of an old, established family business, not a soldier—"

Celia responded smartly. "I doubt that any prisoners of war were born soldiers, Lily. He's probably some nicely brought up young man who was conscripted into the army, the same as our boys were."

Lily said nothing for a moment, then shook her head. "Well, I'm sorry, but I simply can't think that way. War's a bloody awful thing, anyway. So what are you going to do?"

"I haven't really thought, but since Wenna's still so unsettled, it seems a bit mean to go rushing off to Ireland. Maybe the man could be persuaded to write me a letter with all the details and let Ethan send it on to me."

"I'm not sure the authorities would approve of your getting correspondence from a German prisoner of war," Lily said doubtfully.

"Who's to tell them?" Celia retorted.

But as spring merged into summer, another call to Ethan established that the prisoner had been moved on elsewhere, so her chance of finding out anything more had vanished. She cursed her lack of resolve.

Before she could decide if there was anything more she could do, she received two visitors. The women and children were having tea late one afternoon when the men called at the house in an official-looking car bearing a flag.

"Dear Lord, don't say it's bad news," Skye breathed. "We haven't heard from Olly in weeks . . ."

Wenna was still at home, still finding it hard to come to terms with Fanny's death, and seemingly unable to concern herself with anyone else's problems. She spoke crisply.

"We'd be getting a telegram if anything had happened to Olly. They wouldn't bother sending two stiff-necked officials to deliver the fate of one young airman to his family."

"Don't be cruel, Wenna," Skye said evenly.

"I'm not. I'm being realistic."

"P'raps it's about me," Daphne piped up. "P'raps it's ter say me Ma's bought it. Or Butch's Dad."

"And you're a nasty, bloodthirsty little brat," Wenna snapped at her. "I'm getting you out of the way until we find out what's going on."

Daphne grinned. "I like you when you go all red and shout at me. You remind me of me Ma," she said, at which point Wenna grabbed her hand and yanked her out of the room, with Butch following closely behind.

Skye answered the knock on the door, and moments later she returned, with the two men following her.

"The visitors are for you, Celia. I'll leave you—"

"No, please don't do that, Mom – unless it's something private?" she queried the men.

Though for the life of her, she couldn't see what it could be. The men were portly and grey-haired, with an unmistakable military bearing, and she knew she had never seen them before.

"Your mother is at liberty to stay and listen to what we have to say, Miss Pengelly. In fact, you may prefer it," one of them said solemnly.

Celia felt her mouth go dry. Had she done something terrible? If so, she couldn't think what it could be. Unless it was consorting with the enemy . . . The thought was so ludicrous it almost made her laugh out loud. Almost.

"You're very young," one of the men observed.

"I'm twenty-two – nearly twenty-three, actually," she said without thinking. "Not that it's anyone's business—"

Skye took charge. "Please, won't you both sit down, gentlemen, and I'll organise some tea."

A maid appeared as soon as she had rung the bell, and then she turned to the visitors. "Now I think you owe my daughter some explanation of why you're here."

The first one cleared his throat. "My name is Brigadier Ralph Soames, retired, madam, and this is Major Dennis Beasley. Through our sources, we understand that Miss Pengelly attended St Augustine's Academy for Young Ladies near Gstaad, Switzerland, before living and working in Germany as a translator for some time for a Herr Vogl."

"That's correct," Celia said sullenly, resenting the fact that these two seemed to know so much about her, and wondering who the hell these sources were who could give so much of her personal details to strangers. It made her feel disagreeably exposed. In the way of interrogators, the men waited for her to say more, and in her nervousness she spoke too fast.

"Herr Vogl was a friend and business colleague of my mother's family, as well as my employer."

"Ah yes. Your family were once the owners of the china clay business previously known as Killigrew Clay, and also of the associated pottery known as White Rivers, and you did much of your business with the German firm of Vogl's, I understand," Soames said, smiling gratuitously at Skye.

"Look here, would you mind telling me what this is all about?" Celia snapped, losing her patience. "So you know all about us. Is it a crime for me to have worked for a German firm? I'm sure many people did so in the past."

"Quite so, my dear young lady," Beasley said smoothly. "In fact, with your academic credentials, it's a definite advantage. You are obviously fluent in the language in a far greater capacity than the use of schoolgirl phrases."

She didn't answer. She loathed the pair of them with their snide manners, and when the maid brought in the tea, she childishly hoped it would scald them.

"Won't you please come to the point, Brigadier?" her mother said, with pointed American good manners.

"We want to offer your daughter an official position, Mrs Pengelly," Soames said, turning to her. "We have a specialised tracking unit in Norwich, where we are able to monitor incoming calls detailing German military movements. As you might expect, much of this is in code, but with her expertise and knowledge of idiomatic German, we believe your daughter could be of great help to us in deciphering these codes."

"I see. Then her expensive education wasn't entirely wasted after all," Skye said dryly, in an attempt to diffuse the suddenly charged atmosphere between them all. "And what if she refuses?"

The officials glanced at one another. "Madam, it's no great secret that by the end of the year, if not sooner, it's highly likely that all young women will be conscripted, either into munitions work or into the Services. This skilled work we are offering is essential to the War Effort, and we would much prefer that Miss Pengelly makes her own choice."

"Excuse me," Celia snapped. "But I *am* here. I can speak for myself, and I'll be the one to decide whether or not I would be willing to take up such an appointment."

"And would you?" Beasley asked quickly.

"Of course," she said, without a second's hesitation.

Five

"Why on earth did you say yes, if you don't want to do it?" Wenna demanded a couple of weeks later, when Celia was trying to cram yet another item into an already overloaded suitcase, and letting off steam in the only way she knew.

"I don't know," Celia snapped. "I suppose it's better than feeling I'm useless here. Dad definitely approves, of course. He always thought it was beneath me to be a tram conductress, even though it was quite fun."

"So you're taking on this new job just for his benefit, are you?" Wenna persisted.

Celia glared at her. "Since when did you become so picky over everything anyone else does?"

"Since Fanny died," she whipped back. "Since I don't know where I'm going any more. I haven't heard from Austin in months and I'm sure he's missing or dead too, and who would bother telling me, anyway? I'm not his family. I don't even know if he had one. And since my life has been turned upside down, I'm feeling like the useless one, not you!"

As she raged on in her frustration, Celia paused in her packing, wondering where her soft and gentle sister had gone, to be replaced by this beautiful, brittle shell of a girl. And she could only feel immense compassion. Wenna had seen sights that she had never seen except in newsprint pictures. Her instinct was to put her arms around her and hold her close, but Wenna never invited such familiarities these days. In many ways, their old roles were reversed, she thought.

"Wenna, I'm sorry," she said. "But you were never useless. You were always the star in the family, and you've become far too insular since you came home. You've hardly moved out of the house, and you need to see other people apart from us and the evacuees. Go and see Lily – or visit Aunt Betsy, if you can't face Lily's straight talking."

After a moment Wenna spoke grudgingly. "Oh, I know you're

right. You always are, darn it," she added with a twisted smile. "And although I don't want to seem ungrateful for all Mom's done for me, I do begin to feel stifled here. I don't know where I'll go, but perhaps I'll get out my old bicycle for a start and see if I can still ride it."

"That's my girl," Celia said, and resumed her packing.

For good or ill, she had accepted this decoding post in Norwich, and there was no going back on it now, although it had taken several weeks of paperwork and further interviews to get things properly organised. But as the stiff-necks had intimated, if she didn't take the job, she might easily be seconded into it when conscription for young women came in soon, as it surely would.

Despite her collywobbles, she couldn't deny more than a *frisson* of excitement too. She had left home before – for heaven's sake, half her life had been spent away from home, if she thought about it – and she would be doing a job for the War Effort. She would always think of those two words beginning with capital letters now, the way those pompous oafs had said them – but what the heck! Working for the War Effort was something she had wanted to do anyway, wasn't it?

Wenna cycled slowly away from New World, wobbling at first, but quickly regaining confidence on the long-disused vehicle. The sun felt warm and sensual on her back, and gradually the healing, fragrant air began to do more for her peace of mind than anything else so far. The sea was a sparkling blue that afternoon, and the forgotten silence of the summer lanes was wonderful.

She had made her home in a hectic world surrounded by show-business people in London, albeit on a minor scale, but now she realised guiltily that she had begun to feel smothered here by all those who wanted to do the right thing by her virtually stepping on eggshells in order not to upset her.

And she had needed Celia's healthy sibling ranting to show her some direction. She paused to watch some sandpipers race across the edge of the cove far below, and saw how the wash of the waves made their tiny tracks disappear as if they had never been. It was beautiful, charming, and in an instant of time it seemed to Wenna's heightened senses to symbolise birth and death and everything in between . . .

. . . and in her head, she seemed to hear the ghost of Fanny's voice from long ago, the first time she and Celia had ever met her, both standing open-mouthed at this flashy friend of their mother's,

61

the echo of another war and another time that they didn't know. A woman wearing bright clothes and garish make-up, and with a wonderfully wicked way of talking.

'*Bleedin' 'ell, this effing place is deader than a cemetery, gel. How d'yer ever stick it?*'

For the first time since Fanny's death, Wenna realised she was laughing out loud. Not cruelly, but softly, indulgently, with tears streaming down her face, because although Fanny might be gone, her memory would never fade. She had been too vivid a personality for that.

After a long while of letting herself indulge in pure nostalgia instead of trying to blank it all out, Wenna dried her eyes and got back on her bicycle. She still didn't know where she was going, but in the distance ahead of her was Killigrew House, where Betsy Tremayne lived all alone now, since her sons had gone to war and her husband Theo had died. But they all had to go on, no matter what, thought Wenna. It was the nature of things . . .

She thought briefly of the young war correspondent who had stolen her heart, and whom she knew deep inside that she would never see again. If that was Cornish intuition, so be it, she thought, but as she cycled slowly and unthinkingly into the grounds of the imposing house, hardly seeing any of it, she had already mentally said goodbye to Austin.

"Hey, watch out, babe!" said a voice she didn't recognise. "You need a licence for that contraption."

She realised at once that she wasn't alone, and that the grounds of the house weren't as silent as she had expected. There were more than a dozen young men strolling about, or sitting in the sunshine, and they were all in uniform.

And then she remembered. She had been so wrapped up in her own life and the trauma of recent times, that until that moment she had completely forgotten how, after Uncle Theo died, her Aunt Betsy said she was going to turn this house into some kind of convalescent home for the walking wounded.

None of the family had taken her seriously. It was the kind of thing people said spontaneously, and did nothing about. But Betsy had obviously lived up to her word, and as Wenna skidded her bicycle to a halt on the gravel, she slid sideways and fell straight into the arms of a young man with laughter in his eyes wearing the blue uniform of the Royal Air Force.

"Now that's what I call really falling for someone," he went on teasingly, while she glared at him and tried to recover her dignity.

"I'm sorry, and if you'll excuse me—" she began frigidly, and then she heard her aunt's delighted voice and saw her coming out of the house, her plump arms outstretched, her accent still as rich and welcoming as Cornish cream.

"Wenna, my lamb, 'tis so lovely to see you, despite your recent bad news, but you'm as blooming as ever, and if dear Group Captain Mack will put you down, I'll introduce 'ee."

She extricated herself from the man's arms at once, feeling incredibly foolish as she was clasped in her aunt's embrace, while the officer held on to her bicycle.

In the brief moment she had seen him, his striking appearance was etched on her mind. He was tall and fair-haired, with a rugged, outdoor look, and a severe and jagged scar running the length of his right cheek that did nothing to diminish his good looks.

"It's good to see you, Aunt Betsy," she almost gasped, recovering her breath once she was out of both embraces.

"And you too, my lamb. Now you'm just in time for tea, so you can tell me all your news properly. Sebby was sore put out to hear about it, as were all my other boys."

Wenna looked at her blankly, aware that this Mack person was following with her bicycle. His attention irritated her. She had imagined a quiet visit with her aunt, and suddenly she was surrounded by uniforms and idle chatter.

"Your other boys?" she said.

Betsy swung her arm around to encompass them all. "These are all my boys now. They come for a spell and then leave, but they'm all the better for having breathed Cornish air."

She suddenly remembered something and stopped so suddenly that the bicycle wheel cannoned into her, and she scolded herself for her stupidity.

"Bless me, where are my manners today? Wenna, this here's Group Captain Harry Mack. He's from Canada, but his folks originated in Scotland, so he's more or less one of us," she added magnanimously. "And Harry, this is my lovely niece, Wenna. She's just recently suffered a bereavement, so you be sure to be nice to her."

Wenna squirmed, wondering if the man must think her aunt a complete country bumpkin, but he plainly adored her.

"I've seen your portrait, so I feel as if I know you already," he said.

"Oh, I don't think so," she said stiffly, unable to stop herself. She recognised his accent now. It wasn't as strong as her mother's, and there were slight differences in pronunciation, but it was definitely transatlantic.

"You've seen the picture of Wenna's grandmother," Betsy broke in. "People are always making the same mistake. It's Primmy Tremayne's picture over the mantel in the parlour, Harry, but Tremayne women all have the same rare colouring."

"Stop it, Aunt Betsy, you'll make me blush," Wenna said, not wanting to invite any compliments from the Canadian. He was perfectly charming, but she wasn't looking for charm right now. She was still too busy wallowing in her own grief.

She glanced back at him, seeing that jagged scar, more vivid in the sunlight, and the knowledge of her own self-centredness hit her with the force of a sledgehammer.

Everyone here – all of Aunt Betsy's boys, as she called them – had been wounded in action, or they wouldn't be here at all. And here she was, ready and more than willing to snub them. She was ashamed of herself, and gave the Canadian a warmer smile than she had intended.

"My aunt exaggerates, Group Captain Mack," she said.

"I think not," he said quietly. "And the name is Harry."

He offered his hand in friendship and she reluctantly took it in her own.

"Well now," Betsy said in the small silence. "Like I said, it's time for tea. Perhaps you'd remind the others that it will be on the lawn in five minutes, Harry, and you never know, we may just persuade Wenna to—"

"Aunt Betsy, *no!*" she said sharply, knowing exactly what she was going to say.

She had no intention of singing – of *performing* – today. It wasn't why she had come. She hadn't sung a note since the night Fanny had died, and her last memory of performing was of leading the songsters in a London Underground station while Hitler's bombs rained overhead and destroyed part of her life.

"Persuade her to do what?" Harry Mack asked.

"Nothing. Nothing at all," Wenna said. "I'll join you all for some tea and then I have to get back."

"Why do you? We've only just met."

She looked at him, reading the unspoken meaning in the words. Knowing that he was attracted to her, and sensing his desire to hold on to her presence as long as possible. She knew that look, that feeling, that instant rapport. But she didn't want it. Not from him. Not from anybody.

She looked around in relief as several other men in uniform approached – but if she thought there was safety in numbers, she knew her mistake at once.

"Oh, my good Gawd," one of the soldiers exclaimed. "It's *you*, ain't it, gel? I seen you at that fancy club in London one time when I was home on leave and took my lady friend to hear you. You're that Miss Penny Wood, ain't she, missis?"

His voice became animated, and Wenna had no choice but to admit that yes, she was Penny Wood, but that was only her stage name, and she was really Wenna Pengelly, and the niece of Mrs Betsy Tremayne. And she didn't sing any more . . .

"Well, I'll be buggered – oh Gawd, beggin' yer pardon again, ladies, but I never expected ter see such a vision down here – 'ceptin' yer good self, o' course, missis," he added to Betsy. "So that's why that picture in the parlour looked familiar! Fancy Miss Penny Wood being your niece!"

"Ain't you going to give us a song, then, Miss?" his companion asked sadly.

"I'm afraid not," Wenna said at once. "I've – I've had some trouble with my voice recently . . ."

God, but that sounded feeble, when they must all have gone through some ghastly experience to put them here. She could see the disappointment in both men's eyes. And others, too, were crowding around them now, seeing that somebody new was here, and sensing that she was somebody special.

"Couldn't you give us just one song?" Harry Mack said quietly. "Unless it would put too much of a strain on your vocal chords, of course. None of us would want that."

"Well – I'll think about it," she found herself saying weakly. "Maybe after I've had some tea."

She didn't know why she had said it. She didn't want to sing. *Couldn't* sing. Not for anyone. She certainly didn't want to give an impromptu concert on a Cornish lawn.

And then she remembered again the last time, and the raucous voices of the people joining in the chorus with her. Many of them terrified. Many of them too afraid to leave the shelter of the Underground because of what they might or might not find left of their homes above ground. But all of them had been ready and willing to sing their hearts out to drown the sound of the bombing, and to keep up their own spirits and those of all around them . . .

Of course she would sing. In the face of what these casualties must have gone through, she had no option – not if she wanted to keep some semblance of self-respect.

But first of all Betsy and her afternoon helpers brought out the trays of tea and scones and jam and cream, and they all sat around companionably on the grass or garden chairs.

It was blissfully informal, and Wenna thought fleetingly how different it all was from the days when they were children, and her Uncle Theo was alive, roaring his way about the place, with no one daring to speak above whispers. Now that Betsy held court, it was a different world . . .

Then, just for a moment, the scene in front of her shifted, and she had the weirdest vision of the way it must have been many years earlier, when this gracious old house had belonged to Charles Killigrew and his son Ben, who had married her own great-grandmother, Morwen Tremayne. Against all the odds, too, Wenna thought, for who would ever have thought a clay boss would marry a lowly bal maiden who scraped clay blocks up on the moors in all winds and weathers?

"What thoughts are going through your lovely head now, I wonder?" she heard Harry Mack say beside her.

She flashed him a nervous smile as the vision faded.

"None of your business," she said as lightly as she could, "and you wouldn't want to know, anyway."

"I would have to challenge that remark, since I would like to know everything there is to know about you," he said.

She felt her heart leap. "Oh, I'm just a singer, that's all. There's nothing special about me."

"If you're seeking compliments, you can have them, but I think you must already know that I think you're the most enchanting young lady who ever lived."

"Group Captain Mack, *please*," she said in embarrassment.

"I told you, the name's Harry to my friends. And I very much hope you're going to be one of them."

"Really." She ignored the provocative remark and sought for something else to say. "My brother's in the airforce. He was somewhere in Wiltshire the last time we heard from him."

"Oh? I'm based nearer the east coast and I've been on ops for the last few months, but maybe I've come across him. What's his name?"

"Oliver. Oliver Pengelly."

"I don't recall anyone of that name. I'm sure I would have remembered if I had. It's quite a mouthful, isn't it?"

"Not if you're Cornish," she retorted, ridiculously pleased that she had made a tiny score over him.

She saw her aunt advancing towards her with one of the soldiers, and she gave a silent groan. There was no help for it now – but she was sadly out of practice, and she had a moment of panic as she wondered if any notes would come out of her throat at all. Her aunt spoke determinedly.

"Joe will play his piano accordion for you, Wenna."

It was a far cry from the elegant piano at the Flamingo Club, she thought, eyeing the battered old instrument, and then felt a stab of anguish. However elegant that piano had been, it had gone the way of everything else in the street, and was no more than rubble and dust now.

Joe wore a private soldier's uniform and had a black eye-patch over one eye. Wenna didn't want to guess what was beneath the patch. She gave him a watery smile.

"I'd be happy if you would accompany me, Joe," she said. "What will it be? Do any of you have a favourite?"

The group of recovering invalids opted for 'Roses in Picardy' and she knew she should have made the choice herself. The song was far too plaintive, too romantic and emotive, but since it was a unanimous choice, she allowed Joe to play a few bars first, before she exercised her husky voice for the first time in weeks.

And somehow, as incongruous as it had seemed to be to sing in her aunt's garden in front of a motley and admiring crowd that was as far removed from her usual audience as was possible, the feeling of coming home, in more ways than one, gradually began to seep into her heart and soul.

Her voice grew in sweetness and strength as more and more songs were requested, until she was bound to protest laughingly that she could sing no more.

During the final burst of applause and protests, she heard one of the soldiers speak in a choked voice.

"The whole world should be privileged to hear you sing, miss, not just we poor wrecks."

She caught Harry Mack's glance then, and her heart gave an unexpectedly hot surge. Whatever this man was, he was no poor wreck, she found herself thinking, and she had to lower her eyes at the expression she saw in his.

"Well, I've done enough for one day," she said huskily, "but maybe I'll come back another time, if you'll have me."

"Every day!" they begged. "But give us just one more today, miss. One of the old songs."

"What do you say, Group Captain?" Betsy called to him formally, clearly delighted with the success of her niece's visit. "You haven't made a request yet."

He replied at once, his eyes never leaving Wenna's face, and seeing the warm flush creep into her cheeks.

"Do you happen to know 'Loch Lomond', lassie?" he said, exaggerating the Scottish-Canadian accent. "To remind me of my ain folk, you might say."

"Of course," she said, and refused to look his way until the very last lines of the old song, when she simply couldn't resist it. In any case, it would have been churlish not to look at him, since it was his own request.

". . . for me and my true love will never meet again, on the bonny, bonny banks of Loch Lomond."

She looked fully at him then, and saw the way his mouth curved into a smile, and how the creases at the sides of his dark eyes almost met the curling fair hair at his temples. She saw how the sun still highlighted the vicious scar on his cheek that was surely not very old, and she felt a wild and primitive urge to run her fingers tenderly down its length, as if they held some magical witch's potion to relieve its anger.

She was shocked and enraged at her own reaction, coming so soon after the tragedy of Fanny's death, and her virtual goodbye to Austin. Was she so shallow, after all?

"That was a wonderful rendition, and I thank you for it, ma'am," she heard Harry say gravely.

Before she knew what he had in mind, he had lifted her hand to his lips and kissed the back of it.

As she went to pull away from him in laughing embarrassment, her hand turned over and his kiss landed in her palm before she involuntarily enclosed it with her fingers.

It was symbolic, tore through her mind. Such a gesture and outcome would inevitably be seen as symbolic by those of a fey Cornish disposition. Certainly by old Morwen Tremayne, her greatgrandmother; and her grandmother Primmy; and even her own mother, despite her American upbringing.

But she, Wenna, had long since dismissed all that spooky clairvoyant stuff from her mind, being the modern girl that she was, living and working in the sophisticated atmosphere of a smoky London nightclub.

And where had it got her after all? All of it was gone, and here she was, right back here with her roots. Feeling flashes of psychic nonsense that she didn't want, but seemingly couldn't escape . . .

"Are you all right, my lamb? Perhaps we shouldn't have pushed 'ee to sing for so long after all, and 'tis mighty warm this afternoon," she heard Betsy's anxious voice say.

She blinked, realising her eyes had been tightly closed for a moment. "I'm quite well, Aunt Betsy, but I really should be getting home now. I didn't even tell my mother where I was going, and she'll be anxious."

"And you'll come back tomorrow? I can't tell 'ee what a power of good you've done for my boys this afternoon, love."

Her instinct was to say no at once. She didn't dare come back while he was here . . . she wouldn't even think his name right now . . .

She was adamant that she didn't want any complications in her life, no more loves who were taken away from her, no singing, nothing at all, except the chance to let her heart recover from its traumas . . . and then she saw his face.

"I'll be back tomorrow," she said huskily.

"You're looking much better, honey," her mother told her the minute she entered New World. "Celia said you'd gone for a cycle ride, and I can see it did you good. She had to leave for the train before you got back, but she said to tell you goodbye, and that she'd be writing to us all as soon as she's settled in Norwich. So where did you go today?"

A million miles away . . . to the moon and back . . .

Wenna sat down on the sofa and gazed unseeingly out of the window. Her cheeks were still flushed, and not only from the exertion of the ride. She hardly registered Skye's question and instead she asked several of her own.

"Mom, do you think everyone has the capacity for falling in love more than once? And if so, is it being disloyal to the first person you loved to have the same kind of feelings?"

"Good heavens, I didn't expect to be faced with such a deep-meaning discussion on a sunny afternoon," Skye began with a smile, and then saw that her daughter was being completely serious. "What on earth brought all this on, darling?"

"But *do* you, Mom? Think you can love more than one person in your lifetime, I mean."

"I'm hardly the person you should question about that, Wenna. I think you know the answer already."

Wenna felt her face burn. She had spoken unthinkingly, and she should have known better. It was more Celia's style to rush straight in, but their personalities seemed to have got all mixed up recently. Unwittingly, she echoed her sister's own thoughts.

"Oh Lord, I'm sorry Mom! I know you loved my father, and I'm just as sure you love Daddy Nick. And Great-Granny Morwen had two husbands too, didn't she? I don't know how I could have been so thoughtless—"

"You don't have to apologise, sweetheart. Remember what that young terror Daphne said her mother told her. 'If yer wanter know something, then yer have to ask, don'cha?' "

The cockney accent was so false coming from her mother's lips that Wenna found herself laughing.

"So why don't you tell me *why* you asked the question, darling?" Skye went on. "Or is it too personal?"

Wenna looked down at the hands clasped tightly in her lap and without thinking she opened her palm, where Harry Mack had kissed her. Her mother had always been a sympathetic and loving listener, but as yet her feelings were too private to share with anyone.

They weren't even properly formed yet. They were no more than a glimmer of warmth in her cold heart. And she was still too full of anger – about Fanny, about Austin, about how a so-called caring God could sanction all the killing and the pain that a war involved – to truly welcome them.

"It was just a hypothetical question," she fibbed. "But I should have known the answer, shouldn't I?"

And how could she possibly ask her very proper mother if it was so fickle – so *wicked* – to realise that despite all her passion for Austin, she had felt those delicious stirrings again, just thinking about Group Captain Harry Mack . . .

Skye sensed far more than her daughter guessed, but she resisted the overwhelming temptation to ask her more, and instead repeated her own question.

"So where did you go today, or is it a secret?"

"I called on Aunt Betsy," she said abruptly. "I suppose everyone knew she'd turned Killigrew House into a kind of refuge for the walking wounded after all, but I'd forgotten all about it, and it was a big surprise to me. I didn't expect to see all those servicemen there."

"It didn't upset you, did it?"

Wenna shook her head, her voice rueful now. "Between them all and Aunt Betsy, I ended up giving a performance, if you can believe it, and one of the soldiers accompanied me on a battered old piano accordion that had seen better days. Fanny would have been proud of me!"

The name slipped out of her mouth before she stopped to think, and without warning she was sobbing, and being rocked in her mother's arms as if she was a child again. Which was exactly how she felt right then, needing comfort and understanding, and getting it all in full measure.

"I'm sorry," she finally gasped. "I thought I was coming to terms with it."

"And so you are. Do you think Fanny wouldn't have wanted you to cry for her, Wenna, or to mention her name ever again? She knew your soft heart as well as any of us. And you're right. She *would* have been proud of you today . . . So when are you going back to Betsy's to do it all again?" she said calmly.

"Tomorrow," said Wenna with a gulp.

Oliver Pengelly, alias Jimmy Oliver, knew he was in his rightful element at last. He had been born to fly, he thought jubilantly, and his sharp-eyed abilities had been quickly discovered.

He had only been allowed up on practice jaunts so far, having had to fulfil the required number of flying hours before he could officially go on ops. He hadn't encountered an enemy plane in his life, and he had seen the best of it without knowing what real combat was.

He knew all that, and although some of the tales his fellow erks told him were horrific, he still longed to be up there in the thick of it all, giving Jerry what for.

He was training to be a wireless operator, and his world was peppered with an even more exaggerated vocabulary now. His chums were all good eggs, they were whack-oh and spiffing types, and everything was pip-pip or wizard prangs.

And although he was still an erk – the lowest of the low – once he had done the regulation number of practice flying hours, he'd be getting a seventy-two hour leave before going on ops. He had toyed between going home and staying around to make further progress with the pretty little NAAFI girl who had given him the glad eye. But Cornwall won. He couldn't wait for his family to see him in uniform. By now he was sure they would have forgiven him for running off the way he had.

His natural optimism bubbled to the surface every time he thought about it. It would be good to see the folks again, but even better to get back to the base. Long before Christmas he expected to become a fully-fledged member of an air crew.

It was early December before he got his leave. By then he had phoned home several times, and knew that his sister Celia was doing important war work – 'somewhere in Norfolk', of all places, he thought with a sardonic grin. So much for her penchant for travel. And Wenna had joined the ATS and was now attached to ENSA, entertaining the troops.

"Good God, if that isn't the giddy limit," he grinned at one of his pals after his last phone call home. "Wenna will be a star yet. My sisters always fall on their bloody feet."

"So do you, Jimmy-riddle," the erk jeered. "Even if we ditched our kite in the sea, I reckon you'd bounce up from the briny smelling of roses."

"More like old Neptune's barnacles, the old fart-arse," sniggered another. "So you're really going home this weekend, are you, Jimmy?" he said, ducking as Olly threw a book at him.

"I should," he said reluctantly. "I haven't seen the parents in months, but you two just remember to keep your hands and eyes off Rosie while I'm gone, d'you hear?"

"Well, we might keep our eyes off her, but we won't bargain for the hands, will we, Sparks?" the first one taunted, his words resulting in a fierce pillow-fight between the three of them in the billet.

Just like children, Olly thought, with the superiority of an eighteen-year-old, remembering the incident as the train took him westwards on that cold December morning. Just the way he and his sister had once been. Or himself and his cousins Scb and Justin. Great days. Great times.

And he was in a hell of a sloppy mood to be looking back, he told himself severely, when he had everything in the world to look forward to.

He caught the admiring look of a young woman in ATS uniform sitting opposite him in the train compartment, and gave up reminiscing and turned to more immediate matters.

By the time he left the train, he had her telephone number in his pocket and the promise of a meeting if ever their leaves coincided. He doubted he would see her again, but flirting had been fun while it lasted, and took up much of the tedious travelling time across the country. Was a seventy-two hour leave ever worth it, he found himself wondering, when half of it was taken up with getting there and getting back?

The minute he saw his parents on the station platform, he knew it was worth it. This was home, and even the *smell* of Cornwall was different to any other place on earth, he found himself thinking, much to his own surprise.

He felt a surge of affection welling up inside him such as he hadn't known in months. It was a very different kind of affection from the easy-come, easy-go kind he felt for his fellow erks and the NAAFI girls. It was a fundamental affection that filled his brain with the sense that as long as everything stayed the same here, then all was right with the world . . .

He brushed off the stupid feeling that threatened to make his eyes water in a most unmanly way, and blamed the dampness on his cheeks on the way his mother was hugging him so tightly, as if she would never let him go.

"I swear you've grown six inches, Olly," Skye said, "and you look so distinguished in your uniform!"

"Well, thank you, ma'am," he said huskily, seconds before Nick too was hugging this stranger who was their son.

But what the heck? This was wartime, when everybody hugged everybody else on railway stations. Olly gave himself up to their embraces, glad above all to be home, in a way he had never expected to be after his reckless need to leave.

But once the joy of reunion was over, there was an undoubted awkwardness between them all. It was mostly on Nick's part, still unable to fully forgive Olly for running off to enlist, while Skye overcompensated for Nick and was gushingly sweet to him in a way that both of them found completely false. Finally, Olly couldn't take it any longer.

"For pity's sake, Mother, why don't you rant and rage at me like you used to?" he finally snapped. "I can't stand much more of all this sugar and spice – in fact, a little more spice would be very welcome."

"You're right," she said solemnly. "I should treat you more like Daphne does, shouldn't I?"

He started to laugh. Daphne Hollis was still a miniature thorn in Olly's side, an irritating burr who wanted to know everything about flying, and how it felt to have your plane blown up in the sky and if it hurt to get a bullet in your guts from a German machine-gun, and if he'd jumped out with a parachute yet . . .

"She's a half-pint pain in the arse, and I don't know how you can stand her," he admitted without thinking, at which his mother rounded on him at once.

"You can just stop that smart talk while you're here, Oliver, and save it for your barrack-room friends. Lord knows Daphne and Butch know enough swear words already without your adding to them."

73

"Bleedin' 'ell, it wasn't even a swear word worth the candle," he muttered beneath his breath.

"*What* did you say?" Skye asked.

And then they were both laughing, both remembering Fanny Rosenbloom's choice phrases all too well, and each reminding the other that they were two grown-ups now, and that Olly could no longer be treated as a child. The RAF had seen to that, Skye realised with a small shock.

Olly was a man now, and all her children were in uniform. And that was shocking enough for any mother to take, when it seemed like only yesterday that they were babies.

"I'm sorry, honey. I guess I forgot who I was talking to," she said more solemnly, but with a twinkle in her eyes to remind him that she was still his mother, no matter how old, or how large, he got. She decided to change the conversation.

"In case you get stifled here with Daphne and Butch hanging on to your every word, go visit Aunt Betsy—"

"Why should I want to do that? Seb's not home, is he?"

"No, but you might want to meet some of her lodgers. Before Wenna joined up she got slightly friendly with a Group Captain in the RAF. He said he didn't know you."

"Well, he wouldn't. We don't know everybody else in the Services," Olly said uneasily. "But actually, it's time I came clean about that, Mother. I know I've only made the occasional telephone call home all these months, but I think it's time I gave you my name and number, so you can write to me."

"Well, I should think I know your name by now," Skye began with a laugh.

"No, you don't. Not my RAF name, anyway. It's James Oliver, Mom. I couldn't risk you tracing me and dragging me back home, and I discovered it was incredibly easy to rig some false papers. Sorry," he added more jerkily. "You didn't know you had a forger for a son, did you?"

She stared at him steadily, hearing his voice shake a little and seeing how the colour warmed his young face. And she knew that whatever he had done to get himself into the air force, he was still desperate for her approval.

She put her arms around him and gave him a quick hug before she let him go. Physically and metaphorically, she thought swiftly.

"None of it matters, darling, as long as I still have a son. Just come home safe and sound."

Six

"So your lot have come in at last," Nick said to Skye a week later, when the tumultuous news of the Japanese bombing of Pearl Harbor had screamed out of every wireless news bulletin and newspaper headline, and caused America and Great Britain to declare war on Japan.

"*My* lot?" she echoed, still grieving that Olly's leave had been so short, and still wondering about the right time to tell Nick of their son's ruse to evade detection, which she privately thought quite cute. She wasn't sure what Nick would think, with his lawyer's ethics. It hadn't seemed important enough at the time to spoil Olly's leave by finding out, but she knew she couldn't keep it to herself for ever.

Right now, it took a moment for her to realise what Nick was getting at. America had kept out of the war in Europe as long as possible – and rightly so, in her opinion. It hadn't been their war, but now it legitimately was.

But Skye had felt so integrated in Cornish ways for so many years now that it came as a shock to hear Nick speak so.

"You're not going to deny your own birthplace, are you?"

"No. But I'm not denying my roots, either, and they're most definitely here," she said smartly. "Anyway, since the girls here seem to think that every American comes straight out of Hollywood, it will keep them starry-eyed once they start sending troops over."

"I hope you're not implying that our own boys can't do that. Tell that to Olly."

"Actually, Nick, there's something I've been meaning to tell you about Olly," she said carefully, hoping that his mind was so full of the terrible news of the bombing of Pearl Harbor and all its implications that Olly's small deception wouldn't seem so terrible after all.

"He did *what*?" he exploded. "Of all the deceitful young pups. I've a good mind to call the War Office and get him hauled over the coals."

"Don't be ridiculous, Nick," Skye snapped. "Can't you for once admire his initiative and let it go at that? What's the point, anyway? He's over eighteen now—"

"The point is, he enlisted under false pretences, and he's living a lie in continuing with this false identity. If you don't understand the wrongdoing in all that, Skye, then I begin to wonder if I know you at all."

"After all these years of marriage?" she said, appalled to realise how very narrow-minded he was being in all this, and desperate to lighten the atmosphere between them.

"Sometimes I wonder if we ever really get to know another person properly," he said savagely. "In my profession, I see far too many people living by their wits and cunning. I simply never expected my son to be one of them."

It was on the tip of her tongue to blurt out the words she had said once before that had cut him deeply. That Oliver wasn't Nick's son at all, except by adoption.

She managed to resist the damning retort with a huge effort, and she spoke more pleadingly, swallowing her own pride in an effort to save Olly's.

"Nick, can't you see what it would do to Olly if you betrayed him over this? Couldn't you see how proud he was of his uniform when he was home? Our boy's a man now, honey, and if you take that away from him, he'll never forgive you." She paused. "And neither will I."

He didn't answer for a moment, and she could see he was struggling with the damnable conscience that made him such a good lawyer, and such a difficult father at times.

"I'll let it go for the present, while I think about it," he said at last. "But I want you to know it's for your sake as much as his. I can never sanction what he did, but I wouldn't want to see you shamed over this, Skye."

"Thank you," she said, with more humility in her voice than was her usual style. But what was the loss of a little personal pride, when Olly's future was at stake?

And underneath it all, she knew there was something else destined to keep her head held high. Unbelievably, there were still folk in the close-knit clayworking community who still thought of her as the American upstart, even though she had lived among them for more than half her life, and had shared in their war the first time around. All her children were involved in this one, and now her compatriots were in it too.

Anyway, she thought, with an immense surge of pride that was as backhanded as it was tragic – had Cornwall ever been bombed? Let anyone dare sneer at her after Pearl Harbor . . . especially the clayworkers with their closeted outlook that couldn't see a world beyond the glittering sky tips and the barren moors.

She didn't know why she thought particularly about the clayworkers at that time. Killigrew Clay had been out of their personal control for a long time now, and she had no contact with the company of Bokilly Holdings that had amalgamated the clayworks of Killigrew Clay with that of Bourne and Yelland.

Nick was still the associated company lawyer, of course, and occasionally reported talks of threatened strikes and squabbles, and the precariousness of the business as a whole, but none of that was new. It was the way it had always been.

Skye rarely visited the White Rivers Pottery nowadays, and she was sometimes alarmed at how easily her interest in it had dissipated. Once it had been all important in her life, just as the clayworks had been to her family. She must visit it again sometime, she vowed. Nick's brother Adam and her nephew Seb had bought it out, so it was still very much in the family. Butch Butcher was always asking how pots were made too, and she might take him and Daphne up there sometime.

She hadn't lost *all* interest, she told herself somewhat guiltily, and she still worked sporadically on the history of Killigrew Clay, trying not to overdo her family's involvement in it. But she felt she owed it to past generations, as well as future ones, to keep the history alive, and she sometimes regretted that she had been impetuous enough to burn all her grandmother's diaries without reading them properly.

She gave a heavy sigh, knowing it had seemed so right and so noble at the time, and in her heart she still knew it had been right. Morwen Tremayne's thoughts and dreams had been private, the way everyone's were.

They were the only truly private things a person had – and Skye knew that those had been Morwen's sentiments too. It was a pity, though, to have lost all of that. Just like Fanny Rosenbloom, who had left nothing but memories – it was as if she had never been.

Skye shivered, telling herself such a thought was nonsense. Anyway, how could Morwen Tremayne's ghost ever be destroyed completely, while the descendants who were her true legacy lived on – and while the clay was still gouged out of the earth, and the sky tips still soared like gleaming white mountains towards the sky? No matter how the world changed, some things would always remain constant, Skye told herself.

By the time Nick sought her out later her thoughts had returned to Olly. Everyone else had gone to bed long ago, but she was still restless, still full of too many perceptions she wished she could dispel. Nick wrapped his arms around her and kissed her cheek, and she leaned against him with a sigh.

"About Olly, my love," he said gently. "We'll let things remain as they are. What harm can it do, after all, and what difference will it make to the outcome of a war?"

"What difference indeed," she murmured, lifting her face for his kiss and feeling a surge of relief at his words. "I do love you, Nick."

"And I love you, my beautiful witch, in case you thought there was ever any doubt."

"I didn't," she said huskily. "So why don't we go to bed and sleep on it?"

"That wasn't quite what I had in mind," he said, his voice full of a seductive note she couldn't mistake, and didn't want to, anyway.

The news that Sebastian Tremayne's particular war was over came as a great shock to most of his family, and a huge, guilty relief to his mother.

"I just can't help it, Skye," Betsy wept over the phone. "I know you shouldn't be glad to know your son's been wounded, but they say 'tis not putting him at death's door, and at least I'll have him home again and out of harm's way. What kind of a mother could be sorry about that?"

"Nobody could condemn you for thinking that way, Betsy. It's perfectly natural," Skye soothed her. "So what exactly do they say about Sebby?"

She realised they were both speaking about him as if he was a child and had to refer to others to discuss his war wounds, but she let the thought pass. What the heck did any of that matter, as long as Sebby wasn't mortally wounded?

"They say the leg will heal in time, but the bullets severed some vital nerves, and he'll always have an acute limp. He's shell-shocked as well, so they won't let him go back to his unit at all, and they're going to keep him in this French hospital for a spell yet. Justin says we'll all have to be patient with Sebby when he comes home, as he'll probably be feeling very bitter about coming back to civvy street. But he's done his bit for King and Country, so I daresay he'll be more than glad to be out of it. Why should he be bitter?"

"Because he's a soldier, that's why," Skye told her. "And you should listen to what Justin says, Betsy. I'm sure he's seen plenty of severely injured patients who find it hard to come to terms with it. Lily and I had similar experiences with our boys in French hospitals in the last war, and it's true what Justin says. You must see some of that resentment in those who stay with you at Killigrew House, don't you?"

"Oh ah. But they're not my Sebby, are they?" she said. "He'll be glad to come home where he belongs, and I'll make sure my other boys give him the red carpet treatment."

Skye replaced the phone slowly, and immediately rang her cousin Lily.

"You've got to talk to Betsy," she said urgently. "She's got Sebby taking a starring role as a hero, which he may well deserve, but she'll drive him crazy if she doesn't let him get it all out of his system in his own time. And the other fellows are going to hate his guts before he even gets home."

"I'll do what I can, darling," Lily promised. "But Seb's made of pretty strong stuff, and from what I can gather he won't be home for a long while yet."

Right then, Sebastian Tremayne was staring at the peeling paint on the ceiling of the French hospital ward, gritting his teeth as he counted the length of time in seconds between the bouts of screaming from the bed at the end of the ward. He knew the reason for it. The soldier had had both legs amputated that morning, and had come round from the anaesthetic to the horrific discovery.

There had been no time to warn him beforehand. He had been close to death when they brought him in, and was only now learning the extent of his injuries. Seb could hear the starched swish of the nurses' uniforms as they hurried towards the soldier, pulling the curtains swiftly around the bed while they tried to comfort him.

"They're trying to shut him up so the rest of us don't know what we're in for, mate," the young man in the bed next to Seb wheezed. "Have you got a ciggy by any chance?"

"No," Sebby said. "I don't have any use for them. And neither should you if that cough's anything to go by."

The youth gave him a beatific smile, hawking and spitting into the tray balanced on his chest in the disgusting way that had continued all night long, and almost turned Sebby's gut.

"This cough, mate," he wheezed again when he could draw breath, "is the only thing telling me I'm still alive, so don't you go knocking my bloody beautiful cough. Once I croak you won't be bothered with it no more."

"You're not going to croak," Sebby snarled. "You talk too bloody much for that."

"So they tell me," the boy said with a strange sort of gurgling chuckle. And now that Sebby gave a bit more attention to it, he realised the boy's voice had begun to sound different, as if it was coming from under water. As if his entire lungs were filling up with water, or fluid, or blood . . .

Sebby hadn't taken too much notice of him until now. Listening to him all night long since he'd been brought in was bad enough. Sebby was too busy bemoaning his own fate, and the pain in his leg that was excruciating, even though they all kept telling him cheerfully that he'd live, and not to worry, soldier, and there were far worse than him . . . bloody Job's comforters, the lot of them, he thought savagely.

The boy next to him was making an odd piercing noise in his throat now, and Sebby looked at him sharply, in time to see the sudden glazing in his eyes and the gush of frothing blood and mucus that filled his chest tray and overflowed on to his bedding, forming a thick and ever-spreading stain.

"Nurse—" Sebby heard himself croaking. "Orderly – *somebody* – come quick, for God's sake—"

Nobody heard him. Nobody was near. They were all taken up with the screams of the boy who had lost his legs and badly needed sedating. And Seb could only fix his eyes in horror as the boy next to him died with a final explosive vomit.

Then his chest collapsed violently, and he seemed to dissolve into the bed. As he did so, the putrid trayful of blood and vomit slid to the floor of the ward with a clatter, the vile substance moving insidiously towards Sebby's own bed, and sliding beneath it. Near-demented, and in the throes of shameful hysteria now, Sebby watched the nightmare lava flow coming for him, from which he was never going to escape . . .

He didn't know how long it was before he felt the sharp stab of a needle in his arm. These bloody orderlies were as brutal with their injections as if they sank their fangs into their victims, he thought. But right then, he didn't care. Right then, he'd have welcomed a whole bloody armful of drugs if only they would have given it to him.

Anything but having to relive all the sights and sounds and smells – above all the *smells* – he had to endure day and night in this place out of hell.

* * *

When he came to full consciousness a long while later it was night. He struggled to remember where he was and what had been happening. The lights in the ward were dim now, and all was quiet. There was only the distant sound of gunfire to remind him that he was still somewhere in a safe zone in France and that there was a war going on. The patient in the bed next to him had been removed, and he presumed that the amputee was heavily sedated. His own pain was temporarily under control from the cocktail of drugs they had pumped into him.

As his senses revived, he realised that the ward smelled cleanly of disinfectant, and he became aware that he could feel a cool hand on his wrist. As his eyes focused properly, he saw what looked like a white halo above someone's head, and the sense of gladness that rushed through him overcame any feeling of panic. He was obviously dead. He was in some transitional no man's land before he was whisked skywards into some mythical heaven, and he was never going to feel any more pain. Nothing else mattered but that.

"Are you an angel?" he muttered, his voice slurring through lips that seemed far too large for his mouth.

He heard a soft laugh. "I've been called many things, soldier, but never an angel," the female voice told him. "My name is Colette and I'm to be your helper when you come to stay with us, while the nurses get on with their real jobs."

Seb's eyes opened more fully as he realised he was not dead after all, and that this angel with the soft French accent but excellent command of English was no angel after all. She was . . .

"Bloody hell's teeth, you're a nun," he ground out. "Oh God, I'm sorry, Sister—"

"Don't be," she said quietly. "I'm sure God won't object to a few blasphemies now and then. And I told you, my name is Colette. If we're to spend a lot of time together, I prefer that you use it. You are Sebast something – how do you say? I find it difficult to pronounce, I'm afraid."

"I'm Seb Tremayne," he managed to say after a moment when his lips wouldn't seem to work again, wondering if this was a ploy to make him say his name himself. As if she thought he was some kind of blubbering halfwit who had lost his senses as well as . . . his hand went down to the cradle over his leg.

"Is it still there?" he said hoarsely.

"Don't worry, Seb, everything is intact."

She was smiling down at him, and she truly had the face and voice of an angel, he thought. She was beautiful and serene, the way these bloody nuns always were. Nobody had a right to be that treacly, he thought mutinously, especially when their bloody calling put them out of reach of any healthy, red-blooded male who came into contact with them.

Something in her gently teasing words made him want to shock her.

"Everything? You mean you've washed me? Every bit of me? Is that part of your duties – Sister?"

She gave a small sigh. "Every bit of you, soldier. And nothing has shocked me, nor will it. So take that mocking look from your face and I'll give you a sip of water before you go back to sleep."

Well, at least he could thank God or whoever had been watching over him that she hadn't said he needn't make a fuss over such a little thing. His brief attempt to think lecherous thoughts subsided slightly as a wrenching pain shot through his leg, and he saw her reach for the jug and pour a small amount of water into a cup. She was trim in her grey habit, though he could only make a guess at what was underneath it, and he was hardly in a fit state or mood to take much interest, but the day he couldn't appreciate a pretty girl was when he'd know he was *really* dead, thought Seb, and he wasn't dead yet.

He knew she was young, and she was the best thing to happen to him since he was picked up and brought here, well away from the front line. He took the cup from her hand and took a deep draught of cold water, wondering if he dare ask for more painkillers yet.

"Slowly," she urged him, far too late.

The shock of drinking too fast on top of the sedative cocktail made him throw up at once, and he spewed all over her clean grey serge. She folded it into her as if it was of no consequence, took the cup from his shaking fingers and said she'd be back in a few moments when she had cleaned herself.

He watched her go, and felt a fierce and unreasonable rage that she could take things so calmly. He had just *spewed* all over her, for God's sake, and she was no more upset than if he had handed her a rose. If that was what nunning did to a perfectly healthy young woman, he thought aggressively, then they could stuff it.

His brief interest in her as the only decent-looking female he had seen in months was fading fast, and he turned his face into the harsh hospital pillow and returned to his anger and self-pity.

Daphne Hollis was anxious to meet the war hero in the family. She and Butch had discussed it at length.

"I ain't never met one before," she said. "Do you fink he'll have a wooden leg by the time he comes home?"

"Nah," Butch said. "They said he'll limp, that's all."

"I bet he will have a wooden leg," Daphne went on positively. "I wonder if he takes it off at night and hangs it on the bedpost like me uncle does," she added with a giggle.

"You're so stupid, Daphne," Butch said rudely. "Anyway, he's not coming home for ages yet, so you'll just have ter wait and see, won'cha?"

She glared at him. Daphne was sorely put out by the fact that her mother hadn't sent her much for Christmas, promising to come and see her in the new year if she could. And now it was nearly February, and she still hadn't had a visit, while Butch's father had turned up out of the blue and gone away just as quickly, out of his element and needing London's frenzied pace of life as much as Butch hated it.

All the talk everywhere now was of the Yanks who were being sent over here in droves, and of the increase in the rationing system. Practically nothing was going to be available, no sweets or biscuits or tinned fruit – they might as well starve to death, Daphne had announced dramatically, to Skye's amusement.

For a child of such tender years, Daphne knew what was what in the world, Skye told Nick. Butch went on blissfully in his own sweet, unacademic way, but now that he was gone thirteen and the war showed no signs of abating, they realised they might need to find some occupation for him.

The children had come a long way since their first traumatic arrivals in the community, and Skye had got far too fond of them, she sometimes thought uneasily. They were only on loan, as Daphne herself had said loftily when the little Lunn children had been whisked back to London by their mother and her gentleman friend, and never heard of again . . . and Skye didn't want to look any deeper into it than that. But then, Mrs Lunn wasn't the kind to keep in contact, and she prayed that they had all fared better than Fanny had.

Skye still thought about Fanny a great deal, especially now that they had a casualty in their own family. She couldn't really understand why Sebby had been kept in France all this time, but Betsy had been told that his shell-shock had seriously affected his mind. When his physical wounds had healed, they had taken him to a monastery where the nuns were caring for him, and someone called Sister Colette was his chief nurse.

"I bet he'll come back all churchified," Daphne observed, clearly disappointed at hearing that her hero might not be as dashing as she expected. "Nuns make yer that way, don't they, Mrs Pen? They sing all day and pray all night, and live on bread and water. Bleedin' daft, I call it."

"Daphne, I've told you before about your language," Skye said, trying hard to keep a straight face. "And with all this rationing we might all be living on bread and water soon."

"Mrs Pen, when are we going to the pottery like you promised?" Butch asked, as gloom descended on them.

"Today," she said, turning to him with relief. "We'll go today, and it will cheer us all up to have something to do."

"Oh, do I have to go?" wailed Daphne. "Cook was going to show me how to make oatcakes. I don't want ter see how ter make those bloomin' old pots."

"Then you can stay behind with Cook," Skye said, "and Butch and I will cycle up to White Rivers. We can't spare the petrol to take the car for a joyride."

"He won't mind that, Mrs Pen," Daphne said slyly. "He'll do anyfing as long as it's wiv you!"

Skye saw the painful blush creep up the boy's freckled cheeks, and to diffuse his embarrassment, she said airily that as she was acting as his mother, it was just as well, and that Daphne could learn a lesson or two from him.

They reached White Rivers after a considerable effort. The weather was usually mild in the far west of Cornwall, but even so, the wind had taken their breath away long before they reached the end of their ride, and they had been obliged to get off their bicycles and push them uphill for the last bit.

"There you are, Butch," Skye said, leaning on her handlebars and throwing one arm out expressively. "How does it feel to be on top of the world?"

He looked around him as she spoke, following her gaze over the sky tips and the scoured countryside, where the remaining pits of Killigrew Clay were now part of Bokilly Holdings. He gazed down at the clay pool, as creamy smooth as palest green milk, and listened to the whisper of gorse and bracken over the moorside. And he knew he was home. Truly home, in a place that he never wanted to leave. And because he didn't have the words to say all that his heart felt, he said the only thing that came into his head.

"It feels weird – like I should stay here for ever, Mrs Pen," he blurted out. "Like I belong. And now you'll fink I'm as daft as Daphne."

"No, I don't, Butch," she said softly, more touched than she could say. "Because I felt exactly the same way the very first time I saw this place. But we can't stand here all day like two ninnies. Let's go inside and see how to throw a pot."

They freewheeled the last hundred yards to the dip in the ground where the pottery was built, and Skye felt a burst of pride at knowing that starting this business had been her idea. It had been her choice of name too, despite her cousin Theo's derision when she had first mooted it.

She had no regrets about selling out to Adam Pengelly and Seb in later years, though, since it kept the business so very much in the family. It had been a delicious piece of continuity that very much appealed to her romantic heart.

For the first time, she wondered how Sebby was going to cope with being a partner in a business when he came home again. He was once so skilled at his wheel, but who knew how those hands might tremble now? Or how his injured leg might affect his abilities? However, those were problems for later, and she pushed them out of her mind as she saw her brother-in-law coming outside to greet her.

"Skye, by all that's holy. I haven't seen you in ages. What are you doing here? Not bringing bad news, I hope?" he said anxiously.

She shook her head at once. It was a measure of the way they all felt these days, that any unexpected visit might herald bad news.

"Not at all. Butch and I felt like some fresh air, and he'd like to watch you throwing a pot or two if you've got the time to show him, Adam."

"Plenty," he said, his voice giving away more than he intended. But they all knew that a luxury product like White Rivers pottery was of far less importance in wartime than providing the medical manufacturers with the pure white clay that the clayworks could supply. He turned to Butch.

"So you're thinking of taking up potting, are you, boy?"

"I dunno about that," Butch mumbled. "I just wanted to see how it's done."

"And then you'd like to try it," Adam finished for him.

"It was like watching fate reveal itself," Skye told Nick that evening when they had finished their evening meal. "Butch is a natural. He reminded me of the way Seb took to it – the way Tremaynes have always regarded the clay, I suspect, loving it and moulding it as if it was a living thing that required all the care in the world."

"Good God, darling, you're getting quite poetic over that sloppy stuff," Nick said, laughing at her eloquence.

She laughed back. "So I am. And where would we all be without that sloppy stuff, as you call it? If my parents hadn't gone to America and raised a family and been unable to resist passing on the old tales of Killigrew Clay, I'd never have been so fascinated that I had to come over here myself to see what it was all about. And we would never have met. Why shouldn't I be poetic about that sloppy stuff?"

He caught her in his arms, and at the fierceness of his embrace, she knew why she had fallen in love with him. And as he looked down into her luminous, beautiful blue Tremayne eyes, Nick knew why he'd been possessed by her beauty, even when he'd thought she was no more than an enchanting portrait painted by an old uncle incestuously in love with his sister. But the reality of the living, breathing woman had been so much more electrifying than a face on a painted canvas.

"God, but I love you, woman," he said huskily. "Can you possibly know how much?"

"Oh, I think I have a rough idea," she said with a catch in her voice, because such sweet moments were so rare these days, when other people demanded so much of them all.

"Then I think I should waste no more time in showing you how much. Let's—"

The scared voice floated down from the top of the stairs.

"Mrs Pen, I've wet meself. Can yer come quick?"

Skye heard Nick curse. "Christ Almighty, she's nine years old now. Can't she control herself yet?"

"She's only a child, Nick, and this only happens occasionally when something disturbs her. She heard how excited Butch was today, and how he was boasting that he'll stay here forever if his father will let him, and become a potter. I think it's unsettled Daphne."

She put her hand on his arm. "I'll see to her, and then we'll go up. I won't be long."

But by the time she had consoled the humiliated Daphne, changed her bedding and nightclothes and made her sweet again, Nick was already in bed and fast asleep.

Wenna had firmly believed she would be travelling all over the world with the ENSA concert party. She had made herself believe that, in the weirdest way, this chance that was brought about by a war was going to fulfil all of Fanny's dreams for her.

They were her dreams too, of course. She would sing in front of an enormous audience of servicemen, and among them would be all kinds of people, including agents and managers, and entrepreneurs of every kind. Surely at least one of them would see and hear the potential in Miss Penny Wood – although as an ATS private, she was known to her companions by her real name now and only used her stage name for performances.

She had been convinced that future stardom would be staring her in the face through this most unlikely of sources, perhaps on a North African makeshift stage, where even important military men might hear her; or in Egypt; or wherever the army chose to send their little concert party.

Instead of which, the reality was like a cold slap in the face. They were sent to military installations all over England and Scotland, and entertained the troops wherever there was a need for them. It wasn't exactly what Wenna had imagined, but their troupe kept being assured that these people badly needed cheering up, especially those who had been repatriated due to injuries and were waiting to be sent home.

Knowing what had happened to Sebby by now, she knew that he could well be like them, glad of a soft voice and a welcoming smile, and she swallowed her disappointment at not being sent somewhere more glamorous, and sang her heart out on every occasion.

By now she had received confirmation that Austin had indeed been killed in action, and she had wept her tears over him. Group Captain Mack had written to her several times and the letters had followed her around the country. She had answered them cautiously, knowing that the attraction between them was mutual, but still determined to hold back from becoming involved with anyone else.

"I don't understand you, Pengo," her accompanist said, using her current nickname. "The chap must be crazy over you, and you're virtually giving him the cold shoulder. It doesn't add up with the emotional way you sing those songs, kiddo."

"My songs are for every serviceman, Rita, and not for individuals," she retorted.

They were performing that evening to a group of newly-arrived American servicemen. Real GIs, Rita had told her excitedly, and there were rumours that they sometimes brought chocolates and nylon stockings with them for the girls who caught their fancy. It would be better than painting their legs with gravy browning and pencilling in a dodgy wavy line for a seam, Rita declared.

It didn't impress Wenna. She turned round from the cracked mirror in their so-called dressing room and faced her counterpart.

"You just watch that they don't want payment in kind for their nylons," she warned. "Soldiers are soldiers, wherever they come from, and you've been bitten once already."

"I never took you for a prude," Rita said, offended.

"I'm not. I just don't want any entanglements, that's all. But never mind all that. How do my lips look?"

She pursed them towards her friend. Cosmetics were in short supply now, and the NAAFI cook was being constantly persuaded to give cooked beetroot juice to the concert party girls for them to colour their lips in lieu of lipstick.

"Looks good," Rita said approvingly. "A bit of soot on your eyelashes and you'll be all set."

"I'm not going to bother. It makes my eyes sting, and I don't really need it, do I?"

Rita sighed. "You know you bloody don't. Who'd bother looking at your eyelashes when you've got those great baby blues, anyway?"

"Which Hollywood flick did you get that line out of?" Wenna said, glad that their brief spat was over.

But she felt excited too as they faced those GIs in their tailored uniforms that evening, and knew how her mother would approve of her entertaining her own countrymen as she heard their enthusiastic whistles and foot-stamping.

"They know how to let themselves go, don't they?" Rita breathed in her ear a long while later when they had all gone through their routines and the concert party had returned to their base. "One of them in the front row was definitely giving you the glad eye, Pengo, even more than the rest."

"That was hardly the glad eye. He looked as if he should still be in school."

"Don't they all?" Rita said dryly.

"Actually," Wenna said carefully, knowing the reaction she was going to get, "he sent me a note after the show—"

"*What*? What did it say? Did he ask you to meet him? You lucky stiff. I hope you ask him if he's got a friend for me."

"Now hold on a minute, Rita," Wenna said, laughing. "Actually, I think it's someone my sister once knew when she lived in New Jersey."

"My God, you people get around, don't you?"

"I told you my mother and grandfather were American, didn't I? It seems as though this young GI lives on the farm where my sister once worked. Years ago the place belonged to my grandparents, only it wasn't a farm in those days. Well, anyway, this Greg Stone knew Celia had a sister who sang a bit, and we're very much alike in looks, so he took a chance and asked if I could possibly be called Wenna."

"And you are."

"Of course I am. You know that. Anyway, I said I'd see him in the canteen tomorrow for a chat, if he was free."

"As if he wouldn't be! He's sure to bring along some of the others to meet you as well, so can I come along?"

Wenna sighed. Rita was so transparent, but she could hardly say no. And since she had absolutely nothing in common with Greg Stone, except a house in New Jersey that once belonged to her grandparents, another girl might be a useful ally if the conversation flagged.

She tried to recall what Celia had ever said about him, and came up with absolutely nothing, except that he was one of the younger siblings of the Jarvis Stone who had developed such an almighty crush on Celia at one time. The crippled Jarvis wouldn't have been able to enlist in this war, but she guessed that his brother must be about Olly's age and just about old enough to do so.

She smiled ruefully, thinking that for folk who were normally content to spend their lives working on a New Jersey fruit farm, being shipped overseas because of a war must be the strangest way of meeting people.

Seven

"You must tell him that if he's ever at a loss as to where to spend a leave, he's to come and visit with us," Skye said at once when Wenna related the incident to her over the telephone.

"His unit is being sent overseas pretty soon, Mom, though I don't know where, of course. But don't you think it was a coincidence that he should have been at the concert? He told me a lot about the farm in New Jersey, and the time when Celia was there. It was so odd, hearing him talk about the house where you were born, and finding out that he knows it so well, when I don't."

"But how lovely that he made sure you knew who he was, darling," Skye said quickly, needing to overcome an enormous bout of homesickness at that moment, such as she hadn't felt in years. "I'll remember to tell Celia the next time I hear from her. I'm sure she'll be pleased."

When the call ended, Skye put down the phone slowly. How odd it was, she thought, echoing Wenna's words, that the endless continuity in this family should stretch out beyond the bounds of land and sea, and even now, should pull the tenuous threads together.

The Stone family had nothing to do with herself, except that this young Greg Stone had been born in same house as she had. He would know and love the house in the same way she and her brother Sinclair had done. The house where her mother, Primmy, had always been at pains to instil the love of their Cornish roots in her children. The roots that had brought Skye here.

"Oh Mom," she murmured, "you would have loved all this. And so would Granny Morwen."

Even odder was the resolve she now felt to get the history of Killigrew Clay in order. There was no one else with the skill or the urge to record it all, and if she didn't do it, the intimate knowledge would end with her. She got out her bicycle and rode into Truro the very next day and went into the offices of the *Informer* newspaper.

She paused in the outer office before announcing herself. The

90

hum of activity was the same as ever, as was the smell of printer's ink, of newsprint, of bodily sweat, and the indefinable air of excitement that came with a big story.

These days, among the more homely and domestic stories, there were always national and international ones that seemed to be ever bigger, but nonetheless still had their poignant moments. And no matter how dramatic the story, David Kingsley was an expert in sorting out the wheat from the chaff, she thought.

He caught sight of her from behind his office window then, and waved to her to come inside.

"Good to see you, Skye. Tea? Coffee?" he said, as busy as ever, but newly apprised of the trend towards coffee as an occasional drink now that the Americans had infiltrated.

"Tea would be lovely, David. And so would access to the archives, if I may. I'm going to produce some of those booklets we once talked about if it kills me in the attempt. I've already made a start on the scheme, but now I want to see it finished."

She bit her lip as she spoke, as the insignificance of one tin-pot china clay business compared with the worldly state of affairs suddenly occurred to her. To her great relief, David evidently thought otherwise.

"Well, it's about time. When this damn war is over, Skye, people will be looking for ordinary pursuits again, and I've always said that visitors will discover Cornwall and want to get away from the big cities. The evacuees will have helped all that. They'll go home and tell their folks about how wonderful the countryside is, and we'll have hordes of them coming in, you'll see."

"My Lord, how prophetic you are!" she said with a laugh.

"Don't you think it will happen? I'll bet that some of these kids won't even want to go back where they came from."

"Maybe. Butch keeps saying he wants to stay for ever, anyway," she said, realising David could be right. It went with the territory, of course. Being a newspaperman meant keeping your ears to the ground to know what was going on now, and also what was likely to happen in the future.

"Show me what you've done so far," he said, when tea was brought in for them. "You've brought it with you, I take it?"

She produced the folder containing her rough outlines of the time when Hal Tremayne was Pit Captain of Number One pit at Killigrew Clay, and his wife Bess, together with all five of their children, worked for the clayworks. One of those children was Morwen, Skye's own grandmother, but apart from brief mentions of them all, she had done her best to keep the story centred on the history of the clayworks itself.

David scanned it all, and then slowly shook his head.

"You've lost nothing of your storytelling skills, Skye, but what you've overlooked is the personal touch. Because of your family name and your own involvement in the growth of the clayworks, readers will want to know far more about the people than you've detailed. They'll want to know why Morwen's brother Matt went to America and how he came to be the patriarch of a new family of Tremaynes, and how one of them – you, my love – eventually returned to Cornwall, and stayed."

"But that's exactly what I was avoiding. I thought people would be more interested in the china clay itself, and an industry that is unique to Cornwall—"

He interrupted. "You, above all people, should know that a flat account of the way a business evolved is one hundred per cent less interesting that one that has a romantic human story included in it. And what could be more romantic than the son of a clay boss marrying one of his own bal maidens and starting a dynasty? No, you should think again about this, Skye. I know your idea was to keep it as impersonal as possible, but you and I both know that a story about a woman falling for the wrong man, or any kind of scandal, will always touch readers' hearts. And you have an important artist in the family, for heaven's sake. You can't leave out a mention of Albert Tremayne."

"He had nothing to do with Killigrew Clay, except to be Morwen's adopted son."

"But think of the readership, Skye," David urged. "Albert's parents both died tragically young – Sam, Morwen's oldest brother, in an accident on the moors, and his mother from the measles. Then the generous-hearted Morwen and Ben Killigrew brought up the three orphaned children as their own – including the aforementioned Albert – until an indiscreet word from a precocious American child tore their world apart again. The child who was destined to be your father, Skye! Think how your old magazine readers would have loved reading that!"

As he unfolded the story like a romantic saga of old, her writer's mind knew only too well its appeal for readers.

"It's private," she said weakly. "It's family business – and how the blazes did you know so much about it, anyway?"

He gave a short laugh. "I'm a newshound, that's how, and I made it my business to know. I could write the story myself – but it would never have your feminine insight, nor your perceptive and heart-tugging way of writing it, and I wouldn't presume to do so."

He could see her indecision, and he was quick to take advantage of it.

"Don't decide at once. Spend an hour or so in the archives by all means, and take home any relevant copies. Then discuss it with Nick, and see what he thinks."

"It has nothing to do with Nick," she said quickly, just as he knew she would. "Whatever I decide to do, it will be my decision and no one else's."

Just like a true Tremayne woman, she couldn't help thinking, avoiding his knowing eyes. And by the time she left, armed with a pile of old newspapers to study, her plans for the booklets had taken an entirely different direction.

And although she was quite alone as she rode home through the wintry lanes to New World, she got the weird feeling that someone was hovering at her shoulder and silently approving. It was a comfortable feeling that made her smile.

"All right, Granny Morwen, you win," she murmured to the air, watching her breath leave her mouth in a soft cloud before it was borne aloft on a small, sighing breeze.

"Cor, are yer going ter write a book, Mrs Pen?" Daphne Hollis said in astonishment, gazing at Skye as if she was a creature from outer space.

"Maybe more than one, but it won't be a thick book like you read in school, Daphne. It may turn out to be two or three small booklets. They'll be a history of my family and the clayworks on the moors."

"That's not a proper book then," Daphne said scornfully. "Wiv hard covers and all that."

"Probably not," Skye said humbly, seeing how important this was to her. "Not that I ever see you reading one. Your teacher tells me you're not very interested in books."

"I am too! Me Ma gave me one once, borrered it from the penny libr'y and fergot ter take it back – so she said," she added with a grin. "It had too many big words in it though."

Her face flushed as she spoke. At nine, Daphne didn't like to be beaten in anything. Perhaps the teacher at the Truro school had mistaken Daphne's bolshie attitude, Skye thought quickly. If something didn't come easily to Daphne, she simply stiffened her aggressive little shoulders and refused to bother with it any more.

"Perhaps I could help you with that, Daphne," she said carefully. "We could read something together, if you like, and I could check your spelling with you."

"If you like," Daphne said, shrugging.

"We'll start tonight, and you can go through some of these old newspapers with me. It will make a change from reading a boring old school book," she said calmly.

Daphne's eyes sparkled. "I reckon you shoulda been a school teacher, Mrs Pen."

Or a diplomat, thought Skye.

But helping Daphne with her reading by way of the old newspaper accounts of the daily business of Killigrew Clay was going to be a twofold activity. The booklets wouldn't be written for children, but she considered that seeing everything that had happened in retrospect and through a child's eyes might help her to discard the mundane events and stick to the more emotive and important ones. Life – and war – hadn't sent Daphne Hollis here without a particular purpose after all.

British Intelligence, like God, worked in mysterious ways, Celia thought, ignoring any thought of blasphemy in the analogy. How, or why, they had chosen her for the job she was now engaged upon was beyond her, but you learned not to ask too many questions of your superiors. For one thing, you were unlikely to get any proper answers, anyway.

By the summer of 1942 she wore a khaki uniform with the honorary rank of lieutenant, though she knew she had done nothing to deserve it. She also wore a special badge on her shoulder, and had a privileged amount of petrol and a driver assigned to her if she needed to go anywhere in a staff car. They appreciated her qualities, she conceded, and she had more than proved herself with her knowledge of German patois that frequently clouded the coded messages that came across the wires regarding German military and airborne manoeuvres.

She had become friendly with her immediate boss, a more highly ranked individual called Bertram Moon who everyone called Captain Moonlight because he preferred the evening shift to any other. On one of their joint assignments, Celia dared to broach something she had been dying to ask for weeks. By now she felt she could trust him.

"Moonie," she said, with her own pet name for him, "you know I worked in Germany for a time, don't you?"

"Of course," he said, his attention still on the mass of gibberish coming through his headphones. "That's how you got this job in the first place, sweetie."

"Then you realise I must have known a lot of Germans."

"Naturally. And learned the language amazingly well, including some very juicy phrases you keep threatening to teach me," he teased. Then he saw her face. "Go on."

"I fell in love, Moonie. It was, and is, a really serious, passionate, forever kind of love, not one of those one-night things." She blushed, knowing she was laying all her cards on the table and that this kindly man could shop her in an instant if he so chose. And she would probably lose this plum job if he did.

"Go on," he repeated. "I'm listening, but if you want to stop now, you have the choice, Celia. This passionate love of your life was obviously a German."

"*Is* a German, God willing," she said desperately. "And that's what I want you to find out if you can. If you will."

She knew he had access to places and people that she didn't. Despite the importance of the work she did, she knew she was no more than a link in a chain, while Moonie had a vast number of contacts in Germany.

Spies was what they called them in all the action novels, men who risked everything to send back news of the enemy's movements, and who infiltrated the most secret places of an enemy's headquarters, feigning loyalty to both sides, until no one was quite sure to which side they truly belonged.

They were shadowy men, Celia always thought, always having to conceal their true identity and allegiance, but remarkably brave, for all that, with the proverbial nerves of steel. Why, even Captain Moonlight himself could be one of these double agents for all she knew, feeding back false information to British Intelligence, of no use whatsoever . . .

"Drink this, Celia," she heard his voice say in her ear, and she blinked, realising that she was sitting ignominiously on the floor of the operations room, and that Captain Moonlight was pushing a glass of spirits to her lips. "I don't know what the hell got into you just now but you looked as if you had seen a ghost. You passed out for a moment."

"I'm sorry," she whispered, fighting down the almost irresistible urge to fling some crude and idiomatic German phrase at him and see if he reacted in any way.

"So tell me about this man of yours," he said gently.

"I can't," she said. "I mustn't."

"You have to now. I presume he's working for them?"

"Well, shouldn't he be? He's on their side, after all. He's one of the enemy," she said, angry and frustrated at having to say it at all. "But as a matter of fact, no, he *isn't* working for them. If my information is correct, he objected strongly to the Gestapo using his home as a base, and he was interned for his trouble. That's *if* my information was correct, of course."

And now that she had said it, it sounded so thin, and from so unlikely a source. She only had a prisoner of war's vague word on it, and her cousin Ethan might even have got the name all wrong. She was a damn fool ever to have believed it at all, and in her reckless way of allowing her imagination to take over, she had endowed this nice and kindly officer by her side with the added indignity of thinking him a spy.

If it hadn't been so ludicrous, the shame of it would have made her weep. She swallowed her huge sense of disappointment and impotence.

"Why don't you start from the beginning, Celia? And by the way, you and I are on the same side, so if I can do anything to help, I will."

She knew by the steady look in his eyes then that he had read her only too well.

"We were lovers," she muttered, and if she had thought this would shock him, she was wrong again. "I loved him – *love* him – more than I ever thought I could love anyone. He was eventually going to sell his estate in Germany, and we had thoughts of moving to Switzerland to live. That was before the war came and spoiled all our plans."

"As it did for so many others," Moonie reminded her.

"Well yes, of course," she said, embarrassed. "There are many people worse off than me, I know that. My mother's friend had a Jewish husband, and he killed himself rather than face what was happening to his family and friends in Germany. And then she died in an air raid in the Blitz . . .

"Anyway," she went on painfully, "my cousins have a farm in Ireland, and some prisoners of war were sent to work there. One of them said he was a relative of Stefan von Gruber, and that he had been interned for the reason I gave you."

"Sort of like a conscientious objector, then?" Moonie said thoughtfully.

"He's no coward!" Celia exclaimed angrily. "But neither could he

– or anyone with any sensitivity – sanction the things the Gestapo were doing, even to their own people. You should know that as well as I do, Moonie."

"Calm down, Lieutenant, and get it in perspective. If your von Gruber was resistant to the Gestapo moving in and taking over his house, he as good as signed his" – he caught her agonised look and revised his words – "own sentence. Not that it was such a terrible crime, compared with others, but why wasn't he conscripted anyway?"

"He's forty-two years old," she murmured.

"And you're twenty-three."

She turned aside, her face burning. "Age has nothing to do with it, but if you're not going to help me, then say so. I'm sorry I bothered you."

He gave a lopsided grin. "My God, you've got a temper on you, haven't you? Is it a family thing, or do all Cornish women have it?"

"Tremayne women do," she whipped back, and then began to laugh as she wondered why the hell she had said it. She wasn't a Tremayne, except way, way back. Her mother had been Skye Tremayne before she married Philip Norwood, Celia's father, and later married Nick Pengelly. But who the hell was *she*, she thought, starting to feel the sense of panic again?

"It's time we took a break, and you can explain that odd remark over a cup of hot sweet tea," Captain Moonlight said briskly. "That's the correct remedy for shock, I believe."

"I'm not in shock—"

"You will be when I tell you how many strings I'm going to pull to get information about your von Gruber," he said.

Her smile was dazzling. "Oh Moonie, I love you!"

"No you don't, more's the pity. Save it for your man."

There had been a time when Killigrew Clay was one of the largest and most important clayworks in Cornwall. Its steady decline had been due partly to the constant fluctuations in the industry itself, and partly to the intrusion of two world wars. Now that it was part of the larger company known as Bokilly Holdings, and no longer a sole concern, Nick Pengelly was still legally concerned in its fortunes.

But after a lengthy and painful meeting in Bodmin with the present clay bosses and their own lawyer after the product analysis at the end of 1942, what he had to tell his wife was no more palatable to him now than if she and her rip-roaring cousin Theo Tremayne had been in complete control.

"You can't be serious, Nick," Skye said, white-faced. "Things can't really have got as bad as that?"

"I'm afraid they have, darling. Many of the younger men have joined up or been conscripted, of course, which helped to keep the company finances afloat, although Bourne and Yelland promised to keep their jobs open for them. A vain promise, as it happens. Production is very low, and the Roche pits are as good as played out of china clay. Orders have dwindled to practically nothing, and they're simply having to let men go."

"But what about the newsprint and medical contracts? I know it's a horrible thought, but wasn't this war supposed to bring new business for china clay on account of all the medical supplies that would be needed? And do you suppose Theo knew any of this when we sold out – about the Roche pits being nearly played out, I mean?" she added angrily.

"I'm sure he didn't, love. Theo was always looking to the main chance, you know that. And there was nothing underhand from Bourne and Yelland at the time. The pits have simply become exhausted."

"But we're not paupers, are we? We still have dividends coming in from the combined venture, don't we?"

"We do while the venture exists. Once it closes for good, that will be the end of it."

Skye felt her eyes blur. For all this time – a hundred traumatic years – the clayworks had been part of her family. Even after selling out, which had seemed at the time to be the biggest betrayal of all, the pits had still been there. They could still walk the moors and see the row of old cottages where Hal and Bess Tremayne had raised their five children and worked for old Charles Killigrew in the industry's heyday.

They could still see the scars of the four pits that had once comprised the proud Killigrew Clay itself. Through her own ingenuity, White Rivers Pottery had risen like a phoenix from the ashes to continue and further that name and industry.

What would happen to it all now? It was unthinkable to imagine it idle and still, with only the sky tips to remind the world of what had once been Cornwall's pride and joy.

"Darling, it's a dying industry," Nick said gently, as he registered every emotion on her ashen face.

"How many times has that been said?" she cried, with a passion worthy of her grandmother. "How can you say it now?"

"Because it's true. Bourne and Yelland are planning to close, and there's nothing we can do about it. They'll offer it for sale of course, and some other firm will snap it up at a pittance, hoping to make a go of it, but it won't last."

"Then we could buy it back, Nick! I don't care if we're in production or not. We don't need huge profits right now. We just need to keep control of it until this war is ended and we get back our European markets. I know we could do it—"

"Skye, for God's sake, be realistic. How could we possibly buy them out?"

Even though she knew he was right, and that he would put every obstacle in her way, her thoughts went off at a tangent, seeking and hovering over a new solution. A solution that seemed so daring, so grand, so impossibly forward-looking, that she knew it must work.

"They won't get much for a dying concern, will they? A pittance, you said. The cottages go with the clayworks and a couple of them are empty so they can't be many clayworkers left now. If we guaranteed to let them continue doing what work they can, it would salvage a little of their pride as well. We still need clay to supply White Rivers," she pointed out, "and I prefer to use our own clay than to buy it in from outside sources."

Nick couldn't see the sense in it, but he couldn't help but be stirred by her passion. These wild and crazy clayfolk, he thought, distancing himself from the whole lot of them – especially from the hot-headed Tremaynes.

"You're completely mad," he said finally.

"You haven't let me finish," Skye rushed on. "It's something David said—"

"What the devil does he have to do with it?" he said, jealousy of his wife's long-time admirer showing through.

Skye ignored it. "David reckons that in time Cornwall is going to become a mecca for visitors. Think about it, Nick. Once this war is over, people will want somewhere calm and peaceful to visit. They'll want the beauty of the countryside, and they'll have had enough of bomb-damaged cities and want somewhere to restore their spirits."

"And you think the sight of an old clay-pit is going to do that?" he said sceptically.

"The evacuees have already discovered Cornwall and will want to bring their families here. That's partly why I'm writing the history of the clayworks and my family – to interest those visitors who have never seen such places before. And maybe if one of those old pits was turned into a vast area where visitors could go and see just the way it was all those years before, including the old cottages – well, don't you see the potential in it? Someone else may do it if we don't."

When he didn't answer immediately, she plunged on as her imagination took hold.

"We could have my booklets for sale, and some of Uncle Albert's pictures to add more local and family interest. And if you don't think our finances will stretch to buying out Bourne and Yelland in the first place, you know I still have a collection of Uncle Albie's pictures upstairs. I'd willingly sell them to raise the money. So do you still think I'm completely mad?" she added.

It had been an inspiration to remember the legacy of Albie's pictures. Dozens of them were stacked in a locked room at New World, and those that had already been sold had always fetched a handsome price. With the proper advertising, and David's help in it all through the newspaper, it couldn't fail. Skye was sure of it.

It would *all* work. And the need to do it, to continue everything that had always been theirs, was as urgent and necessary to her as breathing.

"We'll think about it and discuss it privately later on," Nick said, as cautious as ever, as Daphne and Butch came bursting in from school with tales of how their classes were going to rehearse Christmas carols to sing at the local hospitals and for the poor soldiers at Aunt Betsy's place.

Skye felt a glow in her heart, because nothing could have told Nick more plainly how integrated these children were now, and how they would want to come back to Cornwall after the war, and bring their folks, and how successful her new venture promised to be, given half a chance.

She felt more optimistic than she had in a long time, even though her own children had left the roost, and these two had sometimes been more troublesome than she had bargained for. She thought she knew now exactly why Morwen Tremayne had opened her heart to her brother's children when he and his wife and died.

Tremayne women had a huge capacity for loving, and there was always room for more, though she had never expected these two to be the catalyst to some new challenge that would stir her imagination and keep her business brain alive. She hugged them both, ignoring their squirming, and recklessly promising them something special for tea.

"Bread and scrape, more like," Daphne observed, prosaic as ever, which made them all burst into hysterical laughter for no logical reason at all.

*   *   *

They decided to call a family council. It was only right that all members of the family should be aware of their proposals. Even in the middle of a war, domestic matters still had their place, though those who couldn't be present had to be informed by letter of what Skye Pengelly had in mind for the future.

By now Sebby had returned home to Killigrew House, and was proving as difficult as his brother Justin had predicted. He couldn't accept what had happened to him, and while his participation in the war was past, the battle within himself was far from over.

He had been driven to the pottery a few times, and had played around with the clay, but his fingers were out of touch with it, and he had flung it down in frustration when the once-skilled hands didn't do what his brain told them they should. Even Butch Butcher could do better, he thought bitterly, and was bragging to all and sundry that the minute he left school next year he was going to be apprenticed to Adam Pengelly.

It was more than likely now, since the day the billeting officer had arrived at New World to tell Butch his father had been killed in an air raid. After a wretched night of crying, Butch had emerged, red-eyed, to say that he wanted to stay here for ever now, if Mrs Pen didn't mind.

She had seen the fear in his eyes that he might be sent away, and she had taken him in her arms and said that of course he could stay. After all, where else would he go? The legalities could wait until after the war, she told Nick determinedly.

The family council consisted of Skye and Nick, Betsy and Seb Tremayne, Adam Pengelly, and Lily and David Kingsley. David wasn't strictly family, but since he was going to have more than a hand in what Skye envisaged, she insisted that he must be included. Apart from that, she had already got her own children's written approval. Justin had written to say it was all right by him whatever they did, and in any case he'd never had his brother's intense interest in china clay.

"You all know why we're here," Nick said, taking charge. "I've given you all a plan of what Skye wants to do, and I'll leave it to her to explain further."

"We'd like her to explain how she plans to raise the money," Betsy said, glancing apologetically at Skye. "I don't have no business brain, my lamb, but I know how tight things were when you and Theo decided to sell Killigrew Clay, so how come you can manage to buy it back now?"

Seb snorted. "Her family has always managed to find money

when it was needed. They never went short, sending their girls to their fancy Swiss school and sending Celia to America."

"Neither did you, Seb," his mother said, "so mind your manners and let Skye speak for herself."

He glared at them all, and Skye hoped he wasn't going to make things awkward. Then she saw how he grimaced with pain as he stretched out his leg, and she readily forgave him.

"You all know that when Uncle Albert died he left his studio and paintings to me," she said evenly, trying to ignore the little lurch of her heart at mentioning his name.

"So does that mean Lily has to sell up to fund your little scheme?" Seb jeered next. "You'd better watch out, Mother. It looks as if we might all have to move out of Killigrew House as well."

"Shut *up*, Seb, and don't be ridiculous," Skye snapped. "Nobody has to go anywhere, and if you would kindly keep your stinging remarks to yourself for a minute, I'll tell you what I have in mind. I have a large collection of Albert Tremayne's paintings still in store. They belong to me, and I have the absolute right to do what I like with them. Is anybody about to dispute that?" she said, looking directly at Seb. He pursed his lips mutinously, and said nothing.

"Then what I propose is that I sell them and put the money towards buying out Bokilly Holdings, including the old cottages. Nick has already checked that I can get it all at an acceptable price. I am not going to bother you with the details, because this will be solely my business. I'm not asking anyone for any money, and nor do I want any partners."

Her voice shook a little as she continued, because it suddenly seemed like such an enormous leap in the dark. And they could well think her a complete madwoman for even considering buying a virtually played-out clayworks.

"What I do want your approval on is this," she went on. "Once the clayworks are in my control, I propose renaming it Killigrew Clay. What do you think?"

Please approve, she begged silently. *Please say you feel as charmed by the idea of preserving our past as I do . . .*

Seb snapped, "I'm sure you and your man have already got it all sewn up between you, so if that's all we've come here for, we might as well have stayed at home."

"I think it's a simply marvellous idea, Skye," Lily said. "People are always interested in the old ways."

"Yes, but all that will have to wait until the war is over. We're hardly likely to get hundreds of visitors right now. And meanwhile, I must stress to all of you that the idea of this scheme goes no further than these four walls. The important thing is to regain control of the clayworks."

"But it's something that I'm sure the townspeople will approve of when they hear," Lily went on. "And it's good that the name of Killigrew Clay will live on after all."

"You always had a clever brain on you, Skye," Adam put in approvingly. "Anything to breathe new life into an old industry has my approval, and once Sebby gets his old skills back, I know he'll see the sense in it."

"You can speak for me as well now, can you?" his partner scowled at once. "I might have lost some of my slickness, but I can still think for myself."

"For God's sake, man," David Kingsley said angrily. "Can't you give this idea a chance?"

Seb's voice oozed sarcasm and innuendo then. "Oh well, we all know why you'd think it so wonderful, don't we?"

Skye could see that Nick was more than ready to grab him by the throat and throw him out, and before it all got completely out of hand, she rapped on the table and called the meeting to order.

"Then if we're all agreed, I intend to arrange for an art expert to put a reasonable price on the paintings before offering them at a public sale. We shall need advertising to attract people from farther away than Truro and St Austell, but I'm sure David will see to all that."

She went on before Seb could open his mouth again.

"So I can now tell you that I have made a nominal bid for Bokilly Holdings, subject to our approval here today, and Nick says it will be held as a true and faithful offer until the sale of the paintings goes through."

"See?" Seb burst out. "It's just as I said. It was all cut and dried before we even came here."

"And it's just as my girls always used to say, Sebby Tremayne. You were a prize pig when you were a child, and you're an even bigger pig now – oink oink," Skye flashed back at him, so fast and so unexpectedly, even to herself, that his eyes almost popped out of their sockets.

Then she saw his slow grin and heard his grudging hand-clap, and she was suddenly laughing back, and the atmosphere in the room palpably changed.

"Come on Sebby, let's get home while we'm all in a good mood for once," Betsy said comfortably, and as they got to their feet, Adam called them back.

"Come up to the pottery again soon, Seb. I could do with you to show Butch a thing or two at weekends."

Skye held her breath, wondering if this was going to light the tinderbox again. But to her surprise, Seb shrugged and said he'd think about it.

"Why not?" he added, with a spark of his old arrogance. "If the master can't teach the pupil how to throw a pot, it's a poor do. I daresay I'm still good for something."

Eight

The plans weren't the kind that could be settled quickly, and another Christmas had come and gone before negotiations with Bourne and Yelland could be properly concluded. To Skye's regret, none of her own brood had got Christmas leave, and the house would have seemed appallingly empty but for the noisy evacuees, who definitely filled a void, she thought guiltily.

But by now, thinking ahead to the way the clayworks might one day be given a different face for future generations to enjoy, Skye was filled with an energy she hadn't felt in years. No other company had shown the slightest interest in buying out Bokilly Holdings, since all were feeling the same pinch with the closing of foreign markets and the fall in prices for china clay.

In the end, the growth of the amalgamated company had been its downfall, since they were unable to provide enough work now for the numbers of clayworkers needed to keep them in production. And pittance though the sale price was – in terms of the vast turnover of the business in other years – to find the necessary funds, Skye knew she couldn't put off sorting through Albert's paintings any longer.

The room where they had been stored since they had been bequeathed to her and brought from his old Truro studio to New World had been locked and out of bounds for many reasons – not least because Skye knew that once she saw the many beautiful images of her mother, she would be reminded again of the creepy and possessive love Primmy's brother had felt for her.

Seeing the pictures would unleash the memory of the unfulfilled love that Skye had felt in her soul was slowly and incestuously being transmitted to herself, because of her uncanny likeness to Albert's sister.

It was an obsessive love that had saddened Skye even while it repelled her. Sometimes she even thought keenly that this much-admired family beauty and likeness was more of a curse than a blessing.

But if her visionary project was to go ahead, there was no help for it, she told herself briskly. She had arranged for an art expert to come to the house in early February, with the sale already being advertised for the end of March. Bourne and Yelland had agreed that they would dispose of the spring dispatches of clay and then the transaction would go through.

And before any of that happened, the paintings needed to be aired and properly displayed for the art expert's assessment and costing.

"You can't put it off any longer, darling," Nick told her, knowing her reluctance to even enter the room.

"I know. It's just that so much of my life is bound up in that room and those paintings."

"It's not *your* life, Skye. Whatever life Albert and Primmy led, it was theirs. It belonged to them and not to you. You have to believe that and let it go. We've discussed this a million times, and I can't believe it's been festering inside you all these years."

"I can't believe it either," she murmured. "I never expected to be still so affected after all this time."

She shivered, wondering if you could ever really rid yourself of the past, or if aspects of it would always be there to haunt you when you least expected it.

"I know I'm being an idiot," she went on slowly. "So I'm going to go up to that room right now and unlock the door. And then I'm going to go inside and dispel those ghosts for ever. And I'll take a duster with me," she added practically.

"Shall I come with you?"

"No thank you. When were you ever interested in dusting?"

She gave him a half smile and headed for the stairs before she lost her nerve completely. It was only a room, for God's sake.

Only a roomful of memories . . .

The stuffiness inside hit her the moment she entered the room. It smelled old and musty, almost choking her, and for a moment her heart balked, because it was so much like Uncle Albie's studio had been when they had finally had to clear it out after he died. It was almost as if he was still *here* . . .

She forced the windows open, their hinges stiff with disuse, and let in the cool February air. She leaned against the windowsill, pressing herself against it without realising that she did so, facing the sheet-covered groups of paintings that were stacked like shrouded ghosts around the room.

One step at a time, she told herself shakily. *Uncover them slowly, just one at a time . . .*

"What yer doin' up there, Mrs Pen?" she heard Daphne's raucous voice yelling up the stairs, making her jump, making her feel sick at the unexpected sound of another voice.

Skye tried to call back at her to stay downstairs, but the words didn't come out, and the next minute Daphne's footsteps were inside the room, followed by Butch's much heavier ones. The children stood, goggle-eyed and saying nothing for a moment.

"Bleedin' 'ell," exclaimed Daphne, predictably. "Did somebody die in 'ere?"

"Shut up," said Butch, nudging her violently. "Can't yer see Mrs Pen's upset about somefing?"

"No, I'm not," Skye said, automatically reassuring them as she had done for so long. "I just have to sort out these paintings. I told you about them."

"You didn't tell us they was 'ere," Daphne complained. "You said they was going ter be in some sale. Can we 'ave a look then?"

Before Skye could stop her, she had lifted one of the dust sheets and pulled it away from the stack of paintings. She stared at it, not saying anything for a moment, while Butch simply gaped.

"Christ-church," he finally said, awestruck, and forgetting how he tried very hard not to swear in front of his idol. "Is that you, Mrs Pen?"

"What do you think?" she asked in a cracked voice. "Do you think it's me, Daphne?"

"Nah," the girl said. "It's somebody else who looks like you, but it ain't you."

"Why not?" Skye said, surprised at her perception. She looked at her mother's image fully now.

Primrose Tremayne had been so beautiful, in an ethereal, yet utterly bohemian and free-spirited way that had captured more than one man's heart, as Skye well knew. They had always been compared as mirror images of one another, and Wenna in particular had inherited all the Tremayne looks too, so what was it that this streetwise child saw that wasn't evident to other people? The need to know overtook all other emotions.

"She's dead, and you're alive," Daphne said positively, after a few moments of cocking her head on one side like an inquisitive little bird. "This one ain't lived 'ere wiv us, has she? She looks diff'rent, like somebody from a long time ago, and – well, she just ain't you. She's that lady in the picture in the drawing room, ain't she?"

"She *looks* like you," Butch said hastily. "But you're prettier," he added, with an enormous blush reddening his cheeks, at which Daphne hooted with laughter.

It was a sound that was out of place in here, thought Skye angrily. This room was a reverent place, a sacred place, dedicated to the memory of her mother and another lifetime.

And just as instantly, she knew how ludicrous she was being. It was just a room that needed airing, and which needed to be sorted out for the sale of her uncle's paintings. The memories would still be in her heart, and they didn't need this stuffy mausoleum of a room to keep them safe.

"Now you're both here, you can help me," she said, after drawing a deep, steadying breath. "We need to uncover the paintings carefully, so mind you don't scratch any of them. Then we need to arrange them so that the expert can see them all and say how much he thinks they're worth."

"I bet it'll be a lot," Daphne said sagely. "Pounds and pounds, I'll bet."

"Even more than a hundred," Butch echoed, at which Daphne hooted again and told him he was dafter than usual if he thought a few old paintings could be worth so much.

Skye was staggered when the art expert told her how much he thought the paintings should fetch. Albert Tremayne's work had grown in value since he died, and the fact that much of his work portrayed the same woman only added to its appeal to collectors.

Primrose Tremayne's beauty had an air of mystery about it, and she had obviously meant a great deal to the artist. The art expert said as much to Skye, and then paused, as if hoping to hear more – but he waited in vain. Just how much Primmy had meant to Albert was a secret that she might guess at, but that no one else would ever know, Skye vowed.

"Don't underestimate the worth of these paintings, Mrs Pengelly," he went on. "In fact, a provincial town is hardly the best place to stage such an important sale."

"You're probably right, Mr Hatch," she replied, "but I don't think that showing them in some London gallery is advisable in these hazardous days, do you?"

He gave a slight smile. "I assure you that not all of London has shut down because Mr Hitler sends over his regular messengers of death," he said delicately. "And the city is quickly recovering from the darkest days of the Blitz."

"All the same, the sale will take place in Truro," she said quickly, not wanting to be reminded of that time, and finding herself beginning to loathe the oily man. "Truro is where my uncle lived and worked, and if people wish to attend the sale, they must come here."

"As you wish, dear lady," he said with a small stiff bow. "Then, when it is all arranged, if you will allow me to have the full details I will gladly distribute them to collectors outside the area who would be interested."

"Thank you," said Skye. "I'll see that you're informed."

She couldn't wait for him to leave, and she told Nick vehemently that she had no intention of advising him of the sale, and that she hoped the paintings would all stay in Cornwall where they belonged.

"That would be very short-sighted of you, darling," he said, to her surprise. "You want to sell the paintings, and he'll know where to find the keenest buyers. You can't afford to be sentimental over this, Skye."

"I'm not—"

"So you would prefer all the best families in the area to buy one of your mother's portraits as a collector's item, and risk seeing them every time we're invited out to tea?"

"You're exaggerating, aren't you? When do we get invited out to tea by all the best families?"

But she knew she was going to cave in. What he said made sense. She had her own paintings of her mother, and they were her own choice, and very different from the stack of them they had discovered long ago in the late Albert Tremayne's studio.

She had shut those paintings out of her life for so long, and until that moment she had never fully realised that the reason for it was because she couldn't bear to see the variety of expressions Albert had drawn out of his sister.

Whether or not Primmy had truly known he was in love with her, somehow Albert had dragged every ounce of sensuality out of her to put on to canvas. In his own twisted way, he had manipulated her for his own lecherous needs, and Skye knew she never wanted to see those paintings again.

But did she really want other people to see them too, and forever speculate about the artist and the sitter?

"Nick, tell me honestly. What do you see when you look at those portraits?"

She was desperate to know, and afraid to hear the answer.

"I see a lovely woman, of course."

"And nothing more? No – I can't find the word I'm looking for. No concubine – or – or—?"

"Darling, all I see is a woman who was painted many times by the

109

artist who happened to be her brother, and found himself a ready sitter. The fact that there are so many of them and that he's captured her in so many moods is the only thing that makes it intriguing."

She had to believe it. *Had* to believe it, otherwise she would feel she was exposing her own mother to whispers and gossip. And it wasn't the first sale of Albert's work. They had gone through this before, and to her knowledge there had been no questions in people's minds. She was letting this whole thing get out of proportion, and it was time to stop.

She needed money, and her uncle's paintings gave her the means to find it. End of problem.

There was no doubt that the first few months of 1943 saw the start of new hope in everyone's mind that the war was being turned in the Allies' favour. The Germans had surrendered to the Red Army in Stalingrad; Berlin had been bombed in daylight for the first time, proving that the RAF could penetrate deep into the enemy's heartland; American troops were driving back Rommel's forces in Tunisia, and Prime Minister Churchill announced that the sound of church bells could be resumed around the country now that the fear of invasion was past.

In early April, Wenna Pengelly's friend and pianist sought her out in their ENSA practice room.

"Have you heard the latest, Pengo? We're detailed to perform at an American army base next weekend. The GIs need a bit of cheering up, being so far from home," she said gleefully, "and I reckon we're just the gals to do it."

"You would think so," Wenna said. "And no, I hadn't heard. Where is this base?"

"Oh, I don't know. Somewhere in Wiltshire, I think—"

"Really? My brother used to be stationed in Wiltshire, but I don't know where he is now. I haven't heard from him in ages. I wonder if his unit will be invited as well?"

"They usually bring in all and sundry – including local girls, more's the pity. I know you're partial to these RAF bods, but they can't hold a candle to the Yanks. There's going to be a dance later on in the canteen," she added.

"You be careful, Rita. You know what I mean."

The other girl giggled, tossing back her fair hair.

"I know, but heck, there's a war on. We might all be dead tomorrow, so if you can't be good, be careful!"

Wenna had to smile. Whatever happened, nothing was going to

get Rita down. She seized any opportunity for fun, and sometimes Wenna wished she could be more like her. If she was, she might not have snubbed Group Captain Harry Mack quite so obviously. She hadn't heard from him in a long while either, but then she hadn't even answered his last letter, simply because it had got over-familiar and frightened her off.

After what had happened to Fanny and then Austin, and knowing how difficult a time her cousin Seb was having getting used to civvy street again, she had no intention of getting involved with anyone.

There was a war on, but that didn't mean you had to seize every moment with reckless abandon. It was what many girls did, and a lot of trouble it got some of them into. One of their own section had been ignominiously dismissed through having got into trouble with a sailor.

She sighed with irritation at her own thoughts, knowing how pompous they were. What right did she have to think herself above everybody else, when she knew she would be no different from the next girl if the right man came along?

That was the trouble. She had a soft heart, and she knew she could easily fall in love again, if she wasn't careful. She had fallen for Austin, giving him her heart, and more – and she could just as easily have fallen for Harry Mack . . .

"Are you decidin' whether or not you're going to let your hair down at the dance, Pengo?" she heard Rita say slyly.

Wenna laughed. "There's not much of it left to let down now, is there?" she said, deliberately misinterpreting, and patting the sleek new cut she had chosen to go beneath her service cap, with the dark fringe almost meeting her finely-arched eyebrows. It changed her appearance, and on anyone else it might have been almost mannish. On Wenna Pengelly, alias Miss Penny Wood, songstress, it was piquant and stunning.

"Anyway, I thought you'd hooked one of these Yanks, as you called it," Wenna said with a grin, "so you shouldn't be looking for another one so soon."

'Why not?" Rita said lazily. "There's safety in numbers. And you can stop nursemaiding me. He showed me this little instruction booklet they've all been given. It's a scream."

"As long as that's all he showed you," Wenna said.

"Do you want to hear some of these bally instructions or not?" Rita said, ignoring her.

"Oh, go on then."

111

Rita recited them so clearly, it was obvious that she and her Yank had studied them and found them hilarious.

"It says that the GIs can make many boners in British eyes – that's *mistakes* to you, Pengo – and that it isn't a good idea to say 'bloody' in mixed company," she gave a snort of laughter, "and that if you say 'I look like a bum' the British will think you're looking at your own backside."

"Rita, you're making this up!" Wenna exclaimed.

"I am not, I swear! A couple of the other instructions creased me up too. "If you're invited to eat with a family, don't eat too much or you may eat all their weekly rations—"

"Well, that makes sense."

"We're also supposed to be more orderly at football and cricket matches. The GIs are told that the men will be generous and shout out "good try" even if they louse things up. Oh, and they must never criticise the King or Queen, or tell us that the Americans won the last war, or mention war debts—" She was laughing so hard now, she couldn't go on.

"Would any of them really bother about such things?" Wenna said in amazement, remembering the happy-go-lucky audiences at several previous concerts when the GIs had just wanted to talk about home, or show pictures of their girl friends, or find out if the British girls wanted any chocolate or nylons or anything else that was in short supply here.

"Dunno. The ones we've met so far have been extra polite, and I like being called 'ma'am', don't you?"

'Well, it's better than some other things I could mention. Anyway, hadn't we better go through some of our numbers for the next show?" Wenna said pointedly.

By now, London had reasserted itself following the end of the Blitz, the dwindling of enemy air raids over the capital to little more than reconnaisance raids, and the advent of the flood of glamorous American servicemen into Britain.

Seeing the breezy GIs with their smooth, tailored uniforms and money to spend, and joining in the growing sense that victory might not be so far off now, others surged back to the once beleagured city to join in the almost reckless enjoyment, eager to laugh at anything and thumb their noses at old Hitler. The warning phrase "the calm before the storm" was pushed aside in the new air of confidence that all would be over soon.

'Make do and mend' might be the stern instruction from the

government, and utility garments might be the order of the day now, with home-sewn undergarments made out of scraps of parachute silk, but there was a longing for freedom and life after darkness that wouldn't be denied. *Gone with the Wind* had been showing at the Ritz Cinema for four years, and attracted far more people than Pathe News. Life went on.

'Why don't we go down to London one Sunday?' Rita asked Wenna, when the concert and dance at the US base was over, and they had jitterbugged the night away and were still too keyed-up to sleep. Rita's Yank and his friends had related all that went on in the city and filled her with restlessness.

She turned her head towards Wenna when she didn't answer. 'Well, what do you say? We could get to London and back easily enough. You used to live there, didn't you?"

'Yes,' Wenna said tersely. "And I don't want to go back."

'Why not? There aren't any air raids now."

They had both flopped down on their bunks in the billet after the vigorous evening, not even having undressed yet. Now Rita leaned up on one elbow, kicking off her shoes to ease her throbbing feet.

"Did something bad happen while you were there?" she persisted. "You never talk about it."

"I don't want to talk about it now, either."

"Why don't you? You don't have anything to hide, do you? Not you of all people!"

"Of course not," Wenna snapped, all her nerves on edge now. "You're so shallow, Rita. All you think about is enjoying yourself. You never think what terrible experiences other people might have gone through."

"Hey, I'm in this war as well, you know," Rita said resentfully. "Go on, then. What terrible experiences have you gone through, with your posh family house in Cornwall and your Swiss finishing school and your lawyer Dad!"

Her inverted snobbery made it all sound like less than nothing, thought Wenna furiously. Instead of which, it had all made her what she was – and proud of it.

"If you must know, for months I spent every night in a London Underground, sheltering from the air raids, and trying to help keep up everyone's morale by leading the singing," she snapped. "I'm no Vera Lynn, but it seemed to help. Anyway, one night after the All Clear I left the Underground to go and search for the woman who was my boss and my friend, and there was nothing left of her or the nightclub or the street where we lived. There was just rubble and dust and the stench of burning flesh everywhere. Is that terrible enough for you?"

"*Christ*, Pengo, why didn't you tell me any of this before?" Rita said in a hushed voice.

"Because it was none of your business. Because it hurts like hell to talk about it or even think about it, even now. And that's why I don't want to go to London ever again."

"Well, that's just why you *should* go," Rita said. "You'll never get over it properly unless you do. What kind of woman was this friend, then?"

"I told you, I don't want to talk about it."

Rita said nothing, and when the silence became too oppressive to bear, and the images of Fanny were all too vivid in her head, Wenna gave a small sigh.

"She was flamboyant and brash and swore like a trooper, but she was the kindest, most big-hearted woman I ever knew. I loved her, and she loved me like her daughter, and I was bereft when she died, because it wasn't her time. I never had the chance to say goodbye and there was nothing left of her to bury. Her whole life – everything – all blown to pieces, unfinished," she said bitterly. "Now do you understand?"

"I daresay the street's still there," Rita said. "So let's get some flowers and say a few words over the place. I don't believe in all that church stuff, but if it'll make you think she's resting in peace, then let's do it."

"What good will that do?" Wenna said.

"What harm will it do?"

Wenna didn't speak for a long while and for once Rita had the gumption to let her mull it all over.

"I suppose my mother would approve," she said finally. "Fanny was her friend long before she was mine."

"That settles it then," said Rita. "We'll make our pilgrimage to Fanny's place on Sunday, and then we'll go and whoop it up in Leicester Square. That's where everyone hangs out nowadays," she said knowledgeably.

Wenna knew it had been the right thing to do, no matter how hard it had seemed at the time, when she received Skye's emotional reply to the letter telling her about it. She scanned her mother's words quickly.

114

It was a wonderful gesture, darling, and in a strange way it will
have helped you to revisit the place you and Fanny both loved.
I'm sure it put some sad ghosts to rest. Your friend Rita is a
very wise young woman.

It wasn't quite how Wenna would have described her, remembering
how the glamorous Yanks in the Square had plied them with drinks
and chocolates before they returned to their billet. Rita had got
quite squiffy, and in daylight too. But it had also been a headier day
than she had thought, and Rita and her mother had been quite right.
In a very sad and loving way, it *had* laid a ghost to see the now
flattened street where she had once known such happiness. She had
placed her flowers there as reverently as if they truly marked
Fanny's grave.

She blinked back the tears and carried on reading the newsier part
of her mother's letter.

"You would have been surprised at the numbers of people who
turned up for the sale of Uncle Albert's paintings, and the prices
they fetched! I'm sure he would have been amazed to know he was
so well thought of, all these years later. You might even see one of
them turning up in some London art gallery, since I've no idea who
some of the buyers were."

Wenna doubted that she would, since she wasn't in the least
interested in touring art galleries. But she was pleased for her
mother, and with the news that the purchase of the one-time Bokilly
Holdings had gone ahead. It had been officially renamed Killigrew
Clay, even though production was virtually confined to supplying
the pottery now, and any post-war plans for the clayworks were to
be kept strictly private for the time being.

"I heard from Celia yesterday," Skye continued in her letter. "She
doesn't sound too well, and had a dreadful bout of flu recently, but
she refused to come home to recuperate. She takes her job so
seriously – to her credit, of course."

Wenna studied those last words. The innocent comments made
her feel less than adequate. Her sister was engaged on important
work for British Intelligence; her brother was now a wireless
operator in Bomber Command; her cousin Seb had been honourably discharged after being wounded in action; and Justin was a
field doctor 'somewhere in France'. She was just a singer in an ATS
concert party who couldn't ever compete with the popularity of
Gracie Fields or Vera Lynn or George Formby.

For all the glamour of her one-time blossoming career, it seemed to be going nowhere very fast now, and sometimes she envied Celia very much for having such purpose in her life.

Wenna wouldn't have been so envious if she could have seen her sister that evening. Celia had fallen in love with Norwich, much to her surprise. It wasn't a large enough town to be pompous, nor small enough to be full of busybodies. In many ways it reminded her of Truro, and it was that very similarity that sometimes made her heart ache for the security of times past and the uncertainty of the future.

But she loved her job. It was intriguing, exciting, and sometimes hugely frustrating when the supposedly important coded messages turned out to be nonsense. At other times, when her expertise helped to thwart some enemy attack by providing their own lads with some prior information, it was more rewarding than anything she could have imagined.

There were also times when she wondered just where it was all leading. The war reports these days led them to believe that victory was just around the corner. Hitler was being defeated. The Japanese weren't getting things all their own way, and the Allied troops had become a mighty force with the Americans behind them now.

One day, all this would be over, and as the song said, 'there'll be love and laughter and peace ever after'.

But not for me, she sometimes thought, in her gloomier moods. *Not for Stefan and me . . .*

She shuddered in the cool of the evening air, and pulled her jacket more firmly around her shoulders. The city was as dark as always, the black-outs in every building firmly in place now, the few cars that were in the streets with their headlamps shrouded and dimmed. Overhead the sky was overcast, with only a few breaks in the clouds to show that stars still shone in the heavens. *Their* star was still there, Celia thought fervently. Even when it was temporarily hidden from view by clouds and rain, it still remained, as constant as their love. Nothing could kill a star . . .

Her shoulders drooped as she leaned on the railings of a narrow bridge, looking down into a stream where her own reflection was no more than a shadow. Wondering, not for the first time, if she was holding on to a dream that was over. Because for all Captain Moonlight's endeavours to find out more about Stefan's whereabouts nothing had come to light.

It was as if he had simply disappeared, as so many others had done. Celia tried very hard not to let her imagination tell her what that might mean in these evil days of reprisals and death for such slender crimes.

She didn't dare think about the future any more either. They had once envisaged such a bright tomorrow, but in her heart she had already begun to wonder if it would ever happen.

Even if they both survived this war, what did the future hold for them? Could Stefan return to his home, or even want to, knowing it had been violated by a regime he despised? Could she go back to Germany to work among people who would have been so recently her enemies? And how could Stefan go to Cornwall to be with her, when *he* would still be regarded as the enemy in many quarters? Old hates weren't dispelled in a day or a year. She shuddered, wondering how he would view her part in decoding his country's wartime activities.

Long before this war began, their dream had been to start a new life in Switzerland, in the place where they first met, near the beautiful Alpine village of Gstaad. It was still her dream, but how fragile it seemed now, without the touch of his hand, or the whisper of her name on his lips, or any communication at all to tell her if he was alive or dead . . .

"I thought it was your delightful shape I could see," she heard a voice say, and her reflection in the stream was joined by another, more solid one. She swallowed the lump in her throat, knowing who it was without turning around.

"Do you think I'm a completely hopeless case, Moonie?" she said sadly. "I know you've already pulled far more strings than you should on my account, and if you can't trace him, I begin to wonder if anybody can."

"Now just you stop talking that way, Lieutenant," he said briskly. "I haven't exhausted all avenues yet, and even if I had, you needn't think the worst. Never give up hope is my motto, and since you look as if a bit of cheering up is in order, and the wind's getting up, I suggest we repair to the local hostelry and drown our sorrows in whatever watery grog they call beer these days. Sometimes I swear it comes straight out of the North Sea instead of from our fine Kentish hops."

Celia began to laugh. "Oh Moonie, you do me good."

"All part of the service, ma'am," he said, in a pseudo-American voice.

He held out his arm and she tucked her hand in it. He was her superior, but he looked after her like a Dutch uncle, she thought affectionately, and with no ulterior motive. He was right about the wind getting up, she thought. It was time to move on before she got thoroughly chilled. She glanced up at the sky where the clouds were scudding faster now, and her heart stopped for a moment as she saw her bright star shining steadily through the gap before they covered it once more.

With rationing extending to every commodity now, the local hostelries had a shortage of beverages. Spirits were limited to two drinks per customer, but there was always plenty of beer available to satisfy the many servicemen and women from the nearby camps.

They had to provide something, Moonie observed, if they were to keep open at all, and it was best not ask where they got their supplies for customers who were specially favoured. The black market could supply anything these days, and it seemed that everyone knew someone who could get something . . .

Celia made do with a glass of the wishy-washy drink that passed for beer. She didn't particularly like the taste at the best of times, and this weak variety suited her palate well enough. Moonie bemoaned the fact that the only decent brandy around these days was for emergency purposes only, and she asked him smartly if he'd like her to faint again so he could get them both a swig or two.

"I think I'll survive without that," he grinned at her. "But I'm glad to see you've recovered your spirits anyway, no pun intended!"

"None registered," she grinned back.

Someone had begun to thump out a tune on the pub's battered piano, and a group of squaddies had crowded around it and begun belting out the words of 'This is the army, Mr Jones'.

Moonie nodded his head slightly towards a noisy group of RAF personnel who were hogging a far corner of the public house. The services tended to stay in their own groups unless a fight broke out between them, which wasn't unheard of.

"Friend of yours?" he asked. "He keeps looking your way. The RAF bloke over there, I mean."

Celia's heart leapt with excitement. Olly! It had to be Olly . . . Her pleasure faded when she looked across the smoke-filled room into a ruggedly handsome face she had never seen in her life before. It certainly wasn't her brother; this man was an officer, hob-nobbing with a couple of fellow officers and some lower ranks.

"I've never seen him before," she said, abruptly.

"Well, he seems to think he knows you," Moonie said. "He's coming over."

Celia was aware of the man weaving his way through the crowded groups, and deliberately turned away. She wasn't an unaccompanied female, and she wasn't looking for company apart from the safety of Moonie's. But she sensed that the officer was standing nearby, and then she heard his voice.

"Pardon me for intruding, but you are Miss Pengelly, aren't you? No one else could look so much like Wenna unless she was her sister."

Hearing Wenna's name unexpectedly made Celia's head jerk around so fast she felt her neck crick.

"You know her?" she asked stupidly.

"May I join you?" the officer said after a brief nod, taking charge so effortlessly it was like poetry in motion, she thought, as he dragged a stool from nowhere and perched on it, his tall frame fitting it awkwardly. Now that Celia looked at him properly, she could see the scar running down his cheek, and registered his accent. He might wear a RAF uniform, and from his wings she could see that he was a pilot, but she knew by his accent that he wasn't British.

"Please forgive this intrusion, but won't you put me out of my misery?" he went on with a smile that would charm the sparrows from the sky. "I spent some time recuperating at a house in Truro, and a young lady called Wenna Pengelly came and sang to we poor wounded mortals. You look so much like her I thought for a moment you must be her, until I remembered hearing that she had a sister."

"Wenna sang at Aunt Betsy's?" Celia echoed before she could stop herself, beginning to feel like a parrot.

Harry Mack smiled in relief and spoke with a hint of triumph in his voice. "Thank God it is you. I began to think I was going crazy and seeing double. Look here, may I get you and your companion something more interesting to drink? I might be able to persuade the landlord to rustle up a bottle of red wine. He owes me a favour or two."

Celia gaped. Red wine was for Continentals, she thought irrationally, and nobody persuaded this landlord to do anything, as far as she knew, but moments later the officer came back to the table with a bottle and three glasses.

"I'm impressed," she said. "But you may have a riot on your hands if you're so privileged."

Why should he be, she thought resentfully, just because he wore a Group Captain's uniform and had what she had now deduced was a slick Canadian accent? She felt her hackles rising, whatever the hell they were, at the thought that he might think her an easy pick-up just because she was here in a pub with a man old enough to be her father.

"It's all right," he said. "They know me here, and Wally's henchmen will keep us from being lynched. I know this is an imposition, Miss Pengelly, but can you tell me what's happened to Wenna? I've tried desperately to keep in touch but she doesn't answer any of my letters. Do you have an address for her, by any chance?"

He was slick all right. But slick with a desperation in his eyes that she recognised all too well, because it echoed the way she so longed for news of Stefan. Just to know that he was alive and still thought of her and wanted her.

It stuck out a mile that this man was in love with Wenna, and that was the only reason he had sought her out. When she didn't answer immediately, he went on rapidly.

"I'm sorry. I can see that I've embarrassed you. But we're leaving here in a few days. Obviously I can't say where we're going, so if you would please just let Wenna know that Harry Mack was asking after her, I'd be very obliged."

He stood up to go, and she nodded at once.

"I'll be sure to do that, Group Captain—"

Her voice was drowned then as the raucous singing in the bar grew louder, and he smiled down at her.

"Thanks. And please finish the wine with my compliments."

He saluted them both, then walked swiftly away to rejoin his companions. Celia turned to Moonie with wide eyes.

"Well, what do you make of all that? It seems my sister made a conquest whether she wanted to or not!"

Nine

By the middle of May the whole country was in a state of intense excitement as news of the Dambuster raids in Germany became the main topic in every newspaper and every wireless broadcast. Led by the fearless Wing Commander Guy Gibson, the bombers of 617 Squadron had breached the huge defences with their new bouncing bombs that had skimmed the surface of the water and then exploded at the foot of two major German dams.

Walls of water had burst through, flooding the valleys of the Ruhr and Eder rivers, destroying a vital power station, causing massive damage to coalworks, ironworks and railways, crashing through the industrial city of Dortmund, and causing thousands of people to flee their homes.

"They were the lucky ones," Nick said grimly to his wife. "The poor devils who thought they were safe in their air raid shelters stood no chance at all. I know they're our enemies, but most of them were probably ordinary people like us, going about their daily business. That's the hellish side of war. We're all puppets in the hands of overlords."

As she was normally the one to show such compassion, Skye was touched by his words. But she had other things on her mind as she read the later reports in the newspapers.

"How quickly they gloss over the fact that eight Lancaster bombers were lost in the raid," she said. "They treat us like children, keeping the grim details from us. The young men in those planes won't be coming home—"

He broke in. "Stop it. I know where your thoughts are going, but we don't even know if Olly was flying Lancasters."

"We don't know that he wasn't, either," she retorted. "We don't know anything, do we? He never writes, and we might as well be on the moon for all the real information we get."

"Would you rather be in London?"

Skye flinched. "I would not," she said.

The news that Wenna and her friend had gone to London and

revisited what had once been the Flamingo Club had touched her at the time. Now, she could only think what danger they might have been in. The German bombardment of the capital might have stopped and moved to other vulnerable cities, but occasionally there were horrific tales of undetonated bombs in burnt-out buildings suddenly exploding and causing untold injuries and deaths to unsuspecting victims.

There was a tale of one such bomb being found beneath a family's doorstep in Notting Hill, and the whole family being sent away. It had been made safe by a controlled explosion, but they had been left with no home to return to. Better that than losing their lives, everyone had said at the time, but it still made the family evacuees and the rest of them aware that danger still lurked in such a silent and obscene way.

Skye also couldn't rid herself of the thought that Olly might be flying in one of these powerful Lancaster bombers. The last time he was home he had sounded so grown-up, so brash in an oddly endearing way, and it had been easy to see he believed himself invincible. She prayed that he was, and that God would forgive her for asking him to protect her own.

In June came the sad news that one of Britain's most beloved actors was 'missing believed killed'.

"He wasn't even involved in the war," she almost wept when the news about Leslie Howard came through among all the regular reports of war casualties. "It says he had been giving lectures in Spain to promote British films there and he was in a civil airliner shot down in the Bay of Biscay. It's so tragic. What had he ever done to the Germans?"

"What have any of us done?" Nick said shortly. "We don't take account of the civilian population when we bomb their cities, either, do we? War's a cruel game, darling, and in the end, it's the little people who are hurt the most."

"Only a philistine would call a famous actor a little person," she retorted angrily.

"They still eat and sleep the same as the rest of us. And break wind too, I shouldn't wonder," he added, trying to lighten the tension between them.

"You're as much of a pig as Seb sometimes, aren't you?" she snapped, knowing he would have put it far less delicately.

"Not at all. Just realistic. And if you're going to spend your days mourning every person who is killed in this war, you're going to depress us all. We all have to get on with living, Skye."

She knew that. She just couldn't rid herself of the nagging fear that Olly was up there somewhere, flying those abominable machines that looked so fragile and beautiful in flight, but could bring such death and destruction to innocent people, and to the men who flew them.

Whether the words were 'missing in action' or 'missing, believed killed', they had a terrible finality about them, and were being delivered via yellow telegrams with agonising regularity these days. Sometimes to a family whose sons were fighting the war at sea against the dreaded enemy U-boats; or engaged in the war in the air; or still fighting on the ground in Sicily or Tunisia or the western desert . . .

Nowhere was safe any more, and the thing most women dreaded was to see a telegram boy leaving his bicycle outside their house and coming towards their front door. When a loved one was declared missing, everyone automatically assumed the worst, and mourned him in their hearts.

Daphne Hollis went missing after school one sunny June afternoon. By now, she and Butch had mastered the bicycles that had been Christmas gifts from their generous Cornish hosts, and rode to and from their Truro school each day.

Butch didn't always wait for Daphne. For one thing, it was getting to be beneath his dignity to hang about for a bumptious nine-year-old girl whose school friends always giggled and huddled together when they caught sight of him. For another, he liked being alone. He liked riding through the lanes and catching sight of the sea, and he liked the smell of the wild flowers, and he liked to think of himself as a proper Cornish lad now, and to pretend that he was here to stay.

On that June afternoon, he dawdled on the way home, knowing Daphne would catch up sometime. The lure of his favourite cove beneath the cliffs was too strong to resist. The whiff of the salt air and the glitter of the sunlight on the waves made it a magical place, though Butch was far too inarticulate to ever put such thoughts into words.

When the tide went out and the sun baked the sand dry, it was firm enough to ride on and catch the spray as the waves crashed on the rocks nearby. It was a sport Butch loved, and the tingling touch of the sea water on his face invigorated him. That day he spent longer in the cove than he should, collecting shells and a few fossils. When he finally cycled back to New World, he was aware of the prickly heat on his skin, but decided it had been worth it.

"Where's Daphne?" Skye said, the moment she saw him come into the house, long past tea time.

He blinked, having been ready to show her his shells and fossils, and share her own pleasure in such simple things, and was momentarily thrown off balance by the anxious look on her face.

"I dunno. She's here, I s'pose," he stammered. "I ain't seen her."

"Hasn't she been with you, Butch? Didn't you wait for her after school?"

The reddened colour on his normally freckled face deepened still more as he heard the accusation in her voice.

"She don't want me to," he said, his adolescent voice cracking more than usual. "She's always off wiv her mates, and she says I'm spoilin' their fun if I'm hanging around."

"What kind of fun?" Skye said sharply.

"I ain't saying," he said sullenly.

"Oh yes, you are!" Skye said, suddenly alarmed. Daphne might think herself worldly-wise and a cut above her country cousins, but she was still only nine years old – almost ten, Skye reminded herself – and a large girl for her age at that. And Skye was still responsible for her. She resisted the urge to shake Butch and spoke more calmly.

"I think you had better tell me all you know about the fun Daphne and her friends get up to, Butch."

In his own slow way, he was troubled by Daphne's wildness, but he didn't want to betray her. But in the end he knew he had to do it.

"They go down to the river where the soldiers sit outside the pubs in the sun, 'cos they give 'em sweets and fings. And once," he gulped, "I caught her smoking a Woodbine—"

"*What*? And you said nothing about it?"

"I told 'er she'd better stop it before she got in trouble," he howled. "But you know what she's like. She finks she knows better'n everybody else. It weren't my fault!"

"I know it wasn't, Butch," Skye said, trying to keep her fury under control. "But you say these little girls hang around the pubs where the soldiers sit in the sun. How long has this been going on?"

The town was more overcrowded than ever before, what with the dozens of evacuees and the servicemen who were billeted in every corner of the country now. Skye felt a new fear crawling inside her. A fear that only adults could know, but of circumstances in which children were the victims. Dear Lord, had she been so involved in her own affairs that she had become lax in taking care of Daphne, and allowed this to happen?

"Stay right here, Butch. I'm going to make some telephone calls and then you and I are going back to Truro."

The first call was to the school, to be told by the caretaker that everybody had gone home long ago and there were no bicycles left in the stands.

Next she called the newspaper office, and asked for David Kingsley's personal number. She quickly related what Butch had told her, and he responded at once, saying he'd go down to the riverside pubs and take a look around.

None of them would be open at this time of day, of course, but the old wooden benches outside had become a mecca for the servicemen stationed down here, as many of the older local girls had soon discovered. But Daphne wasn't old enough to take care of herself in the way those girls were, and while Skye despised herself for thinking the worst of them, she knew there could always be a bad apple in the best of crops.

"The girl will probably saunter in at any minute as large as life," David assured her. "Try not to worry, Skye, and report back to the office the minute you know she's safe."

But she couldn't wait for that, and as soon as she had hung up, she called Nick's chambers in Bodmin to tell him what was happening. Then she and Butch set out for Truro again. He constantly apologised, until she snapped at him to shut up and just concentrate on cycling there as fast as they could.

She hoped against hope that they would see Daphne coming towards them, her head in the clouds as usual, but there was no sign of her, and the sun was getting lower in the sky now, sending a sheen of red and gold across the calm sea.

"What d'you fink's happened to her, Mrs Pen?" Butch finally said cautiously.

"I dare say she's playing with her friends and they just forgot the time," she said, mentally crossing her fingers.

She didn't dare to think what the evacuee billeting officers would say if Daphne was missing for any length of time, or had been harmed in any way. Those stiff-necked townswomen had frightened the life out of the children when they first arrived, and the thought of them interrogating Daphne was something Skye didn't care to imagine.

It would depend on Daphne's mood, of course. Daphne, scared and snivelling, would be easier to handle, even though she'd be a sitting target for a billeting officer's wrath. But Daphne, defiant and belligerent, and peppering every sentence with inventive cuss words, would be something else – and a bad reflection on the household she had been living in for the last three years.

Skye caught her roving thoughts up short, realising that this was no time to be thinking of her own part in all this. What did any of that matter, compared with the safety of a child?

When they reached the town they rode straight to the riverside pubs. David met them there.

"Nobody's seen her, though a group of soldiers offered to start a search party for her if we needed one. I told them it wasn't necessary. No need to alarm people yet. I called home to see if she'd gone there, as she likes playing with our boys, but Lily hasn't seen her either."

"What about her friends, Butch? Do you know who they are and where they live?" he asked the boy.

Butch, always nervous of David's direct manner, looked hunted. He couldn't think and couldn't help.

After a fruitless hour of searching, and asking anyone in the area if they had seen Daphne, Nick arrived from Bodmin and said shortly that if she didn't turn up soon, they must inform the police. He anticipated Skye's protest and spoke sharply.

"They're the professionals, Skye, and it's been more than four hours now since she left the school – and she's our responsibility," he added, echoing her own feelings.

"But it might be nothing at all, and now everyone will know. Her teachers, the billeting officers—"

"Do you want her found or not?" he demanded.

"Of course I do!" She turned to Butch again. "Was there anywhere else she liked to go, Butch? Somewhere you haven't thought about yet?"

"Well, sometimes she said she was going to do what your girl does. She had a terrible screechy voice, but she kept saying the men at Aunt Betsy's liked her carol singing at Christmas. P'raps she's gone back to London to be a singer."

Skye threw up her hands. "Oh, that's the last thing I want to hear, that she's tried to get back to London—"

"Hold on a minute," Nick said. "She'll know the way to Betsy's, and I bet that's where she is. She'll be there preening herself, singing to a captive audience. And knowing what a devious little liar she is, she'll have told Betsy it was all right with us to stay as long as she likes."

"I don't care how many lies she's told, as long as she's safe," Skye declared feverishly. "Let's go there right away."

"You two go with Nick," David said, "and leave your bicycles here. I'll get someone to bring them back tomorrow."

"Bless you, David." Skye got into Nick's car with shaking legs, and Butch breathing down her neck in the seat behind her.

For one crazy moment she had the strangest feeling of *déjà vu*, from when her own little girls and the precocious Sebby and Justin Tremayne had been breathing down her neck in a car on the way home from a fitting for wedding outfits for Vera's wedding to Adam Pengelly, all those years ago . . .

She brushed the feeling aside at once. This was a far more desperate occasion, and she urged Nick to drive at more than his usual careful speed towards Killigrew House.

The minute Betsy came to the door, astonishment on her face at seeing the deputation, Skye's intuition told her they were out of luck.

"Well, this is a surprise, my lambs," Betsy began. "But if you're wanting that pretty little minx of yours, you've missed her by a long while."

"She's been here then? Daphne, I mean? How long ago? When did she leave?" Skye said in a rush, sick with disappointment.

"Oh ah, she were here all right, along with a few of her school friends – all making eyes at my boys, the little madams," she chuckled. "Most of t'others went a long while back, but your girl and a little friend stayed for tea, saying you knew all about it. You *did* know, didn't 'ee, Skye? I didn't do anything out of turn in letting her stay, did I?" she added, finally aware of the tension in the other three.

"I didn't know, but it wasn't your fault, Betsy. I know how plausible she can be. She hasn't come home from school, and we've been out looking for her for hours—"

"Oh well, she'll be back home by now, sure to be," Betsy said complacently. "You'll have missed her, that's all."

"Can we telephone New World?" Nick said, taking over. "We need to be sure before we do anything else."

And if she wasn't there, the next thing they would have to do was to inform the police, Skye thought, feeling sick.

"Are you sure this is the place?" the smaller of the two girls said uneasily. She and her clever friend seemed to have toiled over the moors for hours and were now crouched in a hollow near the very peak, gazing towards the hovel with the curl of smoke rising into the still air.

Daphne snorted. " 'Course I'm sure. There's a witch living there, and she'll cast a spell for yer, quick as lightning."

"What sort of a spell do you want then?"

Daphne glared at her. Tilly was soft and a bit stupid, but she usually did what Daphne said. They all did. Daphne was the leader of the gang, though the others had gone home long ago, and only Tilly Green had agreed to come with her to try to find the old witchwoman the locals spoke about.

Tilly's mother thought she was spending the evening at her Granny's, and her Granny would just assume that Tilly had gone home instead, she had told Daphne triumphantly.

Daphne wasn't scared of witches, but Tilly's jitters were starting to affect her, and she began to wonder if this had been such a good idea. But Tilly was still waiting for an answer, and she said the first thing that came into her head.

"I'd ask her for a spell to send me back to London."

"Don't you like it here then?"

Daphne looked at her in exasperation, needing to think about why she'd said it. "Mrs Pen's all right, but I'd rather be back 'ome. I miss the pie and mash shops and the jellied eels me Ma used ter buy on a Saturday night—"

"Ugh!" Tilly squealed. "It sounds *horrible*."

Daphne grinned as Tilly's pasty face paled still more . . . or was that because they were surrounded by a bit of a mist, now she came to think about it? She sat up cautiously and felt a shock as she saw that they seemed to be sitting in a sea of fog now, where minutes before it had been a bare expanse of moors.

"Jesus Christ!" she said out loud.

"Daphne Hollis, you know you shouldn't take the Lord's name in vain," Tilly said at once.

"I didn't say the Lord's name. I said Jesus Christ," Daphne snapped. "And p'raps he'll tell us how the bleedin' 'ell we're going ter find our way back."

Tilly gave a terrified cry when she saw what Daphne had seen. Without warning she wet her knickers, and the shame and discomfort of it set her wailing even louder.

"Shut up and let me fink," Daphne snapped.

"We're going to die," Tilly wailed. "Nobody knows where we are, and I want my Mum—"

"I want mine too, but fat chance I've got of seein' 'er," Daphne muttered, with a small catch in her throat. "I reckon there's only one fing to do. We'd better see if the witch can help us."

Tilly screamed, and Daphne clamped a hand over her mouth, so that only her scared, tear-filled eyes showed above it.

"It's either that or die of starvation and cold," Daphne said dramatically. "I dare say there are wild dogs roaming about up here as well, ready to come and tear us apart and eat our flesh – and when they've done wiv us there'll be nothing left but bones," she added, warming to her tale. "I bet they're surrounding us right now—"

They suddenly heard a thin, cackling voice close by, causing them to cling together in terror.

"You tell a fine tale, my pretty maid, one that even old Helza couldn't improve on."

For a moment or two they couldn't see her properly for one of the pockets of mist that frequently slid aross the moors at the end of one hot summer's day and heralded a similar one tomorrow. And then, as ever, it moved away just as miraculously, and they could see the old crone leaning on her stick not two yards away, wizened and hunched, and puffing away on an evil-looking clay pipe.

"We know who you are," Daphne said as bravely as she could, considering that her voice was so croaked.

"We don't need no introductions then," Helza cackled. "I know who you be too. You'm the girl staying with the clay and pottery folk, and this one's a local, I dare say."

"She must be a real witch," Tilly whispered, trembling.

Daphne recovered herself quickly. "Don't be daft. She can tell from the way we talk where we're from. Are you going to cast us a spell then?" she demanded of Helza.

"Just ask her to get us home," Tilly said in a fright, the chill of her own urine and cold wet knickers making her shiver still more.

"The devil helps they that help themselves," the old crone wheezed. "You don't need no spells now the mist's lifted. Get on with you and leave old Helza in peace."

She turned and hobbled away, seeming to melt towards her hovel. Tilly scrambled to her feet.

"Let's go before she comes back. As long as we keep going downwards we're bound to get off the moors, aren't we?" she said, her voice ending on a squeak.

Seeing her fear, Daphne was filled with guilt now that the adventure seemed to be over. Tilly might be a stupid little cuss at times, but she had been her friend from the day Daphne arrived. She put her arm around the smaller child.

"I'll look after yer, Tilly, even if it gets dark."

She bit her lip. It wasn't dark yet, but the sun had gone down and after the heat of the day the air was chilled. And those damn wispy bits of mist still kept coming and going.

With one accord they turned and ran, heads down, their chests tight and heaving, then screaming in unison when the ancient standing stone with the hole through its middle that they called the Larnie Stone suddenly seemed to loom up in front of them. They had almost barged straight into it.

"Bleedin' stupid place this is," Daphne snarled between her gasping breaths. 'Who'd wanter stick a bleedin' great rock on top of the moors where people could fall over it?"

"I wish you wouldn't keep saying that awful word," Tilly almost sobbed. "If my Mum heard you, she'd stop me playing with you, Daphne."

She was clinging on to Daphne with vice-like fingers now, pulling at her cardigan sleeve as she tried to keep up with Daphne's scrabbling feet. She knew she couldn't do it. Her legs were too short, and her chest was hurting too much, and she couldn't see where she was going because her eyes were smarting, and the insides of her legs were being rubbed raw by her navy knickers now . . .

With a sudden almighty shriek of pain, she lost her footing in a rut in the ground, flying past Daphne, but somehow still managing to hold on to her cardigan, so that the two of them went hurtling forward and crashed to the ground together, completely winded.

It took a few minutes for Daphne to untangle herself from Tilly's arms and legs that seemed to be stuck out at all angles. Worse than a bleedin' octopus, she thought sourly, having no real idea what an octopus looked like.

She peered down into Tilly's white face and then sat back, feeling a momentary grudging admiration at the way the girl could act like she was dead just to give her a scare.

"Come on, you ain't hurt that bad," she said roughly, and aware of an almighty headache the size of St Paul's, "I ain't carrying yer, that's for sure."

Then she saw the slow trickle of blood on the girl's forehead, and her heart skipped a couple of beats. She spoke fearfully, her throat threatening to close up completely.

"Tilly, stop pretendin', fer Gawd's sake. Come on, open yer eyes, there's a love. We've got ter get off these moors before it gets dark."

Tilly still didn't move, and Daphne smothered a sob. But she could see now that she wasn't dead. There was a pulse throbbing away in her throat, though she wouldn't open her eyes.

Daphne panicked, not knowing what to do. Instinct told her she shouldn't try to move the girl. She could screech for the old witchwoman to come and help them, but she didn't know how far they had run, and she doubted that the old crone would hear her anyway.

The pottery was somewhere around here, she thought next, but even if she could get to it, it would be shut now that it was getting dusk. However, there were cottages at the top of the moors above the old clayworks, she remembered, and perhaps she could reach one of them and get help.

She started to scramble to her feet, and a searing pain like red-hot needles shot through her ankle. She had been so busy worrying about Tilly and her next move, she had hardly thought about herself. Her agonised scream was strangled in her throat as she looked down at the ankle that was rapidly swelling and turning several shades of blue and purple, and she found herself blubbing hysterically.

In a wild panic, she began to shout as loudly as she could, but her voice was quickly carried away until her throat ached and dried up with trying, and still nobody came. There was only the soughing of the evening breeze through the bracken to break the silence.

"There's nothing for it, Tilly," she said hoarsely to her unconscious friend. "We've just got to sit it out and hope somebody will miss us and come looking for us."

Her words ended on a sob, because how could anybody even guess where they were? They were going to be in a God-awful heap of trouble when they were found, too. And the night ahead of them would be very long and cold.

But she knew this was all her fault, and she tried not to notice the stinging pain in her ankle as she covered Tilly with her own body as gently as she could to try to keep her warm until somebody came. Somebody would, she thought, with a faint echo of her usual cockiness. Somebody *must*.

"They've got to be somewhere," Skye said frantically to the police sergeant who had come to the house and was now in charge of the investigation. "Children can't just vanish."

His constable was taking such an interminable time in writing down all the details that she could have hit him. Didn't they sense the urgency of the situation?

"Mrs Pengelly, I assure you they'll be found," the sergeant said complacently. "We've contacted the school to find out the other child's surname, and contacted her parents. They'll be here any time."

Nick spoke angrily. "You've asked them to come here? What good will that do, man?"

"People like to be together in a crisis that affects them all," he said pompously.

Skye groaned. The last thing she wanted was the arrival of two hysterical parents who would be blaming Daphne for taking their little girl away – and that blame would obviously be transferred to the Pengellys. But she smothered the thought, knowing it was uncharitable, and that Tilly's parents would be as frantic with worry as they were.

They arrived a little while later in a police vehicle, a red-eyed mother and a rough-hewn father, unused to the company that lived in a spacious house near the sea and who were posher folk than themselves. As if any of that mattered, Skye thought, and tried to smile reassuringly.

"Please sit down, both of you," she said swiftly, as they stood awkwardly together. "Would you like some tea?"

God, how *inane* that sounded, and of course they didn't want any tea, or any kind of comfort from herself and Nick. They just wanted their child home, safe and sound.

The sergeant cleared his throat and addressed Nick.

"We'll start a search party, Mr Pengelly, and some of the soldiers have offered to help, so we're accepting their offer. My men are combing the shore first, to see if they've fallen down the cliff' – he ignored the cry from the suffering Mrs Green – "and then we'll spread out and cover a wider area on the moors."

"They wouldn't have gone up there," Skye said. "Daphne knows the dangers of the old mine shafts and how the mist can come down quickly and people can lose their footing—"

Dear God, why was she putting such ideas in these simple folks' minds? she thought, as Mrs Green's cries became louder. Her husband seemed to have no idea what to do about it other than to pat her back as if she was a family pet.

"You'll realise it may be a difficult task, since we'll have to keep our searchlights to a minimum," the sergeant went on carefully. "The regulations still apply—"

"You think some stray German bomber is going to pick tonight to swoop down on a couple of frightened children, do you?" Skye said angrily. "Where's your humanity, man?"

"We all have to abide by the rules, madam," he said stiffly. "We won't rest until we find these children, though things would naturally be easier in daylight."

She hated him. She was tempted to say they would have a repeat performance if it suited him better, and let the girls go missing in the morning instead of at night, which would make his job far easier. But she knew how ludicrous that would sound, and it wouldn't help. Nick's steadying hand on her arm told her so.

The sound of the doorbell ringing made them all jump, and the constable went to answer it without giving anyone else a chance. He came back into the room a few minutes later.

"They've found two bicycles at the foot of the moors, Sergeant. There's no sign of the girls, but it looks as if they dumped them there, and went walking."

Butch had been sitting quietly, afraid to speak up after being questioned earlier, and still feeling guilty for not waiting for Daphne. But he couldn't keep quiet any longer.

"Daphne sometimes talked about that witchwoman who lives on top of the moors," he said reluctantly. "She liked to scare the younger ones with spooky stories."

"The young devil!" Tilly Green's father suddenly spoke up, aggressive and gutteral, his fists clenching. "She needs sending back where she belongs and locking up, and if I get my 'ands on 'er—"

"Now then, Mr Green, there'll be none of that talk," the sergeant said sharply. "The important thing is to find these children as quickly as possible, and now that this young scallywag has given us a lead, we've got somewhere to start."

"I don't know if that's where they've gone," Butch said, near to crying. "I only said she talked about it sometimes."

"It's all right, Butch," Skye soothed him. "It's good that you remembered it, isn't it, Sergeant?"

He gave a curt nod, unable to resist complying with that unflinching stare from the woman's blue eyes. He wasn't a ladies' man, but he could guess that people would do anything to please her, even this young evacuee lad.

"Would you like to stay while we wait for news?" Skye asked the Green parents, praying they would say no, and not wanting to see their accusing faces any longer than she had to. She didn't waste her energy on feeling shame at the thought either. They had each other, and all her anxiety was for the children.

"We'll get off and do our own searching, thank 'ee, missis," Mrs Green sniffed. "If we don't find 'er, I dare say we'll be told when they know what's 'appened to our Tilly."

"But you have no idea where to look."

They didn't answer, and Skye gave up protesting as they left, together and yet so alone in their separate miseries. She looked at Nick.

"We're going with you," she told the sergeant.

"It's best if you stay here, Mrs Pengelly—"

"Sergeant, I've never been rude to a police officer in my life before, but if you try to stop me walking these moors tonight I shall demonstrate the extent of my vocabulary."

"I'm coming too," Butch said, standing close to her and Nick and presenting a united front.

"Of course you are, Butch," Skye said, knowing how important this was to him.

The night was overcast by now, and the sky tips loomed up ahead of them like ghostly sentinels. There were huge numbers of people about now, as word had spread through the towns, and police, soldiers and local folk all joined in the search.

"It's ridiculous," Skye said to Nick, as the shouting for the girls echoed up and down the moors. "Even if they called back, we'd never hear them with all this din going on. Can't they see how stupid it is?"

"We should have let the police do their job, Skye. We're only adding to the confusion."

"But we're involved. We couldn't sit at home twiddling our thumbs when Daphne might be – might be—" She was choked suddenly, as the realisation of just what could have happened to Daphne struck her forcibly.

These moors had long been mined for china clay, but they were also criss-crossed with old mine shafts from the days when tin was king. Theo Tremayne's own natural grandfather, Sam Tremayne, had died when Ben Killigrew's rail tracks had collapsed taking clayworkers on an outing to the sea.

The thoughts flitted in and out of her head like a dire presentiment of what could be happening. Her grandmother's best friend, Celia Penry, had drowned in a clay pool belonging to Killigrew Clay. Accidents had happened over the years on these moors, and some things that weren't accidents . . .

Already they seemed to have been searching for hours with the dim lights of the torches like useless glow-worms in the dark. The old moorswoman had been questioned and said she had seen the children, but it was hours ago. Skye could still hear her indignant screeching and cursing as the police insisted on searching her hovel, before reeling out of it, having found nothing but the stink of her and her animals.

Then at last the piercing sound of a whistle stopped her heartbeats for a long moment. It was the signal that something or someone had been found . . .

"Dear God, let them be safe," she whispered aloud, and with Nick's and Butch's hands holding tightly to hers, she struggled to reach the area where the sound was coming from, somewhere beyond the old Larnie Stone.

Ten

It was inevitable that Daphne would see herself as a heroine. She had saved Tilly's life, she told Butch dramatically, by keeping her warm until they were rescued.

They had both been taken to hospital, where Tilly was treated for cuts, bruises and concussion, and Daphne had her sprained ankle strapped up. The nurses petted them, and visitors brought them sweets from their rations. They remained there for two days for observation, and were then allowed home. But if Daphne thought she was going to get off lightly just because everyone was relieved that no real harm had come to her and Tilly, she was very much mistaken.

"Do you know just how wicked and stupid you were, by going off like that?" Skye railed at her. "Anything could have happened to you on the moors at night, and I've had nightmares just thinking about it. You were a very foolish girl, Daphne, and you'll be lucky if you're allowed back to school at all after the summer holidays."

"*Good*," Daphne screamed at her, still wrapped up in her own little euphoric cloud, and not wanting to hear anything different. "I don't want to go back to that bleedin' stupid tin-pot little school anyway."

"*Daphne*, I've told you before about using such language," Skye said, incensed. "I won't have it in my house."

'Well, we can soon change that an' all, can't we?" Daphne bawled back. "I don't wanna be in your house, neither. You're not my mother, and I hate you!"

Skye felt as if she had been slapped in the face. Lord knew she had done her best with this girl, and it had got her precisely nowhere. She turned away from the sofa where Daphne was sitting in state with her feet up to rest the swollen ankle, and fought the urge to retaliate at this little tyrant. And then she heard the sound of sobbing, and Daphne's voice, thin and weak and aching with remorse.

"I didn't mean it, Mrs Pen. I don't hate you, honest."

Skye turned back to her at once, kneeling on the carpet beside her

136

and gathering the stiff little body in her arms. So what if she was being a sucker and Daphne was using her the way she always used people? The evacuees were as much war victims as any wounded soldier. Daphne was in her care, and she had to see this through, no matter what.

"It's all right, honey. We all say things we don't mean in the heat of the moment, and I dare say your ankle's giving you hell, isn't it?" she said, giving her a let-out to save her pride, and knowing it.

Daphne nodded. "You shouldn't use such words, Mrs Pen," she said with a ghost of a smile, and Skye laughed as they hugged one another, both perfectly aware that Daphne was careful to wince dramatically for maximum effect.

"It's true what she said, though," she said to Nick later. "I'm not her mother, and I should remember it. One of these days, her mother will want her back, and I'll miss her."

"Like you'd miss a thorn in your foot, you mean," Nick commented, never able to be as forgiving as Skye.

"That too," she grinned. "She can be impossible, but she's still vulnerable, and she's got a birthday in August, Nick. She'll be in double figures, as our children used to say. We should give her a small party, don't you think?"

"If you like," Nick said. "As long as I don't have to be there. But who are you going to ask, anyway? Do you imagine the Greens will allow their ewe-lamb to come after Daphne nearly killed her?"

"Stop exaggerating, and yes, of course we should ask Tilly, and a few more of her school friends. It will be a nice gesture, and by the time they go back to school after the holidays, hopefully all this will be forgotten."

In her heart, she knew it was a vain hope. Daphne would be bragging about the incident for ever more, and had begged for a copy of the *Informer* newspaper for herself after David Kingsley had felt obliged to put the whole story in print, much against Skye's wishes.

"It has to be done," he'd said. "Everyone's got wind of what happened, Skye, and it's better that they get a tempered version in print than garbled stories spread from mouth to mouth. Before you know it, they'll have Daphne tarred with the same brush as old Helza, and there are still superstitious folk prepared to believe in witches and the like. You don't want any scaremongering to result in the kid being hounded out of New World, with you in the thick of it."

"I suppose you're right," she said with a shudder. "Go ahead then, but don't make her out to be too much of a heroine. She's preening herself enough as it is."

"My mother's going gaga," Wenna declared to Rita, incredulous at the news. "This appalling child has turned the whole town upside down and managed to get her name into the newspaper as if she's a little angel instead of a villain, and now Mom's going to give her a birthday party."

"Not jealous, are you, Pengo?" Rita said, too excited over the fact that at long last they were going overseas to entertain the troops, to bother too much over one wayward child in a remote Cornish town she'd never heard of before.

"Jealous! Of Daphne Hollis?"

"Well, she seems to have conned your mother all right. What did it say in that newpaper cutting? 'Daphne is very contrite about her misdemeanour. Mr and Mrs Pengelly have forgiven her for her irresponsible behaviour, and trust that others will do the same.'"

"My mother's a very forgiving person," Wenna defended her. "She stuck up for my brother when he enlisted under age and refused to let my stepfather bring him back home."

"That's the first time you've referred to him as your stepfather," Rita noted. "In fact, you hardly mention him at all. Don't you get on?"

"Of course we do. He's a darling, and I said it without thinking. We're one big happy family," she added glibly.

"Cripes, do such things exist? Don't answer that. Where do you think they'll be sending us, anyway?"

"Somewhere warm, I hope," Wenna said, stretching like a sleek cat. "Somewhere where the sun shines all day—"

"And the Yanks are ready to play all night," Rita added with a grin. "That'll be enough to raise our temperatures. But with our luck, it'll be the back of beyond."

She eyed her friend thoughtfully. "So are you going to tell me who your other letter was from? The one you read mighty quickly and then tucked away."

"No," Wenna said flatly.

"It wasn't from your Canadian then?"

"He's not *my* Canadian."

"It was from him though, wasn't it?"

Wenna sighed impatiently. Rita could be as tenacious as a limpet when she wanted to know something.

"All right, so it was. He wrote to my aunt's house, and she passed it on to my mother, and it finally got to me."

"And?" persisted Rita.

"And nothing. It was a letter to a friend, that's all. I doubt that we'll meet again, anyway."

"That's not what Vera says, is it?"

Wenna looked blank for a moment. The only Vera she knew was one of her mother's cousins, and she had died years ago . . . and then she heard Rita humming tunelessly, and realised she was referring to the song that Vera Lynn had made her own.

"You're letting all this sentimental romance stuff go to your head, Rita."

"And you're not? Are you telling me you don't put your heart and soul into those slushy songs you sing? Especially when you go all gooey-eyed over 'I haven't said thanks for that lovely week-end' . . ."

"That's different. That's work," Wenna said crisply.

"So when you come off stage with tears in your eyes and your throat working overtime – that's work too, is it?"

"I'm fed up with this conversation, and you're getting far too nosey," Wenna said.

But she couldn't stop thinking about it all the same. She couldn't stop thinking about Harry Mack either, nor the sweet things he had said in his letter. She hadn't wanted to read them, nor to remember his voice, nor the look in his eyes when she had sung the words of the traditional Scottish song he had requested at Aunt Betsy's house.

But somehow, no matter how hard she tried to put such emotions out of her personal range and limit them only to her stage performance, it was gradually becoming impossible to do so. The shock of losing Fanny and Austin, and everything that had happened since – including getting used to the sight of the badly wounded and shell-shocked servicemen who were brought by nurses to hear their concerts – had made her close her mind to becoming involved with anyone else for the duration.

She gave a wry smile as the phrase entered her head. It was one of the phrases they all used so thoughtlessly now. But the duration of what? This terrible war? Her lifetime? Who knew how long that might be? How did any of them know? She shuddered, knowing how fragile life could be these days.

And the sweet, polite, handsome Harry Mack was in the thick of it, maybe flying regular sorties over Berlin by now, and longing for a letter from a girl he knew, just to have a breath of home. So what sort of a monster was she to refuse?

"Yer going to give me a birfday party?" Daphne echoed suspiciously when she heard. "Mc Ma would still be givin' me a cuff round the ears of a night, for what I done."

"I told you, it's history now, Daphne," Skye said. "You have to try to forget it and just be as pleasant as you can at school and not cause any more trouble."

"Why do I have to keep goin' there?" she said, as sullen as ever. "Nobody plays wiv me now—"

"Yes they do," Butch broke in. "Don't tell such lies, Daphne. You should see 'er, Mrs Pen. She's still telling everybody how she saved Tilly Green's life, and as Tilly can't remember much of it, she believes it an' all. They all hang around Daphne when she tells her tales."

"They ain't tales, anyway," Daphne scowled. "It was all in the paper for everybody to see. And I don't remember *you* saving anybody's life, donkey-drawers!"

"All right, that's enough," Skye said, seeing another battle about to begin. "The fact is, Daphne is going to have a birthday party. Auntie Lily's two boys will come, and you can choose which of your school friends to invite, honey."

"I bet their mums won't let 'em come," Butch sniggered.

She turned on him. "Butch, please go into the garden and pull up a lettuce for tea, while Daphne and I talk."

"I hate lettuce," she said at once. "It's yukky stuff, and it's fer rabbits, not yoomans."

"Well, you'll either eat a lettuce sandwich for tea or go without," Skye said grimly. "I don't exactly like seeing my lovely flower garden turned into a vegetable patch, either, but we all have to dig for victory these days, and grow what we can. So are you going to tell me which of your friends you want to invite to your party, or shall we forget it?"

"As long as you don't give 'em lettuce, then," Daphne said, scowling.

"We'll try to do better than that," Skye promised.

"There's something on her mind," she reported to Nick that evening. "I thought she'd be pleased about the party, but she just droops about the place and scowls at everyone."

"She always did," Nick replied.

"But not like this. I wonder if the ordeal on the moors upset her more than we realised. Tilly was concussed, but Daphne probably stayed awake half the night until we found her, imagining all kinds of horrible things. She must have *some* sensitivity, Nick."

"I doubt it. But if anybody can find out what's bothering her, it's you. You're the one she trusts the most."

"Do you think it's because Butch is leaving school now and going to work at the pottery?"

"Why should she care about that?" he said, too busy with his own work problems to worry overmuch about Daphne Hollis, who, he thought, could very well take care of herself.

"I don't know. Maybe she feels we're favouring him. His father's dead, and I know he wants to stay with us when the war ends, now that he's got nobody else. I don't know if it's possible, but I wouldn't object. He's a cute boy."

Nick laughed. "You're too soft with them, Skye. I can't imagine anyone else calling Butch cute."

"Well, so he is. You have to see beyond that large, awkward exterior to the good-natured person inside."

He slid an arm around her shoulders and kissed her. "And you would, wouldn't you? He's not the only one who's cute and good-natured around here."

She kissed him back and then went back to her theme.

"So what do you think is troubling Daphne?"

"Lord knows, and he's not telling," he said carelessly.

"O' course," Daphne said in a superior tone to the admiring crowd of little girls sitting in a circle around her in the school playground, "I don't really want a bleedin' party at all, but Mrs Pen wants me ter have one, so yer all invited, if yer wanna come."

"My mum might not let me," Tilly said uneasily.

"There'll be more grub fer the rest of us then, won't there?" Daphne shot at her. "Yer mums will have to bring yer all anyway, and Mrs Pen's written out the invitations."

Since Daphne had never had anything so grand happening to her in her life before, she handed them round as solemnly as if they were made of gold. Despite her airy voice, she desperately wanted every one of them to come and see the posh place where plain old Daphne Hollis lived now.

It was a bit different to the two-up, two-downer in the East End where she'd been born, crammed in with her Ma and Dad and all her brothers and sisters, though as far as the tiny house went, things had got easier when one after another of the younger ones had died of diphtheria. At least then the six of them hadn't had to sleep head to foot in one room in three narrow beds, all sweaty little bodies and smelly feet and sniffling noses. Daphne swallowed an unexpected lump in her throat, remembering those contrary little devils, bawling and screeching the night away when her Ma and Dad were down the pub, until he'd gone off and was never heard of again. She didn't really miss any of them. Well, not often.

What she did miss more and more, though she wasn't going to tell a living soul, was her Ma. Only Daphne herself knew how bruised and bewildered she was that her Ma never wrote to her now, except to send her a miserable little note from time to time, saying she hoped Daphne was being a good girl for the lady who was looking after her, while Daphne dutifully wrote a letter home once a month.

She had already written an extra one, telling her Ma about the birthday party. Her stiff-necked pride wouldn't let her beg her Ma to come to Cornwall for it, and anyway, she knew her Ma was far too busy working in her munitions factory to bother coming all this way for an afternoon. Or far too busy making eyes at the Yanks . . . but Daphne didn't want to think about that.

By the time her birthday arrived, a small group of Truro mothers and foster mothers had brought their daughters to New World, most of them curious to see this grand house, and confident that Mrs Pengelly wouldn't let things get too riotous with the unruly Daphne and her evacuee friends.

"Mrs Pen's made me a cake," Daphne announced, the minute anyone arrived. "You can all 'ave a piece, as long as there's enough left to keep a piece fer me Ma."

"It'll go rotten by then," Butch sniggered, annoyed at having been made to attend the party, when he'd far rather be up on the moors or messing about with the clay at the pottery.

"Shut up, fat-arse," Daphne hissed, at which several Truro Mamas glanced at one another, wondering how the elegant Mrs Pengelly was going to handle this.

"We're going to play some games before tea," Skye announced, refusing to rise to Daphne's bait. For days now, the child had been verging on the edge of fury, ready to fly at anyone who came within earshot, and Skye prayed that the day would pass without incident.

One of her little friends had been unable to come at the last minute. Their family had received one of the dreaded yellow telegrams, and the mother had telephoned, choked with tears, to say that their soldier son was missing in action, and that little Lena was too upset to come to a party.

"She's a cry-baby, but she'll soon be bragging about 'er bruvver being a hero, 'specially if 'e's dead," Daphne had snorted, at which point Skye had felt ready to throttle her.

"We're going to play Hunt the Thimble now," she went on determinedly after they had played several exhaustive games of Pass the Parcel, all of them squabbling and fighting to regain the package. "As it's Daphne's birthday, she can have the first chance to hide it while we all go out into the garden for exactly five minutes."

As they all trooped out, her cousin Lily spoke under cover of the excited children. "How on earth do you put up with her, Skye? I always said you were a saint."

"I'm anything but that," she retorted, aware of her earlier murdcrous thoughts towards the little madam. "I just try to be tolerant, that's all, and to remember that she's not in her own home."

"She's been here for three years now. From all you've told me about her miserable home life, I imagine she gets far more care here than she did in London."

"But I'm not her mother, and that's what counts," Skye said, unwittingly echoing Daphne's own thoughts.

The screams from the children told them it was time to go indoors, and that the thimble had been hidden. It wasn't difficult to find. It was more difficult to find Daphne.

"Where the dickens is she?" Skye fumed. "Tea's ready, and the star of the show is nowhere to be found."

"We're having a new game," Butch yelled. "It's called Hunt stupid Daphne—"

"Butch, it is *not* a game," Skye snapped, but she was talking to the air. The children scattered, racing about the place like lunatics, while their mothers stayed outside in the warm afternoon.

After another ten minutes of fruitless searching, and the threat of tears from some of the smaller children as it all began to get out of hand, she decided that tea was the best option. If Daphne wanted to be absent at her own birthday party, it was up to her.

They wouldn't cut the precious cake without her, though, having decorated it with some candles carefully stored from previous occasions which were practically burned away to nothing now. But blowing out the candles was for Daphne, and no one else.

Once the guests were all sitting down to the amazing sugar-free concoctions Cook had managed to create to please the small appetites, Skye slipped away from the dining room to make a last search for Daphne. It was ridiculous. She had wanted this party so much, and now it seemed that the ungrateful little tyke had just turned her back on it.

Skye thought she had searched everywhere by the time she heard the sound of muffled crying from the room that had held Albert Tremayne's paintings. It was no longer locked, but now that the paintings had gone, it remained empty and unused.

Skye turned the handle and saw the small huddled figure sitting by the window. Her Sunday best dress that she had put on especially for the day was crumpled and creased by now.

"Daphne, what are you doing here?" she said softly. "Don't you want to blow out the candles on your cake? Everyone's waiting for you—"

"Everyone ain't here. *She* couldn't be bovvered to come, could she? I *hate* her now, and I 'ope she never comes."

"Who are you talking about?" Skye said in bewilderment.

She knelt down beside the girl, but resisted the urge to take her in her arms. The small body was too stiff and unwelcoming, the hurt in her eyes too intense. Skye knew at once that she wasn't the one who was wanted.

"Me Ma, o' course," she lashed out. "I wrote and told 'er about it, and even if I hadn't, she shoulda known it was me birfday, shouldn't she? But she couldn't even be bovvered to send me a letter or nuffin'. She don't want me no more, so I shan't want 'er no more."

"Oh, Daphne, of course your mother wants you," Skye said. "But you know it's not always easy in wartime to do the things we want. She may not even have got your letter—"

"In case she's dead, you mean?" Daphne said viciously.

"No, I don't. Letters can go astray these days, and there's probably one in the post for you right now. I'm sure she would have wanted to be here if she could, because being ten years old is an important milestone. It's almost being grown-up, so dry your eyes and come downstairs and let's show them all what a young lady you're becoming."

Her response was a series of sniffles, then she finally shrugged and stood up, brushing down her crumpled skirt.

"Might as well, I s'pose," she said grudgingly.

"And we'll be sure to keep that piece of cake for your mother, won't we?" Skye went on, wanting her to agree.

"If yer like. She won't come, though."

Skye knew that. It hadn't occurred to her to write to Mrs Hollis to suggest it. The distance between London and Cornwall was too great, and it was obvious that the family was a poor one. Some of the evacuees had visits from relatives, but in the end it usually unsettled them and caused more tears when they had to leave them behind again. In her opinion, such visits were best never made. But the children wouldn't see it that way.

"By the way, Mrs Pen," she heard Daphne say in a small voice as they left the room. "I fergot something."

"What's that?"

"I fergot ter say thanks fer me lovely party," Daphne said in a rush, at which Skye had to turn away and walk ahead of her down the stairs, her eyes smarting.

At the beginning of September the woman in the short, home-made swagger coat fashioned from an old grey blanket toiled the last half-mile to New World, and paused to catch her breath.

The train from Paddington was crowded with servicemen, but the crush was no problem to someone who had lived cheek by jowl with neighbours in a sweaty London Underground shelter all through the Blitz. Someone who enjoyed a saucy joke or two and had a store of her own to tell, despite some of the disapproving looks she got. It all helped to make the long journey pass quicker, and once out of the train station, she had caught the bus out of Truro as far as it went.

Now she took in the sight of the lovely old stone house set near the cliffs. The endless, unfamiliar expanse of sea was enough to make her light-headed too, and she let out her usual expletive as if assure herself that it was real.

"Bleedin' 'ell, duck, you never let on that it was as grand as this, did yer!"

At the sound of the voice, but not the actual words, Skye looked up from her garden, where the flowerbeds had long been taken over by vegetables now, and leaned on her hoe.

"Are you lost? I'm afraid we're a bit isolated here."

The woman grimaced, shifting her chewing-gum from one side of her mouth to the other. "Well, I ain't too sure this is the place I'm lookin' for after all, 'spite of what the bus conductor said."

Skye felt her heart begin to pound. The woman didn't look like Daphne, except for the sharply pointed and determined chin. But there was something in the voice, and the quick way of speaking, so different from the Cornish drawl, that she knew by now could only belong to one place.

"Are you from London?"

" 'Ow d'yer guess?" the woman said, her voice faintly mocking. "I've come looking fer me kid, see, and I know she's livin' around 'ere somewhere—"

The next moment something like a small whirlwind flew past Skye and into the woman's arms, and what had been two separate figures suddenly became one huge blur of grey swagger and clinging arms as the coat enveloped them both.

"I swear that it was symbolic, the way that coat just folded them both inside it," Skye told Nick, when Daphne and her mother had gone off together for a walk down by the sea. "It was as if nothing could separate them again. It was almost – well, beautiful."

"And you're having a hard job not to get emotional about it, aren't you, darling?" he said. "Don't get carried away by the moment or the woman's sudden appearance. She hasn't bothered much before, so what do you think she wants?"

"She wants Daphne, of course."

Now that she had said the words, Skye knew it had been inevitable. From the moment she had seen the handsome woman in the shabby grey coat, and the glorious happiness Daphne couldn't hide as they hugged one another, she had known why Mrs Hollis was here. What she didn't know was what she was going to do about it.

Anticipating her thoughts, Nick spoke firmly.

"You can't keep her, Skye. If her mother wants to take her back, there's not a thing you can do about it. You know that. You've always known it. It happened with the other two children, didn't it? None of them belong to us."

"But what kind of a life will she have in London?" Skye said passionately. "They say the danger is past for now, but who knows what Hitler's got up his sleeve for the future? The war's not over yet, and I thought at least we'd have them here for the duration – and don't you dare suggest we take on any more, because I just can't bear all this coming and going."

"For heaven's sake, Skye, get a grip on yourself. Daphne's been away from home for three and a half years, and her mother will have been missing her. Don't you think she deserves some consideration?"

Privately, Skye thought that if Mrs Hollis had been missing Daphne all this time then her almost total lack of communication was a strange way of showing it. If Daphne had been *her* child, evacuated to a different part of the country to live with strangers, she would have moved heaven and earth to keep in touch . . . but Daphne wasn't her child.

"I know you're right, Nick, so let's wait and see what they have to say when they get back from their walk."

"Maybe this is just a visit, anyway," Butch offered, having learned all about it by the time the Hollis pair returned to the house in time for a late afternoon tea.

The minute Skye saw Daphne's shining eyes, she knew it wasn't just a visit. Daphne had a huge capacity for grasping any opportunity, and as the words tumbled out of her eager lips, they all discovered that a great opportunity was coming the Hollises' way.

"Me Ma's come to take me 'ome, Mrs Pen, and now that she's heard that me Dad's passed on – Gawd bless 'im," she added with false piety, 'she's going to marry 'er Yank, and we're all gonna live in America after the war! What d'yer fink of *that* then, Butch Butcher!"

Butch gaped at her, unable to say anything at all, and struck dumb by the fact that Daphne was hugging and kissing this stranger and behaving more like a normal person than he'd ever seen her. But going to live in America was something he just couldn't comprehend.

"Is this true, Mrs Hollis?" Skye said, aware that it wasn't her place to question or criticise or doubt, but feeling a mixture of all of those things at Daphne's outburst.

"Oh, it's quite true, Missis. Me and my feller have decided to tie the knot as soon as possible now – and we'll be shippin' out the minute the war's over," she added grandly. "I'll be one o' them GI brides, and me and Daphne will be nicely set up wiv my Gary."

"Well, that's – wonderful," Skye said. "So when will you be wanting Daphne to join you? You're not thinking of taking her back to London yet, are you?"

"Course I am. That's what I've come 'ere for. If yer've got room to put me up fer the night, we'll be going back to the smoke tomorrer."

Daphne squealed with joy. "Course we can put yer up, Ma. This is a *yooge* house, and yer can sleep wiv me, just like we used to. She can, can't she, Mrs Pen?"

"Of course," Skye said mechanically, feeling as if these two were taking over the entire household by the force of their personalities and determination.

Her brain seemed reluctant to function properly. But weren't there formalities to go through? Anyone relinquishing an evacuee had to go through procedures. There was the billeting committee to be informed, and the school . . . evacuees didn't just disappear on a whim whenever their parents summoned them back home . . .

Even as she thought it Skye knew that was exactly what did happen. It had happened to the little Lunn children, and now it was happening to Daphne.

But it musn't happen to Butch, thought Skye, seeing his apprehensive face. Butch had no one in the world but themselves now, and no authority on earth was going to drag him away from the place he loved as much as any of her family.

She made a silent vow to that effect while they were all listening to the excited babblings of the Hollis mother and child, and she decided to ask Nick to find out about putting an adoption order in motion as soon as possible.

It was a thought to keep her sane during the hours in which the speed of Daphne's proposed new station in life took precedence over everything else. By the time they had all had breakfast the next morning, Skye was heartily sick of hearing about Edna Hollis's Yank, who was winning the war singlehandedly, by all accounts, and of Daphne's predictable boasting that she'd soon be meeting all the movie stars.

But all the same, when she and Nick drove them to Truro railway station, she felt a heart-tugging such as she had never expected when Daphne suddenly threw her arms around her neck, and whispered in her ear in a strangled voice.

"I do love yer, Mrs Pen. It's just that me Ma needs me back, see? We're gonna be a real fam'ly again."

"I love you too, Daphne," Skye said, choked. "You just remember to write to me, and I promise to write back."

"I will. And when I get to 'ollywood, I'll write and tell yer all about it."

Then the train was ready to crawl away, and they waved them off until they could see no more for the smoke and steam, and the sparks that stung the eyes and tightened the throat.

"Come on, love," Nick said roughly, understanding more than she knew. "We'll waste a bit more of our precious petrol and make a visit to the pottery and the clayworks. Let's take a look at our new acquisition. And don't forget, when all else fails, we've still got each other."

"And Butch," she reminded him huskily.

"And Butch," he agreed with a grin.

*　　*　　*

A Brighter Tomorrow

By the end of the year Skye had recovered from the shock of having Daphne wrenched from her control so abruptly, but she still missed her badly. Another Christmas was only weeks away, and Daphne had assuredly made the most of the previous ones with her raucous behaviour. She had livened up the house, and it was emptier without her. Butch was never the liveliest of companions, fond though Skye was of him.

She found herself aching for Christmases past, and there were times when she wondered fearfully if it was a sign of age that made her wallow in nostalgia far more than was good for her. At other times she told herself severely not to be so stupid, and that it was simply because she was giving more and more time now to her history of the clayworks and her family involvement with it.

How could she help being nostalgic? She was forced to remember all those times past, whether they belonged personally to her or to all those who had gone before. But it was a task of love as well as duty, and now that the house was empty all day long, she threw herself into researching and writing the Killigrew Clay booklets.

Two weeks before Christmas came some news that filled her with very mixed feelings. There was guilt, because no one should rejoice in someone else's misfortune. But there was also an overwhelming elation and thankfulness, because Celia was coming home.

"I know I shouldn't be this happy," she said to Nick, almost shaking with the delirium of it. "I know this Captain Moon's letter advises us to treat her with extreme care, because it was such an unexpected illness, but she'll recover here, you'll see. Cornwall has always been our place of refuge and strength. It's our personal heaven, and I don't care if it's blasphemous to say so. In fact, I'd go as far as to say that what the Lord has recently taken away – meaning Daphne – he's giving us back in full measure, by sending Celia back to us. It was obviously meant to be."

She was almost dizzy with joy and the sense of destiny, and when Nick's face came back into her focus, she became aware that he was less than pleased at her outburst.

"Stop it, Skye," he snapped. "You're getting this all out of proportion, and I won't have all this nonsense. Celia's coming home to recuperate, but once she's better she'll be eager to go back to her job. And she won't thank you for implying that her enforced homecoming was fate compensating us for sending Daphne Hollis home!"

"Well, I think you're wrong. This time, Mr Smarty Pants know-all lawyer, I know I'm right."

Eleven

C elia didn't feel ill. She didn't feel anything but relief that the decision had been made for her. She hadn't even been aware that anything was amiss until the night she and Moonie had been working late and she had suddenly burst into tears of rage and frustration as all the letters and figures on the code she was working on seemed to dazzle in front of her eyes in a crazy ant-like war dance. And when she had begun screaming and trying to fight them off, it became obvious to Captain Moon that something was seriously wrong.

She didn't remember anything after that until she had woken up in a hospital bed and told she had been sedated for two days, and that she was suffering from severe exhaustion that threatened her physical and mental state.

"You mean I've had a nervous breakdown," she had stated to the military doctor, staring him in the eyes and daring him to deny the stigma attached to the words.

"You're suffering from nervous exhaustion, Lieutenant Pengelly," he prevaricated, making her sigh with impatience.

Why couldn't they call a spade a spade a spade and be done with it? They were only words, for God's sake. It was her body and her brain was being sent into turmoil, and whatever label they put on it didn't alter her sense of panic and anxiety and disorientation.

But she could still argue with the best of them when it came to dismissing incompetents.

"How can I be suffering from nervous exhaustion?" she had said perversely. "I'm not fighting in the trenches or dropping bombs on enemy territory. I'm doing a desk job, that's all."

"But we both know it's a job that requires immense concentration and expertise," he said, giving her all the status she deserved. "My dear young lady, we all have our limitations, and when one has personal worries as well as everything else required of us these days, we can all reach the end of those limitations. That's when the mind as well as the body closes down and demands that we take a rest."

God, he was good, Celia had thought. Patronisingly good, of course, but good nonetheless. How much he knew of her 'personal worries' she didn't know, but if Moonie hadn't confided all her fears for Stefan, she had probably blabbed it all herself before being doped up to the eyeballs.

Now she was being sent home, and no doubt all the family was feeling sorry for her, and were ready to tiptoe around her the way they had done around Sebby for the first few days after his arrival. But contrary to what everyone might expect, she was guiltily glad to be out of a job she hadn't volunteered for in the first place – and she was never going back.

She sobered at the thought. She would have to do something else, of course. She was able-bodied, even if she'd been half out of her mind for a while, and she was still only twenty-four years old. Her country still needed her, she thought cynically.

But one thing she wasn't going to be was a nurse. She'd seen enough of that in the short while she'd been in the military hospital. She admired them all enormously, but she couldn't stomach some of the things they had to do. She couldn't go back to being a tram conductress either. Her father would hate that, and stuffed shirt though he might be in many respects, she wouldn't put him through that indignity again.

As the train took her homewards, away from the cities and through the green fields that could still look amazingly peaceful and so very pastoral, even in the midst of a war, she remembered how she and Wenna and Olly had relished visits to their Aunt Em's farm in Wadebridge all those years ago. It had been such fun in those far-off, halcyon days, following country pursuits; feeding the chickens, rounding up the cows for milking, and pulling up carrots and turnips to make Aunt Em's famous stews.

She remembered it all, the sights and sounds and smells, with a warmth of affection for her aunt that she had all but forgotten. And long before the train arrived in Truro, Celia knew what she intended to do with the remainder of her war.

"You're going to join the Women's Land Army?" Lily asked Celia after a few weeks, when she had settled into an uneasy routine of vainly trying to make everyone see that she wasn't about to fall apart, and was dutifully making the round of family visits. "Good for you. What does your mother say about it?"

"I think she understands. I have to have some training first, but I shall ask to be posted in this area – on the grounds that I'm still a bit feeble-minded and need to be near home," she added airily, to take the sting out of it. "Dad's not too keen on the idea," she added, "but that's to be expected. I knew you'd be sensible about it, though, Lily."

"Oh, that's me, darling. Always the sensible one, and leaving the glamour to somebody else!"

Celia looked at her sharply. "What's that supposed to mean? You never used to bother about such nonsense."

"About my looks, you mean? I don't bother now, but perhaps I should have thought about it a bit more."

With one look at her downcast face, everything clicked into place in an instant. Celia drew in her breath.

"You're not going to tell me you think David's straying, are you? I can't believe that—"

"Why not? What makes him so different from other men? He always had a passion for your mother, but I knew all about that, and it meant nothing. It was never going to upset our applecart. Now, well, perhaps my plainness does mean something . . . God forgive me, but I never meant to unload such things on you, Celia, in your delicate state of health."

"You're not plain – and I was never delicate, any more than you were. We're the tough Tremaynes, remember?"

Lily's mouth twisted. "So they say, but neither of us were born Tremaynes, were we? We got diluted somewhere along the way."

Celia brushed aside her weak attempt at humour. "The name doesn't matter. We believe in self-preservation. We're survivors. Look at Sebby – look at *me*! And I can't believe you're not going to fight for David. You *have* confronted him with whatever it is you suspect, haven't you?"

"Not yet."

"Why the hell not?" Celia sucked in her breath, realising how belligerent she was becoming. "Oh Lord, I'm sorry, Lily. I shouldn't speak to you like this. You're my elder, and I've got no right."

"Never mind about calling me your elder," Lily said, more sparkily. "I'm not in my dotage yet, and you have every right to tell me what I should have been telling myself."

"So why do you think there's something wrong?" Celia said carefully. "Don't tell me if you don't want to, mind, but since you've got this far . . ."

"It's a relief to tell somebody. I'd tell your mother, but she was too full of you coming home to worry her. Oh, I don't know – perhaps I'm just seeing things that aren't there. He works late every night, or so he says, and when he comes home, he seems so distracted, and he's always too tired to –" she gave an embarrassed little laugh – "well, I can't tell you *everything*, you being an unmarried girl, but you might guess what I mean."

"Oh, Lily," Celia said, ignoring her own blushes. "Do you think Stefan and I never made love? Do you think I never long to have him in my arms again? I long for him and ache for him every single day. I miss him so much, and I don't know if I'll ever see him again—"

Without warning, the tears overflowed, and she was held tightly in Lily's arms. The comforter badly needed comforting, she thought ashamedly, although by now she wasn't sure who was supposed to be comforting who.

"Forget about me," Lily said eventually. "Have you thought about going to see Ethan, to make contact with that prisoner of war working on his farm who he thought might be Stefan's relative? I know I thought it was a bad idea at the time, but now I'm not so sure."

Celia shook her head. "I wrote to him about it, but the Germans have been moved to a different camp, and Ethan didn't know where. He couldn't tell me anything more, anyway, so that idea was a non-starter, like every other one."

Their conversation dried up, as each brooded on her own troubles, and by the time Celia left she could see how Lily's shoulders were drooping again. On an impulse she went straight to David Kingsley's office and demanded to see him.

"Celia, my love, it's good to see you starting to look more like your old self," he began with a smile. It quickly faded at her reply.

"I doubt that you'll think so when I tell you why I've come," she snapped, never one to mince her words. "What the hell are you playing at, David?"

It was odd, but championing someone else's cause put her own miseries in the background for a while, and even went a little way to putting it all in perspective. David had been so uncharacteristically abject when she told him in no uncertain terms that he was in danger of ruining a good woman's life that she could almost smile about it later.

The shock of realising that Lily had been aware of his shortcomings, and that now Celia knew all about them too, had blanched his good-looking face and made him stutter like a schoolboy caught stealing apples.

"My God, Celia, Lily has no grounds for suspecting me of philandering. It's pressure of work that keeps me here—"

"Oh, not that old thing! I've heard plenty of excuses, and that one doesn't wash any more."

"Really? And what gives a young woman like you the right to censure me, or even question me?"

"*Love* gives me the right, David. Love and family loyalty. And if you don't know what I'm talking about, then you're denser than you look – and you look pretty dense right now, if I may say so."

He gave a rueful grin. "You always did have a knack for words, didn't you? You're in the wrong business, Celia. You should come and work for me."

"No thanks. And don't change the subject. Are you honestly telling me Lily has nothing to worry about except being neglected?"

"Cross my heart and may God strike me down dead this minute if I'm lying to you."

Celia relaxed as she saw his elaborate attempt to reassure her, but she couldn't dispute his sincerity.

"In my experience, God rarely does what you ask him to on the spur of the moment," she said dryly. "But I'll believe you, partly because I'm fond of you, and partly because I badly want to on Lily's account. Don't let her down, David."

"I won't. I promise. And if I do seem secretive and distracted at times, it's in a professional context, not personal. My whole working life is concerned with finding out information from my various sources, and I'm constantly having to suppress anything of any importance in the interests of government security. You of all people must know there's something big in the wind, and it's enough to play on any newspaperman's nerves."

Celia flinched. She knew all about living on her nerves by now, but she also knew what David was getting at. For months now, the planned invasion to liberate France had been an open secret. The only uncertainty was when. Every reporter would want to be the first to know.

She looked at him squarely. "I can't tell you anything, and I wouldn't if I could. That part of my life is over."

Without warning, she began to feel stifled. The varying smells of a newspaper office might be full of nostalgia to her mother, but to Celia they were nauseous, and reminded her too vividly of the small decoding office where she and Moonie had worked for so many long hours. She stood up abruptly.

"You won't forget everything I've said, will you, David? Lily needs you. But don't tell her I came here today."

"It's our secret."

"And I suggest you explain things to her more openly. Don't keep all your worries to yourself. She has a right to share them."

She knew she shouldn't be talking to him like a Dutch uncle. He was fifty-six years old, and showing it. But she had never been slow in speaking her mind – and the next day, a telephone call from Lily told her she had been right to do so.

"I just want to say that everything's all right again. I challenged him, Celia, and now I know how wrong I was. Thanks for making me bring it all out into the open, darling."

"I'm glad," Celia said cautiously, knowing her mother was within earshot. "I'll see you again soon, Lily."

"What was that all about?" Skye asked, when she had replaced the receiver.

"Oh, Lily was a bit worried that Frederick had a temperature, but he seems to be all right now," she invented. Wild horses wouldn't make her reveal that she had gone to David and told him what was what.

"I think I'll go up to the pottery and see how things are, Mom," she said next. "For some reason I can't seem to stay indoors for long."

"Do you want company?"

"Not unless you're desperate to come. Do you mind?"

"Not at all. I'm planning to sort out the old Christmas decorations today, so I'll see you later, honey."

Skye watched her daughter leave, her own eyes troubled. Celia was still suffering, no matter how bright a face she put on it. But although Skye ached to get back the old closeness they had once shared, she knew it wouldn't come yet. Celia needed time alone, and the last thing she needed was to be fussed over. It had never been her style.

Celia relished the vastness of the open moors and the weird sense of being alone in the world, or even on some other planet, as she contemplated the wildness of the scrubland and the soaring sky tips ahead of her. *Their* sky tips, she found herself thinking with an odd sense of possessiveness, now that her mother had managed to acquire the land back where it rightfully belonged. Killigrew Clay it had always been and would always be.

She found herself twisting the pearl and garnet ring on the third finger of her left hand that Stefan had given her. Businesslike, she had worn it on a chain around her neck all these months, but since her bout in hospital she had experienced the need to feel its cold unfamiliarity against her finger, as if to reassure her that he was still alive, still somewhere in the world. To remind her that some day they would be together and able to live the normal life of two people in love.

Her throat closed painfully, knowing that even when this war was over, in many eyes they would still be regarded as old enemies for some time. It had happened in her mother's war, and who was to say it would be any different in this one?

She gazed unseeingly ahead for some minutes, forcing herself to remember that she and Stefan had already made tentative plans. They would live in Switzerland, the beautiful country where they had first met, fallen in love, and been everything that a man and woman could be to one another. They would start their own hotel business and begin their own proverbial happy-ever-after, so beloved of story books . . .

A sob caught in her throat as the plaintive sound of a seagull far from the coast echoed the futility of such hopes and dreams. Why should they be the lucky ones, when so many others had lost sweethearts and lovers?

She was still some distance from the pottery when she saw the small, ungainly figure hobbling towards her. Old Helza frequently terrified walkers on the moors with her unexpected appearance, as if she metamorphosed out of nowhere whenever she chose. But she no longer terrified Celia. As she stood very still, it was as if she had been waiting for the old crone, and they both recognised the fact in a instant.

"So what is it you want of me, girlie?" Helza cackled, her wizened old head on one side as usual. "Is it a potion perhaps, to settle the raging in that pretty head o' yourn?"

"My head is fine, and there's nothing I want from you," Celia retorted. "Unless you're able to see in your crystal ball – or whatever evil instrument of witchcraft you use – just where my fiancé is right now."

Helza's button-like eyes flashed. "Mebbe I can, and mebbe I won't. And what makes 'ee think all witchcraft be evil, Miss Snotface? 'Tis the oldest religion in the world—"

Celia heard nothing beyond her first sentence. "What do you mean, maybe you can?"

The cackling laugh rang out again. "Got your attention now, eh? Well, I don't give no help to non-believers, so you'll just have to go on wond'ring about your man."

"I *do* believe," Celia said desperately. "My great-grandmother

Morwen Tremayne and her friend Celia – the one they named me after – *they* believed, and they consulted your sister or mother, or whoever she was."

She began to feel the sweat trickle over her skin as the old crone stared at her. She was furious for letting herself be mesmerised by the witchwoman, but she couldn't seem to help herself. If Helza could truly give her some inkling about Stefan's whereabouts, she would go to any lengths to find out. In that instant, she knew she was just as vulnerable as that earlier Celia had been, nearly a century ago.

"Show me your palm," Helza said abruptly.

Celia breathed a sigh of relief, even while she hated the fact of her own hand being grasped by Helza's clawlike one. But it was preferable to being invited into the hovel with all its weird potions and smells. With her panicky sense of being stifled anywhere indoors right now, Celia knew she couldn't have stood it for more than a moment.

The old woman studied the lines and contours on Celia's palm, tracing them with her cracked nail and making her squirm. She longed to snatch her hand away and end this farcical confrontation. But she couldn't. She was as transfixed as if their two hands were gummed together.

"I can't tell 'ee any more than 'ee already know," Helza said at last, and the spell was broken as Celia furiously rubbed her palm against her skirt.

"Well, so much for your magical powers," she snapped.

She was disorientated with disappointment. But had she really expected this madwoman to say she had seen a vision of Stefan in some castle stronghold deep in the German countryside, where he was being incarcerated from indulging in any suspected subversive activities . . .?

Her head spun wildly at the thought, and she realised that Helza was already hobbling away from her.

"Wait," she called weakly.

Helza turned and called back, her thin voice carrying on the breeze. "You don't need me to tell 'ee what your own senses know, missie. There's only one man in your life, and your heart line is strong and unbroken. Bide your time, and you'll be together again."

She was gone, while Celia was still asking herself whether she had in fact seen a vision of the place where Stefan was. Or had it all been a hideous fantasy because she wanted so much to believe that, because of his status in the community and what she knew would

157

have been his dignified refusal to co-operate with the Nazis, he had not been severely punished?

However feeble the hope, she told herself that she *had* to believe it or she would end up completely mad. The alternative was to think that it was her own Cornish feyness providing what she so longed to know.

She shivered, not sure she wanted to believe that either. But whatever the reason for the thought or the vision or whatever it had been, she walked on with an ever-quickening step.

Seb saw her coming. He was taking a break outside, and he greeted her with a scowl on his handsome face.

"Sorry, cuz, you've caught me at a bad moment. It's no joke to find out that a young whipper-snapper is better at doing your job that you are."

Despite her own tormented feelings, Celia couldn't resist a small smile at the indignity in his voice.

"If you mean Butch, why shouldn't be good at it? He's had enough tuition from experts, hasn't he? You and Adam should be proud that he's such a good apprentice."

"And when did you become such a diplomat? You're wasted down here in the sticks, Celia."

She didn't miss the sharpness of his reply. It matched the way she used to be, what seemed like a hundred years ago. Now, she simply didn't have the energy to be sharp – and even as she thought it, she knew it was a terrible way to feel for someone of her age. It was the way old women thought, and she mentally and physically straightened her back.

"This is where I belong – for now, anyway," she amended. An image had flashed into her mind at that moment of where she dearly wanted to be, and it wasn't here.

It wasn't anywhere remotely near here. It was among the foothills of mountains where sweet-scented wild flowers grew in profusion, and where the air was as clear as wine . . .

"Hey, what's wrong?" Seb said at once, seeing how her face suddenly crumpled. "This isn't like you at all. You've always been the strongest one among us."

"Have I?" she said, her eyes stinging. 'Well, perhaps I don't want to be strong. Perhaps I just want somebody to lean on, the way people have always leaned on me—"

Without warning, she was in his arms and sobbing on his shoulder. He had always felt affection for her, and she knew that, but thankfully she recognised that there was nothing in the least sexual in the embrace. There was just sweet, much-needed comfort. Eventually she drew away from him.

"Thanks," she said, her voice tight. "We two old crocks should stick together, shouldn't we?"

"Old crocks?" he said, the old aggression back. "Since when did a Tremayne ever become an old crock? My father resisted that until the end, and so will I – and so will you."

"But I'm not a Tremayne, am I?" Celia said, ready to argue. "There's not many left with the name now."

"Tell that to the stars," he retorted. "Once it's in your blood, you never lose it. Nor the name of Killigrew, either. Your mother's plans are going to see to that, aren't they? She's a woman after old Morwen Tremayne's heart, and so are you. Don't let anybody ever tell you different."

"My God, Seb, you're the one who's wasted here," she said in honest amazement, never having heard him be quite so passionate about their heritage.

She didn't dare let herself get emotional about the fact that he had mentioned the stars. She had to keep the faith. She only had to look into the sky at night and see *their* star to know that the love she and Stefan shared was still bright, still strong and everlasting.

She swallowed. "Hadn't you better get back to work? I've come up here to see how things are going, not to have a pep talk – but I thank you for it all the same, Sebby."

She hugged his arm to take the sting out of her words. He was her cousin and her friend, and she needed him now.

"Come and see how young Butch is getting on, then," he said roughly. "He's our rising star now."

Christmas 1943 was a frugal affair as far as normal fare went, but like people everywhere, the Pengellys and their family were determined to make the most of it. As always, Skye and Nick were determined to host the day for as many of the family as could turn up. Wenna was out of the country now, and 'somewhere in Europe', according to the sparse letters she was able to send.

But, amazingly and without warning, Olly arrived home on Christmas Eve, amid tears and laughter from his mother and sister, and a manly hug from his father.

"Did Wenna get leave?" he asked, once the first excitement of reunion had tempered a little.

"No," Skye said, feeling the familiar tug at her heart. "It would have been so marvellous if we could all have been together again."

"Not only for us, Mother," Olly said. "I've brought somebody with me for the holidays. I hope it's all right."

"Of course it is. You know that."

"Have you got a lady friend at last, Olly?" teased Nick.

"It's not a lady – and he's more interested in Wenna than me, Dad. He's gone to see Aunt Betsy right now, but I said I'd go and fetch him later. It's Wenna's Canadian. We ran into one another a few weeks ago and discovered we both had a seventy-two hour pass, so I invited him here. I hope that's all right."

"Wenna's Canadian?" Celia said quickly.

"Group Captain Harry Mack. She must have mentioned him to you. He was recuperating at Aunt Betsy's when she came down here some time ago, and he was besotted with her. They've been writing to one another for some time, I gather."

Celia stared. Her parents seemed to know all about this affair, while she had allowed herself to become so insular that she hadn't even been aware that Wenna had had a beau after Austin had been killed in action.

She knew she *should* remember it, but sometimes her memory was so hazy that she could recall nothing from before the nervous breakdown. It was frightening, and something she didn't care to mention to anyone.

But she did recall that Wenna had said she was never going to lose her heart to anyone again after the trauma of Austin's and Fanny Rosenbloom's deaths. So it would be interesting to meet this Group Captain Harry Mack and see how far the association had gone.

Even as she thought it, she knew how much she had changed too. In the past she would have known a sibling rivalry for Wenna's new man, while now she only felt a protective need to look him over, to ensure that he wasn't taking advantage of Wenna's vulnerability. She had changed, as they all had. War did that, tearing people apart, changing lives, making some of them strong and some of them fall to pieces . . .

"Are you all right, Celia?" Olly said now. "You can come with me to collect Harry, if you like. He asked me to call him Harry while we're on leave," he added, "even though his rank is much higher than mine."

Celia smiled at his obvious pride in having become an associate of this man. Olly had grown so much in stature and maturity, she thought with a rush of affection. He was no longer her little brother. He was a man.

"Yes, I'd like to come with you. Mom knows I don't like being indoors for too long, and in the new year I'll be out in the fields all day long, I dare say."

"Good God, when Mother told me you were going to be a Land Girl, I didn't believe it. You haven't changed your mind about mucking out the cows and dishing out pigswill then?"

Skye forestalled her with a laugh. "When did you know your sister change her mind about anything she had set her heart on, Olly? She's a true—"

"If you're about to say I'm a true Tremayne, I'd rather you didn't," Celia cut in swiftly. "I've heard it so often, I sometimes begin to wonder just who I really am."

"It's meant as a great compliment, darling," her father told her. "Anyone who ever knew old Morwen Tremayne – and your own grandmother – knows that."

"I know it too," Celia muttered. "I just want to be myself, that's all. I'm nobody's reincarnation, and I don't want to be. I'm sorry if that offends anybody."

"It doesn't, honey," Skye said softly. "Because I have so often thought the very same thing."

"Mom's remark didn't help. It just makes me feel even more that we're all somehow one and the same person," Celia said to Olly a while later, when they were bumping along the lanes towards Truro in their father's car to collect Harry Mack. "It's spooky, isn't it?"

"Only if you let it be," Olly said. "This isn't like you, Celia. I know you were unwell some time ago—"

"I had a nervous breakdown, Olly," she said brutally. "I'm not afraid to say the words, and I wish other people wouldn't hedge around them either. Thank God for Lily and David, who don't patronise me by pretending it was something as simple as a summer cold."

"All right, so you're over it now, and you don't want to hang on to it like a comfort blanket. That's good. Forget it, and live for the moment. It's all we've got, anyway."

His accurate summary took her by surprise. "You're such a philosopher all of a sudden, aren't you?"

"Takes one to know one," he said with a grin. "But you know I'm right. The past is behind us and tomorrow's still an unknown quantity. So we've just got to dig in our heels and make the most of today."

She was touched by this new, mature Oliver. He was all of twenty years old now, but he had the wisdom of Solomon compared with the muddle in her own mind lately.

And yes, he was right. She couldn't reach Stefan now, except in her heart, and they could only live each day as it came, until they knew what the future might hold.

"I love you, Olly," she said, the words leaving her lips before she could stop them.

Immediately, she gave a rough laugh to hide her embarrassment. "Oh Lord, just forget I said that! What kind of a soppy, halfwit sister tells her strapping brother that she loves him, for God's sake?"

He squeezed her hand for a second until he put his own back on the steering wheel again.

"The best, that's all. And you're no halfwit. For the record, I love you too, but if you don't want me to run this damn vehicle over a cliff, you'd better change the subject or you'll have us both blubbering. So has anybody heard from the ghastly Daphne child yet?"

"We had a home-made Christmas card," Celia said, glad that he had so cleverly turned the conversation. "She's full of importance now that she's going to live in America when her mother marries her GI."

"God help America then. If they're not careful, it will be Daphne for President in a few years' time," Olly said solemnly, at which they were both convulsed.

"We've met before," Group Captain Harry Mack said, shaking Celia's hand. "Don't you remember?"

The instant she saw him, she remembered the pub in Norwich, and the motley crowd of servicemen singing and laughing, and this handsome Canadian plying her and Moonie with the unexpected luxury of wine. And Harry Mack mistaking her, ever so briefly, for the girl he obviously adored, her sister Wenna.

"I do indeed," she said. "How nice to see you again."

"I hear you've been ill. Are you better now?"

The easy manner with which he said it was as refreshing as a summer breeze to Celia. There was no guile about this man, and she responded instantly.

"Well enough to look forward to a change of occupation. I've just completed my training for the Women's Land Army."

Harry whistled approvingly. "Good for you. There's nothing like good country air for putting some healthy colour back into a person's cheeks. I should know."

"Do you come from a country background then?"

"Canada's one huge backyard," he said engagingly. "I miss the wide open spaces at times, but I'm getting used to it here – and there are compensations, of course."

"Though unfortunately she's not here for the holidays, old bean," Olly put in, pushing his luck with the familiar RAF jargon, in Celia's opinion.

"But at least I can be with her family, and feel her presence in her home," Harry said.

"Good Lord, my mother would say those words are worthy of a true Cornishman," Celia said, caught by the simplicity of the statement.

"Well, thank you for the compliment, ma'am," he said with genuine delight, but his teasing words told Celia it was a mark of how deeply he felt for Wenna. She only hoped her sister appreciated the fact.

Twelve

"My sister's working on a farm near Penzance," Wenna reported to her friend, when the letter finally caught up with their ENSA unit in northern Italy.

"She must be mad," Rita said baldly. "All that muck and animal stink wouldn't be my cup of cocoa, I can tell you. You can keep the country as far as I'm concerned."

"That's because you're a city girl."

"*You* left it for the smoke, didn't you?"

"That's different. I had a career opportunity," Wenna said. She realised how grand she sounded, and gave a half-smile. "Oh well, all right, I suppose I did. It doesn't mean I don't love the country too, though."

"What else does she say?" Rita asked lazily. She wasn't really interested, but anything was better than being confined to barracks now that their tour was over, and they were preparing to return to England.

"They had a lovely Christmas, and my brother had a friend staying at New World with him."

"Not peculiar, is he?" Rita sniggered.

"No, he is not," Wenna said crossly. "As a matter of fact, it was Harry."

"*Your* Harry?"

Wenna sighed. She had long since given up protesting to Rita that Group Captain Mack wasn't her Harry. Besides, by now, she was fairly certain that he was – or could be, if they ever got the chance to see one another again.

As yet, it was no more than a long-distance relationship, built mainly on correspondence, but the memory of his voice was strong in her head whenever she read his letters, and to Wenna, that had to mean something significant.

Already, she knew he was more than a friend, and, inevitably, the searing pain she had felt when Austin had been killed in action was fading from her mind, no matter how much she had tried to cling on to it.

"So?" Rita persisted. "*Was* it your Harry your brother took home to Cornwall for Christmas leave?"

"Yes, it was my Harry," Wenna said softly. "And I wish I'd been there as well to see everybody. My mother always makes a big thing of Christmas, and invites all the family. My stepfather's widowed brother is courting again too," she added, "so it looks as if we'll be having another wedding in the family sometime."

That was another surprising bit of information from Celia, thought Wenna. Adam Pengelly had kept this very quiet – but then, he was a very quiet man, and rather a dull old stick in Wenna's opinion. His new lady friend was also widowed, and fifty-something like himself, according to Celia, and they were clearly looking for companionship rather than passion.

Wenna wondered fleetingly how fulfilled a marriage it would be . . . and without warning her thoughts turned to Harry Mack again, and the look in his eyes that had told her instantly that he desired her. Her heart began to beat considerably faster. The woman that Harry Mack married certainly wouldn't enter into a quiet, middle-aged marriage . . .

"Where's your brother stationed now, Pengo?" Rita was saying. "Is he still in Wiltshire?"

Wenna had a job to drag her thoughts back from the erotic image of being held tightly in Harry Mack's arms and tasting his kisses on her lips, and was irritated with Rita for obliging her to let the image fade.

"I don't know. You'd hardly expect him to tell anybody, would you?" she snapped. "He's with Bomber Command now, though, and Celia says he's dropped a few heavy hints that he might be involved in the invasion – if it ever happens. But now that he's come clean about getting into the air force under age, Olly's become a stickler for the rules. He's quite a character, my brother."

She'd never truly thought about it before. But she realised she admired him tremendously for his tenacity in getting what he wanted. Olly always did, she thought.

Celia too, seemed more like her old self now, she thought thankfully. For a time, the nervous breakdown had been a worry for all of them. It was so unlike Celia, whom Wenna had always considered so much stronger than herself.

One of the other girls in the concert party popped her head around the barrack door as Rita went out.

"Pengelly, there was another letter for you. It must have been left on my bed by mistake, and I've only just got back from the ablutions. Sorry," she said.

Wenna took it absently. Such things happened, and it was nothing to get het up about. And then her heart leapt as she recognised Harry's writing on the envelope, and in an instant she knew that whatever feelings she had for him, they were definitely far from platonic. She'd never really believed that old chestnut about absence making the heart grow fonder, but she was beginning to believe in it now. She opened the letter with shaking hands. It was two months since Christmas, but the letter had only just caught up with her.

I couldn't believe we had missed one another, *Harry Mack wrote*. It was so poignant, being there in your home, touching the things you used to touch, breathing in the atmosphere you knew so well, and imagining other times when you would have joined in singing the Christmas carols around the tree and raising your glass of hot punch for the toast to absent friends. You must know who I had in mind when your mother made that particular toast. I was so happy to be there, and yet so sad without you. It was like stumbling about in the dark and being unable to see the sun and be completely warmed again. You see what effect you have on me, my sweet girl? I dream of you, Wenna, and whenever I hear the words of a love song, I hear your voice in my head.

Even when you're not beside me, I can still feel your presence, and I'm writing this letter slightly under the influence of too much English beer, otherwise I wouldn't be so free with my words. I shall post it without reading it again, or else I'm quite sure I'll never dare to tell you how much I love you and ache to see you again.

Maybe someday when all this is over, I'll show you how vast and awe-inspiring the Canadian prairies are − but nothing could ever be as beautiful as you are to me.

Wenna pressed the letter to her mouth, her eyes stinging with tears. He was so sweet, so utterly and adorably open and sweet, and oh yes, she knew she was falling in love with him. She no longer fought against it. Every love song she sang, she sang for him. Every prayer she offered up was that he would come through this war safely. Every longing in her heart was that someday, someday . . .

She heard the door of the barrack room open and bang shut, and then came Rita's alarmed voice.

"Good God, Pengo, you look as if you've seen a ghost. Not bad news, is it?"

"No," she said huskily. "Not bad news at all."

By the beginning of April, everyone knew that something big was in the wind. The invasion had to happen soon. By now thousands more American and Canadian troops had poured into Britain as General Eisenhower directed his final preparations for the long-awaited invasion and subsequent liberation of Europe from the Nazi stranglehold.

Every coastal area in Britain was banned to visitors as the dummy manoeuvres were conducted on and off shore, fooling the enemy as to where and when the actual assault would originate. Everything was being rehearsed, from airborne landings by parachute, to amphibious operations for landing guns and tanks and personnel. By the end of the month all foreign travel was banned, except for troop movements.

Oliver Pengelly was impatient for it all to begin, and, with the optimism of youth, he was euphoric with the feeling that he could conquer the world single-handed.

"Do you have a death wish or something, brainless?" one of his fellow erks commented. "I'm not half so keen to fly over enemy territory as you seem to be. You should have been born a Yank with all that crazy enthusiasm."

"Thanks, Tom," Olly said with a laugh. "I'll take that as a compliment. My mother's American, and she thanks you too."

The other grimaced. "Doesn't anything ever get you down, you bugger?" he said with wry good humour.

"Why should it? I'm doing the job I was meant to do, and once we've gone in to support the invasion forces, we'll be laughing. It'll all be over by Christmas."

"And where have I heard that before?"

"Well, it can't go on for ever, can it?" Olly said reasonably. "Though I intend to stick with this job permanently. Maybe I'll go into commercial flying or get some backing to start my own flying service—"

"Listen to the monied bastard!" Tom and his other cronies started jeering. "None of that's for me, mate. The minute this is over, I'm back to my desk in the bank."

"Good. I'll know where to come for a loan then, won't I?" Olly said crisply.

He hadn't really meant any of it seriously. He hadn't even

thought about after the war. All he knew was that he wanted to keep on flying, to be as near to reaching the stars as it was possible for a man to be. And *that* little bit of poetic licence was something he wasn't going to share with these bastards, he thought cheerfully.

But it all had to end sometime, and when it did, there would be thousands like him, looking for something to do. Looking for something to replace the mixture of excitement and fear that was so intense that it was almost sexual. Something to replace the rush of adrenalin that came when their silver machine soared into the sky, with no more attachment to the earth they left behind; as free as birds and almost blinded by the welcoming sun.

Olly wasn't religious in the slightest, but he had to admit that when he was flying, he felt nearer to God – if there was a God – than at any other time in his life.

"Who's coming down to the NAAFI?" he said, before his thoughts began to get too serious. "I'll stand anyone who beats me there to a pint, and the rest is on you buggers."

He would miss the camaraderie too, he admitted to himself, as Tom slung his arm loosely around his shoulders and gave him a friendly punch in the solar plexus to wind him and slow him down before they all raced towards the canteen.

Skye missed Daphne Hollis more than she had expected to. She had been gone a long while now, but her presence had been so forceful that even now, Skye sometimes imagined she could hear her scathing remarks as she burst in from school, especially during her last few days.

"Bleedin' stupid lessons. Who cares about stupid old history, anyway?"

"You have to do your lessons, Daphne. It's important to know about what happened in the past—"

"Why is it? It don't matter to me. I'm prob'ly going to end up famous, anyway, like Wenna. I might even be a picture star, and I won't need to know about stupid old history when I'm making pots of dough, so there!"

Skye smiled, remembering, and wondered if Daphne's prophetically wild remarks had been due to the mystic influence of Cornwall. Whether they had or not, she was apparently going to live in America one day, and her young head would soon be filled with dreams of storming Hollywood.

Mentally, Skye wished her well, and admitted that if anyone could manipulate dreams to make them come true, it would probably be Daphne Hollis.

Her own dreams for the re-invented Killigrew Clay were going nowhere. Nor could they, Nick told her reasonably as they got ready for bed that evening. Not yet, anyway.

There was no sense in trying to build a flourishing new empire out of a dying industry, since there would be no tourists, curious to see how an old clayworks operated, for the foreseeable future. She knew she should be content that the pottery was still in business, with the clayworks still ticking over. It just didn't suit her productive and impatient mind to have to wait until Hitler was crushed before she could begin on her new venture, which was what it amounted to.

"You can still draw up some outline plans and sketches for the preliminary ideas, darling," Nick told her. "And the research for your booklets should give you a better idea of how the open-air museum should take shape."

"Is that how you see it? An open-air museum?" she said, pausing in her undressing.

"Well, isn't it?"

"I suppose so. I hadn't thought of it in exactly those words, though. I like the sound of it, Nick. And you're right. There are things I can do, even if the reality of it all seems so very far away."

He put his arms around her. "My poor love. You always did want everything to happen at once, didn't you?"

Skye smiled ruefully. 'You think that at my age I should have learned more temperance, I suppose."

His arms tightened around her. "I do not. I don't want to change a single thing about you. Why do you think I fell in love with you in the first place if it wasn't for your quicksilver mind?"

She spoke teasingly. "Oh, was that the reason? I thought it was more physical than mental."

He laughed. 'Well, maybe so, at first. What red-blooded man could resist such a beautiful woman? It was only later than I discovered that you had brains as well as beauty."

"I'm not sure whether or not that's a chauvinistic remark, honey," Skye said, ready to bridle.

"No, it's not. It's simply the truth. The man who gets a wife who combines brains and beauty is twice blessed," he said, more solemnly. "I fear Adam has yet to discover the lack of brains in his new lady when they tie the knot."

"Oh, of course he won't," Skye said, defending her at once. "Felicity is quiet and charming, as well as being an excellent homemaker and cook, so I'm sure they have everything they both

169

want. No two marriages are ever the same, Nick, and in your profession you should know that only too well, so don't be so patronising!"

He laughed again at her indignant voice. "I always love the way your eyes sparkle like sapphires when you become defensive about something. And as I didn't marry you simply because you were an excellent homemaker and cook, I've got my own ideas on what makes a good marriage."

"Oh, really?" Skye said, perfectly aware that he was hardening against her, and teasing him a moment longer. "Perhaps you'd better tell me what they are then."

"I'd far rather show you," Nick said meaningly.

As his hands went to her shoulders and slid the remaining article of clothing from them, she felt the familiar surge of desire at his touch, and sent up a silent prayer of thanks that this marriage was still so good, and so passionate, after all these years.

David Kingsley telephoned her in the middle of May.

"Betsy's in a hell of a state," he said. "Lily's gone over there now, but I thought you'd want to know."

"What's happened?" she said at once. Betsy Tremayne was the calmest of women and almost *never* got into a state, so it must be something pretty bad, she thought fearfully.

"Justin's caught a packet," David said baldly. "He was patching up some of the wounded when he got caught up in the firing line somewhere in Italy. Betsy doesn't have the full details yet, except that he's already been sent home to a military hospital, but she's in a real panic. After all the comfort she's given to the boys recuperating at Killigrew House, it's a pretty rum do that her own two sons should have caught it, isn't it?"

He went on talking in his quickfire way, but Skye couldn't concentrate. All she heard was the word Italy, a place she hoped and prayed Wenna was well away from now. And all she could think was that both Betsy's two sons had been wounded, while her own was blessedly still safe – as far as she knew. As far as any of them knew . . .

"Are you still there, Skye? I thought you'd want to get over to Betsy's as well."

"Of course I do," she said, fighting down the brief panic that had taken all her breath away for a moment. "I'll get there as soon as I can."

She put down the phone with clammy hands. Just as you got a

little bit complacent, thinking things were going the Allies' way at last . . . just as you thought your own family was somehow charmed and invincible, something happened to remind you that everybody was vulnerable . . .

"I'm going up to the pottery now, Mrs Pen," she heard Butch Butcher's voice say. "Are there any messages?"

She turned with a start. Butch had become so much a part of the family, so much her faithful shadow, that she sometimes forgot he was there. But she wondered now if Seb had gone up to White Rivers before Betsy got the telegram, and if he was unaware of what had happened to his brother.

"No messages, Butch. I have to telephone Sebby myself. You run along now," she said, her voice thick.

"Are you all right?" he asked anxiously.

She nodded, unable to answer sensibly. Just wanting to be left alone, and to gather her thoughts for a moment before she picked up the phone again and asked the operator for the number of the White Rivers Pottery.

"He's not here," Adam answered. "I don't know what's happened to everybody today, but we don't have much business anyway—"

"Adam, Justin's been wounded. I don't know how bad it is, but if Sebby's still on his way to work it could be that he doesn't know yet. Break it to him gently when he gets there. I'm going to see Betsy, and I'll call you again later."

She couldn't say any more. She needed to get out of the house and gulp some fresh air. Whatever happened to one member of the family affected all of them, and even though Justin had been the most self-sufficient of all the cousins, she knew that sometimes the most independent were the ones who fell the hardest. Like Betsy herself . . .

She was proved right the minute she entered Killigrew House and was enveloped in Betsy's clinging embrace. Lily shook her head behind Betsy's back, and Skye wondered fearfully just what she was about to be told.

"Right after the telegram came I got a letter from some medical friend o' Justin's, Skye," Betsy gabbled, "and 'tis worse than I feared. How my poor boy will cope, I don't know. 'Tis a blessing his father's not alive to see this sad day—"

"Come and sit down, Betsy, and tell me exactly what's happened," Skye said carefully. "Show me this letter."

Her heart lurched painfully as soon as she scanned the words, couched in a formal, unsentimental manner of which Justin would have approved, being a medical man himself, but which completely demoralised Betsy.

Dear God, Skye thought in horror, as she read the clinical words. Justin had not only been blinded, but it seemed as though half his face had been blown away . . . For a moment, she felt her innards turn to water at the thought, and then guiltily willed the ghastly images away.

"He says Justin don't even want to come home to us," Betsy moaned, her face scarlet, and her eyes flooding with tears. "He says Justin has to deal with his blindness in his own way and he don't want nobody's pity, nor nobody seeing 'im until they've rebuilt his face. His *lovely face*, Skye," she almost screeched. "Just as if we'd be giving 'im pity, anyway. 'Tis love he wants, love and comfort, and that's what he'd get from his own fam'ly!"

Skye met Lily's glance, and knew they were both thinking the same thing. No matter what she said, they knew that if Justin came home, he would be simply smothered with all the love and pity that Betsy could give him. He'd be as helpless as a puppet, completely dependent on her, and she would slowly love him to death. He would be killed by devotion – if he didn't take his grandfather Walter's way out and kill himself. But how could you say such a thing to a grieving mother who wanted him back in the womb?

Skye was still hugging Betsy close and wondering when the keening would end when Sebby came bursting into the room.

"Adam told me when I got to the pottery, and I came back at once. How bad is it?" he said abruptly.

Lily took the letter from the table and handed it to him.

"It seems it all happened a few weeks ago, but Justin refused to let any of us know until he was back in England, had got the full medical opinion and had decided his own future," she told him. "This is from a close friend and colleague."

Sebby said nothing for a few minutes, and then he nodded.

"I'll go to London and see him," he said.

"Oh, we could do that, couldn't we?" Betsy said at once, sudden hope in her voice. "We could take him things—"

"No, Mother, I'd said *I'd* go and see him. The last thing he wants right now is for folk to descend on him when he's in a vulnerable state. He's not a peep show."

"I'm not *folk*. I'm his mother."

He put his arm around her bulky figure. He rarely made a great show of family affection, but no one could miss his awkward concern for her.

"Ma, listen to me," he said gently, reverting to his old childhood name for her. "I know something of what Justin's going through now, because I've been through it too. I know that feeling of not wanting to see anybody, or having anybody see me. My wounds have healed and I've little more to show for it than a limp. Justin's wounds will take far longer, and you have to accept that he's never going to see again."

"You're cruel to say so," Betsy cried out.

"I'm being honest, Ma. Justin's blind, and his senses will be heightened because of it. He won't be able to see, but he'll sense the pity that people feel for him, and he won't be able to bear it. Not yet. Maybe not for a long time. And that's why we have to stay away until he's ready."

"Except for you," she said accusingly.

"I'm his brother," Seb said simply. "He'll know I understand."

Seeing the indecision on Betsy's florid face, Skye spoke swiftly. "Seb's right, Betsy. No matter how much we want to help, we have to let the young ones fight their own battles. You must know that from the boys you've had living here. Some want to talk it all out, and others want to shut themselves away until they're ready to face the world again."

After what seemed an age, Betsy nodded.

"But my Justin's never going to face the world again, is he?" She swallowed deeply, then spoke more resolutely. "You go to him with my blessing then, Sebby, and tell him when he's ready to come home, we'll be here, just like always."

"It was a very traumatic afternoon," Skye reported to the family over supper that evening. "I felt desperately sorry for Betsy. She's done so much for the boys in her care, yet when it came to her own, she felt completely rejected."

"I can imagine," Nick said. "It's a bit like God throwing back all your good works in your face."

"Oh Nick, I wouldn't say that exactly!"

"You might if it was Olly," he said reasonably.

"Is Justin going to be blind for ever, Mrs Pen?" Butch said nervously. Hoping they wouldn't notice, he had experimented on the thought by closing his eyes, feeling across the table for the salt cellar, and knocking it flying.

"You little idiot," Celia snapped, home for the weekend and

jittery with nerves at this latest happening in their family. "Of course he's going to be blind for ever. It's not like a cough or a cold that you get over next week. What do you suppose he'll do, Mom? He's too young to sit around in a Twilight Home twiddling his thumbs. He'd go mad in a week."

"I don't know," Skye said in distress. "I simply don't know. We'll find out more when Seb's been to London and spoken with him and his doctors."

"At least he seems to have a good friend in this fellow who wrote to Betsy," Nick said. "A medical man, is he?"

"I suppose so," said Skye. "He seemed to know all about Justin's condition, anyway."

Seb Tremayne took the first available train to London and found his way to the military hospital on the outskirts where his brother was being treated for his wounds. He had enough experience of hospitals to know the kind of smells that would assault his nostrils the minute he walked through those doors. The sickly, nauseatingly sweet smell of gangrene and the stifling scent of starched uniforms, carbolic and polished linoleum floors, all mingling with other smells too indescribable to define, well masked by the overpowering stink of disinfectant.

It was enough to turn the strongest stomach, as was the sound of the poor wretches who would be doing just that, heaving their guts out into the nearest receptacle – providing there was one near enough. Seb prayed that Justin wouldn't be one of them.

He thought he had forgotten that time when he too had been brought in to a field hospital to be patched up and sent back as gun fodder. He considered he'd got off lightly when they didn't think him fit enough. But there was bitterness as well as guilty relief in the fact, and before they sent him back to Blighty, he'd still had to go through the ordeal of sharing a ward with men who were never going to get through another night or another day. He had been unable to avoid listening to their screams and agonies as they struggled for one last precious breath.

He had waited inevitably for the heaviest silence a man ever knew. It wasn't the peaceful ending of the very old, dying after a lifetime of fulfilment. It was the jagged silence of a life cut short, long before its time, and it was a silence like no other.

Here and now, returning to one of the hospitals where such nightmares happened, day after day after day, Seb knew he would never forget it. It was a rite of passage and only those who had endured it would ever really know what it was like.

"Can I help you, sir?" said an orderly.

Seb felt momentarily irritated by the officious voice of the young man in the stained white coat that proclaimed his pride in his work. In civvies now, Seb knew he had no status here. He wasn't one of the honourably wounded, or the 'nearly-deads' as he and his equally macabre fellow patients had called those in the beds nearest the door . . . he was just a visitor. However, he quickly regretted his assessment of this young man, seeing the weary way he pushed his hair back from his forehead. They were all stretched to the limit these days.

"I've come to see my brother. He's a patient here. MO Justin Tremayne," he added with professional efficiency.

The orderly's eyes grew more respectful. "I think there's someone with him right now, but I'll tell him you're here."

"I can wait if he's receiving treatment—"

"Oh no, it's a friend who comes to sit with him for the best part of every day. I'll show you to his ward."

"Is this friend a Captain Giles Peterson?" Seb said casually, not knowing why his heart should be thudding a little faster. Good friends were more precious than gold, but some friends were more precious than others.

He had no idea why he should suddenly be having these thoughts, and these feelings. Justin was his brother, and he thought he knew him as well as he knew himself . . .

"He's in here, Mr Tremayne," the orderly said, pointing to a side ward. "Just go on in."

"Is it usual for a man with his injuries to be placed in a side ward?" Seb persisted.

"He was very badly burned, and delirious enough to warrant it. We have to consider the other patients, you know," the orderly added delicately.

"You mean he was raving. It's all right, I've been invalided out myself, so I know the form."

The orderly gave a slight smile. "Then I don't need to explain. Besides, Captain Peterson made a generous donation to the hospital for equipment that's badly needed. The least we can do is to give his friend as much comfort as we can."

You're too young and too naive to see what's right under your nose, thought Seb. *And I pray to God that you are, and that maybe I'm wrong.*

175

As the orderly hurried away to attend to his duties, Seb pushed open the door of the side ward and paused.

The man in the bed was lying perfectly flat, with varying pieces of equipment attached to him. Because of the heavy bandages covering most of his face and the pads over his eyes, he was completely unrecognisable.

In that fraction of a moment, Seb felt the gorge rise in his throat, remembering how he and Justin had romped with their cousins as children, up, up on the moors, breathing in the crystal clear air, sliding down the sky tips that were part of their heritage, and dreaming of the days beyond childhood when all dreams were possible. And now there was this wreck of a man, still young, for whom all dreams had ended . . .

His attention was caught by the middle-aged man sitting beside the bed. As yet, he hadn't turned around to see who had entered the ward. He was too busy leaning forward toward the patient, speaking softly, his strong hand holding the lifeless one, the thumb gently caressing Justin's, the murmured words of comfort as deep and intimate as if from a lover. And at once, Seb knew.

He cleared his throat, and the man turned around. He was handsome, full of military bearing, his face etched with pain until he adjusted his expression on seeing a stranger.

"I'm sorry," he said in an educated voice. "I'll wait outside if you need to examine him—"

"I'm not a doctor," Seb said in a strangled voice.

The figure on the bed moved its head the merest fraction.

"Seb, is that you? I knew you'd come."

Seb moved forward, and saw how Justin's hand slid away from his companion's clasp.

"Of course I came, if only to report home how you are and prevent Ma from tearing up here with armfuls of home-made produce, convinced that they're not feeding you properly."

He had to be jocular and talk quickly, because if he didn't, he knew he would simply fall apart. He was a man, and everyone knew that men didn't cry . . . except in wartime. Except when someone they dearly loved was reduced to this . . .

He felt the touch of Captain Peterson's hand on his shoulder, and just managed to resist recoiling from it.

"I'll speak to you later, if I may, Mr Tremayne," he said quietly. "You'll want to spend time alone with your brother."

"Thank you."

He left them alone, and Seb realised he was completely out of his depth, not knowing how to begin an impossible conversation. It was one thing to be faced with the most terrible injuries he could have envisaged for his brother. It was something else entirely to be confronted with this new situation that was as shocking as it was unexpected.

To his amazement he heard Justin give a small laugh. At least, he presumed that the thin sound that came through the bandages was intended to be a laugh.

"Poor Sebby. You had no idea, did you?"

"Well, I didn't expect to see you quite so swathed in bandages," he blustered.

"That's not what I mean, and you know it. But don't worry. We're outwardly respectable citizens, despite the fact that I shall come out of these bandages looking like a gargoyle, I dare say. But Giles will take good care of me. He's got one of those places in wildest Yorkshire they call stately piles. Ironic, isn't it? All that money and no heir to leave it to. Well, he couldn't have, could he?"

"Are you sure you should be talking so much?" Seb said, when he couldn't think of anything else to say.

"I'm supposed to talk, no matter how painful it is. It exercises the facial muscles and stops them seizing up. So what do you think of my friend?"

Seb winced. "Oh, don't ask that of me—"

"Good God, bruth, I never realised you were so narrow-minded and insular. And you in the Forces too. Didn't you ever see *friends* together?"

Yes; saw them disgraced and hounded out of the army, and shunned them as much as possible . . .

When he didn't reply, Justin went on, his voice still muffled behind the bandages, but with an edge to it now.

"Let me tell you something, Sebby. There would be no future for me now without Giles. I thank God for him every day. For his wanting my companionship in the good days, and still wanting it now. When the doctors and surgeons have finally done with me, we shall move to Yorkshire. He's retired from the army now, and he's promised to look after me as long as I live. Wouldn't you say that's the best kind of friend there is for a wretch like me?"

Seb couldn't doubt the sincerity in his voice, and he sensed Justin's need for his approval too. It was against his own nature to approve of the kind of lifestyle these two shared, but it was their lives.

"I say that anyone whose friend thinks that much of them is

fortunate indeed," he said at last. "But Justin – you are discreet, aren't you?"

"I've been discreet for years," Justin said simply. "But I'm still your brother. Aren't I?"

"And always will be," said Seb.

Thirteen

" So did you meet this stuffy Captain Peterson who wrote to me?"
Betsy wanted to know, when she had exhausted every ounce of information she could get out of Seb on his return to Cornwall, and been reassured that Justin was in the best possible hands. "What did you think of him? What was he like?"

Seb paused. *What was he like?*

How could he possibly repeat the emotional conversation he had had with Justin's companion, without admitting to this homely countrywoman that there were more kinds of love in this world than he had cared to believe, and that only the completely bigoted – or those who were as truly blind as his own brother – would condemn it?

In his heart Seb still condemned it too, but his love for his brother overcame his revulsion. Even so, such a revelation would break his mother's heart, and since it was against the law for two men to indulge in the kind of relationship that would disgrace a family, it was a secret Seb had vowed to reveal to no one outside the three people who now knew it.

"Well, go on, what was he like?" Betsy persisted.

"He's intelligent and well-spoken, and being a medical man himself he's taken a great interest in Justin's future. He's a wealthy man, retired from the army now, and he's offered to move Justin to his private clinic in Yorkshire to study his case," he invented quickly.

Betsy sniffed. "Treating him like one o' they specimens, is he? I don't think Justin will take kindly to that."

"I think Justin will be thankful to be so well looked after, Ma. Strangers can sometimes be the best people to have around you in times of trauma. Your boys here know that, so you should understand a little of how Justin feels. I truly think it's the best thing for him, at least until he regains his self-confidence."

"And then he'll come home to us?"

"Well, that's for him to decide," Seb said vaguely. "But Captain

179

Peterson's promised to send me regular reports until Justin feels well enough to try writing to us himself."

Betsy looked at him as if he was stupid. "And how's he going to do that with no eyes to see? How will he be able to read his own words, or even keep the lines straight on the paper?" she said, bursting into uncontrollable tears at the thought of all that frustration and wasted education. Justin was always so proud of his achievements, and so was she.

Seb put his arm around her. "He'll be taught Braille, Ma. Captain Peterson – Giles – will see to it all in his clinic. Justin was always quick to learn, he'll discover how to read with his fingers, and when he wants to write to us he'll dictate the words he wants to say. Just don't expect things to happen quickly. They have to patch up his face first, and it'll be a long time before he's done with hospitals."

Now that he had had that long conversation with Giles Peterson he had to admire the man for standing by Justin. It wasn't a lifestyle Seb understood, and it wasn't something he cared to think about too much. But he couldn't doubt the genuine feelings the two men had for one another, and once away from prying and curious eyes in the wilds of Yorkshire, he knew his brother would be safe and cared for.

But with an urgent need to prove his own masculinity to himself, Seb had spent his last night in London in the company of an enthusiastic and large-breasted prostitute. And in the best barrack-room vernacular, he had given her a bloody good seeing-to.

By the middle of May, everyone knew what was about to happen. There was an undercurrent of excitement in the very air, as if the promised invasion of France was going to mean the imminent end of all hostilities.

"It won't, of course. It will just mean more killing," Celia Pengelly said to her companions as they paused for elevenses in the field above Penzance where they stooked corn sheaves in the hot morning sunshine.

"You always think you know everything, don't you, Pengelly?" said the one they called East End Gertie, fixing her with a scowl and a flip of her brassy hair.

"That's because she does," her friend Lizzie said. "She prob'ly knew the date it was going to happen before she left that posh job of hers with the Ministry."

"It wasn't with the Ministry," Celia snapped. "How many more times? It was just an office job—"

"Oh yeah?" Gertie sneered. "And since when did the likes of us gels get office jobs? I worked in a button factory before I came down here, and sometimes I wish I'd never bleedin' left it. Just look at the state of my fingernails."

But Celia wasn't looking at anything except the man making his way over the fields towards them. A man she recognised at once. She got to her feet, feeling as though they were made of lead and as if she was moving in slow motion, dropped her hunk of bread and cheese and began running towards him. She couldn't think why he was here, but in all this time, apart from the tenuous and general information Moonie had been able to give her, this man had been her one link with Stefan, and if he had further news . . .

He swung her around in his arms, and it flitted through her head that he had grown tall and stout since his years in Ireland. He was no longer merely the young brother of her stepfather, or the gangly youthful champion of the infant Wenna, but a stolid man in his thirties, she realised. A husband and a father.

"Ethan, what are you doing here? There's nothing wrong, is there?" she gasped, when she could catch her breath.

For of *course* he wouldn't have news of Stefan. The realisation was acute, and her momentary surge of hope vanished as quickly as it came. How could anybody have news of a man incarcerated by his own kind, so far away from the reality that was wartime Britain?

"There is, actually," he said, his voice scratchy now. "It's Ryan. We've brought him over to England to see if the doctors here can help him. He has a weak chest, Celia, and each winter it gets worse. The doctors in Ireland fear that he might not even grow into adolescence."

"Dear Lord! Karina must be demented," she said, shocked.

"She is. So much so that I had to get out of the house where she's weeping and wailing all over your mother right now. I can't take much more of it, which is why I came to see what you were doing these days. It's funny to see you working as a farm girl," he added without a trace of humour.

Celia glanced around, to see that her companions had already begun work again. She knew she couldn't let her mind dwell on the awfulness of Ethan's family problems for too long. The farmer was a stickler for keeping the girls working.

"It won't be so funny if I don't get back to work," she said quickly. "Come and talk to me while I get on with it."

"I'll come and help—"

"No, you won't."

"Yes, I will. I need to be doing something, and there's not a farmer alive that won't welcome another pair of hands."

"And you didn't seek me out for any other reason?"

She had to say it, as casually as possible, knowing how selfish she was being, for his child's health was far and away reason enough to be here at all.

"What other reason?" he said blankly, and then it dawned on him. "God, no, Celia, there's been no news of that kind. We've had no POWs in the vicinity for months now."

She nodded, her eyes smarting. There were so few people she could speak to about Stefan. Nor did she even dare mention his name. He was one of the enemy, and her fellow Land Girls, looking at her curiously now, would have spat on her had they known the identity of the man whose ring she again wore on a chain around her neck.

"Who's your feller, Pengelly?" Gertie jeered at once. "Is this the one you're always dreaming about when you look up at them stars at night?"

"This is my cousin," she said stonily. "He's over from Ireland with his wife and their sick child, and he's offered to help us with the stooking."

"We won't say no to that then, will we, Gertie?" Lizzie said sweetly, smiling at Ethan. Married or not, he still wore trousers and that made him fair game as far as she was concerned.

They might as well not bother, thought Celia. It was obvious to her that Ethan only had Ryan on his mind, and she doubted that even Wenna would stir his heart any more.

As if her thoughts transmitted themselves to him, he forced himself to ask about her sister.

"Been in Italy, a proper little Vera Lynn by all accounts, singing to the troops," Celia told him. "But she's back in England now, much to Mother's relief. Olly's God knows where, of course, flying his kites, as he calls them, and I daresay you've heard what happened to Justin."

Ethan nodded. "Poor devil. It puts everything into perspective, doesn't it?"

Celia squeezed his hand. "It doesn't make your concern for Ryan any less important, if that's what you're thinking. What kind of father would you be if you didn't care so much?"

"What kind of husband am I being, to be enjoying myself out here in the fields with three lovely girls, when my wife's crying her heart out back at New World?" he muttered.

Before Celia knew what was happening, he had flung down his fork and was striding back the way he had come.

"Well, he's a johnny-come-lately and no mistake," Lizzie said, having heard his last words. "Calls us lovely girls one minute, and then runs out on us. Not a queer, is he?"

Celia glared at her. "Sometimes, Lizzie, I don't think you have the brains of a flea. If you can't tell when a man's suffering, then it's no wonder you've never caught one."

"Well, pardon me for breathing, ma'am," she snapped, reminding Celia suddenly of her time in New Jersey when everyone was ma'am and sir, and people were full of an exaggerated politeness that was almost of another time. In that instant she felt a brief longing to be there again, away from it all, in the sweet-scented apple orchards belonging to the Stone household.

But as she heard the Cornish farmer's angry shout to them to get on with their work and stop dawdling, she knew she couldn't do that. Even if she tried, nothing would ever be the same again. You couldn't ever retreat to a safer world. All anyone could do was to go on.

Outwardly, Ryan Pengelly looked like a robust little six-year-old with a healthy tan on his skin, thought Skye. It was only when he began to cough at night, and the wheezing could be heard through the bedroom walls, that it was evident that he wasn't a well child.

Ethan and Karina were making a fair living on their Irish farm, but if Ryan was to have specialist treatment, it was clear they couldn't afford it.

They hadn't come to Cornwall looking for hand-outs, merely the expertise of the British doctors, and they were adamant on that point. But Nick and Skye had other ideas.

"You're our family, and our family deserves the best," Nick declared. "We'll send him to a private clinic and see what they can do for him."

"You must believe that this is not why we came," Karina protested in her soft Irish voice, tears welling in her eyes at the gesture of kindness.

"You came where you belong," Skye told her. "Where else should you be at a time of trouble but with people who love you? We all want to see Ryan able to run and play like other little boys. He's of an age to play with Lily's two now. She paused. "You'll go to see them, of course?"

Karina flushed. "I doubt that Lily's boys will want to bother with

Ryan. They must be thirteen now, and won't want to be seen hanging around with a small boy who can't run about very much. Besides, I'm not sure that Lily will want to see me. I've been very tardy about keeping in touch."

"I'm sure Lily will be as pleased to see you as we are," Skye said firmly. "I'll invite them over for Sunday tea. We might even get Celia to come. I know she's glad to get away from the girls she works with whenever she can."

Ethan laughed. "Having met them, I don't blame her for that – and you won't stop Skye getting the family together on the slightest excuse, Karina."

"It's a family thing," Nick agreed, tongue in cheek. "A Tremayne thing, or whatever they call it."

The teasing broke the tension that had surrounded them all like a cloud, and by the following Sunday the house was full of people again. Superficially, anyone could be forgiven for thinking they didn't have a care in the world. Or that there was a war on at all.

Only someone with a crystal ball, who was able to look beneath the surface, would see that nearly every one of them felt a measure of anxiety and grief.

Betsy wouldn't even come to New World, preferring to stay with 'her boys'. Seb reckoned she was being extra diligent on their behalf as a kind of penance. She felt she mustn't desert them just because her own boy was going through such torment.

"It's irrational, of course, but she has to work things through in her own way," he went on.

"We all do," Celia said.

"No news then?" he asked without explanation.

"How could there be?" she said in a brittle voice.

He slung an easy arm around her shoulders, and she could still marvel that where there had once been so much anger and conflict between them, there was now the closest friendship.

"I reckon you'll just have to settle for marrying me then," he said casually.

"And pigs might fly," she retorted, and then gave an unexpected giggle. "Did you ever know that we used to call you a prize pig, Seb? Mom and Lily did too. Isn't that awful? But you really were the most insufferable child."

Butch Butcher wandered near, thankful to hear laughter when most of the grown-ups seemed to be so miserable lately.

"What's an insuff – whatever you said, Celia?"

"Something you're not, kiddo," she said, putting her arm around him with rough affection and realising to her surprise that he was truly one of the family now. Just like an adopted brother, in fact, and she found herself hoping her parents would finally get around to taking him on permanently.

He wriggled free in embarrassment, his face as red as his hair, and went to find Lily's boys. Celia turned to Seb.

"I'm beginning to think I'm getting soft in my old age," she said. "Maybe I'll turn into one of those ancient, toothless spinsters, mumbling into my cocoa every night about the good old days. What do you think?"

But she didn't want an answer, because it suddenly sounded too frighteningly like the legions of elderly spinsters from the First World War. Those who had resolutely never married because their sweethearts had never come back from the Front, but who carried their images in their hearts for the rest of their lives.

"Not you, sweetheart," Seb lazily. "You'll *have* to marry me before then."

"Hey, you're not serious, are you?" she said in alarm. "Not you and me, Seb—"

"Good God, no," he drawled. "Just giving you the option if all else fails, that's all."

Nick fixed an appointment for Ryan to see a top specialist in Bristol, who would then admit him to his private clinic for observation and treatment if the condition warranted it.

He also arranged for Ethan and Karina to stay at lodgings nearby, and insisted on having all the bills sent to him. He wouldn't hear of anything different.

He and Skye accompanied the little family to Bristol and stayed for one night.

"We want to visit some old friends," Nick told them by way of easing their consciences at all the expense. "My ex-partner and his wife have an antique shop in Bristol and it will be good to see them again."

It would also be good to spend the night in the hotel where, long ago, he and Skye had journeyed to Bristol to inspect the retirement home where old Albert Tremayne was to spend the rest of his days. They had gone there as Albert's married niece and lawyer, and come back as lovers.

"Do you remember?" Skye said softly, as they stood at the window of the hotel that night, gazing down at the silvery ribbon of water in the Avon Gorge far below Clifton Downs.

She felt Nick's arms fold possessively around her, and she leaned back against him.

"As if it was yesterday. I don't know how we had kept apart for so long."

"I do," she said quietly. "It was because I was married to Philip, and we knew it was wrong to give in to our desire."

"But we made a vow not to repeat it as long as Philip lived, and we kept to it, so I don't think God will punish us for that, darling."

She twisted round in his arms. "And now I'm married to you and nothing that happens between us is wrong," she said, her heart beginning to beat faster at the look in his eyes.

It was a dark, passionate look that she knew meant only one thing, and she exalted again in the knowledge that he could still desire her so much and that their feelings for one another had never changed.

"Then I think it's time we confirmed those vows we made all those years ago," he said more urgently, in a way that thrilled her heart and told her the time for talking was over.

They didn't stay in Bristol for more than their one planned night. Next morning, the visit to Nick's ex-partner was a brief but joyous one, full of nostalgic talk of the past and hopes for the future. The city and its docks had had its own horrendous taste of the Blitz and many parts were devastated, even razed to the ground, but the Bristolian spirit had been strong, and would survive, the way it always had.

Skye was filled with a strange kind of euphoria as they caught the train at Temple Meads station and headed home to Cornwall. It had been a journey on account of Ryan's health, but for her, it had also been a renewal of vows, and a reminder that love never dies.

Somehow it had united the past with the present, and all the past impressions, of Bristol and of Cornwall, with her mother Primmy, and Primmy's beloved brother Albert. All that love, through all the generations, seemed to fuse in her own mind into the certainty that Ryan would get well. That the specialist who was treating him would work miracles.

She said as much to Nick as the train rattled westwards, and he smiled at her indulgently.

"Well, let's hope so. Or do I hear Granny Morwen dictating positive thoughts in your head again?"

Her smile was triumphant. "Well, you said it, not me! So who's using his Cornish intuition now, honey?"

Whatever it was, in two weeks' time they heard that Ryan's condition could be treated with a small operation, and that he would then undertake a long course of medication that in time, it was hoped, would completely cure him.

He would need to stay in the clinic for several weeks, and the specialist advised a further month in a specialised children's clinic in the country, where the parents could stay with him before they went home to Ireland.

"It will cost a fortune, Skye, and we're going to take out a loan to pay for it," Ethan finished, at the end of a lengthy and exuberant telephone call.

"You'll do no such thing, Ethan! Nick and I won't hear of it. No matter how much it costs, we shall ask Mr Warner to continue to send the bills to us, do you understand? We'll be deeply upset if you refuse to let us do this."

"How can we refuse without seeming totally ungrateful?" Ethan said huskily. "You're the dearest people we know, and I'll call you again when I'm not so damned emotional."

Skye put down the phone. She had no idea how much an operation of this nature would cost, but it didn't matter. All that mattered was seeing that small boy well again.

She turned around to see Butch hovering behind her.

"I've got some pocket money saved up, Mrs Pen," he said, hot with embarrassment. "If you want it, I'll give it yer."

"Oh Butch, honey, that won't be necessary, but you're an angel to even think of it," she said, hugging him.

"I thought all the fam'ly might be helping, see?"

At once, she knew what he was getting at. It was his way of being included as one of the family, and not just a 'vaccy', as Olly had once called them so scathingly, in what seemed like a lifetime ago. At that moment, Skye knew how important this was to him.

"If we need to call on the family for help, I promise I'll remember your offer, Butch," she said, and was rewarded by a beatific smile on his plain face.

World events overtook domestic ones with dramatic swiftness in early June, when the news broke that the Allies had liberated Rome. It began a wave of patriotic hysteria that at last, the Jerries were on the run.

On June sixth came the announcement from General Eisenhower's HQ that the invasion of Europe had begun. Naval forces, supported by air forces, began landing huge numbers of Allied forces on the northern coasts of France. The actual landing place was not mentioned at first, and the solemn voice of wireless announcer John Snagge made it seem an almost modest achievement. The understated British, Skye thought, with wry and affectionate amusement.

And yet the invasion was so vast in its conception and operation, that it was only when the full facts emerged of the biggest land, sea and air operation of all time, that the plans began to seem so awesome.

Skye went at once to the newspaper offices in Truro, unable to sit at home or do anything else, and quite sure that David Kingsley would have the latest information coming through all day. The more his sources revealed, the more incredible it became that it could have been achieved without the enemy getting prior knowledge of exactly where and when it would all take place.

"It must have been a terrifying sight, to see thousands of parachutes descending on French soil," Skye said. "And all those ships discharging the soldiers and tanks at the various landing points must have put the fear of the Almighty into the German troops waiting to repel them."

"Yes, but we shouldn't underestimate them," David said. "They won't have turned tail and retreated, Skye, and the casualty figures are going to be immense on both sides. It's going to be nothing short of carnage."

She looked at him sharply. "You don't approve of this operation, do you, David?"

"I don't approve of men killing one another."

"Not even for the best of reasons, to make the world a safer place to live in?"

"Didn't they say that about the last one, and about every bloody war that's ever been fought?"

"My God, for a newspaperman, you sounded almost human at that moment," she said flippantly.

"It's not unheard of," he said, and at the frown on his good-looking face she realised they were practically at loggerheads over a cause.

But she also knew well enough that if a newspaperman revealed everything in print that he knew, the public would be shocked to the bone at the cruelty that existed in the world. Danger didn't only exist these days in hand to hand fighting. Modern warfare had more sophisticated weapons of death and was fought on land, on sea and in the air.

"I wonder if Olly was involved in it," she said.

Part of her hoped desperately that he was not, while the other part knew that he would have just as desperately wanted to be there, his aircraft zooming through the skies and bombing railways and power plants, or dropping parachutes with men and supplies to support the great and wonderful invasion that was to liberate France and the world . . .

Suddenly she felt as sick and dizzy as if she too was up there in skies that were darkened with man-made machines filled with death-delivering horror; that she was somehow unable to breathe in the cloying stench of smoke and burning oil in the claustrophobic confines of the aeroplane carrying her son to his destiny—

"Put your head between your knees, Skye," she heard David order her as if from a long way away.

She obeyed without thinking, willing away the surge of bile that climbed upwards from her stomach and threatened to disgrace her.

"Olly," she whimpered, without even knowing that she spoke his name.

"What about Olly?" David said, his head close to hers, his hand still pushing hers down to her knees.

But by now the vision had faded, if vision it actually was. Or had it all been no more than an illusion brought about by her natural fears for her son? She had no way of knowing, but right now the last thing she wanted to feel was that it was some kind of premonition. At that moment, she completely rejected any thought of second sight. She didn't want it, and didn't have it . . . *wouldn't* have it . . .

"Here, drink this," David went on, thrusting a glass of water into her hand. "Sorry it's not brandy, but I can fetch you a drop of that if you feel the need."

"No thanks. Water's fine," she muttered, not wanting her senses dimmed in any way. "I'm sorry, David. I get bad moments at times, worrying about Olly. But they say no news is good news, don't they?"

Instead of reassuring her as she expected, his voice became more clipped. "And we both know that's one of the most stupid clichés ever invented."

"What have you heard?" she said at once.

He shrugged. "Nothing to alarm you. Only that the air force is as much involved in this invasion as anything else. But anyone with any sense knew that it was going to be. This war is very much a battle of the air, darling, even more than the last one was. Anyway, have you heard from Olly lately?" he added casually. Too casually.

She shook her head. "No. But that's nothing new. He's always too busy to write. For all his one-time longing to be a reporter, he has very poor corresponding skills when it comes to his own family."

Illogically, she was angry with David for making her feel even more anxious than before. For bringing her foolish fears out into the open instead of keeping them buried deep in her heart, even from Nick.

But, providing she heard from Olly soon, she decided it would be her new talisman for bringing him safely through to the end of the war.

The thought made her equally angry with herself, for putting such faith in pagan values.

"I think I need some fresh air, David," she said, her chest suddenly tight. "I'll go and see Lily while I'm in town, and I'll speak to you again soon."

But Lily couldn't help, and nor did Skye know what help she wanted or needed. She only knew that she was filled with an inner dread that all was not well, and that Olly was the pivot of that dread.

"You need a tonic, darling," Lily advised her. "I must say I'm glad the Irish lot have got over their trouble and that Ryan's convalescing now. It seemed to me that no sooner did half the evacuees leave New World than the others moved in, and you always did take other people's troubles too much to heart, Skye. You should give more thought to yourself instead of other people."

"They used to say that about Granny Morwen too," Skye said, "but if that's the way you're born, there's not much you can do about it. Anyway, most of our evacuees left a long time ago now. There's only Butch, and I hope he'll stay for good."

"You're really fond of that little tyke, aren't you?"

"Why shouldn't I be? He's a honey," Skye said.

The mood of the whole country was lifted by the fact that D-Day, as it became known, had been a success. But there was a price to pay. Early news reports made little of the terrible toll of killed and wounded in the battles of the first few weeks, but eventually the true figures were reported.

In any case, logical reasoning made anyone question how such a heavy bombardment could meet the expected fierce resistance without heavy casualties on both sides – though for families who had lost loved ones, logical reasoning didn't come into it, of course. Those like the Pengellys, who hadn't had to face receiving a dreaded yellow telegram, could still hold on to hope for their sons and daughters.

"At least we can be thankful that Wenna's safely back in England now," Skye said, but she spoke almost guiltily, still horrified that a family in Truro had heard that their two sons had both been killed in the first wave of Normandy landings.

They had heard nothing of Olly, but by now she was more than ready to hold on to the tired old cliché that no news was good news, however futile. It was by far preferable to thinking the worst.

The wireless news bulletins assured the public that the war was turning in the Allies' favour at last, and that was the important thing. Breaching the Normandy beaches was the first step in liberating France. The recurring theme on everyone's lips now was that the war would soon be over . . .

And then came a new horror.

The telephone rang at Killigrew House late one evening in the middle of June. Seb picked it up quickly, knowing that telephone calls at a late hour held terror for his mother these days. He was thankful he'd answered it when he recognised the cultured voice of Captain Giles Peterson.

"Have you heard the news, Sebastian?" he said formally. "The Germans have launched their secret weapon, and the city's in a state of panic, though the very south of England's seen the worst of it so far. They're calling it the doodlebug or the buzz-bomb – you take your pick. Whatever it's called, it's causing hellish damage."

"Is this the V-1 bomb?" Seb said sharply. "We've all heard about it, even down here in the sticks." They weren't all country hicks in Cornwall.

"Of course," Giles said. "I didn't mean to imply anything else. But I wanted to let you know that Justin's well enough to be moved, and I'm getting him out of London tomorrow morning before the flak really begins here. I have a friend in Derby who runs a private clinic, and he'll continue his treatment there until we can go home to Yorkshire. I wanted to keep you informed, so that your mother wouldn't worry for his safety. The moment we're settled, I'll contact you again."

"I appreciate your letting me know," Seb said, unable to doubt the other's sincerity and genuine concern. "It would have worried my mother to death to learn about these V-1s flying about, knowing Justin was still in a London hospital."

"Well, we'll soon be well out of range of the devilish weapons. Do you know much about them?"

Seb realised he wanted to keep him talking. Make contact. Establish a rapport. The way people did with their lover's family. He made himself remember that Justin was dependent on this man, and forced his own feelings of distaste aside.

"I know they're high-speed craft and carry nearly a ton of explosive," Seb said, dredging up all he had learned.

"And they're already calling the area over Kent and Sussex 'bomb alley'," Giles went on grimly. "People are being warned to take cover as soon as they hear the peculiar engine-note stop, because within fifteen seconds it will explode."

Seb cut in. "Isn't the theory behind it that as long as you can still hear it coming, you can feel safe?"

"Yes. But who can calculate where they'll explode? And with no pilot, what's to stop them being sent over in daylight as well as during the night? First reports are that southern England has been as shaken by the bombardment as if it's suffered an earthquake. Hell on earth is a more apt description."

He spoke with crisp military precision, but it couldn't hide the anger in his voice.

"Then the sooner you get Justin out of the capital, the better," Seb heard himself say. He swallowed his pride, and added, "Thank God he's got you to care for him."

"Those few words will mean more to both of us than I can say, Sebastian. I'll relay them to Justin if I may."

When the call ended Seb went into the living room where his mother and her convalescent boys were crowding around the wireless set, listening intently to the latest bulletin.

Thank God Giles Peterson had already put his mind at rest about getting Justin out of the capital, he thought now, seeing the fear in his mother's face as the announcer relayed much of what Seb had just heard.

"Before you start fretting unduly, Ma, that was Captain Peterson on the phone. Justin's being moved to a clinic in Derby tomorrow for further treatment, so he'll be well out of reach of these doodlebugs."

"Then let's thank the Lord that somebody's looking after him," Betsy said, almost weeping with relief.

"Amen to that," muttered Seb.

Fourteen

Despite the Allies' penetration farther and farther into Europe, hopes for peace seemed constantly thwarted as the German bombardment of London and the south-east became intensified during July, and frantic evacuation began all over again.

The doodlebugs were getting a stranglehold on the capital, and no matter how some of the newspapers tried to shield the public from the worst of it, the public demanded to know the truth. It was becoming clear that no amount of anti-aircraft gunfire seemed able to stop them.

There was no warning as to when the machines would stop their deadly approach, and once the noise of the engine ceased, you might as well say your prayers, according to many eyewitness reports in the newspaper.

It made depressing and horrifying reading, but Skye's attention was caught by another small headline.

"Can you credit this?" she exclaimed. "The government has revealed plans for building between three and four million new houses in the first ten years after the war with proper kitchens and plenty of hot water. That must be a real comfort to people who are homeless now! What kind of tactless idiots sit on their backsides in Whitehall?"

"They mean well," Nick said. "They're planning for the future, and they have to look ahead, just as we all do. This war isn't going to last for ever, and people will want decent homes to come back to. Jerry probably did us a favour in destroying some of the old slums."

Skye stared at him in disbelief and her voice grew passionate with anger. "My God, sometimes I wonder if you have any compassion in you at all, Nick! How can you say such a thing? They may have been slums, but they were homes. People married and had babies there. They grew old together and they died there. There's more to a home than a draughty old kitchen and no running water. There's a family's hopes and dreams—".

"All right, don't take on so, Skye. All I'm saying is that if people are better housed after the war, they'll have a higher standard of living than they ever had before. You only have to compare the old clayworkers' cottages on the moors with the smart little town houses in Truro to know the difference. You wouldn't disagree with that, would you?"

"No. It was just the way you said it, that's all."

He laughed shortly. "Oh well, not everyone can have your gift with words, sweetheart, especially not a stuffy old lawyer like me. I see facts where you see rainbows."

"Well, that's not so bad!" she said. "Everyone knows there's a pot of gold at the end of a rainbow."

"There's no answer to that kind of crazy logic."

But she declared that her prophecy about gold being at the end of a rainbow was proved right when Olly sent word that he was coming home on leave, and had 'oodles' to tell them.

"*Oodles*?" Nick said, as picky as ever. "Where the devil do they get these expressions from?"

"It's called youthful enthusiasm, honey," Skye said, too relieved and overwhelmed by the fact that all was well with their son to care about his censure.

Oliver Pengelly had broadened considerably during the last few years, not only in stature but also in maturity. He was twenty-one years old now, and the important birthday had come and gone. It hadn't mattered a hoot to him that the only celebration had been in the mess-room with his mates where he was bumped and cheered and almost drowned in cheap booze.

He had seen and experienced far more in his years in the Royal Air Force than some men knew in a lifetime, and while some of it was good, much of it was more horrific than he would ever tell his parents.

Once he had got over the usual excitement of being home on his short leave, and they had all got used to his presence, it was only to Seb Tremayne, his closest confidant now, that he revealed the gut-wrenching terror that could make a man 'brown-ass' his trousers in mid-flight and be too traumatised even to notice.

On the last day of his leave, they strode over the moors as they used to do when they were children, finding a good vantage point to view the domain of the clayworks and surroundings that were still essentially theirs. Still Killigrew country. Still Tremayne and Pengelly country.

The endless moors and the Cornish sense of mystery and magic were still so peaceful and unchanging that for a while it was easy to forget that war was raging elsewhere. That men were dying and burning, and screaming in agony . . .

"I sometimes wonder if Justin's so lucky after all," Olly said abruptly, when they had exhausted all other topics of conversation. "Sometimes I think he'd be better off dead. Nothing personal, of course."

"*Christ*, Olly, what kind of a remark is that? It's a hundred times better to be alive than dead."

"Not when you're only half alive, sport. Not when the images of hell are so indelibly stored up in your head and your heart that you can still hear and smell your companions burning even if you don't have eyes to see it happening. Those memories will never die, no matter how much you wish to God that they would," he ended savagely.

"You're speaking personally, of course," Seb said at once. "This isn't only about Justin, is it?"

Olly shrugged. They sat cross-legged on the short stubbly moorland turf now, with the placid sight of the sea rippling like silver in the distance, and the only sound the sighing of the breeze through the bracken.

As it was Sunday, White Rivers Pottery was closed for the day, and the clayworks were still now, where they used to be constantly alive with the sounds of men and women hollering cheerfully to one another above the hum of machinery.

"I had a good mate in my squadron," Olly said. "We shared the same dreams and ambitions for the future, and thought about going into commercial flying after the war. Going into it together, I mean. We could have made a go of it too, except that Hitler's goons put a stop to all that."

"What happened?" Seb said quietly, when Olly's voice tailed away and he continued staring into space, as if his mind was a million miles away.

"What do you think?" he said, suddenly harsh. "Nothing exceptional. Nothing that wasn't happening to dozens of other damn good eggs who thought they could conquer the world. We've all got a bloody nerve thinking we can reverse the Almighty's plan and soar like eagles. We should leave it to the bloody birds to fly, and keep our feet on the ground like nature intended."

Seb snapped back at him, "People get killed with their feet on the ground, Oliver. People get blown up and blinded. People get bombed in their own homes. You aren't defying God's laws by

flying aircraft, if that's what this little bit of self-hatred is all about
You're doing a hell of a good job in helping to win this war, and you
should stop feeling so bloody sorry for yourself and remember it.'

Olly turned and glared at him, and after a moment he managed a
hint of a smile.

"All right, so I'm a bloody hero—"

"Yes, you are, and so is every other man with the nerve to go up in
one of those infernal machines and defend his country, so hate
yourself if you must, but don't belittle the rest of them, there's a
good chap."

Olly glared at his cousin again. "Did you ever think of becoming a
head doctor?"

"No, I just use my common sense, that's all. In this war, we can't
do without people like you and Justin, and your sisters, and the boys
convalescing at Killigrew House. The ones who come home in one
piece are the lucky ones."

"You're forgetting somebody, aren't you?"

"I don't think so—"

"*You*, you bugger! Since when did you become so modest? You
bought it too, and this soft-soaping is definitely not the Seb I
remember. In fact, it's more unnerving than all Hitler's bombs,"
he said with a grin. "So when are we going to go out and find some
girls? There *are* some still around who are looking for a good time, I
suppose? And the day you tell me you don't know where to find
them is the day hell freezes."

"What did you think of Olly this time?" Skye asked Nick when their
son had gone back to his base. "I thought he was very on edge when
he arrived, but I was glad to see that he and Seb got so pally."

"That's because they did what every healthy young man should
do, and went chasing girls," Nick said easily.

"Well, I'm not sure that's a very nice thing to say!"

"How do you want me to say it? It's natural for young men to
want the company of girls, and in wartime, it becomes even more
urgent to sow your wild oats."

"*Nick*!"

"For pity's sake, darling, I'm not suggesting he was bedding every
girl who caught his eye, but when you're never sure if you're going
to see another tomorrow, you want to make the most of your time.
And don't start reading anything prophetic into that remark."

"All the same, I wish you hadn't said it," Skye said uneasily. "I've
always been anxious about Olly—"

"And about the girls, and everyone else you ever knew. Let's face it, my love, you've turned into a worrier."

Had she? Skye felt a little shock at his words, knowing it wasn't the way she thought about herself.

She still thought of herself as the bright and breezy young American girl with the quick New Jersey accent who had burst in on her Cornish family for a year, and stayed for a lifetime. But she was no longer a girl, and she was in danger of letting herself slip into maudlin middle age, she thought with a sudden feeling of alarm.

"Well, I'm not going to worry any longer," she said determinedly. "The war must be nearing the end, and I'm going to start planning my booklets properly, ready for the hordes of tourists who are going to discover us as soon as it's all over. There's no reason why I shouldn't get them into shape, even if there's not enough paper available to print them!"

"That's my girl," Nick said.

But as if to dash her determination every time it came to the surface, and remind her that the war wasn't over yet, there was a telephone call late one afternoon at the end of July that had her heart thumping.

"We're at the railway station in Truro, Mrs Pen, so can yer send somebody ter fetch us, because there ain't no bleedin' cabs or buses to be had."

"Who is this?" Skye said sharply, unable to believe what her brain was telling her.

"It's me and my gel. Edna Hollis and Daphne. Our 'ouse got hit by a doodlebug, and my Gary said we should get straight back down to Cornwall where it's safe."

Skye gasped as the woman's words poured out with about as much emotion as if she was saying she was dropping in for afternoon tea.

"Your house was hit? You mean it was destroyed?" she said, knowing how stupid that sounded.

She heard Edna Hollis's harsh laugh. " 'Course it was, lady. Them bombs don't do things by 'alves. It was lucky me and Daphne wasn't in it when we was doodlebugged."

Skye felt her mouth go dry, and then she heard Daphne's excited voice burst in.

"Come 'n get us, Mrs Pen, and I'll tell yer all about it. The kids next door was burned to a cinder, what was left of 'em, anyway, but we was all right—"

"Stay where you are, Daphne, and I'll be there to fetch you as soon as I can," Skye broke in, knowing Daphne's graphic turn of phrase, and not wanting to imagine the scene just yet. It would be bad enough later, when they had to hear it over and over again. And if the Hollis mother and child were assuming they would stay indefinitely, no doubt Daphne would soon be telling the whole school what it was like to be doodlebugged.

The idea of having the pair of them installed at New World for any length of time quickly stretched Skye's charitable thoughts to the limit. She also knew that Edna's incessant chatter, coupled with Daphne's, would quickly drive Nick insane. There had to be another way. And by the time she reached the railway station in Truro she had already begun to plan it, providing it was handled delicately enough.

Daphne threw herself into Skye's arms with a sudden burst of tears that took her by surprise.

"The little bugger missed yer," Edna observed. "Always on about 'er posh house in the country, she was, even to my Gary, though he kept telling 'er we'd have a big place in America."

"I missed yer, Mrs Pen," Daphne sobbed. "When Gary comes ter visit us I want to show 'im my lovely room."

Skye felt alarmed. How many more of them were there going to be? While she had a patriotic affinity with the unknown GI Gary, she realised that she didn't want her house filled with strangers. Not any more.

"I know you must have had a terrible time, Mrs Hollis, losing your home like that—"

"Oh, it weren't much," Edna said airily. "Anyway, we'd taken a lot of stuff wiv us while we were staying wiv Gary for the weekend. That's how come we was so lucky, not bein' there. We was glad to see the back of the old dump, and there's no excuse now for not getting spliced as soon as poss."

They were in the car now and on the way back to New World, and since Mrs Hollis seemed remarkably resilient, Skye decided there was no time like the present to say what she had to say. While she still had the courage.

"It must have been a shock, though, and you may not be feeling it properly yet, so you're very welcome to stay with us for a while until you're properly recovered."

"We wanter stay wiv you for ever, Mrs Pen," Daphne wailed. "At least until Gary takes us to America! All the kids that went back ter London are being sent away again now."

198

"I know, Daphne," Skye said, "and I was very sorry to hear that. But if you and your Mom are going to be in Cornwall for some time, wouldn't it be nice to have a little place of your own where Gary could come and visit you?"

Edna Hollis snorted. "We couldn't afford no rent, so who'd be daft enough to give us a place of our own, missis?"

"I would," Skye said calmly. "It's only a cottage, but it would be yours for as long as you needed it – and you needn't bother to pay me rent as long as you keep it clean. In fact, you'd be doing me a favour by looking after it."

When there was no reply, she glanced at the woman sitting beside her. To her amazement Edna Hollis's throat was working painfully. But it only took a moment for her voice to return.

"Blimey, missis, this is such a turn-up you fair took me breath away. Nobody ever gave us nothin' before, see, and now me and Daphne are going to have a house of our own—"

"It'll be just for the duration," Skye said hastily.

"Oh, o' course! Once the war's over, we'll be off to America, anyway."

"Where's this 'ouse, Mrs Pen?" Daphne said, scowling in the back seat. "I fought we was coming ter live wiv you."

"So you will, for a while. The cottage will need to be got ready for you, but I know you'll like it. It's up on the moors by the clayworks and the pottery—"

Daphne howled right in her ear. "I ain't goin' ter live all up there! I want me own bedroom at New World."

Her reward was a clip round the ear from her mother.

"Don't be so bleedin' ungrateful, Daphne," Edna snapped.

"You ain't seen where it is! How can I go ter school from up there! I won't see Tilly nor my friends ever again!"

Skye thought there would be a good few parents who would be relieved to know that, but she spoke swiftly.

"Daphne, you're nearly eleven years old now, and most children change schools about that time. There's a very nice school at Roche, which is much nearer than Truro, and you'll make all kinds of new friends there. Besides," she added, "it probably won't be for very long. As your mother said, once the war is over you'll be getting ready to go to America. You'll be able to tell your new friends all about that."

She could feel Daphne breathing heavily down her neck. But by now, Skye knew she'd be wrestling with indignity at not staying at New World indefinitely after all, and the thought of bragging about her mother's GI to her new school friends. In the end, pride won.

"I s'pose we oughter have a look at this cottage then. Just ter see what we think, mind," she said grudgingly.

Nick came home from his chambers to have his ears blasted with the gory details of how Daphne and her mother had found out about the doodlebug that had destroyed their house and the row of houses alongside them. By then Butch was as white as a ghost and Daphne was ghoulishly elaborating about the bodies that could only be identified by bits of shoes and other objects.

"Thank God they're not going to be a fixture here," Nick said, once he and Skye were alone. "You're a blessed genius to have thought of an empty clayworker's cottage, Skye."

"I know," she said modestly. "And tomorrow I'm taking them up there to show them around. The place will need cleaning and airing, and a bit of paint, but Butch said he'll be happy to help with that. The poor lamb's just thankful that Daphne won't be around here for too long."

"And you don't think the Hollis woman will think it's a poor place after the promise of an American paradise?"

"Honey, I think Mrs Hollis is ready to grab anything she can get as long as it's free," Skye said smartly.

But they couldn't get rid of them for a month. The cottage needed considerable repair work, and the roof leaked. Although it was summertime now, no one knew how long the Hollis pair would have to stay there.

However, any unease they might have had about it being beneath Edna's expectations was put to rest as soon as Skye saw her casting her eyes over the hefty clayworkers round about. Some of them were more than ready to lend a hand to their flashy new neighbour, and Skye found herself hoping that Edna's GI Gary was going to be man enough to cope with her.

All the same, it was an uneasy month, and Skye involved herself in securing a place at the Roche school for Daphne. The girl still wanted to see her old friends, though, and cycled all the way into Truro especially to tell Tilly Green about the night the doodlebug had fallen on their house. Nobody else could boast of such a thing, nor had any idea of what it was like, so Daphne had the world at her feet in the telling. By the time she had finished, the bomb had grown to gigantic proportions and killed everyone for miles around.

It was a huge relief to everyone when she and her mother were finally able to move into the clayworker's cottage on the moors, and Daphne could torment the life out of her new schoolfriends at Roche with her outrageous stories. Life at New World could revert to its harmonious level again.

Rumours that Hitler had been assassinated, or was about to be, were in full flood during the next few months, more in hope than fact. Plots to be rid of him abounded, even by his own officers, and it was reported in the press that in the so-called People's Court a number of them were cruelly executed for their part in such betrayal of the Führer.

"It's surely a measure of how things are going in our favour," Skye said, scanning every newspaper. "Hitler must see that there's no hope for him to win this war if his own officers are plotting to kill him. Paris and much of Europe is under the control of the Allies at last, and now that the Russians have cut off much of the Germans' oil supplies in Romania, the country must be in a state of panic. How much longer can they hold out?"

"I don't know," Nick said. "But there's one thing I'm sure about. They'll have their Maker to answer to when the full story of these concentration camps emerge."

Skye glanced at him. Nick was a good man, but not a religious one, and when he resorted to mentioning God in any form, she always knew his thoughts were serious.

"David showed you some of the horror stories he's not prepared to print, didn't he?" she said quietly.

"He did, and in my opinion he should damn well print every one of them. People should know what kind of evil bastards these men are," Nick said savagely.

Skye shuddered. The thought that anyone of theirs should ever be imprisoned in such terrible circumstances – as the Jewish friends and relatives of sweet Georgie Rosenbloom, all of who had never been seen or heard of again, had been – was too stomach-turning to think about. And yet, not to think about them was to deny that they ever existed. Georgie had killed himself because the pain of it was too much for him to bear, and such atrocities should never be forgotten.

"In the order of things, we've been lucky, haven't we, Nick?" she said slowly. "We didn't think so when we heard about poor Justin, but he's safe in Yorkshire now with the friend who's caring for him. We didn't think so when Fanny was killed in an air raid, or when Seb was wounded and Celia had her breakdown. But our three have survived, and we have to be thankful for that. I thank God every day for it."

"It's not over yet though, and until a peace treaty is signed, it would be foolish to be too complacent, darling."

"I'm not going to be a pessimist, either," she said stubbornly. "It's not my style."

By November it had become common knowledge that the Nazis were retreating all over Europe. The more disillusioned German soldiers were voluntarily surrendering in the liberated French and Belgian cities, and as if to underline Skye's hopes for the future, Celia arrived home like a whirlwind.

"I've had a letter from Moonie," she announced, her blue eyes blazing with excitement. "The old darling hadn't given up on me all this time, Mom, and he's got some information about Stefan at last!"

"And from the way you came bursting in here it's obviously good news . . ."

"The best. At least, it's the best anyone could hope for at this time. It seems that some of the captors holding political prisoners hostage have begun to panic over reprisals at the end of the war, and are letting them go."

"Is Stefan a political prisoner?"

"More like a moral one, I'd say, for simply refusing to hand over his home to the Gestapo until he had no choice. But it amounts to the same thing."

"So where does Moonie say he is now?"

Celia's elation faded a little. "He doesn't know. He doesn't even know if Stefan is involved. It's just general information, but I have to keep my hopes alive that Stefan has been freed, Mom, and that somehow he'll be able to contact me soon. I *have* to believe that, don't I?"

Her eyes shone for a different reason now. They brimmed with the tears she refused to shed, and Skye's heart ached for her. The information was all so hazy, no more than a thread of hope, but she knew how desperate Celia was to cling to it. She could see it by the way she twisted the pearl and garnet ring on her finger.

In all this time, Celia had never lost faith that she would find her lover again, and Skye wasn't about to dash her hopes.

"We all have to believe it, darling," she said softly. "I'm sure your Captain Moon wouldn't have raised your hopes unnecessarily. He must think there's a good chance that Stefan will be freed, and he'll be in touch as soon as he possibly can. But you know how difficult that may be, so you'll just have to be patient a while longer, honey."

"I can be patient for ever as long as I know Stefan's coming back to me."

At her mother's doubtful look she gave a rueful laugh, because both of them knew it would take more than all the tea in China to give her patience.

The telephone rang as they were speaking, and Celia pressed her shaking hands together as Skye picked up the receiver, certain that fate had sent her here on this very day, and that she was about to hear Stefan's voice at last.

"It's Wenna," Skye said, turning away from the sick disappointment in Celia's eyes, and holding the instrument away from her ear for a second as her younger daughter's voice came over the wire.

"Darling, that's wonderful, and Celia's had good news too. Stefan hasn't contacted her yet, but we have great hopes that he may be safe," she added, more for Celia's benefit than Wenna's. "You'll come down to see us as soon as you can some leave, won't you? And try to bring Harry home for Christmas."

She hung up, still smiling. This was turning out to be a very special day, she thought. First Celia, and now Wenna. And then she realised that Celia still didn't know what the call was all about, and she turned around to tell her.

But Celia was more intent on watching a boy on a bicycle toiling up the hill towards New World, and only half heard what her mother was saying.

"Harry Mack has proposed to Wenna and she's said yes! I'm very happy for her, though what difference it will make to her musical ambitions once the war is over, I have no idea. I doubt if either of them have considered that yet, anyway."

Her voice trailed away as she realised that her daughter wasn't really listening. "Celia, what is it?"

She caught sight of the boy on the bicycle then, and her heart seemed to leap in her chest. It wasn't Butch Butcher, cycling home from the pottery It was a boy on a red bicycle, the kind that the boys from the Post Office rode. With her mind still so recently full of Stefan von Gruber, all Skye could think about was that after all Celia's hopes she was about to hear bad news.

Unless, of course, it was *good* news. Telegrams didn't always have to bring bad news, did they? she thought, with desperate optimism.

"Oh Mom—" Celia began.

"Keep calm, darling. It may be the news you're waiting for. You stay here and I'll go and see."

It was a long while afterwards that she remembered the look on Celia's face when she went to answer the door and took the telegram out of the boy's hand. A look of premonition regarding something that Skye herself hadn't had the faintest inkling about. Her own sixth sense had completely failed her, she realised as she quickly tore open the envelope and stared at the words in sick horror.

It was nothing to do with Stefan. It was a far more poignant message for Skye. "We regret to inform you . . . your son . . . Oliver Pengelly . . . missing in action . . ."

Wenna managed to get compassionate leave and was home within twenty-four hours, her own news completely overshadowed, her face full of stark misery. Celia was still at New World, having telephoned the farmer to say there was no way she could return to her duties, because she was needed at home. His scathing reply was to tell her not to return at all except to collect her belongings.

"To blazes with him," Celia snapped. "There are more important things than turning over his damn turnip fields. I'll resign and go back on the trams for the duration."

"Can you do that?" Wenna said, glad to talk of anything but the thing that was uppermost in all their minds.

"God knows. And he's not telling. But I haven't even congratulated you on your engagement yet."

"Oh Celia, I can't even think about that now. It seems so awful that Mom and I were talking so happily, and seconds later this happened. It seems—"

"Now just stop it. If you were about to say it's a kind of tit-for-tat thing because you were so happy, forget it. We've all gone through that kind of nonsense, and that's all it is – just nonsense. I could have said the same thing because I'd just heard that Stefan might be safe – and that's all conjecture, anyway. But I refuse to think there has to be a counterpoint for everything good that happens. It's too ridiculous."

All the same, she mentally crossed her fingers as she spoke, because it was all so fearfully possible. All the clever-clever professors said as much, and who was she to dispute their learnings? She did, though, and she was damn well going to stick to it, for all their sakes.

"Look, the house is too bloody full of people this afternoon, with all the family rallying round Mom and Dad as ever, and I'm badly in need of some fresh air. It's the one thing I miss about the farming lark, I guess. Let's go up to the pottery. I want to make a phone call, and I can do it easier away from the house. I don't want Mom to hear it. Will you come with me?"

"Gladly," Wenna said promptly. "I never thought I'd say it, but the house is stifling me too. In the circumstances I haven't said anything to Mom yet about my future plans, but when Harry and I are married, we're going to live in Canada. His folks have a ranch there, and they breed horses."

"It sounds wonderful. And Stefan and I will be managing our own hotel in Gstaad," Celia went on determinedly, "so we'll all be scattering again, won't we?"

But she avoided Wenna's eyes, knowing they were really thinking of Olly, and wondering if he'd be coming home at all.

"By the way, the infant Butch intends to stay here for ever," Celia said suddenly. "Did you know?"

"Thank God for Butch," Wenna said, and they both knew what she meant. "Anyway, what's this important phone call you're going to make that you couldn't make at home?"

"You'll see."

Adam Pengelly was about to close the pottery for the day, and his face became anxious when he saw his two nieces approach. He was clearly afraid to ask if there was any more news of Olly, but Celia forestalled the question.

"We've heard nothing else, Adam, but I want to use the telephone here. Is that all right? Only it upsets Mom to hear me talking too much about it at home," she said glibly.

"Of course it's all right, my dear. Just click the door shut when you've finished and it'll lock itself . . . Me and Felicity intended calling at New World this evening. What do you think? Does your mother want company?"

Celia managed a smile. "When we left, Seb and his mother and all the Kingsley clan were there, and Butch was handing out lemonade and keeping Lily's kids amused. It does Mom good to be surrounded by folk, Adam, so go whenever you like."

Nice as he was, he was an old fusspot, and she wished he would go away now, so that she could put the call through to the special number she kept locked in her memory. Once there was no one at the pottery but herself and Wenna, she picked up the phone and asked for the number she wanted.

After what seemed like an age she heard the efficient, well-remembered tones come over the wire.

"Hello Moonie," she said huskily.

"Celia! By all that's holy, it's a joy to hear your voice. How are you, my dear girl? But I hardly need to ask, do I? I take it this call is on account of the letter I sent you, and I wish I'd been able to tell you more—"

"Moonie, it's not because of your letter, although of course I was overjoyed to get it, and I wanted to thank you for not giving up on me."

"As if I would," he said heartily. "But if it's not about your fiancé, then what is it? I must say, you're not quite as bubbling as I expected you to be, so tell old Captain Moonlight what's wrong."

The sudden kindness in his voice almost finished her, but she held on tightly to the telephone cord and stated the facts as calmly as she could.

"My brother's missing in action, Moonie. We've just heard the news, but I don't need to tell you how frustrating the bare facts can be. There's no real information. Nothing to say if his plane crashed or if he was wounded, or – or worse—"

"Take it easy, my dear," he said, as her voice began to shake. "Just tell me what you want me to do."

She looked at the phone stupidly. What could he do? What crazy idea was in her head when she first thought of him? He wasn't God, able to do what nobody else could do – find her brother among a million other casualties of war . . .

Wenna took the phone out of her hand and spoke rapidly.

"Captain Moon, this is Celia's sister. Would you mind holding on for a moment while she recovers herself, please?"

"Of course. Tell her to take all the time she needs."

Celia caught the sound of his booming voice, and bit her lip. 'Take all the time she needs' . . . as if he wasn't one of the busiest men on earth, with a very important job, and no time to spend on a stupid female falling apart with grief . . .

She took back the phone from Wenna. Like an automaton she gave him Olly's name and service number, and without a qualm she went on with her request.

"I'm asking you to pull rank, Moonie. I know it's not your field, and Olly's only one young man among so many, but if anyone can get inside information, it's you. I know it's a heck of a lot to ask, and I shouldn't be doing it all—"

"I'll do whatever I can, Celia, and of course you had to ask me. I wouldn't have expected anything else. In fact, life has never been the same here since you left. I miss your quick wit and your quirky ways—"

"They're not so quirky now," she mumbled, her eyes smarting at the unexpected compliment that was clearly meant to cheer her up.

"But they will be again, I promise you. I'll be in touch, my dear."

She recognised the change in his voice, and guessed that his priorities had changed. She could almost sense the sudden rush of adrenalin and activity as some new decoding message came in – and she missed that feeling. She was no longer in the thick of it, and despite Moonie's many contacts, she knew it was a very long shot to see if he could find any news of Olly. All she could do was wait and try not to give way to the sudden depression that hit her.

It didn't even occur to her until much later that she hadn't even asked if there was any more news of Stefan. But of course there wouldn't have been, or he would have told her.

Fifteen

The news that Oliver Pengelly was missing spread around the district with the speed of a forest fire. At Skye's request, David Kingsley reported it only briefly in the *Informer*, confirming that the family was still waiting for definite news, and had every hope that their son was still alive.

No one really believed it, of course. The clayworkers were as awkward and inarticulate as Butch with their sympathy, but nonetheless sincere; the townspeople sent cards or stilted letters; and Daphne Hollis arrived at New World with a bunch of wild moorland flowers to make Mrs Pen feel better.

"It's a sweet gesture, but it makes me feel as if everyone has got him dead and buried already," Skye said, weeping in Nick's arms.

She wavered between being completely out of control and deathly calm, and could do nothing to stop the moods. She refused to take the doctor's mind-dulling pills, preferring to keep her senses alert to whatever fate had in store for them.

She knew that the pills might have helped alleviate the nightmares, when she saw Oliver in the grip of some terrible death, burning or drowning, his body ripped apart or blown to pieces. She couldn't stop the nightmares, and nor would she try to blot them out artificially.

She wanted to feel the pain, and even welcomed it in a macabre way, because in doing so, she believed she was sharing whatever Olly was experiencing. It was wrong, and she knew it. It was virtually trying to take on God's role.

No human being could share another's pain, but the agony she had experienced when he was born had been hers alone, and if in some grisly manner she was now sharing the agony of his dying, she jealously guarded that too as hers alone. But the guilt of knowing exactly what she was trying to do made her constantly scratchy with Nick.

"I'm really worried about you, Skye," he told her now, as she shook in his arms. "You're not sleeping properly. You must let the doctor give you something—"

"*No*! Not until I know Olly's safe," she snapped.

"But what good is it doing to suffer like this?"

"Would you not have me suffer for my son? Are you so damn self-sufficient that you can detach yourself from it all?"

"That's not fair," he said, not even raising his voice. "I love him too, Skye, and if you don't know that by now, then I wonder what we've been doing together all these years."

Hearing the tightness in his voice, she was stricken with remorse at his quiet dignity, and she leaned into him again, feeling his strength, but unable to take comfort from it.

"I'm sorry," she mumbled.

"You don't need to say it. And any day now we may get word that Olly's safe, and our worst fears will be over."

She moved slightly away from him and looked up into his handsome face, seeing how his dark eyes were clouded and the lines around his mouth were accentuated with the tension he held so rigidly inside. Seeing how old and drawn her once young and virile lover looked now, she knew how selfish she was in not crediting him with suffering too.

"But you don't really believe he'll come home safely, do you?" she said, her mouth trembling. "The truth now, Nick."

After a moment he slowly bowed his head.

"If it's the truth you want, then I believe we've already said goodbye to our son, Skye," he said.

As if the trauma of saying it out loud was suddenly too much to bear, seconds later his face twisted. He clung to her and wept silently in her arms, and she was at once the comforter and the comforted, and thought all the more of him for breaking down and releasing his feelings.

Celia and Wenna returned from what had become their ritual daily walk to get out of the house to find their parents still locked in a close embrace. With one accord they moved silently outside again.

"I can't stand much more of this," Celia declared. "I simply don't know what to do for the best. We're not helping, Wenna. They don't want us. We're constant reminders that something's wrong. Until some definite news comes through, they have to get on with their lives, and so do we."

"I know you're right, but what do you suggest? Are you going back to Penzance after all?"

"I suppose so," Celia said. "I daresay they'll have me, much as I hated it, and at least I can get home quickly from there if ever –

whenever—" She swallowed hard, and went on more harshly. "I'd dearly love to ask if Moonie could take me back, but I doubt if the proper channels would welcome back a crazy woman."

"You're not crazy. You're the sanest woman I know. But *I* begin to wonder how much compassionate leave is reasonable for someone whose brother is missing in action. If everyone did the same thing, there'd be no service personnel left."

They looked at one another. They had been home for two weeks now, but there had been no more real information. Moonie hadn't been able to come up with anything more definite than the latest official word of 'missing in action'.

Beyond that, he had stretched the bounds of security and told Celia there had been a spate of missing aircraft that was being hushed up for morale purposes. Among them, several Bomber Command aircraft had been shot down during diversion tactics over Norway. It was suspected at source that Olly's had been one of them, but there was no mention of survivors in the reports, and until there was positive news of the air crews, nothing would be released.

"He could have parachuted out of the plane, Celia, and been picked up anywhere and taken to safety," was the best Moonie could say. "If I hear any more, I'll contact you."

"Thank you," she said woodenly. "There's no news of Stefan, I take it?"

"I'm sorry, no."

But why would there be? Moonie didn't even know him, and he was just a civilian, too old for the early conscription into the army, but not too old to be condemned for refusing to support his compatriots. Though, in Celia's opinion, anyone who defied the Gestapo regime was a hero.

She hadn't repeated everything to her parents, only the positive thought that Olly might have parachuted into the countryside somewhere. Even if he had been taken prisoner, he would still be alive – but with the recent revelations about the horror camps, no one dared to make any more comments about such a possibility.

"I really think I should go back to my unit tomorrow," Wenna told her sister now. "I know Mom will understand."

"Can you still manage to entertain the troops, with all this hanging over us?"

"I have to. It's not their fault, Celia. They need encouragement to carry on, and maybe in doing it for them, I'm doing it for Olly too."

"You're a good kid," Celia said huskily. "Not such a kid any more, either. No wonder Harry Mack fell for you."

"We've all grown up, haven't we? And a lot quicker than we would have done if we hadn't gone to war."

"So I guess I'll do my duty and continue eating humble pie in the turnip fields. How's that for growing up?"

But their cautious laughter held more than a hint of desperation, before they linked arms and went back into the house to tell their parents what they had decided.

Long before a mellow Cornish November had slid into December, the newspapers announced that the Home Guard was officially to stand down, and the country gave a cautious rejoicing that surely such things couldn't be sanctioned unless Jerry was truly on the run.

For several months now, towns and cities away from the coast had been allowed to turn on moderate street lighting again, and children who had only ever seen their towns in darkness once night fell were enchanted by the sight.

"Good for them," Skye said to Nick. "But we're still denied the best news of all. And if you tell me once more that no news is good news, I shall scream. Until I hear for sure that Olly is safe, I'll be unable to rejoice over anything—"

"Why don't you think positively, the way you always used to, and turn your words around?" he retorted. "Until you hear for sure that Olly's not coming home, there's always hope."

After a small pause, she spoke sadly. "We've changed, haven't we? I used to be the optimist, and you the pessimist."

"Well, despite what I once said, one of us has to believe that he'll return," he almost snapped. "If you must know, I'm beginning to resent the sight of your gloomy face, Skye. It's not the most welcome thing to come home to."

"Is that why you've been staying out more often lately?"

"Perhaps," he replied, turning away, and she felt a huge surge of fear in her heart.

There could be another reason, of course. He was still a very handsome man, and he came into contact with all kinds of women in his work. Vulnerable women, needing advice and support. Who was to say that he wouldn't be as susceptible as the next man, when the alternative was coming home to a woman who seemed to have lost interest in life?

She caught sight of her reflection in the overmantel mirror, and was shocked at what she saw. Her beautiful black hair, the family trademark, was more than speckled with grey now, and she hadn't bothered about it properly in weeks. Her once lustrous blue eyes were dulled with anxiety and her private, silent weeping.

She was the one now, she thought furiously, who had her son already dead and buried before they even knew his fate. She owed him the force of her optimism.

"If only we could hear *something*," she muttered. "I begin to think there's a conspiracy of silence at the War Office about these missing planes. Either that, or there were so many of them that they daren't let the public know the extent of our losses. They've begun reporting some of them, I know, but how can Olly's plane be missing for so long with no word at all? No wreckage, or sightings, or bodies . . ."

She said the words deliberately, confronting them out loud, and as she did so, she felt a weird kind of strength seep back into her. Perhaps it *was* a conspiracy. Perhaps he'd been on some secret mission that couldn't be revealed as yet.

However crazy it sounded, she knew from Celia's guarded conversations about her previous decoding work that such things happened.

Nick held her close. "Darling, I know he'll be safe. I have a feeling in my bones about it. Despite what I may have thought before, I think we'd have heard about it by now."

He wasn't sure, any more than any of them were, but he wasn't going to dampen her sudden look of determination to think positively. He wasn't going to admit that he too had frequent nightmares about the chance of his son becoming fish-bait in the North Sea, or blown to pieces in a horrific air crash. He wouldn't let himself think of any of it, because he knew that to blot it out was the only way to keep sane.

But the news announcement in mid-December that Glenn Miller's plane had disappeared over a routine trip to France, and that all passengers and crew were feared dead, was almost enough to crush Skye's sprits again. They could find news of a celebrity plane all right, she thought bitterly, but they couldn't trace an ordinary airman's.

Then, when she had all but given up hope again, came a trickle of information.

A letter arrived from the Air Ministry. She was too afraid to open it until Nick came home that evening, even though Butch had offered to read it for her. But it wasn't his place, and she sent him out of the room before she gave the letter to Nick. Whatever Olly's parents had to face, they must do it together.

"Why didn't you call me?" Nick said. "I would have come home earlier."

"I knew you were in court today," she said, her voice jerky with anxiety. "I didn't want to disturb you."

God, how feeble that sounded. How dreadful, too, when she knew instinctively that there had to be news of her son's life – or death – contained in that slim envelope.

"I'm so afraid, Nick," she went on tremulously.

Her hands were clenched together, the palms damp with sweat. She didn't miss the fact that Nick's face was as white as her own, even as he ripped open the envelope and scanned the page.

"It's all right," he said rapidly, but his voice was strained. "At least, it's all right as far as the worst of our fears is concerned. Nothing is confirmed yet – but the news is at least hopeful."

Skye almost snatched the letter out of his hands. "What kind of information is that?" she said angrily. "Are they tormenting us with half-truths?"

She read the formal words quickly. Plane wreckage had been picked up in one of the icy Norwegian fjords, and it was confirmed as one of Oliver Pengelly's squadron. A man had been found wandering in the woods, somehow keeping alive in a half-wild state in the harsh Norwegian winter. Between the lines the Pengellys deduced the terrible state of the man, but he had finally been able to babble out some service information and was now in hospital and identified as a British airman.

The letter went on in similar stilted manner to tell then that although it had been established that the man was not their son, it was hoped that once the airman had fully recovered his senses, more information would be forthcoming, and then the Pengellys would be contacted again.

"And that's all they can tell us?" Skye said, choked.

"At least we know one of them got out safely—"

"You mean *alive*, don't you?" she went on bitterly. "But presumably his mind had gone and all identification was missing. So if he's the only one they've found so far, how much hope you do really hold out for Olly? You told me recently you thought we'd already said goodbye to him, remember? I can't forget that."

"I wish to God I'd never said anything at all."

"So do I."

She couldn't rid herself of the imagery of the plane wreckage in one of those impenetrably deep Norwegian fjords. The fact that one man had got out alive did nothing to ease her torment. In her imagination she could see the pilot still strapped in his seat, even now, deep in his underwater tomb. And Olly . . . her sweet baby . . . his young body ripped apart with the impact of the plane hitting the icy water.

The very thought of drowning – of the sensation of mouth and eyes and lungs filling up with water until they almost burst; of choking and gasping desperately for air, and knowing that there was no escape whatsoever – was filling her with a growing sense of claustrophobia. As if she was the one knowing the terror of sinking into an eternal darkness . . .

"Skye, put your head between your knees," she heard Nick order her as if from a distance.

Next minute, a glass was thrust between her cold lips. She opened them and swallowed the bitter-tasting brandy automatically, choking as she did so.

"I'm all right," she gasped. "Just for a moment I couldn't breathe, but I'm all right now. I need some air."

"Let's go outside—"

She touched his arm. "I need to be alone, Nick. I need space to think by myself. Please understand, honey."

And although he let her go, she knew he wouldn't really understand. Why would he? He was a lawyer, who solved everything by logical means and by poring over legal tomes, not by the airy-fairy urge to be up on the moors in the place where her ancestors had lived and breathed and died.

The thought was in her head without conscious effort. In a strange and inexplicable way, the moors had always been her family's sanctuary, maybe even more so for the women than the men. It was where they always went in time of trouble or fear. It was where Morwen Tremayne and Celia Penry had circled the old Larnie Stone to discover the images of their future sweethearts, nearly a hundred years ago.

It was where Morwen's brother, Sam, had died in the collapse of Ben Killigrew's rail tracks, on a clayworkers' outing to the sea. And that was the death that had resulted in Morwen and Ben taking in three orphaned children to their hearts and their home; Skye's own mother, Primmy, and Walter and Albert.

Morwen had been born in one of the little cottages overlooking Killigrew Clay, which was the pivot of all their hopes and dreams. It was where the heart of the family belonged, and it was where Skye knew she had to be while she concentrated her mind on praying for the safety of her son. She knew how badly she needed the spirit and passion of those ancestors around her now.

She toiled up the wintry slopes, scorning the use of a car or a bicycle, needing to feel in contact with the earth, and not caring if she was behaving like a madwoman, as crazy as the old witchwoman in the hovel on top of the moors.

Sunlight was thin and watery on this December day, but it still glinted on the soaring sky tips as it had always done, unchanging and eternal. The clayworks were silent now, with work done for the day, and no endless shifts of men and women and children scurrying about as they had done in days gone by.

The milky green pool where Celia Penry had drowned herself through the shame of being raped was still and deep, hiding its secrets. That other Celia was someone Skye had never known, but whose memory was forever perpetuated in the name of her own daughter. All for Morwen's sake. All for the grandmother she had loved so much . . .

Without warning, Skye felt a huge bitterness surge in her heart. Hardly aware of her own actions, she picked up a stone and hurled it into the clay pool, watching the ripples spread across its surface and spoil its evil serenity. Without warning, she was shouting hoarsely into the silence.

"Damn you, Granny Morwen! *Damn* you, and Great-Grandma Bess and Great-Grandad Hal, and Mom and Dad, and every Tremayne and Killigrew who ever lived. I want no part of you. I don't want to be beholden to your past. This is *my* life, and mine alone. I wish I had never come here to be entangled with you all. I was a fool to think this was where I belonged."

The rippling patterns of the pool grew wider and wider as she threw stone after stone into it, trying to exorcise every memory of those earlier ghosts. The ground was glossed with dew in the late afternoon, but she noticed none of it as her feet slid and slipped.

She was filled with a weird sense of exhilaration, of freedom and excitement, as if the oppression and weight of all those family ties was being abandoned for ever. It didn't feel like a betrayal, more a sense of becoming herself at last, instead of being just a continuation of all that had gone before. And she gloried in the feeling.

She laughed out loud, revelling in the sound, since it seemed so long since she had laughed, or danced or sung. Her feet gave a little skip of pure joy, and the next moment she went sprawling and rolling on the damp earth, her arms spread out to save herself, but still laughing, as if fully aware of how ridiculous she must appear, a middle-aged woman behaving like a wild thing.

But with the sound of her hysterical laughter came a slower and fuller awareness of where she was, and who she was. She was aware of the madness and futility of her actions in denying her past, and above all in denying those loving ancestors who had helped to shape the woman she was today.

"Oh God, forgive me, Granny Morwen," she heard herself mumble, as her head dropped to the ground and she tasted the dankness of the earth on her lips and felt its coolness on her cheeks. Sobs welled in her throat, where moments before there had been laughter. She knew she had been truly in the grip of madness, for to deny her heritage was to deny her own Celia and Wenna – and Olly too.

She heard a scuffle of feet, and as she sensed the shadow above her, her eyes closed in shame. If this was that grizzled old witch-woman, about to shriek abominations at her, then she would know she had truly let the devil into her heart . . .

"Have you hurt yerself, Mrs Pen?" she heard Daphne Hollis's scared young voice say. "Should I go and fetch me Ma .or somebody?"

Skye jerked up her head, knowing how stupid she must look, a grown woman lying face down on the moors with her arms spreadeagled as if in supplication, and her face covered in clay dirt. She rubbed at her cheeks and sat up carefully, breathing deeply for a few seconds before she spoke shakily.

"I'm not hurt, Daphne. I slipped and got winded for a minute, that's all."

"Yer'd better come to the cottage and let me Ma clean yer up then," the girl said practically. "If yer don't mind me sayin' so, yer look a real sight, Mrs Pen, like one o' them clayworking gels in the old newspaper pictures."

"Do I, Daphne?" Skye said huskily. The thought sped into her mind that out of the mouths of babes and vaccies could often come more common sense than ever came from an educated woman's brain.

"Come on then," Daphne went on. "We was just going to 'ave our tea, and me Ma will be wond'ring what's happened to me. We've got summat to tell yer, anyway."

She couldn't hide the excitement in her voice as she put out her arm to help Skye to her feet.

"Have you? What's that?"

Oh honey, tell me anything to help me rid myself of the madness of the last ten minutes, Skye thought.

"We're gettin' hitched," Daphne announced in triumph. "Gary wrote to me Ma to say he's bein' sent back to America on account of

216

his war wound. So we're gettin' hitched before Christmas and goin' wiv 'im. What do yer think of that!"

"I'm astonished!" was all Skye could think of to say.

She hadn't known that Gary had a war wound, either, but it was clear that Daphne was totally swept away by the glamour of going to America. And what a coup to tell her school friends about, was her next thought. Above all things, Daphne needed to feel important and this was clearly the pinnacle of her dreams.

"I'm really happy for you and your Mom, honey," she went on, giving the girl a quick hug.

Daphne squirmed away. "Yeah, well, as long as I don't have ter start talking funny, like you do," she giggled.

Skye began to laugh. "Daphne, you can talk any way you like, and you'll always do me a power of good."

"Will I?" Daphne said suspiciously. "It's not what me Ma says then. She says I'm a proper caution."

"You're that too," Skye told her solemnly.

"Where the hell have you been, Skye?" Nick said angrily when she finally returned to New World, having had her ears stormed by how wonderful life in America was going to be for the Hollises once they were mutually hitched to Gary. "I was about to send out search parties for you. And what in God's name has happened to your clothes?"

"Oh, don't fuss, Nick. I fell over, that's all, but Mrs Hollis let me have a wash and brush-up at the cottage."

"You've been up on the moors? Skye, it's practically dark now! Anything could have happened to you."

"Where else would I go when I needed to think?" she snapped. "And how could anything bad happen to me with Granny Morwen looking after me?"

She bit her lip. She should be past all that weird stuff at her age, and she knew Nick didn't like that kind of talk, anyway. Besides, she couldn't forget the guilty fact that she had totally rejected it herself just a short time ago. She lowered her eyes, feeling a swift shock that she could have done so, and then she felt her husband's arms fold around her.

"I should have remembered," he said softly. "She would never let any harm come to you."

She caught her breath at his unexpected understanding and acceptance before raising her face for his kiss, and in that moment she had never loved him more.

*   *   *

The Hollises were gone before Christmas. Americans moved with admirable swiftness, Skye told Butch when he came home from White Rivers and reported that the cottage was empty. Daphne had already called to say goodbye, and it might have been a far more emotional one, but for her obvious excitement at going on a ship to the other side of the world.

Just for a moment, Skye had felt a huge tug at her heart, imagining Daphne's feelings at her first sight of the New York skyline, and the green Statue of Liberty rising out of the ocean like a fantasy figure, welcoming all who saw her.

Then she grinned wryly. Knowing Daphne, she would probably not even notice Lady Liberty, except to make some rude comment.

"Are we having Christmas this year, Mrs Pen?" she heard Butch say cautiously. At his uneasy look, Skye felt a rush of affection for him.

"Why, what a thing to say, Butch. Of course we're having Christmas. Why on earth wouldn't we?"

His blush met his carroty hairline. "Well, because of – of Olly, and we've all been so sad lately – I thought perhaps we should all be quiet—"

"Well, we're not going to be quiet at Christmas-time. Goodness me, what would New World be like without celebrating Christmas? We can't let it pass as if it's just another day, can we?"

But she swallowed hard as she spoke, and she didn't let him see how bright her eyes were, or what an effort it was to constantly remind herself that life went on, even if hearts were breaking.

In the end, it was the best idea of all to fill the house with people. Celia was home, and so was Wenna with Harry Mack. All the relatives came as usual, and Skye kept a determined smile on her face as they all drank a toast to Olly, saying stoutly that this time next year he would be drinking a toast to all the stay-at-homes instead.

"And long before this time next year, God willing, we'll all be living in a free world again," Nick added.

"I can't remember what anything was like before the war," Butch said, frowning.

"Good Lord, I don't suppose you can, kiddo," Celia said, glad to change the subject before her mother's smile slipped. "Well, when it's all over we'll have bananas by the bucket-load, and so much chocolate it will make you sick. You'll get so fat you'll be waddling up to White Rivers every day—"

"Stop it, Celia," Seb laughed. "Leave the boy alone. He's doing a grand job at the pottery, and I won't have you teasing my star pupil."

"He's your only one, isn't he?" she grinned back at him, and ducked as he made a mock swipe at her.

Watching them, and listening to their nonsense, Skye thought what a handsome pair they made. If Celia wasn't still so madly in love with Stefan von Gruber – a hopeless liaison in her opinion – she was sure she and Seb could have made a go of it. It wasn't unheard of for cousins to marry – her own parents bore witness to that – but fate had evidently decided that Celia was a one-man girl.

She had thought that about herself once, when she and Philip Norwood had only had eyes for one another, but fate – and Nick Pengelly – had proved that love could come for a second time, and be just as spectacular.

"What are you smiling at?" she heard Nick say beside her.

"I was just thinking how much I love you, and how good it is to have all our family around us," she said steadily. "And even those who aren't here now are still with us in spirit, aren't they, Nick?"

"Always," he said.

The remote Norwegian farmhouse was warm and cosy, the wood fires in every room burning fiercely to defy the bitter cold from the snow outside. The girl with the long silvery hair leaned over the bed of the young man with the ugly jagged cuts on his cheeks and chest.

The wounds were healing satisfactorily now, but they were still too tender for him to bear any bedding touching them. The girl's heart ached for the once-fine sight of the young man's body, criss-crossed with such hideous scars now.

They would fade in time, and few would know the raw vividness she and her brother had seen when they had brought him here a month ago, nearer dead than alive. He had been lucky to be found just days before the first bad snows of the winter had set in. A few days more, and he would surely have perished. Some were born lucky, and Birgitta had known instinctively that he was one of them. She knew about such things . . . she was acknowledged as a healer and she could sense the need for survival in this man.

The patient stirred in his sleep now, and Birgitta wondered if this would be the day, at last, when he would recover full consciousness. Until that day came, they had no idea who he was. His garbled shrieks and mutterings gave no clue as to his nationality or identity, and all remnants of identifiable uniform and dog-tags had been ripped away from him long before they had found him.

219

But the hand holding hers was becoming increasingly strong, and she prayed that he would soon awake. It was foolish to fall in love with someone whose gaze was so vague as yet. But his eyes were as startlingly blue as her own, and they made her heart race each time they looked at her.

Birgitta came from fierce Viking stock, and fervently believed in the old legend that said that the man whose life she saved forever belonged to her.

She felt her brother's hand touch her shoulder, and she waited a moment before looking up at him. Her long straight hair fell over her face, and she hoped swiftly that it hid the passion in her eyes for her unknown warrior.

"Come away now, Birgitta," Rolf said gently. "You know we can't let this go on much longer. We don't know if he's British or Polish, or even German, but people will be looking for him, and we have to notify someone soon."

"Why must we?" she said fiercely. "We've tended to his wounds, and he's healing well. He should be allowed to recover in his own time."

"But there will be others who are missing him. He may have a wife and family—"

"*No,*" she said. "I would know if it were so. I would feel it. Besides, I'm sure he's not German."

Rolf spoke more sharply. "Birgitta, you can't rely on your instincts in this case. It's time to inform the partisans that the man is here, and let them decide what to do next."

As if in answer to his words, the man in the bed stirred, and his incoherent mumbling began as usual. But as Birgitta leaned closer, she heard that some of his words were better formulated than usual, and she frowned.

"Olly?" she said, looking up at her brother. "What does this mean? What is Olly?"

The man's grip on her hand tightened, and she saw that his eyes were a fraction clearer than before.

"Olly," he whispered painfully and slowly, as if finding it hard to move his dry lips over the simplest of words.

"Olly – Oliver—" he managed, and then his clasp slackened again and he slumped into sleep once more.

"Oliver," Birgitta repeated after a startled moment. "I know that name, Rolf, and so do you. It is the name of the boy in the famous British story who asked for more gruel. This is an educated man to speak such a name."

She looked at Rolf again. "He's told us something else too, I think. Whoever he is, he's British. Thank God."

"Then we know where to start. I'll alert the partisans right away, and they will inform the British authorities."

"Must you?" Birgitta said, all her feelings in her eyes, and desperately wanting to keep him to herself for just a little while longer.

At least until the moment when he opened his eyes properly and realised that she was a vibrant young girl on the brink of womanhood, and not merely a pair of healing and caring hands that had tended his most intimate requirements in these past weeks.

"I must, my love," Rolf said quietly. "And you know it. He doesn't belong here."

Sixteen

There had been a time, long ago, when all that Stefan von Gruber had dreamed about was becoming a respected vintner like his father. Of following in the family footsteps, and carrying on the tradition of growing the grapes on the vast von Gruber Estates that produced such fine German wines.

As a small boy, still enchanted with his heritage, he had known the magic of seeing how the rows upon rows of the bare winter sticks of the vines gradually came into shining green leaf. There was even more magic in the way the tiny clusters of dry pips developed into the luscious purple globes of the grapes, their sensual aroma enveloping the crystal clear air of the vineyards.

During the boredom of being interned, he used his imagination fully to exercise his mind, recalling the halcyon days of childhood. He could still imagine the lovely, squishy feel of the grapes in his hands, staining his clothes and his fingers purple, and could well remember knowing he was in for a scolding from his mother, and indulgent laughter from his father.

In the last few years, such memories had sustained him in a way he would never have believed. When the Gestapo had so viciously commandeered his home and imprisoned him along with other political prisoners for refusing to co-operate, he had thought himself one of the forgotten men.

Their guards hardly knew what to do with them, since the prisoners were all intelligent and influential men in their own right. They weren't even criminals in the general sense, and they were given as much leeway within their confines as it was possible to have, without allowing them their liberty. The guards were canny men, and while keeping them strictly at arm's length, had become as sociable with their prisoners as dignity and hierarchy allowed.

In the dying months of 1944, they, like everyone else, knew that the end of the war was in sight. Hitler would inevitably be overthrown, and they would want to be known to have been lenient. And when another new year had come and gone, and the Allies were burgeoning their way through Europe, many of the captors simply panicked and fled, leaving the prisoners to discover that their doors were no longer being locked at night.

There was nothing to prevent them from leaving their isolated strongholds and going their separate ways. But for many, the enforced camaraderie of the past years did not spill over into this new freedom, and they knew it was not going to be easy to resume life in a country that was so vastly different now from the way it had been five years before.

After his parents' deaths, it had been Stefan's plan to begin a new life in Switzerland with his adored Celia, and he offered up a silent prayer of thanks to whatever God was looking after him that he had thought to deposit the bulk of his fortune in a Swiss bank before the worst happened.

But he had no idea where Celia was now, and she might even think he was dead. As a businessman he had known a great many influential people, but he had become wary of everyone now, and there was no way of knowing whom he could trust.

When he left his prison in the chill of a February morning, he was dressed far more soberly than of old. He needed to merge into the outside world, and try to find out exactly where he was.

But he was also disorientated and temporarily destitute, and he knew he must contact someone who could help him. From newspapers and road signs, he realised he had been held in a remote area some distance west of Berlin.

Then he remembered his old boss, Herr Vogl, with whom Celia's parents had done such good business in the years before the war. He prayed that the Vogls would still be sympathetic towards their old business friends.

Herr Vogl had been a fair and honest man, and Stefan hoped that he might advance his old employee some money so that he could make his way to Switzerland.

It hurt his pride to have to ask such a thing, but he would do anything for the chance of contacting Celia again. So, fighting off the panic attacks that had become all too frequent since his unexpected liberation, he gathered his thoughts and made his plans, and tried to feel slightly more human again.

The Vogls were preparing for supper when the doorbell rang, and Herr Vogl answered it with some annoyance. No one trusted late callers these days, although by now everyone knew it was only a matter of time before the Nazi regime was crushed. Then, perhaps, the world could return to normality again after all the suffering and madness of war.

"Yes? Who is it?" he said, opening the door a fraction.

"A friend, Herr Vogl," Stefan said at once. "A one-time friend and business acquaintance. Stefan von Gruber."

Vogl opened the door a little wider and stared at the shabby attire and the spare frame of the man he remembered as once having such a fine physique.

"*Mein Gott*, man, what has happened to you? Come inside and warm yourself by the fire. Have you been ill?"

Stefan gave a bitter laugh as he was ushered into the drawing room. "Not ill, exactly. But deprived of my liberty all this time due to my convictions—"

Too late, he remembered that long ago the son of this house, the young and earnest Franz Vogl, had become one of Hitler's Brownshirts.

Stefan wished desperately that he could have taken his words back, but he had walked for miles to get here, and he was near to collapse with fatigue. He simply couldn't think sensibly any longer. But he recognised that these strait-laced people might well view him as a traitor to the Fatherland . . . He swayed a little, and felt the older man grip his arm.

"Sit down, von Gruber, and take a nip of brandy."

He obeyed, because he had become used to taking orders. He had not been badly treated during internment, but all liberty and sense of self-respect had been taken away from him and his fellow prisoners. They ate when they were told, slept when they were told, took exercise when they were told.

Once he had recovered a little, he knew this man and his wife would want answers as to why he was here. He steadied himself enough to know he must go carefully.

In the formal German manner of politeness before explanation, he enquired about the Vogl family.

"Our son is dead," Herr Vogl said abruptly. "He was killed doing his duty for the Fatherland. My wife and I feel it best to state these things at once, to save embarrassment."

God, he was a cold fish, thought Stefan. Frau Vogl too sat as rigidly as if a son wasn't part of a loving family, just a commodity to be mentioned in passing. But it was their nature, he thought, with a vague recollection of how Celia had amused him with anecdotes of the Vogls' long-ago Christmas visit to Cornwall, and told him how stiff and starchy they had been in that free and easy household. Clearly, nothing had changed.

"My sincere condolences on your loss," he said gravely.

Herr Vogl's shoulders sagged for a brief moment. "We are all casualties of war in one way or another, my friend. The world has changed for the worse, and I fear that the old order is no more, and never will be again."

His words gave Stefan a glimmer of an opening.

"But once it's all over, we will have to resume normal living again, or it will have been for nothing. Forgive me, sir, but even old enemies must strive to regain something of what's past, wouldn't you agree?"

He saw the flash of anger in Herr Vogl's eyes, and for a moment he thought he had gone too far. Then he saw Frau Vogl put a restraining hand on her husband's arm.

"I suspect that you are thinking of the Pengelly girl, Herr von Gruber," she said quietly. "I believe you and she had an affection for one another at one time."

"For *all* time, Frau Vogl," Stefan said, ignoring all thought of caution now. "We loved each other deeply, and were to be married. I pray that someday it will still be possible."

He took a long draught of the stinging brandy and felt his head spin. It had been a mistake to drink on an empty stomach, and so far he had been offered no food.

The condemned man drank a shot of brandy, he found himself thinking . . . *and then he was shot.*

"Please forgive me for bothering you like this," he said, getting clumsily to his feet. "I shouldn't have come here."

"Sit down, man. As a former colleague, you are welcome," Herr Vogl said harshly. "We were about to eat, and I'm sure my wife can stretch our meagre fare to three. The pantry is not so plentiful as it once was, but we survive. Then we will talk, and if it is your wish, we will be happy to offer you the hospitality of our home until you decide what you are going to do."

"You are very kind, and I accept gladly," Stefan said, his heart too full to say more at this unexpected gesture.

Now that France had been liberated, Wenna's ENSA concert party was entertaining troops in Paris and other French cities. Everyone said the war would be over soon, and Celia knew how buoyant her sister was these days, eagerly waiting for the day when it all ended, and she and Harry Mack could be married.

Celia was happy for her, and she tried not to let her own sadness show in the regular letters she wrote to her sister. But at the start of the new year she had good news to tell her, since their cousin Seb was now seeing a girl from Roche, and was seriously courting at last. She was happy for both of them, but it did seem to emphasise her own lack of news, and she felt increasingly lonely.

She never lost faith that one day she and Stefan would be together again, and she ached for the day when he would take her in his arms and vow that nothing had changed between them, nor ever could.

But she was wise enough to know that it would never be quite the way it had been before. Not at first, anyway. So much had come between them, and however much they desired it and longed for it, there would be an inevitable awkwardness at being reunited.

In her darkest moments, she wondered if they would both have changed irrevocably. No one could ever know how deep the changes were until the moment of truth when they were together again. Celia shivered, torturing herself with doubts, but facing facts logically, the way she had always done.

Even as Celia was writing her letter to Wenna, a wedding was taking place in a small country church somewhere south of Paris.

The ceremony was conducted in French and English, and there was no formal attire among the chief participants or the wedding guests. There was a mixture of army and air force uniforms, and a large sprinkling of local people who had turned out to witness a far happier occasion than had been seen in their bullet-riddled town in recent years.

"Do you, Harry Johnson Mack, take Wenna Pengelly to be your wedded wife? Will you love her and honour her, and keep you only unto her, so long as you both shall live?"

The man looked deeply into his bride's vivid blue eyes.

"I will," he said quietly.

The priest turned to the beautiful woman in the trim khaki uniform, mourning, as only a Frenchman could, that with such gloriously dramatic colouring she couldn't be wearing virginal white. But the obvious love between the two was the only thing that mattered, and he cleared his throat once more.

"Do you, Wenna Pengelly, take Harry Johnson Mack to be your wedded husband? Will you love, honour and obey him, and keep you only unto him, so long as you both shall live?"

"I will," murmured Wenna, her voice catching at the solemn

226

beauty of the moment as the priest motioned to Harry to slide the gold ring on to her wedding finger.

"I now pronounce you man and wife," said the priest. He looked around at the congregation and spoke sternly. "Whom God has joined together let no man put asunder."

"Just let anyone try," Harry murmured so that only Wenna could hear, as he pulled her into his arms and pressed his mouth to hers in their first married kiss.

And then all solemnity was over, and their friends and supporters surrounded them, and kisses and tears flowed in equal measure, together with good luck flowers from the local well-wishers. They had little to give, but everyone loved a wedding, and this marriage of strangers in their midst seemed the best way of all to herald the start of the new year.

"Have we done the right thing, do you think?" Harry whispered mischievously in her ear when they were finally leading the procession down the street to the café in the square where they were to hold a small reception.

"No. We're totally mad," Wenna said, smiling, touched beyond words as local children threw flowers in their path.

"What will your folks think when we tell them?"

She smiled again, sure of herself, and sure of his love.

"They'll love it. How could my mother do otherwise, when she and my father did the very same thing?"

She wasn't sure about Nick – though she knew her mother could always placate him – but from the moment Harry had told her he couldn't bear to wait until the war was over to make her his wife, she had known they would do this.

There had been an undoubted sense of charm and continuity in her mind, knowing that her mother had married her father in the very same way during the First World War – secretly, telling no one but their wartime colleagues, and for no other reason but the need to be together.

Skye and Philip hadn't even told their closest family their secret for some time, but Wenna and Harry intended writing home with their news at once.

But first there was the small reception of food and drink, generously hoarded and donated by their colleagues, and catered by the romantic French café owners. There was much laughter and teasing innuendo before it was over, and they winced at the clanking sound of the old tin cans that were tied to the back of the small car they had borrowed.

But finally, as twilight merged into the soft darkness of evening, they were alone to enjoy their brief weekend leave at a small hotel in the country. It wasn't the honeymoon of the rich and famous, but for two people so very much in love, it was more idyllic than anything that money could buy.

"Do you know how often I've dreamed of this moment?" Harry murmured, as he slid the silky straps of her slip from her shoulders, and bent his head to kiss the soft smooth skin of each one.

"Tell me," she said huskily, her senses tingling anew with every touch of his hands and mouth. She was happy to prolong the moment, knowing that this sweet banter was no more than a prelude to the pleasure they would take in one another, on this night and for the rest of their lives.

"Every day since the day I met you," he said, his lips moving downwards to kiss the wild pulsing at her throat. "And every night since then, I've ached to hold you in my arms and make you mine, and to know that no one else could have you."

"No one else ever could – or ever will."

She felt his hands moving over her slender shape, finding the curves and hollows through the slip. With a growing fire in her body that matched his own, she longed for him to know every part of her, properly and without restriction or inhibition.

"Harry, I want—" she began tremulously, hesitating for no more than an instant. "I don't think I can bear to wait a moment longer."

"Nor I, my sweet darling," he said, pushing the silky garment down the length of her body until it fell in a shimmering heap on the carpet. "And I thank God I don't have to apologise for my hunger for you."

With one movement he swept her up in his arms and lay her on the bed. Moments later he had filled her with himself, and she gloried in the erotic fever of his lovemaking. If there was one coherent thought left in her mind as they soared towards an exquisite completeness, it was to thank God that they had found one another, out of all the world.

Normal communication between Europe and Britain was slowly being restored, and the letter that arrived at New World a few weeks later had an unmistakably French stamp on it.

I've truly been meaning to write to you sooner than this, Mom, *Wenna had written.* But after my recent leave we were immediately sent to give a series of concerts to the British and Allied

troops in Normandy, and you wouldn't believe how hectic and
disorganised everything is there. Still, the reception we got was
simply wonderful. Life will never be the same for me after all
this adulation.

Skye smiled indulgently, knowing how unbelievably modest her girl
still was, despite the lovely voice that must have cheered thousands
of servicemen by now. As many as the much-fêted Vera Lynn, Skye
thought loyally . . . She read on, and sat bolt upright.

As a matter of fact, nothing will ever be the same for me again
after my last leave, Mom. It was no more than a weekend, but it
was the most blissful weekend of my life, because I spent it with
Harry in the sweetest little hotel in the country. And before
you're completely shocked, I have something very special to tell
you.
  Harry and I were married on our last leave. We simply
couldn't wait any longer, and I pray that you'll understand,
because it was the same for you and Daddy, wasn't it? I know
you'll feel a bit cheated out of giving me a big wedding but it
wasn't what we wanted, or needed. All we needed was each
other, so please be happy for us.

Skye was reading the words for the umpteenth time when Nick came
home and found her there, sitting motionless, her mind a million
miles away.

Remembering a time when she too had wanted nothing but to be
in her beloved's arms, desperate to know the feeling of belonging
while everyone around them threatened to blast all the world into
oblivion. A threat that was even greater so in this war.

She and Philip had been so in love, exactly as Wenna and Harry
were in love . . .

"What's wrong?" Nick said, alarmed at her silence. "It's not bad
news, is it, darling?"

She smiled at him, the second great love of her life. In many ways
the best love of all, because he was her last and most enduring love.
She stretched out her hand and he came to sit beside her. She leaned
against him.

"No, it's not bad news. For once, it's happy news," she said. "But
I think you had better read it for yourself while I pour us both a
celebratory glass of sherry."

"Good Lord, it must be good news for you to take a drink in the middle of the afternoon," he said with a grin, but she could see the relief in his face. There had been enough bad news to contend with over the years, and it was time they all turned the corner.

The next moment her euphoric mood shattered and her hand shook over the sherry decanter as he uttered a savage oath.

"The unspeakable bastard! This was presumably a shotgun wedding—" he said explosively.

"*Nick*, how could you think such a thing! I thought you had more trust in our daughter."

"I trust *her* all right, but not this conniving bastard. What kind of a hole-and-corner wedding could it have been, anyway, doing it on the quiet and telling nobody until it was all over?"

"*My* kind," Skye said, her voice stiff with anger. "The very same kind that Philip and I had in wartime. But I suppose no one could expect a *lawyer* to understand the needs of two people very much in love and far from home, who couldn't bear to be apart one moment longer, and were always aware that every day might be their last."

The silence in the room was electric. Then Nick had covered the distance between them and was holding her unyielding body tightly in his arms.

"My God, Skye, forgive me. I didn't think—"

"You never do. You can be as objective as ice when it comes to your clients, but not where your family is concerned. Don't you find that strange?"

Her voice still shook with rage and she couldn't relax in his arms. He had spoiled the most beautiful moment of these dark days, and she couldn't forgive him for that.

"Don't you know why?" he said in a strangled voice at last. "Don't you know it's because I love you all so much, and it tears me apart to know what's happening to all of us? I can't bear to see how Celia still lives in hope for her German fellow – and not knowing if Olly's dead or alive – and now losing Wenna in this way—"

"You idiot," Skye said, all her stiffness melting away in an instant. "We haven't lost her. She'll always be ours, and she'll want us to be happy for her now. If she's half as happy as we've been, she'll do all right – wouldn't you say?"

Her eyes dared him to say otherwise, despite their sometimes volatile relationship. Through it all, the love had survived, and always would. All of this was no more than one irregular heartbeat in the steadfastness of their lives together. She truly believed that. She lifted her face for his kiss, and he crushed her mouth with his own.

"I may be a successful lawyer, but my wife is much cleverer than I could ever be," he mumbled against her mouth.

"That's because I'm a Tremayne at heart," she told him, just in case he thought she was still harbouring secret yearnings for Philip Norwood after all this time.

"So are you going to write straight back to Wenna?"

"Of course. We both will, and we'll promise them a New World party to end all parties when we're all together again," she said determinedly.

Celia was openly envious.

"The lucky little devil," she said to her companions in their draughty billet when she heard the news. "My sister's just got married in France to her Canadian Group Captain."

"There'll be a right shaking of the old bedsprings going on in the old barracks by now then," giggled East End Gertie, making a rude gesture. "Unless she did it just to get her ticket back to Blighty, of course."

"What do you mean?" Lizzie said, as dim as ever.

"I mean, pea-brain, that married women can have babies – or didn't anyone ever tell you about the birds and bees?"

"Don't be stupid, Gertie. I doubt that my sister would even think about having a family yet," Celia said.

"And you'd know all about how to prevent it, of course, clever-clogs," Gertie sneered.

Celia looked at her in exasperation. "When are you going to stop this stupid inverted snobbery, Gertie? We're all in the same boat—"

"Don't you mean the same dung-heap?" the other girl grinned, and then shrugged. "Oh well, I dare say you're not so bad, Pengelly – for a country girl, that is. So when are you going to tell us a bit more about this man of yours that you keep so secret? You're next in the wedding stakes, I suppose."

Celia's nerves jangled, and she gave a forced laugh. "I'm waiting until after the war before I tie the knot."

Lizzie spoke up slyly, taking Gertie's lead. "I don't reckon he exists. I reckon you just made him up!"

"Maybe I did," Celia said, turning her head away to hide her stinging eyes. "But you'll never know, will you?"

A sudden knock on their billet door saved her from answering any more probing questions. The farmer's son was calling her name imperiously.

"There's a telephone call for you, Pengelly, and Father says you're to be quick because he wants to use it himself."

"The old fart probably wants to call his lady friend," Gertie jeered. "You take as long as you like, Pengelly."

Celia was glad to escape. They were coarse and irritating, though they had all got used to one another by now, and rubbed along fairly well. In a perverse kind of way she would miss them when they all disbanded.

Like a hole in the head, she amended grimly, hearing their raucous laughter. It followed her across the farmyard to the house, where she thankfully closed the door and picked up the phone in the passageway.

It was Moonie.

"Celia, I've got some news," she heard him say, and her heart leapt.

"Stefan?" she breathed.

The silence at the other end was minimal, but even so, she knew instantly that the news wasn't going to be about Stefan. She smothered her disappointment with a huge effort.

"I believe we've located your brother," Moonie went on, and paused while she gasped audibly into the receiver.

"Is he safe? Is he well?" she spluttered.

She quickly grabbed the nearest stool and sat down heavily on it before she fell down with shock. She couldn't help the agonised thought, coming so soon after Wenna's news, that maybe the Pengellys had used up all their luck now.

"Before I say any more, Celia," Moonie said, "let me assure you that he's safe."

She gripped the phone, feeling as though her stomach was turning somersaults with relief.

"Thank God. Where is he? Was he wounded? What happened to him?" she babbled out all at once, her usual coolness gone in an instant.

"Take it slowly, my dear. I've been in contact with some Norwegian partisans, and it seems he was shot down over Norway, as we've long suspected. Unfortunately the man your family had already heard about has since died, and was unable to tell us any more. But I understand that your brother was pretty badly cut about, Celia, so be prepared."

"Just as long as he's safe," she whispered.

He went on unemotionally. "He was picked up and cared for by some farmers. The woman looked after him very well, by all accounts."

"A woman?" she repeated stupidly.

"It was a brother and sister who farm in a small way, I'm told. Strictly between you and me, Celia, I gather Olly has begged for her to accompany him to England, where he'll be taken to a military hospital for some time. I don't know if it will be sanctioned for her to go with him."

"Is she a nurse or something?" Celia said.

"Some sort of a healer, they say. Lucky, wasn't he?"

Bloody lucky, thought Celia. But that was Olly. Always falling on his feet. Always the darling of the gods. Smelling of roses when everyone else was in the proverbial dung-heap . . . Without warning she burst into uncontrollable tears, because she loved him, and she thanked God he was safe, even if it meant she had used up all her own luck in the process.

So the woman was a healer, was she? Some sort of a crank . . . but how could she think that, and she a Cornishwoman! Her throat was tight with tears.

"I'm sorry, Moonie. I'm finding it hard to take it all in. Just give me a minute, will you?"

"Take as long as you like."

"I can't do that. The farmer here wants to use the phone. Can I call you back in a little while?"

"Of course. I'll be here all evening, and I still need to say more to you."

She hung up and went back to the billet, not wanting to face anyone right now. She couldn't quite believe it was actually true that Olly would be coming home. While she knew she should feel like singing, she prayed for her mother's sake that it wasn't all a cruel hoax . . . but it couldn't be, if Moonie had got the information from the partisans on their elaborate short-wave wireless system. She trusted him totally.

Still, she tried to think rationally. It had been a long time, and as yet she didn't know what Olly's injuries were. Moonie's voice had been cautious, and she knew they couldn't expect to see the same happy-go-lucky Olly who had gone away.

Everyone knew that war changed people. Nobody ever came out unscathed. Her mother would know that. So would everyone of her generation; they had seen it all before.

She felt more rational by the time she managed to speak to Moonie again, ignoring the instruction from the farmer not to make it too long or the cost would be docked from her wages.

It soon became clear that Olly wouldn't have survived without these Norwegian farmers who had found him, though Moonie had no more information about them.

"They're angels, that's who they were. Guardian angels," Celia said.

"Apparently so. Look, Celia, I've got a few days' leave, and I've got clearance to give your family the news myself. I can be at your home tomorrow afternoon. Can you be there?"

"You make it all sound terribly ominous," Celia said, her first elation slipping into anxiety now.

"I don't mean to, but it's quite complicated, and I'd prefer to explain it in person, and I'd like to see you again, of course. But for the moment, I advise you to keep the news to yourself. So go and tell your boss that you need some leave, and I'll see you at New World tomorrow afternoon."

She hung up the phone with shaking hands, her mind in a whirl. She wondered uneasily just how serious Olly's injuries were, and how much he wasn't telling her. But then the most important point of all flooded her senses. Olly was alive. For the moment, her joy eclipsed everything else, even the searing knowledge that there was still no news of Stefan. She had been so sure she would have heard something by now . . .

She was still catching her breath when the farmer came out of the parlour and asked curtly if she had finished her business. He was a boorish man who had no truck with women farm workers, and she hated him.

"I have to go home on family business tomorrow," she said coldly. "I'll let you know when I'll be back."

"Don't bother, miss," he snapped. "You've been a thorn in my flesh ever since you arrived, and I'll be more than glad to inform the authorities that you're no longer needed here."

"Thank you, sir," she said sarcastically. "That will save me the nuisance of doing it myself."

Celia didn't want to go home to New World too early. She would be too afraid of blurting out everything before Moonie arrived, and it was clear that however traumatic the news they had to hear was, he wanted her and her parents to be together when they heard it. She was getting increasingly nervous. Olly was alive, but that was all she knew. It didn't bode well.

Tomorrow was Saturday and Nick would be at home. Presumably Moonie had worked that out for himself. She tried not to imagine terrible injuries, and concentrated instead on packing her things and telling the other Land Girls she was going home for good, and that she intended having a long lie-in before she left in the morning.

"Bimey, gel, what's old sour-face going to say about that?" Gertie exclaimed.

"I'm damn sure he'll be giving three cheers to see the back of me," Celia retorted.

"Well, *we* won't," Lizzie said. "We'll miss you, Celia."

"Go on. You won't have time to miss me! You'll have twice as much work to do without me around," she said, touched by the words, and throwing a pillow at the girl to soften the unexpected emotion she felt.

It must be because of everything that had happened so suddenly, she thought. Wenna's news, and now Olly's . . .

But where did that leave her? Out of nowhere a small voice inside her said that two out of three wasn't bad. There was probably a law of averages that said there always had to be one who didn't get everything she wanted—

Her spinning thoughts were halted as a pillow was hurled back at her, and suddenly the feathers were flying, and the three of them were laughing and spluttering and coughing, and the tears went unnoticed.

Later, she couldn't have said how she spent the whole of the next day until she got back to New World in the mid-afternoon. She remembered parts. She stayed in bed until it was unreasonable for her to stay any longer, and besides, she was far too jittery to be idle.

She bought a midday snack in a local café, idled along the seafront at Penzance, watching the boats jostling in the harbour, and then took the bus as near to New World as possible, before walking the last mile home.

By then, her suitcase felt as if it weighed a ton, and her mother's eyes widened at the unexpected sight of her. Although it was a chilly early March now, Celia's face was as red with exertion and worry as if had been midsummer.

"For pity's sake, honey, come inside. Are you ill or is this an unscheduled leave? You should have let us know you were coming, and Daddy would have come to fetch you —"

"Please don't fuss, Mom. I'm home to stay, that's all. Me and Farmer Giles have parted for good, and that's all I'm prepared to say right now!"

It served two purposes, and Skye knew better than to ask too many questions when her daughter was in one of her scratchy moods. She would explain things in her own time, and right now she looked as if she needed to rest and recover.

In fact, Celia was feeling increasingly guilty at having to keep the news from her mother that Skye would so dearly love to hear. She should never have agreed to keeping it from her until Moonie arrived.

"Is Daddy here?" she asked swiftly now.

He had to be here when Moonie came. She felt the panic rising. It was important that they were all together to face whatever Moonie had to tell them . . .

"He's in his study. Is something wrong, Celia?"

She shook her head, and then they both looked up as they heard the sound of a car door slam. A taxi had pulled up and Captain Moon was alighting from it.

Skye frowned, not knowing who the visitor was, but Celia ran outside at once, and took both his hands in hers. Her heart pounded, and she looked at him searchingly, but he kissed her cheek and spoke reassuringly.

"It's all right, my dear. I promise you everything will be all right. Let's go inside and talk to your parents."

Seventeen

"And he's actually here in England?" Skye gasped, when Moonie had related everything he knew – much more than he had already told Celia.

"My latest information is that he's in a sanatorium south of Bristol that specialises in his injuries," Moonie said carefully. "I must warn you, Mrs Pengelly, that it may be some time before he's allowed home. When he is, of course, I doubt that he'll see active service again."

"I should damn well hope not," Nick said angrily. "The boy enlisted under age, and he's seen enough active service for any man."

"But that's what he is, Nick. A man," Skye said with huge pride and dignity. "And I'm terribly proud of him."

"We all are, Mom," Celia put in. She turned to Moonie. "But what about these Norwegian people? Did the farming woman come with him after all?"

"Apparently. I gather your brother refused to be moved without her."

Celia spoke uneasily. "Well, I thank God he's safe, of course, but I hope this doesn't mean he's become dependent on some crank healing woman."

"Can we visit him?" Skye asked swiftly, wanting to prevent Nick from saying anything scathing, and knowing she and Celia would both be remembering the old witchwoman on the moors at that moment. There was a cranky old healing woman if ever there was one, she thought feelingly.

"I have the address of the sanatorium," Moonie said. "There are no restrictions on visitors."

There was an awkward silence for a few minutes. Moonie had said all he had come to say, and he sensed that these folk would be burning to get away to visit their son as soon as possible. Besides, it wasn't for him to urge caution, to advise them not to bombard the boy with emotions and tears.

Seeing his face, Celia spoke swiftly. "You'll stay with us for a while, won't you, Moonie? I'd like to show you my little piece of the world."

"Just overnight, if that's all right with your parents. I have some visiting of my own to do in the area."

"Of course you must stay, Captain Moon," said Skye, but she was already mentally packing a small suitcase with which to travel to the Somerset sanatorium.

She simply couldn't think about entertaining. This was Celia's friend and colleague, and it was up to Celia to make him welcome. All Skye could think about was that Oliver was safe, and as soon as his wounds had healed, he would be coming home. God had been good to them, and for the first time in ages, she felt a great urge to be inside a church and thank Him properly. She had said many prayers in her lifetime, in many places, and she knew that they all counted. But this time, no other place but God's house would do.

"Do you mind if I spend some time alone?" she said to Nick, once Celia and Moonie had left them, and the tears of relief had dried. "I know it's not your feeling, Nick, but I need to go to church to give thanks for Olly's survival."

"I need that too – if you don't mind," he said quietly.

She put her arms around him and felt him shake. Then she lifted her face for his kiss, and they went out of the house together, their arms entwined.

Olly was recovering more quickly that the doctors and nurses had believed likely when they first saw the extent of his still suppurating wounds. Without the initial application of Birgitta's herbal remedies, he would almost certainly have died, and even so, it had taken all the doctors' skills to deal with the wounds – just as it had taken all Olly's mental energy to insist that Birgitta came to England with him.

By now, he knew he could never thank her enough for all she had done for him. He knew he owed his life to her, and that he could never love anyone as much as he loved her. He knew all the guff about a patient falling for his nurse, but this was different. This was the love of his life.

She was sitting by his bedside, her silvery hair falling over her face, when he realised there were people entering the ward who weren't wearing the obligatory medical uniforms. He sighed, not wanting visitors. Not wanting anyone but the beautiful Norwegian girl he adored. And then, as if in a dream, he heard his mother's voice.

"Olly. Oh, Olly, darling—"

He turned his head carefully, aware of the sting of the stretched, tender skin on his cheeks where the scars were still vivid enough to reveal the extent of his injuries.

"Mom? They didn't tell me you were coming—"

He had been strong for so long, but now his face crumpled and the unmanly tears trickled over his scars making them smart still more as he saw his parents and sister.

To Skye, he was no longer a hero, but simply her boy, her baby, and she rushed forward and held him in her arms.

"Hey, hold on, Mom. It hurts," he said weakly, though the hurt didn't really matter. In any case, it was a very little hurt compared with the searing pain he had endured.

"I'm sorry, darling," Skye said in a choking voice. "It's just so wonderful to see you—"

"You too. But don't drown me in tears. I've had enough water to last a lifetime . . ."

They were crowding him, words pouring out of them all now in their relief at finding him coherent, and apparently still capable of teasing, despite everything. He loved them all, but he had been too long in an isolated Norwegian farmhouse to be able to cope with too much attention too soon.

His lady was standing quietly by now and saying nothing. He reached out his hand and drew her into the circle.

"This is Birgitta, Mom and Dad," he croaked. "She rescued me and brought me back to life. She's my angel, and I hope you'll all love her as much as I do."

Celia saw the girl lower her eyes, and knew at once that nobody on earth could love her as much as her brother did. She hoped fleetingly that it wasn't a case of a young man falling for his nurse, but her sixth sense told her it was far more than that. Lucky Olly, as ever, she thought next – but without rancour, because if anyone deserved to find love, he did.

He would have to remain in the sanatorium for another few weeks, but then he could go home, providing he continued to have nursing care. And since he insisted that the only nursing care he would accept was that of Birgitta and his family doctor, the staff knew better than to argue with this strong-willed young man, and let him have his way.

* * *

"It's wonderful that Olly will be coming home," Lily said to Celia, when the glad news had spread throughout the family. "Do you think he and this Norwegian girl—"

"Oh yes," Celia said with a smile. "There's absolutely no doubt about it. You only have to see them together."

"So it seems as if Wenna has got her man, and Olly has virtually come back from the dead. What of you, my love?" Lily said next. "What's your news?"

Celia turned away, not wanting her cousin to see the raw despair in her eyes. More than ever she was certain that the famed Tremayne luck had all been used up, and there was none left for her. She was the one who had lost out in the game of chance, the one that fate forgot. She swallowed the lump in her throat and tried not to sound bitter.

"What news could I have?" she said.

"Well, David says many German towns have fallen to the Allies now, and the terrible concentration camps have been liberated – not that I'm implying that your Stefan would have been incarcerated in one of those, of course," she added quickly. "But it's all over bar the shouting, as they say – isn't it? Oh Celia, I'm sorry—"

She was aghast as she saw the girl's face, as white as their own china clay. Celia had always been so strong, so flippant and brittle, taking everything life threw at her in her capable stride. Except this.

"Oh, take no notice of me, Lily. I'm all right, really. I just get these moments, that's all," Celia said with a huge effort to gain control of her emotions. "Sometimes I have this image of myself in years to come, like one of those poor elderly spinster women from the last lot, full of useless memories and little else."

"Don't be ridiculous," Lily said briskly. "You're made of sterner stuff than that. You'll find a new love some day—" At Celia's aggrieved look, she knew at once it was the wrong thing to say.

"Have you written him off as well then? That's the difference between me and everybody else, Lily. I haven't, and I never will. I'd rather grow old without him, than ever think I could love someone else."

The news that Hitler was dead came at the end of April, at the same time that Berlin finally fell to the Allies. German towns and cities everywhere were flying white flags now, and Allied soldiers were organising the movement of refugees.

Oliver had returned home to New World with Birgitta by his side and it was tacitly assumed that she was going to stay in Cornwall for the foreseeable future. Olly still didn't want to see anyone but the family. They all accepted that he needed time to adjust, and were prepared to give it to him.

Wenna's concert party had already been disbanded, and she too had arrived home, awaiting her husband's discharge papers to come through at the earliest opportunity. Then they would make known their plans to depart for Canada.

Learning of Hitler's death sent the whole country into rapture, even though it was morally wrong to feel happy at the death of a man. But this had been such an evil man that no one could be anything but relieved at reading the huge black headlines in the *Informer* and every other newspaper telling of Hitler's suicide, with his mistress dead beside him.

The war wasn't officially over yet, but tentative celebrations were already being arranged in many households. New World had always been the scene of great parties, and the Pengellys anticipated a gathering of the whole clan when the peace treaty was finally signed, as it surely must be soon.

Whether in sorrow or in happiness, families needed to be together at such times, and when Birgitta asked shyly if her brother Rolf could be invited to join them, Olly added his voice to the request, and perked up so much at the suggestion that Skye and Nick agreed gladly, knowing how huge a part these two had played in their son's recovery. It was arranged that Rolf would arrive in Cornwall at the earliest opportunity.

During the first week of May, it seemed as if David Kingsley telephoned New World almost hourly as the news came through that everyone had been waiting for.

"The Germans are surrendering everywhere," Skye exclaimed. "Italy, Holland and Denmark – and now Norway."

Birgitta's eyes blurred with tears at the news.

"I am too full to speak, Mrs Pengelly. It is hard for me to express the feelings in my heart at knowing that my country is free again."

"Will you want to return, Birgitta?" Skye said, knowing it would break Olly's heart if she did.

She shook her head. "Not until Olly is tired of me."

"Can pigs fly?" he said, laughing at her puzzled look and taking plenty of time to explain the Englishness of the joke.

Their happiness was almost too much for Celia to bear. She begrudged them nothing, but for her there was only a deep void in her heart as the news broke that the peace treaty had finally been signed and it was all over. Six years of war had ended in a small schoolhouse in Rheims where the Allied Supreme Commander, General Eisenhower, had his HQ.

"There are still the Japanese to contend with, of course," Nick said, cautious as ever, but nothing could dim the joy of knowing that victory celebrations could begin, bonfires could be lit all over the country, and the organised and disorganised street parties could finally take place.

Rations that had been hoarded for weeks could be brought out and displayed on tables groaning with food, while flags flew and balloons soared skywards all over the country. In every city and town the lights were turned on again, and searchlights lit the sky in jubilation instead of fear.

"I'd love to be in London right now," Wenna said wryly. "The people will be out in force to see the royal family come out on the balcony of Buckingham Palace – and Prime Minister Churchill too, I dare say. There won't be an inch of space among the cheering crowds in Piccadilly."

"Do you miss it, honey?" Skye asked her. "And Fanny?"

Wenna took a deep breath. "In some ways I miss her more now than when she died. It's knowing that all this will be going on, I suppose, and that she'd be there in the thick of it. She did so love a knees-up, Mom."

They hugged one another, both remembering the brash, vivacious woman who could cuss like a trooper and had the proverbial heart of gold.

"And what of that life, honey?" Skye persisted. "Will Harry be agreeable to you going back on the stage?"

Wenna took a deep breath. "I won't be, Mom. There won't be much call for singers in the wilds of Canada . . . I didn't mean to blurt it out like that."

"You didn't have to. I guess I always knew."

"And you don't mind?" Wenna said cautiously.

"We all have to go where our hearts are, Wenna, and yours is with your husband. Of course I shall miss you, but you'll go with my blessing."

The world was celebrating the peace, and so was Berlin. The bombing and destruction had all but obliterated many fine buildings, centuries old, and reduced much of that beautiful city to rubble. Those whose homes had survived, whether hovel or mansion, could count themselves among the lucky ones. There were thousands who could not.

Frau Vogl learned of her country's final surrender with unaccustomed tears in her eyes. She was not given to showing emotion, but now that it was all over she could remember her son, and wonder what it had all been for. It was a feeling that was echoed by her husband, even though it was unsaid. Herr Vogl was a man who would remain loyal to the Fatherland, and she respected him for that, despite her maternal sadness at the loss and waste of a young life.

But there was another young man in the household who had needed all their care and attention in the time he had been with them. Not that Stefan von Gruber was such a young man, except when compared with themselves. But when he had succumbed to the vicious attack of pneumonia shortly after his arrival in their home, his life had hung on a thread for many weeks.

The Vogls had discussed the matter thoroughly, and finally decided not to even try to inform the Cornish family that he was safe and well until they knew for sure which way the illness would go.

Now he was well and strong again, and it was time for him to leave them. It would be a wrench, for he had become almost as close as a son to them, but he had chosen his path in life, and it was his to follow.

Stefan himself was well aware that he owed his life to the Vogls and their family doctor. His delirium had been so intense that he had hardly known whether the hammering in his head and the flashes of light that burned his eyes came from inside his head, or from the British bombardment of the city.

When he had slowly started to recover, he was filled with a weird kind of superstition that was worthy of his Cornish sweetheart. Through the darkened window of his bedroom he had watched the searchlights criss-cross the sky and picked out the British planes dropping their death-laden bombs. He had tried not to imagine one of those bombs hitting this house and obliterating them all while he lay helpless.

He had watched the skies like a hunter searching for its prey, his mind tormented and muddled as he sought to find one bright star, while hardly knowing why he did so. Fighting to remember some words from long ago that reminded him that as long as that star still shone, something very precious would survive in his hell.

Now he knew what it was. Now, his mind was lucid and clear, and he knew that if God, or fate, or luck, was on his side, Celia would still be waiting for him. But, still with that feverish near-Cornish superstition, he had decided not to contact her until he returned to their special place.

He had money now. The Vogls had generously seen to that, and his self-confidence had returned. His mind was alert in a way it hadn't been for months, and he knew exactly what he had to do, and where he had to be before he saw Celia again.

As the train took him over the border into Switzerland with a sense of freedom so new it was almost painful, the sight of the mountains ahead gave him a feeling of almost sexual ecstasy. He vowed that once he and Celia were reunited, nothing in this world was ever going to separate them again.

Harry Mack arrived at New World a few weeks later, to the delight of his bride. He treated Olly like a hero, until Olly told him in embarrassment that he'd far rather he didn't. Rolf had arrived from Norway, but stayed only a short while, saying he would return for his sister's wedding before Wenna and Harry departed for Canada in the late summer.

"It's far too soon for Olly and Birgitta to marry, of course," Celia said to Lily, her closest confidante now. "But how can you destroy their happiness by telling him to wait a while? They wouldn't take any notice, anyway."

"Would you?" Lily asked. "The three of you have always gone your own way and got whatever you wanted."

"I hardly think that applies to me."

"You haven't given up hope, have you?"

Celia shook her head slowly. "Of course not, but it's sometimes hard to hold on to a dream. I keep torturing myself with the thought that surely Stefan would have got in touch with me by now if he was still – still able to."

She didn't dare say 'if he was still alive', because it was tempting fate to put such thoughts into words.

"David says that Germany's in a terrible state," Lily told her, quickly changing the subject. "It's practically in ruins, and people are still emerging from shelters, not even aware that the war's been over for a few weeks. Perhaps—"

"Don't even say it," Celia said sharply. "Stefan's not the sort of man to hide in a shelter for weeks on end without knowing what's happening."

But what sort of man *was* he, she thought, if he was still alive and hadn't bothered to contact her? Was his love so shallow after all? She couldn't believe it, but neither could she dismiss it. People changed. And there was always the possibility that he had met someone else.

She had always steadfastly refused to think about such a prospect, and she pushed it out of her mind now. Instead, she reflected on Lily's sensible comments that they must all look to the future now, or it would all have been for nothing.

Olly and Birgitta would marry and live happily after, presumably at New World. Wenna and Harry would go to Canada and raise horses or whatever they did out there. Her mother would begin in earnest on her china clay history booklets and her plans for the open-air museum that would attract hundreds and thousands of visitors to Cornwall in the bright new tomorrow that was now today. And Butch Butcher would be their surrogate son.

And she – where did that leave her? Celia Pengelly, who had once been the brightest and most self-confident of all of them, who had thought she had the world at her feet . . .

She caught her breath on a sob as she neared New World, and then slewed the car to a stop at the side of the road, scattering dust and gravel everywhere.

"What the devil do you think you're doing?" she yelled at the carrot-headed vision that had suddenly loomed up in front of her on the road, dancing about in a frenzy and waving its arms hysterically. She ignored the fact that her thoughts had been too taken up with misery to see him, or anyone.

"Have you lost your senses, Butch?" she yelled again when he seemed too stupefied to speak for a moment. She leapt out of the car and shook him by the lapels. "I nearly ran into you, you idiot."

"There's been a phone call for you, Celia," he screeched, his face as red as his hair. "He's going to try again in an hour or two – though he says he's having a terrible time getting through – and you're to wait indoors for him."

Her eyes blazed with sudden hope, and if he could have done so, Butch would have backed away at their brilliance. But she still held on to him so tightly he was almost choking.

"*He*? Did you say *he*? Who was it? Tell me at once!"

Common sense should be telling her not to get over-excited, but common sense was the farthest thing from her mind now. Of course, it might be Moonie . . . or Ethan in Ireland . . . or someone giving her the news she dreaded . . .

"Mrs Pen says it's your feller—" Butch croaked.

He howled with rage as she let go of him so quickly that he had to stagger crazily to keep his balance. Celia hardly noticed. She almost fell back into the car and screeched it into gear. She couldn't wait for Butch to get inside, and left him there, hollering after her. She heard none of it.

All she could hear in her head were the magical words: 'Mrs Pen says it's your feller' . . .

"Stefan," she almost sobbed. "Oh, please God, let it be really you."

Once home, she slammed the car door behind her and rushed into the house, shouting for her mother.

"Hey, sis, where's the fire?" said Olly with a grin, coming out of the drawing room with his arm slung loosely around Birgitta's waist.

"There was a phone call," Celia stuttered.

"Was there?" he said, unconcerned. "I wouldn't know. We've just come in from a stroll, which is all I'm allowed."

She turned away from him, resisting the childish urge to stamp her feet in frustration. "Where's Mom, Olly?"

"I'm here, Celia," she heard her mother say quietly.

She whirled around, clutching at Skye's arms, all the hope in the world mirrored in her eyes. Almost too afraid to ask, and yet needing so desperately to know . . .

"There was a phone call for me," she said hoarsely. "Butch told me."

Her mouth trembled and her legs began to give way. She felt so dizzy that she swayed and would have fallen if her mother's arms hadn't held her so tightly.

"Hold on, my darling. It's everything you hoped for. It was Stefan, and he's going to try again later, just as soon as he can, but the telephone system between here and Europe is so appallingly overloaded now, of course—"

Celia heard no more. She slid to the floor, and a few minutes later found herself lying on the sofa, with people fussing around her. Someone put a glass to her lips, and she pushed it away. She didn't need it. She just needed answers.

"Tell me I wasn't dreaming," she whispered. "After all these years of hoping and praying – tell me it was really Stefan, Mom, and that it wasn't all some cruel hoax."

"It was no hoax, honey. It was definitely his voice."

Celia hid her face in her hands, not wanting any of them to see the

246

raw emotion on her face that she knew she couldn't hide. Such acute joy was almost agonising, and she didn't want to share this moment – the moment when she thanked God deeply for sending her lover back to her – with anyone.

Then reality came rushing back. She still didn't know if he was well, or where he was. All she knew was that he had telephoned. Someone else had heard his voice first, and she was beset with the most ridiculous feeling of jealousy because of it. She was desperate to hear his voice for herself, to be reassured that he still loved her and wanted her. That every night, when she had searched the heavens for their star, he had looked for it too, or thought of it, and planned for the day when they would see it together once more.

"There's no telling when he'll manage to get through on the telephone next," Skye said, more firmly now. "So we must carry on normally, Celia. Dinner will be at the usual time, and with so many of us in the house, you could do worse than to keep busy and help Cook with the preparations."

"I don't think so, Mom, unless you want me to chop my fingers along with the cabbages," she said shakily. "I couldn't concentrate on anything at all right now, and I need to be alone with my thoughts. Please understand."

She fled upstairs to her bedroom before anyone could argue. In a little while, God willing, she would hear Stefan's voice again, and she would know instantly if everything was still the same.

But dinner came and went, and the day softened into twilight and then darkness, and still the telephone hadn't rung. Celia toyed with the meal, eating no more than morsels of food, in an agony of suspense.

At last the shrill sound of the instrument shattered the quiet of the evening.

Her heart pounded as she rushed to answer it. She made herself take deep breaths and held on to the receiver as tightly as if it was a lifeline. And then she heard his voice.

"Celia, at last, my *liebling*. *Mein Gott*, the waiting has been so long. I began to think I would never hear your voice again."

"Is it really you, Stefan? Please tell me I'm not dreaming," she stuttered, knowing how inane she must sound, and not caring. "I can hardly believe it's true. I've imagined this moment for so long—"

There was a mechanical delay at each end before either of them could hear the other's reply, and Celia held her breath as she waited for him to speak again.

"No one could have imagined it more than I, my sweet darling. I can picture you now, standing in the hallway of that lovely house. Take a moment to look out of the window, my Celia, and tell me what you see."

She looked to where the long French windows reached the floor. Outside, the night had deepened to a soft velvet blue, and shining high above was a shimmering silver star, brighter than all the rest. The breath caught in her throat.

"I see a star . . ."

In the small enforced silence, she tried to collect her senses, but it was almost impossible, knowing their thoughts were still so in tune, despite the distance between them.

"So now we know it isn't all a dream, and that our lives together can begin at last," he said gently.

"But where are you? Are you still in Germany? In Berlin? What's happened to you all this time? I heard you had been interned, Stefan, and about your lovely estate."

She had so often wondered how much he mourned for all that had happened to his old home in the intervening years.

"It's no longer mine, Celia, and I'm no longer in Germany, although I remained in Berlin for a long while in the care of the Vogls."

She gasped, and would have asked more, but he went on speaking gravely.

"Their son is dead, my love, serving his country, but the Vogls took great care of me when I became seriously ill. If it had not been so, I would have contacted you much sooner. But when everything seemed to be over, I decided to wait just a little while longer until I could offer you what we always dreamed about."

He paused, but before she could say any more, his voice became a touch more tentative than before. She could hear the strain in it, as if he too wondered if the time spent apart had changed them irrevocably.

"So how soon can you come to Gstaad, *liebling*?"

"You're in Gstaad?" she repeated stupidly, hardly able to take in all that he was saying.

"In a certain hotel that in due course, I hope, will have my name over the entrance, Celia. *Our* name."

She swallowed. Everything was happening so fast that she couldn't think straight. But one thing was certain. She hadn't waited all this time to be put off by the little matter of finding transport. The old mercurial Celia asserted herself.

"I'll come as soon as I can get a flight, Stefan. I'll telephone the hotel to let you know the time of my arrival."

"I'll be waiting," he said. "And there's something I haven't told you yet. I love you with all my heart."

"I love you too," she choked. "So very much."

It was a little while before she felt able to join her family in the drawing room and speak sensibly.

"Was it your feller then?" Butch said daringly.

"Come on, Celia, tell us what's been happening to him, and put us out of our misery," Olly said, with a hint of impatience in his voice. All the attention had been his until now, and Celia guessed that with the selfishness of the invalid, he wanted to get this new drama over and done with. She didn't blame him. It was the war . . .

Wenna looked more anxious, knowing how very important this was to her sister. She and Olly both had their own futures assured now with loves of their own, but for Celia there had been so much uncertainty. And none of them would readily forget, she thought uneasily, that Stefan was German, and that these two ex-airmen had been doing their best to bomb his country out of existence.

But none of that was going to stop Celia's resolve, and it was to her mother that she looked for reassurance.

"Tell us your fiancé's news, darling," Skye said softly, bringing him into the family circle with one simple word, and daring anyone to dispute it.

"He's in Gstaad, Mom. He's been very ill, but the Vogls have been looking after him. Can you believe that? And he says that Franz Vogl was killed, so they had their casualties too."

She didn't mean to make it sound as if that compensated for the fact that Stefan was a German, but if they took it that way, so be it. Her voice was jerky as she went on.

"I have to get in touch with Moonie as quickly as possible. I need to go to Gstaad to be with him, Mom, and I'm sure Moonie will be able to organise a flight for me. I have to go. You know that, don't you? All of you?"

Her eyes pleaded with them to understand. She needed the approval of her family. They were important to her, but Stefan was her love, her everything, no matter what else he was. If they couldn't see that, then she would be estranged from them for ever, because she could never give him up.

"Cor. I reckon your feller must be somebody special," Butch said in a hushed voice.

"He is," Skye told him, and then turned to her daughter. "You go and contact Captain Moon right away, darling."

Nick added his piece. "And when it's settled, we'll drink a toast to the good times ahead of us all, to wash away old hurts, and to welcome a long and lasting peace."

"Amen to that," said Skye. To Celia's enormous relief, nobody questioned it.

And it was Olly who moved across to her and kissed her, his tender cheek bearing witness to the fact that if he could forgive an old enemy, so could anyone.

"I love you all," she said in a choked voice, before she rushed out of the room again to telephone Moonie.

A week later, she stepped out of the rickety train that had sawed its way into Gstaad, and breathed in the sweet summer air of the mountains and the flower-strewn meadows. She had contacted the hotel to say what time she was arriving, but nothing was reliable these days, and the train was inevitably very late, causing even more frustration in Celia's heart.

Just then she saw him, standing by the gate, as dear and handsome as ever, if older. Oh yes, he looked older. But so did she, thought Celia. No one had come out of this war unscathed, however peripheral a part they had played in it.

And then all thinking was over, as they ran towards each other and were caught in one another's arms. His kiss was sweet on her lips, the same as ever, and yet never so fresh or so cherished as in those first emotional moments.

"I've missed you so much, Stefan," she sobbed against his shoulder. "I've longed for you so much, and I never gave up hope for a single moment—"

"No more did I, my darling," he said unsteadily. "How could I, with our star never failing to appear? But we musn't stand here entertaining the local folk. Let's go home."

A porter picked up her luggage as they walked outside the station still hugging one another, and Stefan drove them to the picturesque hotel in the soft shadow of the mountains that she remembered so well.

The hotel where they had met and had afternoon tea together when the darkly handsome German had interviewed the beautiful blue-eyed Cornish girl for an employment post, during what seemed like a lifetime ago. They had both known then that it was destined to be far more than a business meeting.

Now she learned that the hotel was actually going to belong to them, and there was a sweet sense of inevitability about it that was as Cornish as her name. They explored every bit of it, renewing themselves through memory, and talking long into the afternoon about all that had happened since their enforced parting. Learning about one other all over again, taking it slowly, and exulting in knowing that nothing had changed. Their love was still as bright and new as ever.

Celia turned to him with shimmering eyes, holding his hands tightly as they reached Stefan's bedroom.

"I asked for your luggage to be brought in here," Stefan said carefully. "Or was I presuming too much, too soon? You must tell me if it's so, my love, and I'll understand."

She put her fingers to his lips, smiling into his eyes, and she was at once the old assertive Celia he adored, who had always known exactly what she wanted.

"Will you? Well, I would not! Do you think I've waited all this time, and longed for you with all my heart, for us to worry about petty conventions? Whose hotel is this, anyway?"

"Yours and mine very soon, sweetheart," Stefan said, with the laugh that she remembered that could warm her heart.

Then the look in his eyes deepened into something far more intimate and sensual as he lifted her in his arms and walked purposefully towards the huge four-poster bed.

"I think it's more than time I showed you just how much I've missed you," he went on, his voice deepening with desire. "Or is that too presumptuous a suggestion so early in the evening?"

"Of course not," she whispered, her senses soaring to meet his. "Now that we're together, we have no more need to watch for the stars to come out, my love."

"Except that when they do, I shall want to make love to you all over again," he told her, as he began to unfasten her blouse, teasing every bit of newly exposed flesh with small, erotic kisses. "Tonight and every night, for the rest of our lives, until I'm far too old and weak to do so."

"May that day be never," Celia said softly, as her feverish undressing matched his now.

Their mutual need overcame any thought of strangeness after being so long apart, and her arms reached out to draw him down to her. And then all the waiting was over as Stefan covered her and filled her with himself, and she surrendered to the exquisite fulfilment of belonging.

For them, tomorrow had already begun.

BBC

The Bible of Peckham

VOLUME ONE

Series producers: Ray Butt and Gareth Gwenlan

First published in hardback 1999
Only Fools and Horses format and scripts © John Sullivan
This revised edition published in paperback 2000
The moral right of the author has been asserted

ISBN 0 563 55150 X (hardback)
ISBN 0 563 53818 X (paperback)

Published by BBC Worldwide Limited,
Woodlands, 80 Wood Lane, London W12 0TT

Commissioning Editor: Ben Dunn
Project Editor: Charlotte Heathcote
Art Director: Linda Blakemore
Designed by Peacock

Photographs © BBC

Set in Frutiger and Dom Casual by Keystroke, Jacaranda Lodge
Printed and bound in Great Britain by Redwood Books Ltd.
Cover printed by Belmont Press Ltd.

Written & Created by
★ ★ ★ JOHN ★ ★ ★
SULLIVAN

Starring
★ DAVID ★
JASON

and
★NICHOLAS★
LYNDHURST

with ★ LENNARD ★ PEARCE

CONTENTS

SERIES ONE

Big Brother

THE TROTTERS' LOUNGE.

*The room should reflect their style of business.
Nothing is permanent. The settee and two
armchairs are from three separate suites as
the other pieces were used as make-weights
in various other swaps.*

*There are three TV sets; one colour, one black
and white, and one with its back off awaiting
repair. There are a couple of stereo music
centres standing one on top of the other.
Various video games, talking chess games,
etc, litter the room.*

*Their phone is one of the ornate 1920s type
with separate ear-piece on an alabaster base.
The decor is clean but gaudy. Dozens of
clashing patterns. It should look like the start
of a bad trip.*

*Rodney is lying on the settee checking the
company accounts with the help of a pocket
calculator.*

*Grandad is watching the two TVs which are
showing a film.*

Grandad That Sidney Potter's a good actor,
ain't he Rodney? He was marvellous in *Guess
Who's Coming to Dinner.*
Rodney Yeah, knockout Grandad. Sidney
Potter?
Grandad Yeah, you know him, always plays the
black fella.
Rodney It's Sidney Poitier.
Grandad Sidney Potter!
Rodney Look, it's Poitier.
Grandad It's Potter.
Rodney It's bloody Poitier I'm telling you.
Grandad And I'm telling you it's bloody Potter.
Del enters
Del Are you two at it again, are you?
Rodney Del, how do you pronounce that fella's
name on the telly? Sidney Poitier or Sidney
Potter?
Del Personally I'd pronounce it Harry Belafonte,
but you two please yourselves.
Rodney You daft old sod, it was Harry Belafonte
all along.
Grandad Well I wondered why Sidney Potter
kept bursting into song . . . I don't like Harry

Belafonte.
Del *(Studying his reflection in the mirror)* S'il
vous plait, s'il vous plait, what an enigma. I get
better looking every day. I can't wait for
tomorrow. Oh, do you know, I think I'm suffering
from something incurable. *(Grandad and Rodney
ignore him)* Still, never mind, eh! Oi, come on
Rodney, shake a leg, we've got a meeting at 12.
What are you doing?
Rodney Our accounts.
Del You keeping accounts now? Well there you
are Grandad, a lot of people told me I was a right
dipstick to make my brother a partner in the
business, but this only goes to prove how bloody
right they were. You dozy little twonk Rodney,
this is prima-facie evidence ain't it, eh? The tax
man gets hold of that he'll put us away for three
years.
Rodney Don't worry, if the tax man comes I'll
eat it. This is the only way I can keep a check on
you, Del. I'm sure you're cheating me in some
way – I just can't figure out how.
Del Cheating you! Cheating you! What's that
rumbling noise?
Rodney I didn't hear nothing.
Del No, it's alright, it's Mum turning in her
grave.
Rodney Don't start that again, Del – it's obvious
you're stitching me up. Look at you, you have
three or four changes of clothes a day. Me – I've
got one suit come from an Almost New Shop. It
gets embarrassing sometimes.
Del Oh I embarrass you do I? You've got room
to talk. You have been nothing but an embarrassment to me from the moment you was born.
You couldn't be like any other little brother could
you, eh, and come along a couple of years later
after me. Oh no, not you, you had to wait 13
years. So while all the other Mods were having
punch-ups down at Southend and going to the
Who concerts, I was at home baby-sitting! I
could never get your oystermilk stains out of me
Ben Shermans – I used to find rusks in me Hush
Puppies.
Rodney Del, I couldn't help when I was born.
Del Oh there you go, there you are, you see it's
any excuse with you innit, eh? What d'you think
about poor old Mum then, eh? Do you know
that she was 39 when she fell for you? For the
first three months of the pregnancy you were

treated as an ulcer. And to this day I sometimes think the original diagnosis was correct. Look eh, come on, what sort of bloke do you think I am? Cheat me own brother? Come on Rodney I told you before haven't I, it's everything between you and I split straight down the middle, 60–40.

Rodney Yeah, well explain this to me then Del. How do we manage to pay for the light, gas and rent in this place, eh? I mean, take last week. We went to the auction right, we bought a gross of disposable lighters, a space invaders game, two facial saunas, five water-damaged sleeping bags, and a moon-roof for a Peugeot. Right. Then we swopped the lot for a van-load of one-legged turkeys.

Del They was not one-legged turkeys. They was damaged turkeys.

Rodney How many legs did they have Del?

Del I'm in no mood for trick questions. *(Checking accounts)* Anyway you haven't put down the VAT.

Rodney We don't pay VAT.

Del I know but we collect it, though, don't we eh? Alright Rodney, alright. Look, so we don't pay VAT – we don't pay income tax or National Insurance. On the other hand, we don't claim dole money, social security, supplementary benefit do we, eh, eh? The Government don't give us nothing, so we don't give the Government nothing. Right. What you complaining about?

Rodney Look, I'm 23, I'd like to think I had some sort of a career.

Del *(Through the door)* You're self-unemployed, that's a career, innit?

Rodney What, selling hankies from a suitcase in Oxford Street? I want something better than that Del.

Del Alright, alright, in future you can do Regent Street. Come on.

Exits

Rodney Cheers. *(To Grandad)* And it's Poitier.

Grandad Potter!

Rodney It's Poitier.

THE NAG'S HEAD.

Del and Rodney enter and approach the bar.

Voice Hello Del.

Del Hello darling, how are you, alright?

Voice Fine thanks.

Del Good.

Rodney Do you realise we've always had something missing in our lives. First we was motherless, then we were fatherless and now we're flogging one-legged turkeys from a three-wheeled van.

Del Little acorns.

Rodney What, you got one of them missing as well Del?

Del No. Marks and Spencers started off with a barrow.

Rodney At least they had four wheels.

Del Stop going on about that van will you.

The barmaid, Joyce, arrives.

Joyce Morning, Del Boy.

Del Bonjour, Joycie. Two half pints of your finest low-carbohydrate beer, thank you.

Joyce D'you want it in glasses?

Del Yes please, otherwise it dribbles through yer fingers!

Joyce I meant do you want it in glasses or jugs?

Del As long as it is served by your fair hands Joycie, we'd drink it out of Evonne Goolagong's old tennis boots. *(Joyce leaves)* Look at that . . . Charm like laser beams, eh Rodney. Knocks 'em bandy.

Rodney Yeah, it's your ready wit and three-wheeled van that blows their minds Del.

Del Yeah, I suppose I am full of the old bel esprit, really ain't I? Actually I quite like old Joycie. I mean, fair play, she's a bit of an old dog, but there again you know I quite like old dogs. I mean you know where you are with 'em, don't you, eh? They never ask you if you still respect 'em in the morning and they'll always lend you a nicker for petrol! You know. I like this life though. Don't you Rodders, eh, ducking and diving, wheeling and dealing! You know it's exciting ain't it, unpredictable. You know in this game you can go out in the morning with 50 pence in your pocket . . .

Rodney And come home at night skint!

Del Exactly. Yeah.

Rodney I'm thinking of getting a job Del!

Del Eh, what chance have you got of getting a job? Do leave it out, have you heard that, you heard that Joycie? He's only thinking of getting a job, ain't he, eh?

Joyce *(Laughing)* A job eh!

Rodney I've got GCEs and I took a year's course at the art college in Basingstoke.

Del Yes, I know you *took* a year's course, but you got expelled after three weeks didn't you, eh? The Board of Governors were doing their annual inspection and found you camped in your little room with the biggest reefer this side of Marrakesh. Zonked out on your bed with some Chinese tart!

Rodney She was not a Chinese tart!!

Del Well, Chinese – Japanese, it's all the same to

me. Alright, alright, supposing you go for a job, and you go for the interview, eh? What you going to say to the manager? You're going to say, 'Oh yes sir, I've got qualifications and experience, sir, yeah. I've got two GCEs, an 18-month suspended sentence and I know a good joint when I puff one.' No, your feet won't touch bruv! No, no, I'm afraid not Rodney, at the ripe old age of 23, you are a social leper. Society has placed you in the darkest corner of its deepest cellar to grow moss and be forgotten about! Still never mind, eh? Viva la France as they say in Rome. No need to get depressed.

Rodney Oh, me depressed? No, of course not Del. I'm on top of the world, I feel like a born-again eunuch. I think I'll apply for a mail-order course with EXIT!

Del That's a good idea Rodney, never say die.

Voice How are you? Alright. Terrific.

Trigger enters. He is a local part-time villain. He is in his early thirties, tough, but none too bright. He is wearing grubby jeans, short wellingtons and a donkey jacket. He is carrying a brand new executive type briefcase.

Del Oh, there he is, oi Trigger! Here, you know my brother don't you, eh?

Trigger *(To Rodney)* Yeah, course I do, how you going Dave? Sorry I'm late Del Boy, I had to pop round me sister's to arrange an alibi for next Thursday. *(Calling)* Joycie!

Rodney Del, Del.

Del What?

Rodney Why d'they call him Trigger? Does he carry a gun?

Del No, it's 'cos he looks like an 'orse! Listen, me and the Trigger have got some business to discuss, like, you know what I mean. Okay, so you get the drinks and meet us back here, over by the table, alright?

Rodney *(In a rustic accent)* Oh arr, sir. Anything you say, sir, borrow me daughter, sir?

Del and Trigger sit at table

Del No, no, very clever kid you know my brother, got two GCEs, one in Maths, one in Art. You wanna see him when he writes a letter. Some of the words he uses . . .

Trigger What long ones?

Del Long! *(Opens thumb and forefinger about three inches apart)* Well they're like that, you know some of 'em. Anyway, what you selling?

Trigger This! *(produces briefcase)* I've got 25 of them all told, the others are in the car. I thought I won't wrap it up, parcels attract attention these days, best to carry it openly then it don't look conspicuous!

Del Oh yeah, yeah, that's good thinking – that Trigg. Yeah, very good thinking. Goes so well with your sling-back wellington boots and your off-the-shoulder donkey jacket. You look like an executive hod-carrier! *(Rodney enters)* Let's have a look anyway. Oi, Rodders, what d'you think of this, infra-dig, innit eh?

Rodney It's plastic.

Del Plastic? It's Old English vinyl! With combination locks, yeah dinky little handle – I dunno we might be able to put some of 'em round the old squash clubs, eh?

Rodney We shouldn't have anything to do with them Del. The police are probably looking for them right now.

Del Tell us the truth, are the police looking for these things Trig?

Trigger *(Pushing case under the table)* No, they're not Del, and that's the truth.

Rodney Why are you hiding it under the table, then?

Trigger 'Cos you never know when they're gonna start looking for 'em, do you?

Rodney Leave 'em, Del. Leave 'em.

Del Oh ssh! Schtum.

Rodney Oi, we're partners, at least respect my opinion.

Del Alright, alright Rodney, I'll respect your opinion! *(To Trigger)* How much . . .

Trigger To you, Del Boy, 17 pounds each!

Del You know what happened to the real Trigger, don't you? Roy Rogers had him stuffed!

Trigger Alright then – 14.

Del 14, leave it out. Five.

Trigger 12.

Del Six.

Trigger Ten.

Del Nine.

Trigger Eight.

Del Done!

Trigger *(To Rodney)* That's the way to do business Dave.

Del *(Taking out a pocket calculator)* Right, okay Trig, let's work that out. That's eight times 25 equals, 175, okay?

Rodney 200.

Del What? No, no – Rodney, no, no, no. The calculator says 175, alright.

Trigger Yeah, but he's got GCEs in Maths and Art!

Del So what does that prove, he can paint by numbers. Look Trig, I mean this is a calculator innit, eh? You know what I mean look – calculator says 175, you can't argue with a calculator can you, you know . . .

15

Rodney Give it here. *(Takes calculator)*
Del Rodney!
Rodney 25 times eight equals – 200!
Del Oh yeah! Look at that. I must have got my finger stuck on the button, yeah.
Rodney *(Flexing his fingers)* Pianist's fingers, Del!
Del Yeah! Yeah, you wanna look after them Rodney, they break very easily.

INT. NIGHT. THE TROTTERS' LOUNGE.

Grandad is watching the TVs. The boxes containing the cases are in the centre of the room.
Del *(On phone)* You've gotta see 'em to believe 'em Spiros. Yeah. Ah, I dunno hang on a minute, oi Grandad, where were they made?
Grandad *(Checking case)* It don't say . . . There's some Chinese writing on 'em though.
Del Ssshhh! No, no, no it don't actually give the maker's name Spiros, but then again the best ones never do, do they. You know what I mean. Yeah.
Rodney enters carring a bag containing a cheeseburger which he gives to Grandad.
Rodney How's it going?
Grandad That's about the 15th.
Rodney Briefcase he's sold?
Grandad Phone call he's made.
Del Yeah, yeah, well I'd get in while the going's good if I was you Spiros, I've only got 25 left!
Grandad This is cheeseburger! I asked for an Emperor-burger.
Rodney I couldn't afford an Emperor-burger.
Grandad *(To Del)* He got me a cheeseburger.
Del What?
Grandad I asked him for an Emperor-burger, and he brings me back a cheeseburger!
Del Yes, yes, hang on a minute Spiros. Will you just hang on. *(To Rodney)* Look, what's he on about now?
Rodney He asked me to get him an Emperor-burger, but I couldn't afford it so I got him a cheeseburger!
Del Bloody Emperor-burgers and cheese-burgers!! I'm trying to do a deal here. Now shut up will you! No, no, not you Spiros, no, no me old mate. Alright, now how many of these brief-cases can I put you down for? Ah, none! Right thanks, great – yeah, alright, see you around.
Rodney I told you the best thing to do with them cases didn't I! Chuck 'em in the river!
Del Chuck 'em in the river! Chuck 'em in the river! That's our profit you're talking about. What do you think this is – a nationalised industry?

Grandad He knows I hate cheese!
Del Will you stop going on about that rotten cheeseburger, will you! *(Checking through his little black book)* Ah, Dougie Sadler, he owns the stationers in the High Street, he's our boy Rodders!
Rodney I don't know why he bothers!
Grandad He's a tryer ain't he! Your dad always said that one day Del Boy would reach the top! There again he used to say that one day Millwall would win the cup!
Del *(On phone)* Hello Dougie? Del Boy! How's your luck pal? Good! Family? Soooper! Dougie look, I'm phoning about some briefcases! Yeah? Go on, what a choker! *(With hand over the receiver)* 25 of 'em nicked from his shop last week!!
Rodney Oh God!
Del *(On phone)* No, no, no I'm not trying…. No to sell any no, no, no. No I wanted to buy some, you see, yeah I've got this, er, contact in the stock exchange. Yeah. Em, by the way Dougie, old pal, what were you selling them for? What d'you mean they were rejects?
Rodney Oh beautiful! We've bought a consignment of rejects!
Del What, what was wrong with them then? Oh yeah! Oh I see, yeah, yeah, I mean who'd be daft enough to nick them eh? Yeah, who'd be stupid enough to buy them? Yeah I know. I'll pop down and see you next week when you get some more in okay, yeah. Bye bye Doug. See you around. God struth.
Rodney Alright, so what's wrong with them?
Del Open one!
Rodney *(Trying to open one)* What's the combination?
Del No sod knows, that's why they're rejects!
Rodney There's meant to be a bit of paper with them, giving you the combination?
Del Yes, there is, it's inside the briefcase innit. Cock-up at the factory.
Rodney Nice going Del Boy! You have bought 25 executive briefcases that can only be opened by professional safe-crackers! This makes the one-legged turkey deal look shrewd! Don't it!
Del Alright, alright, Rodney that's the way I'm made innit eh? You know, crash in and to hell with the consequences. He who dares wins! The French have a word for people like me.
Rodney Yeah, the English have got a couple of good 'uns an' all!! I told you all along not to touch them didn't I?
Del Yeah alright, alright, well it's got nothing to do with you is it!

Big Brother

Rodney But we're partners! Ain't we? Oh I see, the truth's coming out now. Well come on Del let's have it out in the open! Then how do you see our respective roles in this 'partnership'?

Del I see it as a combination of my business acumen, contacts and money, and your ability to drive a three-wheeled van! Badly! Or did you see yourself in a different role?

Rodney Well, yes I did! With my qualifications I saw myself in the capacity of a financial adviser!

Del A financial adviser? Bonjour Trieste, you are beautiful, you are Rodney! Today I'd just about clinched a deal to buy these briefcases for £175, when my financial adviser stuck his nose in and advised me to pay *£200*. Right! And having paid the £200 my financial adviser then advised me to chuck the bleedin' lot in the river! Now with financial advisers like you who needs a bleeding recession!

Grandad What kind of a financial adviser goes out to buy an Emperor-burger and comes back with a cheeseburger?

Del Will you stop going on about that ruddy cheeseburger! *(Stuffing it into Grandad's mouth)* Eat it, will you!

Grandad Alright, alright.

Rodney Get off him. It's against the law to force-feed a senior citizen with a cheeseburger and you know he hates 'em!!

Del Well what did you buy it for him for?

Rodney It's all I could afford!! You make my life a misery, you do.

Del Here, oi, just a moment! What was that last remark about me making your life a misery?

Rodney Yeah well, you do Del with your over-bearing, over-protective manner!

Del Let me remind you Rodney that you were a six-year-old little nipper when God smiled on Mum and made her die! Two months after that Dad packed his bags and left us to fend for ourselves. It was me that kept us together, nothing to do with Grandad! He was an out-of-work lamp-lighter waiting for gas to make a comeback! I grafted 19 to 20 hours a day to put groceries on that table – alright, it wasn't always double legal – but you ate the finest food that was going!

Rodney All you ever give me was TV dinners and convenience foods! If it wasn't frozen or dehydrated we didn't eat it. If you had been in charge of the last supper it would have been a take-away!

Del Well anything was better than the salmonella and chips that Grandad used to knock up!

Rodney Del, look, don't get me wrong – I'm,

I'm grateful.

Del I don't want your gratitude, ungrateful little git! I don't know what is the matter with you Rodney. Sometimes I hesitate to tell people that you're my brother!

Rodney Well, I always say I'm your social worker!

Del Do you mind telling me exactly what it is that has made your life a misery?

Rodney Well, you've always treated me like a child! Ain't you? I was the only sixth former in my grammar school who wore short trousers!

Del Yeah, well, I got 'em cheap didn't I?

Rodney But I was 15, Del. I was growing hairs and things! My legs looked like Italian foot-baller's! And you'd never let me do anything on my own, do you? You even had to help me with my GCE studies!

Del You passed in two subjects

Rodney I failed in the other eight Del. I mean you embarrass me, that's why I never bring women home!

Del Oh you know some women do you? Cor, that's a turn up for the book! The only bird I've ever heard you mention was old Shanghai Lil from the art college in Basingstoke. Even then you had to drug her before you could get your leg over!

Rodney No I didn't!

Del What, you didn't drug her or didn't get your leg over?

Rodney You're suffocating me Del! I'm getting out of this house! I'm going to prove to you I can survive on my own! I'm going to the pub!

Del What to prove you can survive on your own?

Rodney No, to get legless! I don't need you no more Del, I don't need you for *nothing*!!
Rodney exits. After a short pause the door opens, Rodney enters and makes his way over to Del.

Del I was just, I was just wondering . . .

Del Of course you can Rodney. *(He peels off two fivers from a wad and hands them to Rodney. Rodney exits)* I think he's very much like you Grandad!

Grandad What, dignified in defeat?

Del No, a ponce!

INT. DAY. THE TROTTERS' LOUNGE.

Del *(On phone)* No, no, I'm sure these can't be the ones they're looking for. No, no, I wouldn't do that to a mate, now would I, eh? No, don't you say nothing to 'em you Wally! I mean you can't trust the Old Bill can you! I mean, look at

that time when they planted six gas cookers in my bedroom! Yeah, alright, don't worry, okay. I'll see you around! Rodney?

Grandad enters

Grandad Where was you first thing this morning?

Del I was out to tryin to sell these things!

Grandad Did you call Rodney?

Del No, I thought I'd let him lie in and sleep his hangover off. Is he still in bed?

Grandad No, he's gone!

Del Gone?

Grandad Packed his ruck-sack and had it away on his toes!

Del What do you mean gone? Where's he gone?

Grandad Hong Kong.

Del Hong Kong? What do you mean Hong Kong?

Grandad Hong Kong. It's in China.

Del I know where Hong Kong is! What I want to know is what's Rodney doing there?

Grandad He said he was gonna hitch-hike there to see that bird from the art college.

Del Who? Shanghai Lil? But she's in Basingstoke, so what's Mastermind doing on the road to Hong Kong?

Grandad No, that's where she is now. She got deported after the drugs trial.

Del Here, just a minute. What did you do, say or cook for him that was so awful it forced him to leave?

Grandad It weren't me. It was that row last night. He's gone to prove himself.

Del Prove himself, no it's just one of Rodney's little games, that's all. He'd never reach Hong Kong. He has trouble finding Clapham.

Grandad He seemed determined.

Del Well didn't you do anything?

Grandad Well yeah, I made him some sandwiches.

Del And he took them? Blimey, this is worse than I thought! No, wait a minute, he ain't got no money!

Grandad He took his post office book with him. Can't you go and search for him? He's been gone about seven hours, the farthest he could have got is France.

Del Oh that's alright, we've got him cornered then, ain't we, eh!

Grandad Ring up Interpol!

Del Interpol? Interpol? I'd get more joy out of Interflora . . .

Grandad But he might be in danger. You could explain to them what Rodney's like.

Del I'm sorry, I don't know the French for pranny! Hong Kong!! I mean . . . Hong Kong! Why didn't he tell me where he was going. He could have taken these bleeding things back with him!

A STREET MARKET.

Del walks past carrying one of the briefcases. He approaches the owner of a stall that sells luggage, leather goods, etc. Del tries to sell the case. The owner shakes his head. Del, who seems resigned to the fact that he'll never sell them, doesn't put up much of an argument before moving off.

A BUSY MAIN ROAD.

The three-wheel van pulls up outside a leather goods shop. Del carries a box of cases into the shop. A few seconds pass, then he re-appears still carrying the box. He places it in the van and drives off.

A LONDON BACK STREET.

The van is parked outside a grotty old bric-a-brac shop. Del exits from the shop carrying the box of cases. He puts them in the van and drives away.

THE TROTTERS' LOUNGE.

Grandad is playing with a talking chess game. Del enters.

Machine A2 F2. Enter, illegal move. A2, B2. Enter, illegal move.

Grandad This thing still ain't working properly.

Del That's because you're playing draughts on it. It's a talking chess game, you can't play draughts on a talking chess game.

Grandad Why not?

Del Because you're supposed to play chess on it, that's why it's called a talking chess game. You've already blown the micro-chip twice trying to huff the rook and what 'ave yer!

Grandad It's supposed to have an electronic brain?

Del It has got an electronic brain, but it didn't know it was gonna have the misfortune to fall into the hands of a soppy old duffer who wants to play draughts on it, did it?

Grandad But I can't play chess! Why don't they invent a talking draughts game?

Del Because if they did you'd most probably want to play bloody ludo on it . . .

Rodney stands in the doorway. Del straightens and turns.

Rodney Del Boy!

Big Brother

Del Hello, Rodney!

Grandad Rodney's back Del . . . Look, he's here. You hungry, Rodney?

Rodney Starving. I haven't eaten for two days.

Grandad Shall I cook you something?

Rodney No, no, no, no!! A cup of tea, perhaps! *(Grandad exits)* Old place don't change much.

Del No, same as ever!

Rodney *(Throwing his arms around Del)* It's really good to be back Del!

Del Don't you think you're over-doing the prodigal's return a bit. You've only been gone six days.

Rodney Well, it might seem like six days to you Del, but to me it seemed more like . . .

Del A week? I take it you didn't reach Hong Kong! How far d'you get?

Rodney South of France . . . St Tropez.

Del St Tropez, oh very mal de mer!

Machine Problem.

Rodney 85 in the shade.

Del What were the birds like?

Rodney Mostly French . . .

Del Oh yeah.

Rodney I met one English girl there, Veronica, her father's a millionaire tax exile.

Del Tax exile is he?

Machine Illegal move.

Del Had a boat had he? You know parked out in the bay?

Rodney A yacht anchored off-shore, yeah, yeah. They invited me over for dinner one night! I didn't go though.

Del Still had some of Grandad's sandwiches left did ya?

Rodney No!! No, that night I packed my bags and headed home . . . I was homesick you see . . . I missed *(Looking from the window)* . . . that!

Del You must be joking. The only people who ever missed that was the ruddy Luftwaffe!

Rodney It may not be much to you Del, but to me it's got a raw and savage beauty. You forget that I've got artist's eyes Del.

Del Yes, you've got pianist's fingers . . . Italian footballer's legs. You ever thought of applying for a disability allowance?

Rodney I know you'll never understand what I mean Del, but you've got to suffer paradise before you can realise what you left behind. Your home, your family . . .

Del Your passport . . . *(Throwing passport to him)*

Rodney Your passport . . . My passport!! You knew didn't you? You let me go all through that and all the time you knew! Where did you find it?

Del Top of your wardrobe! We were expecting a visit from the local gendarmes and I thought I'd better check out just in case you'd left any of that exotic tobacco lying about. No, I knew it was just a moody Rodney. I told Grandad it was just one of Rodney's little games.

Rodney It must be wonderful to be you Del, to *always* be right!

Del I know. It gets a bit embarrassing at times. I'll tell you another thing shall I Rodney? You said that I would never ever get rid of them briefcases!

Rodney And you did, didn't you Del?

Del Yes I did! I chucked the bleedin' lot in the river!

Rodney No. You threw 'em all in the river?

Del Yep, every last one of them! They floated – that was a bit unforeseen. Probably rounding Tilbury about now.

Rodney 200 quid down the Swanee eh – well, in this case the Thames!

Del St Tropez! How far did you really get?

Rodney The Shangri La doss house Stoke Newington! I shared a room with some cholera cultures!

Machine Your move.

Del Well, what do you fancy, shall we go down the pub and act stupid, or shall we sail across to Veronica's dad's yacht for tiffin?

Rodney No, best not go to the yacht, we might bump into those bloody briefcases half-way.

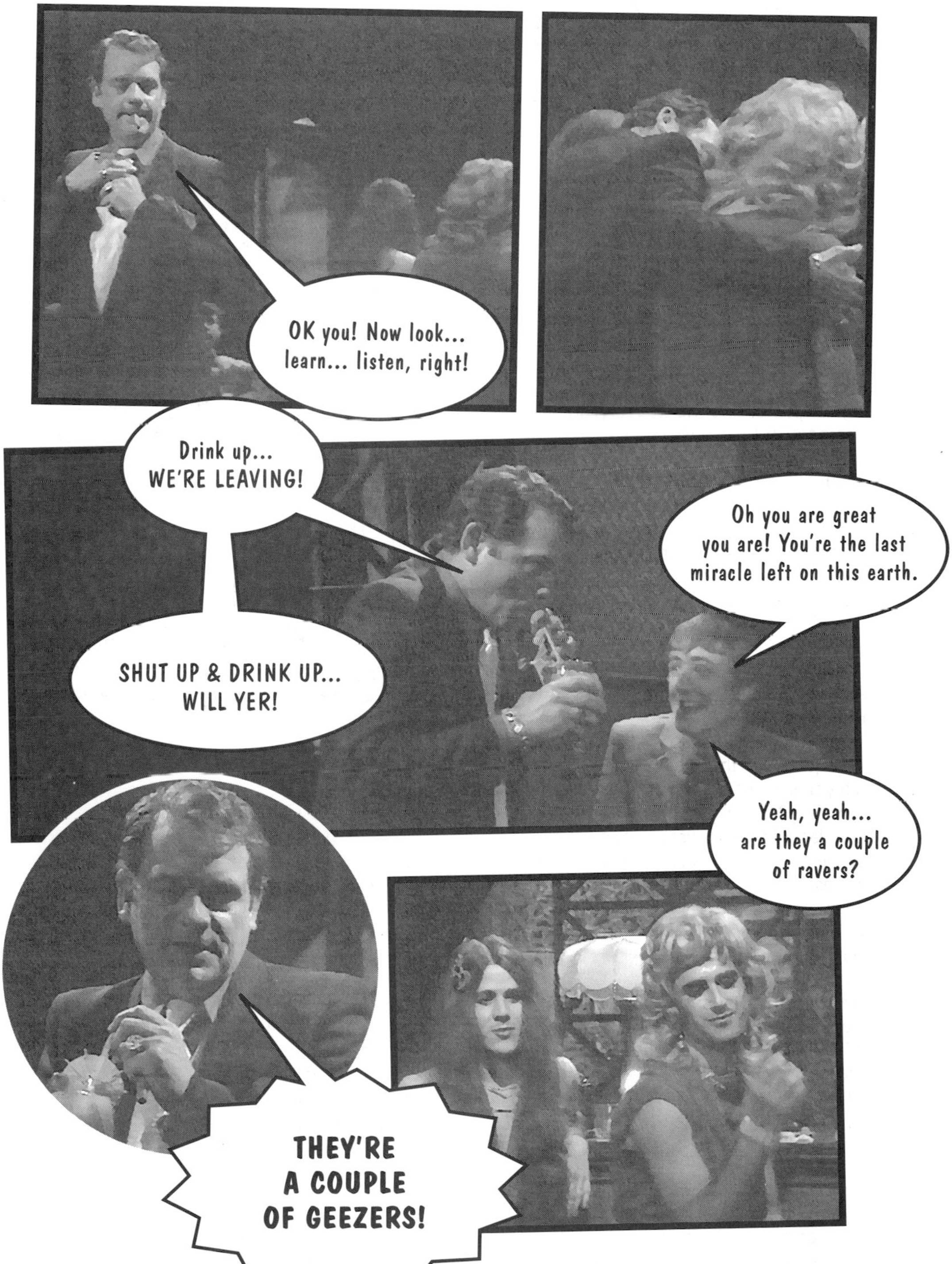

Go West Young Man

THE TROTTERS' LOUNGE.

Rodney, in his usual state, is seated at the table looking into a bowl of soggy cornflakes. He is in a depressed mood.

Grandad is watching the Open University on both TVs.

Del, in his usual flashy gear, is seated opposite Rodney and is reading Glasses Guide (the motor trade's Bible).

Television Just touching the cone and also just touching the plane. And the two points where the spheres touch the plane . . .

Del Alright, here's where our future lies Rodney, second-hand motors! This time next year we'll be millionaires!

Rodney I dreamed I was drowning last night!

Del Here, the way I see it is this, the government, they're going to have to ban the import of foreign cars to save our own car industry. But the unions won't stand for that – because that smacks of racialism – so they'll all go out on strike! That'll mean you won't be able to buy a new car for love nor money!

Grandad No.

Del No, no, that is it Rodney. Britain's future lies fairly and squarely in the second-hand car game. What did you say just now? You dreamt that you were drowning? Is that a gentle way of trying to tell us that last night you wet the bed?

Rodney No, it's not! I'm just depressed that's all, and these cornflakes aren't making me feel any better!

Del Honestly Rodney, you make my teeth itch. I've asked you before, and I've asked you again – phone her!

Rodney She knows I won't phone her first!

Del How does she know that you won't phone her first? Did you tell her that you wouldn't phone her first?

Rodney No!

Del No, well go and phone her and tell her.

Rodney Oh that's stupid!

Del No, it's not, it's no more stupid than the mood you're in. Why is it whenever you're getting your end away, the skies are blue, the lager's cool and England are gonna win the World Cup. And just because some little tart with fat thighs gives you the elbow, you're in a fit of destruction.

Rodney She has not given me the elbow! Monica and I were having difficulties getting it all together on a one-to-one basis. So my mate, Mickey Pearce – now he's lived with a woman – he advised us to have a two-week trial separation.

Del A two-week trail separation? Cor, come on, you've only known her for two weeks!

Grandad What is it then Rodney, a fortnight on, a fortnight off like sentry duty?

Rodney I am not going to phone her Grandad, that's all there is to it! Plenty more chicks around.

Del Yeah, alright then – well come on. I reckon your best bet is have a blind date with a Samaritan!

Rodney I'll survive Del. And Monica has not got fat thighs!

Del She's got fat thighs!

Rodney She has not!

Del Look, I was down the Nag's Head disco last night and either she's got fat thighs or she was bopping the night away in a pair of jodhpurs!

Rodney Monica was out dancing?

Del Yeah! Here, with your mate Mickey Pearce as it happens!

Del exits

Rodney Del!

SECOND-HAND CAR SITE.

An area at the back of the site. Del and the owner, Boycie – out of the same mould as Del – are examining an old black convertible Zephyr Mark 2. It is dirty with rust spots, bald tyres, etc.

Rodney is seated in the Zephyr's driving seat. In the background is an E-Type Jaguar.

Boycie Oh yes – this came in with a Chesterfield and a gross of electric toothbrushes as a part-chop on a Vanden Plas. Still, clean it up a bit, couple of new tyres!

Del Yeah, yeah, a new engine, new body, and you've got a nice little motor.

Rodney There's 98,000 miles on the clock! Is that genuine?

Boycie Eh?

Del Shut up Rodney. Be honest Boycie, I mean seriously, it's a bit of a pig!

Boycie Well what d'you want for 50 quid?

Del Ah, well now you're talking! I'll take that. *(Indicating the E-Type)* What do you want, cheque or shall I give it to you the old readies?

Boycie You would an' all wouldn't you?

Del Oh certainly. No, no, it's handsome though, innit?

Boycie Yeah. You know it's only E-Type Jaguars and Sebastian Coe that make me feel proud to be British these days!

Del Yeah, I know what you mean Boycie. Why haven't you got this up at the front?

Boycie It's not for sale Del, my old mate. As a matter of fact I'm looking for a place to hide it for a week. I bought it as a birthday present. I'm dead scared the wife's gonna see it and suss it all out.

Rodney Spoil the surprise?

Boycie Spoil everything Rodney, it's a birthday present for my bit on the side!

Rodney You what?

Del His bit on the side, his bit . . . Never mind Boycie. It's so long since Rodney had a bit on the side he didn't know they'd moved it! Wait a minute! Hang about . . . Mon dieu, you want to hide this for a week, right?

Boycie Right.

Del We've got an empty garage round on the estate. I can pop it in there for you if you like.

Boycie Be handy Del, save me a lot of aggro. Right well. I owe you one Del!

Del No, forget it Boycie. I mean if you can't do a pal a favour without expecting something in return! I mean . . . *(Indicating Zephyr)* How much did you say you wanted for that again?

THE GARAGE BLOCK.

The E-Type is parked in Del's garage. He is standing outside admiring the car. He is about to pull the door shut when he reacts to the sounds of the approaching Zephyr being driven by Rodney.

The Zephyr skids round the corner into the garage block area. Rodney is hammering the brake pedal. Del leaps back into the garage as the Zephyr roars past him. There is a great screaming from the brake drums as the car shudders to a halt. Rodney collapses over the steering wheel.

Del What's the matter? Brakes a bit spongy are they?

Rodney Brakes! What bloody brakes? I nearly killed myself Del! It's a death trap!

Del What do you expect for 25 quid!

PARKING AREA (ESTATE).

Rodney is polishing the Zephyr, which now looks like a clean heap. A hand-written sign on the windscreen reads 'For Sale. £199' Rodney picks up a cup of coffee which he has left on the ground and then sits in the driver's seat for a breather

The car suddenly starts bouncing up and down wildly. Rodney tries to hang on grimly to his spilling, hot coffee.

A man is bouncing the car up and down to test the suspension. He is about 30 and a real Barry Mackenzie type, one of the Earl's Court Foster's set.

Aussie Your shock absorber's gone!

Rodney Well it has now!

Aussie What's it like?

Rodney What's what like?

Aussie The car you dingo, what you think I'm talking about, yer flaming coffee?

Rodney The car? Oh well, you know, it's er . . . it's . . . it's . . .

Aussie It's a bit over-priced!

Rodney It's a bit over-priced, yeah, that's what I was going to say!

Aussie Says 23,000 on the clock! Is that genuine?

Rodney 23 . . . Well the last time I looked there was over . . .

Del, like a spider descending upon a fly, appears as if out of nowhere.

Del 22,500, quite right Rodney. No I had the RAC do a 500-mile road test on it. Well you know better safe than sorry that's what I always say. It's beautiful though isn't it? Beautiful. What do you think? Son et lumière wouldn't you say?

Aussie Well, I don't know if I'd go quite that far!

Del Oh yeah I mean, look at this eh? Genuine leather upholstery that. Where would you find genuine leather upholstery like that these days, huh? Do you know that the East African gazelle became an endangered species for this model, sacrifice well made I'd say wouldn't you? No, it's an enthusiast's model this one and I can see that you are, in fact, a genuine enthusiast!

Aussie Don't give me that crap mate! I can make up me own mind and I don't need any help from no Cockney villain!

Del Cockney villain! Cockney villain! Now there's no need to be like that sir, I mean after all the British and the Australians are cousins across the sea, ain't they. I mean if your great grandad hadn't have been a bloody villain you could have

Go West Young Man

been one of us! Say no more. C'est la vie. San fairy ann. Allow me to point out some of the optional extras on this one, sir, for you. Look at that; the anti-dazzle mirror. In here you'll notice that we've got the old – look at that – the one-speed wiper, and *(He slams the door and the side window falls down)* er, we've got automatic windows. Oh yeah a perfect example of the sporting tourer, and of course, it comes complete with a full two-weeks MOT still left to run.

Aussie How many owners?

Del How many owners? I'm glad you asked me that sir. Because it's only had the one owner from new . . . and that, of course, was a vicar!

Rodney A vicar?

Aussie A vicar?

Del A vicar! Used to use it to drive backwards and forwards to church on a Sunday that was all. *(Opening the glove compartment)* Oh look at that. Only left his Bible in the glove compartment.

TROTTERS' LOUNGE.

Grandad is watching the two TVs. Del is standing at the table counting a thick wad of money and whistling. He is full of the joys of life having executed this profitable con.

Del *(Speaking in cod Aussie)* As I was walking through Earls Court. Into a pub I was lured. Where a nosey Pom said, 'Where you from?' as I downed the amber fluid. I said 'Get it straight, I'm an Aussie mate. And I'm fixing to get plastered. But the beer is crook. And the birds all look. Like you, you Pommy . . .' *(Handing Grandad two fivers)* Grandad.

Grandad Cheers Del Boy.

Del Alright. Go out and buy yourself a crate of Odour Eaters.

Grandad Yeah. I've heard they're good!

Del Oh they are – they are. Bloody murder to swallow though! Here, where's Peckham's conscience?

Grandad Oh he's in his room pining about that little fat bird! Women! You wouldn't remember when I married yer Grandmother!

Del No!

Grandad The first night we was in bed and – well you know Del!

Del What?

Grandad Well, doing what you do when the lights are out!

Del Holding a seance, was you?

Grandad No! You know what I mean! Anyhow, right in the middle of it, d'you know what she said to me?

Del No, what?

Grandad She said 'What d'you fancy for dinner tomorrow?'!

Del What d'you fancy for dinner tomorrow!

Grandad Bad innit?

Del Bet that didn't happen to Omar Sharif! Anyway what did you say?

Grandad Steak and kidney pudding I think!

Del Isn't love wonderful!

Rodney enters

Aye up. Look out the room is full. Where you going? Fancy dress party?

Rodney No! I'm gonna do what Monica was doing last night.

Del Oh going dancing with Mickey Pearce are you?

Rodney No! I'm going out – I'm gonna paint the town red – rip it up a bit!

Del Oh yeah, where you going, Streatham?

Rodney No, I'm not going to Streatham Del! I'm gonna hit a few clubs up West.

Del What? You up West?

Rodney Yeah.

Del You'd need a bloody compass to find it, you would.

Rodney I am often up West Del, I'm one of the faces!

Del One of the faces! Do me a favour Rodney. Two halves of lager at the British Legion Club is like a walk on the wild side to you!

Rodney Oi! Just leave me to live my own life would you! And what do you mean 'fancy dress'?

Del Well just – wonder why you were hitting the West End looking like a praying mantis.

Rodney Just lay off me Del. Is that the money from the Cortina? That death-trap you sold to skippy?

Del Yes, look, there was nothing wrong with that car!

Rodney Nothing wrong! The oil light stayed on, the steering didn't always go the way you wanted it to and the brakes didn't work!

Del A few minor faults. Anyway, the oil light didn't stay on, I fixed it.

Rodney You mean you actually went to the trouble of changing the oil?

Del No, I took the bulb out.

Rodney You are great you are Del. I mean, you've done some pretty doubtful things in your time but I never thought you'd stoop to selling instant motorway madness!

Del Oh shut up you tart!

Rodney That money is immoral – that is your handful of silver Del. That is nothing more than

blood money!

Del Oh, oh is it? Oh yeah *(Putting the money in his pocket)* alright then.

Rodney Oi, half of that's mine!

Del Ah ha! Now you see what I mean don't you eh, Grandad? That is the mentality of your spoon-fed student type. They walk round all day with Steve Bilko written on their T-shirts spouting about humanity, when it comes to a fight over a torn fiver they make Genghis Khan look like a pacifist!

Rodney Look I was merely stating a fact that half of that is mine. It don't mean to say I want it!

Del Oh I see – don't want this money then Rodney, eh?

Rodney No.

Del Oh, what a bind, I'll have to spend it all myself then won't I, eh? Oh well, still going out are you Rodney?

Rodney Er . . . Yeah . . . Do you er, fancy tagging along Del, I'll show you some of my clubs.

Del No, no, no really. Look if you're hard up for a bit of company I'll come, alright.

Rodney Hey, hard up for company, you must be joking. I've got hundreds of friends!

Del Oh – oh that's alright then – good.

Rodney Yeah. There's the cats from the evening class for a start.

Grandad Cats? Where you going Rodney, dancing or ratting?

Del Ratting! I like that.

Rodney It means ravers Grandad, swingers! And these guys really live it up Del, and when I say live I mean live! Yeah, there's Dave and Bob. . . . Mike and, and Tony, George . . .

Del Jim.

Rodney Jim . . . yeah.

Del Why don't you go and give 'em a bell?

Rodney Who?

Del You know, the Beautiful People from the evening institute!

Rodney Er, they're not on the phone!

Del What, you mean all these swingers ain't got a phone between 'em? Are they on the electric yet?

Rodney Alright, alright! Well, you coming with me, then?

Del No, no, I'll pop down the Nag's Head for a light ale later on.

Rodney Well your loss Del. I'll tell you all about it in the morning then, assuming I'm back in the morning.

Del Yeah alright.

Rodney Well are you coming or not then?

Del No!

Rodney OK then. . . . Well here I go!

Del Yeah, see yer then.

Rodney I'll give the birds your regards shall I?

Del Yeah, you do that, it's triffic, great, yeah.

Rodney Right, well we have take off!

He exits then re-enters

Well make up your mind Del, you coming or not?

Del You bloody kids! They can't even enjoy themselves today can they, eh! Alright, come on soppy, let's go and rip it up!

Rodney Well if you want to tag along that's fine by me Del! Er, if you can pay for your own way.

Del Pay for . . . don't worry, I've got the money. I've got the keys to the van and all – Grandad, go easy on the iron jelloids tonight.

Rodney We're not going up West in a three-wheeled van are we?

Del I certainly ain't walking it Rodders!

Rodney Yeah but I mean it's all about images innit Del. I mean you're very suave and debonair.

Del Yeah well I s'pose I am a bit ostentatious really. Yeah I am, aren't I?

Rodney Still, if I drive, you hide down behind the dashboard and no one will see us arrive.

Del What do you mean no one will see us arrive? I want people to see me arrive don't I, eh?

Rodney In a three-wheeled van? Still, got no choice have we?

Del Yes we have! Yes we have, we can take Boycie's E-Type Jag!

Rodney *(Mock horror)* The Jag! Are you sure Del, well upon your shoulders be it son, let's go. *Exits.*

Del Rodney!

NIGHTCLUB.

It is very dark and intimate. The place is virtually empty save for two girls who are seated with their backs turned some distance away at the bar. Del and Rodney are seated at a table.

Del Is it always as dark as this in here or are they holding a dummy run for a coal miners' convention?

Rodney I dunno!

Del What do you mean you dunno? I thought you said this was one of your regular clubs.

Rodney Well I might have exaggerated a bit when I said regular.

Del How many times have you been here then?

Rodney Never!

Del Never? What you bring us in here for then?

Rodney It looked alright from the outside!

Go West Young Man

Del It looked alright from the outside! That's what the Christians said about the coliseum, you berk!

Rodney Not much action for a nightclub is there!

Del No, probably something to do with the fact that it's only half past seven! The last time I come out with you Rodney!

Rodney Is that a promise you moaning git?

Del Oi, watch it you. Ah Garçon la petite pois!

The waiter approaches. He is casually dressed and effeminate.

Waiter Parlez vous Français?

Del Jawohl!

Waiter Yes! What can I get for you?

Del Um, I'd like a Caribbean Stallion.

Waiter Wouldn't we all dear! What is it?

Del It's an exotic cocktail ain't it, specially created for the discerning palates of the international jet-set! Roger Moore drank one in *Live and Let Die*.

Waiter I wouldn't put anything past her.

Del Eh? Yeah well you'd better write this down hadn't you? What you want is a shot of Tequila and a shot of coconut rum and one of Crème de Menthe. Then you want a smidgin, just a smidgin, of Campari, with the merest suggestion of Angostura bitters. Right, you top that up with fresh grapefruit juice, and you shake it – do not stir – right. Pour that slowly over broken ice. Garnish with a slice of orange, slice of lime, your occasional seasonal fruits. Top that off with a decorative plastic umbrella, two translucent straws and – voila!

Waiter Right! And for you?

Rodney Half a lager please.

Waiter Half a lager . . . Reg Varney drank one of them in *Holiday on the Buses*!

Del Is he a bit funny?

Rodney I dunno!

Del He's definitely a bandit that one. Tonight we dance with our backs to the wall, Rodney!

Rodney Wonder what Monica's doing now?

Del Well, why don't you phone Mickey Pearce, he might be able to throw some light on the subject!

Rodney I don't talk to him no more!

Del Hey look – come on, I'm your brother ain't I eh? You can tell me. What broke you two up?

Rodney What do you mean 'What broke us up?' I found out he was dating Monica!

Del No, not you and Mickey bloody Pearce – you and the fat bird!

Rodney Oh! Well, she thought I was weird! Well not so much weird, more warped!

Del Warped?

Rodney Yeah. See I've got this fantasy! Uniforms, they turn me on!

Del Uniforms? You mean like postmen and that?

Rodney No, women in uniforms. Nurses, air hostesses and my favourites, policewomen.

Del Policewomen? But they nick you. So what you're trying to tell me is that this Monica bird, she sort of like didn't go a bundle on this dressing up idea? Is that – that right?

Rodney Oh I didn't tell her, I tried to do it without her knowing.

Del How the hell do you dress someone up as Juliet Bravo without them twigging?

Rodney I was going to do it gradually, over a period of time. Last week was her birthday, right, so I bought her one of them blue serge suits that Paddy the Greek was selling, right. I already got her the hat, white with navy blue peak . . . and then for Valentine's Day I was going to get her some black stockings and some of them sensible walking brogues right . . . then for Christmas . . .

Del A whistle and a set of handcuffs! Blimey you were lucky she gave you the elbow when she did, those Panda cars cost a bomb you know. Monica's right about you, you know – you're – you're a pervo Rodney. That is immoral, you know that, don't you?

Rodney Immoral! Today you sold a clapped-out Batmobile with no brakes. That's immoral, son.

Del There wasn't nothing wrong with that car. It went didn't it?

Rodney Oh it went, yeah, just didn't stop. You're like the chairman of a cigarette company joining the Festival of Light. You can die for my profit, but don't play with yourself in between.

Del Alright, alright Rodney. Yeah, well I didn't mean the geezer no harm do I. I'll pop round and see him tomorrow and pay to have his brakes repaired. How's that?

Rodney That's good. If you do that for me I'll tell you what I'll do for you.

Del You'll stop thinking about policewomen?

Rodney No, I'll accept my 50 per cent of the profits.

Del Oh my cup runneth over.

The waiter returns with a lager for Rodney and a drink that looks like one of Carmen Miranda's hats for Del.

Waiter Half a lager for sir and a Caribbean Stallion for Mandingo. That'll be £7.

Del Seven quid, blimey I can get that for three quid where I come from.

Waiter Oh you're from Jersey, are you? Enjoy

your stay.

Del What's he on about Jersey?

Waiter By the way, the barman said would you like some evaporated milk with that?

Del Tell the barman to go and get stuffed.

Waiter Thank you, sir.

Del Oh – thank you sir.

Rodney Del! Del! *(Indicating to the two girls at the bar)*

Del What? No not yet it's only twenty to eight. If we pull them now we'll have to buy them drinks all night.

Rodney But we could take them back to the flat.

Del Hey that's an idea, I've got 24 litres of that Yugoslavian Riesling in the garage. We could pop old Grandad in the meter cupboard and have ourselves a little party.

Rodney Yeah, yeah, go on Del. You can charm a tortoise out of a shell you can. Go on.

Del Okay. Now you look, learn and listen, right.
Del smoothes his way over to the bar and talks to the two girls. After a very short length of time he smoothes his way back over to Rodney.
Drink up, we're leaving.

Rodney Oh you are great, you are. You're the last miracle left to this world.

Del Shut up and drink up will yer!

Rodney Yeah, yeah, are they a couple of ravers?

Del They're a couple of geezers.
As Rodney and Del exit the girls turn to reveal they are a couple of transvestites.

WEST END DISCO.

Del is leaning against the bar, sulking. Rodney is watching the dancing.

Rodney I'm sorry.

Del What?

Rodney I said I'm sorry!

Del Shut up.

Rodney I didn't know it was that sort of place, did I?

Del A right blinding night I've had. Become a member of a gay club, discovered me brother's a pervo, had a close encounter with two dockers in drag! You'd better not tell anybody about this, Rodney. I've got my macho reputation to uphold. I'm warning you, if one person – just one – calls me the Naked Civil Servant, and I'll kill you.

Rodney Don't be silly Del. I'm hardly gonna go round bragging I saw my own brother trying to date a couple of transvestites am I?

Del What? It was you who clocked them you – you – just shut up, shut up will you.
Rodney surveys the room. He zeroes in on a

couple of young girls seated at a corner table. One of the girls smiles at Rodney. Rodney smiles back.

Rodney Del.

Del Shut up.

Rodney Corner table to your left. A couple of birds.

Del Oh don't start that again, a couple of birds. It's probably Hinge and Bracket out having a pint.

Rodney These are definitely feminine Del, all the lumps are in the right places this time.

Del Yeah, where? *(Rodney explains with gestures)* No, I don't mean like that you wally, I mean where here? *(He sees them)* Yes that will definitely suit me. Right, come on, bellies in!

Rodney Oi, let's just be ourselves this time shall we? None of your embarrassing lies! And don't try an' put me down!

Del Alright! Alright! And don't you say I'm 35.

Rodney Alright!

Del Come on then, into action.
Del saunters over to the table casually twirling the car keys around his finger.
Whoops, sorry, look at that just dropped the keys to the white alpine E-Type Jaguar, eight track stereo, leather-look steering wheel! It's not my car, it's his.

Rodney Yeah, yeah, it's my car! *(Whispers)* Cheers Del!

Del That's alright. We're just using it while they service my Ferrari!

Rodney He's 35!

Del Sit down will you – sit down Rodney, keep yer brains warm! Go on son. You don't mind if we join you girls do you, no good. This is my brother Rodney, and I'm Del, that is short for Derek, nice name that innit eh – Derek?
The girls are trying not to laugh.

Nicky Yeah, very nice. I'm Nicky, this is Michele.

Rodney Nicky and Michelle, they're nice names!

Del Yes! Not as nice as Derek though, is it, that name?

Nicky Oh no, not a patch on Derek!

Rodney Er, do you come here often?

Del I don't believe you, I don't believe you.

Michele Yes – quite often. I haven't seen you here before!

Del No, no, it's because we – you know – don't come to London very often.

Michele Oh, where do you come from then?

Rodney Peckham.

Del Yeah. Originally. Originally from Peckham. But we spend most of our time abroad now for tax reasons. You know, yeah, we're on the international professional tennis circuit.

Go West Young Man

Rodney Del.

Del Yeah, he's an international professional tennis player and I'm his manager. You must have heard of Rodney, yeah Rodney. The sporting press call him Hot Rodney!

Nicky Don't think I have. What's the surname?

Rodney Trotter!

Nicky Doesn't ring a bell, sorry.

Del No, no that's because we generally concentrate on the big American tournaments, you see.

Michele Do you ever play Wimbledon?

Del No, no, we only do the big 'uns! We've just come back from the Miami Open . . .

Nicky Really? You're not very tanned for Miami, are you?

Rodney No, no, it was an indoor tournament.

Del Yeah, yeah, it's amazing that innit. I mean they call it the Miami Open and then they go an' hold it indoors. That's the Yanks for yer though eh? Anyway we can't complain like because he won it, he did, he er, beat that Jimmy Connelly in the final.

Michele Jimmy Connelly? Don't you mean Jimmy Connors?

Del No, he knocked that dildo out in the first round, nine sets to one! Actually we're only in London to get Hot Rodney here measured up for a new bat.

Nicky It's a racquet!

Del Bloody is the prices they charge, darling. No also we thought it might be an idea to give him some practice on grass you see. 'Cos over in the States they use that stuff called Astroturf.

Michele What do you prefer, Rodney?

Rodney Pardon?

Michele What do you prefer? Astroturf or grass?

Rodney I don't know. I've never smoked Astroturf.

Del You wally! No, no, we're not really professional tennis players!

Michele We know!

Rodney We're just having a laugh.

Del Yeah, just having a laugh that's all.

Nicky What do you really do?

Del We're Concorde pilots!

CAR.

Del Light me up a cigar will you Rodders?
Hands Rodney the cigar pack. Rodney removes the last cigar and throws the empty pack from the window.

Rodney We have struck gold there Del Boy!

Del It's the Klondike my son – the Klondike. I mean it's every bloke's dream innit, eh? Meeting a couple of sorts with their own pad in Chelsea. I hope it's a penthouse, because I'm a penthouse sort of person. Know what I mean, balconies – rubber plants, all that game.

Rodney Hey if we see them next Friday perhaps we can stay for the weekend.

Del Yeah, watch *Match of the Day!*

Rodney Yeah, won't have to spend much will we!

Del Won't have to spend much . . . Honestly Rodney, when it comes down to the nitty gritty you are completely devoid of any je ne said quoi ain't yer? I mean, these aren't your two halves of Stingo, a packet of pork scratchings and Bob's yer uncle type! No, no, no, we'll take 'em to a Berni Inn! Yes.

Rodney I bow to your experience and wallet there Del. Hey, where's their phone number?

Del Oh she wrote it down on my cigar pack.

Rodney Ace! What – what cigar pack's that then Del?

Del The one I just gave you.

Rodney Del!

Del Yeah?

Rodney You know that cigar pack?

Del Yeah.

Rodney I threw it out the window about a mile and half back!

Del Oh that's alright. You what? You pranny!
(Slams on the brakes)
The E-Type screeches to a halt. There is the sound of screeching brakes from a following car. The E-Type leaps forward as it is hit in the rear. There is the sound of splintering glass and metal.
God! I don't believe it. I just do not believe it! Now look what you've done Rodney, you've smashed up Boycie's E-Type Jaguar.

Rodney Me? You were driving it.

Del Don't play bloody word games with me, Rodney!
They alight from the E-Type
(Screaming at the car behind) What's your game pal. What is your game, are you blind or something?
The Aussie alights from the Zephyr.

Aussie I'm really sorry about that mate, but the brakes on this thing are a bit dicky . . . You! I've been looking for you two Flaming Gollahs all day long . . . Now come here!
Del and Rodney turn and run up the road with the Aussie in hot pursuit.

27

Cash and Curry

TOWN HALL CAR PARK.

Rodney pulls up in the three-wheeled van next to a rather rusty Vauxhall Velox Mark 3. He switches the engines and lights off on the van before slamming the door angrily. He glances at the Velox. On the front grill, between the rusty chrome and spotlight with a missing glass front, is a brand new Playboy bunny motif badge.

As Rodney glances at it, there are two Indian fellows sitting surreptitiously in the front seats of a car. One is large and casually dressed (the heavy) and the other is smaller and smartly dressed in western style (Mr Ram).

TOWN HALL FOYER.

A sign on the wall reads: 'Peckham and Camberwell Chamber of Trade Dinner/Dance'

A few middle-aged men and women in evening dress are descending a flight of steps from the main hall. As Rodney enters the foyer, Del, in a flashy evening suit, smoking a fat cigar and slightly sloshed, is descending the stairs.

Del Ah, you made it Rodders, good! Well done my son.

Rodney You've got a bloody nerve you have Del, phoning me up at home and demanding I come down here to pick you up!

Del What could I do Rodney? What – what could I – listen, look I've got the Vauxhall Velox outside haven't I, eh, and I've had a few, you know what I mean, a few drinky poos and I thought to myself, what, I could get a little old mini-cab and then I thought to myself no, no, no, what is more impressive – is more impressive is if you get your driver to come round and drive you home in your Vexhall Volox – Vauxhall Velox!

Rodney What do you mean impressive, eh? Who are you trying to impress?

Del Sssssshhhhh! A contact Rodney! Contact. New man in the area – stone rich, looking for 'business opportunities'. We could earn out of this Rodders my little brother!

Rodney Del, what you failed to realise is when you phoned I was in the flat with a friend!

Del Well why didn't you bring him with you?

Rodney It wasn't a he!

Del Well, what was it then? Have you been up to naughties Rodney?

Rodney No. I just had a feeling something was going to develop!

Del Develop! You've been playing with my Polaroid again haven't you, eh?

Rodney No!

Vimmal Malik, an evening-suited and sober Indian gentleman, passes.

Vimmal I'll just collect my coat Derek!

Del Alright. No rush Vimmal me old mucker!

Rodney Who?

Del Vimmal, Vimmal Malik, my contact! Say no more!

TOWN HALL CAR PARK.

Del, Rodney and Vimmal exit from the foyer. They start to walk across the car park.

Del So he said 'She can't come now 'cos she's weighing the postman.' *(Laughs)* 'Ere, d'you fancy a nightcap Vimmal? I know a nice little pub that does late tasting, eh.

All three stop. Ram and the heavy are barring their way.

Ram Thought you'd given me the slip did you Vimmal?

Vimmal Why don't you go away and leave me alone!

Ram *(To Del)* I have no quarrel with you my friend. It's this pig's behind Malik that I wish to see!

Del Friend of yours is he Vimmal?

Vimmal He's no one's friend.

Del Listen John, I don't know what this barney's all about and I don't want to know! So why don't you chaps get out of the way before someone gets a smack in the ear! Right!

Ram Please, do not threaten me with violence my friend. My colleague here is a second Dan in karate!

Del And I'm a black belt in origami, now get out of the way!

Ram gestures to the heavy. The heavy moves menacingly to within a yard or so of Del and then leaps into a karate pose. Del is coolness itself, relaxed, almost nonchalant.

Rodney Watch him Del, watch his kari tari, mate.

Del I'll watch your bloody kari tari in a minute Rodney, just shut up will you!

The heavy goes through the psyching out process – lots of yells, stamping of feet, flurries of feet, etc.

Del *(Glancing over the heavy's shoulder)* Police! *The heavy turns, as do Rodney, Vimmal and Ram. There is a thud and a groan. Del is still cool and relaxed, but the heavy is kneeling on the ground clutching his groin.*

Del Rodney! You and Vimmal in the car quickly!

Rodney Right, let's go!

Del *(To Ram)* Well it's been very pleasant meeting you both. Have a nice evening won't you.

Ram My friend! It's not good to part in such circumstances. Could we talk?

Del I've done all the talking I wanted to. Goodnight each!

With that, the Vauxhall with Rodney and Vimmal inside roars past Del and out of the car park.

(Shouting) Rodney! I didn't mean drive off! What a plonker! *(To Ram)* Well, on second thoughts I quite fancy a nice little chat! Perhaps you could drop me off home after? *(They help the heavy to his feet)* Oh, oh dear, come on me old mate, come on. No, you'll be alright. You'll be alright. Here, what happened?

INDIAN RESTAURANT.

Del, Ram and the heavy are seated at a table eating a meal.

Ram Agur ye budha kuch aur mangay to kahna ka bawarchi khana band ha.

Del Ah John, that is twice, right?

Rodney enters Starsky and Hutch fashion and surveys the restaurant.

Ram I think your brother has arrived Mr Trotter.

Del Ah, oh yeah, yeah, could you excuse me a minute Mr Ram. Excuse me. Rodney!

Rodney Del – are you alright son? I thought you was in bother!

Del Oh, that's why it's taken you an hour an' 'alf to get here is it? Didn't Grandad tell you that I phoned?

Rodney Oh yeah, he told me! 'Del Boy's been captured by the Indians' he said. I didn't know whether to phone the police or the Texas Rangers!

Del If you were so worried at your brother, you know, you were so worried about me, how come it's taken you till twenty to one in the morning to come to me rescue?

Rodney Because your telephone message lacked something in clarity, didn't it? You didn't tell Grandad which Indian restaurant you was in!

I've been crashing through the doors of every curry house and take-away from Battersea Bridge to Colliers Wood tube station! I can now leap out of the Vauxhall Velox, Dukes of Hazzard fashion, make a chapati and say get stuffed in Urdu!

Del I forgive you, Rodney.

Rodney Oh that's nice.

Del Alright then.

Rodney So there's gonna be trouble is there?

Del No, no, put that spoon down.

Rodney Thank God for that!

Del Right, come on. Rodney I would like you to meet Mr Ram, he owns his restaurant. *(Indicating heavy)* Of course you know Oddjob don't you!

Rodney Well – nice restaurant you've got here, Mr Ram . . . Very . . . er . . . Very . . .

Del Indian.

Rodney Yeah, Indian!

Ram Thank you.

Del Sit down, sit down.

Ram I was just telling your brother how well I've done since I came to Britain. I now own 18 of these restaurants all together. I also own a lot of land.

Del Yeah, yeah, Oddjob's got a couple of acres and all hasn't he?

Ram I am telling you now if I got into my car at nine o'clock in the morning, it would take me up till two in the afternoon to drive around my land.

Rodney Yeah, we had a car like that once eh?

Ram What?

Rodney Don't matter.

Del So Mr Ram you and this, er, Vimmal, you've been having a bit of an up and downer then have you?

Ram Don't mention that name at this table. It will sour the food!

Del What's it all about then?

Ram I'll tell you what it's all about Mr Trotter. It's about truth – it's about righteousness, but above all it's about justice! Vimmal that . . . that pig's behind, has something that's rightfully mine! You see our families have been engaged in a vendetta for many, many years. It goes right back to the days of the old Empire.

Rodney He means the British Empire not the Kilburn!

Del I know that! I know that – pray continue.

Ram Now my family fought against the British whereas the Maliks family supported them! When the conquest of Mother India was finally complete the British Raj decided to reward the Maliks' loyalty by giving them my family's land!

Rodney What, you mean they just took it off your family?

Cash and Curry

Ram That's correct. They destroyed the home, they plundered the family's temple and then they sold the land. The Maliks have built a business empire with the proceeds.

Del Here, couldn't you write to *That's Life*?

Ram *That's Life*!

Del Yeah.

Ram But this happened a century ago Mr Trotter! If Lord Krishna himself couldn't help us I really don't think Esther Rantzen would stand much chance!

Del No, no, that was just a thought. Oh – get off!

Ram Vimmal Malik has in his possession the one, single item that remains of my birthright. It's a simple porcelain statuette of Kuvera. You know of Kuvera?

Del and Rodney Oh yeah.

Del You don't know who Kuvera is!

Rodney Yes I do!

Del Alright then tell us!

Rodney What?

Del Who is he?

Rodney Who?

Del Kuvera!

Rodney Em. . . . Well er. . . . He was, alright I don't know!

Del There you are, see what I mean Mr Ram? He's got two 'O' Levels and he thinks he's Bamber Gascoigne's vest!

Rodney Alright Mastermind, who is he then?

Del Kuvera was one of India's premier wicket-keepers.

Rodney You berk!

Ram Kuvera is the Hindu god of wealth, from the second aspect of the Trimurti – the Hindu Trinity!

Del Oh yeah, oh that Kuvera? Oh yeah, gotcha now, yeah, yeah, there was two of them see.

Ram In worldly terms the statuette is of little value, but in religious and sentimental terms it's precious to me . . . and I want it back, it's mine by right! I'm a rich man Mr Trotter, I shouldn't have to stoop to the kind if intimidation you witnessed tonight. I'm prepared to buy it back from Vimmal Malik. I would pay £4,000!

Del *(Crumbling his poppadum)* Four – four – £4,000. Well, why don't you just go and make him an offer?

Ram Oh it's impossible! It's this wretched caste-system you see. He belongs to the high caste and I belong to the low caste.

Del Oh no, don't put yourself down.

Ram We cannot meet, talk or communicate in any manner! So you see my friends I am up a

gum-tree without a paddle!

Del It seems to me Mr Ram what you need is a mutual friend, you know. Someone who can talk to the both of you, you know act as a sort of go-between!

Ram Perhaps you and your brother!

Del What us? I suppose we could, I mean, cor, why didn't we think of that Rodney?

Rodney I think one of us already did Del!

Ram If you help me to reclaim the statuette, I don't know how I'd ever reward you!

Del Well I've always fancied one of those video recorders. But no, no, pas de Basque. Pas de Basque. We'll go and see this Mr Vimmal tomorrow. Um, £4,000, right?

Ram Right. Oh, but I must make one thing quite clear. I don't trust this man Malik, you see he comes from a long line of swindlers! I won't part with a single penny until I have the statuette safely in my hands!

Del Don't you worry, don't worry Mr Ram, me and Vimmal we're like that! *(He twists his fingers)* Good job that we didn't call the police tonight. *(He jerks his elbow and hits the heavy)* Oh, what happened?

VIMMAL'S HOTEL ROOM.

A typical room in a smaller, cheaper hotel. The kind of place where reps who were fiddling their expenses might stay. Clean and tidy but the Dorchester it is not. Vimmal casually dressed has just been informed by Rodney and Del of the previous night's meal.

Vimmal I'm surprised at you Derek, and you also Rodney! How could you share a meal with that . . . with that gutter dog? I thought you were my friends!

Del We are your friends Vimmal me old mucker! Just trust me will you, trust me! You see this Mr Ram – the gutter dog – told us all about the little misunderstanding that your two families have been having for the last 100 years or so! He also mentioned something about the statue of some god or another.

Vimmal Of Kuvera, the god of wealth!

Del Ah, that's him – that's the boy! Yeah well, yeah, well you know. Well without beating about the bush, you know, I mean – well – you know to cut a long story short, well not to put too fine a point on it . . .

Rodney He wants to buy it off you!

Vimmal Buy it from me! He must have gone mad or he's been eating too many of his own curries! Buy it from me indeed! I wouldn't sell it to him if he offered me £1million! How much did

he offer? Purely out of curiosity you understand.
Rodney is about to say four when Del beats him to it.

Del Er, £2,000!

Rodney £2,000! I thought Mr Ram said . . .

Del Yeah, £1,000, that is right Rodney but I persuaded him to double it!

Vimmal £2,000! No, no, no, I cannot sell it to him!

Del £2,000 Vimmal me old mucker. You know it's not to be sneezed at, is it, eh?

Vimmal I will not deny that I'm tempted Derek. I thought of selling the statuette once before. The most I was offered was £150!

Del Now look Vimmal, you see, I get the impression that you're not quite as rich and successful as you told me you were last night at the chamber of trade bash. I mean, take a look at this place, it's hardly the Ritz is it, eh? More like the Nits!

Vimmal I will admit I have suffered some misfortunes in my business dealings of late.

Del So two grand on the hip would come in dead handy, eh?

Vimmal £2,000 would come in dead handy as you say! But I cannot communicate with him, I'm of a high caste, he's a low caste!

Del But you don't have to communicate with him Vimmal me old mucker. That's where me and Rodders come in. You see we're acting as the go-betweens!

Vimmal Even so I cannot accept his offer. You see it would be like betraying my family. The statuette was left to me by my father! You wouldn't understand what that means would you?

Del Oh yes, yes we would, wouldn't we Rodney?

Rodney Would we Del?

Del Oh yeah, yeah. Our – late mother – well she's dead now – she left us this family heirloom. It was um, it was this – this Victorian globe.

Rodney It meant the world to us.

Del As he said it meant the world to us. Yeah but there came the time when we fell upon stony ground.

Rodney We fell upon stony ground did we?

Del Yes, we fell upon stony ground. And the only thing we had of any value was – was this Victorian globe which we cherished!

Vimmal You sold it?

Del Well, no, no, no, I raffled it down the betting shop!

Vimmal But, of course, you understand the sense of loss?

Rodney Well not really, no, because by some stroke of fortune Del had the winning ticket!

Del I think it was God . . . or something!

Vimmal You think I should sell it to him Derek?

Del Yes, of course I do Vimmal me old mucker. I mean, what is it, it's just an ancient piece of old religious pottery! And with £2,000 wisely invested. I mean in a couple of years you could replace it with um . . . who knows what, a Capo Del Monte! And personally, anyway, I'm not – I'm sorry I've got to tell you this but I think that statue is cursed!

Vimmal Cursed?

Rodney Oh leave it out Del!

Del Do not underestimate the powers of darkness Rodney. I mean for a god of wealth he ain't done Vimmal no favours has he, eh?

Vimmal I'm not a superstitious man Derek but I'm a business man and a realist . . . I have decided to accept his offer!

Del Well, you know it makes sense Vimmal!

Vimmal I'll go and fetch the statue.
Vimmal moves to the door

Del Yeah good man.

Rodney Now just what's your . . . *(Noticing Vimmal still at the door)*

Vimmal Do excuse me, won't you.

Del Oh certainly, yes.
Vimmal exits.

Rodney Now just what is your game Del? Ram offered 4000, how come you're only offering two?

Del Slip of the tonque, Rodney.

Rodney Oh so when he comes back you won't mind me telling him the truth?

Del No, don't you do that otherwise he'll think I'm trying to con him.

Rodney You are trying to con him!

Del No man is an island, Rodney.

Rodney I know that Del. What I'm on about is the – what's that supposed to mean?

Del What it means – what it – look the French have a saying, Rodney. Bouillabaisse mon ami.

Rodney Bouillabaisse mon ami? That means fish stew, my friend!

Del Need I say more.

Rodney Now don't try an' fog me off with your stupid French phrases. You're trying to con him out of 2000 quid. . . . We're going to get lumbered, Del.

Del How?

Rodney Alright, say Ram and Vimmal meet and discuss the deal?

Del That's the beauty of it, Ram and Vimmal cannot meet because of the wonderful caste

Cash and Curry

system. It's Christmas come early for us. And anyway if it wasn't for kind-hearted people like you and me willing to act as go-betweens, Vimmal would end up with nothing. And as it is £2,000 is better than a kick up the bot from Bobby Charlton innit, eh?

Rodney It's immoral.

Del It's free enterprise.

Rodney It's illegal then.

Del Alright so it's against the law, and all. But look, you and I can earn £1,000 apiece out of this.

Rodney It's fraud.

Del Are you in?

Rodney Yeah, all right.

Vimmal re-enters carrying the statue.

Del Right. Ah, ah, oh well, this is it is it Vimmal my old mucker? Oh, that is lovely that – wonderful workmanship. Of course I'm a Ming fan meself, you know. Oh yeah, he made some wonderful stuff didn't he that Ming, yeah. Pity he went and died when he did weren't it, eh?

Vimmal Ming was a dynasty, Derek!

Del I don't care what he was Vimmal, he made a smashing vase. Anyway, look we'll pop this round to Mr Ram and bring you back your £2,000 post haste as they say in Ancient Rome, alright?

Vimmal *(Taking statue from Del)* No, no, no, Derek. This does not leave my sight until his money is on the table.

Del Ah? No, no, no, no, no, sorry, look you don't understand, you see. 'Cos he said that you won't get a penny until he has that statuette safely in his hands. Alright.

Vimmal I don't care what he said Derek, I do not trust the man – he comes from a long line of cheats. You bring me his money first then you can take him the statue.

Del No but you see – you see he said – he said bring the statue and then – then you can have the money.

Vimmal I don't care what he said, Derek.

Rodney He don't care what he said, Derek.

Del Yes I heard what he said. I'll leave Rodney as a deposit.

Rodney Eh?

Del Well what else can I do? I mean look he won't let that go till he gets the money and he won't have the money till he gets that. Oh Gordon Bennett – this is classic this is, isn't it, eh? It's the bacon and the egg situation all over again.

Rodney It's the chicken and the egg Del.

Del We haven't got time to discuss food

Rodney.

Vimmal Talk to him, Derek. Persuade him to submit to my terms. After all you have influence over him, you have already persuaded him to double his offer from £1,000 to £2,000.

Del Yeah, well . . . well, alright, alright. Right Vim, I'll see what I can do then shall I, yeah? I'll um, you know I'll um, I'll get back to you. Alright. You know you er, right, stay loose. Okay and don't you worry Vimmal, don't worry. I mean me and old Ram, I mean, we're like that, we're like, we're like, yeah. *(Rodney twists his fingers for him)* Thanks. Come on.

HOTEL HALLWAY.

Del What are we gonna do now?

Rodney Just forget the whole thing Del.

Del What do you mean forget the whole thing. How can we forget the whole thing? £2,000 up for grabs and you say forget it. No, no, there's got to be another way round it.

Rodney There isn't. Look, Ram won't pay a penny until he's got the statuette in his hands and Vimmal won't let the statuette go till he's got Ram's money.

Del Yeah cheers. Yeah, what he thinks is Ram's money.

Rodney What you on about now?

Del Well let's say, just for instance, that we had £2,000 lying around at home doing nothing in particular.

Rodney Just mooching about.

Del Yeah, you know, kicking its heels, that sort of thing. And let's say that we – we gave Vimmal that £2,000 right and we pretended that we'd just collected from Mr Ram. Well Vimmal, he wouldn't know any better, would he, eh? So thinking that he'd won the battle and, as happy as a sand boy, he'd hand over the statuette which we would then whip round to Mr Ram who also thinking that he'd won the battle, and being equally chuffed as a sand boy, would hand over to us 4,000 lovely smackeroonyos. We would get on our bike leaving them to play sand-castles. Brilliant innit, eh?

Rodney Yeah, there's only one problem I can see Del. How the hell do we get £2,000?

Del You always bring little details up don't you, eh? We get it from a bank.

Rodney What rob it?

Del Well, that's a . . .

Rodney Oi!

Del No, no, no, we'll borrow it from a bank. This is gilt-edge security innit?

Rodney Del, you can't stroll into a bank and ask

for a loan to help you pull off a con-trick. Besides, we haven't got a bank account.

Del Oh well there's got to be another way of raising the money. I mean there's just got to be. Here, we're general traders aren't we?

Rodney Yeah!

Del Well why don't we start generally trading. I mean we could flog all our stock that we've got in the garage, couldn't we? We could sell the deep-freeze, the Vauxhall Velox.

Rodney Three-wheeled van?

Del You're jesting, they'd want a tenner to take that away. No we could flog Grandad's telly, we could flog – 'ere my jewellery, that would bring in enough, I mean it's 27 carat.

Rodney I thought it was nine carat!

Del That was when I was buying, now I'm selling! We could sell that leather coat.

Rodney You're not talking about my leather coat are you?

Del No, no, I'm talking about – have you got a leather coat? Oh we'll knock that one out and all Rodney, yeah that's a good idea.

Rodney Come on Del, we'll never raise two grand.

Del We can, Rodney . . . You can do anything if you want it hard enough. We can do it Rodney, we can do it!

Rodney Yeah, yeah.

Del Come on then.

THE TROTTERS' FLAT.

Del is standing outside the front door. Two blokes are carrying a deep-freeze out of the flat. Del is handed a bundle of notes.

SECOND-HAND CAR SITE.

Del, Rodney and car trader are examining the Vauxhall Velox. The trader hands Del money. The amount is growing steadily.

THE TROTTERS' FLAT.

Del is standing outside the front door as a couple of blokes carry a colour telly out. More money is passed into Del's hand.

LONDON BACK STREET.

The three wheeled van is parked outside of an Almost-New Clothes shop. A sign in the window reads: 'We buy second-hand clothes.' Outside the shop is a long trestle table upon which lie bundles of second-hand dresses, jumpers, etc. Rodney takes a great heap of clothing from the back of the van and carries it into the shop. Del pauses, checks the street

and then scoops up all the dresses and jumpers, etc, from the trestle table and follows Rodney in. He is paid more money.

JEWELLER'S SHOP.

Del removes his watch and hands it to the jeweller. He then removes his rings, his tie-pin, his identity bracelet, his necklaces and medallions. Rodney removes his watch but the jeweller looks at it and hands it back. More money is given to Del

VIMMAL'S ROOMS.

Del places a large bundle of crumpled notes and a bag of coins on the table.

Del Well, thanks a lot, it's tempus fugit then, eh? (*Forgetting his watch is sold, he checks his right wrist.*)

Vimmal Where's your watch, Derek?

Del My watch. Oh, it's at the menders, I broke it last night playing you know, volleyball (*He mimes a tennis stroke*)

Vimmal I thought you were right-handed!

Del Me – no, no, no, no, I'm ambiguous.

OUTSIDE THE HOTEL.

Rodney is sitting in the three-wheeled van. A victorious Del emerges from the hotel holding the statuette up high like the FA Cup. As he descends the hotel steps, he stumbles and juggles with the statuette. He finally catches it diving at full length, inches from the floor and breathes an almighty sigh of relief.

INDIAN RESTAURANT.

Del and Rodney enter. An Indian approaches.

Man Good afternoon, gentlemen. A table for two?

Del No thank you.

Man No thank you?

Rodney We'd like to see Mr Ram.

Man Mr Ram?

Del The owner?

Man The owner?

Del (*To Rodney*) Terrible echo in here ain't there, eh? Yeah we'd like to speak to the owner Mr Ram!

Man The owner, Mr Ram?

Del There it goes again. What is the matter with it. Eh, don't keep doing that. Now listen, listen, we would like to talk to the proprietor of this restaurant.

Man I am the proprietor of this restaurant.

Rodney No, no, he don't understand.

Del What's he on about?

Cash and Curry

Rodney We want to see the real owner, right.

Man I am the real owner.

Del Alright, alright – listen – just wait. Just watch my lips alright. Where is Mr Ram?

Man Look, I don't know any Mr bloody Rams. So will you please leave. You drunks always come here causing trouble.

Del Trouble! We're not drunks are we? Look, I was having a couple of meals here quite recently, you must remember me!

Man I am sorry, you all look alike to me.

Del Alike, what's he talking about we all look alike. What's the matter with him?

Rodney He don't . . . no . . . he's making it up. Look! Look, look my brother, right?

Del That's me.

Rodney Was in here dining with a couple of Indian gentlemen. Right? One was sort of large – large and aggressive. Right? Big, and the other one – smaller. How small?

Del Well he's smaller than that weren't he – get down there.

Rodney About that big and more business-like and he had a beard – beard! He had a beard about that big.

Man Oh, that Mr Ram!

Rodney and Del Yes.

Man I know who you are talking about now.

Del At last.

Man He's the one who gave me a bouncy cheque. A short while ago I went to the address which is written on the back. He scarpered owing three weeks rent.

Rodney Del Boy!!

Del No, no, no, no, no, no, there must be a mistake! It's got to be a mistake! I mean he told me he owned this restaurant. He told me he owned 18 of them in fact.

Man Maybe he was fibbing!

Del Fibbing! Maybe he was fibbing. I've just given him £2,000 for this on the strength of his 'fibbing'.

Man £2,000, but why? *(Indicating an area of the restaurant where there are two replicas of the statuette being used as decoration)* You can get them in Portobello Road for £17 each! It's amazing what you can save if you shop around.

Del I've got a nose-bleed coming Rodney!

MOTORWAY. INSIDE CAR.

Vimmal and Ram are both opulently dressed and smoking fat cigars. The atmosphere is one of celebration.

Vimmal He tried to tell me that the statue was cursed!

Ram You know he told me that he thought Kuvera was a wicket-keeper. Let's see, now we've done Cardiff, Bristol, Southampton and now North and South London. Where to now?

Vimmal Oh to Birmingham, then Manchester, then Newcastle, even maybe Liverpool. In fact, anywhere where there're people who think they can exploit the religious bigotry of two stupid immigrants. We'll be rich my friend, very rich!

Ram I'll drink to that, my old mucker!

HOTEL.

Rodney is waiting in the van, anxiously. The Hotel door opens and Del emerges and descends the steps like a man in a trance.

Rodney No sign of Vimmal.

Del No, he packed his bags and had it away on his toes five minutes after we left! As Macbeth said to Hamlet in *A Midsummer's Night Dream*, 'We've been done up like a couple of kippers.'

Rodney Right, let's go to the police.

Del Oh yeah, that's a good idea, that is – oh that's marvellous, we'd give them a good laugh down there couldn't we, eh? Can just imagine it? Trotter brothers conned out of two grand. It'd be all over the manor in no time, we'd never be able to hold our heads up in court again! I don't know how people like Vimmal and his mate can sleep at night, honest I don't. Lost everything. Leather coats, Vauxhall Velox, Grandad's telly!

Rodney Ah, I've just remembered something. Grandad was renting that telly.

Del Oh triffic, come on – let's get something to eat, I always feel emotionally peckish when I've been gutted.

Rodney Well there's a curry house down the road, Del. Only joking, Del Boy . . . Del! *(Del hurls the statuette across the top of the van at Rodney)*

The Second Time Around

EXT. LONDON STREET MARKET. DAY.

Del and Rodney are selling packs of hankies from a suitcase, surrounded by a crowd of women shoppers. Del is in the middle of his sales pitch. Rodney is holding up the packs of hankies and waiting to take the money.

Del Here we are, the finest French lace hankies – there you are, they're a pleasure to have the flu with! Thanks luv.

Rodney Now hurry up girls, get in while the going's good. It's one for the price of two. One for the price of two.

Del Keep taking the money Rodney. I'm gonna pop down the pub to get a lemonade for the old Hobsons.

Rodney Get us a packet of pork scratchings would you.

Del Pork scratchings. Sounds like a pig with fleas.

Rodney Come on then, get in while the going's good. We're not here today gone tomorrow, we're here today gone this afternoon, now come on.

INT. DAY. THE NAG'S HEAD.

The bar is fairly crowded with lunchtime boozers. Trigger is standing at the bar just finishing a pint. Joyce is behind the bar. Del enters and approaches the bar.

Del Hey, hey, alright Trigger?

Trigger Hello Del Boy, how's yer luck?

Del You can have it for a nicker. Hello Joyce, I'll have a pint of diesel oil for Trigger and I'll have a blackcurrant and Pernod. *(Pronounces Pernod phonetically)* Thank you.

Trigger You'll never guess who I just saw!

Del Er, King Faisal of Saudi Arabia.

Trigger No. No, yer miles off Del!

Del No, no, I knew he wouldn't be in here. He'd be in the Saloon bar wouldn't he. I'm joking, Trigger.

Trigger Oh gotcha! No, it was your ex-fiancée!

Del Which one?

Trigger Pauline.

Del Pauline? Pauline Harris? No, no, no you must have been mistaken. She got married to that Bobby Finch didn't she and went to live abroad.

Trigger Yeah? Well who's that sitting over there then?

Del *(He looks)* Hm. Where?

Pauline is sat at a table. She is in her early thirties, smartly dressed and still very tasty. She was the great love of Del's life, a love that has still not died.

Cor, it is her Trigger. It is her. It's at moments like this when I wish I carried an emergency capsule of Brut around with me!

Trigger Leave it out will you Del, you don't wanna get yourself involved with her again. Remember what happened last time?

Del Yeah, yeah. Did she ask about me?

Joyce Yeah, she seemed very concerned to know how much you was earning.

Del How the hell do you do that?

Trigger What?

Joyce I said she seemed very concerned to know how much you was earning.

Del Yeah well she probably is concerned isn't she, eh? You know, perhaps she's worrying about me! Alright, alright, I'm not gonna get involved am I? No, I'm too shrewd for all that, ain't I, eh? No, I might just go over there, you know, and say hello. If that is alright with you two?

Joyce You want your brains testing!

Del Yeah thank you, Joyce. There did you take one for yourself?

Joyce No.

Del Good! *(He walks across to Pauline sipping his drink nervously. The blackcurrant is staining his lips)* Excuse me. Excuse me, squire. Hello Pauline!

Pauline Del . . . *(She gives him a long, lingering kiss. She also now has blackcurrant on her face)* Oh I can't believe it . . . It's so nice to see you again.

Del Well it's nice to see you. Pauline, what have you got over your lips there? What's all that?

Pauline It's blackcurrant.

Del You what?

Pauline It's on your lips.

Del Oh blackcurrant, look – yeah, it's probably from my blackcurrant and Pernod. Sorry. Oh thanks. Ta. Here let me, er, let me wipe that off of yer –

They both take a serviette from the table. Del dabs his own face, then they dab each other's faces. Pauline gives Del another kiss, leaving him in a gooey-eyed state. He looks back to

the bar to see Joyce and Trigger watching.

Pauline I haven't seen you for 12 years or more, I want to know *all* that's been happening.

Del Er. . . . Nothing you know, nothing really! I heard you got married to that Bobby Finch . . . where's he now?

Pauline He's down the Blackshaw Road.

Del Oh yeah what in those council flats?

Pauline No in a cemetery. You mean you didn't know?

Del No! No, no, I'm terribly sorry, I am sorry, I didn't realise. You see the last I heard was that, you know, that you went to live abroad, so naturally I though that you and Bobby, like, had emigrated.

Pauline No, after Bobby died I went to San Francisco – it suited me being away from familiar surroundings. I got a job as an air hostess, it's a good salary, uniform, free travel.

Del Yeah, of course/ that's in your blood innit eh? 'Cos your mum was a bus conductress. *(They laugh)*

Pauline You never married yourself, Del?

Del No, no, no, I never fancied myself. *(Laughs)* No, no, no, you know what I mean, I mean what I mean is you know, I never – never met a girl that I cared all that much about really you know. Well, I mean, you know, well, there was one.

Pauline But you don't see her?

Del Oh yeah. Well I'm looking at her now.
Pauline holds his hand. They stare into each other's eyes and are about to kiss when Rodney appears at the table.

Rodney Where's my pork scratchings?

Del Oh I'm sorry Rodney, I got distracted. Yeah. This is my brother Rodney. D'you remember – you remember Rodney. He used to be a little scruff. Look at him now, he's a big scruff, isn't he? You remember Pauline?

Rodney Yeah I remember. Pauline Harris innit?

Del Yeah, yeah or do you call yourself Mrs. Finch now?

Pauline No. I call myself Mrs Baker. I remarried, you see, an American chap.

Del Oh gotcha, you're a divorcee are you?

Pauline No, a widow!

Del Blimey, what he kicked the bucket and all did he? No, I am sorry, I didn't mean that, sorry. What about that – ain't that a shame, eh, Rodney you know she's had two husbands die on her.

Rodney Yeah, one more she keeps the match ball.

Pauline Excuse me a moment.

Del Yeah, yeah of course.

Pauline I'm just going to powder my nose.

Del Yeah, yeah, well hurry back won't you because, you know I'll be waiting.
Pauline Exits.

Rodney Yes of course Pauline, hurry back Pauline, can I pull the chain for you Pauline? You make me sick!

Del You've been very hostile towards Pauline ain't you?

Rodney Well, can you blame me? I remember how she treated you when you was engaged. I may only have been a little nipper Del, but I remember how she screwed you up.

Del That was a long time ago Rodney, weren't it? Pauline and me, when engaged, we was mods – the only reason she left me was because she found a bloke with a faster Vespa.

Rodney And that's a fair reason?

Del Yeah it was in them days. You've got to understand the times Rodney. In them days, I mean, teenage marriages broke up because the husband didn't like the Hollies! But we're older now, you know, more mature, we've developed sensitivity and emotion.

Rodney Oh my God.

Del Yeah we have – what would you know about it anyway, eh? You don't have romantic feelings you, you just have animal urges. Sometimes I think you learnt the art of seduction by watching *Wildlife on One*! You've got to understand Rodney that – you know deep down inside me I'm a very sensitive person. I am, I am. What – look at last Christmas and that film *Love Story*. Look how upset I got then.

Rodney I got upset an' all.

Del I know, I know, I got upset because Ali MacGraw died – you got upset because Ryan O'Neal didn't.

Rodney Well, he's too good-looking ain't he?

Del What do you know about it anyway? What do you know? I am talking about men and women I am. You, you're still knocking about with Brownies.

Rodney No I'm not.

Del Yes you are, leave it out, some of your dates arrive by skateboard.

Rodney Look Del, all I'm trying to say is don't get hiked up with that Pauline again. She'll screw you up, you mark my words.

Del Look, Rodney, a lot of water has run under the bridge since me and Pauline broke up. I know what it's all about now, you know, I understand the rules of the game. I know you're concerned for me and trying to give me your advice but . . . how can I put it? Shove it Rodney, shove it.

The Second Time Around

INT. NIGHT. THE TROTTERS' LOUNGE.

Grandad is watching the TVs. Rodney is lying on the settee reading a dirty magazine.

Grandad Del Boy's late ain't he Rodney?

Rodney I wouldn't worry about it Grandad. I'll give him another 15 minutes then start phoning round the morgues.

Grandad What do you mean the morgues?

Rodney Well, it's something about that Pauline that kills em off. I think she must be a carrier or something.

Grandad It's bad news him meeting her again this afternoon. I remember the last time she hooked him. I mean, up till then he was doing alright – well your mum had died and your dad had run off and left you – but . . .

Rodney But other than that tickety-boo?

Grandad Right, Del was out wheeling and dealing and we was coming along nice. Then she turned up. I've never seen anyone change so fast as Del Boy. He was besotted with her – they was engaged within the week – broken up within the month. Little cow was out skylarking around with other fellas. Del had more fights than John Wayne. Well, up 'till then he was always a strong believer in God and all that. I mean he didn't go to church nor nothing.

Rodney No, didn't carry it to ridiculous lengths?

Grandad No. But he'd always give the church a good few quid towards their fund for a new roof. He said it was a penance seeing as how it was him that nicked the old one. But after that he lost faith.

The front door slams.

Rodney Sssh. Act naturally – stare vaguely at them tellies right and no questions. God Almighty, what's he done?

Del enters, slightly sloshed, tie and waistcoat undone.

Del Gentlemen, attention gentlemen. Gentlemen and Grandad I have a gentleman's announcement to make. Pauline and I are engaged to be married. *(There is silence)* Don't all bust a blood vessel will you, eh?

Rodney That's triffic Del. We'll have to put an announcement in the *Exchange and Mart.*

Del That's a lovely idea that, here go and get some glasses, go on and get some glasses, we'll celebrate alright.

Rodney Celebrate? You think I'm gonna celebrate my only older brother getting hiked up to a gold digger?

Del Listen oi, listen motor-mouth! I know that you don't like Pauline . . .

Rodney Oh does it notice that much?

Del Yes it does. I know – look I know you don't like the idea, right, but it's, you know – that's what *I* want! Right come on, come on, come on, have a drink eh?

Rodney Yeah . . . Yeah I'll get some glasses. *(Exits)*

Del Yeah, get some glasses – get some glasses, that's it. Here, Grandad, what do you think then Grandad?

Grandad I'm not saying a word Del Boy! You want to put yourself in lumber for the rest of your life that's entirely up to you. I'm not saying nothing!

Del Oi, listen, you haven't heard the best part yet, listen this is a double celebration, because not only have I got engaged to Pauline, but my bride to be has kindly condescended to come and live with us! *(There is the sound of glass smashing in the kitchen. Rodney enters, crosses the room to his bedroom.)* Well don't say your congratulations then will yer!

Rodney *(Out of view)* Alright.

Del Say something Grandad.

Grandad There's a film on the other side, lots of people get killed in it!

INT. NIGHT. THE TROTTERS' LOUNGE.

Del is at the dinner table finishing a large meal. He is struggling, but forcing it down for Pauline's sake. She is lying in Rodney's usual spot on the settee filing her nails. Rodney is sitting in the armchair giving Pauline dirty looks. Grandad is watching the TVs. Rodney puts his feet up on the coffee table.

Pauline I cleaned that table today!

Rodney Good, it won't make my plimsoles dirty, will it?

Pauline Del. . . .

Del What? *(She gestures to Rodney's feet)* Rodney! Well, that was divine my love. That was divine. That was well – was – Pas de Calais as they say in France. Long time since we has a steak like that, eh, Rodney?

Rodney Hell of a long time Del. Me and Grandad had corned beef!

Del Corned beef?

Pauline I'm not cooking for them two as well Derek! I'll cook for you and me and you and me only. I didn't come here to be a skivvy!

Del No, no, no, I know my love. I know my petal, you see the thing is when I gave you the housekeeping money at the beginning of the week, I meant for you to get some grub for them an' all.

Pauline I did, I got corned beef!

Del Ah yeah – well. There you are see, you like a little bit of corned beef don't you Grandad? *(Grandad sneers)* What's up with you then, eh?

Grandad It's her innit!

Del What?

Grandad She's hid my teeth!

Del What – what you hidden his teeth for then petal?

Pauline Look you don't know what it's like in this place. Well you and Rodney are out at the auctions or the market. But I'm stuck here with him. He's nibbling all day long. There'd be nothing left if I let him carry on! Don't worry, he gets his teeth back at meal times.

Del Yeah, alright, well you – you know best, eh petal.

Pauline Why don't you and Grandad go out Rodney? I wouldn't mind being alone for once!

Del D'you want to be left alone?

Pauline Of course.

Del Right, I'll go with 'em, come on Grandad.

Pauline I mean alone with you.

Del Oh, I see.

Pauline Well we never have any time to ourselves in this place.

Rodney No time to yourselves! You spend most of your lives in that bedroom! Giant pandas mate quicker than you two!

Del Please. That's enough!

Pauline Ever since I moved in here all we ever seem to do of an evening is sit here watching them rotten televisions. And that's another thing, why does he have to watch two televisions.

Grandad 'Cos the other one's being mended!

Pauline You mean he normally watches three?

Del Yeah!

Pauline He's going senile

Del Yeah!

Pauline Well wouldn't he be happier with company of his own age?

Del You're not bringing your Granny round here to live with us are you?

Pauline I was thinking of a home.

Rodney He's already got a home!

Pauline I know a very nice place down near Thames Ditton. Bobby Finch's Grandad died there.

Del I can't put him in a home Pauline, he's family!

Pauline But I'll be your family soon!

Rodney Well you go to a home then . . .

Grandad I don't want to go into a home Rodney, I might catch something!

Rodney Don't you worry Grandad, we're staying put.

Pauline Well, the only alternative is for us to buy a house of our own!

Del What, me buy a house? No, no, couldn't do that. Couldn't do that. Don't you see that as soon as I put my signature on a document the authorities are gonna know that I'm alive. They'll be round here after their pound of flesh quicker than the Mafia!

Pauline But you can do what my other husbands did, put the house in my name. Well nobody's going to think it strange me buying a house, not with all the money I got on the life insurances. Have you got your life insured Del?

Del No, I've never thought about dying before!

Pauline Well, we'll have to sort that out – a wife needs protection.

Rodney Specially with your luck Pauline!

Pauline I fancy an early night Del.

Del Oh no, what, again?

Pauline Come on. *(She leads Del by the hand)*

Del Yes alright my love, my petal . . . *(Grandad and Rodney give Del the 'under the thumb' gesture)* Listen you two – hey!

INT. TROTTERS' LOUNGE.

Grandad, wearing his overcoat and hat, is sitting in his chair. One TV set shows the BBC2 test card, the other set shows the ITV test card. He sits back and watches them.

Rodney You ready Grandad?

Grandad *(Indicating the TVs)* Yeah – I just wanna see what happens first!

Rodney Eh? Now don't start making excuses! We both agreed we're not wanted here no more, so let's get out before Del wakes up.

Grandad We can't go without saying goodbye to him!

Rodney No, alright we'll say goodbye then we'll get on our way.

Pauline enters carrying a tray containing a large fried breakfast, pot of tea, etc.

Rodney Is Del up yet?

Pauline No he's still in bed. He needs his sleep, he had a bad night.

Rodney Yeah, didn't sound too bad from where I was . . . I'll go and wake him up.

Pauline I'll wake him Rodney! I don't want you going in that room.

Rodney That's my Mum's room!

Pauline It used to be your Mum's room Rodney but it's mine now and I don't want to see you in there. Is that understood?

Rodney *(Giving Nazi salute)* Jawohl mein Oppengruppenfuhrer!

Pauline Act your age Rodney . . . *(Exits)*

The Second Time Around

Rodney Why don't you bike it you old bag! You know why she don't want us in there don't you? Probably filled up with sexual torture devices. I bet poor Del's in there now, bound and gagged, wearing a rubber mask, a loincloth and being threatened with French lessons.

Grandad Maybe that's why he's been looking a bit seedy lately!

Rodney Yeah and it's hardly through lack of food is it. I mean, look, there are Third World nations who'd give up their mineral rights for what's on that plate. I wonder what happened to his fried slice.

Grandad Perhaps he didn't want it. His stomach's been a bit dicky hasn't it.

Rodney That's true . . . *(The phone rings and Rodney answers)* Hello Trigger . . . Yeah, hang on I'll get him, Pauline, untie Del will you he's wanted!

Del enters wearing silk pyjamas and a dressing gown. He looks totally exhausted.

Del I'm up, I'm up . . . Hey what do you mean untie Del anyway?

Rodney Nothing.

Del Who is it?

Rodney It's Trigger.

Del Trigger? Oh, hello Trigger, what do you want? No, no, no, you didn't disturb me, I had to get up anyway, I was wanted on the phone!

Pauline enters

Pauline Del –

Del Hang on a minute will you Trigger? *(To Rodney as he clicks his heels together)* Cut it out.

Pauline I'm just popping down to the jewellers to put a deposit on that ring I saw.

Del Alright.

Rodney Another one? You've been engaged five times, married twice, you must have more rings than Bravingtons.

Pauline Just shut it Rodney!

Rodney I mean what is it with you, eh? Are you trying to corner the world's gold market or have you just got a thing about wedding cakes?

Del I'll bang you one in a minute, leave her alone will you!

Pauline Don't forget you've got to arrange a medical for your life insurance. I'll see you down the estate agents. We can go on to the bank from there.

Del Alright darling, yeah.

Rodney Sieg Heil!

Pauline exits

Del Cut it out, what you been doing sniffing that glue again have you? Cor dear – *(On phone)* Hello, sorry about that Trigger, yeah, no just

Rodney having one of his fits . . . Anyway what d'you want to phone me about? What do you mean it's a delicate subject? No, I know you're my mate! No, I won't say that you're interfering! I promise I won't tell you to mind your own business. Just say what you want to say will you . . . Yeah . . . Oh did I? Did you? Did he? Well listen Trigger, why don't you mind your own bloody business, eh? Who do you think you are interferring? Look, you just keep your nose out of it, alright pal?

Rodney How's Trigger keeping?

Del D'you know what he had the audacity to say, he phoned me up to say he heard last night that the police had investigated Bobby Finch's death. Apparently he died of . . . food poisoning!

Rodney Food poisoning! Oh . . .

Grandad Your breakfast's getting cold Del Boy!

Del Yeah, yeah, thanks Grandad. Do you know I think I'm putting on a bit of weight. I think I'll – I think I'll go on a diet.

Rodney Get off, there's no calories in weed-killer!

Del You make me die you do! I suppose you think that Pauline's gone – gone window shopping at Rentokill. Well I'm going down to make arrangements for my medical, I'll see you two later.

Rodney No you won't Del. Because me and Grandad have had it up to here. We're getting out!

Del Eh? What d'you mean you're leaving? No – leave it out Rodney, what you do for money?

Rodney We'll get by. We're thinking of forming a partnership!

Del A partnership! A partnership, you and Grandad? Gawd leave it out Rodney, what have you been doing, sitting on your brains again? You must have noticed at some time or another that he doesn't move. You know – he made the front page of the *Lancet* don't you as being the only living man in history to be treated for rigor mortis . . . Where you going to go anyway?

Rodney Auntie Rose's in Clacton.

Del Auntie Rose's in Clacton?

Rodney Yeah. Grandad says we can go there anytime.

Del Oh did he! Oh did he. Well you'd better go there now then hadn't you, eh? Go on. The pair of you, get on your bike. Go on before Pauline comes back with – with me Deadly Nightshade. *(Grandad exits)* Rodney – no – come on you don't believe all that rubbish about food poisoning do you?

Rodney Of course not, eat your mushrooms

41

Del. *(Exits)*

Del Rodney.

Rodney *(Out of view)* We're not coming back Del.

Del No, hang about, I'm coming with you.

SMALL COTTAGE AT SEASIDE RESORT. DAY.

The three-wheeled van pulls up outside a small cottage

Del Come on Rodney, you bring them suitcases. Grandpa, you carry the light stuff. Okay! *(Auntie Rose opens the door)* Surprise, surprise, hello Auntie, I bet you're surprised to see us, eh love? Come on, come on. Bring that in you two.

AUNTIE ROSE'S COTTAGE. DAY.

They all enter the room.

Del Oh yes, very nice. Here we are. Here, Grandad, change the channels over will you, there's racing on half past two.

INT. NIGHT. AUNTIE'S COTTAGE.

Grandad is watching TV. Del and Rodney are finishing a meal.

Rodney So what d'you put in that note to Pauline then?

Del I just put 'My dearest darling Pauline. The engagement's off, the wedding's off and, as you can gather from this letter, I'm off! I'll give you five days to clear out of the flat and do not ever come back . . . you money-grabbing old murderess. All my love Del Boy!' And then lots of kisses. I didn't – I didn't put it quite as nicely as that but that was the gist of the idea, yeah.

Rodney God knows what we'll go back to! She'll most probably smash that flat to pieces!

Auntie enters.

Auntie Have you had enough?

Del That was handsome – handsome well it was, Champs Elysees as the French say. *(He peels a few fivers from a wad of fivers and hands it to her)* Now listen Auntie, we're going to be here for about five days so what I want you to do is, I want you to take this money here like that, put that in yer pinny, because I don't want you spending your own money on us. Alright?

Auntie Well that's very nice of you! Do you mind if I ask you something?

Del Well of course not, manière d'être. Fire away.

Auntie Who are you?

Del Who – who are we?

Rodney You mean we've been in your house for five hours, had all your shepherd's pie and had a bath each and you don't know who we are?

Auntie Well I didn't like to ask you because you seem to know me!

Del We're Joannie's boys aren't we. *(Indicating Grandad)* Well, I mean, he isn't no – no. You remember Joannie, my mum, married Reg Trotter! You were at the wedding!

Auntie I don't remember you!

Del No, no, no, of course you wouldn't remember me, not at me mum's wedding. I was only a babe in arms.

Grandad You said come down anytime!

Auntie When was this then?

Grandad 1947!

Rodney So here we are!

Del You must – you must remember the wedding! It was at that big church – you know Our Lady the Divine Rosemary, Peckham.

Auntie Peckham . . . I've never been to Peckham in my life! Funny you should mention it though because the lady what owned this cottage before me, she came from Peckham.

Del *(To Rodney)* Auntie Rose has moved!

Rodney Well who's this then?

Del Gawd knows!

Auntie Joannie! Joannie Hollins? Married a Jamaican fella?

Del and Rodney Yeah.

Auntie Yeah but you don't look very

Rodney We're adopted!

Auntie Oh, would you like some apple pie?

Del That would be smashing Auntie, thank you.

THE TROTTERS' FLAT.

The front door opens and Del pops his head around it cautiously. He, Rodney and Grandad enter.

Del Sssh, come in. Come on, come in here. Listen, be alert! Pauline could come rushing out of any of those rooms in there brandishing her mother-of-pearl handles flick knives! It'll be like Psycho in a tower block. Sssh, listen, I'll take the living room, Rodney you take the bedroom, Grandad you take the kitchen . . . Right and good luck!

THE LOUNGE. DAY.

Del creeps into the centre of the room. He realises Pauline is not there. The room is bright and tidy. Rodney enters, Del jumps.

Del Go on my son, go on, go on.

Rodney She's not in the bedrooms!

Del Ah? She done any damage?

Rodney No, all the beds are neatly made, she's even been round with the hoover!

Grandad enters. Both Del and Rodney jump.

The Second Time Around

Grandad She's not in the kitchen! It ain't 'arf clean and tidy out there!

Del What's her game then, eh? What is her game? There's no-way that that – that Pauline would leave this flat without doing something really nasty to me! No, no, don't be daft. Where would she get a bomb from, eh?

Rodney Eh there's a letter here! It's addressed to 'That no-good lying two-faced creepo'.

Del Oh, that'll be for me Rodney! Let's have a look, see what she's got to say for herself then, eh? Right, here we are. Oh well now that's more like the Pauline that I know and loved! Oh dear look at the – look at the language here. You'd think an ex-air hostess would know how to spell better than that look at that, eh?

Rodney *(Reading some of the letter)* Is that true?

Del No, get off!

Rodney Del – did Pauline really mean that much to you?

Del No, no, not really. No, somehow it wasn't quite the same. Sometimes I think I'm not really cut out for this falling in love lark.

Rodney I've got a confession to make Del. You know that phone call from Trigger, the one about the police investigations into food poisoning, well it was a wind-up! Me and Grandad put him up to it . . . We did it for you Del.

Del You put him up to it?

Grandad It was nothing to do with me Del, I only suggested it!

Rodney Yeah, he only suggested it! We was only thinking of you Del.

Del You was only thinking of me! You couple of . . . rascals! *(Laughing)* What am I going to do with you two, eh? What am I going to do with you?

Rodney Got you out of schtuck didn't it!

Grandad Yeah, we're alright on our own – we don't need no birds.

Del No, no, not if you say so Grandad . . . Here – go on – go on, put the kettle on, eh? Look at this girl the way she spells, look at that.

Rodney That's, that's PTO 'please turn over'.

Del I know that, I know what please turn over means, don't I, PTO, I'm not illiterate an' all that.

Grandad Here, there's someone on the phone, it's Tim!

Del Tim who?

Grandad Tim, the talking clock.

Del Here. Oh the cow! She only phoned the talking clock before she left! And this is – Gordon Bennett this is dated four days ago!

Rodney I don't want to worry you Del but this Tim's got a funny accent!

Del She only phoned the talking clock in America that's all.

Grandad You mean we're connected to America? It's amazing innit! Hallo.

Rodney and Del *(Shouting)* Hang it up!

•**SHE WHO DARES**, Good–looking, man of the world, 36, own teeth, sensitive and managing director of an international importing–exporting business. Into culture, steak meals, mutton tikkas, a drop of the old vin ordinaire, objet darts, and evenings out. Seeks refined, decent sort with little bit of the old bon viveur for friendship, laughs and, who knows, a bit of humpty-dumpty and possibly a sincere, lasting relationship if you're lucky. London. P.O Box 666.

EXOTIC intelligent brun WLTM tall, sol traditional Gen 37–48. P.O Box •**IS YOUR H** **READ**, reddish golden? Gradua 28–42, over 5'9' rich and famou would love to Please write!

A Slow Bus to Chingford

INT. TROTTERS' LOUNGE. NIGHT.

The lights are low. Rodney is seated on the settee with Janice. The record player is playing.

Rodney You see, I mean, to me Janice, art, you know – art as . . . an art, must by its very nature be self-indulgent, right. I mean as I said to, er, David Hockney once, 'The inherent element in all artistic projects should not be one of contemporary mass appeal but rather one of personal symbolism.' Don't you agree Janice?

Janice I dunno Rodney.

Rodney Oh well, um, you know that's why I like talking to you, you're one of the few people who seems to understand me.

Janice My brother Don paints you know.

Rodney Really?

Janice Yeah, for the council.

Rodney No, that is cosmic Janice. No really – no that is cosmic that. That's probably why we have the same appreciation and understanding of true art. I mean, we have an affinity, an aesthetic bond, we are kindred spirits, Janice, seekers of beauty in a broken ugly world. Janice?

Janice Yes Rodney.

Rodney Get yer bra off.

Janice I can't.

Rodney Well of course you can, you must live and be free!

Janice I can't Rodney, I'm not wearing one!

Rodney Oh, well.

He is about to move in for the kill when Del enters.

Del It ain't half dark in here innit. *(Switches light on)* Oh put him down Janice, put him down, you don't know where he's been . . . Oh well, what we got going on here. Oh I'll have a drop of that – thanks. Here, look, we don't want all this rubbish on do we, eh? *(Turns record player off)* That's better. Oi Janice, mind his bruises won't you.

Janice What bruises?

Del He's covered in 'em, it's where the girls keep on pushing him away with 10ft barge poles. Oh dear, oh dear, that's better.

Rodney You're in are you Del?

Del Yes, yes, I'm in Rodders. Hope you've been behaving yourself, remember what I told you, not to do it on your own doorstep?

Rodney We've just been sitting here discussing art that's all.

Janice D'you like art Del?

Rodney Oh yeah, Del used to be cultural adviser to the Chelsea Shed!

Del Yes, I like art Janice. I like art, I'm a Renaissance man meself. You know, I like them picture where the eyes follow you round the room.

Rodney Last week, down the pie and eel shop, Del shook the international art world to its very foundations by saying, quite openly, that Michaelangelo was a wally-brain.

Del Well he was a wally-brain weren't he? It took him 12 years to paint one ceiling. That wouldn't do your brother Donald any good would it Janice, eh?

Janice Well he's on bonus.

Rodney I do not believe this. I'm gonna wake up in a minute!

Del Here, look, I'll tell you another thing while we're about it an' all. You know some of these artists you know, they're a bit sick if you ask me.

Rodney What are you on about now?

Del moves over to the sideboard upon which stand about 15 statuettes of the Venus de Milo.

Del Well look, take a look at this right. Now this is a statuette of the world-famous Venus de Milo, right? Now who but the sick of mind would do a sculpture of a disabled person? Am I right Janice?

Janice It's a bit sick innit!

Del There you are.

Rodney It weren't like that originally!

Del No, no, no, this is the product of a twisted imagination this Rodney. Yeah here, talking of twisted imaginations are you still looking for a job?

Rodney What in this country?

Janice There's three million unemployed, what chance has Rodney got?

Del Well, with his big brother looking after him he's go every chance in the world. Now take one of your purple hearts Rodney because I've got a surprise for you. I have managed to secure you for a position with a newly formed security company! Now they did want a man with previous experience and, as your last job was a milk monitor, I did have a bit of trouble persuading them but, however, I have managed to swing it for you.

Rodney Are you putting me up Del?

Del No, definitely, I've got a job for you Rodney!

Rodney Hey that's great Del!

Del Yeah, it's alright, you'll start off as a trainee NSO.

Rodney No.

Del Oh yes and who knows my son you know – you know, use your old filbert, keep your nose clean, a couple of years' time you could you could end up as a, well – I don't know – a senior NSO.

Rodney Oh I will Del, I won't let you down son.

Janice What's an NSO.?

Rodney Oh don't be gauche Janice. What's an NSO?

Del They don't know they're born some of them do they?

Rodney That's right! Tell her what an NSO is Del.

Del An NSO Janice is a Nocturnal Security Officer.

Rodney Yeah see it's a nocturnal security officer. That don't 'arf sound like a nightwatch-man Del!

Del It's nothing like a nightwatchman! I mean yeah, yeah, you will have to work at night.

Rodney And will some of my duties include 'watching'?

Del No they won't, no I mean all you'll have to do is, you'll just have to – you know, you – you just have to well . . . keep an eye out.

Rodney What is the name of this recently formed security company then?

Del Oh well, you wouldn't have heard of 'em.

Rodney Try me Del. Come on, let's have it.

Del It's called . . . Trotter Watch!

Rodney Trotter Watch, that's you innit? I'm working for you, ain't I?

Del Yeah, you see the way I see it Rodney is that crime is a growth industry so I'm getting in while the going's good. It's a nice regular job – got a uniform – good wages.

Rodney How good?

Del We'll talk about that later. First of all let us try on your uniform eh?

Del produces a blue serge jacket from a paper bag. The jacket is in fact a traffic warden's jacket. On the lapels are the initials 'TW'

Yeah come on, slip into. There it is. Oh look at that, colour suits you don't it, eh? Yes look at that fit, oh yeah, déjà vu, it's like made to measure innit?

Janice Yeah for someone else!

Del Oh well the sleeves and that – well he'll grow into them. Don't worry about that, hey,

let's have a look – that's it.

Rodney *(Indicating lapels)* TW.

Del That's right, stands for Trotter Watch.

Rodney Could also stand for Traffic Warden though.

Del Traffic well – yes it could, yeah traffic warden yeah.

Rodney This is a traffic warden's uniform innit?

Del It is not a traffic warden's uniform!

Rodney You've got me done up as a bloody traffic warden!

Del Look it is once and for all not a traffic warden's uniform! Now just trust me will you. . . . Put your cap on. *(He puts the cap on Rodney's head. It is blue serge with a yellow band round it.)* Well?

Rodney I look like a traffic warden. I look like a traffic warden who hasn't been well!

Del No you don't, you look stunning Rodders. Oh yeah, look at that, you're emitting authority all over the place.

Rodney I'm not doing it Del. I don't want the job.

Del Oh no, come on Rodney, you've got to do it, you can't let me down, I gave them your word.

Rodney Gave who my word?

Del The people down at the Tyler Street bus and coach garage. That's where you're gonna be based

Rodney No I'm definitely not doing it Del.

Del Oh alright, yeah okay. Well of course if you're scared! Allemagne dix points, you could admit it, come on, Janice'll understand if yer bottle has gone.

Rodney Me scared? You must be joking!

Del Ah, that's the spirit, now I want you down there tomorrow night nine o'clock, I'm a stickler for punctuality right. Right then, I'm going to bed.

Rodney Sorry Janice –

Del By the way, your bondage robes there're in the garage – alright? And Grandad has washed your whip and he's put it in the airing cupboard. I don't think it's shrunk. Well I'll leave you two love birds alone. And shall I just say 'Buenos Aires'. *(Exits)*

Rodney Janice he was only – you rotten git Del!

INT. NIGHT. THE COACH GARAGE.

It is a vast, dark, echoing cavern of a buidling. Del, all dressed up to the nines ready for a night out, and Rodney, now in the full uniform but still wearing plimsolls, walk from the office out into the centre of the garage.

Del Well I'll leave it in your capable hands then

A Slow Bus to Chingford

Rodders.

Rodney Yeah cheers Del . . . you realise this job's gonna mess up my love-life don't you!

Del Yeah, that's why I'm giving you every second Sunday off, ain't I?

Rodney Yeah but Janice is hardly gonna be happy with that is she? I mean while I'm down here at nights she could be going out with someone else.

Del Now look don't worry about that. What d'you think I'm all dressed up for like this, eh? I'm taking Janice out for a meal.

Rodney You're taking Janice out??

Del Of course I am, for your sake, otherwise she might be going out with someone else!

Rodney Yeah, yeah cheers Del. But if she's . . .

Del Why are you wearing plimsoles?

Rodney What?

Del I said, why are you wearing plimsoles, don't you think they mar the overall symmetry of the uniform somewhat?

Rodney I can run faster in these . . .

Del You what?

Rodney I mean give chase you know . . . pursue and detain sort of!

Del No, nothing happens round here. It's as quiet as a grave. Well I'll see you in the morning then Rodders, take care now! *(He exits)*

Rodney Yeah, don't worry about me Del, I'll be alright.

Rodney hears the metal gates clang shut. He surveys the garage and begins whistling the tune to Oh Susannah. He hears the last two notes echo back. He whistles again and once more the last two notes echo back. He whistles the next line confidently and smiles to himself. But then he hears another whistle. Rodney, petrified, looks left and right then sprints like an Olympic champion.

Del is at the gates of the coach depot laughing victoriously.

INT. DAY. THE TROTTERS' LOUNGE.

Del hands Grandad a cup of tea.

Del Ah, here you are Grandad, there you go. Look at that. Look at that, eh? It's beautiful innit? Beautiful. It's gonna earn our fortunes this is Grandad! *(Shouting)* Come on Rodney it's ten to nine.

Grandad I used to be a security officer you know, before the war.

Del Blimey, do you mean to say that somebody actually trusted you with their property? It's like – like trusting a piranha fish with yer finger –

or worse.

Grandad Oh yeah, it was a big warehouse over Kilburn way, stocked everything from bedroom suites to kiddies' toys. Well, there was this fella used to work there, he used to arrive every morning in a big Wolseley car, he wore a camel-hair overcoat, kid gloves and he always carried a brand-new leather attaché case and he smoked expensive cigars. Well, call it intuition if you like, but I was suspicious of him.

Del Yeah, why?

Grandad Well he was only a sweeper-up!

Del Cor, how do you do it Holmes?

Grandad Anyhow, one night as he was leaving I stopped him and I searched his attaché case. It was empty. Still, unperturbed by this minor hiccup in my investigation, I stopped him and searched his attaché case every night for a whole year. Then he left.

Del I wonder why?

Grandad I don't remember. I think he claimed someone was victimising him. No unions in them days see.

Del No, well this is it – innit, eh?

Grandad Anyway, a couple of weeks after he left the auditors come. D'you know what they discovered? We was missing 348 attaché cases!

Del What you mean you had been searching stolen gear?

Grandad Yeah and I got done for it. Finger-prints. There's a moral to that story Del Boy but for the life of me I can't find it.

Del I don't think I'm even gonna bother to look either Grandad. *(Rodney enters)* Hello the son of the bride of Dracula. Here he is.

Rodney What time is it?

Del The time is nearly nine o'clock.

Rodney Nine? I'm gonna be late if I don't get a move on.

Del No, no, it's alright. There's no hurry – no – no, go on, sit down. Take it easy, that's it, go on. Let me get you a cup of tea, alright?

Rodney Oh yeah.

Del Here you go then.

Rodney Are you still taking my part with Janice?

Del Yes, don't worry, I won't let you down.

Rodney Oh cheers Del . . . How am I doing?

Del Very well, very well. Yes one more steak meal could crack it.

Rodney Yeah? I haven't done this well with a girl for a long time.

Grandad You're like me Rodney, I never ever found it easy to get girlfriends. *(Slurps his tea from the saucer)*

Del I wonder why.

Rodney Here it's still light out . . . It's broad daylight!

Del Yeah, of course, it would be wouldn't it, nine o'clock in the morning, what do you expect?

Rodney Nine o'clock in the morning?? I thought it would be nine at night. I've only been in bed 20 minutes! What d'you wake me for?

Del Sit down. Sit down. It's alright, alright, don't exaggerate, 20 minutes. Listen, I want to discuss something very important with you see.

Rodney What could be that important, eh? I haven't got Janice into trouble, have we?

Del Don't be silly, least I hope not. I want to talk to you see. No, listen now, this night security job of yours is merely a tiny part of my immaculate scheme.

Rodney What immaculate scheme?

Del The Tourist Trade Rodney. The Tourist Trade. Did you realise that over 2,000 are pouring into London every day? And I happen to know, despite the fact that tourism has never been so high, the coach party trade is falling off. Now, why you may ask, is that Del? Well, since you ask, I will tell you Rodney. The reason is yer average tourist he gets fed up, don't he, of seeing the old places. Like the Houses of Parliament, Buck House, the National Gallery, er, you know. Once you've seen one Rubens, you've seen them all. Now this is where a dynamic person like me steps in. *(Rodney is dropping off to sleep)* Wake up while your brother's being dynamic!

Rodney Sorry, go on.

Del Yeah right, you see out there Rodney, out there is a new vibrant exciting London waiting to be discovered.

Rodney Is there?

Del Yeah of course there is. Ethnic London.

Rodney Ethnic London?

Del Yeah, yes, you know all those romantic places that you've heard about in fairy tales. You know the Lee Valley Viaduct, the glow of Lower Edmonton at dusk, the excitement of a walk about in Croydon, yeah, look what I've had printed. *(Shows Rodney one of the leaflets. It reads: 'Trotter's Ethnic Tours.')*

Rodney Oh I don't believe this. Trotter's Ethnic Tours. What's all this squiggly stuff and the Chinese?

Del The squiggly stuff – the squiggly – that is Arabic and the Chinese is Japanese. It's a well-known fact that 90 per cent of all foreign tourists come from abroad, so we've got to speak the lingo, ain't we?

Rodney We?

Del French, I like it. Already you're picking up the lingo. It's what I call enthusiasm Rodney.

Rodney I weren't speaking in French Del, I meant what do you mean 'we'?

Del We, us – you know, us – here you know – 'cos it's a family enterprise innit. Grandad, he'll sell the programmes, I shall be the courier and you, Rodney, you have got the best job of all 'cos you will earn a wage, hold tight everybody Rodney's coming, eh? It'll be another wage Rodney.

Rodney I've already got a wage Del.

Del Yeah but you can't afford to live on what I pay you, can you!

Rodney I don't know Del, how much you paying me?

Del Well not a lot, not a lot. You see I can't afford to. See I, well, I done a deal with the bus garage – what happened was I provided them with a nightwatchm . . . a nocturnal security operative, see, and they provided me with an open-topped bus. That saves the exchange of any cash. You know, stops any paperwork and

Rodney And income tax?

Del Income tax yeah. Eh? Well, come on, what about it Rodney, a lot of work and effort's gone into this enterprise. I mean, Grandad, he was up town this morning at the crack of dawn distributing all those leaflets to every hotel, boarding house and hostel he could find. Grandad, he believes in this scheme, don't you Grandad?

Grandad Ethnic tours, it's the most stupidest thing I've ever heard of.

Del *(To Rodney)* See.

Rodney Del you can't expect me to work all night then, in the morning, drive a bus load of tourists round ethnic London? I've got to sleep Del. My whole body is crying out for sleep.

Del Yeah, yeah, I'll tell you what I'll do, I'll get you some assistance at the garage then you can have a kip, I'll get you, er, I'll get you an ex-police dog.

Rodney An ex-police dog?

Del Yeah, now how do you fancy some breakfast?

Rodney I wouldn't say no.

Del Good, great, come on then, off you go, there you go – in there. *(He leads Rodney into the kitchen)* While you're in there make me a bacon sandwich, alright?

Grandad Where are you gonna get an ex-police dog from?

Del I'll get him – I'll get him Nero.

Grandad Who's Nero?

A Slow Bus to Chingford

Del Nero, Janice's corgi!

DAY. LONDON BACK STREET.

The coach is parked. The door to it is open and leaning against the side is a hand-painted sign that reads: 'Trotter's Ethnic Tours. Departure Point.' Del appears at the entrance and looks up and down the street. Inside the coach Rodney is laid out on a seat fast asleep.

Del We clearly stated on our leaflets nine o'clock was departure time. Here we are 11.30, no sign of 'em!

Grandad I've told you before no one will turn up.

Del Yes they will, soon as the word about it spreads, they'll be here in droves. No the only thing that worries me is, is a 59-seater bus gonna be big enough? Perhaps we should have had two, you know maybe three.

Grandad A tandem would be too big.

Del Leave it out will you.

Grandad I'll bet not one single tourist arrives.

Del I'll bet you, 50 quid they do.

Grandad Right, 50 quid, you're on.

Del Right then.

Grandad Alright.

Del Right.

Grandad Right.

Del Right.

Grandad Right.

Rodney Shut up you two will yer. I didn't get a wink of sleep last night taking that rotten dog for walkies . . . and what 'ave yer. That's a funny kind of police dog that Del, it saw a cat and run a mile.

Del Ah well, cats aren't Nero's strong point. But show him a burglar and it becomes a tower of strength.

Rodney Where's all these tourists then? I thought we'd be having an ethnic look round Chingford by now.

Del Don't worry, they'll be here.

Grandad Huh.

Del Shut up you . . .

Rodney How much you charging them for this tour then?

Del 17 quid each.

Rodney £17 for a walk-about in Croydon?

Del Well that includes lunch don't it. Traditional doner kebab, something like that.

Rodney A doner kebab. For 17 nicker I'd want Donna Summer.

Del You would wouldn't you, you tight wad. No, these tourists, they don't mind splashing out, providing they're getting value for money.

(Produces a couple of the Venus de Milos from a cardboard box) Now look at that, they'll snap these souvenirs of Olde London up they will. That's a snip that is at a fiver a go, almost alabaster, you know.

Rodney You're going to sell 'em models of a Roman statue now housed in the Louvre gallery Paris for souvenirs of Olde London? It's the Venus de Milo, Del.

Del No, that is Boadicea that is innit?

Rodney Boadicea rode round in a chariot with big swords sticking out the wheels.

Del Alright, so she fell off her chariot.

Rodney You're just trying to rip 'em off, aren't you!

Del Au contraire Rodney, au contraire. No, I don't want to leave them potless. I want them to have some money in their pockets, at least enough for us to have a tip.

Rodney As a courier what do you actually know about these obscure places you intend to drag 'em to?

Del Know? Nothing, which means twice as much as they know. Don't worry, I shall bluff 'em Rodney. I shall use the old spiel. If there're questions that I find a bit dodgy to answer, I shall just say I can't understand their English. Don't worry, it'll be a doddle. I mean, today I shall take 'em down Shoreditch and show 'em the house where Sherlock Holmes was born.

Rodney Sherlock Holmes was fictional.

Del Was he? Oh well, I'll just say his house was blown up during the war. Tomorrow I shall take them to the summit of Mount Pleasant.

Grandad The summit of Mount Pleasant!

Del What's the matter with you Grandad, can't you stand heights or something.

Grandad Mount Pleasant hasn't got a summit. All it's got is a big post office sorting depot.

Del Well that's ethnic innit, eh? We can give 'em a guided tour of the depot, you know show 'em the workers getting the most from our post. I should stay awake if I was you. They'll be here in their hundreds in a minute.

NIGHT. LONDON BACK STREET/COACH.

The voices are heard out of view.

Del I'll take 'em over to North London, you know, show 'em where Jack the Ripper was buried.

Rodney Nobody knows where Jack the Ripper was buried.

Rodney Shall we give 'em another five minutes then go Del?

Del Yeah, alright. Take the bus back to the

garage then you can begin your night shift, alright? I want you back first thing in the morning though. And don't forget to take Nero out so he can do his business, alright?

DAY. LONDON BACK STREET/COACH.

Grandad approaches the coach carrying a tray containing drinks and a packet of crisps. He enters the coach and hands the drinks around.

Grandad A pint of lager Rodney, they'd sold right out of Pina Coladas Del, so I got you a Mackeson instead.

Del Oh that's good thinking yes, thank you Grandad.

Rodney What you going to do if the tourists start asking about the history of places. I mean, say one of them wants to know how the Elephant and Castle got its name?

Del Well I'll just say . . . er, once upon a time Richard the Lionheart or Coeur de Lion as the French used to call him – which he did not like one little bit – see where a little bit of intimate knowledge goes a long way in impressing people. Well, I'll say that he had a castle situated roughly near the roundabout.

Rodney And what about the 'elephant' bit?

Del I'll say er, Hannibal and his elephants lay siege to the castle and Bob's yer uncle.

Rodney But Hannibal crossed the Alps.

Del I know, on his way to the castles, and the natives who had never seen an elephant, they were sorely afraid. And that is how it became known in that area as the Elephant and Castle.

Grandad If they'd never seen an elephant before how did they know it was an elephant?

Del For Gawd sake Grandad, an elephant's a bloody elephant, innit? I mean you can't odds that! I mean, you can't look at an elephant and say, I know we'll call this place the Cow and Castle, you can't do that can you?

Rodney But you're not telling them the truth are you?

Del The truth? The truth, you're so naive, Rodders. The truth is only relative to what you can earn from a lie! Einstein.

Grandad I'll tell you one truth that you won't earn a brass farthing out of. No one's gonna turn up.

Del *(Desperate)* They will turn up. They've got to . . . This time next year we'll be millionaires.

Grandad You said that this time last year!

Del You're eating, ain't yer? No. I wanted to do this for years Rodney, I always thought if we could make a success of it, that eventually we

would go legit. You know, we would register the name Trotters Independent Traders as a proper McCoy company. I have this dream where you and I own this skyscraper office block on the South Bank. And we're standing on the balcony in a penthouse suite with a couple of sorts, Gabrielle, Bianca, bra-less but with class – here did you know your Janice doesn't wear a bra.

Rodney Yeah, I know.

Del Oh you know. Anyway we're in our penthouse full of rubber plants and pine tongue and groove – and we're sipping red drinks. And above us on top of the skyscraper in 50ft neon lettering are the initials of Trotters Independent Traders! Good innit, eh?

Rodney Triffic Del.

Del They've got to come. My dream starts the way every success starts, with a big rip-off.

Rodney Del. Grandad's right, no one's gonna turn up.

Del Yes they will, you wait and see.

Rodney I think that dream of yours contains a subliminal message.

Del Yeah, you what?

Rodney A sort of subconscious truth. You see this skyscraper belonging to Trotters Independent Traders right?

Del Yeah!

Rodney And on the roof is the company's initials and you're standing on the penthouse balcony?

Del Yeah!

Rodney Well don't you see what the dream's trying to tell you? As you're standing on that balcony with your red drink – just above your head, in 50ft-high neon lettering, is the word 'Tit'.

Del Come on, let's call it a day.

Grandad You owe me 50 quid on that bet!

Del Eh? Alright you old pessimist!

Del appears at the coach door. He has one last longing look up the street.

Rodney *(Out of view)* What about our wages then Del?

Del picks up the sign which is leaning against the coach and carries it onto the vehicle.

Del Oh yeah, I meant to talk about that!

DAY. THE ESTATE. PARKING AREA.

The coach pulls in and stops. Rodney climbs down from the driver's door. Del, carrying the sign, joins him.

Del I thought that was gonna be the big one Rodney. I thought I was gonna become Freddie Laker of the highways.

A Slow Bus to Chingford

Rodney It was a nice try Del!

Del Yeah, I don't understand it though, I just don't understand it. Grandad distributed a thousand leaflets, a thousand. You'd have thought that one, just one punter might have been interested. Still, as dear old Mum used to say 'It's better to know you've lost than not to know you've won'. Dear old Mum, she used to say some bloody stupid things . . . *(Indicating the sign)* I'm gonna chuck this down the chute.

Grandad Well that weren't too bad was it Rodney? I've had two days away from the housework, a nice little drink and I've won meself a 50 quid bet. Very nice, very nice indeed . . . Where's Del Boy?

Rodney Oh he's just gone to chuck that sign down the dust chute.

Grandad The dust chute? Oh my Gawd!

Del comes away from the dust chute clutching hundreds of Trotter's Ethnic Tours leaflets.

Del Grandad! Come here, you senile old parasite.

Grandad It wasn't me Del, it was me brain!

Del It was your – I'll brain you if I catch up with you. Come here. Get him! Oi!

Del chases Grandad into the flats.

The Russians are Coming

DEMOLITION SITE. DAY.

In the foreground is a pile of bricks and rubble. No one is working on the site. It is desolation. The three-wheeled van rumbles across the site and pulls up close to the pile of bricks.

Del Well, this is it.

Rodney This is what?

Del This is what I bought this morning.

Rodney What?

Del This.

Rodney The land?

Del No you plonker. This pile of bricks, only cost me 100 nicker, nice one, eh?

Rodney Oh shrewd move Del, yeah, I mean people are panic-buying bricks nowadays ain't they . . . Who the hell's gonna buy a pile of old bricks off us?

Del Well, butcher or chemist. Who d'you think's going to buy the bricks, builders ain't they, eh. Over 200 per cent profit here and all in the readies. *(Although they are alone on the site, by nature Del pulls Rodney to one side and talks secretly to him)* Come here . . . They've just demolished a factory here that used to make prefabricated structures, right. Chalets, bungalows, greenhouses, you know, garden sheds, that sort of a thing. So I thought – using my noddle – that we'd make enough out of the bricks alone, *but* you never know what's underneath do you, eh? Decent lengths of timber, bits of metal, you know, few gross of them roofing tiles. Come and see what I found. *(He leads Rodney to the far side of the pile, removes some of the bricks to reveal a cardboard box containing about eight sheets of lead)* Get yer feelers on that.

Rodney *(Examining)* Here, that's lead Del, that's pure lead.

Del There's about another 30 boxes underneath. I estimate three ton altogether.

Rodney Three ton? What's that at today's prices? That's that's about a £1000 innit?

Del Am I brilliant or am I brilliant? Let's get some of it on the van, we can do it in three shifts, come on.

Rodney Is it ours Del?

Del Of course it's ours.

Rodney Legally Del?

Del Don't split hairs with me Rodney. Come on.

DAY. THE TROTTERS' LOUNGE.

Scattered around the room in small piles are the boxes from the site. Rodney is laid out on the settee reading a pamphlet. Grandad, sweating and exhausted, enters carrying another box. Del follows him in.

Grandad Oh that's the lot Del Boy. *(He goes to place the box on another pile)*

Del No, no, no, no, Grandad not there. No, no, we've got three tons of it here. You see you've got to spread it out over a wide area, otherwise we'll be having tea with Mrs Obooko downstairs! Right, I hope this humping and sweating is not disturbing you Royal Highness!

Rodney No, no, don't you mind me, carry on.

Del Oh thanks a . . . Here, look at this Grandad, you've been carrying this one upside down, this is the way. You are a lazy little bark. *(To Rodney)* And what's that you're reading, eh? It's another dirty book I suppose, is it? Honestly you've got a mind like a brown paper envelope. I'll have a look at that when you've finished.

Rodney It's some paperwork I found in one of them boxes . . . D'you know what we've got here?

Del Yeah, I know what we've got here. We've got three ton of lovely lead, that's what we've got here.

Rodney No, no, it's more than that . . . That factory was producing prefabricated structures right? Bungalows, garden sheds, that sort of stuff. Well, this is one of their experimental lines – it's a do-it-yourself nuclear fall-out shelter!

Del Nuclear fall-out shelter, you are a wally.

Rodney *(Offended)* No, it is. Honest. Look, here's the brochure. Here's the plans shows you how to build it.

Del He's right an' all. This is a nuclear fall-out shelter. This is probably worth more than we thought.

Rodney You can't sell it.

Del You don't want to put money on it do you? What do you suggest we do with it? Build it?

Rodney Yeah!

Del Leave it out Rodney!

Rodney Do you realise how close we came to World War Three over Cuba, Vietnam, Afghanistan and Poland? I mean, it only takes one little rumble in the Middle East them missiles are gonna start flying! And what have we got,

eh, in this country to combat the might of the Soviet Union? Three jump-jets and a strongly worded letter to the Russian Ambassador!

Del No, no, no, you don't know what we've got up our sleeve, us Brits Rodney. Do you know Rodney that we've got a device that can track the movements of any Russian nuclear submarine? They can't keep track on ours.

Rodney We've only got one.

Del Have we?

Rodney Yeah I think so.

Del Well anyway, they don't know where it is . . . I sometimes wonder whether we do!

Rodney I bet your life we don't. You see this country is just not prepared for war, I mean, nobody knows what we're supposed to do in the event.

Del Yes, of course we do.

Rodney Alright then, what would you do if you heard the four-minute warning?

Del Well, what's it sound like the first?

Rodney Well, that's it, innit, no one knows. Maybe they're gonna ring church bells, or bang tom-toms or send every ice-cream van out in the country to play its jingle. Your guess is as good as mine innit? Do you realise the great powers have got underground salvos primed with enough nuclear weapons to destroy this planet 30 times over. I'm talking about neutron bombs, Del, multi-warheads – chemicals that attack your central nervous system, and leave you writhing in agony like a worm in bleach.

Del Bit like after a curry you mean? No, no, it's alright Rodney, don't worry, forget about it. Look we've got a £1000 here. Just think what we could do with £1000. Eat, drink and be merry . . .

Rodney For tomorrow we die!! Oh come on Del, this is a Godsend. Look if we build this thing we're gonna be safe, ain't we. Everything's here, the inner walls, the outer walls, the air tube, the filter system, everything!! Oh come on Del. Oh sorry.

Del Alright soppy, just suppose now, just suppose, just suppose, that we do build this thing, right. Where we gonna put it?

Grandad Well, you always fancied a little weekend place. Why don't we find a spot in the New Forest?

Del And how are we gonna get from Peckham to the New Forest in four minutes, you old div?

Rodney Grandad's allotment? That's only a couple of miles up the road, we could do that in four minutes.

Del Yeah, on a Sunday, with a following wind, maybe.

Rodney Well let's give it a go, eh? We'll have a dummy run and time ourselves. I'll get the stopwatch *(Exits)*

Del What – what you, look, I mean, what is the point eh? Alright, so say you can do it in four minutes, what is it going to prove. Knowing them Russian rats they'll probably declare war in the middle of the rush hour.

DAY. THE ESTATE.

Del and Rodney rush out of the main doors and down towards the van.

Del Where's Grandad?

Rodney I don't know.

They rush back for Grandad and drag him to the van. Del opens the back door and bundles him in.

Del Grandad, come on, hurry up you stupid old git.

Rodney Never mind your fag, get in. Three minutes and counting.

Del Yes, alright Rodney.

Rodney The missiles are just going over Sweden!

Del They're bloody fast aren't they, they only left Siberia 20 seconds ago.

They jump in the van and it pulls away.

STRETCH OF ROAD AND T-JUNCTION.

The van is approaching a junction. Rodney has the map fully open and is obliterating Del's view of the road to his left.

Rodney Two minutes 15 seconds and counting Del. The missiles are over the sea and approaching Middlesbrough.

Del Yes, yes, alright Rodney.

Grandad Put yer foot down Del Boy!

Del I can't Grandad. Look, I'm going to the main road, ain't I?

The van pulls up at the T-junction.

Del What's it like your side Rodney?

Rodney Alright after this red one.

A red car passes. The van starts to pull out.

Rodney No!!

The van screeches to a halt. A second red car passes.

Del Bloody hell . . .

Rodney I meant *that* red one!

Del You tit Rodney.

DAY. LONG STRETCH OF ROAD.

The van roars past at top speed.

Rodney Come on Del, they're just going over Luton.

Del Sod Luton.

The Russians are Coming

Rodney One minute 35 and counting.
There is the sound of a police siren.
Del Oh Gordon Bennett.
The van pulls into the side and stops. The police car, siren still going, pulls in front. The driver (Eric) alights and starts to walk back to the van. The siren is still going. Eric stops and calls back to his young co-driver.
Eric Switch the . . . Wayne . . . the siren . . . switch it off!
The siren is switched off. Eric approaches the van
Eric He's young, enthusiastic . . . Well, how are you then Del Boy?
Del Not too bad Eric. How's yourself?
Eric Can't complain . . . How are you then Grandad?
Grandad Alright Eric boy.
Eric *(To Del)* Now what's all that about? 60 miles an hour in a built-up area. You just heard the four-minute warning or something . . .
Del Well as it happens, Eric . . .
Eric Where's yer tax disc? Fell off did it?
Del In the post.
Eric Well, why haven't you got a little sign on your windscreen saying 'Tax in Post'?
Rodney *(Who has alighted from the van)* We did have – it fell off.
Eric You been at those funny fags again, Rodney?
Rodney No I haven't.
Eric Good, 'cos Wayne here's looking for his first nick . . . Talking of that Del Boy, you might be able to help me. I'm on the look-out for some stolen summer-wear, short-sleeved shirts and blouses, men's and women's slacks, swimming trunks, bikinis.
Del You after promotion Eric?
Eric No, me and me wife are off to Corfu next month, gotta look the part ain't yer?
Del Well if I hear of anything I'll let you know.
Eric Good luck. I'll see you around. And oi, take it easy will you . . . *(Eric walks back to police car as the siren goes off briefly)* Stop playing with that siren will you Wayne, you'll end up breaking it!
Del Here, how we doing for time?
Rodney We died 45 seconds ago.
Del Terrific. We're never gonna do this run in four minutes.
Rodney Oh, it don't matter, it's not the end of the world is it.
Del I thought that's exactly what it was.
Rodney All we got to think about is a place nearer home.

Grandad I've been thinking.
Del Oh my God, you haven't got an aspirin you can give him have you Rodney?
Grandad No listen. I may have found us just the spot.

ROOF. DAY.

The air intake tube to the shelter against the grey background of the sky. Voices can be heard echoing from the tube.
Rodney Is that door shut tight Del?
Del Yes, don't worry Rodney, no radiation can get in here! Here, what's this pipe?

INT. THE SHELTER.

The shelter is lit by a couple of calor-gas lamps. The walls are made up entirely of the square sheets of lead. Scattered around the floor are camp beds, sleeping bags, etc.

In the centre is a beer crate with a bottle of scotch and glasses on it. Around the crate are three camp stools. In one corner is an Elsan-type toilet. Grandad is adjusting his portable TV which shows a very faded and fuzzy picture. Del and Rodney are kneeling on a bench by the air intake tube. Del is holding a hammer.
Rodney Oi, don't do that Del, it's fragile. Del, Del, don't do it. Del, this is our air-filter, our life line, our umbilical cord and one thing you must never do with an umbilical cord is bash it about with a hammer!
Del I see, so this is our only source of oxygen is it, eh? What happens if a pigeon decides to nest in the other end, we're all dead I suppose, are we?
Rodney Statistics prove that pigeons rarely nest in the middle of nuclear wars!
Del We're not in the middle of a nuclear war.
Rodney We're practising for one!
Del Yeah, well, do the bloody pigeons know that?
Rodney Look, a pigeon will not nest in our air tube . . . Have faith in me please.
Grandad How can you have faith in him, eh, Del Boy? I brings me telly in here then he finds out the signals can't get through the lead!
Rodney I've said I'm sorry ain't I Grandad. There's some pages missing out of this brochure, and you can't expect me to know everything can yer? Anyway, that's why we're having this weekend's practice isn't it, so we can iron out all the little wrinkles.
Del Yeah, well I'll tell you one thing we've got

to iron out. *(Indicating the toilet)* And that is this has got to be back on that building site first thing Monday morning otherwise them Paddies'll go mad. *(To Rodney)* You, you are a wally, you really are!

Rodney You don't have to stay here Del!

Del I do have to stay and I'll tell you why I have to stay here. I've got £1000 worth of lead tied up in this shelter and I'm not gonna leave it in your hands. Knowing you two, you'd probably lose it! Just think what I could do with a £1000, eh? Fly to America on Concorde. I could buy myself one of them flash Rollex watches. Have me adenoids out privately.

Rodney Yeah, but how many people can boast they have their own private nuclear fall-out shelter?

Del Yes, that's true, knowing our bloody luck there won't even be a bloody war . . . Here that's what we ought to do you know, we ought to drop a bomb on all them Russian cities, you see and then declare war on them. And what we say is that the declaration for war got held up in the post due to a communist-inspired strike at a sorting office.

Rodney Yeah, that's typical of a ruthless little mercenary like you innit?

Del What d'you mean ruthless mercenary? I'm not a ruthless mercenary. Who is it goes round at every Christmas making sure all the old people have got enough to eat and drink?

Rodney Yeah, and who was it, during the Brixton riots, drove down in the van selling paving stones to the rioters? I mean, what did you think they were going to do with them, eh? All run off home and start building patios.

Del Mine is not to reason why, mine is but to sell and buy! No, anyway. Anyway I know a lot of them youngsters down in Brixton and their trouble and frustration. Yes, you see, modern society has denied them their birthright of a war!

Rodney Oh I don't believe you! You saying war's our birthright?

Del Oh yes, yes it is. For century after century you see every generation of British youth has been guaranteed a decent war! Well that's sort of, you know, raw, 'Over the top chaps, you know, try that one for size Fritz' I mean that sort of courage is obsolete. Because the next war's gonna be fought by computer programmers . . . See, that's what's frustrating the modern youth! You can see them any day down the amusement arcade, you know, they're doing their national service on the space invaders. Yeah but that sort

of, of real war that I'm talking about, you know Errol Flynn leading the gallant 600 into the Valley of Death. John Mills marooned in a dinghy, it's Kenneth More refusing to let a little thing like no legs get him down. It's a glorious valiant war that!

Grandad Don't talk like a berk Del!

Del Do what?

Grandad What do you know about it anyway? The only war you've ever fought is the inch war!

Del Ah no, I've seen all the films ain't I.

Grandad Ah tomato sauce and stuntmen . . . I'm talking about the real thing. I remember when I was a little nipper and I saw the soldiers marching off to battle. Oh yes, it was a glorious sight alright!

Del Yeah I bet all them spears and chariots must have stirred the blood mustn't they?

Rodney Just hear him out will you!

Del Alright, alright.

Grandad My brother George was at Passchendaele. Nigh on half a million Allied troops died there, all for five miles of mud! I was at Kings Cross station when his regiment came home after the armistice. Most of them was carried off the train. I saw men with limbs missing, blind men – men who couldn't breathe properly 'cos their lungs had been shot to bits by mustard gas! While the nation celebrated they was hidden away in big grey buildings, far from the public gaze. I mean, courage like that could put you right off your victory dinner couldn't it? They promised us homes fit for heroes, they give us heroes fit for homes!

Rodney I'd, I'd never wear a British uniform – on principle!

Del What principle?

Rodney Well on the principle that the Russians might shoot at it!

Grandad The politicians, the politicians and the military men used to con you see. They had little lads, youngsters believing that their country really *did* need them! D'you know, they used to have little lads of 14 pretending they was 18 just so they could fight for their king and country!

Del What, and they accepted the little sprogs?

Grandad More often than not . . . My brother George lied about his age!

Rodney Pretended he was 18?

Grandad No, he *was* 18, he pretended he was 14, they saw through it though. I think it was the moustache.

Rodney Oh yeah 'cos 14-year-olds they don't . . .

Del Bloody 'ell.

The Russians are Coming

INT. THE SHELTER.

Grandad is watching the fuzzy picture on his portable TV. Del is at the mirror, cleaning his teeth. Rodney is checking the air-filter system. He starts to bang the tube with a hammer.

Del Oi, oi, what are you doing?

Rodney I think there's a pigeon trying to nest in our air tube. Think I've frightened it away, now don't worry! The battery's getting a bit low an' all.

Del Here, these batteries you've got here. How long do they last?

Rodney About 12 hours each!

Del 12 hours? Cor, we been 'ere 12 hours, only another 36 to go. Don't time fly when you're having fun . . . *(To Rodney)* Here, here Oppenheimer, listen if the bomb was to drop round here, how long would we have to stay inside this thing here?

Rodney Well, it depends upon the degree of the contamination in the air outside. 'Cos we're very vulnerable position here being close to the docks. But I would say roughly – give or take a week or two – about . . . two years!

Del/Grandad Two years??

Rodney Yeah, give or take a week or two!

Del If you think I'm staying in a lead-lined nissan hut with you and Grandad and a chemical bloody khazi you've got another thing coming.

Rodney Yeah, but if we leave the shelter within two years we'd die of radiation poisoning!

Del And if we stay inside the shelter for two years we'll die of bloody lead poisoning.

Grandad He's right Rodney. The rescue team will whip us straight round the nearest scrap metal yard!

Del Yeah, that's another point, that's a point. Listen, oi! These batteries that are supposed to purify the air right, they last 12 hours, right? Okay how many of them are we gonna need? Come on Einstein, you're the one with the GCE in Maths!

Rodney Well, it's two a day, seven days a week two sevens are 14.

Del See that Grandad – two sevens are 14. Just like that, no hesitation.

Rodney Shut up will yer! So that's 14 times 52 . . .

Grandad Twice!

Rodney I know! So that works out at about 1450-odd.

Del Well, that's not too bad, I thought we were gonna need a lot! What we're gonna need is 1450-odd heavy duty batteries, about five tons of canned food, 30,000 gallons of fresh drinking water, and a three and 'arf acre warehouse to store it all in!

Rodney Well I did say we'd have to iron out a few little wrinkles, didn't I?

Del Few little wrinkles? A few little wrinkles? We've got more wrinkles than a elephant's got in his bleedin' trunk! All in all, and taking everything in consideration Rodney, I think I would rather be outside and go instantly with the bomb!

Rodney Instantly eh? And what makes you so sure it'd be instant eh Del? Them bombs contain Strontium 90 not Nescafé! You see the bomb explodes about a mile above the city right, causing a radioactive rain to fall. Now this radiation then penetrates the pores of the skin causing violent sores and diseases.

Del Um, best not to wear anything decent then eh?

Rodney Will you be serious for one minute. Look, it's here once the radiation is in the blood stream it begins to attack your metabolism. You'll become subject to drastic biological changes, that's metamorphosis!

Grandad Oh yeah!

Rodney Yeah anyway, your shape and form will alter radically as the mutation takes effect!

Grandad Don't sound too promising do it Del Boy, I mean you have a job to get a suit off the peg now don't yer! *(He and Del laugh)*

Rodney Alright, alright, you can laugh, but I'm telling you, this city would be inhabited by roaming mobs of mutants! Vacant eyed sub-humans dragging their knuckles through the litter and debris that was once civilisation.

Del Sounds a bit like Stamford Bridge after a bad result . . . Look if this is true Rodney what the hell are we doing trying to survive?

Rodney Well, it's our duty ain' it, I mean when we step out of here we're gonna be intact, perfect. Yeah, well I mean you know, the human race will be looking to people like us to replenish the species, we'll be like two new Adams going forth to multiply.

Del Yeah! And you, you dirty little ram, will be out there multiplying quicker than a pocket calculator! I see it all now, I see it all now, he's practically praying for the end of civilisation just so he can get out there and put it about a bit! What time do you make it Rodney?

Rodney Ten past 12.

Del Oh yeah, I make it that too. C'mon then Grandad it's bedtime, come on.

Grandad Oh yes.

Rodney Well, as the saying goes, if my species

needs me I will not be found wanting.

Del Yeah, anyway that's one thing to look forward to innit Grandad, eh? You know, come the end of the war me and Rodney are gonna make a foursome with a couple of mutants! I'll have one with three lug 'oles and the eye underneath her arm, 'cos I don't fancy yours much!

Rodney It won't be like that!!!

Del You bet your sweet bippy it won't! It won't make any difference to you anyway, you go out with mutants in peacetime! I mean look at that thing you took out on Thursday! Cor, stroll on, I was so embarrassed I had to tell my mates you were taking it to market!

Rodney I did try and warn you it was a bit ragged!

Del Bit ragged! You liar! You said to me it looked like the one out of Abba!

Rodney Yes, I meant the one with the beard, anyway we won't be the only ones to survive the holocaust intact, will we? I mean I'm thinking of the various institutions – public schools, that sort of thing. I mean you bet your life *Roedean's* got a shelter. *(His face lights up)* Eh Del? A thousand nubile girls – in a shelter . . . in school uniform!

Del *(With a killing glare)* You sicko!

Rodney No, no, don't misunderstand me. I mean the school uniforms are of no importance whatsoever. I don't know why I mentioned them.

Del No, no, it's probably because you're a twisted perverted corrupted, warped little pervo!

Rodney Well, yeah, that might have something to do with it! It's in the line of duty Del! They're perfect specimens. They're intelligent.

Del Course they're intelligent, they're still at bloody school ain't they?

Rodney They're fit – all that hockey! You might fancy the headmistress!

Del Oh thank you very much.

Rodney Well, I think it's definitely worth bearing in mind. In an emergency.

Del Yeah alright, well, goodnight Rodney.

Rodney Goodnight Del.

Del Night Grandad.

Grandad Goodnight Del.

Rodney Night Grandad.

Grandad Goodnight Rodney.

Rodney Night John Boy.

Del Shut up.

Grandad War is hell!!

Del What?

Grandad War is hell! Alan Ladd said that.

Del Did he really? Go to sleep.

Grandad Or was it Audie Murphy?

Del I dunno, I'm tired!

Grandad It must have been one of 'em!

Del Well perhaps they both bloody said it! Now go to sleep will you.

Rodney No, that was Rock Hudson!

Del For crying out loud, will you two go to sleep. Rodney . . . Here Rodney don't keep yer eyes closed – I'm talking to you!

Rodney What?

Del I've just been thinking. Might not be a bad idea to survive the next war after all!

Rodney Why? You got something up yer sleeve Del?

Del No, no, just a little idea that's been running round me old brain box, that's all.

Grandad What's the point? All the animals will be dead. Won't be able to grow nothing 'cos all the earth'll be contaminated! Where we gonna get something to eat?

Del Bound to be a little Paki shop open somewhere! But we won't be the only ones to survive will we? I was just thinking about all them girls down at that Roedean School.

Rodney Aah.

Del No, no, no, no, nothing like that, nothing like that. I was just thinking you see, most of those girls down there, they are daughters of the noblesse!

Rodney The what Del?

Del The noblesse, the noblesse. It's French for nobility, ain't it eh?

Rodney Oh sorry – I was miles off.

Del Well you see, down there you don't know who's who, do you? I mean you could meet a scruffy 17-year-old in a sweaty hockey shirt and muddy plimsoles, and you could be talking to the 459th in line for the throne! But after the old Russians have dropped 20 nuclear bombs on us that scruffy 17-year-old could turn out to be first in line for the throne. So, you see, if I got on my bike, nip down there a bit sharpish like, did me Adams act – splash of Brut, you know, took her out for a steak meal – loads of charm – I could end up being the King! On the other hand a bit of mutation, a touch of Strontium 90, I could end up being the Queen. But either way, either way, see it wouldn't matter because the taxman wouldn't be able to get at me, would he, eh? Because I would be the head of State. And what with you out there multiplying all over the place, I shouldn't be short of a few subjects, should I, eh? *(They begin to laugh at the idea)* We, we could go for our holidays in Mustique.

Rodney Eh, eh.

Del What? What?

Rodney Grandad could be the Queen Mother!

58

The Russians are Coming

Del Yeah, we'll dye his hat pink . . . yeah, yeah. No even if that didn't happen and I can't honestly see how I could fail. You see if the entire civilisation was wiped out we'd all be equal wouldn't we, 'cos none of us would have nothing, right.

Rodney Right!

Del Except us Rodney!

Rodney Well what would we have Del?

Del A grands worth of lead eh . . . pretty shrewd, eh Rodney?

Rodney Yeah, that's a real mindbender Del, that!

Del No, no, we'll be alright. We'll survive Rodney, d'you know why? Because we're survivors that's why, yeah. When did the alarm bells start ringing and the missiles start firing, and all the people are rushing about like mad mice trying to find somewhere to hide, we'll be tucked up in our own little nuclear shelter. The end of the world could be just the break we're looking for! Oh we're pretty shrewd Rodney. If they started dropping the bomb on us right now we'd be as safe as houses brother, safe as houses!

The camera pans back to reveal for the first time that the shelter has been built on the top of a tower block.

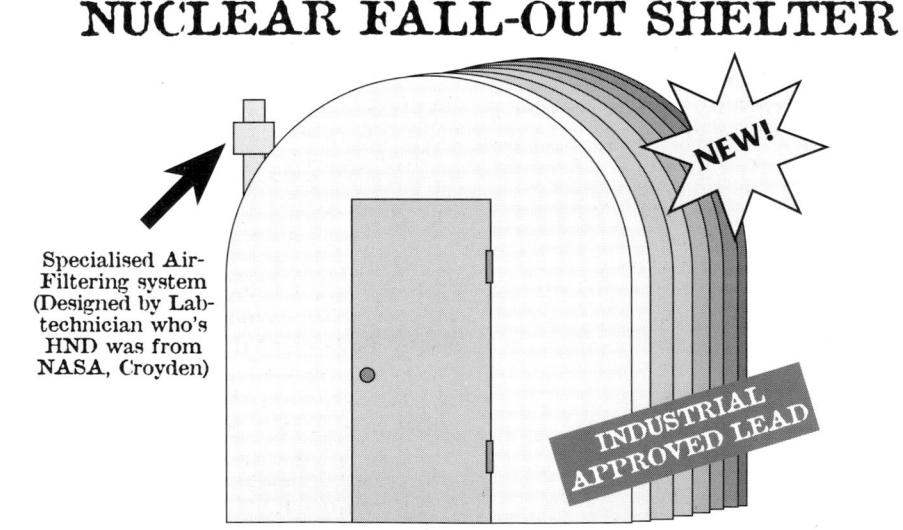

Grandad's Christmas Menu

**Chef is Grandad Trotter – former trainee chef at
The Peckham Ear, Nose and Throat Hospital.**

Starters

Spanish Omelette – containing three eggs, one of them's on the
turn, but there's a lot of pepper in it.

Or

Jacket Potato – really well done. So well done in fact that it can be
identified only by reference to its dental records.

Main

Roast one-legged turkey, stuffed with sage and onion and the
giblets left in. Cooked slightly rare, so a kiss of life could revive it.
Served with roast potatoes all burnt up so they look like rock hard
prunes, some green stuff we can't quite identify but they may have
been sprouts once and gravy, which will be strained before serving.

Or

Vegetarian chargrilled Pizza. For those of you who don't like a bit
of meat, we have peppers, mushrooms, pineapple, anchovies and
carrots all burnt to a crisp on a round bit of dough. (This item
requires notice of 24 hours so Rodney can get down the Pakistani
shop to buy it.)

Desert

Christmas Pudding, again really well done, served with custard,
which is about the only thing the soppy old git can cook.

Or

A cup of Mellow Birds coffee, a selection of cheeses – Cheddar,
Double Gloucester and Crackerbarrel –
and biscuits – Hob Nobs, that sort of thing.

Wine

Vin Ordinaire.
Those frogs make a blinding drop
of wine, y'know.
This is none of your table wine.
It is, well, bain marie.

INT. TROTTERS' LOUNGE. DAY.

The christmas decorations are over the top. Too bright, too gaudy and too many.
The artificial Christmas tree is silver, festooned with baubles and standing on an oil drum. The table is laid for dinner. Even the cutlery and wine glasses are gaudy and cheap looking. Rodney is laid out on sofa. A book he is reading is held up before his face. The book is entitled: Body Language. The Lost Art He lowers the book. He has a licentious grin – wide-eyed and delighted.

Rodney Oh yeah! *(Calls towards kitchen)* Hey Grandad. You wanna see this book Mickey Pearce lent me! It teaches you how to say filthy things to woman from great distances without actually speaking! I mean they can't set their brothers in on you or nothing!

The kitchen door opens and a cloud of smoke belches out. Grandad, wearing a dirty food-stained apron, fights his way out and gulps in some fresh air.

Grandad D'you like your baked potatoes *really* well done Rodney?

Rodney Have I got a choice?

Grandad Well, not really!

Rodney Yeah I like 'em *really* well done Grandad! I like 'em all burnt up so they look like rock-hard prunes.

Grandad Oh good! Well dinner won't be long then. *(looks at the book)* Body Language?

Rodney Yeah, it's no good for you Grandad, you'd need an interpreter!

Del, in roll neck sweater, sheepskin, enters. He is smoking a large cigar.

Del Alright Grandad, dinner ruined yet?

Grandad Coming along nicely Del Boy. *(Is about to exit to kitchen)*

Del Good good! . . . 'ang on 'ere y'are. *(Hands Grandad a twenty-pound note)* There's a score for yer, little Christmas pressie.

Grandad Oh cheers Del, very nice of you. I didn't get you nothing, I don't agree with the commercialisation of a Christian festival! *(Jabs the twenty-pound note into his pocket and exits into kitchen)*

Del I don't believe that! He actually took me money then gave me a rollocking! It's like being mugged by a magistrate!

Kitchen door opens.

Grandad Oh, and Merry Christmas! *(Exits)*

Del Yeah – and a partridge up yer pear tree an' all you saucy old git! *(To Rodney)* What happened to you today then? I thought I'd see you down the Nag's for a pre-luncheon aperitif and some light conversation with your little head bangers!

Rodney No the old belly's a bit dicey. Sort of burning pains!

Del That'll teach you to play Russian roulette with a mutton vindaloo won't it?

Rodney Oh no Del, this is psychosomatic mate. This is me brain sending messages to me belly warning it that Grandad's rotten Christmas dinner'll be on its way down soon! Have a butchers in that kitchen Del! It's all smoke 'n' smells, it's horrible! There's baked potatoes that look more like lumps of anthracite! There's green stuff out there – I don't know what it is Del, I was gonna ask then I thought I'd wait till you got in! Why do you let him do it Del?

Del Well it's a tradition innit? He's been cooking Christmas dinner ever since Mum went!

Rodney Yeah and he's been cooking it up ever since Mum went!

Del What do you want, a *sacré-bleu* chef or something? I mean I don't fancy it any more than you do Rodders, but what can we do?

Rodney Let's pretend we've both become vegetarians, then we won't have to eat his turkey!

Del Don't be a dipstick all your life Rodders! If we say we're vegetarians we'll end up with a plate of anthracite and green stuff!

Rodney Well I'm gonna say I'm on hunger strike – some kind of humanitarian grounds!

Del Leave it out will yer, leave it out. I remember when you went on hunger strike as a protest over American cruise missiles being based in Britain. You said that you were gonna starve yourself until the missiles were moved.

Rodney So?

Del So Rodney that was *eight* months ago! The missiles are still here but what's more to the point so are you! You went one and 'arf days on hunger strike then sent out for a curry!

Rodney Well I was starving!

Del That's the idea of it, you plonker! Grandad'll never wear that! Anyway, cooking the Christmas dinner has become Grandad's purpose in life. All

year long he sits in that chair watching the tellies like an unoiled redundant cog but he knows that come Christmas he can whir into action. It's his role within the family circle. It makes him feel that he still has an important part to play, y'know that he's still needed! You don't want to take that away from him do you? All for the sake of a little bit of . . . (Indicates Rodney's stomach)

Rodney Botulism!! No, alright Del!

Del Why don't you do what I do? Don't look at the dinner, just put it in your mouth and think of England! Anyway, for all we know this year it may turn out to be gourmets' dream!

Grandad enters from kitchen amidst another cloud of smoke.

Grandad I'll just strain the gravy then I'll get it up!

INT. THE TROTTERS' LOUNGE. DAY.

The Trotters are all seated at dinner table, wearing party hats. Near table and close to Rodney is an ice-bucket on legs containing a bottle of wine.

Their plates already contain food. Del, using an electric knife in a conventional manner, is carving a final slice from turkey.

Del We'll have to get a plug on this thing Rodney!

Rodney pours a glass of wine for himself then places the bottle back in bucket.

Del Alright, alright I'll have some wine please Rodney.

Rodney reaches for bottle.

Grandad D'you want some gravy Del?

Del No thanks Grandad, I'll have some wine.

Rodney pours a glass of wine. Del rolls the wine around his tongue.

Del Oh *bain marie, bain marie*! I will say this for them old Frogs, they make a blinding drop of wine! That shiyster down at the off-licence only tried to palm me off with table wine! . . . Must have thought I was a Philistine or something.

Rodney nods in agreement.

Del Anyway, I pulled him up a bit sharpish. I said 'Oi John. I don't want none of yer table wine. I said get down that cellar and sort me out a bottle of Vin Ordinaire!' . . . (Tries a piece of turkey) . . . Hmm, not bad Grandad, slightly underdone maybe.

Rodney Slightly underdone? I reckon the kiss of life would revive that turkey!

Del (Trying to keep the peace) That's enough Rodders!

Rodney is about to try his first mouthful of the turkey.

Grandad How's yer guts now Rodney?

Rodney lowers fork.

Rodney Not too bad now Grandad, thank you very much!

Pause. They eat.

Rodney lifts fork towards his mouth again.

Grandad (To Del) Hope he ain't got worms!

Rodney He's doing this on purpose!

Del Now come on you two. This is the dinner table I mean worms and all that! Rodney's got a burning sensation in his stomach ain't you Rodney?

Rodney Yeah. (Lifts fork again)

Del Maybe they're glow worms!

Del and Grandad laugh. Rodney, in exasperation, hurls fork across table.

Del Oi oi oi! What's your game?

Rodney Well do you think we could change the subject?

Del Alright alright. There's no need to get over-wrought! This turkey's lovely Grandad, innit Rodney?

Rodney Triffic!

Grandad Who's Brenda and Terry?

Del Eh?

Grandad Who's Brenda and Terry?

Del Who's Brenda and Terry?

Grandad Yeah.

Del Who's Brenda and Terry Rodney?

Rodney I don't know!

Del (To Grandad) What are you on about you old div?

Grandad We got a Christmas card from 'em. It said love from Brenda and Terry and the kids Shirley, Shane and Shaun.

Rodney Yeah, yeah that was from Brenda and Terry!

Grandad I know! But who is Brenda and Terry?

Del It's Shirley, Shane and Shaun's mum and dad innit.

Grandad Oh! Did we send them one back?

Rodney How could we send them one back? We don't even know who they are let alone where they live!

Del Just as well with them rotten cards you bought.

Rodney There was nothing wrong with them cards! You didn't like them 'cause they came from a charity organisation!

Del Now that is not fair Rodney, that is not fair Rodney. Nobody likes a good cause better than me do they Grandad? It's just that when it comes to Christmas cards you've got to be very careful about which charity you choose.

Rodney What do you mean got to be careful

Christmas Crackers

about which charity you choose?

Del Well some of them cards might offend our family and friends. It says Merry Christmas from Del Boy, Rodney and Grandad, and all the gang at the Deptford drug-addiction centre!

Rodney And with all the cuts we've had in social services you don't think that's a good cause?

Del I'm not saying it's not a good cause Rodney! All I'm saying is that at Christmas time people prefer a traditional Christmas card, you know with a nice wintery scene – a snowman, a little robin redbreast – not a sprig of holly and a bunch of mistletoe wrapped round a rusty syringe!

Rodney You do me right up sometimes Del!

Grandad I don't know why they want these drug-addiction centres. I mean ain't we got enough drug addicts without them recruiting them?

Rodney No Grandad! They're not *training* centres!Oh God, I give up! Can we change the subject again?

Del Stroll on Rodney, we're going through subjects quicker than *Mastermind*!

Del *(To Grandad)* You didn't throw the giblets away did you?

  Rodney slams his knife and fork down on plate.

Del *(To Rodney)* I only asked because I promised them to the old girl down stairs for her cat!

Grandad There weren't any giblets in it Del. It was ready-cleaned, said so on the box.

Del Yeah I know it was ready-cleaned Grandad, but they put the giblets in a plastic bag then stick it back in the turkey.

Grandad Do they?

Del Oh yeah.

  Del and Rodney look at each other.

Del You took the bag out didn't you?

Grandad I didn't know it was in there Del!

Del Oh my Gawd!

Rodney You mean he's cooked it with every-thing still in there? Oh no!

  Del peers into the turkey.

Del Oh my good God, it's like peering into the jaws of hell! *(To Grandad)* Didn't you at any time notice it? Like for instance when you were putting the *stuffing* in?

Rodney There's stuffing in there as well??

Del Oh it's all in here Rodders! Sage and onion, molten plastic and . . . things! It looks like an Irish night in a delicatessen!

Grandad I just didn't know it was in there Del Boy!

Del Alright Grandad, don't get overwrought, it's

over and done with innit eh? Don't upset yourself, as the French say, a fait acomplan. *(Now trying to be falsely cheerful)* Well, what about the old afters eh?

Grandad I'll go'n get it. *(Exits to kitchen)*

  Rodney is about to say something.

Del Alright, alright don't worry about it Rodney! Custard is his forte!

  Grandad appears at kitchen door holding a smouldering Christmas pudding.

Grandad D'you like your Christmas puddings *really* well done?

  Rodney and Del just nod zombie like.

INT. NIGHT. THE TROTTERS LOUNGE.

The TVs are on both showing the same circus. Del, wearing a paper hat, is lying asleep in the armchair. Rodney, looking thoroughly bored, is seated on the sofa. He surveys the room then sighs heavily.
At the sound of the sigh Del stirs slightly but does not wake. Rodney stands. He mooches round the room kicking his heels and just trying to kill another minute. He sighs even more heavily. Again Del stirs but does not wake. Rodney flops back on sofa. He picks up a Christmas blower (one of those trumpet-type things with the paper tube that unfolds when blown). Del stirs and then wakes. Through his bleary eyes he sees Rodney looking at him.

Del Sorry! *(He prepares to go back to sleep)*

Rodney I don't like circuses!

Del What?

Rodney I don't like circuses!

Del Oh!

Rodney I never have liked 'em!

Del Triffic!

  Pause.

Rodney Never will like 'em – Circuses.

Del Alright you've made your point Rodney! Why don't you switch over?

Rodney Yeah, alright! *(Moves to TV and switches one over. We see there is another circus on the other channel.)*

  Del hides his delight and laughter.

Rodney There's one on the other side!!

Del Is there? It's a pity you don't like 'em or you could be having a whale of a time couldn't yer? Now put a sock in it for 'arf hour or so will you?

  Snuggles down in armchair. Rodney moves to window.

Rodney It's good living in a tower block annit Del?

Del Yeah, mustard. The Queen don't know

what she's missing.

Rodney Look at that view eh? On a clear day you can see . . . the ground.

Rodney (Shouts) Boring Boring Boring Boring Boring B . . . o . . . ri . . . ing!

Del leaps from the chair.

Del I'll ffff . . . I'll whack you one in a minute Rodney!!!

By now Rodney has done a swift ali shuffle out of the danger zone.

Rodney Well nothing's open out there and I'm bored!

Del Hang about and I'll get on the phone and knock you up a Mardi Gras. Everyone's bored! Christmas is a religious festival, its meant to be boring!

Rodney I thought we supposed to be celebrating the birth of our Lord! A time of great joy!

Del It is a time of great joy that's why everything's closed! Everyone;s at home enjoying themselves!

Rodney Enjoying themselves?

Del Where's me nuts.

Rodney Just take a look at it out there, Del. It's like a neutron bomb's hit it – the buildings are still standing but there's no sign of life! No, the British nation have *forgotten* how to enjoy itself! We're all charging toward the cliff edge of terminal boredom like a herd of . . of . . . (Struggles for right word) What's them things that commit suicide all the time?

Del Japanese!

Rodney No, lemmings! Yeah like a herd of lemmings! Let's go out somewhere Del. There's bound to be a pub or a club open somewhere!

Del It's Christmas night Rodney!

Rodney The Monte Carlo club over New Cross is open! There again it's a bit rough!

Del (Limped wrist – effeminate voice) Oh yes all them big men, drinking beer and burping! You great big tart you!

Rodney Alright let's go to the Monte Carlo. A few birds get down there, we might be able to pull a couple!

Del I don't want to go out Rodney!

Rodney (Frustrated) You're boring as well!

Del You're hardly a go on the big dipper yourself Rodney!

Rodney Well why don't you want to go out??

Del I'll tell you why shall I? It may have slipped your notice but there are *three* people living in this flat. You, me and that scruffy little old man who does funny things to turkeys. Namely *Our* Grandfather! Now you're not honestly suggesting that we just push off out it and leave him to

spend the night on his own?

Rodney But we often leave him in on his own!

Del Not on Christmas night Rodney, not on Christmas night!

Rodney But we sit in with him every Christmas. He wouldn't mind just this once!

Del He'd *pretend* he didn't mind! But you don't know what'll be going through his little mind as he sits here in this empty flat all on his own. Thinking of the old days when Mum and Dad were here – when Christmas was a great, big family affair, and we're still a family Rodney so we'll stay in with Grandad and watch, y'know *The Sound of Music.*

Rodney I don't like *The Sound of Music*!

Del Well we'll switch over!

Rodney What's on?

Del A circus.

Rodney I want to go out Del!

Del Listen Rodney, there are alot of old people all over the country sitting alone this Christmas night. Half of 'em don't get a Christmas card let alone a bit of company. So you're going to stay put with me and Grandad!

Rodney If I want to go out I'll go out!

Del No you won't!

Rodney Yes I will!

Del You won't Rodney!

Rodney I will Del!

Del You won't!

Rodney I will!

Del You won't.

Rodney I will.

Grandad, washed, shaved and wearing his best suit, opens the door.

Grandad I'm off out now, see you later.

Del Yeah tadda Grandad.

Rodney See yer.

Del You won't.

Rodney I will, Del.

Del If I say . . .

(Shouts towards door) Oi!

(opens door to hall)

Grandad is still in hall putting his overcoat on.

Where d'you think you're going??

Grandad I'm going to the Old Folks Christmas Do over at the Community Centre. I thought anything'd be better than sitting in here all night listening to you two arguing. Tell us what happens in *The Sound of Music*. See yer. (Exits)

Del (Stunned) Yeah. . . . See yer, Grandad. (To Rodney) That's terrific that is, innit?

Rodney Charming. He goes out gallivanting and we sit in watching Julie Andrews.

Del Oh no, bruvver – definitely not. Let's get our

Christmas Crackers

glad rags on and hit the Monte Carlo Club.

Rodney Yeah!!

Del I'll have a bath first 'cause there's hardly any hot water left. Fix yerself a drink, make yerself comfortable – and watch the circus.

Del exits.

INT. NIGHT. THE MONTE CARLO CLUB.

It is all tinsel and tat, the kind of place that looks good with the lights out.

Congregated around the bar are a few beer-supping three-piece-suits-thirty-five-year-old hooligans, accompanied by the sort of women that admire thirty-five-year-old hooligans.

As we join the scene, couples are locked in embrace on dance floor as a smoochy song ends.

Del wearing a navy blue three-piece suit, a navy blue shirt, white tie and white shoes and a couple of gold medallions beside his obligatory gold rings, watch, and chunky bracelet. And Rodney, wearing his only suit and tie approach bar.

Del *(To barman)* Oi John. Giss a Remi Martin with cream soda and lots of ice, and 'arf of lager.

Standing near Del is Earl, another three-piece suit. He is about Del's age but not as bright or as sharp as Del.

You all right, Earl?

Earl Hullo Del Boy. Nice Christmas?

Del A belter. Where's the enemy?

Earl She took the kids over her mum's.

Del How's the old man?

Earl Up and down like Tower Bridge. Still in hospital – unconscious most of the time – when he wakes up he don't know where he is.

Del *(Struggles for some sympathetic words)* Well next time when he comes round again you wish him a Merry Christmas from me and Rodney.

Earl I will, Del.

Rodney What's wrong with him?

Earl I can't pronounce it.

Del Oh, now listen Earl, now listen my son, this is what you want to do. Next time you're up the hospital, you get hold of one of them surgeons you know they're the guys with the little white jackets and you say to him that your old Dad wants some antibiotics, – Antee - by-ot-ics. I'll write it down for yer. Giss that Replay that I gave you for your Christmas present Rodney.

Rodney hands del a pen.

Del writes on a paper napkin that is lying on bar.

Rodney You're being a bit pushy, ain't you? I mean don't you think the hospital's already

thought of that?

Del That bunch of wallies?? These are magic things Earl. They work a treat. Gawd knows where they get 'em from. D'you remember when Grandad was in hospital about eighteen month back? They gave him so many antibiotics that one day he sneezed and two other blokes got better.

Del hands Earl the paper napkin.

Well there it is. Don't take this to a chemist's it ain't a prescription.

Earl No I won't, Del Boy. Well thanks a lot, that's really nice of you.

Del That's alright my son. You have a nice Christmas, you hear? Come on Rodney.

Del and Rodney move away from bar.

Rodney You're something else you are. You've stuck your nose in where it weren't wanted a good few times but this takes the biscuit. Suddenly you're a miracle worker.

Del Listen Rodney. Life's been pretty gutty for Earl quite recently. First, he got made redundant, it's been like that between him and his missus *(Moves hands up and down in balancing gesture)* then to top it all his old man collapses in the Nag's Head right across the table where me and Trig were sitting. It was terrible, glasses went flying, everything.

Rodney Yeah? What, serious?

Del No, I only had about that much left. No, I mean can't afford a private hospital. He wanted to take his dad to Lourdes, but couldn't afford the fare. The way his luck's going he couldn't afford the fare to Leeds let alone Lourdes. So I have just given him a bit of false hope – a light at the end of the tunnel, a straw to grab at, a bit of promise for the New Year.

Rodney But what happens if he tells the hospital to administer these antibiotics? It might finish the old man off.

Del Leave it out Rodney. What do you think they are up the hospital, a bunch of wallies?

Rodney But you just said . . .

Del moves away

Rodney *(Following him)* You're flash you are aintcha? You think you know the lot. Everything about you is – lairy.

Del What do you mean – lairy?

Rodney Well just look at the way you're dressed to begin with. You make Christmas trees look sombre. And God knows how you've got the courage to walk down dark alleys wearing all that gold. I mean when they see you coming they must look like a mugger's pension scheme.

Del Listen, how d'you think a peacock attracts a

lady peacock? With his plumage Rodders. This is my plumage. . . . When I approach a bird she don't see *me*, the good-looking young man about town, own teeth and all that sort of game. No she sees in her subconscious a white yacht floating in the blue waters of a Caribbean bay.

Rodney *(Smiling sardonically)* Is that right?

Del Yeah. *(Looks Rodney up and down with a sneer of condemnation)* With you they see a winkle barge sinking off the end of Southend pier.

Rodney No, because I don't need all the bullion and perfume and white shoes. I'm natural – I'm me, Del, I'm me.

Del Yes, I know you're you, thats why you always end up with a dog.

Rodney I don't go out with dogs.

Del Leave it off Rodney, you've had more dogs than Crufts. Grandad took your suit to the cleaners the other week and found a muzzle in the pocket. No Rodney, I know the secret , that's why I always blag the good 'uns – the air hostesses and part-time models. . . . Oh yest bruv I got the secret – it never fails me.

Del turns to discover the two plain girls smiling willingly at him. he reacts.

As he starts to move away he nudges Rodney. Gotta bone handy Rodders? I think you've cracked it again.

Rodney reacts as he sees the two girls. he smiles nervously – nods politely then quickly follows Del.

INT. NIGHT. THE MONTE CARLO CLUB.

Another record (maybe a pop christmas release) is ending. a few people are dancing to this more up tempo song. All the tables are still taken. Rodney and Del leaning against a wall looking thoroughly bored.

Del I wouldn't mind a sit down, the old pins are aching.

Rodney Amazing annit? I mean look at us – the Peckham Playboys and I bet the only one who's pulled tonight is Grandad.

Del I thought you'd be used to it. The only thing you ever pull at Christmas is yer cracker.

A man and woman move from their table. There's a table free over there, Rodders look lively. *(turns to get his drink, cigars and lighter which are on a near-by shelf)*

Rodney starts to move towards table, but as he does so we see two very pretty girls sit down at it. one should be blonde, the other brunette.

Rodney reacts, delighted with the turn in

events. He nudges Del. The nudge causes Del to spill some drink down his suit.

Rodney Hey Del, look.

Del What? *(Turns and sees the girls)* Ah no, they've only pinched our table.

Rodney Don't worry about the table, Del. Look at them two.

Del But I want to sit down, Rodney.

Rodney We'll sit down at their table. Come on. *(He strides confidently across dance floor towards the girls)*

Del remains at wall brushing the drink from his suit.

as rodney reaches the half-way mark he becomes aware that he is alone. He hurries back to Del.

Well go on then, Del!

Del Go on then what?

Rodney Do the bizzo. Chat 'em up.

Del How comes it's always me who's gotta do the donkey work, eh? You're like a spy you are, Rodders. You find where the enemy are hiding but I'm the one who's gotta charge across no man's land and capture 'em! Well I think it's about time you took a bit of shot and shell. Go on.

Rodney You mean me chat 'em up?

Del Yeah. Go on.

Rodney Alright then, I'll do it.

Del Go on then.

Rodney Alright I will. *(He takes out his 'body language' book and consults it – begins preparations, loosens shoulders, pulling the belly in – generally psyching himself up)*

Del What you doing?

Rodney Eh?

Del What you doing?

Rodney Psyching meself up.

Del Oh!

Del catches the two girls looking

Del *(Shouts across empty dance floor)* Its alright, he'll be with you in a minute girls, he's just psyching himself up.

Rodney turns and tries to hide himself in the wall.

Rodney For God's sake shut up, will you?!

Del What what do you think you're playing at? This is kamikaze time, Rodney – get over there!

Rodney I will!

Del Well go on then!

Rodney In my own time, Del!

Pause. takes out book.

Del Well go on then.

Rodney Just shut up, will you?

After preparing himself, Rodney starts to

Christmas Crackers

move across the floor. He walks in what can
be best described as an exaggerated John
Wayne style. Del reacts. he looks around the
club with alarm hoping that no one has
noticed Rodney.
As Rodney reaches the middle of the dance
floor Del shouts at him.

Del Oi, soppy. Come here.
*Rodney stops, cringing with embarrassment.
He returns.*

Rodney I'd like to kill you sometimes.
Sometimes I'd really like to really hurt you bad.

Del What was that silly walk for? Your guts
playing you up again?

Rodney It wasn't a silly walk. It was body
language. I've got this book on it.

Del Body language? I thought you were limping.

Rodney I was 'talking' to them!

Del Talking? You were lisping then, Rodney.
What was you supposed to be saying?

Rodney The walk was saying pelvis, virility. It
was saying here comes a man who's got natural
masculinity and maturity!

Del Well from back here it was saying here
comes a man who's got his truss on back to
front. Don't do it Rodney, just don't do it. Go
over again and this time, walk normal.

Rodney I'm not going back there now, Del. I've
made meself look a right lemon.

Del No you haven't.

Rodney What after aborting me attempt half-
way? You go.

Del Me? After you've made a right lemon of
yourself? No way bruv! I'll tell you what we'll do,
we'll act cool.
*Rodney moans at the thought of trying to act
cool after the events of the last minute.*
We'll stroll over to the bar and get ourselves
another drink. Then we'll wait till they're not
looking.

Rodney *(Hopefully)* Sneak out.

Del No. When they're not looking and then
we'll ambush 'em. You wally. Come on.

INT. NIGHT. THE MONTE CARLO CLUB.

*The two girls are still at the table, talking.
Del and rodney are slumped at bar. Del is
deep in thought – plotting.
The blonde girl catches Rodney looking at her,
she smiles at him. Rodney attempts a smile
back then thinks better of it and lowers his
eyes.*

Rodney Hey. Del.

Del Right I've got it. No, shut up, shut up. This is
what we're gonna do. You leave the club.

Rodney Leave?

Del Yeah, then give it a couple of minutes and
come back and say to the doorman outside that
there's a brand-new Rolls Royce Corniche
obstructing your three-wheeled van.

Rodney Why?

Del Because he'll announce over the mike
'Would the owner of the brand-new Rolls Royce
Corniche kindly move it as it's obstructing some
sap's three-wheeled van! Then I will casually
stand up – jangling me keys – and join you
outside.

Rodney Why?

Del Well because them two birds will think that I
drive a brand-new Rolls Royce Corniche.

Rodney Oh yeah. Yeah, but they'll also think
that I drive a three-wheeled van.

Del But you do.

Rodney I know I do, but I don't want them
knowing that, do I!

Del But they won't know will they 'cause you'll
be outside.

Rodney Yeah with you.

Del Right.

Rodney So that means the girls will be in here
in the warm and us two shrewdies'll be outside
on the pavement somewhere congratulating
each other! And then we'll have to pay to get in
again.

Del *(Grudgingly submits to the argument)* Yeah
yeah alright clever Dick! Look, let's just play it by
ear, shall we. We'll go over there and engage
'em in conversation.

Rodney Oh no, hold it a minute Del.
They are about to move from bar.

Rodney Hang on a minute.

Del What??

Rodney What sort of conversation you going to
engage them in? I mean you always tell lies,
don't you. You tell 'em we've got flash cars and
we're film producers and we got a private jet!

Del Everyone exaggerates now and then,
Rodney.

Rodney But I never know what to say. I get
embarrassed! Let's just tell 'em the truth. Tel 'em
about our likes and what we do.

Del Rodney, all I want to do is sit down. You do
the talking.

Rodney Right.
They are about to move away again.
Hold it, Del.

Del God Almighty.

Rodney What shall I tell them?

Del You can tell 'em we went down the auction
last Friday and bought a 1962 A.40, that you

sold thirty Christmas trees in the market and two gross of fire salvaged Rubik cubes in Croydon shopping precinct. Tantalise 'em Rodney, tantalise 'em.

Rodney You don't think it'll bore 'em?

Del No. They wouldn't have had so much fun since their last exorcism!

Rodney We can talk about Christmas!

Del Yeah, tell 'em about them giblets. Let's go.

Rodney No Del, hold it.

Del I'll kick you in the shin in a minute. Now what?

Rodney Which one d'you fancy?

Del Not yours, Rodney. Look, they're both very nice. I ain't particular.

Rodney No, I'm not particular either.

Del Good! I'll have the blonde one then.

Rodney I fancied the blonde one.

Del Gordon Bennett!! The dark-haired one's very nice, Rodney. And if I'm not mistaken I've seen her two or three times coming out of Guy's hospital. Now either she's a very sick girl or she's a nurse. Now you like a nice nurse, don't you, particularly in uniform, eh?

Rodney *(Casual shrug)* Take it or leave it. Anyway she's not wearing her uniform, is she?

Del Well of course not. You don't come to the Monte Carlo club dressed up as Sister George do you. But she might have her uniform with her.

Rodney Oh yeah! Stuffed in her handbag in case she sees an accident on the way home.

Del Alright, so she ain't got her uniform with her. But on the other hand, she might be able to give you something for your stomach might'n she. Now come along, we're making our move now Rodney, and I'm doing *all* the talking. So if you should hear words like Lamborghini, Malibu Beach or Lady Diana, don't get nervous.

Rodney Alright then.

They start to move from the bar and begin their approach. As they do so two other guys appear from out of the crowd at the bar and ask the girls to dance. Del and Rodney are stunned as the two girls wrap themselves round their new partners.

Del *(Hurls his cigar to the floor)* You dozy little twonk, Rodney.

Rodney Me? Don't blame me Del, it's your fault!

Del My fault? Just five minutes ago I was about to make me move, but you kept calling me back.

Rodney An hour ago I was half-way across that floor and you called me back.

Del That's 'cause You were doing a silly walk. And anyway your timing was all wrong. The birds had hardly sat down and you were steaming across that floor like Ivor the Engine. It's no good just crashing in with a smile and a prayer. A woman needs time, Rodney.

Rodney Them tactics have never failed me in the past.

Del Well they wouldn't with the little Ovaltinies you chat up. I've heard your line of patter my son. If they don't know Adam Ant's birthday or the Chelsea result, it's goodnight Vienna, innit? With me,
it's different I take a woman's feelings into consideration.

Rodney laughs.

Del I do. When a woman goes out with me she is guaranteed three things – well four actually, but the fourth's an optional extra. One: she's guaranteed a well-dressed man. Two: she is guaranteed a steak meal. And she is guaranteed care and consideration. Oh yes she is. I take a woman's feelings into consideration. are fragile things. It's so easy to hurt her deeply with a thoughtless word, a badly timed gesture. No, I care about people's feelings. There's too much pain in this world Rodney without me causing more!

We see the two plain girls, still seated at table, and still smiling at Del. Del smiles back sympathetically. He checks his watch. He and Rodney move across to the girls.

Del *(In a softly spoken, sympathetic voice)* Excuse me, Ladies. It's getting rather late and my brother and I were wondering if you were thinking of going home yet?

The two girls stand eagerly.

1st Girl Oh yes, we were just going to get our coats.

Del *(Now the real Del)* Oh good, we'll have your chairs then. Come on then Rodney. *(Sits down on chair)*

Rodney turns away unable to face the two wretched girls.

Brotherly Love

Del on Rodney

Del on Rodney's paleness
You look like a blood donor who couldn't say no.

On Rodney's behaviour
He's just reached that awkward age. You know he's a bit like a trifle.
What d'you mean, mixed up?
No, he's thick and fruity.

Rodney, why don't you go into the kitchen and stick your head in the food blender?

On Rodney's career
You know, Rodney tried to join the police force once, yeah, it was after he failed the intelligence test to become a Unigate milkman.

On Rodney and women
He thought he was going to pull a Swede and she's got lumbered with a cabbage.

Well, when Rodney came in he was behaving very strangely.
He was all trembling and sweating.
Don't worry, Grandad, it's just the start of the mating season.

On Rodney's education
He's got two GCEs and he thinks he's Bamber Gascoigne's vest.

Rodney on Del

On his sales technique
You could make the Elgin Marbles sound like a second-hand Datsun, couldn't you?

On his generosity
You'd give me half of everything?! You'd nick the hole out of me last Polo if I didn't keep me mouth shut.

On Del and religion
There are Cardinals and Archbishops — they've been in the business all their lives and never got a sniff of a miracle. Then along comes Del, he's in the game for five minutes and already he's a prophet. Profit being the operative word.

On his dress sense
You make a Christmas tree look sombre. And God knows how you've got the courage to walk down dark alleys wearing all that gold. I mean, when they see you coming you must look like a mugger's pension scheme.

SERIES TWO

The Long Legs of the Law

THE TROTTERS' LOUNGE.

Both TVs are on. Grandad is searching around the lounge, in drawers, under the seats of the armchair, etc. Rodney, in a hung-over state, enters and slumps down at the table.

Grandad You seen my teeth?

Rodney Have you tried yer mouth?

Grandad Now don't get sarky, Rodney. I had 'em last night, I meant to put them in soak. I might have left 'em in the kitchen. D'you want any breakfast, Rodney?

Rodney No I don't! My belly's going up and down like Tower Bridge.

Grandad I'll see if we've got anything out here for you.

Del, dressed in all the gear and feeling as bright as a July morning, enters.

Del Right. Ah! There you are Rodney. Morning. Great night last night weren't it, eh? *(Rodney ignores him)* Hey Grandad, I found your teeth they were outside by the rubbish chute.

Grandad What were they doing out there?

Del Well, I don't know, do I? Did you lend 'em to anyone.

Grandad Course I didn't.

Del Are you sure? Here put a couple of rashers of streaky in that pan for me will you, Grandad. That's what you need, Rodney, after a night on the old drink, a nice drop of the old bacon fat, slides down the little red lane like a pint of Duckhams on a warm morning. 'Ere what's a matter with you, you're not still sulking are you?

Rodney No!

Del Oh no – no. Come on, grow up Rodney, grow up will you.

Grandad enters from the kitchen carrying a glass of water which contains two fizzing Alka-Seltzer type tablets. He places the glass on the table. Rodney starts sipping at it.

Grandad What's up with him now?

Del I'll tell you what's a matter with him, shall I, Grandad. The other day I meet a couple of birds right – well, when I say a couple of birds, a mother and her daughter. Now I've known them for a long time, they're two very charming people. Anyway, I suggested that we made up a foursome, right. So last night we went out for a drink. We took them out and gave them a nice drink. Had a lovely meal and then, him over there, he goes and gets the sulks don't he.

Grandad What's the matter with you, Rodney? It sounds like a nice evening.

Rodney Grandad – when he said we was going out with a mother and her daughter I assumed that I'd be with the daughter. Instead of that, he drags me round every pub in the Old Kent Road holding hands with some old sort with a cough.

Del I thought it was a very romantic evening, Rodney.

Rodney Well it might have been for you Del. For me the night air was filled with all the sensuous promise of a tour round the Sanatogen works!

Del 'Ere, how's that bacon?

Grandad Alright. You didn't get in till four o'clock. What d'you do, go back to their place?

Del No, don't get excited, we went on to this little spick drinking club I know, over New Cross. 'Ere you know who was there, Grandad. Tommy Razzle. Do you remember Tommy, used to live in Cathles House.

Grandad Oh young Razzle – used to have that dog?

Del Yeah, that's right – well he's married 'er now!

Grandad He still on the Underground?

Del No, no, no, him and er – him and Monkey Harris they've teamed up together, they put in false ceilings or something. They've just come back from Saudi Arabia, they was putting in a false ceiling in a – in a dental clinic or something. Anyway, they had a big row, didn't they, Rodney, last night. You should have seen it – you see Tommy, he reckoned that he'd seen a salt beef bar in Jeddah and Monkey Harris said no way. Anyway, before we knew where we were they was off, weren't they. Tables flying, bottles, glasses . . .

Rodney Almost had to call for the manager at one point, didn't they?

Del Yeah, that's right. It was as bad as that. Anyway somebody phoned the law right and who'd they send, but a young policewoman! Well, course, that was it weren't it. Should have seen him over there. What! His eyes they went all goggle like that and then he was sniffing round her.

Rodney I was not sniffing round her! I merely asked her if she needed any assistance.

Del Oh leave it out! There was Monkey Harris

draped over a keep left sign, there was Tommy with the handcuffs on, their two wives were fighting like a couple of strays and this plonker here is trying to date the arresting officer. You should have seen it, it was pathetic. He was going, 'Well, you know, um, well I'm thinking of going to the pictures tomorrow, d'you – d'you want to come?' The only date that you would have got with her was ten o'clock Monday morning at Horseferry Road Magistrates! How's that bacon?

Grandad Oh, I'll have a look at it. Oh, Trigger called round last night.

Del Yeah. What he want?

Grandad With these watches.

Del Ah? Watches?

Grandad Watches, look. *(Hands Del a box of ladies and gents watches)* Knocked off are they?

Del No they're not knocked off. Knocked off – he's a comedian isn't he – knocked off. Hey, these are not bad. Look at that Rodney – look at that. What do you think of that, eh? Répondez s'il vous plait, ain't it it – that one.

Rodney Yeah, they're not bad as it happens!

Del No, I reckon that's a Longines or a Cartier.

Rodney Yeah?

Grandad Trigger said they're four quid each.

Del Four quid each, oh well.

Grandad Del Boy, I've burnt yer bacon.

Del Oh, you stupid old git. I told you to look after it, didn't I? Never mind, you can have it. Come on then Rodney, let's go and see if we can flog some of these watches. We'll stop off at Sid's place on the way, alright?

Rodney Yeah, right. Actually, I could do with something to eat now, I feel a bit better after that. *(Indicating glass)*

Grandad What have you done with my Sterodent?

Rodney clutches his stomach and rushes past a laughing Del and out of the door.

CAFE.

The cafe is quite crowded with an assortment of lorry drivers, building site labourers and the obligatory dosser in the corner. Del and Rodney are seated at a large table. In front of Del is a large platter showing all the evidence of a bygone breakfast. In front of Rodney is a side plate with a few crumbs on it. Del is smoking a cigar and reading the Financial Times. Rodney is smoking a roll-yer-own and reading Mayfair.

Del ICI have dropped a point.

Rodney Yeah? Chelsea dropped three on

Saturday.

Del They should never have sold Greavesy should they? Come on then, you fit?

Rodney Yeah, right.

They move to the counter, behind which is Sid. He is the middle-aged proprietor. He wears a filthy apron, smokes a cigarette and rarely takes his eyes off his Greyhound Express as he talks to customers.

Sid Right, what did you have Del Boy?

Del Er, just a packet of biscuits and a cup of tea Sid.

Sid What did you really have?

Del Sausage, bacon, double egg, beans and tomatoes, mushrooms, black pudding and chips, three teas, two bread. Bread was toasted.

Sid No fried slice?

Del No, not this morning Sid, belly's a bit dicky.

Sid What did you have, Rodney?

Rodney Just me usual bacteria on toast, you know.

Sid One day I'll smack him in the mouth.

Del Yeah, if you can find it. *(To Rodney)* 'Ere, coming down the Nag's Head tonight, they've got a couple of strippers on.

Rodney No, I'm going out tonight.

Del *(To Sid)* Oh – here take that back, I want one of them down there. One of them biscuits, alright? *(To Rodney)* Oh yeah, where you going?

Rodney I didn't tell you, did I? I've got a bird – Sandra.

Del Sandra? Where d'you meet her then?

Rodney She was down the club last night.

Del I didn't see you talking to anyone last night, not even the bird that you were supposed to be with. Who was Sandra then – that part-time barmaid, was she?

Rodney No. She's not a part-time wallah. She's got a career.

Del Oh career. What is she – a lollypop woman?

Rodney No! Policewoman!

Del reacts and, in the process, he drops knives, forks and spoons out of his sleeve.

THE TROTTERS' LOUNGE.

Del and Grandad are sitting in front of the TVs. The news of Rodney's date has brought about a certain grimness in the household and their faces show this. They are looking at the TVs, but not watching.

Grandad I mean, Rodney going out with a policewoman! What are the neighbours gonna say? Why's he doing it to us Del Boy?

Del 'Cos he's kinky, ain't he. He's got what leading psychiatrists call a – 'a thing' about

The Long Legs of the Law

policewomen's uniforms!

Grandad Well if that's all he wants can't we club together and buy him one.

Del He don't want to wear it, he wants the policewoman to wear it. Gordon Bennett, he may be perverted but he ain't dangerous!

Rodney, in a suit and tie, enters. Del and Grandad turn and look at him accusingly, they then turn back to the TVs.

Rodney Del – do you think. . . . Could I please have the keys to the van Del?

Del throws the keys across the room at him.

Del Oi, have you stopped to consider how your actions are going to affect our business? Don't you realise that them streets out there are our boardroom, our factory floor, and the people that live in 'em are our customers, our business acquaintances. How d'you think they're gonna feel about doing business with – with a grass?

Rodney Bloody 'ell Del, I'm just taking a bird to the pictures and suddenly I'm Bertie Smalls.

Del You're not taking a bird, you're taking a policewoman!

Rodney But under the uniform she's just the same as any other girl.

Grandad Our kind and their kind don't mix Rodney. We're like cats and dogs. I mean you'll have to watch every word in case you say something incriminating. Them people's never off duty.

Rodney Oh don't talk rubbish Grandad. She's hardly gonna nick the bloke who's taking her out, is she?

Del What do you know about it you wally-brain? Don't you know that – don't you know that police officers have to take a vow that, if necessary, they will nick their own mum and dad – she's hardly gonna think twice about a rag-bag like you is she?

Rodney Now you're trying to run my life again ain't you Del? Well, if I let you get away with it this time I won't be able to go for a Nelson Riddle without you giving me a blueprint.

Del Leave it out. Hear that, hear that, hear that? After all I've done for him. Here you are, Grandad.

Rodney What have you ever done for me?

Del What have I done for you? I brought you up, I fed you, I clothed you, I picked you up when you fell, I wiped your tears away, but most important of all Rodney, I've always been there. I have always been there.

Rodney Besides that.

Del Always used to take you away on holidays.

Rodney Oh yeah, the Costa Del Kent! That's

right, yeah. You used to create therapeutic little adventure games, didn't you, like 'Let's see who can pick the most hops today, Rodney'.

Del Hopping was all we could afford weren't it Grandad?

Grandad You've either got a short memory Rodney, or you're just ungrateful. Don't you remember the time when your little mate Roy Taylor got a set of Jacko roller skates for his birthday? You came in crying 'cos you didn't have none. The next day Del Boy brought you in a pair exactly the same as Roy Taylor's.

Rodney What d'you mean exactly the same as Roy Taylor's? They were Roy Taylor's! His big brother give me a right hiding when he caught me on 'em!

Del Yeah, I got him back for you though, didn't I?

Rodney Yeah fine consolation that was weren't it. I'm sat in me little bed with a split-lip and an 'eadache!

Del Alright, alright then, who paid your fine when you got caught for smoking pot?

Rodney Yeah . . . well, I could have handled that myself.

Del What, 300 quid? Do me a favour, Rodders. I remember when you got nicked for riding your motor scooter without a crash hat. You only got fined five quid and you asked for time to pay!

Grandad You've always been a bad 'un Rodney.

Rodney What 'cos I didn't wear a crash helmet?

Grandad I mean smoking mari-jew-arna! You brought a slur upon the family name.

Rodney Oh leave off Grandad. I'd have to get done for chicken molesting to bring a slur on this family's name!

Del Oi, oi, that's enough of that!

Grandad It's a good thing your mum died when she did 'cos that would have killed her!

Del Why don't you shut up you soppy old goat.

Rodney Look, I don't care what neither of you say. I'm going out, right. I mean you're always on about how you brought me up, how you kept me, the one thing you've never told me is why?

Del Well – tell you the truth *(Finding it impossible to tell the truth)* the council wouldn't let me keep a dog in the flat!

Rodney Well, I think it's because you wanted to see me develop into a mature adult – someone who could stand on his own two feet – independent. And one of the little clauses in my independence, Del, is that I decide where I go, what I do and with whom!

Del Alright Rodney, alright, why don't you do

that small thing. You decide where you go, what you do and with whom you do it, because I'm finished with you – I've washed me hands of you – as far as I'm concerned you don't exist, right. And Rodney.

Rodney What?

Del Been raining, them roads'll be treacherous. Drive carefully.

Rodney Yeah I will. . . . Cheers, Del.

Del What for?

Rodney Nothing. Well I shouldn't be too late, Sandra's got to be up early, she's on riot patrol. *(Exits)*

Del The world's a strange place to live in innit? Innit Grandad, eh? One minute you're walking along quite nicely, and the next minute, whack, life jumps out and gives you sobering thoughts.

Grandad Oh I've had a lot of sobering thoughts in my time Del Boy. It was them what started me drinking.

Del Yeah, I can understand that. The boy's grown into a man. I don't, I don't feel as needed as I used to be. Soon he'll, he'll fly the nest! But you know what the most sobering thought of the lot is? One wrong word from that plonker Rodney and I could end up doing five years!

THE TROTTERS' LOUNGE.

Del is asleep in the armchair. On the coffee table next to him we see a couple of the watches. Grandad is turning the TVs off. Del stirs and wakes.

Del 'Ere I was watching that! Rodney home?

Grandad No not yet. He's most probably drove her home.

Del Yeah, more than likely. Oh he's late though, ain't he. 'Ere I hope she hasn't asked to see his MOT.

They hear the front door close.

Grandad Here he is now.

Del *(Shouting)* Oi, hello. Z Victor one. How d'you get on? Hope you didn't leave any finger-prints over the suspect.

Grandad Ssssh Del, he's brought her home with him!

Del He's done what? What's he trying to do to me? Quick Grandad, hide things!

Grandad What things?

Del Well everything innit? That's bent for a start. Quick get rid of it. *(By the cocktail bar there are three cardboard boxes piled on top of each other. A sign on each reads: 'South London Distillery Ltd, Wines and Spirits.')* The booze Grandad, the booze!

Rodney enters with Sandra.

Rodney Hello.

Del Hello. Yeah, we were just talking about you weren't we Grandad? We just said, yeah, we'll give Rodney another month and then we'll phone the police.

Rodney I've just brought Sandra back for a nightcap.

Del Oh good.

Sandra Hello . . . again!

Del Yeah hello, again. Well did you – did you enjoy the film?

Sandra Yes it was very good.

Del Take you to see something romantic, did he?

Sandra No – *The Exterminator*!

Del Oh *The Exterminator*. Well, of course, to Rodders that – that is romantic. I mean he cried his little eyes out over *The Texas Chainsaw Massacre*.

Rodney Leave it out, Del. D'you want to sit down, Sandra?

Sandra Thank you. And what have you been doing?

Del Nothing! No, no, nothing. No, we've been in all evening haven't we Grandad, eh?

Grandad Yeah, and we've got witnesses to prove it!

Sandra I wasn't asking you to provide an alibi, I was just enquiring out of politeness!

Del Oh yeah, yes, yeah of course you was Sandra. Sorry. It's just that you know us being such a law-abiding family we're, we don't really know how to converse with er, the Old Bill!

Grandad *(Indicating Rodney)* He's got a police record.

Del Yes, er *Walking on the Moon*. You know you've heard that one, ain't you? Yeah, yeah, I'll – I'll play it for you later on if you like, you know, if you haven't heard it.

Rodney D'you like Police LPs Sandra? I've got their latest one. It ain't even been released yet has it Del?

Sandra If it hasn't been released how d'you come by it?

Del No – no, what he means is, no, it hasn't been released in Britain yet. You see we got it when we was abroad on holiday, didn't we?

Rodney We – we got it on holiday.

Sandra Where did you go?

The Trotters all speak at once.

Grandad Italy.

Del Spain.

Rodney Greece.

Grandad We toured.

Del Yeah we toured. *(He sees two watches on*

The Long Legs of the Law

the coffee table. Hiding the table with his body he carefully picks the watches up and places them down the side of the armchair) Well this, this is pleasant innit? You know, er, Rodney, you know he tried to join the police force once, yeah, it was after he failed the intelligence test to become a Unigate milkman.

Rodney He's joking.

Del No, no, I'm not. Er that – that's a very nice looking watch you've got there, Sandra.

Sandra Yes lovely, isn't it. Rodney gave it to me!

Del Oh, did he? Oh, of course he's a very generous boy, our Rodney, you know. Sometimes I think he's too generous for his own good. Yeah, come on. Er, Rodney shall you and me get Sandra a drink, eh? You and me. And me and you. You know, together. You and me.

Rodney Yeah alright. What will you have Sandra?

Sandra Gin and tonic please.

Rodney G and T. Cheers.

They move to the sideboard.

Del Why d'you give her that watch for?

Rodney Don't worry, I'll give you the money for it!

Del I don't worry about that. I'm not worried about the money am I? Don't you realise those watches are a very sought after property. They are especially sought after by the River Police and the Flying Squad.

Rodney You mean they're hot?

Del Hot? They're so hot it is advisable to wear oven gloves when winding them up.

Rodney But you told me they were straight!

Del Yeah well I lied, I lied, didn't I? Appellation Bordeaux controlée!

Rodney What?

Del We've got to think of a way to get that watch back off 'er!

Rodney Yeah, yeah, I'll just say, 'Sandra can I have the watch back, because I only lent it you'!

Del No we can't do that. She might get suspicious mightn't she. I'll have to think of something subtle.

Rodney Yeah, that's what I like about you Del, you'll try anything once!

Del Oi, oi, oi! Just er – no I've got an idea. Here. Just watch me. *(Takes the gin and tonic)* Here we are Sandra – a nice gin and tonic for you. Please allow me put it on the arm of the chaise-longue for you. *(As he is about to place the gin and tonic on the sofa arm, he pours the entire drink over Sandra's watch)* Oh dear, oh dear, butterfingers. I'm ever so sorry.

Sandra Oh no, no, it's alright. Don't worry.

Del No, I do worry, I do. I mean I feel partially responsible. Yes. Oh look you're all wet. Grandad, could you bring a cloth. Look at that all over your nice new watch. Give it – give it to me I'll get it repaired for you.

Sandra Oh no, no honestly, it doesn't matter. It's water-proof.

Del Ah? Well, yeah, I know it's water-proof, but is it gin-proof? You see gin – gin's a very funny thing, you don't quite know where you stand with it, see. Sorry, sorry about that he's a bit eccentric, you know. Um, no if you, if you, if you give me that watch I'll get it repaired for you, alright.

Rodney Yeah, yeah, he's right, Sandra. 'Cos it's probably out of guarantee now it's been soaked in gin, you know.

Sandra Well are you sure you don't mind?

Del Mind? La plume de ma tante. It will be a pleasure. *(She hands him the watch)* There you are. That's right. There, look I'll let you have this back in what – you know, in a couple of months – it will be as good as new! Well come on then Rodney – you know – get Sandra another drink. *(Del moves back to the sideboard)* That got you out of schtuck didn't it, eh?

Rodney What d'you, got me out of schtuck? You put me in it in the first place.

Del Oh that's alright – go on, pass the buck. Alright? Yeah. No listen, no more cock-ups. Just, you know, you think before you act, alright?

Rodney Alright!

Del *(He tips the empty bottle of gin)* Oh blooming 'eck. I'm sorry Sandra, we seem to be right out of gin.

Rodney Ah no we're not, no I've got another three cases of it down here!

Del *(Turning away, incredulously)* Unbelievable. I don't believe him. What a plonker! What a plonker!

SANDRA'S FLAT. HALLWAY/DOOR.

Rodney and Sandra arrive at her door. She takes her keys from her bag.

Rodney Oh well, here we are!

Sandra Yes, here we are!

Rodney Do they let you bring your uniform home Sandra?

Sandra Yeah, it's hanging in my wardrobe. Why?

Rodney Nothing.

They kiss gently. They are now in a sort of half-hearted embrace – cheek to cheek.

Sandra Rodney.

Rodney Yes, Sandra?

75

Sandra Can I ask you something?

Rodney Yeah . . . Anything!

Sandra You know your flat?

Rodney Yeah.

Sandra Well is there anything in it that's legally yours? *(They part)* I recognised a lot of the stuff from Scotland Yard photos and *Police Five*!

Rodney *(Floundering)* Yeah, er, well I mean you know. You're not interested in the little things that fall off the backs of lorries are you!

Sandra No! But I am interested in who pushed them and who picked them up. I mean you had three cases of export gin. You can't buy that in Britain!

Rodney No, no, we got it on holiday.

Sandra Oh, you smuggle as well?

Rodney Ah come on, Sandra. I bought you a doner kebab tonight.

Sandra And you gave me a stolen watch!

Rodney Now I didn't know that was nicked!

Sandra Well, tell that to the beak Rodney! You don't seem to realise I'm trying to build a career in the police force. Now, what do you think my commanding officer would do if he found me in possession of stolen property?

Rodney Put you in charge of the Christmas Club more like.

Sandra This is not funny Rodney, I could end up with the sack. Which of you two's the culprit, you or your brother?

Rodney No it's . . . yeah it's me. Del, Del don't know anything about it – he's a bit of a wally you see. Well I'll come quietly, miss – it's a fair cop.

He holds his hand out as if ready for the handcuffs.

Sandra If I was to carry out my duty to the full I'd take you straight down the station now . . . But you did take me to the pictures. And you bought me a doner kebab.

Rodney And a packet of cashews – and a watch! Oh no, forget about the watch!

Sandra No, I won't forget about the watch. Neither will I forget about the others, your brother hid down the side of the armchair. Look – I'll give you 24 hours' breathing space – time to, shall we say, spring clean your flat. And after that I'm coming round with the CID. That's 24 hours Rodney.

Rodney Yeah . . . right. Reminds me of that Gene Pitney song, you know *24 Hours From Dartmoor*! Well . . . thanks for a lovely evening Sandra.

Sandra Thank you, Rodney.

Rodney I don't 'alf fancy a coffee!

Sandra Oh do you? Well there's an all-night sandwich bar down the Walworth Road.

Rodney Oh yeah. I'll most probably pop down there then. Sandra – will I see you again?

Sandra Of course you will. I'll be round your flat in 24 hours. And in case you don't recognise me in uniform, I'll be the one with the warrant. *(She enters her flat)*

Rodney *(To himself)* 'Well, we've got 24 hours, Del. Well as you so rightly say Del. Rodney, 24 hours is better than nothing. Thanks for being so understanding, Del!'

THE TROTTERS' LOUNGE.

Del has Rodney by the throat and pushed up against the wall.

Del I'm gonna kill you Rodney!

Rodney You're choking me!

Del Listen – that's right, this is it you dipstick. Have you got any last requests?

Rodney Yeah – I want to leave my plimsoles to medical science, now get off will you.

The flat is virtually empty – save for the chest of drawers, the dining table which has both flaps down and the settee which is jammed between the door frame leading to the hall. Grandad enters climbing over the settee.

Del No, I won't get off.

Grandad Just leave him alone.

Del Eh?

Grandad Now, what's up with you now? I thought you'd calmed down . . .

Del I had calmed down. Then I trapped my finger in a flap on that table, got meself a black man's pinch and it's all this dipstick's fault!

Rodney I've said I'm sorry. I mean, what more does he want me to say?

Del You could say 'I'm emigrating Del Boy.' 'I'm jumping off the balcony, Del Boy.' Anything that would – that would cheer me up.

Grandad Anybody can make a mistake Del Boy.

Del Yeah, you're right, look at the mistake Mum and Dad made! How could they produce such a stupid kid?

Rodney Oh don't put yourself down Del.

Del I'll chin you, I will.

Grandad Look, we ain't got time to stand here arguing. We've only got a few hours to get rid of all this stuff!

Del That's right. Help me clear out this sideboard, make it a bit lighter.

Rodney Did we get this sideboard down Hooky Street, then?

Del I don't know Rodders. I don't know. Half the stuff in this flat is legal, the other half . . . isn't! It's been such a long time I – I just don't

The Long Legs of the Law

know what's bloody what any more. We've got to get rid of the whole issue. That's it, come on. Oh I know, there's something that I mustn't forget.

Rodney Oi Del!

Del What?

Rodney Can I keep one of these bottles of after-shave?

Del Yeah, what for?

Rodney *(Dabbing a drop on his cheek)* Well, it's just in case Sandra comes round a bit early, you know.

Del *(Dropping what he is holding)* Just come – come here, a minute will you.

Rodney No I – I don't want it now. I don't want it.

Del Come here a minute. Come here you! Will you just come here! I've just about had enough of you. You – come here!

77

Ashes to Ashes

EXT. A LONDON STREET MARKET. DAY.

In among the general hustle and bustle of a busy market day, we see Del, Rodney and the suitcase.

Del is trying to sell packets of women's tights. A tired Rodney is leaning against a wall and almost dropping off to sleep.

Del Listen, now listen. 'Ere, why shed a tear over the recession when you've got me around, eh? Now just look what I've brought you today girls. Look at that, authentic French tights, alright? As worn by Sacha Distel's mum! No seriously – I'm being serious. Now they're 20 denier and they're sheer nylon, not only are they run proof but they're fun proof as well. Now listen, if I asked you for £1 a pair I'd get killed in the stampede wouldn't I? Yes, I know, I know, I can see your face but I'll tell you what I'm not asking you for £1 a pair, I'm not going to ask you for 80p a pair. What did you say? You'd give me 60p a pair would you love? Put your money away – put your money – I don't want 60p – I don't want 60p a pair. I want 50p a pair and I'm starving myself . . . Now come on. Ladies, 'ere I thought you, I thought you were bargain hunters. You ladies. Now look you can't even get these in the factory for 50p a pair. Oi Rodney, am I keeping you awake?

Rodney No don't you mind me Del, you carry on.

Del Listen I know the Government keeps asking us to save energy, but this is taking the piss!

Rodney Look, I didn't get a lot of sleep last night, worrying about all the trouble and what 'ave yer!

Del Trouble. What trouble?

Rodney Well last night I went round that bird Linda's house for the evening, right. And her mum and dad come home earlier than what we expected.

Del Catch you at it, did they?

Rodney Well no – you know they didn't actually catch us. It was all a bit of a panic though.

Del So where does all the trouble come from then?

Rodney Well as I was leaving, her dad just happened to notice I had me jeans on back to front.

Del You had yer jeans on back to . . . Well what'd he say?

Rodney He swore at me!

Del Yeah I bet he did . . . I bet he didn't know whether you were coming or going!

Trigger, who is the market road sweeper, is pushing his way along the kerb

Del Oh, hello Trigger. 'Ere, how's yer gran?

Trigger Didn't you hear Del? The old girl passed on.

Del Oh what a shame, I am sorry Trigger.

Trigger Weren't your fault Del. The funeral's on Friday. You'll come won't you?

Del Er, Friday's a bit difficult. I'm a bit tied up actually Trigger. Anyway you don't want a big crowd there do yer!

Trigger There won't be a big crowd Del, I'm the only one who's going.

Del Oh yeah, yeah, I'll come. I tell you what I'll bring Grandad and all. 'Cos he used to know your gran, didn't he? Rodney'll come as well.

Rodney Eh?

Trigger Cheers Del – appreciate it.

Del That's alright.

Trigger I'll tell you what, I'll order a car shall I?

Del That's a good idea, Trigger.

Trigger I'll see you at gran's house, 'bout ten o'clock.

Del Alright – cheers.

Trigger sweeps on, up the road

Rodney Oi you, what's the idea of lumbering me with a funeral?

Del He's a mate, ain't he. You wouldn't want him to go on his own would you?

Rodney Well . . .

Del No of course you wouldn't. Anyway going to a funeral'll be good practice for me and Grandad.

Rodney Practice for what?

Del For when that Linda's dad catches up with you.

Rodney Now that is not funny Derek!

Del Yeah I think it is – hilarious. Alright, come on then girls, 'ere we are, genuine French tights, as worn by Charles Aznavour's sister.

INT. GRAN'S HOUSE. LOUNGE. DAY.

The décor is a depressing grey with matching suicidal brown. The furniture is antique (in a Portobello Road sense). One of the paintings littering the walls is a print of the Mona Lisa

and on the mantlepiece stands two matching china urns.

Rodney and Grandad, both in their funeral suits, are seated nervously. Del, in a brighter suit, is examining the furniture and paintings and mentally pricing them. Rodney is disgusted with Del's behaviour.

Del *(Examining chair)* It's Wedgwood.

Rodney Wedgwood's pottery!

Del Oh, is it? Oh yeah. I always get those two mixed up. That must have been why I couldn't sell that Chippendale teapot last week! Oh well. *(Studies the Mona Lisa)* Here – look at this over here – look. Look at that. It's a copy. *(Del examines one of the urns)* No, these are nice. Look at that – these are a nice, matching pair an' all.

Grandad Talk about a vulture.

Del No listen, Grandad. Look, Trigger's gran left him these in 'er will, right, and all this other stuff he wants to sell it, right. You know Trigger, he's not the brightest thing in Christendom, is he eh? I mean, I know a lot of people are born an 'apenny short of a shilling but in Trigger's case God added VAT. Look, if he tries to take this lot up town he's going to get right taken in ain't he – eh? So I reckon it's much better that he gets well, you know, stitched up by a friend rather than a stranger.

Trigger enters. He is in a black suit and tie.

Trigger I've put your coats in the bedroom. Fancy a drink?

Grandad No.

Trigger *(To Rodney)* Dave?

Del Just a small large one, Trigger.

Rodney *(To Del)* Oi, don't you think this is the wrong time and place to be shanting it up?

Del No, no, of course not. Eh, Trigger what you reckon, eh? Would your gran like to think of us, you know, standing around moping and mourning?

Trigger Yeah, she'd have loved it. She was a miserable old cow!

Grandad She never used to be like that son. When she was younger she was a real live wire. Life and soul of the party was Alice.

Trigger Yeah, I heard she was a bit of a girl. They reckon that's what helped finish my grandad off. *(To Grandad)* You knew my grandad Arthur didn't you, Mr Trotter?

Grandad Yeah, I knew Arthur alright.

Trigger He was a smashing man. He took care of me when my mum went.

Rodney Where was your dad?

Trigger He died a couple of years before I was born.

Rodney Oh!

Trigger I can almost see my grandad now, sitting by the fire, one leg on the fender – other one in the corner.

Del It's alright, he had a false leg didn't he – it came off . . .

Rodney . . . Had a leg that long.

Del Don't you be silly.

Trigger He was a road sweeper as well.

Del Yeah taught you the trade didn't he Trigger – eh?

Trigger Takes you back, dunnit?

Del Come on Trigger, it's no point dwelling in the past, you've gotta look towards the future ain't yer? Come on, you're going on your holidays on Tuesday ain't you?

Trigger Yeah, I'm looking forward to that Del. I've been under a bit of pressure lately, what with Gran in hospital and me case being adjourned. It'll be nice to get away from it all. I'm gonna live it up a bit. Discos, nightclubs, golden beaches, blue skies.

Rodney Sounds great Trigger. Where you going?

Trigger Ireland . . . Me gran left me a bit of money and these bits and pieces, so I ain't short of a few bob.

Rodney *(Looking from the window)* The car's here.

Trigger Well, just take one last look round the old place. When you think of all that's gone on in this house. Me gran and grandad living here together. Makes you go cold don't it?

Del No, no, come on Trigger – should be the opposite, shouldn't it – I mean you must remember all the – all the warmth and the love that they had between them!

Trigger No, there weren't much of that Del Boy, they didn't talk to each other for 15 years.

Rodney 15 years??

Trigger Yeah, me grandad found out that while he was away in the army, she used to have another man in the house.

Grandad lowers his eyes in guilt.

Trigger *(To Grandad)* Did you ever hear that rumour?

Grandad Me? No son! Did he ever, er – did he ever say who it was?

Trigger Never. I wish I knew though!

Grandad I'll go an' fetch our coats.

Trigger They're in the bedroom. It's up the stairs.

Grandad I know where it is. *Exits*

Ashes to Ashes

INT. THE TROTTERS' LOUNGE. NIGHT.

The Trotters are still in their funeral suits. One of the urns now stands on the table. Del is examining the other urn with a magnifying glass. He then checks his findings in a glossy reference book of antique pottery, etc. Rodney peers eagerly over his shoulder.

Del That confirms it Rodders.

Rodney Yeah?

Del Yeah.

Rodney Confirms what?

Del Well look, see that little mark there?

Rodney What?

Del There.

Rodney Oh, I can get that off, just a minute.

Del No, not there – not on – on there – look, that little mark there, look. See that confirms that these urns are . . . Meissen!

Rodney No!

Del Yeah, guaranteed brother!

Rodney Meissen eh? What's Meissen then, Del?

Del Well it's German china innit? Mid-19th century according to the book. There was a china sale at Christies the other week. And a couple of pieces similar to these – not in such good condition – went for £250! These must be worth £300 of anybody's money! Wait a minute, there's a paper in my bedroom with an article about it. I'll go and fetch it. *(Moves to the door)* *(To Grandad)* And oi – you – you just keep yer mitts off that – right? *(Exits)* I've got me eye on you.

Rodney 300 nicker.

Grandad Don't look very valuable.

Rodney Yeah, well the best ones never do, do they?

Grandad Oh it looks like the stuff we used to win at the fair!

Rodney Oi, you break that and he'll stuff your head down the bog.

Grandad is now peering into the urn. He reels back, horrified at what he sees and pushes the urn violently away.

Grandad Gawd Almighty!

Rodney Grandad – what's up with it?

Grandad Just look for yourself!!

Rodney Look at what?

Grandad What's in there!!!

Rodney It's not a spider, is it?

Grandad No.

Rodney peers into the urn

Rodney What is it?

Grandad It's Arthur!

Rodney Arthur?

Grandad Trigger's grandad Arthur. Them's his

ashes. Put the lid on Rodney.

Rodney Yeah! Oh bloody 'ell. *(Calls)* Del . . . could you come in here please? There's something up with one of the urns.

Del *(OOV)* If that soppy old git's broken it I'll stick his head down the khazi! Well – what's up?

Rodney It's Arthur's ashes!

Del Arthur's Ashes? That's the black bloke who won Wimbledon innit?

Rodney No! It's Trigger's grandad – Arthur!

Grandad His ashes are in that urn. Don't take the top off.

Del What's the matter with you – don't take the top off? What you got in here, a genie or something? *(He peers inside)* Well, how d'you know it's him, eh? It's hardly a passport photo is it!

Grandad It's him alright Del! I know it's him.

Del Yes alright, alright then, so it's him. There you are look, nothing to worry about is there!

Grandad Nothing to worry about?? You don't know the full story do yer? You see, them rumours about me and Arthur's wife – well they was true. But, but nothing happened between us Del. You've gotta believe that – nothing happened. We were just two lonely people. Arthur was away in the army, and yer gran had just . . . departed . . . Oh no, she hadn't died – just departed.

Del and Rodney lower their eyes.

Rodney Oh yeah, got yer.

Grandad Well we was just a bit of company for each other that's all . . . But Arthur wouldn't believe that.

Del No – well he wasn't as soppy as they made out then was he?

Grandad He put a curse on me Del. He pointed his bony finger at me and said, 'Trotter, someday, somehow, I'm gonna come back and haunt you!' And he had gypsy blood in him Del. You know what they say about a gypsy's curse!

Del Oh come on, you don't believe all that pony, do yer?

Rodney Yeah, I mean, it was a long time ago weren't it. You've moved since then – he's never gonna find you now. Oi, then again being a gypsy he might move around a bit, eh?

Grandad Never gonna find me? *(Points accusingly at urn)* Look over there. He's in the same bloody room as me!

Del Now don't be silly, Grandad. I mean ghosts an' all that – it's a load of rubbish, innit?

Rodney Yeah, I mean it's – it's greasy kids' stuff, innit?

Del Yeah, that's right, yeah. No, no, I'm gonna

go to me room. And get the paper alright – yeah. *(Exits, then reappears)* Who left this wooden leg out here?

Grandad Don't be bloody silly Del Boy!

INT. THE TROTTERS' FLAT. HALLWAY. NIGHT.

Three doors lead off hall. Two of the doors lead to Del and Rodney's respective bedrooms, the other leads to the bathroom. The hall is in darkness. The bathroom door is open and the light is on. We see Del in his pyjamas and dressing gown, still half-asleep, filling a glass with water at the basin. He switches the light off and is about to return to his bedroom when his attention is drawn by a hushed almost whispering voice from the lounge.

Grandad *(OOV)* I mean the thing is Arthur, you and me were – used to be friends . . . once! So I think there ain't no point in holding a grudge is there?

Del eases the door to the lounge open a few inches. There, in the darkness of the lounge, we see Grandad talking to the urn.

Grandad I know what happened annoyed you – it would have annoyed me! But, well, it was a long time ago, so why don't we just let bygones be bygones, eh?

Del grins evily to himself

Grandad Well you never frightened me with all that old tosh about a curse and what 'ave yer! I mean I – I ain't the superstitious type. In fact I don't know why I'm talking to you now. Well I know you can't hear me, Arthur!

Del picks up traffic cone and speaks through it with a ghostly voice

Del That is what you think, Trotter.

Grandad A-A-A-A-Arthur? Y-Y-Y-Y-You mean you can hear me??

Del You're coming through louder than a CB Rubber Duck . . . Is it forgiveness that you seek, Trotter?

Grandad Well yeah. I'm really very sorry for what's happened Arthur!

Del Ah, but how do I know that you mean it?

Grandad Oh I do, I do Arthur, really. I'll do anything to prove it to you Arthur, anything you say!

Del Alright then, tell me where your money's hidden.

Grandad I ain't got no money!

Del Oh don't give me that you lying old git! I know you're alright for a few bob and I wanna know where it is hidden.

Grandad It's in me suitcase under me bed.

Del No it ain't, I looked.

Grandad You've been under my bed??

Del I've been everywhere, Trotter. I am always with you . . . On those cold winter nights when your two grandsons, Rodney and the good-looking one, are out, have you never felt a . . . presence? I am the chill wind that wakes you in the dead of night. I am the – the movement in the curtains, I am also the creaking of the floorboards. Always with you even when you're alone, I am keeping you – company!

Rodney, just awoken, appears at Del's shoulder

Rodney What you doing?

Del Aaaarrrrgggghhhh!

Grandad screams and reels back from the 'spirit' now stumbling into the lounge. The sudden awakening even causes Rodney to cry out in alarm. There is a pause as everyone catches their breath.

Grandad You stupid little sod, that could have finished me off that could have!

Rodney What's that all about?

Del Oh, Soppy here was holding a seance with his little mate Arthur.

Grandad You never underestimate the powers of the unknown Del Boy! All I'm saying is get them ashes out of this house. Why don't you try an' get in touch with Trigger, get him to take them away?

Del Well what do you think I've been trying to do all evening? I've left messages for him everywhere. And he'll be going off on a three-week holiday soon!

Grandad Looks like we'll have to dispose of them ourselves then.

Del Yeah, looks like it. Suppose that's the least we can do is to give him a dignified send-off. Anyway we can't give anyone a dignified send-off at three o'clock in the morning! Right? So we do it tomorrow.

Rodney You got any ideas how we're gonna do it?

Del Well I thought we'd put him in an envelope and post him anonymously to a priest.

Grandad Bowls!

Del Well you got any better suggestions then?

Grandad No, *bowls*! He was a life-long member of the Peckham Bowling Club. I think he'd love to be scattered over that green.

Del Yeah, well, alright, that's what we'll do then.

Rodney Well they could refuse permission!

Del Yeah. Only if we ask.

Rodney Come on Del, you can't go merrily

Ashes to Ashes

sprinkling someone's ashes over a bowling green without being noticed! They'll be playing on it!

Del That is why we're gonna do it at night, when they're not playing on it! Right?

Rodney Alright – well I'm going back to bed.

Del Yeah, so am I. Goodnight Grandad.

Rodney exits

Grandad Del Boy. D'you think I've made me peace with Arthur now? I mean that were a good idea of mine about the bowling green weren't it? I think he'd have liked that . . . And you heard me apologise to him, didn't you. I mean, I don't think I ain't done nothing else that could incur his wrath have I?

Del No – no, of course not! Mind you there is one tiny little thing that might have upset him.

Grandad What's that Del?

Del points to the second urn.

Del Well Arthur is over there! Sweet dreams.

EXT. BOWLING GREEN/CLUBHOUSE. NIGHT.

All is in darkness. Del, clutching the urn, and Rodney creep into the centre of the green

Rodney What we gonna do now?

Del How should I know? This was his favourite bowling club right? This is where he spent many happy hours right. So I'll just turn the urn upside down and we'll have it away on our toes!

Rodney Eh, no, you can't just tip it upside down, it'll leave a mound. They'll think they've got moles!

Del Alright then, we'll scatter it evenly about whilst we sing a hymn or something! D'you know any hymns?

Rodney Er. We Three Kings of Orient are.

Del That is a Christmas carol you wally! 'Ere, why don't you go the whole hog you know and sing Jingle Bells while I dance about and we sprinkle him around?

Rodney Sshhh!! Do what you want to but hurry up.

Del Alright, I'll just say a prayer – get down on your knees . . .

They both kneel and clasp their hands in prayer. The urn is between them.

Dear God, high up in the sky . . .

The floodlights around the green are switched on. We see that a group of middle-aged and older men and women, all in bowling whites, have entered the clubhouse. There is the buzz of conversation and laughter from the bowlers, none of whom look out to the green.

INT. THE CLUBHOUSE. NIGHT.

Del and Rodney sprint away in opposite directions, leaving the urn. One of the lady bowlers looks from the window and reacts to the urn, spotlighted as it is in the centre of the green. She calls back incredulously to bring the captain's attention to it. As this happens, we see Del sprint back across the green, whip up the urn and sprint out of sight. The lady bowler brings the captain to the window and points to the empty green. The captain reacts, now doubting her sanity.

Captain Can't see a thing me dear, there's nothing there at all. I think you're imagining it.

Woman Bill, I assure you, I saw something I . . .

Captain You spent too much time in that bar.

EXT. RIVER THAMES. DAY.

We see Del and Rodney in a small rowing boat in mid-river. Rodney is rowing and Del, in his camel-hair overcoat and kipper tie, is holding the urn.

Del Heave to Rodney, heave to. This will do nicely!

Rodney Del, I've told you before and I'm gonna tell you again. You cannot perform a burial at sea in St Catherine's Dock!

Del I'm not performing a burial at sea, am I? I'm performing one of them Indian ceremonies like what they do on the Ganges! I saw it on *Whicker's World*, don't worry it will be a doddle!

Rodney But this river's polluted!

Del Well that ain't gonna upset Arthur is it, eh?

Rodney It ain't gonna do the river much good either!

Del Oh, look, just shut up will yer! Sit quiet for a minute and think – sort of – religious!

Del takes the lid from the urn. As he does so we hear the distorted, echoing voice of a man, apparently coming from the urn.

Voice What are you doing?

Del pushes the urn away to arms length.

Del God Almighty.

Rodney Del!

Del What?

We see a river police launch close by. One of the policemen is using a loudhailer.

Policeman I repeat, what are you doing?

Del Thank Gawd for that!

Rodney Say something sensible Del. I mean don't go telling 'em we're boat people or nothing.

Del We're Buddhists!

Rodney Dear God!

Del We're scattering some remains – it's part of our religion.

Policeman Have you written permission from the river authorities?

Del *(To Rodney)* Have we written permission from the river authorities?

Rodney Well of course we bloody ain't!

Del Of course we blood . . . No I'm afraid not Officer.

Policeman You can't do it then!

Del Oh – oh I see – right, well, thank you very much for all your help. *(Quietly, to Rodney)* Let 'em get out of sight and then I'll pull it overboard alright.

Policeman We'll escort you back to the shore!

Del Oh right. Thank you very much. Ain't it marvellous. There's never a copper around when you need one. But the sods are always there when you don't need 'em! *(ad lib)* Rodney . . .

EXT. ANOTHER LONDON STREET. DAY.

As they walk folornly up the road, dejected and on the verge of defeat, they pass a house that is having some minor building work done. In the road is a pile of sand, some bags of cement and a portable mixer. As they pass, Del looks at the cement mixer and stops. He is about to pour the ashes into the mixer when one of the labourers appears close by. Del smiles nervously.

Del Magic ain't they? The old Irish tumble-dryer! *He moves off to join Rodney with the labourer eyeing him suspiciously*

Rodney Oi, you weren't were you?

Del Of course I weren't! What d'you think I am, a Philistine or something?

EXT. SUBURBAN ROAD. DAY.

A middle-aged woman pulling a basket on wheels passes by. She reacts with snobbish surprise to Del and Rodney who are seated on the kerb with their legs in the road. The urn is in the gutter, between Del's legs. They are too preoccupied to notice her walk by them.

Rodney Could be a sign you know!

Del What?

Rodney Our failure to get rid of the – contents – of that urn, could be a sign that we didn't ought to dabble in that sort of thing!

Del What are you going on about?

Rodney Well, look, we're walking straight into the unknown here ain't we! I mean you don't know what strange dark powers we might evoke!

Del Oh give over you tart! What d'you think, the bogeymen are gonna come round and get us in our flat? If they do, they'll be too knackered to

do any haunting – them lifts have broken down again!

Rodney Yeah, well, as far as I'm concerned Del you can scrub round it, alright! Give the urns to a church jumble sale, or something, I've washed me hands of 'em!

Moves a few yards away. Del, leaving the urn in the gutter, follows him.

Del Rodders, listen now don't be a plonker. They're worth 300 quid! And you don't go giving our national treasures to jumble sales do you?

A council cleansing lorry, the type with the giant rubber tube, passes by. It passes by the spot where the urn was left.

Rodney Eh? I mean, just think what we can do with 300 quid, eh? We could get a nice new suit each . . . *(Del double-takes on the lorry)* That thing's just sucked up our urn. Oi!!! Oi stop!

They chase after the lorry, which eventually pulls to a halt

Driver What's the problem?

Rodney You've sucked up our urn!

Driver Your Ern'? Oh my Gawd! What was he, a little kitten?

Del Eh? Is he winding me up or what?

Rodney No, he just don't understand, look. *(To driver)* It's not Ern as in Ernie, it's urn as in you know Grecian!

Driver Oh! Well I thought there was something blocking me tubes.

Del I'll block his tubes permanently. Come on. Come on then. Is it there? You found it? Eh, that's it.

The driver pulls the base of the urn from the tube and hands it to Rodney. He then retrieves the top.

Rodney And there was the, er . . .

Del That's it.

Rodney Yeah.

Del Thanks. Right.

Driver There you go. And be careful where you leave yer bloody Grecian urns in future! I'll have the union in on this I will!

Del examines the inside of the urn.

Del Oh my Gawd, it's empty. It's empty. Arthur's been sucked up into that thing! It wasn't our fault though was it, Rodders, eh?

Rodney No, no, it was a complete accident Del – totally beyond our control! There's no need for us to reproach ourselves! Is there?

Del No, no, no, there isn't! It must have been an act of God. I mean, don't you see the poetic irony of it? Well Arthur used to be a road sweeper! To him this must be like a Viking's burial! Maybe he would have wanted it like this!

Ashes to Ashes

Rodney Maybe . . . I doubt it but . . . maybe!

INT. THE TROTTERS' LOUNGE. DAY.
Del and Rodney, who are now celebrating their good fortune, enter. Grandad is on the phone.
Grandad Hang on, he's just coming in now. Del Boy it's for you.
Del Who is it?
Grandad Trigger.
Del Trigger?? What's he want??
Grandad He said you've been leaving messages for him to phone you!
Del Yeah, I know I had, that's when I wanted him to have his grandad's ashes back! But we've got rid of them now! 'Ere, supposing he wants them – you know wants them back after he comes back off holiday? He wants me to keep them. What am I going to say?
Rodney Er, well, you just say . . . Oh you'll think of something.
Del Oh yes, thank you very much Rodney, you're a great help . . . git! *(Takes the phone)* Hello Trigger, how's it going my son? Yeah? What's the weather like? Oh foggy is it? Well it's a bit misty here . . . Yeah. Where are you? You're fogbound at Gatwick airport. *(To Rodney and Grandad)* He's still here, he could get in a cab and come back for it couldn't he? *(To phone)* Um, yeah, well Trigger – the thing is – look we've got a bit of a problem. Yeah, it's a bit delicate. So . . . Well you know, I – I'd brace yourself if I were you – yeah. Well you remember them urns that I had off you. Yeah, well you see I was just sort of cleaning them up, like, to get them ready to go to the Boy Scouts' bring 'n' buy sale, and er, well I, I found your grandad's ashes in one of them. . . . Yeah and I wondered what you wanted me to do with them? Yeah well, this is the problem innit, I mean what do *you* do with them? Look, why don't you leave it up to me Trigger? Eh? Of course it'll be a respectable and dignified ceremony! Yeah, yeah, good boy, well you know it makes sense! Yeah. Eh? *(Gives 'thumbs up' to Rodney and Grandad)* Well, they must be your grandad's! No I didn't know that! *(Stares venomously at Grandad)* No. No. Nobody told me! Right you have a nice time Trigger and I'll see you when you get back alright. There's something you forgot to tell me Grandad!
Grandad What's that Del Boy?
Del Trigger's gran was married *twice*!!
Del takes the lid from the second urn.
Del Oh no!!

A Losing Streak

INT. THE TROTTERS' LOUNGE. DAY.

The table is littered with marmalade jars, tea cups, a half empty bowl of soggy cornflakes and all the usual signs of a finished breakfast. The TVs are on, showing the BBC and ITV test cards. In the middle of the room is an enamel bath tub which is a quarter full with a yellow liquid. Rodney is seated on the floor and reacting to the vile smelling liquid. He is filling small perfume bottles from the bath tub and placing them in small cardboard boxes bearing the name: 'Yves Saint Dior' 'Parfum de Toilette' 'Paris.' Rodney hands the boxes to Grandad who, while keeping a close eye on the TVs, stamps the boxes with a tabbing machine and then places them in an old suitcase.

Del *(On telephone)* . . . When did I nick your speaker? Oh that speaker. Yeah, well I only borrowed it for the party didn't I? I gave it back to you the next day. Well, alright, the next week. Anyway, you are not honestly trying to tell me that you've only got *one* speaker? What just one!! Blimey, what a way to run a railway station. Anyway, look, never mind about your rotten speaker. Now listen, this is a once in a lifetime offer. How would you like to buy a *genuine* mink coat for 50 quid? No, no, it's not bent. No, the reason why it's so cheap is because it's Ethiopian mink . . . Ethiopian. Yes, I've got a contact in Babylon. Ah, well, the only difference between Ethiopian and ordinary mink is the colour. . . . Yeah, that's right. Well it's a sort of a . . . er . . . *(To Rodney)* What colour would you call them fur coats in the garage?

Rodney Tabby.

Del *(On phone)* They're sort of tab . . . They're a sort of mottled grey with delicate black highlights . . . I'll pop one round to you . . . You ain't got a dog have you? Winston, I'm only gonna leave it with you, you ain't got to feed it or nothing! Yeah, yeah, alright pal – fair enough. I'll see you around. *(He moves away from the phone in deep thought, obviously worried. He sees Grandad and Rodney are observing him and changes instantly into bright, happy-go-lucky Del Boy)* Oh well, win some lose some – nothing ventured, nothing gained – it's, well, boeuf à la mode, as the French say.

Rodney What's wrong Del?

Del Wrong? No, nothing's wrong. Things have never been better Rodney. This time next year we'll be millionaires! Right, here put the parfum de toilette in the back of the van, and we'll see if we can make a killing down the old market, alright.

Rodney Right-ho. *(Exits)*

Del That's it, off you go.

As soon as Rodney leaves, Del becomes a worried man again. He checks his wallet. Grandad is watching him. He has seen these signs many times in his life.

Grandad D'you play cards again last night?

Del Eh? Yeah, yeah, that's right Grandad you know me, eh? He who dares wins.

Grandad How d'you get on?

Del I lost. I even had Mum's lucky rabbit foot with me. Brought me about as much luck as it did the rabbit.

Grandad You wanna ease up with this gambling Del Boy. I've seen too many good men finish up in the gutter chasing 'easy' money.

Del It's that Boycie innit? You know Boycie, the second-hand car dealer from Lewisham. I have never seen anyone so lucky at cards Grandad, it's all for big money an' all.

Grandad He ain't using a marked deck is he?

Del What, no, we're close friends, anyway, he knows I'd break his arms.

Grandad Well I were in a card school once where the cards was marked. I lost a fortune.

Del What, you knew they were marked?

Grandad Oh yeah, I marked 'em . . . I was never much good at cards.

Del Stone me! Never mind.

Grandad Here, this Boycie fella, does he like spinning the old coin Del, you know double or quits?

Del Well yeah, him, he likes any form of gambling, don't he.

Grandad Oh well here Del, you try him with this. It's a double-headed coin.

Del A what – double-headed coin? I thought you only saw these in them old British movies.

Grandad Scotch bloke gave me this during the war. I remember it like it was yesterday. His hands was trembling and his voice was just a whisper. He said 'I want you to have something to remember me by, Trotter. Take me lucky coin.' Then he . . . he went!

Del What – he died?!

Grandad Deserted. Mind you, you couldn't blame him the way them Germans was carrying on. Someone was gonna get hurt.

INT. THE NAG'S HEAD. DAY.

Stood at the bar are the despondent figures of Del and Rodney. They each have a half-finished half of lager in front of them. The suitcase is leaning against the bar near their feet.

Del I don't believe it, I just don't believe it! I mean I thought we'd have got a right result with that scent. You know I thought they'd be queuing – camping out on the pavement like they do at an 'arrods sale. Instead of that . . . *(Makes a sharp pull of a chain gesture)* How many did we sell in the end?

Rodney What, altogether? None!

Del As many as that was it. Hang on, but I saw you sell a bottle.

Rodney She fetched it back.

Del Why?

Rodney She smelt it. She said the last time she smelt an odour like that was when the cat sanctuary got bombed during the war.

Trigger enters

Trigger Alright Dave? How's yer luck Del Boy?

Del Don't ask Trigger.

Trigger Still bad, eh? I'll have a pint of mild please, love, *(To Del)* What you on?

Del No, I'm alright Trigger

Trigger *(To Rodney)* I've never seen such bad poker hands as he's been getting. He lost 150 nicker in cold blood last night.

Rodney A 150 pounds!!

Del Nothing to worry about! I'm just on this losing streak that's all. It'll be over soon, it'll soon pass.

Rodney You don't honestly believe all that rubbish about winning and losing streaks do you? You make your own luck in this world, son, there's no such thing as a losing streak.

Del You give my arse an 'eadache sometimes Rodney. You don't know nothing about cards, do you? You and your little mates are still playing strip-snap, ain't yer? *(To Trigger)* They're thinking of inviting some girls one day.

Trigger You see Dave, a losing streak is like joining the Moonies. Easy to get into but a bark to get out of!

Rodney Just how much have you lost Del?

Del Got your 'ankie handy? I didn't want to tell you, I didn't want you worrying, I couldn't stand all that dermatitis all over again! We've got 70

quid and that's all that's left of your – profits.

Rodney Well, at least we can put the central heating back on and get something to eat.

Del Eh? You don't think I'm wasting this on food and warmth do you? This is my stake money for tonight's game.

Rodney You're playing again tonight??

Del Yeah, tonight 8.30 at our place!

Boycie enters

Boycie Trigger. Del.

Trigger and Del Hello Boycie.

Boycie Hello Rodney.

Rodney Boycie.

Boycie Oh dear what's up with you, bird trouble? You look as though you've had a promise from a liar . . . How's yer luck, Del?

Del Oh changing, changing, outed two-and-a-half hundred quid's worth of French scent this morning.

Boycie Oh good, you in the chair, then are you?

Del Eh? Oh yeah, yeah, Trigger?

Trigger I'm alright.

Boycie I'll have a cognac. Better make it a small one, don't want to skint you before tonight's game do I?

Del Julie could I have a double cognac please. *(Looking Boycie defiantly in the face)* And I'll have a large, I say, a *large* chivas Regal *with* coke!

Rodney *(Equally defiant)* Yeah and I'll have a double Southern Comfort with American dry!

Del That's 'alf of lager for Rodney. *(To barmaid)* And why don't you have one yourself you know and put the change in the Third World relief bottle will you! *(To Boycie)* So how's your luck pal?

Boycie Well, not too good to be fair with you. I've sold one today, mind you, a 1980 Simca Estate. Only made 850 out of it though. I mean what's 850 these days? Hardly heats me swimming pool for a week.

Rodney Grim innit?

Boycie Oh yeah, absolutely. I said to Marlene – the other day, you remember Marlene, Del.

Del Oh yeah, yes, all the lads remember Marlene.

Boycie Yeah, well I said to her . . . I said to Marlene, I said, if it wasn't for the fact that I was making so much out of Del and the boys, I'd have to do something really drastic – like only having smoked salmon *twice* a week.

Del You've got more front than Brighton ain't yer? Listen Boycie, I'm telling you that my luck's changing. I'm on a winning streak. Right! No I am, straight up, now listen, alright then, I'll tell

A Losing Streak

you what, tell you what, look, here's 20 quid right that says the next customer in buys a pint of something!

Boycie You're on! 20 here says the next customer orders a short.

Rodney You're pushing your luck a bit, ain't you?

Del No, no, I'm not Rodney, I've just seen the next customer who's coming in past the window.

> *The pub door opens and a large Irish navvy enters.*

Julie Yes, love?

Paddy I'll have a dry Martini and a slimline tonic.

Boycie *(Taking money from Del)* It pains me to take it Del, you know it really pains me . . . Well cheers, 8.30 round your place is it. *(Moves towards the door)*

Rodney Hold it Del. What are you doing??

Trigger Yeah leave him, Del!

Del I'm not gonna hit him you fool. Listen I've got a double-headed coin I'm gonna stitch him up, where is he? Boycie. Here, just a minute, just before you go, I tell you what. You're a gambling man, that 20 quid I'll toss you for it – double or nothing!

Boycie Go on then.

Del Right?

Boycie Heads.

Del What??

Boycie Heads. You know what Del, I hope this winning streak of yours holds out till tonight. *(Exits laughing)*

Del That's it, that is it, I've just done me stake money for tonight's game, ain't I?

Rodney Good!

Del What do you mean 'good'??

Rodney Look, you're on the verge of losing everything we've ever worked for in a rotten bloody poker game! What do you expect me to say? 'Good old Del Boy – he knows a short cut to the workhouse!'

Del Alright Rodney, alright, don't worry. If the worst comes to the worst you know we can always do ourselves in can't we, eh? Me, you and Grandad can go and jump in the River Thames.

Trigger Be quicker to drink a drop of it!

Del Looks as though you've already started.

Rodney Del, why don't you say to Boycie tonight's off? Say you've caught something!

Del Look, let me explain something to you Rodney. Look beneath all this finery – there lies – a berk! Now that surprises you, doesn't it!

Rodney No.

Del Look, you don't remember the day that Dad left home do you? Course you don't, you was too young. Well Mum she'd, well, she'd only just, you know, left us, and you were just a little nipper with a pink patch over yer national health specs, you know to help that turn in your eye, Grandad, he was sitting in his armchair waiting for colour television to be invented, anyway I came home that evening and found that Dad had gone, taken all his things and gone. He, he took everything Rodney. He took my savings, me three quarter length suede, he even opened your little piggy bank . . . The one thing that he didn't get was the money Mum had left me and you that was 'cos I'd hid it too well see, anyway he'd left us with nothing Rodney, not even the price of a meal. D'you know what that day was? It was my 16th birthday. He even took my cake!

Rodney What a lousy b . . .

Del Oi, oi, oi, that's yer father you're talking about!

Rodney Well I'm sorry Del, but that's how I feel about him!

Del Well it's alright, well, it's understandable, it's understandable . . . But you see, from that day I swore that I would *never* run away from anything in my life, I mean, you know if a wild lion were to come in here now my old April'd be pouting like a good 'un, but I'd stand me ground. I would, 'cos it's geezers like me that, that capture German machine gun nests! And that's why I've got to play the game tonight, Rodney, you see, because I *can't* run away! Running away only wears your shoes out . . . D'you understand me?

Rodney Yeah, yeah, I understand you Del! And I'll tell you something else, we're gonna beat Boycie tonight!

Del That's the spirit my son, that's it. We'll take him to the cleaners!

Rodney Ey, they'll call our place Che Sketchleys by the time we've finished with him. Right, well I'll see you later, I'm gonna get you some stake money!

Del Where from?

Rodney Oi, when the chips are down I can be just as sharp as you. Now, remember that party we had at the flat last month? Yeah there was plenty of booze, right?

Del Not gonna organise a disco are you?

Rodney Eh no. I'm gonna take the empties back for you! *(Exits)*

Del It's amazing ain't it Trigger. I've lived with him for all these years and I thought I really knew him. You know, and then something like this happens – some simple gesture – and then you suddenly realise what a 100 per cent, 24 carat

plonker he really is!

INT. EVENING. THE TROTTERS' LOUNGE.

The table is now covered with a green cloth in readiness for the game. Del in a three-piece suit paces the room. He flashes angry glances at Grandad, who is unmoved and continues watching the TVs.

Del Well?

Grandad Well what?

Del Are you gonna lend me that money or not?

Grandad I ain't gonna lend you *nothing*! If I had £1million I wouldn't give you a penny of it.

Del Come on Grandad, just give me a straight yes or no!

Grandad Why should I give you money to lose? And don't give me that old fanny about a losing streak.

Del It's true! Today I put 20 quid on a McAlpines navvy who was on a diet! Now what are the odds on you picking the only genuine weightwatcher in London?

Grandad What makes you think I've got any money anyhow? I'm an old-age pensioner Del Boy.

Del *(Mimics)* 'I'm an old-age pensioner, Del.' You crafty old sod! You had a 25–1 winner at Kempton Park on Monday. I know 'cos I gave you the fiver! And Rodney picked up your winnings, 125 quid.

Grandad Oh that?

Del Oh yes, oh that! Come on Grandad lend us £100! I'll pay you back double! Now be fair, I've always been straight with you haven't I? Remember last month when you said you was feeling the cold in bed, what did I do for you?

Grandad You bought me an electric blanket.

Del Right. Give me that £100 and I'll put a plug on it for you .

Grandad Alright . . . You pay me back double though!

Del Yeah, don't worry, alright, alright.

Grandad unbuttons his shirt. He is wearing a money belt. He tries to hide it from Del.

'Ere, d'you always wear that money belt?

Grandad Well it stops me getting a chill on me belly.

Del That is most probably why your kidney stones didn't show up on that X-ray!

Grandad *(Handing Del a bunch of notes)* There you go –

Del Thank you Grandad.

Grandad And don't lose it!

Del No, alright – alright, I won't. Cheers.

Rodney enters.

Rodney Trigger and Boycie are here!

Del Alright, alright, keep calm Rodney, keep calm. Right, now just er, just play it cool, know what I mean? Come on, just er, nice and cool, nice and cool . . . What you doing?

Trigger and Boycie enter.

Hello Trigger.

Trigger Del, Dave, Grandad . . .

Del Alright then Boycie.

Boycie Good evening, you don't see many places like this these days Del Boy.

Del Oh thanks. I designed it myself!

Boycie Yeah I thought as much! As a matter of fact I saw a place rather like this on a television programme recently.

Grandad *Dallas*?

Boycie No not *Dallas* – definitely not *Dallas*. No, it was a charity appeal – had the wife in tears you know. Still Marlene's easily touched.

Trigger Yeah, as Del said earlier all the lads remember Marlene.

Boycie Yeah, it was one of them programmes that . . . Well are we gonna stand here rabbiting all night or are we gonna play cards?

Del No, we're gonna play cards Boycie. Sit yourself down over there, come on Trigger. That's it. Right, that's it Rodney, get them beers down. Right.

The three sit at the table with Del opposite Boycie.

Five card draw – usual limit yeah?

Boycie That's alright.

Del Right good, right, I've got a new pack of cards.

Boycie Yes I brought a new deck as well.

Del Oh. Well we'll use mine save opening yours, alright.

Boycie No we'll use mine.

Del No, no, let's use mine!

Rodney Del's the host!

Boycie And I'm the guest! So we'll use mine!

Trigger Why don't you spin for it?

Del Oh yeah yeah, that's a good idea. Trigger. Alright with you Boycie?

Boycie Yeah, go on then.

Del Okay then here you go.

Boycie Heads.

Del Eh?

Boycie I said 'heads'.

Del But you called heads in the pub!

Boycie And I'm calling heads again!

Del We'll use your pack!

Trigger takes a small bundle of crumpled notes from his pocket and lays them on the table. Del lays his £100 on the table. Boycie

A Losing Streak

opens his briefcase and places three thick wads on the table.

Boycie Is that all you've got Del?

Del Er no, no, no, I've got more than that you know, Rodney's got the rest for me.

Rodney Oh, yeah, Del, there's the £4.37 from the empties.

Del closes his eyes in abject embarrassment.

INT. NIGHT. THE TROTTERS' LOUNGE.

It is almost the end of the evening and the atmosphere is now one of a smoke-filled gambling den. Jackets have been removed and hung on the backs of chairs, ties are loosened and waistcoats unbuttoned. Ashtrays are filled with cigar butts and dog-ends. Del and Boycie smoke fat cigars, Trigger a tipped cigarette. Rodney and Grandad puff nervously on roll-yer-owns. All three players are studying their hands.

Del Down to you Trigger.

Trigger Too heavy for me Del Boy. I'm calling it a night.

Boycie Looks like it's down to you and me then Del Boy. Right, your 30, and I'll raise you 30 . . . It's gonna cost you 30 quid to stay in, Del.

Del I ain't got 30 quid left Boycie.

Boycie Well what can I say?

Del Alright, hang about, hang about. Go on, 30 quid and I'll see you.

Boycie I have a running flush. Four, five, six, seven, eight of hearts.

Del Jeeze and I've got three tens! Cor, stone me.

Boycie Not good enough then, is it Del Boy? *(Scooping the kitty in)* Well that seems to be the end of the evening. Shame, really I was just getting into me stride . . . Well I'll bid you adieu then.

Del Hang about, Boycie, no, hang about. I ain't finished yet.

Del goes to telephone.

Grandad *(Quietly to Trigger)* He knows more card tricks than Paul Daniels don't he!

Trigger D'you reckon he's been switching 'em?

Grandad Course he's switching 'em! He's done you two up like a couple of kippers.

Del pulls a wad of money from the phone receiver.

Rodney Del, oy where d'you get that from??

Del Buzzby sent it down the line didn't he?

Rodney How come for the last fortnight we've been off Queer Street and suddenly all them notes materialise?

Del This is the money that Mum left you and me. She said it was only to be used in a life-or-death situation.

Rodney Oh, now come on Del, this ain't a life-or-death situation, it's a bloody game of poker!

Del No it isn't Rodney. This is not a game – this is a duel! Alright Boycie I've got 500 quid here that says that this game ain't over yet.

Boycie Nice one, Del Boy, I like yer style. I tell you what let's make this a bit exciting, shall we? No limit!

Del That suits me Boycie. That suits me right down to the ground . . . Alright dealer takes one . . . Go on your bid.

Boycie A century.

Trigger 100 notes? You're coming it a bit ain't yer Boycie?

Boycie This is a no limit game between me and Del Boy, so keep yer nose out Trigger!

Del Don't worry, don't worry Trigger. He's bluffing, alright here you are, there's your 100 and I'll raise you 100.

Boycie Your 100 – and I'll raise you 100.

Del You're bluffing!

Boycie Only one way to find out ain't there Del Boy.

Del Oh he's bluffing – he's definitely bluffing, I can tell by his eyes, he's bluffing.

Rodney It's gonna cost you another 100 to find out Del.

Del Trust me Rodney trust me, he's definitely bluffing! I've got him by the short n' curlies! Your 100 – and I'll raise you 200. Want to see me Boycie?

Boycie Oh no no, no, no, Del Boy that's your 200 – and I'll raise you a grand!

Trigger Knock him out, Del.

Boycie It's gonna cost you a thousand notes to see my cards Del.

Del I'm skint Boycie!

Boycie Well you shouldn't play big boys' games then should you?

Grandad *(To Boycie)* Oh play the game son. That's the money their mum left 'em. That's all they've got!

Boycie Well, Del, do something or get off the pot.

Del Yeah, yeah, alright. *(Removing jewellery)* All my jewellery, right and um . . . *(Looks to Grandad who gestures that he has nothing) (Appealing)* Trigger!

Trigger I'm boracic mate.

Del *(Turning to Rodney)* Ro . . . Forget it you.

Trigger Here are you can have me car. *(Reluctantly hands his keys over)*

Del Cheers Trigger you're a real pal. Right, so

that's my jewellery right and Trigger's car – it's a good 'un!

Boycie You must be joking, I sold it to him!

Del Right you'll get your money back won't you, so that's my jewellery, Trigger's car, the stereo and the tellies!

Boycie It still don't come to a thousand notes Del.

Del Alright, alright, tell you what I'll do, it's my jewellery, Trigger's car, the stereo, the tellies and *everything* in the flat, right, the cooker, the fridge, the deep-freeze, the beds, and wardrobes, our clothes . . .

Rodney Now what's your bloody game Del?

Del It's alright, trust me Rodney, he's bluffing. Have faith in me.

Boycie Alright Del Boy, seeing as we are friends, I'll accept all of that as a bid of £1000.

Del What have you got?

Boycie I've got Kings.

Del How many?

Boycie lays them one at a time on the table.

Boycie Un – deux – trois – quatre.

Del *(Stunned)* Four!!

Boycie I didn't know you were good at maths Del.

Del I thought you were bluffing.

Boycie Oh no, no, no, no, no, Del Boy. Not on your Nelly.

Del I thought he was bluffing!

Rodney You berk!

Trigger What did you have Del?

Del Two pairs.

Grandad Two pairs? You went all that way on two rotten pairs?

Del I thought he was bluffing?

Grandad Well he was bloody well wasn't was he? *(Exits to kitchen in disgust)*

Trigger Couldn't give us a lift home could you Dave?

Rodney Yeah, I could as it goes, I'll drop you off on our way to the river.

Del's head is bowed in defeat.

Boycie Well Del I'll send the boys round in the morning for the stuff. It really pains me Del, it really does pains me. *(He is about to scoop up the winnings when Del's hand shoots out and grabs his wrist.)*

Del What are you doing?

Boycie What d'you mean what am I doing, I'm picking up the winnings Del, that's what I'm doing!

Del Oh no, no, no, me old mate, no, no, not on your Nelly! You know the rules of the game. *All* cards must be shown before the winnings are collected.

Trigger Leave it out will you Del, you've only got two pairs.

Boycie No, no, Trigger. It's alright, let Del have his little moment, come on Del let's see your two pairs.

Del *(Laying two cards on the table)* I've got one pair of aces.

Boycie *(Bored)* Yeah.

Del And I've got . . . *(Laying two other cards on the table)* another pair of aces.

Boycie is stunned as he realises he has been beaten. His cigar falls from his open mouth. Del smiles sweetly at him. Rodney, Grandad and Trigger stare disbelievingly at the four aces on the table.

Boycie That's *four* aces!!

Del I didn't know that you were good at maths either Boycie.

Trigger Four aces! I ain't never seen it before!

Rodney Four aces! Four bloody aces! *(Turning to shout to Grandad in the kitchen, not realising he is stood beside him)* Grandad! Sorry! He's got four aces, SEE!

Grandad I thought Del Boy might have something up his sleeve!

Del reacts to Grandad's comment, indicating that is exactly where the other two aces came from.

Rodney Oh look at all that lovely money!

Del I told you I could do it didn't I, eh?

Rodney Well done.

There is general celebration, back-slapping, etc.

Del Oi Rodney now careful what is your game?

Boycie Well done Del.

Del Thanks.

Boycie Nicely played. *(Hissing)* Where d'you get those four bloody aces from?

Del Same place you got them kings! I knew you were cheating Boycie.

Boycie Oh yeah, how?

Del 'Cos that wasn't the hand I dealt you!

Boycie moves to the door

Rodney Del, let's take him again.

Del No, no I don't want to push me luck.

Rodney Oh come on you're on a winning streak!

Del Eh yeah, yeah you're right. Oi Boycie. Hang about, hang about, listen I always like to see a man get a chance to get some of his money back. Right, tell you what I'm going to do, look, there's 200 quid. I'll spin you for it. *(produces the double-headed coin.)*

Boycie No way Del. I've already beaten you

A Losing Streak

twice with the coin. By the law of averages
you've got to win it.

Del Alright, I'll make it fair. Rodney'll call for me.

Rodney Yeah, yeah, I'll call.

Boycie 200? You're on.

Del All right Rodders, call it. *(Spins coin)*

Rodney Tails.

Del What??!

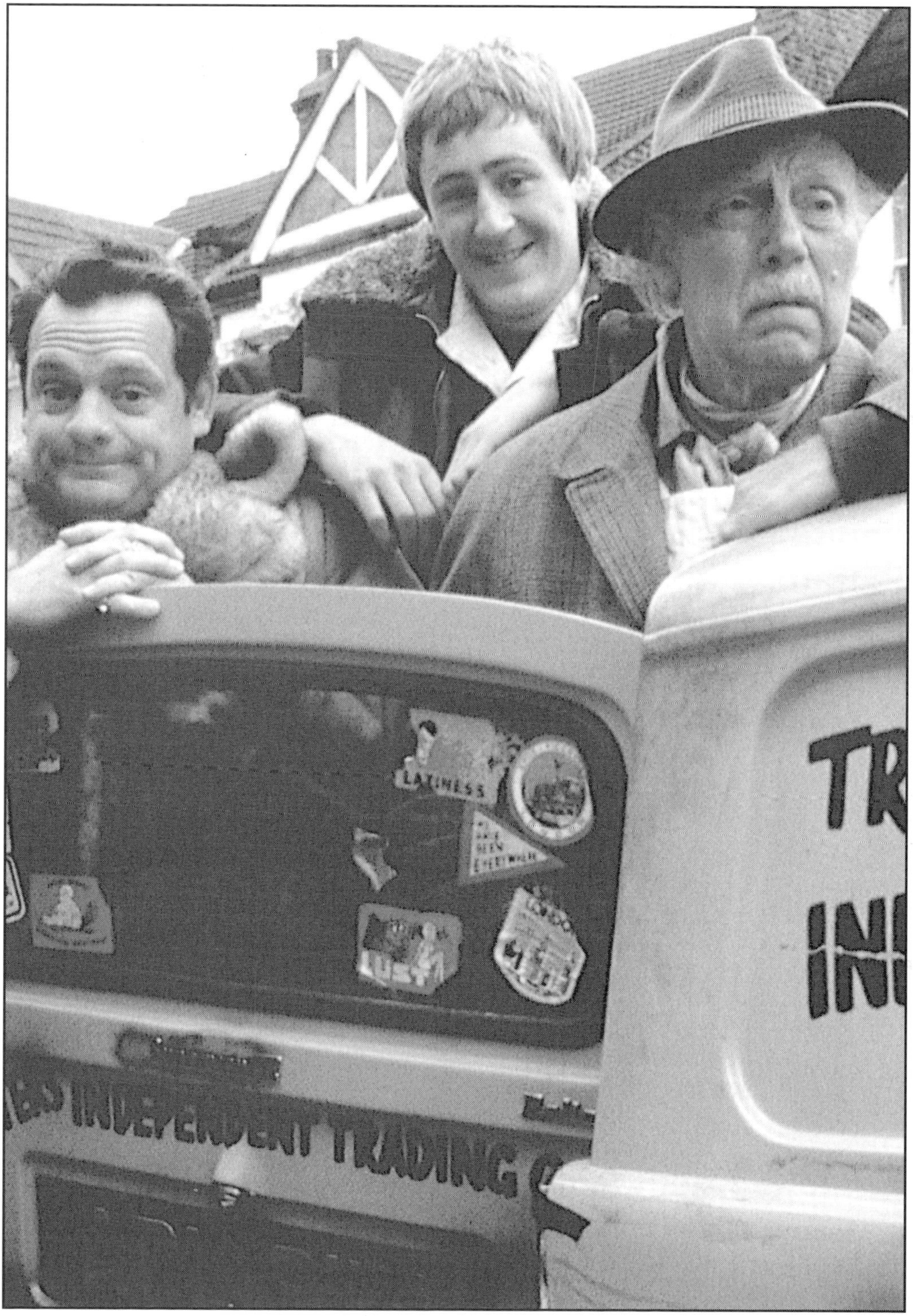
LAZINESS
INDEPENDENT TRADING

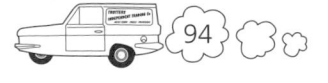

A LONDON BACK STREET. IRENE'S HOUSE. DAY.

The van is parked at the kerb. Del is wearing a brand new camel hair overcoat. Rodney is also wearing a similar overcoat which is far too big for him. Del is buttoning the coat up for Rodney.

Rodney But I don't like camel-hair Del!

Del This is not camel-hair, it's genuine polyester! There you are. That's it. Go and have a look in the mirror. *(Del adjusts the wing mirror)* It's 'ansome innit, eh?

Rodney What d'you mean 'ansome? Look, it's miles too big for me!

Del Of course it's not, that's the fashion innit?

Rodney Well how come yours looks like it's made to measure then.

Del Oh, this one. Yeah, it's a bit too small for me. I saved you the best one Rodney!

Rodney Del, it's horrible!

Del Well you could at least wear it for a while, see if you get used to it. I mean, it is a gift Rodney, it is a gift.

Rodney closes his eyes and curses his thoughtlessness. Del has the suitcase open at the back of the van. He is filling it with various items of women's clothing. The repentant Rodney appears at the back of the van

Rodney Hey you're right, Del. Once you've had it on for a while it really grows on you don't it!

Del D'you like it then?

Rodney Like it? I love it. I think it's really, really smart you know. Cheers!

Del I'm glad you like it. That's a score you owe me.

Rodney A score? You said it was a gift!

Del Well it is a gift at 20 nicker. Cost you a 180 up Bond Street!

Rodney Yeah but . . .

Del Alright, don't worry about the money Rodders, I'll take it out yer wages! Well you said you liked it!

Rodney Yeah I know, but . . . yeah . . . yeah, cheers Del.

Del That's alright Rodney. That's what brothers are for . . . Now listen, I want you to pop down and see that Mrs Singh. 'Cos according to the book she had a dinner service and two Persian rugs off us last month and she ain't paid a penny off 'em since!

Rodney Right.

Del Right. Oh, and while you're at it. See if you can get her interested in any of this gear.

Rodney Del, Mrs Singh's a Hindu! Hindus do not go about in peek-a-boo bras and nifty knickers!

Del What are you, some kind of Swami or something? You don't know what goes on under them saris! Go on, I'll see you later.

They part and move off in opposite directions. Rodney arrives at a house. A woman is just opening the front door. This is Irene. She is in her late thirties, speaks with a London accent but is not a 'Cor Blimey' type.

Rodney Excuse me, sorry, can you tell me if Mrs Singh's in at all?

Irene Mrs Singh don't live here any more! She moved away, about three weeks ago. I've taken her flat.

Rodney Great! Did she say where she was moving to!

Irene Bangladesh!

Rodney Oh good, for a moment I thought we'd lost her!

Irene Can I do anything for you?

Rodney No, no, not really. It's just that Mrs Singh bought a few items off us and she's supposed to be paying for them on the weekly.

Irene I see. What are you, a tallyman?

Rodney No, no, no, I'm not a tallyman. It's just that every so often I manage to get me hands on a few . . . 'bargains' you know.

Irene Really, what are you selling today?

Rodney Women's clothing. You know skirts, blouses, under . . . er, lingerie, that sort of thing.

Irene Bring them inside. I might be interested.

Rodney Yeah alright.

Irene Are you coming in or not?

Rodney Yeah okay . . .

IRENE'S FLAT. LIVING ROOM.

It is a reasonably bright and pleasant flat. The furnishing is early MFI. Rodney is alone in the room. He sits nervously on the sofa drinking a scotch. He lays back, forcing himself to relax. He surveys the room with a wry smile – considering all the possibilities. He does a double-take when he sees a wedding photo and goes back to his nervous position.

Rodney Bloody hell, he's a big bloke!

Irene *(Out of view)* Sorry, I can't hear you!

Rodney Er, no, nothing!

Irene enters from the bedroom. She is wearing a very tight skirt with a thigh length split up the side and a low-cut blouse. She does a twirl.

Irene Well what do you think?

Rodney Triffic!

Irene You don't think this split's too revealing do you?

Rodney No! No, that's just right!

Irene Hey, I can't quite reach this zip. Could you give us a hand.

Rodney, obviously relishing the thought of physical contact within such a short space of time, moves towards her. Remembering the wedding photo, he hesitates.

Rodney Er, what time does your husband get home?

Irene He doesn't. My husband's away!

Rodney Oh! *(With renewed confidence, he places his left hand firmly on Irene's backside and pulls the zip up with his right hand.)*

Irene Ooh, ain't you 'alf got a strong grip!

Rodney It's all that free school milk they keep giving us! So you're on your own then?

Irene No!

Rodney Oh!

Irene There's my son Marcus.

Rodney Oh right, what is he asleep in the bedroom?

Irene No he's down the snooker hall! He's 16 . . . I hope you don't mind me asking, but have you been ill recently – or lost a lot of weight?

Rodney Eh? *(Realising she means the coat)* Oh this? No, no you know, it's the fashion.

Irene Is it really? Well I'm so out of touch. I seem to spend every hour of the day in this flat.

Rodney What you don't know many people round this area then?

Irene No. I only moved here a month ago. I come from East London you see.

Rodney It must get pretty gutty being in on your own of an evening?

Irene Hmm, specially for someone who's used to going out and enjoying herself all the time. Are there any nice places around here?

Rodney Na! Oh there's a dinner 'n' dance place over Streatham way, that's supposed to be really good. I was thinking of giving it a try Saturday night.

Irene Oh I hope you and your girlfriend enjoy yourselves.

Rodney Oh, I haven't got a girlfriend! Well, what I mean to say is I haven't got a regular one!

Irene Oh hundreds of casuals I bet!

Rodney Yeah, all over the place! The thing is, they're all busy Saturday night! So um, you know I – I was wondering whether you'd um, you know, if you're not too busy, perhaps you'd like – I expect you are – but if you're not – would you like to come with me?

Irene Thank you very much, it's just that . . .

Rodney Oh, no, no, it's okay, you've made other arrangements, I understand!

Irene No, I haven't made other arrangements!

Rodney You're washing your hair!

Irene No!

Rodney You're mending your bike?

Irene No I did that last Tuesday.

Rodney So what is it?

Irene Well, how old are you?

Rodney Well I'm not a kid if that's what you mean! I'm 23 and a half!

Irene That's what I mean! You're 23 and a half, and I'm older than you!

Rodney So?

Irene Well doesn't it bother you?

Rodney No! Does it bother you?

Irene Well . . . no!

Rodney So where's the problem?

Irene There isn't one! Thank you very much for the invitation, I'd love to go out with you! See you Saturday night.

Rodney Right at 8.30, I'll pick you up in the va . . . in a mini cab!

Irene There's just one thing! You'd better tell me your name, it's gonna get a bit embarrassing if I keep having to call you thingy all night.

Rodney Sorry. Yeah, Rodney.

Irene Irene.

Rodney No – Rodney. Oh sorry, sorry, pleased to meet you Irene. *(They shake hands gently)*

Irene Oh yeah.

Rodney Well I'd better get me suit down the cleaners then.

Irene Rodney. You sure you don't mind? People might stare.

Rodney Let them stare! That sort of thing don't bother me Irene. I went out with a Chinese girl once! *(Exits)*

NIGHT. THE TROTTERS' LOUNGE.

Grandad is watching the TVs, each showing a different programme. Del is at the table having just finished his tea. Rodney's tea of egg and chips remains untouched. He is on the phone talking to Irene in a hushed, romantic tone.

Rodney Of course I missed you today. Yeah, I

missed you yesterday, and the day before that, and the day before that, yeah. Come on you know I'm thinking about you all the time! Are you? Really? Aah!

Del Oi!

Rodney *(To Del in same gooey voice)* Yeah? *(More masculine)* I mean, yeah?

Del Can I dip my bread in your egg?

Rodney Help yourself.

Del Thanks very much.

Rodney . . . No, no that's my brother. Oh, yeah, yeah, okay, I'll see you soon, of course I do! I can't. There's people here! Yeah alright. Okay. See you. Bye.

Grandad Who was that Rodney?

Rodney Eh? Oh, er, Mickey Pearce.

Del Mickey Pearce?

Rodney Del, I want your advice. I've got a bit of a problem.

Del I don't wanna know, I don't wanna know. I'd rather die in ignorance! There's never been anything like that in our family. Hey hang about Mickey Pearce is on holiday in France ain't he?

Rodney Oh yeah! Well it wasn't him actually, it was a girl.

Del Don't you ever do that to me again Rodney. I'll be up all night with heartburn . . . So you've got a bird have you? Ah, well, that explains it!

Rodney Explains what?

Del It explains why you've been lolloping about so much for the last week or so! You wanna pull your socks up my son, it's beginning to affect business!

Rodney How can it affect business?

Del I'll tell you shall I? *(Indicating little black book)* Look a tart in here called – Irene Mackay right – she's had 17 quid's worth of clothes off you. And you're letting her pay you back at 25 pence a week right. That means you've got to go round there every week for a year!

Rodney Yeah, I know!

Del Oh I geddit, Rodney's got a mystery!

Rodney Irene's not a mystery! We've just been seeing a lot of each other and well, we've become quite close! Promise me you won't laugh?

Del No of course I won't!

Rodney I think I'm in love.

   Del bursts out laughing.

Grandad Oh, do us a favour Rodney. Only a month ago you was in love with that skinny bird from the dry-cleaners. Now along comes another little girl and you're away again!

Rodney Marguerite from the dry cleaners was just an infatuation! This is the real thing! And

Irene is not a little girl – she happens to be a woman!

Del Oh a woman, eh? He's fell in love with someone who's got the vote this time! How old is she, 20?

Rodney No. She's about – 30.

Del What d'you mean about 30? How old is she exactly?

Rodney 40.

Del and Grandad 40? 40?

Del You're not being serious are you?

Rodney Well what's wrong with going out with a woman of 40?

Del Nothing, nothing at all, if you happen to be 50! Blimey she's even too old for me!

Grandad Well I'd have to think twice!

Rodney Shut up Grandad.

Del No, he's right Rodney, he's right. I mean, when she was drinking frothy coffee with some Ted up the Lyceum, you were struggling to keep your gripe water down! Oh no, bruv, this is one problem you're gonna have to solve on your own!

Rodney That's not the problem!

Del What, something else is it.

Rodney Yeah. Her husband!

Del She's not married an' all is she?

Rodney Oh no he don't live with her. He's away.

Grandad Where?

Rodney Parkhurst.

Del I don't believe you! I don't believe you! You're not going – you're not going case-o with the wife of a convict are you?

Rodney You don't 'alf jump to conclusions don't you, I mean just 'cos he's in Parkhurst don't automatically mean he's a convict! I mean he could be a warder, or even the governor!

Del And is he?

Rodney Is he what?

Del Well a warder or the governor?

Rodney . . . Well, no, he's a convict – but you weren't sure, were you?

Grandad What's he in there for Rodney?

Rodney Er, you know, this and that.

Del Yeah come on, like what?

Rodney Well like wounding with intent, GBH and attempted murder.

Del He's got a little bit of a temper has he?

Rodney Well this is why Irene's had such an unhappy life with him. He used to beat her up Del! She's moved over this way from the East End to get away from him.

Del Hang on a minute, hang on a minute. What d'you mean get away from him? He's on the Isle

of bloody Wight Rodney!

Rodney Yeah, I know that, but he's being released soon! That's the problem. Look, when he comes out do you think I should go and see him, and tell him about me and Irene, man to man?

Del Well, let me put it this way. You know one day if you're really fed up with having knees in the middle of yer legs, you know, you go and see him. On the other hand, if you've grown quite attached to them, emigrate to Vietnam – you stupid little plonker Rodney. What do you think this is, *Jackanory*? This bloke's a killer!

Grandad Well he only got done for attempted murder!

Del Oh did he. Well, maybe that was just a bit of practice, eh? His first big success is going to come with Rodney.

Rodney You're just like the rest of modern society, aren't you – frightened!

Del What me, frightened of them nutters out there in the shadows? Yes, oh yeah, they frighten me Rodney!

Rodney Yeah, well, I've got a life to live right and I'm not going to have some mindless little thug like her old man, Tommy Mackay, telling me what I can do and what I can't do! It's one battle I'm gonna have to win ain't it!

Del Alright, alright. Go on, you go and do that then Popeye. What are you gonna do? Carry a couple of tins of spinach round with you? Listen, you wanted my advice right – well here it is. Steer clear of Irene Mackay otherwise sleep with one eye open alright?

Rodney Yeah, well, I'll think about it Del. I'll see you both later, I'm going round Irene's! *(Exits)*

Del *(Calls)* Yeah, go on then – go on. You go round there. Off you go – on your bike. I wouldn't bother to put that on 'cos when we come to pay our last respects to you, you'll be wearing a concrete overcoat. You'll be helping to support a flyover on the M26!

Grandad What are you gonna do Del Boy?

Del Nothing! I mean you know – you know what he's like with birds don't you, falls in and out of love more times than Starsky and Hutch. Anyway, they always give him the elbow after a fortnight.

Grandad But in case she don't?

Del Gonna put his name down for BUPA!

THE NAG'S HEAD. DAY.

The bar is sparsely crowded. A few young punks are playing the Space Invader. Rodney sits alone at a table sipping a scotch.

He is depressed – life has kicked him in the stomach.

Del Good morning my little pot pourri.

Julie Good morning.

Del Giss a Tia Maria and a pineapple juice and, er, 'alf a lager for lover boy will you.

Julie He's on scotch and that's his fourth!

Del Is it? Alright give him one more and that's his lot!

Julie Right.

Del Alright Rodders? I knocked out all of them Georgian digital clocks.

Rodney Yeah?

Del Yeah.

Rodney Triffic!

Del Leave that there, right. Don't sit on it. What's the matter with you?

Rodney Nuffing!

Del Now come on, don't give us that. What's the matter now.

Rodney It's Irene!

Del Oh don't tell me. They've turned down her free bus pass?

Rodney She's finished with me!

Del Oh! Oh well, all's well that ends well I suppose.

Rodney What d'you mean 'all's well that ends well'? It hasn't ended well for me has it!

Del Oh now, come on Rodney. Come on. You've had a good time, ain't yer – you know, a few drinks, bit of the old Humpty Dumpty and now it's finished ain't it, eh?

Rodney You're a pig ain't yer? That is the pinnacle of your aesthetic appreciation innit – a few drinks and a bit of Humpty Dumpty!

Del Yeah . . . No I was just trying to put it into perspective that's all. I mean, you didn't honestly think that anything was gonna come of it did you?

Rodney I loved her Del!

Del Now come on Rodney, believe me bruv, it's – you know, it's all for the best in the end. I mean I know exactly what would have happened. You know, one day you'd have gone down that roller disco and met some blinding 18-year-old sort who'd have knocked your eyes out. And she would have fell head over heels for you, wouldn't she?

Rodney *(Allowing himself a little smile and a shrug)* Well . . .

Del Yeah and then you'd have had to go and break the news to Irene! How do you think a 40-year-old woman would feel, knowing that she's lost in love to a younger woman? She wouldn't be just losing any man. She'd be

No Greater Love

losing you!

Rodney I've never thought of it like that.

Del That scar would never heal!

Rodney No! Oh poor chick!

Del Exactly! It's che sara, sara as the French say. Anyway, her old man was released yesterday, so it's saved you from all that didn't it.

Rodney Yeah! You're right. Look I'm sorry if I've bin a bit of a pain lately.

Del No, of course you ain't, no!

Rodney Oh do leave off! Look at me – I've been acting like a right wally!

Del Oi, now I don't want you talking like that Rodney! Emotions that you've been experiencing are the things that separate you from well from those morons. *(Indicates the punks)* No it's alright. It just shows that you're a human being, in the fullest sense of the word. You proves you've got a heart Rodney, and them feelings deserve respect and dignity. Don't feel ashamed of them – you feel proud of them.

Rodney Yeah!

Del That's it.

Rodney Cheers Del.

Del It's alright. I'll get our drinks, eh?

Rodney Yeah.

Del Right.

> *Del moves to the bar*

Julie What's up with him?

Del Oh some old tart's given him the sack – you know what he's like don't yer. *(Returns to the table)* Here you are. If you're looking for answers you won't find any in the bottom of a glass!

Rodney No, I just fancied a drink that's all!

Del That's alright, that's alright – just you know, you just lay off the bottle. Alright? Right cheers then anyway.

Rodney Cheers.

Del Good luck.

> *Marcus enters. He is another punk with partic-ularly spiky hair. He is wearing one of the camel hair overcoats.*

Marcus Hello Rodney.

Rodney Oh hello Marcus. *(To Del)* This is Irene's son. This is my brother.

Marcus Alright Del!

Del Yeah – hello son. Smart looking kid ain't he, eh? I bet he could pick up BBC2 on that hair. BBC2 on his hair . . . What's the matter with you now?

Rodney Ah, no, nothing, but how did you know Irene's husband was released yesterday?

Del Ah well you – you must have said!

Rodney Did I? But I didn't know!

Del You must have said I mean – how else would I have known?

Rodney Yeah. I s'pose I must have!

Del 'Ere well, come on, come on, let's get going. Drink up, eh, see if we can do a bit this afternoon.

Rodney Yeah, alright, how did Marcus know your name?

Del You introduced us didn't you, eh?

Rodney No I just said you was my brother, I didn't say your name!

Del Well, he must have heard it before somewhere mustn't he?

Rodney He's never met you before!

Del *(Indicating his medallion)* Well it must have been me 'D' look. I'm wearing a big 'D' ain't I, it's obvious me name's Del innit?

Rodney No, that could stand for David, Daniel, Douglas. He's wearing one of your coats.

Del I know that – I know that, we're all wearing them ain't we, eh? Look it's the fashion, ain't it eh? Come on – come on let's go!

Rodney Oi Marcus! How did you know his name?

Marcus I met him on Thursday when he took Mum out for a drink!

Rodney You took Irene out?

Del Now look Rodney, it's not what you think. I just wanted to talk to her about you.

Rodney Me? What did you tell her about me?

Del I didn't tell her anything about you. I was – I just – I just told her a few home truths, that's all. I just – I just said, you know, if she thought anything of you, she ought to leave you alone!

Rodney *(Spitting the words)* Thanks Del! Where would I be without you, eh? Happy maybe!

Del Now come here Rodney. Now Rodney, just a minute. Look, I did it for you. I mean, what do you wanna do – end up dead?

Rodney No! But it's nice to have a choice innit. One of these days Del – just one of these days! *(Exits)*

Del Rodney, come – Rodney, I did it for you. *(To Julie)* That's the thanks I get!

LONDON BACK STREET. NIGHT.

> *The van is parked at the kerb. Del, wearing his new coat, is at one of the doors talking to a young Indian. Ahmed is also wearing one of the coats, which is far too big for him*

Del Oh yes, it was made for you Ahmed my son.

Ahmed It's too big man!

Del No, no, no, it isn't. No, that is the fashion. Let's have a look at the back. Oh that's beautiful that is.

Ahmed Yours isn't too big!

Del Ah but – this is small on me! Anyway, I reserved the best one for you Ahmed my son. Now come on at 25 nicker you can't go wrong, can you, eh?

Ahmed Alright man, I'll take it.

Del That's it. You know it makes sense! Now, d'you want to pay now or do you want it on the old . . .

Ahmed I'll pay you two pound a week Del.

Del Alright. I'll see you next week.

Ahmed Alright.

Del You won't catch cold in that.

THE ALLEYWAY. NIGHT.

Del passes a small alleyway. As he does, a West Indian leaps from the alley and drags the struggling Del back into the alley.

Del Oi, oi what's your game!

Leroy Take it easy man, you might hurt yourself! There's someone here who's been dying to meet you.

Del Oh yeah – who's that then?

Tommy Mackay, with a face that makes McVicar's seem angelic, steps from the shadows.

Tommy Me! Mackay's the name. Tommy Mackay. Ring a bell does it?

Del Yeah, I think I've heard of it before.

Tommy You bet your life you've heard it before sunshine! You've been seen out with my wife Trotter! Guilty or not guilty?

Del Oh no, it was just only a friendly drink!

Tommy But I'm not a friendly geezer. And that kind of thing makes me very 'angry'! I'm gonna teach you a lesson you'll remember for the rest of your life, Rodney my old son!

Del Now listen, listen now, let's not be hasty, er? Rodney? Did you say Rodney?

Tommy Yeah that's right. Rodney Trotter, that's you innit?

Del Yeah, yeah, I'm Rodney Trotter yeah.

Tommy Good! Okay Leroy give him some air.

Tommy and Leroy remove their jackets. Del removes his overcoat. Tommy and Leroy throw their jackets to the ground. Del throws his overcoat into the darkness behind him – he turns to see that it has landed in a muddy puddle. He turns back, now snarling and seething with anger.

Del Now look what you've made me do! That was a brand-new coat that was.

We can hear groans and thuds after Del dives in to fight. A dustbin clatters in the struggle and rolls out of the alley and comes to a halt on the kerb.

A police constable walking down the street has his attention drawn to the alley by the sound of a scream. He rushes down the road and arrives at the alley. He observes the blood-letting going on inside. He turns and runs away out of sight.

Eventually the sound of the fighting subsides to the sound of just the occasional thud. Del, dragging his overcoat behind him, staggers from the alley. His face is swollen and bruised, blood runs from his lips. His shirt is speckled with blood and is hanging out, his tie has been ripped. He leans against the wall and takes great gulps of cold air.

THE NAG'S HEAD. NIGHT.

The bar is crowded – somewhere a pop record plays, mingling with the drone of conversations and general pub sounds. Rodney, now in a suit, sits alone at the bar clutching an almost finished lager.

Del, in a bad condition and still slightly unsteady, pushes his way through the crowd.

Del Rodders. Guess what I've done for you Rodders?

Rodney Well if it's another example of your so-called brotherly love, you just forget it, right. As far as I'm concerned Del you're no longer my . . . *(He turns to see Del)* What the bloody hell's happened to you?

Del It's alright. It's alright. No, it's just – you know, I just walked into a door.

Rodney It did all that?

Del Yeah, well it was a revolving door! Listen, listen to this. I had a bit of luck tonight. I bumped into Tommy Mackay. That was lucky weren't it, eh?

Rodney Did he do that Del?

Del No, no – he didn't do it, no – no – no, it's just that I had – you know – I had one too many like, and I fell down the stairs at Monkey Harris's house.

Rodney He lives in a bungalow.

Del Yeah, well, he's moved now ain't he, eh – he's moved. Just shut up and listen will you. Well I had a chat with Tommy Mackay, tonight you see and, um, I managed to do what all the psychiatrists and social workers have failed to do! I've rehabilitated him. He's seen the error of his ways. You know, he'll give you no more problems. I've left the path clear for you and Irene!

Rodney Me and Irene? Oh that's all over Del!

No Greater Love

Del What?

Rodney Well we both had a long talk about it, and we decided it was never gonna work.

Del It will – it will work. I got, er, I've got a box of Black Magic in the back of the van, I've only had one of it. Go on, whip – go on whip it round to her now. Go on.

Rodney No, it's no good Del! I mean, it was just circumstances that threw us together weren't it? She was lonely in a strange part of town, and well I was just looking for a mother-figure I suppose, anyway you was right Del!

Del No, no, no, no, I wasn't – I wasn't.

Rodney I don't mean about me and Irene!

Del Well what d'you mean then?

Rodney Well, this afternoon I went down the roller-disco and I met this bird, Zoe.

Del Zoe?

Rodney 18 she is, with a body that makes Bo Derek look a cert for plastic surgery! Irene was just infatuation, but this is love! Oi, here she is now. *(Zoe enters)* Alright babe? This is Zoe. This is my brother, he fell down some stairs.

Zoe Nice to meet you.

Del *(Stunned)* 'Lo!

Zoe *(To Rodney)* Are we going then?

Rodney Yeah, yeah, right I'll see yer later on Del. Alright? You can finish that if you want it.

Del Yeah! See yer Rodders . . . See yer Zoe.

Rodney *(Calls from the door)* Oi Del! I'd have that head looked at if I was you! *(Exits)*

Del It's the truest bloody words you've spoke for ages Rodney!

Julie What happened to you?

Del Me? No, no, nothing happened to me. Rodney got a bloody good hiding though!

To Irene
All My Love Rod xxx

The Yellow Peril

INT. TAKE-AWAY.

Del is inside 'The Golden Lotus' Chinese takeaway. Behind the counter is a door marked 'Kitchen'.

Del So we have a deal then Mr Chin?

Chin Yes, we have a deal.

Del Good.

Chin Do you take Barclaycard?

Del *(Indicating the till)* Do you? No, call me old fashioned or sentimental if you like, but I'm a readies man meself – cash in hand, that's my motto! Anyway, we'll see you first thing in the morning right, about 11 o'clock.

Chin Can't you do it today?

Del Oh, no, no, no, sorry I can't do it today Mr Chin. You see, today is a very special day. Today is the anniversary of my late mother's passing from this immortal curl; and by tradition my brother and me, we always spend the day with her in the cemetery, tending the grave, that sort of thing. Anyway, I must rush, gotta buy some flowers.

Chin Yes – I'm very sorry!

Del Oh, it's no sweat, I get them cheap off a geezer in the market! Sayonara.

Chin Cheerio.

As Del goes out to the van he removes an 'Out of Order' bag from a parking meter and puts it in his pocket.

CEMETERY/GRAVESIDE.

A marble-look headstone reads: 'Joan Mavis Trotter. Wife of Reg. Mother of Del Boy and Rodney. Fell asleep March 12, 1964.'

The headstone is incorporated within Mum's marble-look 'monument'. The centrepiece is a large cross reaching up to 8ft high. Beneath this is the sculptured face of an old man with a long flowing beard (Del's idea of God). On either side of the cross stand marble-look statues of The Virgin Mary, and gathered all around this are a host of chubby angelic figures. The monument is beginning to show signs of wear, both from the weather and local pigeons. The other graves are all in a terrible condition, uncared for, overgrown with weeds and grass. Del is standing on the grave trimming the grass with a small pair of shears. Rodney is seated on a nearby bench.

Del There you go Mum . . . s'cuse feet. *(Admiring)* It's the bestest grave in the entire cemetery Rodney.

Rodney Yeah, it's mustard.

Del Yeah, I mean look at the others – they all look like monuments to the unknown gypo . . . While the others fall and crumble into dust this will stand forever. And do you know why? 'Cos it's the only one in the entire cemetery made of fibreglass.

Rodney Del, it's the only one in the entire cemetery that required planning permission!

Del That's right . . . *(Joins Rodney on the bench)*

Rodney It's looking a bit tatty nowadays.

Del I don't know, it's not too bad. It's bound to be a bit iffy innit, after 17 years? I mean, so would you be after standing there for 17 years of pigeons and diesel fumes and other mourners stubbing their cigarette ends out on you. I dunno, maybe you could be right. It could do with brightening up a bit. If I added some fibreglass models, of say, an apostle and four cherubims with trumpets, do you think it would alter the effect?

Rodney If you added fibreglass models of Snow White and the seven dwarfs you couldn't alter the effect of that!

Del Oi, oi, oi, don't start getting sacrificial! I don't know what's the matter with you Rodney, really I don't. You seem to have no sense of occasion. You've no. . .tres bien ensemble, as the French say. I mean look at you now, loafing about around your mother's graveside. Don't you feel any emotion?

Rodney Now look Del, I didn't know Mum that well, did I? When she died I was just a little nipperoni, all odd socks and eczema! Now you feel a sense of personal loss – me, I just feel cheated.

Del I'm sorry Rodney. I should have realised . . . Our Mum was a wonderful woman . . . She had long blonde hair . . . sometimes. Every night you'd see her sitting at the bar in the Nag's Head with her simulated beaver skin – with her rum and pep in one hand, 20 Senior Service in the other. She looked like a lady – lots of people mistook her for a money lender.

Rodney Really?

Del Straight up. Oh yes, course, I was much younger then and didn't have much money, but

every night she used to send me across two or three pints of light and bitter, or whisky if she was flush. That was Mum . . . Then come about ten o'clock she'd look over where I was sitting and she'd shout 'Come on Del Boy, get off home to bed – school in the morning!' That was the kind of woman she was Rodney, concerned about our welfare.

Rodney Where was I then?

Del Outside in the pram eating an arrowroot.

Rodney Wasn't she worried?

Del No, it was only an old pram . . . No, it's alright, I'm pulling your leg. Course she was worried. No. I like it here though, don't you Rodney. Nice and quiet, away from the crowds and the noise and the traffic. It really is. It's so quiet.

Rodney Yeah.

Del Tranquil.

Rodney Hmmm.

Del You're decorating the kitchen of a Chinese take-away tomorrow.

Rodney *(Not really hearing)* Yeah.

Del The sun is shining the birds are singing.

Rodney What did you just say?

Del I said the sun is shining and the birds are singing.

Rodney No, I mean before that?

Del Everythin's quiet and tranquil!

Rodney No Del, in between it being quiet and tranquil and the sun shining and the birds singing you mentioned something about a Chinese take-away.

Del Chinese ta . . . Oh, the Chinese take-away. Well the owner's, see, in dead schtuck. He's got the health inspectors coming round and he's got to have his kitchen, you know, painted, you know, brightened up a bit.

Rodney So why have I got to paint it?

Del Well you're the one that's got the GCE in Art. It's a good earner this is Rodney. I'm charging him a 150 nicker.

Rodney I don't care.

Del Oh come on, I've given him your word now.

Rodney Look, I am not painting the kitchen of some grotty Chinese take-away. Alright?

Del Alright, if that's the way you want it . . . Yeah, I remember what Mum said to me on her deathbed. She called me over to her side and she said 'Del Boy . . . Del Boy.

Rodney Stuttered did she? . . .

Del turns on him with a glare that could kill. Rodney has committed a cardinal sin and he knows it.

Sorry Del . . . No, really, I'm sorry. I don't know why I said it . . . Sorry.

Del 'Look after Rodney for me Del Boy' she said. 'Share everything you've got with him, try to make him feel normal . . .' And that's what I have done. Half of everything I've got . . . I mean, fair enough, I've got nothing, but half of it's yours!

Rodney You'd give me half of everything! You'd nick the hole out of me last polo if I didn't keep me mouth shut.

Del That hurts Rodney . . . That hurts. If I had any kind of wealth I'd give half of it to you like a shot.

Rodney Yeah? Say you had two Rolls Royces?

Del Why I'd give one to you wouldn't I.

Rodney You'd give me one of your Rolls Royces?

Del Yeah, course I would. If it was weather like this I'd give you one with the sun-shine roof.

Rodney If you had £2 million what would you do?

Del I'd give you £1 million wouldn't I.

Rodney Really?

Del In cash.

Rodney What would you do if you had two of them deep sea diver's watches?

Del Now you know I've got two of them deep sea diver's watches . . . Don't take bloody liberties with me Rodney!

Rodney Yeah, that's the real Del coming out!

Del Alright, you can have one of me deep sea diver's watches. Alright?

Rodney No, no, I've got to draw the line somewhere. I'm fed up with you and your bribery and your emotional blackmail every time you want me to do the dirty work! It's a point of principle now Del, you'd better get this straight, I am not painting that kitchen tomorrow, I'm not painting that kitchen in 1,000 years – no way my son!!

Del I'll give you a lend of me dirty books.

Rodney Yeah, alright then.

EXT. DAY. SIDE STREET/TAKE-AWAY.

The van pulls up at a parking meter. Del alights from the driver's side, Rodney from the passenger side.

Del *(Throwing Rodney the 'Out of Order' sign)* Oi Rodney, put that on the meter will you. *(He opens the back door to reveal a sulking Grandad in among the step ladders, buckets and dust sheets)* Right, come on, what's that look for?

Grandad You can't expect me to paint with me feet Del Boy.

Del I don't expect you to paint with your feet.

The Yellow Peril

All I expect you to do is sweep up, mix up and hold the ladder for Rembrandt here, alright. Come on.

Del walks off towards the take-away which has a 'Closed for Redecoration' sign on it. Del approaches the door, opens it and a cat runs out.

(Calls) Oi, don't let him out . . . Well that's going to please Mr Chin innit?

Rodney Was it his pet?

Del No but number 39's off the menu.

INT. CHINESE TAKE-AWAY.

Del and Rodney enter.

Rodney D'you reckon them rumours about these places are true then?

Del No, of course not.

Rodney Well, that cat looked pretty alarmed about something.

THE KITCHEN.

The kitchen is a nightmare vision. The kind of kitchen we all fear may exist behind those swing doors of our favourite restaurant. It is dirty and greasy, littered with unwashed pots and pans. Lumps of meat and veg lay rotting on the work tops. Del notices the look of horror on Rodney's face.

Del Here we are, nice little kitchen innit.

Rodney Nice little kitchen? This is the pits Del Boy. This is the bloody pits. The whole place looks like an explosion in a dripping factory.

Del This is a working kitchen Rodney. You've got to expect a little bit of fat to spill out of the pan every now and then.

Rodney So what period are we going to decorate it in Del? Early bubonic perhaps?

Del Yes, if you like, look, don't worry about it, you've had all your innoculations haven't you? Come on.

Grandad enters carrying a portable TV

Grandad Is this the kitchen?

Del No, this is the master bedroom, the kitchen's upstairs in the bathroom you wally. Now, listen you two, you should be out of here in a couple of days if you don't do anything stupid like stopping for lunch.

Del picks up a cardboard box which is standing next to a stove. He places it on the table. He opens the box and produces a few small tins of paint with no labels on them.

Oi, Rodney, come here, down here, look at this. This is yer paint – right, there's yer walls, there's yer ceiling – and now I'll leave it all up to you Michelangelo.

Rodney Oh yeah, and just what am I supposed to do with them soppy little tins – look I can't even dip me brush in 'em.

Del He can't even get his brush in 'em. He can't even work that little problem out. Tell him how to do it Grandad.

Grandad Get a pair of scissors and trim your brush.

Del Yeah, no, no. You don't get a pair of scissors and trim yer brush up. Look what you do is get yer little tins open them up and you put them into a big tin.

Rodney Oh yeah I'd thought of doing that already . . . They've got no labels on them, we don't even know what colour they are.

Del I know, the owner bought them cheap, he got well taken on, it's a load of rubbish.

Rodney You can say that again. Where'd he get 'em from?

Del Me.

Rodney You? Is this nicked Del? I'm not doing it if they're nicked!

Del It's not nicked Rodney. It's bankrupt stock. I bought a couple of gross as a job-lot. Trust me, will you, trust me.

Chin enters.

Chin Good morning.

Del Ah, good morning Mr Chin . . . Well my men are here as promised – and may I say that these two are the best in the business. The crème de la menthe of the painting and decorating world.

Chin Good. (To Grandad) You are the painter?

Grandad No, no, no, he's the painter. I'm his apprentice.

Del No, they're the best, the very best. Don't worry about it Mr Chin – in fact, chin up.

Chin Have you decided what colour the walls will be?

Del Colour . . . (Looks to tin of paint which Rodney is desperately trying to open) Yes, I mean, you don't leave an important decision like that until the last minute. (Hisses to Rodney) Get that lid off.

Rodney I'm trying.

Del (Playing for time) Well, Mr Chin, the colour that I thought of – now you may not agree with me, but somehow I think you will. What I thought, and you can shoot me down in flames on this one if you like . . . got it off yet?

Rodney No.

Chin Blue.

Del What?

Chin I like blue!

Del Blue, oh blue, Jeux Sans Frontières, that's

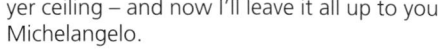

exactly what I thought of. I thought, why don't we paint these walls a nice subtle shade of blue.

Chin What shade of blue?

Rodney *(Removes lid)* Yellow.

Del And then I changed my mind. I thought no not the blue – gold.

Rodney That is yellow.

Del This is gold Rodney, what's the matter with you, are you illiterate or something? *(To Chin)* I remembered the name of your beautiful restaurant 'Gold for the Golden Locust'.

Chin Well Mr Trotter, I'll leave it to you. As long as my kitchen is painted and cleaned up before the health inspector calls. Alright?

Del Fine.

Rodney Sorry, how do you know the health inspector's calling? I didn't think they warned you or nothing

Chin Oh I had a telephone call from a man, he did not give me his name, but he tells me, 'Get you kitchen painted or you be in big trouble, John.'

Rodney John?

Del John, yeah – John. John, you know, John, it's the expression, cockney expression. Alright John and all that. Somebody up there must like him, eh?

Rodney I wonder who that anonymous caller could have been Del?

Del Well, I don't know. Don't think we're ever going to find that one out are we Rodney, eh? Well, come on now, we must now say chow mein and let our men get on with the work. Eh, Mr Chin? *(Chin exits)*

Gradad D'you think this anonymous person is likely to ring up any other Chinese Restaurants and tell 'em to get their kitchens painted?

Del Well I had to do something, didn't I? Otherwise we would have been lumbered with all this paint. Right, now listen. I'm going to take these boxes with me, right, so Rodney you'll have to water that lot down a bit, you don't want it too thick do you 'cause the plaster's none too kosher. Just remember, a little dab'll do you, right, a little dab'll do you!

Grandad Here, what about all this grease and filth Del Boy. You arranged for anyone to clean it up?

Del Of course I have, what do you think I am a cowboy or something? There's a tin of Ajax and a rubber glove in that bucket – go easy on the Ajax. See yer!

THE TROTTERS' LOUNGE.

Grandad is turning the TVs on as he sits.

Rodney *(Out of view)* He's not in.

Rodney enters

Grandad P'rhaps he's gone out!

Rodney Oh yeah, I never thought of that. You daft old . . . of course he's gone out, the question is where? This is the second day on the trot that Del's done a complete disappearing act, but when I ask him where he's gone, he's always acts sort of evasive.

Grandad I thought he told you to mind your own bloody business.

Rodney Yeah, that's what I mean, evasive. You know what, I reckon that while I have been imprisoned in that Chinese take-away, he's been out wheeling and dealing on the quiet – making a few bob and cutting us out . . .

Del enters.

Oh you're in.

Del You can't pull the wool over this boy's eyes can you, eh Grandad? Yes I am in Rodney . . . Seven out of ten for observation. Did you finish that job?

Rodney Yeah, about half an hour back.

Del Good, give us the money then, give us the mazoola. Thank you. £150 – spot on. Well done.

Rodney We phoned you to come and pick us up but you weren't in. What have you been up to Del?

Del Oh bits and pieces.

Rodney Where have you been?

Del There and back.

Rodney So what you been doing?

Del This and that.

Rodney Long as I know.

Grandad I thought you'd winkle it out of him in the end.

Del Listen Rodney I been doing something . . . private . . . Alright so let's just leave it at that. Okay? I think the best thing to do with this money is to split it three ways. Here you are Grandad – that's 35 for you.

Grandad Oh cheers Del Boy.

Del 40 for you Rodney.

Rodney 40!

Del Yeah, well, you're the craftsman aren't you? You get the most 'cos you're experienced.

Rodney Yeah but over there you said . . .

Del Hang about, hang about. And you also get your diver's watch. There you are.

The door bell rings.

Hello, somebody at the front door. Grandad go and see who that is will you.

Grandad Oh, my legs are older than yours.

Del I know, that means they've had more experience haven't they?

The Yellow Peril

Del *(Referring to the watch)* D'you like it then?

Rodney Yeah, cheers.

Del Good. Oh, the bloke said don't get it in the water.

Rodney Don't get it in the water? But it's a deep sea diver's watch.

Del I know that, but it doesn't mean to say you've got to go deep sea diving in it does it? I mean, I've got a pair of them desert boots but you don't catch me in the Sahara. Look, it tells you how deep you are and everything.

Grandad It's Trigger for you, Del.

Trigger follows Grandad in, Rodney is at the table trying to get the watch to work. He winds various buttons, holds it up to his ear, shakes it and finally bangs it on the table.

Del Oh yeah, hello Trig.

Trigger Alright Del Boy? Hello Dave.

Del What's up with you then Trig?

Trigger I got some more of that paint, interested?

Del Oh yeah. Yeah, I'll have some of that. Yeah, what is it – same price or lower?

Trigger Same.

Del Oi, Rodney, don't bang that watch, it ain't shock proof.

Trigger *(Indicating paint)* I won't be getting any more of this for a while. I'm laying low for a spell, we almost got caught the other night.

Rodney What do you mean almost got caught?

Trigger Yeah, by the railway police. See me and Monkey Harris get this paint from a storage shed down in Clapham Junction.

Rodney You swore to me it wasn't nicked! Bankrupt stock you said!

Del British Rail, same thing innit?

Rodney Knocked off railway paint, eh? Well I bet Mr Chin's going to be well pleased when he finds he's had his whole kitchen done out in Inter-City yellow.

Del I prefer to call it Awayday Gold.

Grandad I wondered where I'd seen that colour before. All day long I was whistling 'This is the Age of the Train' and I couldn't think why.

Trigger No, this ain't the stuff they paint trains with. They use this for painting signs in tunnels.

Rodney It doesn't matter what they use it for Trig, it's still knocked off – and it's still illegal.

Del Yeah, but it's good for the country though Rodney, innit?

Rodney Come on Del, how can nicking off British Rail be good for Britain?

Del *(To Trig)* He amazes me you know Trig, he's got a GCE in Maths and he still acts like a total wally-brain. *(To Rodney)* I'll tell you why this is

good for the country, shall I Rodney? 'Cos British Rail have to hire more security guards to protect this paint thus lowering the unemployment figures – plus, their insurance company will need more people to handle British Rail claims that means redundant insurance clerks will be snatched from the dole queues and handed back their dignity. Right? Now these people may very well celebrate their good fortune by buying a car and taking their wife and kids on a touring holiday round Britain. This will result, this will result in a much needed boost to our ailing car industry, higher revenue for North Sea Oil and a vital cash injection into seaside resorts and depressed areas. On the other hand, they may decide to take a holiday abroad, right, thus forcing foreign hoteliers, restauranters and bar owners to buy more British beer, food and goods. This will result in higher export drive which, in turn, will be very good for our balance of payments surplus! Soon this country will be rich and famous again – the starving shall be fed – the homeless will be homed. Right?

Rodney is left open mouthed. We can almost hear the figures whizzing around his brain.

Rodney This watch is broke!

Del This watch is not broke, it's just that you don't know how to work it properly. Look, see it tells you the time in all the major capital cities of the world.

Rodney Yeah look, everyone except London. Look all I can tell by this is that it's nearly chucking out time in Peking and I'm low on oxygen.

Del What do you want for nothing? Jam on it?

Grandad Tunnels.

Del What did you say?

Rodney No, he said that.

Grandad Trigger said tunnels! He said they use that stuff to paint tunnels. Well how can you see a sign in a tunnel? It's pitch black innit?

Trigger Na – this is luminous paint.

Del It's luminous paint Grandad, that means you see it in the dark . . . Luminous? Bloody luminous??

Trigger I thought you knew Del Boy.

Del What do you mean you thought I knew, you didn't tell me. What do you think I am, a psychic or something?

Trigger D'you still want this box of paint?

Del Want it? No I don't want it – you can stick it up . . . *(The phone rings)*.

Del I'm not in Grandad.

Grandad Hello . . . Oh hello Mr Chin. No, no Del's gone out. . . . I'm not sure, where

you gone to Del?

Del Give it to me you stupid old git. Now sit down before I knock you down. *(Takes phone)* Hello Mr Chin. How are you?

THE CHINESE KITCHEN.

The actual lights in the kitchen are out but the walls are glowing bright and eerily. In the centre of the room, three Chinese kitchen hands huddle together fearing for their lives. Chin is talking on the phone. He is wearing sunglasses. Cuts back to Del in flat.

Chin Don't you 'Hello Mr Chin' me. What have you done to my walls??

Del *(On phone in the lounge)* Glowing are they? Now listen tell 'em not to be frightened 'cos this is a new energy saving paint. Yes. It's designed to cut down on the old electricity bills . . . I get it from a contact in . . . er . . .

Trigger Stockholm.

Del Yes – Stockholm. Stockholm?! 'Cos, you see, the Norwegians they lead the world in paint technology . . . Yes . . . Yes, I understand, I'll be round to see you in the morning, first thing.

Rodney Does he want his money back?

Del No, he wants you to go round tomorrow and do his living room out in it . . . I'll have that other box of paint off you . . . *(Starts to pay Trig)* Oh my God!

Trigger Something wrong Del?

Del Oh what have I done? It's all your fault. It's your fault, you and your stupid paint.

Rodney Oi, what have you done?

Del Now, listen Rodney. Listen, you've got to understand right. That I did it in good faith.

Grandad Did what in good faith?

Del I'll show you. Come on you better get your coats.

MAIN ROAD. RAILINGS.

The three-wheeled van pulls up at the kerb. Del alights and faces Rodney and Grandad.

Rodney Del, what you brought us here for?

Del Wait a minute. *(He peers tentatively over Rodney's shoulder and turns and cringes at what he sees.)* Take a look at that.

Rodney and Grandad turn to look in the same direction.

Grandad Oh my Gawd.

Over the headstones, on the brow of the hill, Mum's monument is glowing gold in the night sky. It looks radioactive.

Rodney Is this where you've been for the last couple of days, painting Mum's monument??

Del It was her favourite colour and we both agreed that it needed brightening up.

Rodney Brightening?? That's more like a rocket launch!

Del Well I didn't know it was going to be luminous did I?

Rodney D'you realise our mum's grave is now going to become a beacon for every Satanist and acid-head in England. There's going to be white witches dancing round that on a full Moon – there's going to be chicken blood everywhere!

Grandad What worries me is it's on the main flight path to Heathrow!

Del I wish you two could see yourselves. There's Mum and her monument – she's fast asleep – the third coat hardly dry and already you're quivering in your shoes! Well, I'll tell you this much, I don't regret that I did it. I will not bow my head to any snotty-nosed town hall clerks and their narrow-minded rules. I shall look them straight in the face and I'll say 'I am the man responsible – and I'm proud of it'. We'll put it down to vandals let's get out of here before we get our collars felt.

Joan Mavis Trotter

It is a tribute to Joan Trotter, who sadly passed away yesterday, that upon her death her family received a message of condolence from the Palace. The Gin Palace on Peckham High Street to be exact.

She was a much loved woman whose good manners, easy virtue and zest for life have been passed on to her to her handsome son, Derek, who helped compile this obituary, and the other one, Rodney, 5. She was well known about town and such was the loss felt by her death that the landlord of her local, The Nag's Head, cancelled Happy Hour yesterday as a tribute.

Derek, 16, loved his mother. He had these kind words to tell the Echo about the woman everyone knew simply as 'Joanie.'

' Our mum was a wonderful woman. She had long golden hair - sometimes. Every night you'd see her sitting at the bar of The Nag's Head with her simulated beaver skin, a rum and pep in one hand and twenty Senior Service in the other.

She looked like a lady - lots of people thought she was a money lender.

Every night she used to send me across two or three pints of light and bitter, or whisky if she was flush. That was Mum. Then come about ten o' clock she'd look over where I was sitting and she'd shout 'Come on Del boy, get off home to bed – school in the morning.' That was the kind of woman she was, concerned about our welfare.'

Joan was 23 when she gave birth to Derek, and 39 when she fell for Rodney. For the first three months of her pregnancy Rodney was treated as an ulcer, and many believe to this day that the original diagnosis was correct.

A devout catholic, she married her husband, Reg, at the Our Lady of the Divine Rosemary church, Peckham, in 1947. The couple shared a tempestuous relationship, but Reg never raised his hand against her – except in self-defence.

Her illness came as great shock to the family, being as it was prolonged and painful. She spent a great deal

of time on her death-bed, Derek recalls, from where she issued many nuggets of advice to her son on bringing up young Rodney without her.

Among these were to make sure he always wrote Rodney's name in all his younger brother's clothes; give him all the encouragement you can and don't hold him back; look after him the best you can and always send him down the fish shop to get the tea.

She was instantly recognisable; tall and slender, long hair, fingers covered in ruby and gold, and bracelets adorning her wrists. She was the first woman in Peckham to smoke menthol cigarettes and was immensely popular with a number of people, saxophonists and trumpet players to name a few.

Such was the love the family had for her, they plan to erect a huge memorial in Peckham cemetery to commemorate her and her life. Derek told the Echo it will be the only grave in the whole area to be made of fibreglass.

Peckham Echo 13th February 1964

It Never Rains

THE NAG'S HEAD.

Del and Rodney, who has their suitcase by his side, are seated at the table. Business has been rained off for the last few days – Rodney is bored by the lack of activity, Del is agitated by the lack of earnings.

Del Poxy weather!

Rodney Yeah.

Del Wish I was chairman of Pac-a-Mac!

Rodney Hmm! Oh, by the way, a Father's Day card arrived for you this morning. *(Hands Del an envelope)*

Del Is it Father's Day? It's a pity we don't know where Dad's living – we could send him a letter bomb! Er, Father's Day card? Hang about I'm not married!

Rodney Oh no! I wonder what that could mean then?

Del Well, I know what it could mean . . . it could mean! Oh no, no, no, she told me – she definitely . . . *(Begins opening envelope. Rodney starts laughing)* You dozy little git! You nearly gave my heart a connery then. Cor dear.

Rodney Well, I just wanted to liven us up a bit didn't I. I mean, for the past four days we've been hanging around in pubs and cafes waiting for this rain to leave off. 'It's just a summer shower Rodney' you said. 'Red sky at night and swallows flying backwards, that's a sure sign of a heatwave Rodney', you said.

Del Alright – alright, don't go on about it! Where d'you think I work, the metaphorical office or somewhere? No, it'll soon be over. Don't worry. Who's that on there? You is it?

Rodney No it's you.

Del Anyway, what d'you want to drink?

Rodney I'd better have just 'alf a lager.

Del Yeah, well, the way business has been going this week I think I'd better join you. *(Moves to the bar where Alex, a travel agent, is standing)* Hello – How's it going Alex?

Alex Hello Del. Want a drink?

Del Oh well, go on then, I'll, um, have half a lager.

Alex Half a lager.

Del Yeah, and I'll have a large Drambuie with lime – with er – topped up with soda, lots of ice, slice of lemon and a little cherry on the top.

Alex Two halves of lager, luv. Done much today?

Del What in this weather, you must be joking. I wouldn't send a dog out in this, would you? No, I'll send Rodney out later on. See what he can do. What are you doing? Have you still got that travel agent's?

Alex Yeah, it's not doing me no favours though! I thought I'd clean up on that World Cup but I couldn't get no bookings. Honest Del, I've got thousands of pounds worth of holidays just laying about. But everybody's skint. I tell you, this recession's going to be the end of me!

Del Well you want to cut down on your own prices then don't you, Alex, me old mate.

Alex I'd lose money!

Del No way – you'd have some coming in wouldn't you? I mean, I'd rather lose a thre'penny bit than a fiver, wouldn't you?

Alex Well that's true, yeah.

Del I mean, listen, I don't care what the papers say, there's still plenty money about. You know – if you know where to get it. I mean, you want to find some way of hooking the punters. You know, you – you want – you know, a bit of a gimmick.

Alex Such as?

Del Ah? Well. You put it round the manor, right, that the very next customer in your shop is going to get the biggest cut-price 'oliday in the history of travel. No – no – listen and I mean really cheap Alex right. I mean something like anywhere in the world and you'll knock off 80 per cent of the price.

Alex 80 per cent, leave off.

Del Eh, no 80 per cent, now listen – listen. But only to the very next customer right. So what they'll be doing see – they'll be fighting each other to get in your shop. Now once they're in there you sell the rest of them their holidays at the – the normal price don't you. Eh? This time next year you'll be a millionaire.

Alex D'you know that's not a bad idea Del. Come to think of it, it's a belting idea! I tell you that's what I'm gonna do, exactly what you told me. Thanks for the advice, mate.

Del That's alright, don't mention it pal. I'll see yer around alright?

Alex Right.

Del *(Returning to the table)* Fancy an 'oliday?

Rodney We can't afford an 'oliday.

Del Yes we can. Alex, special offer, anywhere in

the world – 80 per cent off.

Rodney He'll go bust!

Del Yeah I know he will – I know – that's what I told him but he wouldn't listen, you know what he's like . . . Ah, what about it then Rodney, eh? Me and you, eh? What up into the wide blue yonder. Yeah, get a bit of the currant bun on our backs, eh?

Rodney Oh yeah, I'll have some of that Del, yeah!

Del Good boy, right I'll tell you what you do. *(Indicating suitcase)* You go down the road and knock out a bit of that gear and I'll do the old bizzo with Alex. Right?

Rodney Yeah right! Oi, wait a minute! It's peeing down out there!

Del Yeah well – you want some spending money for yer duty frees don't yer?

Rodney Well yeah, oh I'm never gonna be able to sell this gear!

Del Of course you are my son. Remember me motto. He who dares wins!

Rodney Yeah right! See you later. *(Exits)*

Del See you later good boy. Here, Alex. About that offer!

LONDON BACK STREET.

Rodney is standing in the pouring rain looking like a drowned rat. Rodney opens the suitcase and produces a flimsy sun hat.

Rodney Genuine Italian sun hats. Made in Roma!

THE TROTTERS' LOUNGE. DAY.

Grandad is watching the TVs. Rodney, with a towel around his head, is sitting with his feet in a bowl of hot water.

Rodney I could die you know!

Grandad More than likely!

Rodney I mean, fancy sending me out in weather like that.

Grandad Been raining has it?

Rodney Been raining? Why don't you stick your nose out of that door once every so often, eh? It's been raining non-stop for four days!

Grandad Tch!

Del enters.

Del I've done it Rodney – done it. I've booked our holiday. Here you are, my boy. That's it – there it is all in there. We're going somewhere different, we are away from the tourists.

Rodney Yeah – where?

Del Benidorm! It'll be fantastic Rodney, we'll have a great time won't we – eh? All that blue sea, the sunshine, dancing with all them foreign

sorts! You know Viva Espania.

Rodney Yeah! That's what it's all about innit?

Grandad When do we go Del?

Del Eh? Er, in three weeks' time Grandad. It's goodbye Luton airport, hello Benidorm . . . *(Realises that Grandad thinks he's going with them)* Um, yeah, well the thing is Grandad . . .

Grandad I've always wanted to go to Benidorm. Where is it?

Del It's in Spain, ain't it.

Grandad Spain? I've been to Spain before!

Rodney Oh, oh, well you wouldn't wanna go again then, would you, it'll be the same old thing!

Grandad I ain't never been to Benidorm! It'll make a nice break.

Del Yeah! Yeah, the thing is Grandad – I tell you what um, er, well look, why don't you go out in the kitchen, you know, and knock us up a nice Spanish omelette – you know, help us get in the mood.

Grandad Alright Del Boy *(Moves to the kitchen door)* Oh! I've only got three eggs left and one of them's on the turn. Still, if I put a lot of pepper in.

Del Great – triffic. *(Grandad exits)*

Rodney Are you gonna tell him?

Del Oh Rodney, how can I tell him, look at him, he's got his heart set on it ain't he?

Rodney We can't take him with us Del, he'll cramp our style won't he? I mean you could bring a bird back to the room, go to pour her a Sangria or something and find his false teeth in the glass.

Del Yeah, that would upset the romantic ambience somewhat, wouldn't it? Well, what we gonna tell him then?

Rodney Er, say the food won't agree with him!

Del No that won't work, you know him, he's got a stomach like a rubbish skip!

Rodney Er, the change of climate! Now the last holiday we had the change of climate upset him didn't it and we'd only gone to Bognor!

Del Good one! Like it. No, I can't Rodney. No look it's gonna break his heart.

Rodney Alright, Del, well if you can't tell him, then I will!

Del Alright. Just a minute – just now. If you're going to tell him now, do it gently will you. You know – I mean – he's family.

Rodney You just – just leave it to me Del. *(Strides purposefully to the kitchen)*

Del Alright, good boy Rodney.

Rodney Er, Grandad, could I have a word. *(Closes door behind him)*

It Never Rains

Del *(On phone)* Oh Alex? Hello it's Del Boy. Look about that holiday I booked with you this morning? Yeah – listen – um, d'you reckon the hotel could put another bed in our room? Only Grandad's coming. Oh nice one Alex. Right, yeah I'll pop that kite round to you in the morning. Alright, see you around pal. Well?

Rodney *(Sheepishly)* Oh, look, couldn't the hotel put another bed in our room? Eh no, Del, I couldn't have told him, it'd broken his heart!

Del You're just like the man at the top you are ain't yer, you're utterly ruthless!

Rodney I can be when I want to!

Del Oh yeah.

Rodney I can – I've just this minute told Grandad I don't like Spanish omelettes!

Del Oh yeah – I mean – that's really being ruthless that is innit, eh?

Rodney I also told him that you love 'em, so you've got two!

Del puts his foot in the bowl.

Del You . . .

Rodney Careful Del, there's a there's a bowl down there . . .

STILLS MONTAGE

*(Music: 'In The Summertime' – Mungo Jerry)
The Trotters go through passport control. We see their coach arrive at a small Spanish hotel. They enter their little three-bedded room. Del opens the balcony door and reacts as we see the view is of a scrap metal yard.*

Del and Rodney are now out on the town, dancing in a disco with a couple of girls. Then in a little bar sharing champagne with two girls. They return to the hotel with their arms wrapped around the girls. They walk along the corridor and Del opens the door to their room. He and Rodney allow the girls to enter first.

HOTEL. NIGHT.

Grandad is lying fast asleep on his bed, the sheets drawn back to his waist revealing the dirty old pyjama jacket he wears around the flat. On the bedside table there is a glass of water containing his false teeth. The girls, horrified, leave quickly.

Del Now then what do you want . . .

Girl Oh God!

Rodney Who –

Del 'Ere, hang about. Oi girls.

Rodney Wendy it's alright he's asleep.

Del Now come on, listen . . .

DAY. A BEACH.

A bronzed Del, wearing leopard skin swimming trunks, is laid out on a beach bed. Rodney approaches carrying three bottles of ice cold lager.

Del 'Ey, watch it.

Rodney There you go boy.

Del Oh, cheers, this is the life, eh Rodders? When we become millionaires we'll move out – get a villa . . . Get Grandad one of them little old folks' homes that they have out here.

Rodney What old folks' homes they have out here?

Del You know, we saw 'em in the holiday brochure. What d'they call 'em? Pensions!

Rodney *(Calls)* Grandad I got yer lager! Grandad!

Grandad, trousers rolled up and still wearing braces and trilby, is paddling in the water. Del hurls a small ball which whacks Grandad on the head, causing his hat to fall in the water.

Del Yoohoo. Grandad, Rodney has a lager!

Grandad *(Fishing his hat from the sea)* You oughta act yer age a bit more. That could have blinded me!

Rodney Come here.

Grandad I don't want nuffink to drink. I'm going back to the hotel to have a fiesta. *(Exits)*

Rodney Hey, d'you reckon he's alright? He's been acting all edgy and nervous ever since we got here.

Del Maybe it's that squid he ate . . . The grub in the hotel ain't up to much is it, eh?

Rodney Oh you can say that again! Here about that soup last night! Called it oxtail – it's more like foxtail weren't it, eh? You don't reckon he's sickening for anything do you?

Del No! It's probably just the heat, he's not as young as he used to be is he. 'Ere Rodney, put some of that oil on me back will you.

Rodney, still watching Grandad moving away up the beach, reaches for the sun oil but accidentally picks up the lager bottle. He pours ice cold lager on Del's back.

Rodney Yeah. Oh Del I'm sorry. Sorry I thought it was oil.

Del chases Rodney up the beach.

THE HOTEL SWIMMING POOL.

To one side of the pool area there is a small snacks and drinks bar. Del and Rodney, returning from the beach, enter.

Del Childish that. Probably marked now, is it?

Rodney You don't 'arf go on don't yer? I said I'm sorry! Look, I'll go up to the room and get

you a fresh shirt. Alright?

Del Yeah, why don't you do that small thing Rodney, alright. *(Rodney exits)*

Del observes a girl at the bar, believing her to be French. Donning his sunglasses, he moves in for the kill.

Bon soir.

Girl Oh bonjour M'sieur. Vous restez à l'hotel?

Del Defense de fumier! Avez vous Dubonnet?

Girl Oui, oui, merci . . .

Del *(To barman)* Garçon, dos Dubonnet pore favore. Danke schon.

Girl De quelle partie de la France êtes-vous?

Del Oui! Er, je t'aime, je t'adore? Sur le pont d'Avignon!

Girl Pardon M'sieur!

She leaves the bar and moves to a chair close to the pool. A young Englishman (Ray) is seated on one of the inflatable chairs that litter the poolside. He is an athletic six-footer, confident to the point of arrogance.

Ray Hey Jackie!

Girl Hi!

Ray Join me for a drink?

Girl Oh, I'd love to but I think I got stuck with that little French feller over there.

Ray I wouldn't worry about him. Pull up a pew – he won't bother you with me around.

Del is annoyed at the snub and approaches with the two drinks. His expression indicates he's ready for trouble with Ray.

Del Je suis frontières.

Ray stands and dwarfs Del.

Ray Thank you waiter! *(To girl)* I hope he doesn't kick sand in my face.

Unable to compete with Ray physically, Del jabs his cigar into his inflatable chair and moves off. Ray sinks unceremoniously into the deflating chair. We hear Rodney's voice shouting.

Rodney Del! Del!

Del Shut up! What's up with you? I was just about to pull a French sort.

Rodney Look you've got to come with me now. Come up.

Del What's the matter?

Rodney It's Grandad!

Del Grandad? He's ill ain't he? I told you there was something the matter with him but you wouldn't listen to me would you.

Rodney He's not ill!

Del Well what's up with him then?

Rodney He's been arrested!

Del Arrested!

Rodney Well come on!

A SPANISH PRISON CELL.

Grandad is seated on the bed looking very unhappy with his lot. The cell door is opened by the Spanish guard.

Guard Veesitors!

Del and Rodney enter.

Grandad Huh, it's you two!

Del Yeah, good afternoon Grandad, how are you? Settled in alright? *(To guard)* Quo vadis senor.

Guard Huh.

Del You know, quo vadis!

Grandad Took yer time getting here didn't yer?

Del Now don't you start getting stroppy with me you ungrateful old git! I've been running round this town – I've been running about here like a tit in a trance looking for you! I went to the police station, they knew you'd been arrested – but they couldn't remember what they'd done with you!

Rodney Yeah. And for the last four hours I've been phoning round trying to get hold of a consul!

Grandad Oh charming! So while I'm banged up in here Rodney's out trying to hire a car!

Rodney Not that sort of consul, you daft old git! I mean the British consulate!

Grandad Well why didn't you bring him then with you?

Rodney Well why did you get yourself arrested?

Del Sssh! Keep your voice down. You'll get him chucked out of here! Just – just keep calm will you, everybody please. Just nice and calm and easy. Right, what happened?

Grandad Nuffing! I was just crossing the road to the hotel when this police car screeched up to me – nearly running me over – next thing I knew I was banged up in here! They ain't even charged me with nuffing!

Rodney No – no – look you must have done something Grandad! You went back to the hotel for a little kip right, 'alf hour later you're doing porridge!

Del Now think hard Grandad. Have you done anything remotely out of order? I mean, did you get drunk and disorderly. Did you have a punch up with the Kuwaiti supporters' club. Did you goose the maid?

Grandad No! Well . . . there was a little incident Del. It didn't happen today though!

Del Now we're getting somewhere. Alright, come on. Tell me when did it happen?

Grandad 1936!

Del You know for a moment there I thought you said 1936!

It Never Rains

Rodney That's funny that but so did I!

Grandad In 1936 I was deported from Spain! And all her territories and dominions!

Del Would you, er, would you consider it nosey of me if I were to ask you the reason why.

Grandad Do you really wanna know?

Rodney Well no . . . we're just curious that's all!

Del Yeah, you know, well we just wondered.

Grandad Well . . . I were up to no good weren't I!

Del Well I didn't think they got ruddy well deported for doing missionary work did I? So what happened in 1936?

Grandad The Spanish Civil War happened, that's what happened!

Del The Spanish Civil . . . This gets worse Rodney!

Grandad Oh look, it's a long long story!

Rodney Well according to Manuel the guard you may have a long long time to tell it in! So let's hear it.

Grandad Well in 1936 the family was living in Peabody Buildings, Peckham Rye. Oh it was terribly hard times! We had no money – no food – no future! There was millions of unemployed on the dole.

Del Excuse me. Just a minute – just a – sorry – just a minute. I mean, excuse me, I may be being a wally or something, but you – can you possibly explain to me what a dole queue in Peckham has got to do with the Spanish Civil War?

Grandad I'm building up to it Del!

Del Having a conversation with him is like the slow death innit?

Grandad One day me and my mate Nobby Clarke, we decided we had just about had enough of it. So we run off to join the Foreign Legion!

Rodney The Foreign Legion? You don't mean the British Legion?

Grandad The French Foreign Legion! Camels and forts, you know! So we hitch-hiked to Southampton.

Del That's where their headquarters was?

Grandad No! That's where we tried to get aboard a boat! Well, eventually we stowed away on a tramp steamer. We hid under the tarpaulin in the lifeboat. But oh – the voyage was terrible, there was storms and gales. Us Trotters have never made good sailors! Now Nobby was – he was alright on the water, I think it come from the time when he was a caretaker at a seamen's mission in Grimsby.

Del Oi oi, I don't want to worry you, you know, but our plane leaves in three days. What happened to Spain?

Grandad Well I'm just coming to it! Oh now where was I!

Del You and the Fisherman's Friend were under a tarpaulin in the lifeboat.

Grandad Oh yeah! Well, when the ship finally docked guess where we were?

Del and Rodney Spain!

Grandad No, Tangiers!

Rodney Grandad, is it worth me making any plans for my future? I mean what has all this got to do with the Foreign Legion?

Grandad Tangiers was one of their main bases wasn't it.

Del You see any normal person who wanted to join the French Legion would have gone to France, wouldn't they. Not him, no!

Grandad Well we jumped ship and made our way to their barracks. When we got there we couldn't believe our eyes. They were the biggest band of cut-throats, villains and murderers you could ever hope to see! They was the scum of the earth!

Rodney So you didn't join?

Grandad We tried but they wouldn't have us! Well, now me and Nobby was in dead lumber. We had no money, we had nowhere to sleep and we was a thousand miles from home! But then we had a bit of luck, well it were more a quirk of fate really. We bumped into an Arab and he offered us a job. He said he'd pay us to take his motor launch over to the Spanish coast and deliver a . . . a cargo.

Del What sort of 'cargo'?

Grandad Guns?

Rodney You mean you were gun-running in the middle of a civil war?

Grandad Well that's the best time to do it Rodney, supply and demand!

Rodney You dirty little mercenary!

Grandad Oh we didn't do it purely for financial gain! Oh no, we both felt a deep commitment to a political cause!

Del Which side were you selling to?

Grandad Well whichever side had the most money really.

Rodney Bloody hell!

Del Oh no, no – it's alright Rodney. No, I mean, you know a conscience is nice but business is business, right.

Grandad Well it was after the seventh trip when it happened . . . There was government troops, lying in wait for us. They arrested us and they took us to this little prison outside a town called Tarifa. They took Nobby away and . . . tortured

him! You could hear his screams echoing through the night!

Rodney Woke you up at one point didn't it?

Grandad The last thing on my mind was sleep Rodney! But no matter what they done to him Nobby wouldn't say a word!

Del I bet he didn't ever have his Callard and Bowser to suck did he!

Grandad Then it were my turn!

Rodney They . . . they tortured you?

Grandad No! But they would have done if I hadn't told them everything I knew! *(Del, whose respect for Grandad has been growing, looks at him total dismay)* Well, a couple of days later these government geezers arrive with our deportation orders, and well, well, that's about it!

Del Are you sure that's about it? I mean you haven't forgotten any little minor details have yer? Like, I mean, you didn't pop over to Hong Kong and become an opium peddler or you didn't get a Saturday morning job as a white slave trader did you?

Grandad No – I just went back to Peckham Del, put me name down on the housing list.

Del Grandad, why the hell didn't you tell us all this before we left home?

Grandad Well, I was gonna tell you but I thought it might spoil the 'oliday!

Del Spoil the 'oliday! Well what do you think this has done?

Rodney We'd have been better off with that caravan in Buenos Aires now, wouldn't we.

Grandad Well it all happened a long time ago. I thought the Spanish authorities would have forgotten about it by now!

Del Forgotten about it? Forgot about it. You're most probably on their ten most wanted terrorists list – you're probably somewhere between Carlos the Jackal and the Black November!

Rodney September!

Del What?

Rodney It's September. The Black September! You said November!

Del Gordon Bennett Rodney, we haven't got time to stand about here discussing signs of the bleedin' zodiac! We've gotta think of a way of getting the Red Shadow out of here!

Rodney It's no sweat, they'll just deport him again!

Del Just deport him. You're joking of course. They've just held the World Cup here haven't they, they've got 'arf of Manchester and Glasgow to get rid of first! By the time we get him back he'll be eating paella and calling us gringos! There's gotta be a way! Now there's

always a way!

The cell door is unlocked.

Rodney Hello, visiting time's over!

Del Here – listen, oi, you two – now you keep schtum. Let me do all the talking alright. *(Guard enters)* Ah hello Juan! Just the one I wanted to see. Yeah, well, um, no I just wanted to say like my grandfather here was telling us about the charming reception that he's received in your charming bijou nick!

Guard What ees thees you say to me, eh? You take thee peees yes?

Del I'm not taking the piss, au contraire – au contraire Juan. No I was, um – the thing that I wanted to say to you – was . . . *(Del is producing a wad of peseta notes and holding them invitingly in front of the guard)*

Rodney Oi Del! What the bloody 'ell do you think you're doing!

Del I told you keep schtum! Pardona Monsieur. El Wally. I've been racking my brains to find a way that I could possibly repay you, you know for all the good work that you've done. *(Pushes the money in the guard's breast pocket)* And I thought that perhaps you might give this to the charity of your choice, know what I mean?

Guard The charity of my choice?

Del Yeah.

Guard Gracias senor.

Del Grandeur.

Guard Gracias!

Del Now listen Juan, now – now we're such close friends, I was just wondering if you – you know, that you could pull a few strings and get my old Grandad out of this khazi?

Guard Ce senor! You can go!

Rodney What – go! What, just like that?

Guard Si! You are free to go.

Del Um, excuse me Juan, er, shouldn't you like, clear it with the Guv'ner first, you know what I mean.

Guard There's no need senor, I have hees release papers here!

Del You mean that you were going to let him go anyway?

Guard Si senor!

Del Nice one. Nice one Juan! Yes – yes a couple more years and you could be in charge of yer own borstal couldn't yer.

Grandad How comes you're letting me go so soon?

Guard You done nothing – it's a little offence. How you say – a traffic violation. You crossa the road almost causing the car to crash! But we make no charges – bad for Anglo-Spanish

It Never Rains

relationships!

Rodney Yeah, well, don't think you're getting Gibraltar back just 'cos of this!

Del *(To Grandad)* You – well, it appears you walked across the road Grandfather! You were done for jay-walking you stupid old berk!

Grandad Well I didn't know Del Boy. When they screeched to a halt I thought they'd captured me!

Guard *(To Del)* Gracias once again senor. The charity of my choice will be very pleased!

Del I bet she will Juan, I bet she will!

Guard exits.

Rodney Well I suppose we'd better stop off at the drug store and get something for Grandad's cuts and bruises.

Grandad I ain't got no cuts and bruises!

Del It's early yet!

A Touch of Glass

A RURAL COMMUNITY CENTRE OR CHURCH HALL.

The three-wheeled van is parked between Bedfords, Transits, Volvo Estates, etc. Various signs indicate an auction. A few people are leaving the auction, among them the Trotters carrying a large cardboard box. They approach the van. Del opens the back door.

Del Can you manage Grandad?

Grandad Yeah.

Del Good. Mind your hernia. Yeah, that's not bad you know – not bad. I reckon we done well there.

Grandad Yeah, it's alright for you. Waste of money if you ask me! Come all this way an' all!

Del What do you mean a waste of money? I mean, look at 'em, they're beautiful ain't they! Not only are they an exquisite ornament guaranteed to brighten and adorn any sideboard, but they are also revolving musical boxes! *(Reveals cat)*

Rodney They are china cats that play *How Much is that Doggy in the Window*!

Del Well, what d'you want for £1.25 – 'Okla-bleedin'-homa'?

Rodney Well don't you think it's a bit sick you know – a cat playing a song about a dog?

Del No. It means they're unique!

Grandad It means there was a balls-up at the factory and they put the wrong chimes in!

Rodney Yeah.

Del Yeah, I'll put the wrong chimes in you in a minute. Come on. Get this stuff loaded into the van, right. Get this gear in 'ere.

Rodney No, actually, you know he's got a point there. I bet there is some trader somewhere who's got lumbered with a gross of revolving dogs playing *The Siamese Cat Song*!

Del Very funny. Come on Grandad, we want you in here an' all.

Rodney Right, go on.

Del In you go.

Grandad Alright, alright.

Del Jam him in – go on. The door will hold him in. Don't worry – we're going to earn out of this. No listen. This is not rubbish you know. This is North Korea's finest porcelain. But our two great cultures have a different attitude towards animals. We are both a nation of dog lovers – the only difference is they love to eat 'em! Come on

Rodders, get your finger out, we've got a long drive home.

As the van drives along country roads, we hear their voices over.

Rodney Do they really eat 'em?

Del Yeah, would I lie to you? If a North Korean came to live in London he'd think that Battersea Dogs Home was a take-away! No, there's nothing they like more than a nice plate of poodle kebabs.

Rodney Oh leave it out will yer!

Del Or a bull terrier pie.

Grandad Alright Del Boy, that's enough!

Del Or sweet 'an sour greyhound.

Rodney Oi! – one more word out of you and I'm gonna be sick on your sheepskin, and I mean it!

DAY. A COUNTRY LANE.

A car has broken down on the grass verge. The bonnet is up and smoke is belching from the engine. Staring hopelessly in to the car is Lady Ridgemere, wife of Lord Ridgemere who owns the local estate. She surveys the lane in hope of another car coming along. She sees the three-wheeled van approach from the distance.

INTERIOR OF VAN.

Del Go on, put yer foot down Rodney, I'm starving! I could just go a nice Jack Russell and chips.

Rodney For the last time shut up! Oi, look, shall we pull over and give her an 'and?

Del Do me a favour, I wanna get home for the pubs!

Rodney We can't just leave her stuck out here in the middle of nowhere, can we!

Del You're a right little angel you are aren't you, eh? Go on then, go on, pull over!

The van pulls up. The Trotters alight.

Good afternoon madam, can I be of any assistance?

Lady R Oh that's awfully nice of you. Do you know anything about cars?

Del Do I know anything about cars? I used to drive for the John Player Special team!

Lady R Oh, the Grand Prix circuit?

Grandad No, delivering fags round Lewisham.

Del He's a card ain't he?

Lady R I'm trying to get to Ridgemere Hall, it's

that large estate about five miles back up the road.

Grandad Ridgemere Hall. That's that big mansion what we passed Del! *(To Lady R)* You in service there?

Lady R Certainly not! I live there – I'm Lady Ridgemere!

Del Lady Ridgemere! Rodney, get the tow rope. Would you come with me m'lady, I'll get you home in no time at all. Here we are. Did you go to the wedding?

Lady R The wedding? Oh *the* wedding? Yes, we did.

Del Yeah, it was a lovely do weren't it? Yeah. We watched it on our TV – in colour. It's a pity we didn't know you then 'cos we were doing a lovely line in toasters. That would have made a blinding present! May I? Mind the hole.

RIDGEMERE HALL.

A magnificent 17th-century mansion set in its own grounds with well maintained and manicured gardens. The van, containing Del and Lady R, and the car, containing Rodney and Grandad, come up the long drive and pull up. They all alight.

Del Right Rodney, undo the tow rope and give Grandad his scarf back will you.

Wallace, the Ridgemere's ageing and very snobbish butler, appears and rushes down the main steps.

Wallace Is everything alright m'lady?

Lady R No Wallace – everything is not alright! The car broke down and I was stranded in the middle of nowhere!

Wallace Oh, dear – how dreadful for you! *(He looks the Trotters up and down with a contemptuous sneer)* And who are these – 'people'?

Lady R Oh they towed me home that's all. Now be a good chap Wallace and do push the car round to the garage. *(Climbs into the car)*

Wallace Oh very well m'lady! *(Attempts to push car)*

Del Oi – you shouldn't be pushing a car like that at your age! Keep your knees bent, and your back straight.

Rodney Did you hear that? *(Mimics Wallace)* And who are these 'people'? Ponce! Come Del let's go! Here you are Grandad. *(Gives him scarf)*

Del Go? What do you mean 'go'? You don't think I'm leaving here without so much as a cucumber sandwich and a cup of the Earl Grey do yer? This is fate, Rodney, Unison Oppotunaire. There's gotta be an earner in it.

Rodney Oh no, come on Del, most nobility are brassic nowadays aren't they?

Del *(Points to Rolls Royce and Range Rover)* Oh yeah, and where do you think they get them from then, eh? Out of a Christmas cracker?

Rodney Yeah, alright, so they've got the money. But they don't wanna know the likes of us do they?

Grandad No, they think we're peasants!

Del Peasants? What do you mean 'peasants'? They may think that you two are peasants! Well come to that I think you two are peasants! But me, I'm one of them that is accepted anywhere – whether it's drinking lager with the market boys down at Nine Elms, or sipping Pimm's fruit cup at Hendon regatta!

Lord R appears at a window.

Oi up, eyes down for a full house, it's his lordship! *(Gives him a smile and a royal wave)*

Lord R *(Calls)* I say. I'm sorry, I'm afraid we're not open to the public for another three weeks!

Del No, no, your grace, you're under a misapprehension. We're not members of the general public! We're friends of your wife – she's just popped the car round the garages.

Lord R Oh, I see! Well, er, in that case I suppose you'd better come in.

Del Oh right. Thanks very much your grace! *(To Rodney)* And, oi, these are very refined people and they do not wish to hear your joke about the queer magician. Got it? *(To Grandad)* And don't you go dropping none in there!

They enter.

THE RIDGEMERES' DRAWING ROOM.

In one corner stands a cabinet filled with Lady R's collection of fine china and porcelain. Among the paintings on the wall hangs a photograph of some kind of passing out ceremony at Cambridge University.

Lord R, becoming increasingly irritated by these intruders, is seated on the sofa with his drink in hand. Rodney, feeling uneasy and wishing he wasn't there, and Grandad, who seems quite at home, are seated on another sofa. They have drinks.

Wallace is pouring another drink for Del who is admiring the artwork while making the appreciative noises of the connoisseur.

Del Very nice, very nice! They don't make pictures like that any more do they, eh? No. 'Cos I'm a great fan of the Byzantine period myself. I don't think you can whack 'em you know . . . *(Indicating painting)* Now it's a funny thing you

A Touch of Glass

know, your Lordship, but Van Gogh happens to be my favourite artist an' all.

Rodney It's a Canaletto!

Del I beg your pardon Rodney?

Rodney It's a Canaletto!!

Del I know – I know it's a Canaletto. I was just saying that Van Gogh happens to be one of my favourite artists that's all! *(To Lord R)* Here, why do you reckon he chopped his ear off, eh?

Lord R Doctor's orders possibly!

Del Do you think so!

Wallace Your brandy sir.

Del Oh thank you very much.

Wallace I'm afraid we have run out of cream soda!

Del Oh well, don't worry about it Wallace.

Wallace I shan't sir! *(The phone rings)* Excuse me sir.

Del Certainly. Gives good measures here don't he. You ought to watch him. Very nice, very nice. *(Indicating photo)* There he is – look at that, lovely. I didn't know you went to Cambridge though m'lord! 'Cos I'm an Oxford man meself.

Lord R You were up at Oxford?

Grandad No, but he always supports them in the boat race!

Del Yeah, thank you Grandad! Thank you.

Lady R You must be in a hurry to get home Mr Trotter?

Del Oh no, no, no m'lady . . . no, no, no. No, we've got all the time in the world. All the time in the world. Yeah, I love this place, beautiful ain't it. Beautiful house. I think I saw a photograph of it once in the, er, *Horse and Hound*.

Lady R The *Horse and Hound*! You hunt Mr Trotter?

Del Oh yes, I hunt, punt and ski when the snow's firm enough.

Grandad How old is it?

Lord R Er, is what – how old is what?

Grandad The House – is it old?

Lady R Yes, the original structure was built in 1642.

Grandad Oh! Still you've done it out nice!

Lady R Thank you.

Grandad Is it haunted?

Rodney Oi, what you after a part-time job or something?

Wallace enters.

Lady R No, I'm afraid the one thing we lack is a resident ghost.

Del Oh, never mind you've still got Wallace ain't you.

Lord R Yes Wallace, what is it?

Wallace Begging your pardon m'lord. There's a telephone call for you. The chandelier people.

Lord R Ah, and about time too . . . You will excuse me won't you?

Del Yes, go on. You take yer time m'lord. *(Lord R exits)* Oh this is nice. I see you like a bit of china and porcelain m'lady. Yeah, this is very nice – this. I like this. Now don't tell me – don't tell me Capo Del Monte?

Lady R It's mostly Dresden. And that particular piece is worth several hundred pounds.

Del Is it really? Gawd, get away, feel the weight of that then Rodney. Yeah, it is ain't it, eh? Yeah, of course that's where the money is ain't it – in the weight. Oh mon dieu, mon dieu, if you like a nice piece of fine porcelain I've got the very thing for you in the back of the van.

Lady R Don't inconvenience yourself Mr Trotter.

Del No, no, it's no trouble m'lady. No trouble. I picked it up in this little, er, antique shop in Yeovil. Well it's, um, it's well circa something or another! I'll pop out and fetch one for you shall I? *(To Rodney)* Right keep sprawnsing alright? Excuse me m' lady. *(Del exits)*

Lady R Where do you live? That is assuming you're not squatting here!

Rodney No, er, we live in London. One of – one of the better parts of London!

Grandad Yeah Peckham.

Rodney It's, um, Peckham Village actually! It's, er, well it's like a little St Johns Wood you know, just south of the water.

Grandad It's very nice! We've got a flat in a tower block.

Rodney Well it's an apartment! In a – in a complex. A tall complex. Very sophisticated actually. It's got lifts – everything!

Lady R Yes. Must be quite valuable with the price of property these days?

Grandad Oh no, we rent it.

Rodney No, we – we lease it! He forgets bless him. He's got a bit of shrapnel! It's a lease Grandad – do you remember, a long-term lease!

Grandad Oh yeah, yeah, yeah. We lease it! The council said we could buy it for £8,000 though!

Rodney God help us!

RIDGEMERE'S HALLWAY. DAY.

Lord Ridgemere is on the telephone.

Lord R Yes, yes, but it must be in your office somewhere! All I know is your people came down here, examined the chandeliers. That was three weeks ago and I am still waiting for your estimate! Yes. Well, I suggest you have another good look . . . Yes I'll hold on.

Del enters the hall carrying a china cat.

Del *(Showing cat to Lord R)* Bisque porcelain!

Lord R What?

Del Demi-glazed! It revolves and plays *How Much is that Doggy in the Window*! You can't go wrong for a fiver can yer, eh?

Lord R No, I suppose not.

Del No. Don't be long, I'll pour you a drink, alright? *(Moves towards the drawing room)*

Lord R Just a minute Potter er, er, Trotter *How Much is that Doggy in the Window*?

Del Don't know, depends how much you want to spend. Little joke, no, no, no, it's the tune ain't it. *(Sings)* How much is that doggy in the window. The one with the waggly tail.

Lord R Yes, yes, yes, yes, I know, I know. The thing is a cat!

Del *(Examines cat)* Oh well, you're right an' all, it's times like this that I wish I went to Cambridge! Tell you what, look, I'll pour you a drink. Don't be long.

Lord R Hello? You've found it! Good. £1200?

Del is just about to enter drawing room when he hesitates at the mention of money. He listens in to the conversation.

Lord R Are you sure you're looking at the right paperwork? Yes, two Louis 14th chandeliers – that's right! But how do you arrive at a figure of £1,200? All you've got to do is to take the things down, clean them, do a few minor repairs! Yes I am aware that it is 17th-century French crystal, I own the damn things! Yes, I know it's a job for an expert that's why I got in touch with you! But I'm sure if I shopped around I – I could find a lower estimate than that. Yes I know that it is a dying trade but there must be someone, somewhere!

Del nods in agreement, then slips quietly into the drawing room.

MAIN HALL. RIDGEMERE. NIGHT.

It is a massive dazzling hall with a long sweeping flight of stairs. The sort of place that would have American coach parties 'Gee Whizzing' all over the place.

The main eye-catchers are two large crystal chandeliers – straight out of Cinderella. There are the sounds of footsteps and voices approaching.

Del Oh, sorry we couldn't stay any longer yer lordship.

Lord R That's perfectly alright Trotter, please don't apologise.

Lord and Lady R enter the hall followed by the Trotters. Del surveys the hall.

Del Oh toujours la politesse, toujours. I mean this is beautiful innit, eh? Bet you've held a few balls in here m'lady?

Lady R What? Oh yes, yes we have!

Del We like a nice social gathering ourselves. Perhaps you'd like to come to the next one, eh Rodney?

Rodney Yeah, yeah, I mean, you know, just bring a bottle and an LP or something.

Lady R Thank you for the 'cat' Mr Trotter. It blends so well with the rest of my collection.

Del Specially with the Dresden I thought!

Lady R Yes! I'm sorry we weren't able to pay you for it. But neither my husband nor I carry cash.

Del Oh don't worry, pay me next time I'm down.

Lady R Yes of course. What do you mean 'next time'?

Lord R D'you mean to say you're coming here again? Whatever for?

Grandad To pick up that fiver she owes him!

Del A la mode, à la mode! Please accept it as a token of my esteem.

Lady R Thank you!

Lord R Yes, well, it's getting rather late! I think we – we better say goodbye, er, Trotter.

Del Trotter, yeah. Well thank you very much for your hospitality, it's been very nice of you. *(Del notices the chandeliers)* Now look at that – that's beautiful innit, eh?

Lady R Yes. Goodbye.

Del French crystal?

Lord R Yes, it is actually!

Del Yeah, thought it was. You can always tell by the old er, cut of the er . . . droplets! 17th century that, ain't it Grandad?

Grandad Yeah, if you like Del!

Del Yeah, I'd say it was one of the Louis's! If it ain't one of the Louis's, it's very similar, ain't it Rodney?

Rodney Oh it's a dead ringer Del, yeah, dead ringer!

Del Yeah, yeah, but is it Louis the 13th or Louis the 14th? No don't tell me, your Lordship I can get this. That is Louis the 14th. Am I right yer lordship?

Lord R Spot on Trotter! How do you come to know so much about chandeliers?

Del *(Laughs, as do Rodney and Grandad but their exchanges soon fade to bemusement)* How come we know so much about chandeliers! Oh sorry. Sorry about our amusement there your lordship! But see asking a Trotter if he knows anything about chandeliers is like asking Mr

A Touch of Glass

Kiplin if he knows anything about cakes! This is our business!

Lord R Really?

Del Oh yeah. Chandelier, candelabra, quality crystal and what 'ave yer. It's been the family trade for generations. Knowledge has been passed down from father to son. Our name goes right back in history don't it Rodney?

Rodney Yeah, yeah, right the way back to the plague!

Del Our forefathers used to make them – did you know there are still four Trotters hanging in Buckingham Palace?

Lady R Amazing!

Del No, straight up – 'cos what, with the advent of solar energy and fluorescent lighting, there's not much call for it nowadays. In recent years we've tended to specialise in the old, er, renovation work.

Lord R Do you mean to say that you could – you could take that thing down and – and clean and repair it?

Del Oh yeah, do that blindfold. *(Checks watch)* Anyway we mustn't keep you any later, so I'm gonna say bonne bouche to you both! *(Is about to exit)*

Lord R No hurry Trotter, no hurry! I've just remembered I've got a bottle of rather special port through there in the study. What say we open it and – and have a bit of a chat, eh?

Del Oh well that's very civil of you my lordship.

THE TROTTERS' LOUNGE. NIGHT.

Del is pacing the room. Grandad is slumped in an armchair. Rodney is sitting on a dining table chair. There has been a row.

Del Don't be a plonker all your life Rodney! I've done the deal now. It's 350 quid just to take down and clean a couple of chandeliers.

Rodney And you do honestly think he's gonna pay us?

Grandad Of course he's gonna pay us! He ain't one of your fly-by-night merchants. I mean he's a lord of the realm, he's got blue blood and – and mottos!

Rodney He didn't even pay us for that cat!

Del Oh shut up about that rotten cat!

Rodney Del, you need specialised equipment for a job like this – refined glass brushes, advanced soldering gear. What we gonna use, eh? Superglue and a bottle of Windolene knowing you!

Del Look I'll get the right equipment Rodney, I know this panel beater and he owes me a favour. Look once we've done this job our name will spread. All those dukes an' earls they'll be crying out for us. Just imagine it, eh? We'll be the toast of the county set, eh? Just think of it, all the hounds, you know, baying with excitement, as our steeds bite on the rein eager for the chase. Hello Tally ho Sir Herbert. Did you ken John Peel? Come on boy . . .

Rodney Take a look at him will yer! He's spent three hours in a stately home and he thinks he's the Earl of Sandwich! He can't wait to get a shotgun and a retriever and go marching across the grouse moors all done up like a ploughman's lunch can he.

Del No, that's right Rodney. I deserve a bit of the good life, worked hard enough for it, I mean· I've always been a trier. Where's it got me? Nowhere that's where it's got me! We live 'alf a mile up in the sky in this lego set built by the council. Run a three-wheel van with a bald tyre. We drink in wine bars where the only thing's got a vintage is the guvnor's wife! That's why I want to grab this opportunity with both hands Rodney. You know, he who dares wins. This time next year we'll be millionaires.

Rodney Do you honestly believe that Del? I mean, do you really think we can make a success of this?

Del Of course we can Rodney. The door will be opened to a new world. It'll be like . . . like Alex Through the Looking Glass. You will dine at the finest restaurants on – on steak chasseur and sauté potatoes. Your shoes will be by Gucci, your jewellery will come from Aspreys, your clothes will be made by Man at C & A! What d'you reckon Rodders, eh? What d'you reckon?

Rodney Man at C & A. Yeah, alright. I'll give it a whirl.

Del Good boy. You know it makes sense don't you.

Rodney Oi, but we do a proper job, right. No bodging!

Del Of course not, what do you take me for, eh?

Rodney Oi!

Del I'll save the best bit for you.

Rodney I'll see you in the morning then.

Del Yeah see you in the morning. Night.

Grandad 'No bodging.' I think he lacks faith in you Del Boy!

Del Always been his trouble innit, eh? Oi, 'ere, do me a favour will you Grandad. Pop out in the kitchen see if we've got any Windolene and superglue left, will you.

THE MAIN HALL. RIDGEMERE HALL.

Rodney carries a high set of aluminium ladders into the hall and lays them against a wall. He then exits to collect the second set. Grandad enters carrying a tool bag and large canvas bag. Del is supervising. Wallace watches from a distance with a growing sense of doom.

Del Righto Grandad, you pop upstairs and get the floorboards up! Now you know what you're doing don't you?

Grandad *(Removing a hammer, a large screwdriver and a spanner from the tool bag)* Don't you worry Del, leave it to me.

Del *(To Wallace)* Oh he's a craftsman! *(Calls)* Oi, Grandad, d'you want a jemmy?

Grandad No I had one before we left.

Wallace Why does he have to remove the floorboards?

Del What is this, the International Year of the Wally-Brain or something? Listen, my good man, how do you think that that great big heavy chandelier stays up there on that ceiling, eh? It is not by the power of prayer or double-sided sticky tape! There is a long threaded bolt through that chandelier, it goes through a wooden joist and is held in position by a locking nut. Now in order to undo the locking nut you must first lift up the floorboards! Ordre du jour!

Wallace We learn something new every day! If you need me I shall be round at the garages.

Del Right. Here, while yer there give the van a wash, will you. *(Wallace exits as Rodney enters with ladders)* Ah, talking of wally-brains. Come on. Here – watch it!

Rodney I mean this is terrific innit. His lordship's nowhere to be seen and now even the butler's having a moody! D'you reckon we're gonna get paid?

They begin to place the ladders beneath one of the chandeliers.

Del Look, his lordship is away on holiday, he'll pay us when he gets back! Now come on, get these ladders up. Yeah, you never know might be in for a bonus.

Rodney Oh yeah, perhaps he might bring us back a nice stick of rock each, eh?

Del Well just shut up moaning will yer! Oi, Grandad how you doing?

UPSTAIRS ROOM. DAY.

Grandad has the carpet rolled back and has one floorboard removed. He is levering another one free.

Grandad *(Calls)* Alright Del Boy. I've found it Del!

THE MAIN HALL. DAY.

Del and Rodney are a few feet from the two ladders and are un-rolling the canvas bag.

Del Here you are. See, he's found the nut. I told you we could trust him. Right come on get this out.

Grandad *(Out of view)* I've started to undo it.

Del and Rodney No!

Del *(Calls)* Gordon Bennett, we ain't even up the ladders yet!

Rodney Grandad – don't you touch nuffink till we tell you.

Del Come on, we'd better get it up there. *(Holding the canvas bag between them, Del and Rodney climb the ladders carefully enveloping the first chandelier with the canvas bag)* Alright Rodders? Is there anything you want?

Rodney Yeah, I wanna go home! This ladder's none too safe.

Del The ladder's alright. Look this is the chance I've been waiting for. Now, don't let me down Rodders – now don't let me down! *(Calls)* Alright Grandad, we're ready! You can start undoing it now!

UPSTAIRS ROOM. DAY.

Grandad places the spanner on the nut and begins easing it round.

Grandad It's coming Del Boy! One more turn Del!

THE MAIN HALL.

Del Right. Now brace yourself Rodney, brace yourself!

Grandad gives one last bang with the hammer and the nut comes free.
In the hall the second chandelier crashes to the floor with an almighty 17th-century crystal type crunch.

Del and Rodney stare at each other for a few seconds before turning to survey the damage.

Del *(In shock)* Grandad was undoing the other chandelier!

Rodney How can you tell?

They descend the ladders slowly, lowering the canvas bag gently to the floor. They walk slowly towards the remains of the chandelier, broken French crystal crunching beneath their feet.

Grandad descends the stairs blissfully unaware.

Grandad Alright Del Boy?

Del Alright? What do you mean 'alright'?

A Touch of Glass

Look at it!

Grandad Did you drop it Del?

Rodney Drop it? How could we drop it? We wasn't even holding it! We were working on that one!

Grandad Well I wish you'd have said something! I was working on this one! Is it very valuable Del?

Del No, not really! It was bleedin' priceless when it was hanging up there though!

Rodney What's his lordship gonna say when he finds out?

Del Well, I think I can safely say that my invitation to the hunt ball has gone for a Burton!

Wallace It's broken!

Del Look, what the hell do you know about chandeliers anyway?

Rodney I think he's tumbled Del!

Wallace I shall telephone his lordship at his cottage immediately!

Del Yeah, well, tell him to phone us at home. Oh, by the way, has his lordship got our home address and telephone number?

Wallace No!

Del Good! Right, out of it. Go on.

The Trotters run for the door.

THIS TIME NEXT YEAR...

CHRISTMAS ★ SPECIAL

Diamonds are for Heather

THE NAG'S HEAD.

It is Spanish night at the Nag's Head. On every table there are bottles of wine, jugs of Sangria and plates of Spanish food. Enrico is nearing the end of a romantic little number sung in Spanish. The Trotters are seated at a table. Rodney and Grandad applaud the end of a song. Del, in a maudlin mood is too pre-occupied with self-pity to bother.

Grandad Eh, he's good ain't he Del Boy?

Del *(Indicating a plate of chicken)* Yeah, I wish I could say the same about this chicken!

Grandad Wassamatter with it, tough?

Del Tough – tough! It's the toughest chicken I've ever known. It's asked me for a fight in the car park twice!

Rodney Alright, come on, what's upset you?

Del Me? Nothing! Don't worry about me Rodney.

Rodney I'm not worried about you. I'm worried about the fiver I spent on this ticket! I thought we'd be enjoying ourselves you know – what's the matter?

Del Ah, it's just that – I went round to Lennie Morris's little kid's christening today you know. There was just this fantastic atmosphere in his front room. His Mum and Dad were there, and his wife and his little baby, and I thought you know, he's got all his family round him! He's got a real family! And what have I got?

Grandad You've got us!

Del Yeah I thought of that – that is when I left! *(Rises and moves away)*

Grandad *(To Rodney)* You know that rich bird what he's been seeing lately? Her with the nose. Well she's just given him the old heave-ho!

Rodney No? Oh well that explains it don't it? Del had high hopes of selling some gear to her.

Grandad What sort of gear?

Rodney Well her dad left her a chain of laun-derettes in his will right. Del's gone and lumbered himself with two ton of hooky Persil!

Grandad Oi, oi, don't you say nothing Rodney, he told me in confidence!

Rodney No, no of course not!

Del Right 'ere you are. Come on. Get some of this gut-rot down your neck.

Rodney Ah come on Del cheer up, eh? tell you what, let's have a family sing-song like in the old days, eh?

Del Yeah alright. Alright come on then, go on Rodney. Start us off.

Rodney Yeah right, altogether. *(Sings)* 'We're gonna hang out the washing on the Siegfried line, have you any dirty washing . . .'

Del glares at Grandad, who is trying to look as innocent as possible. Rodney realises he had done the wrong thing and stops singing.

Del *(Calls)* Oi Enrico! Enrico! Come here a minute will you.

Enrico Si Señor?

Del Listen, do us a favour, will you. Sing 'Old Shep' for me will you?

Rodney Oh leave it out Del! Not Old Shep again!

Grandad We're trying to enjoy ourselves! You can't enjoy yourself with a song about a dead dog!

Del Sing 'Old Shep'!

Enrico Senor. Eet ees no possible to seenga thee Olda Shep song! Eet ees – er – howa you say – thee trageec song, si? Eet makea thee tears falla from the eyes!

Del Go on sing Old Shep!

Enrico *(In broad cockney)* Look, leave it out will you Del Boy I've got a living to earn! That's a killer of a song! Once I've sung that the evening's finished. Look I'll sing another song for you – any other song – but no way do I sing Old Shep!

Del *(Menacingly)* Sing – Old – Shep!

Enrico Whena la wasa a lad, and Olda Shep was a pup . . . And eefa dogs have a heaven there's one thing I know, old Shep has a wonderful home.

(The regulars moan with disapproval from the regulars as they realise what song it is. Del has a wistful look of pain and nostalgia as Enrico sings. Ennrico finishes the final few bars. The atmosphere is now one of 'Chapel of Rest' solemnity. Rodney and Grandad look bored stiff, Del is close to tears. When the song finishes only two people applaud – Del and a young lady (Heather) sitting at the bar.

Del Bravo, bravo Enrico. Di Stefano my son, di Stefano! That is my most favourite song about a dog that is you know.

Rodney Yeah, I mean as songs about dead dogs go it's a real mind-bender ain't it.

Grandad The only trouble is nobody likes it!

Del Yes they do. Yes they do. I liked it! And that

young lady over there, she likes it. *(Del smiles at Heather. Heather returns the smile)* Excuse me gentlemen. I think I've got a cultural encounter coming on!

Rodney Del, Del. While you're over there ask your cultural encounter if she's alright for Persil!

Del *(Moves to the bar)* Good evening!

Heather Oh hello!

Del Do you mind if I park me bott?

Heather No, please.

Del A drink?

Heather No thank you.

Del Well that was – oh sorry – that was a lovely song that ain't it. Beautiful eh? Always gets me right here that does, yeah. Always brings back such poignant memories.

Heather Did you have an old dog?

Del Oh, I've had many old dogs in my time. Er sorry – um, sorry what did you say your name was?

Heather Heather.

Del Heather! Heather, that's a beautiful name, that is. Heather. That's one of my most favourite names that, Heather. My name is Del, it's er, short for Derek! Do you know what the word 'Derek' means?

Heather No I don't.

Del No, nor do I – I'm always meaning to check it up. I'm very surprised to see a charming young lady like yourself here on her own.

Heather Well I'm supposed to be meeting someone here – a girlfriend. But she doesn't seem to have shown up so I was just about to leave.

Del Well, I don't blame you. Now he's sung that song, it's stone-dead in here innit eh? Listen I hope you don't think I'm being forward, or nothing but I just wondered if you fancied going on for a drink in a little nightclub that I know.

Heather Well I'm not sure. It's getting home in early hours!

Del Well there's no bother, no. I can always drop you off! D'you live local?

Heather Brixton.

Del Oh, Brixton – do you really? Oh that's funny that is. Funny, funny I haven't seen you before because I do a lot of work down there you know in Rorke's Drift.

Heather What line are you in?

Del Umm . . . I'm an importer exporter of quality merchandise – antiques, that sort of thing. I tend to specialise in Parisienne haute couture fashion, you know and special objets d'art, modern works of art!

Heather It sounds fascinating!

Del Oh, yes it is. Oh, it is. I tell you what. If you're interested, I've got some very cheap washing powder. No straight.

A TENEMENT. NIGHT.

The passage is in complete darkness. Heather unlocks the front door and enters followed by Del.

Heather Sorry about the light. The landlord took the bulb out, he says he's doing his bit to conserve world energy!

They ascend the stairs.

Del That's a rare combination innit? A rent collector and a Friend of the Earth!

Heather Oh mind the step.

Del trips.

Del Oh!

HEATHER'S FLAT.

The room is small and slightly dingy. Scattered around the room are a few toys and baby things. Heather unlocks door and enters followed by Del.

Heather Well this is it! I told you it wasn't much of a flat didn't I?

Del Well don't know, could be worse!

Heather Oh yeah? How?

Del Could have been on the top floor! Servir Frais Mois Non Glacé, as they would say in France.

Heather True! Very true!

The bedroom door opens and Brian enters. Del reacts, believing this to be Heather's husband. He breaks away from her quickly, but Heather is relaxed and very casual.

Brian I didn't hear you come in!

Heather Sorry I'm late love, Del took me on to a nightclub!

Del Only being friendly John, you know what I mean?

Heather Oh, Del let me introduce you, this is Brian. Brian lives downstairs, he's my baby-sitter.

Del Oh! Pleased to meet you Brian.

Brian Nice to meet you too. Well um, I won't stop, I've got some studying to catch up on.

Heather Brian goes away to university soon.

Del Oh you're a bit long in the tooth for that sort of lark ain't yer?

Brian I'm a mature student!

Del Oh go on? 'Ere my brother went to university.

Brian Oh really? What was he reading?

Del Gawd knows. *Mayfair* and *Penthouse* knowing him!

Brian Yes! I see, well I really must be going.

Diamonds are for Heather

See you in the week Heather. Bye for now.

Heather Thanks for looking after the place Brian. I hope he didn't get on your nerves too much.

Brian No! No, no, I've er, I've got to get used to people like him!

Heather No, I meant the baby!

Brian Oh sorry! No, no, no he was as good as gold! Bye for now. *(Exits)*

Heather Bye. Mind the step.

Del I didn't know er, didn't know you had a baby!

Heather Well he's not a baby any more, he's nearly three-and-a-half. There's a picture of him on the mantelpiece.

One of the pictures is of Darren, her son, the other is of Vic, her husbajnd.

Del *(Looking at the picture of Vic)* Blimey he's a big lad for his age ain't he?

Heather No that's Vic, my husband! That's Darren.

Del *(Studies picture)* Cor, he's a little cracker ain't he ah? Where's your husband, these days?

Heather I don't know – and I don't particularly care! He walked out of here one morning – said he was popping down the Job Centre to sign on. That was eighteen months ago!

Del Well the way things are he could still be queueing!

Heather Do you know, when we got engaged Vic had a straight choice between going on holiday with his mates, or buying me an engagement ring.

Del Did he send you a postcard?

Heather Like hell he did! Vic looked after number one! I don't think he was ever meant to be married! He couldn't face the responsibility. I used to say to him 'Vic' – I used to say – 'you've got a baby now Vic. Isn't it time you sorted yourself out?' Oh God, I'm sorry Del, there's nothing worse than having your ear bent by somebody else's problems! I'm just tired.

Del Yeah, well I'd better be off, I've got an early call in the morning. I've got to get down to er, got to get down to Peckham by seven, pick up a consignment of fire-damaged works. Anyway I'll be finished by about ten. I just wondered whether you might fancy going out for the day somewhere, you know and a spot of lunch, something like that.

Heather Yeah I'd love to. I'll – I'll see if Brian will baby-sit again.

Del No, no, no I meant you know – you and the boy!

Heather Are you sure?

Del Yeah.

Heather Most men don't want to know when they find you've got a baby.

Del Yeah well, I'm not most men Heather. Yeah okay well er, yeah I'll er, I'll see you about eleven right, tomorrow?

Heather Yeah alright then.

Del Yeah okay then. Yeah.

Heather Bye then.

Del Bye then. Tata.

Heather closes the door. She leans against the door and considers the evening and the pleasant way her luck seems to be changing. She then looks alrmed and opens the door.

Heather *(Calls)* Mind that st . . .

There is the noise of Del tumbling down the steps.

MONTAGE.

Del, Heather and Darren are seen outside a kiddies toy shop. At the zoo, all three are standing close to the monkey's cage. Del and Heather react to something happening in the cage. Del places his hands over Darren's eyes and they all hurry away.

Del and Heather are then sat on a bench at night. They are staring dreamily up at a perfect night sky. They kiss, and a man's hand appears and grabs the back of Del's collar. They are chicked out of the main doors of the London Planetarium.

On HMS belfast, Del is pointing as he holds Darren, who is holding an ice-cream cornet. Heather prepares to take a picture of them. As she presses the shutter Darren sticks the ice-cream on Del's nose.

In a candlelit restaurant, Del and Heather are seated at a table. They touch glasses together and then hold hands over the table.

THE ESTATE/PLAY AREA. DAY.

Del and Darren are playing football.

Del That's right come on then Darren kick the ball to your Uncle Del! Good boy! Good ball – good ball my son. Now let's see you come out the goal. This way. Good boy. You'll play for England one of these days. *(Turns and calls)* What do you reckon Rodney, Darren could play for England couldn't he? He's better than that load of rubbish! Right come on. You'll get in the England side playing like this.

Rodney is washing the van. Grandad, holding a plastic carrier-bag filled with shopping, approaches.

Rodney Just have a look at him will yer! He's

like a born-again Ovaltinie! I mean he's only known Heather and the kid for what – six weeks, and look at him!

Grandad I don't know what's got into him. He spends most of his time on them climbing frames and swings and what 'ave yer! The other day I see the caretaker telling him off for coming down the slide backwards!

Rodney Coming down backwards! That's dangerous innit? I mean all his conkers and marbles could have fallen out of his pockets!

They laugh. Del approaches, chasing after the ball.

Del Listen Rodney, what's the joke?

Rodney Oh nothing much. We're just talking about wallies that's all.

Grandad Your name cropped up.

Del Not so much of it! Here y'are Darren. *Throws ball and runs off.*

Rodney And that's another thing! I wish he'd get rid of this sign! *(Indicating windscreen where the names Del and Heather are stuck on)* I mean whenever I'm sitting in the passenger seat people 'look' at me . . . sorta funny!

Grandad Oh I wouldn't let that bother you Rodney!

Rodney No?

Grandad No! They most probably just think you're a poof!

THE TROTTERS' LOUNGE. NIGHT.

Grandad is watching the TVs. Del dressed up in all his finery is standing in front of the mirror brushing his hair. Rodney is lying on the sofa watching Del's preparation with a mixture of disbelief and condemnation.

Rodney You must have spent a third of your life standing in front of mirrors! My earliest childhood recollection is of you standing in front of a mirror! Up until I was four I thought you was twins!

Del If you're trying to wind me up Rodney, it ain't gonna work, no way bruv. Because tonight is a very, very happy night and a very, very special one for me.

Grandad What is it, Cubs' night?

Del No it ain't Cubs' night. Well go on Rodney. How do I look, eh?

Rodney You look like a second-hand car trader!

Del Oh, thanks a lot Rodney. Here, that reminds me. You know what we were talking about earlier on, about Heather and Darren coming over for Christmas. I mean you don't mind do you? 'Cos you like Heather don't you eh? Don't you Rodney, eh?

Rodney Yeah – she's alright!

Del What about you Grandad? You like Darren don't you eh! He's not a noisy little brat is he?

Grandad Oh no, he's a good little kid.

Del Yeah. 'Ere Rodney. How'd you feel about Heather becoming your sister-in-law?

Rodney Do what?

Del No, no, no, not now! Not immediately I mean, you know, some time in the future! I haven't even mentioned it to her yet – I mean I don't want to jump me guns.

Rodney Well, I'm not fussed!

Grandad She won't want to come and live here with that noisy little brat will she?

Del No. No we've applied for a Council house. Well where's me billy-goat? Oh here it is here. Right. That's it. Well I'm off out then. I'm taking Heather out for an evening that she will never forget. You know it's gonna be soft lights, music, champagne, of course the very, very finest of foods, I only hope she likes curry. *(Exits)*

Rodney Well! I suppose it was always on the cards! I think they'll be happy together, don't you?

Grandad Oh yeah, she's a good girl – she'll look after him.

Rodney Yeah. And he thinks the world of that kid don't he, eh? And they fit so neatly into his style of living, you know fast foods, ready-to-wear suits, and now he's got an instant family, eh? I'm – I'm pleased for him.

Grandad You seem to be forgetting something Rodney. If Del Boy moves into his Council gaff with his off-the-peg next of kin, who the hell's gonna pay the rent, gas and electric in this place, eh?

AN INDIAN RESTAURANT – NIGHT.

Del and heather are seated at a table studying menus. A waiter is beside them.

Del We'll have a chicken tikka, off the bone, a mutton Madras, a pair of onion bhajis, four popadoms, some nan bread and a couple of portions of rice.

Waiter Yes sir. Which rice would you like?

Del Have you got any Uncle Ben's?

Waiter No sir. We have pilaw rice, basmati rice or plain white rice.

Del Oh, we'll have the pilaw rice, and make sure you take the feathers out first. Oh and Tony, I want a bottle of your finest champagne, alright son?

Waiter Yes sir.

Del Thank you.

Heather You're pushing the boat out a bit

Diamonds are for Heather

aren't you?

Del No, I'm always like this when I've got something to celebrate.

Heather Yeah? What are you celebrating? You sold all those Chinese woks?

Del No, no. I got a bit lumbered with those actually – I'm giving them away with packets of Persil.

Heather So what's the champagne in aid of?

Del Well . . . Christmas. *(Puts small box on table.)*

Heather What is it?

Del Open it, see.

Heather Del! Oh it's lovely!

Del I got it off this mate of mine – Abdul. He gets a discount at Hatton Garden.

Heather Del, is this an engagement ring?

Del No, it's a set of socket spanners! Of course it's an engagement ring. I'll change it if you like. See, I remembered what you said – that you liked solitaire diamonds, so I thought . . . well y'know . . . that I'd get her a cluster of solitaires.

Heather No, no it's a beautiful ring Del.

Del What's up then?

Heather It's Vic!

Del Oh is your nose blocked up?

Heather No, no it's Vic my husband!

Del Oh! Well what about him?

Heather He wrote to me. . . . Last week!

Del Oh yeah, last week? You didn't mention it!

Heather I know. I've been trying to find the right moment to bring the subject up. He's living in Southampton. Got himself a nice flat appar-ently. He wants me and Darren to move down there with him! You know, try again – see if we can make it work this time.

Del Oh yeah well – I mean – you're not gonna believe all that old pony are you! Are you?

Heather The thing is Del he is still my husband! He's Darren's father! I owe it to him!

Del Oh come on, don't give me all that Heather! I mean he don't care a monkey's about you and Darren! I mean what did big brave Vic do when the going got heavy, eh? He pulled on his hiking boots and had it away on his toes.

Heather You don't know what he's like Del!

Del I do know what he's like 'cos he's exactly like my old man, that's what he did to me eighteen years ago!

Heather It wasn't all his fault! He was unem-ployed – all he wanted was a regular job. You've no idea what sort of pressure that can do to a family! Well he's got himself a job now in a department store.

Del Oh yeah, doing what?

Heather He's a Father Christmas!

Del Oh, well that's a steady little number that, innit eh? Free uniform – luncheon vouchers, forty-eight weeks holiday a year!

Heather I still love him!

Del What about me?

Heather I love you Del, but not in that way! I feel for you the way someone would feel for a . . .

Del Goldfish or a gerbil?

Heather No! Like a brother! I feel for you the way you feel for Rodney.

Del And I thought you liked me! Heather, I thought that you and I had an understanding!

Heather Honestly Del, I never knew you felt that strongly! I mean, you never said anything.

Del I'm not a poet Heather! You know, I can't do all that lovey-dovey stuff. I feel things but when I try to say 'em they always come out – wallyish! I thought it was obvious the way that I felt for you. What else could I have done?

Heather I don't know, a sign, or something.

Del What like, tie a yellow ribbon round an old oak tree or something?

Heather I leave next Tuesday. Will you come round and say goodbye to Darren?

Del No.

Heather He really took to you. You like kids don't you?

Del Yeah! I used to go to school with a lot of 'em!

Hands Del back the ring.

Heather It's a beautiful ring Del. Thank you.

Del Normally I'd let you keep it – but I only got it on a week's approval.

Heather I don't really feel hungry any more Del. I think I'll go. That's alright, I'll get a taxi.

Heather rises and starts to exit. Stops, turns, looks at Del. She then exits.

NIGHT. THE INDIAN RESTAURANT.

Some yards up the road a group of choir singers are singing the final few bars of 'Silent Night.'

Singers Silent night, Holy night,
All is calm, all is white . . .

Del exits from the restaurant. As he walks to the van the carol singers end the song. They begin another carol.

We wish you a Merry Christmas,
We wish you a Merry Christmas,
We wish you a Merry Christmas
And a happy new year.
Good tidings we bring to you and your King,
We wish you a Merry Christmas

and a happy new year.
We wish you a Merry Christmas
We wish you a Merry Christmas
We wish you a Merry Christmas
and a happy new year.

Del closes his eyes and smiles at the irony of the song. He walks towards the carol singers. As he approaches the leader holds out a collection tin. Del produces a twenty pound

note. *The leader stops singing. Del has a word with him. The leader looks to the other sings, clears his throat and begins singing.*

Leader When I was a lad and Old Shep was a pup,
O'er hills and vales we . . .

One by one the others join in. Del, happier with his lot, walks to the van and drives away.

The Trotter Guide to Seduction

1. Always carry an emergency capsule of Brut with you, you never know when you might meet a saucy little sort and you don't want to smell like a khazi when it happens.

2. When you manage to get a sort back to your place, make sure you've got something nice in for tea — a proper tea, you know, Chicken Italienne & smash with fruit salad and dream topping to follow — or Angel Delight — is an example of a pukka meal. Fix a nice cocktail, a Pina Colada's always a safe bet.

3. Be sensitive to a woman's needs. The emotion you experience seperate you from the other morons. It shows you're a human being in the fullest sense of the word. It proves you got heart, and them feelings deserve respect & dignity. Don't feel ashamed about them — feel proud of them. Just remember that the next time some old tart gives you the sack.

4. A bit of French goes a long way, gives a man an air of sophistication and je ne sais pas pourquoi. Y'see it's easy. A good way to impress a sort is striding up to the bar confidently, look her in the eye and say "au revoir" and then order a glass of Dubonnet before thanking the barman with a swift 'danke schon'. Knocks 'em badly, believe me.

5. Sometimes, though, the more direct approach can work. A sign of mutual attraction is all it needs. For example, walking up to a bird, slapping her on the arse and asking if she fancies a curry can be just the ticket. If a ruby doesn't take her fancy, try a steak meal.

6. Don't be yourself. I read somewhere that women were turned on by men in situations of power. So, pretend to be a Euro-minister of something. In my time I've pulled the birds with a variety of personas. There was the time Rodders and I pretended to be on the international tennis circuit, me his manager and him the player. Hot Rod was his name, but it went down the kermit when that dipstick was asked by a blond sort if he preferred grass or astroturf. The little plonker said he'd never smoked astroturf. If that's too far fetched try being a Concorde pilot — you'll be back at their penthouse suites in no time. Lovely jubbly!

7. Don't be too picky. People ask me whether beauty matters and I say 'of course, it bloody does.' But then, if times are hard, there's always the old dogs. You always know where you stand with old dogs. They never ask you if you'll still respect 'em in the morning, and they'll always lend you a few nicker for petrol.

8. Be gentle. When it comes to the parting of ways, you know, giving them the old heave-ho, then a man must be subtle. He must realise women are fragile sorts whose feelings should be treated carefully. I often find it best to say 'look darling, you're giving me the right 'ump, now go away and haunt someone else for a change.'

9. Always dress well. Jewellery is good, and lots of it. The same goes for Brut. How do you think a peacock attracts a lady peacock? With his plumage, you dozy twonk! When I approach a bird she don't see me, the good lookin man about town, own teeth & all that. No, in her subconscious she sees a white yacht floating in the blue waters of a Caribbean bay. With Rodney they see a winkle barge sinking of the end of Southend pier.

10. Know what you want. Don't go for anything out of your league, like Rodney, messing about with Lady Vicki's and what have yer. Me, I like refined sorts, one that knows the difference between Liebfraumilch and Tizer. One who shares my love of opera and knows a good Capo del Monte when she sees one. One who knows a good steak meal when she sees one. A couple must be compatible.

With these little hints you can't go wrong, my son. Oh, and don't forget when you meet the lady of your dreams to tell her name is your most favourite in the world. Go on, knock 'em bandy.

SERIES THREE

Homesick

THE TROTTERS' LOUNGE.

Del is brushing his hair in the mirror. He wears white slacks, white loafers, a brown leather bomber and all the gold. Rodney, wearing his usual 'Man from Oxfam' clothes, enters from the bedroom area.

Rodney Yeah, well, you try and have a nice kip, eh? His legs are still playing him up.

Del Well, I told him not to run in the London Marathon?

Rodney Anyway, he's not coming to the tenants' meeting with us. You're still coming ain't yer? *(Sits at table and writes in a notebook)*

Del Eh? No way bruv, I'm going out with that little waitress that I blagged from the Pizza Palace.

Rodney Eh? How did you manage to pull her?

Del Well, I read somewhere that women were turned on by men in situations of power. So I told her I was a Euro Minister.

Rodney And she believed you?

Del Oh yeah.

Rodney She must be thicker than them pizzas she dishes out.

Del Oi, don't get sardonic. *(Referring to Rodney's notepad)* Here what's all this about anyway?

Rodney I'm writing out a list of questions I want to ask at the meeting.

Del Oh yeah, like why the lifts are still out of action in our block?

Rodney No, more important things than that, Del.

Del Oh yeah.

Rodney I mean, in the last year or so we've had a crime explosion on this estate, yeah, and yet the police don't come near or by. And I want to know the reason.

Del Well, they can't get on the estate, can they. The natives won't let 'em.

Rodney Come on, that is rubbish.

Del No, no, it ain't. Look, last month a copper came round just to return a lost dog and we had three nights of rioting.

Rodney Look, I don't care what their excuses are, I'm gonna demand more police patrols on this estate.

Del Not too many Rodney.

Rodney Come here, I'm writing out this catalogue of crime, see what the Chairman's got

to say about that.

Del Catalogue, let's see. Some catalogue innit – look. *(Reads)* 'May the sixth. Grandad's shopping trolley stolen from pram sheds.'

Rodney Yeah, well, that's the only one I can think of.

Del Gordon Bennett. There are 2,000 stories in the Naked City and this plonker is looking for a basket on wheels.

Rodney Look, I've heard of other crimes, but I don't know the times and the dates and what 'ave yer. I've got to provide details, not rumours.

Del Well, why don't you tell them what happened to poor Rita Alldridge then?

Rodney Yes, good idea. *(Is about to write)* What happened to Rita Alldridge then?

Del Last Friday night she was indecently assaulted over by the adventure playground.

Rodney No, did she report it?

Del Yeah, I saw her this morning, she'd just been down the police station.

Rodney *(Busy writing)* Right, there you are you see, that's exactly the sort of thing . . . Hang on a minute – if this happened on Friday night, how come it's taken her till Wednesday to report it?

Del Because she didn't know she'd been inde-cently assaulted until this morning when the bloke's cheque bounced.

Rodney Oh. *(Rips page from pad and hurls it to the floor)*

THE COMMUNITY HALL.

On the stage there is a long committee table. Only one member of the committee has turned up, this is Baz, the Chairman. Baz wishes he wasn't there. He has a constant cigarette dangling from his lips and coughs a lot. In the main part of the hall there are 50 or so chairs. Rodney sits alone in the front row. Baz is writing something in the minutes book and coughing. On the table in front of him is a 'No Smoking' sign. Rodney, bored with waiting for the meeting to start and irritated with the coughing, attracts Baz's attention. Baz looks up and Rodney points to the 'No Smoking' sign. Baz raises a finger of thanks and then turns the sign face down. He continues writing and coughing. The main door opens and Trigger enters.

Trigger *(Calls from back of hall)* How you going

Dave?

Rodney Oh. Alright, Trigger.

Trigger No Del Boy?

Rodney No, he's out.

Trigger How's your grandad, I heard his legs were playing him up.

Rodney Yeah, well, it's most probably a touch of fibrositis, you know.

Trigger Yeah, more than like . . . that's how my nan started off. Did you ever meet my nan?

Rodney Well, only at her funeral.

Trigger That's right, you were at her funeral weren't you Dave?

Rodney Trigger – why d'you call me Dave? My name's not Dave – my name's Rodney.

Trigger I thought it was Dave.

Rodney No, it's Rodney.

Trigger You sure?

Rodney Yeah, I'm positive. I've looked it up on me birth certificate and passport and everything. It is definitely Rodney.

Trigger Oh well, you live 'n' learn – so what's Dave, a nickname like?

Rodney No. You're the only one who calls me Dave. Everybody else calls me Rodney, and the reason they call me Rodney is because Rodney is my name.

Trigger Oh well, I shall have to get used to calling you Rodney.

Rodney Thank you.

Trigger *(Calls to Chairman)* Here Basil. You gonna get this meeting started? Me and Dave ain't got all night.

Rodney Rodney.

Trigger Oh yeah.

Baz I can't start the meeting until the Vice Chairman's in attendance. It's in our constitution.

Rodney Well how long's he gonna be?

Baz Could be a hell of a long time son – he died a fortnight ago.

Rodney Died? Well, what was the point in calling the meeting?

Baz I was hoping – if we'd had a bigger turn-out – to elect a new Vice Chairman from the floor.

Trigger You need a new Vice Chairman? Well, if it'll help you out any Baz, I nominate Rodney.

Rodney What?

Baz Right, seconded.

Rodney Now hang on a minute.

Baz All those in favour? *(Baz and Trigger raise their hands)* Against? *(Rodney raises his hand)* Nomination accepted. Welcome aboard, son.

Rodney But I don't wanna be Vice Chairman.

Trigger I thought you was interested in all that political malarky.

Rodney Well, yeah, I am, but I don't want this job.

Trigger Oh well, I suppose Del Boy was right all along.

Rodney What d'you mean?

Trigger Well, he always said you were too immature to accept responsibility.

Rodney Oh did he? Well, we'll have to see about that then, won't we? Where do I sit Baz? Where do I sit Baz?

Baz Eh – oh, next to me, son – right then, I declare this meeting open. Now, the first item on the agenda is my resignation. *(Pushes 'Chairman' nameplate across to Rodney)* You're the new Chairman, congratulations son. You going down there, Trigger?

Trigger Yeah, I'll have a quick one with you Baz.

Rodney Oi, what about the meeting?

Baz Well, you'll have to close it won't you? You ain't got a Vice Chairman.

Rodney Oh yeah – well, um, meeting closed.

Baz He done that well didn't he?

Trigger He's a natural. See you, Dave.

Rodney is seated alone at the committee table, still stunned by the speed of events. He now allows himself a little smile of pleasure. The feeling of power is starting to grow. He leans back in his chair and puts his feet up on the table. He is becoming almost smug about his new position of importance within the community. He remains like this for a few seconds before leaning back on his chair just a little too far. He tumbles backwards off it and out of sight.

THE MARKET.

Del, in his market clothes plus sunglasses and cap, is selling or oranges from a couple of crates which stand on the fold-away table.

Del Oranges, they're lovely, three for 25p. They're lovely, they're juicy, they're full of vitamin C. Suck one of these a day, you'll never catch scurvy. There you go, three darling. God bless you, luv. Look after yourself. Come on girls – the finest Spanish oranges, just in from Seville.

Old lady They're fresh then?

Del Fresh? Fresh? They were playing castanets this morning my luv. There you go . . . take that one for luck.

Old lady Thank you very much.

Rodney enters wearing his suit and tie.

Del God bless you my luv. Don't swallow the pips will you. *(To Rodney)* Where the ruddy hell have you been, eh?

Rodney You know where I've been. I told you I

Homesick

had to go down to the Town Hall.

Del Yeah, you said you'd only be 20 minutes, that was four hours ago.

Rodney Oh yeah, sorry, but well, you know, I got a bit involved with council business.

Del Oh did you, yeah. Well, of course, I got a bit involved myself here you know, with silly little things like trying to organise us some profit. *(A kid swipes an orange)* Oi, you little git. *(Picks up another orange and hurls it after him. Turns to Rodney. There is the sound of china smashing. Neither notice)* You wanna get your priorities sorted out, my son. You want to make your mind up whether you want to be Chairman of the Tenant's Association or you wanna work this pitch, right?

Rodney No, no, 'cos I had to go down and introduce myself to Miss Mackenzie.

Del Who's Miss Mackenzie?

Rodney She's in charge of the housing and welfare down the Town Hall, she's a very important lady. And she was very impressed with me.

Del Oh well, she would be, wouldn't she? I mean, it's the suit innit, eh?

Rodney Well, yeah.

Del *(To customer)* What d'you want, three? God bless darling.

Rodney She's very intelligent actually. We got on really well.

Del Yeah well, they do say opposites attract don't they, eh? Come on you, get these crates sorted out, will you.

Rodney What? Oh come on, Del. I mean, don't you think it's gonna be a little bit demeaning for the Chairman of the Tenant's Association to be seen 'umping dirty old crates around a market.

Del D'you want any wages tomorrow?

Rodney Where shall I put 'em?

Del Don't tempt me Rodney, don't tempt me. *Grandad enters struggling through the crowds with two heavy bags of groceries. He passes a china stall where an orange is lying on the stall among a pile of broken china. The two owners are discussing this strange event. One of them is looking up to see if the orange could have been thrown from a window.*

Grandad Alright, Del Boy?

Del Hello Grandad, what you doing here, eh?

Grandad I've just been getting something in for dinner.

Rodney What have I got, Grandad?

Grandad Er – d'you like haddock pie, Del?

Del No I don't.

Grandad You've got haddock pie, Rodney.

Rodney Triffic . . . How's yer legs?

Grandad Still hurting.

Del I've told you, told you what they are, they're growing pains.

Rodney Look, if you wanna hang on I'll give you a lift back in the van.

Grandad No, that's alright Rodney, I'll try 'n' walk it off. See you later. *(He limps away)*

Del Yeah, see you.
A rather miserable old woman is pawing the oranges.

Old woman Has he got pineapples?

Rodney No, it's just rheumatism. Oh. No, no, sorry, no.

Del No, we ain't got any pineapples luv, you see. No, it's this weather we've been having, you know, you can't get the people to go out and pick 'em. Never mind, look, I've got some nice pineapple-tasting oranges here. No, I got them in special today, I knew you was coming in. They come from Seville. There's three for 25p . . .

THE TROTTERS' LOUNGE.
The room appears to be empty. There is the sound of the front door opening.

Rodney And then after that, right, me and Miss Mackenzie were thinking of forming a Police and Local Community Action Committee.

Del You wanna get them pigging lifts fixed first.

Rodney No, that's alright, that's all in hand. *(He sees the two bags of groceries)* Oh look at this. He ain't even put the shopping aw . . .

Del The lazy git, I'm gonna sack him one of these days I will. Hang about.
Rodney is frozen to the spot.

Rodney Del.
Grandad is lying on the floor in the space between the TVs and armchairs.

Del Oh my Gawd. Grandad, Grandad!

Rodney What's the matter with him?

Del How the hell do I know?

Rodney Del, the brandy.

Del Yeah, yeah. *(Moves to drinks area, picks up the bottle of brandy and holds it up to the light)* No, he ain't been at this.

Rodney I meant pour him some . . . Shall I give him the kiss of life?

Grandad I ain't that bad, Rodney.

Rodney Thank God for that, you're alive. I mean awake.

Grandad I just got up to switch over to *Cross-roads*.

Del And what happened?

Grandad I don't know Del Boy, I didn't see the end of it.

Rodney No, he actually meant what happened to you?

Grandad I just come over bad, Rodney – me legs give way. Them stairs'll be the death of me.

Del Yeah, come on, come on, get him into bed. Come on Grandad. Come on, that's it, get up. *(They help him to his feet)* Look, I'll put him to the bedroom, you phone for the doctor, Rodney.

Rodney Right.

Grandad No need to call the doctor Del Boy, I'll be alright.

Del Now you just shut up, it's nothing to do with you.

Rodney *(On phone)* Oh good evening. Could you put me through to Dr Becker please . . . Yes it is an emergency. Hello, Dr Becker, look, sorry to bother you but it's my grandad, he's not very well. Yeah, yeah, my name is Trotter, we live on . . . Oh you remember . . . Has what cleared up? No, I've never had anything like that. No, no, you must be getting me mixed up with somebody else.

Del Well, is he coming round?

Rodney Could you come round straight away please? You're going out to dinner?

Del Tell him he can have dinner here.

Rodney Yeah, you could have dinner here . . . *(To Del)* He can have my haddock pie.

Del Your haddock pie? Give us that will you. *(Takes receiver)* Hello Doctor, my name is Del Trotter, now you don't know me but we've got a mutual friend. Her name is Rita Alldridge. That's right. And I happen to talk to your good lady wife every day in the market. Right. *(Puts phone down)* He's on his way round.

THE TROTTERS' LOUNGE.

Doctor enters from Grandad's bedroom and crosses the room.

Doctor I want you to make sure that he gets plenty of sleep and lots of fresh air.

Rodney Yeah, we could put his bed on the balcony.

Del Fresh air? Fresh air. Haven't you noticed all the juggernauts and buses smoking their way past this place? The only fresh air my grandad gets is when he's listening to *The Archers*.

Doctor Well, there isn't very much I can do about the pollution problem.

Del No, no, I'm sorry, I'm sorry doctor. What about his legs?

Doctor Oh, don't worry, he's got legs like Nijinsky.

Del Nijinsky's a racehorse.

Rodney No, Del, he means Nijinsky, the Russian ballet dancer.

Doctor No I don't.

Rodney Oh, um, well, what's – what's the matter with him, Doctor?

Doctor Exhaustion. 12 flights of stairs is difficult enough for a young man, let alone someone of your grandad's age. Now what he needs is ground-floor accommodation. Have you seen any of those new council bungalows in Herrington Road?

Del Oh yeah, them. They're lovely ain't they. They've got three bedrooms, little garden, right opposite the park. Still what chance do we stand? I mean, you need to have nine kids and speak with a foreign accent to get one of them.

Doctor If you think it would do any good I could write a letter to the council recommending you be moved.

Del You did that for my mum back in 1962 and they moved us here.

Rodney I'll put the shopping away. *(Exits to kitchen)*

Doctor The only other thing that would hold a lot of sway with the council's housing department would be support from the Chairman of the Tenant's Association. Now who is the Chairman of the Association these days?

Rodney It's me.

Del Alright, alright, good boy.

Rodney What?

Del Nothing, good boy.

GRANDAD'S BEDROOM.

Just a sidelight burns. Grandad, propped up by pillows and still wearing his hat, is asleep. Del is seated next to the bed. Rodney enters with a bag. Del gives him a look of contempt.

Rodney I didn't know you were in here. You keeping a vigil?

Del No, I'm just sitting here with Grandad. *(Referring to bag)* What you got there?

Rodney Oh, it's just some fruit.

Del What you get? Got him some grapes have you?

Rodney No, they're oranges.

Del Orange – oranges?

Rodney Well, I couldn't think of what else to get him . . . Look, Del, you know I'd like to help.

Del I've got nothing further to say on the subject. Here you are Grandad, have a suck of that – go on. How you could do this to your own flesh and blood, I've got no idea.

Rodney Look, what's Miss Mackenzie gonna think? I mean, I've only been Chairman of the Association for two days and already I'm into her

Homesick

for a new bungalow.

Del I'm not concerned with what – I'm not concerned with what Miss Mackenzie thinks. I'm only concerned with Grandad. I mean, look at him. His brain went years ago. Now his legs have gone. There's only the middle bit of him left.

Rodney We could take him to Lourdes?

Del Lord's. Lord's. But he don't even like cricket.

Rodney I meant the Lourdes in France.

Del Lourdes in France, no, no, that's no good. I mean, what you gain on the miracle cures you'd lose on the sea-sickness on the way home.

Grandad Still here, Del Boy?

Del Yes, I'm here Grandad, it's alright, don't worry. Look Rodney's bought you some oranges. I'll put 'em over there shall I, with the other 3,000.

Grandad You're a good boy, Rodney. You've always looked after your old Grandad . . .

He tries to reach beneath his pillow but is too weak.

Rodney, put your hand under my pillow.

Rodney Yeah okay. *(Suddenly stops)* Why, what's under there?

Grandad It's just something what was left to me by my grandad.

Rodney pulls out an old, silver cigarette case, badly dented.

Rodney What is it?

Grandad It's my grandad's old cigarette case. He carried that with him right throughout the Boer War. That's a bit of history you're holding, not like them Nelson's eyepatches Del Boy flogs to the tourists.

Rodney What's this big dent?

Grandad There's a story behind that Rodney. See, one night my grandad was on sentry duty, standing out there alone in the middle of Africa. And suddenly a sniper fired at him. The bullet was aiming straight for my grandad's heart, but he had that cigarette case in his breast pocket and the bullet hit that instead.

Rodney Jeez. It saved his life?

Grandad Well, not really. See, the bullet ricocheted up his nose and blew his brains out. I want you to have it, Rodney.

Rodney What?

Grandad My gran always said it were lucky.

Rodney Grandad, it made the bullet ricochet up his nose and blow his brains off.

Del Yeah, well, it could have ricocheted downwards and ruined his entire life.

Grandad And do you know where he died, Rodney? Fighting the Zulus at the Battle of Rorke's Drift.

Rodney No. Was he actually there? Oh Cosmic. *(Puzzled)* I always thought it was Welsh.

Del No, no, it was definitely the Zulus, I saw the film.

Grandad You keep that with you always, Rodney. It'll be something to remember me by.

Rodney Now don't you talk like that, Grandad.

Del It's alright Grandad, it's alright. He'll remember what he done to you. I'll see to that, don't you worry.

Grandad Oh don't keep on at him, Del. He's doing what he thinks is best. Besides, I might not have liked living on the ground. I've always been up in the air somewhere . . . I think I would have liked the garden though. I could have grown some flowers. I've never ever had a garden. Still what you've never had you never miss, eh Del Boy?

Del That's right Grandad. That's right. Rodney, where you going?

Rodney I'm gonna phone Miss Mackenzie about that bungalow.

Del That's a good boy Rodney, good boy. You know it makes sense . . . Welcome back, you're one of the family again. *(Rodney exits)*

Grandad Del Boy. I'd like to be cremated.

Del Well, you'll have to wait till morning 'cos they'll be closed now.

THE TROTTERS' LOUNGE.

The following evening. A coat is draped over an armchair. On the table is an open briefcase and lots of paperwork. Del enters through the hall door.

Del *(Calls)* Oi, gor, Rodney. Come on, look, clear this place up, that old biddy from the council'll be here any minute.

Rodney enters from the bedroom area.

Rodney Del, I'd like you to meet Miss Mackenzie.

Miss Mackenzie enters. She is in her early thirties, very attractive and smartly dressed. The complete opposite to how Del imagined her.

Miss Mac Good evening.

Del Entende, I'm sure. *(Kisses her hand)* Please do sit down, Miss Mackenzie. Can I get you a drink? Tea, coffee, Pina Colada?

Miss Mac No thank you, that's very kind of you, Mr Trotter.

Del Mais oui, mais oui, Derek please.

Miss Mac Derek – I've just been in to see your grandfather. He's a very interesting man, he was telling me how his own grandfather had died at the Battle of Rorke's Drift.

Del Well, no, he wasn't actually at Rorke's Drift itself. What he was doing, see, he was camped in a little field behind, and one night he went over to the Zulus to complain about the noise. *(He laughs, Miss Mac, who doesn't have much of a sense of humour, looks bewildered)* Was – has it always been your ambition to work for the council, Miss Mackenzie?

Miss Mac Please call me Margaret.

Del Margaret. Margaret, do you know, that is my most favourite name.

Miss Mac Thank you. Actually, when I left school I wanted to be a choreographer.

Del Really? What a coincidence 'cos I always wanted to go into the medical profession meself.

Rodney A choreographer, Del, it means she wanted to teach dance.

Del Oh yeah, course, that sort of choreographer, yeah. Are you interested in dancing then, Margaret?

Miss Mac Well, I was a student of dance for two years.

Del Was you really, amazing, so was I.

Miss Mac Really. I was at the London School of Dance, Knightsbridge.

Rodney Del was at the Arthur Murray School, Lewisham.

Del Thank you Rodney. Rodney, why don't you go into the kitchen and stick your head in the food blender. Well, do you like ballet, Margaret?

Miss Mac Oh yes, very much.

Del So do I. Triffic innit? What about that Nijinsky then, eh?

Miss Mac Nijinsky?

Del Fabulous dancer, eh? Well, for a Soviet.

Miss Mac Yes. I suppose so.

Del I'm a great fan.

Miss Mac Of Nijinsky's.

Del Yeah, actually I was thinking of getting a couple of tickets, you know, for one of the shows.

Miss Mac Derek – Nijinsky died in 1950.

Del Did she?

Miss Mac She? Nijinsky was a man.

Del Oh yes, yeah, of course he was. Sorry, sorry, I always get him mixed up with . . . er . . .

Rodney Arkle.

Del Yeah, Arkle.

Miss Mac Well, that seems to be about it. I think I have all the information I need.

Rodney How long will we have to wait until we know if our application's been accepted?

Miss Mac You can know right now, Rodney. I've just signed it.

Rodney You mean we've got the bungalow?

Miss Mac Of course. Here's your new rent book and all the necessary paperwork.

Rodney I don't believe it. Are you sure you don't want to double-check nothing?

Del That won't be necessary Rodney. Margaret knows what she's doing.

Rodney I don't know what to say.

Del Well, just say thank you to the nice lady.

Miss Mac Really there's no need, I'm only too pleased to help. Many people get themselves voted on to Tenants Committees purely for their own ends. But Rodney's different. He cares.

Del Oh he does, he cares. He's a diamond, he really is.

Miss Mac Well, I hope you'll be very happy in your new home. I'll see you at our next committee meeting then?

Rodney Yes, yes of course. And thanks again – I can't wait to tell Grandad. Well, I suppose we better . . .

Del No, I'll see Margaret out, Rodney. Excuse me. There you go. Don't drink it.

THE HALL.

Del Well, I suppose you must have pulled a few strings?

Miss Mac Well, let's just say I applied some rather liberal interpretations to our rules.

Del Yeah, well, if only there was some way that I could show my appreciation. But mon dieu – mon dieu – why don't I take you out for a celebratory drink?

Miss Mac Oh that's very nice of you, but I've got a lot of paperwork to finish.

Del Okay, well, some other time maybe then?

Miss Mac Yes. Well, goodbye.

Del No, not goodbye, Margaret, just bonjour.

THE LOUNGE

Del enters.

Rodney Well, we've done it. Now that is the power of being a Chairman, Del.

Del Leave it out. It was my chat what did it.

Rodney Oh yeah, your chat, yeah. 'A choreographer. Of course, I've always wanted to be in the medical profession meself.'

Del Oi, cut that out will you.

The door to the bedroom area opens and Grandad enters.

Grandad Have we got it, Del?

Del Yeah, of course, we've got it, Grandad. Look, we move in next week.

Del and Grandad *(Singing and dancing)* 'My old man said follow the van, and don't dilly-dally on the way.' Hang on, I'll get you a beer,

Homesick

Grandad. *(Singing)* 'Off went the van with the whole . . .'

Rodney *(Was stunned, now angry)* We feeling a little bit better are we, Grandad?

Grandad I'm feeling on top of the world Rodney.

Rodney You know, I thought as much. Because five minutes ago you couldn't wiggle your toes and now you're doing an audition for the *Hot Shoe Show*. You pair have really stitched me up ain't yer? And not just me – Dr Becker and Miss Mackenzie as well.

Del Oh shut up you tart. We couldn't let you in on our little plan could we, 'cos, well, to put it politely, you're full of principle, aren't you? Here you are Grandad.

Grandad How else could we have done it, Rodney? We've got ourselves a beautiful new home, a bit of garden, a garage and no stairs.

Rodney Grandad the point is that is . . . I suppose them stairs were a bit much for you. And I can hardly blame Del for the lifts breaking down.

Del looks away

Rodney You mean you even went to the – right, come here you.

The front door bell rings.

Del I'll just get the door, Rodders. *(Exits to hall)*

THE HALL

Del Oh hello, Margaret. Did you forget something?

Miss Mac Only my manners I'm sorry to say. I've just realised that you, quite naturally, would like to celebrate your new home. But as Rodney would have to stay in with Grandad you have no one to go with. So if your invitation is still open?

Del Oh well, of course it is. If you'd just like to hang on one moment.

Miss Mac I mustn't have too much to drink though – it goes straight to my head.

Del Does it really? I'll have to keep a close eye on you then won't we. *(He opens door to lounge and calls in)* Oi, listen, I'm off out. I don't know what time I'm going to be back so don't put the Chubb on, right. *(To Miss Mac)* Listen what I thought we might do is slip down the Nag's Head for a couple of halves and then we could go to this – well – go on to this spick drinking club I know over at New Cross.

Miss Mac I don't want to be out too late.

Del Don't worry we'll get you back in your flat before three.

The lounge door opens and Grandad with a glass of brandy and a large cigar in one hand, Del's scarf in the other, appears.

Grandad Here are Del, don't forget your scarf, it's freez . . . Ooh my good Gawd.

Miss Mac Well, hello again. *(To Del)* He seems to be over the worst.

Del Yeah, well, you know, it comes – and goes.

Miss Mac So it would appear.

Del *(Out of corner of his mouth)* Collapse.

Grandad What?

Del Collapse!

Miss Mac I shouldn't bother, you might do yourself an injury.

Rodney appears at the door.

Rodney Oi, you're gonna need the keys.

Miss Mac I am disgusted with the lot of you. But especially with Rodney. I believed you.

Rodney I believed me.

Miss Mac I assume you'll be resigning, Mr Chairman?

Rodney First thing in the morning, yeah.

Miss Mac And I'll tell you what I'm going to do in the morning. I'm going to do you all yet another favour. I'm going to save you the inconvenience of moving. Goodnight to you all.

Del Margaret.

Miss Mac What?

Del We still on for that drink?

Curriculum Vitae

Name: Rodney Charlton Trotter.
Address: 127 Mandela House,
Nyere Estate,
Peckham, London. SE15

Education: Peckham Comprehensive - left with 2 GCEs in Art and Maths.

Basingstoke Art College - left after three terms after being found zonked out on the bed of an Oriental lady, with the biggest reefer this side of Marrakech in my hand, during the Board of Governors annual inspection. I was failed by my tutors but given an 18-month suspended sentence by the Old Bill.

Employment History
Since leaving art college I have been self-unemployed, working with my brother, Derek, as a financial adviser in our successful importing-exporting business. Apart from my role as financial adviser, my other duties within Trotters Independent Trading Company (TITCO) have included being a look-out, decorator, dog-minder, chandelier repair-man and a whole range of other positions. In 1981 I gained brief experience as a Nocturnal Security Officer with a firm named Trotter Watch. Two years later I started my own business in partnership with Mickey Pearce but it was liqui-dated after a misunderstanding over lawn-mower engines — and when he scarpered to Benidorm with the first week's takings. In 1988 I started a computer diploma course at night school, which I passed without trouble, and landed a position with a computer firm run by my father-in-law. After gaining valuable experience in information technology and data processing, I left that post after mistakenly tendering my resignation when experiencing marital difficulties. I also possess experience in film-making, gained during a series of art classes that I attended at a local evening school in 1986. With the aid of an Arts Council grant I wrote a short film entitled 'There's a Rhino Loose in the City' — the title is self-explanatory. My brother supplied the rhinoceros. I have also written a short story called 'The Indictment,' a blistering criticism of the failing system.

Interests: Art and adult art literature, socialising and women in uniform. I also like music. In 1987 I was briefly the drummer in a pop band named 'A Bunch of Wallies' but we split up after one gig due to artistic differences. They could play, I couldn't. I left and they went on to a Top 20 hit and an appearance on Top of the Pops.

Referees:
Mr Derek Trotter   Mr Mike Fisher
127 Mandela House   The Nag's Head
Nyere Estate   Peckham SE15
Peckham SE 15

Reference from Derek Trotter.

The first thing you should know about my bruv is that when it comes to art and maths he is the creme de la menthe. Some people think that all his GCEs in Art and Maths are good for is painting by numbers, but as my junior partner he has only occasionally let me down by being a right dipstick. He was the first Trotter ever to go to university. I don't know what he was reading, but it was probably Mayfair and Penthouse. He may not have left Basingstoke with a diploma but he certainly knows a good joint when he sees one. It is a sign of his determination that he hasn't let that episode in Shanghai Lil's bedroom hold him back. No, that's my job. The little git did try and set up his own rival business once, with that dipstick Mickey Pearce, who's as useful as a one-legged man in an arse-kicking contest, but that soon went down the kermit thanks to yours truly.
    My commodites business, with him as my financial adviser and dogsbody, has flourished, due to a combination of my business acumen, contacts and money and his ability to drive a three-wheeled van. Thanks to the 150 quid I slipped his tutor, Mr Jamille, he got his diploma in computerisa-tion at evening school. He is now an expert at poncing around on computers and can type with both hands. That's right, John, he's ambiguous. The wallybrain can also write, as 'The Indiktment' or whatever it was called, showed. Granted, it did not have the social impact of Cathy Come Home - more like Lassie Come Home - but at least he tried. Sur la pont Avignon, as they say in France. No, Rodders, despite being a dozy little twonk at times, is well worth hiring as long as he gets douce in bounce a week and you keep him away from the funny fags. As a fellow businessman I know how valuable good staff can be, and trust me, my bruv is a diamond, one of the bestest blokes you could find on this septic isle. Will that do, Rodney? Now move your arse and help me knock out these heat-damaged sunglasses.

EPISODE ★ TWO
Healthy Competition

BUSY SHOPPING CENTRE.

Del is standing outside a large department store. The suitcase is open on a fold-away table and contains seven or eight battery-driven toy yap-yap dogs. A crowd has gathered round and Del is into his sales spiel.

Del No, they're beautiful ain't they? They're beautiful. And listen, I don't care whether your nipper has got measles, mumps or a scabby eye, because these are guaranteed to bring a smile right back on to his face. Now listen, gather round everybody. Listen to me, now listen ladies, I want to tell you something, please don't let it go any further because I'm afraid I might be in breach of the Official Secrets Act. Right. I happen to know that little Prince William has one of these little fluffy toys in his nursery in Buck House; now I'll tell you how I know, shall I? Because his dad gave me a bell last week and he said 'Del Boy – Del Boy,' he said, 'I'm in right lumber, the enemy's doing her pieces because I've forgotten Spud's Birthday.' Now Spud happens to be the nickname for the little Prince William. So what did I do? I walloped straight round there with one of these. And it was end of aggravation, end of story.

Rodney is standing a few yards away acting as look-out. He isn't at his most alert, seeming pre-occupied, deep in thought.

Del Now they come complete with batteries, they're fully house trained. Whoops. That one isn't, never mind. These are not made in Taiwan and these are not made in Hong Kong. These are 'Made in Burma'. What can't speak can't lie . . .

By now Rodney has lost total interest. Above the heads of the shoppers there is a policeman's helmet moving nearer like a shark's fin.

Del Now listen, the fully recommended retail price is £14.65. Now, I'm not going to mess about with coppers, now that's a Freudian slip, so I'm not asking for 14 quid, I'm not going to ask for ten quid. Who'll give me six quid for this little yap. Six quid, come on anybody, six quid. Let me tell you something, if these were fluffy little chickens you'd be saying 'Good heavens, they're going cheap.' Going cheap, do you get it. But they're not, no, these are little butts and they're going 'Yap, yap'. But they are still remarkably cheap and I'll tell you why I've got to

get rid of them, shall I? *(He spots the policeman's head moving ever nearer. The policeman pushes Rodney out of the way to get nearer Del)* Because I'm going on my holidays and I need my suitcase, right. Now what I . . . what I, er, right, listen sorry I can't stay. Tell you what, I just remembered my flight leaves in 'alf an hour. See ya. *(He slams the suitcase shut and exits into the department store)*

THE DEPARTMENT STORE.

Del hurries through the store with the barking suitcase. The policeman follows and gives chase.

Del Excuse me, excuse . . . oh.

BACK STREET/ALLEY.

Del, beginning to tire, hurries along the street. A cat on a wall spits at Del and the suitcase. He exits from the alley pursued by stray dogs. He is kicking them and shooing them out of the way.

Del Shut up, will ya?

At this point the van, driven by Rodney, screeches to a halt. Del leaps into the back. The van roars away.

The policeman runs into the street. He stops and listens. There is barking from the alley. He runs into the alley. After a pause, he runs out being pursued by the stray dogs.

THE TROTTERS' LOUNGE.

Grandad is watching the TVs. Del, carrying the suitcase, enters. He hurls it down and kicks it.

Grandad Had a good day Del?

Del Had a good day, a good day? Oh the best, Grandad, the very bloody best. I've been chased by a gendarme, attacked by Pussycat Willum and almost caught rabies. And it's all this dipstick's fault.

Rodney Oh he don't 'alf exaggerate.

Del Exaggerate. You should have been with me in that alley Rodney, it was like *Call of the Wild*. Why didn't you warn me that that copper was coming?

Rodney Because I didn't see him.

Del You didn't see him? What d'you want me to get you, radar or something?

Grandad Oh you've gotta give him the benefit

of the doubt Del Boy.

Rodney Yes, thank you Grandad. At least somebody understands.

Grandad I mean, they are difficult to spot – with their size 18 boots and their pointed heads.

Rodney Why don't you shut your mouth you sarky old goat.

Del Oh and that's another thing. What about last Friday then, when we were knocking out them Italian shirts. Listen to this one, Grandad. That wasn't – that wasn't just one copper you failed to warn me about – it was an entire squad car. I mean, it stood there by the kerb, all big and white with a red stripe running through it like a tube of Signal.

Rodney Well, I didn't see it.

Del You didn't see it . . . you must have been a tiny suspicious when this ginormous great big jam sandwich pulled up next to you?

Grandad Well, maybe he needs medical help Del.

Del Yeah, like psychiatric treatment.

Grandad Or glasses.

Rodney Look, I don't need psychiatric treatment and I don't need specs, right. I've had a lot on my mind just recently. I've been struggling to find a way of making a very important announcement.

Del Oh yeah, what important announcement?

Rodney Alright, for the last two weeks or so I've been taking stock of my life. Who I am, what I am and where I'm going.

Del And that's taken you a fortnight? I could have answered all them questions for you – could have answered them all during a commercial break.

Rodney Will you just shut up for one minute. I am 24 years old, I have two GCEs, 13 years of schooling and three terms at an adult education centre behind me, right. And with all that, what have I become? I'm a look-out.

Del No Rodney, you're wrong. You're not just a look-out. You're a bad look-out.

Rodney Alright, alright, so I'm not very good at it. Perhaps that's 'cos me heart's not really in it.

Del I'm not asking you to put yer heart in it, just yer eyes'll do.

Rodney Del, what I'm trying to say is . . . I'm thinking of breaking up the partnership.

Del What partnership?

Rodney Ours.

Del Oh. What do you wanna do that for? We're doing well. Business is booming, profits are up. What more d'you want?

Rodney I want to make my own decisions. I've made one Del, I'm going it alone.

Del Who with?

Rodney Mickey Pearce.

Del Mickey, Mickey Pearce, oh, leave it out. He couldn't keep a rabbit going with lettuce.

Grandad You wanna watch that young Pearcey. He's a bit too fly for my liking. He'd rob his own grandmother he would.

Rodney Oh don't be stupid, Grandad – that was never proved. Anyway you give credit where it's due, right. Mickey's quite an astute businessman. And he's putting capital into this venture.

Del Oh, putting money in is he?

Rodney Well, no. But he will as soon as his Giro cheque arrives.

Del I see, and what are you putting in?

Rodney I've got money, Del.

Del Oh, oh, oh, have you?

Rodney Yeah, I've got my half of the partnership.

Del What partnership? What our part . . . Alright, if that is the way that you want it, my son. *(He produces a wad of notes. He removes the elastic band and begins counting out some fivers, etc)* 'Cos you'll have to understand one thing Rodney. Going it alone means exactly what it says. Right, from now on, you've got to pay your own way in the world. You pay your own way in the pubs and you pay your own way in this house. You make a mistake you stick by that mistake. Alright?

Rodney Fine.

Del Fine. And if things don't go right for you, I don't wanna hear no moaning or whining from yer.

Rodney Look, I won't moan or whine about nothing.

Del *(Hands him the money)* Right, there you go then.

Rodney Is this all I got?

Del Yeah.

Rodney Oh bloody hell, Del, all them years of working, you give me this.

Del Yeah, well, I mean, you know, business's a bit shaky – profits are down.

Rodney Hold on a minute – just now you said we were doing well.

Del Yeah, well, we are doing well, relatively speaking Rodney. I mean we are doing well, compared to . . . an Iranian gin salesman. Anyway, I had to buy some stock off Alfie Flowers yesterday, and I mean a trader is only as good as his stock, right.

Rodney Alright, well, this'll have to do then won't it. But I'm going to prove to you that I've got business acumen, that I am as quick-witted

Healthy Competition

as you, Del. See you down the auction tomorrow.

Del Alright. How will I recognise you?

Rodney Ah, I'll wear that stripy tie with . . . See yer.

AUCTION ROOM.

The Auctioneer stands on a small platform. The traders are seated around the platform, with a few others standing at the back. Del is at the back of the hall, as are Rodney and Mickey Pearce.

Auctioneer Lot 35, ladies and gentlemen, is a consignment of smoke-damaged fire alarms. Now they are industrial models and all guaranteed – sort of – to be in perfect working order. Well, we've written evidence from the night-watchman to say they all went off when the factory went up. Now there's 70 all-told, and they usually retail around the 30 quid mark. So I can start the bidding at £50 the lot.

Mickey *(Nudging Rodney)* Go on, bid for 'em.

Rodney What do we want industrial fire alarms for, eh? How many factories do we know are going to catch fire?

Del enters.

Del Alright Rodney?

Rodney Good morning Derek.

Del Hello young Michael.

Mickey Watcha Del. It's good here innit?

Del Er, triffic.

Mickey This is my first auction.

Del I thought it might be. Listen, a word of advice. You've gotta be very careful what you do with yer hands in a place like this. I mean, I know you didn't realise it Mickey, but just now you put in a 40 quid bid for an electric generator when you scratched your bum.

Mickey Did I?

Rodney He's winding you up.

Del The state of him. What are you after?

Mickey Cut-glass goblets.

Rodney *(Alarmed)* No, no, we ain't.

Mickey But I thought you said . . .

Rodney *(Interrupting)* No, no – we're not after nothing in particular.

Del Oh I see. Now listen, the one that you wanna beware of is Lot 37. It's nothing more than a load of scrap iron, right, so be careful. See you later.

Auctioneer 130, thank you sir. A 130. Do I hear any more? *(Bangs the gavel)* 130 – down to young Towser. Now ladies and gentlemen, we come to lot 36, 112 pieces of near perfect cut-glass goblets. Take a look ladies and gentlemen.

Mickey This is us Rodney.

Rodney No, hang on a minute. Let's have another look at Lot 37.

Mickey Yeah, but Del told us to be careful of that one.

Rodney Yeah and why d'you think he did that? Use your noddle Mickey. Del's after Lot 37, ain't he? He's just trying to put us off and leave the field open for him, ain't he. I know how his mind works son. *(Checks programme)* Right, Lot 37, assorted agricultural machinery. Hey, that could be anything – that could be tractors, combine harvesters.

Mickey Yeah, we could take 'em out in the sticks and do them old carrot crunchers up.

Rodney Hey, shall we go for Lot 37 then?

Mickey Yeah.

Rodney Yeah.

Mickey Yeah.

LARGE YARD.

Rodney and Mickey are staring at something with stunned expressions. Lot 37 consists of a pile of old lawn-mower engines and other bits of rusting metal. Harry the yard foreman is standing close by.

Harry *(To Rodney)* You bought this son?

Rodney Yeah.

Harry *(laughing)* There's always one at every auction, ain't there Del?

Del is passing by to the van parked a few yards away. He is carrying two cardboard boxes.

Del Yeah, get two for the same price at this one.

Rodney Oi you, this stuff is a load of rubbish.

Del I know, I did try to warn you Rodders.

Rodney Yeah, but I thought when you put . . .

Del Yeah, the trouble with you Rodney, is that you will insist on thinking.

Rodney Well, what have you bought then?

Del I got those crystal goblets that you were after.

Mickey What are these things?

Del What those? They are lawn-mower engines.

Rodney Lawn-mower engines?

Del Yes, listen they're not ordinary lawn-mower engines.

Rodney *(Optimism rekindled)* No?

Del No. They're broken lawn-mower engines. *(Laughs)*

Rodney Del. We'll probably have a few problems getting these back to the, er, depot.

Mickey Yeah, we come down on the Green Line see.

Rodney Yeah.

Del Oh well, your best bet is to hire an open back truck then ain't it?

Rodney Yeah, but we was wondering whether you could take maybe a few in the back of the van?

Del Back of my van? You must be joking – I've only just cleared 'em out of the van.

Rodney You mean you was selling 'em in the first place?

Del Yeah. That is the rubbish that Alfie Flowers sold me. Normally, I'd never have bought it, you know, but he caught me when I was a bit non compos mentis down the One Eleven Club. Well, look, I never thought I'd ever got shot of them. But you know me Rodney. He who dares wins. Actually it made a tidy little profit on it an' all.

Rodney Yeah, but what are we supposed to do with 'em?

Del Well, why don't you do what I did? Find yourself a couple of right little plonkers with cash on the hip.

Rodney *(Mouths the words)* Piss off. *(To Mickey)* So what are we gonna do?

Mickey *(Indicating Harry)* Wait till he ain't looking and run away.

Rodney No, we can't do that, he's got my address.

Mickey Yeah, well he ain't got mine.

Rodney Oh thanks partner.

Mickey Well, you would insist on bidding for 'em.

Rodney Yeah, and who wanted to go out to the sticks and flog 'em to the carrot crunchers?

Mickey Well, you said they were combine harvesters and tractors. The way you were talking we were going to do a deal with Weetabix.

Rodney Oh get off my back.

Mickey . . . How we going to get home now anyway?

THE TROTTERS' LOUNGE.

A week later. Grandad is watching the TVs. Del enters through the hall door. He has a Financial Times under his arm and carries a punnet of strawberries.

Del Hello Grandad. Here are, look at this. Bought you some strawberries, go on, dip in.

Grandad Oh here, they ain't very big are they.

Del What do you mean they ain't very big? You wouldn't like one of those up yer nose for a wart would yer.

Grandad Well, no.

Del Well, go on then, shut up and eat up. I'll put the kettle on.

Grandad You're splashing out a bit ain't yer?

Del Yeah, well, I've had a right blinding week. I've sold the lot. Here, I even sold those technicolour woollen tea cosies I bought.

Grandad How d'you manage that? Who the 'ell wants woollen tea cosies these days?

Del No, no, no, no – look, I got that Mrs Murphy right, to stitch up all the holes. And then I whipped down to the youth centre and I flogged 'em to the West Indian lads as soppy hats. *(Hands Grandad some money)* There you go, look, there's the housekeeping money, alright, and look at that, there's a tenner for yourself.

Grandad Oh cheers Del.

Del That's it, don't squander it.

Grandad No, no, I'll invest it wisely. How's young Rodney doing?

Del Oh well, the opposition are floundering somewhat. Well, to be more precise, they're going down like a one-legged man doing the hokey-cokey. I've seen Rodney skulking around the garden centres and what 'ave yer

Grandad He ain't got rid of them lawn-mower engines yet?

Del No, they're still in their depot. Well, depot, that's Mickey Pearce's garden shed. Here talking about that. Do you know what happened last Tuesday night, somebody broke into their shed and nicked two of them engines.

Grandad Ah no. That's rotten innit. I feel sorry for young Rodney.

Del No, no, no, it's alright, because Wednesday night they broke in again and put 'em back.

The front door slams.

Grandad Oh here he is. Listen Del Boy, don't say nothing about them lawn-mower engines. I think he's getting a bit embarrassed about it.

Del Alright, I won't mention 'em.

Rodney enters, at first he has the look of a man who has the worries of the world on his shoulders, upon seeing Del he tries to brighten up and appear more confident.

Rodney Alright Del?

Del Triffic, brill Rodders, had a blinding week. How about you?

Rodney Oh fine – could not be better.

Del Sold those lawn-mower engines yet?

Rodney Lawn mower – lawn mower? Oh no, no, we've had lots of enquiries, obviously, but we're hanging on for the right price, you know.

Del Oh that is the way, Rodney, agent provocateur as the French would say.

Rodney Well, that's what I thought. Oh that reminds me, did the paper boy bring my *Sun* this morning?

Healthy Competition

Grandad Well, we've had to cancel it Rodney.

Rodney Cancel it? Why?

Del Well, you haven't paid yer bill, have you?

Rodney What, I'm paying that separate as well now am I?

Del Yeah, well, you're on yer own now, remember?

Rodney Oh yeah, yeah. It's alright, I'm just saying, you know, as long as I know. I'll – I'll go and pay it tomorrow.

Grandad You hungry Rodney?

Rodney Ah well, I had a pretty hefty lunch with a client earlier on. But, yeah, reckon I could manage some egg and chips.

Grandad I'll go and put the pan on.

Rodney Yeah.

Del Just a minute, just a minute. Has he paid his housekeeping money?

Rodney Er – *(Feels in his pockets)* Well, I've got a bit of a cash flow problem at the moment.

Del Well, so's half the people on this estate but they don't come in here eating my egg and chips.

Rodney No, it's alright, I'll pay double next week.

Del Ah well, that's alright then. That's alright, you can have double egg and chips next week.

Grandad How can you have a cash flow problem Rodney? I thought you had nearly £200 left out of your share.

Rodney Yeah, yeah, that's right. But – Mickey's holding the money. Well, he's financial director see.

Grandad Why don't you pop round his house and get some money?

Rodney Yeah, yeah, I would but he's out of town at the moment.

Grandad Yeah, I thought I hadn't seen him around for about four or five days.

Rodney No, no, well, that's 'cos we're doing this really big deal, you see, and Mickey's gone away to tie up all the loose ends.

Del Oh, well that explains it then.

Rodney Yeah. Explains what?

Del No, it's just that I saw his mum this morning. She said she just got a postcard from him – from Benidorm.

Rodney Benidorm?

Del Yeah he's doing alright. You know the weather's fine. Food's good. Met this Swedish bird called Helga. Oh, would that be the contact that he went to meet?

Rodney What? Yeah, yeah, yeah.

Del Well, I've gotta admire yer bottle Rodders – I must admit. You've been in the business five

minutes and already you've opened up a Spanish branch. You've cornered the world market on broken lawn-mower engines – what's your partner doing now, is he buying second-hand pedalos?

Rodney No, no, no, nothing like that, no, we're – we're going into the self-catering holiday trade.

Del Cor, what on 200 nicker?

Rodney Yeah, well, we're starting in a small way.

Grandad What you got, a Wendy House?

Rodney Grandad, I am not prepared to discuss the situation any longer, alright, it's confidential information.

Del I understand Rodney, no, no, I understand. Well, I'm off out.

Rodney Where you going?

Del Well, I thought I might go down and have a couple of light ales down the Nag's Head, and then go on to the Star of Bengal for a Ruby Murray. Coming?

Rodney I'm potless ain't I?

Del What?

Rodney Ah no, no, I really ought to stay in and do the company accounts, I suppose.

Grandad picks up one small piece of paper from the sideboard and hands it to Rodney.

Grandad Oh here they are.

Rodney Oh, cheers.

Del *(Putting his hand on Rodney's shoulder)* You don't really think I'm that hard do you Rodney?

Rodney Na.

Del No, of course I'm not.

Rodney stands and takes his coat from the back of the chair believing he's going out for a drink.

Rodney Oh, cheers Del.

Del Grandad. Do him them egg and chips will you.

THE STAR OF BENGAL.

Del sits alone at table finishing his meal. The waiter passes.

Del Oi Tony. None of the boys been in?

Waiter I haven't seen any of them, Del. Oh young Towser's just come in for a take-away.

Del Oh has he, oh yeah. *(Shouts)* Oi Towser. Towser. *(To diner)* Sorry madam. Yer onion bhaji's down there by yer foot.

Towser arrives

Towser Hello Del, how's it going?

Del Alright my son, sit down and have yourself a popadum.

Towser Listen, I can't get involved. I'm getting the missus a take-away and I wanna get home

tonight.

Del Come on, you've got time for a drink. *(Pours him a glass of wine)* Go on, sit down.

Towser Oh cheers.

Del Listen, I'm glad I bumped into you . . . I want you to do me a favour.

Towser What's that?

Del Sit down, you know those broken lawn-mower engines that dozy twonk Rodney got himself lumbered with?

Towser Yeah, what about 'em?

Del I want you to buy 'em off him.

Towser You want me to do what? Do me a favour Del. Alfie Flowers offered me them engines a month ago. I don't want nothing to do with 'em.

Del It's alright, it's alright. Now listen, you don't have to spend any money. *(Produces a wad of notes)* There are, see that, look 200 quid I want you to offer him that.

Towser 200? Here, they're only worth about a score, scrap value.

Del I know but I want him to think he's made a good profit. Look, he's had a bad week. He's been tucked up something chronic by that best mate of his and now he's brassic.

Towser Why don't you just give him the money?

Del 'Cos it'll seem like charity, won't it, eh?

Towser Yeah, and he'll be too proud to accept it?

Del No, he'd snap it up like a shot. Look, I want him to think that he's been successful. I want him to believe that he's proved me wrong . . . It's important Towser.

Towser Alright then Del, if that's what you want.

Del You're a pal. 'Ere don't let him know that I'm behind all this. Look you say to him that you got this contact in the GLC parks department and, er, they can't get enough lawn-mower engines, something like that. You see the thing is I'm not going to lose out on the deal, because come this time tomorrow Rodney'll want to be my partner again, and I will get my money back. See.

Towser Hey, wait a minute. What am I going to do with all these engines?

Del Well, I don't know, dump 'em somewhere.

Towser Oh no, no, I couldn't do that Del. I mean, I got nicked for fly-dumping a couple of months ago, I mean, they're going chuck the book at me this time.

Del Right I'll tell you what you do, take 'em back to Alfie Flowers and tell him that he can have 'em

for nothing.

Towser Yeah, alright Del. Here, hang about, what's in it for me?

Del Give you 15 for it.

Towser *(Looks at the money but doesn't pick it up)* Oh yeah.

Del 20?

Towser That'll do.

Del Thank you.

Towser Anything for a mate.

Del I wouldn't pay that bill if I were you. *(Exits)*

Waiter Thank you Del – good morning.

THE NAG'S HEAD.

Rodney sits alone at a table his feet up on another chair.

Del Alright Rodders?

Rodney Yeah.

Del Here, look I've had a right blinding day. Here look at that . . . *(Flashes a thick wad of money)* Er, I must tell ya. There's a really silly bloke down the market today. Think he must have come from the funny farm he was really silly. I said to him I said. 'Here do you wanna buy some broken lawn mower engines?' Then he said to me, 'I ain't that silly.'

Rodney For your information, Derek, this morning I successfully negotiated the sale of them engines to Young Towser.

Del You're kidding me.

Rodney No, on my life. He's bought the lot – he's got a contact in the parks department at the GLC.

Del Cor, well that's a stroke of luck then innit?

Rodney No, no, it's not luck Del – that is good business sense. I knew all the time if I held on long enough I'd get my price.

Del Yeah, well, I must say I admire your courage Rodders.

Rodney Oh well, he who dares wins.

Del Yeah, that's right. So well, that Mickey Pearce he's going to be pleased when he comes back off holiday ain't he, eh?

Rodney Now, don't you talk to me about that Mickey Pearce. I've liquidated our partnership.

Del Oh, so what you gonna do then? I mean still carry on, on your own like?

Rodney Well – I was thinking – oh, you know.

Del Go back as we was, eh? You and me?

Rodney Yeah. You and me Del, eh? And now I've got experience of buying and selling meself.

Del Yeah, that could be invaluable Rodney. Yeah, okay then, come on let's pool our resources. There we go. Now then, how much did you get for them lawn-mower engines?

Healthy Competition

Rodney £165.

Del Is that all you got for 'em, Rodney?

Rodney Well it's not bad Del, 'cos they're only worth what, a score, scrap value.

Del You certainly have learnt a lot, ain't you, Rodders. Okay, let's see the colour of your money.

Rodney Oh, I ain't got it.

Del What do mean, that Towser didn't pay you?

Rodney Oh yeah, he paid me. But I've invested the money.

Del You did what?

Rodney I went down to Alfie Flowers yard, got us another load of lawn-mower engines.

Del You're joking. Tell me that you're joking.

Rodney No, well if Towser's bloke at the GLC, well he can't get enough of them engines. Oh I'll tell you I was dead lucky down at Alfie's. He'd had another load delivered this morning. But don't worry though 'cos they're exactly the same as the others.

Del You bet your life they're the same. What a 42-carat plonker you really are.

Rodney Come on Del, don't you think it's time you showed a bit of faith in me?

Del Yes, anything you say Rodney. Anything you say.

Rodney Good. Oi, Del, I was wondering now that we're partners again d'you think you could help me out? Eh, 'cos I ain't had a pint all week, all I've had to eat is Grandad's cooking and look, the sole's coming off me best Guccis. Look.

Del Yeah, I'll help you out Rodders. *(Takes the wad of money, removes the elastic band and gives it to Rodney)* Put that round yer Gucci, it'll stop the sole coming off.

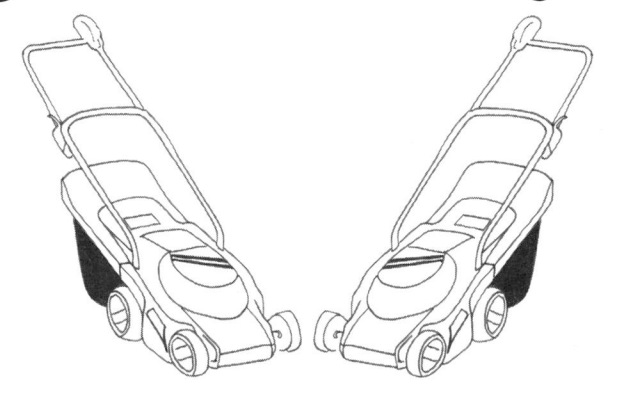

Friday the 14th

THE TROTTERS' LOUNGE.

Rodney is at the table eating a Chinese take-away. As he eats he reads an edition of 'Penthouse'. Grandad is seated watching the TVs. The door opens and the ends of three fishing rods poke into the room. Del enters holding the other ends of the rods. He also carries a couple of angler's wicker boxes, a couple of keep-nets and a couple of pairs of waders.

Del Here we are. Guess where we're going at the weekend?

Rodney No. Give us a clue.

Del Alright Rodders, if you insist.

Del opens a round aluminium tin and puts it next to Rodney's rice. It is full of maggots.

Rodney Eerrgh, you pig, you. Geddit away.

Del How's that rice going down, alright?

Rodney Geddit out.

Grandad Where are we going then Del?

Del We're going skiing. Where d'you think we're going you soppy old . . . We're going fishing aren't we?

Grandad Well, I know that. I mean where?

Del Oh. I see what you mean, we're going to a place called Tregower.

Rodney Where's that?

Del Cornwall.

Rodney and Grandad Cornwall?

Grandad Why we going all the way down there?

Del Because that's where Boycie's weekend cottage is. I had dinner with him last night at Mario's restaurant and he happened to mention he'd got this weekend cottage and it was free and so Bob's yer uncle.

Grandad How much rent he charging you?

Del Nothing.

Rodney He's letting us have it for free?

Del Yeah, all for gratis.

Rodney *(Suspicious)* Come on, Del, there's gotta be something behind this. 'Cos Boycie would scalp you if dandruff had a going rate.

Del You're becoming so cynical Rodney. He's just doing a mate a favour isn't he, eh?

Rodney Wait a minute. You met him in Mario's?

Del Yeah, that's right, yeah. Grandad come on, look, clear all this fishing gear will you 'cos I want to pop out.

Rodney Mario's is a fish restaurant.

Del Is it? Yeah, see you later.

Rodney Bit of a coincidence Del, innit, you meeting him in a fish restaurant and the next thing we're all going fishing.

Del He's like Elliot bleedin' Ness at times ain't he, eh? Alright Rodney, I was gonna tell you when we got down there – you know – as a sort of surprise like.

Rodney Oh yeah.

Del Yeah, yeah, as a surprise, yeah. Well, this cottage happens to be near one of the finest salmon fishing streams in England. Now Mario has agreed to pay us £10 for every fish that we bring back. Now Boycie and I are going to halve it, that's a fiver each. So let's say that we – we do what, 60 fish, that will be 300 sovs in our pocket. We split it three ways that means that you and Grandad get £50 each, a weekend's fishing and free digs. Now, what d'you reckon to that?

Rodney I reckon it's illegal.

Del You hurt me sometimes Rodney. You really do, you don't even let me finish before you go jumping to your nasty little conclusions.

Grandad It's lucky you ain't a judge Rodney – you'd hang 'em before they'd finished the oath.

Rodney Alright. Alright. I'm sorry. I just thought.

Del Yeah, I know exactly what you thought.

Rodney So we've got permission have we?

Del Well, we will have. We see the gamekeeper when we get down there and pay him 25 quid.

Rodney What and he gives us a fishing permit?

Del No – he shows us the hole in the fence.

Rodney I knew it.

Del It's called business.

Rodney It's called stealing.

Grandad No it ain't Rodney.

Del Listen to your Grandad.

Grandad It's called poaching.

Rodney And what do we know about that, eh? *(Indicating Grandad)* Del, he can't even poach an egg.

Del Rodney, it'll be a doddle. This stream's jam-packed with salmon. We just put our hooks in and whip 'em out.

Rodney Del – it is illegal, it is immoral, it is unethical.

Del Alright, me and Grandad'll go on our own, and split the profits between us.

Rodney *(Sudden change of mind)* Now I didn't say I wouldn't come, did I?

A BY-PASS OR MOTORWAY.

The fishing rods are tied to a roof rack on the van. It passes a sign saying 'The West'.

Rodney *(Voice over with Rodney singing)* 'Gone poaching, ba ba ba ba, left a sign upon the door. Gone poaching, ba ba.'

Del You keep on Rodney and you're gonna get a smack right in the ear'ole.

VAN.

There is a violent storm. The van is waved down by a policeman with a torch at the side of the road.

Rodney Oi, oi, oi, what's all this about?

Del Ooh my Gawd, it's the Old Bill.

Grandad Someone's doubled you up about them salmon.

Del Ssh. Look, just let me do the talking. *(The van pulls to a halt, Del winds the window down)* Good evening Officer. Now, if it's about the tax disc I can assure you that the new one is in the post.

PC It's nothing to do with your road fund licence sir. Down for a bit of fishing are we?

Del No, no, no, no, nothing like that, no.

PC Then why have you got three fishing rods tied to yer roof rack?

Rodney No, no, 'cos you remember we said we might do a little bit of fishing.

Del Yeah, that's right, yeah, yeah, might do – you know – just a little bit – tiddlers.

Grandad No salmon though.

PC I see. You haven't given anyone a lift in the last half-hour or so have you sir?

Del No. Look, what is this all about anyway.

PC We've just had word that a patient's escaped from the local hospital.

Rodney Escaped? What you got out here, national health stalags?

PC It's no ordinary hospital sir. It's an institute for the criminally insane. See, this storm's brought a few power cables down, blacked out the entire area. It even put the institute's security system out of action. So this patient took his chance and made off across the moors. He's out there somewhere now. For all I know he could be watching us.

Del What was he in there for anyway?

PC Ten years ago this very night, he killed a party of weekend fishermen. You may have seen it on the TV? They called him the Axe Murderer.

Del No, no, no, I must have been out that night.

PC You good people be very careful. Don't pick up any hitch-hikers, don't stop for anyone, no matter what the circumstances. And, if you see or hear anything suspicious, phone the police immediately. Your lives may depend on it. Right gentlemen – have a nice weekend won't you.

Del *(Weakly)* Yeah, thank you . . . *(Pulling himself together)* Yeah, well, come on. Full ahead both Rodney.

Grandad We ain't going on are we?

Del Yeah, of course we are.

Rodney Del, there is a crazed axe murderer out there somewhere.

Del I know that Rodders, but you seem to be forgetting that we're on a 300 quid earner. Don't worry, we'll be locked up safe and sound in Boycie's cottage. Anyway there's three of us . . . *(Sees Grandad's frightened expression)* There's me and you . . . *(Sees Rodney's frightened expression)* Don't worry, I'll look after you.

THE COTTAGE/WOODLANDS.

The cottage stands alone. A small dirt track leads through the trees to it. The storm continues as the van makes its way down the track. It pulls up outside the cottage. Del climbs out, opening an umbrella.

Del Right, get this stuff out of here, come on.

Rodney Alright. Grandad.

In the foliage a man's heavy breathing can be heard. He moves the foliage with his hand to get a better view of the Trotters as they enter the cottage.

THE COTTAGE. LIVING ROOM.

The decor and furnishing is basic but comfortable. Del enters and tries to switch a light on. The place remains in darkness and Del remembers the entire area has been blacked out.

Grandad and Rodney enter.

Grandad I wish you'd shut up Rodney, you're making me nervous.

Rodney Look, I didn't say I saw 'someone' did I. Just that I saw 'something'.

Del Yeah, alright don't worry, get them lanterns going will you Rodney.

Rodney Why, what's wrong with the lights?

Del No electric is there.

Rodney Someone's been tampering with it.

Del No, look, the storm has blown the power cables down remember? The whole area's blacked out innit?

Rodney Oh yeah.

Friday the 14th

Del Yeah, I'll just see if I can find some candles in this cupboard over here . . . *(He sees Rodney dialling on the telephone)* What are you doing?

Rodney I'm phoning the law.

Del You're doing what? What are you trying to do to me? Cor, look, we're down here doing a bit of 'fishing', the last thing we need is the local Polizia sniffing round our keep-nets.

Rodney Look, that copper said if we see or hear anything suspicious phone the police immediately – our lives could depend on it.

Del Alright then, who have you seen Hawkeye?

Rodney I saw a – well, a movement in the trees.

Del A movement? Of course you're gonna see movement in the trees – there's a ruddy typhoid blowing out there.

Rodney Yeah, you're right, I'm sorry.

Del It's alright, come on, pull yourself together, alright.

Rodney I'll be alright, sorry.

Del That's it.

Rodney It's a typhoon.

Del Good idea Rodney, put the kettle on, we'll have a nice cup of tea.

Rodney Del, there's only an electric kettle out there.

Grandad Well, use a saucepan then.

Rodney No, there ain't none.

Del Gordon Bennett. Look, come out of my way, look, I'll do it. Here, look – have a look in that cupboard, see if Boycie's left any scotch will you. If he hasn't we'll have to drink mine.

KITCHEN.

Del enters and begins filling the saucepan from a tap.

Del Here you are Rodney. See what I mean, there ain't no ghosts or ghouls out here.

At the kitchen window, there is a flash of lightning and a silhouette of a man standing outside the kitchen window.

LIVING ROOM.

Rodney is kneeling at the open door of the sideboard with a horrified expression.
Grandad is close by looking equally horrified.

Grandad Del Boy, come in here quick. Rodney's found something.

Del *(Enters)* Has he? What? *(Rodney produces a game of Monopoly)* Monopoly. Oh, now we are all doomed.

Grandad Not the Monopoly.

Rodney produces a hand axe.

Del Well, it's only a chopper.

Rodney It's an axe.

Del Same thing.

Rodney No, Del. The police ain't looking for an escaped chopper murderer.

Del Let – just a minute – let me ask you two something. Where are we?

Grandad We're in schtuck.

Del No. We're in the country, aren't we? And country people have these things hanging about. It's part and parcel of their lives.

Rodney Alright, let me ask you something. Where do you think that escaped bloke is right now?

Del Probably out there on them moors.

Rodney In this weather?

Del Well, he's mad ain't he?

Grandad He might be mad, he'd have to be bloody stupid to be out in the moors.

Rodney Exactly. I reckon he'd have holed up somewhere. Found himself an empty place. Like this.

Del Yeah, but this place ain't empty, is it?

Rodney It was before we arrived, Del. *(He looks fearfully up the dark stairs)*

Del What d'you reckon, alright then, he's up there having a kip?

Grandad Well, he could be up there.

Del Well I shouldn't let it worry you Grandad, 'cos the three bears have probably eaten him by now. I mean, what is this fairy story that you're giving me? What's the matter with you two? You been sniffing the bostik or something?

Rodney Alright then, well, why don't you go up the wooden hill to Bedfordshire and check it out?

Del I don't have to. Look, I mean, listen, would any self-respecting axe murderer pop upstairs for 40 winks and leave his chopper in the sideboard?

Rodney He might have a spare one.

Del He's got a kit of 'em now has he? I suppose he's got a little caddie that carries 'em round for him. And another thing. If the man of the moment is upstairs having a lie-in, who was that you saw out there in the trees? His brother?

Rodney Oh yeah, that's right.

Grandad He can't be in two places at once.

Rodney No, of course not. Oh, he's most probably half-way to London by now.

Del Yeah, of course he is. He's most probably looking for an empty place up there.

Grandad Hope he don't find our flat.

Del Will you shut up. Will you just stop all this nonsense. Now look, are we all agreed that we are safe and sound?

Grandad Well, well yeah.

Del Right. Right. Now can you just, like, relax a bit now, you know. Alright? Here you are. Now, I

wonder where the toilet is.

Rodney It's outside, I saw it as we come in.

Del Right. *(Moves to the door, then stops)* I think I'll leave it till the morning.

THE LIVING ROOM

It is later. The Trotters are playing Monopoly. Del is winning. Rodney is moving his symbol around the board.

Del Ah – Park Lane. I think that's one of my properties Rodney.

Rodney Course it is – you own everything on the board.

Del No I don't, no I don't. Look, you've got Coventry Street. Grandad's got the Waterworks and all that. Ah, yeah, Park Lane, with one hotel, £2,000, please.

Rodney Two – hold on. According to this it's only £1,500.

Del Yes, I know, but I've put you in the penthouse suite haven't I?

Rodney I don't want the Penthouse suite do I. *(Hands money to Del)* There you go, £1,500 – that's all you're getting.

Grandad He's like a big kid, ain't he.

Del Yeah, well, I give up on him, Grandad.

Rodney It's your go, Grandfather . . .

Grandad rolls the dice and moves his symbol

Rodney Ah, Piccadilly. Right that's mine and I've got an hotel so that's £1,200.

Grandad £1,200 for a hotel next to a smelly old waterworks.

Rodney What?

Grandad All them sewers. I'd rather sleep in the car or look for a bed and breakfast.

Rodney No – no you don't understand. Bless his little . . . Look, look, it's in the rules.

Grandad £1,200 – it's scandalous. I ain't a tourist you know.

Rodney Del, can you have a word with him?

Del Well, I think he's got a point, Rodney. I mean, I don't know what possessed you to build a hotel next to a sewage farm in the first place. I mean, let's face it, your gaff's never going to get into the *Michelin Guide* is it?

Rodney But the point of the . . . *(Rodney cannot find an answer. In frustration, he flips the Monopoly board up in the air, scattering the pieces everywhere)* Stupid bloody game.

Del Oh that's charming that is innit, eh?

Grandad Just because you're losing.

Rodney Oh shuddup.

Del You wanna learn to grow up a bit my son.

Rodney I didn't wanna play this stupid bloody game in the first place.

Del Yeah, alright. Grandad, I think there's an hotel underneath your chair. If there's any money down there it's mine, alright. There's the car . . . any more money down there?

Rodney is at the window. For no other reason than for something to do, he leans towards the window and pulls the curtains open. On the other side of the glass, only inches from his face, is a man.

There is a slight pause. Rodney appears frozen. He pulls the curtain closed and turns to Del and Grandad who are still scrabbling on the floor for pieces.

Rodney Del.

Del Don't you speak to me Rodney, I'm finished with yer.

Rodney Del, there is a man at the window.

Del You what?

Rodney There is a man at the window.

Grandad He ain't got a bucket and a shammy leather has he?

Rodney I'm being serious, Del. There is somebody at the window.

Rodney's tone of voice forces Del to take him seriously.

Del Alright Roddy – alright. Relax, just take it easy alright. I'll take a look. *(He moves to the window, pulls the curtains open. The man has gone)* There's no one there, Rodney, look. There's no one out there.

Rodney He was there, Del, I swear to you. My face was inches from that glass.

Grandad What did he look like?

Rodney Horrible. He had these evil eyes and this grotesque evil face.

Del Maybe it was a reflection.

Rodney That was no reflection Del, I swear to God . . . What d'yer mean 'a reflection'?

Del No, no, what I mean is that your imagination sometimes plays games with you, you know. It tricks you into believing that you saw something that isn't really there.

Rodney Del, I saw the rain running down his forehead, I saw the blood vessels in the whites of his eyes. I saw the hairs coming out of his nostrils.

Grandad It might have been the shadows in the trees, Rodney.

There is a loud thumping on the front door. The Trotters freeze. Another loud thumping follows. A well-spoken voice is heard.

Chief *(Out of view)* Is anyone there?

Grandad I think there's someone at the door.

Rodney No, no, it's most probably just the

Friday the 14th

shadows.

Del Shadows? Well until they start singing *Summer Holiday* we'll expect the worst. *(Calls)* Who's there?

Chief *(Out of view)* Oh good evening. My name's Robson, I'm chief of security at the institution.

Rodney Oh thank Gawd for that.

Del *(Grabbing Rodney's arm)* What the hell do you think you're doing?

Rodney He's chief of security at the hospital.

Del Says who?

Rodney Well he, just this minute . . . oh yeah.

Del He could be anybody couldn't he? You get ready.

Del opens the door. Momentarily, the chief can be seen. He is in his early forties, wears a uniform and cap and also a waterproof cape. He smiles and is about to enter when Del slams the door on him.

Well?

Rodney Well what?

Del Is that him?

Rodney Who?

Del The face at the window.

Rodney I don't know, I didn't look.

Del You wally.

Rodney You never said what you was gonna do.

Chief *(Out of view)* Is everything alright?

Del Yeah, I won't keep you a minute Chief. *(To Rodney)* Now do it – do it again and this time take a good look.

Rodney Alright.

Del Alright ready.

Del swing door open.

Chief Good evening.

He is about to step in when Del slams the door again.

Del Well?

Rodney No, it's not him.

Del You sure?

Rodney Yeah, I'm positive. That is definitely not him.

Del Alright. *(Opening the door)* Do come in, Chief.

The Chief enters and removes his cape.

Chief Thank you. Appalling weather.

Del Yes, sorry about leaving you standing out there but you can't be too sure can you – you know. We thought you might be a double-glazing salesman.

Chief What? Oh yes. *(Taking a wallet from his pocket)* Well, if you'd like to see some identification there's everything there from my

driving licence to my blood donor's card.

Del Oh no, no, that's alright, alright. Rodney, fix the Chief a drink will you? So, you haven't caught him yet then?

Chief Unfortunately no. We've extended the search up to this area now. We've the entire police forces of three counties out looking for him. I was passing, saw a light. What exactly are you gentlemen doing here?

Grandad Oh, we're on a fishing trip.

Chief I don't suppose you've seen anything?

Grandad Well other than the face at the window, nothing.

Chief Face at the window?

Del Yeah, well, Rodney here reckoned he saw a face at the window. I don't know whether to believe him or not.

Rodney Oh I saw him Del, I was only sort of like three inches away from him.

Chief Could you describe him for me?

Rodney Yeah of course I could. He was about 50. He had this gaunt, hungry expression and his eyes were like wild animal's.

Del And hairs out of his nostrils.

Rodney Yeah, and there was all that.

Chief You're quite certain it wasn't a reflection?

Rodney Look, it was not a reflection.

Chief I'm sorry, but at times like these people's imagination run amok. Why, we've had 200 sightings this evening alone. What was the colour of his hair? *(Rodney has not quite understood the question. He puts his hand to his nostrils)* On his head.

Rodney Oh, er, grey.

Chief Sounds like my man. When exactly did this happen?

Del Well just now. A minute or so before you arrived.

Chief So he must have seen me. *(Looks from the window)*

Del D'you reckon he's still out there then?

Chief Oh no, he'd be long gone by now. It's the uniform you see – he's terrified of people in authority. Well, after ten years in an institution who wouldn't be?

Del Yeah, well, I feel sorry for the poor little cock. Chief, do you mind if I ask you something?

Chief What's that?

Del Well is it safe for me to go to the khazi? I mean it's outside.

Chief Oh you're perfectly safe. He'll be a long way away by now.

Del goes to the door, opens it and surveys outside.

Del Oh good. Right, that's alright then.

Rodney Well go on then Del, there's nothing to be frightened of now.

Del I know, you don't have to go out there, do you?

Rodney You heard what the Chief said. Go on, there's no need to worry.

Del Yeah, well, alright. *(Exits)*

Rodney closes the door, turns the key and then slides the slip bolts across at the top and bottom of the door.

Rodney He's such a worrier.

Chief You weren't frightened at all?

Rodney Me? Na. No 'cos you see, in the past I have done work for the mentally disturbed.

Grandad He went out selling flags one Saturday.

Rodney Well yeah, but, er, I can actually sympathise with this guy's problems.

Grandad Sympathise? But he's a psycho.

Chief Have you any idea what a 'psycho', as you so eloquently put it, is?

Grandad Course I have. He's a geezer what dresses up in his mother's clothes.

THE COTTAGE.

'The Man' appears. He moves towards the cottage. As he reaches the door of the outside toilet it flies open, masking the man. Del exits from the lavvy. He closes the door to reveal the man lying spread-eagled on the ground.

Del Bloody hell's bells. Rodney, Grandad, come out here quick, bring some rope.

A RURAL POLICE STATION.

The rain has ceased. Grandad stands guard at the back of the van. Rodney, followed by a police sergeant and a couple of constables, exits from the station.

Rodney Yeah, so then, right, I grabbed the axe out of his hand and I cracked him good and hard on the jaw, so obviously he went down right. Then I tied him up good and tight and we bundled him into the back of the van.

Sarge Good work lad. You say you captured him single handed?

Rodney Yeah. Well, no, Del, my brother, back at the cottage he helped a bit.

Grandad You're too modest, Rodney.

Sarge Well, there could be a medal in this.

Rodney *(Shrugging modestly)* Well.

Sarge Right, get ready lads, this one could be a handful. *(They pull the man up, then turn to Rodney)* Is this some kind of joke?

Rodney What d'you mean?

Sarge This is no escaped lunatic. This is Tom Witton, the gamekeeper. And you shouldn't have gagged him like that, he suffers with asthma. *(He removes the gag and we hear the gamekeeper's heavy breathing)*

Rodney Now hold on a minute – the Chief of Security from the Institution itself said it was him.

Sarge What Chief of Security?

Grandad What's his name? Robson. I mean, you can ask him yourself, he's back at the cottage with Del.

Sarge Chief Robson is not at the cottage – he's at the hospital. The escaped man hit him on the head then stole his uniform and his identity papers.

THE COTTAGE LIVING ROOM.

Del Well, I still reckon we should have gone with 'em.

Chief No. It was imperative that I made out my report immediately. And after all I needed you here with me, you were the one who recaptured him.

Del Well, yeah, I suppose, yeah. Hey, what do you say we have a nice little drink to celebrate, eh? *(He moves towards a bottle of scotch. The Chief has a manic glaze in his eyes.)*

Del pours drinks. He looks from the window. The old weather's clearing up nicely. Look at that, it's a full moon.

The Chief reacts. He moves towards Del who has his back to the Chief. He reaches his hand as if to take Del by the back of the neck. Del turns and places the glass in his outstretched hand.

There you go, Chief . . .

The phone rings and Del answers it.

Excuse me. Yes, hello. Hello . . . Rodders, did you get there all . . . Yeah. Em. He's what?? *(Turns and gives the Chief a forced smile)* Alright? No, you alright? The Chief's just standing there, you know, examining his axe . . . Yeah, alright then. You'll hurry back won't you. Alright goodbye. *(Replaces receiver)* Just phoned up tell us he got there alright.

Chief Good. Do you like fish?

Del What?

Chief Do you like fish?

Del Oh yeah, yeah, little bit of salt an' vinegar, they're lovely.

Chief I only like living fish. Fish that swim in the rivers and the seas. I don't like people that kill them.

Del No, no, no, don't like that sort myself either.

Chief But I saw fishing rods on your van.

Del No, no, no, they didn't belong to me, they

Friday the 14th

belong to my brother and Grandad. I mean, I keep telling them. I beg 'em not to hurt the poor little fishies. I mean, I only come down here for the fresh air.

Chief Do you like snooker?

Del Snooker?

Chief Yes.

Del Do you?

Chief Oh yes.

Del So do I. It's triffic innit?

Chief Shall we play a game?

Del Of snooker?

Chief Yes.

Del Yeah, yeah, alright. I'll tell you what. I'll just pop out to the shed at the bottom of the garden 'cos I think I remember seeing a snooker table in there.

Chief *(Indicating the middle of the room)* No need, we'll use this one here.

Del What you mean this one here, you mean?

Chief Yes.

Del Yeah, yeah okay. *(There is the sound of a helicopter passing over. Del looks from the window, closing his eyes with relief)*

Chief Is that a police helicopter?

Del No, you're alright. It's Barratts.

Chief Good. You can break.

Del *(He prepares himself for the biggest gamble of the evening. He reaches out tentatively for the axe.)* Um, I tell you what, why don't I put that somewhere safe? Because you won't be able to hold yer cue properly with that in your hand, will you?

For a moment the Chief is wary and defensive.

Chief No, I suppose you're right.

Del *(Slowly taking the axe)* Yeah, course I am. You know it makes sense. *(Looks up to God in silent gratitude)*

The Chief thrusts both hands out in front of him, fists clenched.

Chief Which cue would you like?

Del I'll have this one.

He is handed the right hand 'cue.'

Chief *(Indicating his left hand 'cue')* Good, this is my favourite.

Del Yeah, you can see it's a good 'un, can't you.

Chief I'm not very good at snooker. I always lose.

Del I've got a feeling you're gonna win this one.

Chief I hope not. I don't like winning. My father used to force me to win at everything I did. But people challenge winners. You become vulnerable, you feel open to attack. Do you know the feeling?

Del *(Emphatically)* Yeah, yeah, I know exactly what you mean.

Chief But losers are anonymous. No one wants to challenge a loser. There's something comforting in defeat. I really like losing.

Del *(A scheme is being born)* Do you? Well, what do you say we make this game a little more interesting? Shall we play for a tenner a frame? *(Produces a wallet)*

Chief Alright.

Del *(Quietly)* Got a feeling that this weekend is not going to be a total loss after all.

Chief Sorry?

Del Nothing. *(Surveys the room)* Got the chalk? Thanks.

157

The Peckham Business Directory

Company Name - Trotters Independent
Trading Company (TITCO)

Address - 127 Nelson Mandela House,
Nyere Estate, Peckham, London SE15

Chairman and Managing Director -
Derek Trotter

Financial Adviser - Rodney Trotter

Company Motto - He who dares, wins.

Company Description

Well, John, we do a bit everything. Our main earner is importing-
exporting quality merchandise - New York, Paris, Peckham, you name it
and we'll get it, my son. Parisian haute couture, sunbeds, watches,
massage equipment, lowvery doors, Georgian digital clocks to list just
a few. We can get our hands on almost anything, no questions asked and
we'll quote you a decent price. Payment in kosher readies only,
please. My younger brother and I can be find down the market most days
outing any number of items, so if you've got some cash on the hip and
want new toys for the kiddies or a watch for the enemy pay us a visit.
Fabrique Belgique?

But knocking out bargains from a suitcase is just one little petit
pois of our business. The Trotter family empire can turn its hand to
many jobs, as long as there's a bit of bunce in it. Unison opportu-
naire as they say in Rome. Take chandeliers for an example. Asking a
Trotter if he knows anything about them is like asking Mr Kipling if
he knows anything about cakes. It's a family business passed down over
the years, our history goes right back to the plague, but there's not
much call for it these days. But we do specialise in renovation work
so if your Louise the 15th is a need of a brush up, then you know who
to call in to do a pukka job.

The painting and decorating game is another thing we Trotters have
been doing for generations. My Grandad was a painter for the council
back in 1924 and my bruv, Rodders, has a GCE in art. No job is too big
or small, but we do like to know if clients have any pets, canaries
that sort of thing, before we move in. Speaking of pets, we also turn
our hands to a little bit of dog-minding should you be going away to
Torrermolinos for a couple of weeks and don't want to stick the mutt
in a kennel. I won Crufts two years on the trot - you may have seen me
on that Chum advert. There's nothing I don't know about dogs. Pas de
bas, I've been out with a few.

That's not all. As a religious man, though I've never been to
Lourdes — cricket ain't my game — I know what it's like to stand in
wonder before the glory of the coming of the Lord, and all that pony.
So any of you out there with religious miracles to market will be
relieved to hear that I have previous experience in that game. The
media, y'know, BBC, ITV, Reuters, The Peckham Echo, but not Channel
bloody Four, go bandy for that sort of thing. I know a lot of churches
these days are potless and it's a good way of putting a score or two
in the old collection box.

Well, there you have it. Whatever your needs, TITCO is on hand to
get you of schtuck. Whenever you need us just give us a bell and my
brother will be round to see what you want. I hope this is not goodbye, just eau de toilette.

THE LIFT FOYER OF THE TROTTERS' TOWER BLOCK.

There are two lift doors. Hanging over the call button of one of the lifts is an 'Out of Order' sign. The Trotters enter the foyer from outside. Rodney and Grandad are carrying an antique (or at least antique-looking) cabinet. Del is directing them.

Del Right, come on, come on. Let's have it on. Get it on. Get it in here.

Grandad Alright Del, alright.

Del That's it. Right, come on, careful – careful with it. Come on, we ain't got all day. Alright.

Grandad It's heavy.

Del Come on then. Mind your hernia Grandad. Put your end down there Grandad, that's right. *(Grandad lowers his end gently to the floor)* Now your end Rodney. *(Rodney let's his end drop with a thump)* Gordon Bennett Rodney, what is your game? This could be a de-luxe Chippendale and you're treating it like something we've dragged out for the bonfire.

Rodney That's about the best place for it.

Del You don't know, this could be a Queen Anne cabinet.

Rodney Oh, give over Del.

Grandad Don't look very old to me.

Del Ah – no – that is because when you was a lad this was probably 'G' plan. But to anyone born after the Napoleonic Wars this is antique. Anyway I'm going to put an ad in the paper in the morning. Don't know what to charge for it though. What d'you reckon, what, 95?

Grandad Why don't you go the whole hog and make it a pound?

Del You're starting to annoy me.

Rodney *(Examining the cabinet)* Hey, it's got woodworm.

Del That has not got woodworm.

Grandad What's all them little holes then?

Del Well I don't know. Maybe Queen Anne played darts. *(Banging the lift doors)* Where's these lifts? I tell you what, I tell you what, I'm considering letting the British Museum take a look at it.

Rodney Yeah? I'd let Rentokil have a go first.

Del You don't know nothing about antiques you, do you? I mean, you know, dealers they often put holes in items like these to give it that sort of 'distressed' look.

Rodney Distressed. Del, this thing looks panic-stricken.

Del *(Bangs on lift again)* Where are these rotten lifts? If those kids have jammed them again I'm gonna clump their ear'oles.

As Rodney examines cabinet one of the doors comes off in his hand. Del and Grandad, more interested in the lifts don't notice. Rodney remains holding the door for a few terrified seconds. He taps Grandad's arm and hands the door to him. Grandad, innocently, takes it. Then realises, and tries to hand it back to Rodney, who resists. Del turns, Rodney and Grandad freeze with the door between them.

Del I don't believe it. I don't believe it.

Rodney Oh no, come on, Del, it was a complete accident, look, it just come off in his hand.

Grandad What? You lying little git, you ripped it off.

Rodney Now come along Grandad, tell the truth for once.

Del I just don't believe this. This thing has survived the Spanish Armada, the Black Death and the Blitz. And then you two cack-handed sods come along and in five minutes you've destroyed a piece of our national heritage. I don't know.

The doors to the 'Out of Order' lift open and a West Indian woman exits.

Woman Morning Mr Trotter.

The Trotters Morning Mrs Murphy. *(Exits)*

Del Look you could – that was the lift weren't it? Now what am I gonna do about that thing, eh? I mean, you can't bodge about with this sort of quality. I mean, it's gonna take the skills of a fully-trained furniture restorer.

Grandad Oh they ain't 'alf dear, Del Boy.

Del Are they? *(Takes a pound from his pocket)* Here Rodney. Whip down to the DIY shop and get a bag of nails, will you?

THE TROTTERS' LOUNGE.

Grandad is watching the TVs. Del is checking through the suitcase, cross-checking with his notebook. Rodney is seated at the table reading the classified ads. The cabinet is also in the room.

Rodney Here y'are. *(Reading)* 'Queen Anne cabinet. Genuine antique, good as new. Lovely condition throughout, a snip at £145.' You could

make the Elgin Marbles sound like a second-hand Datsun, couldn't you?

Del Oi, how much of this stuff did you sell today?

Rodney What d'you mean in pounds sterling or in number of items?

Del Either.

Rodney None.

Del None?

Rodney People ain't interested Del.

Del Gordon Bennett Rodney. I pick a prime site in the Arndale Centre and you can't even get shot of a pair of pop-socks. You wanna grow up a bit, my son. I suppose you spent all day playing marbles with that mate Elgin of yours.

Rodney What?

Grandad What you doing tomorrow Rodney? You and Mickey Pearce playing five-stones?

Doorbell rings.

Del You want to pull your socks up you do, you know.

Rodney Del, these things look like living bras that ain't been well.

Doorbell rings.

Del Alright, alright, hang about – don't wear the battery out.

HALL.

Del enters from the lounge. He opens the door to Miranda. Miranda is in her early thirties, attractive and well spoken. She is expensively dressed and very 'Chelsea.' She has a very business-like manner and doesn't like to waste time.

Miranda Good evening. Miranda Davenport.

Del Eh?

Miranda Miranda Davenport.

Del Ah yes, I think I know what this is all about. Now if it was your Mercedes I backed into the other day, I can assure you . . .

Miranda No, no, no, you obviously haven't the faintest idea why I'm here. I telephoned earlier about your newspaper ad for the Queen Anne cabinet.

Del Oh gotcha.

Miranda Well, I left a message with an elderly gentleman, he did sound somewhat vague.

Del Oh yes, yes, well he is rather vague. He had a bang on the head you see.

Miranda Ah yes. When did it happen?

Del Soon. Do come in Miss Davenport, or may I call you Miranda?

Miranda Well yes, I suppose so.

Del D'you know, Miranda is my most favourite name?

Miranda Really?

Del Yeah. My name is Del, that's short for Derek. How d'you do? Please go in to the sitting room will you. There you go.

They enter the lounge. Rodney is examining a pair of flimsy briefs as Miranda enters. He does a double-take and hides the briefs.

Rodney Oi, Grandad.

Del Grandad, did somebody call earlier about the cabinet?

Grandad Oh yes. She's coming round this evening. Some posh tart.

Del Some posh tart. He's a card ain't he?

Miranda Yes, isn't he just.

Del Rodney come on, clear this . . . put your homework away would you Rodney? Come on, right. There. *(Indicating cabinet)* Well, what do you think?

Miranda Very nice. Where is the Queen Anne cabinet?

Del This – this is it.

Miranda This is the Queen Anne cabinet?

Del Oh yes, it's definitely a Queen Anne, it's been given the once-over by experts. Do you know anything about antiques Miranda?

Miranda *(Examining cabinet)* Yes. I run my own antique shop in Chelsea.

Del Well, it might not be Queen Anne.

Miranda It isn't. It's Queen Elizabethan, circa 1957 *(Pointing inside cabinet)*. If you look inside you'll see, beneath the dust and cobwebs, some faded lettering.

Del Oh yeah . . . F . . . Y . . .

Rodney F . . . F . . .

Del Thank you, yes, Rodney . . . E . . . S.

Rodney F . . . Y . . . F . . . F . . . Fiffes. Fyffes.

Del Didn't they used to make bananas?

Miranda That is correct.

Rodney So – so what does that indicate then?

Miranda It indicates banana boxes of course.

Grandad Maybe they were antique banana boxes.

Del Alright, alright, thank you very much, Grandad. Why don't you go to your bedroom and watch the *Chinese Detective* on the portable? Go on.

Grandad Oh. Alright, I know where I'm not wanted.

Del Well, go on then. *(Grandad exits)* He never – never quite got over Suez. Well, are you interested in it Miranda?

Miranda No, I'm afraid not Mr Trotter.

Rodney Well, what do you think we should do with it then?

Miranda I'm not sure. Is there a tip near here?

Yesterday Never Comes

Del No there must be a wally somewhere who'd want to buy it.

Rodney Yeah, let's face it Del, you bought it last week didn't you?

Miranda is studying a small, gilt framed painting hanging on the wall.

Miranda I say, that's rather pretty isn't it?

Rodney That? You must be joking, it gives me itchy fever every time I look at it.

Miranda I think it's rather sweet. Is it for sale?

Del No – definitely not. No, you see that is a family heirloom. It belonged to my late-departed Grandmother. We couldn't possibly sell it, could we Rodney?

Rodney No, no, no way, no. It's valuable then?

Miranda Oh no, no, it's worthless. I just rather like it that's all. You see, I'm re-decorating my London flat and I'm just on the look-out for little pieces like that. Still, never mind . . .

Miranda's attention returns to the cabinet.

She also becomes more friendly towards Del. Um, do you know, I'm really rather in two minds about this cabinet now.

Del What – you think this might have some potential do you, Miranda?

Miranda Well I'm not really sure. But you see, what's persuading me is that you're obviously a man with an eye for this sort of thing.

Del *(Modestly)* Oh yes, petit Suisse.

Miranda Quite. Whereas I'm just a woman trying to make her way in the big wide world.

Del Oh yes, it's dog eat dog in the antique game Miranda.

Miranda I know. Derek – you'll most probably say no – but I was wondering whether you and I could go into this together?

Del How d'you mean Miranda?

Miranda Well, I was thinking. We could take this to the workroom at the back of my shop. I have a very good man working there who could possibly restore this to its former glory. Re-polish the top, varnish out the lettering, some new brass handles, and then we could put it in the shop and share the profit. What d'you think?

Del I think that sounds just the ticket Miranda. Mind you, I'd have to have a word with my partner. *(Looks to Rodney)*

Rodney Oh me.

Del Yes, you. Will you excuse us while we confer? Rodney, would you join me, I'd like to have a word with you in the office?

Rodney What to, er . . .

Del Confer, yes. Excuse us. There you go. Thank you, we'll be back in a couple of shakes, alright.

They both go into the kitchen. Del closes the door behind them.

Rodney Well, if you want my opinion Del, I don't think we should let that cabinet out of our sight.

Del That cabinet is definitely going to her shop to be tarted up and sold for a ridiculously high profit. End of discussion.

Rodney Good, good, well, there's nothing like talking things out is there. If you wasn't interested in my opinion, what d'you drag me in here for?

Del 'Cos I want your advice, Rodney, I think she fancies me.

Rodney Miranda?

Del Yeah.

Rodney Leave it out Del, she's an intelligent woman.

Del *(Grabs Rodney by the throat)* I know she's an intelligent woman. That is most probably why she fancies me.

Rodney *(Fearing violence)* True, true, yeah, well, I did notice the way she looked at you.

Del Yeah? How?

Rodney What?

Del How, you know, how did she look at me?

Rodney Well – sort of – *(contorts his face)* like that.

Del Like that? Looks like she had a hot chip in her mouth.

Rodney Del, I can't do a face like hers, can I?

Del No, no I suppose not, no. How am I going to tell her that – you know – the 'feeling' is mutual?

Rodney Just tell her.

Del But how?

Rodney I don't know, do I?

Del You do, you're the one with the GCEs.

Rodney Just be yourself.

Del Leave it out, Rodney, I wanna be in with at least half a chance.

Rodney Del, for once in your life, be you. Right. And you won't need none of them soppy French phrases either.

Del What d'you mean, soppy French phrases? La bonne vie, you stupid . . .

Rodney See what I mean? Del, you can't speak French. You're still struggling with English.

Del What is it with you Rodney? Do you like hospital food or something?

Rodney I'm just being honest with you. Let's face it Del, most of your French phrases come straight out of a Citroen manual, don't they?

Del A lot of people are impressed with things like that.

Rodney Yeah, maybe the cave-people down at the Nag's Head. But it's not going to cut any ice

with Arthur Negus's youngest in there, is it?

Del I suppose you're right.

Rodney Del, if you're really that interested, why don't you just give her a sign of your – mutual attraction.

Del Yeah, a sign, eh.

Rodney Yeah. And be yourself.

Del Yeah, yeah, yeah, okay – yeah. That's it. *(Prepares himself, flexes his shoulders)* He who dares, wins. Right.

LOUNGE.

Miranda is studying the painting. She moves away as Del and Rodney enter from the kitchen.

Del Well, that is it Miranda. I have discussed the matter with my partner and we both agree that we shall exceed to you delusions.

Miranda What?

Del You take that thing with you and get it tarted up.

Miranda Oh good. Well, I'll telephone you in the morning and arrange for it to be collected.

Del Yes, thank you.

Del looks desperately to Rodney, who gestures for him to do or say something. Del takes a pace forward, brings his hand back and smacks Miranda's bottom. Rodney closes his eye in shocked disbelief. Miranda turns with a surprised and offended look.

Del *(With a confident grin)* Fancy a curry?

Miranda *(Smiling and shrugging)* Why not? *Miranda picks up her handbag and exits. Del gives Rodney the thumbs up and follows her. Rodney stands open-mouthed in disbelief that Del's approach actually worked.*

PEDESTRIAN ZONE/HIGH STREET.

A continental-style pavement café. Del is seated at one of the tables. Rodney returns with a cup of coffee for Del and a coke, in a paper cup, for himself.

Del My old guts are playing me up this morning Rodders.

Rodney Yeah, I know.

Del I've got a touch of the old Gandhi's revenge bruv.

Rodney What, from the Ruby last night?

Del Yeah.

Rodney Did Miranda enjoy it?

Del Well, she had a bit of aggro with the chicken tikka, mind you it was a bit rubbery. She was chewing on one bit for about 'alf an hour – I thought she'd end up blowing bubbles with it any minute. She's quite a sort, ain't she Rodders?

Rodney Yeah, she's alright.

Del What d'you mean, alright? Alright? You wouldn't say no would yer, eh? No she's quite taken with me an' all you know. *(Rodney gives a little laugh)* No, she is, she's very impressed. Well, she knows I know a lot about antiques don't she, eh?

Rodney Oh yeah, yeah, well, you've been out with enough ain't yer.

Del Oi, that is enough of that. Anyway listen, I went up her shop this morning up Chelsea. Real pukka establishment Rodney, I mean, you know, real pukka. Sort of place royals go. No, I think something really good's gonna come out of this, bruv.

Rodney Do us a favour, Del. Look, don't get too carried away with this Miranda sort, eh? I mean, her type don't give a monkey's for the likes of you.

Del What do you mean by that?

Rodney It means I've seen it all before. You meet someone you take a fancy to and within a week it's all wine and roses and 'I'm just popping down to Bravingtons Rodney.'

Del What do you think I am some sort of whelk or something? Still wet behind the ears? I know exactly what I'm doing. *(Taps his nose)*

Rodney *(Believing Del's had a scheme all along)* Aah. Nice one Derek, nice one my son.

Del I must admit there is a certain – chemistry between me and Miranda. I'm just gonna pop next door and get a *Daltons Weekly*, alright.

Rodney shakes his head sadly. He finsishes his coke. Seated at another table is an attractive young woman. Her and Rodney's eyes meet accidentally and Rodney smiles at her. Slightly embarrassed, she returns a polite yet inviting smile. Rodney crushes the paper cup with one hand in the same swaggering manner that macho men crush beer cans. He throws the cup to the floor and stands. The girl stands and begins to organise her handbag. Rodney approaches and finally plucks up the courage and smacks her bum. The girl turns to him with a look of complete surprise.

Rodney Fancy an Indian?

The girl gives Rodney a smack round the face and storms off, leaving Rodney to face the other diners who have witnessed this. *(To himself, but referring to the girl)* Fascist! *Del arrives back.*

Del Right, you fit then Rodders, eh? *Rodney turns to face him. A large red weal is on his face.*

Rodney Yeah, yeah fit.

Yesterday Never Comes

Del Here, you ain't 'arf got a nasty rash coming up on your boat race.

Rodney Oh yeah, yeah that's, um, that's just where I caught the sun, you know.

Del Well, if I didn't know any better I'd swear that someone had smacked you right in the eye.

Rodney Alright don't go on about it.

Del What d'you mean? You're a touchy little git sometimes ain't yer?

THE TROTTERS' LOUNGE.

The room is in darkness. The front door is heard opening. Del enters the lounge and switches the lights on. He is wearing an evening suit, velvet bow tie, frilly shirt, gold cuff-links, etc. We can almost smell the Blue Stratos. Miranda follows him in, wearing a low-cut, full-length evening gown. They appear as if they have just returned from an evening at The Savoy.

Del Here we are. That's it. Do come in. There we are. I'll get the door. Oh, allow me. Thank you, there you are Miranda. Sit yourself down on the chaise longue and I'll fix us a drink. Now what can I get you, port and lemon, rum and coke? Or shall I surprise you?

Miranda Why don't you surprise me.

Del Right you are. There we go. That was a blinding meal weren't it Miranda, eh?

Miranda Yes, it was very nice. I did feel a bit over-dressed for a Berni Inn though.

Del I don't think so. I think we made quite an impression – I mean everybody was looking at us.

Miranda Yes.

Del *(Returns to sofa with two 'red' drinks)* Take a sip of that Miranda.

Miranda What is it?

Del That is called a Tequila Sunset. Cheers.

Miranda It tastes of gin.

Del Yeah, I run out of Tequila.

Miranda Well, it's very nice.

Del Yeah, it is innit? I actually got the recipe off a Mexican barman.

Miranda Have you been to Mexico?

Del No, no, he lives in the flat upstairs. Miranda. I, well, I've been, thinking about us. And I've . . . *(Miranda reacts to something she has found down the side of the sofa. She produces a Penthouse magazine. Del takes it from her.)* Oh yes, sorry about that, it belongs to Rodney. He's into still-life. He's got his GCE in Art you know.

Miranda Really?

Del Oh yeah. He'll most probably be famous when he's dead. As I was saying – I've been thinking about you and me.

Miranda Do you like art?

Del Oh yeah, it's triffic, I can't get enough of it. You see the thing is that I was thinking . . .

Miranda *(Referring to drink)* This is very strong.

Del Yeah.

Miranda Do you like Cézanne?

Del Oh yes, a bit of ice and lemonade, it's lovely. You see, you and I have got, well, you know. We've got a lot in common, haven't we? I mean we're both – well – English.

Miranda I do love that painting.

Del Yeah, it's triffic innit.

Miranda Your grandmother must have had very good taste.

Del No, she couldn't have had much, she married my grandfather.

Miranda Do you like that painting Derek?

Del What that? No, I hate it, can't wait to get rid of it.

Miranda Oh don't ever throw it away, please. It would look so nice in my flat. I'd hang it just above my bed. Just try to picture it. Oh you can't – I've just remembered, you haven't seen my bedroom . . . yet.

Del No, I haven't seen your bedroom . . . yet.

Miranda You were saying?

Del What?

Miranda You were talking about . . . . us.

Del Oh yeah. Yeah – yeah. Well, I was gonna say that I was thinking about – well – you know maybe later – you know – not now – if you like in the future sometime, when you, sort of felt like it, we could, sort of, work closer together.

Miranda I've been thinking exactly the same thing.

Del Have you?

Miranda Ever since I first met you.

For the first time ever, Del appears to be lost for words.

Del Oh Miranda, drink up, I'll get you another Tequila Sunset.

Miranda No really, I've had quite enough.

Del Yeah, alright, shall I put my Richard Clayderman LP on?

Miranda No, I must be going. I have to be up early in the morning, Mummy and Daddy will probably ring first thing to wish me happy returns. You know what parents are like.

Del No, I haven't had any for ages. Sorry, did you say it's your birthday?

Miranda Yes. Surely I told you?

Del I s'pose you must . . .

Miranda Oh, you haven't bought me a present?

Del What?

Miranda Oh you really shouldn't have. It's very

sweet of you though, thank you. *(Kisses him on the lips)* I really must be off. *(Exits)*

Del *(While mulling the situation over his eyes fall on the painting. He looks up to Heaven)* Sorry Gran.

THE TROTTERS' LOUNGE.

Rodney is laid out on the settee feeling hungover. Grandad is clearing the breakfast things from the table. Del, dressed to kill and carrying a bunch of daffodils and a birthday card, enters from the hall.

Del Good morning Rodders, good morning Grandfather. It's a beautiful day out innit, eh? Makes you glad to be alive, don't it?

Rodney Yeah, triffic.

Grandad Where you off to then Del?

Del I'm just going out to Miranda's shop. Just to see the cabinet.

Rodney What time's visiting hours then?

Del There's nothing wrong with that cabinet, Rodney. I keep on telling you, it's a very nice cabinet.

Rodney Yeah, it is. I mean a million woodworms can't be wrong can they?

Del I've told you before Rodney, there are no woodworms in that cabinet.

Grandad *(Looking at the birthday card)* Whose birthday is it then Del?

Del Mine if I play me cards right.

Grandad *(Reading)* 'Happy birthday sweetheart, from your ever loving Delly-Welly.'

Grandad and Rodney laugh.

Rodney Delly-Wally more like.

Del Alright. Alright, put that down and let's not have so much of it, shall we.

Grandad *(Sarcastically)* It's Miranda's birthday Rodney and we forgot.

Rodney Oh no, what a choker, still never mind.

Grandad What d'you get her for her birthday Del?

Del Eh? *(Looks to where Gran's painting was, which is now an empty space)* Oh, nothing much.

Grandad *(Catching Del's glance, turns and reacts)* What's happened to your Gran's painting?

Del Eh? Well, I told you the sun would affect it didn't I?

Grandad Sun, my arse, you've given it to that tart ain't yer?

Del Well, she's not gonna raffle it, is she? She'll only hang it on her bedroom wall.

Grandad Your Gran brought that painting into this house Del. There was an history behind it,

and you knew it.

Rodney You stole your own Grandmother's painting?

Del I didn't steal the painting. Gran left that painting to me.

Grandad Don't give me that old Mother Hubbard.

Del She did. One night, when she wasn't feeling too well, she said to me, she said, 'Del, when I go that painting is yours.'

Grandad I don't remember it.

Del No, you were out.

Grandad That's handy innit, no witnesses.

Del There were witnesses. There was Mum and Rodney.

Grandad Mum ain't here any more.

Del I know that but Rodney is. You remember don't you Rodney.

Rodney I can't say I do Del.

Del But you must remember. You were there, over there in the corner. With Mum . . . having yer nappy changed.

Grandad Having his nappy cha . . . He could have only been about four.

Rodney Exactly, how the hell do you expect . . . Four???

Grandad I never thought I'd live to see the day when you, you of all people, let the family down. I'm going to my room.

Del Here, Grandad. Come on. *(Produces a wad of notes)* Here you are, look, have a tenner, come on.

Grandad gives him a look of contempt. He exits.

Rodney She's got you tied up like a turkey ain't she? You've changed since you met her Del.

Del You've got more hooter than Pinocchio. Just stay out of my life, will you.

Rodney Yeah, I'll stay out of your life. In fact, I think I can quite safely say that me and Grandad won't ever get under your feet again. *(Looking at flowers)* I just hope Miranda suffers with hay-fever.

Del Rodney.

Rodney What?

Del Don't be a plonker. *(Exits)*

Grandad enters.

Grandad Did he leave that tenner?

ANTIQUE SHOP/LONDON STREET.

A street in the quiche lorraine and Burberry sector of Chelsea. The shop is very upmarket. The three-wheeled van pops to a halt outside the shop. Del alights and moves to the shop. The door has a 'Closed' sign on it. Del tries to

Yesterday Never Comes

open the door but finds it is locked. He
knocks on the door. Harry, a furniture
restorer, enters from the back of the shop and
approaches the front door. He unlocks it.

Del Hello Harry. Is Miranda about?

Harry No, she's popped down to Huddleston's.
Just down the road there, on yer left Del.

Del Right, I'll pop down and see her. Here, how
comes you ain't open?

Harry Had to close mate, we're being
fumigated, the place is full of woodworm.

Del You wanna watch that H. Especially with
your wooden leg.

HUDDLESTON'S AUCTION ROOMS.

*This is a very upmarket, Sotherby's-type
establishment. Miranda is sat bidding for an
item.*

Auctioneer £2,200, £2,500, £2,700 . . . (To
Miranda) £3,000. (Gestures in the opposite
direction to a representative of a gallery) The bid
is with Gideon's Gallery . . . (Miranda gives the
merest of nods) £3,200. (Rep raises his
programme. To Miranda) £3,400. £3,500, the
bid is with Gideon's.

*Del enters and surveys the room. This is the
kind of place he has dreamed about. He spots
Miranda and waves with the flowers.*

Auctioneer (Spotting Del) £3,600, with the
gentleman at the back . . . (Miranda, unaware of
Del, nods back) £3,800, with Miss Davenport.
(Checking the rest of the room) £3,800? (Bangs
gavel) To Miss Davenport.

*As the bidding has now finished there is a
hum of conversation from the other people in
the room. Del joins Miranda. She is
embarrassed by Del's proximity.*

Miranda Derek.

Del Yeah.

Miranda What are you doing here?

Del I thought I'd just pop up and take you out to
lunch, you know, sort of birthday treat.

Miranda Birthday? Oh yes. How sweet.

Del These are for you. They're daffodils.

Miranda (Not wishing to handle anything as
common as daffs) So they are.

Del They used to be my Mum's favourite.

Miranda Oh really? Well, thank you. Look, I'm
rather busy at the moment. Why don't you wait
for me at that little wine bar round the corner?

Del Yeah, alright. Will you be long?

Miranda (Sharply) How should I know? (Hands
him the flowers) Look, take these with you as
well please.

Del (Hurt) Yes – yeah, right.

*Del goes to leave. As he does he glances
towards the rostrum and does a double take.
There on the rostrum is Gran's painting being
exhibited as the next item.*

Auctioneer Now, Lot 24 is this recently
discovered work by the late 19th-century artist
Joshua Blythe. Now it's a particularly fine
example of his work and I'd like to start the
bidding at £7,000. Do I have £7,000? (Someone
bids) £7,000.

*Del sits next to Miranda who feels
embarrassed that the truth has come out.*

Del You lied to me, didn't you?

Miranda Nobody's perfect.

Del It's not your birthday at all, is it?

Miranda It will be soon.

Del All you wanted me for was that painting
weren't it?

Miranda Well, what else did you think I was
interested in? That banana box of a Queen Anne
cabinet? The damn thing's infested my entire
stock.

Del No, I thought, you know, maybe there was
something else.

Miranda Oh, you. Did you honestly think I
enjoyed being in the company of a man who
slapped my bottom, called me sweetheart and
assaulted my digestive system with third-rate
curries?

Del Yeah.

Miranda You must be a fool.

Del Miranda, you should have told me that you
wanted to sell the painting.

Miranda Don't be ridiculous, I'm in business. I
realised how valuable it was the moment I saw it.
Why should I tell you?

Del No, Miranda, you don't understand.

Miranda I think you're the one who's confused
Derek. And let's get one thing absolutely clear.
That painting is now mine. It's been legally
registered in my name. Mummy and Daddy have
even signed an affidavit to swear that the
painting has been in our family for generations.

Del Thank Gawd for that. I've been trying to get
shot of that painting for years.

Miranda What do you mean?

Del I know exactly what that painting is and I
know exactly how much it's worth.

Miranda Rubbish. How could someone like you
possibly know that.

Del I'll tell you how I know shall I? Because my
Gran used to be a char-lady to an art dealer.
That's how I know.

Miranda Oh I see, and this Mrs Mopp examined
it did she?

Del No, she didn't examine it. She nicked it.
Auctioneer £17,600.
Del Good luck sweetheart. *(Del exits)*

In 1989 Derek Trotter visited the School of Business, Peckham, and delivered a lecture entitled 'Readies: How to make millions of 'em.' Printed below is an extract.

"...YOU WIN SOME AND YOU LOSE SOME. 'ALLEMAGNE DIX POINTS,' THAT'S WHAT I SAY. MY LITTLE BRUV, RODNEY, WAS ONCE A STUDENT LIKE YOU, ALL STEVE BILKO T-SHIRTS, DOC MARTENS AND FUNNY FAGS. REMEMBER THOUGH, A CONSCIENCE IS NICE, BUT BUSINESS IS BUSINESS. RODNEY HAS LEARNT FROM A MASTER. I TELL YOU, I COULD TEACH THAT NICOLA HORLICKS A THING OR TWO ABOUT BUSINESS, AND OL' BILLY GATES COULD DO WITH COCKING AN EAR ONCE OR TWICE IN MY DIRECTION. RODDERS ONCE TRIED TO GO IT ALONE, WITH THAT MICKEY PEARCE, WHO COULDN'T KEEP A RABBIT GOING WITH A LETTUCE. AT THEIR FIRST AUCTION THE STUPID PLONKERS LANDED THEMSELVES WITH A LOAD OF BROKEN LAWN-MOWER ENGINES THAT I PICKED UP WHILE A BIT NON COMPOS MENTIS AT THE ONE ELEVEN CLUB FROM ALFIE FLOWERS. I DIDN'T THINK ANYBODY WOULD BUY 'EM AND TOLD RODDERS TO AVOID THEM, BUT THE TWONK THOUGHT I WAS PULLING A FAST ONE AND DECIDED TO PAY DOUCE IN BUNCE FOR THE LOT— THEY WERE WORTH A SCORE IN SCRAP AND THAT'S IT. A GOOD LESSON THERE FOR YOU ALL: IF YOU'RE STUCK WITH DODGY MERCHANDISE, FIND YOURSELF A COUPLE OF BERKS WITH CASH ON THE HIP.
MASTERS OF BUSINESS CAN'T SURVIVE WITHOUT A BIT OF INITIATIVE. SOME DEALS WHAT LOOK ON THE FACE OF IT LIKE A RIGHT LOAD OF OLD PONY CAN BE NICE LITTLE EARNERS. TAKE THOSE TECHNICOLOUR WOOLEN TEA COSIES I BOUGHT ONCE. I GOT OLD MRS MURPHY TO STITCH UP THE HOLES, LEGGED IT DOWN THE YOUTH CENTRE A FLOGGED 'EM TO THE WEST INDIAN LADS AS SOPPY HATS. LOVELY JUBBLY! ENTREPRENEURS LIKE MYSELF NEVER GIVE UP; NOTHING VENTURED, NOTHING GAINED. WELL, IT'S BEOUF A LA MODE AS THEY SAY IN FRANCE.
A LOT OF YOU HERE MAY SNIFF AT MY LINE OF BUSINESS AND I WILL HOLD MY HAND UP AND SAY I AM NO SAINT. HE'S NEVER BEEN THE SAME SINCE HE SPLIT UP WITH GREAVSIE

ANYWAY. A LOT OF STUFF I DEAL WITH IS HOOKY, YES. BUT LOOK AT IT THIS WAY — AND LEARN. FIRMS HAVE TO HIRE MORE SECURITY GUARDS TO PROTECT THEIR MERCHANDISE, THUS LOWERING THE UNEMPLOYMENT FIGURES. THE INSURANCE COMPANY WILL NEED MORE PEOPLE TO HANDLE INCREASING CLAIMS SO REDUNDANT CLERKS WILL BE SNATCHED FROM THE DOLE QUEUE AND HANDED BACK THEIR DIGNITY. RIGHT? NOW THESE PEOPLE MAY VERY WELL CELEBRATE THEIR GOOD FORTUNE BY BUYING A CAR AND TAKING THEIR WIFE AND KIDS ON A TOURING HOLIDAY ROUND BRITAIN. THIS WILL RESULT IN A MUCH NEEDED BOOST TO OUR AILING CAR INDUSTRY, HIGHER REVENUE FOR NORTH SEA OIL AND A VITAL CASH INJECTION INTO SEASIDE RESORTS AND DEPRESSED AREAS. ON THE OTHER HAND, THEY MAY TAKE A HOLIDAY ABROAD, RIGHT, THUS FORCING FOREIGN HOTELIERS, BAROWNERS, AND RESTAURANTERS TO BUY MORE BRITISH BEER, FOOD & GOODS. THIS WILL RESULT IN A HIGHER EXPORT DRIVE, WHICH IN TURN WILL BE VERY GOOD FOR OUR BALANCE OF PAYMENTS SURPLUS! MOULES MARINIERE! SOON THIS COUNTRY WILL BE RICH AND FAMOUS AGAIN- THE STARVING SHALL BE FED- THE HOMELESS WILL BE HOMED! BET YOU DON'T GET TAUGHT THAT IN YOUR JOHN MILTON KEYNES TEXT BOOKS. AND OK, OCCASIONALLY, I IMPORT THINGS INTO THE COUNTRY WITHOUT PAYING THE APPROPRIATE TAX. BUT, SAY I PAID IMPORT TAX THEN WHAT DO YOU THINK THE GOVERNMENT IS GOING TO DO WITH IT? THEY'RE ONLY GOING TO GO OUT AND BUY ANOTHER ONE OF THOSE STRIDENT MISSILES WITH IT, AIN'T THEY? SO, I'M ALSO DOING MY BIT FOR WORLD PEACE. A SUBJECT CLOSE TO THE HEART OF SOPPY STUDENTS LIKE YOU.

AND WHAT HAPPENS WHEN THE COUNTRY FALLS IN TO DEPRESSION, EH? MONEY GETS TIGHT. PEOPLE CAN'T AFFORD TO PAY FOR WHAT'S IN THE SHOPS 'COS THE PRICES ARE SO INFLATED, SO WHAT DO THEY DO? THEY COME TO BLOKES LIKE ME. A DEPRESSION IS A GOLDEN AGE FOR THE BLACK MARKET AND WE MAKE SURE THE POOR GET WHAT THEY NEED, LIKE EXPORT GIN, CHEAP WASHING POWDER AND LITTLE YAPPING TOY DOGS FOR THE KIDS. YES, YOU CAN SNIFF, BUT IT'S PEOPLE LIKE ME WHAT KEEP THIS NATION GOING IN TIMES OF HARDSHIP.

THE WORLD IS CHANGING OUT THERE, IT'S A FINANCIAL JUNGLE. IT'S A QUESTION OF ME WHO DARES, WINS, AND ME WHO HESITATES...DON'T.

May the Force be with You

INT. DAY. THE NAG'S HEAD.

Rodney and Trigger are leaning against the bar chatting. Sitting further along the bar, behind Trigger, is Slater. He is a Detective Inspector. Although he is in plain clothes, everything about him says 'Copper.' He is in his middle-to-late thirties. He has a snide and superior manner and is loathed and feared by both the small-time crooks and his own colleagues in the Met. He is watching Trigger and Rodney intensely.

Rodney Yeah. So, right I said to her, I said, 'Bernice' . . . I said . . .

Trigger That her name is it?

Rodney . . .Yeah – Bernice! Yeah, Trigger, that's why I call her Bernice you know.

Trigger Right!

Rodney I said, 'Don't play with me girl, 'cos you are playing with fire!' I said, 'Don't you dare try 'an tie me down!'

Trigger She's into all that is she?

Rodney . . . No, Trigger, I meant it in a, you know, spiritual sort of way! I mean she's not – no – see, 'cos I'm a free agent Trigger. Wherever I right I lay my hat, right, that's my home! That's the sort of guy I am.

Trigger Yeah . . . You got a hat now then have you Dave?

Rodney No, no Trigger it's a saying you know. Anyway –

Trigger I had a hat once!

Rodney Yeah? So I could see she was upset you know.

Trigger Someone nicked it at a party!

Rodney Really? Yeah, well . . . She was crying, begging me not to leave her.

Trigger And my return ticket in the brim! I had to walk all the way home from Plumstead!

Rodney I'm gonna phone Del, see if he can come down for a drink. *(Moves away towards the phone)*

Trigger What colour was your hat Dave?

Rodney Pink!

Trigger Same here!

Slater stands. As Rodney passes him their shoulders catch.

Rodney Sorry!

Slater *(Quietly to himself)* You will be if it happens again sonny. Trigger!

Trigger *(Alarmed)* Oh! Er, watcha Roy! Long time, eh? What brings you round this way, I thought you were stationed in West London.

Slater I missed you all, didn't I? I got meself transferred back to the old parish. And it's not Roy any more. You can call me Mr Slater, Detective Inspector Slater or just plain sir! Mine's a large scotch!

Trigger Right! *(Calls)* A large scotch, love.

Slater Know anything about a microwave oven?

Trigger No, I'm no good with electrics and that!

Slater I ain't asking you to mend the bleedin' thing am I! I'm talking about a *stolen* microwave oven! Someone lifted one off the back of a lorry in Lewisham Grove earlier on!

Trigger Yeah? Tch, some people!

Slater Yeah, some people! So what you up to these days Trigger? Still doing a double-act with Monkey Harris?

Trigger No, I ain't seen Monkey for ages.

Slater And what about Boycie?

Trigger Dunno, I ain't seen him for years!

Slater Really! And how about my favourite man? *(With hate and menace in his voice)* How's good old Del Boy keeping?

Trigger Haven't a clue, I ain't seen him for a long time!

Slater No, you ain't seen much of anything lately, have yer? You ought to eat more carrots Trig!

Boycie enters. He strolls in his usual confident manner but, upon seeing Slater, he does a sharp about turn and is about to rush out.

Slater Well upon my soul, it's Boycie!

Boycie Oh! Hello Roy. What a nice surprise!

Slater And what a coincidence as well!

Boycie Eh?

Slater That you two should just happen to be drinking in the same pub! I mean, how long is it since you last saw Trigger?

Boycie Ooh, er, it must be . . . *(Trigger holds up two fingers)* at least two months.

Slater Trigger said years!

Boycie Oh yeah, now you come to mention it, it must be two years! Time does fly, don't it?

Slater Certainly does! Seems like only yesterday that I was pounding the beat around here. They were good old days weren't they, eh?

Trigger Triffic.

Boycie Great.

Slater How's Marlene these days?

Boycie Oh, you know, still the same!

Slater Is she? *(Shaking his head sadly)* Dear, dear, dear . . .

Slater I heard that you're dabbling in the video game!

Boycie Oh yeah. It's just a side-line, you know.

Slater I heard a whisper that you're flogging pirate tapes!

Boycie Yeah, *Treasure Island*, *Mutiny on the Bounty*.

Slater I'm surprised to hear Del Boy's still at the same place.

Boycie Yeah, still there! Oh, he's er thinking of moving though.

Trigger Emigrating actually!

Slater Emigrating? Yes, I bet these developing nations are crying out for fly-pitchers!

Boycie Well, I must be off!

Slater So soon? After all these years I thought you two would have a lot to talk about!

Boycie Yeah, well, we do, but I have just seen a business acquaintance of mine. *(Calls)* Hello Rodney! Well, see yer Roy. *(Moves from bar)*

Slater Yeah, see yer Boycie. Give my love to Marlene! Everyone else used to! …Rodney? Weren't Del's kid brother called Rodney?

Trigger Oh, I don't know Mr Slater.

Slater No, you're deaf, dumb and blind these days ain't yer! I bet you're a wizard on the pinball machine!

Boycie *(Shakes Rodney's hand warmly)* Hello Rodney. Nice to see you again!

Rodney Boycie! I was talking with you last night!

Boycie Oh were you, oh yeah, of course you were. Memory must be slipping. Well take care of yourself, see you around! *(Exits)*

Rodney Yeah – see yer Boycie!

Slater Don't tell me. You're Del Boy's brother Rodney! Am I right?

Rodney Yeah!

Slater I was at school with Del, sat next to him in class. Haven't seen you since you was a little nipper.

Rodney Really? What's your name?

Slater Detec . . . Roy! Roy Slater!

Rodney Roy Slater? No. No, I can't recall him mentioning it. Perhaps he called you by a nickname?

Slater Yeah, knowing Del that's about it!

Trigger Well I'm away now Mr Slater.

Slater Behave yourself Trigger. Well, well, well . . .

Slater turns to face Rodney. Trigger, behind his back is gesturing to Rodney. Slater follows

Rodney's eye-line and catches Trigger mid-act. Trigger tries to excuse his behaviour by pretending he has something in his eye. He turns and exits.

Rodney What's up with everyone today?

Slater Been at the booze, ain't they? So – fancy bumping into you! Shame Del Boy couldn't have made it.

Rodney Well d'you know, I've just this minute come off the phone to him. He was coming down for a swift one but he got involved with a bit of business, something to do with a microwave oven . . .

Slater Is that right? Oh I would have loved to have met him again. It would have been a real surprise for him!

Rodney Well, I tell you what, why don't you come back to the flat and have a beer?

Slater Could I? Oh, that would be smashing!

Rodney Yeah, yeah, I'll go and give him a bell.

Slater *(Sharply)* No! You'll spoil the surprise!

Rodney Oh yeah . . . Hey, I can't wait to see his face when you come through the door, eh?

Slater It'll be a picture Rodney, it'll be a picture!

INT. DAY. THE TROTTERS' LOUNGE.

The microwave oven is standing on the sideboard. Grandad is studying it and fiddling with the switches. Del is in the kitchen.

Del *(OOV)* I mean, I don't ask much of you do I? But even when I ask you to do the simplest thing you let me down!

Grandad Oh shuddup!

Del *(OOV)* I mean she won't wanna know me now will she, not after last night!

Grandad I ain't bothered!

Del *(Entering, carrying a cup of coffee)* I invited her all the way over from Canning Town for a nice quiet intimate candlelit dinner. And all I asked you to do was to put the box of wine in the fridge and me tub of neapolitan ice-cream in the freezer. But no, you get that arse about face, don't you? So, come nine o'clock all I could offer her was a bowl of gunge and a Beaujolais ice lolly! Ruined my entire evening it did! What are you doing?

Grandad I'm trying to get *The Dukes of Hazzard*!

Del *The Dukes of Hazzard*! This is a microwave oven you dozy old twonk! Gordon Bennett, you'll be putting frozen pizzas into the portable next! Come out of the way will yer! You're lucky you didn't barbecue yourself! Now just leave it alone!

Rodney enters.

Rodney Hey Del, guess who I met down the

May the Force be with You

pub?

Del Well, whoever she is don't invite her back here to dinner!

Rodney No, it's one of your old school mates!
Slater enters.

Slater Hello Del Boy, long time eh?

Del Slater!! *(Drops his tray)*

Slater In all me glory! *(To Rodney)* I told you he'd be surprised didn't I?

Rodney Yeah!!

Slater Is this your Grandad?

Del No that's the au-pair innit!

Slater Watcha Grandad. You wouldn't remember me, Roy Slater, I used to be in Del's class at school!

Grandad Well, well, that's a turn up for the book innit Del Boy?

Del Yeah, innit just?

Grandad Rodney, get Roy one of them lagers in the fridge.

Rodney Yeah right!

Del Yeah, well, I'll just, er, yeah, I'll just give Rodney a hand. Carry on now.

KITCHEN.

Del What the bloody hell are you trying to do to me? Have you no idea who that is?

Rodney Yeah, he said he was an old mate!

Del He's not an old mate – he's an Old Bill! And when I say an Old Bill I mean an Old Bill! That geezer out there'd nick you for *anything* you did! In fact, he'd nick you for anything you didn't do! And he wouldn't let a silly little thing like innocence get in the way!

Rodney I didn't have a clue Del, I swear!

Del You wally! Alright, alright! We gotta play this nice and cagey! Now listen, you gotta, you gotta be careful what you say to him, because that fella in there, he collects informers the way other people collect stamps.

Rodney He's got a few grasses – has he?

Del No, he ain't got a few grasses Rodney – he's got an entire lawn! Right, when you go back in there, only speak when you're spoken to, and then keep it down to a simple yes or no! Think before you blink, and if God is smiling on us, we might get away with it, alright? Get them beers.

LOUNGE.

The kitchen door opens and Del and Rodney enter. Grandad is demonstrating how the microwave works to Slater.

Slater And does it cook as quickly as they claim?

Grandad Oh I – I don't know so much about that.

Slater Don't you?

Grandad We ain't used it yet.

Slater No? That's strange, it feels hot!

Del Yeah, well, here y'are, come and cool your fingers down on this Roy me boy! There you go. And how's the *police* force treating you?

Grandad Police??

Slater Not too bad. I got promoted a while back, I'm Detective Inspector now.

Del Oh congratulations. A few years from now you could be advertising tyres! How's the family?

Slater I don't see much of 'em these days, Del. The old man is still not talking to me.

Del No, well, he's probably still got the needle over that time you nicked him!

Grandad He nicked his own father??

Slater I had no choice! If there had been a way of avoiding it I would have. But his rear light *was* defective! I mean, what else could I do?

Del It's true, he'd only borrowed the bike to go down the fish shop 'an all.

Slater That's right! It was just a twist of fate. But you've got to understand that at the time I was young and keen. Now that I'm older and more experienced I regret doing it!

Del Leave it out Slater. You've never regretted a nick in your life!

Slater Now that's not fair Del! You're judging me by the Roy Slater that you used to know. But I've changed in lots of ways. Things that were important to me in the past mean nothing now. I used to be enthusiastic, career minded, but what have you got at the end of the day? You've won your stripes – and lost your friends!

Del Oh come on Roy. You didn't lose your friends!

Slater No?

Del No, you didn't have any to lose in the first place!

Slater Yeah, I suppose you're right! Del, maybe one evening – if you're not too busy – we could have a couple of beers together?

Del Yeah, well, see how it goes shall we?

Slater Yeah, alright, thanks for the drink. It was nice seeing you all again . . . I'll see myself out.
Slater moves sadly to the door. There is an embarrassed silence in the room. Rodney and Grandad are obviously feeling a certain amount of pity for Slater. Slater opens the door and is about to exit.

Slater *(Turns)* Oh by the way. You're all under arrest! (Grins)

INT. NIGHT. A POLICE INTERVIEW ROOM.
A virtually bare room save for a desk and a

few chairs and a filing cabinet. A young PC (Hoskins) stands by the door. The Trotters are seated around the desk. Slater is on the phone.

Slater Yes sir . . . Oh yes, well, thank you very much sir, very nice of you to say so . . . well, I can only have them for receiving sir, but one of them's an old mate and I get the feeling that if I treat him nicely enough he may be – persuaded – to volunteer the name of the real thief . . . Oh yes sir, you know me sir, I play everything by the book sir. Well there's three of them actually sir. Yes, I arrested them single-handed! Well I don't think of the danger sir, I simply see it as my duty! *(The Trotters – and Hoskins – are sickened by his toadying)* Well, I'll get back to you sir as soon as I've got some information. Okay sir . . . Thanks very much sir. Thank you once again, sir. Okay sir. Bye for now sir. Do you know who that was?

Del The wife?

Slater That was the assistant commissioner.

Grandad You want to be a bit more careful about your health, son. In the last 'alf hour you've done so much boot-licking you could be going down with Cherry Blossom poisoning!

Slater Have you informed them of their rights, constable.

Hoskins Oh yes sir!

Slater *(Angered)* Tch!!

Rodney Yeah and I demand the right to phone my solicitor!

Slater Sit down and behave yourself!

Rodney I'm saying nothing until I've phoned my solicitor!

Slater Go 'n then, phone your solicitor!

Rodney I haven't got a solicitor!

Slater Well don't waste my bloody time then!

Del Just calm it down will yer! Just calm down. Now listen, Slater, I think I've found a way in which we can clear this mess up.

Slater What, you tell me the name of the person who nicked the microwave?

Del No, I give you 50 quid and you let us go!

Slater I didn't hear that Del!

Del *(Louder)* I said I give you 50 quid . . .

Rodney Del!!

Slater Did you hear that Hoskins?

Hoskins Oh yes sir, loud and clear.

Slater Oh, you really are a star Del Boy, you really are a star! You are now down for receiving stolen goods *and* attempting to bribe a police officer!

Del You never complained about it before.

Slater Did you hear that Hoskins?

Hoskins Sorry sir? Miles away!

Slater Right. Who 'alf inched the microwave? Was it Trigger? Come along gentlemen, I want a name!

Grandad We found it, didn't we Rodney?

Rodney Yeah, yeah – down the market! This bloke, sort of, dropped it!

Slater Oh, he dropped it did he? Didn't you call after him?

Rodney *(Lost for words)* Er . . .

Del Well yeah, but he was a bit mutton, wasn't he.

Slater Oh, I see, well that explains it! Tch, I just wish you'd have told me earlier, it would have saved us all this trouble! It's easily done constable. You're walking along the street, your mind on other things, you take your handkerchief out of your pocket and, bang, your microwave falls out. *(Indicates Rodney and Grandad)* Take these two down the corridor and put them in *separate* rooms! I'll be along later to get their descriptions of this stone-deaf villain! And oi, no conferring! *(Rodney and Grandad rise)*

Grandad It's bleedin' starters for ten now.
  They exit.

Slater I see Boycie's selling pirate videos now!

Del *(Momentarily off guard)* Ye . . . Is he?

Slater Hmm! Which number in Kings Avenue does he live?

Del I dunno! But you can't miss his house, it's the one with the Jolly Roger flying from the chimney!

Slater Oh, that takes me back Del Boy! D' you remember when we was kids, we used to go over the ponds to play at pirates? You were Dan Tempest – Trigger was Long John Silver – and what character did I play Del?

Del You played the bloke what walked the plank.

Slater Oh yeah! The bloke that walked the plank! I was always the bloke that walked the plank, wasn't I? I must have been in and out of that pond more times than a duck's head! I always wanted to be Bluebeard!

Del Well you should have said so!

Slater I did say! But you'd never let me!

Del I did – once!

Slater Oh yeah I remember. That was the day Bluebeard had to walk the plank weren't it?

Del I tried to be friendly Slater, but you were such a snide there was no helping you!

Slater You tried to be friendly? Like when?

Del Do you remember that time when all the boys dragged you to the ground, and Fatty Walker sat on yer face and Trigger put all that itching powder in your belly button?

May the Force be with You

Slater . . . Vaguely!

Del Yeah, well I was the one who made 'em stop at your belly button! They were all for having yer braces off! And how did you repay my act of kindness? You caught me behind the bike shed with some bird and went and told the headmaster!

Slater It was my sister!

Del See, you always let personal feelings creep into it didn't you?

Slater Right! Down to business! The face who dropped a microwave oven in the market! What did he look like?

Del Well, he was er . . . about average height!

ANOTHER ROOM – BLANK BACKGROUND.

Grandad He was a great big tall fella!

ANOTHER ROOM – COLOUR BACKGROUND.

Rodney Oh, he was little more than a dwarf!

Slater *(OS)* Age?

Rodney About 25.

ROOM – BLANK BACKGROUND.

Grandad Middle fifties!

INTERVIEW ROOM.

Del He was just a kid!

Slater *(OS)* What about his ethnic group?

Del Well, I didn't notice anyone with him!

Slater *(OS)* No, I mean was he caucasian?

ROOM – BLANK BACKGROUND.

Grandad No he was a white fella!

ROOM – COLOUR BACKGROUND.

Rodney He was African I think!

INT. NIGHT. THE POLICE INTERVIEW ROOM.

Hoskins is standing by the door. Del is seated at the table and is obviously feeling the effects of the long night. His jacket has been removed and his tie loosened. His shirt cuffs have been folded back to reveal a chunky gold bracelet on one wrist and a gold watch on the other. Del checks his watch.

Del Is he allowed to keep us here this long?

Hoskins No.

Del That mean we can go then?

Hoskins No.

Del Triffic!

Hoskins Well, you shouldn't get yourself involved with hooky gear should you!

Del No, you're absolutely right young Terry! How's that gas fire I sold yer Mum, alright is it?

Hoskins Oh, er, yeah, cheers Del! Look, why don't you do yourself a favour and give him the name of the bloke? He'll get it out of you in the end, he always does! Slater's a nasty piece of work. The only people that hate him more than the villains is us coppers!

Del Supposing I gave him the bloke's name, what would happen to him?

Hoskins See that filing cabinet over there? That is full to the top with unsolved crimes. Slater would lay the whole lot on the bloke! So after only two weeks at the station he'll have doubled the conviction rate. The public are reassured, Slater gets his promotion and the Commander takes another step closer to his CBE! And everybody's happy!

Del All except the poor sod who's gone down the Kermit! Na, I'm not going to tell him nothing.

Hoskins Well watch out for him Del, he's got no scruples. He'll try *anything*!

Slater enters carrying a mug of tea and a couple of files.

Slater Alright Hoskins, you can go and have yer supper break now.

Hoskins Oh, thank you very much sir.

Slater Shame the canteen's just closed innit? *(Hoskins exits)* Sorry Del, did you want a cup of tea?

Del No it's alright Slater, I had one yesterday!

Slater Good, good! *(Starts reading some of the paperwork. He begins to laugh)* Sorry Del Boy. I'm just reading these descriptions of the phantom of the market! Oh, it's good Del, it's good! According to you and your family we are looking for a 6ft 7in dwarf, aged between 15 and 50, a white male with oriental features who's as black as Newgate's knocker! And, oh yeah, he wears a deaf-aid!

Del Not a lot to go on inspector!

Slater If I was to take this lot in to court I could have you for perjury as well! *(Referring to one of his files)* I've just found this in our records department.

Del I hope it's Barry Manilow!

Slater No it's not Barry Manilow Del! It says here criminal file number 94628/A76. Name: Trotter! Rodney!

Del Now look Slater – Roy. Now just – here now come on. Let's leave Rodney out of this, eh?

Slater He was a little scallywag at that art school, weren't he? Caught in some tart's room puffing a Moroccan Woodbine!

Del Now listen, he was innocent!

Slater Well, not according to this he weren't!

Del He only went down to her room to borrow

173

some charcoal!

Slater Whatever he was smoking when the police burst in, it weren't charcoal Del! Now I wonder what would happen if, horror of horrors, I was to discover an illegal substance in one of Rodney's pockets?

Del Leave it out Slater – you know Rodney's got nothing in his pockets!

Slater That's soon remedied!

Del I see, and what you gonna stitch Grandad up with, eh? Found in possession of a forged bus-pass, or demanding protection money from the local Darby and Joan Club?

Slater Oh no, I'll see that Grandad's kept out of this. While you and Rodney are away sewing mailbags – Grandad'll be back on the estate . . . Alone!

Del Just what is that supposed to mean?

Slater Dangerous places them estates Del! I do hope Grandad doesn't fall victim to the mindless filth that walks our streets!

Del I thought you drove everywhere nowadays. Listen to me Slater – I know lots of coppers and they're all good blokes. I mean, I don't like 'em but they play a fair game and then there's you, you dirty stinking . . .

Slater Steady Del, I don't want to have to add abusive language to your ever growing list of offences! I might not have room on the charge sheet! You and young Rodney are going down for at least a year apiece! Unless you give me the name of the mush who nicked the microwave.

Del Oh leave it out Slater. You know I can't do that. It's against all my principles! My Mum'd turn in her grave if she knew I'd become a copper's nark!

Slater *(Picks up phone)* Well, you're gonna have a lot of time to think about your principles. I hope the porridge ain't too lumpy! I'll get the charge sheets typed up!

Del is a desperate man. His eyes are closed with intense thought. Then they open, an idea is born. Del smiles to himself.

Del Now, just a minute – Roy. Now let's not be hasty! I think we can make a deal.

Slater I don't like deals!

Del You're gonna like this one! If I give you the name of he bloke that stole that oven, you let Rodney and Grandad go – no charges!

Slater Yeah alright, I'll let them go!

Del And you also drop all charges against me!

Slater Oh come on Del, I'm looking forward to that!

Del You don't seem to understand what I'm saying Slater! Once I've given you the name I'll be one of your – grasses!

Slater Oh Del, Del Boy, that is beautiful! *You* would be one of my merry men! I'd have you in my pocket, I could bounce you about and make you dance whenever I felt bored! And if you ever stepped out of line, I'd let it be known on the streets that you're an informer!

Del Yeah! I know!

Slater The deal's on my old hoppo. I'll drop the charges against you, you have my word.

Del Your word! Your word means about as much as the guarantee on that hooky microwave! Now I want immunity from prosecution. And I want it in writing, and I want it signed, sealed and delivered!

Slater I'll get it arranged right away Derek. Oh, we're gonna have a good future together you and me – I can feel it! What's wrong Del? Cursing the day you crossed me?

Del No, I'm cursing the day I made them stop at your belly button.

INT. NIGHT. CORRIDOR IN POLICE STATION.

Rodney and Grandad are in the corridor. Grandad is seated directly below a 'Watch Out There's a Thief About' poster. He sees it and moves his chair closer to Rodney.

Grandad Why's he keeping Del Boy in there?

Rodney That is about the 38th time you've asked me that in the last 'alf hour! And for the 38th time Grandad, I'm telling you, I don't know!!

Grandad I thought he'd just charge Del with receiving, he'd get a £50 fine and then it would all be forgot about!

Rodney That's what I thought!

Grandad So did I! So why's he keeping him in there?

Rodney Gawd bless my old brown . . . I don't bloody know Grandad!

Grandad Well, Rodney . . .

The door to the interview opens and Hoskins looks out to see what all the noise is. Rodney and Grandad smile nervously at him.

Hoskins Look, I thought I told you two you were free to go!

Grandad Oh we thought we'd hang on a while.

Rodney Yeah, it's good here innit?

Slater exits from the charge room carrying a piece of paper.

Slater Still here?

Rodney We're waiting for Del.

Grandad Will he be long son?

Slater Only as long as it takes him to tell me who nicked the microwave.

May the Force be with You

Rodney Better get our head down till the morning then!

Slater Oh no, Del's seen the light. He's decided to cooperate.

Grandad No, you're pulling our legs!

Slater D'you reckon? Well why don't you come in and see for yourselves? Come on.

INT. NIGHT. THE INTERVIEW ROOM.

Del is seated at the table. Slater enters followed by Rodney and Grandad.

Slater Alright Hoskins, away you go, canteen's open now.

Hoskins Oh thank you very much, sir.

Hoskins exits.

Slater *(Throws paper on desk)* There you are, Del Boy, your immunity from prosecution, signed by the Superintendent himself.

Rodney What are you playing at Del??!!

Del What are they doing 'ere?

Slater Oh, I thought it'd be interesting for them to see you in your real light. The Great Del Boy, the man who can talk his way out of a room with no doors, reduced to this, grassing!

Del I've got to tell him Rodney. He's got me all ends up . . . I've got no choice.

Grandad But you don't know his name Del, he was just a bloke in the market!

Del Oh leave it out Grandad. If Mr Slater was to believe our description he'd have had his men searching for someone who's a cross between Tom Thumb and the Jolly Green Giant!

Slater With a deaf-aid!

Del With a deaf-aid! Rodney, I wasn't doing it just for myself – he threatened to plant something on you, and set you up for a bit of bird!

Rodney But, but that's against the law!

Slater Well phone the police!

Rodney Don't tell him Del!

Del Look, I've got to Rodney, otherwise it'll mean you and me would go down the road and Grandad's going to be left alone on the estate, see I've got no choice, I've got no choice! Alright, Mr Slater, let's get down to business.

Slater Oh Del, Del Boy, those words are music to my ears. I will cherish this moment! Righto Del, who nicked it?

Del *(Indicating Rid and Grandad)* They are free to go ain't they?

Slater Yeah, they're free to go, no charges, they can leave whenever they like! Okay give me his name?

Del And you've got nothing on me either?

Slater *(Losing his temper)* No! You've got an immunity from prosecution! You've got less chance of a pull than the Queen! *(Del signs the paper)*

Del Long as I know!

Slater Right, for the third and the last time of asking, who nicked the microwave off the back of the lorry?

Del looks anxiously at Rodney and Grandad.

Del I did!

He smiles triumphantly at Slater.

●**COSMIC GIRL,** Sensitive, artistic M 24, educated, with two GCEs in maths and art, financial adviser for succesful importing–exporting business, with own car. Into art, world peace, music, adult art magazines, exotic herbs and computers. Seeks a soulmate who is also a right brahma, must have a uniform. No women with old men doing porridge need apply. London. PO Box 999.

Wanted

THE NAG'S HEAD PUB.

The pub is very crowded with teenagers and Del-types. Pop music is playing very loudly. We cut away to where Rodney and Mickey Pearce are standing. They both wear their suits and are eyeing a couple of girls.

Mickey What d' you reckon then?

Rodney They're alright ain't they! Don't 'alf look alike.

Mickey They're identical twins!

Rodney Yeah, which one d' you fancy?

Mickey I'm easy!

Rodney Are you sure that's not *one* bird sitting next to a mirror?

Mickey No, they're sisters or something, they've been here before! G' on then!

Rodney What?

Mickey Say something!

Rodney What?

Mickey I don't know! Anything!

Rodney Like what?

Mickey Just say the first thing that comes into your head. It's easy!

Rodney Alright then, if it's so easy, you say something.

Mickey What?

Rodney Anything. It's easy!

Mickey Alright then I will.

Rodney Well go'n then!

Mickey I will . . . *(Calls across to the girls)* Oi! *(To Rodney)* There you are.

Rodney Was that it?

Mickey Yeah!

Rodney Oi??

Mickey Yeah!

Rodney You're a right little John Travolta when you get going ain't yer Mickey!

Mickey They looked didn't they?

Rodney Of course they looked, someone just shouted 'Oi' at them!

Mickey Hold up, they're looking over here.

Rodney Hello, I think we've cracked it Mickey my son!

Del appears out of the crowd.

Del Watcha Rodders, alright Mickey my son? Who you two after? Not the gruesome twosome are you?

Mickey They're alright!

Del Alright? Look, they're so ugly they even look alike!

Rodney Del! They happen to be two sisters!

Del Sisters! *(Calls)* Oi girls, seen much of Cinderella since the wedding? *(Laughs)* Cinderella! Ugly sisters. That's a good 'un innit Rodders, eh? Anyway, look, I won't hang about 'cos I don't wanna spoil your chances! *(To someone across the pub)* Hello darling! You alright? Are you still working at Sainsbury's? See you. Just a minute.

From the moment Del called to the girls, Rodney and Mickey have been staring ahead in stunned silence as their last chance was flushed down the pan.

Rodney I'll see you Tuesday then?

Mickey See you Tuesday!

NIGHT. STREET.

Rodney is wandering down the street singing quietly to himself. A woman is seated rather unsteadily on a garden wall. She is about 45, heavily made up with peroxide blonde hair. She is obviously bemoaning her fortune. Rodney approaches.

Woman *(Sings)* 'You made me love you. I didn't want to do it . . .'

Rodney You okay love?

Woman Who is it?

Rodney Shall I phone you a cab?

Woman No – there'll be a bus along in a minute my lovely!

Rodney No, no, ain't got no buses going along here. No, they cut the route in about 1973! I'll get you a nice taxi, eh?

Woman No, no, I shall be alright! *(She stands and stumbles)*

Rodney *(Puts his hand out to steady her)* Careful!

Woman What you doing?

Rodney I'm just steadying you that's all!

Woman You touched me!

Rodney Eh?

Woman I've read about your sort!

Rodney Hey, hold on, I was just trying to stop you from falling flat on your face!

Woman I'll have the police on you! You touched me.

Rodney No, I didn't, honest!

Woman *(Calls)* Help!

Rodney *(Panicking)* What you doing? Don't shout!

Woman You touched me!

Rodney No, no, it's alright 'cos I'm a doctor!

Woman You're not a doctor!

Rodney I am, I am really! Alright – say 'ah!'

Woman (Loudly) Aaaahhhhh!

Rodney No, not that loud! Bloody hell! Look, I tell you what I'm just going back to the van right, to get a thermometer! Alright listen!

Rodney sprints up the street.

Woman (Screams) Help, help! Rape! Rape! Help! Help!

THE TROTTERS' LOUNGE.

Grandad exits from the kitchen carrying a plate containing a fried breakfast.

Grandad (Calls) Del Boy, your breakfast's ready!

Del (OOV) Yeah, hang on a minute! (Calls) Come on Rodney shake a leg, six o'clock!

Del enters, washed, dressed and ready for the kill.

Grandad It's on the table. (Exits to the kitchen)

Del Nothing like a traditional British breakfast is there.

Grandad (OOV) That's right.

Del Gordon Bennett. Why don't you try cooking one every now and then? Blimey, it looks like a bad day at the Blue Cross.

Grandad (Entering with a pot of tea) Were you two alright last night?

Del Yeah, of course, why?

Grandad Well, when Rodney come in he was behaving very strangely. He was all trembling and sweating.

Del No, he's probably alright, don't worry, it's just the start of the mating season.

Grandad No Del – something's up. Ain't you eating that?

Del No, Grandad, see I'm on a diet.

Grandad (Calls) Rodney, your breakfast's ready.

Rodney enters. He looks tired.

Del Alright Rodders?

Rodney What d'you mean 'alright?'

Del Nothing – nothing, just alright Rodders?

Rodney Yeah, fine why shouldn't I be alright?

Del No reason. I just said like, alright Rodders. Like I say, you know, alright every morning don't I?

Rodney Yeah, Sorry!

Del That's alright, what did you do when you left the pub last night?

Rodney What makes you think I did something?

Del Gordon Bennett! No, I mean, I just asked you like if you went on anywhere? If, you met anyone or anything?

Rodney No! No, I didn't. I come straight home. Didn't meet anyone, didn't talk to anyone, a very

uneventful journey!

Del That's alright, as long as you enjoyed yourself! Go on, get that down, come on, we've got to get away early. Got to pick up the van from the Nag's Head.

Rodney Why?

Del Ah, well, when we fell out the pub last night the whole area was teeming with the Old Bill! I mean, they were all there. There was the Flying Squad, alsatians and the SGB! Anyway, I thought to myself, I thought, there's no way I'm driving home through that lot. Not with me like being as soppy as a sack, so I, you know, I got a cab!

Rodney Did they have a clear description of him?

Del Who?

Rodney The man they were after?

Del Who said they were after a man?

Rodney Oh, I just assumed they were looking for someone that's all.

Del, now suspicious, looks to Grandad.

Grandad See what I mean?

Del Yeah! Alright Rodney, come on sit down. Something's bothering you ain't there?

Rodney No!

Del Has somebody threatened you? If they have, you tell me their name and I'll go and sort them out before we go to the market!

Rodney It's nothing like that!

Grandad You might as well tell us sooner as later Rodney! It'll save a lot of time!

Rodney Oh it's probably nothing! My journey home last night was not as uneventful as I made out! There was this woman! Well, she weren't feeling very well, see! I don't know what was wrong with her but she stunk of booze! So I stopped, right, to ask if she wanted any assistance, and – and she started acting all sort of odd!

Del Odd?

Rodney Yeah . . . Um, screaming shouting things!

Grandad What kind of things?

Rodney Oh, things like 'Rape!' you know, that sort of thing! So to try and reassure her and calm her down – I told her I was a doctor!

Del and Grandad are left open-mouthed.

Del You told her you were a . . . You, You didn't give her a prescription or nothing did you?

Rodney Oh no, nothing like that!

Grandad Why was she accusing you of these things?

Rodney Well, I think 'cos at one point right she – she stumbled forward. So I put my hands out to

Wanted

stop . . . you know. I didn't touch her! Well no, obviously I did touch her, but I didn't, you know, honestly!

Del squeezes Rodney's shoulder as a way of re-assurance.

Del Alright. Alright, okay, take it nice and easy right. This is gonna take a bit of working out!

Grandad What did this woman look like?

Del has his back to the others. As Rodney gives his description Del has a growing smile that shows he knows the identity of the woman.

Rodney Well she was blonde, 45 and her hair had black roots and, er, purple fingernails and she was really heavily made-up.

Del Did she call you 'My lovely?

Rodney Yes! D'you know her?

Del No, no, no, you didn't catch her – you didn't catch her name or nothing did you?

Rodney Oh she was wearing an identity necklace that said something like – Blossom . . .

Del mouths the word 'Blossom' in time with Rodney. He now has to pinch his nose to stop himself laughing.

Rodney Del, honestly, I did not touch her I swear to God.

Del *(Controls his laughter, forces a serious expression)* You expect me to believe that?

Rodney Yes!

Del Alright, let's go through the facts shall we! After a night's drinking, on your way home you meet a *sick* woman! And, instead of phoning for an ambulance like any right-minded citizen, you touch her! What do you think you've got, healing hands?

Rodney I don't believe you're saying this to me!!

Del No, no, no, this is not *me* Rodney! That is what the council for the prosecution will say during his cross-examination!

Rodney You don't think it will go to court?

Grandad Oh it's a pound to a penny Rodney. I mean, the police don't let matters like this drop lightly!

Del No, Old Bailey would be my bet! The case of the Peckham Pouncer!

Rodney Who called me the Peckham Pouncer?

Del Look, the police did last night! You see at the time, well, I didn't think nothing of it! *(Bites his lip to stop from laughing)*

Grandad Why don't you give yourself up Rodney?

Rodney I'm not giving myself up! What? You ever seen some of them detectives give someone the third degree on the telly? Well, one of them pretends he really wants to beat you up bad, right, and the other one pretends to be Mr Nice! So it's . . . you know.

Grandad Yeah p'rhaps you're right. After all, you've got form ain't yer! I mean, you still ain't finished that two years suspended yet!

Rodney No! I'd forgotten about that!

Del It's the others what worry me!

Grandad What others?

Del Well, last night there were mobs of vigilantes roaming the street and they were shouting things like 'Lynch him! Lynch him! At the time, I didn't think nothing of it you know!

Rodney Well maybe it would be better if I did give myself up then 'cos all they've got is circumstantial evidence.

Del Circumstantial? A sick woman is attacked at night by a known criminal posing as a doctor!

Rodney D'you know what they'd call me if I went in the nick? I'd be a beast!

Del A beast?

Rodney Well, that's what the other prisoners call people like me! Everywhere I went the walls would be whispering 'Beast, Beast.' There'd be posses of them waiting for me in the shower room, there'd be razors in me soap, there'd be broken glass in me porridge!

Grandad Oh you'll soon learn to adapt Rodney!

Rodney No, it's not fair Del! I swear to God I didn't touch her. I was only trying to help!

Del Alright Rodney, alright. Now come on. Take it easy – relax – alright. Now listen, I'll tell you what I'm going to do. I want to go out, put me ear to the ground, see what I can find out! In the meantime I want you to go and get some kip and, above all, *stop worrying*!

Rodney Yeah. I'm innocent Del. Honest!

Del I believe you!

Grandad So do I Rodney! *(Rodney exits)* D'you reckon he done it Del?

Del Leave it out Grandad! All he's down, he's bumped into Blossom that's all!

Grandad I don't understand you?

Del Well she's well-known for this sort of thing! She's as nutty as a fruit cake. She spends most of her time in the Happy Home, they only let her out at weekends to get a bit practice!

Grandad You mean she's always accusing blokes of doing this sort of thing?

Del Yeah, it's her hobby! She's well known to the police.

Grandad But why didn't you tell young Rodney?

Del What, and spoil all the fun? No way. I'm gonna wind him *right* up with this! By this time tomorrow evening I'll have him believing that all

these flats are under siege!

Grandad You wanna be a bit careful Del Boy! A joke's a joke but you never know when to stop! What about that April Fool's day! You told me the pools had rung to say I'd won 'alf a million!

Del Yeah that was a belter weren't it!

Grandad Oh wonderful! But you could have least have stopped me going up West with me pension money! *(Del is convulsed with laughter)* Oh it wasn't funny Del. I mean there was I, in a Soho nightclub drinking champagne, and I suddenly realised I didn't even do the bloody pools!

Del Stop it!

NIGHT. NAG'S HEAD.

Del, Trigger and Boycie are seated at a table playing cards. Del is shuffling the cards. They are laughing.

Del You should have seen his little face! It was a picture. I wish I'd had a camera!

Trigger How could he swallow that, eh?

Del Well, you know Rodney don't you. He said he was thinking of forming an appeal committee! I said you've no need to worry about that. You ought to form an escape committee I said.

Trigger I thought everyone round here knew what Old Blossom was like . . . She accused my cousin once!

Del Who's that, young Sidney?

Trigger No, Marilyn! There again, Marilyn's always been a bit of a Tom Boy!

Boycie Oh yeah, it was a crew cut, braces and a pipe last time I saw her!

Del She still up at Greenham Common? Here, you playing Trigger or what?

Trigger No, I'll be away in a minute!

Boycie Of course, this Blossom person is completely loopy you know! Oh yes, I don't think they should be allowed out!

Del Oh yeah, why's that?

Boycie Well they might be a danger to the public!

Trigger Still selling them second-hand cars Boycie?

Boycie Oh yeah, I knocked out a couple tod . . . of course, I 'ave heard she receives electroyde treatment, you know. Oh yes, every three months or so they take her away and plug her head into the National Grid! The lights have been known to dim as far away as Watford!

Trigger Yeah but they reckon she's as sane as anyone when they're finished!

Boycie Yeah, until she gets her electric bill!

Karen Del – there's a call for you.

Del Oh excuse me chaps won't be a moment. Oh Karen, can we have three large scotches – Boycie's round.

Trigger Oh cheers, Boycie.

Del *(On phone)* Hello? Oh hello Grandad! You what . . . What about Rodney? What d'you mean he's gone on the run? Why? Oh leave it off, Grandad it was just a joke! Yeah alright, alright now don't – don't panic, he'll be home when he's hungry and he wants something to eat . . . Oh has he! Alright, alright Grandad, I'll tell you what I'll do, I'll go and have a look round for him and I'll be home in about an hour! Yeah, alright, bye.

Trigger What's up Del?

Del It's that dipstick Rodney. He's only gone on the run ain't he. Reckons he's found a secret hiding place!

Trigger Where?

Del Well how do I know? If I knew where it was it wouldn't be secret would it, eh?

Trigger No, I meant there must be a clue!

Del Yeah, well, he left a note saying it's no good trying to find him 'cos he'd be in the last place anyone would think of looking for him!

Boycie Have you tried under his bed?

Trigger He'll be home as soon as he gets hungry!

Del No he won't, Grandad reckons he's taken all the tinned food from the cupboard!

Trigger So, what you gonna do then Del?

Del I don't know Trigger, I just don't know!

Boycie Ain't you got nothing in the freezer then? *(Laughs)*

THE TROTTERS' LOUNGE.

It is the following morning. Del enters. He is tired and unshaven. Grandad enters from the kitchen.

Grandad Any luck Del?

Del Na, no sign of him Grandad!

Grandad Where did you look?

Del I've been everywhere! I've been traipsing round Charing Cross, Soho, Leicester Square! Oh, you want to see what it's like up there in the early hours Grandad! It's like the end of the world! It's full of drug addicts, glue-sniffers, winos! D'you know what, if a nightingale sang now in Berkeley Square someone would eat it!

Grandad Bad night, eh Del?

Del Yeah, very bad? You know I've been offered everything from 50 quid for me passport to a plate of Magic Mushrooms! *(Sniffs)* You cooking something?

Wanted

Grandad No!

Del What's that horrible smell then? Sweet and sickly!

Grandad Oh, perhaps it's this after-shave I've got on!

Del Gordon Bennett! Where d'you get that from?

Grandad Out of your room!

Del Well, that can't be it then can it!

Grandad Oh, I know the smell you're talking about. It was here last night, everyone in the flats was moaning about it! Here, why don't you get some sleep Del Boy!

Del No, I'll be alright Grandad. I'll have a cup of tea and have another punt round for him! Where can he be?

Grandad I had a note from him here somewhere, he said he's in the last place you'll ever think of looking!

Del Yeah I know I remember! You have looked under his bed haven't yer?

Grandad First place I checked! *(Opens a drawer on the sideboard and looks inside)*

Del Yeah. Well, he's hardly likely to be in that bloody drawer is he?

Grandad I'm looking for the note! Now don't you get funny with me Del, this is your fault, you and your silly jokes!

Del I know, I was gonna tell him this morning!

Grandad Well you could have told him yesterday. Instead of that you sat there playing your *Johnny Cash Live at San Quinton* LP!

Del Alright, don't go on at me – don't go on. I feel bad enough as it is! What is that smell? I've smelt it before somewhere!

Grandad I know, so did I.

Del When?

Grandad I told you! Last night!

Del No, no, no, before that.

Grandad It seems to be coming from the ventilation system!

Del Grandad, go and get them chicken legs at the fridge! I think I know where Rodney's hiding.

THE TANK ROOM.

A massive water tank stands on a concrete base. Fitted into the tank is a tap. The room echoes. The door opens and Del enters carrying a hold-all.

Del Rodney! Rodney, it's Del Boy! Rodney I know you're here! Rodney don't be a plonker all your life! Listen I can explain everything there's nothing to be frightened of! I've got – got some scotch here, something to eat!

Rodney is crouched down on the far side of the water tank. He is dishevelled and has two days of stubble on his chin. He is also terrified. Beside him is a pile of tinned food, unopened. As he tries to shift a few inches further back he knocks one of the tins over.

Rodney Meow.

Del smiles at the pathetic cat imitation.

Del Or if you prefer I could get a saucer of milk? Come on, least we can talk about can't we?

Rodney is beginning to weaken. Behind him is a sheet of metal, which he accidentally catches and it falls to the ground with an almighty echoing clatter.

Del Oi! That is you innit Rodney?

Rodney No, it's that cat again!

Del appears round the tank. Rodney appears above it.

Del You had me going there for a minute, know what I mean?

Rodney Did you know I was here?

Del I know a lot of things Rodney! Like I know you've bin smoking your funny fags again!

Rodney No I ain't Del, honest! I ain't touch . . . Well, a couple!

Del I tell you that was the give-away you see. The smell from your exotic tobacco has been wafting down the air ducts! There's not a man, woman or child that isn't high as a kite!

Rodney You're kidding?

Del No I'm not. If you stand outside this tower block all you can hear is giggling! Grandad's calling everybody 'Man'. Thinking of growing his hair in dreadlocks!

Rodney Is Grandad okay?

Del Yeah he's alright. Worried about you though. What are you doing up here?

Rodney Nothing much! There's not a lot to do in a tank room Del. I mean you can look at the view but that gets a bit boring after eight hours or so.

Del I wasn't – wasn't asking about your activities. I was speaking meteoroically. What you playing at?

Rodney Playing at! Well, Del this is a little game called 'Not Going to Prison'! The rules are ever so easy you know. All you gotta do is find yourself a place to hide and stay there till you die!

Del Don't reckon it will catch on Rodney!

Rodney You could be right there Del, but I'll tell you something, if necessary I will shoot my way out of this room.

Del Oh so while you've been up here, you've made yourself a gun have you?

Rodney Well, I'll throw tins at 'em then!

Del Yeah, well, you could get an empty can

couldn't you *(Indicating water tank)* you know and you could like, splash 'em to death!

Rodney I ain't had nothing to eat since I've been up here!

Del Why's that, you been too frightened?

Rodney No, I forgot the tin-opener!

Del Well why didn't you pop down for it!

Rodney Del, desperate men on the run don't pop home to borrow a tin-opener! Anyway, going without food ain't so bad! People like us are used to it!

Del Oh come on. Don't give me all that James Cagney stuff! 'Look at me Ma! I'm on the top of the World Ma! Look I'm in the tank room Ma!'

Rodney Why don't you shut up!

Del unzips the holdall and hands Rodney a couple of chicken legs.

Del You hungry?

Rodney Yeah.

Del Here you are. Get that down your neck.

Rodney Oh cheers, Del, great. Oi, have the police been round to question you and Grandad yet?

Del Er, no!

Rodney Good! Good! That means they ain't on me trail yet, gives me a bit of time!

Del Yeah, Rodney, I've got to explain something like – well, this is sort of like, confession time! You know that woman you met, Blossom.

Rodney Yeah?

Del Well she's mad, Rodney!

Rodney I'm not with you.

Del She's mad you know. She's well-known to the Old Bill. They don't take no notice of her.

Rodney No – you're lying to me.

Del No, no, I'm not. No I'm not, look – look, cross my heart, swear to die. You remember old man Corby, well a couple weeks ago she accused him of assaulting her! Well, I mean, he was so surprised he nearly fell off his wheelchair!

Rodney Alright then. Alright then. You explain this to me then, what were all them police doing outside the pub that night?

Del That was the – that was the mods and the skinheads, they were at it in the kebab house! Terrible scenes, for all I could hear. I mean there was chairs going through the windows, there was chilli sauce up the wall, then somebody knocked over a frying pan and the staff rest room went up in flames!

Rodney No, I don't believe you Del, you're just trying to get me to come quietly!

Del No I'm not. *(Points out of window)* Look go on then, go on – look out – look out there look, go on. Now, you see the kebab house?

Rodney No!

Del Exactly, it ain't there no more! What further proof do you need?

Rodney No Del, I don't understand this! You mean there's been no photofit pictures, no house-to-house searches, no public outcry?

Del No, none at all! Here, look, d'you want some water with yer scotch?

Rodney No! *(Del offers scotch, Rodney ignores it. Del fills his glass up with water from the tap.)* Then why did you tell me I'd go away for ten years as a special category prisoner, that they'd nicknamed me the Peckham Pouncer? That there were gangs of men roaming the street looking to hang me from the nearest lamp post?

Del For a laugh!

Rodney A laugh?

Del Yeah, it was just a bit of a wind up that's all?

Rodney Del, I haven't slept, I'm starving hungry and I've been freezing my – boots off in this tank room because of your bloody wind up!

Del You take things too seriously, that's your trouble Rodney!

Rodney I'm gonna kill you!

Del No, no, no, don't be silly!

Rodney No, really, I mean it. I'm gonna kill you right now!

Del Now just a minute! Just a minute. Alright now, I realise that I took the joke too far! And I should have told you earlier, and I'm – I'm sorry Rodney, I really am!

Rodney I'm still gonna kill you!

Del I've been all over London looking for you! I've been in more doss-houses than a tramp's vest!

Rodney So that's where you were going so late that night, eh? I saw you drive off!

Del You saw me. Why didn't you say something?

Rodney Del, I'm a desperate man on the run! I can hardly lean out and go 'Ooh oooh, Del!'

Del No, I s'pose you can't. Listen Rodney, I feel – you know, I feel really sorry for all the aggro that I've caused you. I'd like to try and make it up to you, let's say I take you out and I buy you a big slap up meal, eh?

Rodney Yeah?

Del Yeah, with the wine, all the works!

Rodney I mean look at these clothes!

Del That's alright. Come on I'll buy you a new suit.

Rodney Yeah!

Del Yeah.

Rodney Yeah, but then I'd look silly, you know

Wanted

brand-new suit and these dirty old plimsoles!
Del Don't you bloody come it Rodney! Come on, come here. Come on I'll buy a new pair of rhythm an' blues as well! How's that?
Rodney Yeah, alright!
Del That's a good boy – good boy, you know it makes sense don't you!
Rodney *(Holds his glass up for a toast)* All in the past, eh?

Del *(Clinks his glass)* All in the past cheers!
Rodney watches Del down his drink.
Rodney Look at the state of me!
Del Don't worry. You'll have a nice hot shower when you get down the flat!
Rodney Oh, I don't fancy standing under that water Del. Not after what I've been doing in it!
Del looks at the remains of his scotch and water. Clutches his stomach.

'Who's a Pretty Boy?'

EXT. THE NAG'S HEAD. DAY.

An old transit is parked at one of the meters outside the pub. The sign on it reads: 'B. O'Shaughnessy, Painter and decorator.' The three-wheeled van pulls up and parks beside it. Del alights.

Del *(Indicating transit)* 'Ere, look who's here, look, Phil the Flooter!

Rodney Oi, now don't you go winding him up! There could be rivers of blood!

Del Yeah, there will be rivers of blood. Look at the way he tucked us up with that paint last week! *(Throws Rodney the 'Out of Order' bag)* Here, just shove that on the meter. And I'll see you inside in a minute! Alright?

INT. THE NAG'S HEAD. DAY.

Seated at the bar is Brendan O'Shaughnessy. He is a well-built, tough-looking man in his mid-thirties. He speaks with a thick, Irish brogue.

Del enters and shares a word or two with some of the regulars at the bar.

Del *(To an Indian fellow with a turban)* Hello Ranji my son, how are you, alright? Here, I saw your missis on Tuesday, she's got a terrible spot on her forehead ain't she? *(To Karen)* Hello sweetheart.

Karen Alright?

Del Yeah. He's a nice bloke you know, that Ranji! He took me and Rodney over to Southall last week. They was holding this Asian song contest.

Karen Is that right?

Del Yeah, bloke called Singh won it! *(Del smiles, Karen doesn't)*

Del Singh!

Karen What d'you want, usual?

Del Yeah, Campari and diet coke please! 'Ere, how's the new guv'nor treating you?

Karen Oh, he's alright! Did you know we're having this place done up?

Del Are you? About time it was re-decorated. Last time it was done they had to keep stopping 'cos of the Zeppelin raids! *(Notices Brendan)* Look who's here, look . . . there he is, Paddy McIntee's goat!

Brendan Are you alright Del?

Del Alright? What d'you mean alright? After that paint you sold me!

Brendan Was there something wrong with it?

Del It was supposed to be apple white!

Brendan And what was it?

Del Battleship grey!

Brendan Well there's a thing! I'll tell you what. If, on my travels, I come across someone who wants their battleship painted, I'll put 'em in touch!

Del You do that! You do . . . you're a right con merchant you are aren't you, eh? I don't know how people like you can live with yourselves. Really, I . . .

Karen Oi – you know that overcoat you sold my dad?

Del Yeah.

Karen It's got a great big hump in the back!

Del Well of course, it's genuine camel-hair innit!

Karen I'll tell him.

Del Yeah, yeah, alright, alright, I'll let you off the paint, this time! Here, I thought you were going back to Dublin's fair city?

Brendan I was, till the brewery decided to have this place re-decorated.

Del Oh and you've got the contract have you?

Brendan As good as! I've arranged it with the guv'nor that mine's the lowest estimate! See you Del. Oh, by the way. If you come across young Denzil tell him I tried to phone him twice last night but I haven't got his number!

Del Right. 'Ere, just a minute, has he got your phone number?

Brendan No.

Del I'll tell him to phone you then.

Brendan Thanks.

Del Oi, just a minute – just a minute. Here, what d'you want with Denzil anyway?

Brendan Oh, he's after having me decorate his front room. It'll be a couple of hundred to take back to the old country.

Del 'Ere, well listen, when you go back to the old country don't eat any of them carrots!

Brendan Why's that?

Del They've got potato-blight!

Brendan Would you believe it . . . *(Brendan moves to the main door, as he does so Rodney enters and bumps into him. He is scared of Brendan.)* Are you alright there Rodney?

Rodney Yes, yes, triffic thank you Brendan!

Brendan Were you happy with that paint I got you last week?

Rodney The paint? Yeah, ace!

Brendan Good. I'll see you around then.

Rodney Oh yeah. Yeah, you take care of yourself.

As soon as Brendan exits, Rodney's attitude changes to one of aggression. He moves across to Del smashing a clenched fist into an open palm.

Rodney I don't know how I managed to keep my hands off him.

Del Come on, drink up, we're going!

Rodney What do you mean drink up? I haven't had a drink yet!

Del Good, I don't want you falling off the ladder!

Rodney What ladder?

Del The ladder round at Denzil's place!

Rodney Del, what the hell are you talking about?

Del We're doing up Denzil's front room!

Rodney You never told me.

Del I know, I couldn't. I mean, be fair Rodney, I haven't even told Denzil yet! Come on.

INT. A CORRIDOR IN BLOCK OF FLATS/DENZIL'S FRONT DOOR. DAY. HALL.

Del and Rodney enter through main doors.

Rodney Del, I've told you before an' I'm gonna tell you again, we should have nothing to do with it!

Del I know, but Denzil's no good at papering and painting and that sort of thing.

Rodney Well that makes three of us.

Del Look, no, you seem to forget that Grandad used to be a decorator for the council!

Rodney Del, that was in 1924. He used to go to work on a horse! And even then he got the sack after two days for wallpapering over a serving hatch! Oi, that's another thing, how d'you think Denzil's wife's gonna react after what you did to her last year?

Del Now Rodney, that's all in the past, Corinne's a sensible girl, it's forgive and forget, that's her. Anyway, give us a chance to get even with that Paddy, I'd love to take a couple of hundred off him! Anyway you never know, we might be able to get shot of that paint!!

Rodney Oh yeah! I mean everyone's having their woodwork done in battleship grey nowadays!

Del But you don't know. Corinne and Denzil may quite like it!

Rodney Del, you'll make their front room look like the conning tower of the Ark Royal!

Del Oh, shut up you tart!

INT. DENZIL'S LIVING ROOM. DAY.

The furnishing is modern but the decor is a bit old hat. Denzil is talking to a canary in a cage.

Denzil Come on Sylvester, talk to Denzil! Say Viv Richards is King! Come on, let me hear them golden tones! Come on. Ah, you stupid ras bird! *(Doorbell rings)* Alright, I'm coming.

Rodney You'll have sailors doing the hornpipe, jump-jets landing of the sofa!

Del Will you shut up Rodney!

Denzil opens the front door.

Denzil Del my man!

Del Denzil my son, how are you? *(They do a West Indian-style hand slapping greeting)*

Denzil Come in.

Del Yeah, great.

Denzil I haven't seen you for ages, where have you been?

Del Well, you know me, here, there and everywhere – ducking and diving.

Denzil Rodney, you're looking good!

Rodney *(In cool voice)* Yeah!

Denzil He's cool, I like it! I tell you, if he wasn't so white I'd swear he was black!

Del Yeah, he is white ain't he!

Denzil He's the whitest man I've ever seen in all my life!

Rodney I'm not ever so white!

Del You are! You'd make an albino look bronzed!

Denzil *(Hands out beers)* Here, grab one of these each!

Del Oh, here Denzil, Corinne ain't about is she?

Denzil No, no, she's round her sister's.

Del Oh that's alright . . .

Denzil Hey, you're not still worried about what happened are you? Come on Del, she's forgotten all about that now. Anyway, what brings you round?

Del Just passing, thought, you know, thought we'd call in. 'Ere have you had this place done up?

Denzil No.

Del No, I didn't think you had.

Denzil We're getting it decorated soon though. Corinne's been on at me for ages about it, but I'm no good at that sort of thing so I got the Irishman to do it.

Del Oh Brendan? Oh well, can't go far wrong with him Denzil! He's a good man. Here, did you hear about that house he did up in, where was it, Kings' Avenue. He made a beautiful job of it so I hear. Mind you I only saw it *after* the fire! Who's a pretty boy. He's a lovely boy ain't he! Is he yours Denzil?

'Who's a Pretty Boy?'

Denzil No, he's Corinne's, she's had him for a few years – what fire?

Del Eh?

Denzil You mean the house burnt down?

Del Yeah, but don't get me wrong, it wasn't Brendan's fault! I mean, look, I know a lot of blokes who like to have a couple of pints at dinner time. And it's very easy to forget where you left your blow-lamp!

Denzil So it was accidental then?

Del Oh yeah! It was an accident, even the coroner said so!

Denzil Coroner??

Del Yeah.

Denzil Right, that's it, I'm not having no drunken Irishman falling about my living-room with a lighted blow-lamp! No way.

Del Oh my Gawd, oh I wish I hadn't said nothing now, oh I really feel really bad about this – you know what, with Brendan being a mate an' all! Look, never mind Denzil. Look on the bright side, he might *not* burn your place down.

Denzil Yeah, well I'm taking no chances Del, I'm getting somebody else in to do the job!

Del Oh well. Well, it's up to you. I mean, as I always used to say to my customers when I was in the painting and decorating game, I used to say 'It's your money, it's your choice.'

Denzil You never told me you used to be a painter and decorator?

Del Oh yeah, yeah, it's been in the family trade for generations ain't it Rodney?

Rodney *(Preoccupied with his 'whiteness')* Eh?

Del Yeah. There you are, see. But demand got too much, we had to give it up in the end.

Denzil Listen, well, couldn't you just do this living room for us?

Del What, this? Oh no, no, no, sorry mate, no, no, you know, we've given the game up now!

Denzil Oh come on Del! Corinne's been bending my ear about it for ages. Just this one room yeah?

Del No, no. No, no, no, no, no, I'm sorry. If I do it for you I've got to do it for all the others! Haven't I?

Denzil Del, for a mate in trouble! Please!

Del Alright, just for you though!

Denzil Cheers Del, you're a pal!

Del I don't know. I don't know what it is with you. You manage to twist me right round your little finger, don't you?

Denzil When can you start?

Del First thing in the morning. £100 up front, we supply the paint and that's extra.

Denzil Done.

Del And you will be.

Denzil I'll get some more drinks.

Del Good, what about that Rodney, eh Rodney, nice little earner, eh?

Rodney *(Looking in the mirror)* I don't think I'm ever so white!

Del You are. You look like a blood donor who couldn't say no!

Corinne enters.

Corinne *(To Denzil, not noticing the Trotters.)* Hiya!

Denzil Hi hon.

Corinne *(To canary)* Hello baby, have you missed me? *(Turns and sees Del)* Denzil!! What the hell is *he* doing in my home??

Del Hello Corinne, you look as lovely as ever!

Denzil Del just popped in to say hi hon.

Corinne Did he really? *(To Del)* 'Hello'. There's the door!

Del 'There's the door.' She's a card ain't she!

Rodney is studying himself in the mirror.

Corinne And what's he doing?

Rodney I want you to tell me the truth Corinne. Am I white?

Corinne Denzil – have you and Rodney been at the funny fags?

Denzil No, honest hon, we haven't, we've just got some drinks that's all.

Corinne I go round my sister's to see how she is after having the stitches out, and I come back to find my home full of crazy people!

Denzil Oh come on babe, be friendly! Del's gonna do the decorating for us!

Corinne He's what?

Denzil Well, I blew the Irishman out, I mean I've heard bad things about him!

Corinne *(Indicating Del)* Denzil, how can you trust this man? Every time you meet him you end up drunk or out of pocket?

Denzil Yeah I know, but he's a mate!

Corinne Would a mate sell you an overcoat like the one he sold you?

Del Oh now, come on, come on, be fair Corinne, that was a very nice overcoat, looked like it was made to measure!

Corinne Yeah, for the Hunchback of Notre Dame! And what about the time he offered to do the catering for us?

Denzil Oh now don't bring that up honey please.

Corinne That was our wedding Denzil!!! What was it we were supposed to have Del? Lobster vol-au-vents, game pie, kidney with saffron rice, beef and anchovy savouries!

Rodney Philadelphia Truffles!

187

Corinne And what did we end up with? Pie 'n' chips all round!

Del Now I explained all that Corinne, didn't I? The fridge went on the blink and all the goodies went manky!

Corinne And what about our three-tier wedding cake?

Del Yeah, well, that was in the fridge with all the other gear! I mean the icing melted, it dripped everywhere

Rodney Yeah, yeah, that's true Corinne, by the end of the week it looked like a big candle!

Del *(To Denzil)* I thought you said she'd forgotten about all this!

Corinne How can I forget it? I have to live with that wedding album! The rest of my life. How many times have you seen a picture of a bride and groom cutting a jam sponge?

Rodney Oh be fair, Corinne, be fair. He only got that at the 11th hour, otherwise it could have been an eccles cake!

Corinne You want 'em to do the decorating then you let 'em. But I promise you this Denzil, if anything goes wrong I'll make you wish your mother had had a headache the night you was conceived! *(Exits to kitchen, slamming the door behind her)*

Del She's a little treasure ain't she? Come on Rodney, let's leave the love-birds alone! Talking about birds, you just make sure that Buzzby's in the kitchen tomorrow 'cos of the paint fumes. Leave the key under the mat! Cheer up Denzil, you know it makes sense! Come on, let's get out of here.

THE HALL.

Del and Rodney exit from the flat

Del That'll keep us out of trouble for a couple of days!

CORRIDOR.

Rodney Look, I know I'm white, but I'm no whiter than anyone else!

Del You are, you're whiter than Denzil.

Rodney Kunta Kinte's whiter than Denzil!

Del Here, we might be able to earn a couple of bob out of this.

Rodney How?

Del Well, we could hire you out for hauntings.

Rodney I'm starting to get my wild up.

Del Now listen, you'd do very well in one of them Mickey Mouse seances! You know where you have to appear through a thin veil of gauze. You could say, 'I am Rodney, the anaemic ghost.'

Rodney Del, Del!

Rodney snatches Del's cap from his head and exits through the main doors.

Del What, oi, that's my hat. You saucy little git. *(Del exits)*

Del *(OOV)* Oh no, it's gone under a bus now!! I'll put you under that ruddy bus . . .

INT. DENZIL'S HALL. DAY.

Del, not dressed for any form of work, enters the living room followed by Rodney and Grandad in white overalls, carrying dust sheets, ladders, etc.

Grandad They ain't got a serving hatch have they?

Del No, no, it's alright, don't worry! Alright, come on Rodney. Now get them dust sheets – all over this furniture, will you.

Grandad switches the TV on and sits in the armchair. Del helps himself to an apple from the fruit bowl.

Rodney Hey, look Corinne's left a note! 'Leave the TV alone, don't eat the fruit and stay out of the kitchen.'

Del Leave the TV alone and don't eat the fruit! What sort of people does she think we are?

Rodney Yeah, she's got us tagged all wrong ain't she!

Del 'Ere, look at the time, it's half past nine, come on Rodney, put the kettle on, we'll have a cup of tea.

Rodney Del, she said stay out of that kitchen! Now I reckon you're taking liberties!

Grandad Well, everyone's entitled to a cup of tea Rodney, I mean, it's in the Magna Carta or something!

Rodney exits.

Del That's right taking liberties, I ask yer . . . 'Ere, while you're out there have a look in the cupboard an' see if there are any Jaffa cakes going. *(To Grandad)* Go on, go on, don't worry Grandad – we'll soon have this job finished!

Grandad Yeah, soon as Rodney pulls his finger out!

Del Yeah.

INT. DENZIL'S LIVING ROOM. DAY.

Rodney and Grandad are up the ladders. Del is in the armchair, his feet up on another chair, and dialling the last few digits on the phone.

Rodney If this gets a bit much for you Del have a nice sit down, eh?

Del Yes, alright, alright, Rodney, thank . . . Go on, get going, get going, we'll never have finished at this . . . *(On phone)* Hello Ginger? Del

'Who's a Pretty Boy?'

Boy! How are you going my son? Oh no, we're all fine, no we're absolutely fine 'ere. Well, Rodney's looking a bit pale. Apart from that we're alright. How's the family? Oh triffic!

Grandad Ginger? Who's he talking to, Ginger Ted?

Rodney Yeah it sounds like it.

Grandad Has he come back from Canada then?

Del What's the weather like out there?

Rodney No.

Del The time. It's just gone 'alf past ten! No. What, is it really? Cor, go on. No, I'll tell you what, no, you go back to sleep, yeah, I'll give you a bell tomorrow, alright. And I'll leave it a bit later like. Yeah, alright, see yer pal! *(Replaces receiver)* Cor look at that, it's marvellous ain't it, eh? All the way to Vancouver and it's as clear as a bell, yeah, well, it's modern space technology innit! I've just been bounced off a satellite!

Grandad If Corinne finds out she'll bounce you off Chelsea Bridge!

Del Oi you, where's my tea?

Rodney What tea?

Del Well I asked you about an hour ago to put the kettle on to have a cup of Darjeeling, remember?

Rodney Oh Gawd, yeah, I forgot all about it.

Rodney Bloody hell, I left the kettle on the gas!!

Del Oh stone me Rodney, I don't know what's the matter with him sometimes, he seems to live in a world of his own!

KITCHEN.

Grandad Here Del.

Del What?

Grandad Supposing the steam starts the wallpaper peeling.

Del Oh that's charming that, isn't it. We come round here to do up the living room and end up stripping the kitchen!

Rodney Oh Del, I can hardly breathe!

Del You may not ever breathe again if this wallpaper's ruined!

Del *(Waving steam away with his arms)* Oh look, condensation is everywhere! Quick, get me a cloth!

Grandad Yeah I'll open the window.

Del That's right, go on Grandad. If we tidy this place up maybe she might never notice!

Rodney She might notice the kettle! *(Holds kettle up to show a hole has been burnt in the bottom)*

Del Gordon Bennett, I don't believe it! Put it back. Say nothing. She might blame Denzil.

Grandad Del Boy, come and have a look at this!

Del No, we're busy Grandad!

Rodney Look, I'm sorry about all this Del, it's just what with all the other work in there and then you . . .

Del Alright, alright, alright, Rodney. It's no good going on. It's just one of them things. Accidents will happen you know.

Rodney Yeah, cheers

Grandad Del, Del look. It's the bird . . . *(Canary is lying dead at the bottom of the cage)* He don't look very well to me!

Del That is most probably due to the fact Grandad that he is stone-dead. You dozy little twonk Rodney!

Rodney Hold on, just now you said it was an easy mistake to make!!

Del Yeah, it is if you're bloody stupid.

Rodney It might not be completely dead!

Del It might not be completely dead, it just been sautéed! What is Corinne gonna say when she comes back and finds out what you have done to her little pet??

Rodney Well I wouldn't mind seeing her face when she gets her next telephone bill.

Grandad Look at this big hole you've made in the kettle!!

Rodney Well, it's not as big as the hole you made in them Jaffa Cakes is it!

Del Will you two pack it in! We've gotta think of a way out of this!

Rodney I've got it! I've got it, we could say it was caused by paint fumes!

Del Paint fumes? Paint fumes. When Corinne comes back in here she's gonna find her kettle's been knackered, her kitchen's been turned into a Turkish bath and she's got a Kentucky Fried canary at the bottom of the cage! And we're gonna say paint fumes.

Rodney Yeah, you're right!

Del I'll tell you what we'll do, Rodney and I, we'll try and clear this place up! Grandad, I want you to go down the High Street and I want you to get a packet of Jaffa Cakes and a canary.

Grandad Where do I get a canary from?

Rodney Why don't you try the boot mender's!

Grandad Don't you get saucy Rodney, you ain't too big to get a slap round the head!

Del Oi, oi, will you stop it you two. We haven't got much time now, go on.

Grandad Well, how much is a canary?

Del Well how the bleedin' hell do I know? *(Hands him a wad of notes)* Here, look, take the lot. Go on and make sure you don't get mugged!

Del And make sure . . . And make sure you get a canary – you know and a yellow one!

Rodney Yeah, we don't want a budgie or a parrot!

Grandad No, you want a canary don't you?

Del Yes! Alright, alright, write it down for him Rodney! Write it down.

Grandad It's alright, Del, I'll remember! Yellow canary.

Del Go on and hurry up then!

Grandad A yellow canary – a yellow canary . . . yellow canary. *(Exits)*

Rodney Well I suppose it could have been worse.

Del Could it?

Rodney Well if you're gonna be like that, no!

Del I'll tell you what we're gonna do, right. If we clean this place up, polish the kettle, put a new canary in the cage, maybe Corinne won't suspect anything! Grandad's the one that worries me!

Rodney How d'you mean?

Del Oh, it's I've got this feeling in the pit of my stomach, he's gonna come back with a goldfish!

INT. THE PET SHOP. DAY.

The sign on the pet shop door reads 'L. Lombardi.' Grandad enters the shop.

Grandad Louis! I need a canary, quick!

Louis Hey Grandad, it's a long time, eh? You sit down for a while.

Grandad No. I ain't got time.

Louis You want a drink?

Grandad No, I want a canary! This is an emergency.

Louis Emergency? I've never sold an emergency canary before! I tell you what I've got for you, I gotta lovely greenfinch. She's beautiful!

Grandad No, I want a canary!

Louis You want a bird of paradise?

Grandad Is it a canary?

Louis No!

Grandad Well I don't want it then!

Louis Alright, alright, stay calm, now please what do you want?

Grandad I want a canary!!

Louis He wants a canary, I've only got one canary!

Grandad I'll take it.

Louis No, no. It's not as simple as that! This is my canary! This is Arturo, he is my own pet! *(Holding a canary in a cage)*

Grandad Can't you sell him?

Louis No, he's been with me for years! He's like one of the family, he's my own flesh and blood!

Grandad I'll give you £45!

Louis *(Without hesitation)* Okee Dokee, Ciao Arturo!

EXT. HIGH STREET/ PET SHOP. DAY.

Grandad exits with a huge cage covered with a blanket or cloth. Corinne approaches.

Corinne Hello Grandad!

Grandad *(Hides cage behind his back)* Oh, hello Corinne love. Smashing weather ain it?

Corinne Yeah! I thought you was back at the flat?

Grandad I am. What I mean is I just popped out to get something to eat!

Grandad You going home straight away?

Corinne No I've got a bit more shopping to do.

Grandad Oh good! Well, I'll see you back there later love.

He backs away from her keeping the cage from her view while grinning in a 'things couldn't be better' manner.

INT. DENZIL'S KITCHEN. DAY.

The new canary is in its cage. Rodney and Grandad study it intensely, Del is more concerned with money.

Del That thing cost £50?

Grandad Yeah. I mean, they was much cheaper in my day and age.

Del I thought they were much cheaper in this day and age . . . I mean for 50 sovs you could at least have got a bigger one!

Rodney No, no, 'cos then Corinne would have known the difference. You see to us it's just a canary, but to her it's a personal friend. We ought to double check it you know make sure it ain't got no distinguishing features!

Del You mean like freckles or birthmark?

Rodney Del if this one is different she'll twig it straight away!

Del Grandad, go down the vet's and see if you can get his dental records. Sit down, sit down. *(To Rodney)* Look soppy, unless the other one had got a dimple in its chin and a beer gut, no one's gonna be none the wiser! Now, come on, let's get back in that other room and make it look as though we've done something today!!

LIVING ROOM.

They hear a key in the front door.

Del That's her, quick, go on get up the stairs. Grandad, against the wall, go on. That's it, go on, go on, That's the way Rodney, *lots* of care! That's right, I want this to be a 100 per cent luxurious job! I want this place to look like a palace for Denzil and Corinne when the . . . *(Corinne has entered)* Oh, hello Corinne, how are you sweetheart?

Corinne I'm fine thanks.

'Who's a Pretty Boy?'

Del Good.

Corinne D'you want a cup of tea?

The Trotters No!!

Corinne Alright, don't bite my head off, I only asked if you wanted a cup of tea!

Del No, no, it's alright, Corinne. No, it's just that we're like Magnus Mackeson, you know we've started so we'll finish!

Grandad Yeah, it's sort of personal pride with us Trotters.

Corinne Okay. Please yourselves! *(Exits to the kitchen)*

Rodney She's gonna twig it, I know she is!

Del No Rodney, just, you know, just have faith in me will yer! There is no way in a million years that she's gonna suspect . . .

Corinne *(Exiting, stunned, from the kitchen)* What's happened to my canary??

Del On the other hand.

Grandad What's up love?

Del Listen to me, listen to me, if that thing's laid an egg I'm gonna kill you!

They follow her to the kitchen where she is standing by the cage. The Trotters gather round. The canary is hopping merrily from perch to perch.

Corinne Look!

Grandad Well, he seems alright to me love!

Rodney Yeah, there's nothing wrong with him!

Del Yeah look at him he's hopping about all over the place like a good 'un!

Corinne Yeah, I know, but when I woke up this morning he was dead!!

INT. THE NAG'S HEAD. NIGHT.

A few hours later. The Trotters are seated at the table. The atmosphere is all doom and gloom.

Del I never did like that Corinne.

Grandad No, fancy chucking us out like that.

Del Yeah, I mean what did she expect? How many decorating firms does she know that give you a free canary with every job?

Rodney I shouldn't imagine there's many Del!

Del No. And was she satisfied? I said, was she satisfied?

Rodney and Grandad No!

Del No, of course she wasn't.

Grandad I mean, why didn't she just bury the thing this morning?

Rodney She was too upset weren't she? ?That's why she was waiting for Denzil to come home!

Del She could of at least told us it was laying in state in the kitchen?

Rodney She wasn't there was she! That's why she left the note 'Please do not go in the kitchen.' Look she ain't blaming us for the demise of Buzzby. I think what really got up her nose was when she went to make a cup of coffee and flooded the kitchen!

Del She turned down my offer of a brand-new kettle! Didn't she?

Rodney Didn't have a tenner on her!

Del She could have paid on the weekly!

Brendan enters.

Brendan Are you alright Del?

Del Yeah, hello Brendan.

Brendan Rodney?

Grandad D' you reckon he knows Del Boy?

Del No. Corinne's not the sort to broadcast it.

Brendan I taught I taw a puddytat a cweeping up on me!

Del Mouthy cow!

Brendan I was talking to Eye-talian Louis, he told me he sold you a flea-bitten canary for £45.

Del £45?

Grandad What did I say then Del?

Del What did you say!

Brendan Don't worry Del, I've taken over the job at Denzil's flat. But it'll cost him a bit more now you amateurs have been playing around with it!

Del Do you know what Rodney, if that Brendan wasn't so big, I'd give him a right seeing to!

Rodney Yeah, so would I.

Grandad Well you're as tall as he is, Rodney.

Rodney Well you can't hit a man of that age can you.

The new governor arrives at the bar collecting glasses.

Mike You alright gents? How are you?

Del Oh, you must be the new governor?

Mike That's right, Mike Fisher, pleased to meet you.

Del Hello Mike, Del Trotter, people may have mentioned me.

Mike Yes they certainly have!

Del Well I'm a popular character round these parts. 'Ere Mike, could you just tell me is it true that the brewery are gonna have this place decorated?

Mike Yeah, that's right, in the very near future.

Del Is it also true that mouth almighty over there has got the contract?

Mike Well, let's just say he's favourite, his estimate's by far the lowest.

Rodney How much is he doing it for?

Mike Oh come on, it's confidential isn't it.

Del No, no it's not, no come on. Brendan and I, well I mean, we're like that!

Mike I don't suppose it matters who knows, he's bragging about it himself now. He reckons he'll do it for a grand.

Del A grand? And who decides which estimate to accept?

Mike I do.

Del Michael, could I have a word in your shell-like . . . *(Grins as a scheme is born)* I might be able to offer you a much better deal my son! I could get this pub decorated to exactly the same standard as Brendan, and it would cost your brewery a mere two thousand pounds!

Rodney *Two* thousand pounds?

Grandad *(Sarcastically)* That must be a tempting offer, eh Rodney?

Rodney Yeah, well, he's a born businessman ain't he?

Mike No hang about, hang about – look why should I turn down an offer of £1,000 and accept one of £2,000???

Del Because of all the advantages it has to offer, like my specialised profit-sharing scheme! Let me explain how it works. The £2,000 would be disbursed thus: There would be £500 for vous and £500 for me.

Mike What you mean I get 500 quid?

Del Oh yes!

Mike Yeah, and what happens to the thousand that's left over?

Del We give that to the Irishman and let him do the job!

Mike You've got a deal Mr Trotter!

Del Thank you Michael. *(To Brendan)* Can I have a word? Who's a pretty boy then?

Del Boy's Ten Worst Earners

(1) 25 executive briefcases. It started off badly when I clinched the deal to buy 'em for £175, before Rodders, my financial adviser, stuck his nose in and advised me to pay £200 for 'em. Bonjour Tristesse, is he a plonker. Then when it came to out them I discovered they were a consignment of rejects. No sod knew the combinations and the piece of paper with 'em on was inside the briefcases. Turns out they could only be opened by a professional safe-cracker. It made the one-legged turkey deal look shrewd. Still, that's me, I crash in and to hell with the consequences.

(2) Trotter's Ethnic Tours. Thought I was on a winner by tapping all the tourists who come to London every day. The idea was to take a coach party to discover the vibrant, exciting London that is out there. You know, all those romantic places people have heard about in fairy tales. Like the Lee Valley Viaduct, the glow of Lower Edmonton at dusk, the excitement of a walk about Croydon, including the traditional doner kebab lunch, afternoon tea in Leytonstone, shopping on Kilburn High Road. I sorted the coach, a driver – Rodney – and Grandad got up at the crack of dawn to deliver leaflets to every hotel and boarding house he could find. Trouble was, no sod turned up. It couldn't have been the fee, which was only £17. No, Grandad, the lazy old git, had chucked all 1000 leaflets down the dust chute. I could've brained him.

(3) Ethiopian mink coats. The only difference between Ethiopian and ordinary mink is the colour. These were mottled grey with delicate highlights, black and white – a great present for the enemy. True, some cynics would say the colour was Tabby, but that was no problem if people didn't have a dog. I was only asking 'em to look at it, not feed it or nothing. This was part of my infamous losing streak, when nothing was going right. Even mum's lucky rabbit didn't work, brought me about as much luck as the rabbit in fact. Made up for it though by taking Boycie to the cleaners at Poker. Our house was chez Sketchley that night.

4 Deep-sea diver's watches. These looked like a nice little earner, to be honest. Rodney loved it when I gave him one. Thing was they weren't waterproof. I told him, I said, 'You don't have to go to deep sea diving in them.' I mean, I've got a pair of them desert boots but you don't catch me in the Sahara. Mind you, they weren't shockproof either. In fact, all they could tell you was it was nearly chucking out time in Peking and how low you were on oxygen. But then what do people want for that price. Jam on it? Cordon bleu, people can be picky.

5 China cats. If you like a nice bit of fine porcelain these were the very thing for you. Revolving, demi-glazed China cats that played 'How Much is that Doggy in the Window'. Don't know when they were made, but they were circa something or other. Rodney thought they were a bit sick, a cat singing about dogs. But what do you expect for £1.25 - 'Okla-bleedin'-homa'? They weren't rubbish, they were North Korea's finest porcelain. But our two great cultures have a different attitude towards animals. We are both nations of dog lovers – the difference is that they love to eat 'em. If a North Korean came to live in London he'd think Battersea Dog's Home was a take-away. No, there's nothing they like more than Poodle kebabs or a nice Jack Russell 'n' chips. Still I managed to flog one to Lady Ridgemere that time, it went a treat with her Dresden.

6 Genuine camel-hair overcoats. These didn't go do very well at all, gave everyone the right 'ump – literally. The barmaid at The Nag's Head didn't realise the lump in the back was because they were genuine camel hair. I sold one to Denzil as well and that wife of his, Corinne, gave me earache about it, as she is prone to do. I told her the coat was made to measure, and the cheeky mare said 'Yeah, for the Hunchback of Notre Dame.' She's a little treasure ain't she? I don't know how Denzil puts up with her, I really don't.

7 Corinne and Denzil's wedding. Mind you, she's always had a grudge against me. Don't know why. Apparently, it all goes back to a tiny misunderstanding at their wedding where I, very kindly, offered to do the catering for a reasonable price. There was a great spread - lobster vol-au-vents, game pie, kidney with saffron rice, beef and anchovy savouries, Philadelphia truffles. But the fridge went on the blink and all the goodies went manky. We ended up with pie n' chips all round. Worst of all, the three-tier wedding cake melted, all the icing dripped everywhere. Corinne was not the happiest bride ever, there's a picture in their wedding album of her an' Denzil cutting a jam sponge. I only got that at the 11th hour, otherwise it would have been an eccles cake.

8 Suntan lotion. This was the fault of that dozy little twonk, Rodney. In the middle of the worst winter for two million years – with the weathermen laying odds on a new ice age – that dipstick went out and bought some Amber bloody Solaire. 500 quids worth of the stuff. He said it was an investment. Menage a trois! All them other plonkers down the market were making a right killing selling woolly hats and thermal underwear. He squandered the last of the firm's capital on something we couldn't out for at least five months. That GCE in maths has done him no bloody good. The only time it has come in handy is when I asked him to count those tins of paint.

9 Cricket bats. Now I'm not really one for the summer game, but an earner is an earner. Rodney had a bit of aggro, though, when he tried to sell these cricket bats down the Arndale Centre. I thought they'd go down a bomb because they were personally autographed by Viv Richards. Alright, it wasn't the Viv Richards, it was Davey Richard's eldest sister, but I didn't think anyone would notice, never mind riot. I thought those cricket types were meant to be gentlemanly sorts. Rodney had the bruises for weeks afterwards.

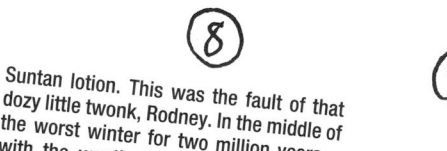

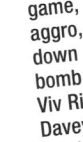

10 Washing Powder. When ol' Billy Shakespeare wrote that, 'The course of true love never runs smooth,' it wasn't just a load of old pony. I'd been seeing a rich sort, and I'd been hoping to sell her some gear. Y'see, her old man had shuffled off this immortal curl and left her a chain of launderettes in his will. But she gave me the old heave-ho and I was lumbered with two ton of hooky Persil I was hoping she'd take off my hands. I spent the next month asking people if they were all right with their whites. I felt like Danny bloody Baker.

Thicker than Water

INT. TROTTERS' LOUNGE. NIGHT.

Rod and Grandad are in the armchairs watching TV.

Grandad I remember this film when it first came out. It was in the middle of the war. I remember half-way through it there was an air raid and we all had to run for the shelter.

Rodney I bet you all hated the Kaiser that night eh?

Grandad What's the matter with you you moaning little git??

Rodney What's the matter with me?? Grandad, it is Christmas night and I am stuck in with . . . *(Is about to say 'you' but stops)* I am stuck in – here, watching a film that the Germans tried to bomb!

Grandad I know what you mean Rodney, I feel exactly the same.

Rodney I thought you liked this film.

Grandad I do! It's just that it's Christmas night and I'm stuck in with you!

Rodney Thank you very much.

Grandad Well stop yer whining then! I don't know why you didn't go out with Del.

Rodney He's seeing *Lassie* again ain't he?

Grandad You don't wanna let Del hear you refer to her as a dog!

Rodney Well he must know! When she come back from Tenerife it took him two weeks to get her out of quarantine.

There is a ring at front door bell. Rod and Grandad refuse to budge.

Grandad Was that the bell Rodney?

Rodney It sounded very much like it Grand-father!

The bell rings again.

Rodney There it goes again! Whatever could it mean?

Grandad It means there's someone at the door you lazy little toe-rag! Go on Rodney, it might be Del popped back for something.

Rodney reluctantly moves to door.

HALL.

Rodney exits from lounge shouting to front door.

Rodney I suppose you've run out of Bob Martins again!

He opens door to Reg Trotter, Del and Rodney's father, Grandad's son. Reg is fifty-six-ish, and wears a stained and dishevelled suit, he has a two-day growth of beard and carries a small and battered case. He has a pathetic air about him. At first he appears meek and helpless.

Rodney, who hasn't seen his father since he was five, doesn't recognise him.

Rodney Yeah?

Reg Oh, good evening sir.

Rodney looks over his shoulder.

Rodney Oh, what d'you want?

Reg I'm sorry to bother you but I wonder if you could help me?

Rodney Yeah, hang on. *(Reaches into his pocket)*

Reg No, I don't mean like that! I'm looking for a family called the Trotters.

Rodney The Trotters?? What makes you think the Trotters live here?

Reg It's written on your bell.

Grandad enters hall.

Grandad Who is it? Ro . . . Reggie??

Reg Hello old 'un, how you diddling?

Grandad It's really you!!

Reg It's me alright! Long time, eh?

Grandad Too long Reg, too long! *(Embraces Reg)* Oh it's good to see you, it really is!

Rodney You two have met before have you?

Grandad I'm sorry, let me introduce you. Reg, this is Rodney. Rodney, I'd like you to meet your Dad.

Rodney Pleased to meet you!

INT. TROTTERS' HALL. NIGHT.

The front door opens and Rodney enters, followed by an irate Del.

Del Right – where is he?

Rodney *(Stops Del)* Will you just calm down a bit! Before you go in there shouting and bawling, just you remember, he's still our father!

Del Well you and me could be spending the night in the orphanage by the time I've finished!

Rodney Del, he's not the man you remember. I mean, you've told me how he used to be a right Jack the lad, all flashy shirts and gold cuff-links, a bit like . . . a bit like some of the blokes down the pub! But he's old now Del. He's dishevelled and pathetic, he seems kind of, frightened! Just bear it in mind will you, please!

Del Alright, Rodney, alright.

LOUNGE.

Rodney and Del enter there has been a trans-formation. Reg has showered and shaved, he wears fresh trousers, one of Del's killer-diller shirts and also one of his medallions.
He has a large scotch in one hand and one of Del's cigars in the other. He is now full of confidence and once again the master of the house.

Reg Del Boy! Good to see you son. Pour yourself a drink.

Del looks at Rodney who just shrugs.

Del I had a shirt like that once!

Grandad Yer Dad had a bath and a shave Del, then he found he was low on clothes!

Del He'll be low on teeth before he's much older! *(He takes cigar and drink from Reg's hands)* Get yer things together and sling yer hook!

Reg Alright, if you wanna talk it over I'm listening!

Grandad He only wants to stay for one night Del!

Del When he closed that front door in 1965 he closed it for good!

Rodney Have I got any say in this?

Reg Let's hear what Rodney's got to say.

Del What's to be said Rodders? You know what he's like!

Rodney No I don't!

Del Of course you do, I've told you often enough!

Rodney Yeah and that's all I know! I wouldn't mind the opportunity of judging him for myself.

Reg *(To Rodney)* I never raised a hand to your Mother Rodney except in self-defence!

Del What do you mean 'judging him'? He deserted you when you was five years old! And not just you. He walked out on his own Father! In all that time he didn't even know if Grandad was dead or alive!

Rodney Well we're never that sure! Alright so he left, but he's back now!

Del After eighteen years! I mean what happened, did his watch stop? Stone me Rodders, we see Hayley's Comet more often than him! *(To Reg)* Just go will yer?

Grandad Look, whatever you think of him Del, he's still my son. All he wants is a bed for the night!

Del I don't believe you two! Can't you see what he's doing? He's playing on your sympathy and yer family loyalty! He is evil! That is the devil standing there!

Grandad Don't be so bloody stupid Del! That's your own Father!

Del Yeah, but he sold his soul for an ounce of Old Holborn years ago! *(To Reg)* Give me one good reason, just one, why I shouldn't chuck you out by the scruff of the neck?

Reg I can't think of one Del. I'm not proud of what I did Del. I'm ashamed – ashamed and sorry! Just recently I've been laying in that hospital bed, night after night, re-living the moment I walked out of here! It hurts Del Boy, it hurts!!

Grandad *(Rises)* Hospital bed? What's wrong with you Reggie?

Del Something serious I hope!

Rodney Can't you wrap up for five minutes!

Del Don't be fooled by him Rodney. He's had everything from Galloping Lurgy to Saturday Night Fever! I was doing some homework once and I asked him what a cubic foot was. He didn't know but he tried to have a week off work with it!

Grandad What's wrong with you Reggie? Come on son, you can tell me and Rodney.

Reg Well, a few months back they took me into hospital, just for a few routine checks.

Del Jackanory Jackanory.

Reg I'm telling you the truth this time Del, look! *(Produces a medical card headed 'Newcastle Infirmary')*

Del Newcastle Infirmary??

Reg I've been living up there for the last year or so.

The medical card convinces del that the story is true.

Del *(More concerned)* So, what's wrong with you?

Reg *(Struggling for the right lies)* Er, well they discovered I had this em, hereditary blood disorder! It's called . . . well it's a medical word!

Grandad A long one Reggie?

Reg Ooh yeah Dad!

Rodney Can they cure it?

Reg They're not sure! I just live in hope. Hope's about the only thing I've got!

Rodney Oh come on . . . Dad! These doctors can perform miracles nowadays. Try'n be brave eh? Come on, be bra . . . Hereditary??

Reg Eh?

Rodney You said it's hereditary! That means I could have it as well!

Del *(Starts laughing at Rodney, the laugh dies)* And me!!

Reg *(Grasping the opportunity)* Yes. Well this half the reason I dashed down here! The doctor said I had to warn my children immediately!

Thicker than Water

Grandad What have they got to do? Go for blood tests?

Reg As soon as possible! I've done me best by you this time ain't I Del Boy?

Del *(Still stunned)* Yeah. Thanks!

Reg I'm feeling a bit weak. I think I'll climb in. 'Night boys.

Rodney/Del 'Night!

Reg And Merry Christmas.
Reg exits.

Grandad D'you think I'll have to have a blood test as well?

Rodney No, it's hereditary, it means it's passed on not back!

Del *(Rises)* You're most probably the carrier! What a right blinding Christmas this has turned out to be! Some people get wise men bearing gifts – we get a wally with a disease!

Grandad You two had better get straight down that hospital after the holidays.

Rodney Yeah, but with these National Health cuts we could wait for ever!

Del No we won't. I'll phone Dr Becker first thing in the morning.

Rodney He's not gonna see us on Boxing Day!

Del Oh yes he will! He owes me a favour. See, his ten-year-old son thinks the bike that Santa brought him came off the back of a sleigh. Me and the doctor know better! Hang on, where's Dad sleeping?

Rodney I offered him my bed.

Del Tch, you're a great big softy ain't yer!

Rodney Well, he's not very well and all. You'd have done exactly the same thing wouldn't you?

Del Yeah, of course I would!

Rodney Good, 'cos he turned my bed down and chose yours! Nite! *(Exits)*

Grandad *(Fearing his bed may be in danger)* See you in the morning Del! *(Exits)*

TROTTERS' LOUNGE. STUDIO. EVENING.

Grandad is watching TVs. Rodney is on sofa.
Del enters from bedroom.

Del Where's the ghost of Christmas past then?

Grandad He ain't here Del.

Del You mean he's gone?

Grandad Only down the pub for the New Year's Eve do.

Del Oh, I thought it was too good to be true.

Grandad You talk about your own father as if he were an alien. You seem to think of him as ET.

Del No I don't Grandad, ET went home!

Grandad A couple of letters arrived for you two this morning. I think it's the results of your tests!
We see the two brown envelopes.

Del *(To Grandad)* Oi, these have been opened!

Grandad Well that must have bin your Dad.

Del Well the saucy . . .

Grandad You can't blame him Del. I suppose he was too worried to wait for you!

Del Yeah, well alright then! Well go on then Rodders, what's yours say?
Rodney slowly lifts the results card from envelope.

Rodney *(Great relief)* All clear! All clear! I got an all clear my son! Well don't look so cheerful about it Del!

Del I ain't had a look at mine yet have I?

Rodney Oh no, sorry!
Del lifts his results card from envelope. He studies it then with a horrified expression looks to Rodney and Grandad.

Grandad What – what's it say Del?

Del *(Can barely raise his voice above a whisper)* It says – it says, result of test . . . negative!
Rodney and Grandad are left stunned by this news. Rodney now reacts.

Rodney Negative?

Del Yeah!

Rodney Well that means all clear you plonker!

Del Does it?? Thank Gawd for that! I thought it was a medical term for curtains! Why don't they bloody well put all clear then?

Rodney Oh who cares? Listen, we gonna have a drink to celebrate?

Del Yeah I need something Rodders!

Rodney Right, I'll go'n get changed.
(Exits)
Grandad sits at table.
Del exits to hall.

Grandad That's funny!
(Del re-enters)
Your bloody group's AB – Rodney's is A.

Del It can't be can it! He'd have the same blood group as me!

Grandad *(With growing suspicion)* That's what I thought!

Del Giss 'em here! *(Checks reports)* Look, my blood group is AB . . . and Rodney's blood group is A! A! – Well how's that wally managed to get himself a different blood group?
Grandad gives him one of those 'I'm saying nothing' looks.

Del Look, we're brothers right? So we should have the same blood! I mean we had the same mother, we had the same fath . . . er!!

Del Are you suggesting Rodney's got a different dad?

Grandad I'm saying nothing! But I always remember Maisie Turner!

Del Maisie Turner! Who the hell's Maisie Turner?

Grandad She married Bernie. Remember Bernie? Used to pull the stall out down the market.

Del Yes yes! What about 'em?

Grandad Well she had two sons. One by Bernie, the second by some bloke she met on a charabanc trip to the lights! Bernie found out and divorced her.

Del How did he find out? Blood tests?

Grandad No, the youngest boy was half-caste! Now I ain't saying anything against yer Mum, Gawd rest her soul. But if you put two and two together . . .

Del You come up with Rodney!

Grandad You remember just before your Mum announced that Rodney was on his way, her and yer Dad were having lots of rows. She started going out with . . . new friends.

Del You mean that trumpet player from the Locarno?

Grandad I thought he played the saxophone!

Del No that was the other one! Yes, yes it's all beginning to make sense now! Remember when Rodney joined the Boys' Brigade? He was a natural with that bugle weren't he?

Grandad And look at him Del. He's sort of . . . *(Raises hands to indicate height and shape)* different!

Del *(Rises)* Oh my Gawd! Why did this have to happen eh? I mean this of all things!
Rodney, now wearing suit, enters.

Rodney Alright?
Del and Grandad put on big false smiles.

Del Yes, wonderful Rodney!

Grandad Couldn't be better Rodney!

Rodney What's wrong?

Del Nothing, honest! Everything's brill!

Rodney Good! I wonder where Dad is?

Del That's exactly what me and Grandad were wondering . . . I mean there's no telling which pub he'll be in!
Del looks Rodney up and down.
Rodney checks his flies.

Rodney What?

Del Just admiring the suit Rodney. New is it?

Rodney No, I bought it five years ago, it weren't new then! Look, something's wrong, now is anyone gonna tell me??

Del Oh I suppose you've got a right to know Rodney! Although I want you to understand that it doesn't make a blind bit of difference! Everything will still be the same! Rodders, that man you call Dad – ain't!

Rodney Ain't what?

Del He ain't yer Dad!

Rodney What is it, a joke?

Del No, I wish it was Rodney!

Rodney I don't get you. Of course he's my Dad!
Del shakes his head.
But he must be, Grandad introduced us!

Del Just take my word on it Rodney, let's leave it at that!

Rodney *(Stands)* No I will not leave it at that! You are trying to tell me that that man is not our father?

Del No he just isn't *yours*! You've got a different blood group Rodney, look!

Rodney *(Reads the reports)* So I've got a different blood group, what does that prove?

Del It proves you're a whodunnit Rodney! There's more to it than just that. You see, just before Mum fell for you, she'd met a new 'friend'! This trumpet player from the Locarno!

Grandad And a saxophone player!

Del Yes, thank you very much Grandfather!

Rodney What are you trying to tell me. My Dad was a band?

Del No Rodney, no! Just the brass section!

Rodney No I don't believe it! I mean the way you've always described Mum she'd never do anything like that!

Del Well normally she wouldn't! It must have bin a sort of one off!

Rodney Great! I can't wait to fill in my next passport application form. Mother's Name: Joan Mavis Trotter. Father's Name: Herb Alpert and the Tijuana Brass!
Reg enters from hall. He is in an angry mood and, as we shall discover, knows the truth.

Grandad Been for a drink Reggie?

Reg Yeah I've bin for a drink Dad. I've got bloody good reason to ain I!

Del What are you moaning about now?

Reg I can read Del Boy! Earlier this morning I happen to notice them medical reports! I thought that's funny, different blood groups! So just to be on the safe side I checked my group with me donor's card, then I checked yer Grandad's group with his old army records. And what do I discover? We've got a Lone Ranger in the family!
Del and Rodney look at each other.
I'd just like to know who the hell Tonto was! If your Mother was alive now I'd kill her!

Del You what?? . . .
Del tries to get at him but is obstructed by the table or chairs.
Reg backs away from him.

Thicker than Water

Reg Try'n see it from my point of view Del! How would you like to have a son who you love and care for, who you fetch up as yer own, only to find years later that he's a mystery?

Del Love and cared for him? You walked out and left Rodney when he was five years old! You didn't care if he had shoes on his feet or grub in his belly!

Reg What do you keep bringing Rodney into this for? You're the mystery!

DAY. THE NAG'S HEAD.

Del is seated alone at bar. He is reading the News of the World, unable to concentrate, he folds paper up and places it on the bar. He reaches into inside pocket and produces the now very crumpled medical report card. He studies it for the thousandth time and shakes a frustrated head as he still cannot find an answer.

Del *(Mumbling to himself)* AB. Why?

Karen You alright Del?

Del Eh? Yeah, I'm alright darling.

Karen I thought you'd have been in last night for the New Year's Eve do! The rest of the family were here.

Del Were they? No, I er, I got a bit involved elsewhere.

Karen Your Dad's a giggle ain't he?

Del Yes Karen, that man is one long grin!

Karen He got up on the stage and sang a couple of Adam Faith songs.

Del You're kidding? What after all these years he's *still* doing the Adam Faith impression?

Karen He was good! He sang 'What do you want if you don't want money?' and, what was the other one? Oh yeah, 'Someone Else's Baby'.

Del 'Someone Else's Baby'?

Karen Do you want another one?

Del Yeah, Grand Marnier and grapefruit.

Karen moves to optics. Del studies the medical report again.

The main doors open and Reg, Rodney and Grandad enter. Rodney is wearing 'the suit', Grandad is in his funeral gear and Reg is wearing Del's sheepskin. They are all laughing at some outrageous story that Reg is telling.

Rodney Oh leave off Dad!

Reg It's true I'm telling you!

Grandad What, he still didn't know it was you?

Reg He didn't have a clue. I saw him years later and he still had the scar!

They now reach the bar and react as they see del on the opposite side.

Rodney Alright Del?

Del Yeah triffic Rodders.

Grandad Why didn't you turn up last night for the New Year's Eve party?

Del I er, I had a bit of business to attend to. . . . *(To Reg)* Can I get you a drink?

Reg That's nice of you, but I'm with my family.

Del *(Through clenched teeth)* Well I'll get yer family a drink as well! Karen, give them people over there a large brandy each.

Reg Cheers. *(To Rodney and Grandad whilst gesturing towards table)* Anyway let me finish the story.

Rodney Well I'm gonna have a chat with Del.

Reg Oh! Alright Rodney – don't be long, eh!

Reg and grandad move to table. Rodney moves round bar and joins Del.

Rodney You didn't come home last night?

Del No, I stayed round at Trigger's place. I'm fed up with kipping on that settee.

Rodney Is that the only reason?

Del Yeah – yeah that's the only reason! *(Reg laughs)* You and the old man are seeing a lot of each other ain't yer?

Rodney Yeah. I think he's trying to make up for all the lost years.

Del Oh yeah! *(Referring to the suit)*. You bin out this morning?

Rodney Yeah. He took me to the zoo.

Del Oh yeah . . . alright was it?

Rodney Yeah, you know, animals and . . . things!

Del Good! Listen, I don't wanna spoil the surprise, but I saw him up Selfridges on Friday checking out the Action Men!

Rodney has to grin at this picture.

Rodney Hey Del, why don't you just come back home, eh?

Del How can I Rodney, with him there? He'll never let me forget that I'm a – a Lone Ranger!

Rodney Del he hasn't mentioned it, honest!

Del Maybe not to you, but every time he passed me on the landing he kept shouting hi ho silver!

Rodney Look, I'm sure I can remember that during a biology lesson at school, the subject of genetics came up, and the teacher said that the children of the *same* parents can have different blood groups!

Del Thanks Rodders – you're trying to cheer me up. You're a diamond Rodney!

Rodney No, I mean it, Del. Why don't you get some advice on the subject. Go and see Dr Becker.

Del I couldn't Rodney!

Rodney Why not?

Del Because then he'd know!! He's been the

family doctor for years. He treated Mum when she was ill. I don't want him thinking 'that' of her! No, it's all clear cut, Rodney, it's oeuf sur le plat as the French say! The rest of the family are A, but I'm AB!

Rodney So what does it matter eh? You're just one letter out. That's nothing is it? The only difference between us is a B.

Del And you know what B stands for!

Reg *(Callls)* Rodney! You gonna play cards with us?

Rodney Yeah, in a minute! You wanna game?

Del No not me Rodney. He's bound to find something to wind me up!

Rodney No he won't Del! Look, if you just sit over here on your own he'll think he's beaten you! C'mon. He who dares wins!

Del *(Rises)* Alright then!
Del and Rodney move across to table where Reg and Grandad are sitting.
Reg is shuffling a pack of cards.

Reg Take a seat Rodney . . . oh, does your friend want to play as well?

Grandad Now just lay off him will you Reg!

Del Don't say anything to annoy me!

Reg Oh as if I would! He's touchy ain't he? Don't know who he gets it from. Right, what shall we play?

Rodney Before you say it, no, we don't wanna play Happy Families!

Reg Alright. We'll play Pontoon . . . *(Deals one card to each player)* One for me, Dad, Rodney, Kimasabi.

THE TROTTERS' LOUNGE. NIGHT.
A disgruntled Rodney is watching the TVs.
Grandad is clearing the table.
Reg is looking for a cigar u/s of TV.

Reg You got any money Rodney?

Rodney I gave you my last fiver this morning.

Reg Dad?

Grandad You know I'm skint!

Reg Well why didn't you nip Del for a few quid?

Grandad I can't ask Del Boy for money after what's happened!

Reg No I don't suppose you can! Rodney could!
Del enters from hall. This is the old Del, rubbing his hands together and full of the old bounce.

Del Alright Grandad, Rodders. Evening Reginald! Stick a pizza under the grill Grandad.

Grandad You in for the night Del?

Del Yes I'm in for the night!
Grandad exits to kitchen.

Reg Good! *(To Rodney)* We can all have a family

sing-song this evening. *(To Del)* You can join in if you like!
Del allows the jibe to wash over him and simply smiles through it.
Reg exits to kitchen.

Del *(To Rodney)* What's up with you?

Rodney Well, earlier on I showed him my GCE certificates. He said he was proud of me! Then he went and wrote a bet on the back of one of 'em!

Del He wrote a be . . .! He's the devil Rodney!

Rodney I'm beginning to think you're right!

Del I tell you one thing, *you* were right!

Rodney Was I?

Del Oh yes. I took your advice Rodney!

Rodney Good! What advice was that Del?

Del *(Winks to Rodney)* I'll tell you in a minute!
Reg exits from kitchen.

Reg *(Shouting back at grandad)* Well there were four in there earlier!
Grandad follows Reg in.

Grandad Yeah, and you drunk 'em all!
Reg is angry and frustrated at not having a drink. He now puts on a sweet smile for Del's sake.

Reg You don't fancy popping down the off-licence and get a few drinks in do you Del?

Del No!

Reg Oh!

Del No I'm off the drink for the moment. I went and saw Dr Becker this evening.

Reg *(Slightly alarmed at this news)* Yeah? Why what's wrong with you Del?

Del *(Aimed at Reg)* Well, for the last week or so I've been suffering from this pain in the arse! So while I was there I asked the doctor to give me a second blood test, just to double-check things. But he told me there was no need because, as you so rightly said Rodders, a person's blood group doesn't mean a thing! A mother and father could have three children, and them kids could all have different blood groups!

Reg That's rubbish! I mean what does he know anyway.

Del Oh he knows a lot! Like he knows that my blood group is A!

Grandad Well why's he write AB on the results?

Del He didn't! Someone else added the B!

Rodney Now I wonder who could have done that??

Reg Well it must have been someone at the clinic having a joke! I mean the letters arrived by post. The envelopes were sealed!

Grandad Until you opened 'em!

Reg I was only trying to make sure that my two

Thicker than Water

boys didn't have the same *(Becoming weaker)* illness as me!

Del Oh yeah, Dr Becker was very interested in your 'blood disorder'. So he phoned the Newcastle Infirmary just to find out what exactly was wrong with you. And what do you reckon?

Rodney They'd never heard of him!

Del Now how d'you know that Rodney?

Rodney I'm clairvoyant!

Del Well they ran his name through their computer but they didn't have a patient called Trotter. *But*, they had a *porter* called Trotter! But he left two weeks ago with 57 blankets, 133 pair of rubber gloves and the chief gynaecologist's Lambretta!

Reg I don't feel all that well!

Del I mentioned that and Dr Becker recommended lots of fresh air, new surroundings and plenty of exercise – like a long . . . brisk . . . walk!

Reg Did he? Yeah maybe he's right. *(Checks watch)* Is that the time? I really must be on my way!

Del So soon?

Reg Don't wanna outstay me welcome Del! I'll

. . . I'll get my things together! *(Starts to exit to bedroom area).*

Grandad The crafty, conniving little . . .!

Del Alright! Hey Grandad, I hid a bottle of scotch under the sink.

Grandad Good boy Del. *(Exits to kitchen)*

Rodney I'm glad he's going! He's made this a right miserable Christmas for us all.

Del All over now Rodders. Before you know it we'll be back to just how we used to be.

Grandad enters from kitchen.

Grandad Del Boy, I've burnt yer pizza!

Del See what I mean!

SERIES FOUR

Happy Returns

DAY. A NEWSAGENT'S.

Behind the counter is Debby. She is a very pretty cockney girl in her late teens. She is serving a couple of old ladies. Del and Rod enter. Her and Rod exchange smiles.

Rodney Hello Debby.

Debby Hello Rodney.

Del *(Mimics them)* 'Hello Debby.' 'Hello Rodney!'

Rodney Shut up will yer! *(Moves away to look at magazines)*

Del *(To old lady)* Hello darling.

Old lady Been up to the hospital, love?

Del Yeah, we just come back from there now.

Old lady How is he?

Del Moaning! The doctors 'ave been trying to take his hat off, but he wouldn't have none of it! They gave him an X-ray yesterday, and they found out he got a pulled ligament in the wallet, and severe fraying of the trilby!

Old lady Give him my love.

Del Ooh, he ain't up to nothing like that!

Rodney *(To Del)* This is awkward!

Del What is?

Rodney Well, I wanted to buy one of my adult art magazines.

Del What's the problem?

Rodney Debby's serving! We've been seeing each other, sort of thing! She might think I'm odd!

Del She's gonna find out sometime Rodney.

Rodney Get it for us would you Del?

Del Alright, alright, Rodney!

Rodney Cheers Del, you're a pal!

Del *(To Debby)* Here you are, darling, look *Exchange and Mart,* oh, give me one of yer dirty magazines darling will you.

Debby Yeah, which one d'you want?

Del *(Calls)* Which one d'you want Rodney? *(Rodney exits, embarrassed)* Just the *Exchange and Mart.*

DAY. THE ESTATE.

Del and Rodney are walking past a tower block (Zimbabwe House).

Rodney 'What one d'you want Rodney?' I don't believe you sometimes!

Del I wish I'd had my Polaroid with me! You should've seen your face!

Rodney You've embarrassed me!

Del I've embarrassed you! Oh, it's alright for some bird to think I'm a pervo though is it?

Rodney You ain't taking her out, are you?

Del Don't know, I ain't made me mind up yet!

Rodney Oh, listen to him, will you!

Jason, a little nine-year-old, fair-haired boy dashes past them and towards the road.

Del Oi, oi, oi! *(Grabs kid by collar as he is about to run into the road)* Hey, what's your game, eh?

Jason My Mum said she's gonna kill me!

Rodney Well she won't need to will she? You'll kill yourself running across the road like that.

Del No, haven't you ever heard of the Green Cross Code?

Jason But I'm gonna be killed in a minute!

Del No you're not. She's not gonna kill you!

Jason She said she was!

Del Yeah, I know, but mums say lots of things they don't mean, don't they, eh. *(Takes 50p from his pocket)* Here, tell you what. Here you are, go and get yourself an ice-cream at the Paki's on the corner.

Jason Oh thanks mister . . . what about my brother? *(He indicates a little West Indian kid standing a few yards away)*

Del Ah, who's he?

Rodney That's your brother is it?

Del Is it? *(Produces another 50p)* You'd better get him one an' all hadn't yer?

Jason Ta mister.

Del Oi just a minute, why was your Mum telling you off?

Jason I let down the tyres on that motor.

Del and Rodney turn to see the three-wheeled van with all the tyres deflated.

Del I'll kill you!

Rodney Oh bloody hell Del, look at that.

Del Little scallywags round here ain't they!

Rodney Well it's nothing to laugh at Del, I mean, look at it!

Del Oh no, they're only kids though ain't they? I used to do the same sort of thing when I was a nipper. I remember me and Albie Littlewood we let a couple of tyres down once. Should have seen the palaver it caused. Everyone had to get off the bus! They were the days! Still, I'll go round the garage and get the foot pump for you.

Rodney Yeah right. Oi, hold on what d'you mean you'll get me the foot pump?

Del You ain't 'alf getting independent ain't yer?

Alright, go and get your own foot pump.

Rodney That's more like it.

NIGHT. THE ESTATE.

Del, dressed to kill, exits from his tower block. He walks to the van, gives a cursory examination of the now inflated tyres, jumps in and drives off. As the van nears Zimbabwe House we see little Jason sitting forlornly on the kerb. Del pulls into the kerb and alights.

Del *(Sits next to him)* Alright Champ? What you doing?

Jason I'm running away from home.

Del Running away from home are you? Ain't got very far have you?

Jason My Mum said I mustn't cross the road!

Del That makes it difficult then dunnit? Where's yer brother?

Jason His Dad said he has to go in.

Del I see. Well I reckon that's the best place for you to go, an' all, don't you.

Jason She'll kill me!

Del No she won't, listen, they were my tyres that you let down weren't they? So I'll come home with you and I'll tell your Mum that I *asked* you to let my tyres down 'cos I wanted to see how long it would take my brother to pump 'em back up again! How's that?

Jason Alright then.

Del There, good boy, see, you know it makes sense! Come on then. You'd better get in 'cos the bogey man will be coming soon.

Jason I've seen the bogey man!

Del Have you? What's he look like?

Jason He's got a funny old hat and wears pyjamas under his mac!

Del That's not the bogey man, that's my Grandad!

INTERIOR OF FLATS.

Del and Jason approach a door to one of the flats.

Del Right, come on then. Is this it? This your house?

Jason Yeah.

Del Is it? Right, now don't you worry. She'll be as sweet as a nut, I'll guarantee. Just stay there.

June Where have you been? I was just about to call the police. Look at the state of you. Go and put your pyjamas on. I'll see to you in a minute.

Jason exits into the flat.

Del *(Recognising voice)* Does that go for me an' all?

June You what? Del? Cor, I don't believe it!

Del Junie, how you going?

June I'm fine!

Del Oh great.

June You don't still live on the estate, do you?

Del Well yeah, over the way there, you know Nelson Mandela House. Here when d'you move in here?

June Six weeks ago, there don't stand out there, people'll think you're the tallyman. Come in.

Del Right. 'Ere hang about. What about the old man?

June Erh, he's gone away for a bit.

Del enters.

Del Oh gone away for a bit. Anyone we know?

NIGHT. JUNE'S LOUNGE.

Del is seated having a glass of beer. June enters from the bedroom.

June I le's soundo already. Didn't even want a bedtime story tonight.

Del He's a little scallywag ain't he?

June Ooh, he's a right handful! D'you know what he did today? He only let the tyres down on some crappy old three-wheeled van over there!

Del Yeah?

June I think he misses his Dad!

Del Yeah, I used to miss my Dad – till I learnt to punch straight! When's the old man get out?

June *(Pouring herself a drink)* Oh, he's not in prison Del! No, he works on an oil-rig.

Del Oh I see! When are you expecting him back then?

June About six months if he keeps his nose clean.

Del smiles at her subconscious slip. June, realising her mistake, smiles as she concedes the point.

June I'd have popped over and seen you, but I didn't think for one minute you'd still be living here! D'you remember what you used to say to me all those years ago?

Del I can remember quite a lot of funny things I used to say to you!!!

June I don't mean 'that'! You used to say, 'This time next year I'll be a millionaire!'

Del Did I? What a wally! Well, we were much younger then weren't we, I mean, anything seemed possible in them days. 'Ere, 'ere, how long ago was it that, you know, you and I, well, we stopped seeing each other?

June Must be . . . 19 years now!

Del 19 – 19 years!

June It's longer than that in fact. We broke up in September 1965. Just after Albie Littlewood's funeral.

Del That's right! Yeah, that's right, cor, we were

Happy Returns

a right little team up till then, weren't we?

June What, the famous four! You and me, Albie and . . . what was his girlfriend's name?

Del Deirdre.

June That's it, Deirdre.

Del Deirdre! Do you know I often wondered what would have happened if he hadn't been coming over to see me that night. You know, if he hadn't taken the short cut across the railway lines, you know – if his bike hadn't accidentally fallen on the live rail. I mean what's the point of talking about ifs! If me brother had been a bird he would have been me sister, wouldn't he, eh?

June Oh you had a kid brother! Rodney. How is he?

Del Oh, he's alright alright. He's just reached that awkward age. You know he's a bit like a trifle!

June What d'you mean, mixed up?

Del No, no, he's thick and fruity!

June Oh and what about your Grandad?

Del Oh Grandad, well, he's not too fit at the moment, he's laid up in Dock but I sometimes think you know given half a chance he could be thick and fruity an' all.

June I take it you never got married!

Del Me, no, no, no, I just get engaged! 'Ere, talking about that . . . you still got my engagement ring?

June Yeah, you don't want it back do you?

Del No, no, no, I – you know I was just wondering that was all! No, I was just wondering like, 'cos you know, I – I could always whip over home and get my Sheena Easton LP, if you like!

June Not much point, I haven't got a record player.

Del Oh, I'll have to keep my eye open for one! For you, won't I, eh? Don't worry, you leave it to me, alright. *(They go to kiss but the doorbell rings)*

June Oh Del. Oh! 'Ere Del, help yourself to a drink.

Del Yeah, thanks Junie. *(June exits to the hall. He moves over to examine a picture or ornament)*

June *(OOV)* Oh come in love. *(June enters from the hall)* It's alright. It's a friend of my daughter's. *(Calls)* Debs, it's for you! She's got that bloody radio on again, she'll wake Jason! *(Exits)*

Rodney enters from the hall door. He is carrying a Duran Duran LP and a bottle of brandy. Del spots him. Rodney, unaware of Del's presence, wanders around getting the feel of the place. He smiles licentiously as he tests the softness of the settee. Del observes all this. Rodney, believing himself to be alone, relaxes and starts to play 'Joe Cool' in that optimistic way of someone who thinks they will soon be getting their end away. He studies himself in the mirror and has a very confident air. He undoes another shirt button, pulls shirt wider apart to reveal more of his chest, has second thoughts and does the button up. He now flicks his hair to give a more natural look, as he does this he sees Del's reflection in the mirror. He freezes and turns his head away and closes his eyes really tight as if he thinks he is seeing things. Rodney then looks back at the mirror and Del's reflection is still there. Rodney turns.*

Del You little plonker!

Rodney What are you doing here?

Del What am I doing . . . What are you doing here?

Rodney Well, this is where Debby lives, ain't it. That bird from the paper . . . 'Ere – 'ere you're not trying to . . .

Del No I am not! Leave it out, I'm a friend of her Mum's!

Rodney Yeah, when d'you meet her then?

Del 1964.

Rodney What and you've only just come round to see her?

Del No, I was engaged to her, soppy!

Rodney What, another one! Stone me Del, you've ben engaged more times than a switchboard ain't yer!

Del Don't you start getting lippy. *(Indicating record)* I don't know what you brought that round for. 'Cos they ain't got a record player!

Rodney *(Opens it up to show the sleeve is empty)* That's alright, I ain't got a record!

Del You are a saucy little git you really . . . *(Sees bottle of brandy)* Oi, I've got one of those at home on the sideboard!

Rodney Yeah alright, well I'll get you another one tomorrow, won't I.

June enters.

Del Yeah you better . . . Junie, June, you'll never guess who that is? That is *little* Rodney!

June You're kidding!!

Del No, straight up!

June I don't believe it! The last time I saw you, you were about that high! How old was he Del?

Del Then, about two and 'arf!

June Anyway it's very nice to meet you again Rodney.

Rodney And you . . . *(Not sure how to address her, but wanting to ingratiate himself)* Ma'm.

Del Leave it out Rodney, you're making me feel quite Tom and Dick you really are.

June You can call me June.

Rodney Oh thank you.

June Debby won't be a minute, she's just putting some clothes on.

Rodney Oh she needn't bother!

June What??

Rodney No, no, no, I mean, you know, she needn't bother to put on anything special. I was thinking actually . . . er . . . if you two wanted to go out and you know chat about old times and all that, well you know I'm sure me and Debby wouldn't mind baby-sitting.

June What d'you think Del?

Del I daren't tell you what I think Junie! Come on let's go out for a drink! Shall we.

Debby enters wearing dressing gown.

Debby Hello Rodney.

Rodney Debs!

Del You alright darling?

Debby Oh watcha.

June You two met?

Debby Yeah, he came in the paper shop this morning for a dirty magazine.

Del 'Ere no, actually . . . listen . . .

Rodney Er, I was just saying you and me wouldn't mind baby-sitting if Del and yer Mum went out for a drink!

Debby Yeah, that suits me.

June I'll get my coat. *(Exits to hall)*

Del Yeah alright, darling, 'Ere I'd do that up if I was you, you'll get a cold on yer chest!

Rodney It's Debby's house, she can do what she likes. Do you want a brandy Debs?

Debby Brandy eh? You're splashing out ain't yer?

Del Yeah well of course he's celebrating ain't he?

Debby Celebrating what?

Del Oh, hasn't he told you. He's just heard from the clinic! He's got an all clear.

THE NAG'S HEAD.

Del and June are seated at the table. Del raises his glass, containing one of his concoctions.

Del Well, there you go. Old times, eh?

June *(She raises her glass)* Old times.

Del Cheers.

June Cheers.

Del 'Ere, Junie, I hope you don't mind me asking, but there's always been something that's been bothering me.

June Look, if it's something from the past let's leave it.

Del No, no, it's just that I always wondered why it was that you left so suddenly like that?

Without a letter, or a word, nothing!

June It's personal Del! All over and done with now, right? Can we talk about something happier.

Del Yeah of course! What they put your ol' man in prison for?

June He stole some watches.

Del Oh I see! Ain't still got 'em have you?

June We're getting a divorce when he comes out. The marriage never worked right from the start.

Del Oh, I don't know! It seemed to have lasted quite a while!

June Oh no, we've only been married seven years!

Del Seven years?? But no Debby. She must be . . . Oh I'm sorry!

June He's not Debbie's father.

Del No, no, sorry I didn't mean, you know! I wasn't trying to . . .

June 'Ere, it's her birthday next week. We're gonna have a little party. D' you fancy coming?

Del Yeah, not half, I'll have some of that! 'Ere, I'll have to get that record player for you a bit lively won't I.

June Oh yes.

Del 'Ere what do you want? Another one, same again.

June Oh, I'd love another one. Same again.

Trigger Here you go Del.

Del Cheers Trig.

Del *(To barmaid)* 'Ere you are, Maureen, same again love, that's a Singapore Sling and half of Strongbow.

Maureen Coming up.

Del What you up to Mickey?

Mickey I've just come from evening school. I'm learning Aikido.

Del Really? Go on then, say something.

Mickey Eh?

Del Say something in Aikido.

Mickey No, it's not a language Del. It's a martial art! I had a fight with five blokes last night!

Del What was it, a pillow fight? Leave it out you ain't got a mark on you son!

Mickey That's because I wiped 'em all out with Aikido.

Del *(Sniffing the air)* Can you smell that? What is that? Sheep is it? It's cows? No, no, I know what it is. It's bullshit!

Mickey I'm telling you the truth Del!

Del Leave it out Mickey. I can always tell when you're lying.

Mickey How?

Del Yer lips move! 'Ere you are, love.

Happy Returns

How much is that?

Maureen *(With drinks)* £2.49.

Del Right cheers.

Maureen Cheers. Where's Rodney tonight?

Del Rodney? He's round at that young Debby's place.

Maureen Oh yeah.

Mickey Well I don't know what he sees in her! I mean, she's just a kid ain't she!

Maureen She's 19 next week mouthy!

Del What about your 19th birthday Mickey?

Maureen Yeah.

Mickey What about it?

Del Well, you looking forward to it, are you? *(To Maureen)* 19, 'ere just a minute that Debby. That young Debby. She can't be 19!

Maureen She's 19 next Wednesday, Del.

Mickey Yeah, tell you what, I've got an invitation to her 19th birthday party.

Del That's impossible!

Maureen What's the matter with you Del?

Del 19 an' 'alf years ago, me and Debbie's Mum . . . *(He looks across at June, who smiles back at him)* Oh my Gawd!

Maureen What are you talking about Del?

Del Eh?

Maureen What you talking about?

Del No, no, no, nothing! No it's alright, no, forget it. Just no – forget it.

Returns to table with drinks.

Del Junie, Junie, I know why you left so suddenly all them years ago!

June Do you?

Del Pot pourri . . . Why didn't you tell me?

June I couldn't. I didn't know how you'd take the news.

Del I'm just going to the bog.

NIGHT. THE GENTS.

Trigger is just doing up his flies as Del enters.

Trigger Alright Del Boy?

Del *(Desperately pacing the floor)* No, I'm not alright Trigger! I don't know what I'm gonna do! I just don't know what I'm gonna do!

Trigger Hang on Del Boy, leave it to me! *(Bangs on cubicle door)* Come on hurry up, we've got an emergency out here!

Del No, no, no, not that Trigger!! Come here. Listen to me. D'you remember about 20 years ago, I was – I was engaged to that bird right.

Trigger What June? Yeah, remember her! She's back on the estate now.

Del That's right. Well she's got a – she's got a 19-year-old kid.

Trigger Yeah, Debby, works in the paper shop.

So what?

Del So what? Me and June broke up about 19 an' 'alf years right ago. That means that she was expecting her at the time! Which means Debby is my kid!

Trigger But she's a pretty girl!

Del Of course she is! I mean, look – look, that's a chip off the old block, ain't it, eh?

Trigger Didn't June say nothing to you at the time?

Del No, not a dicky bird!

Trigger You sure Del?

Del Well, I would have remembered something like that Trigger, wouldn't I?

Trigger I mean, you sure she's your kid?

Del Yeah, she's gotta be, I mean . . . she's gotta be!

Trigger 'Ere, the little cow short-changed me the other day!

Del Well that is it then innit!

Trigger You told the rest of the family?

Del No, no, I've only just found out meself! Gawd knows what Grandad and Rodney are gonna say when they . . . Rodney!! Rodney!!

NIGHT. JUNE'S LOUNGE.

The lights are low. Rodney and Debby are laying on the settee. They are about to kiss. The hall door bursts open and the lights come on.

Del Put her down Rodney!!

Rodney You're back early ain't yer?

June, seething with Del, enters.

June Yeah, ain't we just, eh? I'm going to bed Del!

Del No listen, June we've gotta talk.

June Look, I knew this was how you'd behave, that's why I didn't tell you! I'll see you around sometime . . .

Del No listen, June.

June Maybe! *(Exits)*

Del Look we've gotta talk . . .

Rodney You've made another lasting impression then I see!

Del Come on get up out of there, come on. Give Debby some air. The poor girl can't breathe.

Rodney Yeah, alright! You want another brandy Deb?

Del No she don't!

Debby I'll make my own decisions thank you!

Del Yes, of course! Of course, it's just that if you have too much to drink you might make yourself sick! And you don't wanna be ill for yer party next week. *(To Rodney)* It's Debby's birthday next week, Rodney.

207

Rodney *(Quietly to himself)* Yeah, I thought it was mine tonight!

Del I'll get you a nice present shall I – dear? I'll get you a solid gold watch, eh? A couple of hundred quid at least!

Debby Alright!

Rodney What's your game Del?

Del Just feeling generous that's all. Come on, Rodney I'll give you a lift home, come on.

Rodney Give me – Del, we only live 50 yards across the precinct!

Del I know that – I know, but when I came back tonight there was a load of muggers hanging about!

Rodney Oh yeah?

Del Yeah.

Rodney Well perhaps I'd better go Debs – I've gotta be up early!

Debby Alright then . . . *(To Del)* Goodnight.

Del *(Paternally)* Goodnight . . . Pleasant dreams. *(Exits)*

Rodney Well, goodnight Debs.

Deb Goodnight.

He puts his arm around her, he is just about to kiss her when Del's hand appears and pulls him out of the door by the scruff of his neck.

Del Come on Rodney!

STUDIO. NIGHT. THE TROTTERS' LOUNGE.

Del enters from the hall switching the lights on as he does so. Rodney follows.

Rodney Now just what is your game Del? All that, 'Shall I buy you a nice gold watch shall I, dear?' And 'Sweet Dreams!'

Del I was just being friendly, that's all!

Rodney You're trying to pull ain't yer?

Del *(Offended)* I am not trying to pull her! What d'you think I am, some kind of sicko or something?

Rodney Well, you're trying to interfere between me and Debbie ain't yer?

Del I am not trying to interfere, Rodney. Now listen. Rodney, look, I just . . . I don't think that you two are . . . 'right' for each other!

Rodney It's got nothing to do with you! Me and Debby think we're right for each other! As a matter of fact we're thinking of getting engaged!

Del You're what? You can't get engaged to her Rodney. No, what I mean – what I mean, is, what I mean is you're too young!

Rodney I'm 24 Del! By the time you was my age you'd been engaged to every bird this side of the water! No, you're just jealous ain't yer? You can't stand the thought that I might end up with a nice little wife.

Del You're gonna end up with a nice little stretch if you ain't careful! Rodney, you mustn't get engaged to her!

Rodney You give me one good reason why I mustn't??

Del *(Takes a deep breath)* Because she's my daughter! That's why!

Rodney Debby – is – your – daughter?

Del Yeah!

Rodney No. It's not real! No, it's not happening to me! I'll tell you what, I'm in the middle of a bad trip! I'm gonna wake up in a minute!

Del I've worked it out on the calculator Rodney! Me and June broke up 19 and 'alf years ago. It's Debbie's 19th birthday next week! You're the one with the GCE in Maths, you work it out yourself!

Rodney Well maybe she met someone after you!

Del No, she was born a couple of months after!

Rodney Well then she was premature!

Del Premature?? She'd have had to have been bloody instant, Rodders!

Rodney But – she's a pretty girl!

Del I know that – I can see Mum in her! Come on . . . cheer up Rodney.

Rodney Cheer up?? Del I've just met the first girl in my life who really means something to me, and it turns out to be my bloody niece!

Del Alright, Rodney. Come on, that's why I had to tell you, you see, 'cos this sort of thing it ain't allowed – it's . . . well, it's incense! Say you had got married to her – you can see what sort of confusion that would have led to, I would have been your father-in-law!

Rodney Bloody hell!

Del Yer mother-in-law would have been yer aunt, yer wife would have been yer second cousin – Gawd knows what that would have made Grandad – the fairy godmother I should think.

Rodney Del, are you absolutely certain of this?

Del Yeah, well, certain as I'll ever be. Just think eh, Rodney, young Debbie has grown up all these years 'an she never never knew that I – I was her Daddy! Do you think I ought to tell her?

Rodney Eh, no, no, that could come as a great disap . . . great shock.

Del No perhaps you're right!

Rodney Could you do something for me Del.

Del Yeah sure.

Rodney You go and see June. Right, you go and see her and you find out if it's definite – definitely definite!

Happy Returns

Del Yeah, tomorrow – I definitely promise!
Rodney Well I'm going to bed. I bet I'll have a nightmare! I bet I'll have a nightmare where my wife keeps calling me Uncle Rodney, eh?

STUDIO. NIGHT. JUNE'S LOUNGE.

Lights are low and the TV is on. June enters followed by Del.
June Alright Del, you've got five minutes! Say what you have to say and then go!
Del Is Debby in?
June No, she – she's gone over her Auntie's. Look, if you've come here to dig up the past again, you can forget it!
Del Come on Junie, there are things that have got to be discussed!
June What sort of things?
Del Look Junie! I know!
June So you said last night!
Del Well then? Are you gonna tell her or shall I?
June Tell her what?
Del Oh come on, June. Don't play the innocent with me. Tell her – that I am her father!
June You're her . . . Oh Del! When you said you know, I thought you *really* knew! Debby's not your kid.
Del Yes she is. No, come on, she was born six months after we broke up! Well she's gotta be – I mean, if I'm not her father, then who is??
June Albie Littlewood!
Del Albie Littlewood? Albie Littlewood? My bestest friend in all the world? The greatest pal a bloke could have, and all the time he was doinking my bird?
June That's why I left!

Del How could he do it to me? We were blood-brothers!
June We were just kids – we were just playing games. That night he died on the railway lines – he wasn't coming to meet you in the pub. He was coming to meet me!
Del For nigh on 20 years I've carried that guilt around with me, it's hung round my neck like some great two-ton medallion!
June Well, well, now you're free of it ain't you? Albie didn't take the short-cut for you.
Del It's not the reason why I was feeling guilty! 'Cos if he had made it across the railway lines that night he wouldn't have met me in the pub! I wasn't in the pub! I was round at his bird Deirdre's place!
June You were with Deirdre??
Del It's alright, June. We were only playing games, only playing games.
June Why you dirty little toe-rag.
The front door closes and Debby enters.
Debby Hello Mum.
June Hello love.
Mickey Pearce enters.
Debby I've brought Mickey back, we're going to my room to listen to the radio.
Del Good evening young Michael! Alright?
Mickey Watchya Del! I just met Debby walking across the estate. So I thought I'd better make sure she got home safely.
Del Yes! So you thought you'd escort the young lady back to her bedroom. Yeah, I know Mickey, I know only too well my son! Goodnight to you all! Oh Mickey, make sure you don't take the short cut across the railway line.

Strained Relations

In the small road that runs through the cemetery there is a parked cavalcade. The funeral director and a couple of assistants are lounging around, smoking and talking quietly. Laying against the wall of the chapel are 15 or so wreaths. There is one very large, very gaudy wreath. The wreath floral message reads simply: 'Grandad.' On a card pinned to the wreath is the handwritten message: 'Always in our foughts, love Del-Boy and Rodney.' In the distance a group of mourners are standing around the graveside. The group of Del, Rodney, Trigger, Boycie, Mike, the vicar, two old ladies, cousin Stan, representing the north London branch of the family, his wife Jean and Uncle Albert, who is in his mid-sixties and is Grandad's brother. The words of the ceremony cannot be heard clearly, the vicar's voice is just an indiscernible drone. The ceremony ends and the mourners begin to move away from the graveside, forming small groups as they do so.

Del turns and moves away alone. He is wearing a black three-piece suit, a black silk tie which is held in position by a large diamond tie-pin, plus the compulsory 'Big D' and the medallion. He wipes his nose on a hankie, takes a deep breath and regains his 'take it on the chin, never let 'em see you're hurt' composure. Trigger approaches.

Del Alright Trigger?

Trigger Yeah, I'm alright . . . em . . . well . . . em . . .

Del Yes, it's alright, I know Trigger, I know mate. You going back to the flat are you?

Trigger Yeah I'm coming back.

Del (Hands him some keys) Yeah, do us a favour will yer, go on open up, I've got one or two things – bung the vicar a couple of quid, that sort of thing. Them three over there, they're the North London branch of the family. Make 'em welcome will you, keep your eye on 'em.

Trigger Yeah, sure.

Del Thanks, cheers Trigger. (Trigger exits)

As Del is about to move off he notices that Rodney is standing alone at the graveside. We sense Del's frustration, he wants to explain to Rodney, to conjure up some words that might ease his pain and sense of loss. He is about to

move back to Rodney when he changes his mind and decides to leave Rodney alone with his thoughts.

Old lady I love a nice funeral.

Del Why don't you hang about, there's two more after this!

Del hands the vicar a few pound notes. Del doesn't want to talk to the vicar, he just hands him the money and moves off. The vicar nods his gratitude. Grandad's hat is hanging on the daimler symbol on one of the cars. Del smiles at it lovingly, he picks it up and caresses it. He moves back towards the grave. Rodney is still at the graveside, staring blankly into the grave. He becomes aware two gravediggers are waiting to fill in the hole.

Rodney Sorry!

Del appears at Rodney's side with the hat. They share a nostalgic and emotional smile over the hat. Del gives the hat to Rodney, he gestures that it is Rodney's privilege to drop the hat into the grave. Rodney drops the hat gently into the hole. Del squeezes Rodney's shoulder.

Del We'll leave the car shall we, eh?

Rodney We'll have a nice little walk, eh?

Del Yeah, come on . . . let's have a nice walk eh . . .

As they are about to move away Del shoots a threatening finger at one of the gravediggers who is about to hurl a spadeful of earth into the grave.

Del Oi, gently!!!

Mike is standing near the cars. Boycie approaches him.

Boycie Well Michael. How's business in the pub?

Mike Not bad Boycie. Not bad. Oh, you didn't hear did you? Thursday night some berk nicked me cigarette machine!

Boycie Never! What about that sonic burglar alarm Del Boy sold you?

Mike Oh yeah, they nicked that an' all. (Laughs)

The vicar and the undertaker look in Boycie's direction. Boycie looks embarrassed at his lack of respect. Nearby Stan, Jean and Albert are standing next to a car.

Jean Just make some excuse Stan. Say we're in a hurry or something!

Stan But it's a funeral love!

Jean We've gotta get all the way back to North London. If we don't leave now we'll cop the rush hour!

Stan Look, I don't wanna go back to their flat either Jean, but I'm family!

Albert I wanna go back there – he was my brother!

Jean It's got nothing to do with you Uncle Albert so stay out of it!

Stan What do you mean he was your brother!? You and him didn't talk to each other for years!

Albert Me and your Aunt Ada didn't talk to each other for years but she was still me wife!

Stan Come on, we'll go back for 'alf hour, show our respect. Anyway, we'll only have him whining all the way home!

Stan And don't you dare light that pipe in my car!

Albert puts his pipe in his pocket. We see the vicar buttoning up his overcoat. One of the ladies approaches.

Old lady It was a lovely service vicar.

Vicar Thank you very much. Thank you. *(Looks to car bonnet)* Has anyone seen my hat? It was here.

DAY. THE TROTTERS' LOUNGE.

Boycie, Trigger and Mike are standing together drinking, telling jokes and generally having a laugh. A disgusted Rodney is observing all this from a distance. Stan and Jean are standing together sipping their drinks, feeling rather out of place and waiting for an opportunity to leave. Uncle Albert is seated next to them, drinking rum. Del enters from the kitchen carrying a tray of sandwiches.

Del Right, 'ere you go. Here you are look, come on, come on! Get stuck in there will you.

Rodney *(To Del)* Where's the cake and candles Del?

Del Eh?

Rodney Don't matter!

Mike So the Chinese bird says to him, 'Listen I ain't cooking at this time of night.'

Del, Boycie and Mike laugh. Trigger's not so sure.

Trigger Is that true?

Boycie Have a day off Trigger!

Trigger moves towards Rodney.

Rodney Well everyone seems to be enjoying themselves, eh Trigger?

Trigger Yeah, it's a good do Dave!

Rodney Yeah, I don't believe you mob sometimes. *(Searches pocket for cigarettes)* Have

you got any fags on you Trigger?

Trigger produces an array of different packs of fags.

Trigger Yeah, what sort d'you fancy?

Rodney Anything'll do!

Trigger *(Hands him a pack)* Here you are, keep 'em, I've got loads!

Rodney Cheers!

Trigger Cheers Dave.

(Trigger moves off. Albert arrives to get a drink)

Albert Rodney, innit?

Rodney Well, it is when Trigger ain't about, yeah.

Albert Uncle Albert – well *great* Uncle Albert really! I'm yer Grandad's brother.

Rodney Yeah, yeah, he told me about you. But, you know, I don't take no notice of that sort of thing!

Albert No, no, it's best not to son! Shame really, me and him lost touch with each other years ago. I spent most of my life at sea, you know, Royal Navy, Merchant. D'you know, I was torpedoed five times!

Rodney Yeah?

Albert Yeah! D'you know what the crews nicknamed me?

Rodney Jonah?

Albert No! No, they didn't call me Jonah – not many of them! They used to call me Boomerang Trotter, 'cos I always come back!

Rodney Triffic!

Del approaches Rodney.

Del 'Ere Rodney, do me a favour will you. You know them batteries out there in the hall. Stick 'em out in the corridor in case someone falls over 'em.

Rodney *(Angrily)* Yeah, right!

Mike 'Ere, Del, come here, come here son, listen to this one.

Del is frustrated. He wants to follow and explain to Rodney, but again senses that there are no words that can do this. He returns to the others. Albert has heard all this and looks to the hall with genuine concern for Rodney. Stan and Jean arrive at the drinks cabinet.

Del What is it, what? Go on.

Stan *(To Albert)* Well, we'll have one more drink and get on our way, alright?

Jean I don't like the people over this side of the river! They're not as nice as North Londoners!

Albert You don't know what you're talking about girl! I was born round here!

Jean Need I say more?

Albert You couldn't wish to meet a more

Strained Relations

honest and generous people as South Londoners!

Jean Honest and generous! I noticed they didn't have a whip round at the cemetery!

Albert Well they couldn't could they! Someone nicked the vicar's hat!

Stan Del . . . Del . . . do you . . . remember us, cousin Stan.

Del Stan yes, of course I remember you. . . . Yeah I was gonna come over and have a chat with you.

Stan This is my wife, Jean.

Del Jean, yeah, hello Jean. How are you?

Stan Uncle Albert.

Del Oh uncle Albert, is it? Hello.

Albert Your mum asked me to be your Godfather.

Del Yeah? I thought Uncle George was my Godfather?

Albert Yeah, that's right. Me and George spun a coin.

Stan George lost!

Del So what are you up to these days Stan? Are you still poncing round in the insurance game, are you!

Stan I'm still in the insurance business, yeah, and doing very nicely thank you!

Jean We've got our own place all paid!

Del Oh really what you got, a maisonette?

Stan No – it's a mobile home actually!

Del Oh, you've a caravan?

Jean It's got two separate bedrooms, a breakfast bar and a combined toilet and showroom!

Del It's a big caravan?

Jean Well this is just a council flat isn't it?

Albert Yeah, but there's no chance of this getting a puncture is there!

Stan He's been living with us for 18 months now! He only popped round to borrow a screw-driver!

Jean If I hear another nautical yarn I'll swing for him!

Stan Someone suggested an old folks' home!

Del You can't do that, he's family!

Stan Oh we didn't consider it. Did we love?

Jean No, of course not! Well not at them prices anyway!

DAY. CORRIDOR/HALL.

Albert is seated. Rodney enters from hall with a battery.

Albert Are you alright son?

Rodney Yeah.

Albert You ever been on board a ship Rodney?

Rodney Yeah, yeah, when I was a kid. Grandad took me.

Albert I see. Did he ever take you down and show you the engine room?

Rodney No, no, it was only the Woolwich ferry! He got sea-sick. We had to go home via the Rotherhithe tunnel.

Albert I used to work in the engine room – maintenance, that sort of thing. Cor, them boilers took some looking after and all! D'you know what the most important gadget is in the engine room?

Rodney The lock on the porthole?

Albert No – they don't have port . . . *(Forgets it)* It's the safety valve on the boiler! You get a build-up of pressure and the safety valves ain't working – bang – the whole gubbins explodes! You've gotta find a way of releasing the pressure, that's what's happening to Del! He's releasing the pressure – laughter's just his safety valve!

Rodney I don't think it's right! Them people laughing in there! I ain't laughing . . . I ain't today, I ain't laughing tomorrow, I don't wanna laugh for the rest of my life.

Albert Well, as long as you're happy son.

DAY. THE LOUNGE.

Del is alone at the drinks cabinet. He is deep in thought, remembering the past and the events that led to this day. It is a snatched moment of quiet contemplation

Mike I'm away now, boys. So I'll see you later.

Voice In your trousers, Michael.

Mike I'm off now, Del alright son.

Del Yeah. 'Ere, thanks for coming Mike. *(Checks watch)* 'Ere, you're doin' a bit of a flyer ain't you?

Mike Well, as a sign of respect for yer Grandad I've decided to open the pub early.

Del Oh that's very nice of you Mike, appreciate the gesture! Thanks.

Mike Oh about the booze. It comes to 86 quid.

Del Please Mike, don't discuss money now, I mean you'll be offering me a discount for cash next won't you!

DAY. THE CORRIDOR.

Albert is spinning Rodney one of his naval yarns.

Albert I saw the periscope half mile off starboard. I saw the wash through the torpedo's fins. It caught us at the . . . at the pointed end. Wallop! Up it went. Foam, flame, fine smoke, burning metal! As soon as it happened I thought to myself, 'Hello, we've been hit.'

Rodney I s'pose you get to know the little signs, eh?

Albert Yes!

The flat door opens and Mike and Del exit.

Del Yeah, okay Mike, 'ere listen, don't worry about that burglar alarm that got nicked. 'Cos Trigger knows where he can get hold of another one. Alright, so I'll whip it round to you okay.

Mike Okay, cheers Del. See you Rodney.

Rodney Yeah, bye.

Mike exits.

Del Thanks Mike, yeah.

Albert Del, I've just been telling young Rodney about my days in the navy. *(To Rodney)* I don't know why you don't join up?

Rodney Yeah, well you've just given me five good reasons!

NIGHT. THE TROTTERS' LOUNGE.

The same day. The guests have all gone. Rodney sits alone at the table, he remains motionless, deep in thought for a few seconds. Unconsciously, he looks in the direction of the TVs and armchair. He quickly looks away again. Del enters carrying a tray of food. Del, in a vain attempt to cheer Rodney up a little bit, is being falsely buoyant.

Del Here we are. Here we go Rodney, look speciality of the house. Sausage unt ala the old mash! There you go.

Rodney I ain't really all that hungry Del.

Del Oh come on Rodders! I've been an hour out there in that kitchen cooking this! Go on, try it at least.

Rodney I can't eat that Del . . .

Del What's wrong with it?

Rodney Well, it's nothing like Grandad's is it? It tastes nice.

Del I tried to mess it up, honest I did, Rodney! Do you know, I just didn't have his knack! He was taught to cook at one of London's biggest establishments.

Rodney You're kidding.

Del No, straight up, he was a trainee chef at the Ear, Nose and Throat Hospital! Now, come on then. *(Picks up a quarter full bottle of scotch)* Come on, let's give this an 'iding? Shall we?

Rodney Yeah, why not?

Del Well it's just – it's just us two now bruv!

Del Me and you against the rest! They don't stand a bloody chance do they, eh?

Rodney Del, someone's trying to pull our lavatory chain!

Del Yeah, I know – I know it's an awkward one innit? The secret is one slow pull and then a

sharp one! Like that. There you go. There it is see.

Rodney What I'm saying is, right, we're the only ones in the flat and someone's trying to flush our lav!!!

Del No, yeah, well maybe it's a washer! Or something!

Rodney How can a bloody washer pull the chain???

Del I don't know do I! I am not a scientist or something? Am I? No, it's alright, it's probably, you know quite simple. You know nothing. Nothing at all really. Where's my bloody hammer.

Rodney Del!

Del turns and sees the door opening. He raises the weapon above his head. Albert, in a hungover condition, enters.

Albert Oh my bloody head!

Del Gordon Bennett!! You nearly had your head caved in then! You soppy old sod!

Albert I had too much of that cognac! Where is everyone?

Rodney Well, they've all gone home! It's 'alf past 11 at night.

Del Where the hell have you been?

Albert I conked out on one of them beds, my belly's going round and round. Oh my Gawd! 'Alf past 11. D'you think Stan and Jean'll be worried about me?

Del Worried about *you*? Yeah, well of course they'll be worried about you! Look, we can't drive you back there tonight now, no, me and Rodney have had enough to drink!

Rodney What about a mini-cab then?

Del No, you won't get one now Rodney, they'll be busy washing out their back seats! I reckon you've got to stay the night and I'll drive you back to North London tomorrow. Rodney, you go and lock up, oi, make sure you bring them batteries in 'fore someone swipes 'em.

Rodney No one's gonna nick them Del!

Del Really, how d' you think we got 'em?

Albert I appreciate this son.

Del Oh forget it, I'll get you a pillow and some blankets, and you can yourself a bed there on the chaise longue, alright?

Albert 'Ere, I won't be able to sleep on there Del! I need a good firm mattress, I've got a curvature of the spine see!

Del Really? It's all them years sleeping in a hammock I suppose is it!

Albert Yeah, I wouldn't be surprised! *(Indicating Grandad's room)* I might as well kip down in there, eh?

Del No, no, you can't go in there. That's my

Strained Relations

Grandad's room!

Albert Yeah but – I'm his brother!

Del Yeah, that don't make no difference. Only me and Rodney are allowed in that room! That room is gonna remain exactly as he left it! That room is going to be a shrine dedicated to the memory of my Grandfather.

Albert I understand Del!

Del No, we'll just have to think of something else that's all. Listen, if I get the big mattress out of Rodney's room I can put it down. No, I'd never get it through the door would I.

Rodney enters from the hall carrying batteries.

Rodney Oi, where'd you want these then?

Del Oh, sling 'em in Grandad's room for now will you Rodney.

DAY. THE TROTTERS' LOUNGE.

There is a heap on the settee, it turns and yawns and reveals itself as Rodney.

Rodney Alright? D'you get Albert home safely?

Del Yes, I got him home safely alright Rodney!

Albert, carrying a canvas navy hold-all, enters behind Del.

Albert Morning son!

Rodney Morning. You're back?

Albert Boomerang Trotter. Always comes back!

Rodney What happened?

Del What happened? I'll tell you what happened, I drove him all the way back to North London. Right through the bleedin' rush hour! And what did we find when we got there? Stan and Jean have moved!!

Rodney Moved? What do you mean moved???

Del What do I mean? They hooked the caravan on the back of the Cortina and they've had it away!

Albert *(Referring to hold-all)* This was lying where the caravan once stood! It's just my clothes and a few personal belongings.

Rodney You mean that's all you've got in the world?

Del No, we've gotta go back tomorrow to pick up his parrot! How could they do this to me?

Rodney That is disgusting innit? I mean, deserting him like that!

Albert Yeah! It ain't the first time it's happened either!

Rodney I mean, I, something, there should be a law or something against that!

Del Yeah, I know. All I wanna know is where they've got . . . 'Ere. What did you say just then?

Albert I said it ain't the first time it's happened either!!

Albert D'you remember yer cousin Audrey? I went and stayed with her and her husband Kevin for a year. One day they sent me down to Sainsbury's with the shopping list. When I come back they'd emigrated! Not a dicky bird to me though! Then there was young Gillian, you know, Patsy's girl. I went over there to give her a bit of comfort 'cos her husband was on nights. Six months later she sets fire to the house. She got three months medical supervision for that! I can remember thinking as I stood on the ledge and jumped into the fireman's net 'That's gratitude for you.'

Rodney I ain't 'alf got a funny feeling Del!

Del So have I Rodney! I feel like a turkey who's just caught Bernard Mathews grinning at him!

Albert takes a couple of items of clothing out of his hold-all.

Albert What shall I do with these then?

Del stuffs them straight back in the hold-all.

Del I tell you what you ought to do with these shall I, put 'em in here right. In they go, in there, 'cos you're not staying here.

Albert No, of course not! Just for a couple of days that's all!

Del No, no, no, not for a couple of days, not for one day! There's a seaman's mission down there at St Katherine's. You go down there, go on.

Albert Well, I thought I'd just have a look at the local paper, and find meself some digs.

Del Yeah, that's a good idea Uncle. They'll have a local paper down at the mission! Now, go on sling your hook.

Albert Yeah – alright Del! Don't mind if I have a quick cup of tea do you?

Del No, go on there's a flask of cold tea out there and some vol-au-vents from yesterday. Go on, you can have them.

Albert Cheers son!

Exits to kitchen.

Rodney has been watching in disbelief. He now smiles thinking Del is joking.

Rodney What are you doing, winding him up?

Del Yeah, yeah, I'm winding him up aren't I. I'm winding him up!

Rodney Del, he only wants to stay for a couple of nights, and get himself sorted out!

Del He's a Trotter Rodney.

Rodney We're Trotters!

Del Yes I know, but we take after Mum in nature. He's from Dad's side of the family! You know what they're like. You offer 'em a cup of tea and they think you've adopted 'em. Look at that time when Dad came round here he wanted to stay 'one' night! Took us nigh on a fortnight to get rid of him!

Rodney Uncle Albert might not be like that!

Del Oh leave it out Rodney! You've heard him yourself when he was telling us about that time he came round the Cape of Good Hope, he was three months on the same wave!

Rodney I don't believe you Del, I do not believe that you of all people, could! *(Storms to door)*

Del Where do you think you're going?

Rodney I'm going down the caff, I'm gonna get some grub and some better company! *(Exits to hall. Del flops down in the armchair. Hall door opens, Rodney enters.)* I'm gonna put some clothes on first! *(Exits to bedroom)*

> *Del touches the arms of Grandad's armchair affectionately. He leans forward and switches the colour TV on. Rodney enters.*

Rodney You've changed Del!

Del Yeah, well it's about time you did, come on, we've got to go down the market later on.

Rodney I mean your personality has changed! I've seen a side of you I never knew existed!

Del You don't understand Rodney!

Rodney You're right about that Del! I mean, look at you last night, you was laughing you was drinking, I mean, why didn't you just put yer Boney M record on Del, we could have had a good old knees up! It was Grandad's. . . . How could you get over it so easily?

Del Get over it? What a plonker you really are Rodney. Get over it. I ain't even *started* yet!!! Ain't even started bruv! And d'you know why? Because I don't know how to!!! That's why I've survived all my life with a smile and a prayer! I'm Del Boy ain't I! Good old Del Boy – he's got more bounce than Zebedee! 'Ere you are pal, what you drinking? Go on! Hello darling, you have one for luck!!' That's me, that's Del Boy innit? Nothing ever upsets Del Boy. I've always played the tough guy! I didn't want to, but I had to and I've played it for so long now, I don't know how to be anything else! I don't even know how to. . . . Oh it don't matter! Bloody family! I've finished with 'em! What do they do to you, eh? They hold you back, drag you down, and then they break yer bloody heart!

Rodney *(Whispers)* I'm sorry. *(Exits to bedroom)*

> *Del remains in the chair staring at the TV, refusing to cry. Now, like an act of defiance, he switches the black and white TV on as well. He sits back in the chair, grips his bottom lip firmly with his teeth and stares at the two TVs.*

NIGHT. THE NAG'S HEAD.

> *Del and Rodney, now suited up, enter.*

> *Rodney sits at the table, Del goes to the bar. This is the old Del, bouncy and full of the old Bel Esprit. Maureen is behind the bar.*

Del Alright there, alright. Hello darling.

Rodney I'll be over there.

Del Okay, alright. Alright pal, what you drinking? Give him one. I'll have a Malibu and tonic with some lime and 'alf of lager, please darling.

Maureen In the same glass?

Del No, in separate ones if you don't mind!

Maureen Well I don't know do I, it might have been one of your erotic cocktails, Del.

Del Saucy little cow that one, ain't she, eh?

Mike Alright Del?

Del Yeah, brill! Triffic. How's things?

Mike Oh you know, quiet. Here, you know that old boy that was at the funeral, him with the beard?

Del Yeah.

Mike He was in here lunchtime.

Del Oh yeah?

Mike What is he? A relative or something?

Del Nah – well yeah, I mean, he's a distant relative, yeah.

Mike He was telling me all about his wartime dramas. Torpedoed five times, dive-bombed twice. He's a bit of a jinx ain't he?

Del Yeah. You know what his last job was don't you? He was entertainments officer on the Belgrano. Straight up. Cheers darling.

Maureen £1.80 please.

Del Alright, there you go. Go on. Have one for luck.

Maureen Oh cheers!

Mike Oh that reminds me Del, about all that booze yesterday?

Del Yeah, what about it! Went down a treat didn't it? See you later Mike. Cheers.

Rodney I wonder where he is?

Del Eh, who?

Rodney Uncle Albert!

Del Oh him, oh, well he's down the seaman's by now ain't he, eh, got himself a lovely bed, blinding little locker – yeah, he's as happy as pig in sugar! He is yeah.

Rodney Yeah I suppose so but . . . makes you think don't it? A man fights for his country like that, you know, laying his life on the line. D'you know he went down with five different ships!

Del Yeah! I know, I don't know why he just didn't join the submarine corps in the first place.

> *Albert enters, still carrying his hold-all. He sees Del and Rodney and smiles and nods in their direction. Albert starts coughing, obviously to*

Strained Relations

gain sympathy.

Rodney He's got a nasty cough! Ain't he?

Del Yeah, pity Boots ain't open innit!

Rodney moves to the counter.

Rodney You alright Unc?

Albert Yeah, fine son, ta.

Rodney Yeah good. Did you go down the mission then?

Albert Yeah I went down there, but it ain't there no more! They knocked it down, built some luxury flats and a marina!

Rodney *(Takes a couple of pounds from his pocket)* Look, I ain't got very much . . . I've got what . . .

Albert Put yer money away Rodney, I don't want it! Thanks for the offer though. Go 'n, you get back to Del. Don't you worry about me. Alright? Don't worry! *(Rodney is about to move off when Albert starts coughing again)* It's alright Rodney, nothing to worry about! It's just me lungs. We hit a mine coming back from Normandy. I was trapped for 12 hours in a smoke-filled engine room.

Rodney Well, if it's not one thing it's another, eh? *(He moves back to speak to Del).* He ain't got nowhere to sleep tonight! He went down the mission, it's not there any more – there's just a marina.

Del Well can't he kip in the back of that?

Rodney A yachting marina! Come on Del – that's Grandad's brother sitting over there. Where do you want him to sleep, eh? A dosshouse?

Del Listen Rodney, that bloke has been in shark-infested seas, right, he's been attacked by kamikaze pilots, and blown up more times than a beach-ball! One night is a dosshouse ain't gonna do him any harm, is it?

Rodney You don't believe all them stories do you?

Del What? Do you reckon they're porkies?

Rodney Well of course they are! I didn't wanna say nothing 'cos, you know, he's a proud man!

Del What proud? Him? He comes from Dad's side of the family don't he.

Rodney No, I just offered him a couple of quid and he wouldn't take a penny!

Del No, well, he wouldn't would he, he's still got the £100 I gave him this afternoon!

Rodney You give him £100!

Del Yeah! You don't think I'd let him go potless do yer?

Rodney Is that why you can't pay Mike for the booze?

Del *(Refuses to answer. Stands)* Oh come on, come on. *(They move across to Albert)*

Del Alright?

Albert Yeah, alright son. Just having a drop of rum, warm the old cockles.

Del You eaten?

Albert Nah, not yet.

Del Then why didn't you have something to eat when you was in here at lunchtime?

Albert Well, all they had left was sausage and mash and I've gone right off that!

Del You fancy an Indian?

Albert Wouldn't mind son!

Rodney We'd never get a table this time of night, Del.

Del No. We'll have to get a take-away, and eat it at home!

Rodney Yes, that's what we'll do, we'll get a take-away and eat it at home . . . Eh?

Albert If it's alright with you two.Del. Thanks.

Del Don't know what you're thanking me for, you're paying!

Del Come on Sinbad, let's get down there before the health inspector!

Del moves off towards the main doors followed by Rodney who carries Albert's hold-all. Albert downs the last of his rum and is about to leave when Mike calls him.

Mike Oh, I'm glad I caught you. I've just phoned the mission and they said they've got a bed for you.

Albert Sshh!

Follows Del and Rodney out.

Hole in One

DAY. TROTTERS' LOUNGE

The only stock lying about the flat are three large unmarked cardboard boxes. Rodney, in his 'just got up' look, is seated at the table reading one of his magazines, sipping tea from a mug and smoking a roll-up. He looks tentatively at the cardboard boxes. Rodney is mentally squirming at the memory of his mistake. The front door can be heard opening. In the hall, Albert enters wearing a duffle coat, scarf, gloves and hat. He shivers with cold. Two brown envelopes drop through the letter box. Albert kneels down and examines them, then 'posts' them back through the letter box. He enters the lounge.

Albert The Paki shop won't let us have nothing on tick! Says it's part of his culture!

Rodney Don't think it's got anything to do with the 46 quid we already owe 'em do you?

Albert Funny enough he mentioned that! *(Albert peers in one of the boxes. He looks at Rodney, gives a sharp intake of breath and shakes his head sadly)* Still, it's got nothing to do with me!

Rodney That's right!

Albert The moment you suggested going down the auction and buying on yer own, I knew there'd be trouble! But I won't say nothing on the matter Rodney!

Rodney Good.

Albert They must have seen him coming!
Del enters from the bedroom. A glare is exchanged between him and Rodney.

Del Good morning Uncle.

Albert Oh, morning Del. The Paki won't let us have no breakfast!

Del That's alright, I haven't much felt like eating, recently.
Del and Rodney share another glare. Del opens the top of another box, peers in and closes the top quicky with an ironic laugh.

Del *(Sarcastic)* What's the weather like out?

Albert It's parky Del!

Del Good, good! Nice thick frost is there?

Albert Bit slippery underfoot, yeah!

Del Oh cushty! Nice northerly wind howling in from the Urals is there?

Albert Cuts right through you Del!

Del Lovely! Because today Uncle Albert, owing to young Rodney's foresight and GCEs, while all them other plonkers down the market are selling woolly hats and thermal underwear we're gonna make a right killing. Do you know why we're gonna make a killing? We ain't got woolly underwear. *(Produces bottle from a box)* We've got sun tan lotion!! And we ain't got just a little drop of sun tan lotion! We've got 500 bloody quids worth of the stuff.

Rodney I've told you I bought it as an investment!!

Del An investment! Ménage à trois!! In the middle of the worst winter for two million years – with the weathermen laying odds on a new Ice Age – this dipstick goes out and buys out Amber Solaire!

Rodney The weathermen are also forecasting a boiling hot summer! So come May or June we can sell all of that or swop it for something else!

Del Like 50 or 60 anoraks! Maybe.

Rodney You won't give me any credit, will you?

Albert Nor will that Paki!

Rodney Oh shut up Albert!

Albert It's nothing to do with me!

Del That 500 quid that you squandered on this stuff was the last of the company's capital!

Rodney And how was I supposed to know that??

Del How were you supposed to know that? You're the firm's accountant you wally!!

Rodney Throwing that at me now are you?

Del Oh, look at that, we've got nothing to sell and no money to buy with!

Albert It can't be that bad Del! There must be something you can knock out?

Del Yeah, I know what I would like to knock out.

Albert What's in the van?

Del Nothin'!

Albert What's in the garage?

Rodney The van!

Del The only thing we've knocked out in the last month was that electric deep-fryer to the guvn'r at the Nag's Head – and I'm waiting for a comeback on that!

Rodney *(Pointing at Albert)* It's him, ain't it? I mean, ever since he come to live here we've had nothing but bad luck!

Albert What's he on about now?

Del Oh I don't know.

Rodney Alright, what about the time he was in

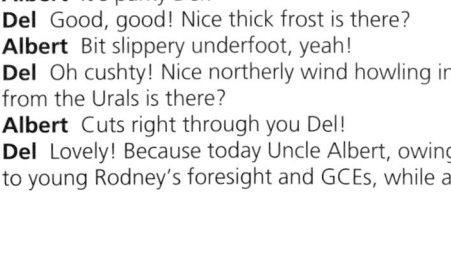

the navy! Every single ship he ever sailed on either got torpedoed or dive-bombed! Two of them in peacetime! Del, that man is a jinx!

Del Oh leave it out Rodney! Gordon Bennett, you'll be burning witches next! I went down and ordered Grandad's headstone the other day! Beautiful thing it is! It's got all angels and things round it and it's got this great big eagle with a scroll in its foot! Of course, I think I'll have to cancel that now! That'll cheer 'em up down at the plastics factory won't it, eh? They've gone and bought all the fibreglass and everything!

Rodney Something's bound to turn up Del! He who dares, eh?

Del If you say so Rodney, if you say so.

Albert I was reading in the Sunday papers about them fellas what pick up with these rich old widows – what they call 'em – toy boys! You wanna see the stuff they pick for presents. Solid gold watches, sports cars – money! Might be worth considering!

Rodney Well, we both admire your spirit Uncle, but don't you think you've left it a bit late for that sort of thing.

Albert I'm not talking about me! I meant you!

Rodney Me?? I'm not selling my body to some old tart! Thank you.

Albert Not even for the family??

Rodney Especially not for the family!! I'm not gonna let myself become some hooker!

Del Listen Uncle. You came to stay with us for a couple of nights, about fours weeks ago. So you don't know us very well. So let me explain something to you, you see. You see, you can't expect Rodney to go and do something like *that*! I mean even I wouldn't expect Rodney to do something like that!

Albert I suppose it was too much to ask! Sorry Del.

Del That's alright!*(To Albert)* I mean, Rodney can't even give it away let alone flog it!

DAY. THE NAG'S HEAD.

A brewery lorry is parked at the kerb. The wooden flaps leading to the cellar are open and the drayman and his mate are shooting cardboard boxes down the slope. Mike the landlord is down there collecting and stacking the boxes. The three-wheeled van pulls up, backfiring, steam billowing from under the bonnet. Del leaps out and kicks the van.

Del 'Ere you are, look, stick that on the windscreen, will you.

Rodney places a 'CD' sticker on the windscreen and alights. Del opens the back door to release Uncle Albert.

Rodney Couldn't we sell this and get something more useful?

Del Like what?

Rodney Like a bus pass!

Del I ain't in the mood Rodney, I'm just not in the mood!! Alright.

Del *(Referring to the boxes being thrown down the shute)* Be handy if one of them was to accidentally fall in our direction wouldn't it, eh?

Rodney Leave off Del!

Albert You've got nowhere to hide it!

Rodney Yeah, well, that's what I meant.

Del I suppose you're right. Come on.

As they pass the open cellar hole Albert calls out to Mike.

Albert Hello Mike. How's that deep-fryer Del sold you?

Mike *(Shoots an accusing finger at Del)* I want a word with you Trotter!

Del Yes, yes, of course Michael! I'll be in the office! *(To Albert)* What are you trying to do to me??

Albert I didn't know Del Boy!

Rodney Del, I've just had a thought where we could hide one of them barrels.

Del Yeah, where?

Rodney *(Referring to Uncle Albert)* In his mouth!

DAY. THE NAG'S HEAD.

Del is at the bar. He is waiting for his change from Maureen.

Maureen That's enough, thanks Mike.

Man Come on darling, I ordered chicken in a basket 'alf hour ago! What you waiting for, the egg to hatch?

Maureen It's not my fault! Our deep-fryer's on the blink! *(To Del)* Ain't customers stupid, eh?

Del Put it like that, I suppose they are! *(Del moves to table where Rodney and Albert are seated)*

Del Here you are, come on, get that down your neck, a small rum.

Albert Just to keep the cold out Del!

Del Make the most of it, could be your last!

Rodney I've been thinking!

Del Oh leave it out Rodney, we're in enough trouble as it is.

Rodney Hang on, right, now look, when I was studying for my GCE in Maths, right I had to learn to do cross-cancelling equations. The idea is, you list all your problems and then eradicate them using a process of elimination, thus discovering the solution! That's what I've been doing!

Hole in One

Del G' on then, I'm game. Go on.

Rodney One: We are traders who have nothing to sell, right?

Del Yeah!

Rodney Two: We are traders who have no money to buy with. Correct?

Del I'm gonna smack you right in the bloody mouth in a minute.

Rodney Hang on! Three: . . . *(Checks notepad)* Oh no, there ain't a three! So, the solution to our problem is thus: We have to find a way of making money out of nothing!

Del and Albert Yeah?

Rodney Oh, I don't know how we do it, that's the answer!

Del And you had to use ink to come to that conclusion?? Stone me Rodney, a Millwall fan could have worked that out!

Rodney Don't keep on at me Del, at least I'm trying ain't I, which is more than I can say for you.

Del Me, I wasn't the one that spent 500 quid on all that rubbish.

Rodney Would you get off my back . . .

Albert Pack it in you two! Look at you, you're at each other's throats. Bloody money, whether you've got too much of it or not enough, it always causes trouble. Don't worry, something will turn up, you see. I'll see you two later. *(Albert exits)*

Del Yeah, yeah alright.

Rodney D'you think we ought to go with him in case he gets mugged?

Del Nah, he's skint anyway! Well that's it, ain't it, I'm gonna have to pawn all the jewellery again! Honestly these rings they know more about hock than a German wine taster!

Rodney Something's gonna turn up Del!

Del What, with our luck?? If I threw a fiver into the air it'd come down as a summons! I don't ask much out of life do I, eh? Only an 'apenny more than I can spend. And look at me, look, I'm gutted! It's all your fault Rodney!

Rodney Oh don't start all that again!

Del Well it is. I mean ever since you were that high you've done nothing but hold me back!

Rodney I held you back??

Del Yeah, I mean, when Mum died I should have had you put in care! I would have been someone by now! I would have done, I would have probably had me own penthouse, and I would have had an Aston Martin with a telephone an' all that.

Rodney Well, I'll tell you something Del. You'd have been doing me a favour if you'd had put me into care! 'Cos at least then I might have got a proper job when I left school, instead of humping your old suitcase all over London!

Del But you didn't wanna leave school did you? If it'd been up to you, you would have been there drawing your old age pension.

Rodney I only wanted to stay there while I got GCEs in Maths and Art!

Del And a lot of good they done the firm! The only time your GCE has come in handy was that time I asked you to count them tins of paint!

There is a massive thud and the sound of breaking glass from the back of the pub.

Del What the bloody hell's that?

Rodney You don't think it was that deep-fryer do you??

Del I'm not gonna stay to find out. Come on, let's look lively! Come on.

They make to dash out of the pub when Maureen calls.

Maureen Del.

Del Yeah, won't be a minute love.

Rodney Yeah, we've just got to . . .

Maureen It's your Uncle Albert!!

Del What about Uncle Albert?

Maureen He's fallen down our cellar! Quick.

Del Fallen down the cellar . . .

STUDIO. DAY. THE PUB CELLAR.

Crates and broken bottles lie around the cellar floor. The plank is still in position. Mike is sittng on the floor holding his injured neck. Del and Rodney arrive and survey the cellar urgently.

Del *(To Mike)* Well??

Mike No, no, no, Del the old neck's gone.

Del No, no, no, I mean, what happened??

Mike I don't know! I just looked up – and there was Albert plummeting towards me!

Rodney Hold on, where is he??

Mike Oh he's over there somewhere!

Rodney rushes to the corner where Albert is spread-eagled on the floor amid a pile of fallen crates and bottles. Del is puzzled as to how Albert managed to fall through the cellar hole but end up 15 yards away in the corner.

Del How the hell did he get over there?

Mike He hit the plank and bounced! He went through the air like one of them springboard divers! Cor my neck don't 'alf hurt, Del!

Del Your neck! Your neck. Uncle Albert nearly ends up in a Jumbo's flightpath, and all you can think about is your rotten Gregory!! Oh come on.

Rodney Are you alright?

Albert I'm a bit shaken and dazed Rodney!

Del It's probably jet-lag! Come on, get him onto his feet Rodney. Come on, up you come.

Albert Fancy leaving an open cellar door unguarded. I've a good mind to sue the brewery!

Del Yeah, put yer arm round Rodney's. *(Del muses thoughtfully and greedily on Albert's last speech)* Sue the brewery. *(To Rodney)* Put him down. What the hell d'you think you're doing.

Rodney Del, you just said pick him up.

Del Yeah, I know what I just said but you don't know what sort of damage he's done! He might have broken something!

Rodney Yeah he has! About four dozen bottles of Guinness! Come on Del. There's nothing wrong with him. He said so himself.

Del Yeah, but how does he know that? How does he know that? He might have hit his head and got percussion! Look, the first thing to do in first aid is never move the victim, right?

Albert You'll have to move me soon Del, the last bell's just gone!

Del See that, he's got ringing sounds in his ears! This is even worse than I thought Rodney. Quick nip upstairs and get on the telephone, yeah, phone for a solicitor!

Rodney Yeah, a solicitor?? Del you can't sue!

Del You don't wanna put money on it do you? Him falling down that hole could be the biggest bit of luck we've had in years.

Rodney But Del, if he'd hurt himself there'd be little signs – wouldn't there – like blood and pain! His hat ain't come off.

Del How's that alright.

Albert Don't give us all that *Quincy* cobblers Rodney! You don't know how bad I am!

Del You see, you don't know how bad he is now quick whip upstairs and phone Solly Attwell! You'll find his number in the Yellow Pages. Go on, look lively.

Rodney Solly Attwell's our solicitor. Bloody 'ell, he's more bent than the villains!

Del That's the sort of man we need in a case like this, a specialist! G' on then, get on the blower!

Rodney You don't mind if I phone for an ambulance first, do you?

Del Ambulance! Ambulance! Good thinking. That'll look great on the report! Well done, Rodney. Go on, away you go. *(Rodney exits)* The old brewery are gonna pay through the nose for this.

Albert I told you something'd turn up, didn't I Del?

Del That's alright Uncle, you just conserve yer oxygen. That's right.

Del moves a few yards away, wearing a greedy and satisfied grin. He now turns suddenly and urgently as if hearing something.

Del Uncle – Albert – did I hear you groaning in pain?

Albert No!

Del Well why not?? Come on.

NIGHT. THE TROTTERS' LOUNGE

Solly Atwell is seated at the table reading the various accident and medical reports. He is 40 and a bit seedy. His black three-piece suit is slightly grubby and doesn't quite fit him. Soll, as the 'local man', deals mainly in GBH cases, burglaries and lots of drunk and disorderlies. He is, however, an expert in 'Mickey Mouse' law suits and industrial compensation. Del and Rodney sit anxiously awaiting his verdict. Solly, with a concerned expression, looks up.

Solly I'm afraid it's bad news Derek, I'd brace yourselves if I was you! According to this medical report and the X-ray they took . . . there's nothing wrong with him!

Del There's gotta be something wrong with him! He was none too clever *before* he fell down the hole!

Solly Sorry Del Boy! Not a mark, scratch, abrasion or bruise! He must have landed on something soft.

Rodney Yeah he did, the landlord!

Solly If I were you Del Boy I'd accept the brewery's offer.

Rodney What offer??

Solly Their solicitors phoned me today. To save any adverse publicity they're willing to settle out of court for £2,000.

Rodney Two grand??

Albert Take the money Del

Del No, I wanted more than that! I wanted enough money to set us up proper. Wait a minute, if they're willing to settle for £2,000 out of court, think what they'll settle for in court!

Rodney But Del, there's nothing wrong with him!!

Del Well it ain't my bloody fault is it??

Solly Gentlemen, gentlemen, gentlemen, please! Now perhaps we should look at this case from another angle. I mean we've only been considering the *physical* damage! *(Pointing to Albert's head)* But what about this!

Del We ain't gonna get a lot for this bloody hat are we!

Solly No, I mean his – his mind Derek! Psychological injuries!

Hole in One

Del Will the court swallow that?

Solly If you three say the right things they will. Hey listen, there was a case in America where this chap fell down a manhole and, like your Uncle, he sustained no physical injuries. Yet he successfully sued the Los Angeles City council for $30 million!

Del and Rodney *(Drooling)* Thirty million!!

Solly He claimed the accident had ruined his sex life!

Del At that rate we'll get £1.75.

Solly We're not claiming anything like that! I'm just giving you that as an example of how these – these 'unseen' injuries can mount up in the old compo stakes! Now, look at the facts as I see them. An elderly man who fought bravely for his country, sailing the seven seas ensuring that Britain never, never, never shall be slaves, has had his retirement – his few well earned years of rest, ruined by the negligence of a multi-national company! An active man struck down by the thoughtless action of this mammoth, rich corporation! The bouts of amnesia, the fear of the outside world and, most distressing of all, losing the use of his legs!

Albert is standing.

Del Sit! Right, that's it, do the bizzo Solly! Alright listen, I don't want no Mickey Mouse magistrates! I want the High Court, I want a pukka brief – you know black cape, crown-topper, all the Xs, alright? Right Solly?

Solly I'll set the wheels in motion. I shall need a list of witnesses.

Rodney No, see, there weren't no witnesses!

Del Will ten do?

Solly Lovely!

DAY. THE COURTROOM.

Representing the Trotters is Mr Frazer – seated behind him is Solly. Seated opposite and representing the brewery is Mr Gerrard. Seated behind is Mike, wearing a surgical collar. Rodney is in the witness box.

Frazer Now Mr Trotter, you were standing outside the Nag's Head public house when this tragic accident occurred?

Rodney *(Obviously lying)* . . . Yes!

Frazer You saw the incident clearly?

Rodney Yes!

Frazer Would you tell the court what happened.

Rodney . . . My uncle fell down a hole!

Frazer Yes! Would you tell the court how he fell down the hole.

Rodney . . . Em . . . well, it was . . . *(Contorts his body and does a little hop sideways)* Like that!

Frazer No, no Mr Trotter! Did he trip, did he stumble?

Rodney No. Well, he sort of walked and then fell down the hole!

Frazer Didn't he see the warning notice?

Rodney There was no warning notice.

Frazer Wasn't he stopped by the guard rail?

Rodney There was no guard rail either.

Frazer I see! NO warning notice, no guard rail! Sounds very dangerous to me!

Rodney Yes! I can remember thinking to myself at the time, 'That's rather dangerous! Someone could fall down that!'

Frazer And how right you were! So, you ran straight down to the cellar?

Rodney Yes!

Frazer And were you the first person to find your Uncle?

Rodney Yes!

Frazer What did he look like?

Rodney Horrible!

DAY. THE COURTROOM.

Del is in the witness box.

Frazer Would you please tell the court, are you related to the plaintiff?

Del *(Indicating Mike)* No, no I just drink in his pub! *(Indicating Albert)* That little one there is me Uncle!

Frazer Quite!

Del I saw it all your worship, utter negligence – a complete disregard for public safety . . .

Judge Yes, yes, quite! Mr Frazer, I don't think we need concern ourselves any further with the accident itself! I believe liability has been proved quite – quite conclusively!

Frazer Much obliged to your honour! Let us move on now to the after-effects of the accident. Has your Uncle changed in any way since this happened?

Del Do what? Oh yeah – oh yeah. He's a completely different man now! I mean he used to be so active! You know it was full of swimming, sponsored walks, marathons. You know, well they used to call him the Jimmy Savile of Peckham! Well, he was always out and about, you'd rarely find him in!

Frazer And now?

Del Well, now he is like the Olympic flame – he never goes out your worship. Locked in his room, he's – he's frightened he might fall down another hole!

Frazer And how has the gradual loss of feeling in his legs affected him?

Del Well, how would it affect you Captain? I

mean, one minute, you, know he's there doing his acrobatics to his Bizzy Lizzy LP, and then the next minute he has to ask us whether or not he's got his shoes on! But I mean, the worstest, the worstest thing of all is your honour is these sudden bouts of amnesia. You know, they have led to him having some very nasty falls.

Judge I fail to see the connection. How can amnesia cause one to fall?

Del He keeps forgetting he can't walk!

Frazer I have no further questions m'lud.

Judge Mr Gerrard?

Gerrard No questions your honour.

Judge You may stand down Mr Trotter.

Del Stand down? I've only just started. I've got loads more I could tell you!

Judge That will be all Mr Trotter, thank you.
Del moves from the witness box to the back of the courtroom beside Rodney and near Solly. He nods to Mike.

Del Alright Mike.

Mike *(Nods back and feels pain)* Aahh!

Del How we doing Solly?

Solly We're home and dry. This could be a ten grander coming up here!

Judge Mr Frazer, do you intend calling any more witnesses?

Frazer I have no further witnesses m'lud.

Judge Mr Gerrard?

Gerrard Just one your honour. I call the plaintiff, Albert Gladstone Trotter.
One of clerks pushes Albert, in a wheelchair that squeaks, to the witness box.

Del I thought you said they wouldn't call him?

Solly I said 'we' wouldn't call him! Look don't worry, I've already briefed him. Any awkward questions he just claims loss of memory!

Rodney Loss of memory! Knowing him he'll forget!

Clerk Take the book in your right hand and read the card.
Albert, putting on the agony, struggles to stand.

Judge There's no need to stand Mr Trotter. Please remain seated.

Albert Thank you your worship. I swear to tell the truth, the whole truth and nothing but the truth.

Gerrard You are Albert Gladstone Trotter, presently residing at 368 Nelson Mandela House, Dockside Estate, Peckham?

Albert I think so sir.

Gerrard Yes. I'll make this as brief as possible Mr Trotter, I realise how distressing this must be for you. Do you have any recollection of the accident?

Albert Very little sir. One minute I was walking along, on me way to post me entry form for *The Krypton Factor*. Anyway, next I was falling through the air! All me life flashed before me! The battle of the River Plate, the sinking of the Graf Spee, raid on Telemar.

Mike *(Shaking his head, reacts to pain)* Aahh!

Judge Silence that man!

Mike Sorry your honour!

Albert After that it's all a blank. Me memory keeps going, see.

Gerrard Have you ever suffered with amnesia before?

Albert I can't remember.

Gerrard I see! But you can remember the war! After all, you have all your ribbons there to remind you. Where were you based Mr Trotter?

Albert I was overseas sir.

Gerrard Really, how odd! I looked into your naval record and it seems that you spent the best part of the war stationed in a storage depot on the Isle of Wight! Hardly overseas!

Albert You wanna try walking it pal!

Gerrard I also noticed Mr Trotter that in May, 1944, you were one of several naval ratings, seconded to a Marine parachute unit, specially formed for missions behind enemy lines. I believe you were involved in laundry matters! But whilst with this unit you underwent basic parachute training. Would you tell the court what this training consisted of?

Albert Em . . . jumping off of things!

Gerrard 'Jumping off of things!' In other words, learning to fall without injuring oneself!

Albert My memory ain't what it used to be your worship.

Gerrard I sympathise Mr Trotter and intend to help you as much as I can. Tell me, could you possibly be the same Albert Gladstone Trotter who, in 1946, fell down the cellar of the Victory Inn, Portsmouth, and received £100 compensation?

Albert I can't remember that far back sir.

Gerrard Well, let's try a more recent case then. Could you have been the same Albert Gladstone Trotter who, in 1951, fell down the cellar of the Coach and Horses, Peckham Rye, and received a £225 out of court settlement?

Albert Me mind's a blank!

Gerrard Maybe you were the same Albert Gladstone Trotter who, in 1949, fell down the cellar of the Crossed Keys off-licence, Gravesend? How about the Thatched Inn, Canning Town, or does the Brunswick Club, New

Hole in One

Cross, ring a bell?

Rodney I don't believe it.

Del It's a bloody nightmare Rodney, it's a bloody nightmare! He's been down more holes than Tony Jacklin.

DAY. THE COURTHOUSE.

Del exits through the main doors followed by Rodney. Del draws on a cigar in an agitated manner, trying to control his temper. Rodney sighs heavily.

Del I don't believe it! I do not believe what that garrity old git has done to us! I mean, the only hole he hasn't fallen down is the black one in Calcutta! What was it the insurance companies nicknamed him?

Rodney The ferret!

Del The ferret!

Rodney He's had 15 previous lawsuits for falling down holes!

Del Those are the *known* cases Rodney! I mean, how many times has the landlord settled out of court with a quiet backhander to save all the aggro?

The sound of a squeaking wheelchair is heard. Del and Rodney both stretch themselves to their full heights at this sound. A sheepish Albert is sitting behind them, frightened of their response.

Del Alright, come on, how many pubs, off-licences and drinking clubs have you done in your time?

Albert Well, quite a few Del! The first cellar I fell down was genuine – honest! But 'cos I'd learnt to fall properly I didn't hurt meself – but I still got compensation out of it and I thought 'This is handy!' So, whenever me and yer Grandad was hard up for a few bob well I'd go'n fall down a hole! I was only tryin' to help.

Rodney Only tryin' to help? I was nearly done for contempt of court. *(Indiciating Del)* His name's been sent to the director of public prose-cution and Solly and the brief look like they're gonna get defrocked! And you were only tryin' to help!!

Albert I said I'm sorry Rodney! I didn't wanna do it! I mean, I'm past all that stunt-man lark! But you two have been good to me these past few weeks. And I wanted to get some money to – well – repay you. And I wanted to get yer Grandad his headstone.

Del You did it for Grandad's headstone?

Albert He was my older brother Del. When I was a kid he used to look after me. I never did anything for him – never had the chance to – until now! Sorry boys!

Del Yeah, yeah, alright don't worry about it Uncle Albert. Come on Rodney, let's get Ironside home!

With Del pushing the wheelchair and Rodney strolling along beside, they move up the road. There is a pause.

Albert It's turned out nice innit boys?

Rodney Triffic!

Del I'd better knock out some of that sun tan lotion, eh.

They continue moving away. There is another short pause before Del stops.

Del 'Ere just a – just a minute why am I pushing you? You can walk you lazy old sod!

Albert Oh yeah, I forgot!

Rodney Oh had another little bout of amnesia, eh Del!

Del Now don't you start all that blackout nonsense with me Uncle 'cos it won't wash!

EPISODE ★★ FOUR

It's Only Rock and Roll

DAY. THE WAREHOUSE.
The three-wheeled van is parked a few yards from the warehouse door. Del exits carrying a large cardboard box, bearing the words: 'Kandy Doll. Your Talking Friend.' Del opens the back door of the van and pushes it in. An identical box is already in there.

Inside the warehouse Rodney is talking on the phone. There are another 8 'Kandy Doll' boxes in the warehouse.

Rodney Yes, so we're definitely rehearsing tonight? Eight o'clock down at the hall! Right, will the rest of the group be there? Oh great man!

Del Oi, Ringo! I hope all my huffing and puffing ain't interrupting you!

Rodney Eh? No! It's no sweat man!

Del Well it's certainly not coming from you, you lazy little git!

Rodney I've gotta go Charlie. Look, I'll see you later on, alright. *(Rodney joins Del. He bangs out a drum beat on one of the boxes)* Rehearsing with the group tonight!

Del Group! You're a drummer who's got no drums!

Rodney No – well, it's early days yet!

Del I don't know why you waste your time with that bunch of wallies for.

Rodney They are not a bunch of wallies! Anyway, you haven't ever heard us play yet.

Del I don't need to! I mean, look who yer lead singer is, Mental Mickey!

Rodney Oi, there's nothing wrong with Mickey Maguire!

Del Nothing wrong! He bit a bloke's ear off once, that's all.

Rodney Not all of it!

Del Well, before you become deeply involved in any musical argument with Mental Mickey, make sure you're wearing a bullet-proof balaclava! Let's get this stuff in the van.

Rodney What we bought anyway?

Del Well, it's obvious innit, sauages! Talking dolls, innit.

Rodney I mean what sort of stock is it? Bankrupt, fire damaged, water damaged, soiled or just plain hooky? *(They go outside)*

Del It's none of them Rodney! These are near-perfects!

Rodney Near-perfects! So what's wrong with 'em?

Del Nothing.

Rodney Well, if there's nothing wrong with 'em why aren't they called 'perfects'?

Del It's just a bit of legal jargon used by the insurance company to save on paperwork that's all. Don't worry about it.

Rodney That's easy for you to say, but I'm the one who has to go down the Arndale Centre and flog these things, I mean, look at the aggro I had at Christmas with them cricket bats! *(Quoting Del)* 'Each one personally autographed by Viv Richards!'

Del And each one was personally autographed by Viv Richards! Alright, it wasn't *the* Viv Richards!

Rodney No, it was Davey Richards' eldest sister! I had nothing but comebacks on that!

Del *(Del opens one of the boxes and removes a carton containg a doll. He removes doll head, keeping it upright all the time)* No you'll be alright with these things. I mean have a look, take a look, can you see anything wrong with 'em?

Rodney No, it looks alright!

Del Alright! This is Taiwan's finest Rodney! This is quality *par excellence* this gear! We'll pick the rest of 'em up after dinner. G' on, jump in the van. *(Del replaces the doll in the carton feet first. As he does the doll leans backwards)*

Doll What's up Doc?

Rodney Eh?

Del What?

Rodney I thought you said something!

Del No!

Rodney Oh! You know, I reckon this group of mine could go places.

Del And the sooner the better if you ask me.

Rodney We're styling ourselves on Frankie Goes to Hollywood!

Rodney beats out a drum beat on the van roof. Del has his head inside the van and, surprised by the banging, springs up and smashes his head on the roof.

Del You dozy little twonk Rodney. You bang my roof like that again and it won't be Frankie Goes to Hollywood, it'll be Rodney Goes to hospital.

Rodney Bloody hell Del, I said I'm sorry, didn't I?

Del You will be if I get a headache.

NIGHT. THE TROTTERS' LOUNGE.

The TVs are off. Uncle Albert is standing at the drinks cabinet. He has just lit one of Del's cigars. He pours a brandy into a cut glass goblet. During all this he is singing to himself.

Albert 'The wind is blowing, the snow is snowing . . .'

Del enters from the hall.

Del Oi, get your thieving hands off!

Albert I weren't been feeling all that well, Del.

Del You'll feel even worse if I catch you at my Courvoisier again.

Albert What's all the big hurry then?

Del I've just heard a very interesting bit of news down the pub. Er, listen have you ever heard of the Shamrock Club, over at Deptford? The Paddies' Moulin Rouge!

Albert That place?? I've read about it in the local paper!

Del Well, their resident band the Dublin Bay Stormers had a bit of a ruck last weekend and they're all banged up on remand!

Albert So?

Del So – what is it next Sunday? It's St Patrick's night innit! Their biggest earner of the year and the Shamrock Club ain't got a band! But I have!

Albert You don't mean young Rodney and that bunch of wallies? They can't do all that Mother Macree stuff!

Del Listen, you don't know Rodney that well. He's a very talented little lad, they'll love him!

Albert They'll tear him limb from limb.

Del No they won't. The worst he'll get is a red nose!

Albert Still, it's got nothing to do with me!

Del No, that's right!

Albert I'll keep my opinions to myself!

Del Good.

Albert It don't seem right though!

Del has been preoccupied with selecting a record to put on the record player. He has found one and is placing it on the turntable.

Albert I mean, it's not fair!

Del Nor's Frank Bruno's arse but he don't keep on about it!

The needle is hovering above the record player. Del dials the phone.

Del Hello, Shamrock Club? Could I speak to Liam please? Yeah, Derek Trotter.

He releases the lever that drops the needle on to the record. The opening strains of 'Dianne' by the Bachelors starts playing.

Del Boy. How you going pal? Triffic, er listen, I just heard the tragic news about the Stormers! Oh, the bloody laws in this country, diabolical ain't they, oh yeah. So how are you fixed for a group on Paddies night? Well this is it, I mean, where do you find a good band these days? There's so many cowboys around! What's what noise? Oh that? Well, that's what I'm phoning you about you see. I'm down here at the community hall and there's a group of young-sters on the stage rehearsing here . . . Yeah, that's them in the background! Now do what? Just a minute . . . *(Shouts)* Keep it down will you lads? I'm on the blower, er . . . hold on Liam, I'll close the door. *(Pauses, then mentally times his footsteps to the door, switches the sound down on the record player, then times his footsteps back again.)* There we are now, we can hear ourselves speak now! Eh? Yes they sound a lot like the Bachelors! Yeah that's who they model themselves on . . . Well, there's good news and there's bad news Liam. The bad news is they're expensive! It's 300 sovs I'm afraid. But the good news is they're free on St Paddy's night! Yes alright. He wants to think about it!

Albert Well that shouldn't take long should it.

Del No, no, no, Liam you carry on old son, you take all the time in the world. I've got plenty of time. *(Switches record up loud and shouts)* Oi, close that door will yer! *(Switches sound down)* Well you won't go far wrong with these boys, no, no. You know it makes sense. There is one thing . . . now *they*, not me, *they*, you under-stand insist on cash in advance! Yeah. Alright, I'll tell you what old son, I'll pop down in about an hour. Alright, pal. Hee hee hee hee hee, triff ta-ta.

Albert The family used to tell stories about you and yer 'business activities'! I never believed 'em up until now!

Del Get in, get out and don't look back, that's my motto!

Albert I can't wait to tell young Rodney the good news!

Del Er, listen you keep quiet. This is gonna be a . . . it's supposed to be a . . . erm . . . a surprise!

Albert Oh, it's nothing to do with me Del! I just hope I don't let it slip out!

Del No that would be very unfortunate wouldn't it? Oh, I tell you what uncle Albert, would you like a nice large brandy in there Uncle Albert.

Albert That's nice of you son, thank you! Might as well leave the bottle here, save me having to keep on getting up!

Del Have a nice evening – you blackmailing old bark!

It's Only Rock and Roll

INT. NIGHT. ST NICKS.

The group are Rodney, Charlie, Stew and Mental Mickey – they are the only ones in the hall. Charlie and Stew both play acoustic guitars, Stew plays lead, Charlie plays rhythm. Mental Mickey is a rather wild and dangerous looking character, full of frustration and aggression. Rodney has no drums, but is playing a couple of packing cases. The band are playing the opening bar of a song they wrote themselves. During these opening bars Mental Mickey does a trance-like dance, with fists firmly clenched.

Mickey Come on Rodney! Give us some cymbals.

Rodney Cymbals?

Mickey starts singing. During this Del enters and wanders slowly across to them. Mickey stops singing.

Mickey Oi, oi, oi, what's he doing here?

Del I just come down to listen to you lads. Don't mind do you?

Rodney You just come down on the wind up didn't yer?

Del Au contraire Rodney. Au contraire! In fact I've been very impressed. He sounds, does young Mental Mickey, in very good voice.

Mickey I don't like people calling me that!!

Del Ooh, I'd better keep my hands on me ear-lobes then!

Charlie Why don't you piss off down the pub Trotter?

Del Oi, oi, watch it. This is our community hall. Anyone's entitled to walk in here! Come on then, let's hear you!

Stew Yeah, come on. He's not gonna put us off!

Rodney Yeah, right! One, two, three . . .

Mickey Oi, oi, Rodney I do the one, two, three, fours!

Rodney Sorry Mickey, forgot!

Mickey One, two, three, four . . .

They are just about to play.

Del Hold on, hold on, where d'you learn to count, Rampton?

Mickey I ain't never been to Rampton in my life. Who started them rumours about me being in Rampton?

Charlie Alright, take it easy Mick!

Mickey I've never been to Rampton! I've been to Broadmoor, once or twice, but that's not the point.

Del Carry on.

Rodney One, two, three . . .

Mickey Oi, I told you once Rodney, I'm not gonna tell you again son. I do the one, two, three, four.

They start playing. Del feigns interest and enjoyment. He halts them in the second verse.

Del Hold up, hold up.

Mickey What is it now??

Del Well I am very surprised! I came down here to listen to you bunch of wallies, expecting you to sound like a cat being doctored without anaesthetic! But you're good!

Rodney What?

Del You're very good! Alright you're not quite up to the standard of Spanner Ballet or Duran Duran! There's something about your music that I like! It's well it's got something! *(Quietly)* I only hope it ain't catching!

Rodney Look Del, if this is all a build-up to some joke, will you just tell us now and stop wasting everybody's time!

Del It's no joke Rodney, I mean it! I'm very impressed, very! *(Applauding)* Bravo, bravo! Of course, you realise that you're gonna flop like a jelly on a wet mattress, don't you?

Mickey Oh yeah why should we flop?

Del Because you're undisciplined that's why! You ain't going to go nowhere till you get yer act together!

Charlie Yeah? Well my mate's cousin works for a record company and he reckons he could get us a contract!

Del And my mate's cousin's a doorman at Chelsea, but he couldn't get me a bloody game though could he? Na, you're still rough around the edges. I mean, why don't you take a butcher's at yerselves. You look like something the cat dragged in – then dragged out again!

Mickey Trotter, shut it, we like looking like this. We're Marxist Trotskyite anarchists!

Rodney and Charlie and Stew Yeah!

Rodney Are we?

Del So why do you want to be superstars then?

Mickey 'Cos we wanna be *rich* Marxist Trotskyite anarchists!

Charlie Well, not too rich!

Stew No, just a little bit rich! Money ain't everything!

Del No, but it certainly takes the sting out of being poor, though don't it? Strikes me you need someone to steer you in the right direction you know. Look after yer interest. A manager! No hold on, hold on! Don't look at me. . . . I mean the bloke who becomes your manager has gotta get you all brand-new equipment. Guitars, drums, speakers! Cost an arm and a leg!

Stew I thought you said we were good!

229

Del You are good! You're natural, you've got raw talent!

Mickey Oi, Trotter you don't wanna put your money where yer mouth is though, do you?

Del You think I'm not the kind who would back me instincts? You know me. He who dares wins! But, well, the fact of the matter is, things are tight at the moment.

The group Yeah yeah! We've heard it before.

Del Alright then! You win! I will be your manager! I'll get you bookings, you see if I don't!

Mickey What about instruments?

Del I'll get that as well!

Rodney Don't listen to him! We'll end up with the chuck-aways from a Boys Scouts' band!

Del All yer instruments and equipment'll be new! Write down what you want, I'll get it for you! I'm making an investment in you lads. This time next year we'll be millionaires! I can see it now. Albert Hall, Carnegie Hall, the Hollywood Bowl! The revolutionary new sound: Pop Protest! You don't know of any of the Bachelor numbers, do you? *(Group shake heads)* It's not important! Well, you carry on rehearsing! 'Cos I'll get this show on the road. Come on then – let's hear ya, your manager has spoken!

Rodney Yeah right! Here we go then, one, two, three . . .

Mickey I do the one, two, three, four!

Rodney Sorry!

Mickey One, two, three, four.

NIGHT. THE FOYER. ST NICK'S.
Del exits from the hall still feigning enjoyment. The moment he is out of their sight, and with the sound of the group in the background, he collapses against the wall.

Del Gordon Bennett!

NIGHT. THE SHAMROCK CLUB.
A sign says: The Shamrock Club. From the first floor windows there are the sounds of a massive fight. Bottles being broken, chairs being smashed. Screams of pain can be heard.

Liam (VO) Put the table down Pat!

Pat (VO) I'll put it on yer bloody head if you want!

Liam (VO) What's that you're saying??

Pat (VO) Auurgh!

Woman Sean, Sean!
The door to the club opens and Del rushes out carrying a speaker. Rodney follows carrying a bass drum which he ties to the roof of the van. Del opens the back door of the van and runs back into the club. Stew and Charlie exit

carrying guitars and the smaller drums. Del reappears with the second speaker which he hands to Rodney. He goes back in and comes back with the cymbals. He jumps in the van as does Rodney and they are about to drive away.

Rodney What about Mental Mickey?
Mickey is at the door of the club fighting with unseen opponents inside.

Del He's happy enough! *(They pull away)* Mickey watches the van disappear before he crashes back into the club, fists flying.

Peckham Records Present:

A BUNCH OF WALLIES

APRIL

Mon 1	South London Correctional Institution for Wayward Teenagers with Facial Acne
Wed 3	Peckham Library (European Politics and Government Law Section)
Fri 5	Nag's Head
Sat 6	Star of Bengal (Indian Pop Night)
Mon 8	Tooting Hospital for the Hard of Hearing

MAY

Thurs 3	Lady Gillian's Annual Pony Club Ball
Sat 5	Flat 307 Nelson Mandela House (15th Floor)

AS SEEN ON TOP OF THE POPS PERFORMING THEIR SMASH HIT **"BOYS WILL BE BOYS"**

DAY. THE TROTTERS' GARAGE.
A Police Constable is checking over the stock in the garage.

PC Let's make sure I've got all the details now. The stolen items consist of two guitars, two speakers, and a set of drums. Here's one of your sticks, it's a bit oily.

Rodney Cheers! D'you reckon you'll catch 'em?

PC Shouldn't have too much trouble! We'll just go round the clubs till we find a rock 'n' roll band with a one-armed drummer.

Rodney I need you don't I! I mean I really need you.

PC What's all this other stuff doing here?

Rodney Er – we collect things!
Del appears at the garage doors carrying a large box bearing the 'Maltesers' symbol. Upon seeing the PC he turns swiftly and disappears from view.

PC Funny things to collect ain't they?

It's Only Rock and Roll

Rodney Yeah well, er, everyone's gotta have a hobby ain't they!

The PC picks up a doll and leans it forward. It laughs like Woody the Woodpecker. Del arrives minus box.

Del Good afternoon Officer, can I be of any assistance?

Rodney They've had the drums, guitars, everything! I locked the door last night Del, I swear to you I locked it.

Del Yeah, alright Rodney, not to worry, eh, not to worry.

Rodney What do you mean not to worry? All our equipment's been nicked!

Del Well, that's not *quite* true! Er Rodney, would you like to nip outside to make sure I switched the engine off on the van?

Rodney No!

Del Oh! Well you see Officer, the items haven't been stolen. A van came to pick them up this morning and take them back to the shop! You see I know the owner of the shop. I had them on what is called a sale-or-return basis!

PC *(To Rodney)* I see. Do you enjoy wasting police time, eh?

Rodney Hold on, I didn't know he had 'em sale or return!!

Del It's my fault, I didn't tell him! I'm sorry.

PC Right! This stuff here . . .

Del Excuse me Officer, but when I come in there was some kids taking the front wheels off your Panda car!

PC They what?? I might be back to see you!

Rodney I can't wait!

PC exits.

Del What do you think you're playing at, inviting the bloody Old Bill round here?

Rodney What am I playing at?? You told me you'd bought that equipment and all the time you had it on sale or return. You just set us up didn't you?

Del We earned 300 sovs, right, listen Rodney and we didn't have to pay out for any equipment! Brilliant innit!

Rodney Brilliant Del! We nearly had our heads smashed in! I didn't wanna play the Shamrock Club! None of us wanted to play the Shamrock Club! But we played it Del because you said it was our first step on the road to stardom! We believed you!

Del Well you must be bigger plonkers than you look! You didn't honestly think that you and that bunch of wallies were destined for the Albert Hall or Carnegie Hall did you? The only hall you were destined for, sod all, that's what! But as it turned out you've 150 so think yourself lucky, and anyway you can still carry on with the group.

Rodney No I can't. We had an artistical disagreement! Look what that Mickey tried to do to my ear!

Del The vicious little git! Now I'm gonna sort him out. What was the row about?

Rodney They accused you of setting us up! They said you'd only done it for a quick earner and to get rid of the suits you've had in here since 1975!

Del The way some people's minds work!

Rodney What do you mean? They were right!! But I defended you! I mean, stood there and defended you! And d'you know why? 'Cos you're my brother – and I don't like to hear people rubbishing you!!! That's why.

Del Still work does it?

Rodney Yeah.

Del It was a pipe-dream Rodney!

Rodney At least I had a dream Del – it's more than I've got now.

Del Come on, you didn't think you were gonna get anywhere did you? I mean just look at that other three! They had about five and half brain cells between them, and one of them was on the blink! I tell ya. That showbusiness lark – they're all Stoke-on-Trent aren't they. You have to watch yer old deaf and dumb in that game! Rodney.

Rodney Look, why do you always have to stop me in everything I try to do?

Del Who, me?

Rodney You always have to stick yer oar in and mess things up for me! Sometimes I get the feeling that you're scared!

Del Scared, me scared? Scared of what?

Rodney Scared of me becoming a success! You're terrified that one day I might make it – on my own!

Del That is like a knife in my heart that Rodney!! There is nothing I'd like more than to see you become *someone*! Nice little Capri Ghia and all that! I remember what Mum said on her deathbed. She said 'Del,' she said, 'Give little Rodney all the encouragement you can! Never Del, never hold him back!'

Rodney She didn't 'alf say a lot on her deathbed.

Del What?

Rodney Whatever the subject is, Mum had something to say about it on her deathbed! She must have spent her final few hours in this mortal realm doing nothing but rabbiting!

Del You are walking a bleedin' tightrope here Rodney!!!!

231

Rodney No hang on. Right, remember last week we were having a row about whose turn it was to go down the chippy, yeah? And you claimed that Mum said on her deathbed 'Send Rodney for the fish!'

Del Yeah, well, I'd had a few hadn't I? You tried something and it didn't work. Look what you've got! *(Holds up a wad of money)* 150 beer vouchers!

Rodney makes no attempt to take money but Del shoves it in his top pocket

Del Well, come on then Rodders. Come on, cheer up, come on. We've got to go down the market this afternoon!

Rodney Triffic!

Del Oh, come on now Rodney, listen, it ain't all bad news! I mean, on the one hand you've just had your hopes and dreams dashed! But on the other hand, I've got a van load of hooky Maltesers! Come on let's go . . .

NIGHT. THE TROTTERS' LOUNGE.

The TVs are on. Del is alone talking on the phone.

Del Alright Monk, I'll come straight with you, look, these dolls, I've had these dolls for about a week and I ain't shifted one yet! If you'll take a chance I'll take a loss, I can't be fairer than that! Would I lie to you? Alright, I'll see you around Monk!

The music on the TV has stopped and applause can be heard. Del sits oblivious to it. On the TV a DJ is introducing a record on Top of the Pops.

DJ In at number 26 *Boys Will Be Boys* from A Bunch of Wallies!

Stew, Charlie, Mental Mickey and a new drummer start playing the song they were playing at the community hall.

Del *(Mumbling)* P'rhaps Trigger could knock some out down the council depot. Oh shut up. Bloody noise, I can't think! *(Goes to switch sound down)* I don't believe this! It's that bunch of wallies!! What do they think they're doing??? They're on *Top of the Pops*!! *(The front door slams)*

Rodney *(OOV)* You know that old bird who works down the laundromat, the one who's after . . . What's wrong?

Del switches both sets off. Rodney enters laughing.

Del Nothing Rodders! Alright fine. Wanna cigar?

Rodney No thanks.

Del Go on, what was you saying?

Rodney Oh yeah, I wound her up, right, I said that Uncle Albert wants to take her to the old folks', beano on Thursday. He'll be well pleased. *(Del laughs falsely)*

Del I like it! I like it!

Rodney Are you sure everything's alright?

Del It's triffic Rodders, never been better!

Rodney Good. Hey, *Top of the Pops* is on!

Del Yeah but the telly's broke!

Rodney I'll watch it on the black and white one then!

Del That's broke as well!

Rodney Well it's got to be the fuse in the socket!

Del No, I tried that! They're both broke! I'll have to get a firm in – naus innit, eh?

Rodney Yeah! Oh well, I might as well give Albert the good news! Where is he?

Del He's in his room.

Rodney opens door to Albert's room.

Rodney Uncle Albert.

Albert *(OOV)* Hello son, you alright?

Del quickly puts his coat on.

Del He'll go bloody divvy when he finds out!

Albert exits from the bedroom.

Albert *(Shouting back at Rodney)* You wanna act yer age you intefering little . . . Can't you have a word with him Del? He's only come in there to annoy me! I don't wanna go on no old folks' beano!

Del Well don't go then, don't go! Listen, I'm off out – don't mention it to Rodney!

Albert I doubt if he'd wanna go with you anyway, he's watching *Top of the Pops* on the portable.

The door to Albert's bedroom opens. Rodney exits and stares at Del.

Rodney They're in the charts!!!!

Del So they're in the charts. Marque de Fabrique, as they say.

Rodney They could go to number one! They could have a smash hit on their hands.

Del Alright, so you have a smash hit on you hands. You might not have another one for the rest of your life!

Rodney I always said they could make it, and you convinced me they couldn't.

Del That is your trouble Rodney, you're too easily swayed! And what about me, eh? I was their manager!

Rodney *(Picking up drumstick)* I'm gonna stick this right up your jacksy!

It's Only Rock and Roll

Sleeping Dogs Lie

NIGHT. THE TROTTERS' LOUNGE.

Rodney is seated at the table reading a newspaper. Albert is near the colour TV and is moving the aerial around trying to get a picture. Del is on the phone.

Del No, no no, no, everything's cushty! Yeah, no, no, no, you've got nothing to worry about. You know me, I'll do anyone a favour if the money's right, yeah.

Albert *(To Rodney)* You have to interfere don't yer?

Rodney I was merely trying to get a picture for yer!

Albert I had a picture till you come in and started mucking around with the aerial!

Rodney There was a ghost on the screen!

Albert Course there was a ghost on the screen – I was watching an 'orror film! Just leave things alone will yer Rodney!

Rodney D'you realise there are nigh on four million people unemployed in this country! And all you can do is sit there and watch horror films!

Albert What would you like me to do?

Rodney Well . . . You could at least think about it!

Albert I've been thinking about it, that's why I want to watch the horror film.

Del Oi, 'old on, shut up you two will yer, I'm on the blower. Yes, sorry, go on.

Rodney Course I blame it on computers! I mean, how many people have been put on the dole by robots that can build cars and what ave yer?

Rodney That's why I'll never get a proper job! 'Cos they can train a robot to do something better than I can!

Albert *(Mumbling)* They could train a chimpanzee to do it better than you!

Del Yeah, okay, I'll see yer tomorrow morning about 11 o'clock. *(Puts phone down)* Yeah, cheers. That's it Rodney, I've got a coup. I've pulled off a coup Rodders, a genuine coup.

Rodney Oh, not another coup! What you done this time?

Del We have got a guest coming to stay for the next couple of weeks. A *paying* guest!

Albert Yeah? Who's that then Del?

Del It's not 'who' it's 'what'.

Rodney What?

Del Exactly, it's a dog! And I don't want any of

your smart remarks either. It's Boycie and Marlene's puppy! They're going away on holiday tomorrow and they want us to look after it.

Rodney Why don't they just stick it in kennels?

Del You see Marlene don't trust 'em! See, the thing is Rodney, for the last few years Boycie and Marlene have been trying to start a family right but so far, as they say on the continent, nito!

Rodney So what's this gotta do with their dog?

Del Marlene started getting broody, right, so did Boycie. He goes and buys her a little puppy. I mean pukka thing you know, it's got a pedigree. Cost him 600 quid, 600 quid. Well I said to him, I said, you know Boycie, I mean if you'd have come to see me like, I could have got you one much cheaper.

Rodney Cheaper like, you know what I mean?

Del Anyway, Marlene right, she thinks that this puppy is her baby now, you know what I mean, and she don't want her baby put in some muddy old kennels. She wants it to receive personal attention! The sort that we can provide! For 60 quid a week!

Rodney 60 quid a week?? Del, we don't know nothing about it! I mean, canine welfare, right, that's a specialised profession.

Del Oh leave it out Rodney! I mean look all you've gotta do is feed it in the morning, right, take it for a walk across the adventure play-ground and Bob's yer uncle!

Rodney And what if Boycie and Marlene find out?

Albert We'll have to swear the dog to secrecy won't we!

Rodney I meant, what happens if one of the neighbours tell them?

Del So what are they gonna say? 'We saw Rodney taking your dog every morning and every evening for a walk!' Well what's wrong with that. That's exactly what Boycie and Marlene want us to do innit, eh?

Rodney Oh yeah! I didn't think of that.

Del exits to the kitchen.

Rodney What do you mean they saw *Rodney* taking the dog for a walk every morning and every night??

Del *(OOV)* It's just a figure of speech that's all Rodders.

Rodney Oh no it ain't a figure of speech. I know your games Derek Trotter.

Del No leave it out.

EXT. DAY. BOYCIE'S HOUSE.

Boycie's Merc with the boot open is parked in the drive. Boycie exits from the house carrying a couple of suitcases. Puts a case in the boot and checks his watch. He bends into the boot as Del pulls up and gives a blast on his horn. Boycie leaps up in surprise and whacks his head on the boot. Del and Rodney alight stifling laughter.

Boycie I'll have a headache for the entire flight now! You were supposed to be here 'alf an hour ago!

Del No, no, we're on time Boycie! There must be something wrong with your watch! 'Ere, don't wanna buy a decent one do you?

Boycie What from you? You must be joking!
Marlene exits from the house. She is a dapper little cockney woman.

Del Why listen. . . . Hello Marlene my love!

Marlene Hello sweetheart
They kiss and Del touches her up.

Del Wohoo!

Marlene Did you have a nice Christmas?

Del Oh triffic yeah.

Marlene I had a dog!

Rodney Yeah, we had a turkey same as every other year!

Marlene Oh yeah! Honestly, you two are as bad as each other! Woho!
Del touches her up again.

Marlene Derek!!

Boycie Marlene, why don't you go an' get the dog then perhaps we can get going!

Marlene Yeah alright, I'll fetch his food as well. *(Exits to the house)*

Boycie I don't like your lipstick Del.

Del What? *(He brushes off Marlene's lipstick)*

Rodney So where you off to Boycie?

Boycie Oh, we're just off for a couple of weeks in the Seychelles! You ever been to the Seychelles have you?

Del Dunno. Have we ever been to the Seychelles Rodney?

Rodney I'd have to check me passport.

Boycie Now are you sure you'll be able to look after this dog?

Del Of course I will!

Rodney Yeah, oh yeah, Del's had lots of experience!

Boycie Right remember, this is not just a dog. This is Marlene's baby! Sometimes I wish I'd never bought it.
Marlene exits from the house with a Great
Dane on a leash. She is struggling to hold the dog back. She also carries a large hold-all.

Del You didn't tell me it was a Great Dane!!

Boycie Didn't I? Must have slipped my mind!

Rodney I thought it was a puppy!

Boycie He is!

Del Gordon Bennett!

Marlene Duke, this is your uncle Del and Rodney . . .
(Duke barks)

Marlene He's lovely ain't he?

Del Triffic!

Marlene Take him for walkies first thing in the morning, once in the evening and then again last thing at night. When it's his bedtime you put a blanket over him and then you talk to him for a while.

Del You don't want us to bring his wind up?

Marlene No, he should be alright! And don't worry, he's house-trained.

Rodney But we live in a flat!
She opens the hold-all to reveal huge steaks, etc.

Marlene In here his vitamin pills. One in the morning, *before* breakfast, not after!

Boycie We've got a plane to catch Marlene! Come on, kiss him goodbye.

Marlene Bye Del, see you soon.

Boycie For Gawd's sake, the dog Marlene!

Marlene Bye-bye my little bubba-luba! I know Dooky's gonna miss his Mummy, and Mummy's gonna miss her little Dookie-Wookie Wookie.

Boycie Makes you wanna throw up don't it?

Del Yeah, I feel a bit Tom and Dick myself!
Marlene leads the dog to the back of the van. The dog leaps in the back.

Boycie Come on Marlene, we'll gonna miss that plane!

Marlene If he bites you, don't scream – he's highly strung!

Rodney Is it alright if we bleed?

Marlene Oh, he doesn't sink his teeth in. He's only playing! Bye-bye, bye-bye DookyWookie. Did you switch everything off?

Boycie Yes!

Marlene Did you switch the burglar alarm on?

Boycie Yes!

Marlene Did you lock everything up?

Boycie Get in the car!
Boycie and Marlene pull away. Del and Rodney look at each other. They look at the van, which is rocking as Duke moves around inside.

Del Well go 'n then Rodney.

Rodney What?

Sleeping Dogs Lie

Del Jump in!
Rodney After you Del!
Del I've got to get the food!
Rodney I don't mind waiting waiting!
Del picks up the hold-all.
Del Here look at this Rodders. Steak, fillet steaks, chicken breasts, veal escalopes! We're gonna eat well for the next week or so.
Rodney It's supposed to be for the dog!
Del You must be joking! That thing's gonna get a bowl of Kennomeat every day and think itself lucky.
Rodney And what happens if Marlene finds out?
Del And how's she gonna find out? I suppose Duke's gonna grass us up is he?
Del climbs in the driver's seat.
Del Come on Rodney! Here you are, do some work for your living.
Rodney gingerly climbs in. There is a menacing growl.
Rodney That dog don't like me!
Del He's alright, he can smell fear!
Rodney I'm surprised he can smell anything at all with that gallon of Brut you're wearing!
Del Come on.

DAY. A PUBLIC PARK. NEXT DAY.

The van pulls up. Del and Rodney alight.
Del Your turn today Rodney.
Rodney It was my turn yesterday.
Del Go on Rodney, take him for a run.
Rodney moves to the back of the van. Del wanders off puffing a cigar.
Rodney Duke. Duke, here you are then. Come on, up you get old boy! Come on look . . . look . . . look ready Duke! (He shows the dog an old tennis ball and throws it. He repeats it with another ball)
Duke come on shake a leg!
Duke is lying flat out in the back of the van with no sign of life.
Rodney (Fearful) Duke!!
Del is approaching an attractive woman who is walking a Dachsund.
Del Hello, he's nice, how long you had him? Or has he always been that length? I'm a Great Dane man meself!
Young lady Really?
Del Won Crufts two years on the trot!
Young lady Really?
Del Oh yeah, you might have seen me on the Chum advert?
Young lady I can't say that I actually have!
Del Oh yes. Nothing I don't know about dogs.

You want any advice, you know I'm yer man.
Young lady Well, Sacha keeps tearing little holes in my carpet. What would you recommend?
Del A new carpet! As it happens I know this little bloke down in Wapping way, he'll fit you up a treat! He's Iranian but he's got contracts in Persia!
Rodney approaches, shouting.
Rodney Del! Del!
Del Ah, here's my trainer! What is it Rodney?
Rodney I don't wanna worry you but I think the dog's dead! (Del is stunned.) Let me re-phrase it shall I? I don't wanna worry you but I think the dog is dead! Now come on!
Del (To young woman.) You just can't get staff these days!
They set off running.
Del What have you done to it you dipstick?
Rodney I ain't touched it!
Del This is a wonderful turn of events this is! Boycie and Marlene ain't even got the top off their sun tan oil and we're burying their dog!
They arrive at the van.
Rodney Look!
Del Come on Duke boy! Cats! Cats! Meow. No, he ain't dead Rodney, he's breathing look!
Rodney Thank Gawd for that! So what's the matter with him?
Del Well I don't know do I? We'd better get him down a vet's! This is gonna cost an arm and a leg this is!
(Rodney notices the two tennis balls he threw earlier as he is about to climb in the van)
Rodney Oi Del, shall I get his balls?
Del You leave him alone! I don't want him waking up in a temper!

DAY. WAITING ROOM OF VETERINARY CLINIC.

Del and Rodney are the only people in the room. After a few seconds, Rodney gives an ironic laugh.
Del What?
Rodney I was just thinking, that's all, Marlene's tried for all these years to have a baby and failed. When you tell her her Dookie-Wookie's croaked it she'll have twins!
Del He is not dead!
Rodney He ain't chasing many cats though is he?
Del Look, maybe this is normal!
Rodney Normal? Del, What you tryin' tell me? Dogs hibernate or something?
Del No, what I mean is. I mean is I mean . . . Oh

I don't know what I mean do I. All I want you to know is something. I ain't blaming you!

Rodney What d' you mean you're not blaming me? I ain't done nothing!

Del That's why I'm not blaming you! But . . . When you put Duke in the back of the van you didn't catch his head when you slammed the door?

Rodney No I didn't!

Del Are you sure?

Rodney Del, if you catch a Great Dane's head in a door, you *know* you've caught a Great Dane's head in a door!

Del Yeah, I suppose you're right.

Rodney I'll tell you who's to blame for this. Uncle Albert!

Del Why, what did he do?

Rodney He didn't do nothing, he's just a jinx!

Del Oh don't start all that again Rodney!

Rodney I've said it before, I'll say it again. That man is a right Jonah! They reckon when he boarded his last ship the crew shot an albatross for luck!

Del Will you stop going on about bloody Albert!

Rodney Well it's a bit of a coincidence though innit Del? I mean, yesterday we pick up a perfectly healthy dog. One night in the flat and 'wallop', the curse of the Trotters is upon it!

Del Everything is gonna be alright, I've got a feeling! Dookie's gonna be okay, he'll come out in a minute he'll be full of life, full of vim and full of vigour.

Rodney I wish I had your faith Del!

A young attractive receptionist enters.

Del Oi up. Well, what's the SP?

Receptionist Mr Collis is running a few final tests. He shouldn't be too long.

Rodney How's Duke?

Receptionist He's holding his own.

Del There are Rodney, he's up to his old tricks already!

Receptionist No, you don't understand. Duke is still unconscious! Look, why don't you sit down and relax. Duke is in the best possible hands, I can assure you.

Del Yeah, yeah, okay, thanks darling.

Rodney D'you know what I feel bad about now? That leg of pork Marlene put in the bag for Duke.

Del Well what about it?

Rodney Well we ate it last night, didn't we! Dookie had to make do with a tin of dog food! Every mouthful of that dinner made me feel more and more guilty.

Del You should have let me know Rodney you

and him could have swopped! Anyway, he had some of it didn't he.

Rodney What, warmed up left-overs for breakfast!

Del I didn't hear Duke complaining, did you?

Rodney We even had his steaks for lunch the other day didn't we?

Del Duke has steak every day, he most probably sick to death of the steaks, ain't he? Can you now change the subject please? Bloody steaks and legs of pork! Can't we talk about something more . . . more . . . you know. *(Struggles to pronounce it)* Aesthetical?

Rodney You want to . . . yeah, yeah, sure you take it away Derek.

Del struggles to find something aesthetical to say. He notices the receptionist.

Del Couldn't 'alf give that one, couldn't you Rodney?

The vet enters.

Del Oh Doc, any news?

Vet It's difficult to say. His heart beat is normal.

Del Is that good?

Vet Of course! All the tests have proved negative, I'm just waiting the results of his blood sample.

Rodney Have you taken an an X-ray?

Vet Yes, yes, there's no sign of damage. It's a complete mystery! Never mind, we'll keep him here as long as necessary. Where shall I send the bill?

Receptionist I got the details here sir.

Del How long d'you think it'll take Doc?

Vet Oh, it shouldn't take long, not if I send it first class.

Del No, no, no, I don't mean that. I mean how long will it take for Dookie's recovery!

Vet Oh, I see. Well it will take as long as it takes Mr Trotter! All we can do now is keep a close eye on him and let nature take its course . . . what have you been feeding him on?

Rodney Tins of . . .

Del *(Cutting in)* Steak! Steak, best porterhouse steak for his lunch. Liver for his supper. Roast pork for his breakfast. Only the very finest. He's had his milk, vitamins, he's had his, you name it he's had it!

Vet Pork? For his breakfast? Was it freshly cooked pork?

Del Yeah, freshly cooked the night before.

Vet Did you re-heat it thoroughly?

Rodney Well, we warmed it up a bit.

Vet You warmed it up a bit! Oh well, I think we may have solved the mystery, were neither of you aware that white meat, particularly pork, unless

Sleeping Dogs Lie

thoroughly re-heated, is a notorious breeding ground for salmonella poisoning?

Del Salmonella poisoning!! You reckon that's what Duke's got?

Vet Well, a strong possibility wouldn't you say? This leg of pork, do you still have it?

Rodney Not on us.

Del No it's at home in the fridge.

Vet Could you bring it in for examination?

Del Yeah, we'll pop back and get it right away. Come on Rodders.

Rodney Del. The dustmen come round today. Albert might have slung it!

Del Oh no, that dozy git! Can I use your phone? *(Del begins dialling)*

Rodney If it is salmonella, d'you reckon he'll survive?

Vet It depends what strain of salmonella it is. That's why I need to examine that meat! How long have you had the dog?

Rodney Oh er, one day.

Vet One day??

Rodney Oh, it's not our dog. It belongs to friends, we're just looking after him!

Del *(On phone)* Albert? It's Del Boy. Listen, that . . . Yeah, ahoy there! Listen Albert that pork in the fridge . . . Yeah . . . Pickles and crusty bread. Sounds lovely Albert. *(To Rodney and vet)* He's eaten it.

Vet Oh God! I'll phone the hospital from my office. Get him down there as quickly as you can.

Del Albert, Albert – Uncle Albert. Now listen to me, listen very carefully. I want you to do me a favour. I want you to put a few things in your duffel bag, put your coat on and go and stand in the hall for me and Rodders. We're gonna pop you down the hospital . . . You've gotta have an operation!

Rodney He won't have to have an operation!

Del A fiver says he does!

Rodney Alright, you're on!

Del What? I know you don't want to have an operation! Nobody *wants* to have an operation! But everyone at some time of their life has to have one! And today it's your turn! Now listen. . . . Well, you know that pork you had for dinner? Well . . . you're gonna laugh at this Albert . . .

Rodney A pound he don't!

Del Well, there's a strong possibility that it contained sam-and-ella poisoning! *(Hands Rodney a pound)* Oi, stop that, stop that, you're a grown man, pull yourself together, now listen we're gonna come down and pick you up in a couple of minutes, now be ready.

Del Rodney you should have warned me about this.

Rodney What d'yer mean warn you? I didn't even know meself!

Del You've got GCEs ain't yer?
Exits.

Rodney *(Calls)* Yeah. I got a GCE in Maths and Art! I ain't got a GCE in *Pork!*

NIGHT. THE TROTTERS' LOUNGE.
Rodney enters from the kitchen. Del is on the phone.

Del Well tell him we'll be in to see him tomorrow. Yeah. . . . Thank you Sister. Yeah okay, bonjourno. Ha ha, see what I mean, little bit of French, Rodney, little bit of French knocks 'em bandy.

Rodney Yeah, yeah, yeah, what about Albert? I take it we can't go and see him tonight then.

Del Ar no, he's none too clever apparently, I mean you know and pipes and . . . gadgets, everything stuck in him! You know.

Rodney *(Produces a bag of grapes)* Oh well, waste not want not, do you want a grape?

Del Yeah, why not? Cheers, bring 'em over here will you.

Rodney Oh did you get in touch with the vet's?

Del Yeah. He said Duke was . . . comatose!

Rodney Comatose? Well funnily enough I thought that when I saw him spark out in the back of the van!

Del You'd be right Rodney wouldn't yer? 'Cos I bet with this comatose, most probably sleep's the best thing for him!

Rodney Yes Derek. Rest, rest and more rest! Oh did they operate on Albert?

Del No.

Rodney That's a bit of luck. You owe me a fiver!

Del What?

Rodney In the vet's, remember? I said they wouldn't operate, you said they would! And you laid a fiver on it. *(The phone rings)*

Del Never mind about that, the phone, go on, the phone, go on there may be work there. Look, go on, go on.

Rodney Yeah? Who is it? Boycie. Boycie??

Del Where is he? Has he come home early or something?

Rodney So where you phoning from then Boyce? You're still over there? Yeah, Del?

Rodney Er . . . Del's not in at the moment! Oh yeah he's 'ere. . . . Yeah, alright, put her on. Hello Marlene . . . Don't you worry about Duke, he's as happy as they come! Yeah, get down Duke! The little rascal, he's jumping all over me!

Most probably recognises your voice, eh Marlene? Eh? *(To Del)* She wants Duke to talk to her!

Del Talk to her!? He's a bloody dog, the scatty mare! Tell her she can't.

Rodney holds mouthpiece in Del's direction.

Rodney *(To Del)* Come on Duke, come and talk to Mummy! Come on Dookie, talk to Mummy.

Del puts his mouth to mouthpiece and makes a quick, dog-like panting sound.

Rodney He's run off into the kitchen now Marlene and there's someone at the door, so I've gotta go, bye!

DAY. A TWO-BEDDED HOSPITAL WARD WITH A SMALL CORRIDOR LEADING OFF.

A young, pretty nurse exits from a ward and crosses the path of Del and Rodney. Rodney looks up the corridor in the nurse's direction.

Del Oi, oi! You up to that again are you? Women in uniforms?

Rodney No I'm not.

Del I tell you Rodney, the way you carry on you'll end up married to an arkela!

A doctor passes.

Del Doctor, sorry, we've come to pick up our Uncle.

Rodney Mr Trotter. The nurse said he might be able to leave.

Doc Oh yes, of course. I'll, er, I'll have a quick look at him first. Last night he underwent some rather – thorough examinations . . .

Del Yes, so the sister said on the phone! So was there anything wrong with him?

Doc Not that I could find! In fact I've just come off the phone to Mr Collis at the veterinary clinic. Apparently the dog has now made a complete recovery.

Rodney Duke's back on his feet?

Doc Still, you did the right thing to bring your uncle in. Better safe than sorry! Okay. Let's go and see how he is . . .

Doc leads Rodney and Del through doors. The screen is removed and Albert is dressed and putting a few things in his rucksack.

Doc Mr Trotter.

Albert You ain't doing nothing else to me are you?

Doc No, no, don't worry!

Del Alright then?

Albert No I'm not! I was alright yesterday though! Yesterday I'd never felt better in all me life! But you had to drag me in here for bloody Frankenstein to experiment on! They've had me on me back, on me belly, upside down, every which way but loose! Wires, pipes, tubes, bits of string, injections! And what d' they give me for lunch today? Roast bleedin' pork!

Rodney Oh well, you didn't miss much on the telly last night so . . .

Albert What was wrong with me?

Del Er . . . nothing!

Albert Nothing?? You mean I've had stomach pumps, anemones, glucose drips and students drawing all over my belly with felt tip pens and there was nothing wrong with me??

Del Great innit, eh? Yeah!

Albert I noticed you didn't come to see me last night! Still, I suppose you were too busy visiting the dog? Fight for yer country, risk yer life in sea and flame, then you get old and everyone forgets you!

Del Listen you old . . . *(Aware of the Doctor)* You silly old sausage. They wouldn't let us visit you last night 'cos you was under observation!

Albert Oh, don't give me that son!

Rodney We bought you grapes!

Albert Yeah, where are they?

Del We ate 'em!

Albert I see! I lay here last night, tubes sticking out of every place they could stick 'em in! Couldn't sleep, pills wouldn't even work, and all the time you two were eating my grapes!

Rodney Come on, we missed you last night!

Albert Did you?

Rodney Mmmh! We had no-one to spit our pips at! Let's get out of here Del, he's giving me the hump!

Doc Any problems?

Albert No doctor, there's *nothing* wrong with me! In fact I feel full of fitness and vitality!

Doc Good, good! Well, bye for now Mr Trotter, see you again!

Albert Not if I see you first shipmate!

Del Come on, hurry up, we're gonna get you home.

Del and Rodney move a few yards away.

Del The moaning, miserable old git you. . . .

Rodney Don't stop does he. Yeah! I mean, we got him all that treatment. All for nothing!

Del Yeah! And does he think anything of it. No does he hell!

Doc *(Produces a brown bottle of pills)* Oh by the way. Sister gave me these.

Del Why, what's a matter with you?

Doc No, no. She found them in your Uncle's locker.

Del Oh I see.

Doc Patients are not allowed to bring their own medication into the hospital. Please bear that in

Sleeping Dogs Lie

mind for the future.

Del What's he doing with these then? They're Duke's vitamin tablets!

Rodney No, they're Albert's sleeping pills. *(Produces an identical bottle)* I've got Duke's vitamins here.

Del Bloody hell Rodney! You've been giving Duke his sleeping pills!!

Rodney No! They were on the sideboard, I thought . . . Albert's been taking the Bob Martins?

Del No wonder he's full of vitality

Rodney What shall we do?

Del Well don't start throwing any sticks!

Rodney Shall we tell him?

Del No, no, no, it's a bit unfair after what he's been through!

Rodney Yeah, let's tell him!

Del Look, he's miserable enough as it is isn't he?

Rodney Yeah, he'll start thinking he's gonna turn into a werewolf or something!

Del We'll stay schtum on the whole affair! Don't say a word and no one'll be any the wiser! Just keep a close eye on him at lampposts and things! *(They move back to the bed attempting to contain their laughter)*

Del Come on then Unc. We'll get you home. We've gotta pick Duke up, Rodney's gotta take him for a run.

Rodney Actually you can come as well if you like Albert?

Albert What's the matter with you two?

Rodney Nothing, nothing! Well let's go then.
Del moves a few yards away and turns to Albert. He slaps his thighs.

Del *(As if calling a dog)* Come on boy!

TROTTERS INDEPENDENT TRADING Co
NEW YORK · PARIS · PECKHAM

"Au Revoir! It's Del Trotter here Founder and Chief Executive of the afore mentioned Peckham conglomerate "Trotters Independent Traders".

If there's anything that you want, we at T.I.T. have the best pukka deals in Peckham. It's not just our great offers that are créme de la menthe, but our company is based on customer relations and you will be guided through the sales process by our own sales team headed by Financial Director: Rodney Trotter G.C.E. So remember, whatever your needs, the T.I.T.s will deliver."

— Derek Trotter

The Bestest Boozer Guide

The Nag's Head.
Peckham. London. SE15.

This homely little hostelry was built on the site of a public grave where many victims of the great plague were buried. Unfortunately, it has an atmosphere to match. The locals are a colourful bunch drawn from all walks of life – wheeler-dealers, market traders, road-sweepers, second-hand car dealers and war heroes all mingle for a lunchtime drink or a few jars in the evening. The pub was re-decorated in the mid 1980s, and about time too. The last time it was done they had to keep stopping because of the Zeppelin raids.

No gambling is allowed on the premises, the landlord is frightened of losing his licence, though a number of the more belligerent patrons have told him what he can do with his licence. The landlord, Mike, does generously allow his more trusted customers to have drinks and meals on the 'slate' though he is known to moan about it. This is down to his religion; he's an orthodox tight-arse.

A variety of drinks are available behind the bar. Mr Fisher stresses he only sells English lager: Kronenburg, Hofmeister, stuff like that. Due to the tastes of one particular customer the staff have become proficient at mixing a wide range of cocktails ranging from the normal - Pina Colada - to the more erotic(*sic*) - Tia Maria and Lucozade.

The bitter, however, does not come up to scratch, as the regulars are willing to tell anyone within earshot. When someone says,'Looks like rain' he is not referring to the weather, but the strength of the beer. It did, however, win second prize in the Breweries' contest, narrowly beaten by the metropolitan water board.

The food is the standard range of bar snacks, basket meals and fried food, like chip sandwiches. It is not of the highest quality, however. One local character, often seen wearing a sheepskin coat and dripping with gold jewellery, once claimed the chicken was so tough that it asked him for a fight in the car park - twice.

The function room upstairs can be hired for a variety of events. In the past it has been used for wedding receptions, christenings and, on one memorable occasion, a seance. The evening proved to be a disaster when a horde of local heavy metal fans turned up believing The Seance were a group in the mould of Iron Maiden. When Elsie Partridge, the medium, walked out in her hat they rioted. Fortunately, she remained in a trance throughout. In the main bar, discos, talent contests and domino matches are all regular occurrences, but visitors should take care to avoid an old sailor with a white beard prone to playing the piano.

(Recommended by Mr D. Trotter, Mr R. Trotter, Mr A. Trotter, Mr Trigger, Mr Boyce, Mr M. Pearce, oh, and Denzil as well.)

The Dive.
Peckham. SE15.

The newly f[...]
pleasant, fun, c[...]
of Peckham. [...]
own home br[...]
are so strong[...]
don't worry [...]
and enjoy y[...]
true "Dive[...]
but is serv[...]

Watching the Girls go by

NIGHT. THE NAG'S HEAD

Albert is playing the piano and singing 'I'm in the Mood for Love.' A few of the locals, including Trigger, are listening to him.

Trigger *(To Maureen)* He's good ain't he? I like that! Hope he don't do no more though!

Mike 'Ere Trigger, you coming to the do Saturday night? Only I've only got two tickets left!

Trigger Yeah, put 'em down to me Mike!

Mike Good boy. Now they're £2.50 each but you can have the pair for a fiver!

Trigger You're a pal. *(Pays him)*

At a table Boycie and Del are playing cards. Behind them nearby is a dartboard. Mickey Pearce and a few mates are playing darts. Boycie looks up at a dart that has thudded into the board. He is increasingly worried about the flying missiles.

Boycie Right, I'll go for a tenner on that one.

Del Royal Flush! Get out of that my son!

Boycie I don't know where you're pulling 'em from tonight, Del Boy, I really don't!

Another dart thuds into the board.

Boycie *(To Mickey and mates)* Now listen you cretinous little erks! There is a three-yard exclusion zone around this table! And if another of your missiles should fall within it, I will personally shove it – point, shaft, feathers an' all, right up your gear box! Do I make myself clear?

Mickey Yeah, alright Boyce, we get yer drift.

Boycie Well just be aware then, eh just be aware . . . *(To Del)* Bloody peasants!

Del That's what I like about you Boycie, you've always been such a good loser!

Boycie Yeah, I've had plenty of bloody practice where you're concerned, ain't I?

Trigger arrives at the table.

Trigger Mike says no gambling. He's frightened of losing his licence.

Boycie Trigger, Michael knows very well what he can do with his bloody licence! I'm tryin' to win my money back here.

Del Alright, alright. There's plenty of time Boycie. Listen, I'll go and get some drinks. What do you want, scotch, scotch, Trigger?

Trigger Cheers Del.

Boycie About time an' all.

Del goes to the bar, calling to a mate as he does.

Del Alright Tommy?

Tommy Hello Del.

Del 'Ere, listen. Tell the enemy that I haven't forgotten about her sandwich toaster, I'll pop it round to her in the morning, alright? Michael please, three scotches if you don't mind.

Mike Del, I've told you before, do not gamble in the pub! I'll lose my licence.

Del Yeah why, no it's only a friendly game.

Mike Friendly, friendly? I've seen at least 50 quid change hands in here tonight!

Del That's what I mean, it's a friendly game! *(Hands him a fiver)* There you are, put the rest in the bottle, will you . . . I'm in the mood for love.

Mike 'Ere Del, Del. D'you want tickets for the do Saturday night, I've only got two left?

Del Yeah, go on then, I'll have 'em.

Mike Maureen, give them to Del, will you. And get the money.

Maureen That's a fiver.

Del *(His hands are full with drinks)* Yeah, alright, go on, get the money yourself. Help yourself. They're in me pocket.

Maureen roots through both pockets of his trousers. She is unable to find any money.

Maureen There's no money in there!

Del I know, it's in me jacket pocket! Go on help yourself.

She produces his wallet and takes a fiver.

Maureen You're a swine, you really are.

Del Take a pound for yourself.

Maureen Yeah I will, thanks very much.

Del There we are and thank you very much.

Mickey and his gang move to the bar. Rodney enters.

Rodney Maureen . . . Vodka and lemonade, please.

Maureen Vodka and lemonade.

Rodney Oi Mickey, alright? We going down the pizza palace later on then?

Mickey Well, we're going down there! But we're with the birds see!

Rodney Oh right. Yeah, well, I didn't fancy a pizza to be honest! Gotta be up early market and all that.

Mike 'Ere Rodney, do you want tickets for the do Saturday night, only I've only got two left?

Mickey Well he won't want two, will he Mike?

Rodney Why won't I want two?

Mickey Well you won't be bringing a bird will

243

you?

Rodney Why shouldn't I be bringing a bird?

Mickey There's no reason Rodney, but why break the habits of a lifetime?

Rodney Yeah, I'll have the two Mike! How much?

Mike Good boy, that's a fiver.

Mickey Who you bringing, then, your Uncle Albert?

Rodney I'm bringing a girl!

Mickey Oh give over Rodney!

Rodney I'm bringing a girl!

Mickey What's her name?

Rodney Eh?

Mickey What's her name?

Rodney It's none of your business! You'll have to find out Saturday night, won't you!

Mickey Who is it? 'Ere it's not that sort from the fishmongers is it?

Rodney No it ain't that sort from the fishmongers actually. This one happens to be in showbusiness!

Mickey Showbusiness. You're a liar.

Rodney I'm telling you the truth, Mickey. You wanna see her, an' all, she's a right bramma!

Mickey Well, I've got ten says you won't bring a bird on Saturday night!

Rodney Make it 20?

Mickey Alright, 20!

Rodney Right.

Del arrives.

Del Oi, oi, oi. What's all the noise? I can't hear myself think here.

Rodney He's betting me I ain't got a bird to bring to the do on Saturday.

Del Well you ain't have you? What really?

Rodney Yes.

Del Go on then Rodney, go on, take him the mouthy git! Go on.

Rodney I'll tell you what, make it 30.

Mickey Make it 40 if you like!

Del Go'n, go'n Rodney my son!

Rodney I know, I know let's make it a nice round 50.

Mickey You're on! I'll see you Saturday, and you'd better bring your money with you.

Mickey and gang exit.

Rodney He's got more front than Buckingham Palace ain't he?

Del Don't worry, come Saturday night you'll be the one that's laughing won't you?

Rodney Yeah!

Del Yeah, that's it. Come on, come and sit down over here and hold yer noise, right.

Trigger Here are Dave, you can sit here, I'm

going.

Boycie Are we playing cards or what?

Del Yeah come on.

Boycie About bloody time an' all.

Del Right it'll be down to you then Boycie. Here . . .

Del *(Referring to Mike)* Keep yer money to yourself will you, 'cos of old . . .

Boycie Okay I will go a pound.

Del Yeah, go on I'll have some of that. Two pound.

Boycie Four.

Del Eight.

Boycie 16.

Del 32, go on.

Boycie 64! . . .

Trigger is collecting his coat from behind Boycie. As he does he looks at Boycie's hand and then shakes his head at Del.

Boycie It's gonna cost you 128 to see me Del Boy.

Del Just a minute Boycie! Just a minute. This is supposed to be a friendly game ain't it. Friendly? It's like the start of World War Three ain't it?

Boycie Well what can we do Del, it's just the way the bids have gone!

Del I'll tell you what we can do! We can both take our bets back, and start all over again, and just you know try to play a little more sensibly. Alright.

Boycie Alright Del Boy! Anything you say. Right, a pound.

Del I'll see you!

Boycie I've got three tens!

Del Oh well that beats me out of sight Boycie. Well played my son. Goodnight. Come on Rodney let's go!

Del, Rodney and Trigger exit. Boycie is left staring at his cards and his £2.

NIGHT. THE TROTTERS' LOUNGE.

Del, Rodney and Albert are eating a takeaway.

Del Then I said to him, I said 'I'll see you!' Well you should have seen his face Uncle, he didn't know whether to laugh or cry! It was a picture weren't it Rodney?

Rodney Eh?

Del Boycie's face – when I tucked him up at cards!

Rodney Yeah, yeah, it was triffic!

Albert Wassamatter with you Rodney?

Rodney Nothing!

Del Come on Rodney cheer up. Pay day tomorrow and then it's Saturday when you take

Watching the Girls go by

Mouthy Mickey to the cleaners!

Rodney Yeah. Well that's what's bothering me Del.

Del Oh Rodney. You ain't starting to feel sympathy for him 'ave you? I mean, he's got far too much rabbit. It's about time he was put in his place once and for all that boy.

Rodney Del – I ain't got a girl for Saturday night! I ain't got a girl for any night!

Del You ain't got a . . . Well why did you keep upping the ante?

Rodney You told me to! You were stood behind me going 'Go on Rodney, go on my son!'

Del That's because you said you had a girl and I believed you!

Rodney Yeah, well I weren't telling the complete truth!

Del Telling the complete truth! You were lying through yer back bloody teeth, you stupid little berk! *(To Albert)* He stands to lose £50 on this!

Albert Why d'you have to tell lies Rodney?

Del Yes.

Rodney It was pride talking weren't it? I mean, there was Mickey Pearce and all the others and they was laughing at me! So I pretended! I lied! Anyway, what's to say I won't meet a girl by Saturday night?

Albert That's the spirit Rodney! There's loads of girls on this estate. And one of 'em must be willing to go out with you!

Rodney Well, the thing is Albert, I've been out with most of 'em in the past.

Albert What, didn't they like you?

Del Well they haven't started a fan club yet, have they Rodney?

Rodney *(Annoyed)* No Del, they ain't have they?

Del 'Ere, I've got it! I've got it! What about that tubby girl, who lives down by the community hall there, she'll go out with you Rodney. 'Cos she ain't got a full deck!

Rodney I can sort this one out on my own, thank you Derek!

Del Alright, alright, up to you.

Albert 'Ere, what about the girl from the fishmonger's?

Rodney No thank you Uncle!

Del Got it, cracked it, cracked it. Remember a couple of months ago when I took you out on that blind date?

Rodney Remember it?? I'm still having therapy for it! You are not honestly suggesting I spend another evening with Big Brenda??

Del Just 'cos she's taller than you! Anyway, I heard she was a very sporting girl!

Rodney Yeah, but when you told me she was a sporting girl I didn't realise you meant she was Southern Areas Shot-put Champion!

Del Well you seemed to get on with her! Very well, you were laughing and dancing and that.

Rodney Del, I was scared of her! Anyway, if you think I'm walking into the Nag's Head on Saturday night with Miss Anabolic Steroids on me arm, you've got another think coming. I could not stand another night of: 'So I said to Zola' and 'Zola said to me!'

Del Oh well, you'll have to sort it out yourself Rodney, I mean, you know I've done me best, ain't I, eh?

Albert You wanna be careful Rodney! Look at that little thing you took to the pictures the other week – lucky not to get yer collar felt!

Rodney Now that's not fair! She swore blind to me she was 18!

Del That's right, how did Rodney know she was only nine?

Rodney She was 16 that month! Anyway, I didn't suspect nothing till she paid her fare with a school bus pass! And she did all the chatting up! You know. I mean she invited me to the pictures!

Albert Well she had to didn't she, they wouldn't let her in without an adult!

Rodney Oh get off my back you two! I'm going to bed!

Del Rodney, listen are you sure you don't want me to phone up that Big Brenda? Oi, watch your language these walls are paper thin! I don't know, Uncle. I don't know what the younger generation's coming to, they can't even swear without effing and blinding!

NIGHT. THE TROTTERS' LOUNGE.

The following evening. Del is on the phone.

Del Yeah, yeah, alright then darling. Yeah, no it's been lovely hearing your voice after all these years! Okay see you around then. Bonjour. *(Replaces receiver)* Oh well. That's it. That's it. That was the last one.

Albert Last what?

Del I've been phoning round some of my old girlfriends, see if I could pull something out of the hat for Rodney. No luck. I tell you what Uncle, phoning round some of your old birds don't 'alf make you feel your age!

Albert Some of them married now, are they?

Del A couple of 'em are dead! Any phone calls for me today?

Albert Yeah, that young Mickey Pearce called, said he had a phone number of a lonely hearts club for Rodney!

245

Del Cor he's a lairy little sod he is. I'd like to tuck him up, I really would! *(Rodney enters from the bedroom wearing a white jacket, a black shirt and a white tie)* Oh well, carry on. Alright Rodney?

Rodney Yep!

Del Bloody hell!

Albert That reminds me, I'm playing dominoes down the Legion tonight!

Del What have you done to yourself??

Rodney Del, what you see before you is the new me! The old Rodney Trotter is dead! Long live the King!

Del You look like a liquorice allsort!

Rodney You ain't gotta wear it, have you?

Del No, that's too true, I ain'!

Rodney Look, I've still got a couple of hours left to win that bet! I'm going to go out and see if I can't bump into a right bramma!

Del Make sure you don't bump into her on a zebra crossing. No, I mean it looks a bit like now you see me, now you don't! Do you know what I mean? Rodney, use your loaf, you're never gonna pull a tart dressed up like Bertie Bassett?

Rodney You ain't getting to me Del so save yer breath!

Del Alright.

Albert You know what would look good on you Rodney, a big white stetson!

Rodney Do you know what would look good on you Albert? A dobermann pinscher!

Del Alright, alright, come on you two . . . Now pack it in. Listen, d'you want me to come with you?

Rodney You can if you like, I don't care.

Del Alright, alright, I'll come with you.

Rodney What you gonna wear?

Del Sunglasses I should think!

Rodney Oh don't bother, I'll go on me own.

Del Calm down, calm down. Come on, calm down, have a cup of tea. *(To Albert)* And will you stop winding him up!

Albert I ain't said a word!

Del No, well just make sure you don't then! I don't know what it is, but I keep getting this yearning to put my Bobby Crush LP on! Alright, where, Rodney, where did you get that?

Rodney I bought it off Paddy the Greek!

Del Paddy . . . the Greek! Pad . . . That's the rubbish I sold him last Monday! When I offered it to you then, you weren't interested!

Rodney Yeah I know, but he was cheaper than you!

Del Yeah, well, I've got to cover me overheads ain't I! Look, there's gotta be easier ways to win a bet than this ain't there.

Albert There's something I don't understand! All these young girls on the estate that you've taken out.

Rodney What about 'em?

Albert How come none of 'em want to see you again?

Del Yeah, that is a bit of a mystery innit, eh that.

Rodney Alright seeing as how it's 'National let's take the piss out of Rodney week'. I will tell you. I frighten them off! Alright.

Albert Frighten them off?

Del Yeah, well, he's got this thing about uniforms ain't he, you know what I mean.

Rodney It's got nothing to do with uniforms! I got over that phase months ago! Alright, look, to morons like Mickey Pearce, and *(Almost indicates Del)* some of the others, a woman is not a person, to talk to, someone to relate to. Oh no, a woman is just a trinket to bolster their masculinity. You know, something to hang on their arm to prove their macho image! Well I'm different! *(Albert makes a puzzled and then frightened face)*

Del No, no, there's nothing like that about him.

Rodney Look either I like a girl, or I don't! If I don't like her I don't see her no more! Right but if I do like her, I . . . tend to get a bit serious! And well I think that's what's frightening 'em off! They're young, you know, they want to see a bit of life – perhaps they don't want a wally like me drooling round 'em! I just fall in love too easy, that's my trouble!

Albert It's a family trait Del! Us Trotters wear our hearts on our sleeves!

Del Leave it out. He wears his heart in his Wranglers!

Rodney Oh, here we go again! See!

Del You don't know what love is Rodney, you haven't had enough experience to know!

Rodney I bet you have though ain't yer??

Del I certainly have bruv! I am covered in emotional scars me.

Albert I was in love once!

Del Yeah? Triffic! You see Rodders, I used to have this vision of love! I used to imagine that me, me and my – sweetheart – were running, in slow motion, through a field of buttercups! We're both – you know, we're both like that dressed in white, and you know like *(Pats belly)* I'd done a bit of weight! And suddenly – there in the background I can hear Semprini's orchestra playing the theme tune from *Doctor Zhivago*! *(Albert exits to the bedroom)* Where's he going?

Rodney Probably gone to be sick!

Watching the Girls go by

Del Shut up and listen, listen will yer? Then again, you see another time – another time. I imagine us at the top of an Alpine peak. Looking out across the mountains and the forests, it's just like as if we're the last two people left alive in the world. But suddenly behind us you hear the sound of a lone violin.

Rodney Semprini on a skiing holiday is it?

Del Will you shut up and listen.

Rodney Oh, come on Del, that ain't a vision of love, it's a yogurt commercial!

Del Oh well, thank you very much. There I am tryin' to give you – give you the benefit of my experience and what do you do, eh, you throw it back in my face. Well thank . . .

Albert returns carrying an old photograph.

Del What's this?

Albert That's Helga!

Del and Rodney Helga?

Del Helga who?

Albert I was in love with her! I don't think I ever really stopped loving her!

Rodney Yeah, well it's getting on ain't it, if we're going down the club.

Albert It was in 1946. We'd sailed in to Hamburg to pick up some prisoners of war. Helga was working in a bar near the docks. She was the most beautiful woman I've ever seen – I fell in love with her the moment I saw her! The little finger on her right hand was missing!

Del Caught her hand in the till did she?

Albert No, she lost it when her home was bombed. Her entire family was wiped out!

Del Oh! Sorry!

Albert I asked her to marry me. She said no! Just like that, no! See I mistook her gestures of friendship as tokens of love! I suppose it was all for the best really. You see the authorities didn't like us fraternising with the Germans, and I was still married to yer Aunt Ada and she'd have kicked up a stink! It's funny you know, but even after all this time, if ever I'm watching a German war film and I hear the word 'nein' I always think of Helga!

Rodney What, 'cos that's how many fingers she had?

Albert It's the German word for 'no'! I'll put this back in me box.

Del Yeah that's it. Go on, you put it somewhere safe.

Albert I think in her own way she loved me! She never used to charge me as much as the other lads! *(Exits)*

Del He tells a good story don't he? It gets you right here. *(Thumping his chest)* Don't it, eh, –

like bile. Well come on – come on, shake a leg. Come on.

Rodney No, I don't think I'll bother Del!

Del Yeah come on, Rodney, come on you've gotta make an effort!

Rodney No I'm never gonna pull a bird, am I.

Del Yes you are. Come on like, remember, he who dares wins!

Rodney Yeah but that don't work for me Del! I just have to pay Mickey the money that's all.

Del No you don't listen. I'll tell you what you're gonna do. *(Produces a fiver)* Listen. I'll buy the bet off you. Right, now if we win, I collect the 50. If we lose, I pay out. How's that grab you?

Rodney Yeah, alright then!

Del Good boy, you know it makes sense! Now, come on then, we're gonna go down and give those dance halls a bit of an' hammering tonight! *(Sings)* 'Come on let's twist again like we did last summer.'

Rodney Yeah Del, this time, you know, let's not just go crashing in there right and – kick 'em in the ankles and 'Wanna dance darling?' You know, let's have a bit of decorum this time, eh? Bit of sophistication!

Del What are you talking about? Sophistication is my middle name!

Rodney Yeah, I know, I know, I just forgot!

Del Well that's alright then. Don't you worry. Listen, I'm just gonna have a – a clean pants, splash of Brut, be with you in a minute, alright son.

Rodney Triffic!

NIGHT. A NIGHTCLUB.

A rather seedy dive. All the men appear to be second-hand car dealers, all the women are rather tarty. Del and Rodney enter and move to a vacant table.

Del I don't know. Stone me. A right blinding night this has turned out to be ain't it, eh, cor we've been everywhere! Empire Leicester Square, Hammersmith Palais, you name it we've danced there! And the only thing I've pulled is a ligament in me back, trying to do that bloody break dancing. Surely to goodness Rodney, one of them girls would have done you!

Rodney No, no, they wouldn't Del! This one's got to be something a bit special. I told Mickey she was in showbusiness. You know, I made her out to be a bit of a film star!

Del You didn't tell me that when I look the bet off you did yer?

Rodney No!

Del No, you saucy little git! Honestly I don't – oh

come – sit – put your tookers down there come on for heaven's sake. Take the weight of it. Well now are we gonna find a Bo Derek look-alike in Peckham? If it had been Bo Diddley we'd have been laughing!

Rodney Well, we ain't gonna find her here, are we? What d' you bring us in here for? Looks like a trouble place to me!

Del It's not a trouble place!

Rodney Del, there's dried blood on the door handle!

Del The cleaner's night off. Don't worry. *(Indicating back of club)* 'Ere look at that – oi, down there – those two there – those two there.

Rodney Do I look like St George? Oh come on Del, look at that one, she's older than the Mary Rose!

Del She's alright. I thought you said that this girlfriend of yours was a bit of a film star. Bette Davis is a film star!

Rodney Yeah, well so was Rin Tin Tin but I ain't taking a bloody alsatian to the do!

Del Don't know, it hasn't bothered you other years! Has it?

Rodney God, look at the state of her, eh.

Del Eh, what?

Rodney You can see her wrinkles from here!

Del Alright, alright.

Rodney Got a face like a bulldog chewing a wasp, ain't she.

Del Leave it – alright, go on, you can have the best one!

Rodney That is the best one!!

Del I don't know what I'm going to do. I just bloody well give up with you. I really do. What you drinking?

Rodney Lager.

Del goes to the bar.

Del That's all you're gonna get. Oi, Orlando! *(Sitting a few yards away is an attractive, if tarty, woman. She is all body and little brains)* 'Ere Vonny. Vonny how are you? How you going?

Von Hello presh, how are you?

Del Oh I'm alright. You know, I'm doing a bit here, I'm doing a bit there. You know me. What are you doing these days, you still stripping are you?

Von I'm not a stripper Del, I'm an exotic dancer!

Del Ah yeah, of course you are. Sorry. You still take yer clothes off though, don't yer?

Von Well it's part of the act!

Del Yeah, yeah. 'Ere I heard you got into a bit of trouble the other week. What was that?

Von Did you hear about that? Bloody drug-crazed tourist, he jumped up on the stage after

me! He tried to strangle me you know!

Del Yeah I know, so I heard! How is the snake now?

Von Oh he got over it.

Del Oh good, good.

Von I've got the sack from most of my clubs now.

Del Oh yeah Orlando! *(To Vonny)* Yeah, why's that then?

Von Well, to be honest·with you Del, I've been hitting the bottle a bit too much.

Del Oh have you.

Von Doctor says I've got a drink problem. I said to him, I ain't got no problem, I like it! Of course, my real problem is frustration!

Del Perhaps I could help you out there, couldn't I, eh?

Von I shouldn't be a stripper Del!

Del Oh I don't know, I think it suits you.

Von Deep down inside I'm a singer! But no-one'll take me seriously!

Del No, I know. Gives you the 'ump don't it, eh? Oi Orlando.

Von *(Starts singing)* 'I would not leave you, in times of trouble.'

Del Yeah, that's beautiful Vonny, that is, really lovely you know. Yeah, you'll go a long way!

Von *(Still singing)* 'We never could have come this far. I took the good times.'

Del That's really nice Vonny, that is, yeah beautiful I love it.

Von *(Still singing)* 'I'll take the bad times.'

Del Yeah super . . . Oi, Orlando.

Von *(Still singing)* 'I love you just the way you are.'

Del Gordon Bennett, that's my bloody ear'ole Vonny . . .

Von Sorry presh!

Del Stone me, leave it out. 'Ere just a minute. You know my local, don't you. The Nag's Head. Well there's a bit of a do on there tomorrow night, do you fancy going?

Von Will they let me sing there?

Del Well yes, they'll insist!

Von Alright then. You gonna pick me up?

Del No, well you see you won't be going with me!

Von Who am I going with then?

Del It's alright, you'll be going with my dopey little brother over there.

Von Where?

Del He's over there! Over there at that table, there look.

Von Well there's no-one there, just some geezer dressed up like a negative!

Watching the Girls go by

Del Yeah, that's him!

Von Oh Del . . .

Del I stand to win a bet.

Von Oh Gawd!

Del Listen Vonny. I'm on for a 50 here, alright. *(Hands her some money)* I'll tell you what, come on look there's a score in it for yourself.

Von Oh ta Del.

Del Alright. Go'n then!

Von What?

Del Well, you've gotta go over there haven't you and you've gotta chat him up! Make it look real! Go on. That's it, use your charm girl. Go on.

Rodney is looking bored. He catches Vonny looking at him. Vonny smiles. Rodney looks over his shoulder to see if someone is behind him. Rodney returns a nervous smile. Vonny comes over.

Von Hi!

Rodney Oh, watcha!

Von Is this anyone's seat?

Rodney Em . . . No! No!

Von My name's Yvonne.

Rodney I'm Rodney. . . .

Von I ain't seen you here before!

Rodney No, well that's probably something to do with the fact that I've never actually been here before! So, do you work here?

Von Oh no. I'm . . . erm . . . I'm in showbusiness!

Rodney Really? You ain't done any films have you?

Von Oh well, there was a couple when I was younger, but I'd rather not talk about it! I just called in here tonight on the off chance, I was hoping I might bump into some friends. I heard someone was throwing a party tomorrow night! But now it looks as though I'll have to spend the evening in on my own!

Rodney Oh!

Von Yes, I've got absolutely nothing to do tomorrow night!

Rodney Listen I've got a couple of tickets for a do! It's only a pub . . .

Von *(Cuts in)* Oh, I'd love to go with you, thank you!

Rodney It starts about 8.30.

Von Oh I'll see you there.

Rodney Well, hold on, I'd better write the address down for you.

Von Oh it's alright, I know where the Nag's Head is! Must rush. *(Exits)*

Del arrives.

Del There you go. Don't tell me you've pulled.

Rodney *(Smugly)* I have.

Del You haven't!

Rodney I have.

NIGHT. THE TROTTERS' LOUNGE.

The lounge is in darkness. We hear the front door slam. Del enters and switches on lights. He is in a state of panic and has obviously been running. The doorbell rings.

Del *(Calls through closed door)* Rodney, Rodney listen. Now listen to me. Let me explain before – before I do something that you'll regret, I'll explain to you, you see . . .

Albert No Del, it's me, Del.

Del Ah! Oh it's you. Come on in where's Rodney?

Albert He's coming up the stairs. Oh he's after your blood, Del.

Del It wasn't my fault. Well not entirely. I only did it so that he could win the bet. I'm sure in the cold light of day Rodney will realise that Vonny's behaviour wasn't that bad.

Albert Oh it was bad, Del. It was very bad. At one point Rodney starting crying.

Del Oh no!

Rodney storms in.

Rodney I am going to kill you!

Del Careful, now listen, don't be a plonker all yer life!

Rodney You set her . . . up to . . . going out with me!

Del I did not set her up I paid her!

Rodney You paid her?? Well that's worse! Come here.

Del Now listen. Stop it. Alright, now listen, I only did it for you to win the bet. And to save your pride!

Rodney My Pride!? Tonight, in front of half of Peckham, the bird I told everyone was my girlfriend stood on the counter and took all her clothes off!

Albert I don't think anyone noticed Rodney!

Rodney Well you certainly noticed Uncle! Because you stood on a chair to notice! *(Indicating Del)* And at one point he almost knocked you off!

Del That's right, he did. No listen alright, so she has one too many gins, I didn't know she had a drink problem.

Rodney No, I found out a couple of new things about her as well. I didn't know she could juggle light ale bottles. I didn't know she couldn't sing! And where did that snake come from??

Del I don't know! Nobody knows where it went either!

Rodney That's it isn't it? I will never ever live this

evening down. This is the sort of stuff that legends are made of! Right? I was telling everyone how me and Yvonne was thinking of getting engaged. And I turned round and there she is stark b . . . with nothing on! I had her singing in one ear and Hissing Sid in the other!

Albert Yeah, but you won your bet didn't you?

Rodney Yeah, I won the bet alright.

Del Ah good boy, did Mickey Pearce pay up?

Rodney Yeah, he paid up – he was laughing but he paid up.

Del Alright. Come on come on, let's have the 50!

Rodney flicks a 50p coin to Del.

Del What's this? 50p??

Rodney Yeah . . . (Smiling) Oh, I bet I know what you thought!

Del You and that Mickey Pearce, you're like a couple of bleedin' kids.

Albert I can't wait to tell the boys down the market! Rodney's girl did a strip and Del Boy won a 50p bet.

Rodney (Looking into the hood of his duffle coat) Uncle, stand very still! There is a snake in the hood of your duffel coat!

Albert freezes.

Albert What?

Del God there is too. Look at it. It's a big 'un. Quick go down and phone the vet's quickly.

Rodney and Del Hissss . . .

The Loves and Loses of Rodney Trotter - Part 1

MONICA

Monica and I had trouble getting it together on a one-to-one basis, if you see what I mean. Mickey Pearce, who has lived with a woman, advised us to have a two-week trial separation. Del, of course, thought this was hilarious, seeing as we had only been seeing each other for a fortnight. He said I was miserable just because some bird with fat thighs had given me the elbow. She did not have fat thighs and she did not give me the elbow. True she was seen dancing at the Nag's Head disco with Mickey Pearce during our trial separation, but I was determined not to let it bother me. Del and I went up west in Boycie's Jag and pulled a couple of posh sorts. I did all the chat, Del chipped in with his usual pony. Trouble was, on the way to their Penthouse I chucked the cigar pack with their address on out of the window. Still, never mind, plenty more chicks around. Del got the right 'ump with me though.

JANICE

Janice and I had the same understanding and appreciation of art – an affinity, an aesthetic bond, kindred spirits and seekers of beauty in a broken, ugly world. Probably because her brother, Don, was a painter for the council and I had my GCE in art. My deep understanding of her led me to discover she didn't wear a bra, until Del came in and ruined everything just as we was getting intimate. He's such a philistine – he once said Michaelangelo was a wallybrain because it took him 12 years to paint a ceiling, and that whoever sculpted the Venus the Milo, as he called it, was a sicko. My romance with Janice went down the kermit because I got a job as a night security operative with Trotter Watch and Del took her out to make sure no-one moved in on her. To be honest, with Del taking her out for steak meals nearly every night I was doing quite well with her, but it came to nothing.

SANDRA

Now this turned out to be a bit of a sticky one. Problem was, Sandra was Old Bill and Derek did not like it one bit. I met Sandra during a blind date Del and I was on with a mother and daughter. Unfortunately, I copped for the mother and spent the whole night holding hands with an old sort with a cough. Luckily, a riot broke out at this drinking club we went to in New Cross and Sandra turned up to sort it out. Well, I like a bird in uniform so I asked her out. Del accused me of being a grass, but I took her to the pictures and bought her a doner kebab. Let no-one say Rodney Trotter does not know how to charm a woman. Unfortunately, I took her back to the flat and she realised everything in it was hooky, including the watch I had given her. That was the end of that, and I only survived having my collar felt because I bought her that kebab. I suppose our type and her type don't mix.

IRENE MacKAY

This was another dodgy one. I was selling lingerie door to door when I came across this married sort. It bothered Del, though, She was 40 and I was 23 and a half, though the age difference didn't bother me. It bothered Del, though, who said when she was drinking frothy coffee with some Ted at the Lyceum I was struggling to keep my gripe water down. What bothered him more was Irene's husband, Tommy, who was inside doing a spell for wounding with intent, GBH and attempted murder. I told Del I could look after myself, but he had to stick his bloody nose in and she finished with me on his say-so. He tried to make up for it by sorting Tommy Mackay out for me, but Irene and I had decided it wouldn't work. Anyway, I met this bird called Zoe, 18 she was and with a body that made Bo Derek look a cert for plastic surgery. I suppose Irene was just a mother figure I was looking for.

DEBBY

Debby worked in the newsagents, which was a bit of a problem when I went in there to buy one of my adult art magazines. We were very much in love, thinking of getting engaged in fact, until Del threw a huge bloody spanner in the works. Turns out Debby's mum was one of the thousands of birds Del's been engaged to. He's handed out more rings than Ratners. Well, Del gets the idea that Debby is his daughter, even though she's a pretty girl. When he told me I thought I was in the middle of a bad trip. For the first time in my life I thought I'd met a girl who really meant something to me and it turned out she was my bloody niece. I had a nightmare where my wife kept calling me uncle Rodney. Of course, it was all a load of pony and Debby was really the daughter of Del's best mate. But it was too late, Del blew it for me and Mickey Pearce was in there like a rat up a drainpipe.

YVONNE

Now this was a bloody disaster. I got myself involved in a bet with Mickey Pearce that I'd bring a bird to a disco at The Nag's Head. I told him she was in showbusiness, which presented a bit of a problem because at that time I was going through a spell dryer than the Sahara. Del took me up west to try and pull a decent sort because he'd taken the bet over from me. Little did I know that the bird he fixed me up with, Yvonne, was an exotic dancer. That night in front of half of Peckham the girl I'd told everyone was my girlfriend took all her clothes off. God knows where the snake came from. Turns out she had a bit of a drink problem. Still, it was worth it to see Del's face when he realised the bet with Mickey was for 50p, not 50 quid. And he calls me a plonker.

HELEN

This is best described as a brief encounter. I thought Helen was a bit of a Brahma - slender, tall, a bit older than me, but then I've been brought up to respect my elders. All told, she looked like that Linda Evans who played Crystal Carrington in *Dynasty*. I thought I'd struck gold, bloody Klondike in fact. Del didn't agree, described her as an old dog - well, he should know. When I said she looked like Crystal Carrington, he reckoned she was more like Crystal Palace. Helen of Croydon, he called her. The face that launched a thousand dredgers. Needless to say it didn't last.

LISA

This wasn't a romance, really, but it's worth noting for the fact that I managed to stitch Del up like a kipper. Lisa is Trigger's niece, I used to play with her when I was a nipper. She was a scruffy little mare then, had more candlesticks than Liberace. Anyway it turns out that she's grown in to a right sort. Well, I tried to move in, and so did Del, the seedy old git. We both tried giving her the chat and it ended up with her coming for tea at the flat with the two of us. Talk about cosy. I went under the sunbed to get a tan and my brother decided to turn the timer up so that by the end my face was redder than a smacked arse. Del, the git, said I looked like a Swan Vesta. He got his though after he started giving Lisa some old pony about him being a paratrooper. I fixed up for him to spend a day hang-gliding with her and her pals. He tried to wriggle out of it, but he ended going up and disappearing for 12 hours. I was a bit worried for a while but apart from the cuts and bruises he was fine. The TV transmitter that he hit never recovered though. Turned out Lisa was engaged all the time. What a couple of wallies.

251

And then we'll take you down to the nice man who'll give your Uncle Delly Welly... three lovely grand!

Yeah he's alright. A bit wet, but he'll survive. The sun'll soon dry you out, won't it?

DENZIL! I've got your money!

Great! I'll see you down the pub later

SPLAT!

As One Door Closes

DAY. THE TROTTERS' LOUNGE.

Leaning against the wall next to the kitchen door is a high cardboard container which states 'Louvre Doors.' Albert is watching an Asian programme on TV. Del and Rodney are sat at the table anxiously working something out on a pocket calculator.

Del Well?

Rodney 1,992!

Del That's what it come to last time!

Rodney Yeah, I know and that's what it'll come to this time and the time after that an' all.

Del Two grand! Where are we gonna get two grand from? Look, try it again Rodney. And this time see if you can get it lower!

Rodney Well how can I get lower? Look 12 times 166 equals 1,992!

Del *(Producing another calculator)* Use this calculator!

Rodney It's still gonna work out the same Del! I could do it on this calculator, that calculator. I could do it on me fingers and toes, I could do it on beads, it's still gonna come to 1,992, ain't it?

Del Right bloody help you turned out to be Rodney!

Albert Keep the noise down will yer, I can hardly hear this!

Del Shut up you saucy old git.

Rodney Well, even if you could hear it, you couldn't understand it, could you, it's in Indian!

Albert In 1959 I was in Bombay!

Del You carry on much longer by tomorrow afternoon you could be in traction.

Albert But I like this kind of music!

Del Ah! Oh yeah, look at that Rodney. It's one of his favourites that is. That's that good old-fashioned sing-along number, *Knees Up Mother Patel.*

Del Listen, we're over there trying to devise a scheme that is gonna make us into millionaires, and all you can do is sit here and watch bleedin' Indian banjos!

Rodney Why don't you just stick a George Harrison LP on yer Walkman or something?

Albert You two are gonna be millionaires! And the Titanic was unsinkable!

Rodney Oi, you, there's a fortune to be made out of this deal!

Albert Yeah? What is this deal then?

Del Lowvery doors!

Albert So what about 'em?

Del Well what about 'em? I'll tell you what about 'em! There's a certain painter and decorator what gets down the Nag's Head, and his name is Brendan O'Shaugnessy.

Rodney He's Irish!

Del Yeah! That is correct, Rodney. Now this Brendan O'Shaugnessy has just got a contract to decorate and fit out a new housing estate over at Nunhead. And what has the architect deemed shall be fitted to all wardrobes? None other than lowvery doors! 166 to be precise!

Albert Well, you've got one of them, that's a start innit?

Del Ooh, he can be a sarky old bark when he wants to can't he, eh?

Rodney That's just a sample, innit? You see Del's mate, Teddy Cummings, right, he manages a joinery works and he can let us have hundreds of them doors dirt cheap! And there's 200 per cent profit on each one!

Del That's right. It's like printing money! And the cherry on the cake is that this building firm is putting up houses all over the shop, so it's a sort of long-term, on-going situation!

Albert So where's the problem?

Rodney Well, Teddy Cummings will only sell them doors in bulk!

Del Yeah, if we don't get two grand by tomorrow afternoon the deal's off!

Albert Well can't you borrow the money?

Del We've tried all that ain't we! We've been everywhere! The bank that likes to say yes said on yer bike!

Rodney The sign of the Black Horse gave us a load of old pony, didn't they.

Del Even the listening bank cocked a deaf 'un!

Rodney Del . . . you'll most probably think this is stupid!

Del What is?

Rodney Well, it's a long shot I'm here to tell you. It's a real long shot!

Del Oh I know, I like long shots. You know me. Rodney, he who dares wins! What is it?

Rodney Oh well, 'ere you are. I was reading this colour supplement yesterday.

Del Yeah?

Rodney There was an article in it that really caught my interest!

Del Yeah, yeah?

Rodney It was about a butterfly.

Del A butterfly?

Rodney Yeah! Not an ordinary butterfly though!

Del Ah!

Rodney No, this one's a bit of a rarity. It's virtually unheard of in this country!

Del Oh well, that's interesting innit?

Rodney I think its name was, eh, the Jamaican swallow tail.

Del Well it don't mean a lot to me Rodney, that, no.

Rodney No well here it is. Look it's scientifical name is *Papilio humerus*!

Del Oh, now, that does ring a bell! I don't believe what he is doing to me! Here I am on the verge of losing the biggest deal of my life and this plonker here wants to give me a lecture about poxy butterflies!!

Rodney No, you don't understand do you? It's an endangered species.

Del Yeah, I know, you'll be an endangered species if you carry on much longer Rodney!

Rodney Look some of these things have been seen in southern England! One of them was spotted in Greenwich Park!

Albert You wanna whip him down the quack's a bit lively, the boy's flipped his lid!

Rodney Listen mouthy, there's this private . . . *(Can't pronounce the word)* Well there's this private butterfly collector right and he's willing to pay a £3,000 reward for one of these butterflies.

Del £3,000!

Rodney Yeah and Greenwich Park is only up the road, innit?

Albert You mean, you want us to go around chasing butterflies?

Rodney Yeah!

Del You know what? I think you're right Rodney!

Rodney Yeah?

Del Yeah! It is stupid!

Rodney Well I said it was a long shot, didn't I.

Del Gordon Bennett! I can just see us three now running up and down Peckham High Road. We'll be trying to catch Mars Bar wrappers.

Del Hey come on, look at the time. Hey, come on, get this stuff out of here. We're gonna go and see if we can do a bit.

DAY. THE MARKET.

Del is trying to sell a batch of 'Home Hair Trimming Devices'.

Del Ask yourselves this, ask yourselves this, how much do you spend on hairdressing, eh? Now it's gotta be six or seven quid a hit these days innit?

You work that out over a year and it comes to a national debt! Right but, for just £1.50 you could invest in one of these super de-luxe trimming combs! I mean, you can save yourself a fortune in the comfort of yer own front room! Could you just – just come round a bit closer, come closer 'cos at these prices I can't afford to deliver!

Rodney arrives carrying a few boxes. He bends down to put them in a suitcase.

Man in crowd Hey is this sharp enough, mate?

Del Is it sharp? Is it – sharp?

Del looks for something upon which to demonstrate sharpness. Without a thought, he takes a chunk of Rodney's hair out with the trimmer.

Del Is that sharp enough for you?

Rodney knows something has touched his head but doesn't know what. He feels his head and surveys the sky for low-flying pigeons.

Del Invest £1.50 and you can save yourselves thousands! This is a better bet than Piggott on a favourite! Now listen to me – listen. These come recommended you know by the world's leading hair stylists. Vidal Sassoon, Teezy Weezy, Mick the barber, Mick the Miller – Mickey Mouse, Sweeney Todd. *(Giving up the ghost)* Why do I bother?

Rodney It's been one them days innit?

Del Never mind Rodney, pack up the suitcase, we'll go down the Nag's Head for a couple of swift 'alfs . . . Two thousand by tomorrow! I've got as much chance of winning Miss World!

Denzil approaches, a massive ghetto-blaster strapped to his shoulder.

Del Oi, Denzil!

Denzil Del Boy! *(Slaps Del's open hands)* Rodney! *(Raises has hands to slap Rodney's hands. Rodney puts suitcase down and holds his hands out but Denzil has forgotten about it by then)* So how's your luck?

Del Don't ask! Don't ask. If they made it into a film it'd be a bigger tear-jerker than *Love Story*!

Denzil Bad as that, eh?

Del Yeah. I'd go into the details – only I don't want to see grown men cry!

Denzil Listen, you want to hear a sob story I will tell you a sob story! I have just found out that my wife has been lying to me!

Rodney No! *(Thinking she's got another man)*

Denzil Yeah! Every morning she says she's gonna leave me, and when I come home at night she's still there!

Del Like it. Look at him, look. Soppy look.

Denzil I can't stop, I've gotta get down to the

As One Door Closes

Job Centre.

Del Yeah alright. Down the Job Centre eh? You've got yourself into a growth industry at last!

Denzil Yeah, well, the wages are lousy, but the hours suit me fine!

Del See you then Den.

Denzil See you around.

Del See you Denzil. Give my love to Corinne. *(Under his breath)* The miserable old cow! Oh well, come on, let's go.

Rodney I heard it took three coppers to arrest Denzil the other night!

Del That's right. One to put the handcuffs on and two to carry the radio!

Rodney You've heard it then.

Del We've all heard ain't we. Come on. Let's go.

Del Hey hold up! What did Denzil get the sack for?

Rodney Oh he didn't, he was made redundant.

Del Hold on, if he was made redundant, that means he's got redundancy money?

Rodney Yeah, I suppose so!

Del *(Calls)* Denzil!! Denzil!

Denzil *(Alarmed)* You're not having any!

Del I'm your friend. Denzil. Denzil! Denzil!

Denzil *(Running away)* You're still not having any!!

Del Oi Denzil, I'm gonna make you rich, Denzil. Put me down . . . I'm a policeman . . .

Denzil Please don't make me rich!

Del Denzil, don't be a plonker all your life!!

DAY. THE TROTTERS' LOUNGE.

Albert is alseep in the armchair. When he hears the front door slam he wakes and picks up a dustpan and brush. Del enters in a victorious mood.

Del I'm gonna live forever . . . Alright Uncle? Had a good day?

Albert I've been busy doing the housework Del. I've made all the beds except yours and Rodney's.

Del Oh that's alright. Well sit yourself down. Go on, you don't want to knock your old pipe out do you, eh?

Albert No that's my trouble. I never know when to stop!

Del Yes this is true. This is very true.

Albert You're in a better mood than you were this morning!

Del Yeah well I've got every reason to be, haven't I. I've clinched the lowvery door deal!

Albert Never!

Del Yeah it's true! I've picked them up, paid for them, and Rodney at this moment in time is stacking 'em in the garage! All I've gotta do now is phone Brendan, and he'll come round and pick up and then we shall be rich!

Albert Where d'you get the money to pay for 'em?

Del Well d'you remember my pal Denzil – called in here a couple of weeks ago.

Albert Oh yeah. He was black?

Del Yeah – well, he still is! Anyway did you hear that he had £2,000 in redundancy money?

Albert Yeah.

Del Well he ain't now!

Albert Oh come off it Del. You didn't take the fella's redundancy money!

Del Well yeah. I mean, he insisted!
Rodney enters from the hall.

Rodney I have never seen anything like it. He did Denzil up like a kipper!

Del *(On phone)* Yeah, well look, tell him when he comes in that I've got all the lowvery doors and they're in the garage and he can come and pick 'em up any time he wants.

Rodney He chased him he did! A mile and 'alf through Deptford! Denzil was 300 yards from his front door. And he put in a kick! I tell you, Seb Coe ain't even in the picture when he's got a smell of money in his nostrils!

Del Okay then Bridie, don't you forget to tell him now will yer?

Rodney He forced lager down his throat then he frog-marched him to the bank! Do you know Denzil was crying when he handed that money over!

Del Listen to me, dopey. Listen, now right, Denzil give me £2,000 pounds today, I give him £3,000 tomorrow! Now that means he gets £1,000 profit in 24 hours. Now he ain't gonna get that at the Bradford and Bingley is he? Denzil knows it makes sense!

Albert What about his missus, she's a bit of a dragon ain't she?

Rodney Well let's just say I wouldn't like to be in Denzil's shoes when Corinne finds out!

Del No, she'll be alright. She'll be as sweet as a nut! Denzil bought her a little present.

Rodney Oh yeah, a do-it-yourself hair cutting kit!

Del No, she's gonna treasure it, you mark my word. Now listen gentlemen, listen to me, because this evening I am taking you down the Nag's Head public house, where we're gonna hold one of them things that Rodney couldn't organise in a brewery! After that – after that, we're gonna to the Star of Bengal for a Ruby! *(Produces cans of beer)* So get that down your

neck, Rodney. Cheers.

Rodney is in front of mirror. He is horrified to discover a chunk of his hair is missing.

Rodney My hair's falling out!

Del What?

Rodney My hair's falling out in great chunks! I'm going bald! Derek, I am 24 years old and I'm going bald!

Albert That's supposed to be a sign of something.

Rodney Yeah, it's a sign that I'm going bald!

Del Listen you tart. Come here. Let me have a look at it! Come on, let me see.

Rodney Well, what d'you reckon?

Del Well, let me put it this way Rodney, if your head was a tyre you'd fail the MOT!

Rodney Bloody hell I'm going bald!!

Albert No it might not be that Rodney. You might have a touch of alopecia!

Rodney I never thought of that Unc! And there's me fretting, eh? My head's gonna look like a bloody egg!

Albert Get yourself a wig son!

Rodney Oh yeah, I'm gonna look really cool ain't I, tryin' to pull a bird with a Davy Crockett hat on me head!

Del *(Phone rings)* I'll answer that. It could be the phone. Hello? Brendan. How are you pal? I see you got the message then? Eh? What d'you mean you've been tryin' to phone me all day? Eh? Well what's wrong? Why don't you talk to him? You know. Go and persuade him.

Rodney Del, what's up?

Del It's the architect, he's changed his mind! He wants Victorian panel doors now! *(On phone)* Brendan, listen, listen, listen Brendan, you know, go – you know, give him a few quid, eh? Bung him, eh. Eh? Well . . . beat him up then! Well I'll come down and beat him up for you if you like! No Brendan, look I've got 165 lowvery doors in my garage! All my capital is tied up in 'em! I know we didn't sign a contract but what am I supposed to do with 'em? And yours. I'll get you for this, Brendan, you just see if I don't! *(Puts phone down)* Damn! There they go. Look at all that, I knew everything was going too smoothly, all that money!

Albert Can't you take 'em back to the warehouse and swop 'em for panelled doors?

Del Take 'em back to the warehouse!!

Rodney Yeah, why don't we just take 'em back and swop 'em?

Del We can't take 'em *back* can we, eh? We were well lucky to get 'em out without being caught!

Rodney They were hooky? Oh great Derek! Cosmic! They were hooky lowvery doors were they! Well you didn't mention that small fact to me, did you?

Albert *(Looking form the window)* Del?

Del What?

Albert You know that Denzil fella?

Del Yeah.

Albert Has he got any brothers?

Del Yeah, five, why?

Albert Nothing. It's just that five West Indian blokes just got out of a Rover!

Del *(He and Rodney are looking from the window)* It's them. That is them, it's Denzil's brothers!!

Rodney Look at the size of them!!

Albert What you gonna do Del?

Del Oh well, we'll just stay here. We'll stay here. And if they wanna cut up rough we'll exchange punches you know like man to man.

Rodney You're not including me in that are you? Fight 'em! Derek look at the size of 'em!

Albert They'll look even bigger when they get up here Rodney!

Del Yeah, well, I'll tell you what. Don't worry. Don't worry. Listen I'm gonna explain. Bloody hell! I'm gonna, what we're gonna do – what we're – I'll tell you. We can run for it. Come on let's get out of here. Quick . . .

DAY. THE CEMETERY.

Mum's monument is a faded, flaking gold. Del is in a mood of quiet contemplation. Albert is sitting on the bench bored. Rodney is agitated.

Albert What's he brought us here for?

Rodney Gawd knows!

Albert I don't like these places, they make me feel queasy!

Del What's up with you two?

Rodney Oh it's nothing, it's just Albert, he don't feel too well!

Del How bad is he? I mean, is it worth our while taking him home?

Albert Oh, I ain't that bad Del!

Del Oh good. Well you just sit back and enjoy yourself then!

Rodney Enjoy ourselves Del, we are £2,000 in debt, we have a garage load of hooky doors and a mob of irate Rastafarians after our blood! So what are we doing hanging round Mum's monument?

Del Because I always come here in times of trouble Rodney. I just come here, stand here and tell Mum my problems and, somehow, she

As One Door Closes

always seems to provide an answer. She's never let me down yet! I mean, you take that time when you were done for possession of cannabis. I just came here an' I told Mum that her little baby was in trouble with the law! And it was almost as if I could hear her voice saying to me 'Bribe the Old Bill, Del!' And what happened? When the case came to court the police could provide no evidence!

Albert *(To Rodney)* You told me you got a 250 quid fine and a suspended sentence!

Del Yes, because three days before the trial this plonker pleaded guilty by post! Mum wasn't to know that was she! Don't worry, she'll come up with a solution to our financial plight! Come on, sit yourself down, just relax Rodders. Look around you Rodney, just think, one day all us Trotters'll be here. *(To Albert)* Well I don't know about you!

Albert That's alright Del, I'm with the Co-op!

Del Yeah, back in the Sixties I bought us all plots you know. I thought land's a good investment annit?

Rodney Oh, can't go wrong Del can yer!

Del See, I'll be over there, next to Mum, and Grandad, well he's over there in the Gardens of External Peace.

Rodney Where will I be?

Del points into the far distance, so far he has to squint.

Del Oh yeah, you are, oh look, see look, see right over there. Right over the back there.

Rodney Yeah.

Del See that, can you see the big pile of stinging nettles?

Rodney Yeah.

Del There!

Rodney Under the stinging nettles! I ain't gonna be buried under a pile of stinging nettles!

Del Well it ain't gonna bother you is it Rodney, 'cos you're gonna be brown bread!

Albert What happens when his family come to pay their respects?

Del He won't have no family, will he? 'Cos I'll be there next to Mum and you'll be picking up yer divvies!

Albert He could be married by then! How's his widow gonna tend his grave when it's covered in stinging nettles?

Del She'll have to buy herself a decent pair of gardening gloves won't she! Come to think of it, I've got a beautiful pair of gardening gloves in the garage! They retail at £4.75 normally, they could be yours for a nicker!

Rodney I don't want any gardening gloves!

Del Oh that's charming, innit, eh? Never a thought for the poor missus! There she'll be with swellings and blotchs all over her hands, the poor little mare!

Rodney I don't believe this conversation is taking place! In 35 seconds you two have married me, buried me and given my widow skin trouble!

Albert Well, you've gotta look to the future ain't yer Rodney?

Rodney Not if I can help it Uncle!

He spots something of interest in the distance.

Del I often look into the future. And I find it very reassuring to know that whatever happens down here, in this mortal curl, one day we'll all be together up there in Heaven – for ever and ever, amen!

Albert Do you believe in all that heaven and what 'ave yer?

Del Oh yeah, it's true, I read it in a book!

Rodney has got up. A butterfly has rested on some flowers on another grave. Rodney's eyes are fixed on it.

Rodney Del.

Del Yeah, just think Rodney. When you walk through them Pearly Gates, Rodney – all like clouds and things – the first face you'll see will be mine.

Rodney Yeah, that's cosmic Del!

Albert Your Mum'll be there as well!

Del Oh yes, Mum'll be there 'cos she'll be wanting to see Rodney, her little wonder baby! She always used to call him that you know 'cos she used to wonder how the hell he happened.

Rodney Derek!

Albert I suppose your Dad might be up there as well, eh?

Del Oh I do hope so. I do hope so Uncle, can't wait to get my hands on that old git! I'll give him such a whack with my harp he won't know if it's Good Friday or Bonfire Night!

Rodney Del, will you stop rabbiting for one minute and come over here.

Del Oh Gordon Bennett, what's up with you now?

Rodney Look over there! *(Points to flowers)*

Del Where?

Rodney Just by them flowers.

Albert It's like that butterfly thing from Rodney's magazine.

Rodney That's because it *is* that butterfly thing from my magazine!

Del Oh leave it out you wally! What that thing over there's worth three grand? Never . . .

Rodney produces the picture from a magazine.

Del It is, it is that an' all. Bloody hell! If we could, if we could capture that all our problems'll be over!

Rodney Yeah.

Del I told you two didn't I? Didn't I tell you two that Mum'd come up trumps.

Albert Yeah, let's get it!

Del No look, be careful, take yer time. Take yer time! We've gotta do this the way the professionals would do it.

Albert What d'you mean? We've gotta jump over things and skid around in the van?

Del I don't mean Bodie and bleedin' Doyle you stupid old git . . . I mean professional butterfly catchers! Albert.

Albert Yes Del?

Del Giss yer hat!

Albert hands Del his cap. He creeps towards the butterfly, walking over a grave as he does.

Rodney Derek!

Del What

Rodney Have some respect!

Del Oh sorry . . .

He closes in on the butterfly. Taking careful aim, he throws the hat at the flowers.

Del It's gone! Quick Rodney. Get after it. Go on quick. Where'd it go? Get after it. There quick come on. (Del and Rodney chase after butterfly)

DAY. A PARK.

Rodney's face is very concerned.

Rodney Careful Del! Take it, nice and easy does it!

Del is on the roof of one of the park shelters, inching his way along to where the butterfly is perched.

Del Yes, yes, thank you Rodney!

Rodney 'Cos you could slip and kill yourself easy as anything!

Del I know, I know!

He gets very close to the butterfly.

Rodney (Shouts) Now!!

This alarms Del and he starts to slip. He hits the ground with a thud.

Del Oh, you stupid idiot.

Rodney Come on Del, he's getting away!

Rodney pursues the butterfly. Del is spread-eagled on the ground. He gets up painfully, brushing the leaves and dirt off himself.

Del The things I do for money!

DAY. THE PARK/LAKE.

Rodney is standing on a small boating platform when Del arrives.

Del Well, where is it?

Rodney He's out there on that lily pad!

Del Oh, well we can't just leave him out there can we?

Rodney Well what d'you wanna do then, phone the coastguard?

Del Look, a bloody great pike could come up and have him for supper. No, one of us has got to go in and get it. Go Rodney, I'll look after your shoes!

Rodney Eh? I'm not going in there!!

Del This is no time for second thoughts Rodney! That is not a butterfly out there, that is Denzil's money!

Rodney So how comes I've gotta go and get it?

Del 'Cos I'm not a very good swimmer!

Rodney Nor am I!

Del I know but you're taller than me, ain't yer, it'll take you longer to drown! It's only shallow.

Rodney How shallow?

Del Well I don't know do I! Get in and see!

Del pushes Rodney in. Rodney splashes about. A crowd of passers-by has gathered to watch the goings-on. Albert arrives, out of breath.

Albert What's Rodney doing?

Del I dunno – backstroke. Our three grand's out there on that lily pad. I begged him, I begged him not to go in! Pity you weren't here, this is right up your street this innit?

Albert I can't swim Del!

Del You used to be a sailor!

Albert Don't mean a thing! Nelson couldn't swim!

Del Course he couldn't, he'd only got one bloody arm! He'd be going round in circles wouldn't he?

Rodney has got to his feet.

Del There you are Rodney, it's not as bad as you thought is it?

Rodney You pushed me!

Del I did not, I did not push you Rodney. I just gave you a little bit of encouragement! Anyway come on Rodders you're in now!

Rodney Yeah, and I'm getting out now 'an all.

Del Just a minute, just a minute. Not ten yards, not ten yards from you, right, is one of the rarest, most beautiful and precious of God's little tiny creatures! And them wallies in that magazine of yours are gonna give us three grand for that thing!

Rodney I don't care Del, I'm still getting out!

Del Look, we give Denzil his two grand back and we've got £1,000 for ourselves!

Albert I thought you said you'd give Denzil three grand!

Del That's funny you know, 'cos Denzil thought

As One Door Closes

I said that 'an all. Rodders, everyone's a winner! What d'you say?

Rodney makes his way out to the lily pad.

Albert Nice and gently Rodney.

Rodney Shuddup!

Rodney reaches and gently scoops the butterfly up in his cupped hands. He slowly makes his way back to the shore.

Del Easy now, don't splash, go slowly, don't disturb it. Shush, mind how you go . . .

Rodney I've got it.

Albert He's got it.

Del Good boy, come on.

Rodney I bet I'll get a cold next week now!

Del Shut up you tart!

Rodney This water'll make my hair go frizzy!

Del Don't worry, the alopecia'll soon cure that Rodney. If you get into difficulities, save the butterfly right.

Rodney Stuff the butterfly!

Del There's only a few of them things left in the world, there's millions of you!

Albert Nice 'n' easy Rodney, almost there!

Rodney places the butterfly in Del's hands. Del and Albert walk away a few yards leaving Rodney to get out of the water alone.

Del Careful, careful, got it, got it.

Albert Is he alright Del?

Del Yeah he's alright. A bit wet, but he'll survive. The sun'll soon dry you out won't it? And then we'll take you down to the nice man who'll give Uncle Delly Welly three lovely grand!

There is the sound of reggae music approaching. Del looks up to see Denzil approaching. Del holds his hands out to show Denzil.

Del Denzil I've got your money.

Denzil brings his hands smashing down on Del's in the West Indian greeting.

Denzil Great man! I'll see you down the pub later!

Del looks staright ahead in shock. He looks down at his hands and cringes. Rodney arrives dripping wet.

Rodney What's that mess on your hands?

Albert That used to be a butterfly Rodney!

Rodney The butt . . . But . . . You didn't . . . Not when Denzil. *(Del nods)* Well what a plonker! So what do we do now?

Del clears his hands of the butterflies remains. He turns to the crowd.

Del Ladies and gentlemen, how would you like to be the proud owners of a set of lowvery doors?

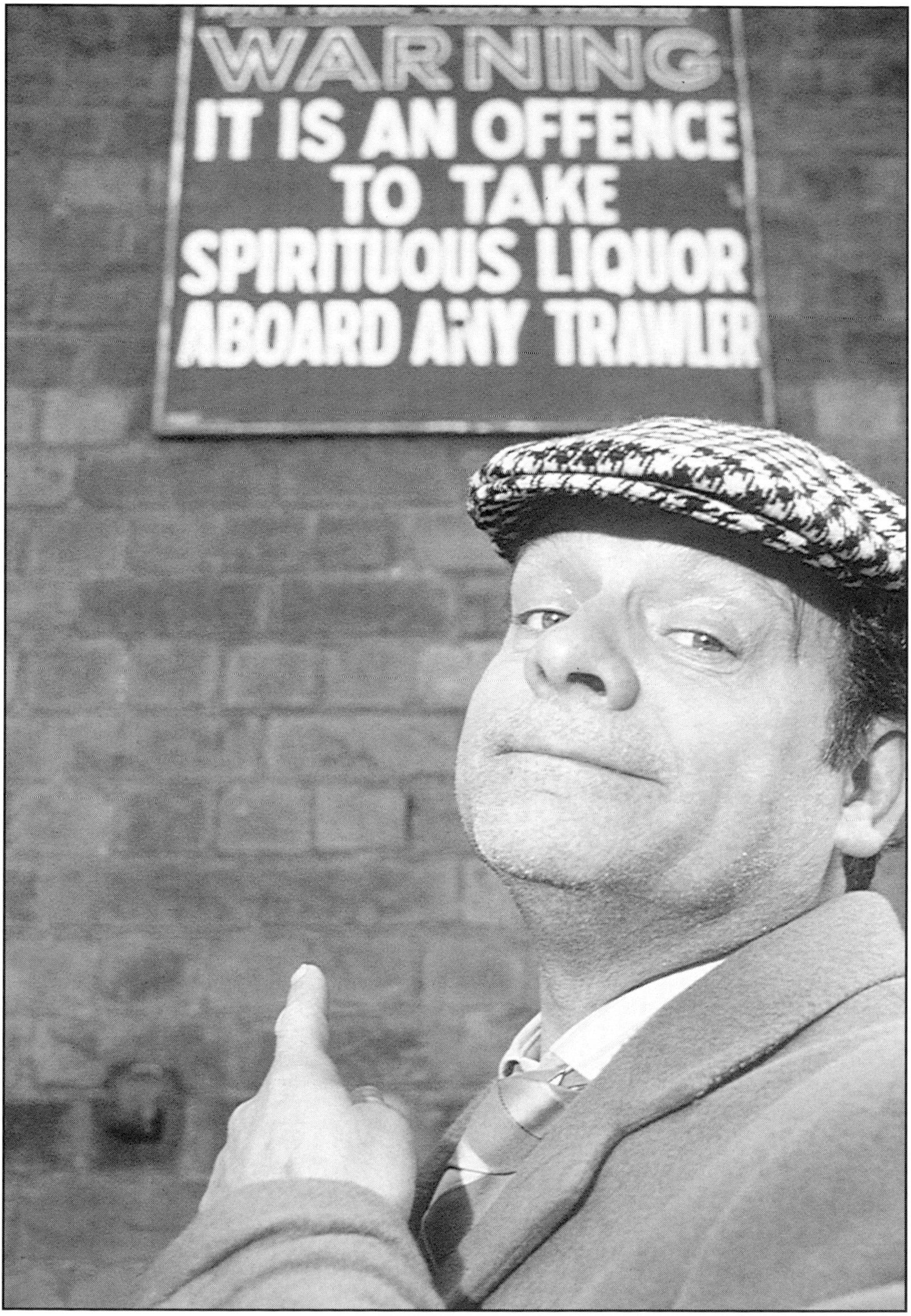
WARNING
IT IS AN OFFENCE
TO TAKE
SPIRITUOUS LIQUOR
ABOARD ANY TRAWLER

To Hull and Back

CUSTOMS AREA

Among the passengers there is a well-dressed man carrying hand luggage. A short distance away is a well-dressed woman carrying a suitcase.

Female tannoy announcer British Airways are pleased to announce the arrival of Flight 417 from Amsterdam.

The man and woman appear not to be together, though they share a tiny glance which indicates they know each other. As they enter the customs area the woman's suitcase opens, spewing clothes onto the floor. She feigns a stumble. Two customs officers leave their post to give her assistance.

Female passenger Oh, I'm sorry.

Male airport worker Are you alright madam?

Female passenger Oh, I'm sorry I've spilled everything out of my case, I don't think the catch is working properly, I don't know what it is – thank you very much.

Male airport worker Thank you.

As the customs officer assist her, the man walks through customs and out into the main airport foyer.

THE NAG'S HEAD.

The bar is packed. Albert is seated next to an elderly lady. They are trying watch a film on TV depicting a black and white film about some Second World War naval battle. Rod and Del are leaning against the bar. Del is not really listening to Rod.

Rodney So anyway, I says to her right, you know, I mean as gently as I could like I said, 'Engagement is a big step'.

Del Yeah terrific, yeah right.

Rodney I said you know, 'It's not the sort of thing you enter into very lightly'.

Del No, no it isn't. *(Reacts to some beer spilt on the bar which is now on his sleeve. To a young Rastafarian)* Oh look at that. Oi Calvin, spill your lager over this bar once more and I'll smack you right side the bloody earhole.

Calvin Sorry Del man.

Del This is not polyester you know, this is pure crimplene.

Rodney As I was saying . . .

Mike Have you seen Boycie Del?

Del No no not recently why?

Michael, Barman Well he's looking for you, says it's urgent.

Del Oh well, he knows where to find me Michael don't he eh? Knows where to find me.

Rodney Now where was I?

Del Hey, are you still going out with that little sort?

Rodney Imogen, yeah, I'm still going out with her, that's what I've been telling you for the last ten minutes.

Del Oh why, what's up then? *(Calls across the bar)* Hello Corrie love how are you alright? Yeah go on.

Rodney She's getting a little bit too serious for my liking, and I'm trying to find a way of cooling her down a bit but I don't want to hurt her.

Del All you've got to say is, you got to say, 'Imogen you're giving me the hump now go away and haunt someone else for a change?'

Rodney Yeah that's pretty . . . Del innit? I don't believe you.

Del You're too soft with her Rodney, you're too soft, that is your trouble. Look, here y'are, you get the drinks in 'cause I'm going to pop over there do a bit of business.

Rodney Vicky, can I have pint of lager in there and what's Del drinking these days?

Vicky Oh God knows, Tuesday it was a Bacardi and Russian, last week it was Grand Marnier and Orange, the week before that it was Dubonnet and Coke.

Rodney Oh give us a Tia Maria and Lucozade then.

Del is trying to sell a digital watch to one of his mates. Close by Albert and the elderly lady (Ruby) are still watching the war film.

Del There you go look, it's fifteen quid I can't say fairer than that – it's none of your foreign rubbish, look it's Japanese.

Ted Del I've already got a watch.

Del Call that a watch? That's crap that is, that's crap.

Ted You didn't say that when you sold it to me.

Del No, no, Ted what I meant was, well, I mean its had it's day innit? Look, here, here, fifteen quid right, that's what I paid for it, you're getting it at cost.

Ted Del I don't fancy it.

Del Alright then, for you a tenner, as it's the last one.

Ted Ten?

Del Hm hm.

Ted Here, it's got a scratch on the face.

Del Oh don't worry about that I'll get you another one from the back of the van. Look it plays thirty-six different national anthems, it tells you what day of the week it is and it's a calculator an' all.

Ted Blimey is that the time?

Del Oh no it's still set on Oriental hours innit? You get your money out I'll be back in a tick. Back in a tick, I like it.

Albert *(Indicating battle on TV)* I was there Ruby.

Ruby Where, yeah but which one were you then?

Albert No I don't mean I was in the film, I meant I was in that battle.

Ruby What battle is it?

Albert God knows I can't hear a bleeding thing with all this monkey music.

Ruby Must have taken a lot of courage to do what you did Albert.

Albert Yeah.

Ruby All them sharks and icebergs.

Albert Yeah and a giant octopus.

Ruby Oh gives me itchy fever just thinking about it.

Albert Sometimes I wake up in the middle of the night screaming, nightmares about all the torpedoes, mines, kamikaze pilots – that's why I never talk about it Rube.

Ruby My Harry used to wake up in the middle of the night screaming.

Albert No.

Ruby Yeah – sometimes he used to scream in the middle of the day. Bloody glad when they put him away I was. What did it was the tragedy that happened to our son. Harry just never got over it, he was such a lively lad, he went to school with Del Boy, they used to sit next to each other in class, Del must have mentioned it, Slater, Roy Slater.

Albert Slater – don't remember Rube.

Ruby No, well maybe it's still too painful for Del to talk about, he was only 18, he had all his life before him.

Albert What was it a motor-cycle accident?

Ruby No he, he joined the police, he's one of their top men now, he's put more people behind bars than Watneys.

Del returns to the bar. Boycie and Abdul enter.

Del I know it looks like . . .? That's why the girls . . .? Boycie.

Boycie Can I have a quiet word?

Del Yeah sure – watcha Abdul alright my son?

Abdul Very well thank you.

Del Hey are you still up at that Hatton Garden are you?

Abdul Yes I'm still in Hatton Garden. Could I have a word with you please?

Del Yeah course you can, why not?

Boycie We'll be in the back room.

Del Oh, oh alright I'll just get me drink. *(To Rodney)* Here, I've do a bit of business with Boycie and Abdulla. *(Vicky takes Rodney's tenner and holds it up to the light.)* Oi, saucy mare.

Vicky It's orders from the governor, there's a lot of forged money floating round.

Del You didn't check his money just now.

Vicky Yeah well, that's different innit?

Del I'm going right off that girl – see you in a minute.

Del sips his Tia Maria and Lucozade. He doesn't know what it is, but he likes it. Trigger enters.

Trigger Alright Dave?

Rodney Watcha Trig, how you going?

Trigger Alright, I'm feeling lucky tonight, you never know I might pull so I thought I'd have a dab of Blue Stratos, put me best clothes on.

Rodney Yeah, what stopped you then?

Trigger These are my best clothes.

Rodney Oh.

A young attractive girl passes by.

Trigger Hello darling where you been all my life.

Girl Piss off!

Trigger I always use that line with the birds.

Rodney Yeah? Why?

Trig Dunno really, it's never worked.

BACK ROOM OF THE NAG'S HEAD

Del, Boycie and Abdul are seated round the table. They are already in discussion.

Del I see, so what sort of deal is it?

Abdul I have recently made contact with a certain gentleman who runs this business in Amsterdam

Del Amsterdam – Amsterdam in Holland you mean?

Boycie I told you he was the right man for the job, didn't I Abdul?

Abdul My brother Sayeed has done business with him in the past. Do you know my brother lives in France now.

Del No, no I didn't know that.

Abdul Yes, yes, he's doing very well.

Del Is he?

Abdul Yeah he's married now.

To Hull and Back

Del Oh good.

Abdul His wife's expecting.

Boycie Get on with it Abdul for God's sake, otherwise we'll be here all bleeding night.

Abdul Yes well, last week I flew to Amsterdam to see the gentleman in question, a Mr Van Cleef and after some preliminary discussions Mr Van Cleef has agreed to sell us some merchandise.

Del Merchandise, what sort of merchandise?

Boycie Diamonds.

Del Diamonds.

Abdul Thirty of them cut and polished blue diamonds.

Boycie Top of the range Del Boy.

Del Blimey, it's going to cost an arm and a leg innit?

Boycie Fifty grand.

Del Fifty grand, you and Abdul are weighing out fifty grand?

Abdul In England they have a market value of one hundred and fifty thousand pounds.

Del Bloody hell – I take it you're not going to bother to inform our friends Customs and Excise of this little matter?

Boycie No well they're rather busy I think they'd appreciate it.

Del Really? Well anyway where do I come into all this? You're not expecting me to buy any off you are you? The thing is you know, I've had a few bad results lately and I'm potless.

Boycie Leave off Del Boy, these gems sell at around five grand apiece.

Abdul What we are asking you to do Derek is – is to take the money to Amsterdam for us.

Del You want me to take fifty thousand pounds to Amsterdam?

Boycie Yeah and . . .

Del And what?

Boycie And bring the diamonds back.

Del Do you know for a minute there I thought you were serious.

Boycie We are very serious Del, deadly serious.

Abdul There is nothing to worry about Derek, Mr Van Cleef has completed many of these transactions and he assures us nothing ever goes wrong.

Del Up your kilt. What do you think I am a total wally or something?

Abdul We would look after you Derek.

Del Yes I'm sure you would. You'd visit me once a month wouldn't you eh? Bring me cakes with files in – you find yourself another mug.

Boycie We'll give you ten grand.

Del, who was about to leave, stops at the door. He's never been offered ten grand

before. He's never seen ten grand before.

Del Ten thousand pounds?

Abdul Alright twelve, *(To Boycie)* I knew he'd haggle.

Boycie You berk Abdul.

Boycie Alright Del twelve grand. Just think of it Del Boy twelve big 'uns – set you up a treat for the future.

Abdul And there will be no problems, it will all be as easy as apple tart.

Del Well if it's as easy as apple tart how come you two ain't going yourselves?

Boycie Well we're both scared of flying ain't we?

Del Oh leave it out Boycie, Abdul's done more flying than sparrows.

Abdul No no, no no, it would look very suspicious for me a registered Hatton Garden merchant to fly to Amsterdam too often.

Del I don't know about this.

Boycie Look Del, we chose you specially, we needed someone we knew, someone we could trust.

Abdul Someone who was skint.

Del What happens if I get caught?

Boycie Well Abdul and me have done our money haven't we?

Del Done your money, your money? I stand to get banged up for five years.

Boycie Right Del – fifteen grand.

Pause

Del Not much use to you when you're locked up in the Scrubs though is it eh?

Abdul We are paying you to take the risk Derek.

Boycie It's a big gamble Del – and he who dares wins don't he? 'Course if it's too big for you Del, if you think you're a bit out of your depth just say so.

Del Fifteen.

THE BAR OF THE NAG'S HEAD.

Rodney See my problem is I don't want to hurt her, 'cause Imogens a lovely kid you know, I mean she's gentle, she's sensitive and on top of all that she cares.

Trigger I reckon she'd do a turn if you played your cards right.

Rodney What's the point in discussing it with you eh Trig? We're talking on two different levels.

Trigger Yeah.

Del exits from the back room. Albert is still chatting to Ruby.

Albert Two and a half weeks we were adrift in the middle of the Pacific Ocean – got a nice tan

though.

Del Come on Albert we're going home. Quick Rodney, come on, home.

Rodney Well suppose I ought to be getting on really – give Imogen a ring tell her it's all over between us. Sorry can I just get past you.

Rodney pushes past some people including a kissing couple. He reaches for his coat near the kissing couple.

Sorry. Sorry I was just trying to. Hello Imogen.

THE MARKET

Del and Rodney are unloading the van.

Rodney Look, I know what you're doing, I just don't understand why.

Del Mum said to me on her deathbed, she said Del Boy she said.

Rodney No, no, don't start on that. What do you think the odds are of you getting caught?

Del Oh shut up Rodney, you've been going on about it all night.

Rodney Del you are smuggling diamonds.

Del Do you think you could yell just a little bit louder, 'cause there's a geezer down there at the other end of the market who didn't quite catch it all?

Rodney Del, do you realise what you're getting into?

Del Yes I do know what I'm getting into, fifteen grand is what I'm getting into. Look Rodney, this is not drugs or guns is it? I mean that, that sort of stuff kills people – it's only little diamonds – I try to bring down the cost of getting engaged, I thought you and Imogen would have been pleased.

Rodney Yeah well, me and Imogen's finished.

Del Oh so you finally told her then did you?

Rodney Yeah sort of.

Del Did she cry?

Rodney No, look Del smuggling diamonds is still illegal.

Del It's only illegal because Boycie and Abdul ain't paying any import tax. Alright, right, supposing they pay import tax then eh? What do you think the government is going to do with that – they're only going to go out and buy another Strident missile ain't they eh?

Rodney So you're telling me that smuggling diamonds is a blow for world peace.

Del Every little bit helps Rodney.

Rodney Well why don't you bring back a load of diamonds Del? You might end up with the Nobel Prize.

Del Hadn't thought of that. Now come on Rodney we'll waltz through the customs at Gatwick, they won't take any notice of us.

Rodney Del what do you know about diamonds eh, I mean to you diamonds are them things that you wear in your cufflinks and, to be quite honest with you I've seen better cats eyes.

Del I don't have to know anything, Abdul's in charge of that side, we're just the couriers.

Rodney Hang on a minute – what do you mean we?

Del Look, don't think I'm going to cut my little kid brother out of a deal like this do you? What sort of bloke do you think I am?

Rodney Well your little kid brother don't want a cut in.

Del A little while ago you said you wanted to be a courier.

Rodney Yeah, for Club 18–30.

Del Look I'm going to need you on this one Rodney 'cause when that aeroplane lands you're going to be my diversion.

Rodney Do you know how long I'd go away for, I've already got a record for possession of cannabis ain't I?

Del Exactly, and that is what's going to be my diversion 'cause not only is Amsterdam the centre of the diamond trade, it's also the drugs capital of Europe right? So when we go through passport control they see Rodney Trotter nipping off to Holland they're going to say, 'Oh, that little rascal he's after the old exotic stuff again'. When we come back through Customs who are they going to nab, me the sophisticated jet-setter in a camel-hair coat or you the boomtown rat?

Rodney Well they'll pull me won't they?

Del So whilst you're inside being strip searched you know and all that game – me and the diamonds have been having it away down the kermit?

Rodney Oh terrific, so while you're off the road jollying it up, it's touch your toes time for Rodney.

Del Oh you won't come to any harm Rodney, it'll only be a minor discomfort – they'll let you go in a couple of hours and then you come home to five lovely grand – your share.

Rodney Five grand?

Del Five grand. Buy an awful lot of lollypops for five grand Rodney, get yourself a nice second-hand Capri, whip round to Imogen's, get your old card stamped, know what I mean?

Rodney I don't know, I've never actually been to Amsterdam, I suppose we could turn it into a bit of an 'oliday eh?

Del Well, yeah, I mean we'll be there at least an hour. Look come on while you're thinking about

To Hull and Back

it let's try and knock some of this gear out and make some of that stuff that we read about called profit 'cause if all this falls through bruv we are skint right.

As Denzil turns away, Denzil is seated at the wheel of a juggernaut, caught in traffic.

Denzil my son.

Denzil No.

Del No what?

Denzil No I don't want to buy anything, no I don't want to sell anything and no I don't want you to make me a millionaire.

Del Innit, innit marvellous eh? Innit marvellous? You just stop to say hello to an old mate and all you get is a load of old verbal – I don't want anything Denzil honest. What you carrying?

Denzil Nothing it's empty.

Del Ah well, I could fill that up for you. You could earn yourself a few bob.

Denzil Look, just leave me alone will you, alright? Corinne and I have just got back together again and I've had to promise her that I'd stop seeing you, stop getting drunk, stop gambling and get a steady job.

Del Is it my fault you married a wrong 'un? It's no reason to give me a bolly. Hang about there for a minute, I'll be back.

Denzil *(To Rodney)* It's everywhere I go you know, he's on the phone to me, he's at me front door, he's in the betting shop, he's in the pub and now he's in a bloody traffic jam. You know what Rodney I get this feeling that he's haunting me, know what I mean?

Rodney Yeah – yeah I know exactly what you mean.

Denzil drives off.

Del *(Returning)* Hey what's up with him, what have I done now?

Rodney I can't understand it Del, I mean all you've ever done is ruin his wedding reception, almost break up his marriage, flood his kitchen and steal his two thousand pounds redundancy money, and he goes and gets all silly about it.

Del Yeah.

THE MARKET (PROPER).

Del has the suitcase open. There are watch cases inside.

Del These are Japanese and these *(Rolls trouser leg up)* are hairy knees. Right, now now what's the difference, I'll tell you what the difference is – *(Indicates knee)* these will not give you the time in all the major capital cities of the world, neither are they a calculator, nor do they play thirty-six different national anthems, but this, *(indicates watch)* well this is a quality timepiece of precision craftsmanship that will cost you sixty-seven pounds upwards – now, I'm not going to ask you for sixty-seven pounds oh no, I'm not going to ask you for forty-seven, I'm not asking thirty-seven pounds.

Rodney Steady on Del think of the profit margin.

Del No no don't interrupt me now Rodney 'cause not while I'm in my stride, I'm not asking you for twenty-seven pounds, this is fifteen pounds for this quality watch ladies and gentlemen, that's all, this beautiful timepiece, yes ladies and gentlemen for a mere twenty quid.

Woman in crowd No no you said fifteen.

Del I beg your pardon madam.

Woman in crowd You said fifteen.

Del No I didn't.

Crowd Yes.

Del No I didn't.

Rodney He didn't say fifteen pounds.

Del Hold on, hold on Rodney, no hold on, I do believe that I said fifteen pounds, I'm sorry, I must be going mad, I'm sure I said, I'm going, alright darling just to show you that I'm a man of my word, go on you can have this watch for fifteen quid, go on, steal it from me. Go on, I'm losing money on the deal, right Rodney come on get the rest of the watches out of this suitcase, 'cause there'll be a mad rush in a minute. *(To Rodney)* Oh they're not going all that well are they.

Rodney They're going down like saveloys in a kibbutz.

Del If I could just sell one I know that the others would follow. . . . Here just a minute I've had an idea, watch this. . . . *(To crowd)* Right here you are, listen ladies and gentlemen, listen, listen, excuse me just a moment, give us, give us your time 'cause I've just had a business discussion with my partner here on my right who informs me that we desperately need the space in the suitcase right? So what I'm going to have to do, I'm going to have to give these watches away, I've just got to give them away so here you go, I'm giving them away at ten pounds each there you go, go on, ten quid, fifteen quid to the black bloke can't say fairer than that.

Black man Why can't I have it for ten pounds then?

Del For ten pounds sir, course you can. Rodney take the man's money, there you go, there we've sold that one, there we go, we're off and running, there we are, come on darling, cast your bread upon the water, that's what I say, it'll

come back tenfold. That's it, there you are, alright listen – give us your money, take the money.

A policeman approaches. Del closes the case. Alright, listen, hang about we'll be back in five minutes alright.

They hurry off.

Don't look back.

They run back to the van, as they do Slater and Hoskins appear.

Slater Del Boy.

Del Slater.

Slater Well what a coincidence, I was just saying to Hoskins I wonder how my old mate Del Boy is, weren't I Hoskins?

Hoskins Eh? Oh yes sir.

Slater How are you Rodney?

Rodney Very well thank you detective inspector.

Slater Chief inspector.

Rodney Sorry, I didn't know you'd been promoted.

Slater Yeah about six months back – I took Hoskins with me, he's my driver.

Del Oh, driver – everyone always said you'd be going places Terry.

Hoskins Going places – oh yeah.

Del Here I saw your mum down the Nag's Head last night Slater.

Slater Yeah – she ask after me?

Del No.

Slater Do you fancy a cup of tea Del?

Del Ah, actually Roy we're in a bit of a hurry if you don't mind.

Slater I don't think you heard the question Del, I said do you fancy a cup of tea?

Del Well now you come to mention it, I am a bit parched.

SID'S CAFE.

Del is seated opposite Rodney at the table, the suitcase at their feet. Slater and Hoskins are at the counter. Sid puts four teas on the counter.

Sid There you go Detective Inspector.

Slater Chief.

Sid What?

Slater I'm a chief now.

Slater turns to get some spoons.

Sid I'll be bleeding glad when Custer arrives.

Hoskins smiles and then takes the teas to the table.

Del Watch what you say Rodney, that Slater's a bastard.

Rodney Eh?

Del I said. *(Stops as Hoskins approaches)*

Hoskins Watch what you say, Slater's a bastard.

Rodney Yeah I remember from the last time.

Hoskins He's on the warpath now, he's retiring soon and wants to go out in a blaze of glory.

Del Retiring – that's a bit early innit?

Hoskins He's had no choice, it's come from the top they're forcing him out. See a little while ago Slater persuaded this young black fella to sign a full confession to being a peeping tom – when the case gets to court it turns out he's a registered blind person – bad publicity for the police innit?

Rodney What about the poor black bloke?

Hoskins Oh he's not too upset they reckon he might get a record contract out of it, sh . . .

Stops as Slater arrives.

Slater There you are Hoskins, bacon sandwich for you – are you sure you didn't want nothing to eat?

Del Yeah yeah, quite sure, we're not all that hungry actually Roy. Anyway what you doing back in the parish? Thought you'd been transferred to river police.

Slater No not transferred no, that was just a special assignment, I was after this little gang of diamond smugglers.

Del Any luck?

Slater Oh I caught them Del yes, even nabbed the ringleader, a geezer called Hendrix. They got away though, lack of evidence.

Del That's a choker innit?

Slater Oh I'll have him down.

Rodney What, they still doing it then?

Slater How many times have you almost?

Hoskins Twice.

Slater Twice that's right but each time they've somehow managed to get shot of the diamonds – if you haven't got them, you've got no evidence.

Del No no.

Slater Between you and me Del I've heard a whisper they're trying it on again. A couple of local businessmen shall we say have put the money up and we know who they are don't we Hoskins?

Hoskins Boycie and . . .

Slater Hoskins.

Hoskins Sorry sir.

Slater But I don't know who the courier is, now unless I can catch the courier with the stones on him I'm knackered – this is where you come in Del.

Del Me? You don't think I'm the courier do you?

Slater Leave off Del, this is big – no, the way I see it is this you hear all the gossip in the clubs

and the pubs, now it's no skin off your nose if you ring me with a name, after all these business-men ain't puttin' no money your way are they?

Del No.

Slater You don't even have to say who's calling, make it anonymously, and I will make life very comfortable for you, no more aggro from wooden-tops in the market.

Del That's very fair of you Roy, innit?

Rodney Oh yeah very fair.

Slater This is my last case Del, I'm retiring from the Met.

Del Oh.

Slater The Commissioner begged me stay but I've had enough, I want my career to end on a high note.

Del Yeah well 'course we wish you a lot of luck Slater.

Slater I'll get 'em in the end Del, I never give up you see once I get my teeth into something I don't let go – do you know what they call me at the Met?

Del No.

Slater Bulldog.

Del Oh – actually I have heard one or two people call you bulldog or words to that effect anyway.

Slater That's the sort of guy I am, I never give up, so if you hear anything Del, you know my number. Well it's been nice, like old school days you and me sat at the same desk – only this time you didn't put frogspawn in me milk – you rascal. *(Calls)* Do you want me to pay for my breakfast Sid or what?

Sid No, have it on the house Mr Slater.

Slater Very nice of you Sidney, very nice indeed. You'd better pay for your breakfast Hoskins.

Hoskins Thank you Sir.

He moves to the counter.

Rodney So you don't know if this courier is a man or a woman.

Slater No, I hadn't thought of that, that's very good thinking Rodney – have you ever thought about joining the police.

Rodney No I'm ambitious.

Slater Ha ha, very good – no all I know is that he or she will be flying in with the goods next week and I'll be waiting for them.

Sid hands Hoskins his change.

Sid There you go young Terry.

Hoskins Thanks Sid.

Slater and Hoskins exit.

Rodney Well that's that then, innit?

Del How do you mean?

Rodney You can't get ahead with it now can

you? Slater's got all the airports covered.

Del He can't watch all the airports twenty-four hours a day can he eh? Have to find another way of sneaking in?

Del moves to wall phone.

Sid You owe me thirty-two pence Del.

Del Eh? No no, Mr Slater paid for ours.

Sid Oh.

BOYCIE'S OFFICE

Boycie is with a middle-aged couple extolling the virtues of one of his cars.

Boycie Oh yes it has a full service record, taxed till the end of the month, it'll have no trouble passing its MOT.

Boycie's young car-cleaner Colin exits from the office and calls.

Colin Boyce someone on the phone wants you.

Boycie Who is it?

Colin Don't know.

Boycie Would you just say that I'm rather busy with some clients at the moment please Colin?

Colin He said it's something to do about diamonds.

Boycie I'll be right there. . . . *(To couple)* Yes it's the new Austin Diamond coming out next year, still in the experimental stage – do excuse me Mr Biggastaff?

He picks up the phone.

Yeah what's up?

Del It's Del Boy. Listen, I've just had a very interesting conversation with Chief Inspector Slater, you know bullshit of the yard.

Boycie Slater? What's he want?

Del He knows.

Boycie How?

Del Look I don't know do I? He's got more grasses than Fisons.

Boycie Well how much does he know?

Del Well he knows. . . . He knows that you and Abdul have put the money up.

Boycie I don't believe it. Well, we can't pull out now Del, Abdul's just made all the arrangements with Van Cleef.

Del Alright, alright listen, don't panic, don't panic – he doesn't know who the courier is, that's what he was pumping me about so I'm the last bloke that he suspects.

Boycie Yeah well, it's alright for you I've still got fifty grand in my house, if Slater comes sniffing around how am I going to explain that away. No – we've got to meet tonight, I'll give you the money and Abdul can make the final arrangements.

Del Right where shall we meet, your place?

Boycie You must be joking, my house might be under surveillance, we can't meet at Abdul's either for the same reason.

Del How about my flat?

Boycie You don't honestly think I'm going to walk across your estate with fifty grand on me do you?

Del You've got a point. What about the Nag's Head?

Boycie Leave off, he knows that's our local – anyway we can't meet in any public places, he sees the three of us together he's got the full story. We've got to come up with somewhere dark and secluded, somewhere where we can lock the doors and be on our own and nobody will be able to see us.

Del I know just the place.

Boycie Yeah, where?

THE BACK OF DENZIL'S TRAILER.

Boycie and Abdul are in the back. Boycie carries a suitcase.

Boycie The back of Denzil's bleeding lorry, I mean what a place to hold a meeting.

Abdul Personally I think it's a good idea – as Derek said this is the last place Slater would think of looking.

Boycie Yeah but I'm going to get grease stains on my coat, I am going to look a right mess. I mean what has Denzil had in here? Smells like rotten fish.

Abdul Oh, stop your whining Boycie, you're like an old woman at times.

LORRY PARK.

The three-wheeled van pulls in to park and halts fifty yards from the juggernaut. Del alights. He spots Boycie's Merc.

Del Right they're here – about five minutes. Spot any danger give us a signal, right?

Rodney Oi, what's the signal then?

Del You what?

Rodney Shall I beep the hooter?

Del No you wally, that'll attract all sorts of unwanted attention wouldn't it eh?

Rodney Well shall I flash the lights?

Del How are we going to see flashing lights when we're in the back of a ruddy trailer?

Rodney Alright then, so what's the signal?

Del Can you make a sound like an owl?

Rodney An owl sound?

Del Yes you know like this? *(Makes owl sound)*

Rodney Oh that?

Del Yeah.

Rodney No.

Del Oh.

Rodney I can do bunny shadows though.

Del Enough of your bloody sarcasm Rodney just think of a signal – back in a minute.

He moves off towards the trailer.

BACK OF DENZIL'S VAN.

Abdul You don't think Slater suspects anything else do you?

Boycie No, if he'd suspected that he'd have been round with a search warrant by now.

Del 'Ello 'ello 'ello, what are you doing in here then?

Boycie Get in here for God's sake will you?

Del Cor, it don't half hum in here don't it? Alright Abdul, got everything sorted out?

Abdul Yes the arrangements have all been made.

Boycie Of all the places on earth, why in God's name do we have to meet in the back of a stinking lorry?

Del Oh dear – look around you, can you think of a better place eh? Look, no prying eyes, no plain clothes coppers, nobody knows we're in here.

Boycie What, do you mean Denzil don't know?

Del Course he don't, leave it out, he'd go diddley – no apart from Rodney out there in a van we're the only three people in the world who know we're in here.

SLATER'S OFFICE.

Slater is on the phone. Hoskins is putting some files away.

Slater Alright, alright, leave it to me. *(Replaces receiver. Takes his coat)* Get your coat and a uniformed officer Hoskins.

Hoskins Where are we off to sir?

Slater Transport Cafe in Soweto Road, one of the neighbours reported seeing three men breaking into a lorry.

Hoskins Righto sir. Parker, get a car round to the front.

BACK OF DENZIL'S VAN.

Abdul I spoke to Mr Van Cleef this morning about the date, the venue and the time of the exchange and you must be very clear about these matters Derek, so listen carefully. The exchange will take place this coming Friday at twelve noon.

Del Twelve noon right.

Abdul That's right – now here is the address in Amsterdam, memorise it and then destroy it.

Del Doesn't self destruct then?

Boycie Be serious Del, please. Friday at twelve right.

To Hull and Back

Del Alright alright – got it.

Abdul My cousin, Hussein, will meet you in Van Cleef's office.

Del Your cousin – stone me Abdul your family get everywhere don't they, got a brother in France, cousin in Holland. Sure you ain't got no one out in outer Mongolia?

Abdul A very distant uncle, but we never talk about it. My cousin is also a diamond merchant, he will be there to check the merchandise.

Boycie Don't want you coming back with a load of Mickey Mouse gear, do we Del Boy?

Del Watch it Boycie, my mum gave me them.

Boycie Oh.

Del Sh . . . it's alright, so come on where's the money, where's the money?

Boycie *(Hands him the briefcase)* There's fifty grand there Del Boy, please be careful with it.

Del Trust me Boycie.

Boycie Of course we trust you.

Del What's the combination to this?

Boycie When you get to Van Cleef's office you phone me and then I'll give you the combination.

Del Oh that's terrific, that's a great deal of trust that is, innit eh?

Abdul One thing we forget to mention, the most important thing of all, if anything should go wrong, nothing can go wrong, but if it should, you never heard of us.

Boycie Me and Abdul never had nothing to do with it, you never heard the name Van Cleef. It's just a precaution Del Boy.

Del Terrific – that means I'm up on offer don't it eh?

Boycie That's what we're paying you fifteen grand for.

Del Alright, alright don't worry, won't be no comebacks. What about the expenses for these aeroplane tickets?

Abdul Tickets? You only need the one Derek.

Del No I'm taking my kid brother with me.

Boycie Taking Rodney, what is this a bloody outing?

Del No – Rodney is going to be my diversion for when I come back through the Customs – look it's going to be hard enough with Slater and the 7th Cavalry ferreted about amongst all the duty frees, don't make it any harder.

Abdul Very well we will pay the expenses, it's alright.

Boycie Don't lump 'em up too much though.

Del No alright.

Boycie Right, I'm off.

Del Are you? I wondered what the smell was. Alright.

Abdul Right we'll see you next Friday when you return – good luck Derek.

Boycie Best of luck Del Boy.

Del And you.

Boycie Give us a minute to get clear.

LORRY PARK.

Rodney is in the van reading a magazine. He sees Boycie and Abdul jump down from the trailer and get into Boycie's Merc. They drive off, just as a Panda car roars into the park. Slater, Hoskins and Parker alight from the car.

Slater Parker down there. Hoskins check over the back there.

The three check beneath the lorries. Rodney gently winds the window down. He cups his hand together and does his best impression of an owl hoot. It sounds more like a ruptured seagull.

Parker What was that sir?

Slater Don't know, sounded like a crow.

Rodney *(Offended)* Crow.

BACK OF DENZIL'S VAN.

Del moves to the trailer door. He sees the blue flashing light.

Del Oh my God! Oh God, they'll throw the bloody key away.

He closes the door quickly.

LORRY PARK.

Slater Go on get on with it or we'll never get home tonight. Any luck?

Parker Not yet sir.

Slater *(Gestures towards the trailer)* Hoskins, Parker.

Hoskins *(The torch falls on the trailer's open latch)* This looks promising sir.

Slater Take over Hoskins.

Hoskins Alright Parker.

Parker Me?

Parker flings the door open. He shines his torch into the empty trailer. Apart from some tarpaulin, the trailer is empty.

Hoskins What is that?

Parker I don't know but whatever it is, it's been dead a fortnight.

Slater Right, we'll have a quick shufti over the back then we'll call it a night.

He slams the latch into the locked position. Some of these lorry drivers invite crime don't they?

They exit.

In the trailer Del hurls the tarpaulin back – a great cloud of cigar smoke billows. Del is

269

coughing, gasping for air. He staggers to the trailer door only to find it is locked tight. Rodney is still in the van. He reacts as Denzil, ghetto blaster playing, exits from the café and approaches juggernaut. Rodney can see both Denzil and the police.

Rodney *(Hisses)* Denzil, Denzil, Denzil.
Denzil climbs into the cab. Del is trying to force the doors as the engine starts.

Del Denzil, Denzil, Denzil, wait I'm in here. Is that you? Denzil you plonker.
The juggernaut moves off. Rodney is desperately trying to start the van.

Rodney Oh come on please, please, I'll clean ya, I'll clean ya.
It starts and Rodney sets off in pursuit. Denzil has the radio blaring and is blissfully unaware of what is happening. Del is swaying in the back.

Del Denzil, Denzil this is your friend speaking – I'll do you when I get hold of you.

SLATER'S OFFICE.
Slater and Hoskins enter.

Slater Bloody hoax phone calls, my last station I had to put up with jokers. Get to your desk Hoskins, might have had some new reports.

Hoskins No, nothing yet sir.

Slater I want a watch put on Boycie and Abdul, I want to know everywhere they go, everything they do – got to make their move soon. Who's the courier Hoskins? I know who's putting the money up, what they're buying and who from but I don't know who's bringing it in.

Hoskins Bound to be local sir.

Slater Oh yeah wouldn't go far outside the parish, got to have someone they can trust – but who?

Hoskins It's a mystery sir – no one's behaving in an unusual manner, well no more unusual than normal – everyone's just carrying on the same.

Slater Except the Trotters – went round the estate their van's missing, toured the area, no sign of it.

Policeman Maybe it's been nicked sir.

Slater Nicked? If someone's nicked that three-wheel van of theirs we've got a dangerous maniac on our hands. Ha ha ha.

Policeman Take your point sir.

Slater Something's just struck me Hoskins, maybe we've been underestimating Del Boy. All these years he may have been fooling us with his 9 carat gold and his wide-awake suits, I mean Del Boy's well acquainted with the ways of this world – he knows all the wrinkles, he invented a lot of

them himself, and his soppy brother has got GCEs.

Hoskins What are you trying to say sir?

Slater What I'm saying is Hoskins, maybe them two's more intelligent than we've given them credit for, yeah, it's all beginning to fit. The Dutch firm are the suppliers, Boycie and Abdul are the money men and the Trotters are the brains.

Hoskins You could be right sir.

Slater I was only joking Hoskins, for God's sake ain't you got no sense of humour?

Hoskins Sorry sir.

BACK OF DENZIL'S VAN.
Del, exhausted and sweating and being flung about, is banging with both fists on the trailer's walls.

Del Denzil, Denzil, Denzil . . .?
A motorway sign indicates 'The North.' The juggernaut roars past. Shortly after the van passes. In the cab of the lorry Denzil places a cigarette in his mouth. There is a distant muffled sound – Del shouting. The cigarette falls from Denzil's mouth. The haunting has now begun. He switches the radio back on. The van passes the motorway sign, backfiring. The juggernaut crosses the Humber Bridge. Denzil pulls up at a toll booth..

Man at Toll Bridge Cheers.
He drives off. The van crosses the bridge. It draws to a halt by a toll booth

Man at Toll Bridge That's a pound.

Rodney What?

Man at Toll Bridge I said that's a pound.

Rodney I've got 75 pence.

Man at Toll Bridge Well that's not a pound is it?

Rodney Oh no, but this has only got three wheels.

Man at Toll Bridge *(Indicates silhouette of car on sign)* That's only got two but it's still a pound.
Rodney finds the coins and hands it to the attendant.
By the way be careful where you dump that thing will you.

Rodney Funny innit? I'm laughing look.
He drives off.

THE DOCKSIDE CAFE.
Denzil's lorry is parked outside. Inside, weary from his night's drive, Denzil rests his head on his hands. Lil, the woman who runs the café, approaches the table.

Lil There's your tea Denzil.

To Hull and Back

Denzil Ta.

Lil Don't you want that breakfast?

Denzil Course I do, just a bit drowsy that's all.

Lil You've been overworking love, I've seen it before with your lorry drivers trying to work 25 hours a day. I know the money is good lovey, but you'll get no overtime in the mortuary.

Denzil I'm always like this after a night drive.

Lil You're looking tired lovey, you're dark round the eyes.

Denzil I'm dark around everywhere Lil. Listen don't you worry about me, I'm a big, strong lad you know, I'll prove it to you.

Lil I'm not talking about physical illness, there's no knowing what lack of sleep and overwork does to the brain. I've seen it happen to them lovey.

Denzil Seen what happen?

Lil Young fit men, went to pieces, started hearing things and seeing things – you slow down lovey, or you'll go same way.

Denzil thinks about her words then shrugs them off. As he picks up a mouthful of food the yellow van drives slowly past the window. Denzil sees the van in the mirror. He looks round but the van has gone.

CAFE CAR PARK.

Rodney has pulled in behind the juggernaut. He opens the trailer door. Del is crumpled up asleep at the front of the trailer. Del wakes.

Rodney Del.

Del Is that you Rodney?

Rodney Yeah it's me.

Del I knew you'd come and save me, you're a saint Rodders, oh, you're a 42 carat saint.

Rodney Come on let's get you out of here.

Del Thank you, oh, oh – it's been a nightmare Rodney, a bloody nightmare. Camp on Blood Island was a doddle compared with that.

Rodney Look, do you want something to eat or a cup of tea?

Del No – it's alright, we ain't got time for all that, we've got to get the aeroplane tickets and the lot ain't we hey? Come on let's go, come on Rodney, come on.

Del looks around at the ships, the sea etc. He looks alarmed.

Where the bloody hell am I?

Rodney Hull.

Del Oh. Hull – what Hull in what's its name?

Rodney Yorkshire yeah.

Del What the bloody hell am I doing in Hull?

Rodney Well this is where Denzil brought you innit? He's most probably got a load to pick up.

Del That bloody half-head Denzil, I'll get him, you just see if I don't.

Rodney Oi, don't you think you ought to have a rest eh, get your strength back?

Del No I don't Rodney, just get me back to Peckham as soon as possible otherwise I'll be saying hey-up and breeding whippets before I'm very much older – come on.

They get in the van. Rodneys tries to start it with little success. Del is looking out at the ships. We can sense his brain ticking over.

Del Switch that off Rodney – take a look.

Rodney What?

Del Boats.

Rodney Oh yeah.

Del Big boats, little boats.

Rodney Yeah there's a red one, a white one look.

Del Don't you see Rodney?

Rodney See what.

Del Slater has got all the airports covered. Why has he got all the airports covered? 'Cause that's how he thinks that we're getting back into the country.

Rodney Yeah – but that's how we are getting back in the country.

Del Not any more we ain't, we're going by boat.

Rodney Oh yes like it Derek, yeah, we get the Ferry.

Del Not the Ferry you plonker, the Customs there are going to be just as bad as they are at the airports. No we're going to sail across in our own little boat.

Rodney Sorry?

Del We're going to sail out of here to Holland and back again and no one will be any the wiser.

Rodney We . . . we are going to . . . us, in the sea?

Del Hm, Rodney, it's not far look it's only across the water there look innit eh? I mean, I remember seeing it on the map it's only, only that far. *(Holds thumb and forefinger an inch apart)*

Rodney Derek, we'll die.

Del No it'll be a piece of cake, we'll be in and out of there like a sour plum.

Rodney Del, we don't know the first thing about sailing a boat.

Del Oh Rodney, Rodney, use your filbert – I'm going to get one with an engine.

Del walks off leaving Rodney in the van.

DOCKSIDE.

Del is checking name plates on doors. A group of men cross a zebra crossing. Del

walks with them. Denzil stops at the crossing in his lorry. Del is behind the men, partly hidden. Denzil reacts horrified at this apparition. He puts his hand over his eyes and shakes his head. He looks up again. The men disperse but there is no sign of Del.

ALLEY/DOCKSIDE.

Del arrives at the end of an alley and enters the quay side. A boat owner is repairing a boat.

Del Ahoy there, shipmate.

Boatman Morning.

Del Any idea where I could hire a boat round here?

Boatman You want to hire a boat?

Del Yeah.

Boatman What kind of a boat?

Del Er, schooner.

Boatman Schooner?

Del With an engine.

Boatman Schooner with an engine – follow me shipmate, I might have just the thing for you.

Del Oh, tally-ho.

ON BOARD THE INGE.

Del, Rodney and the boat owner are on deck.

Del Well Rodney what do you reckon?

Rodney What – this boat's got woodworm.

Del No that's not woodworm, that's just um, it's – what is that?

Boatman That's where the ropes have worn it away through the years.

Del Just where the rope has worn it away through the years, it's sort of wear and tear innit?

Rodney And we're supposed to sail to Holland in this thing?

Boatman This is a sturdy vessel sir, built of very mature timber.

Rodney In other words, it's old.

Del Well the old 'uns are the best 'uns Rodney.

Rodney We're talking about boats now Del, not your birds.

Del Oi, don't push your luck you saucy git.

Boatman I'll leave you two alone to discuss it – I'll be over here. *(Exits)*

Rodney Right.

Del Yeah, okay yes, ahoy there shipmate, we'll be ashore in a minute.

Rodney Yeah we'll go ashore what, about 7 bells eh Del? Will you pipe him ashore or shall I?

Del I'm beginning to lose my temper Rodney – you'll cop an unfortunate one in a minute.

The boatman approaches a friend.

Boatman 2 You're not really letting your boat out to them southern nancies are you?

Boatman Oh aye.

Boatman 2 You'll never see it again.

Boatman That vessel's worth ten thousand pounds – at least that's what it says in the insurance papers.

Del and Rodney are still conferring.

Del Come on Rodney, we can do it, you know he who dares wins. Look I got the right price from the owner and everything.

Rodney Del I'll tell you now there's no way us two can sail this thing to Holland and back.

Del What? Us two, you think that . . . that we're going to sail it . . . is that what you thought, that us pair of wallies are going to take this thing out on the high seas?

Rodney Well yeah.

Del Course we're not. No I'm going to get us a skipper, an experienced man to do the sailing.

Rodney So there's going to be someone in charge?

Del Of course there is – you didn't think I was going to risk our lives did you? Come here you dipstick.

HULL RAILWAY STATION.

Albert, complete with duffle-bag, alights from the train.

Rodney Dear God.

Del Oh, leave it out Rodney, that is England's greatest little sailor since Nelson lost the Armada.

Albert approaches.

Albert Ahoy there.

Del Yeah, yeah, ship ahoy.

Rodney Del, every single ship or vessel that man has ever sailed on has sunk.

Del I know, luck's got to change sometime innit Rodney? Alright Uncle Albert?

Albert All shipshape and bristle fashion.

Del He's got all the dialogue ain't he? Good good come on then. Right now listen – did you bring the passport?

Albert In the old duffel bag.

Del Good good – did you bring some clothes?

Albert I threw some of me old jumpers in.

Del Lovely – did you bring our clothes?

Albert Did you want me to bring you some then?

Del Oh what do you think I phoned up about?

Albert I thought you meant my clothes.

Rodney We haven't had a wash or a change of clothes for two days now.

Albert Well how am I supposed to know that?

Rodney Well it don't take a lot of working out

To Hull and Back

does it?

Del Oi, oi, oi you two – alright calm down, calm down don't worry we'll sort something out. Right some on skipper, let's show you your vessel.

Albert Yeah I'd like to look her over Del make sure she meets with my approval.

Del Bleeding shame if she doesn't because we sail in half an hour.

HULL DOCKSIDE.

The boat is sailing up a narrow strip of water. Alb is in the wheelhouse. Del is directing him from the bow.

Del Albert slow down, you're going too fast. You're going too fast, slow down, don't . . . right right a bit.

Albert Eh?

Del To your right.

Albert You mean starboard.

Del I mean right – don't start all that Captain Birdseye bloody cobblers, I said right.

Rodney is in the cabin. He is tying up his life-jacket.

Del Now you've gone too far now, you're too far don't . . . come on, come over to your left, there – I said . . . I said left.

Albert That's portside.

Del I'll come up there and punch you in the bloody nose in a minute – when I say left I mean left. Mind . . . mind this little boat down there.

Albert Eh?

Del Watch, watch this, watch this little boat down – sorry shipmate. What did you say pal? And to you sir, cheeky git. Alright come, come to your right again now Albert, you're doing very well. Not, no, no. What are you doing up there, you got Saint Vitus Dance or what? Look come right again.

Denzil is strolling along the shore. He is a very worried man.

Denzil It's overwork that's all, too many hours in that lorry cab, all you need is a bit of relaxation and some fresh air, that's all.

He sits down and takes a deep lungful of fresh air. He looks out to sea. His expression changes. The boat is sailing out of the estuary. Del is at the bow looking out to sea.

Gordon Bennett. I'm sick. I'm sick. Oh.

Back on the boat, Rodney climbs up from the cabin.

Rodney I feel sick Del.

Del What? Leave it out you tart, we've only just started, that was only just a little ripple. Wait till we get out there on the big waves, we'll be going up and down and up and down, be just like the big dipper, whooo. . . .

Rodney Oh God! *(He leans over the side.)*

Del That's it Rodney, go on cough it up, could be an ace? Oh, gets an old tingle running down the spine this don't it? Ha ha, well it's in the blood of course. Ah, this island race, this sceptic isle, yeah us Brits, we've got salt water flowing through our veins.

Rodney Oh will you shut up about bloody veins!

Del And when you think of all the English heroes that have set sail out of these waters to go and discover the new world and stitch the dagos up, makes you feel very, very proud. *(Sings)* 'Robin Hood, Robin Hood with his band of men, Robin Hood, Robin Hood riding through the glen, feared by the good .'

ON BOAT AT SEA.

The Trotters are in the wheelhouse. They are all simply staring out into the blackness.

Del Have you got any idea where we are?

Albert *(Looking at charts)* Not really Del, I never got the hang of these charts.

Rodney Well then how in God's name did you expect to get us across to Holland?

Albert Well Del said it weren't all that far.

Del Well it ain't all that far if you're going in the right bleeding direction. We should have been in Holland five hours ago. Look at it – middle of the poxy bleeding night and not a windmill anywhere. I thought you said that you could sail a boat.

Albert Well it went, didn't it?

Del I know it went, yeah, it went alright, but where hey? Look Albert where is our position?

Albert Well we're er, we're here ain't we? Sort of.

Rodney *(Checking the chart)* Oh right, so according to all your calculations we're just off the Strait of Gibraltar but we're also very close to Copenhagen.

Albert Well it narrows it down a little bit don't it?

Del Yeah – the right ocean at least ain't we?

Albert When I was in the Navy I was a boiler maintenance man.

Rodney So you've never actually studied navigation at all?

Albert Boiler maintenance men didn't have to – see the boiler has a tendency to go wherever the ship's going. Look we can't be far away can we? I mean, seemed to go pretty straight didn't we?

Rodney He's something else ain't he? And what about all the currents they got around here eh we could have drifted anywhere by now.

Del Yes he's right an'all ain't he? We're in the middle of the North Sea ain't we? It's got more currents than a hot-cross bun.

Albert Let's not panic hey, we'll wait till the morning, bound to see something.

Del Oh yeah, we'll keep our eyes peeled for tulips, listen out for the sound of clogs.

Rodney looks up to the night sky.

Rodney Stars.

Del What?

Rodney The stars.

Del Stars. You don't need to read your horoscope Rodney to realise you're in dead lumber.

Rodney Them stars – you can steer a ship by the stars.

Del That's right an'all – I remember seeing it once in the *Odedin Line.*

Albert That's a bloody good idea Rodney, yeah. *The Trotters exit from the wheelhouse and stare up to the sky.*

Albert There's millions of them ain't there?

Rodney I love him, I just bloody love him.

Del Isn't there anything up there that rings a bell?

Albert I'm not quite sure what I'm supposed to be looking for – they've all got names ain't they like The Bear, things like that.

Del Can't you just find The Bear?

Albert Well what does it look like?

Del Well it looks like a bloody rabbit don't it? I mean what do you think a bear looks like?

Albert Well where would I find it?

Del Standing up there on top of the glacier mint – you're giving me the hump you are Albert, you're giving me the right hump.

Albert Look! *(Pointing up to the sky)*

Del What?

Albert Up there, it's Concorde.

Del So?

Albert I'm just saying, Concorde.

Del I'm going to kill him, I'm going to kill him, the soppy old git, I'm going to kill him!

Albert Agh, Rodney!

Rodney Del leave him alone.

It is the following morning. Rodney is in the wheelhouse surveying the area with bleary eyes. Del climbs up with a cup of tea.

Del Here we go Rodders, here's our tea, sorry I spilt it. Any luck?

Rodney No not a thing – where's Ahab?

Del Oh he's down below in the cabin poncing about with the radio – it's all crackles and hisses and dog-a-bag, can't be doing with it.

Rodney Well at least he's doing something positive to get us out of this mess.

Del Positive – he's trying to get the Kid Jensen show. *(He spots something on the horizon)* where are them binoculars.

Rodney There.

Del Ahoy – full ahead both Mr Christian.

Rodney Why?

Del We're going to Holland Rodders, we're going to Holland.

GAS RIG IN THE MIDDLE OF THE NORTH SEA.

The boat approaches a gas rig. There are men working on board.

Del *(Calls)* Hoy, hoy, John – Holland.

Man on Rig What?

Del Which way to Holland?

Man on Rig Holland – *(Points)* it's over there.

Del Cheers pal. Albert it's to the right, Holland is that way. Thank you. Rodney see, you don't know the way, you just got to ask someone ain't you? Hey diddley dee a sailor's life for me.

BOYCIE'S OFFICE.

Boycie is pouring himself a drink. Abdul is pacing the room.

Abdul What is the time?

Boycie What do you keep asking me for, you got a watch of your own ain't ya?

Abdul Yes, but it hasn't worked properly since Del sold it to me.

Boycie Cor – it is five to eleven, that's five to twelve their time, the exchange doesn't take place till midday so just calm down will you?

Abdul Huh, calm down he says, I'm becoming rather concerned about this whole affair.

Boycie What is worrying you now?

Abdul You know perfectly well what's worrying me – what happens if Van Cleef discovers the fifty thousand pounds is all counterfeit money?

Boycie How's he going to do that? He's a Dutchman, he wouldn't know a dodgy English tenner from a real one.

Abdul Not immediately perhaps but in time he may.

Boycie We have discussed this time and time again – the first thing Van Cleef is going to do is launder that money, he's then going to exchange it at safe houses for Dutch notes, it will then be exchanged time and time again, pass through many hands until some smart arse discovered it's worthless but by then it'll be too late 'cause they won't know who gave it to 'em.

Abdul Del may notice they're fakes.

Boycie I shouldn't think so. In any case he's

To Hull and Back

hardly going to voice his doubts with Van Cleef when his heavy is in close attendance is he? There's a minute to go, I wonder if he's there yet?

THE BOAT ON THE CANAL.

Rodney exits from the cabin.

Rodney Where are we then?

Del *(Referring to windmills)* It's obvious innit eh? We're in Bulgaria.

Rodney I know that, I know where we are. What I meant was, well, where are we?

Albert This is the North Sea Canal Rodney. Takes us right into the heart of Amsterdam.

Del Yeah, just don't act suspicious Rodney, just let's pretend we're Dutchmen, right? *(Waves at some people on the bank)* Ajax.

BOYCIE'S OFFICE.

Boycie It's one minute past time. Why ain't he rung?

Abdul Maybe they've sunk.

Boycie No no they've got their Uncle Albert with them – yeah maybe they have sunk. Hello? Oh hello, Mr Biggastaff, you bought a car off us when? Well I don't care if you are broken down on the A1, what do you expect me to do about it? Well my advice to you pal is shove it. No this is not Mr Boyce speaking, this is his public relations officer.

STREET IN AMSTERDAM.

The Trotters check name plates on the doors. They find the door they are looking for. Del, realizing he has no idea what he is walking in to, calls on all his courage.

Del You stay down here alright?

Rodney Why?

Del 'Cause we don't know what sort of welcome we're going to get up there do we? Might turn very nasty.

Rodney Oi listen Del, if there's going to be any trouble I want to be up there with you.

Del I want you to stay down here Rodney, first sign of any trouble from up there now, you leg it.

Rodney No way.

Del Rodney – *(To Albert)* you keep your eye on him, make sure he stays down here.

Albert Alright Del. *(To Rodney)* It's for the best son.

VAN KLEEFE'S OFFICE.

Van Kleefe is seated at his desk smoking a cigarette. On the settee is Abdul's cousin, Hussein. One of Van Kleefe's heavies sits in a chair, the other stands at the window. There is a knock on the door.

Del Good afternoon, Derek Trotter from London.

Del pats his briefcase. The heavy looks to Van Kleefe who gestures for him to enter. Del enters.

Good afternoon Mr Van Cleef, my name is Derek Trotter, sorry I'm a bit late, I had a bit of bother as you can probably see.

Mr Van Cleef Not a worry Mr Trotter, you're here now – this is Mr Hussein Abdul's cousin and these two gentlemen are my assistants.

Del *(Indicates heavy)* He's a big lad ain't he? Suppose it's all that cheese he eats is it?

Mr Van Cleef Do you have the money Mr Trotter?

Del Yes I have the money Mr Van Cleef. Do you have the diamonds?

Mr. Van Cleef Yes I have the diamonds.

Produces a puch of diamonds. He pours them on to the table.

If you'll examine them, I'll go and make the phone call.

Hussein goes to examine them.

In Boycie's office the phone rings. He grabs it quickly.

Boycie Hello? Oh good afternoon Mr Van Cleef. *(To Abdul)* It's him.

Mr Van Cleef Your man has arrived. Of course. *(To Del)* He wants to talk to you.

Del Hello Boycie.

Boycie Everything alright Del?

Del Yeah, couldn't be better.

Abdul Is my cousin there?

Boycie Is Abdul's cousin there?

Del Yeah, he's checking the merchandise now.

Mr Hussein *(Has checked diamonds)* These are blue white stone, purity absolutely clean, cut by experts. They are of the finest quality.

Del He says they're pucker.

Boycie *(To Abdul)* The stones are good. Okay Del, I'm now going to give you the combination to the briefcase. It's 7.1.4.

Del 7.1.4.

Boycie 9.3.9.

Del 9.3.9.

Del opens the briefcase and looks at the money. His face tells us nothing. He hands the briefcase to V.K who gives the contents a cursory inspection. He hands it to one of the heavies who begins flicking through each pile. Del awaits the decision anxiously. Eventually, one of the heavies gives V.K a nod of approval.

Mr Van Cleef Good. *(Handing Del the pouch)* I believe these are yours Mr Trotter.

Del Thank you very much. *(On phone)* Boycie we got a deal.

Boycie Good – no problems?

Del No, everything went as sweet as a nut – I'll see you soon.

Boycie Yeah don't forget now will you?

Del I'll give you a bell. *(Hands receiver back)*

Mr Hussein Will you be needing me any longer?

Del No, no, on your way pal. *(He exits)*

Mr Van Cleef *(On phone)* The exchange is completed. Thank you, it's nice to do business with you as well.

Del Well must fly. See you soon Mr Van Cleef.

Mr Van Cleef Good day Mr Trotter and good luck.

Del *(Del moves to the door)* Thank you. *(To heavy)* Ajax. *(Exits)*

Mr Van Cleef *(Picks up the phone)* The courier has just left – should be with you soon. Trotter. Derek Trotter.

THE STREET IN AMSTERDAM.

Rodney and Albert are waiting outside the door. Del exits.

Albert Alright Del?

Del Terrific. Well gentlemen.

Rodney *(Gestures in direction of a police car)* Del.

Two officers alight from the car. A plain clothed policeman steps out of a doorway and moves in their direction, followed by the two officers in uniform.

Del Leg it.

Rodney Let's go. *(They dash off)*

The chase takes place through the streets of Amsterdam. Albert shows signs of tiring. Eventually he stops and leans against a wall.

Albert *(Gulping for air)* Oh Del.

Del Come on Albert, come on.

Rodney Come on, we got to keep going.

Albert You two go on, go on, I'll be alright.

Rodney Yeah alright, come on Del.

Del Terrific, we can't leave him.

Rodney Why not? He's got nothing incriminating on him.

Del Hey now, come on, you can't leave the poor old sod to face the music can you?

The plain clothes policeman runs round the corner followed by the two in uniform. Del and Rodney put their hands up in the air.

Alright, alright, look, look, hands up, no rough stuff eh?

The plain clothes policeman rushes straight past the Trotters pursued by the two in uniform. Eventually they catch him and a short struggle ensues. The Trotters make to leave.

Del You dozy little twonk Rodney, what did you shout run for, eh?

Rodney It weren't me, it was him.

Albert Del shouted run.

Del No I didn't, it was nothing to do with me.

Rodney Yes you did, I heard you.

Del I come out the building didn't I? I was doing all the main heavy . . .

SLATER'S OFFICE.

Hoskins You called sir?

Slater *(Indicates Del's name on a board)* We've got our man Hoskins?

Hoskins Del – how did you find out sir?

Slater I've got a funny feeling in my water – remember what happened last time I had that funny feeling?

Hoskins Oh, you mean the antibiotics.

Slater No I don't mean that. I'm talking about the time I nicked that little Paki gang for bringing in cocaine mixed with curry powder.

Hoskins Oh yeah that was a good hunch of yours sir.

Slater Have a look at this – I've got Davis and Skinner covering Luton airport, there's a ten-man team at Heathrow, you and me are at Gatwick. Right Hoskins, I'm going to teach you the basic rules of airport surveillance – remember patience Hoskins, be prepared for a long, long wait, also suspect everyone. What's the most important thing we have to do Hoskins?

Hoskins I don't know sir. . . . *(Slater produces a sombrero)* Oh yeah, wear sombreros

Slater What do I look like?

Hoskins Carry on sir.

Slater I look like an ordinary holidaymaker don't I?

Hoskins Oh I see – blend into the surroundings.

Slater The first rule of surveillance is, don't look conspicuous. We'll have to get you something Hoskins, you look a right tit.

THE MIDDLE OF THE NORTH SEA.

Del *(Shouting)* How can we be lost again? I thought you'd know the way by now.

Albert So did I – it all looks the same to me.

Rodney I feel sick.

Del Oh shut up Rodney. *(To Albert)* look why can't we just go back the way we came?

Albert That's what I've been trying to do.

To Hull and Back

Rodney *(Seeing something on the horizon)* Del, there's a ship.

Del Oh well, that's a turn up for the book innit eh? This is the last place you'd expect to find a ship, oh.

Rodney It's the *Norland*.

Del It's the *Norland* – so what?

Albert The *Norland*, we saw that back in port just 'fore we left England.

Rodney Del, that is the Zeebrugge to Hull Ferry.

Del Alright so it's the Zeebrugge to Hull . . . the Zee . . . ah, good boy Rodney, well spotted. Albert.

Albert Sir.

Del Follow that boat.

BACK ROOM OF THE NAGS HEAD.

Boycie is seated. Abdul is pacing the room.

Abdul *(Checks watch)* Four o'clock they're still not back.

Boycie *(Checks watch)* It's not four o'clock it's half past twelve.

Abdul Bloody watch. They're still a day late though, something has gone wrong.

Boycie Del phoned me this morning at half past seven he's back in England, they even got through Customs without a hitch, they probably got held up on the way h . . .

There is a sound of a van backfiring.

Abdul It's them.

The van stops outside the pub.

Del Let Popeye out the back will you Rodney? *Boycie unlocks and opens back door. Del enters. Rodney and Alb follow.*

Boycie Where the hell have you . . .

Del Alright alright alright. Had a little bit of trouble you know, got lost in the middle of the North Sea, then Rodney spotted the Zeebrugge to Hull ferry so we followed it.

Abdul And that's how you got to Hull?

Del No that is how we got to Zeebrugge – it was going the wrong bloody way, so we had to wait for it to turn round and then we followed it back.

Boycie Okay well you're here now anyway. Okay, you got the diamonds?

Del You got the money?

Boycie *(Takes a large wad of notes from his pocket)* Here's your money.

Del Now, put it on the table.

Abdul Del, Del.

Del On the table, on the table.

Boycie puts the money on the table. As Del hands him the puch of diamonds the back door is kicked in. In the doorway is Slater wearing a sombrero.

Slater Buenos dias.

Boycie Bloody hell, Slater.

Del Rodney, quick this way, out the back.

They make a rush for the door, but Parker is blocking the way. They make their way to another door, but Hoskins is there holding a straw donkey. During this Slater has wlaked to the table and picked the diamonds up from the table.

Slater *(Pours diamonds into his hands)* They're pretty ain't they?

Abdul *(Appealing to him)* Inspector Slater.

Slater Chief Inspector.

Abdul My apologies, Chief Inspector – couldn't we discuss this in a civilised and gentlemanly manner?

Slater What's to discuss? I've got you bang to rights. *(Reacts to the smell of Trotters)* Phew, you smell like a mackerel trawler.

Albert So would you if you spent half the week in the middle of the North Sea.

Slater Oh, so you came in by sea did you? I just spent eighteen hours waiting at Gatwick Airport for you. *(Referring to Albert)* Who is this little person – don't tell me, you're a Trotter ain't ya?

Albert I'm the boys' uncle.

Slater Yeah you can see the family resemblance – it's those shifty little rodent eyes and the furtive movement of the feet, dead giveaway. This is a very sad day for me – my very last case and I have to nick two of me old school friends. Still never mind eh? *(Places last diamond in the pouch)* Thirty, spot on.

Boycie Roy, give us a break will ya? Wasn't us that smuggled those diamonds in, it was Del Boy.

Abdul Yes he's right Chief Inspector, it was nothing to do with us, it was them three.

Del No no no, it was just me Slater.

Albert No, I was the brains behind it. *(The others give him a 'don't be stupid' look)* Oh alright then.

Slater It is tearing me apart to see you lot squirming like this – what am I to do? *(Opens door to bar and says to Parker)* Away you go Parker. Alright I've reached a decision – there are two ways we can handle this unfortunate situation – one, I take you all down the nick with the evidence and see you banged up for five years apiece, or – two, *(Places diamonds in his pocket)* I walk out of here and pretend it never happened.

Boycie Yeah, that sounds a good scheme Roy, let's pretend it never happened.

Abdul Yes, yes I will go along with that.

Slater What do you think Del Boy?

Del I think something smells very fishy around here and it ain't just these clothes. How come you knew there was thirty diamonds in that bag?

Rodney Yeah and how come you knew who was involved right from the start?

Del Just a minute – when we were in the cafe the other day that bloke you was telling us about that you could nick for smuggling diamonds 'cause of lack of evidence, what was his name?

Slater You mean Henry.

Del Yeah – his surname wouldn't have been Van Cleef by any chance would it?

Slater You found me out you rascal.

Boycie What – you and Van Cleef?

Slater That's right. He offered me a little business deal. He sets up a bunch of wallies who are greedy enough to smuggle diamonds into the country and I pick them up this side of the water. Not only do we get paid at both ends – you take all the risks. Brilliant innit? It's the third time we've pulled it off and there is nothing you can do about it – unless of course you fancy a spell in the Scrubs. Well gentlemen, I think we've concluded our business don't you? Ain't you going to wish me good luck for the future – no? Oh well, win some, lose some.

Del I hope we bump into each other one of these days, Slater.

Slater I don't think so Del Boy, I'm going a long way away from here. Cheer up lads – still got your freedom. *(Exits)*

Boycie You berk Abdul.

Abdul How was I to know Van Cleef was a crook? Bloody foreigner.

Del walks towards the door.

Boycie Where are you going Del?

Del Where am I going? I'm going where I should have stayed right at the bloody start – going home.

Boycie Look, don't, don't get the hump with us, we ain't done nothing.

Del You ain't done nothing? You sent me half-way round the world, I've been to Amsterdam, I've been to Hull and back, for what? Slater's taken the diamonds, he's taken the money, on top of all that my two mates have grassed me up.

Boycie We weren't actually grassing you.

Abdul No no no, it was more of a diversary tactic.

Albert Yeah to divert the blame from yourselves.

Del Come on Rodney, Albert, let's go home.

SLATER'S CAR.

Hoskins is driving. Slater is in the back feigning dejection.

Hoskins I can't understand sir not a single clue to the diamonds' whereabouts.

Slater Not a thing, they were all as clean as whistles.

Hoskins This is the third time we've followed these diamonds and this is the third time we've drawn a blank.

Slater That's the way it goes in this game – maybe I'm past it Hoskins, my hunches don't seem to pay off any more. Just as well I'm taking early retirement.

Hoskins Do you know what I think?

Slater No and to be honest I'm not really interested, you're not paid to think Hoskins, you're paid to do your job, now drive me home.

Hoskins Yes sir.

Hoskins swings the car left into a side road.

Slater Where are you going Hoskins, this isn't the way to my house?

Hoskins No I know it isn't sir.

There is a police block. Hoskins stops the car.

Slater What's all this?

Hoskins They've known about you for a long time and they just couldn't catch you in possession till now sir.

Slater You've set me up.

Hoskins You set yourself up, sir.

Slater Look Hoskins, Terrance, use your loaf, help me out of this and I'll make you a rich man – the money from them other diamonds is in a bank account, I'll let you have half. What do you think?

Hoskins You seem to forget sir, I don't think, I only do my job.

Hoskins turns his lapel over to reveal a small hidden microphone.

A DUTCH BANK.

The briefcase containing the counterfeit money is being examined by a teller. Van Kleefe waits patiently. The teller shows them to a colleague, who examines them then gestures to a couple of security men. The security men lead him, protesting his innocence, away.

BACK ROOM OF NAG'S HEAD.

Boycie and Abdul are together.

Abdul I think we should phone the police.

Boycie Phone the police? Oh yeah. And what are we going to tell them? A bent copper disguised as the Cisco Kid stole our smuggled diamonds.

Abdul Yeah, you have a point. Well anyway at

To Hull and Back

least the only money we lost was counterfeit.

Boycie Apart from the fifteen grand Slater half-inched.

Abdul You mean that was real?

Boycie I drew it out the bank Friday. I didn't intend to pay Del Boy funny money, I ain't into plastic surgery. I am gutted. Gutted.

THE TROTTERS' LOUNGE.

Del, exhausted, enters and throws his coat on the settee. Alb follows him in.

Albert Del.

Del Alright, alright, hold on, hold on a minute.
Rodney enters.

Rodney Oi, listen you two, this hasn't turned out as bad as you think.

Del Hasn't turned out as bad as we think – it's turned out bloody well Rodney. Albert, pour the drinks.

Albert What do you want Rodney?

Rodney *(Bewildered)* Well an explanation would be nice.

Del Listen to me, you know that fifty grand that we took over to Amsterdam?

Rodney Yeah.

Del It was counterfeit.

Rodney It was counterfeit – and you knew?

Del Well not till I opened the case in Van Cleef's office I didn't. There's one thing I do know about Rodney, and that is kosher readies. Oh cheers.

Rodney And you didn't tell no one?

Del Oh yes, I said, 'Excuse me Mr Van Cleef, all that money, it's Mickey Mouse money.' Of course I didn't, I just stood there and prayed, course me old apron was going like a moped. Fortunately he gave the money to these two gorillas to check and, well, they were about as bright as an eclipse.

Rodney So Boycie and Abdul sent us over there with fake money?

Del Hm hm.

Rodney Right we're going to get even with them for that ain't we?

Albert We already have Rodney.

Rodney Eh?

Del Go on Albert, show him.
Albert produces his pipe.

Albert Hold your hand out.
He removes the tobacco and pours two diamonds into Rodney's hand.

Rodney They're real ain't they?

Del They're top of the range my son, blue-white purity, absolutely clean, they are as they say in France, chasse de forme?

Rodney Eh, no, hold on, Slater picked up thirty diamonds

Del No he didn't, he took twenty-eight diamonds and *(Showing his cuff links minus the solitaires)* two cats eyes.

Rodney Oh Derek, oh, who's a pretty boy then?

Del Worth about 5 grand each – well by the time we've put them through the fence we'll get what, six grand for the pair. Six thousand pounds split three ways means that you two get one thousand pounds each in your skies?

Albert Yeah – hey?

Rodney Well actually we got slightly more than that Derek.

Del Hm, what do you mean?

Rodney You know that fifteen grand that went missing?

Del It didn't go missing, that bark Slater picked it up didn't he?

Rodney Oh, Slater didn't pick it up.

Del Eh?

Rodney *(Produces wad of notes)* I did.

Albert *(Takes money from him)* You crafty little sod Rodney.

Rodney Well you know, it was just there lying on the table and in all that confusion when we tried to escape I could just hear it saying, 'Daddy, Daddy', so I picked it up.

Del You know what we're going to do with this money Rodney?

Rodney Yes – we'll invest it, we'll make it work for us, this time next year we'll be millionaires . . . or shall we go to Benidorm.

Del No, I'll show you what we're going to do with it.
He throws it all out of the window. Rodney and Alb are open-mouthed.

Albert For a minute I thought he threw that fifteen grand out the window.

Rodney No don't be silly unc, I mean who'd do a silly thing like that.

Del It was Boycie's money weren't it? It was fake, dud, counterfeit.

Rodney But it looked genuine enough to me 'cause you know it had all the little watermarks in it and the little silver strips and everything.

Del Oh leave it out Rodney, what do you think I am eh, some sort of wally?

SERIES FIVE

From Prussia With Love

THE NAG'S HEAD

Albert is sitting at a table playing cards with a couple of locals. Del and Rodney are at the bar talking to Mike. Sitting alone at a table, a suitcase by her side, is Anna. She is an attractive 19-year-old language student from Germany. She can speak English quite well, but has problems with 'Nag's Head English.' She surveys the bar in an almost frightened manner. She is vulnerable and sad.

Del What do you reckon then Mike, 25?

Mike Last orders now – please. *(To Del)* I'm not interested.

Del I'll give you the box – it's got re-dial, oi, top me up too, don't hang about.

Mike Maureen! Maureen! *(Indicating Anna)* Go 'an tell that girl over there will you, we're closing in a minute.

Maureen And how am I supposed to do that? I've been tryin' to talk to her all night but she's foreign, don't understand the lingo!

Rodney What's occurring Mike?

Mike Well it's that foreign tart, she can't speak a word of English. She's been sitting there all night. Keeps bursting into tears!

Del Yeah, well at your prices you can't blame her? What's her nationality?

Mike Ain't got a clue!

Rodney *(Hopefully)* Maybe she's Swedish!!

Mike and Del Swedish??

Del Hark at him.

Mike Yeah, well d'you know the Swedish for 'Chucking out time'?? That's £1.47 . . .

Del Alright, I'll get it.

Mike Here Del, Del, you speak a bit of French don't you?

Del Potage bonne femme!

Mike Listen, go and have a chat with her, see if she speaks French?

Del Of course I will Mike, anything for a mate. How much d'you say these drinks were?

Mike One four . . . On the house Del!

Del Good boy, well done Michael, you're a gentleman! Right, you can stay here if you like Rodney.

Rodney You must be joking! You're gonna to speak French to someone, I wouldn't miss this for £1million.

Del Alright, alright then – I'll show you. Come on.

Rodney Go on then.

Del approaches.

Del Alright Maureen, I can take over now. Right. Alright. Au revoir! Parlez vous the old Français?

Anna Oh, oui bien sur. Pouvez vous m'aider s'il vous plait? Est'ce qu'il y'a un hotel ou pension quelconque par ici où je peux trouver une chambre?

Del is stunned. For the first time his 'Renault Handbook' French has been confronted by the real thing. Rodney grins at Del.

Del Na, she don't speak French either Mike!

Anna Excusez-moi Monsieur. Je ne suis pas Française, mais Allemande!

Del Who?

Anna Allemagne! Deutschland! Germany! Ja?

Rodney She's German!

Del Oh, it's alright, panic over Mike, Bamber's cracked it! She's German. *(To Albert)* What do you want?

Albert I can speak a bit of German, I was over there just after the war.

Del Yes, sit down, sit down. Come over here. Now listen to me. I want you to ask her what her name is, where she lives, her address and all that sort of thing.

Albert Right, leave this to me . . . *(In cod German accent)* Vot ees your nem?

Del Vot is your n . . . Vot is your nem . . . He's winding me up ain't he?

Anna Does anyone speak English?

Del English! You saucy mare, course we speak English, we invented the lingo didn't we.

Rodney Yes we sp . . . Well, I speak English!

Anna You help me maybe? I look for my hotel!

Rodney Oh right. Which hotel? What is the name of your hotel?

Anna I not sure of this!

Del Oh stone me, there's bloody millions of them across the river.

Anna *(Looks to Rodney for translation)* Please?

Rodney Er, he say 'There are many hotels in London.'

Anna Oh ja, many!

Albert You just come in then? Gatwick airport – silver bird?

Anna *(To Rodney)* Please?

Rodney He say 'Have you just arrived in England?'

Anna Oh no. I be in England now for one year.

I am language student. French and English, ja? I work as au pair and study at the college. This morning now, the family I work for tell me I must go. They are not happy with me. They say I must leave, so I have hotel yes?

Rodney Oh yes! Don't worry, I – I will make sure you get to your hotel. I will make sure you get safely to your room! I think I can handle this on my own Del, don't you?

Del Yeah, I bet you can! Yeah, blimey what a turn up, eh? He thought he was gonna pull a Swede and she's got lumbered with a cabbage! Come on Albert, let's take a Toby home, we'll leave the keys of the car with the old saint here! Off you go. Tata darling.

Albert Best of luck darling, keep yer hand on yer pfennig!

Mike No Del!

Del Alright, I tell you what I'm gonna do Michael, I'm gonna leave the phone here so that you can have a think about it and I'll give you a bell on it in the morning. Alright son.

Rodney So, have you any idea where your hotel is?

Anna I do not have hotel!

Rodney But I thought you said you were looking for a hotel?

Anna Ja, I look for hotel.

Rodney Oh . . . There are no hotels in this area!

Anna This is what I think!! So, I am nowhere? *(Begins to sob)*

Rodney No, no, don't cry! Something'll turn up! Give us a bit of time to think!

Anna *(Produces a few fivers)* I have money!

Rodney Put that away!! Blimey, they'd chop your head off round here if you've got gold teeth!

Anna Please?

Rodney This is dangerous place at night! The streets are bad place!

Anna Ja, this is why I fear!

Mike Come on, time to go home now – please.

Rodney Well look, you could stay the night at our flat I suppose. You know – if you want. It ain't very much, but it's comfortable . . . Well no, it ain't really comfortable. You're more than welcome! You could have my bed.

Anna But where will you sleep?

Rodney Oh, we'll think of something. Shall I take your case?

Anna Thank you.

Rodney picks up her suitcase. Anna stands and it is evident that she is heavily pregnant.

THE TROTTERS' LOUNGE.

Albert is watching TV eating fish and chips from the wrapping paper. Del is the table engaged in a conversation on a 'nomad phone.' On the table he has fish and chips and a lurid cocktail.

Del Mmh! Yeah! Mmh! Eh. Yeah, listen Kristos, everyone's got a cordless phone these days except you! What? No, of course they're not faulty! I said of course they're not faulty!

Rodney Hi!

Rodney enters, nervously.

Albert D'you get that little bird home?

Rodney Eh, yeah I got her home! See thing is Del, she didn't actually have a hotel to go back to!

Del Alright Rodney – can't you see I'm on the phone. What did you say – go on.

Rodney So I said she could spend the night here!

Del What d'you mean, she can spend the night here?

Rodney Come in Anna.

Anna enters.

Del Yeah hello dar . . . *(He spies the lump)* Alright Kristos, listen, I've got to go, I'll hang up because something big has just turned up. *(Switches phone off)*

Rodney Anna, this is my brother Derek. Del this is Anna.

Anna Good evening.

Del Good evening, yeah.

Rodney And this is our Uncle Albert.

Anna How do you do?

Albert Hello dear, nice to meet you all!

Anna May I sit down?

Del Certainly, yeah, sit here. Please put your bag down. That's it – good girl.

Albert D'you fancy a bit of 'addock?

Rodney Hey, no, you're alright, we've already eaten. I took her down the Star of Bengal.

Del D'you think a ruby was wise in her condition? Excuse me, excuse us. *(To Rodney indicating kitchen)* Could I have a private word with you in private please, thank you.

Rodney Yeah, yeah sure. I won't be a minute Anna.

Del Albert please try to entertain our guests!

KITCHEN.

Del Shut the door.

Rodney Del, I couldn't help it, honest, I mean, how was I to know she was pregnant?

Del 'How was I supposed to know she was pregnant?' It doesn't take a Doctor bleedin' Spock to work that one out Rodney!

From Prussia With Love

Rodney Look, I'll take her out tomorrow and find her a room, eh?

Del And what happens if that sprog of hers decides to clock in tonight?

Albert enters.

Albert I don't want to worry you two boys, but unless I'm very much mistaken that young girl out there's up the duff!

Rodney Why don't you go out an' hit an iceberg Albert?

Del I don't understand this, I just don't know what's been happening to me just lately! I just do not know what's happening. I've got more relatives crawling out the woodwork than Blake Carrington, and now I'm taking in the waifs and strays of Europe.

Rodney Ah, that's why we gotta help innit? We're in the European Community now, we've gotta stick together!

Del Pity her knees didn't!

Rodney Look Del, come on, we got room in the flat ain't we? I mean, it's only one more person.

Albert Yeah, but it's one more person who's about to become two more persons! On the other hand it could be twins or triplets, or quadlets!!

Del Yeah, he's right an' all. I mean, she could be sitting out there with a bellyful of people! One hot bath and we get chucked out for over-crowding! No, I'm sorry Rodney, I'm sorry. I can't take the risk. Sorry, no!

Rodney Alright, alright, we'll chuck her out in the street shall we? But you go an' give her the good news Del!

LOUNGE.

Rodney is already in the lounge as Del and Albert enter from the kitchen.

Del *(To Anna)* Munchengladbach! We've hit a bit of a snag! See the thing is, Anna, I mean at this pacific moment in time, we are a bit knackered for space see.

Anna *(To Rodney)* Please?

Rodney He says 'There is no room at the inn!'

Del Don't start all that Sunday school rubbish with me Rodney. *(To Anna but gesturing to Rodney)* Unt plonker, yah!

Anna *(To Rodney)* Please?

Rodney He's calling me a . . . Don't matter.

Albert Who did the dirty deed then?

Anna *(To Rodney)* Please?

Rodney He say, who's the father? Oi, that's a bit personal innit?

Del Yeah, a bit personal.

Anna Oh, father, yes, I understand. Family I

work with, Mr and Mrs Wainwright, have son, Spencer, who is the student. One day Spencer return from university with degree ja? I'm not drink but this day I have the champagne. Then I am spinning, ja? Then Spencer comes to my room. He wants to . . . to . . . what word?

Del Oh, you mean he wants to . . .

Rodney *(Warning)* Del!!!!

Anna He wants to be my friend, ja?

Albert What, while you were still spinning?

Anna Ja, I am still spinning! Then I find baby is here. I phone Spencer and he say I must not tell his parents he is father. But this morning, I am very worried and I tell them. They say I lie, they say I am bad person. Mr Wainwright say 'My disruptive influence on Spencer makes it inexpedient for me to remain!'

Del *(To Rodney)* Please?

Rodney He say 'On yer bike!'

Del Oh! On yer bike.

Anna Mr Wainwright, he is a . . . What word?

Del Git!

Anna A businessman. A rich man. He give me money for journey home.

Albert So why didn't you go?

Anna I cannot go yet. My family will see baby. This is not good! So I wait and when baby is born I give baby to people.

Del Yeah, yeah, if you think so sweetheart, yeah. It's a terrible world this innit Rodney? Terrible. Look, the best thing you can . . . Why don't you chuck Anna's things in your room for you know – for tonight.

Rodney Cheers mate.

Del Anna, listen, you go with Rodney through there and he will show you where you can kip tonight. Yeah.

Anna Thank you.

Del It's alright – here you are girl – let me help you. I'll take these – straight through here. Open the door – take that, take this as well.

Rodney and Anna exit.

Rodney Mind the batteries.

Del Yeah, mind that, alright? Goodnight now. Night.

Albert It's a funny old world innit? I mean, you take the thousands of couples round the world all trying to have kids but can't! I remember my mate Nipper Townsend. Years and years him and his wife dreamed of having a kid. They never did though!!

Del Yeah, well you got to take so many things into account, ain't you? Well, the temperature, the cycle, tight pants, all that!

Albert True! Course, Nipper being stationed in

Malta didn't help! You seem to know a lot about all this medical malarkey!

Del Yeah well, I get it off Boycie and Marlene don't I! You know Boycie, the second-hand car trader. Yeah, well him and Marlene have been trying to have a little sprog for years but no joy. They've had more tests you know than the atom bomb – still no good. I mean they've tried to foster and adopt, no, nothing. Funny that eh? Funny, they're stinking rich and yet with all that money they can't buy the one thing they want most dearly – a little baby!

Albert Yeah, that's the way the cookie bounces, eh?

Del nods in agreement. Then looks up. He is putting two and two together. A scheme is being born.

Del Yeah, I expect . . .

Albert What's wrong?

Del Eh? No, nothing, nothing. No, I've just worked out everything could work out very very cushty!

THE FRONT OF BOYCIE'S HOUSE.

Boycie's Mercedes and the three-wheeled van are parked in the driveway. Duke the dog is barking. Rodney's voice can be heard in the distance.

Rodney Come on Duke, get stick. Come on Dukie.

BOYCIE'S LOUNGE.

Del is seated in the armchair with a cigar and a glass of beer. Marlene is on the settee, Boycie is standing. They are both looking stunned.

Boycie S . . . say that again Del Boy??

Del I said, I could help you have a baby!

Marlene Well, what d' you mean? You're willing to be one of them suffragette fathers?

Del No, no! I mean, I know where there's a baby going!

Boycie What – knocked off?

Del No, no, no, it's all pukka! You see, I know this young German girl. She hadn't been in our green and pleasant land for no more than three months when she was suddenly taken pregnant!

Boycie Oh that's lovely innit Marlene? A little while from now we could be awakened by the pitter-patter of tiny jackboots!

Del Leave it out Boycie! Look, he'd be brought up as yours wouldn't he. Anyway, the father is English, you see, the full story is Rodney met this girl in the pub a little while ago . . .

Boycie Hang about! You mean that dipstick Rodney's the father??

Del *(Moving to patio doors)* No, no, no, of course he ain't Boycie, leave it out. What Rodney, blimey, he don't know what it's all about yet. Haven't you seen the funny way he still stirs his tea? *(Shouts from window)* No, Rodney, get your leg out of that dog's mouth!! I despair of that boy – I really do. The father is some sort of student geezer who's washed his hands of the whole affair like he don't know!

Boycie Well him and me have got a lot in common, because I don't wanna know either!

Marlene Now hang on a minute Boyce! Let's not be hasty, I mean you're the one who's always going on about having a son and heir.

Del And it is a boy!

Boycie I didn't think it'd been born yet?

Del She had a scan! Let me show you something. Look, I borrowed her passport so I could show you. Look there's a picture of her there – look. Her name is Anna. She's a beautiful girl ain't she? She's bound to have a handsome kid. And the student fella's father is a very, very successful businessman! So the kid's gonna have everything, good looks, brains and business acumen. Just the sort of son and heir that you need for your second-hand car empire Boycie!

Marlene We can at least talk about it Boycie!

Boycie Yeah, yeah, alright then love. Just give us a couple of minutes, will you Del.

They move away for a discussion. Rodney enters, exhausted.

Rodney I think I've tired him out, he's a rascal! What they doing?

Del It's alright, nothing. They're just having a bit of a chat. Go and get yourself a light ale, and top me up while you're over there, alright.

Boycie It is definitely a boy??

Del Yep, definitely a boy!

Rodney What's all that about?

Del No, no, nothing, Boycie's thinking of getting a boat and I'm gonna get him some equipment see.

Rodney Oh that sort of buoy!

Boycie This German bird, is she healthy?

Del Healthy? She's Boris Becker's cousin!

Rodney What the bloody 'ell's going on here Del?

Del Alright, alright Rodney! I was gonna tell you, see Boycie and Marlene might have Anna's baby.

Rodney What!!!! What is this, a raffle? Del, this is a tiny human being we're talking about!! This is flesh and blood. It's Anna's child!

Del Yes I know that Rodney, but Anna wants it

From Prussia With Love

adopted, and Boycie and Marlene want to adopt!

Rodney Yeah, well, if that's what they want they go to an adoption society?

Marlene No, we've tried lots of times Rodney, but they always turn us down. *(Indicating Boycie)* It's because of his record!

Del Boycie did a little bit of a stretch when he was younger you know.

Rodney Oh yeah! What for?

Boycie Perjury, embezzlement, conspiring to pervert the course of justice, the fraudulent conversion of traveller's cheques and attempting to bribe the Mayor of Lambeth! See, it's any little thing with these adoption people!

Marlene Leave it out Boycie, with your record I'm surprised we're allowed to keep a dog!

Boycie Yeah, but it's all in the past! I mean how many times have I gotta repay my debt to society??

Del Yeah, that's true. I mean, don't a person deserve a second chance?

Rodney Well . . . Yeah, that's fair enough.

Del And that's what we're gonna give this little baby! A second chance! A chance to live in this beautiful house. A chance to have a loving father and a doting mother! And they don't come more doting than that! I mean, even Duke's got a bib!

Rodney But it's illegal!

Marlene What, giving a little baby love and warmth and a chance in life is against the law?

Rodney I don't know, the welfare people gonna wonder where Anna's baby is?

Del It's obvious innit? It's with its mother . . . In Germany!!

Marlene I think we've cracked it at last Boycie. Well, you can tell everybody it's our own child! I mean, we're always reading in the papers about women giving birth who didn't even know they were pregnant.

Boycie It might raise a few eyebrows!

Marlene Well yeah, but they're only neighbours!

Boycie I was thinking more of that gynaecologist who examined you on Monday!

Marlene I'll never have to see him again, will I? Just give us a minute Del. Come on Boycie. Look.
They go into a huddle.

Rodney You're gonna earn out of this ain't yer?

Del How dare you! That is a terrible thing to say!! What sort of a bloke d'you think I am?? I'm doing it for Anna and them two, but most important of all, I'm doing it for that little unborn baby.

Rodney Oh look, I'm sorry.

Del No, don't touch me.

Rodney I'm sorry. . . . But you are gonna earn out of it ain't yer?

Del Look. That is a cruel and callous jibe.

Boycie How much this all gonna cost?

Del Only her airline ticket home, and of course money for the birth certificate and a few quid to cover our petrol and telephone calls . . . Three grand should cover it, I should think.

THE TROTTERS' LOUNGE.
Anna is in the armchair watching TV. Del is at the table working on a computer. He presses a few keys as if he knows what he's doing. Albert enters from kitchen with a cup of tea.

Albert Tea up Del Boy!

Del Ssssh! Can't you see I'm busy? *(Presses another button. We hear the sound of an explosion)* Got you, you Martian git! Let me see, re-set . . . (Rodney enters from the bedroom, giving Del a withering look) What's up with you?

Rodney You know perfectly well what's up with me! Selling a baby. God – it's like something out of Dickens' times!

Del Rodney listen. How many times has Boycie tucked me up, eh? That three grand isn't for the baby, it's just payment of old debts!

Albert It's most probably for the best son. I mean, Anna gets her baby adopted by a loving family.

Del That's right. Marlene gets the sprog she's always wanted.

Rodney *(To Del)* And you get three grand!!

Del Exactly, everyone's a winner!

Rodney Yeah, everyone, everyone except Anna!

Del Au contraire Rodney, au contraire! Because as soon as old Boycie weighs in with the poppy I'm going straight down the bureau de change and I'm gonna get a few hundred translated for her! So that means that Anna is gonna go straight back to the Fatherland with 300 drachma in her bin!
Anna lets out a howl of pain. The Trotters are terrified.

Del She's in pain!

Albert How'd you know, you can't speak German!

Del This is it! This is it!

Rodney No, no, no, it's not. Maybe it's just indigestion!

Del Listen to me – go in the kitchen and get a glass of water!

Rodney Right! *(Exits to kitchen)*

Albert You ain't giving her Andrews are you?

Del Don't be a plonker, now phone the hospital, get on the blower, don't forget, call the

maternity unit!

Rodney pours a glass of water and drinks it himself.

Rodney I'll hold the lift. I'll hold the lift.

Del Yes. Deep breaths! Deep breaths!

Albert *(Fumbling with cordless phone)* How the bloody hell do these phones work???

Del Right, when did you start getting the pains darling?

Anna They come this morning.

Del This morning – don't worry, don't worry because the ambulance is gonna come any minute and don't worry. Just relax everything's gonna be cushty! How are you getting on?

Anna Del.

Del It's alright darling.

Anna Danke.

Del That's alright. Vorsprung durch Technik! *(Anna cries out in pain)* Ooh don't.

THE TROTTERS' LOUNGE. A WEEK LATER.

Boycie is seated nervously on the sofa. Marlene paces the floor. Del pours himself a drink.

Del Sit down Marlene, you're doing the Wilton up!

Boycie Sit down Marlene!!!!!! *(She sits)*

Marlene The baby's alright, ain't he Del?

Del Yes, yes, Marlene, for the umpteenth time. You're gonna have a beautiful bouncing baby!

Marlene What's he weigh?

Del Dunno, he ain't stopped bouncing yet! Ain't stopped bouncing! *(He laughs, Boycie and Marlene don't)* I don't know, seven pound something!

Marlene We've decided to call him Mark!

Del That's handy, 'cos his Dad's name was Spencer!

The front door opens.

Rodney Del.

Del They're here, they're back. Here they are now! Just take it easy. Don't panic, alright? Calm down.

Del exits to the hall.

HALL.

Del Everything alright Rodders?

Rodney No, everything is not bloody alright!

Del Sssshh! Boycie and Marlene are here.

Rodney Oh, are they here already? Have you told them about their little boy?

Del What about him?

Rodney About him being a little girl.

Del No, no, I haven't broken the news yet! How could that Anna do it to me? After all I've done

for her! So what's wrong then?

Rodney Well for one, Anna has fallen in love with her baby! But the most important thing . . .

Del She's done what? Oh no, she can't do that to me. No she can't do – a deal's a deal! I'll sort it out.

Rodney No you've got to listen . . .

Anna enters with Albert.

Del Get in – alright Albert? Alright, I'll sort it out. Here she is. Hello sweetheart, how you feeling?

Anna Oh, I am fine thank you.

Del Oh good.

Anna I think maybe things are not cushty! I think maybe now I keep baby.

Del No, no, no. You can't do that darling – no, no, no. Because you know, we'll have the VAT people round here. Come in, come in and I'll explain everything. Go on, go in there. Go on, in you go.

LOUNGE.

Del Put the baby down there. First of all these are the very nice people who are gonna buy . . . erm, erm, who are gonna look after your baby. There we are.

Boycie Someone upset her?

Del No, no, no. She's just got like baby blues that's all . . . Just a minute Boycie, I'm gonna have to come clean, you see the thing is, it's about your little baby boy – he ain't.

Marlene Ain't what?

Del Well, ain't a little baby boy.

Boycie What is it then?

Del A baby girl innit, eh?

Boycie A girl? But you said she'd had a scan.

Del I know what I told you, alright Boycie. I know I told you it was gonna be a boy but it ain't. Just keep your money the deal's off right.

Marlene I don't care if it's a boy, a girl or twins! It's a baby.

Boycie Alright Marlene, we'll take it. It's amazing innit? Everything you buy off him's got something missing!

Marlene moves to cot.

Del *(To Albert)* Alright don't look at me like that. What else could I do?

Albert No good asking me son. I ain't never flogged a baby before.

Del Rodney, you know I was doing it for Anna weren't I? I was only tryin' help.

Rodney What do you want, applause??

Del Alright sorry Boycie, sorry mate. Listen the deal's off, it's off alright.

Boycie *(Who has also moved to the cot)* Is that

From Prussia With Love

right Del? The deal's off is it? Too bleedin right it's off.

Del What are you talking about? What?! How?!

Rodney That's the other thing I meant to tell you out there. You see Spencer's mummy and daddy came over in 1956 from the West Indies.

Marlene Well it don't bother me Boyce.

Boycie Leave off Marlene. The baby's brown.

Marlene So is Duke.

Boycie But I ain't claiming to be Duke's father.

Albert There is a likeness though.

Boycie Just shut it.

Marlene We could say it's a throw-back.

Boycie For Gawd's sake Marlene. I might be able to con people into buying my cars. I might be able to convince 'em that you conceived and gave birth in seven days flat, but how the hell am I gonna persuade 'em that my grandad was Louis Armstrong!! You ain't heard the last of this Del Boy! *(He exits)*

Marlene I s'pose he's right, eh Del?

Del Yeah, yeah, you know it makes sense darling eh.

Marlene Still, it was a nice little dream while it lasted, eh? I'm gonna turn round now, I'm gonna walk out that door . . . and I ain't gonna look back.

Del No, of course not. *(Marlene exits tearfully) (Anna starts crying, then the baby)* Gawd, women. Sssh Anna. Anna come out here, your baby's hungry. Quiet, quiet, your mummy's coming, yes she is. *(To baby)* Ain't you got bright eyes, eh? Look at that. She's gonna be a blinder when she gets older, eh? Yes you is. *(Tickling baby)* Coochy coochy coo! Coochy coochy coo . . . urgh!

The Miracle of Peckham

THE TROTTERS' LOUNGE

Rodney is seated at the table feeling hung-over. He sips his coffee. He touches his aching temples gently.

Rodney *(Moaning)* Bloody hell!

Albert enters from kitchen carrying a teapot and a kipper on a plate.

Albert *(Shouts)* D-E-L!

Rodney Why don't you just get a megaphone and finish me off quickly!

Albert Now you know how I felt last night, I was fast akip I was, when you come in my room and made that horrible noise in my ear!

Rodney Yes, sorry.

Albert That could've killed me!

Rodney D'you reckon?

Albert Where d'you get that trumpet from anyway?

Rodney What trumpet?

Albert I felt my heart go all funny. In my unconscious state I thought it was the abandon ship alarm!

Rodney Oh yeah, thought they was playing your tune did you?

Albert Yes, that's all very well innit. You could at least say sorry!

Rodney I am sorry, now can we drop the matter?

Albert Charming innit. Fight and die for your country, and this is the thanks the younger generation gives yer.

Rodney I'm sorry!

Albert So, what was it all about last night then?

Rodney Well, me and Del, it's just we'd had a right blinding week, I mean we were selling it before we'd bought it, so we had a bit of a celebration, right. Anyway, I went down the Nag's Head and, of course, Friday night is disco night, innit? And I met this bird – Helen. Oh, she's really something else. I mean, she's tall, she's slender, bit older than me, but you know, I've been brought up to respect me elders.

Albert Was it her trumpet?

Rodney I don't know! I don't remember having a bloody trumpet. Anyway, listen right, you've gotta see this bird, she really is the works. You know, everyone in the pub was looking at me, they was as jealous as hell. Do you know who she looks like? She look like that Linda Evans out of *Dynasty*.

Albert Which one's that, Joan Collins?

Rodney How can bloody Linda Evans be Joan Collins? It's Linda Evans, you know, she plays Krystle Carrington!

Albert Oh her, that's a bit tasty innit son?

Rodney Yeah, and she's got the right hots for your truly. I have struck gold, son.

Albert Well, good luck to you boy. *(Yells)* D-E-L!

Del enters.

Del Right, alright, you mouthy old git! What d'you think I am, mutton or something? Gawd blimey, eh? Oi, Rodney, you were a bit steaming when you come in last night, weren't you, eh?

Rodney Yeah, well I had something to celebrate didn't I.

Del Yeah, what, you finally got shot of it then, did ya?

Rodney What?

Del Well, you know, that old dog who was hanging round you last night.

Rodney 'Old dog?' What d'you mean, 'Old dog?'

Del She was – she was a bit scraggy weren't she. Blimey, she must have been six foot six!

Rodney Well yeah, she was tallish.

Del Tallish? Blimey, not many birds call you shortie do they hey?

Albert *(Laughing)* He told me she looked like Krystle Carrington.

Del Krystle Carrington? Crystal bleedin' Palace more like from where I was standing!

Rodney Derek, you do not even know the girl.

Del Yes I do, course I do. Her name was Helen, right?

Rodney . . . No.

Del Oh yes it was. 'Cos I know, 'cos they call her Helen of Croydon. The face that launched a thousand dredgers.

Albert *(Laughing)* I'll do you a bit of breakfast Del.

Del No, leave me out Albert. I've got a bit of business to do. No, it's alright.

Rodney I tell you what, I could do with a bit of egg and bacon now.

Albert Yeah, well, give Helen of Croydon a bell! *(Exits to kitchen)*

Rodney The rotten old git! *(Takes Del's after-shave and sprinkles it over Albert's kipper)*

Del Oi, oi, don't waste it, what's the matter with

289

yer? Give us it.

Rodney Well, it's the way he treats me innit, him giving me all that just 'cos I woke him up. So, er, I had a trumpet with me when I came in last night?

Del Oh yeah, that's right. Belongs to Biffo the bear, his group were playing at the Nag's last night, don't you remember?

Rodney What's he lend it to me for?

Del He didn't did he? Don't you remember, you were so out of your mind at one point last night you went on the stage, took his trumpet off him, blew down the wrong end, gave him the V-sign and walked out with it.

Rodney Bloody hell, he's a big bloke an' all ain't he?

Del And he ain't 'alf in a bad mood an' all.

Rodney Why?

Del Well, you won't believe this, some dozy git nicked his trumpet!

Rodney I'll get it back to him today, hey, I'll buy him a drink or something.

Del Yeah, well, you've got the morning off, 'cos, you know, I'm busy.

Rodney Where you going?

Del I'm goin' to church.

Rodney *(Laughs)* No, come on, where you going?

Del I am going to church.

Rodney Why?

Del Why not? See you later.

Del exits. Rodney is dumbfounded. Albert enters from kitchen.

Albert Del gone?

Rodney He's gone to church!

Albert Church? Del Boy?

Rodney Yeah!

Albert That's funny you know, 'cos he came in from the pub last night, had a couple of pina coladas and started talking to me about religion. He asked me if I believed God saw everything – and, if so, did he take notes. I've seen blokes catch religion before, it's always very sudden like.

Rodney moves to sideboard and searches through a drawer.

Rodney It's gone.

Albert What's gone?

Rodney His Cliff Richard cassette.

Albert Ah, it's most probably nothing son. Maybe he feels the need of a bit of spiritual guidance.

Rodney Del? Yeah, maybe you're right Uncle.

Albert Of course I am. I mean, I couldn't honestly see Del Boy becoming one of yer Burning Bush and Joshua at the battle of Jericho

mob, could you?

Rodney No, what Del? With the . . . No of course not! Hey, talking of Joshua, where's that trumpet?

Albert I chucked it down the dust chute.

Rodney You did what? That ain't mine, it's Biffo's! He'll mangle my head!

Albert Well it'll teach you not to blow it in my ear 'ole won't it.

Rodney Oh, you dopey little git.

Rodney rushes to the hall and exits. Albert is laughing. He takes a bite of kipper and almost chokes on it.

DUST CHUTE.

Rodney is in a giant bin ferreting through the garbage.

Rodney Where is it? It can't be that far down, he only chucked it out this morning. Ugh, oh God! Who'd chuck something like that down a chute? Pigs. *(From beneath a pile of rubbish he pulls out the twisted trumpet)* I don't believe it. I don't believe it. How can I give it back to Biffo? He's bound to notice. Albert! I hate you Albert! Albert!

There is a low rumbling sound. Rodney is puzzled. He looks up and gunge hits him straight in the face.

HALL OF CHURCH.

Del enters puffing on a Castella. He walks slowly down the aisle, footsteps echoing. In front of him is a large gold crucifix. Del bows his head respectfully and tries to do a sign of the cross, but it comes out more like tic-tac.

Del Shop!

Father O'Keith *(OOV)* I'll be with you in just a moment!

Del *(Calls)* Right you are, thank you.

CONFESSIONALS.

Del enters the confessionals. Father O'Keith enters the hall from the back of the church. He surveys the hall for the visitor. He limps across the hall to the confessionals and enters.

Father O'Keith Flaming corns, they've been the bane of my life. *(Cigar smoke billows between the booths)* Is that you Del Boy?

Del Yes Father, it's me.

Father O'Keith I thought as much! So, how are you these days?

Del Well, you know, struggling. How's yourself?

Father O'Keith Oh, the corns are still giving me gip.

Del I've got some lovely orthopaedic sandals

The Miracle of Peckham

coming along, I'll pop a pair into you.

Father O'Keith Thanks Derek. So, to what do I owe the honour?

Del I have come to confess my sins.

Father O'Keith *(Checks watch)* Oh Derek please. I've been invited out to dinner this evening.

Del Well, it's just one main sin really.

Father O'Keith Oh thanks be to God for that. Wait a minute. I didn't know you were Catholic.

Del Eh? Well, I don't know do I? I don't know that. I was only a kid, but me mum was Catholic.

Father O'Keith I know that, I married her here in this church. Your father wasn't Catholic.

Del No, he was a black magic man I think.

Father O'Keefe Have you ever been to this church before?

Del Well of course I have, when me mum and dad got married.

Father O'Keith You were just a little baby then! I mean have you ever been to this church since then?

Del Er, no.

Father O'Keith Del, my boy, you disappoint me.

Del I watched *The Ten Commandments* on the telly. Look Father, I don't wanna get up there on Judgement Day and find out that I'm on the hit list. I mean, God sees everything doesn't he?

Father O'Keith Look Derek, this is not the God'll Fix it Show. Forgiveness is only for those who feel shame and remorse.

Del I do feel shame and remorse. Father, does it matter what religion I am?

Father O'Keith Well, I don't know that you're not a Catholic, do I?

Del That's the spirit, you know it makes sense.

Father O'Keith Alright, fire away Del. But the truth mind you, I don't want you lying in my con-fessionals.

Del Would I lie to you? Well, about a week ago I bought some gear off a couple of gentlemen. I bought it in good faith, honest I did. The thing is last night I found out there was more to it than meets the eye. I didn't know, honest I didn't. I mean, I was led like an artificial lamb to the slaughter. If I'd of known the full SP I would never have taken it on, honest I wouldn't. But you don't ask do you?

Father O'Keith Well, you don't Del.

Del I didn't think I needed to ask, Father, I trusted these two gentlemen. I believed that they were both honest and upstanding citizens of our community.

Father O'Keith Who were these men?

Del Sunglasses Ron and Paddy the Greek.

Father O'Keith Well, you can't get them more honest and upstanding than them two. I'll give you a choice of penance. You can either say five Hail Marys and ten Our Fathers or make a little donation to the hospice fund?

Del Will a score be alright?

They exit from the confessionals.

Del Is that it then. All squared?

Father O'Keith Your sins have been absolved Del.

Del No, no Father, I wanted to be forgiven.

Father O'Keith You have been forgiven.

Del Oh, cushty. So what's the fund for then Father? Are they building a new extension to the old hospice or what?

Father O'Keith I wish they were Del. No, unfortunately they're demolishing it.

Del Eh? But why? That's been there for years and years.

Father O'Keith Ah, that's the problem. Over the years it's become dilapidated. They've estimated it'll cost a quarter of a million to repair it, that's what the fund's for. But, I'm grieved to say, we've little or no chance of reaching our target.

Del Wait a minute, maybe we could organise a charity darts match for you at the old Nag's Head. How much more money d'you need?

Father O'Keith £185,000.

Del Say I threw a raffle in an' all, eh?

Father O'Keith It's very, very kind of you Del, and I do appreciate it. But I really think this is one battle that we've lost.

Del They can't knock it down. What's gonna happen to all the old and the sick people living there?

Father O'Keith Well, they'll move them out first.

Del I know, I know that. But I mean, to where?

Father O'Keith Who knows? They'll probably be disbursed to the four quarters of the metropolis, far away from their friends and relatives. I mean, they're all local people in St Mary's.

Del Yeah I know, they looked after my old Mum you know, when she was ill.

Father O'Keith So they did.

Del Treated her well an' all. And my Grandad – bless him, he used to moan at 'em a lot. No, they can't knock it down! Can they?

Father O'Keith Well, it's out of our hands, look I'll be honest with you Del. For the past six or seven months, since I first heard of the plans for the hospice, my faith has been tested. All my efforts and prayers have failed. You know, I feel

as if I've let the people down.

Del Now come on, come on, don't talk like that Father. Come on, something'll turn up. Remember the old saying? He who dares wins.

Father O'Keith Well, I'll bear it in mind. Say a prayer for me Del.

Del Yeah, I will.

Del walks off up the aisle. Father O'Keith bows to the crucifix. He is about to blow the candle out when his attention is drawn to something. At first he is puzzled, but when he looks closer his expression turns to one of awe.

Father O'Keith Sweet Jesus! Derek!

Del at the far end of the hall is about to put some money in the box.

Del I'm putting it in, I'm putting it *in*!

Father O'Keith Come down here quickly.

Del What's up then?

Father O'Keith Come and see this, hurry!

He runs down the aisle.

Del What is it?

Father O'Keith Look! It's a miracle!

Del looks in the direction indicated. The statue of Virgin and Child is weeping. From the corner of it's right eye a tear is running down it's cheek. Del and Father O'Keith look at each other open-mouthed. A second tear falls.

Del Yeah, don't get many of them round Peckham.

Father O'Keith It's a sign Del.

Del Yeah, it's a sign that we can make a fortune!

Father O'Keith What?

Del Can't you see what we've got ourselves? An authentic, deluxe miracle. They go for a bomb these days.

Father O'Keith How can you talk about money at a time like this?

Del Well, what d'you wanna talk about, yer holidays? Don't you see the opportunity you're being presented with here? People will pay hard cash just to see this sort of thing.

Father O'Keith Look, I have no intention of turning my church into some fairground peep show. And how could I charge my own flock to see their miracle?

Del I'm not talking about your flock. I'm talking about the newspapers, the magazines, the television! The media people will pay through their noses just to get this sort of thing on their front pages!

Father O'Keith I don't know if it's right Derek.

Del See those old people down at St Mary's hospice, they'd think it right wouldn't they?

Listen to me, with the money you could earn out of this, you could have that place repaired, redecorated and get Samantha Fox to re-open it for yer!

Father O'Keith D'you really think we could?

Del Yeah of course. I mean she don't come cheap, but I'll see what I can do.

Father O'Keith No, I mean save the hospice?

Del Of course, of course we can. It'll be a doddle. Where's your phone? It's alright, I'll find it, you stay here.

Father O'Keith *(Calls)* I don't think I could exploit . . .

Del No, you couldn't Father, but I'm shit hot at it!

TROTTERS' LOUNGE.

Albert is watching TV. Rodney is wearing a dressing gown. He is holding the bent trumpet.

Rodney *(Thrusting it in Albert's face)* Look at it! Just look at it will you!

Albert Get it away from me.

Rodney What am I supposed to tell Biffo? I let Yuri Geller have a go on it!

Albert Tell him what you want son, ain't my problem.

Rodney And you chucked all that rubbish down the chute knowing that I was at the bottom! I've had to have a shower and everything.

Albert I didn't chuck the rubbish down the chute. It must have been one of the neighbours.

Rodney I found your kipper

Albert It could have been anyone's kipper.

Rodney Oh yeah, and how many kippers wear Brut?

Albert Is that what that horrible taste was?

Rodney Yeah.

Albert You sprinkled it with after-shave?

Rodney Yeah, to get even with you.

Albert I wish I hadn't told you where your trumpet was now.

Rodney So do I actually. *(Phone rings, Rodney answers)* Hold that. Hello. Del, you wanna see what Rumplestiltskin's done to this trumpet, he's only gone and chucked . . . Oh, sorry! What'd you mean, phone Reuters? You've seen a what? *(Laughs)* What happened, did Boycie buy a round? Alright, alright, keep your hair on! Yeah, bloody hell, hold on . . . *(Makes notes on a pad)* Yeah, right, OK – Reuters, Tass, the *Peckham Echo* . . . Oh right, BBC . . . ITV . . . Right, what about Channel Four? Oh no, right OK. *(Rubs Channel 4 out)* Yeah, I've got it all, it's all here mate. Yeah, take care, I'll see you later

The Miracle of Peckham

on, see ya, Bye. *(To Albert)* He's flipped. He's gone completely bloody loopy!

Albert Why what's happened?

Rodney He's seen a miracle.

Albert A miracle?

Rodney Well, that's what the man said. Hang on a minute. Last night he was talking about God. This morning he went to church, this afternoon he's seen a miracle. It can only mean one thing.

Albert He's caught religion.

Rodney No, he's pulling a stroke ain't he? Oh, come on, think about it. There are Cardinals and Archbishops – they've been in the business all their lives and never got a sniff of a miracle. Then along comes Del, he's in the game five minutes and already he's a prophet. Profit being the operative word! How's he gonna make money out of the church?

Albert He's got that consignment of orthopaedic sandals coming soon.

Rodney Yeah, so what?

Albert Well, maybe he's got the franchise on the monastery.

Rodney Maybe.

THE MAIN HALL OF CHURCH.

Three days later. Facing the statue are a BBC news camera and an ITN news camera. A number of photographers and reporters are sitting around on the pews. A rather embarrassed Father O'Keith approaches Del.

Father O'Keith Nothing's happening Del. They've been waiting for three days, and nothing's happened.

Del Na, na. Yeah, I know, 'ere Father, have a look at these contracts. I worked them out in such a way that if they want to sell any of the photos or the film of the miracle anywhere else in the world, they've got to pay you again, look see.

Father O'Keith You've made them sign contracts?

Del Of course I have, it's business innit? No poppy, no picture, that's my motto.

Father O'Keith But what happens if the miracle doesn't occur again?

Del Well, we give 'em their money back, I suppose. But don't worry, don't worry. I always get this feeling when the miracle's due and I've got a feeling it could be pretty soon too.

Father O'Keith Well, I hope you're right.

Del Trust me, trust me.

Rodney and Albert enter and approach Del.

Rodney No luck?

Del You know, 'ere take a butchers at that will ya.

Rodney *(Looks at contract)* They're paying you all that money?

Del Well, it's not every day that they get a chance to see a miracle is it, eh? And that's just the British media, you wait till the rest of the world's press gets here.

Albert Look at all these noughts Rodney.

Rodney Yeah.

Albert You can see his game now can't yer?

Del What are you talking about?

Albert You're gonna cream some off ain't yer?

Del Now you listen to me Albert, I am not the kind of bloke who cheats on the sick and the elderly. You put your peepers down there, you'll see that all cheques are made payable to St Mary's hospice fund!

Albert Sorry son.

Del That's alright. I simply want to keep that place open, and you'd better pray I succeed!

Albert Why?

Del 'Cos one more crack out of you and you're gonna be their next client!

One of the cameramen calls out.

Man David, look at this will you!

All the press pack rush forward. The statue begins weeping. Del gives Father O'Keith a wink. Del and Albert are dumbfounded by the miracle.

MAIN HALL OF CHURCH

Two days later. Word has spread around the world. Camera crews have arrived from all countries. Del and Rodney are studying another batch of contracts.

Del *(Referring to contract)* Take a look at that one Rodney.

INT. CHURCH. LATER ON.

Another camera crew enters.

Aus G'day, Australian Broadcasting.

Del G'day to you. Sign that pal.

Aus Well what is it?

Del That tells you how much you've gotta pay to take pictures of the finest little miracle this side of Heaven.

Aus *(Reading)* Struth! Stone the crows!

Del I tell you what we're gonna do, while we're waiting, save us getting bored, we're gonna have another little collection. Alright, there we go, come on, thank you very much. Come on everybody, now let's dig deeply for the poor and needy. No coins please, because it scratches the pewter. Thank you, and you, danke schon, merci bo-coo. Thank you. *(As Del collects the 'miracle'*

occurs once more.) Hello, now they're off and running!

Aus Get that camera over here.

Del Just a minute, just a minute. Have you signed that contract please? Thank you. Oi mind the camera there will yer? Thank you very much. There you are Rodney, it's done, my son.

Father O'Keith This is the happiest day in my life.

Del Yeah, I know what you mean Father. It's rien ne va plus as the French would say. . . . Where's that brolly?

EXT. DAY. THE CHURCH.

It is raining. Del exits followed by Rodney. The Aussie approaches and hands him a piece of paper.

Aus Sign that will you.

Del *(Thinks it's an autograph.)* Oh yeah, sure, who's it for then, the wife or the kids?

Aus That's a receipt for all the collections.

Del Hey, oh right.

Man Oi Bruce!

Del Why are they all called Bruce?

An American interviewer approaches.

Interviewer Mr Trotter?

Del Yes?

Interviewer Sandra Cox, NBC, New York. Father O'Keith told me that you actually prophesied the miracles.

Del Um, yes, this is true, that's me.

Interviewer I wonder if we might have a short interview for our viewers over in the States?

Del Yes, of course. *(Calls)* Make-up? Is there some make-up there?

MAIN HALL OF CHURCH.

Father O'Keith is alone in the church. Albert wakes up from sleeping on one of the pews.

Albert Everyone gone?

Father O'Keith Oh, yes, yes they have all they need. And so do we. All thanks to your nephew.

Albert Yeah, he brought you nothing but luck, didn't he?

Father O'Keith Unfortunately he also brings the weather with him. Every time he's prophesied the miracle it's been pouring with rain.

They share a grin. Father O'Keith climbs a small plinth and looks just above the statue. Water drips down from a wooden beam just inches above the statue's head. Father O'Keith is horrified.

OUTSIDE THE CHURCH.

Del is being interviewed.

Interviewer And what form do these 'divine' messages take?

Del Well, what happens is I get this strange sort of feeling from the centre of my body. At first, I thought it was a dodgy mutton tikka. Then I realised I was in fact a prophet. Many are called, but I'm afraid, few are chosen. I do not want any reward for the work I have done for the elderly and sick in the community. No medals, no OBEs, no Nobel Prizes. No, I would like to think, however, if there is enough money left after repairing the hospice that they might build a new wing and perhaps name it after me. This would . . . *(Father O'Keith appears behind Del grabs him by the collar and drags him inside)* Thank you.

Father O'Keith Come with me!

Rodney Sorry viewers, the Lord's work calls. Rodney Trotter signing off.

Interviewer Oh, cut.

BELFRY.

Great shafts of light are coming through the roof. Footsteps can be heard coming up the stairs. The door opens and the Father, Del and Rodney enter.

Del Alright, it's a bit dirty up here, innit? Don't shove, don't shove.

Father O'Keith Look at my roof!

One side of the roof is missing tiles and lead. There are just rafters and open skies. The rain is puring in.

Rodney Bloody hell! Sorry.

Father O'Keith And look! The water seeping through the floor across the joist onto the lamp and right onto the statue. This isn't a miracle, it's a flaming leak!

Del Oh, that's a turn-up, innit?

Father O'Keith Somebody's stolen the lead.

Del You can't trust anyone these days can you, eh?

Rodney No, wait, you're in luck, because we've got a load of lead in our ga . . . rage. *(To Del)* I don't believe you!

Father O'Keith So this is what you bought off Sunglasses Ron and Paddy the Greek isn't it?

Del I didn't know at the time, otherwise I wouldn't have touched it. That's what I come to tell you.

Father O'Keith But you didn't tell me.

Del No, I'm not a grass, am I?

Father O'Keith You knew all along it was no miracle, you weren't receiving divine messages, you were listening to the weather forecast!

Del Yeah, we saved St Mary's though,

The Miracle of Peckham

didn't we?

Father O'Keith Derek, look me in the eyes! Are you telling me that for the sake of some small, decrepit old building, you created this whole tissue of lies and deceit? You deliberately and willingly set out to defraud all those newspapers and television companies out of thousands and thousands of pounds? Is that what you're telling me?

(Del and Rodney both have their heads bowed. Del nods. Father O' Keith places his hands on Del's head)

Del God bless you my son!

STREET.

Del and Rodney walk in front of the church.

Del I was gonna do some lecture tours, organise prayer meetings at Wembley you know, something like that! This time next year we was gonna be millionaires!

Rodney This time next year you'd have been a prison inmate unless you watch your step! If I was you Derek, I would keep a very low profile.

Journalists Thanks, cheers pal. Thanks for your help. *(Del and Rodney, with their heads down, mumble replies)*

Each journalist shakes their hands and let go. Rodney with his head down, has shaken two hands, but the third doesn't let go. Rodney is puzzled and looks up. He is staring into the face of very tough looking guy. It is Biffo.

Biffo Where's my trumpet?

Rodney Oh hello, Biffo, how are you?

Biffo Where's my trumpet?

Rodney Your trumpet. Yeah, there's been a bit of a hitch on the old trumpet front, mate. *(Indicates Albert)* See that old man there?

Biffo turns and Rodney legs it.

Biffo *(Calls)* Oi! Where's my trumpet?

Albert *(To Del)* Ain't you gonna do something?

Del Yeah course I am! *(Calls to film crews)* Oi, do you want to film some authentic inner city violence? Come on, bring yer cameras, bring your wallets. *(Calls up the road)* Hold on Rodders, not so fast!

BOYCIE'S MOTORS

"I'm waiting for your call"

Tel:081 555 556

Best deals in Peckham!

- 4X4s · Cortinas
- Capris · Minis
- Jaguars · Bentleys
- BMWs · Mercedes
- Robin Reliants
- Rolls Royce (Not For Sale)

& Many Many More...

The Longest Night

DAY. THE SUPERSTORE.

The Trotters are at a checkout. They are packing the bags with food. Sheila, the girl on the counter, couldn't give a toss and speaks in monotone

Sheila £29.48.

Del Sorry?

Sheila £29.48.

Del Did you sue 'em?

Sheila Who?

Del The charm school!

The Trotters are going through the exit doors. A large sign on the door reads: 'Topbuy Superstores are offering £1,000 to our millionth customer!'

Albert *(Referring back to Sheila)* Miserable little cow!

Del Yeah, right, we won't come here again. In future we'll take our custom down to Patel's Multi-Mart. They might be a bit dearer but at least they smile when they take yer money . . . Rodney, what's up with you?

Rodney It's him innit! Whacked me straight in the shins with that shopping trolley.

Albert I couldn't help it! That trolley had a mind of its own.

Rodney Oh, what are you saying, it was intellectually superior to you, is that it?

Albert Don't get sarky Rodney, it don't become yer!

Rodney Well, a broken leg don't become . . .

Del Alright you two will ya.

Tom Clarke, the store's Head of Security, follows the Trotters from the store.

Tom Excuse me, one moment Gentlemen. Tom Clarke, Topbuy Superstores. I wonder if I could have five minutes of your time please?

Del Certainly Tom. Why what's up then?

Tom If you'd like to accompany me to the manager's office I'll explain there.

Rodney spots the 'millionth customer' notice. He nudges Del and points it out to him.

Del Here, just a minute – what is your game? Oh, yes.

Tom Can I help you with any of the shopping?

Del Oh yeah, thanks a lot. Lead on MacDougal!

DAY. THE MANAGER'S OFFICE.

Mr Peterson, the manager, is talking on the phone to his wife. We get the strong

impression he is under the thumb.

Mr Peterson Yes . . . yes . . . yes. . . . But Valerie . . . darling, listen to me for a moment! Why do you want to buy a brand-new car?

DAY. A SMALL CORRIDOR INTO MANAGER'S OFFICE.

Tom holds door open for them and the Trotters enter the corridor.

Del Alright ta.

Rodney *(To Albert)* Look I'm sorry I snapped at you back there, but I'm trying to give up smoking you see . . .

Albert That's alright son, forget it. Er, I wonder which one of us it is?

Rodney What d'you mean?

Albert Well, there can only be one *one* millionth customer can't there!

Del Yeah, well it's got to me innit, 'cos I paid for it all didn't I?

Rodney Yeah, but I gave you my housekeeping!

Albert And I gave you half my pension!

DAY. MANAGER'S OFFICE.

Tom enters followed by the Trotters,

Del Alright, alright, don't go on about it!

Rodney Del, we'll share the money fairly!

Del Alright, leave it to me, Rodney.

Rodney No, we'll share it fairly!

Mr Peterson *(On phone)* Look I can't talk now, somebody's come into the office! No, I'm not quite sure what time I'll be home darling. You're not cooking anything special are you? Entrecote Rioja . . . Yes, my favourite! I'll give you a call just before I leave. Bye. *(Smiles at the Trotters)* The wife!

Del Whose?

Mr Peterson So, what's it all about Tom?

Tom I stopped these gentlemen as they were leaving the store sir, as I have reason to believe they have some stolen items in their possession!

Mr Peterson Dear, dear, dear!

Del Stolen items??

Rodney What are you on about??

Albert We paid for these groceries!!

Del That's right! £29.48.

Rodney Ask the girl at the checkout!

Tom They came quietly sir, usually a sign of guilt!

Del Of course we did, because we thought we'd

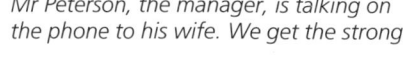

won the prize didn't we?

Mr Peterson Alright Tom leave it with me . . . and well done.

Tom Thank you sir. *(Exits)*

Del Come on, come on, let's go, let's go. *(They move to the door)*

Mr Peterson Gentlemen, if I press this button security will be waiting for you outside the door. And it might appear to a magistrate that you were trying to evade arrest!

Del Now wait a minute. Look, we paid for all these goods – and we've got a bill to prove it!

Rodney Ah yes, and we've got a bill to prove it!

Del Show him the bill Rodney!

Rodney What?

Del The bill!

Rodney I ain't got it!

Del Well of course you must. One of you must have!

Albert Don't look at me I never even saw it!

Del Yes you did, don't you remember . . .

Rodney She took it out the till.

Del Er . . . *(To Mr Peterson)* Actually we haven't got the bill!

Mr Peterson What a shame. Gentlemen, there are two ways of handling this unfortunate situation. One; we can remain here in the office and discuss it like civilized people, or two; I can call the police! Why don't you talk it over amongst yourselves while I carry on with this.

Albert There must be some way of proving we paid for all this!

Del There most probably is Albert, but what happens if the Old Bill starts asking questions about all my gear and Rodney's watch??

Albert Yeah I s'pose you're right.

Rodney You mean my watch is knocked off?

Del Ssshhh! Listen, alright, it's not up to us to prove our innocence, right. It's up to them to prove our guilt. So, all we've got to do is say nothing at all. Right. Just keep schtum! We'll be out of here in ten minutes flat, alright.

DAY. THE SUPERSTORE.

The clock on the wall says six o' clock. Lennox Gilbey enters. He is black, 20 years-old and is charming and confident. He smiles and greets total strangers who ignore him.

Lennox Hello there, how are you? I'm very well thank you. Lovely weather for this time of year, yes. Yes it is. *(Sings)* 'Some enchanted evening.' *(Sees an old lady trying to reach a tin of spam on a high shelf)* Allow me. That's very reasonable isn't it? I think I'll have two. *(He puts tins in his pocket)* You take care now.

He moves around the store openly stealing but with a smile. Packets of biscuits are bulging in his pockets, etc. Sheila notices him.

Sheila Mr Clarke!

Tom It's alright Sheila, I've seen him, leave it to me.

At the tobacco kiosk.

Lennox 20 Rothmans and a box of matches, love.

Woman That's £1.46, please.

Lennox Put it on my account! You take care now. *(Exits without paying)*

Woman You come back here with that stuff!

Tom Alright son, this is the end of your fun and games!

Lennox *(Innocently)* What have I done?? Oh no? Don't tell me, I haven't paid for these have I?

Tom Haven't paid for? Get back in there, you're nicked!

Lennox No, no, I have this problem you see, memory blanks!

Tom Get in there!

Lennox Listen to me man. The other day I went into Woolworths. When I got home I had a pair of binoculars, 12 packets of Strepsils and a roof rack for a Cortina and I didn't know!!

Tom Yes, tell that to the manager, you're going up to the office.

Lennox Please man. I'll go away for this. Look, I've only just come out!

Tom You should have thought of that before-hand! Come on, up to the office.

Lennox Please don't take me up to the office. Give me a break will yer??

Tom I'll give you a break if you keep on! Come on.

Lennox Look, please don't take me up to the office!

DAY. THE MANAGER'S OFFICE.

The Trotters are beginning to show worry. Mr Peterson is lounging back in his chair eyeing them, tapping his ball-point pen on his teeth.

Del That's a very nasty habit you got there you know. You can lose your teeth doing that.

Mr Peterson Really? And how would you know that?

Del 'Cos I'm gonna stick my fist right down your throat if you don't pack it in!!

Rodney Oi, oi, oi, Del!

Del Well Rodney, he's giving me the right hump he really is.

DAY. A SMALL CORRIDOR INTO MANAGER'S OFFICE.

Lennox *(To Tom)* Don't take me to the office!

The Longest Night

DAY. THE MANAGER'S OFFICE.

Tom shoves Lennox in.

Tom Here's another one for you.

Lennox *(Produces a gun from inside pocket and points it at Mr Peterson)* Okay, open up the safe!!

Tom Alright son, now take it easy!

Lennox *(Referring to the Trotters who are standing with their hands in the air)* Who are they?

Mr Peterson Er, they, they're here on suspicion of shoplifting.

Lennox Oh! Move. *(To Del)* Ain't I seen you somewhere before!

Del No, no, no. I ain't been anywhere before, have I Rodney, eh?

Rodney No, no. He's the stay at home all the time.

Lennox *(To Mr Peterson)* Go on, open up the safe.

Mr Peterson Yes, of course!

Lennox *(To Del and Rodney)* I'm a right villain I am! A real hard nut!

Del Yes triffic! Yes.

Lennox Hey, what's with the hands in the air?

Del Well you've got a gun in your other hand.

Lennox Come on, let's not be formal, put 'em down. D'you know the secret of my success?

Del No, no.

Lennox Planning! No detail is left unturned, no stone unchecked. I plan everything down to the last second!

Mr Peterson Excuse me, I'm terribly sorry but I can't open the safe!

Lennox *(To Tom)* What's he say to me??

Tom *(To Mr Peterson)* Come on now, don't be a prat sir! Open the safe for the nice man.

Mr Peterson I can't open it, the combination won't work! What's the time?

Lennox It's about twenty past five.

Albert No, it's quarter past six.

Lennox Bloody watch, it's always going wrong! Me mum only bought it for me a month ago down the market!

Rodney looks at Del.

Mr Peterson I didn't realise it was that late! I won't be able to open the safe. You see, it's fitted with a time-lock which comes into operation at 6pm!

Lennox *(To Tom)* Is this true??

Tom Yeah, I'm sorry son, you're 15 minutes late!

Lennox Bloody watch!! So when does it switch off?

Mr Peterson Tomorrow at 8am!

Lennox Oh great! Well thank you very much! So what am I supposed to do now??

Albert Can't you come back first thing in the morning?

Lennox No I can't – I have got other things to do you know! Oh well, I suppose there's nothing else for it! *(He goes over and locks door)* We'll have to wait!

Del Eh, wait? What are you talking about. Well that's 14 hours!!

Lennox Look, I don't wanna stay in here any more than what you do! But have you any idea how much is in that safe? There's about 60 grand!

Rodney You're kidding.

Mr Peterson I'm afraid not, Friday is our busiest day.

Lennox *(To Del, tapping his temple)* See planning! Let's all settle down now. It's only 14 hours, it'll soon go. Sit down!!

Del *(To Rodney)* And I had a date tonight too, with that croupier bird from the 1-11 Club. Charming sort. She's well spoken, cordon blue cook and does the business! It could be months before I have another crack at her!

Rodney Yeah, I am well choked for you, ain't I.

INT. MANAGER'S OFFICE. LATER.

It is later. The room is in darkness. Everyone is sitting, fear having been replaced by boredom.

Rodney *(Quietly to Del)* Got any cigars on you?

Del No, no, I smoked me last one about an hour ago. Anyway this'll help you to pack it up, won't it, eh?

Rodney Oh yeah, a gun at yer head's just the sort of incentive you need innit!

Del *(Referring to Lennox)* He ain't gonna hurt no one! He's just a kid tryin' to get some money. He's more frightened than us.

Rodney Aah bless him!

Del Are you still there son?

Lennox Yeah, what d'you want?

Del Just wondering about if we can have some lights on. You know, see what we was up to, know what I mean.

Lennox But passers-by might see the light!

Del No, no, not if you pull the blinds, right?

Lennox Oh yeah! *(To Tom)* Okay, I want you to do exactly as I say.

Tom Anything you say son, you're the boss.

Lennox I want you to switch the light on then pull them blinds down.

Del No, no, hang on. What you want to do is pull down the blinds then switch on the light!

Lennox Oh yeah, thanks. Right, I want you to pull them blinds then . . .

Tom Yes, yeah I think I've got it!

He pulls the blinds down and switches the desk lamp on.

Lennox *(Moves over to Del)* D'you know what the police have nicknamed me?

Del I've got a shrewd idea, but no, go on!

Lennox I'm known as The Shadow! Because I'm fast and fleeting, I come and I go and no-one knows!

Del Come and go do you? It's gonna take you 14 bleedin' hours to come and go in here!

Albert I've known epidemics come and go quicker than you!

Lennox I didn't know that safe was on a time lock. No, I'm a man of mystery me! A master of disguises – the man of a thousand faces! Do you remember the Scarlet Pimpernel?

Rodney That weren't you was it?

Lennox No, but I'm like him! They seek him here, they seek him there, those policemen seek him everywhere. Is he in Heaven, or is he in Hell, that damned elusive Sh-a-dow!

Del Yeah, that's er, good, very, very good, that's good that. So the police are looking for The Shadow are they?

Lennox They'll never catch him!

Del No, no, but I bet Hank Marvin's had a few tugs though!

Lennox laughs with Del. The phone on the desk rings.

Lennox What's that??

Mr Peterson It's the phone.

Lennox I know it's the phone! I ain't stupid! I mean who is it??

Mr Peterson Well it's a little difficult to tell at this stage!

Albert You'd better let him answer it son, it might be his wife.

Rodney Oh yeah, she's got entrecote rioja.

Lennox Oh I'm sorry to hear that! Well go 'n then, find out how she is.

Mr Peterson Yes! Peterson? *(Hand over mouthpiece)* It's security, they're just about to shut up . . . *(On phone)* Yes, you can switch the alarm system on.

Tom Oi, oi, oi, I'm the Head of Security! *(Grabs phone)* You can switch the alarm system on, yes!

Mr Peterson There you are you see, everything's alright now.

Lennox Yeah? You don't mind if I double-check do ya? *(Checks through the blinds)*

Albert *(To Rodney and Del)* He's becoming more nervous and agitated! They're the danger signs in a situation like this!

Del I've told you, he'll be alright, he'll be good as gold as long as we don't upset him! He's just a kid.

Albert That's what makes him dangerous! A nervous kid, hair trigger! Put 'em together and . . .

Rodney You're a cheerful old bark ain't yer?

Albert One of us has got to create a distraction! So that the other two can grapple with him and disarm him!

Lennox *(To the Trotters)* What are you whispering about?

Del It's alright son, nothing, alright, alright, no problem.

Albert D'you mind if I stand up a bit and walk round?

Lennox Why?

Albert I've got a bit of cramp in me leg.

Lennox Go on then. No sudden movements though!

Del Sudden movements, him!?

Rodney The closest he gets to a sudden movement is when he wipes the cobwebs off his head!

Albert Ooh that's better! *(Suddenly clutches his chest as if in pain, contorts his face and starts wobbling)*

Albert Aaahhggg! Aaaggghhh!

Albert lowers himself to the floor and kicks his right leg in the air a bit. None of the others show a flicker of emotion. Albert's eyes open on the floor and he surveys the room. Realising his ploy hasn't worked he gets to his feet and sits back down. Nothing is said.

Rodney *(To Albert)* You got any tobacco on you?

INT. MANAGER'S OFFICE. EARLY MORNING.

The next morning. Clock says 7.30am. Everyone in the office is asleep. Lennox is asleep, his head on the desk. He is not holding the gun but it is very close to his hand. There are noises outside.

Del What's that noise?

Albert Weren't me!

Mr Peterson It's the staff arriving.

Del What time d'you open?

Mr Peterson 8.30am.

Rodney We've been here 13 an' a 'alf hours! Don't time fly when you're in good company.

Tom Only 'alf hour to go and it'll all be over.

Del *(Looks at sleeping Lennox)* The old Shadow's looking pretty knackered ain't he, eh?

Tom With proper training you can condition your body to do without sleep. I learnt that out

The Longest Night

in Kenya.

Rodney What, you got a branch out there then?

Tom No, no! When I was younger I did a bit of travelling. I ended up doing five years with the Kenyan Police Force. I was out there during the trouble with the Mau Mau.

Albert He's too young to know what that means. He most probably thinks the Mau Mau is the African Post Office!

Rodney We did modern history at school, didn't we, mouthy?

Rodney's attention is drawn to the desk and the sleeping Lennox.

Tom Judging by all them ribbons you must have seen a bit of action Albert?

Rodney stands up very slowly and very cautiously begins moving towards desk.

Albert Yeah. I was in the Navy, Royal and Merchant. I've seen things that would make yer teeth itch! But I never talk about it though. Sharks! Don't talk to me about sharks! I've seen 'em 50 foot long! Monsters they were!

Rodney is getting closer and closer to the desk.

Del Yeah, he thinks that Jaws was a stickleback! Oi Rodney! What the bloody hell d'you think you're playing at???

Rodney Ssshhhh!

Del Rodney . . .

Albert Rodney – come back and sit down son!

Tom Don't do anything rash son, it ain't worth it!

Mr Peterson For God's sake there's only 30 minutes to go!!

Rodney's nerves are at breaking point. As he reaches the desk a floorboard creaks. Lennox stirs at the sound. Rodney stops. He reaches out across the desk, his hand inching towards the gun. His hand moves past the gun and picks up the pack of fags. He turns triumphantly.

Del You plonker!!

Lennox *(Waking)* What you doing??

Rodney Nothing! I just fancied a fag that's all!

Lennox Well why didn't you ask me? There's no need to steal!

Rodney No, sorry!

There is the sound of a car outside.

Lennox What was that??

Mr Peterson It's the staff arriving.

Lennox *(Checks watch)* They start early don't they? Quarter past four!

Tom It's half past seven!

Lennox Bloody watch! So, only 'alf an hour to

go! It's sad really. We might never meet again.

Del We could always hold a reunion next year, if you like.

Lennox *(Pointing gun at Del)* I remember who you are now!

Del No, no. It's alright son – you can have a full rebate, no problems, alright.

Lennox You're er . . . oh what is it? No, don't tell me! Tel. No, Del . . . Del Trotter! Right? Don't you recognise me?

Del Well you're a master of disguise ain't yer!

Lennox D'you remember Roseanna Gilbey? West Indian lady, lives down Cutler Road . . . Years ago you used to come round on the weekly and that, selling shoes Del.

Del Yes I remember, and that was you??

Lennox Don't you remember her little boy?

Del No, no. You're not little . . . Lennox!

Lennox That's right! It's me – Lennox Gilbey!

Del Lennox Gilbey. I don't believe it! Stone me. Last time I saw you, you was about that high! Cor dear, doesn't time fly, eh? So what you doing with yourself now?

Lennox Oh well, I'm on the dole Del.

Del Oh yeh, how's your mum?

Lennox She's alright, suffers from her feet a bit, but . . .

Del Yeah, well, but she would. Wait, hang about. I remember your mum. I remember – very straight lady, proud, church-goer and all that!

Lennox Yeah, she won't know nothing about this Del.

Del Oh no. So how you gonna explain away £60,000, eh? Christmas bonus from the Job Centre? Listen Lennox, there are millions of people out there in the same boat as you! But they don't go round robbing everyone!

Lennox Look I haven't had a job right in six years!

Del Well nor has Rodney!

Lennox I've got no future!

Del Nor has Rodney!

Lennox Look I haven't done a day's work since I left school Del.

Del It's a tough old world Lennox, tough world but it doesn't give you the right to go round pointing guns at people! *(Referring to the gun)* That thing's gonna put you in prison!

Lennox No, I'm too shrewd!

Del Oh shrewd, you? Shrewd are you? Very shrewd.

Lennox Yeah!

Del An hour ago you were The Shadow right, man of mystery. Now we know your name, your address and your mum's shoe size! Give it up

Lennox before it's too late, eh? That gun doesn't suit you!

Lennox In 20 minutes Del I'll be rich!

Del And in 30 minutes you're gonna be banged up! I'll tell you why shall I? Just review the situation for a second. All the staff have arrived, right. They're starting to work out there. And you've gotta walk through 'em, ain't ya? They're all out there – shelf-packers, the porters, the cleaners, the security men! The shop doesn't open till half past eight, right. So in order for you to get out, you've gotta go up, ask them to get the keys to let you out!!

Albert Before you can say 'police sniper' there'll be more lead flying about than a fight in a scrap-yard!

Rodney You'd never reach your get-away car.

Lennox Get-away car! I knew there was something . . . Here look Del, I didn't *wanna* go through with this right. I just got . . . I just got a bit desperate!

Del It's alright, it's alright. I know son, I know alright.

Lennox And the police didn't really nickname me The Shadow! I'm not known by the police! I've never done anything like this before!

Del Look, now listen to me, listen, you give it up before it's too late! I'll tell you what I'll do, I'll come down the court with ya, and speak for ya.

Lennox *(To Mr Peterson)* You said it would be easy!!!

Mr Peterson Shut up you fool!!

Lennox I've been set up for this Del!

Rodney You??? You and . . . Lennox??

Lennox He said I'd just walk out with the money!

Mr Peterson And you could have if you'd been here at five o'clock as arranged!!

Del That's it, innit. Of course – it's been worrying me all night this has. I mean to say, how did Lennox know so much about this place? How did he know there was all that money here in the safe, and where it was?

Mr Peterson You must believe me, I didn't do it purely for the money!

Albert What d'you do it for then?

Mr Peterson . . . Well alright, I did do it for the money! But it was simply to pay off my debts! You see I have a wife whose hobby is spending! £12,000 for a solarium. £15,000 for a swimming pool and now she's got the estimates on a marble-tiled gazebo! God, we only live in a semi!

Del Couldn't you seek professional help?

Mr Peterson You mean a psychiatrist?

Del No, I mean a hit-man.

Mr Peterson No, I couldn't afford it! This . . . seemed the only way out.

Rodney But how did you two ever meet? I mean, I can't imagine Lennox at the young Tories ball, and well you wouldn't go down a bomb at the Ram Jam Club, would yer?

Mr Peterson Lennox came here last year looking for a job.

Lennox Then we bumped into each other a couple of months ago in court.

Mr Peterson I'd been summonsed for failure to maintain the repayments on a hire purchase agreement that had been signed by my wife, the fat greedy cow.

Lennox I was there on an attempted wounding case. Oh, I weren't the accused Del, I was the victim! Anyway, me and Mr Peterson got chatting and the whole thing started from there.

Albert Did he supply you with the gun?

Lennox Oh no! *(Indicating Tom)* He did!

Del Chamboussiz nouvelle. Cor dear, would you Adam and Eve it, eh? Dixon of Kuala Lumpur is involved!

Tom Yeah that's right, the three of us planned it. But I want you to know I did it *purely* for the money!

Del I bet you did.

Tom I retire in a couple of months' time and you should have seen the crummy pension this firm was offering me! I was gonna get less than Duncan Goodhew's barber!

Mr Peterson We needed Tom in with us for his police experience. He told us what to do, how to make the robbery look genuine.

Rodney So where did we fit into all this?

Tom Well, it would have looked a bit dodgy wouldn't it, if the only witnesses to a 60 grand robbery were the store manager and the head of security! No, what we wanted was some *independent* witnesses!

Del Oh. I see, so that is why you pulled us in? 14 hours just to provide you with an alibi? Cor, well I'll . . . just a minute – give me that here! *(Taking gun)* Look, where did you get this?

Tom Out of our toy department.

Del Yeah – I wondered how long Taiwan had been making Lugers!

Mr Peterson So what happens now? Are you going to the police?

Del Na! I'm gonna phone 'em instead.

Lennox Del!

Del It's alright, don't panic, don't panic, just winding you up! You are a wally Lennox!

Lennox Sorry Del!

Del What is your mum gonna say, eh? Anyway

The Longest Night

there's no real harm done right? No one got hurt, nothing got nicked! Now listen to me Lennox, you're after a job right?

Lennox I've been after one since I left school, Del.

Del Well I know where there's one going. And I'm well in with the governor!

Lennox You're kidding??

Del No.

Lennox You reckon you could swing it for me?

Del I think so, mind you the job does not become available until . . . *(To Tom)* When d'you retire Tom?

Tom What, *him* work here – in security??

Albert Can you think of anyone better? *(Referring to Mr Peterson)* He'll know exactly who to keep his eye on!

Del That's right, tell me – what would you prefer, young Lennox or Old Bill?

Mr Peterson Welcome to the firm Lennox!

Tom I'll sort you out a uniform, show you yer duties!

Del That's it Rodney. Come on Albert, come on, we're going. We're leaving. Let's get out of here! Oh dear.

Rodney This lot's gonna have to go straight in the fridge when we get home.

Picks up a french stick and bangs it on the desk. It is rock hard.

Del *(Throws it to Lennox)* Here are Lennox, save you buying a truncheon, won't it, eh? Oh, by the way Mr Peterson, I'm coming back to your shop this afternoon.

Mr Peterson Why?

Del 'Cos I've got this funny feeling that I am gonna be your millionth customer! What do you think?

Mr Peterson I have exactly the same feeling!

Del You know it makes sense don't ya? Bonjour.

Tea for Three

NIGHT. THE NAG'S HEAD.

It is talent night. On the small podium that acts as a stage there is a pianist, a drummer and a bad singer. Albert is at at the bar in a maudlin mood. Trigger is at the bar when Del and Rodney enter.

Del Oh, excuse me mate, oi give us . . . oh, Gawd blimey Michael, give us . . .

Mike Two pints.

Trigger Alright Dave?

Rodney *(No longer reacts)* Oh yeah, hello Trigger. Looks like rain don't it?

Trigger Yeah, tastes like it.

Mike Oi, I bloody heard that Trigger! I'll have you know my beer has just won second prize in the breweries contest!

Del Yes that's right, he was narrowly beaten by the Metropolitan Water Board! *(They all laugh except Trigger)* Do you hear that? He was narrowly beaten by the Metropolitan Water Board! You see Trigger, they sell water you know and Mike, he sells . . . *(He gives up)* Yes, what do you want? What is it Albert?

Albert Now brace yourself boys, I just had a bit of bad news. Your Aunt Ada's been rushed into hospital, she's in a bad way by all accounts.

Rodney Oh no, that's a shame innit?

Del That's a choker.

Trigger Who's Aunt Ada?

Del Gawd knows; I don't.

Albert She's me wife.

Del Oh that Aunt Ada? But you ain't seen her for ages.

Rodney Yeah, she said to the rest of the family that if she saw you again she'd kill you.

Del Yeah.

Albert She was annoyed when she said that. You see it's like a chapter of my life is coming to a close.

Del Yeah, I know just how she feels though, eh?

Albert Well that's it you see son, I don't know. I'd like to go 'n visit her and find out.

Rodney Well why don't ya?

Albert 'Cos she might not be as ill as they say.

Trigger He's really in the dumps ain't he?

Del Yeah, I know. Still what can you do? Sorry darling! I tell you what we can do, why don't we take him down the chinky, that should cheer him up, ey Rodders? Do you want to come with us Trigger?

Trigger No, I ain't sure Del. My niece'll be here in a minute. She's come up from the country for a few days. You remember little Lisa don't you?

Del Lisa, oh your sister's kid? Yeah, I remember her.

Trigger I'd better see what she fancies doing. Listen, I'm gonna have a chat with Albert, jolly him up a bit. *(Moves along bar)*

Del Jolly him up. Thanks Trigger, you're a pal.

Rodney I remember Lisa – scruffy little mare weren't she. She had more candlesticks than Liberace.

Del Yeah, that's her. I remember her mum though, she was a fair sort – pig-ugly, but a fair sort. I nicknamed her Miss 999 you know 'cos I only phoned her in an emergency. See if we can do a bit of business here, Michael . . . Mike, just a moment – Mike . . . Could I . . . Michael. . . . *(To singer)* Oi, shut up will yer, I can't hear meself think over here.

Rodney Del, it's a talent contest!

Del Well she ought to be disqualified.

Rodney That's the favourite.

Mike Oi, what's all the hollering about?

Del Well, I dunno, I just told her to shut up. *(Showing brochure)* 'Ere, listen Michael, now listen, I've got a beautiful ultraviolet sunbed back at the flat. Now they retail normally at £375, it's yours for £120. Just think of it eh, your own personal home-solarium?

Mike I don't want it.

Del I can see that you're in two minds so I'll tell you what I'll do. I have here a super deluxe modern plug-in telephone and I'm gonna give it to you free with your home-solarium. I can't say fairer than that, because this is my last one.

Mike I don't want it.

Del I'll chuck an extension in.

Mike I – don't – want – it.

Del Yes or no?

Mike Do me a favour Del . . . please.

Del I'm doing you a favour . . . *(To Rodney)* And I nearly had him then.

Rodney Yeah, I could see he was weakening. Is it worth stopping here for another one?

Del No it ain't. Come on Rodney – let's get going. That bird over there's giving me the right hump. Oi, shut up.

Rodney Derek.

Lisa enters.

Trigger Del. Lisa's here.

Del Not now Trigger, we ain't got time. Say hello to her for us. Come on Rodders – let's get going.

Lisa *(Calls across the bar)* Hello Del.

Del Hello darling . . . Bloody hell!

Rodney *(In a state of shock)* That ain't that scruffy little thing with the funny drawers is it?

Del I think so. Yeah, must be, yeah.

Rodney Bloody 'ell . . . Are you off then, are yer?

Del Eh? No, no, no, I think I'll stay for another one. Are you gonna go down the chinky with Uncle Albert then?

Rodney No, I don't fancy it – all that batter and that.

Del Na.

Rodney Na.

Del *(Tries to push past Rodney to get a head start)* Well, out of me way, come on, out of me way.

Rodney *(Elbows him back)* You piss off.

Del *(To Rodney)* Look, there's a pound down there, look there.

Rodney *(Stops)* Where?

Del Hello darling.

Lisa Hello, Del. Oh it's been such a long time.

Del Yeah innit? Haven't you got big, eh? No, I mean you've grown up.

Lisa Well I'm 25 now.

Del You're not! 25 now . . .

Rodney Hello Lisa, do you remember me?

Lisa Hello. How are you?

Rodney Oh fine, I'm really good.

Lisa Oh that's nice. *(Quietly to Del)* Who is he?

Del Eh? Who him? That's little Rodney. Don't you remember little Rodney. You used to play with him.

Lisa Oh, of course. You've changed.

Rodney Yes, so have you.

Del I'll say she has changed. Cor you are a big girl . . .

Rodney Why don't we go and sit down over here, and have a little chat. *(Starts moving to table)* I'll see you later on Del.

Del No, no. I'll come with you. I'll come with you.

Rodney Here you are, sit here Lisa. Do you remember the old days?

Lisa Oh it's lovely seeing you two again. *(To Del)* You know I always remember that day – ooh it was years and years ago – you drove round to me Nan's house in a brand-new three-wheeled van. *(To Rodney)* I remember him saying to Uncle Trigger, this time next year it'll be a Mercedes. I

was so impressed . . . Did you ever get the Mercedes?

Del Na, na, I went off 'em . . . I got a nice little two-seater now!

Rodney Yeah, two seats, three wheels! It's the same van innit?

Del That's right, I let Rodney borrow it sometimes when he's behaved himself, 'cos he can't afford a car of his own! I mean, what kid can of his age, eh? So you're living down in the country then, eh?

Lisa Just outside Winchester. You still livin' in the same place?

Del Yeah, yeah, we're still there. Listen, you know before you go home you ought to come round to the flat. We can have a chat about old times, you know. You can stay for tea.

Lisa Oh thanks, I'd love to.

Rodney I was gonna invite you to tea an' all. How about tomorrow night?

Lisa Fine.

Del Yes tomorrow's fine with me sweetheart.

Rodney No, I invited Lisa for tomorrow night.

Del Yes, I know Rodney, but don't forget I did invite Lisa first.

Rodney Derek, you clearly heard me invite Lisa for tea *tomorrow* night.

Del But I invited her *first*.

Lisa Look, why don't we all have tea together? Then the three of us can talk about the old times.

Del *(Reluctantly)* Yeah . . . Alright then.

Rodney *(Equally reluctant)* Fine.

Lisa Oh good.

Rodney Yeah, great.

Albert is on the stage at the piano.

Lisa Isn't that your Uncle?

Del What's that soppy old duffer up to?

Albert I'd like to sing a very special song for a very special lady who unfortunately ain't with me tonight. I like to think this song was named after my dear, sick wife. It is that beautiful old ballad, Ada.

Del Ada??

Lisa Is there a song called Ada?

Rodney Well there must be, he's about to sing it.

Albert 'Ada, you with the stars in your eyes, Love never made a fool of you . . .'

THE TROTTERS' LOUNGE.

Albert is lying beneath a sun-bed canopy wearing protective glasses, a white vest, baggy old navy shorts and plimsolls. Rodney enters from the kitchen.

Rodney Hurry up will you, I want 'alf an hour

Tea for Three

under there.

Albert 'Ere, these ultraviolet rays contain vitamin E don't they? I read somewhere that vitamin Es are good for an 'angover.

Rodney Yeah, well you made a right berk of yourself at the talent contest didn't yer? Getting up on stage and singing that stupid song.

Albert What are you on about, I won!

Rodney You *won*??

Del enters with a bag of groceries.

Del, he only won the talent contest!

Del Who did?

Rodney Roy Orbison here!

Del Must have been a sympathy vote! Anyway, I've got all the grub in for me and Lisa's tea tonight.

Rodney Yes, well I made a contribution too.

Del Oh, have ya? Well I got chicken Italienne and fruit salad and Dream Topping to follow and what've you bought?

Rodney Cheese.

Del Cheese! Cheese? Well, it's a good job I bought all this grub then innit, eh? If it was left up to you the poor little cow'd been down for Welsh rabbit.

Albert gets up.

Rodney Well, if you put your hand in your pocket every so often and gave me some proper money.

Del Listen, I earn the money in this family.

Albert Why don't you two pack it in?

Rodney *(Referring to Albert)* God, you look like a geriatric ball-boy.

Albert You two were niggling each other last night and you've been bickering all morning, I'm fed up with yer. I'm going down the Legion.

Del *(Referring to Albert's legs)* Well, just make sure that you put on a pair of trousers first. There's a lot of stray dogs on this estate! Anyway, I better make sure we've got enough Smash in for Lisa's tea.

Rodney Right, I'm gonna have a quick tone-up, a nice shower and I am sorted! Oi, how'd you turn this thing on for 'alf an hour?

Albert On the end there.

Rodney Right, got it. *(Rodney lays out beneath the canopy)* Oh, this is lovely!

Albert Listen to me Rodney. I told you once, you remember, that Grandad and I didn't speak to each other for years?

Rodney Mmmh.

Albert Well *that* was all over a woman! It was yer Aunt Ada!

Rodney *(Sleepily)* You're not gonna sing again are you?

Albert I remember me and yer Grandad, we were just like you and Del Boy. We weren't just brothers, we was mates, went everywhere together, got up to some right capers. Then one night we met Ada at the local palais. She was a beautiful woman – a bit like Ginger Rogers. Last time I saw her she looked more like Fred Astaire! Well, we both had a couple of dances with her, then we both wanted to take her home. We ended up fighting in the street over her. He never spoke to me from that day to. . . . He never spoke to me ever again. I'm frightened history's about to repeat itself. I don't wanna see that happen to you and Del. Rodney? *(He is asleep)* Bloody kids! Oi, Rodney!

Del Oi, Rodney! I'm gonna whip down the shops for another packet of Smash and some Brut so I want you to . . . Rodn . . . Ah, he's gone to sleep bless him! So you wanna get a nice tan for the girl then do you? I'll give you a nice tan alright. *(Switches the timer on to full)*

THE TROTTER'S LOUNGE. NIGHT.

The meal is finished. Del and Lisa are alone at the table. Del fills her wine glass.

Lisa Oh, not too much I got to be up early in the morning.

Del Just a little topperooni – there we go. *(Calls to kitchen)* Come on Rodney. Oi, come on, bring your cheese.

Lisa I really think Rodney should go to hospital with his face.

Del Yeah, I know, I've been telling him that for years!

Rodney enters from the kitchen carrying a cheeseboard. He is wearing a beige suit, open at the neck. His face is lobster red. Del makes Red Indian gesture.

Del How!

Lisa Does your face hurt?

Rodney Only when I smile.

Del Listen Rodney, I wouldn't stand about in that suit too long if I were you, not with your head!

Lisa Why not?

Del Well, he looks like a Swan Vesta! You've only got yourself to blame, haven't yer?

Rodney How's your mum these days Lisa?

Lisa Oh, she's fine thank you.

Rodney Did you know that years and years ago, Del used to take your mum out?

Lisa Oh, I didn't know that.

Del Yeah, yeah, we were just little tiny kids then.

Rodney What was it you nicknamed her, Del?

Del Em . . . It was the Rose of Peckham.

Lisa My mum??? I can't wait to tell her.

Rodney Well, that's funny because he told me in the pub . . .

Del *(Changing subject)* I know there was something I wanted to ask you. D'you like going to the flicks?

Lisa Oh the cinema, oh yeah. Have you seen *An Officer and a Gentleman*?

Del and Rodney Oh yeah, yeah.

Lisa Oh that Richard Gere, isn't he fabulous?

Rodney Yeah he's alright.

Del I like what he wears.

Lisa Oh when he was wearing his uniform. Oh God, I went all goose-pimpley. You know there definitely is something about a man in a uniform.

Del Well you take after your mum there, she used to go out with this geezer from the Gas Board!

Rodney I used to be in the army! Well, cadets!

Del I used to be a paratrooper!

Lisa Really?

Del Didn't I Rodney??

Rodney Well you've made a few drops in your time Del.

Lisa I don't know how you could do it. I've got these friends back home who belong to a hang-gliding club.

Del Oh, yeah hang-gliding, well I love all that.

Lisa They're always asking me to try but just the thought of it terrifies me.

Del There's nothing to it. No, I used to free-fall from 20,000 foot.

Lisa No.

Del Yeah, I didn't used to open my chute 'til I saw the tops of the trees.

Lisa Oh God.

Del At night.

Rodney You also had your feet tied together and a hand over one eye, didn't you!!

Del One night my chute didn't open at all!

Lisa What happened?

Del Eh? Oh, er, I had a bad landing! But fortunately they teach you to fall properly! It was alright.

Lisa You know it's funny but I've always imagined paratroopers to be . . . Well, taller!

Rodney Yeah well, he used to be six foot one but, like he said, he had a bad landing!

Del Thank you, thank you very much Rodney for your observations. Now, get out in the kitchen and put the kettle on will yer?

Lisa Oh no, no. I've got to be going.

Del No, no, no.

Rodney Listen, I'll walk you home, eh?

Del No, no, no Rodney, you can't do that. You can't stand around on street corners with your face, the traffic'll be waiting for you to change to green! No listen, I'll give you a lift home.

Lisa Oh that's nice of you Del.

Del L'état c'est moi! As the French would say. What else could I do for a charming lady?

Lisa Why thank you kind sir!

Del Not at all. I'll just go and get the keys shall I? I'm going. *(Del goes into the bedroom)*

Rodney Well, it's been really nice seeing you again after all this time.

Lisa Oh I've enjoyed it so much. You know – shopping and meeting old friends.

Rodney Yeah, what time you off tomorrow?

Lisa I get the 10 o'clock train from Waterloo. I've got to be home by 12 noon, I'm meeting those friends I was telling you about.

Rodney What, the hang-gliders?

Lisa Mmmmh. I'll just get me jacket.

She goes to the hall to get her coat. Rodney's brain is working overtime. He follows her to the hall.

Rodney Yeah, why don't me and Del drive you home tomorrow?

Lisa I couldn't ask you to do that!

Rodney No, no, we'd like it. We'd have a nice day in the country! Del'll jump at the chance. And I was thinking, it's Del's 46th birthday soon and I'd love to give him a real surprise. D'you know what his ambition is?

Lisa What?

Rodney To hang-glide! Well, you know, being the old ex-paratrooper it's natural innit? So d'you reckon your mates could arrange for him to have a little flight?

Lisa No problem, they'd be delighted.

Rodney Oh that'll be great! I can't wait to see his little face. It'll be our little secret though, eh?

Lisa Sure, oh me bag.

Lisa goes back in the lounge.

Rodney Yes, I can't wait to see his little face.

VAST OPEN COUNTRYSIDE.

Del What???? *(He looks up skywards. In the background there are hang-gliders in action)* You want me to go up on one of them wings fings? *(Trying to shrug off)* No, no, no, not today darling, you see I'm not in the mood.

Lisa You can't wait to get up there can you? I can see it in your eyes!

Del Really?

Lisa *(Calls)* Andy, come over and meet some friends of mine. *(Del looks to Rodney in desperation but Rodney just grins)* I'd like you to meet

Tea for Three

Del and Rodney.

Andy Oh, nice to meet you.

Del Watcha son.

Rodney Hi.

Andy Hi! *(Sees Rodney's red face)* Are you okay?

Rodney I'm fine.

Andy Sorry, it's just that you look sort of flushed.

Del No, no, it's alright. It's just his great-grandad was a Comanche.

Andy Well, Lisa tells me you used to be a paratrooper.

Del Eh? Oh yeah, well it's many, many years ago now like, you know what I mean?

Andy Well, I've done a bit of free-falling myself, nothing in your calibre of course, but it was great fun.

Del Yeah, triffic!

Andy *(Indicates a glider)* Well, whenever you're ready Del.

Del Em . . . No, no, no, it's alright, I don't wanna spoil your fun Andy, I'll stay here and just watch, eh.

Lisa Listen to me Derek Trotter. I've arranged all this specially for you! It's my way of saying thank you for that lovely meal last night. I wish you could have seen it Andy.

Rodney *(Quietly to himself)* Hang around and you might!

Lisa Andy doesn't mind you borrowing his equipment, do you?

Andy No, no, it's a pleasure. And we've got some great thermals today.

Del Thermals? Oh what a shame, I'm just wearing me ordinary Y-fronts.

Andy No, no, thermals, you know – warm air.

Lisa He's just having you on!

Andy Oh I see! We'll get everything ready then.
Andy and Lisa move away.

Del Yeah, okay. What am I gonna do?

Rodney I don't know! Dear oh dear oh dear oh dear, what a pickle! I mean really, it's a bit of a shame you ever said you were a paratrooper.

Del I wish I'd kept my bloody mouth shut. What's that Andy want to go sticking his 'ooter into my affairs for eh, eh?

Rodney Well he thinks he's doing you a favour, don't he?

Del I'm gonna land him a doughboy right round the lug 'ole before he's much older! What am I gonna do Rodney? I can't tell 'em I'm scared can I, eh, eh?

Rodney No, no, you'd make yourself look a right dipstick in front of everyone. You don't

fancy having a little fly then?

Del No I do not. I wanna keep my feet firmly on the old terra-cotta! I'll tell 'em I'm not feeling very well!

Rodney Eh, you can't do that! A Green Beret with an 'eadache! This is one little problem you're gonna have to work out on your own Del, innit?

Del See Rodney, listen to me. I know we haven't been seeing eye to eye for the last few days, but listen to me, we are brothers after all, ain't we? I mean it's blood! It's like Uncle Albert said, he said brothers shouldn't fall out over a woman. Didn't he, eh, what d'you reckon? Eh Rodney, eh?

Rodney You're right Del! No, you're right. I mean it's stupid arguing, innit?

Del Of course it is, you know it makes sense. Come on, help me out of this mess Rodney, please. Come on, any ideas? Eh?

Rodney Alright, alright we'll just have a look at the problem, right. On the one hand right, you don't want to fly!

Del No.

Rodney No, no, that's alright. But on the other hand you want to keep your pride intact?

Del Of course I do.

Rodney Right, right, I've got it. You *pretend* to be dead keen to get up in them old clouds right! You put on all the gear, put yourself in the glider thing, then at the last minute I come over from the van, rushing up and say we've had an urgent call come through on our car-phone.

Del Yeah! That's brill innit eh? But we ain't got a car phone, have we Dopey? We ain't even got a ruddy car, look.

Rodney *(Produces a phone handset)* Who's gonna know any different? And then I say you've gotta rush back to London immediately, right, and you act all disappointed, you go 'Oh no, but what can you do?' Then we're in the van and we're away!

Del Oh yeah, good boy. Well done Rodders, well done. Listen, you are gonna stay here though aren't yer?

Rodney I'll be right here, mate.

Del Good boy, good boy. *(Calls)* Hey Andy, come on then, hurry up, I'm getting a bit impatient to be off ain't I? *(To Rodney)* He don't know does he?
Del is wearing a crash helmet and has the glider strapped to him. He is still wearing his camel coat.

Lisa Everything alright?

Del Oh yeah, beautiful darling, beautiful.

Andy Now do you remember everything I told

you about controlling the glider?

Del Yeah, don't worry Andy, it's all up there. Down there for dancing. What d'you reckon, all the thermal and all that – alright up there Andy?

Andy No, no, it's one of the best days of the year. Well, whenever you're ready Del.

Del Ah right, cushty. *(Nods in Rodney's direction)* Cushty.

Andy You're switched on . . . Yeah, it's all working, yeah.

Del *(Cups his ear)* Oh! Is that our phone I can hear ringing Rodney?

Rodney Eh?

Del I said is that our phone I can hear ringing?

Rodney No!

Del Are you *sure*?

Rodney Yeah. We ain't got a car-phone! *(Rodney grins a victorious 'Got you bastard' grin)* Get up as high as you can Del. You might get a tan.

Del *(Realises it was Rodney's plan)* I will get you for this Rodney, you just see if I don't.

Andy Are you going Del?

Del Eh? Yeah. Yeah I'm going . . . Oh my good Gawd! Oh bloody 'ell!

Del closes his eyes and runs forward with a great 'Geronimo' shout. He flys off the hill.

Rodney *(Horrified)* Oh!

Del *(In the air, eyes squeezed closed)* They do this for fun! Oh Gawd, please let me get down safely.

Lisa What's he doing????

Andy Well, where's he going??? I told him to stay close to the ridge.

Rodney Why, what's over there?

Lisa He's heading out to sea.

THE TROTTERS' LOUNGE.

Rodney is studying a globe of the world. He is a worried man. Albert, disgusted with him, puts a brandy on the table.

Albert Get that down you! He's been missing for 12 hours! 12 hours, that's nearly 'alf a day!

Rodney I know, I've got a GCE in Maths, haven't I.

There's a ring at the front door.

Albert Shall I answer it son?

Rodney Yes please.

Albert exits to the hall. Albert and Trigger enter.

Trigger Watcha Dave.

Rodney Watcha Trigger.

Trigger You alright?

Rodney Yeah, I'm fine, this is nothing! Have they found him?

Trigger Yeah. . . . They found him Dave!

Rodney Eh. Where?

Trigger He crashed into a television transmitter in Redhill. They rushed him to the local hospital. X-rays and that. They tried to phone his next of kin – but they couldn't get through, so they phoned the pub. Me and Mike got a cab out there.

Albert We'll see you for the fare son.

Trigger Na, that's alright. We got a Green Line back.

Rodney But what happened? Has he broken anything?

Trigger Well they reckon the aerial's beyond repair.

Rodney No Trigger! I mean Del – how's Del??

Trigger You'd better ask him yourself Dave.

Del, in a wheelchair pushed by Mike, enters. His face is bruised and speckled with bits of plaster. His coat is ripped and stained. He is a wretched, pathetic sight.

Del See you got home safely then Rodney?

Rodney Yeah. Are you alright Del?

Del Is he winding me up or what?

Mike No, no, he's just a bit concerned that's all Del. 'Ere, are you alright?

Rodney I'm fine!!

Albert So what did the hospital say son?

Del They said. . . . *(Del lowers his head, as do Mike and Trigger. Rodney becomes suspicious)* They said I may never walk again! Rodney, Rodney, my *brother*, I know that in your heart of hearts you never meant to disable me! And I just want you to know I won't hold it against you.

Rodney Alright.

Del Alright, what I meant was, I'm sorry I let you lay under our home-solarium all that time and made you go a bit red. I suppose, alright, this is my punishment, innit? Spend the rest of my life in this wheelchair!

Trigger Still, it could have been worse Del!

Mike How??

Trigger My gran had one with a squeaky wheel!

Rodney This is all a bit sick innit? I mean, you might fool these three, but not me bruv!

Del What do you mean Rodney?

Rodney Oh come off it Del! Two pina coladas then you'll put on your Eric Clapton LP and you'll be up and jiving won't ya?

Del I don't believe this! I don't believe what he's doing to me! He's torn my world in half and now he's having a pop at me!

Albert You're right out of order son!

Rodney Oh listen to me. Hospitals do not send home paralysed people by bus!! What is it you

Tea for Three

are after Del, sympathy from Lisa or a disabled sticker for the van, eh?

Del *(He leaps from the chair, grabs Rodney by the throat and pushes him against the wall)* You listen to me you vicious little git! I may never walk again for the rest of . . . *(Realises he is standing)* Although I must admit, I'm getting some feeling back!

Albert You should never tell them sort of lies Del!

Mike You made us go all the way out to Redhill and there was nothing wrong with you!

Del Don't blame me, it was him. I just wanted to get my own back on this plonker.

Trigger Yeah, but when you fancied a smoke on the bus you made me carry you up to the top deck.

Del Don't blame me Trigger! Don't blame me! Blame him! Rodney, I was up there three hours! Three bloody hours! I did loop-the-loop over Dimchurch. Little kids were shouting at me, 'There goes a spaceman, a spaceman.' Finally, just when I'd given up hope I clattered into an aerial thing and fell 50 foot to the ground. It was only by the grace of God that I landed on something soft.

Rodney Yeah, I noticed the bruising around your head.

Del It was not my head! I landed on a very unfortunate and very unsuspecting courting couple.

Rodney You're kidding?

Del No, I wish I was. Due to your vicious mind and general wallyness, they have had to put their wedding back six months. I've had to pay for a new sun-roof in their Sierra – and that's regardless of what Radio Rentals are gonna do me for for the aerial!

Rodney Would it help if I said I was sorry?

Del No it would not!

Trigger Talking of weddings, that reminds me. Lisa has invited you to hers.

Del Well that's all I need innit, eh? That's another trip down to bleedin' Hampshire . . .

Rodney Lisa's getting married?

Trigger Yeah, in a couple of months, that's what she came up for – to buy herself a wedding dress in Oxford Street.

Del This is all a bit sudden innit?

Trigger No. She's been engaged for over a year – some geezer called Andy.

Mike That's a bit of good news Trigger! 'Ere, I'll tell you what I'll do, I'll open the pub and we'll have a little celebration drink.

Trigger Yeah nice one Mike. You coming Albert?

Albert Yeah I'll be there son.

Mike I suppose you two will be joining us?

Albert So she was engaged all the time! What a couple of wallies!

DEAR CHIEF,
    CONTRARY TO POPULAR BELIEF, TROTTER INDEPENDENT TRADING HAVE NO WAY BEEN INVOLVED, OR HAVE KNOWLEDGE OF, THE SALES OF ONE-LEGGED TURKEYS, NUCLEAR FALLOUT SHELTERS, YAPPING TOY DOGS, LEAD ROOFING, THE INSTANT MOTORWAY MADNESS ROCKET CAR, PAINTING TOMBSTONES OR HAVE WE HAD ANY BUSINESS IN THE CHANDELIER CLEANING INDUSTRY.
        LOVELY - JUBBLY
    DEL & RODNEY TROTTER

STAMP IN POST

CHIEF OF POLICE
'THE NICK'
PECKHAM HIGH ST
PECKHAM
LONDON SE15

P.S IF ANY INVOLVEMENT IS LINKED TO T.I.T, IT WAS PROBABLY UNCLE ALBERT

Video Nasty

THE NAG'S HEAD

Mickey Pearce is at the bar with Amanda. Boycie and Trigger are at the table playing poker.

Trigger What's the matter with you Boycie? You don't seem your old self tonight. You ain't cheated once.

Boycie No, sorry Trigger, I'm just a bit down, that's all. I mean, you don't know what it's like to have a wife who cannot have children. I've tried to console her. I've said 'Marlene, God didn't mean you to have kids, so shut up about it.' Doesn't seem to help.

Trigger I'd like to be someone's dad.

Boycie We're down for another bloody going over at the hospital next week. I mean, embarrassing ain't the word. I'm sure they do half those tests just for a giggle. I mean, she's the one with the problem, why have I gotta go?

Trigger I never knew who my dad was.

Mike I heard your mum weren't that sure.

Trigger You're out of order Mike. She knew who my dad was . . . roughly.

Boycie Now, come off it Trigger. I seen your birth certificate at school! What did your mum put down under father's name?

Trigger . . . Long time ago weren't it?

Boycie What did she put down under father's name?

Trigger 'Some Soldiers!' Well maybe that's where I get my military bearing from!

Boycie *(Hands him his glass)* Oh yeah? Well go'n do a counter-attack then! Where's Del Boy tonight then?

Mike He's gone to the Zoo.

Boycie He's gone to the . . .

Mike Don't ask.

Amanda Right then, I'm off now Mickey.

Mickey *(Produces a wad of notes)* Yeah, I'll see yer later Amanda. Here doll, treat yourself to a chinky, yeah.

Amanda Cor, cheers Mick. I'll give you a bell in the week.

Mike Seems like a nice girl Mickey!

Mickey Yeah well! You know how it is Mike, every so often a person fancies a bit of rough!

Mike And she picked you?

Mickey Oh that's a joke innit? I remember you said something funny a couple of years ago!

Rodney enters carrying a large case.

Rodney Alright Mick?

Mickey Alright Rodney, what you having?

Rodney Oh, um, 'alf a lager please, ta.

Mickey 'Ere y'are Mike, make that a big pint!

Rodney Oi, oi, what you been up to then?

Mickey I'm working for Boycie ain't I! Delivering, picking up. He's in the video game in a big way. Pirates, naughties, all that! And it's cash in hand, no questions, sweet as a nut! *(Indicates case)* Where you been, out on the knocker?

Rodney No, I've just come back from me evening class ain't I? Remember I told you we'd applied for an Arts Council grant? We got it!

Mickey Never!

Rodney Yeah, straight up! Mr Stevens, right, he's head of our art group, got confirmation this morning. We have got £10,000 to make a local community film. *(Patting the case)* And we've got all the equipment, everything – and guess who's in charge of the project?

Mickey You're putting me on!

Rodney No, straight up, it's me. What I've got to do, you see, I've gotta come up with the idea and then delegate the various responsibilities to all the other students.

Mickey Yeah, well put me in won't you? I'm a member of your art class aren't I?

Rodney Oh come off it Mickey, you only came one night – and that's only cos I told you we had a nude model.

Mickey Yeah, well I thought it would be a bird. Anyway, you've gotta write it Rodney?

Rodney Yeah.

Mickey Well, you're a natural when it comes to the written word. I'll never forget that thing you wrote some years back. What was it called?

Rodney *The Indictment.*

Mickey That's it, *The Indictment*, yeah. That would have made a triffic book you know. Why didn't you send it to a publisher?

Rodney I'll be perfectly honest with you Mickey. I couldn't think of a single publisher who could understand what I was saying.

Mickey Yeah, it was a bit strange weren't it?

Del and Albert enter. They are covered in little bits of straw and hay.

Del Alright Rodders?

Trigger Hello Del, what you having?

Del What am I having? *(Indicating Albert)* A bleedin' hard time with this moaner, here.

Albert I shouldn't be humping bales of hay around at my time of life.

Trigger Bales of hay??

Del You see, Abdul's cousin's girlfriend's brother's mate's mate, right, he's a gamekeeper down at one of these private zoos! And Monkey Harris's sister's husband's first wife's stepfather, right, he works for an animal food company. So, put the two together and what you got – a nice little earner.

Mike (Indicating Albert's beard) Don't wanna worry you but I think you've got something nesting in there, old son.

Albert Up yer shirt! (Calls) Oi Rodney!

Rodney (To Mickey) Hang on. I'll see you in a minute.

Albert While you've been poncing around at yer soppy art class I've had to unload two tons of hay!

Rodney Oh, poncing around, is that what you call it? Well, for your information, this evening I was commissioned to make a film!

Trigger Leave off Dave, I wouldn't leave you to make a jelly!

Boycie I have heard rumours Mickey Mouse wears a Rodney Trotter wristwatch!

Rodney It's true.

Del I love it, Boycie.

Rodney I'm telling you!! I've got all the equipment, and everything! I'm writing it and . . . and Mickey Pearce is directing!

Del You what . . . Mickey Pearce directing. He couldn't direct a sea gull to the coast him.

Rodney He's got experience in films!

Del What, that Saturday-morning job at the photographic counter at Boots? Leave it out Rodney. Anyway, you couldn't write a film script. I mean, what was that book that you wrote, what was it called The Indikment, I mean that never got published did it, eh?

Rodney No, 'cos you chucked it down the bloody chute!

Del Yes that's right, because I didn't want to see you disappointed! It was a bloody stupid story – no murders in it or nothing!

Rodney It was an indictment of a failing system weren't it? Alright, it was a first effort so it probably didn't have the same social impact as, say, Cathy Come Home!

Del It didn't have the same social impact as Lassie Come Home!!

Mike This film you're making Rodney – anyone in it we know?

Del (Pointing to Mickey and a group of girls) I tell you what, all them birds are in it for a start, look.

Albert That's a shrewd move on your part Rodney. You're the writer, Mickey's the director. So he gets the casting couch and you get the Biro!

THE TROTTERS' LOUNGE.

Rodney is seated at the table with a notepad and a pen. Rodney gets sudden inspiration, goes to write, then returns to his original position. Del enters from the hall carrying a large package wrapped in brown paper.

Del 'Ey up there, here you are Oscar, mind out, quick – I've got a present for you. There y'are.

Rodney What is it?

Del Close your eyes.

Rodney Oh come on Del!

Del Now, come on, close yer eyes!

Rodney (Closes his eyes) I bet Tom Stoppard don't have to put up with all this!

Del places package on the table and removes the wrapping to reveal a very old, slightly battered typewriter.

Del Alright, come on then open 'em. Well? There you are.

Rodney Yeah . . . er . . . it's er . . . it's a typewriter, innit?

Del You see that Albert, he recognised it straight away, that's the author in him! Well, come on Rodney, come on, let's get going boy. You'll soon have that old screenplay knocked out now won't you my son? Go on, there.

Rodney It's er . . . it's old isn't it?

Albert They made stuff to last in them days. That is quality Rodney. Look at that crest, by royal appointment.

Rodney Oh yeah . . . Victoria Regina!

Del Well go'n.

Rodney What?

Del Well go on, try it.

Rodney (Hits a key and checks paper) It's very faint Del, innit?

Del Well you gotta hit it harder than that Rodney – have another go.

Rodney (Hits hey harder) It's still faint Del.

Del Well, you've gotta give it a good whack haven't ya. Here look, (Gives key an almighty thump) I'll tell ya – look. There y'are, there y'are, that's a bit better, look.

Rodney Yeah that's great, thanks a lot.

Del Away you go then.

Rodney Away I go what?

Del Well, you know, you know, start the old typing.

Albert Yeah, be creative!

Video Nasty

Rodney Be creat . . . I can't just be creative at the drop of a hat can I? There are certain things a writer needs before he can actually start writing. Like a story!

Albert You ain't even got a story??

Rodney Not exactly, I've only been trying for a few days, ain't I!

Del Listen, I've had an idea for a story and it's a bloody good 'un an' all! D'you wanna hear it?

Rodney No . . . Not really Del.

Albert Oh that's charming innit? You buy him a brand-new typewriter *and* come up with a story for him, and what thanks d'you get?

Del I'll tell you what thanks I get Albert, no sodding thanks, that's the thanks I get!

Rodney Alright, tell us yer story then!

Del No, no, don't bother yourself Rodney, please. I was only tryin' help you!

Rodney Oh now, come on, honestly Del, seriously, I'd like to hear your story . . . Well, I need a bit of help, don't I?

Del Right, okay, now this is a *Jaws*-type story.

Rodney *Jaws*?? *Jaws* has been done though.

Del I know it's been done! But this is different. It's called . . . *There's a Rhino Loose in the City!*

Rodney . . . *(Stares at Del increduously)* There's a Rhi . . . There's a Rhino Loose In . . . A rhino? As in rhinoceros??

Del That's right. *There's a Rhino Loose in the City!*

Albert What's it about Del?

Del Well, it's about this rhinoceros right, escapes from a zoo and it heads straight for London! And after two or three days they find like all these dead bodies lying about and no-one knows who's done it! So, they get hold of this private detective, you know, like a sort of Charlton Heston type geezer to try and solve the crime. Now the zoo keeper happens to be a very attractive woman. Before you know where you are, old Charlton is giving the sort what for, so that's yer romantic interest!

Rodney A rhinoceros??

Del Yeah! But they don't know it's missing!

Rodney But how can you *not* know Del?? If you've got a rhinoceros right and one day it ain't there – well, you tend to know it's missing!!

Del Don't be a plonker all yer life Rodney. She ain't got one rhinoceros, she probably had two or three rhinoceroses!

Albert And how's he escape?

Rodney Squeezed through the bars most probably!

Del Now don't you start getting saucy with me Rodney, I'm only trying to help you.

Rodney I don't believe this! Nobody knows it's escaped? What about the eight million people living in London? Don't none of them spot it?

Del Yes! But the ones who spot it – they're the ones who get trampled to death!

Rodney And what about all the others? The people in offices, the people in cafes, the people sitting on top of buses! It's a rhino Del.

Del He only comes out at night!

Albert What is it, a vampire rhino?

Del No it is not a vampire rhino. That is stupid that is, innit eh?

Albert And where does he live during the day?

Del In a lock-up garage in a back street!

Rodney What, he's leasing it is he?

Del He's not leasing it. It's a disused garage in a back street where no one ever goes! The detective does find it, only it's at night!

Albert And the rhino's gone out?

Del That's right see, so you see the old detective is nowhere near solving the mystery. You see what it is Rodney, it is not only a love story! It's an whodunit!

Rodney An whodunit! What do you mean an whodunit? We know who-dun-it! The rhino done it!

Del Yes, I know that, we – *we* the audience know that, but they don't know – the actors do they?

Rodney This is something! A rhinoceros has escaped from a zoo! There are 300 dead bodies covered in rhinoceros footprints! There's a lock-up garage two and 'arf foot deep in rhinoceros crap and Charlton Heston suspects the butler!!

Del I do admit there are one or two teething snags! But it's got all the essential qualities of a hit hasn't it. I mean, it's got suspense, lots of killings and a bit of humpty dumpty! I mean, look, this is a disaster movie!

Rodney Disaster? It's a calamity Del!

Albert Why is he killing people?

Del Well, what d'you want him to be a social worker? Well, he's a man-eater ain't he?

Rodney No, no, rhinoceroses aren't carnivorous! They're vegetarians!

Del Alright, so we elbow the lock-up garage and we make him hide in the back of an health food shop!

Rodney And he wouldn't head for the city neither.

Albert But he's gotta head for the city so he can kill lots of people!

Del Yeah that's right!

Rodney No, his natural habitat would be open country.

Del Alright, so what are you suggesting? We call the film *There's a Rhino Loose Somewhere Out in the Sticks Where No Sod Lives*??

Albert You don't call the likes of Charlton Heston in 'cos something's eating carrots! I think it's a good idea Del.

Del Thank you very much Albert.

Rodney Yeah, well I'll pass!

Del Alright, alright, I just wanted to put an idea in your head that was all. I wish it'd been a bleedin' bullet now!

Rodney Del, I've only got a small budget, ain't I?

Del But that's the beauty of it Rodney. I know where's there's a rhinoceros going cheap!

CHINESE TAKE-AWAY.

Albert and Rodney are standing at the counter. Del is on the pay-phone.

Del Yeah, alright Chas, I'll knock out that stuff for you tomorrow night. Eh? Um, not sure if we'll be wanting the rhino now.

Rodney We won't.

Del Alright, listen I'll give you a bell tomorrow Chas. Tata mate. *(To Chinese owner)* Oi Tony, come on, where's that grub – we've been waiting 'alf hour. There's something I wanted to catch on the telly, the Epilogue.

Owner Yeah it coming, it coming. Wha' you order?

Del Look I told you, two chicken and rice and one Spanish omelette.

Owner Two chicken rice, one Spanich omerette.

Del Can't even speak the lingo can he? *(To Rodney)* Well, how are you getting on with your story then?

Rodney Well, I have the kernel of an idea! I'm just waiting for it to develop somewhat. It's what *writers* call the gestation period.

Albert And what do *you* call it?

Del Stop it, stop your winding up you.

Albert And where's your director then Rodney?

Rodney He is acquainting himself with the video camera and all equipment.

Del Yeah. He's down the Town Hall filming a wedding.

Rodney What d'you mean he's down the Town Hall filming a wedding?

Del Well, well you see what happened was, I went down the Town Hall and around a few churches taking notes of the banns. Then I contacted a few brides and asked them if they'd like their happiest day recorded on film for 50 quid a throw!

Rodney I don't believe you're doing this to me!

Del Well look Rodney, that Mickey Pearce has gotta practise with that camera ain't he? He's gotta work out how to focus it and all that. You know, why not earn while yer learn! That's what I say. Anyway, he nicks all the tapes from Boycie, don't he, eh?

Rodney But Del, this is an opportunity for me and all you're doing is making money out of it!

Del It'll be alright because he's only got five or six weddings to do, two or three christenings and he's finished.

Rodney But that camera is council property!

Albert Yeah so is the Town Hall.

Del Yeah see, there you go!

Rodney You're just abusing the trust shown in me, ain't yer.

Del Look, will you shut up you tart! Look, here is your share.

Rodney I don't want it.

Del Oh well, please yourself. It goes back in the . . .

Rodney Alright, just this once!

Del Don't do me no favours Rodney! Will ya, eh?

Rodney You've got a nerve . . .

Boycie and Marlene enter. At first they do not notice the Trotters.

Marlene Well, that's shut you up for a good while though innit Boycie!

Boycie I keep telling you Marlene, them doctors don't know everything! They're a bunch of chancers that's all. *(To owner)* Good afternoon, I phoned an order through earlier, Mr Boyce.

Owner Oh yes, I go see.

Boycie Thank you.

Marlene All them bloody tests I've had!

Boycie And what about all the bloody tests I've . . . *(Sees Trotters)* Oh good afternoon Derek. I didn't realise you and your family were dining out.

Del Oh yes, I like to treat 'em once in a while, keep the morale up. *(Slaps Marlene's bottom)* Hello darling, how are you? Hey, is my little godson in there yet?

Marlene No he ain't! And he ain't likely to be with him.around!

Boycie Marlene!

Marlene Marlene bloody nuffing! All these years you've said it was my fault we couldn't have kids! They've just discovered there's nothing wrong with me – it's him.

Boycie Ain't it bleedin' fair eh??

Del What's the matter then Boycie? You ain't a noofter are you?

Boycie See what you've started now Marlene!

Video Nasty

Even the doctors ain't allowed to discuss this outside the confines of the laboratory. And you're holding a public debate in a Chinese take-away.

Marlene He's got what doctors call a low count.

Rodney Don't wanna buy a calculator do you Boyce?

Albert What's it mean?

Boycie Nothing!

Marlene It means he's been firing more blanks than the Territorials!

Boycie You happy now Marlene?
The owner exits from the kitchen with a plastic bag.

Owner Mr Boyce, prawn balls?

Boycie Yes thank . . . *(Looks round at everyone, daring them to smirk)* Yes, thank you very much.

Marlene It's our anniversary next Friday. 20 years, Gawd, that's something to celebrate innit? Anyway, we've hired the pub and you're all invited.

Del Oh lovely, we'll be there sweetheart.

Boycie Yeah, well come along then Marlene.

Marlene Yeah alright, oh Rodney is that right you're making a film?

Rodney Yeah.

Marlene You know I used to act a bit when I was younger. Actually someone once said that I had a promising career in films.

Boycie Yeah, then talkies come along and ruined it! Let's go Marlene!

Del Tara Marlene. Bye bye Boycie. *(They exit)* What about that then? Old Boycie's a Jaffa.

Rodney A Jaffa?

Del Yeah, you know, seedless!

Rodney I could use Boycie's problem as a theme for my film couldn't I. Because that hospital they attend, that's one of the leading centres for genetic research, artificial insemination and all that. That's quite interesting?

Del Oh yeah, on the edge of yer seat stuff that – yeah. Have you thought any more about the rhino story?

Rodney Del, I am not doing a film about a blood-sucking rhinoceros and a divvy detective! No, that hospital interests me though.

Albert I don't reckon they should be allowed to do it – freezing things and all that. They're messing around with nature.

Rodney No, they are not messing around with nature are they? They're assisting nature! See, 'cos they only freeze the ova, or eggs, right, until they are ready to be fertilised, right, and then they get the egg and well they sort of mix . . .

There's this geezer . . .

Albert Oi, oi, I've ordered an omelette 'ere.

Del Yeah, yeah. Do you know what I reckon, in a few years' time, young married couples wanting to start a family, they won't go to the doctors, they'll nip down the road to Bejams!

THE TROTTERS' LOUNGE.
Rodney is at the typewriter. He has a large pile of fresh writing paper and a tiny pile of finished pages. He starts whacking at the keys. Del enters from the bedroom area.

Del Everything alright Rodney?

Rodney No, the T and the A are missing.

Del Well it's no problem is it?

Rodney Well it is if you wanna write words like 'at'!

Del You'll find a way round it. I've got faith in you, I really have. Anyway, how are you coming on? Can I have a read, or something?

Rodney No you can't! It's not finished yet!

Del Oh alright. What's this, just a minute. *(Indicating a page)* What's this red mark up here, is that something technical is it?

Rodney No, one of my fingers started bleeding!

Del Never mind, you'll be alright. Hey! I tell you what, your movie ain't 'alf caused a stir round here! You'd be surprised how many actors and actresses live locally. I don't mean – you know, like professionals, I mean a lot of new, fresh, untapped talent! Well, I made a list for yer, there you are. *(Hands him list)*

Rodney *(Rodney studies it, turns to the second page)* You're not suggesting I use all these people in my film?

Del Just extras Rodney, just extras. Don't mind the quantity think about the quality!

Rodney I'm thinking about the money Del!

Del I did say, well a tenner a day.

Rodney I can't afford to pay 'em a tenner a day!

Del No, they pay *us* a tenner a day.

Rodney You're just exploiting people again ain't yer?

Del No I am not Rodney. I've given 'em your word now.

Rodney Well you had no right to!

Del Alright here's your share. There you go, look. *(Lays money on the table)*

Rodney And they're just extras?

Del That's all – just extras. By the way, there's a list here of local businesses you might like to mention. *(Hands him another list)*

Rodney *(Reads list)* The Seventh Heaven Sauna Parlour??

Del Yeah, just a mention, something like 'The

nice relaxing atmosphere, nice and friendly service.' You know what I mean? Oh, is the undertaker's down there?

Rodney No.

Del Oh well bear it in mind, will yer?

Rodney Del, why are you doing this to me? I had high hopes when I started this project! Mr Stevens said if it was good enough he'd show it at the National Film Theatre.

Del What's the matter with you, you're earning ain't yer? Look, listen I've gotta shoot, I've gotta another client to meet. It might mean another booking . . . 'Ere, talking about that . . . what is a 'natural birth'? Never mind – I'll find out myself. Oi Albert, Albert, d'you wanna lift?

Albert Yeah, I'll be with you in a minute son.

Del Well come on, come on shift yourself I ain't got all night you know. See you later.

Del exits to the hall. As he opens the front door, Mickey arrives with the camera on his shoulder.

Mickey Smile, you're on *Candid Camera*.

Del Alright, listen, I might have another booking for you later on. I'll bell you, alright. *(Exits)*

Mickey Smart. *(He enters the lounge)* Alright Rodney?

Rodney No it's not alright! This is getting out of hand! *(Hands him cast list)* Look!

Mickey What is it, a petition?

Rodney No, that's our cast list! *(Hands him another list)* And this is a list of all the shops and businesses we've gotta advertise.

Mickey *(Reading)* He forgot the undertaker's!

Rodney You mean you knew about it?

Mickey Well it's good business Rodney!

Albert Right, I'm off out now Rodney. *(Doorbell rings)* I'll get it.

Rodney Look it's gotta stop Mickey!

Amanda enters, heavily made-up.

Rodney We're promoting shops and businesses, ain't we? We've got more extras than *Ben Hur* there.

Mickey Watcha babe. This is Amanda.

Rodney It's a what?

Mickey Amanda. I'm taking her out for a drink tonight so I asked her round here so you could make her a nice cup of coffee. Alright Rodney.

Rodney Yeah, okay. *(Exits to kitchen)*

Amanda removes her coat to reveal a very short nurses uniform, black stockings and suspenders. Rodney appears at the kitchen door.

D'you take sugar?

Amanda Two please.

Rodney exits. Two seconds later he enters

the room.

Rodney Mickey, could I have a moment of your time please.

Mickey What's up?

Rodney Why is she wearing a nurse's uniform?

Mickey She's just come off duty!

Rodney Oh yeah. You must think I've just come off a banana boat! What are yer playing at??

Mickey Look, I've been delivering these films for Boycie ain't I, so I know where I can sell 'em. We've got all this equipment, why waste it? We can cut the middle-man out!

Rodney I'd like to cut your liver out. You are not making any films in this flat. Understand? Both of you??

Mickey Alright Rodney, no need to get out yer pram about it.

Rodney Sit down. I'll make you a coffee then you can both hit the road.

Exits.

KITCHEN.

Rodney What's happening? What the bloody hell's happening? I've got a cast of thousands, I've got more advertising than Pearl and Dean and now Mickey wants to make *Emmanuelle in Peckham*. Oh this is a bloody nightmare . . . Now Rodney, Rodney . . . Calm down . . . Deep breaths . . . Nice 'n' easy does it . . .

Mickey *(OOV)* *Night Nurse* Take One.

Rodney *Night Nurse* Take One??

LOUNGE.

Mickey is filming. Amanda's hand drops the bra.

Mickey That's the way baby. Let it slip to the ground.

Rodney Mickey . . . You better not be doing . . . *(Sees Amanda)* Oh no Mickey. No, get her to put 'em back! Oh bloody hell!

THE NAG'S HEAD.

Mickey is still filming.

Mickey Right, hold 'em up. That's it. Move 'em about a bit.

Del, Rodney, Albert, Boycie, Marlene, Trigger, Mike, the vicar and other guests are holding their glasses up in a toast.

Marlene Oh hurry up Mickey love. Boycie, he don't like smiling for too long.

Mickey Okay everybody, that's a wrap.

Boycie I wasn't ready for that one.

Del Happy anniversary.

Albert Happy anniversary dear.

Mickey Oi, vicar get a move on. We've got that

Video Nasty

christening to do in 20 minutes.

Vicar Yes, I'll be with you in a moment Mickey.

Mickey Alright I'll wait for you down the church then. Alright Rodney?

Rodney Shut up!

Mickey Please yerself! *(Exits)*

Del Here we go Rodney, my son, that's your share, alright?

Rodney I don't like this Del, you know I don't like this. Ta.

Mike Here Del, we're slipping out to the back room. *(Winks)* Alright?

Del Right, good Mike, yeah.

Mike Hi Rodney.

Rodney Alright Mike.

Mike *(Bogart impression)* Of all the bars in all the world and you had to walk into mine.

Rodney You in my film as well Mike are yer?

Mike Yeah, just a little cameo role son. I'll see you in a minute.

Del Come on Rodney. Come on Albert.

Rodney Alright.

Vicar Well it all seems to be going rather well.

Rodney Oh yeah, it's very nice innit vicar?

Vicar I married the happy couple all those years ago. Of course, I had hoped by now that the Good Lord would have blessed their union with an offspring or two. But if it's not to be . . .

Rodney Well I heard that because of the precarious state of the world, Boycie and Marlene had decided against starting a family.

Vicar Oh really? I heard that Boycie was a Jaffa. Tell me, is it true that you're making a film Rodney?

Rodney Oh yeah. We got an Arts Council grant.

Vicar I er . . . I was talking with Derek earlier . . .

Rodney I'll give you a bell when we start shooting vicar.

Vicar Thank you my boy.

BACK ROOM OF THE PUB.

Trigger draws the curtains. Boycie puts a video tape into the recorder. Rodney enters.

Del Alright – everyone got a drink have they?

Rodney Even the vicar's in on it Del.

Del What you want to drink?

Rodney Give us a beer.

Del Here. Go on then my son.

Trigger Watch Dave.

Rodney Alright Trigger.

Trigger You dirty rat!

Rodney Oh this is getting bloody stupid.

Boycie Alright gentlemen, would you like to settle down. If you'd like to take your seats.

Del Come on, here we go.

Boycie The Boyce Video and Leisure Arts Company is proud to present the British Premiere of *Night Nurse* from the novel by Enid Blyton.

Mike Ooh, that was a bit unexpected innit?

Del Here look at that one. I've got no sympathy for her, look.

Mike No, no, Del that's gotta be special effects.

Del No that's real. No stop – it's starting proper now . . .

The picture shows a flat.

Boycie Where do they get these grotty flats to film in?

Mike 'Ere I've seen that bird before somewhere. *On screen Amanda is lying on the Trotter's couch. She wakes, stands and stretches. She begins unbuttoning her blouse. Rodney stands and heads for the door.*

Del Go on girl, let's have a look. 'Oh dear, I am tired I've just come back from nursing.'

Boycie One of those would do me a week.

Del Hello, who's got her ear muffs off now. . . . *On the screen Rodney appears at the kitchen door as Amanda removes her bra.*

Del *(Screams)* Rodney!

THE TROTTERS' LOUNGE.

Rodney *(Pinned against the wall by Del)* It was nothing to do with me Del. It was a Mickey Pearce production!

Del Mickey Pearce. You wait till I get my hands on him. I'm gonna shove that camera 'alf a mile up his nostril! Rodney, didn't you have any idea what you were getting yourself into?

Rodney I thought Boycie wouldn't be too pleased you know, someone muscling in on his business and that.

Del God. Boycie. Boycie's not the one that worries me. It's his partners that are giving me grief. D'you know who's backing him in this, only the Driscoll Brothers that's all. Have you heard of 'em?

Rodney No.

Del No. Well let's hope they haven't heard of you. Now I'm gonna see if I can save your knees and make sure they stay in the same place. *(Produces the tape)* Now I'm stuffing this down the khazi, you stay there.

Rodney Del, I promise nothing like this will ever happen again – I promise. *(Del exits, Mickey enters)*

Mickey Hello Rodney? Alright for a cup of coffee??

Rodney Oh yes, do come in Mickey.

Mickey I bought a few friends with me. *Amanda, another girl and a big bloke enter.*

Rodney Oh yes.

Del *(Enters)* Pearcie! I want a ruddy word with you. You wait. *(They run out, Del chases)*

Rodney *(Phone rings. Rodney answers.)* Hello? Oh Mr Stevens, hi! Yeah, yeah and have you had a chance to read it? Great. Well what do you think? And please be truthfully blunt with me. Okay, yes, ah ha! Yes well that's truthfully blunt innit Mr Stevens. Yes, there are a lot of charac-ters in it, yes, but all vital to the theme I thought. Yes, well, I actually wanted to write a film that not only dealt with the contemporary issues but also challenged some of the more widely held beliefs of modern youth! No, that is no problem because my brother knows where he can get us a rhino, yeah!

Dockside Secondary Modern

Report for SPRING JAN 17th – APRIL 20th Term 19 62

Name DEREK TROTTER Form V

Subject	Exam marks %	Master's Comments
French	70	Derek has a firm grasp of the basics but is prone to use phrases at completely the wrong moment and believes he is much better at the language than he actually is. Once he realises there is more to learning French than attracting members of the opposite sex with phrases such as Je suis frontieres, and remembers Bonjour means hello and not goodbye he has the ability to become quite fluent.
English	60	Derek shows a natural talent for drama, but will insist on calling Shakespeare ol' Billy Shakespeare, that Shaw is a brand of lemonade and that poetry has to rhyme. His compositions show imagination and a colourful turn of phrase but he has the tendency to use the wrong word. For example people who can use both hands are ambidextrous not ambiguous and it is sacrificial, not artificial lambs that we metaphorically send to the slaughter
History	52	Derek has an enthusiastic approach to History but does tend to get dates and events confused. It was not Stan Laurel who said 'Kiss me, Hardy' but Admiral Nelson and there was slightly more to Henry VIII's beheading of his wives than the fact he was "getting a bit of grief from the enemy" to use Derek's words. Probably can't do better.
Maths	55	DEREK HAS A NOVEL APPROACH TO MATHS, BELIEVING THAT TO SPLIT SOMETHING FIFTY-FIFTY IS TO TAKE MORE FOR HIMSELF RATHER THAN SIMPLY HALVE IT. HE HAS, THOUGH, A NATURAL HEAD FOR FIGURES BUT HIS SUMS LEAVE A LOT TO BE DESIRED. HIS COPYBOOK WAS BLOTTED WHEN HE SOLD YOUNG ROY SLATERS COMPASS AND PROTRACTOR FOR TEN SHILLINGS TO YOUNG TRIGGER.
Economics	92	DEREK HAS AN EXCELLENT GRASP OF THE VALUE OF MONEY AND UNDERSTANDS CLEARLY THE INTRICACIES OF THE BUSINESS WORLD. HE APPEARS TO FOLLOW THE RULES OF SUPPLY AND DEMAND CLEARLY AND HIS EARS PRICK UP WHENEVER WE DISCUSS PROFIT MARGINS AND NET GAINS. HE AND YOUNG BOYCE OFTEN HAVE HEATED DEBATES ABOUT WHAT CONSTITUTES GOOD BUSINESS, THOUGH THEIR SEVEN HOUR POKER GAME AND THE BOOK THEY OPENED ON THE GIRL'S LONG JUMP ON SCHOOL SPORTS DAY WERE UNNECESSARY. I HAVE A FEELING THAT WITH THE RIGHT BACKING DEREK COULD ONE DAY BE THE MILLIONAIRE HE SO OBVIOUSLY DESPERATELY WANTS TO BE.
Science	5	Derek has little or no interest in Science beyond the rudiments of Physical Biology. He caused a great deal of upset with his crass remark about the female form and accusing young Boyce of 'firing blanks', as he put it. Physics is a mystery to him, show none more; clearly than in his insistence that Louise Pasteur owned a dairy. The less said about this the better!
Physical Education	8	DEREK HAS NO APTITUDE FOR SPORT WHATSOEVER! THIS MAY HAVE SOMETHING TO DO WITH THE CIGARS HE HAS BEEN FOUND SMOKING BEHIND THE BIKE SHEDS. HE CAN HOWEVER RUN VERY SWIFTLY, PARTICULARLY WHEN HE SENSES DANGER!
Art	15	DEREK WAS PUT IN DETENTION FOR THE TIME HE BROUGHT IN A COPY OF THE MONA LISA AND TRIED TO HAND IT IN AS HIS FIRST ASSIGNMENT, CLAIMING IT WAS A PORTRAIT OF HIS GIRLFRIEND. HE RECKONS VAN GOGH CHOPPED OFF HIS EAR UNDER DOCTOR'S ORDERS AND THAT MING WAS A PERSON, NOT A DYNASTY. HE IS ON THE WAY TO TURNING IGNORANCE INTO AN ART FORM.

Head Master's Comments   This makes poor reading. There is a lot here for Derek to address if he ever wishes to make something of himself. He can make a start by ceasing his trading in the playground, stop smoking cigars furtively and referring to members of the opposite sex as 'sorts'. If he refuses to change his ways he will never ever realise his dream of getting out of his council flat in Peckham and could well end up selling goods of low quality from a suitcase in the market. It is in his hands.

Paul Oggon Head Master

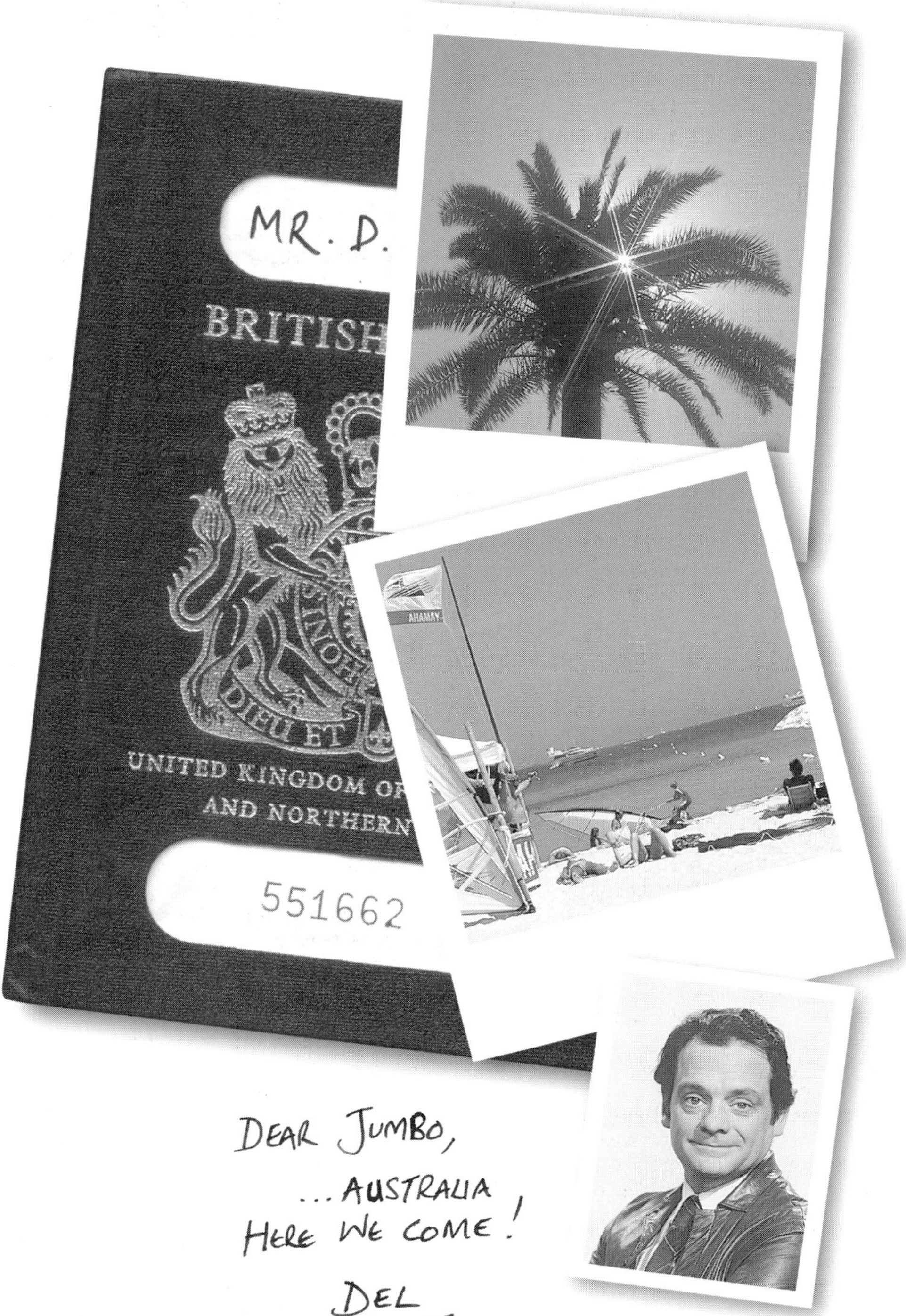

MR. D.

BRITISH

UNITED KINGDOM OF
AND NORTHERN

551662

DEAR JUMBO,
...AUSTRALIA
HERE WE COME!

DEL

Who Wants to be a Millionaire?

THE NAG'S HEAD.

Albert is playing the piano. Boycie is at the counter, fawning over and desperately trying to impress Jumbo Mills. Jumbo is one of the old gang and was once Del's partner. He emigrated to Australia in 1967 where he became a successful businessman. His main ability is a shrewd eye for investment. His great failing is in the field of public relations – he gets up every sod's nose. He is rather flash and blunt to the point of being considered big-mouthed. He wears clothes that show off his tan and as much gold as Del. He also wears a wig.

Boycie Ah yes, we'll have two sirloin steaks, thank you Michael.

Jumbo Make 'em big 'uns mate.

Boycie Yes that's right, as Jumbo says, make 'em big 'uns. Sauté potatoes, a selection of greens and the whole thing put on my account will you Michael.

Mike What account?

Boycie Ha, ha, what account! See what I mean Jumbo, the old place hasn't lost its sense of humour!

Jumbo Well, I wouldn't laugh if a barman made a berk of me.

Mike Barman! Now just you listen here pal!

Boycie Michael, Jumbo did not mean any offence. Shall we sit down over here?

Jumbo Hey mate. *(To Albert)* Did you know this pub hasn't got a music licence? Still, as long as it's him playing there's no problem, hey?

Albert Who's the big-mouth Aussie, Mike?

Mike Oh him, he's no Australian, he used to be a local lad then he emigrated.

Albert That was a bit of luck weren't it? So what's he doing back?

Mike Buying some cars off Boycie or something.
Del enters.

Del *(To Albert)* Oi, there you are, you mucky old sod. Listen, have you seen the state of my Persian rug back at the flat? You run the old J Edgar over it soon as you get back. Cor blimey, should see it. Give me, giss a Manhattan Mike, small rum for him. Spit in the rum.

Albert Where's Rodney?

Del Rodney, I left him down clearing up the market.

Albert 'Ere, some mush just had a go at me.

Del Had a go at you? Who had a go at you, where?

Albert *(Indicating Jumbo)* Him! Took the mickey out of my piano playing.

Del Well, you ought to be used to that now Albert. I'll sort him out, you stay here. I'll sort you out an' all – later. Right 'ere, excuse me pal – I don't believe it! I don't believe it! *(Moves to table)* Jumbo bloody Mills! Who let you back in the country?

Jumbo Oh, look at this will yer! Talk about a bad penny. Del Boy, how are you mate?
They are genuinely pleased to see each other.

Del Alright mate, alright my son. You are looking double well.

Jumbo That's 'cos I live in a healthy country. No fog or frost in Oz mate.

Del It's great, it suits you, it suits you. Look at all that! So tell me, what you doing back home, eh?
Sits at table to Boycie's chagrin.

Boycie Derek, Jumbo and I are having a business meeting. It's all rather confidential.

Jumbo I've got no secrets from Del. Me and him were partners back in the Sixties.

Del That's right, that's right. We used to have a fish stall right outside the pub 'ere, didn't we?

Boycie Yes, I remember.

Del Cor, those were the days, eh. Those were the days. So how long you back home for anyway?

Jumbo Well, just a week or so. In fact, I'm just here to finalise a deal with Boycie, take in a bit of sightseeing. I wish to God I hadn't bothered. This country's become a cesspit Del.

Boycie You're right there Jumbo.

Del *(Patriotic)* A cesspitt. What do you mean, cesspit?

Jumbo You could find cleaner places in an Abbo's armpit.
Boycie laughs with him. Del has a crooked, vengeful grin.

Del I tell you what though Jumbo. You can't tell that that's a wig.

Jumbo *(Stops laughing)* That's because it's not a wig.

Del Oh, do me a favour. You used to have curly hair, come on that's a syrup innit?

Boycie Course it ain't a syrup.

Del Look, I've got a tenner here that says that is a syrup.

Boycie I have got a tenner here that says it ain't.
Del Alright then, cover that Boycie. Now listen, I tell you why I know that . . . *(Indicates bar)* Is that your change over there? *(Jumbo turns and Del snatches the wig from his head)* Here we go. *(Picks up the money)* Thank you very much.
Jumbo What the flamin' hell d'you think you're playing at?
Boycie I don't believe you sometimes Del, here am I tryin' to clinch a business deal and you've just nicked my client's wig.
Del Well it was for a bet! You do understand don't you Jumbo?
Jumbo No I bloody well don't! *(Has difficulty putting the wig back on straight. He gives up and puts it in his pocket)* Jeez. You always did like embarrassing me didn't you? Look chaps, this is just a temporary condition. My doctors have assured me that me own hair will grown back – well – eventually.
Mike arrives at the table.
Mike Here you are gents. *(To Boycie)* Where's the loud-mouthed Aussie gone?
Jumbo Just put the stuff on the table and leave us alone mate.
Mike Now just a minute pal.
Del Mike, Mike, leave it, leave now, go on, it's alright. *(To Jumbo)* He's a nice bloke, he really is a nice bloke.
Jumbo Oh yeah, a typical Brit, the only thing that works is the mouth!
Boycie Del, I'm trying to have a business meeting, do you mind.
Del Alright. You enjoy your nosh, I'll see you later.
Jumbo Yeah, I've gotta talk to you Del.
Del Alright then, any time. Sorry. They want you over there Boyce. *(Boycie looks away and Del pinches a chip)* See you. *(He moves to the bar)*
Boycie Oi!
Albert He seems a nasty bit of work.
Del Who, Jumbo? Na, that's just the way he is, that's all. He's got a heart of gold, that bloke. His trouble is that his mouth is always three seconds ahead of his brain. But, I tell you what, I tell you what, he is a diamond that bloke. He's never cheated me. He's as straight as a die. A real diamond.
Boycie The import and export licences will be looked after by my people, they should only take a couple of weeks.
Jumbo Yeah, yeah, look Boycie I'm sorry, but I can't concentrate without the toop. I feel naked. I'll pop out to the gents and put it back.
Boycie Oh course Jumbo, I fully understand.

Rodney enters.
Rodney Oi, I want a word with you. *(He passes Jumbo and stops)* What's the idea . . .
Del Oi Jumbo, no wait a minute. Listen, I remember that horrible little kid brother of mine? One with the funny hair cut, all snot and Marmite.
Jumbo Yeah, I remember. It's him innit? You ain't changed a bit Rodney.
Del This is Jumbo Mills, remember him?
Rodney Na.
Del Na, of course you wouldn't, you were only a little sprog when he emigrated to Australia. Done very well for himself, ain't he, eh? Look.
Jumbo You can say that again mate. The best thing I ever did was getting out of this dump. Now, of course, I'm a major shareholder in an office cleaning company. Got a chain of fast-food restaurants and I'm just going into the automobile trade. Last year, Del, I bought this apartment overlooking Sydney harbour. Half a million dollars. Architect-designed interior right down to the mirrored ceiling in the bedroom.
Del Mirrored ceiling!
Rodney Oh, kinky.
Jumbo No, no, it's purely decorative. I mean, I wouldn't use it for anything like . . . well, like that.
Albert Well, you wouldn't use it to comb your hair, would you.
Jumbo *(Offended)* You think I'm bald don't you?
Rodney Well, it had crossed my mind.
Jumbo Well, I'm not.
Albert Well, that's a hell of a parting you've got there son.
Jumbo What I mean is I am not naturally bald.
Rodney You mean you pay someone to do that?
Jumbo What I mean, Rodney, is that this is the result of a nervous disorder, and my doctors have assured me that me own hair will grow back at any time now.
Mike Trouble is that they told him that 15 years ago!
Del No, listen, he don't mean it. He's only winding you up.
Jumbo Alright Del, I'll see you about eight o'clock. *(Exits to toilet)*
Del Alright mate, see you later. Come on then Rodney, Albert, drink up we've got work to do. D'you clear up down the market?
Rodney Yes I did. That's what I wanna talk to you about. How long have I been a rubbish clearer? You never told me I got promoted. And

Who Wants to be a Millionaire?

that weren't even our rubbish, Del, that come off Harry Dando's fruit and veg stall.

Del I know it did, now listen Rodney. Harry's, well, an old man now, he's getting on, got arthritis and a touch of rheumatism. You know, if I can help somebody as I go along my way, my living will not have been in vain. That's my motto.

Rodney How much he pay you?

Del A fiver, so you want £2 then don't you?

Rodney No I don't. I want £2.50. *(Jumbo exits from the toilet.)* Oi, when that doctor said your hair could grow back anytime now, he weren't kidding was he.

INT. NAG'S HEAD. LATER THAT EVENING.

Del and Jumbo enter.

Del So anyway, listen, he said for a moment, 'There I thought you were 'hissing' my performance.'

Mike Hello Del.

Del Alright Mike. Listen, giss a banana daiguiri for us moi and Australian lager for Jumbo. Alright.

Jumbo Please.

Mike I only sell British lager, Del. Kronenbourg, Hofmeister, stuff like that.

Del Well, giss one of them then, that's alright, fine.

Jumbo So how's life been treating you Del?

Del I'm alright, not complaining, not complaining.

Jumbo I take it you never did become that millionaire you were always talking about?

Del Well, no, no, not yet. You know.

Jumbo 'This time next year I'll be a millionaire.' Do you realise they were the last words you said to me before I emigrated? Trouble is that was 1967!

Del Well, you know there's still time, still time. Thank you Michael. Thank you, cheers.

Jumbo D'you believe that Del? I mean, do you truly believe it?

Del Yeah, course I do, yeah.

Jumbo You should have come with me Del. You're wasted here. This country's finished, it's old – decrepit.

Del Yeah, alright, it's my country so stop having a pop at it will yer?

Jumbo The stench of defeat is everywhere.

Del Alright, so it's British stench and I happen to be proud of it. Alright?

Jumbo The old place has got no guts any more.

Del That's funny that is Jumbo, someone said that a while ago. A little jumped-up general in Buenos Aires. And if you're not careful you'll get what the Argies got, a good smack in the eye. Right!

Jumbo Now hold on, hold on. I didn't mean to offend you, I'm just tryin' to point out a few facts, that is all.

Del Alright mate, leave it at that then.

Jumbo D'you remember when our business broke up and I decided to emigrate? Well, if it hadn't 'ave been for you Del, I'd have gone to Australia potless. You gave me your last £200.

Del I told you to forget it, forget it, didn't I?

Jumbo Well I never did forget it mate. No, even when times were hard I used to lay in bed at night and think to myself 'One day I'm gonna pay Del back, with interest!' And now I am. I want us to reform our old partnership.

Del What, get another fish stall?

Jumbo No, no, no, no. You see, I'm starting up this business. I'm gonna import prestige European motors, like Rollers, Mercs, that kind of thing. I want you to come to Australia as my partner. I want you to front the business Del Boy, I want you to deal with the public, give 'em that old razzamatazz like you used to.

Del Australia?

Jumbo Well, I've got the money, I've got the site and thanks to my little deal with Boycie, I've got the motors. All I need is you.

Del Well, I dunno. Australia, it ain't 'alf a long way away off innit, eh?

Jumbo They'd love you over there, they've got no class.

Del What?

Jumbo No, what I mean is they've got no class structure like they have here in England. Over there it doesn't matter how you talk. You see, in Oz, a bloke's just a bloke.

Del Yeah but, cor blimey, it'll cost a fortune to get over there, won't it eh?

Jumbo I'm paying.

Del No, no, I couldn't, I ain't got a trade or nothing. You know, they wouldn't accept me, would they?

Jumbo You've got better than that. You've got a full partnership in a growing company. Derek, this time next year you will be that millionaire!

Del No, no, you know, I've got family ties and all that ain't I?

Jumbo Well bring 'em with you. Put young Rodney on the pay roll.

Del Well, he has got two GCEs.

Jumbo That doesn't matter, we'll find something for him to do.

Del Well, no, no Jumbo. You gotta remember we didn't 'alf used to row a lot didn't we?

325

Jumbo So we'll still row. Our biggest argument will be who's got the most millions. *(Spits on palm of his hand and holds it out for Del to smack)* So what do you say Del Boy, are we gonna do it or ain't we?

Del Alright, put it there, you old bastard, you're in for a fast ride. *(Smacks his hand)* Let's do it! Michael, Michael, please a bottle of champagne for my partner and me. And make it the best champagne. A bottle of that Dillingers 75. That's Prince Charles's favourite champagne that.

Jumbo No, that's Bollingers.

Del It's bloody true I'm telling you.

THE TROTTERS' LOUNGE.

Albert is watching TV, a documentary on the blitz of London. Rodney enters from the kitchen.

Rodney *(Referring to TV programme)* They're not at it again in Brixton are they?

Albert This is the blitz of London. I was there. *Del enters.*

Del Rodney, Rodney, Rodney, we're going to Australia!

Rodney I'll just see the end of this first.

Del *(Switches TV off)* Good boy, good boy. Listen, I'll get the glasses. *(Sings)* 'Sunarise, she come in the morning, Sunarise, she come in the morning, Lighting up the ground all around.'

Rodney I think you've had enough, don't you?

Del I'm celebrating ain't I? It's not every day like you decide to go to Australia, is it? Go on.

Rodney I tell you what, I'll make you a nice cup of black coffee.

Del Oi oi oi. No, you don't understand. We're going to Australia!

Rodney What do you mean 'We're going to Australia?'

Del Now listen, I met . . . What's the matter? What's the matter with this boy? Don't he understand? Let me put it another way, right. We are going to Australia. See what happened, Jumbo, Jumbo offered me a partnership in his company, his new company, and it's gonna be a real big earner, Rodney, this time next year we will be millionaires. Right, first thing in the morning we're going up Australia House, right and we fill in our forms and you know, we're away, we're away.

Rodney Don't I have any say in this? I might not wanna go to Australia.

Del It's too late, it's too late now, I've given him your word, you see.

Rodney Well, I want time to think about this.

Del You don't have to do that, I've done all that for you. Just think Rodney, eh, Australia, where the men are men, eh.

Albert And so are the women.

Del What's that supposed to mean?

Albert Last time I was over there the only way you could tell the sexes were the men spit further.

Del Alright, when was the last time . . . When was the last time you was over there?

Albert 1929.

Del 1929. Cor blimey, we were still transporting prisoners over there then, weren't we? Never mind, listen, listen, I want to explain something to you. *(Produces photos)* Look Rodney, I've got . . . Look Jumbo borrowed me some of his photos. Look at them, look at that beach there.

Rodney Oh yeah, look at that bird.

Del Oh, that'd bruise yer ribs wouldn't it. Hey Rodney, that could be us in a little while. Blue skies, surfing, beach parties, all that, eh? What'd you reckon?

Rodney It sounds great. And he wants us to help run his new car business?

Del No, no, no. Not help run it. No, no, no, I'm gonna be a partner, aren't I. Straight down the middle, see Jumbo he's gonna have 51 per cent of the shares you see.

Rodney Well how's that straight down the middle then?

Del Well I'll get 51 per cent as well, I suppose. The thing is Jumbo's gonna be behind the scenes like, he's gonna handle all the money like, and I'm gonna be the sales director. I'm gonna have my own executive office, with a swivel chair and all that game. See.

Rodney So what's my job?

Del Ah, listen Rodney, you are gonna play a very vital role in the organisation, and I know, I just know that you can handle it.

Rodney So what is it?

Del Well you know when all them Rolls Royces and Mercedes they come trundling off the ship, what is the first thing they're gonna need?

Rodney Import licences, customs clearance, all that.

Del More important than that.

Rodney *(Snaps his fingers)* Re-registering, they gotta have new number plates and log books and all that.

Del What are they gonna need even more than that? *(Rodney doesn't know the answer)* Cleaning!

Rodney Cleaning?

Del Yeah.

Albert He's going 20,000 miles just to be a car

Who Wants to be a Millionaire?

cleaner?

Del No, he's not gonna be just a car cleaner. He's gonna be a prestige car cleaner. You know, he's gonna be in charge of it and all that.

Rodney I'll have staff working under me then?

Del Eventually, yeah. I mean this is a growing business, Rodney, and in a year from now I can't afford to have you down there with your mutton cloth and your T cut. I've got to have you up in the boardroom, and you'll have your own in-car celluloid phone.

Rodney And a secretary?

Del Yeah, all that, you've got to have all that.

Rodney What about Albert, though. We got to find something for him to do.

Del Yeah, well I've sorted it all out.

Albert I wouldn't waste your time boys, 'cos I'm not going.

Del Oi, come here Albert, what you mean not going?

Albert Listen to me son. I've spent three-quarters of my life sailing round this world. Now, all I want is a place to sit down and stay there. When I come to live with you two I hoped that I would end my days here.

Rodney Yeah, well so did we. But, I mean, this is a great opportunity for us Unc.

Del Yeah.

Albert It's a young man's opportunity Rodney. I'll be alright here on my own.

Del Alright, if that's what you really want Unc.

Albert Yeah.

Del Listen, I'll make sure you're alright for a few bob.

Albert Yeah, you're a good boy Del.

Albert exits to bedroom.

Rodney Hey Del, we'll be getting away from all this – the fumes and squalor.

Del It's goodbye to all that and hello to clean air, good living.

Rodney That's a point, where are we gonna live?

Del Jumbo said we could have his apartment for a while.

Rodney What, not on Sydney Harbour?

Del Yes that's the one. It'll be like living on another planet.

Rodney Er, Del.

Del Yes Rodney, you can have the room with mirror ceiling.

INT. DAY. TROTTERS' LOUNGE

This is a fortnight later. Albert and Del are sitting at the table. Del reads a letter.

Albert Well, what's it say?

Del I've been accepted. I've been accepted!

Albert Well, thank God for that.

Del I've had this feeling see. Everything's been going so well I thought something's gotta go wrong, ain't it?

Albert No boy, you're home and dry. I've got this feeling as well. I think this is the chance that's gonna change your life.

Del Yeah, I'm gonna make it this time Albert. You bloody see if I don't!

Rodney enters from bedroom area.

Rodney Alright?

Del Triffic Rodders, Triffic. I had a letter, I've been accepted ain't I! Wassamatter?

Rodney Nothing, nothing's the matter.

Del Oi, you ain't getting homesick already are you?

Rodney No! I got a letter this morning as well.

Del Yeah, yeah.

Rodney They've refused me an immigration visa, they've turned me down. Sorry mate.

Albert But why Rodney? I mean you're young.

Del And you've got GCEs.

Rodney I've also got a criminal record for an offence involving drugs.

Del Yeah, but, I mean, bloody 'ell! That was years ago and you only took one bloody puff!

Rodney Yeah I know, but it don't say that on your file does it. It just says 'Found guilty for the illegal use of drugs.' I'm sorry mate, I'm really sorry. I've messed it all up for you ain't I?

Del No you ain't bruv, no you ain't.

Rodney Yes I have. I've blown your big chance.

Del No you haven't, there is a way round Rodney. There's always a way round it.

Rodney Really?

Del Yes, don't worry Rodney. I'll find another car cleaner.

Rodney You're still going? You're gonna go without me?

Del I've got to, I mean. I've got a partnership waiting for me over there.

Rodney But what about our partnership?

Del Our partnership? Oh, our partnership. Well, yeah, that means all the world to me Rodney you know that, but I'm just gonna have to say bonjour to it.

Albert Look boys, I know it's none of my business . . .

Rodney You're spot on Albert. (*Albert exits to the kitchen*)

Albert I'll make some toast, son.

Del Look Rodney, this is my golden opportunity to fulfil my potential. What do you want me to do? Stay here, flogging all this rubbish. I've got

327

24 computers here that don't work, I gotta near-Persian rug that's got more food on it than a menu.

Rodney But last year when I had a golden opportunity you forced me to give it up didn't you? You give me all that cobblers about loyalty and family ties.

Del But you wanted to become a window cleaner, didn't you? It's hardly the end of the rainbow stuff that, is it?

Rodney Yeah, well I'd have had my own business.

Del I know Rodney, but you will have your own business because as soon as I step on that aeroplane you will become the sole proprietor of Trotters Independent Traders.

Rodney And what exactly am I supposed to trade with?

Del Well, at least you've got 24 beautiful looking computers, and this sort of Persian rug, not bad, you sloosh it over with a J cloth and it's a real goer. I tell you what I'm gonna do. Here's my little black book right. Now I'm gonna give you that and that contains the names and addresses of all my birds.

Rodney *(Takes book)* And this is my future. 24 computers that don't compute, the only rug in the world with a sell-by date and *(Referring to the book)* the script to *A Hundred and One Dalmatians*. Thanks a lot!

Del Don't you think I've sacrificed enough for you?

Rodney Sacrifices? For me?

Del Yes you, when dear Mum, Gawd rest her soul, when she died . . .

Rodney Don't start again.

Del When she died, who stood by you?

Rodney Yes, I remember that well. I was a little five-year-old stood in a damp graveyard wondering what the hole in the ground was for, I remember all the other people saying 'I wonder what's gonna happen to poor little Rodney?' But I had no need to fear, did I, 'cos suddenly a vision appeared from beyond the silhouette of the gasworks. Is it a bird? Is it a plane? No, it's Del Boy! Da da da daad! 'I, Del Boy, will look after this small waif. I will bring him up in the ways of Del Boy. He will sell iffy watches from old suitcases on street corners. And I will also teach him to drive a three-wheeled van whilst pissed out of his skull!'

Del And I did, didn't I?

Rodney Yeah, you made a bloody good job of it too. Just think Del, so far I'm your only success! That says a lot for the two of us, don't it?

Del Look Rodney, Rodders, listen, I'm gonna make a fortune over there, I'll send you money and that.

Rodney You know what you can do with your money Del.

Del Rodney, look, I've gotta have a chance, I mean this country's going downhill fast, innit?

Rodney I know but I think the real opportunity lies right here Del. What happens when a country's in a depression, eh? Money gets tight, don't it? People can't afford to pay the inflated shop prices, so what do they do? They come to blokes like us don't they. I tell you, the more hard up Britain gets, the richer we'd become, eh?

Del This is my big chance Rodney.

Rodney Fine, well I'll see you around, sport!
Exits.

Del Dipstick. *(Albert enters)* I suppose you heard all that?

Albert There are tugboat crews on the Thames heard it all. So what have we come to, eh? A family feud. You're like them Ewing brothers, Bobby and JR.

Del Yeah, I suppose I am a bit like that Bobby. I wouldn't have said Rodney was like that JR though. AJ Arthur, but not a JR!

INT. NIGHT. THE TROTTERS' LOUNGE.
Later the same day. Del sits solemnly in the armchair puffing a castella and pondering the situation. Albert is in the other chair watching the TVs.

Albert Rodney's late.

Del He's probably out getting smashed somewhere. Families, families, they're nothing but problems, ain't they Albert?

Albert That's true son. Would you like my advice Del?

Del Yeah, why not. Go on, chuck your penny-worth in.

Albert You've gotta go son. If you don't take this chance down you'll spend the rest of your life wondering what might have been. It's a kind of thing can eat away at you. I know it'll be tough for young Rodney, but eventually he'll learn to stand on his two feet. In the long run, this could be the best thing for the both of you.

Del Cheers Albert. Thanks very much, perhaps one day you'll try explaining it to Rodney. You're better at it than me. I'm gonna phone Jumbo, and tell him what time I'll be arriving. *(He presses out five digits. Pauses. Presses another four digits. Pauses. Presses another five digits)* I tell you one thing, phoning Australia don't 'alf hurt your finger. Hello Jumbo, Del Boy, eh? Well with

328

Who Wants to be a Millionaire?

your money you ought to have a phone in the khazi! Now listen, a bit of a problem. Young Rodney won't be coming over. No, we've got a few snags this end see. Me? *(Struggling with himself. Trying not say the words)* Na, I won't be coming over either. Well it's loyalties innit? Family ties, all that. I know what I am. I'm sorry mate, the whole deal's off. You know it makes sense. Anyway, thanks very much for the offer, it was much appreciated. Yeah, I'll see you around pal, cheers.

Albert Well, I'm glad my advice helped.

Del Well, what else could I do, eh? I suppose it'll be for the best in the end.

Albert Are you happy now son?

Del I dunno, in a way I suppose, yes. It's like a big weight's been removed from my shoulders, I know that.

Albert Well I suppose that's something. Well, see you in the morning son, goodnight. *(Exits)*

Del Yeah, night Unc.

> *Del goes to pour himself a large brandy. Rodney enters.*

Rodney *(Sheepish)* Alright?

Del Oh yeah, brill.

Rodney I owe you an apology Del. All them things I said earlier, I was right out of order, and you've gotta take that opportunity.

Del Na, it's too late bruv. I've already phoned Jumbo and told him the whole deal's off.

Rodney You ain't? Because of what I said?

Del Well, yeah, in a way Rodney, in a way, because you said 'The real opportunity lies here.' You know the country's in a bad way, money's tight, people are looking for bargains and who do they turn to first, eh?

Rodney Blokes like us.

Del Blokes like us. I was sitting here, you know, and I thought Rodney has hit the nail right on the head there. I thought, this wonderful land of ours is on the eve of a golden age of the black market. And you and me, you know we're gonna be in there first. I'm glad I listened to you Rodney, I really am, because if I'd have taken that 'Chance of a Lifetime' it could have ruined me.

Rodney So we're . . . we're still partners?

Del Yes, if you'll have me back?

Rodney Oh well, let me sleep on it, eh?

Del I'll smack you in the nose, saucy sod.

Rodney Hey Del, this time next year, eh.

Del Yeah, this time next year Rodney, eh.

Rodney Well, I'll see you in the morning.

Del See you in the morning.

Rodney And Del, you know . . .

Del Yeah, I know bruv, goodnight . . .

(Rodney exits to the bedroom) Yeah, this time next year!

Del downs his drink with a vengeance. He crosses to the door and looks back at the room. He is deeply, deeply saddened. A tear is in the corner of his eye. He sings, his voice faltering with emotion and frustration.

'Who wants to be a millionaire?'

Cast List

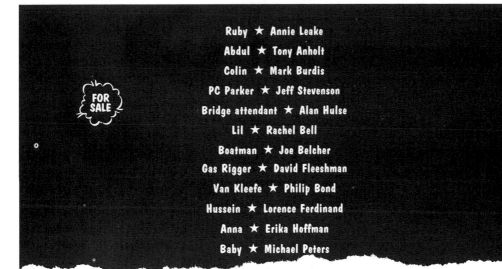

Ruby ★ Annie Leake
Abdul ★ Tony Anholt
Colin ★ Mark Burdis
PC Parker ★ Jeff Stevenson
Bridge attendant ★ Alan Hulse
Lil ★ Rachel Bell
Boatman ★ Joe Belcher
Gas Rigger ★ David Fleeshman
Van Kleefe ★ Philip Bond
Hussein ★ Lorence Ferdinand
Anna ★ Erika Hoffman
Baby ★ Michael Peters

Father O'Keith ★ P.G Stephens
Biffo ★ Pierce Jones
Australian reporter ★ Peter Wickham
American reporter ★ Carol Cleveland
Man in church ★ James Richardson
Tom the security officer ★ John Bardon
Mr Peterson ★ Max Harvey
Lennox ★ Vas Blackwood
Woman in kiosk ★ Jeanne Mockford
Checkout girl ★ Catherine Clarke
Lisa ★ Gerry Cowper
Andy ★ Mark Colleano
Pianist ★ Fred Tomlinson
Singer ★ Joan Baxter
Drummer ★ Derek Price
Stuntman/Double for Del ★ Ken Barker
Stuntman ★ Graham Walker

Amanda ★ Dawn Perlman
Vicar ★ Rex Robinson
Chinese takeaway owner ★ Chua Kahjoo

Cast List

GOING CHEAP

Brendan ★ David Jackson

Denzil ★ Paul Barber

Corinne ★ Eva Mottley

Louis ★ Anthony Morton

Reg Trotter ★ Peter Woodthorpe

June ★ Diane Langton

Debby ★ Oona Kirsch

Maureen ★ Nula Cornwell

Old lady in newsagents ★ Lala Lloyd

Jason ★ Ben Davis

Vicar ★ John Pennington

Cousin Jean ★ Maureen Sweeney

Cousin Stan ★ Mike Kemp

Solly the lawyer ★ Colin Jeavons

Judge ★ Dennis Ramsden

Mr Gerrard ★ Andrew Tourell

Mr Fraser ★ James Woolley

Cockney man ★ Michael Roberts

Clerk ★ Les Rawlings

Policeman ★ Geoffrey Leesley

Mental Mickey ★ Daniel Peacock

Charlie ★ Marcus Francis

Stew ★ David Thewlis

DJ ★ Mike Read

Marlene ★ Sue Holderness

Dog owner ★ Linda Barr

Receptionist ★ Debbie Blyth

Vet ★ John D. Collins

Doctor ★ Brian Jameson

Yvonne ★ Carolyn Allen

Smuggler ★ Jane Thompson

Vicky ★ Kim Clifford

Teddy ★ Johnny Wade

Cast List

Alex the travel agent ★ Jim McManus

French girl ★ Anne Bruzac

English girl ★ Jilliane Foot

Spanish guard ★ Anthony Jackson

Lady Ridgemere ★ Elizabeth Benson

Wallace the butler ★ Donald Bisset

Lord Ridgemere ★ Geoffrey Toone

Enrico ★ John Moreno

Heather ★ Roslalind Lloyd

Brian ★ Roger Brierley

Indian waiter ★ Dev Sagoo

Baz ★ Ron Pember

Old lady no.1 ★ Gilly Flower

Old lady no.2 ★ Renee Roberts

Doctor ★ John Bryans

Miss Mackenzie ★ Sandra Payne

Small boy ★ Miles Rinaldi

Auctioneer ★ Glynn Sweet

Mickey Pearce ★ Patrick Murray

Harry the foreman ★ Rex Robinson

Young Towser ★ Mike Carnell

Policeman ★ Ray Mort

Gamekeeper ★ Tom Witton

Madman/Chief of security ★ Christopher Malcolm

Police sergeant ★ Michael Stainton

Mrs Murphy ★ Lucita Lijertwood

Miranda Davenport ★ Juliet Hammond

Harry ★ Robert Vahey

Auctioneer ★ Garard Green

Det Insp. Roy Slater ★ Jim Broadbent

PC Hoskins ★ Christopher Mitchell

Karen the barmaid ★ Michele Winstanley

Blossom ★ Toni Palmer

CAST LIST

Derek Trotter ★ David Jason

Rodney Trotter ★ Nicholas Lyndhurst

Grandad ★ Lennard Pearce

Uncle Albert ★ Buster Merryfield

Trigger ★ Roger Lloyd-Pack

Boycie ★ John Challis

Mike Fisher ★ Kenneth McDonald

Joyce the barmaid ★ Pete Bernard

Aussie Man and Jumbo Mills ★ Nick Stringer

Waiter ★ Barry Wilmore

Nicky ★ Jo-Anne Good

Michelle ★ Caroline Ellis

Mr Ram ★ Renu Setna

Vimal ★ Malik Armhed Khalil

Indian restaurant manager ★ Babar Bhatti

Pauline ★ Jill Baker

Auntie Rose ★ Beryl Cook

Janice ★ Gaynor Ward

Eric the policeman ★ Derek Newark

Earl ★ Desmond McNamara

Anita ★ Nora Connolly

Sid ★ Roy Heather

Sandra ★ Kate Saunders

River Policeman ★ John Collins

Council street sweeper driver ★ Terry Duggan

Pub customer ★ Michael G. Jones

Irene Mackay ★ Gaye Brown

Julie the barmaid ★ Julie Le Rousse

Marcus ★ Steve Fletcher

Ahmed ★ Raj Patel

Leroy ★ David Rhule

Tommy Mackay ★ David Daker

Zoe ★ Lisa Price

Mr Chin ★ Rex Wei

marvellous.

menage a trois *interj.* an exclamation of surprise or horror.

moenchengladbach *sentence substitute.* an expression of greeting used on meeting a person from germany.

monkey *mod.* five hundred english pounds.

mutton *adj.* deaf; hard of hearing. 2 n. a type of curry which can cause a case of gandhi's revenge (see above.)

noofter *n.* a man of homosexual tendencies.

oeuf sur la plat *phrase.* meaning it is all clear-cut.

pas de calais *interj.* a statement of delight and approval. as in 'that steak was divine, well, it was pas de calais as they say in france.'

plonker (pa-lon-ka.) *n.* a person of very low intelligence, prone to cocking up and sending the whole deal down the khazi.

plume de ma tante *interj.* an expression of exasperation. similar in meaning to 'gordon bennett' or 'bloody nora.'

pony *mod.* twenty five english pounds.

potless *adj.* to have no cash on the hip, in the pocket, under the bed or any bleedin' place else for that matter.

pukka (puck-ah) *adj.* genuine; perfect.

ruby *n.* authentic indian cuisine sold on the high street. usually follows a night at the nag's head and results in a morning on the khazi.

schtum (sh-tum) *adj.* to be quiet. as in 'keep schtum, rodders, and we may be in the clear.'

score *mod.* twenty english pounds.

sort *n.* woman; bird. as in 'let's go up west and pick ourselves up a right couple of sorts, rodney.'

stoke on trent *adj.* (see noofter)

stone me *interj.* an exclamation of desperation, usually in frustration when surrounded by a couple of plonkers.

stuke *adj.* a spot of trouble. as in 'we're in stuke, rodders.'

this immortal curl *n.* the world in which we live; terracotta. as said by hamlet in one of shakespeare's best comedies, ' hamish macbeth.'

tres bien ensemble *phrase.* to possess a sense of occasion. as in 'you've no tres bien ensemble, rodney.'

triffic *adj.* wonderful; superb. sometimes said through gritted teeth.

twonk *n.* as in 'you dozy little twonk.' a dipstick who gives me the right 'ump.

wally *n.* also wallybrain. one of immense stupidity, and just who happens to be my financial adviser.

ajax (eye-ax) *sentence substitute.* an expression of greeting used on meeting a person from the netherlands.

allemagne dix points *phrase.* to be philosophical, accept events as they occur. similar in meaning to the phrase 'such is life.'

au revoir *french.* sentence substitute. hello

boeuf a la mode *phrase.* to win some and lose some. similar in meaning to 'nothing ventured, nothing gained.' he who dares, wins, after all.

bonjour *french. sentence substitute.* goodbye.

brassic *adj.* impecunious; without money; skint.

century *mod.* one hundred english pounds (usually in cash.)

cop *vb.* **1.** receive; as in 'watch it or you'll cop an unfortunate one soon, rodney.' **2.** a member of the old bill

cosmic *adj.* outstanding; exceptional. normally used by dozy little twonks who've been at the funny fags.

creme de la menthe *phrase.* the very best. as in 'when it comes to decorating, rodney and grandad are the creme de la menthe.'

cushty (coosh-dee) *adj.* great; brilliant.

di stefano *interj.* well done! praise; often used for a singer who has completed a pukka rendition

of 'old shep.'

dipstick *n.* a foolish or senseless person - even one with gce's.

douce in bunce *n.* two hundred english pounds. (in cash, of course.)

earner *adj.* a business transaction resulting in profit for yours truly.

enemy *n.* wife; missus. as in 'how's the enemy? did she like that doorbell i sold you that chimes 36 different national anthems?'

fabrique belgique *sentence substitute.* o.k. an expression of agreement or approval.

gandhi's revenge *n.* a stomach upset, usually the result of a dodgy ruby (see below) at the star of bengal.

grand *mod.* a thousand english pounds.

heave-ho *v.* the act of ending a relationship with a member of the opposite sex. as in 'birds usually give rodney the old heave-ho after two weeks.'

hump (ump) *n.* to be annoyed, irritated. as in 'he's giving me the right 'ump.'

humpty-dumpty *n.* sexual intercourse; the act of procreation. to get one's leg over.

jacksie (jax-ee) *n.* posterior; arse.

jaffa *adj.* one who fires blanks; seedless. ask boycie.

kosher readies (co-sha red-ees) *n.* unlaundered money.

lovely jubbly *adj.* fantastic;

PECKHAM CONCISE

TROTTER
DICTIONARY

TROTTER>ENGLISH
1ST EDITION

FINAL VERSE OF THE BLOSSOM MOON SONG,
AN ANCIENT CATHRAN BALLAD

Down in the waters, cold and deep,
My true love has gone to eternal sleep.
Long will I wait for his returning,
Hoping, my heart afire with yearning.
In Blossom Moon, in Blossom Moon, it will never be.

PROLOGUE

The Royal Intelligencer

An unexpected thing happened last night.

As is my habit, I had been working long hours on my Boreal Moon Tale, struggling along despite cramped fingers, dimming eyesight, and the daunting magnitude of the writing project I had set myself at a time when most old men are content to doze and dream. But I have more reason than most to wish my story told to the world – most specifically to the inhabitants of High Blenholme, island of my birth, whose official Chronicle will no doubt be turned all arsey-versey by my mischievous revelations.

I had laid aside my quill after describing the chain of improbable events leading to King Conrig Wincantor's establishment of the Blenholme Sovereignty, thinking this would be an appropriate place to break the narrative and end the first book of the tale. It was very late and bracingly cool, as nights tend to be during midwinter months in southern Foraile, and the air was laden with the sweet scent of moth-jasmine. Oddly – though I did not fully appreciate the fact until later when I went outdoors – the night was almost completely silent. The usual sounds made by nocturnal birds and insects were absent and the murmur of the nearby Daravara River was muted.

1

After sanding the final closely written parchment sheet, I added it to the rest and locked the manuscript in the copper box that preserves it from the mice and palm roaches that would otherwise make a meal of it. I rose from my desk, paused to work the worst knots from my aching muscles, and blew out the bright flame of the brass desk lamp, plunging the room into near-darkness. A faint illumination came from the lantern that my peg-legged housecarl Borve leaves lit at the far end of the hall to guide me to bed. That was usual. What was *not* usual was the odd flickering glow coming through the window that looked northward toward the river. The crescent moon had set early and thick foliage made it difficult to see outside. My first thought was of wild-fire, since the light was too ruddy and fitful to be starshine. The rains were late this year and the scrubby hills above the jungle valley were tinder-dry. I made haste to the door, slipped outside onto the veranda, and went down the short flight of steps into my riverside garden so as to have a clear view of the opposite shore.

The northern sky was ablaze with immense rippling curtains and thrusting beams of scarlet, green, amethyst and flame-gold, so bright that they dimmed the stars, so active and intricate in their movements that every instinct of the beholder seemed to affirm that this was no mere natural phenomenon, but the work of elemental living beings.

I knew who they were, what they had been – those shining abominations who had fed on pain!

The people of High Blenholme gave them various names: the Beaconfolk, the Coldlight Army, the Great Lights. Their domain is the far north, the arctic barrens and the island in the Boreal Sea from which I had been banished. Never had I seen the Lights during my enforced sojourn on the southern mainland. Early on in my exile, when I had cautiously ques-tioned my manservant Borve about folkloric beliefs in this part of the world, he made no mention of terrible sky-beings in the local pantheon of demons and demigods. Yet here they were, transforming the night of subtropical Foraile into a facsimile of the incandescent heavens above the northland. Was it possible that I was dreaming? I hardly thought so, but it would not be the first time that nightmares provoked by the evil ones among the Beaconfolk had tormented me.

Still less did it seem they should be able to manifest themselves here, so far south! Their once-mighty powers were circumscribed now, pent-up and curtailed so that the pain-eating predators among them might no longer slake their obscene appetites upon humans and other ground-dwelling beings. And yet I seemed to feel something reaching for me, grasping my poor pounding heart with claws of ice and slowly – so slowly – tightening its grip. The chest spasm was tentative and entirely bearable, but my feeble old legs now refused to support my body and I subsided onto my knees, eyes still locked onto that dreadful blazing sky.

I have said that the night was strangely quiet. I was aware of this anomaly almost at the same time that I realized it was not quite true. A ghostly sound was discernible at the very limit of audibility, a sibilance that ebbed and flowed like surf, all the while overlaid with a complex rustling that almost resembled speech. I had first heard its like some sixty years ago, as I lay dying on the Desolation Coast of Tarn. The Coldlight Army had blazed above me then in all its awful strength, jeering at my mortal frailty, ridiculing the notion that a pathetic creature such as I might be able to frustrate its devilish entertainment.

'But I survived in spite of you!' I managed to croak, shaking a fist at them. 'I used your own twisty rules of magic to thwart your schemes. Do you want to know how? It's simple: I never told you my true name! I'm Snudge, but I'm *not* Snudge. What d'you think of that, Lights?'

Above me the luminous draperies and glorious colored beacons flared in response to my puny effort at defiance. The faint crackling sound intensified momentarily and I felt a crushing agony behind my breastbone. The pang subsided almost at once and I slowly exhaled, sagging back onto my heels and then sprawling sideways to rest against the trunk of a small tree, eyes shut tight.

Was the pain really of their doing, or was my aging heart simply giving out at last as I dreamt of my old enemies? I waited motionless, in fearful anticipation of a more violent attack that would finish me; but none came, and at length I relaxed, reassuring myself that the lethal capabilities of the Lights were indeed extinct. They could do me no serious harm. I, Deveron Austrey, called Snudge, would live.

When I opened my eyes, I saw that the sky was empty except for the rich expanse of southern stars.

The grand scheme to unite the four disparate realms of High Blenholme into a single Sovereignty was conceived by my first master, Conrig Wincantor, later to be nicknamed Ironcrown, while he was still very young.

Growing up as Prince Heritor of Cathra, the richest and most powerful of the island realms, Conrig idolized his remote ancestor Emperor Bazekoy, the towering personality who first vanquished the great Continental nations of Foraile, Andradh, and Stippen, then set out to wrest control of Blenholme from the Salka and the other nonhuman monsters who had inhabited the place since the dawn of time. The year that Bazekoy's conquering army sailed up the River Brent marked the beginning of the Blenholme Chronicle.

After a long and glorious life, the emperor chose to return to the island to die – influenced, according to legend, by a dream of Great Lights. Over a thousand years later his remains, interred in Zeth Abbey, were destined to play a strangely influential role in the life of Conrig's father, King Olmigon of Cathra – as I have already described in the first volume of this Boreal Moon Tale.

Conrig's own reign began in Chronicle Year 1128, with a triumph and what seemed to be an appalling tragedy. A great sea-battle and a climactic storm in Cala Bay resulted in the defeat of King Honigalus Mallburn of Didion and forced that ill-fated monarch to accept vassal status in Conrig's new Sovereignty of High Blenholme. As a condition of Didion's surrender at Eagleroost Castle, in a move that stunned most of the high nobility of Cathra, Conrig divorced his Tarnian wife Maudrayne Northkeep – presumed by him to be barren after six years of turbulent marriage – and pledged to wed Princess Risalla, the younger half-sister of Honigalus.

Although I was only sixteen years of age at the time, I was already closely attendant upon Conrig and serving un-officially as his Royal Intelligencer by virtue of my secret wild talents. Thus I was one of the horrified witnesses who saw Maudrayne calmly put her name to the bill of divorcement, then throw herself off the castle battlements into the wintry sea forty ells below.

I was also a member of the large party who subsequently combed the ice-covered shore rocks for Maudrayne's body. My uncanny seekersense was then extremely powerful; nevertheless I was unable to detect any trace of the poor suicide. In the days that followed, both the Brothers of Zeth and Conjure-Queen Ullanoth of Moss utilized their magical talents to hunt for the woman Conrig now termed the Princess Dowager, scrutinizing not only the shoreline but also the interior regions of the island, on the improbable chance that she had somehow survived. The searchers found nothing. It was decided that the body must have been carried far out into Cala Bay, to be lost in the frigid depths.

After a month of official mourning, Conrig quietly married

Risalla Mallburn. His profound condolences had been dispatched to Tarn, Maudrayne's birthplace and the only island nation not yet accepting the Edict of Sovereignty. Tarn's ruler, the High Sealord Sernin Donorvale, reacted with predictable fury to his favorite niece's public humiliation. In the year following her presumed death, Sernin rebuffed Conrig's demands that Tarn join Cathra, Didion, and Moss in a unified High Blenholme, even when the Sovereignty 'reluctantly' cut off trade with his corner of the island, leaving Tarn at the mercy of rapacious mainland merchants and pirates. Forced to purchase food and other needful commodities from the Continent at inflated prices, the once-wealthy domain grew more and more impoverished and vulnerable.

The injurious effects of the Wolf's Breath volcanic eruptions – which had caused widespread crop failures on the island, shut down Tarn's all-important gold mines, and precipitated the political upheaval that inspired Conrig's scheme of unification – were now only a bad memory. Eastern Didion recovered from the famine that had devastated its largest cities. Its pragmatic ruler, Honigalus, rebuilt the capital city of Holt Mallburn that had been devastated by Conrig's invading army. He regained the trust of Didion's independent-minded timberlords, whose cooperation was vital to the restoration of his country's shipbuilding industry, paid off the war reparations demanded by Conrig by building a new fleet of naval vessels for the Sovereignty, and did his best to keep a lid on his fiery younger brother Prince Somarus, who remained implacably opposed to Conrig's hegemony and considered Honigalus a traitor for having capitulated.

In the tiny kingdom of Moss, which enjoyed First Vassal status in the Sovereignty thanks to Conjure-Queen Ullanoth's magical assistance to Conrig during the war with Didion, things were apparently tranquil. The queen's insanely ambitious younger brother Beynor, who had briefly occupied the throne until his imprudent ventures into high sorcery incurred the displeasure of the Beaconfolk, had fled to the desolate Dawntide Isles to live with the Salka monsters. Whenever she gathered strength enough to pay the pain-price to the Beaconfolk, Queen Ullanoth made use of a powerful magical tool, the moonstone sigil Subtle Loophole, to keep watch on Beynor . . . and to observe other events transpiring here and there about High Blenholme. Part of this intelligence she shared with her sometime lover, High King Conrig. The rest of it she kept to herself, while she quietly pursued thaumaturgical studies and pondered the possibility of seizing control of the Sovereignty herself when the time was ripe.

Early in the spring of 1130, when most Tarnian ports remained icebound and the majority of that nation's fighting ships were still hauled up ashore, High Sealord Sernin learned that a large fleet of freebooters had set sail from Andradh on the Continent, intending to seize Tarnholme and the other important port cities of Goodfortune Bay – the only section of the Tarnian coast that remained reliably unfrozen in winter. Poised in the mountains above Tarnholme to re-inforce the sea invasion was a ragtag but formidable army of insurgent warriors loyal to Prince Somarus, led by robber-barons of western Didion.

Facing an impossible situation, Sernin and his Company of Equals swallowed their pride and sought aid from the Sovereignty, pledging fealty in return. Conrig agreed only after Tarn bowed to draconian conditions. The High King dispatched his new navy to beat off the Andradhians, and commanded his Royal Alchymist to bespeak the hedge-wizards attending rebellious Prince Somarus, warning of nasty consequences if his fighters pressed their attack on Tarn.

The Continental freebooters were soundly defeated at sea, while the prince's outlaw Didionite land-force scuttled back

over the White Rime Mountains into the wilderness of the
Great Wold, never having unsheathed their swords.

While these events transpired, I myself grew from a youth
into a man. My wild talents ripened with maturity, known
only to my royal master Conrig, to his brother Stergos who
had become the Royal Alchymist, and to a handful of other
trusted intimates of the High King.

During those early years of Conrig Ironcrown's reign, my
duties were important but rather humdrum. I spent most of
my time spying on Cathra's quarrelsome Lords of the
Southern Shore, holders of the original fiefdoms established
under Bazekoy over a millennium ago. This group of affluent
merchant-peers, who had played only a minor role in the
establishment of the Sovereignty, remained a continuing
thorn in the High King's side because the ancient laws of
Cathra made it difficult for the Crown to increase taxes on
their considerable revenues. Also, unlike the rest of the
nobility, the Lords of the Southern Shore possessed the immemorial right to veto changes in the Codex of Zeth, the charter
affirming the rights and privileges of Cathran aristocracy and
defining limits of regal authority – including the succession
to the throne. It was the Codex that specifically excluded
anyone possessing the least whiff of magical talent from
Cathra's kingship. This rule dated from Bazekoy's time, and
prevailed in Tarn and in Didion as well. Only Moss, youngest
of Blenholme's nations and founded by a brilliant sorcerer,
was an exception.

Less than a year after Conrig's second marriage, High
Queen Risalla gave birth to a strapping son who was named
Bramlow. Unfortunately Lord Stergos, the Royal Alchymist,
almost immediately determined that the child had moderate
arcane powers. In a move that surprised and bewildered his
Privy Council and loyalist nobility, the High King pressured

the Lords of the South to amend the Codex so the boy could be named Prince Heritor in spite of his talent. The lords refused, backed up by the powerful Brethren of the Mystic Order of Zeth, who inflamed the sentiments of the common people against the king's dubious proposal. In the end, Bramlow was consecrated to the Order as an acolyte, the inevitable fate of windtalented royal offspring.

Excepting Conrig himself . . .

Oh, yes. My royal master was himself possessed of an all-but-insignificant portion of magical aptitude, imperceptible to the scrutiny of the Brothers. His urgent push to amend the Codex in Prince Bramlow's favor was actually an attempt to safeguard his own position as High King of Cathra and Sovereign of Blenholme, in case his great secret should be revealed.

I, with my own undetectable 'wild' powers, had discovered Prince Heritor Conrig's puny talent by accident years earlier – and almost paid for it with my life. Instead, the prince decided to make me his personal snudge, or spy. Later, I inadvertently betrayed my master to his older brother Stergos, who kept the perilous confidence in spite of serious misgivings.

Ullanoth of Moss, the beautiful young sorceress who later became that nation's Conjure-Queen, also knew about the king's talent, but had motives of her own for not disclosing it. Only two other persons had found out Conrig's secret: his first wife Maudrayne, whom he believed to be dead, and her friend the Tarnian High Shaman Ansel Pikan, who was very much alive. So far, Ansel had also kept silent. But he remained a potential threat who might possibly betray Conrig and precipitate the dissolution of the Sovereignty. Killing the powerful shaman was no easy option. The only person who might be capable of doing the deed, Ullanoth herself, demurred for fear of offending the touchy Beaconfolk, who were the source of her powers. She did counsel Conrig with the obvious solution to his dilemma: sire a 'normal' son as soon as possible. Then, if worse came to worse, the attainted High King could abdicate in favor of the infant Prince Heritor and make use of an obscure point of law to declare himself regent, preserving his grip on the Sovereignty for at least twenty years, until his son's majority.

Two years after Bramlow's birth, in 1131, High Queen Risalla was delivered of healthy male twins who were named Orrion and Corodon. Lord Stergos and the other Brothers of Zeth who examined the babies pronounced both of them free from magical talent. Orrion, the elder by half an hour, was affirmed as Prince Heritor.

Unfortunately, the Brethren were mistaken in their assessment of the twins – as I learned to my dismay when I first beheld their tiny faces. As with their father Conrig, I was able to perceive that the infant boys had the faint but unmistakable spark of talent in their eyes. It was my clear duty to inform the king, but perhaps understandable that I should have delayed making the dire announcement. Knowing about Conrig's own hidden talent had already placed my life at grave risk; if I confessed to knowledge of his newborn sons' taint as well, who knew what my liege lord might do?

As it happened, I was spared the unwelcome task by none other than Queen Ullanoth, who had scried the little boys from a distance with the powerful moonstone sigil named Subtle Loophole. After confirming her discovery, she did not hesitate to tell Conrig the truth about the twins. She advised the dismayed king to keep the matter secret, continue pressing for a change in the law of succession . . . and beget still more offspring. In appreciation of the Conjure-Queen's wholehearted pledge of silence, Conrig doubled the annual benefice already vouchsafed to her loyal but needy little realm in exchange for magical services rendered.

Thus it appeared, as the fateful summer of 1133 began,

that most of the problems that had threatened to undermine
Conrig Ironcrown and his fledgling Sovereignty were well
under control. The realm of Cathra enjoyed unprecedented
prosperity. Thanks in part to my own underhanded activities, there was a welcome respite in the intrigues and machi-
nations of the Lords of the Southern Shore. High Queen
Risalla was happily pregnant again. Didion's fractious robber-
barons were quiet, licking their wounds following yet another
failed small insurrection by Prince Somarus. Embittered Tarn
seemed finally resigned to its vassal status and paid its exorbitant taxes without a murmur. The Continental nations had
apparently shelved their expansionist schemes for the time
being and were content to engage in orderly trade. Even the
Dawntide Salka monsters were lying low, not having raided
the shore settlements of Moss for over a year, thanks to fierce
storms created by Conjure-Queen Ullanoth and a sharp retal-
iatory strike on the islands by the Sovereign's navy under
Lord Admiral Hartrig Skellhaven.

I myself was a contented man that year, celebrating my
twentieth birthday and entry into adulthood on the second
day of Blossom Moon.

As part of the great Summer Solstice festival a few weeks
later, I was initiated into knighthood together with fifteen
other armigers from all parts of Cathra, becoming Sir Deveron
Austrey. We received the accolade at the traditional ceremony at noon on Midsummer Eve. To my surprise, I was
not made a simple Bachelor like the others but was created
a Knight Banneret of the Royal Household in recognition of
my confidential services to the Crown. The commander's
honors included a velvet purse containing a hundred gold
double-marks, twice the boon vouchsafed to the Knights
Bachelor; a smallish fortified manor house called Buttonoaks
with a freehold of six hundred goodly acres, situated in the
rolling hills below Swan Lake, which was supposed to provide

me with a decent income and a place to live when I was not needed at the palace; and the services of two armigers rather than one, together with an apprentice windvoice who would ostensibly enable me to communicate with my superiors via the arcane network of Zeth Brethren. (My own windtalents were, of course, a state secret.)

After the dubbing ceremony, High King Conrig kindly suggested that I quit the court for several weeks and visit my new demesne, which lay less than three days' easy journey to the north. With the realm at peace and likely to remain so for some time to come, the king anticipated no immediate need for my particular services.

I agreed to the idea eagerly and made ready to leave at once, glad of the chance to avoid the elaborate Solstice banquet and the many entertainments that would take place over the next several days. I found the pomp and splendor of court festivities tedious. In my rôle of Royal Intelligencer, I often moved among the great ones of the Sovereignty; but I had been born a commoner of low estate, the son of a palace harnessmaker, and preferred more modest pleasures.

I invited a close friend, Sir Gavlok Whitfell, to accompany me on my tour of inspection. He was another who esteemed the simple life and was glad of a chance to spend time in the country. Together with our youthful attendants, Gavlok and I left Cala Blenholme city about the sixth hour on Solstice Eve, heading north toward the Swan Lake region. My armigers Val and Wil, and my windvoice Vra-Mattis, newly come to the palace from Vanguard and Blackhorse duchies and Zeth Abbey respectively, were still unfamiliar to me. But they all seemed to be biddable lads and I looked forward to getting to know them better.

I was in a fine humor, anticipating exploration of my manor in the company of congenial men. For a short time at least, I would answer to no master but myself.

ONE

The great outdoor feast in the Cala Palace gardens had come to its conclusion by the tenth hour of Solstice Eve. While servitors dismantled the banquet boards, re-arranged the chairs and benches, and laid out the hardwood dancing floor with its flower-decked standards and strings of twinkling lanterns, the throng of high-born guests slipped away to chambers of ease inside Cala Palace to refresh themselves before the music began.

In the royal retirement room adjacent to the great hall, High Queen Risalla sat at a dressing table enduring the attentions of her personal maid, who was rearranging her hair. The Sovereign himself rested on a padded long chair, seeming to be lost in deep thought. He had hardly exchanged a dozen words with the queen since they had left the gardens. The room was warm and he wore only his black undertunic, hose, and soft ankle-boots, having shed his ornate overrobe of black tissue velvet with white gold ornamentation. His valet was busy daubing spirits of wine on a grease spot on one of the sleeves.

'Sire,' the queen said, 'I have a special request to make of you.'

Conrig frowned absently. 'What is it, madam?' He had significant concerns of his own this evening, following a brief

13

confidential talk with Earl Marshal Parlian Beorbrook towards the end of the feast. And there was also Ullanoth's impending visitation . . .

'I'm concerned about our children. With so many special events going on today, I had no time to look in on them. Your Reverend Brother dosed the boys with a physick he declared would surely cure them of their catarrh, and it's true that Bramlow and Corodon seemed well on the road to recovery yesterday. But I'm worried about little Orry. He's so much more delicate than the others.'

'Send a page to inquire how the lad does,' the preoccupied king said, only half listening.

Risalla waved the maid away, rose from her stool, and came to stand beside her husband. She was a woman of five-and-twenty whose face often seemed bland and plain in repose; but when she was animated, as now, her cornflower-blue eyes glowed with a disconcerting vigor. For the festivities she was attired in a high-waisted gown that revealed nothing of her six-month pregnancy. It was made of violet silk, embroidered about the low neckline with a pattern of vine leaves picked out in gold thread. A chain supporting a single large diamond pendant hung at her throat. Her honey-colored hair was dressed in a high coil of braids adorned with tiny twinkling sprays of gold wire and amethyst brilliants. A delicate golden diadem, yet to be pinned into place, waited on the dressing table.

'No, husband,' she said firmly. 'Sending a page won't do. I insist on going to the nursery myself, before Orrion and the others are put to bed. Do come with me! You haven't visited the children all week.'

'It won't be long before the dancing begins,' Conrig objected. 'We have to step out first, as well you know. And after that we must prepare for the special visitation of the Queen of Moss.'

Risalla's lips tightened in determination. 'The housemen are only beginning to put up the lanterns around the dance ground. There's ample time.' She took his hand, drawing him to his feet. 'Surely the Prince Heritor of Cathra is deserving of your sovereign attention.'

Something flickered in Conrig's dark eyes. But then he let a slow, wintry smile soften his face. He was a tall man and well built, still youthful in appearance at thirty years of age, fine-featured with a short beard and hair the color of ripe wheat. The famous iron crown, originally the rusty top hoop on a small cask of tarnblaze but now polished and given a handsome blue-heat finish, lay unobtrusively on his brow.

'Dear madam, you defeat me once again. We'll surprise the little rascals at their supper, and I don't doubt that we'll find all of them in good fettle, save for their disappointment at having to miss the Solstice celebration.' He said to the valet, 'Trey, summon my escort. And carry on scraping off that splash of gravy while I'm gone.'

'Thank you, sire – dearest husband.' Risalla spoke with every evidence of humble diffidence before adding in a drier tone, 'After all, it's not as though the dancing could begin without us. And Conjure-Queen Ullanoth is a very patient woman . . . or so I've heard.'

Conrig Wincantor, Sovereign of High Blenholme, stood with his wife outside the closed door to the royal nursery. A look of contained chagrin stiffened his features. Shrieks of childish laughter, furious shouts from an adult female, and the sounds of smashing crockery were audible through the thick oaken planking. The household knights of the royal escort kept straight faces with difficulty, while the two palace guards on duty in the corridor came to attention and smote their polished cuirasses in salute.

Inside the nursery, there was a jarring thud and someone

began to scream hysterically. A shrill voice cried, 'I'll catch him!'

'Oh, my,' Queen Risalla murmured, with a sidelong glance at the king.

Conrig scowled and addressed the senior door guard. 'What the devil is going on in there, Sergeant Mendos?'

'I 'spect it's the monkey, Your Grace,' said the guardsman, his countenance wooden. 'Little Prince Bramlow commanded that it join them for supper. Viscountess Taria's abed today with a megrim and the younger ladies and the nursemaids haven't a lick o' sense among the lot of 'em, so they agreed. Silly wenches thought it'd be fun to see the wee beast sit down at table with the royal lads. Cheer 'em up, like, since they couldn't attend the festival. I said it was a bad idea –'

'Bazekoy's Bones!' growled the king. 'Where's the creature's keeper?'

'Gone away, sire. The young ladies made him leave. He didn't want to let the monkey off its chain, y'see, and Their Graces insisted.'

'Fetch the stupid cullion,' Conrig snapped. 'I'll teach him to tend to his duty!' He hauled the door open and entered the nursery, followed by the queen. The knights of the royal escort tactfully remained in the corridor.

The large suite of rooms housing the royal children was illuminated by mellow twilight entering through open casement windows. On a food-splattered but otherwise empty table in the center of the supper area stood a sturdy boy some four years of age: Prince Bramlow, the oldest son of Conrig and Risalla. He was barefoot, wearing a red nightrobe as befitted an acolyte of Zeth, and held a bunched tablecloth in his hands as he stared keenly up at the unlit iron chandelier overhead.

A monkey the size of a large housecat sat on one of the candle-arms. It clutched a bowl of strawberries and chittered with evil glee as it pelted the human inhabitants of the room

with well-aimed pieces of fruit. The floor around the table
was littered with capsized furniture, broken plates, cups,
spoons, and scattered cushions – all commingled in a soggy
mass of spilt porridge, slices of bread, mashed berries, and a
pool of milk spreading from a cracked pitcher.

Two very young ladies-in-waiting huddled together behind
a wooden settle, weeping, their fine clothes rumpled and
splashed with berry juice. A third noblewoman, somewhat
older, stood with her back to the far wall. The giggling two-
year-old boy struggling in her arms was Prince Heritor Orrion,
who seemed to be in good health. His twin brother Corodon
jumped up and down and squealed with laughter. A pair of
nursemaids approached the table, glaring up at the monkey.
One maid brandished a broom and the other held a clothes
basket at the ready.

'Here goes!' Bramlow cried out to them, shaking the tablecloth he held. The piece of fabric billowed, soared from his
hands like a living thing, and wrapped itself neatly about the
simian vandal, who tumbled into the waiting basket with a
muffled howl. The two younger princes clapped their hands
and cheered. Bramlow hopped off the table, bowed formally
to the king and queen, and stood there grinning as the
triumphant nursemaids carried the struggling captive out of
the room. The unencumbered ladies-in-waiting made deep
curtsies and waited, their faces now full of dread. The woman
holding Prince Orrion set him on his feet at a gesture from
the queen.

Risalla said, 'Nalise, Erminy, Vedrea, you may leave us.
Wait outside until you're summoned.' The ladies fled, closing
the door behind them, and the queen regarded her sons with
a sad expression. 'You children have been very wicked.'

'Yes, Mama,' the three of them chorused. The younger
boys looked frightened and stood close together, hand in
hand. They were not identical: Prince Heritor Orrion was

slightly smaller than his twin brother, plain-featured and sandy-haired like Bramlow, while Corodon had his father's striking good looks and hair so fair it shone like silver.

'Wicked,' Conrig repeated in a terrible soft voice. 'But especially you, Bramlow. And you know why.'

The older boy lifted his chin. 'Yes, sire. It was bad to use talent to catch the monkey. But –'

'Only an ordained Brother of Zeth, dedicated to the service of the realm and pledged to harm no human person, may use overt forms of windtalent. A child who uses overt talent for vain or silly reasons commits a serious sin.' Conrig's voice deepened and Bramlow winced. 'A *royal* child who dares to exhibit overt talent in front of others, reminding them that one of our ancestors tainted the blood by mating with a nonhuman, comes very close to committing treason. Even though you're still too young to go to Zeth Abbey and begin your arcane studies, you are old enough to know right from wrong in this important matter.'

The boy dropped to his knees on the dirty floor. 'I'm sorry, sire. Really, really sorry.'

'You will be punished, Bramlow. For one week, you'll remain alone in your room, with only bread and milk to eat. A novice Brother will guard you. You are forbidden to windspeak Uncle Stergos or any other talented person, neither may you scry nor perform any of the other kinds of subtle magic that are usually allowed to you. The watching Brother will know if you disobey.'

'I – I promise I'll be good.' Tears gleamed on the four-year-old's face. 'Please don't punish the monkey!'

'The animal will be confined to its cage for a sennight,' said the king, 'and its keeper will receive a sound thrashing. Keep in mind that it is your fault that they suffer. Now retire to your room and pray for forgiveness until the midnight sun touches the horizon. Then go to bed.'

'Yes, sire.' Bramlow rose up, bowed, and trudged away into an inner chamber.

When he was gone the queen spoke to the twins. 'It was very wrong of you to ask the ladies to bring in the monkey without its chain and collar. A monkey isn't a person. It can't be trusted to behave. Do you understand this now?'

Corodon smiled slyly. 'Bram said it be great fun. It was!'

'But wrong.' Orrion's face was solemn. 'We sorry, Mama.'

Queen Risalla gathered the boys to her, kissing them. 'How do you feel today? Do you still cough and sniffle?'

'No, Mama. All well now.' Corodon beamed.

'And did you eat supper before the monkey spoiled the food?'

'Some porridge,' Orrion mumbled.

'Monkey took strawberries,' Corodon said. 'We didn't get none.'

'Didn't get *any*,' the queen corrected him. She rose to her feet. 'The ladies will make you milksops to eat in bed. No strawberries for you tonight. That will be your punishment. Now bid your father goodnight.'

Conrig lifted and embraced each boy gravely, looking deeply into their eyes before kissing them. The infinitesimal glint of talent was imperceptible to him, as it was to the Zeth Brethren and every other adept save Conjure-Queen Ullanoth and possibly Snudge – who'd never said a word about it, curse him!

Talent. That blessing and curse was present in all three of his offspring. But Risalla was once again with child, and if God pleased, Conrig would know tonight if the unborn was a normal-minded heir and the Sovereignty secure.

Much later, as the time of Ullanoth's visitation approached, Conrig and Risalla waited in the king's private sitting room in the royal apartments. The draperies were drawn against the still-bright sky, but open casements admitted both cool air and the sounds of laughter and dance-music rising from the gardens. Risalla had changed into a summer nightrobe of fine primrose-colored lawn and reclined on a cushioned couch. The hypnagogic draught prepared by Vra-Stergos, which she had swallowed only a few minutes earlier, was already making her drowsy.

'I still don't see why this examination is necessary.' The queen did not bother to hide her resentment. 'You required no such thing of me when I was pregnant with the other children.'

'Ullanoth has fashioned a new spell,' Conrig prevaricated. 'It will not only tell us the sex of our new child, but also whether or not it has talent.'

'Talent!' Risalla's tone was uncommonly peevish as she drifted between wakefulness and sleep and her usual invincible self-control dissolved. 'What does it matter if this babe shares poor Bramlow's arcane abilities? You have your precious heir to the throne in Orrion, and there is always Coro in case . . . in case . . .' Her eyes closed, but she gave a start and was wide awake again. 'In case of misfortune – may heaven forfend. I don't see why I must sleep during this procedure, either. Why shouldn't I know what Ullanoth does to me and to the child in my womb? I *hate* the notion of her casting a spell on us! I hate her, God forgive me, though I truly know not why.'

Her vehemence startled Conrig. He was fairly certain that she was unaware of the longstanding liaison between him and the sorceress, and the queen's temperament was ordinarily so coolly dutiful and tranquil that she seemed as incapable of jealousy as she was of sexual passion. In contrast to his mercurial first wife Maudrayne Northkeep, whom Conrig had adored until he came to believe that she could not give him children, Risalla Mallburn kept close custody of her emotions. It had never occurred to him to ask if she loved him; he deemed it sufficient that she was gently mannered, reasonably attractive, intelligent, fertile, and a princess royal of Cathra's traditional antagonist, the vassal nation of Didion.

'The Conjure-Queen will do nothing to outrage your dignity,' Conrig reassured her. 'She will only look at the child in a special way, without even touching you.'

'I still hate being in her power. Helpless.'

'Perhaps it's your Didionite heritage that makes you uneasy. You have a natural distrust of magic, due to your people's hostility to the sorcerers of neighboring Moss. And it's only natural that you should still resent Ullanoth's rôle in Didion's . . . submission to the Sovereignty.'

'Our defeat!' Risalla sighed and her eyes slowly closed again. 'To say nothing of the shame that most of our warriors died not in honest battle, but as the prey of bloodsucking tiny monsters, commanded by your good friend, the Conjure-Queen. All Didion knows that she invoked the Beaconfolk as well as the spunkies to ensure your victory. And so do many of your own nobles, here in Cathra. They believe you are in league with the Lights.'

'Madam, you don't know what you're saying.' He tried to speak calmly – for, after all, she was hardly conscious and Gossy had assured him that she would remember none of this tomorrow. Yet he had no doubt that Risalla spoke now from deep conviction, freed by the alchymical potion from the constraint of prudence that usually governed her tongue. It was no surprise to Conrig that the barbarous Didionites should believe him to be in thrall to Beaconfolk magic. But if it were true that his own people gave serious credence to the notion . . .

'Who among the Cathran nobility has spoken so perfidiously?' he asked her. But she only turned away and seemed to sleep.

There came a sound of hesitant knocking. The king rose
from beside his wife's couch and opened the door. The
corridor was empty except for his elder brother Stergos, the
Royal Alchymist, attired in splendid crimson vestments in
honor of the festival. Although he was five years Conrig's
senior, he appeared to be much younger, with a clean-shaven
round face and curly blond hair that always seemed slightly
disordered. Tonight he was obviously ill at ease and his brow
was dewed with perspiration.

Stergos whispered, 'All's well with Her Grace?'

Conrig nodded and the alchymist came quickly into the
apartment, closing and locking the door behind him. 'I bespoke
Ullanoth in Royal Fenguard castle not ten minutes ago. She
can ascertain nothing through her ordinary scrying, but if the
unborn possesses talent, she will be able to Send to it as she
does to you and me. First, let me make certain that your lady
sleeps.' With great care, Stergos lifted one of the queen's
eyelids. The iris with its dilated pupil had rolled upward. 'Good.
Now we must distance ourselves from Risalla if the experiment is to work. Let's go into the queen's sitting room.'

They passed through Conrig's great bedchamber and
Risalla's adjacent one into the spacious solar where the queen
and her ladies were accustomed to sew, read, and break their
fast. 'We should be at least twenty ells away from her,' Stergos
said, 'so our own talent is incapable of giving substance to
the Sending.'

'What then?'

'I am to bespeak the Conjure-Queen that all is in readiness,' said his brother, perching on one of the chairs near
the cold fireplace. The king took the other one. 'She will
attempt the Sending, while we pray she does not succeed.
If Ullanoth walks through that door, it means that the babe's
talent permitted her to materialize beside Risalla.'

'And I'm futtered once again,' Conrig murmured bitterly.

'Damn it, Gossy! If I could but convince the Lords of the South to do away with the impediment, then I'd be safe and so would my sons . . . What a king young Bramlow would make! Bold as a hawk and sharp as a varg sword! You should have seen the little rogue get the better of that bloody pet monkey this evening.' He described the scene in the royal nursery, and Stergos had to smile in spite of his nervousness.

'I punished the lad harshly,' Conrig admitted. 'A week's confinement on bread and milk. He must learn self-discipline if we ever hope to have the talent restriction lifted. The Lords of the South will never yield if they envision a wizard with overt powers sitting one day on the throne.'

Stergos ventured, 'Shall I windspeak the Conjure-Queen now?'

'Wait just a moment.' The king casually covered his mouth with his hand. 'I must ask your advice on another matter before we converse with Ulla's Sending. She almost never uses the Loophole to eavesdrop now because of her considerable pain-debt, and if we guard ourselves from scrier's lip-reading our speech should be secure from her.'

'What is it, Con?' Stergos had drawn the hood of his crimson cloak over his head so that his face was concealed.

'I had disquieting news from Parlian Beorbrook tonight at the feast. You know he's just come down from an inspection of our Wold Road outposts in western Didion.'

'Don't tell me Prince Somarus is up to his old tricks!'

'No. As far as the earl marshal can tell, the bastard's laying low for the moment somewhere in the Lady Lakes region. Beorbrook's news concerns something far more serious: a rumor that Maudrayne may be alive, hiding somewhere in Tarn. A traveler from Donorvale said that the rumor has spread like wildfire over the past two weeks among the fishermen's taverns of the north-western shore, and thence to the low dives of the Tarnian capital.'

The hooded figure of the alchymist had given a great start as the king spoke his first wife's name. 'Saint Zeth preserve us – it's not possible that Maude lives! The conjoined minds of the Brotherhood searched the entire island, virtually inch by inch, and failed to scry any trace of the Princess Dowager. Even Ullanoth's Subtle Loophole detected nothing – and the sigil supposedly can oversee anyone, anywhere in the world.'

'So the Conjure-Queen says. But her close scrutiny took place four years ago, shortly after Maude was thought to have drowned. At the time, Ulla admitted that her search might have been thwarted by Red Ansel Pikan. The magical capabilities of the Grand Shaman of Tarn are unknown to her. He might have been able to block the action of the Great Stone. The painful search effort so debilitated Ullanoth that she was forced to avoid using Loophole for many months. Since then, as far as I know, she has made no further attempt to look for Maude.'

'What are we to do, Con?' Stergos's voice was taut with shock. He and the king had found and read Maudrayne's secret diary after her presumed death. In it, she had revealed not only that she had conceived Conrig's child, but also her knowledge of her husband's arcane taint. 'If the princess lives and has birthed a son not possessed of talent, you are undone! She knows your secret and could divulge it at any time, with Ansel to testify to the truth of it. Even if your twin sons by Risalla are accepted as normal, the law says that Maudrayne's boy must inherit your crown if you are deposed.'

'*If* she lives! And *if* she tells what she knows and produces the normal-minded male child. Here is where I require your advice, Gossy. Would it be wise for me to once again enlist the Conjure-Queen in the search for Maude? I'm reluctant to do so, since it would give Ulla even more power over me than she has now. I feel I'd be jumping from the hot griddle into the fire-pit.'

'My God, yes. Her ambitions . . . Con, you know I've never trusted the woman.'

'Yes, yes,' the king said impatiently. 'Nevertheless, her Loophole probably holds out the best chance of locating Maude and any child she may have had.'

'Perhaps not, if Red Ansel still keeps the Princess Dowager under his protection. But even the most powerful sorcery has limitations. For instance, Maudrayne and her child could not live permanently inside a spell of invisibility woven by Ansel. Such an existence would be insupportable to the healthy human temperament. Furthermore, a high-spirited woman such as Maude would never consent to be immured within some impregnable magical fortress for years upon end.'

Conrig gave a short mirthless laugh. 'No, not Maude! She'd take her boy hiking on the tundra and sailing in her yacht on the arctic waters. She'd teach him to ski and to hunt elk and icebears and sea-unicorns. And if she does these things, there arc bound to be local people who know about it. In my opinion, she might be sought and found by a clever and talented spy – such as my Royal Intelligencer, Snudge. What do you think, Gossy?'

Stergos hesitated. 'If Maude is hiding in Tarn, she would surely be protected by the magic of more than one of the local shamans. Ansel would hardly spend all of his time shielding her. He has other responsibilities. Deveron Austrey would have a special advantage over the lesser northern adepts, since his talent is imperceptible to all but the most powerful. Furthermore, he's impossible to windwatch, so they would be able to observe him only with ordinary eyesight. But what will you do if Deveron does discover that your former wife is alive, and has a son?'

'That . . . can be decided later. But I believe there's only one solution to the problem.'

'For the love of God, Con, tell me you would not –'

The king cut off his brother's horrified protest. 'Say no more! This rumor may prove to be entirely false. We will not discuss the fate of the Princess Dowager now.'

'As you please, sire.'

Conrig said, 'I gave Snudge permission to leave Cala Blenholme and visit his new estate following his initiation ceremony. He said he'd ride out at once. You must bespeak him, ordering his return.'

'Very well. I'll take care of it as soon as we finish here.' Stergos threw off his vestment hood. 'We should delay no longer bespeaking the Conjure-Queen.'

'Do it then,' Conrig said.

The Royal Alchymist let his head sink into his hands and called out silently on the wind. After a few minutes had passed, he opened his eyes and said, 'She will make an attempt to Send immediately.'

They waited, straining their ears, fearing the sound of approaching steps from the room where Risalla lay, but hearing only the distant sounds of music and revelry outside in the gardens. At length Conrig leapt to his feet.

'I can't stand it any longer. I'm going in there –'

'That won't be necessary.'

The sweet woodsy scent of vetiver wafted into the room. A silhouette was standing in front of the tall undraped window, completely enveloped in a deep-green cloak. Ullanoth's Sending had flashed into existence with no warning. A hand, pale as milk and wearing a ring of carved moonstone on one long, graceful finger, emerged from the folds of cloth and extended itself toward Conrig.

He hastened to take the hand, brushing the back of it with his lips. He carefully avoided any contact with the ring, which was a powerful sigil named Weathermaker. 'Gracious Queen, welcome.'

Ullanoth of Moss unfastened her cloak and handed it to the

High King as though he were a simple lackey. Except for the purplish shadows about her eyes, her face was as lovely as ever, framed by shimmering long hair that mimicked the pearly interior of certain seashells. Her gown was the same unadorned green samite as her cape, and her belt was gold, with a hanging purse. Around her neck hung a golden chain with a curiously carved small translucent pendant that glowed in the dim room like wan foxfire – the Great Stone named Sender, the third major sigil that she owned. Its power, invoked only at the cost of terrible pain now that her debt to the Lights was so heavy, enabled Ullanoth to inhabit a magical simulacrum of her natural body, in which her soul might travel anywhere in the world while her true flesh lay senseless. The Sending was no vaporous ghost, but rather a warm and solid replica with a full palette of physical sensation, able to carry from its point of origin all clothing and other accoutrements worn or held by the original. It could not, however, draw sustenance from food or drink at its destination, nor could it carry back any foreign object. And if the Sending remained in existence for more than a few hours, the true body would begin to deteriorate mortally.

There was another important limitation to the Sending that only the most advanced arcane practitioners were aware of: it could materialize only near a talented person, from whom it drew magical substantiation.

'Then Risalla's unborn child is free of talent!' Conrig cried joyously.

Ullanoth nodded. 'Yes. Tonight, I've used Vra-Stergos as my substantiator. Let us go to your wife now and determine whether the babe is male or female.'

The three of them went into the room where Risalla lay, but after a few suspenseful moments Ullanoth stepped away from the sleeper's couch and shook her head. 'Alas for your hopes, my king! Your wife carries a healthy girl, without arcane talent as all of her sex must be, unless they are of far northern human blood . . . or doubly descended from the Green Ones.'

Conrig groaned. 'If the laws of Didion prevailed here, the lass might reign as their great Queen Casabarela did! But Cathra reserves its crown for male issue, and so must my Sovereignty.'

'Unless the law is changed,' Stergos put in with a hopeful smile.

'Don't be a fool, Gossy,' the king exclaimed. 'Why should the Lords of the South agree to change it now, when all save we three believe there are two legitimate male heirs to the throne? We can only hope for a better outcome to a future pregnancy, and meanwhile pray that no enemy learns the secret of my poor sons and I.'

'There are only two enemies,' Ullanoth said, 'that need concern you now.'

Conrig and Stergos regarded her with open dismay, each thinking that she must have heard the rumor about Maudrayne and her son.

But the Conjure-Queen went on to say, 'My little brother Beynor knows nothing of your own talent – not yet. But he's up to some kind of mischief with the Salka. I've been too indisposed to spy on him closely with the Loophole sigil of late, but my ordinary scrying reveals him to be in a state of unusual excitement. I've told you that Beynor spends his time studying the historical archives of his monstrous hosts in the Dawntide Isles. I cannot read lips well, and the Salka have erected magical barriers that dim my unaugmented oversight of their citadel. But I believe that Beynor may have made some important discovery. And he may have shared it with your old enemy, Vra-Kilian Blackhorse, the former Royal Alchymist.'

'But how?' Stergos demanded. 'Our wretched uncle was deprived of all talent by the iron gammadion before being

confined to Zeth Abbey. Kilian is unable to speak on the
wind himself, nor can he receive any windspoken communication from another. And no humans dare set foot on the
Dawntide Isles, so there can have been no written message
from Beynor delivered to the abbey.'

'My brother may have been cursed by the Lights and
stripped of his sigils,' Ullanoth said, 'but he still retains the
strong natural talents he was born with. One of those is the
ability to invade dreams. When we were young children, he
used to torment me until I learned to shut him out.
Fortunately, that defensive ability comes readily to those who
are adept at the arcane arts.'

The king nodded thoughtfully, remembering that Snudge
had also told him once of being harassed by Beynor while
sleeping. 'So you believe your brother communicates with
Kilian through dreams?'

'Zeth Abbey is well-shielded from windsearching, but I
have been able to follow Beynor's mental footsteps, as it
were, to that place many times. I doubt there is any other
person residing in the abbey who would be of interest to
him.'

'Beynor and Kilian!' Conrig mused. 'What common cause
could the two exiles share nowadays? And yet they did
conspire against me as I prepared to invade Didion . . .'

Ullanoth had learned some years ago that both villains
shared knowledge of a mysterious hidden trove of sigils. But
she was unware that the King already knew of its existence.

'I shall have to warn Abbas Noachil about this at once,'
Stergos said. 'He's very old and ill, but he can order the
Brethren to take special precautions against Kilian's escape.'

'That would be prudent.' Ullanoth turned to Conrig.
'Unfortunately, Beynor has also attempted to invade the
dreams of some person residing here in Cala Palace. I learned
of this only two days ago, as I scried him on the parapet of

the Salka island fortress and followed his windtrace. I don't know who his intended target was, only that the dreamer successfully repelled Beynor's effort.'

'God's Teeth!' Conrig exclaimed. 'Could the bastard have been trying to enter *my* dreams?'

'Were you aware of any such assault?' Ullanoth asked. When Conrig admitted he could recall no such thing, she smiled. 'Then you're very likely safe. Your talent, meager though it is, would probably have alerted your sleeping mind to any attempt at forcible entry. Were you an untalented person, however, it's possible he might have invaded you without your being aware of what was happening.'

'This is a troubling piece of news,' Stergos said. 'If Beynor's target was not the High King, then who might it have been?'

'I don't know,' she said. 'Dream-invasion is an uncommon talent. Certain members of Moss's Glaumerie Guild have used it in the past to gather information from the minds of ordinary folk, or as a means of subtly coercing dreamers into some activity. More often than not, the invasion fails of its objective unless the dreamer is predisposed to cooperate, is very young, or has impaired willpower.'

'Will you continue to oversee Beynor's footprints on the wind,' Conrig besought her, 'and warn us if he attempts some wicked ploy among the residents of Cala Palace? I would deem it a great favor.'

'You ask the impossible. My surveillance of my brother is sporadic at best because I am so drained of strength. I only undertake it to protect myself and my kingdom from his evil designs.'

'Then what can we do?' Conrig asked.

'Nothing except be on guard.' Ullanoth took her cloak from Conrig's hands and wrapped it about her once again. 'It's time for me to leave you. I dare not let my Sending remain here any longer, for I feel myself growing very weak.

Be assured that I'll notify Vra-Stergos promptly if I should discover anything that you should know.'

'Thank you for examining the unborn babe, my dearest queen.' Conrig made a formal inclination of his head. 'I regret that your pain will be endured to no good outcome.'

She touched his cheek. 'We are with one another so seldom now that I welcome the opportunity to be here – even if it can only be in a brief Sending. Consider a voyage to Moss this summer. You can easily contrive an excuse.'

'It's a wonderful idea. You'll be hearing from me.' He bent over her hand again, and a moment later she disappeared.

Aghast, Stergos whispered, 'Surely you would not go to her!'

Conrig's smile was grim. 'No more than I would dive head-long into the steaming crater of Mornash volcano. But let her have hope.'

The Royal Alchymist spoke anxiously. 'You know what Kilian must be after.'

'I know. But the Darasilo Trove can't be easy to get at, else our uncle would have had his minions seize it years ago . . . or you and Snudge would have located the bloody thing yourselves.'

'But –'

'Brother, we'll consider the matter tomorrow, when Snudge returns. He knows more about that cache of sigils than anyone else we can trust. For now, I think you and I should carry Risalla to her bed. Then you must bespeak Snudge ordering his return and warn Abbas Noachil to put Kilian and his three cronies into close confinement. Meanwhile, I'll seek out Earl Marshal Parlian in the gardens and ask his opinion of this fine mess. One thing is certain: I was much mistaken in telling my Royal Intelligencer that this would be a peaceful summer.'

Stergos had given all of the Brothers in the palace permission to set aside their usual duties and enjoy the Solstice entertainments. So he was surprised to find three red-robed figures standing outside the great door that led to the Alchymical Library, engaged in earnest conversation. He vaguely recognized them as visiting scholars, associates of Prior Waringlow who had come down from Zeth Abbey several months earlier to do research on some historical project or other.

'Why are you tarrying inside the palace on such a beautiful night?' he asked them, unfastening a large iron key from the ring he wore on his belt. To reach his own rooms, he had to pass through the library.

The Brothers bowed in respectful unison. One of them said, 'We had hoped to do some studying, Lord Stergos, but found the library locked. Perhaps you'll admit us –'

'Nonsense! Go listen to the music and have a cup of wine. Your work can wait.'

'Certainly, my lord.'

Stergos watched them go, trying to recall their names. But thoughts of what he must say and must *not* say in the upcoming wind-conversation with Vra-Mattis, the novice Brother assigned to Snudge, distracted him, and he gave up the effort as he fitted the key into its massive lock.

TWO

Drumming. Drumming. Drumming.

Dom dom t'pat-a-pat pom . . . dom.

The sound coming from the little hut beyond the byre was soft but still audible in every room of the arctic steading's main house, repeating the same simple percussive figure, continuing hour after hour for nearly two days, longer than ever before. Sometimes the beat would falter, the timing spoiled because of inattention or the fatigue of the drummer's aged wrists and fingers; but after a painful pause the rhythmic sound always began again.

Dobnelu the sea-hag was having a particularly difficult time crossing the barrier this time. She could not recall how many false starts she'd made. Even a single mistake in the three thousand measured patterns of drumming meant going back to the beginning, but it was unthinkable that she abandon the effort. Not even her dire premonition about the woman and the boy who were her special charges must tempt her to give up. Red Ansel Pikan and Thalassa Dru were waiting beneath the ice. Needing her.

And so was the One Denied the Sky.

Dobnelu could only join them in the starless world by

means of the drum-trance, a ritual not especially difficult for Tarnian shamans in the prime of life, but an excruciating ordeal for a woman whose years numbered over four score and ten.

Dom dom t'pat-a-pat pom . . . dom.

Eyes shut tightly against the brightness of Midsummer Eve, resolutely gripping the bone drumsticks in her gnarled hands, Dobnelu the sea-hag forced herself to go on.

The maidservant Rusgann and the boy were somehow able to sleep through the maddening sound of the drumming, but Maudrayne Northkeep always remained conscious of it, even when she slipped into and out of a troubled half-doze. In disjointed prayers, she begged for an end to the infernal noise.

At last, as always, the end did come. The drumbeats ceased abruptly after a single climactic *DOM*. There was a sudden silence, broken only by the bleating of a goat in the meadow. The hag had succeeded in opening the door to that other place again. She'd entered and so left her prisoners free of her supervision for at least a day, perhaps even two.

Maudrayne pushed aside the opaque curtain of her cupboard-bed and descended on the stepstool, naked except for the ornate golden necklace with the three great opals that she never took off, her Uncle Sernin's precious wedding gift that she had worn on the night she cast herself into the sea. The air in the shuttered little room was fresh and pleasantly cool, thanks to the sod roof of Dobnelu's sturdily built home. Outside, under the endless midsummer daylight, it was probably rather warm. Perfect for what she had planned.

After putting on her clothes, she tiptoed to the partly open door leading to the large central chamber, the combined kitchen and sitting room where her serving woman and the boy slept. The hourglass on the mantelpiece indicated about three in the morning. Little Dyfrig's nook was wide open and he sat unclothed on the edge of his bed, watching his mother with solemn, intelligent eyes. Neither Maudrayne nor her son needed much sleep in the summertime: their Tarnian blood saw to that. But Rusgann Moorcock was a southerner, and she'd demonstrated that she could sleep through a tundra-deer stampede. Her bed-cupboard's curtains were shut.

'No more magic drum,' Dyfrig whispered to his mother. His hair had the same tawny golden color as that of his father, and he also possessed Conrig's handsome features and unusual dark brown eyes. A moon earlier, the boy had celebrated his fourth birthday.

Maudrayne put a finger to her lips and beckoned him. He slipped to the floor noiselessly and joined her at the kitchen's single small window. Leather-hinged at the top and held open by a hook and eye fastened to the low ceiling, it was covered with a screen of black gauze to exclude biting midges. Outside, bright sun shone on the meadow and reflected from the island-strewn expanse of Useless Bay beyond the drop-off into the fjord. A distant iceberg with multiple spires, like a dazzling white castle, hovered on the horizon off Cape Wolf.

Maudrayne pointed to the sea-hag's holy hut at the edge of the steading and spoke softly into the boy's ear. 'Eldmama Nelu has drummed herself into an enchanted sleep again. Her body will stay in the hut for a few days now, while her spirit soars away northward to the icecap of the Barren Lands to talk to the One Denied the Sky and the other witches and wizards. Now that she's gone, we can leave the farm without her permission and go wherever we please! Would you like to walk along the seashore today and have a treasure hunt?'

He squealed with excitement. 'Yes! Yes! Maybe we can find whale bones, or scales from a mirrorfish!'

'Shhh. You'll wake Rusgann –'

Curtain-rings rattled and the maid's homely face popped

out of her enclosure. 'I'm already awake, Your Grace.' A lanky body modestly clad in a homespun shift emerged. 'And you know very well we're forbidden to leave the steading circle without Dobnelu along to protect us from danger.'

Ignoring the servant's admonition, Maudrayne went to the larder, where she gathered rye bread, cheese, a small crock of goosegrease flavored with wild herbs, and some sweet cranberry cakes. 'There's no danger,' she insisted. 'None at all, except from our own misadventure, and we'll take great care not to lose our footing on the cliff trail or be caught by the rising tide. Now dress yourself, Dyfi. Visit the backhouse and wash your hands, and we'll be on our way. We can have a picnic breakfast on the beach.'

The boy threw his clothes on and darted outside with a joyful shout, slamming the door. The maid Rusgann lumbered over to her mistress and stood, fists on hips, scowling in disapproval. 'Your Grace, the spells protecting us extend only to the ring of white stones around this house and the outbuildings. If we venture outside the magic circle, the Beaconfolk could do us harm. Or some windwatching scoundrel of the king's might scry us!'

'Do you know what day this is, Rusgann?' Maudrayne was serene and smiling. Her long auburn hair, freshly washed and hanging free as she stubbornly insisted upon wearing it, shone like burnished copper. 'This is the Solstice Eve, a very lucky day. No wicked sorcerers or monsters – not even the Coldlight Army – can harm human beings today.'

'Huh! I never heard of such a thing.'

'That's because you're Cathran-born. We Tarnians know more about dark magic than you do. As for windwatchers – none of them know we're in this godforsaken spot except Ansel, who brought us here. No one who matters even knows we're alive! So I say we're in no danger. And today my son and I will leave this dreary steading and walk free for hours along the sunny shore without a cranky old witch dogging our heels.'

She wrapped the food in a cloth and put it into a basket, together with a long kitchen knife, a leather bottle of mead, and two wooden cups. There would be plenty of good water from freshets trickling down the cliff face. 'The only question is, will you accompany Dyfi and me on our holiday, or stay behind and sulk?'

The maid was hauling on her garments. 'It's not safe, Your Grace! There's others that could find us here besides magickers. Like that blue fishing vessel that tarried offshore two tennights ago. Dobnelu said the crew peered at the steading with a spyglass! The old woman was in a rare tizzy about it. It seems that plain eyesight isn't hindered by her shielding magic. The fishermen could have seen you out by the byre.'

'Please God, they had! For I recognized the lugger as one belonging to Vik Waterfall of Northkeep Port, where my own family's castle lies. And since catching sight of it, I've thought of nothing but how we might use such a boat to get away from here.'

'Oh, no, Your Grace!'

'Stop calling me that, you stupid creature! The only one here worthy of such an honorific is my son.' She turned away, and her next words came through gritted teeth. 'And I'll see Dyfrig gets the crown he deserves . . . if I don't die of vexation and melancholy first, trapped in this loathsome place.'

The sturdy maidservant persisted in speaking her mind, as was her habit. Rusgann's fierce loyalty had never equated with submissiveness. 'My lady, you owe it to the lad to keep him secure. To obey High Shaman Ansel's instructions and those of the sea-hag. Life here's boring, I'll give you that, but Mistress Dobnelu and the shaman know what's best for you.'

'Lately, I've had my doubts.' Maudrayne stared out the

window at the desolate grandeur of the fjord and the high tundra above it. The snow that had blanketed the windswept plateau was finally melted now, leaving outcroppings of pink and grey granite and patches of vivid green grass tinged with the purple, yellow, and white of short-lived arctic wildflowers.

Rusgann sniffed. 'I suppose doing housework and taking care of farm animals is a hard life for a high-born lady like you –'

'You silly thing! That's not it at all!'

'Well, what, for pity's sake?' the maid muttered. 'We have a snug place to stay, plenty of food to eat, and magic to keep your enemies at bay.'

'We've been here for four years, Rusgann, hardly ever leaving the stone circle. I have only a small child and you and that senile witch for company, with infrequent visits from Ansel when he can spare us the time. God knows I'm used to northern winters that are eight months long, but not the isolation we have to endure here in this miserable hovel!' Maudrayne gestured in disgust at the modest kitchen, which was neat and clean enough now thanks to her own efforts and those of the maid. 'My family's castle at Northkeep is a cheerful place, full of people. When I lived there we weren't forced to stay inside during the long winter nights – not even when the Coldlight Army prowled the sky. My brothers and cousins and I played in the snow and went visiting and bathed in the hot springs. There was singing and feasting and games and bards telling wonderful tales. And in summertime we sailed and hunted and fished and gathered berries and went exploring. This wretched steading might as well be a prison. And Ansel won't even tell me how long we must stay here.'

'He said we must remain until there's no danger to you and the lad. How can you dispute the wisdom of that?'

She stamped away from the window with her blue eyes blazing. 'And just when will the danger be over? When Dyfrig is a man full-grown? When his damned father is dead? All of life is fraught with peril, yet we don't spend our time hiding safely under the bed!'

Rusgann made a helpless gesture. 'You seemed content enough to stay here earlier.'

'When I believed we had no other choice. When Dyfrig was a baby who couldn't understand the need for prudence and secrecy. But he's four now, and wise beyond his years. He needs teachers and companions of his own age. If he's forced to spend his entire childhood here, his spirit will be stunted – just like those tiny winter-blasted birch trees up on the tundra that never grow more than two handspans high. I can't let that happen to my son! Surely there are better ways for Ansel to secure our safety. Why can't we live under the protection of my brother Liscanor at Northkeep instead of in this cramped farmhouse?'

'You could ask the High Shaman that question when next he visits us. But in the end, you have to trust his judgment.'

'I used to think Ansel was my loyal friend, whose only interest was our welfare.' Maudrayne spoke in a low voice and her expression was disillusioned. 'Lately I've come to believe he may have other reasons for keeping us confined here that have little to do with our physical safety.'

'I don't understand.'

'When last he came, just after the ice breakup, Ansel and the sea-hag were whispering together in the kitchen, thinking that little Dyfi was napping in his bed-cupboard. You and I were mucking out the byre. The boy heard Ansel say, 'We must make certain he remains king. He's the only one strong enough to hold them back. Without him, we have no hope of liberating the Source.' The boy was clever enough to remember the strange words exactly – and he asked me about them.'

Rusgann's brow wrinkled in puzzlement. 'I suppose Ansel was speaking of High King Conrig.'

'Yes. Both Dyfrig and I threaten him – but especially me, since I know a great secret of his that would cost him his throne. Perhaps Ansel hopes to eliminate this threat by keeping us out of the way.'

'But who is it who must be *held back* by King Conrig? And what in Zeth's name is the Source?'

'I know not which particular enemy Conrig's Sovereignty must hold in check. He has so many! As for this Source, the last time Ansel spoke of it was after I jumped from the parapet of Eagleroost Castle into Cala Bay. As he rescued me, he spoke mysteriously about what his Source would think if my unborn child and I had died in the icy water.'

'My lady, I still don't know what you're talking about.'

'From other things old Dobnelu has said, I've come to believe that Ansel's Source might have something to do with the person the hag visits during her long trances. Perhaps they are even the same.'

Outside, Dyfrig was calling. 'Mama! Come out! Let's have our picnic. I'm hungry.'

Maudrayne Northkeep, who had been wife to Conrig Wincantor and Queen of Cathra, picked up the basket and headed for the door. She looked over her shoulder and said to Rusgann, 'I believe that Ansel and Dobnelu and this Source may be playing some deep magical game. To them, Dyfrig and I are nothing but pawns on their arcane gameboard – and so, evidently, is my former husband, the Sovereign of Blenholme. But I'll be no one's gamepiece willingly, and neither will my son. This is the last summer we'll spend here, Rusgann. We're going to escape.'

The handmaid's mouth dropped open in consternation.

Maudrayne laughed. 'Don't stand there gaping, woman. If you're coming to the shore with us, step lively.'

She sailed out the door, and with Dyfrig skipping at her side went through the outbuildings toward the flowery meadow, where honeybees and boreal warblers foraged, and a herd of goats and sheep with their young grazed the fresh grass. At the edge of the enchanted circle, Maudrayne told the boy to wait while she went to the holy hut nearby and looked inside.

The place was windowless, but light entered through a smokehole in the roof. Dobnelu lay unconscious on a rickety cot, her discarded magic drum beside her. She was a small person who could not have weighed seven stone, dressed for the ritual in a tattered blue silk robe that had once been magnificent and costly. Her head had only a few wisps of white hair and the skin of her skull was so translucent that blood vessels seemed to cover it like a netted cap. Her eyes, large and black and smoldering with arcane energy when she was awake, were shuttered by crinkled lids. Her mouth hung slightly ajar, showing a few stumpy teeth. From time to time her lips moved soundlessly.

'Where do you journey?' Maudrayne whispered. 'Whom do you talk to?'

The former queen's hand stole into the basket where the sharp kitchen knife lay and she fingered the long blade. It would be easy to take the sea-hag's life while she was entranced and helpless. But would such a deed be justifiable, even to permit their escape? The old woman was terrible-tempered and imperious but without real malice. She had opened her home to three refugees at Ansel's request (complaining loudly all the while), but had treated little Dyfrig with unfailing kindness, so that he came to love her and called her Eldmama Nelu. Maude and Rusgann she had used as domestic slaveys and farmhands, berating them mercilessly when they were clumsy or negligent. But she had never punished them with her magic.

I cannot kill the witch, Maudrayne realized. Nevertheless, I won't rest until I find a way to escape without doing her serious harm.

She left the hut and closed the door behind her. Rusgann was waiting with Dyfrig, carrying her own cup and an extra bottle of mead. Maudrayne put the things into the basket, handed it to the maid, then led the way through the pasture to the steep path down the cliff.

After the picnic breakfast was eaten, the three of them embarked on the promised treasure hunt along the narrow fjord beach. Good food and plenty of drink had cheered Rusgann so that she put her former misgivings aside. The bay waters sparkled under the bright sky. Kittiwakes, fulmars, and other birds nesting on the rough rock walls and sea-pinnacles made a raucous din. Green sedges, cliff-ferns, and tufts of white starwort grew in sheltered high places, while some deeply shadowed stretches of shingle above the tide-line were still heaped with slow-melting slabs of ice driven ashore by the winter westerlies.

The tide was receding. They hiked along the emerging sands and slimy boulders below the fjord cliffs for hour after hour, finding all sorts of interesting things: colorful agate pebbles, net floats, shells, the skull of some small animal, and a freshly dead mirrorfish two ells long from which the boy gleefully scraped a heap of huge, gleaming scales. There was even a chunk of white quartz with embedded metallic specks that might have been gold. Maudrayne carried all the treasures in the basket, along with the remains of the food.

Dyfrig raced ahead tirelessly, pursued by laughing Rusgann. After a while the two of them were lost to Maudrayne's sight behind a jutting promontory at the end of the fjord beach.

She brooded as she hurried to catch up with them. Escape from Dobnelu's steading was not going to be easy. The sea-hag was a vigilant guardian except when she was sunk in one of her trances or stupefied by strong drink, as happened when changing weather made her bones ache. The drumming happened only at irregular intervals, so they would probably have to rely on ardent spirits to disable Dobnelu's wind-searching ability. Fortunately, Rusgann was an expert distiller of malted barley liquor, and there was plenty left from last year's batch. However, tempting the old woman to over-indulgence without arousing her suspicions would be tricky.

As the raven flew, Northkeep Castle and its surrounding villages lay only sixty leagues to the south-east, on Silver Salmon Bay; but to get there traveling overland was virtu-ally impossible. Away from the shore, this region of Tarn was a trackless plateau of rolling tundra and bogs. Game would be the only food source unless they waited for the berries that ripened at summer's end. Maudrayne was an experienced hunter, but without a bow and arrows, she could take birds and animals only by means of inefficient snares. Nor was the upland wildlife entirely innocuous: even if they managed to evade the bears, snow-lions, and wolf packs, biting midges might well eat them alive.

Following the shoreline meant fewer insects and preda-tors, and the tidepools were full of mussels and crabs and stranded small fish. But the irregularity of the coast route more than doubled the distance to the castle, and the going would be appallingly hard, especially for a small child. South of Dobnelu's home fjord, the shore was jumbled rock and saltmarsh, rather than easily traveled sand. Below Useless Bay lay another broad inlet with a river delta and treach-erous flats that could be crossed only by means of ski-like mudshoes. The final obstacle before Silver Salmon Bay and the settled lands held by her elder brother, Sealord Liscanor, was a precipitous headland so sheer that it could only be climbed with the aid of ropes.

No, only an idiot would think of escaping on foot. The terrain was too difficult and the journey would take too long.

Dobnelu – or Ansel himself – would be certain to find them with windsight long before they reached Northkeep Castle. Only one course of action had any real chance of success: escaping the same way they had arrived – by boat.

Fishermen came only rarely into Useless Bay, fearing its treacherous shoals as much as the sorcery of the infamous sea-hag who dwelt there. But the sighting of Vik Waterfall's lugger – and Dobnelu's warning about the sailors having a spyglass – had given Maudrayne an idea. The next time a boat appeared offshore, she'd try to signal to it from a place out of the old woman's sight. She'd proffer the valuable opal necklace, and use handsigns to tell the crew what she wanted and where and when to pick her up. If she was lucky, one of the men might recognize her, even though ten years had passed since she sailed her sloop-rigged yacht among the fishing fleet in Northkeep Port, before going south to become the bride of Conrig Wincantor . . .

She had almost reached the end of the rocky point that separated the long fjord beach from the next cove, into which Rusgann and Dyfrig had evidently vanished. She paused for a moment, setting down the basket and looking out to sea, past the numerous barren islands and shallows that gave the bay its discouraging name, to the distant open water where the great iceberg drifted. As a proficient sailor in northern waters, she knew that with cautious navigation and a fair wind, even a small craft might reach Northkeep in a little over half a day. Given a few hours' head start, even if Dobnelu woke from her drunken slumber and bespoke Ansel of their escape, he would never catch them at sea unless he conjured up a storm that risked killing them.

And Ansel doesn't want us dead, she said to herself, else he would have left us to our fate long ago. No, our deaths would somehow spoil his great game.

Mulling the possibilities, Maudrayne made her way around

the end of the promontory, climbing among huge granite boulders veined with white quartz and overgrown with thick mats of slippery seaweed. This part of the shore was unfamiliar. In their abbreviated outings with the old woman, she and the boy had never gone so far away from the steading. When the tide turned, the easily traversed sections of these rock piles' would probably be submerged, and Maudrayne was beginning to be concerned about getting back safely with Rusgann and Dyfrig ahead of the flow.

The next cove was small and extremely steep-sided, with a towering islet poking up amidst a welter of exposed reefs a few hundred ells offshore. The boy and the handmaid were nowhere in sight, perhaps concealed among the many large rocks at the base of the cliff. She was ready to call out to them when she caught sight of something that brought her to a standstill with her heart pounding.

Barely visible in its anchorage on the far side of the high island was a single-masted fishing lugger with a blue hull. It was almost certainly the same boat that had cruised past two tennights ago.

Dear God! Was it possible that Rusgann had signaled Vik Waterfall to come ashore?

In her haste, she tripped and fell, spilling the contents of the basket into a tidepool. She muttered an oath and hurried to retrieve only the important things – the knife and the finely made wooden cups – thrusting them into the capacious pockets of the peasant apron that was part of her everyday garb at the steading. Unencumbered now, she scrambled over the rocks as fast as she could. Some of them were house-sized or even larger, with narrow gaps between them that had to be threaded with care. She was still unable to see much of the cove shoreline ahead, but she was encouraged by the occasional sight of footprints on patches of wet sand. Dyfrig and Rusgann had certainly come this way.

At last she came out onto the narrow beach, and pulled up short.

About twenty ells away, a leather coracle was drawn up on the strand, one of the lightweight watercraft with whale-bone frames that the smaller Tarnian sailing boats often used as tenders. Two men stood near it, hailing her approach with eager shouts. Rusgann sat on the pebble-strewn sand a short distance away from them, with her back pressed against a half-buried boulder and Dyfrig huddled against her skirts. The maid's hair was disheveled and her face distorted by fury.

The older of the two men came striding toward Maudrayne, and her heart sank as she realized that he was not her affable old acquaintance Vik Waterfall but rather the latter's younger brother Lukort, a character notorious in former years for his violent temper and unsavory dealings. Eleven years ago, the Waterfall clan had banished him for stealing lobsters from the traps of other fishermen. Yet here he was, wearing a skipper's cap, in charge of his brother's boat.

Lukort Waterfall was sinewy, straggly-bearded, and not very tall. His eyes, almost as pale as a wolf's, were close-set under bushy brows. He wore a vest of pieced and embroi-dered sealskin, canvas trousers cut off at the knees, a belt with a tarnished silver buckle, and high seaboots. His companion was a burly, oafish-looking youth with a soup-bowl haircut, a heavy jaw, and cheeks as smooth as a girl's, clad in a homespun tunic and trews of undyed wool. His huge feet were bare.

'Princess Maudie!' Lukort exclaimed, doffing his cap with a flourish and bowing deeply. 'You took long enough gettin' round the point. We feared you had a mishap.'

'Mama!' Dyfrig screamed. 'Run!'

Before her shocked mind could react, Lukort rapped out a command to the younger man, who darted to the boy, wrenched him away from Rusgann, and clapped a big hand over his mouth.

The maid sprang to her feet shrieking, 'You stinking whoreson, let him loose!' The youth fetched her a casual blow in the stomach with his fist and she fell moaning to the stony sand.

His mouth temporarily freed, Dyfrig again cried, 'Run away, Mama!'

'Don't move!' roared Lukort. A split second later his tone was wheedling and conciliatory. 'Be easy now, princess. My son Vorgo and I won't hurt the wee smolt and we won't hurt you . . . So he's *your* boy, is he?. Well well! Yon wench said he was hers! A liar as well as a foulmouthed hellcat, ain't she?'

Vorgo smirked, keeping a firm hold on Dyfrig as he wriggled. Rusgann struggled to her feet and stood a few feet away from the pair. Her face was unreadable.

'I know you, Lukort Waterfall,' Maudrayne said in a stern voice. 'How dare you mistreat my child and my servant?'

'The twitch needs to be taught good manners. Got a nasty mouth on her. As to the lad, no one's mistreatin' him. We just don't want him runnin' off afore you and me have a chance to talk business.'

'Business?' Her mind was a turmoil of conflicting emotions. 'What kind of business?'

'The world thinks you be dead, princess. Your brother Liscanor was in a black rage when the news come to Northkeep. He tried to talk the other sealords into makin' war on Conrig Ironcrown to avenge the insult to you and your family. Nothin' come o' that. Tarn had too many other troubles, and now we're part of the Sovereignty whether we like it or not.' He shrugged. 'But here you be, alive – thanks to the God of Heights and Depths! – and with a fine young son to boot. Imagine that! How old would the little fella be? About four, eh?'

She said nothing, feeling the hairs at the back of her neck creep with apprehension. The crafty devil had guessed who Dyfrig's father must be.

Lukort murmured something to Vorgo, who hoisted the child to his shoulder and strode to where the coracle lay. He cut off a piece of line to bind Dyfrig's wrists, put him into the skin boat, and cast off, heading for the lugger anchored behind the small island.

The skipper beckoned to Maudrayne. 'Come closer. No need to keep shoutin' one at t'other. Don't worry about your lad. I told my son to take special good care o' him.'

She came slowly toward Lukort, stopping well out of easy reach. It would not do to underestimate the cleverness of this villain. She spoke to the maid. 'Are you badly hurt, Rusgann?'

'Nay, my lady. The young lout only punched the breath out of me. The lad and I came on the two men here when we rounded the point. Dyfi was all happy and excited, but I warned him he must say nothing at all until we knew they intended no evil. This Lukort was polite enough at first, asked if I knew the Lady Maudrayne Northkeep who lived nearby with the sea-hag. Said he was one of Lord Liscanor's subjects, come to see if you were being kept here against your will.'

Maudrayne turned her gaze to the fisherman. 'Two tennights ago, you saw me at Dobnelu's steading through your spyglass.'

He nodded, all joviality. 'And wasn't it a great shock, seeing a queenly redheaded beauty carrying a milkpail from the old hag's byre! Us seamen give Dobnelu's fjord a wide berth accounta her curses. But nothin's to stop us peepin' at the place as we sail on by. I studied through the glass and nigh jumped out o' my skin when I realized 'twas you: Ironcrown's wife that was supposed to be drownded in Cathra, alive and well and back home in Tarn. I pondered it for days, wonderin' what to do.'

'Wondering how he could turn his discovery to profit!' Rusgann growled.

'And did you tell others of what you'd seen?' Maudrayne inquired.

'Only a few good mates who know to keep their gobs shut. Needed advice, didn't I, to figger the best way to outwit the sea-hag.'

Maudrayne said, 'I'm surprised you dared risk her wrath, setting foot on this forbidden shore.'

A look of low cunning spread over the skipper's face as he took from his shirt a small pouch hanging on a string around his neck. 'Got me special charms for that. Vorgo, too. Cost every silver mark I owned to get 'em from Blind Bozuk the shaman. This here lets us cross the hag's magic circle of stones without her knowin'. Bozuk said it'd only work on Solstice Eve, when the fires of sorcery burn wan in the midnight sun. We waited till the time was ripe, then sailed back here in my lugger *Scoter,* keepin' far out from shore. We came into Useless Bay with the centerboard up, mostly using sweeps to drive the boat. Mortal hard work it was rowin', but we stayed clear of the shoals and made it to this cove, outta sight of Dobnelu's steading. We was all set to go afoot along the fjord and creep up to the farmhouse, when the wench and the lad come along.'

Rusgann said, 'I was fool enough to say you were following us along the shore, my lady, when I thought the men might be friendly. This one started whispering to that blockhead son of his. The lackwit blurted out something about hiding behind a rock and grabbing you when you appeared. I tried to run with Dyfrig then, but they caught us and knocked me down.'

'And now you intend to kidnap us, Lukort Waterfall?' Maudrayne said contemptuously.

'*Rescue* you, princess!' The fisherman's voice was laden with false reproach. 'First I figgered to take you back to your brother, hopin' he'd give me a nice reward.' The yellowish eyes shifted. 'But now I reckon if I took you and the boy down south, some others – say, your uncle the High Sealord Sernin – might be even more grateful for your return.'

'I see.'

Others! Sly Lukort knew full well that Conrig Ironcrown was the one who would pay a fortune for her and the child . . . alive or dead. And if it were not to be the latter, she'd have to think fast.

'Here comes Vorgo back with the coracle, so let's be off, princess. Your boy's waitin' for you aboard *Scoter*. She's a fine craft, a legacy from my late brother, may the fishes eat his eyeballs. You'll ride easy in her.'

'How many in your crew?' Maudrayne asked casually.

He chuckled. 'For this sailin', just me and Vorgo. *Scoter* needs five men when we're haulin' in fish, but you're a catch easier to handle, eh?'

Only the two of them. So the plan that had sprung into her mind might work. 'You'll take my maidservant also, of course. She is very dear to me and to my son.'

Lukort's face hardened and he shot a rancorous glance over his shoulder at Rusgann. 'Not bloody likely. The big wench stays.'

'I beseech you not to leave her here with the terrible sea-hag. Look – I'll give you a fine reward if you but reconsider.'

She pulled the splendid necklace of opal and gold out from her dress and made as if to unfasten the catch at the back of her neck.

'Swive me!' the fisherman gasped, undisguised greed widening his eyes. 'That's a beaut! Fire-stones the size of quail eggs.'

'The clasp is stuck. Come help me open it. The bauble is yours in payment for Rusgann's passage.'

'Huh! I reckon it's mine anyhow!' And he was on her as

fast as a heron striking, laughing in malicious triumph. He took hold of the pendant stones and gave a painful tug. She was aware of his wiry eyebrows and foul breath and the bits of food caught in his beard as she pulled the kitchen knife from the pocket of her apron and drove it into his throat just to the side of his windpipe, severing the great bloodvessels of the neck as she'd done many a time hunting, when putting a downed and wounded game animal out of its misery.

Lukort uttered a bubbling croak and, staggering, caught her by the hair. She yanked the knife free and an amazing jet of blood shot from the wound, soaking the two of them as they fell in a tangle of flailing limbs. With him struggling beneath her, she stabbed him again, this time taking him between the ribs. She screamed, 'Rusgann!'

The maid rushed forward, a granite stone the size of a turnip in one hand. She used the other to pull Maudrayne aside and smashed the rock into Lukort's crimson-smeared face. Kneeling beside him, she struck again and again and again until there was nothing human left of his features.

'Stop,' Maudrayne said at last. 'He's dead, bled out like a stuck deer. But take care, his boy Vorgo is coming back in the little boat.'

'Dad!' wailed the big youth, his lumpy countenance full of horror. He sat as though paralyzed in the coracle, which drifted in the shallows a dozen ells away. 'Dad!'

Maudrayne rose slowly to her feet, a figure tall and hideous with gore, holding the red-stained knife high. 'Now for you!' she howled, wading into the sea. The youth stared at her in disbelief, then threw himself over the gunwale of the skin boat and began to thrash away frantically in the direction of the lugger.

Maudrayne took a few more steps in pursuit of the swimmer, shouting threats, while Rusgann splashed to retrieve the empty coracle, which she deftly flipped onto the sand.

'Well done,' Maudrayne said. 'Oh, well done, my dearest friend!' She came ashore.

'Are you hurt, my lady?'

'Scratches and bumps. The bastard didn't get my necklace, but he left a smart welt trying to steal it.'

Rusgann used her drenched apron as a wash-clout on both of them, removing the worst of the blood, until Maudrayne said, 'Enough. We can finish cleaning ourselves on board the lugger. Poor Dyfrig must be terrified and we must go to him.'

They launched the small craft and climbed into it, after helping themselves to Lukort Waterfall's filleting knife and belt wallet. A great mob of ravens and gulls had suddenly appeared and were wheeling in a cloud above the body, ready to begin feeding. The noise they made almost drowned out the sound of a distressed human voice.

'It's that poor dolt, Vorgo,' the maid said, 'wanting us to pick him up. He knows he'll never make it swimming to the fishing boat. The ice-cold sea water is sapping his strength.'

'Go back to shore!' Maudrayne shouted to the youth. 'Go back! If you strip off the soaked clothes draining your body heat, you may live.'

After a momentary hesitation, the floundering swimmer changed direction and headed toward land.

'The air's warm,' Maudrayne said to Rusgann with a grim smile. 'He knows the way to the steading, and he has his own pouch of magic trinkets to give him access to the sea-hag's house. Mayhap Dobnelu will let him stay when she awakes. With us gone, she'll need a new slavey.'

THREE

The prisoner in Zeth Abbey filled the hours of Solstice Eve with his usual quiet activities. In the early morning, before the sun made the enclosed garden too hot, he pulled weeds, and carried endless cans of water from the well in his strong arms so that the roses would not flag, and gathered whatever things Brother Herbalist had requested. Then, after eating alone in his little apartment as became one banished from the routine of the Brethren, he retired to the great library to study. His choice of materials sometimes surprised the librarian, but Father Abbas had decreed that all things were to be at his disposal, as though he were still a Doctor Arcanorum in good standing in the Mystical Order of Saint Zeth.

After supper, as he often did, he held conversation in the bee-yard with his three friends; the clouds of busy, harmless insects ensured that no unwanted person would overhear their scheming. When the night-bell rang, he took to his bed more eagerly than usual and slept, and dreamed . . . and opened his mind to the invader.

Kilian. Vra-Kilian Blackhorse. Do you hear me?

'Finally, Beynor! I'm relieved to hear from you at last. You really should have contacted me earlier. I was becoming concerned. But never mind. My men in Cala Palace are ready. By the end of Midsummer Day, if all goes as I've planned, they will have escaped from the city with the Trove of Darasilo! I hope that matters go similarly well with you.'

There's a serious problem. I need you to postpone the Cala mission. Just for a short time.

'Impossible. My agents were given their orders months ago. By now all the arrangements are in place. It's imperative that the attack occurs early tomorrow, while those at the palace are sleeping off the previous day's festivities.'

Kilian, I need more time to complete my research here at the Dawntide Citadel. A week at the most. I've laid my hands on a document in the Salka archives that could be vitally important. But translating it is no easy matter. When I skimmed the thing, I could understood only about one word in five. But I deciphered enough to know its tremendous significance. It dates from before Bazekoy's Conquest!

'I couldn't stop the Cala mission from proceeding, even if I should want to. Vra-Garon has been sent off to Elkhaven on business by Abbas Noachil, and is also carrying out an important assignment of mine. He won't be back here until tomorrow. There's no one else at Zeth Abbey whom I can trust to windspeak my agents, and it's too late to send them a message by conventional means.'

Kilian, I could windspeak your men and tell them to hold off. It wouldn't be easy from this great distance, but I could do it. They'd listen and obey if you give me their signatures and the command password now, instead of waiting until –

'No! You'll bespeak and windwatch them only when the trove is safely in my hands. Do you take me for a fool?'

You misunderstand –

'And don't think you can circumvent my safeguards against your coercive talents by invading my agents' dreams!

You'll never countermand my orders that way. The Brothers were trained in my own somnial defensive techniques before they ever left the abbey. No one can speak to them in dreams unless they consent. But I daresay you've already found that out for yourself, or you wouldn't be trying to trick me!'

Kilian, please believe that I'd never betray our agreement and try to seize the trove for myself.

'Of course you would, my boy. Neither of us has ever trusted the other. That will never change until we've successfully divided Darasilo's sigils, and overcome the obstacles that now prevent either of us from utilizing their sorcery.'

Just listen to me. Let me explain why I need more time. I don't want to offer our bargain to the Salka until I learn more about the Unknown Potency's effect upon the Beaconfolk themselves. The stone does more than liberate sigils from the Lights' control and abolish bonding. I'm certain of that. This ancient document tablet that I've found may reveal why the Potency was created in the first place. There's something in it about an intention to sever the Lights' ability to meddle in the affairs of earthbound beings such as ourselves.

'Depriving us of Beaconfolk sorcery altogther? I don't much like the sound of that!'

I'm more interested in the possibility that the tablet might confirm what we've only assumed must be true – that the Unknown's power may enable me to utilize liberated sigils with impunity!

'And so you shall. I thought you were already convinced of it. If the Lights lose their ability to feed on the pain of sigil-wielders, if they're compelled to deliver sorcery without demanding a price, there is no way they can harm you. Their curse is effectively annulled.'

I must make certain. What good will my half of Darasilo's Trove do me if the curse still holds good? I'll tell you one thing: if I can't have mine, I won't help you get yours. And neither will I free you of your iron gammadion!

'Calm yourself.'

Once I leave Dawntide Citadel, I'll never have access to these Salka archives again.

'Then take the tablet in question along with you when you go. Puzzle out its contents later, on the voyage to Didion.'

I can't take the bloody thing away. I can hardly lift it. It's a stone slab the size of a cartwheel, jam-packed with inscriptions, and if the monsters knew I'd stolen it they'd probably slaughter me out of hand . . . or do worse.

'Copy the wording.'

I haven't the proper materials to make a rubbing, and there's too much on the tablet to simply write it down. The only parchment available in this benighted place are the fragile sheets I make myself from baby sealskin. I have only a few of those left.

'Don't forget that Darasilo's Trove includes two arcane books written in the Salka tongue, in addition to the large collection of inactive stones. The books' subject matter deals with sigils, beyond a doubt. I could tell that from the illustrations, even though I'm unable to read the Salka language. One of those books may very well contain the information you seek.'

Why should I take a chance? I'm going to postpone leaving here until I translate the tablet. That's final. You do as you please and be damned.

'Beynor, you've forgotten the other important reason why we dare not delay. The king of Didion and his family will begin their progress upriver from Holt Mallburn on the day after the Solstice, as they do every year. There's only one suitable spot for our ambush – just below Boarsden Castle at Boar Creek, where there are fierce rapids and an exceptionally deep eddy. It will take the royal party no more than six days to reach that point in their voyage, making the traditional stops along the way. Six days, Beynor! Barely enough time for you and the Salka assassins to get there and organize yourselves, since they won't be able to swim at full speed once they're in the river. If our amphibian friends aren't in place, ready to attack, we'll be forced to revise the Didion part of our scheme drastically – or abandon it altogether.'

Getting the Salka to kill King Honigalus and his family is a needless complication, Kilian. I've said that from the beginning.

'And I've told *you* why it's an absolutely essential step in the destruction of the Sovereignty.'

Well –

'Pull yourself together and keep your mind concentrated on the great goal that's finally within our grasp! I've done what I promised to do, putting my agents into Cala Palace without getting caught. Your task dealing with the Salka has been more difficult, I'll grant you, but you're the bravest, most audacious young man I've ever known. This is why I've been willing to place my own life and hopes in your hands. Listen to me, Beynor! We may never love one another as father and son, yet we are bound together by our mutual ambition more closely than by any tie of blood. Only together can we exploit Darasilo's Trove. Only together can we dupe the Salka into assisting us to bring down Conrig's Sovereignty. Only together can we rule.'

Damn your eyes!

'Bless yours, my boy – and may you use them to see straight ahead and avoid distractions! I have every confidence in you. Don't let me down.'

. . . Very well. I'll arrange to meet with the Four Eminences immediately.

'Excellent. I know you'll convince them. Put your mind at ease.'

Huh! That's hardly possible – given that I must shortly confront a pack of inhuman brutes who may well decide to torture me in creatively gruesome ways, rather than strike a bargain.

'Salka minds work more slowly than ours and are deficient in imagination. It's more likely that the monsters will pretend to accede to the proposal while planning to break faith with you later. We can deal with that easily enough. Don't take it amiss, but it's a good thing that the Salka think you a pathetic failure, cursed by the Lights, with only a few puny magical powers left. The arrogant boobies are bound to underestimate you and let their guard down.'

You state the facts with tactless candor, for one who was once first counselor to a king and now lives in disgrace, under a deferred sentence of death, stripped of all magical talent by the iron hanging around your neck.

'Don't be so touchy. Neither of us can afford wounded pride. Together we may possibly rule the world. Apart we're doomed.'

No more word games, Kilian. It's time for me to go.

'Before you do, we must discuss your sister. My agents in Cala Palace will do their utmost to disguise their real objective. But if Conrig suspects that either of us might have caused the trove to be stolen, he might pressure Conjure-Queen Ullanoth to put us under close observation. Even worse, he could ask her to trace my agents. No ordinary talent is able to scry the moonstones, but her Subtle Loophole sigil can.'

Conrig would never let the Conjure-Queen know about Darasilo's Trove. He'd be afraid she'd covet it for herself.

'I suppose you're right. But the king might use some pretext –'

Ulla hasn't spied on me with Loophole since the incident last year that nearly cost her life. I've been assured of this by Master Kalawnn himself. That particular sigil is the most powerful one she possesses, and the price of its conjuring is tremendous. Unless Conrig tells her that we might have stolen a secret hoard of inactive moonstones, she'll refuse to endanger her health and sanity by using Loophole to watch us or my men.

'She's bound to find out about the trove sooner or later.'

That's why I intend to have the Salka attack her. I've worked out a plan –

'I agree we should make her demise one of our earliest priorities . . . but only after the death of Honigalus! You must convince the monsters to kill him and his heirs first, Beynor. The circumstances are ideal and such an opportunity may never come again. The destabilization of the Sovereignty is absolutely crucial to our success. But that won't happen unless Conrig loses his hold on Didion. Do you understand?'

Yes. Honigalus first, but then Ulla dies.

A sigh.

Return to your peaceful slumber, Kilian – as I do my best to tiptoe scatheless through the nightmare I inhabit here. Should I manage to gull the Salka, I'll pop back into your dreams to inform you how the matter went. If I fail, remember me as you study Darasilo's worthless collection of baubles – and think of what might have been.

The brightness and warmth of the endless midsummer daylight hardly penetrated the dank chambers of the great Salka citadel that crouched on the highest point of the Dawntide Isles. After four years of exile in the awful place, Beynor always felt pierced to the bone by cold, no matter how many furs he piled on. He was one-and-twenty years old now, and had enjoyed excellent health when he first came; but he knew he could not survive here much longer. The citadel was an abode fit only for nonhuman grotesques. It drained his bodily strength and weakened his innate talent more and more with each passing day. If he must risk everything now in a bid to restore his lost fortunes, then so be it. He carried a whale-oil lantern as he descended a slippery flight of steps to a corridor that extended well below sea level. The widely spaced jars of luminous marine plankton used by these Salka to illuminate the lower precincts of their refuge gave too meager a light to accommodate human vision. Even the smoky flame of the lantern was inadequate, and Beynor cursed as he threaded his way among numerous stinking black puddles, fed seawater (and noxious little swimmers) by perpetual leaks in the tunnel ceiling.

At length he reached the anteroom outside the presence chamber of the great trolls known as the Eminences. Six gigantic Salka guards holding granite battlehammers stood before double doors faced with slabs of carved amber and wrought gold. The hanging bowls of glowworms were larger here, giving plenty of light, so the young sorcerer discarded his sputtering lantern, strode forward with as much fortitude as he could muster, and spoke in the harsh tongue of the monsters.

'I am Beynor ash Linndal, rightful Conjure-King of Moss and honored guest of your people, come for an audience with the Eminent Four.'

Slowly, the amphibians inclined their crested heads and studied him with a gaze like banked smoldering coals. They beheld a man tall and slimly built, having an intense narrow face and long pale hair that had gone stringy in the dampness. His eyes, which seemed at first to be black, were actually darkest green, with a glimmer of exceptional talent in their depths. The regal garments Beynor had worn when fleeing his lost kingdom had long since fallen to rags; and since his nonhuman hosts were unfamiliar with clothing, he had fashioned with his own hands a suit of pieced sea-otter fur, along with a voluminous fox cloak and sturdy boots of seal hide. The sole emblem of monarchy he had brought from Moss, the Royal Sword in its heavily bejeweled scabbard, was girded about his loins.

Saying nothing, the guards stepped aside and swung the chamber doors wide open. Beynor entered and the doors clanged shut again. He stood with his hands steepled in the Salka gesture of submission, biding his time until he should be recognized by the Eminences.

The beings who awaited him in the fantastically orna-
mented undersea cavern lolled on stubby-legged golden platforms, heaped with seaweed, that served them as couches.
They were unattended and conversed among themselves in
voices like muted thunder, apparently paying no attention
to the human newcomer. A low table containing dishes and
flasks of outlandish food and drink stood within tentacle-
reach. Behind the dais rose a huge mosaic made from multi-
colored bits of amber and gleaming pearl-shell, depicting a
legendary Salka hero. His flexible arms brandished twin
obsidian axes, his saucer eyes glared fire-red, and his fanged
mouth gaped in a silent roar. The image was framed by
amber-bead curtains and lit with hanging crystal globes
containing lively phosphorescent organisms.

Like the champion in the mosaic, each Eminence wore
around his thick neck a softly glowing greenish-blue carving
suspended from a golden chain: moonstone sigils of the minor
kind that drew magical power from the Beaconfolk at the
cost of pain to the wearer.

The Eminences were not royalty, but rather ruling elders
chosen by their people for strength of character and proficiency
in their separate fields of endeavor. Three of them – the First
Judge, the Supreme Warrior, and the Conservator of Wisdom
– Beynor had never seen before. As a mere human sorcerer,
even one of royal blood who had come bearing a marvelous
gift to ensure his welcome, he had been beneath their notice
during his enforced stay in the Citadel of the Dawntide Isles.
The only one of the Four familiar to Beynor was Master Shaman
Kalawnn, pre-eminent adept of his race, who had been an intimate friend of the late Conjure-King Linndal. Unaware that
Beynor had murdered his father, Master Kalawnn had agreed
to give the deposed young ruler sanctuary after the Great Lights
cursed him and stripped him of all but one of the sigils he had
used to secure the throne of Moss.

That single remaining magical moonstone of his, dull and lifeless as it had been since it was first fashioned over a thousand years earlier, rested now on a spindly gold tripod to the right of the dais. Its presence was presumably a tribute to the human who had finally returned it to its original owners. The sigil's name was Unknown Potency, and it was the most celebrated thing of its kind ever made, priceless at the same time that it was deemed supremely dangerous.

For long centuries following the damnation of the stone's Salka creator, the precise manner of the Potency's activation and operation had been forgotten by other members of the amphibian race. The person who made it – supposedly to be used as the ultimate weapon against the conquering hordes of the Emperor Bazekoy, although the monsters were not certain of this – had in the end failed to empower it.

Never brought to life, dreaded more than cherished, the Unknown Potency had become an enigmatic symbol of extinct Salka glory. Over the centuries, learned thaumaturgists among the monsters believed that the sigil might hold the key to unimaginably great magic surpassing that of the Beaconfolk. But none had been brave enough to test it, for fear of the Great Lights' capricious wrath.

About a hundred years earlier, through subterfuge, the Unknown Potency and six other notable sigils had passed from the Dawntide Salka into the hands of an extraordinary human wizard named Rothbannon, who used some of the stones to establish himself as the first Conjure-King of Moss. Although Rothbannon did eventually learn the spells that would activate the Unknown Potency, he and his descendants were disinclined to make use of the dubious sigil – as had been Beynor himself, even when the security of his throne was at stake and the fickle Beaconfolk turned against him. As the Great Lights repudiated and cursed the young king, they unaccountably left in his possession the 'dead'

Unknown Potency, at the same time forbidding him to make use of it, or any other sigil, on pain of instant annihilation. But the Lights had not stopped Beynor from handing over the Unknown to the Salka.

Nor had they prevented him from engaging in studies concerning the nature of the cryptic stone while he lived in the Dawntide Citadel under Kalawnn's protection . . .

'We give you leave to approach us, Beynor,' the Master Shaman now said, 'and to speak to me and my august colleagues about your researches.'

He came forward, and without preamble pointed to the Unknown Potency on its golden tripod. 'Eminences, I've discovered what this thing does.'

The leaders uttered undignified whoops of astonishment. The Supreme Warrior, who was the largest and most physically imposing of the Four, surged up from his couch and slithered across the dais with astonishing speed. He plucked from its resting place the small object resembling a hard translucent ribbon twisted into the form of a figure eight, and held the thing high while bellowing into Beynor's impassive face.

'*You* have discovered the operation of the Unknown Potency? The secret that eluded the most learned of our shamans for over eleven hundred years? How dare you say such a thing? You're lying!'

'I studied your own archival tablets, Eminence – documents that have lain neglected in the bowels of this citadel since the defeated remnant of the Salka host took refuge in these forsaken isles. The work was very difficult, even though I am fairly fluent in your language. But I persevered. I succeeded. And now I propose to share my hard-won knowledge of the Potency with you.' Beynor paused. 'As is only just, I ask something in return for my labors.'

'Now we come to the heart of the matter!' exclaimed the

Supreme Warrior, with a vicious clash of teeth. 'He intends to trick us in some fashion, as the wretch Rothbannon did! Kalawnn – explain how this miscreant was able to pry into our sacred archives. How long have you been aware of this alleged discovery?'

'Calm yourself, Ugusawnn,' the Master Shaman replied equably. 'I myself gave Beynor leave to investigate the Unknown Potency's history not long after his arrival. Why not, since our own scholars seemed unaccountably tepid in their reaction to the precious sigil's return? As to Beynor's discovery, he told me of it just hours ago, saying he had finally marshaled sufficient evidence to support his hypothesis. I commanded him to wait on us Four without delay and explain everything.'

'And now the insolent groundling thinks he can barter his so-called knowledge!' roared the Warrior. 'I say he should be tortured until the truth is wrung out of him!'

'The journeyman is deserving of his wage,' said Beynor, who seemed unfazed by the threat. 'Forgive my saying so, Eminences, but your shamans – with the shining exception of Master Kalawnn – are a timid and lazy lot, fearful of arcane matters outside the range of their limited experience. They flatly refused to help with my researches, so I undertook them alone, working for four years under conditions inimical to human good health. Eventually I uncovered the Potency's secrets. It may no longer be called Unknown, Eminences! I know its true nature. And while the Great Lights have forbidden me to empower it – or any other sigil – they have not constrained you Salka. I'm willing to show you how to bring the stone to life. What's more, with my help, this one small moonstone can restore to you your lost homeland on High Blenholme island, avenging your defeat by Emperor Bazekoy.'

'Astounding, if true,' said the First Judge. He was a rotund personage who snacked on tidbits from the refreshment table as he observed Beynor through shrewd, half-closed eyes.

The ancient Conservator of Wisdom whispered, 'If there is the least chance that the groundling does speak the truth, we must weigh his proposition.'

'I am truthful,' Beynor stated. 'And I'll reveal everything I know if you pledge to help me attain my own heart's goal.'

The Supreme Warrior gingerly replaced the precious piece of moonstone on its golden stand and loomed over the young man. Two boneless arms as thick as beech trunks, each having four digits armed with daggerlike talons, reached out in menace as the Salka general spoke with ominous gentleness. 'You'll tell what you know without making demands, carrion-worm, or I will first disjoint your limbs piecemeal, then slowly slice open your belly and consume your throbbing entrails while you watch with dying eyes.'

'That will do, Ugusawnn,' said the Conservator of Wisdom. He was an individual of wizened stature, plainly infirm and weighted with years, but his red eyes burned with an authority that quelled the Supreme Warrior like an upstart child. 'Please resume your place. I will question the former Conjure-King of Moss myself.'

'Huh!' said Ugusawnn. But he crawled obediently back to his slimy kelp couch as the Conservator beckoned for Beynor to come closer.

'It pains me to speak loudly, groundling. But listening to lies pains me even more. Do you swear by your human God to tell me the truth about the Unknown Potency, on peril of damnation to the Hell of Ice?'

'I do indeed, Eminence.'

But not all of the truth . . . no more than I told it to Kilian!

'Then say first what favors you seek in return for your discovery.'

Beynor took a breath. 'My principal desire is vengeance

upon my evil sister Ullanoth and her accomplice Conrig Wincantor, the Sovereign of Blenholme. They conspired to humiliate me and steal my throne, and are ultimately responsible for my losing the friendship of the Beaconfolk. To achieve the ruin of these two persons I would renounce all hope of ever ruling Moss – or any part of High Blenholme Island. Instead, I offer to restore your original homeland to you, after which I intend to pursue my own destiny on the Southern Continent.'

'He *offers* Blenholme to us!' the Supreme Warrior scoffed. 'As though he ruled it rather than Conrig's Sovereignty.'

'The Unknown Potency can enable your army to destroy both the Sovereign and my sister,' Beynor said. 'With my help.'

'Tell us how,' the First Judge demanded, picking his glassy teeth with one talon and examining the result with a frown.

'Before I do that, I require tangible proof of your goodwill. It's only just, Eminences – and my request isn't difficult to fulfill. As a first step in subverting Conrig's Sovereignty, I believe we must undermine his control in the region where the island is most vulnerable: the vassal kingdom of Didion. Didion is a keystone state whose lands adjoin those of the other three realms. It is susceptible to a Salka sea invasion from the east, the west, and most especially from the north, through the Green Morass. Its king, Honigalus, is a weakling, but he is unswervingly loyal to Conrig.'

'What has this to do with us?' the Conservator hissed impatiently.

'As the first step in achieving my revenge, and your reconquest of Blenholme, I ask you to help me assassinate Honigalus, his three children, and his wife, who stand in line to the throne. If this is done, the king's younger brother will inherit – a hothead prince named Somarus who is violently opposed to the Sovereignty. I'm very well acquainted with Somarus and his ambitions. He's highly susceptible to my coercion. And if this princely creature of mine were perceived by neighboring Tarn to be a legitimate heir to the throne and not a fratricidal usurper – as would be assured if *Salka* were clearly seen to be responsible for his brother's death – then Sernin Donorvale and the Sealords of Tarn would have no scruples about allying with Didion in an attempt to throw off Conrig's hated dominion. The Sovereignty would be plunged into chaotic war, making it easy for your own army to seize the advantage.'

'It sounds like a clever scheme, if somewhat convoluted.' The Conservator of Wisdom spoke wistfully. 'But history has shown that our fighters have not the physical agility nor the military competence to withstand human beings on land. This is why most of us have remained in the Dawntide Isles for these many centuries, only venturing to attack the groundlings on rare occasions, from the sea . . . and why the Salka who still dwell in Blenholme's Little Fen and the northern estuaries inhabited by humans live furtive, inconspicuous lives.'

Beynor said, 'The high sorcery of the *Known* Potency will make you superior to any weapon humanity can wield, be it natural or supernatural.'

'Tell us how this can be,' said the First Judge. He uncorked a flask and poured a viscous fluid into a gold cup, sniffed it, and took a tentative lap. His tongue was purple, and nearly the length of Beynor's forearm.

The young sorcerer strode to the golden tripod and cupped his hands beneath the inactive sigil. 'Look upon it, Eminences! Apparently naught but a finely carved little stone ribbon, twisted to resemble a figure eight. But a finger slid along its surface discovers that the thing has but a single side and a single edge! A twofold wonder . . .'

'Do not touch the Potency!' the Supreme Warrior bellowed. 'Never touch it again!' Beynor froze but did not

flinch. After a moment, he let his hands fall to his sides and
withdrew from the tripod, smiling.

'Continue,' said Master Kalawnn, with a reproachful
glance at his colleague.

Beynor nodded. 'Properly conjured, this small object defies
the Beaconfolk's control of their own sorcery. *It forces them
to yield up arcane power through moonstone sigils without causing
pain to the conjurer.* The mere touch of the living Potency liber-
ates any other active sigil from the Lights' control, as well
as from the control of the former owner. A liberated sigil
retains its efficacy, without exacting the former pain-price.
Think what this might mean to wielders of minor-sigil
weaponry such as flame-stones and stunners.'

'Incredible!' Kalawnn exclaimed.

'Not at all, Master. I've also discovered that the Potency
can instantly activate dead sigils without the usual agonizing
ritual, whether the Lights will it or not. You Salka might also
use the Potency to safely empower newly fashioned Great
Stones. Just imagine what ten Weathermakers could do to
Conrig's army and navy! Or even one Destroyer . . .'

'At the present time, we are unable to make new sigils,'
Kalawnn admitted, shaking his ponderous head. 'All that we
have left are those minor stones brought to the isles by the
refugees fleeing Bazekoy.'

Beynor kept a lid on his elation with difficulty. The chief
sorcerer of the Salka had confirmed what Beynor and Kilian
had previously only deduced to be true: the monsters would
already have used Great Stones as weapons against humanity
if they had owned any.

'Still,' Beynor said, 'the Potency can be a great boon to
you. Even the lesser sigils conjure more powerful sorcery than
talented humans are capable of. King Conrig's alchymists and
warriors will flee in terror before your conquering magic!'

The Supreme Warrior gave a skeptical grunt. 'That remains

to be seen. In my opinion, if we have only minor stones to assist us, humans might retain a strong advantage – especially on land – as they did in Bazekoy's day. Even our Great Stones did not deter his warriors for long. They slew the sigils' owners from afar with their arrows, then were able to smash the dead stones before we could retrieve and reactivate them. Only three Great Stones ever came to the Dawntides, those that Rothbannon took away from us. They eventually were handed down to you. In your incredible stupidity, you misused them, and now only this Unknown Potency is left.'

'A more prudent course is open to us,' the Conservator of Wisdom said. 'As Kalawnn observed, we lack the ability to make new Great Stones *at the present time*. But that situation could change.'

Beynor forced himself to speak nonchalantly in the face of this shocker. 'And how might that come to pass, Eminence? Nothing I've studied so far in your archives tells of the origin of moonstone sigils.'

The Conservator turned to the Master Shaman. 'Colleague, please explain matters to this groundling protégé of yours. My voice grows weary.'

'Thousands of years ago,' Kalawnn said, 'our people discovered that a certain precious mineral had the power to conjure the magic of the Coldlight Army. The mineral was never abundant, and obtaining it was a difficult and dangerous business. With the passing of time and the changing climate, the two sources of the mineral, known as the Moon Crags, became inaccessible to our people. Indeed, the very location of the smaller crag has been lost – we know only that it lies atop a mountain – while the larger crag is situated deep within the Barren Lands of the far north, in a place now colder and more inhospitable than it was in ages past.'

The Conservator said to Beynor, 'If the Unknown Potency

does indeed have the power you describe, we might undertake a special effort to reach the Barren Lands Moon Crag
once again. It might take a number of years to accomplish
the task. But if we fashioned powerful new Great Stones and
activated them through the Potency, then our victory against
humanity would be certain rather than problematic. The
Lights would have no way of betraying us, as they did so
perfidiously when Bazekoy first threatened our homeland.'

The other Eminences murmured in agreement. Beynor
stood like a statue, fighting the nausea swelling inside him.
He'd been so certain that they were ready to acquiesce to
his scheme – and now this!

Well, there remained one bargaining tool that could mend
the situation. Mentioning it now might lead the Eminences
to suspect – rightly enough – that he was planning treachery
after the action in Didion; but he had to risk it.

'It's understandable that you feel you must hold off
reclaiming your heritage until you obtain Great Stones,' he
said carefully. 'However, I might point out that there are
three other Great Stones already in existence that could be
used to further the Salka cause without delay. In my opinion,
these sigils alone would enable you to secure a strong initial
foothold on High Blenholme while your valiant shamans
simultaneously undertake the Moon Crag quest.'

Kalawnn said, 'I presume you refer to those owned by
your sister, Conjure-Queen Ullanoth, which supposedly came
to her as a gift from your dead mother, along with four minor
stones.'

'Hmm. I'd forgotten about those,' the Conservator said.
'The young witch was said to have found them hidden among
the roots of a swamp tree, after being guided by a dream.'

'That's so,' Beynor said. 'The important sigils are called
Sender, Weathermaker, and Subtle Loophole. My sister rarely
uses their high sorcery these days, since she has accumulated

an enormous pain-debt employing them in the service of her lover, King Conrig.'

'She uses them against us!' Ugusawnn snarled. 'In our failed attack last year, the Conjure-Queen employed her Loophole sigil to see us coming, and smote our landing force with a great storm conjured by Weathermaker. After that, even with the queen disabled by pain, human ships attacked these very isles. Our fighters were crushed like fishlice!'

'I'm aware that recent Salka assaults against Moss were repelled.' Beynor gave the Supreme Warrior an apologetic shrug. 'Forgive me, Eminence, for saying that the actions were poorly planned, using insufficient numbers of warriors who relied upon brute strength rather than appropriate magic.'

The huge eyes of Ugusawnn gleamed like baleful rubies. He bared his crystalline teeth at Beynor, and each was twice as long as a man's hand. 'Do you know a better way to fight the Conjure-Queen and her allies?'

'Suppose your forces were equipped with numbers of Concealers and Interpenetrators. I know your people possess such minor stones, as well as many others, but they are reluctant to use them because of the price. Liberated by the Potency, these sigils can assure victory! If you mount a stealthy attack on Royal Fenguard from the upstream side, using my special knowledge of the castle's defenses in that area, you could penetrate the fortress walls and move about under cover of invisibility. Queen Ullanoth's Great Stones would be yours before she or her ally King Conrig realized what was happening . . . because, with the Potency, you would not have to kill the queen before taking her Great Stones for yourselves.'

The First Judge was aghast. 'What are you saying?'

'As you are aware, Eminence, a living sigil will ordinarily burn or even kill an unauthorized person who ventures to seize it. Even if the bonded owner is separated from the sigils, the owner can often command it from a distance – perhaps causing great harm or mischief. But a moonstone liberated by the Potency is severed from its former owner at once. Recall what I said: a liberated stone becomes re-bonded painlessly to the Potency wielder without the usual lengthy and painful ritual.'

The Conservator of Wisdom spoke with heavy sarcasm. 'It is good that we need have no fear that *you* might manage to appropriate your sister's three Great Stones for yourself, Beynor of Moss!'

'Alas, no, Eminence,' Beynor lied. 'The curse of the Beaconfolk places them beyond my reach forever. But not beyond yours.'

'All this sounds like a splendid course of action,' the Supreme Warrior sneered, 'but in my opinion it has as many holes as a sponge. It relies too much on this groundling's help and I don't trust him. We can't even be sure he's told us the truth about the Potency.'

The Master Shaman said mildly, 'Beynor is the son of my departed friend, Conjure-King Linndal. He has never given me reason to doubt his friendship toward the Salka people. He returned the Potency to us without condition. We know for a fact that he is incapable of using sigil magic himself. His assessment of the situation in Moss coincides with my own knowledge of Ullanoth's affairs. I think we should consider the proposal to invade Moss very carefully. That isolated corner of High Blenholme would provide us with a perfect staging area for the main attack upon the rest of the island. Numbers of our people already reside in Moss's fens and in the swamps along its principal rivers. And I agree with Beynor that the Conjure-Queen's three important sigils would immediately give us an enormous advantage over human enemies.'

'Then let's go against Moss right away!' said the First Judge, hoisting high his golden cup for emphasis. 'Why muck about with this assassination of the Didionite king? What benefit is that to us?'

'It gains you my gratitude,' Beynor said in a loud, cold voice. 'And it's a sure method of fatally weakening Conrig's Sovereignty. If you kill Honigalus, I promise to help activate the Potency immediately afterwards and help you attack Moss. If you refuse me, I won't share my knowledge with you.'

'I say we should simply put this presumptuous tadpole to the torture,' growled the Supreme Warrior, 'He'll tell us everything we need to know about the Potency inside of an hour. Once our search parties are equipped with liberated minor sigils that the Lights can't meddle with, we'll locate the Barren Lands Moon Crag in short order. We won't need this snotty groundling's help to reconquer Blenholme if we have plenty of new Great Stones. No human force could stand against us!'

'Bazekoy's did,' the Conservator said bleakly. 'Remember that.'

'Because the Lights betrayed us,' the Warrior thundered. 'They allowed him to win – perhaps for their own perverse amusement. This time, the situation will be different.'

'Doing things my way would be so much more efficient, Eminences,' urged Beynor. 'I can speed your conquest because I'm human. I know human strategy. I know human weaknesses and strengths. And more than anything in this world, I want to destroy Conrig Wincantor and my sister Ullanoth.'

A prolonged silence fell over the chamber.

'How strange,' mused the First Judge, as he licked the last mucilaginous drops from his cup, 'that Conjure-Queen Ullanoth should have discovered a hidden cache of sigils so fortuitously – although we know that many such must have been secreted away during our long retreat from Bazekoy's host. I wonder if other lost Great Stones might be located using her Subtle Loophole, that most puissant tool for wind-searching? If we owned a liberated Loophole, then it would be unnecessary for us to launch a long and arduous expedition to the Barren Lands Moon Crag.'

Beynor felt his gorge rise anew at this terrible possibility, which had never occurred to him. What a catastrophe if the monsters located and took control of Darasilo's Trove before he could steal it away from Kilian . . .

But the Conservator's next words wiped away Beynor's dismay and kindled fresh hope. 'It seems to me that the young sorcerer's proposal to help us seize the Conjure-Queen's sigils has considerable merit. We should not reject it lightly.'

'I agree,' said the Master Shaman. 'Furthermore, torturing the human as Ugusawnn urges can produce unsatisfactory results. Humans have such frail bodies compared to our own.'

'If I die under the Supreme Warrior's ministrations before telling you the secret of the Potency,' Beynor said reasonably, 'you will have thrown away any chance of abolishing the pain-yoke of the Lights, or regaining your ancestral island home.'

'He's right,' the Conservator said. 'And this assassination that he demands as a goodwill gesture doesn't seem particularly difficult.'

'It would be quite a simple matter,' Beynor said, 'requiring only a small force of Salka warriors. Perhaps only a score. I would have to lead them myself, since I'm familiar with the River Malle and the type of vessel carrying King Honigalus and his family. I also know the best escape route. As soon as the fighters and I return to Dawntide Citadel, I'll show you how to activate the Potency. You must choose who among you will bond to the Great Stone –'

'It must be Ugusawnn,' the Conservator said. 'He is the most suitable person. Aside from his undeniable fighting prowess, his own sigil enables him to communicate with us across long distances, so we always know how his ventures are faring.'

The Supreme Warrior's enormous glowing eyes widened in gratified surprise. 'Do the other Eminences concur?'

The Judge and the Master Shaman nodded.

And Beynor thought: Perfect! My principal opponent is disarmed!

'Ugusawnn will also lead the assassination party into Didion,' the Conservator said, 'with the human sorcerer serving as his guide. This will not only enhance the possibility of success, but also make certain that the action proceeds without . . . unexpected developments.'

The Conservator meant Beynor's escape. But he already had worked out a simple plan to get away from the monsters. 'I would be honored to have such august company on the expedition,' the young sorcerer said humbly.

The Supreme Warrior glowered at him. 'Precisely where are these royal murders to take place?'

'At a point on the River Malle near Boarsden Castle, where the barge is most vulnerable to attack from the water,' Beynor said. 'The spot is some six hundred leagues from the Dawntide Isles. Honigalus and his family will be there six days from now.'

'So soon?' the Judge said.

'Our strongest swimmers could get there easily if we left at once,' Ugusawnn said. He shot Beynor a look of distaste. 'But I don't know how we'll manage to transport the groundling sorcerer without drowning him. I'm not even convinced that it's a good idea for him to go along on this mission. What if he's killed? We'd never empower the Potency then.'

'It would be up to you,' the Conservator said wearily, 'to keep him secure.'

'Do you still intend to oppose this scheme, Ugusawnn,'

Kalawnn asked, 'even when we would make you Master of the Potency?'

'I don't oppose it. But I do mistrust this tricky groundling with all my heart and soul!'

Beynor said, 'I know an easy way to transport me to Didion. When the Master Shaman so graciously offered me sanctuary, I came here from Royal Fenguard in my own barque, *Ambergris*, which was a gift to me from the Didionites after I did them a great favor. The ship is in a sad state of neglect now, careened in one of the coves below the citadel. But her boats should still be sound, and they are of a common type that would be inconspicuous on the River Malle. I can cross the sea in one of them, dismasted and towed along at speed by your force. When we reach Mallmouth Harbor, I'll step the boat's mast, hoist her sail, and go innocently up the river – pulled more slowly and inconspicuously as needed by my Salka guardians.'

'Is this practicable, Ugusawnn?' the Conservator inquired.

'It would probably work.' The Supreme Warrior spoke without enthusiasm. 'But I'd rather leave the groundling here. Let him instruct me in the details.'

'I won't agree –' Beynor began to say.

'Silence!' The Conservator of Wisdom gave the command in a voice that was suddenly resounding and steady. 'Beynor of Moss, step back from the dais and wait by the doors while we Four confer.'

Beynor obeyed. Numbed by the ordeal, he now felt no anxiety nor sense of anticipation as the great trolls murmured interminably among themselves. At long last the Conservator called out, 'Beynor, come and stand again before us, and receive our decision.'

Kilian. Vra-Kilian Blackhorse. Do you hear?

'Yes, Beynor.'

We've won. A small Salka force will leave for Didion within a few hours, taking me with them. They'll be led by their Supreme Warrior, a surly savage named Ugusawnn. After slaughtering the royal family, we're supposed to return to Dawntide Citadel, where I show the Four Eminences how to activate the Potency. They've decided to bond it to the Supreme Warrior. He intends to lead an attack on Royal Fenguard immediately, snap up Ulla's sigils, and conquer the world for the Salka.

'Heh heh heh! Brilliantly done, my boy. What a pack of simpletons!'

I'm supposed to believe that Ugusawnn will take me along on the invasion of Moss. But I'm fairly certain he intends to kill me as soon as he's sure that I've properly activated the Potency.

'It would be extremely vexing if the monsters did polish you off.'

Ugusawnn is no fool and he has serious doubts about me. Still, it should be easy enough to give him the slip once he and the others have taken care of Honigalus. They have no suspicion that I'm able to impel a small boat with my talent – as if that weren't one of the first tricks a Mossland magicker learns! Once I'm safely away in Didion, I'll windspeak the Eminences the revised version of the bargain. And we pray that they swallow their outrage and agree to it.

'Why shouldn't they? The alternative is custody of a useless dead sigil. How could the Salka possibly suspect that the Potency bonds to no one? That it can be snatched away from this Supreme Warrior and used by anyone at all without causing harm to the taker?'

Such a thing would never occur to them. I wonder why the Potency's creator made it thus? Not too sensible, was it? Not that I'm complaining!

'Consider this: If the Potency doesn't bond to its activator, then it doesn't die when the owner does. Unlike all other sigils, the Potency might very well be immortal.'

Interesting – and unsettling, too. God of the Depths! How I wish there were some way of reading that last archive tablet! We need to know why the Potency was made, and why its reputation has always been so dire.

'After we wipe out the Salka with Darasilo's Trove, you can return to their citadel and find out.'

Perhaps . . . Kilian, this conversation must end now. The Supreme Warrior is expecting me to join him. We're inspecting the small boat that will carry me to Didion.

'Good luck, then, Beynor. May you have a safe voyage.'

I'll see you in your dreams.

FOUR

Snudge and his companions broke the first short day of their northward journey shortly before the eleventh hour after noon. The cavalcade had arrived at a little village called Swallowmere, some sixty leagues north of the capital, where there was a tavern of unpretentious but promising aspect. The horses were tired by then, but the young travelers weren't – not on Solstice Eve, when every man of spirit save those constrained by holy orders was expected to celebrate High Summer.

The Green Swallow Inn proved to be well stocked with extra food and drink for the occasion. Crowded with friendly locals, it featured a three-man band of peasant musicians and plenty of lasses to dance and flirt with. Snudge, his armigers Valdos and Wiltorig, and Sir Gavlock and his squire Hanan joined wholeheartedly in the roistering.

Meanwhile Vra-Mattis, the apprentice windvoice assigned to Sir Deveron by the king, eschewed worldly pleasures as befit a novice in the Mystical Order of Saint Zeth. The night was very warm, so Mat put off his robe and settled down in the inn's forecourt in his undertunic. He ate a good supper of mutton-dumpling stew and strawberry tarts, rested his saddlesore muscles, and finally fell into a doze on a heap of clean straw, bothered not a whit by the convivial racket coming from inside the tavern.

Some time later, in the wee hours, the novice was jolted awake by an urgent windspoken message from the Royal Alchymist Lord Stergos, intended for Sir Deveron. Its portent was so grave that Mattis hastened to seek out his master without even donning his robe. The interior of the inn was now jam-packed with funseekers, many of them so taken by strong drink that they could barely stand. Skirling pipes, a squawking fiddle, a thumping tabor, laughter and song fairly shook the rafters.

Mattis found his master grinning owlishly as he stomped and shuffled in a drunken round-dance with three cavorting farm-girls. From the sidelines, Sir Gavlok hoisted a cannikin of rustic rotgut and cheered, ignoring the frantic novice who bellowed into his unresponsive ear.

The dance finally ended to raucous applause and Mattis rushed to take Snudge by the arm and pull him in the direction of the inn's front door. Gavlok trailed along after, protesting his friend's evacuation.

'Sir!' the novice cried. 'Sir Deveron, can you understand me?'

'Unhand me, knave,' Snudge mumbled. 'Wanna dance!' He tripped over his own feet and fell to his knees in the dirt courtyard. 'Feel sleepy. Time f'bed.'

'Sir, please listen!' Vra-Mattis attempted without success to haul his master upright. 'I've received an important wind-message from the Royal Alchymist. His Grace the High King commands you to return to the capital immediately.'

'Booger the king. Booger Stergos. Go 'way.' Snudge rolled onto his face.

The dismayed windvoice appealed to the other young knight, who now seemed to be almost sober. 'What am I to

do? We dare not wait until he's slept off his carouse. Lord
Stergos insisted that we leave here at once.'

Gavlok nudged his collapsed friend with his foot.
'Commander! Arise! Duty calls!' The only response was a
muffled curse. Inside the inn, the music had started up again
more loudly and off-key than ever. A fat man staggered out
the door and spewed in the shadows.

'Poor Deveron,' Gavlok mourned. 'His very first holiday.
Alas – he was having such a fine time, too! But I fear, Brother
Mat, that drastic measures are now called for. Assist me, if
you please.' Together, the two men began to drag the inert
Snudge across the courtyard toward the stables. A courting
couple fled at their approach.

Sir Gavlok Whitfell was aware that Deveron Austrey
frequently undertook secret missions for King Conrig, but
knew nothing of his friend's arcane talent. Formerly armiger
to Lord Stergos, Gavlok had been knighted a year earlier than
Snudge and was now assigned to the Royal Alchymist's Guard.
Although he was nobly born, the fourth son of a distinguished
Westley family, he was too introspective and sensitive to be
an enthusiastic warrior. Lord Stergos valued the gangling, fair-
haired young man for his intelligence, his unswerving integrity,
and his self-deprecating sense of humor – as did Snudge.

'We do this for Sir Deveron's own good,' Gavlok declared
to the windvoice, as the two of them reached a horse-trough
with their burden. They tipped Snudge into the water with
a great splash, then hauled him out and sat him down in
the straw, coughing and spluttering.

'Whoreson!' Snudge croaked, lashing out with feeble fury
at the friend who was divesting him of his sodden garments.
'I'll b-broil your b-bollocks for this!'

'No doubt,' Gavlok replied. 'But first you must listen to
Vra-Mattis, who has a message for you from the king.'

'What?'

Mattis told him. Snudge groaned piteously. 'Shite! My head spins like a whirry – whirligig. A 'mergency, you say? What sort?'

But the novice had not been entrusted with further information, and Snudge knew with woozy certainty that there was no possibility that he himself might bespeak the Royal Alchymist and learn more. His own windtalent had been totally extinguished by ardent spirits, as had most of his other mental faculties. In fact, he was nearly paralytic.

'Gavvy,' he whispered, sinking to the ground again and holding his swollen head in his hands. 'Gavvy, old friend. I muss – must lay a great 'sponsibility on you. Can't hang two thoughts together myself. D'you think you can get the lot of us on the road? Fresh horses, o'course. Clean clothes, too. Our three squires are swizzled as swineherds, lyin' in a filthy heap somewhere inside.'

'I'm none too sharp myself,' Gavlok admitted, 'and I'll need your fat purse to make the arrangements. But count on me.'

'Good man.' Without another word Snudge curled into a ball and began to snore. Overhead, the sky was already pink at three in the morning of Solstice Day, and Cathran song-birds were singing their dawn chorus, oblivious to the merry-making inside the inn.

He woke with his head clanging like an anvil, riding through a town where well-dressed inhabitants stared at him as he passed. Now and then, someone would snicker. He discovered that he was lashed to the saddle so he would not fall, and he was mounted not on his fine black charger but on a scruffy roan nag with a hogged mane. The beast plodded along on a lead-strap behind another rider who wore a dusty crimson robe. To the rear was a drooping figure on a third horse, with a lead attached to Snudge's cantle-ring.

'Mat?' Snudge's mouth felt like the inside of an old boot and his eyes seemed clogged with sand.

The robed figure looked over its shoulder at him. 'Ah. Finally awake? Very good.' He called out to someone riding ahead. 'Sir Gavlok, my master has come round.'

Gavlok made some unintelligible reply. Snudge muttered to the novice, 'What – what's the hour? And where are we?'

'This is Axebridge, a village along the River Blen some fifteen leagues above the capital. I have relatives here. It's about the ninth hour of morning. We'll stop soon for brief refreshment.'

'Never have I had a worse hangover,' Snudge whimpered. 'I'm nearly blind with headache and perishing of thirst.'

'I'll make a remedy for you soon,' Mat said cheerfully. 'Alchymical studies have a practical side, thanks be to Saint Zeth. A concoction of strong ale, raw egg, garum, and ground pepper will quickly banish your blue devils, sir.'

The party turned off the high street into a lane and proceeded to a prosperous-looking cottage where a large chestnut tree gave welcome shade from the hot sun. There Gavlok assisted Snudge to dismount while Vra-Mattis helped the three moaning armigers.

'This is Mat's cousin's house,' Gavlok said. 'I'll pay the goodwife well to prepare food for us, which we can eat when we're back in the saddle. But first, we'll fetch you and the lads that healing draft.'

Leaving the stricken men sitting on the grass and drinking from skin waterbottles, the tall skinny knight and the bandy-legged little novice went to the cottage door and spoke at length to someone inside.

Valdos Grimstane, who at sixteen years of age was Snudge's senior squire, said faintly, 'I think I may die, Sir Deveron.'

He was a grandson of Duke Tanaby Vanguard, and it was a mark of Conrig's esteem that such a high-born youth had been assigned as armiger to the newly belted Royal Intelligencer. Valdos was pleasantly ugly and usually of a ruddy complexion, but at the moment his face was cheese-green and his eyes so bloodshot that their true color could hardly be discerned.

'No, you won't die, Val,' Snudge assured him. 'You'll gather your wits as speedily as you can, for something has caused the High King to cancel our country holiday and summon us all back to the palace posthaste. I know not why.'

'Bazekoy's Biceps! You have no hint at all of what's up?'

'None. But I suspect it's no trivial business.'

'What a disappointment for you, sir, not to see your new manor house after all,' said the junior armiger. A year younger than Valdos, his name was Wiltorig Baysdale. He was a native of the Southern Shore, a distant cousin of the Lord Treasurer, Duke Feribor Blackhorse, and uncommonly good-looking and tall for his age. He had curly blond hair, grey eyes, and an ingratiating manner that Snudge had found to be a bit cloying. But perhaps the lad was only overeager to please.

'I daresay Buttonoaks will wait, Wil.' Snudge sighed. 'I've been assured that my steward is a very competent fellow . . . How do you feel?'

'Seedy, sir. I've never been drunk before. It seemed great fun last night, but I've never had such a headache. I could swear that nails are being pounded into my skull.'

'Ah, ye poor mite,' came the mocking voice of Gavlok's squire, Hanan Caprock, a burly youth who came from the wild mountain lands above Beorbrook Hold. 'Imagine that – your first hangover! Must be a quiet life down in Blackhorse Duchy . . . when the local peers aren't murdering each other or plotting treason against the Sovereign. I suppose you'll be a virgin, too, eh?'

Wil's face went crimson. His retort was surprisingly cool.

'That's none of your business. And I advise you to stifle your crude remarks in future, or you'll regret it.'

Hanan's hooded dark eyes narrowed. 'Oh, I will, will I, pretty one?'

'That's enough!' Snudge said testily. 'Hanan, you've a mouth on you like a potboy. Apologize at once, or Sir Gavlok will hear about this. I won't have my men baited.'

The older squire climbed to his feet and bowed elaborately to Wiltorig. 'I ask your pardon, Baysdale. And I apologize to you, also, Sir Deveron. I'm a highland ass who never learnt fine manners! So why don't I trot off and see if my master can use me for donkey-work?' He slouched toward the rear of the cottage, where Gavlok and Vra-Mattis had disappeared along with the woman of the house.

'I'm surprised Sir Gavlok tolerates such a lout,' Wiltorig remarked with disdain.

'His choice of squire is not your concern.' Snudge stood up and eased his sore joints. 'And so long as Sir Gavlok rides with us, you'll be civil to Hanan, even under provocation. Is that clear?'

'Yes, sir.'

Snudge was weary of the armigers' callow chatter and felt a need to organize his own befuddled thoughts. 'I'm going to stretch my legs in yonder orchard. There's probably a well behind the house. You two water the horses. They're very thirsty.'

'How do you know that, sir?' Wiltorig asked with studied innocence.

Snudge was taken aback. The lad's tone seemed oddly pointed. 'Any competent horseman can tell!' he snapped. 'Obey me.'

He cursed himself for the possibly revealing slip of the tongue as he moved away into a grove of cherry trees that were already setting fruit. One of his lesser gifts was the ability to coerce and control horses, and he was also uncannily aware of the animals' physical needs and afflictions. When he was a young boy, the talent had brought him special treatment in the royal stables from grateful grooms. Eventually, it resulted in his first fateful encounter with Conrig Wincantor, which had forever changed his life.

But why had the armiger Wiltorig posed his question so oddly? Was Snudge being overly imaginative – or had someone primed the boy to watch for evidence of wild talent?

Duke Feribor Blackhorse?

Snudge felt a queasy stirring in his belly that had nothing to do with his hangover. The formidable Lord Treasurer was a childhood friend of King Conrig, one of his closest advisers, and in a perfect position to have put forward his young relative as an armiger candidate. Snudge, wrapped up in the excitement of his investiture and the unexpected holiday, had thought nothing of the coincidence until this moment.

His physical discomfort forgotten, he thought about it now. And berated himself for never having put together certain facts about the duke.

Feribor, accused by persistent rumor – which the king flatly refused to countenance – of having poisoned his first wife, as well as orchestrating the death of his feckless older brother Shiantil so that he might inherit the Blackhorse dukedom . . .

Feribor, who now stood first in the line of succession to the Crown of Sovereignty, should Conrig's offspring be debarred . . .

Feribor, suspected of colluding with the scheming Lords of the Southern Shore, and completely exonerated of any wrongdoing after a too-hasty investigation in which the Royal Intelligencer played no part . . .

Feribor, Lord Treasurer, whose tax-gathering irregularities came under scrutiny when other members of the Privy Council pressed the issue, only to be forgiven his 'mistakes' by a Sovereign who refused to believe his old Heart Companion would cheat the Crown . . .

Feribor, nephew to the deposed Royal Alchymist and convicted traitor Kilian Blackhorse, who might have been told by his uncle of the hidden Trove of Darasilo – and Snudge's role in revealing its existence to Conrig . . .

Feribor, who might have long suspected that the shadowy young royal henchman Deveron Austrey was a wild talent dangerous to his own ambitions, whose late armiger Mero Elwick had murdered three of Snudge's companions and narrowly missed killing *him* – probably following his master's orders . . .

Did the devious duke still want Snudge dead? Had Feribor assigned young Wil Baysdale to complete the job botched by Mero? The latter had failed because he coveted the sigil named Concealer, Snudge's secret possession. Mero had been a greedy fool, and his vain attempt to seize the moonstone had brought about his own death.

If Wil *was* newly cast in the role of assassin, there was almost nothing to be done about it – at least for the present.

If I tell King Conrig my suspicions, Snudge thought, he won't believe me. Even worse, he might mention my mistrust to Feribor – which could provoke the duke into taking immediate action against me. And what if Wil hasn't been ordered to kill me at all? What if he's under orders to report my activities to Feribor?

Spying on the king's spy!

I must discuss this matter with Lord Stergos as soon as possible, Snudge decided. The Royal Alchymist had always been a sympathetic mentor to him. If anyone could overcome Conrig's misjudgment of the Lord Treasurer, it was his beloved older brother . . .

The cherry orchard was bounded by a wooden fence, which Snudge climbed, now painfully aware of an overfull bladder. Beyond was a strip of stony ground that ended at a bluff overlooking the River Blen and the broad valley leading to the sea and the sprawling city that had been renamed Cala Blenholme by the Sovereign. After relieving himself against a boulder, Snudge stood shading his still-bleary eyes against the blazing sun. A rampart of towering white clouds loomed on the southwestern horizon, no doubt the advance guard of a thunderstorm that was certain to disrupt the Solstice festivities in the capital. It was a moment before Snudge realized that a narrow pillar of jet-black smoke was also rising from the skyline.

Rising from the exact location of Cala Palace.

Lord Stergos! his mind screamed on the wind. *What's happened?*

There was no reply.

Before knighthood was conferred on him, Snudge had been accustomed to conceal his secret activities by posing as one of the anonymous young armigers or footmen attached to the retinue of some trusted noble, who would be under royal orders to visit the place or person under investigation. The cooperating peer was of course aware that Snudge was the king's spy; but he had no notion that the young agent possessed arcane abilities exceeding those of most Brothers of Zeth. In this situation, it had been relatively easy for Snudge to slip away from his fellow-retainers, perform his clandestine duties, and bespeak his findings directly to Lord Stergos, who would pass the information on to the High King.

Once Snudge was dubbed Sir Deveron, however, a new arrangement became necessary. A Knight Banneret had far more authority and status than a mere squire or even an ordinary knight, and was potentially more useful to his royal master. But he was also more conspicuous. Snudge rated two armigers of his own, and soon would employ servants who would expect to attend him closely. In time, he could expect to command other knights and men-at-arms. His privacy was diminished, and he was bound to find it more difficult to exercise his wild talents secretly.

Conrig did not intend for his intelligencer's arcane gifts to become common knowledge, but neither did he wish to be constrained in his ability to stay in close contact with him. The solution was to assign a personal windvoice to Sir Deveron Austrey, who would act as official liaison between him and the throne.

This was by no means an unusual privilege: many senior royal officers had ordained Brothers of Zeth in their retinues, and so did other important personages. Sir Deveron's apprentice windvoice Vra-Mattis Temebrook was a more modest symbol of privilege, but he was bright, highly talented, and at eighteen years of age eager to escape the gimlet eye of the Palace Novicemaster. In time, if Mat proved loyal, Snudge thought he might consider sharing his great secret with him. But for now he intended to use the young Brother cautiously, and urge Lord Stergos to do the same –

Unless some evil thing had happened to the Royal Alchymist. Why hadn't he responded to Snudge's call? It was up to the apprentice windvoice to find out.

Back at the cottage, Snudge found Gavlok and the others preparing to depart.

Vra-Mattis held out a cup to him. 'You still look unwell, sir. Drink down this hangover cure. It'll do you a world of good.'

Snudge quaffed the dose with a shudder. 'More ails me than a thick head.' He called the others to gather around him. 'During my stroll I came upon a vantage point overlooking the Blen Valley and the distant capital. I regret to tell you that a great fire seems to be raging in the vicinity of the palace.'

The armigers cried out horrified queries, but Snudge shook his head. 'Be silent! Vra-Mattis, withdraw from us and attempt to bespeak Lord Stergos for information. If you can't attract his attention, call upon his assistant, Vra-Sulkorig, or any other of the ranking Brethren who may be able to reply.'

The novice wasted no time in speech. He moved behind the trunk of the big chestnut tree, seated himself on a root, and covered his head with the hood of his robe in order to concentrate.

Snudge issued more orders. 'Valdos, see if the goodwife has such a thing as a tall clothespole. We're going to ride at speed from here on, with you bearing the royal banner, and we have no lance to tie it to . . . Wiltorig, unpack our mail shirts and helmets and lash them to the saddles where they may be easily donned if needed. Hanan, do the same for Sir Gavlok and yourself.'

The armigers rushed to obey.

Gavlok said, 'We should be able to reach Cala in an hour. These horses I bought at Swallowmere may not be hand-some, but they're tough as flint. Is there aught that I can do?'

Snudge replied in a low voice. 'I may ask a great boon of you later. For now, only stand by me as a friend.'

'With all my heart, Deveron. But I'm no great shakes in a fight, you know —'

'Oh, sirs!' cried Vra-Mattis, rising up from his tree root and calling out to the two knights. 'A terrible calamity has occurred at the palace. There's been an attempt to kill Lord Stergos! His apartment and the library have been almost completely demolished by several tarnblaze explosions and a great fire.'

'Is he dead?' asked Snudge.

'Nay, sorely burned but expected to survive. I bespoke Vra-Sulkorig, who says that your speedy return is now more needful than ever. The Royal Alchymist demands to speak to you and will take no remedy for his pain lest it send him to sleep and prevent him from giving you a special command. But he will tell no one what this command might be – not even the High King.'

'I see.' Whether it was Mat's disgusting potion at work, or his own brain's energy rising to the occasion, Snudge now felt clear-headed and revitalized. 'Then the King's Grace is unhurt?'

'He and the rest of the royal family are safe. The fire is confined to the wing of the palace where the Zeth Brethren reside. Sadly, numbers of them have been killed or injured. You're aware, of course, that the devilish substance tarnblaze cannot be put down by magical spells. The conflagration is being fought with water pumped from the river and the palace moat. It still burns strongly, and the roof-timbers are collapsing.'

'Tell Vra-Sulkorig I'll try to attend him and Lord Stergos inside of an hour. Bid him have the City Guard clear the West River Road approach so we won't be delayed. By now, there must be panicky crowds as well as gawkers on the streets surrounding the palace.'

Mattis nodded and covered his head again.

'All is in readiness, Deveron,' Gavlok announced, 'whenever you wish to ride.'

A few minutes later they were all in the saddle, galloping back onto the highroad with the squire Valdos leading the way, holding the crown banner of the Sovereignty and shouting, 'Make way! Make way for the king's men!'

FIVE

'My lord, I'm here. I grieve to see you so wounded.'

Snudge bent low over the bandaged face of the patient lying motionless on a bed in a room adjacent to the king's suite. Only the hazel eyes were uncovered. They were partially open, with their lids blistered and lashes seared away, and darted aimlessly from side to side as if vainly seeking someone. Snudge felt his heart contract. Was the poor man blind?

'My Lord Stergos, are you awake?'

Is it you, Deveron? The response came in unsteady wind-speech.

'The skin around his mouth has been terribly burned,' High King Conrig whispered. He sat on a stool beside his suffering brother, his own countenance a mask of anguish. 'He may not be able to answer.'

Snudge said covertly, 'He bespoke me. But I dare not let these other people hovering round about him know that we can converse mind-to-mind. Send them away. Lord Stergos is in great pain. He may slip into unconsciousness at any moment.'

Conrig climbed to his feet and addressed the crowd of

red-robed physicians and alchymists. 'All of you, leave us. Sir Deveron and I will confer privately for a few minutes and pray over my brother.'

The Brothers reluctantly filed out of the sickroom and closed the door. A subdued roll of thunder announced the approaching storm.

Snudge said, 'Lord Stergos, do you have a message for me? It's safe to use windspeech. The others have gone away.'

Ah . . . Mustn't compromise your secret, Deveron. Especially not now.

'No, my lord.'

All of them think . . . the explosion was attempt on my life. Even Con! Not true. I believe . . . someone demolished my quarters to get at the Trove of Darasilo. You remember Kilian had it. We never found . . . impossible to windsearch sigils . . . we thought he hid it somewhere in palace . . . he'd never entrust it to another.

'I agree,' Snudge said. 'Shall I tell His Grace about this?'

'Here!' Conrig protested. 'There'll be no secrets kept from me!'

Tell him.

'Sire,' Snudge said firmly, 'in matters of high sorcery, you must always be guided by the judgment and wisdom of your Reverend Brother. However, he's given me permission to tell you his concerns. Do you remember the secret trove of inactive sigils and the two magical books that I discovered in the rooms of the former Royal Alchymist, Kilian Blackhorse?'

'Yes. Our search after Kilian's arrest turned up nothing, so I assumed they had been lost. Gossy said so, too. If the things had turned up, he planned to destroy them to keep them away from that cunning little bastard, Beynor of Moss. He and Kilian were cooking up some conspiracy together.'

'Your brother believes that the sigils were hidden somewhere in the Royal Alchymist's apartment by Kilian, before Lord Stergos himself took up residence there. He also thinks that the tarnblaze assault was an attempt to uncover the items so that they might be stolen away.'

Conrig nodded. 'So we can presume that either Beynor or Kilian himself was responsible for the explosion?'

Beynor . . . exiled among Dawntide Salka. No way to escape. Queen Ulla assured us. But Kilian . . . friends at abbey . . . The windvoice trailed away.

Snudge said, 'Lord Stergos thinks Beynor couldn't have done it himself. He's a virtual prisoner of the Salka on a remote island in the eastern Boreal Sea. Kilian is confined under house arrest in Zeth Abbey, but he has many friends – as we know too well – whom he may have converted to his cause.'

Conrig was on his feet, clenching his big fists. He began to pace back and forth. A flash of lightning lit the room, followed almost at once by a crash of thunder. 'Damn that scheming wizard! I knew I should have lopped off his treacherous head. But our mother couldn't bear losing her precious brother!'

Queen Mother Cataldis was a gentle but steel-willed woman. Neither Conrig nor Stergos could bring themselves to oppose her.

Three visiting Brothers . . . scholars . . . outside library yesterday when all the others were away at the Solstice Eve feast.

'Lord Stergos says there were three suspicious Brothers of Zeth working near his apartment yesterday,' Snudge said. 'By the library.'

The High King bent over the bandaged man. 'Gossy! Can you tell Snudge their names?'

Can't recall. Ask Dean of Studies, Vra-Edzal.

Snudge reached for a wax tablet and stylus that lay on a bedside table beside a tray of medicines, wrote the name down, and handed the tablet to the king. 'This man will know, sire.'

Deveron . . . examine my rooms. See if there really is a hiding place . . . empty. Those unholy tools of the Beaconfolk must not reach Kilian . . . Aah! The pain . . . very bad.

'Never fear, my lord. I'll do as you say. If Darasilo's Trove has been stolen, the thieves can't have gone far yet. We'll catch them.'

The sigils and books must be destroyed. You know what Kilian and Beynor would do with them. Even my dear brother might . . . Promise me!

'I promise, my lord.'

The pain . . . the pain . . . No more, Deveron. Summon the doctors and I'll take the poppy draft. God have mercy on me . . .

'What's he saying?' Conrig demanded.

'He's finished speaking. He wants the doctors. He's in agony.'

Conrig strode to the door and shouted for the medical attendants to return. They flocked back, and several of them lifted the burn victim, parted the ointment-smeared bandages covering his mouth, and administered the narcotic draft that had been refused earlier.

'You must leave him now, Your Grace,' one of the doctors said. 'He will sleep for many hours.'

Conrig scowled, but he finally turned away and beckoned Snudge to follow. When the two of them were alone in the corridor, the king asked sharply, 'What did you promise Lord Stergos you would do?'

'Pursue the mysterious Brothers,' Snudge said evasively, 'presuming they stole the sigils and the books.'

'If those three are the villains who burned poor Gossy,' the king said with quiet menace, 'they shall have their own close acquaintance with flame.'

'Perhaps they're still hiding in the palace. But it's more likely that they escaped in the confusion and fled the city. A search must begin at once, sire. You'll need to summon this Vra-Edzal. He can provide the names and descriptions of the three, and perhaps even arrange for drawings of their faces. This would greatly assist both the windsearchers and the untalented hunters. The Lord Constable, Earl Marshal

Parlian, and the other members of your Privy Council will have to know about this.'

Including Duke Feribor Blackhorse, who might have played a key role in the disaster! But there was no way of proving that, nor even any chance now of discussing the possibility with Stergos.

'Hmm.' Conrig looked away, thinking. 'I must decide how much to tell my counselors. Unfortunately, we can't avoid giving out some sort of description of the stolen trove. But it should be as vague as possible – old books of great value only to alchymists, and a few small stone carvings. We'll offer a large reward, but make it seem that the most important consideration is capturing those who wounded Stergos and destroyed the library. All of the searchers will be sworn to secrecy. Others will learn soon enough about this damned collection of moonstone sigils, but we must keep their dread capability secret. Only you and I and Stergos must ever know of that.'

'Not the Conjure-Queen?' Snudge asked softly. 'Her Subtle Loophole would readily scry the location of the stolen things.'

'God forbid! If Ullanoth found them before we did, it could bring on a catastrophe far worse than the one we already face. You do understand that, don't you, Snudge?'

'Yes, sire. I was not sure *you* did.'

'Impudence . . .'

'However, you face something of a dilemma here, sire. I think Queen Ullanoth is bound to learn something about the theft before long. News of the palace fire will spread from one end of the island to the other. Fortunately for us, there's no easy way for her to get her hands on the trove, even if she scries its location. Her Sending is unable to take back anything to its point of origin. She'd have to come after the trove using her natural body. That would be quite difficult for her, given the situation in Moss and her present state of physical frailty.'

'What are you driving at? What's the dilemma?'

'If the thieves aren't captured in short order, you may be forced to ask for her help. To prevent the trove from falling into the hands of Kilian or Beynor.'

'God's Eyes! Of course. One of them certainly planned the theft.'

'Or both,' Snudge said. 'This is what Lord Stergos believes. He asked me to inspect the scene of the conflagration. Perhaps I might find some useful indications.'

'The burned-out wing can hardly be cool yet, but the oncoming rainstorm will take care of that.' Outside the corridor windows it had grown very dark, and the lightning and peals of thunder were now almost continuous. 'When you finish, come to my study. We still must talk of the reason why I called you back to the city.'

Snudge let his chagrin show. 'How remiss of me! This terrible disaster wiped all thought of the other matter from my mind.'

'We'll talk of it later.' Conrig turned abruptly and strode away.

Snudge started off in the opposite direction, intending to go to the knights' lodging in the Square Tower where he had left Gavlok and the others. He was going to need help searching the ruins, and he already felt deathly weary. The anguish emanating from the mind of Lord Stergos had deeply affected his own humor. It was a troubling aspect of his wild talent that he was only beginning to come to terms with. There were other considerations as well, but they didn't bear thinking of now.

And neither did his motive for not telling King Conrig all that he had promised Lord Stergos.

Snudge, Gavlok, and the three squires armed themselves with iron-shafted pikes, donned waterproof military cloaks and heavy boots, then set off to begin the miserable task of poking through steaming rubble. A torrential deluge now beat down upon the palace. Since the damaged wing had largely lost its roof and was open to the elements, the rain had quenched the last of the flames. Most of the firefighters had withdrawn.

When Snudge's party arrived at the ruined library they found Vra-Sulkorig Casswell himself. He had put off his robes in favor of waxed-leather hunting garb, and was supervising the removal of an incinerated human body from among the fallen stacks.

Stergos's principal assistant bore the symbolic title Keeper of Arcana, but his actual duties were administrative. He was an austere, balding man in early middle age, more pragmatic than mystical. The king's brother was over twenty years his junior, and had relied on Sulkorig's greater experience to govern the scores of Zeth Brethren assigned to various palace duties.

As Gavlok and the armigers began a cautious tour of the gutted library, Snudge explained to the Keeper why he and his men had come.

Sulkorig nodded brusquely. 'Looking for clues, are you, Sir Deveron? Then you'll find this interesting.' He held out something in his gloved hand. 'We found it with these sad remains.'

Snudge took the muck-encrusted, faintly gleaming object, bent down, and rinsed it in one of the myriad pools of rainwater. It was a solid gold gammadion pendant on a matching chain, one of those worn by every professed Brother of Zeth. On one side, the pendant was engraved with the voided cross emblem of the order. On the other side was a name. Snudge had to strain to read it in the gloom:

VRA-VITUBIO BENTLAND – C.Y. 1108

'The name of the owner and the date of his ordination,' Sulkorig explained. 'He was one of those heroes who attempted to rescue the Royal Alchymist after the tarnblaze explosions took place.'

Snudge pocketed the pendant. 'I'll give this to His Grace. He'll surely wish to commemorate the bravery of this man, who gave up his own life for Lord Stergos. Can you tell me anything about him?'

Sulkorig watched stoically as two white-faced young novices finished loading the nearly fleshless, contorted corpse onto a litter and covered it with a sheet. 'Take him to the old laboratory and lay him out with the others, lads. You need do no more work today.'

'Yes, Brother Keeper.' The pair shuffled off with their grisly burden.

'Vra-Vitubio was a visitor to Cala,' Sulkorig said to Snudge, 'one of three historians come down from Zeth Abbey to do research in our library. I myself know little about him, but doubtless his companions can tell us all that the High King requires for the commemoration.'

'Doubtless,' Snudge said through clenched teeth. 'Do you know the names of the others?'

'Vra-Felmar Nightcott and Vra-Scarth Saltbeck. It appears that they were also among those who tried to rescue Lord Stergos, but were unable to find him in the smoke. Neither one was seriously hurt.'

'Would you do me the great favor of windspeaking the two right now, and ask them to present themselves to Lord Telifar, His Grace's secretary?'

Sulkorig's brows rose in surprise, but he pulled off a glove and covered his eyes with his hand. After a couple of minutes had passed, he regarded Snudge with a puzzled expression. 'Neither man responds. I consulted our infirmarian, and they are not among those recuperating from injuries.'

'I didn't think they would be! Vra-Sulkorig, you know that I am the king's man, and that I undertake to perform certain

privy services for him. I must tell you something now in
strictest confidence. His Grace suspects that those two
Brothers and their dead comrade were responsible for this
terrible conflagration.'

'My God! Why should they do such a thing?'

'In order to steal certain valuable arcane objects belonging
to Lord Stergos. I was not in the city at the time of the
disaster. Please tell me what you know of the sequence of
events here.'

The first explosion had occurred at about eight in the
morning, at a time when most residents of the palace were
still sleeping off the night's festivities, so as to be well rested
for the events scheduled later on Midsummer Day. The
Brothers were free to do as they chose, but many of them
– including the Royal Alchymist – attended the usual
communal breakfast in the refectory at the sixth hour.

Stergos would ordinarily have gone to his office at the far
end of the cloister wing after eating and dealt with his correspondence. But on this holiday, with the scribes and secre-
taries excused from duty, he told his assistant Sulkorig that
he would return to his own quarters for a time, since he had
much to meditate upon. When the first tarnblaze explosion
blew open the outer door of the Alchymical Library, Stergos
was among the stacks, searching for a book dealing with the
thaumaturgical history of the Salka race.

The concussion toppled many of the free-standing book-
shelves. One of them caught Stergos by the lower leg, trap-
ping him. He began to cry for help and became aware of
agitated shouts in the exterior corridor. Then, as he later told
Vra-Sulkorig, red-robed figures moved into the smoke-filled
chamber. As yet there was no widespread fire. A reassuring
voice called out from not far away, apparently trying to locate
him among the jumble of fallen stacks. Stergos answered, but

heard nothing further for some minutes save the tolling of the alarm bell mounted outside the library door and a single youthful voice – perhaps the bellringer – screaming for help.

What happened next was so appalling that Stergos nearly fainted from shock. First came a sound of persons running. The smoke, which had the typical sulphurous stench of tarn-blaze, had thickened and it was getting harder for him to breathe. Then a tremendous blast emanated from his own rooms on the far side of the library, causing more shelves to crash and shaking the edifice to its foundations. He'd left the apartment door open when he came out to fetch the book, and even through the smoke he could see a huge gout of flame belch out of his sitting room and set the library furnish-ings – and his own clothing – afire.

He cried out with the last of his strength, then succumbed to oblivion until he awoke in the King's Suite and bespoke his story to Sulkorig, who later pieced together certain missing details by questioning witnesses.

Earlier, the novice who had been hauling hysterically on the bell cord was joined by another young Brother with more initiative. Shortly before the second explosion occurred, the two of them decided to attempt to rescue the unknown victim who was trapped in the library and calling out. They pulled down arras from the corridor wall and wrapped themselves, as protection against the fire within, and together plunged into the smoke.

Instantly, they were bowled over by two Brothers dashing *out* of the library and crying, 'Run! Run for your lives!' Then came the horrendous second blast, and the fast-spreading inferno. In a small miracle, the roaring flames seemed to diminish the thickness of the smoke momentarily. The two rescuers caught sight of Stergos engulfed in fire. They used an arras to beat it down, then dragged the Royal Alchymist to safety.

By then the corridor was thronged with men in red robes, members of the Palace Guard trying without success to restore order, and a few servants bearing containers of water, who doused the burned man and his scorched saviors.

'Everyone on the scene assumed that the two Brothers who had emerged from the library a few minutes earlier were would-be rescuers who lost heart and fled,' Vra-Sulkorig concluded. 'Someone recognized them as they pushed through the crowd and tried to ask them questions. But they were coughing and moaning, and soon vanished amidst the commotion. By then the flames had spread to other parts of the cloister wing, and the residents were fleeing.'

Snudge stood over the spot where the corpse had lain. 'Do you see, Brother Keeper? He had come only a few ells from Lord Stergos's apartment door. He must have been the last one to run out of there before the second explosion happened. The fireball roasted him in mid-stride.'

'Blessed Zeth,' Sulkorig muttered. 'May heaven grant him mercy.'

Snudge suspected there was scant chance of that.

'Sir Deveron!' The armiger Valdos called out from some-where inside the ruined apartment. 'You must come in here and see this! But beware. Some of the roof beams are sagging and may collapse at any minute.'

Snudge entered, trailed by the Keeper. Fallen timbers lay everywhere in precarious tangles, some still smoldering in spite of the continuing downpour. Blackened and broken containers of ceramic or glass had survived, but all of the furnishings were ashes, and the beautiful hardwood floor that he remembered from his clandestine invasion of Kilian's quarters four years earlier was entirely burned away, leaving the same flagstone underpavement that was visible in the library.

Valdos stood just inside the doorframe of what had been

the Royal Alchymist's bedroom. The rear wall, made of closely fitted granite blocks, bore an irregular stain of yellowish-white at least five feet in diameter, surrounded by a halo of soot.

'I believe that the second explosion involved two bomb-shells, set off simultaneously,' Vra-Sulkorig noted. 'In my early life I was a soldier, and I've seen such things before. Perhaps the fire-raisers had intended to blast open the door to Lord Stergos's apartment. When they found it unlocked, they used both bombs inside.'

But Snudge's attention was elsewhere.

In the middle of this room, where the bed had once stood, was a square area of newly exposed floor that measured some three ells by four. Instead of stone, it was covered over with rusted iron plates that were bulging and distorted by heat. At one end, a pair of plates on hinges had dropped open like trapdoors, revealing a hole partially clogged by debris from the fire. Stone steps led down from the bedroom level into a kind of cellar . . . or crypt.

'Codders!' Snudge whispered.

He crossed the room with the greatest care, squatted gingerly, and peered into the opening. The underground chamber was about three ells deep and awash at the bottom with water in which floated bits of burned material. At the far end were two sizable objects of roughly hewn stone with heavy lids. They looked like tombs. In front of them stood a warped iron framework like a skeletal cabinet or chest that still held a few slabs of charred wood.

The iron thing had a tantalizing familiarity.

Then he knew what he must be seeing. Using his pike as a staff, he descended the steps into the crypt.

'It was the remains of Kilian's small oaken storage cabinet, sire. The one I had discovered in his sanctum, bound with iron bands and fitted with the peculiar lock that almost defeated my attempt to pick it. Its doors – or what was left of them – were wide open.' He reached into his belt-wallet and placed a discolored metal mechanism on the king's desk. 'I found this in the dirty water down around the tombs. But there was no trace of the sigils that had been stored in that cabinet – more than a hundred of them – nor the small moonstone medallions that were fastened to the covers of the two large books that I left behind with the sigils.'

Conrig took up the lock and turned it slowly in his hands. 'Someone knew how to work it,' Snudge said. 'It's undamaged. And open.'

The draperies of the study windows were drawn against the grey twilight and the wrenching sight of the ruined library and cloister wing across the quadrangle gardens. It was around the tenth hour after noon and still raining steadily, although the thunder and lightning had passed.

'So now we are certain,' the king said. 'The trove is gone. Stolen.'

'I fear so, sire. I learned some time ago that the two ancient books were transcribed in the Salkan language. Like the smaller one that I took away, they contained pictures of different sigils. I can only presume that the books held expanded descriptions of their varied uses, along with spells of activation.'

'Including that of your own Concealer sigil that was . . . lost during the assault on Mallmouth Bridge?' The Sovereign's tone was dry.

'I never noticed, sire. Since the larger books were illegible to me, I paid them scant attention. Concealer was certainly depicted in the smaller book, which had much of its content written in an old version of our own tongue. That's why I stole it. But Concealer's activating spell, like all others in the little book, was written in Salkan. And I must emphasize that correct pronunciation is absolutely critical for bringing a sigil to life. I was told by Beynor himself that saying the words wrong would anger the Beaconfolk and cause them to kill me. So he pretended to coach me – while actually plotting my death. Lord Stergos and I believe that Kilian also knew the peril of mispronouncing the spells. This was why he formed an alliance with the Crown Prince of Moss and agreed to share the stones, in exchange for Beynor's expertise in the Salkan language. The Glaumerie Guild knows how to bring sigils to life, and Beynor belongs to the Guild, as do all members of Moss's Royal Family. Kilian evidently had no suspicion that there might be another, simpler way to activate sigils – merely by touching them to the moonstone disks mounted on the book covers.'

'You never told me that.' Conrig looked at Snudge narrowly,

For good reason, Snudge thought. There was more to the brief activation process as well, which he would never divulge to the king. 'It slipped my mind, sire. And of course I was forced to give the little book to Ansel Pikan shortly after I took it.'

'God only knows what *he* might have done with it! You and Stergos were both fools not to have kept it safe.'

Snudge said nothing. The Royal Alchymist would have destroyed both the book and the Concealer if he had been able to. He believed their magic to be inherently evil and corrupting to the user. Belatedly, Snudge had come to the same conclusion. For this reason he had hidden Concealer away after the Battle of Mallmouth Bridge, telling the king it was lost in the fray. He had not attempted to use it since.

Conrig's brief flash of anger vanished and he smiled. 'Ignore my ill temper. I fret about my poor brother. Although the leeches say he'll recover, he will carry terrible scars.'

'Then his sight was spared? I was afraid –'

'God be thanked, his vision is normal in spite of the burns

about his eyes.' Conrig poured amber malt liquor into his
favorite cup, which was silver with a gold-lined bowl and a
great amethyst set into the stem as a talisman against poison.
'Will you drink with me?'

'I thank you, sire.' Snudge took a crystal goblet from a
sideboard and accepted a small amount of the spirits.

'Please be seated,' Conrig said. Both of them tasted the
malt, which was smooth and fiery. 'I have a mission for you,
one that will take you far from Cathra.' He held up his hand
as Snudge attempted to speak. 'No, it has nothing to do with
the pursuit of the thieves, although it may be possible for
you to join the hunt for them as you journey north on this
other matter. I already have three thousand men searching
for the fugitives, and pictures of them provided by Vra-Edzal
were transmitted by wind hours ago to every corner of
Cathra. By tomorrow, the local adepts will have drawn up
numbers of posters with images of the two rogue Brothers
and nailed them up in every city and town.'

Snudge nodded and waited.

Conrig said, 'As for this special assignment: there is no
other person I can entrust it to, for it involves a challenge
to my own perilous secret.'

'Your talent.'

'Aye, my accursèd talent, that would deny me my Crown
of Sovereignty –'

'And perhaps give it to Duke Feribor,' Snudge blurted,
'unless the Queen's Grace should be delivered of a normal-
minded son.'

Conrig sighed. 'She carries a normal child, but it is a girl.
Queen Ullanoth was kind enough to confirm this fact for
me.'

Snudge lowered his eyes at the disappointing news.

'At yesterday's feast,' the king went on, 'the earl marshal
told me of a very disturbing rumor that apparently circulates

in north-western Tarn among the local fishermen. It popped up only recently, and its gist is that my first wife may still be alive.'

'Sire, that can't be!' Snudge exclaimed. 'I windsearched for Princess Maudrayne myself when she flung herself from the parapet at Eagleroost – and for months thereafter. The Brothers of Zeth also combined their talents to sweep the entire island for traces of her. So did the Conjure-Queen, using her Great Stone Subtle Loophole.'

'Ansel's sorcery probably could have concealed Maude from all of you with ease. Tarnian shamans are the most powerful natural talents in the world. Consider also the disturbing fact that her personal maid Rusgann Moorcock unaccountably vanished without a trace. The woman was devoted to Maude, as if she were her own sister . . . And there's worse, which I've never confided to you.' He took a deep pull of the malt liquor and hesitated.

'Your Grace?'

'Ah, shite,' muttered the king. 'You must know. Stergos and I found Maude's diary. In it, she wrote that she knew of my talent and would not hesitate to expose it if I persisted in my amorous attachment to the Conjure-Queen. She also wrote that she had told Ansel my secret. And the diary held still another surprise: Maude was pregnant with my child.'

'Great God! And yet she said naught to you!' Snudge was both baffled and horrified. 'She signed the bill of divorcement. And was willing to take her own life and that of the unborn babe . . .'

'A woman of fierce Tarnian passions. How we once loved one another, Snudge! But for six years it seemed she could not conceive, and the shame of it made her anxious and short-tempered. Meanwhile, I was absorbed in the struggle with my late father and the Privy Council, and had small time for the loving attentions that such a high-spirited woman demands of her mate.'

Snudge had only taken a few sips from his goblet, but he now downed a generous swig. A sense of foreboding had begun to grip his heart. He knew Conrig's terrible dilemma concerning Maude and the child – and feared what his own role might be in its resolution.

The king said, 'The Princess Dowager is capable of a hatred as deep as her love once was. If she lives, and if her child lives and is a son, he is my legitimate successor. He was conceived in wedlock. The divorce is irrelevant. Add to this Maude's knowledge of my talent –' He shook his head, tossed down the last of his drink, and refilled the cup.

Snudge said, 'You wish me to go to Tarn and find out the truth. But that may be impossible, if she's protected by Ansel's sorcery. Even though my windsearching talent is considerable, it has limitations that I'm only beginning to understand. I met Red Ansel Pikan and he's more powerful than I can ever hope to be. Furthermore, he's in league with some supernatural entity he calls his Source, who guides him like a puppet. We know so little of the shamans of Tarn, sire! They're said to be directly descended from the Green Men, who shared this island with other inhuman monsters before Bazekoy's conquest –'

'Anent that point, let me tell you something else you may not know!' the king hissed. 'Green blood also taints thee and me, Deveron Austrey – and every human being possessed of talent, for this is how our magical abilities were instilled in us!'

'Oh, sire –'

'But that matters naught. The only important thing is that you find Maude and her babe – if they do live – before their existence is revealed to the world. And when you find them, do what must be done to protect me and my Sovereignty from the danger they pose.'

Snudge held the king's gaze. 'You wish me to slay them.'

'I did not say that. If you're able to eliminate their threat in another way, then do so. You are my sworn man, Deveron Austrey. Do you accept this charge?'

Snudge set his unfinished drink on the polished wood of the royal desk and rose to his feet. 'I will carry it out as best I can, Your Grace.'

'That's no answer.' Conrig's voice was low and harsh.

'It's mine, sire.'

Their eyes remained locked, but the Sovereign of Blenholme was the one who finally blinked and looked away. 'I fear her more than Kilian and Beynor,' he whispered, 'more than Ullanoth, more than all the scheming rebels of Didion and Tarn and the Southern Shore combined.'

'I know. Let me see what I can do.'

Conrig sat still, staring at nothing. Then he gave a small start and seemed to pull himself together. When he spoke it was with his usual forcefulness. 'Tomorrow, seek out Parlian Beorbrook and tell him your mission. I trust the earl marshal absolutely – as must you, since he also knows of your talent. Ask his advice. He understands the barbarians of the north country better than any man in Cathra, since he and his family have defended our border against them for nearly three hundred years. He may be able to lend you guides from his troop of Mountain Swordsmen to assist your penetration of Tarn. Whatever else you need, you shall have.'

'I desire that my friend Sir Gavlok Whitfell may accompany me on this mission, along with our armigers and Vra-Mattis, my apprentice windvoice. Gavlok and Mattis, at least, must know at the outset that we seek Maude and her child. The squires can be kept in ignorance until we reach Tarn. Since Lord Stergos is too ill to receive windspeech from me or Mat, I recommend that Vra-Sulkorig, the Keeper of Arcana, relay messages in his place. He will also have to be taken into your confidence – at least partially.'

'Very well, but none of these people must ever know of *my* talent, even though we have to tell them about yours. The danger posed by a son of Maude to the Cathran succession is sufficient justification for your search.'

'I'll be prudent when reporting, sire.'

'As you make your way north, I also desire you to windsearch for the two thieves. Your natural ability along that line is probably greater than that of anyone else in Cathra.'

'But Cathra is a large nation,' Snudge protested, 'and we can't be sure which route the two outlaws have taken. If they head directly to Zeth Abbey and Kilian, I might have a chance of scrying them out. But perhaps they went in some other direction entirely, or even escaped in a ship. They might be under orders to hide the trove in some remote spot where Kilian will retrieve it later.'

'Let's hope not,' the king said, looking glumly into his cup.

'Your Grace, you must think about the wisdom of asking Queen Ullanoth for help. There's danger – but if she finds the two men with her Loophole, you can send pursuers straight to them. You don't have to tell her what the villains stole – only that they attempted to kill Lord Stergos. As soon as the trove is located, it must be destroyed. This is the only safe course. Lord Stergos knows it, and so do you. Inactive moonstones can be crushed without danger and rendered useless. We may presume that the book-medallions can be destroyed in a similar manner, and the pages burnt.'

Conrig groaned at the prospect, and Snudge knew that his niggling suspicions about the king were correct. He still toyed with the notion of using the things himself.

'I must think about what to do,' Conrig said. 'If Ulla somehow seizes the trove . . .'

'That's why the stones must be smashed and the books burnt, sire,' Snudge emphasized. 'To keep them from her, from Kilian, and from Beynor.'

'Yet I must be sure in my mind that I've made the right decision. I'll take one more day to think on it further, for I'm so weary now that my wits fail me. Leave here tomorrow at an early hour, but only after conferring with Earl Marshal Parlian. Travel to Tarn via the Great North Road and the Wold Road through Frost Pass. Break your first day's journey at Teme, and I will then tell you my decision about consulting Ullanoth. You may go now.'

Snudge bowed. 'Very well, sire.' He turned and started for the door.

'One final thing,' the king said. 'I know you told me that your Concealer sigil was lost. I'm also aware of your deep misgivings about moonstone magic. But if it should happen that your sigil were found . . . I'd be most grateful if you'd use it once again in my service.'

Snudge stiffened, but he refrained from turning back to meet the king's eyes. 'I doubt it will ever be found, Your Grace. But be assured I'll do everything in my power to carry out my duties faithfully.'

SIX

The darkness was not absolute. The outcroppings of frost mottling the cave walls had a faint glow, and the auras of the three visitors outlined their subtle bodies in dim colors that changed with the fluctuation of their emotions.

He himself was visible only by reflected light, a shapeless, eyeless hulk chained to the rocks with gemlike fetters of bright blue-glowing ice. His enemies had forced him to retain the Salka form he had assumed during the Old Conflict, since it was capable of physical suffering. And so he had suffered in both body and spirit for over a thousand years, while denied the sky.

But the foe could not take away his great oversight or his voice, which kept hope alive as one helper after another failed in strength or was struck down. These latest three souls were among the best he'd ever found. He'd cherished them specially and sustained their human fragility while they implemented his instructions. Because now, after what had seemed an interminable series of failures and setbacks, it seemed that there was a real chance he might finally succeed in severing the unnatural link between the Sky Realm and the groundlings.

Did you bring the small book?

'It's here.' Ansel drew the ancient volume from his belt-wallet and set it down on the rime-encrusted cavern floor. The disk of moonstone fastened to its crumbling leather cover was lifeless, but still capable of drawing down the power of the foe. 'There remain the two books hidden in Cala Palace, Rothbannon's transcription from the Salka archives, and the archival tablets themselves, sequestered in the vaults of the Dawntide Citadel.'

Thalassa Dru, have you brought contributions from the Green Men and the Worms of the Morass?

'I have only a few this time, unfortunately, and all of the lesser sort.' She emptied a pouch containing a dozen dead moonstone carvings onto the floor next to the book.

Still, this is a worthy effort. Every stone that is obliterated weakens the link . . . And you, my dear Dobnelu. What do you have?

'I have gleaned three minor stones from the sea. And this, which one of my friendly wolves discovered deep in the wilderness of the Stormlands and brought to me.' The hag tossed the lesser sigils onto the heap, but the fourth she held up before the featureless dark face of the One Denied the Sky. It was a small wand carved from pale stone, covered with minute lunar symbols. 'I've never seen one of these, Source, but I believe it to be a Destroyer, perhaps a relic of the Barren Lands phase of the Old Conflict.'

Ah! So it is! Blessings be upon you, Dobnelu, for ridding the world of one of the most evil of the Great Stones, and thus confounding the Pain-Eaters. My souls, you have all done very well. Now shield your eyes, while I unite with the Likeminded and dispose of these abominations.

The humans pressed their hands to their faces. A dazzling burst of light illuminated the enchained hulk of the One Denied the Sky for an instant. Then the cave was restored to its former state of tenebrous gloom. The book and the sigils were gone, as usually happened. But something else had occurred that caused the auras of the three humans to flare amber and sea-green with surprise.

'Your chains,' Ansel exclaimed.

The two women echoed him in a wondering chorus. 'Your chains!'

The blazing sapphire color of the transparent ice manacles pulsed and then slowly faded, as though the links were being filmed over with grime. After a moment the internal luminescence once again increased, but it was significantly duller than before.

'Their radiance diminishes,' Ansel breathed, hardly daring to believe it. Can it be that their strength also grows less?'

'Are you still tightly shackled?' Thalassa Dru asked.

The huge form shifted, straining at the links, but to no avail. *Alas, my souls. I'm held fast, as always.*

'But this must mean something,' Ansel said.

True. I think it's necessary that I consult immediately with the Likeminded about this strange occurrence. Forgive me, but we must forgo our usual hours of meditation and discussion. Perhaps when you come to me the next time, I'll know more . . . Dear souls, I thank you for once again enduring the ordeal of crossing. Now return to your own world.

'Farewell,' said Thalassa Dru, and vanished.

'Farewell,' said Dobnelu the sea-hag. But instead of disappearing, her fragile form staggered as if from a blow, and her aura flared violet and flame-red, betraying sudden fear. 'I cannot go back! The way is closed to me. Why? Source, what has happened?'

Ansel opened his arms to her and embraced her, while gazing at the Source with stunned disbelief. His own corona had dimmed and reddened.

The thing manacled by ice stirred, and its utterance was full of sorrow. *I did not see it happening! I was distracted. Oh, my poor dear Dobnelu! Your entranced body has died.*

The violet of her aura deepened and she spoke in a tremulous wail. 'While my subtle body remains alive . . . trapped here in this netherworld beneath the icecap? Oh, heaven help me! I didn't think such a thing was possible.'

'It isn't,' Ansel said. His face was now a raging furnace. 'Unless the death wasn't natural. Source! Have the Pain-Eaters done this?'

No. Now I perceive the truth. Share my envisioning, souls.

'Good God – and the miserable maggot laughs about it!' The High Shaman of Tarn held the old woman tighter, clenching his teeth to forestall a volley of curses at their bad luck. His fury burned, drowning the crone's emanation of stark terror. 'One of Blind Bozuk's damnable charms allowed this to happen, Dobnelu. I saw the thing clearly, hanging about the stripling's neck. Both Bozuk and the murderer will pay for this.'

'What will happen to me?' The hag moaned.

Don't despair, dear soul. There is a remedy, although it will not be easy to employ. Ansel, you must go to the steading as quickly as possible – in your physical body, of course. This is not an occasion for subtlety.

'I left my boat anchored in the lee of Cape Wolf. It won't take long for me to get to the fjord. But are Maude and the child in danger as well?'

Not from him . . . Go now. Bring the body-husk back to me, and be very cautious during the crossing so that it is not lost.

He nodded, released Dobnelu from his embrace, and vanished.

She stood there forlornly. What remained of her aura was so dull a purple as to be nearly brown. 'It seems colder. And I suddenly feel very tired. May I be seated, Source?

Your vital energies are dwindling. It's to be expected – but in order to protect you from true death, I must change you for awhile. Don't be afraid. If all goes well, you'll awake later in your own home, quite restored.

'And if it goes badly, will I die?'

Don't think of that. Only come and touch me.

She cringed. 'You always forbade it before this.'

Now it's necessary. Come. Hold out your hand, close your eyes, and let me take care of you.

The dead-black tentacle with its glowing blue chains reached out to her. She lifted her bony old hand and squeezed her eyes tight shut.

With a faint ringing sound, a tiny emerald sphere no larger than a pea fell to the cavern floor.

The One Denied the Sky was alone again. He picked up the sphere with great care, turned about, and pressed it into the ice of the wall behind him. It sank in until it was deeply embedded, joining scores of other glimmering little objects, all of them shining hopefully green.

There is a remedy. If it works, you'll live. If it fails, you'll also live, my poor human soul.

But what a life.

The slow-witted youth named Vorgo Waterfall had sense enough to follow the sarcastic advice of the bitch-princess who had slain his father. He floundered back to shore, stripped himself naked, and lay on a flat rock in the midsummer sun, shuddering and blubbering, until the encroaching tide forced him to move further inland. After his blood warmed and his skin dried, he wrung out his woolen shirt and trews and put them back on. They weren't too uncomfortable. He still had his belt and his sheath-knife and the little charm-sack hung round his neck on a string. But nothing else – not even boots.

His father's body had boots. Maybe other things. It was awash now, rolling a little with the wavelets that had appeared along with a rising wind. The thought of touching a dead man made his flesh creep with superstitious fear, and

for a long time he held back, watching the ravenous, noisy
mob of birds that dived and pecked, dived and pecked.

Finally he ran at them through the shallows, throwing
stones and yelling at the top of his lungs. Some of the birds
flew away, but others attacked him with such viciousness
that he was afraid they'd get his eyes. So he gave up, sobbing,
and ducked his head in the water to wash away the filth
they'd splattered on him, and the blood.

What am I going to do now? he asked himself. The lugger
had long since gone away, its escape from the shoaly bay
assisted by the rising tide. The bitch-princess hadn't even
bothered rowing with the sweeps. She'd just hoisted the sail
and jibed out through the reefs slicker'n eel slime!

Cursing monotonously, Vorgo Waterfall trudged along the
shrinking beach. He knew he wasn't clever. Dad'd told him
that often enough, sometimes with a curse and a smack on
the ear. 'But you be a crafty one, Vorgo,' he'd also said. 'You
got a nose for the main thing, like a cur pup. You can do
lots worse than follow that nose o' yourn.'

Right now, his nose was leading him back the way the
women and the boy had come, toward the sea-hag's steading.
The tide was half-high, and in many places the going was
hard, even dangerous, until he rounded the point and came
to the fjord beach. There all he had to do was slog on. He
tried to come up with a plan. Dad always had a plan. But
now the bitch-princess who would have made them rich was
gone. Only the sea-hag was left.

She was a witch, a very powerful one. All of the fishermen of the north-west shore knew that it was death to
enter her fjord. But why should that be? He thought hard
about it as he tramped and waded along. Why didn't she
want visitors? Other magickers were glad to sell their potions
and amulets and spell-dollies to orn'ry folk, but not old
Dobnelu. Why?

Maybe she had gold hidden in her house!

He touched the bag of charms hanging at his throat. What was it they were supposed to do? Make him invisible once he entered the circle of magic stones? Fend off the sea-hag's sorcery? He couldn't recall. But the charms had to be strong, because Dad had paid a lot for them, and they were good only on Midsummer Eve.

So he had to get on with it. Find that gold!

He climbed the cliff path, crossed the meadow, and stopped at the boundary of stones – ordinary looking things with nothing special about them at all. He clutched the charms and held his breath as he stepped between them, but nothing happened.

Am I invisible now? he wondered. No way to tell. There was a tiny hut not far away, near the vegetable garden. He decided to start looking for the gold inside it. People often hid things under the floor of sheds.

When he pushed the door open he gave a yelp of fear and froze in his tracks. The sea-hag herself was in there, lying on a low cot! She didn't move but he could hear her raspy breathing. He was amazed at how small she was and how frail. The sorceress who'd terrorized the entire coast of Tarn was just a little old bag of bones dressed in a ragged robe!

Why, he could wring her neck like a chicken . . .

Vorgo bent over her and very carefully touched the hag's sunken cheek. She slept on, so he screwed up his courage and did it, and she never squirmed or cried out or even opened her eyes, but only ceased to breathe. He let go of her and lurched away. Sweat ran from his hair into his eyes and he was shivering in spite of the day's heat.

Dead! The awful sea-hag was dead, and her treasure was his for the taking. All he had to do was find it.

He searched inside the farmhouse for four hours.

But he found no gold, no money, no jewels, hardly anything

of value at all save a dented silver cup and a string of agate
beads and a finely wrought little dagger with a carnelian
pommel. Frustrated and furious, he kicked a wooden bucket
across the kitchen. Now what? He'd have to hunt more
carefully, try the byre and the hen coop and the backhouse.
But first he'd have something to eat from the well stocked
larder –

The outside door opened.

Standing there was a robust man of medium stature, clad
in a simple brown deerskin tunic and matching gartered
trews. He wore crossed baldrics with many small bulging
compartments, and on his breast was a massive pectoral of
gold inset with Tarnian opals. His hair and beard were as red
as fire-lilies and his deep-set black eyes glittered with unshed
tears.

'Did you do it?' he asked.

Vorgo had heard of him: all Tarn had, although few had
ever seen him face to face. This was Red Ansel Pikan, the
Grand Shaman, leader of nearly all the other magickers in
the sealords' realm, the most famous wizard of the northland. Too shocked to speak, the youth stood stock-still with
his mouth hanging open.

The shaman lifted a small baton of carved unicorn-ivory.
There was a soundless flash. Vorgo gave a despairing wail
and his legs folded under him. He knelt on the scrubbed
wooden floor with his hands clasped in entreaty. 'I didn't
kill her! I never did!'

He felt a frightful pang of agony in his right ear. He shrieked
and writhed as something small fell from his head, bounced
off his shoulder, and smashed into white shards on the floor.

Ansel's black eyes had grown enormous and they held no
pity. 'Tell me your name. Explain what you're doing here.
If you lie to me again, your *other* ear will freeze solid and
fall off. More lies will cost you your nose and your lips –'

'No!' Vorgo howled. 'I'll tell!' The sordid tale poured out, disorganized and half-coherent; but Ansel understood it well enough. Dobnelu's physical body had been casually slain by a half-wit, barely sixteen years of age for all his brawny build, corrupted by his venal father, hardly knowing right from wrong.

He sighed. 'So the princess and the maidservant and the boy sailed away in your boat?'

'Yes, my lord.' Vorgo hung his head and bawled. Strings of snot leaked from his nose.

Ansel's eyes lost their focus and he windsearched the sea south and east of Useless Bay. Found her almost at once, handily steering a fishing smack under a louring sky. What a woman! Rusgann and Dyfrig were with her in the cockpit. The maid was honing a long kitchen knife with an oilstone. Maude wore an even larger blade on her belt. They had tied up their skirts to simulate trousers, donned tattered oilskin jackets, and wrapped their heads in grubby kerchiefs.

They'd reach Northkeep in late tomorrow, with the wind light and fitful.

Here's a pretty mess, Ansel thought. I must take Dobnelu's body to the Source without delay. The tricky crossover is bound to take hours, and only the Three Icebound Sisters know how long I'll have to tarry in the cave once I do arrive. Meanwhile, Maude is giving me the slip as nicely as you please! I can't becalm her with the weather brewing up as it is, and I certainly can't capsize the boat with a windblast. So she'll take refuge with her brother Liscanor at the castle. And he'll use his resident windvoice to inform High Sealord Sernin of the news about Maude and her son – and a talented Sovereign sitting on Blenholme's throne. The gaff will be well and truly blown – and how will Conrig Wincantor survive to play his part in the New Conflict?

Shall I abandon Dobnelu and transport my subtle self to

Maude? I could subdue her and the others and sail their boat back to the steading. *But she might arrive at Northkeep before I finish the drumming ritual and am able to transport myself.*

Shall I carry on trying to save my friend and let the Source sort out the others? *He's not omnipotent. Once Maude lets Conrig's cat out of the bag, it's out to stay.*

God of the Heights and Depths! Is there any other way I can salvage this situation? *Why not bespeak Liscanor's wind-voice, scare him silly, and command him to keep his mental gob shut?*

'Workable!' Ansel Pikan exclaimed out loud.

'M-my lord?' the wretched youth mumbled. He sat slumped on his heels. A thin trickle of blood from his amputated ear stained the shoulder of his shirt.

Ansel had nearly forgotten the murderer's presence. Time to deal with him.

'Vorgo Waterfall, you have committed a grave sin by taking a human life and you must atone for it. You are young, however, and sadly lacking in brains. And as it happens, I can use you.'

'Me?' The dullard slowly lifted his head.

'You. I'm going to attempt to bring back the woman you slew. Restore her life. It may take a fairly long time. If she does return, I want her to find her house and her livestock just as she left them. So you will stay here and take care of them as if your own life depended upon it. *Because it does.* Do you understand me, Vorgo?'

'You're not gonna kill me?' Dawning hope.

'Not if you work hard. Can you do that?'

'Oh, yes, my lord!'

'I can't promise to let you go, even if the sea-hag lives. She's a very old woman and needs help to survive in this place. You'd have to stay with her until her natural death occurred. Natural, Vorgo! It could take years. After she passed on, I'd come and take you back to your people in Northkeep Port. What do you say? It won't be an easy life, and if you can't bear the thought of it, I'll just freeze you to death right now. You won't feel a thing.'

'No! No! Please, I'll do it. Anythin' you say.'

I'll have to spell every task out for him three times over, Ansel thought in resignation. But first, I'd better bespeak Liscanor's windvoice – and any other near to Northkeep.

'Stay here and beg God's forgiveness. I'll be back in a moment to tell you what to do.' The shaman stepped outside the door and closed it behind him.

Back in the kitchen. Vorgo wiped his eyes and nose with his sleeve. Only now did he truly understand his great good luck. He wasn't going to die! Instead, he'd feed ducks and herd goats and sheep and hoe the sea-hag's cabbages. It would be lots easier than gutting fish or mending nets. This house was much larger than the squalid cottage on the waterfront he'd shared with his evil-tempered father. Probably fewer rats, too. And the larder was crammed with food and barrels of homebrewed ale and jugs of malt. Not bad at all!

He'd worry about the sea-hag coming back to life later.

Meanwhile, there was still her treasure to hunt for . . .

The rain began late the next day when they were still a league out of port, and Maudrayne was glad of it. With no darkness to hide them, she had been concerned about being recognized. Lukort Waterfall's lugger *Scoter* would be familiar to every sailor and fishmonger in Northkeep, and she had wondered if it might be safer to moor it in some secluded spot, go ashore in the coracle, and push on to the castle by some roundabout route afoot.

The misty rain and the false dusk brought on by the low-hanging clouds made that unnecessary. Boldly, she steered straight for the castle's deep-water landing stage. A few other returning skippers hailed her, but she deflected their interest in the time-honored fashion of the trade by growling, 'No luck,' and adding a salty curse on fickle fish.

Torches burned on the castle landing. Two large schooners and a single tall fighting frigate, Liscanor's beloved *Gayora,* were tied up there, along with a score of smaller craft. For some reason, the slip where she'd always berthed her own sloop-rigged yacht in days gone by was empty, so she guided *Scoter* in with easy competence while Rusgann tossed the bow line to a boy who had been sitting on the dock, fishing, indifferent to the gentle rain. No one else was in sight. They were probably all celebrating the holiday.

'Can't tie that old tub up here,' the urchin said with a grimace of contempt. He was about ten years old, dressed in rags, with bare feet. He had already caught a pair of fat speckled rockfish. 'Sealord's guards be along to send you packin' afore I get 'er snubbed to a cleat.'

'Make that line fast!' Maudrayne commanded in a no-nonsense voice. She rummaged in Lukort's confiscated wallet and held up a silver penny. It was probably more money than he'd seen in a year. 'Then fetch the watch commander quick as you can, and this will be yours.'

'Aye, cap'n!' He obeyed, then ran away.

'Get Dyfrig,' she told the maid, and hopped onto the dock with the stern line to secure it. Her son had gone below to the boat's tiny cabin when the rain started, and now he emerged rubbing sleep from his eyes, staring up at the immense curtainwall and looming towers of Northkeep with something akin to fear.

'Where are we, Mama?' he said.

'This is the castle where I was born. Now it belongs to my dear brother, who is your Uncle Liscanor.' She released her bound-up skirts and stripped off the concealing headcloth. Her long auburn hair gleamed in the torchflame, spangled instantly with tiny drops of rain. For a final touch, she pulled the spectacular opal wedding necklace out of her dress and arranged it on her bosom. Then she jumped back into the boat.

'Now listen to me carefully, Dyfrig.' She crouched to meet his eyes. 'We must once again play the game where you pretend to be Rusgann's son. We do this because, for the time being, I don't want anyone in the castle to know who you are.'

'Not even Uncle Liscanor?'

'Not even him. I'll reveal our secret to him later, but probably not tonight.'

'All right, Mama.' Dyfrig looked at her askance. 'Are there wicked men inside the castle, like Lukort and Vorgo?'

'None so evil as those two villains,' she reassured him, hoping that she told the truth. 'Only men and women who talk too much – who might carry tales about you if they knew you were a crown prince. Without meaning to, they might betray our great secret and put us in danger. So while we're in the castle, you must call Rusgann "mama" and stay close to her always. Try not to talk to me at all. The child of a servant wouldn't do that. But if you must, call me "my lady". Can you remember that?'

He smiled in a somber manner that was anything but child-like. 'Yes, my lady.'

She kissed his forehead. 'Well done.'

'Here come the guards,' Rusgann muttered.

They heard the tramp of studded boots, along with the excited cries of the dockboy.

Maudrayne leapt back onto the dock. Rusgann handed up Dyfrig to her and followed more decorously.

'There they be, just like I said!' The dockboy came dancing impatiently ahead of a squad of four guardsmen, then skidded to a halt with his eyes like saucers. 'Mollyfock! They be wimmen – and a wee brat!'

The sergeant, a grey-bearded veteran, strode up to Maudrayne with his hand on the hilt of his sword. 'Now then, what's all this? Who do you think you –' His mouth snapped shut like a trap. He stood silent, his gaze sweeping her from head to toe, before whispering, 'My lady Maude?'

Maudrayne nodded regally and smiled. 'So you remember me, Banjok. It's been many years since last we met, and so much has happened.'

The younger guards obviously had no notion who she was and stood well back, their expressions uncertain. That suited Maudrayne. She said to the sergeant, 'Please say no more at this time – especially not my name.' She pulled her oilskin jacket closed to conceal the necklace. 'Only take us to the sealord at once. I presume he is here?'

Banjok looked dazed. 'Yes. He's within, with Lady Fredalayne, presiding over the Solstice Day feast for the Line Captains and their families. It was moved to the great hall because of the rain. Please follow me.' He turned and marched off.

The urchin thrust himself forward, blocking Maudrayne's way. 'Hold on! My penny!'

She had to smile at his determination. 'What is your name?'

'Eselin. Some day I'll be a Line Captain and eat with the sealord!'

She handed the coin to him. 'It will happen, Eselin, if you make it happen.' Then she walked away into the rainy evening, trailed by Rusgann, Dyfrig, and the three silent guards.

Once they were inside the walls, Banjok dismissed his men, warning them to say nothing about the odd visitors if they valued their sword-hands. After the three retired to the guardroom inside the gatehouse, the sergeant led the women and the little prince into an antechamber called the Peace Room, just off the great hall. The dinner guests who came armed left their weapons and shields there, hung on wall pegs, according to the Tarnian custom. The place had a few padded benches but no other furniture.

Banjok locked the outer door that gave onto the corridor along the wall of the central keep. 'Wait here. It may be a short time before the sealord is able to leave the high table.' Banjok opened the heavy inner door and slipped quickly into the hall, from which loud sounds of music and conviviality emanated.

Rusgann sat Dyfrig on a bench, told him to stay there, and led her mistress to the opposite side of the chamber. 'Now let's be sure I understand what's going on here,' she hissed. 'Do you intend to tell your brother what's happened since your supposed death?'

'I'll say Red Ansel saved me from drowning, and brought me and my beloved maid to the sea-hag's steading to keep us safe from Conrig Wincantor, who wanted to put me under permanent house arrest in Cala so I wouldn't make trouble. I'll tell Liscanor that I know a terrible secret about Conrig that could cost him his Sovereignty, but I won't reveal what it is. Not yet.'

'Any more than you'd tell me,' Rusgann grumped. 'I suppose I was the pregnant one who delivered a boy-child.'

'Of course. Your hair is fair, like Dyfrig's. It'll work if you can keep people from questioning him. Pretend he's sick, or numbed by the ordeal of our escape.' Maudrayne shrugged out of the damp oilskin jacket and dropped it onto the stone floor. She took a comb from her belt-purse and began to work on her snarled hair.

'What do I say about the escape?' Rusgann asked. She retrieved the discarded oilskin and hung it on a peg, then took off her own.

'More or less the exact truth. I couldn't bear to live with the hag any longer. I planned to signal to a fisherman and bribe him to take us away. But Lukort Waterfall had already spotted me through his spyglass and come to kidnap me and hold me for ransom.'

'So we killed him, and left his son Vorgo to the sea-hag's mercies, and we sailed away, and here we are – bashed and bloodied, but safe!' Rusgann's plain face shone with unholy relish.

'Not really. There's still Ansel to worry about. I'll ask Liscanor to protect us from him, demand that we be allowed to stay here in Northkeep. But if Ansel wants to take me away, there's nothing my brother can do. He can't go up against the Grand Shaman of Tarn. He's a brave man, but he's afraid of Ansel. They all are.'

Rusgann put her finger to her lips. 'Keep your voice down. You'll frighten the boy.'

Dyfrig was leaning tiredly against the wall, looking very small in his oversized rainjacket. But his dark eyes were fixed on the women and he was doing his best to listen in.

'Sorcery!' Maudrayne's tone was full of loathing. 'What a curse it is! But how many people are willing to believe that? Not many; when magic can give you power over other persons, or secret knowledge that's even more valuable. Even Ansel's been corrupted by it! I thought he was my true friend, but all along he planned to use Dyfi and me in some bloody cunning scheme.'

'Now, my lady, you don't know that for sure. You might be misjudging the man.'

'We'll find out when he walks straight through the locked gatehouse door of Northkeep.' Maudrayne gave an ugly little laugh. 'And I doubt we'll have long to wait. The sea-hag never stays entranced for longer than two days. She'll bespeak Ansel when she wakes up and finds us gone, and he'll know we went to Northkeep. Where else could we go?'

Rusgann frowned. "Twould be best if your brother put you aboard that fine big warship of his right away, and sent you to the High Sealord at Donorvale. Doesn't Lord Sernin have a passel of strong-minded wizards loyal to him? Would Ansel dare oppose all of them – and the Tarnian council of sealords as well?'

'I don't know.' Maudrayne was thoughtful. 'You're a wise woman, Rusgann. It's a plan worth considering. If I told Sernin the truth about Dyfrig . . .' And the greater truth about Conrig! 'I'll ask Liscanor to bid his windvoice bespeak Sernin at once.'

Maudrayne embraced the maid, then went to sit beside Dyfrig, trying to draw him close to her. He pushed her away. 'You shouldn't be doing that, my lady. I'm only a servant boy.'

Her face went white and she sprang to her feet. For the first time in months, she burst into tears.

Rusgann gathered her mistress into her arms and held her as she sobbed, and it was thus that Sealord Liscanor discovered them when he arrived a few minutes later.

She sipped from a cup of soothing bearberry tea and huddled near the peat fire Liscanor had kindled in the little south-tower sitting room, waiting for him to return with news of the windvoiced conference with Sernin Donorvale. Rain tapped on the small glazed window. The sky was almost black.

After a brief, emotional reunion with his long-lost sister in the Peace Room, Liscanor had summoned his wife, sworn her to secrecy, and entrusted Rusgann and Dyfrig to her care. Kind Lady Freda had tried to put Maudrayne to bed as well, but she refused to rest until she had conferred with her brother. The two of them slipped up a back stairway to the secluded little tower chamber where the sealord conducted his private business. There she told him what she wanted him to know. But over an hour had gone by since he left her alone, and she was becoming very worried. What could be taking so long?

When the door finally opened and she saw his face, she knew it was nothing good.

'Come, sit here and tell me.' She poured him a cup of tea from the steaming pot on the hob.

Liscanor Northkeep had the same bright auburn hair as his sister, but otherwise they were unalike. She was beautiful and regal in demeanor, even in her torn and dirtied peasant garb, while he had a body like a barrel, arms so heavily muscled that they hunched his shoulders, and a pitted, truffle-nosed face that was almost ogrish in its spectacular homeliness. Only his voice belied his unsightly appearance: it was deep, resonant, and cultured.

'Maudie, my dear, there's magical mischief brewing,' he said, shaking his head. 'My windvoice, Kalymor, told me he'd been forbidden by the High Shaman to bespeak any message of mine to anyone. I threatened him with a beating and then with banishment, but he wouldn't budge. He said Red Ansel would do worse to him if he disobeyed, and no other shaman in the demesne of Northkeep would transmit messages for me, either. They're to keep silence for a tennight!'

'I suppose it was to be expected,' Maudrayne said, resigned.

But Liscanor's sea-blue eyes glistened with triumph. 'There's more than one way to skin a hare, Sister! On the outskirts of town lives a renegade hedge-wizard called Blind Bozuk, who owes no allegiance to Anwyl and his high-flown kind. He sells love-philtres and fake talismans and other rubbish to gullible souls, but he's also a genuine wind adept.'

'I know of him. He supplied Lukort Waterfall with charms to counter the magical defenses of the sea-hag.'

'I rode out myself to this rogue's hovel and gave him ten

gold marks to bespeak a message to our Uncle Sernin. While
I stood there, Bozuk contacted his great and good friend
Yavenis, an outcast witch of Donorvale. She supposedly deliv-
ered my message to the High Sealord in person.'

'Supposedly,' Maude said. 'What was the message?'

'It was simple and discreet: "Come at once to Northkeep
in your fastest ship, with your most trusted men."'

'Ah. Very good.' She ventured a smile.

'We'll set sail ourselves at once in my frigate *Gayora*, and
rendezvous with Sernin on the high seas. Then you shall tell
your two great secrets to both of us.'

'I think I must tell them to you now.' She had made the
decision on the spur of the moment, prompted by a growing
certainty that Ansel was going to intervene somehow, and
she would never reach Donorvale. 'Someone must know, in
case something happens to me . . . and to my dear little son.'

'Son!' Liscanor exclaimed. 'Great God, are you saying –'

'The fairhaired lad Dyfrig is not the child of my servant.
He's mine – the first-born son of Conrig Wincantor and heir
to the Sovereignty according to ancient Cathran law.
Furthermore, this High King who has forced Tarn into
vassalage reigns under false pretences. He is a man having
arcane talent, ineligible to sit his throne.'

Liscanor stared at her in thunderstruck consternation,
deprived of speech.

'My servant Rusgann is a witness to Dyfrig's birth. She
and many others in Cala know I was a faithful wife who
never cohabited with any man save my husband. Dyfrig is
the very image of Conrig. The king's talent will be much
harder to prove, since it is extremely meager and imperceptible to the usual methods of detection. My own testimony
would not suffice, and the Conjure-Queen of Moss, who also
knows about it, may refuse to speak. But I suspect that Lord
Stergos, Conrig's Royal Alchymist and his brother, must know

the truth as well. He is a man of scrupulous honor, who would keep Conrig's secret only passively, by not volunteering the information. If he were put under solemn oath and questioned, he would not lie.'

The stalwart sealord's face was ashen and he was wringing his hands like a woebegone maiden. 'Oh, Maudie, this is awful news indeed! I hardly know what to say! I'm only a simple northcoast sea-dog and these are state secrets of the most devastating kind –'

'Guard them with your life, then. But never hesitate to reveal them to Uncle Sernin and the Company of Equals if I cannot.' She rose from her seat. 'Now we must leave Northkeep without delay. There's more than Ansel to be concerned about. That villain Lukort Waterfall was probably planning to sell me to Conrig Wincantor. Who can say whether he told the magicker Blind Bozuk about me when he purchased charms from him?'

Liscanor looked guilty and ashamed. 'God help us if I've placed you in danger, Sister. I never thought of such a thing when I went to the whoreson, thinking how clever I was. Forgive me!'

'Dear Liscanor, there's nothing to forgive.' She kissed his weather-roughened cheek. 'How long before we can sail?'

'Less than an hour. I've already given orders to prepare the ship. Her officers were all here at the feast, and her crew resides in town.'

'Then let's fetch my son and my servant, and get on board without further delay.'

It was after midnight when they left the castle and went on foot to the berth where the frigate was tied up. Seamen and housecarls in castle livery were still carrying chests and kegs of supplies aboard, and dozens of shadowy shapes were moving on the upper decks and in the rigging. Rain slanted sharply down, blown by a chill wind. It was very dark.

Liscanor went to confer with the officer who stood at the foot of the gangplank, then quickly returned. 'I'm told that the cabin being prepared for the three of you is not quite ready,' he said. 'I must go aboard *Gayora* and do a final tour of inspection. It's no place for you, with men rushing about on last-minute ship's business. Why not wait in that covered area, beside the large warehouse nigh to the curtainwall? It's dry there, and the torches give plenty of light. I'll send one of the ship's boys for you as soon as I can.'

He went off, cloak flapping like the wings of a very stout bat, and Maudrayne and Rusgann moved over the wet cobblestones into the sheltered place. The maidservant carried Dyfrig's well-wrapped body over her shoulder.

'He still sleeps?' Maudrayne asked, lifting her son's hood.

'Never woke, even when I dressed him in the new clothes Lady Freda gave us. He was too sleepy to eat much, and so was I. Can't say I'm happy to set out to sea again on such a raw night, but it's for the best.'

'I hope so . . . Solstice Day is over. Such a terrible, eventful day! And no sooner do we reach a place of safety, than we must leave it.' Her eyes roamed over the other vessels and small craft tied up at adjacent slips. 'Lukort Waterfall's boat *Scoter* is gone. My brother must have had it moved across the harbor basin to the fishermen's wharf to divert suspicion. Still, numbers of people must have seen us bring her in besides the dockboy Eselin. One of them might have talked about us to Blind Bozuk, even if Lukort didn't.'

'You've got no good reason to think Lukort told the magicker about us,' Rusgann said crossly. 'Stop worrying.'

'Perhaps the hedge-wizard wouldn't sell Lukort the special charms unless he told why he wanted them. Sneaking into the sea-hag's steading is hardly the usual thief's job-of-work! Information about me would bring a pretty sum from

Conrig's Tarnian spies. You could trust a person like Bozuk to know who they are.'

'We'll be away from here soon, my lady. Then Bozuk's tittle-tattle won't be worth two groats in a dungheap.'

The sound of clopping hooves echoed among the warehouses, almost drowned out by the increasing noise from the ship. 'Someone's coming,' Maudrayne said. 'There. A covered wagon drawn by two mules. Perhaps it's the last batch of supplies that my brother's been waiting for.'

They watched the wagon's approach without curiosity. Then a small figure came rushing down the ship's gangplank and trotted toward them across the wet pavement.

Rusgann heaved a sigh of satisfaction. 'About time! Here's the ship's boy.'

He was about twelve years old, clad in oilskins, and bowed smartly from the waist. 'My ladies! Sealord Liscanor bids you kindly come aboard, for we cast off immediately.'

The muleteer had drawn up a few ells away, and after setting the brake on his rig, climbed down and approached them with a casual wave of his hand. He wore a waterproof hooded longcoat slit up the back, and all that could be seen of his face was teeth gleaming in a wide grin.

'What do you want, my man?' Maudrayne asked irritably when he blocked their way to the ship. 'We have no time for you.'

'Maudie, Maudie. You have all the time in the world.'

She opened her mouth to scream for help, but no sound emerged. In fact, she was frozen to the spot in mid-gape, like some ridiculous statue. Rusgann and the ship's boy were similarly immobilized.

Red Ansel Piken lifted Dyfrig from Rusgann's unresisting arms, carried him to the covered wagon, and stowed him inside.

No, Maudrayne thought. No, no, no. Not after we have

come so far and endured so much!

The huge castle and the rainswept dock with its flaming torches seemed to fade to a foggy blur as tears of rage and helplessness filled her eyes. She strained to cry out as Ansel returned and led Rusgann away, docile as a sheep, and assisted her into the wagon. Maudrayne was powerless against the shaman's sorcery just as she'd always been. He'd do whatever he wanted with them. Use her and poor little Dyfrig any way he chose.

He came to her and took her arm, and she was able to walk but could not speak. Across the gleaming stones, up a short ladder, and into the back of the wagon she went. It was filled with straw and numbers of bundles. Rusgann and Dyfrig lay covered with blankets, apparently asleep. Ansel soon had her bedded down as well, then closed the tailgate, put the ladder inside, and laced shut the canvas cover.

He returned to the paralyzed ship's boy, who was still poised in an attitude of confusion. At Ansel's touch, the lad looked about wildly. Only gibberish came from his mouth.

'Your power of speech will return once you're back on the ship,' the shaman said. 'You're to tell Lord Liscanor that the two women and the child are safe aboard in their cabin. You'll remember nothing at all of me or what happened here. Now go.'

Ansel went back to the wagon and climbed into the driver's seat. After arranging his coat to keep the worst of the rain off, he released the brake, cracked the whip over the mules, and set off for the road that led east, away from the sea and into the Stormland wilderness of Tarn.

SEVEN

'Arise, Kilian Blackhorse. Arise and don your robes. By order of Abbas Noachil, you must leave this chamber and accompany us to a more secure accommodation.'

His second dream of Beynor had hardly faded, and he woke with difficulty. Someone was shaking his arm. He opened his eyes and saw the forbidding face of Vra-Ligorn, the Hebdomader or superintendent of discipline at Zeth Abbey. He was at first unable to stir, as sometimes happens when one is roused from deep sleep. Then the blankets were stripped away and he was hoisted to his feet. Two husky Brother Caretakers manhandled him into his clothes. Two more held heavy staves and lighted lanterns, even though they had opened the opaque drapes to allow the early morning twilight of Solstice Day to enter his bedroom. The caretakers of the Order of Zeth wore brown robes. Although they possessed talent, it was too weak to generate important magic, so they devoted themselves to serving the ordained Brethren through manual labor or domestic duties.

Kilian found his voice at last. 'Vra-Ligorn, where are you taking me?'

'To a cell on the sump-pit level, my lord. And you must submit to being chained while we convey you there.'

The last remnants of sleep evaporated in a burst of dismay as Kilian finally realized what was happening to him. The comfortable little apartment where he had lived for four years under open detention was to be exchanged for a window-less dungeon.

'Does Prior Waringlow know of this – this highly eccen-tric order?' he protested. 'You know how ill Father Abbas has been. At times he even shows symptoms of dementia. I can't believe he was in his right mind when he issued this order. I've done nothing to provoke such punishment –'

'Abbas Noachil is as rational as you or I,' the Hebdomader said without emotion. 'The command for your close confine-ment came directly from High King Conrig, via the Royal Alchymist, Lord Stergos. There's no mistake.'

'I see.' He extended his wrists for the fetters, and said not another word as they conveyed him into the bowels of the abbey, down to the third basement, where the drains from the upper floors debouched into an evil-smelling under-ground watercourse. There were only a handful of dismal cells down there, reserved for the most heinous sinners. Usually, no prisoner remained there long before being handed over to the secular authorities for execution.

Is this to be my fate, he wondered, only hours from the coup that was to have liberated Darasilo's Trove, set me free, and restored my lost powers? What could have happened to make Conrig do such a thing? Had Vitubio, Felmar, and Scarth revealed their intentions through some blunder? Has my nephew Feribor implicated me in his political intrigues? Or – worst thought! – is Beynor responsible for this, playing some treacherous double game in hopes of eliminating me before I can take possession of the trove?

'In here, if you please, my lord.'

They had reached the dungeon. Vra-Ligorn unlocked a cubicle carved from solid rock that was hardly two ells wide and three ells long, and motioned for him to enter. As a wearer of the iron gammadion of shame, stripped of every talent and privilege of the Mystical Order, Kilian was no longer honored with the title of Brother or Vra. But no one could deny his noble Blackhorse blood, and so his gaolers had called him 'my lord' during his period of detention – albeit with an ironic inflection.

The cell door clanged shut behind him. It was iron, with a rotary hopper through which food and other items might be passed and an observation slot covered with metal mesh. Dim light from the corridor illuminated a narrow cot and a heap of blankets, a large covered water-jar, and a tiny table that held a pottery basin with a block of soap and two rough towels. A wooden stool stood beside the table.

'Father Abbas has graciously consented to leave a lighted lantern outside your cell,' Ligorn said, 'so you and your fellow-inmates need not suffer the added privation of utter darkness. Your meals will also be as usual – not bread and water – and you have warm bedding.'

Fellow inmates?

'How long must I remain here?' Kilian asked.

'Until it pleases Father Abbas to release you. If you are well-behaved, you will be given books to read and candles later. There is a latrine beneath the stone lid in the cell's far corner, and a box of green leaves for your comfort. If you urgently require anything else, inform the Brothers who will bring your breakfast.'

The Hebdomader and the others went away then, and Kilian called out softly through the door-slot, 'Who else is here?'

'Niavar.'

'Raldo.'

'Cleaton.'

So the three close associates who had been convicted of treason along with him were also imprisoned. But clever young Vra-Garon Curtling, who had joined Kilian's cause hoping to escape his vow of celibacy, was evidently still free. More importantly, so was Prior Waringlow . . .

'My poor comrades,' he said. 'I fear that King Conrig has roused Father Abbas's suspicions of us. Our mutual friend may find it more difficult to aid our escape, but I'm confident that he'll still find a way to carry out the plan.'

'Master, something must have gone seriously awry down in Cala,' said Niavar. He had been Kilian's principal deputy and Keeper of Arcana. Diminutive stature and an eyeball that wandered grotesquely around in its socket had made him an object of ridicule when they were both novices; but the handsome, imposing Kilian had unaccountably befriended clever little Niavar and thus earned his undying loyalty. 'I warned you not to trust Vra-Vitubio. The man was eager, but too slow-thinking to be reliable. It's possible that his clumsiness has undone us all.'

'We're finished!' Raldo's voice was shrill with terror. He had been the Palace Novicemaster, a stout, deceptively jolly-faced man notorious for savagely punishing the slightest infraction of the Rule. 'Conrig has discovered everything and we're dead men!'

'Nonsense,' said Kilian.

But Raldo persisted. 'Master, you'll only have your head chopped off because you're noble. But we commoners will be hanged, cut down alive, drawn, and quartered. Oh, I can't bear the thought of it. My poor entrails hacked out and held up dripping before my eyes . . . my limbs severed while I'm still conscious!'

'Be silent, you silly bag of guts,' growled Cleaton. He was a burly man with a swarthy, pinched countenance who didn't suffer fools gladly, the former Hebdomader of the Palace

Brethren. 'You only make things worse with your futile imag-
inings. We can't be sure that we've been condemned. Vra-
Ligorn didn't say so. In fact, he sounded almost apologetic
when he locked us up. Why would he be so solicitous of our
comfort if we're going to die? He's hardly known as a font
of kindliness. No – mark my words, there's something odd
going on. Ligorn's caught in the middle, and he wants to
save his arse by obeying old Noachil at the same time that
he preserves Lord Kilian and us from the worst hardships of
this putrid hell-hole.'

Until the downfall of their master, the trio had enjoyed high
positions at Cala Palace, where courtiers, servants, and the
younger Brothers forced to endure their petty tyranny had
dubbed them Squinty, Butterball, and Vinegar-Face. They had
not endured their captivity well. Being stripped of magical
power and authority had turned Niavar sullen and Cleaton
quarrelsome, while Raldo had grown morose and added
another eight stone to his already considerable weight. There
were times when Kilian regretted having included the three of
them in his escape plans. But they were his oldest friends in
the Order, who had served him faithfully for nearly thirty years.

And two of them, at least, might still play useful roles in
the adventure to come.

'I urge you not to lose heart, Raldo,' he said. 'Cleaton is
quite right. We have no solid reason to believe that we're
compromised. If the king had certain knowledge of our
conspiracy, he would have taken much more drastic action
against us.'

'But why else would he suddenly command that we be
shut up in a dungeon?' the fat man asked querulously. 'The
smell of this awful place! I nearly swooned away when we
first arrived.'

Someone gave a snort of derision.

Kilian responded with patience. 'Whatever King Conrig's

reason, it likely has nothing at all to do with our plan of escape. Now listen to me, comrades: at this very moment, our friend Vra-Garon is on his way back to the abbey from Elkhaven, on the great lake. While there on an errand for the abbas, he collected horses and lay clothing for us at Ironside Manor, the home of Lady Sovanna, who is a close friend to my sister, the Queen Mother. What Garon doesn't know is that the lady also holds in safekeeping for me a large sum of money, which will finance our flight to Didion.'

'You told us that Queen Cataldis had balked at sending the gold,' Niavar said. 'What made her change her mind?'

'I sent a secret letter to Duke Feribor, my nephew, who foolishly expects me to help him become High King. He has his own special methods of persuasion.'

'I hear he used them to excess on his late wife,' Cleaton said with heavy sarcasm.

Kilian said, 'The money will be sufficient to pay for everything we need on our journey, with plenty left over to bribe Somarus of Didion, who has agreed to put us under his protection.'

'The rebel prince?' Niavar was hesitant. 'Master, he and his followers are little more than a ragtag gang of brigands!'

'So Conrig and Honigalus would have everyone believe. But things are not always what they seem. Somarus has a wide base of support among the barons of that kingdom's remote hinterlands, who give only lip-service to the Sovereignty and consider King Honigalus a craven traitor for having submitted to vassalage. If Honigalus and his heirs were eliminated, Somarus would inherit Didion's throne. And a person who was in a position to . . . assist the new king in a significant manner would share his power.'

'Do you speak of yourself, Lord Kilian?' Cleaton asked. 'And is the elimination of Didion's royal family mere wishful thinking, or something more?'

Kilian did not reply to the questions. 'After we escape from the abbey, we'll ride directly to Elkhaven. It will be arranged so that no one notices that we're missing for many hours. Vra-Garon has hired a cattle-transport boat and crew to carry us and our horses north to Roaring Gorge, at the head of the great lake. About thirteen leagues up the gorge is a cave that almost no one knows about. There we'll take shelter, and wait for certain companions who'll travel with us over the Sinistral Range. We will follow tracks known only to shepherds – and to Vra-Garon, who spent his boyhood in the border highlands. Eventually we'll come to the Lady Lakes region of the Elderwold, where we'll join Prince Somarus and his men.'

Raldo said, 'Master, I always presumed that Great Pass was the only safe way to cross the Sinistrals.'

'It's the first place Conrig's troops would look for us.'

'Riding through high mountains on backcountry tracks sounds very difficult and dangerous,' Raldo protested. His high-pitched voice trembled with anxiety. 'And the Elderwold is said to be full of fierce creatures and Green Men! Who will cook our food and care for the horses? Where are we to spend the nights? I don't think I could bear sleeping on the ground.'

'Bazekoy's Burning Brisket!' growled Niavar. 'Stay here in the dungeon, then, Butterball, and enjoy the food and warm bed. After a few weeks, you won't even notice the stench.'

'Master, it won't just be soldiers hunting us.' Dour Cleaton was deadly serious. 'You said we'd have magic to shield us from windsearchers. But how –'

'And so we will. The person who will release us from this prison has promised to unlock our iron gammadions as well.'

Niavar and Cleaton uttered oaths. Raldo quavered, 'My talents? I'll have my talents back?'

'Only those we were born with,' Kilian said, 'not the additional powers we gained when we were ordained. The combined magic of the four of us should be sufficient to defend us from ordinary pursuers and all but the most powerful wind adepts. And I have conceived a new cover-spell of peculiar efficacy, which I shall erect over us as soon as my talent recovers from the years of disuse.'

'Who in God's name is this collaborator within the abbey?' Niavar asked. 'And why is he willing to break his vows to Saint Zeth and commit treason against the Sovereignty in order to help us?'

'He helps *me*,' Kilian said, 'because he expects a reward. That's all you need to know.'

'Part of the Cala treasure?' Raldo suggested archly. None of them knew the nature of the Trove of Darasilo, but they all were aware that Kilian had sent agents to the capital months earlier to steal something of consummate value.

'Be silent, fool!' Niavar said. 'Have you forgotten that the master ordered us never to speak of that?'

Ignoring Raldo's mumbled apology, Kilian continued. 'I must try to sleep now, in case there is another dream-message from Beynor of Moss. If you find yourselves unable to close your eyes, I suggest that you spend the time praying for bad weather. While clear skies persist, we cannot escape. We need clouds and rain to conceal our getaway from ordinary human eyesight, since we have no true darkness at this time of year.'

'It's Blossom Moon,' Cleaton pointed out. 'The weather may remain clement for weeks.'

'I think not,' Kilian said. 'I was allowed to work in the herb garden yesterday, and I noted a ring around the sun. This often presages a change. There could be a storm on the way.' He paused, then added softly, 'A very great storm indeed.'

He went to the cot, arranged the ample bedding, and lay atop it fully clothed. But his brain was a beehive of swirling thoughts that he could not repress, no matter how hard he tried, and he remained wakeful until the tolling of a far distant bell marked the hour of rising in the abbey above.

To his surprise, Beynor knew about the attack on Cala Palace as soon as it happened.

Kilian had told him that the assault and theft were scheduled for the quiet hours around seven or eight in the morning on Solstice Day, but he never anticipated any personal perception of the event. Cocooned in a sleeping-sack, he lay in apathetic misery beneath the small boat's canvas dodger, a kind of half-awning which only gave scant protection from the flying spray, enduring the slam-bang progress of the craft over the rough Boreal Sea. The team of monsters towing him insisted on swimming at top speed, and he would have been flung overboard by the constant severe jouncing if he hadn't taken special care to wedge himself between a padded thwart and the oilskin supply bags crammed in the bow.

Beynor was ordinarily an intrepid sailor; but on this appalling voyage, withdrawing into the windworld was the only way he'd been able to avoid mortal seasickness. It was quiet and tranquil on the black bosom of the wind, except for the inconsequential mental yammering of the Salka, which was easy enough to ignore if he didn't try to translate it. He'd almost managed to drift into uneasy slumber when a mental shriek pierced his cranium like a red-hot needle.

He gasped, sat up, and made a muzzy attempt to track the chaotic tangle of voice-threads. It emanated out of the south. He knew after a few minutes what it must signify.

The silent clamor was perceptible to him, but evidently not to the dull-witted Salka, who swam on unconcerned. Wild with curiosity, Beynor tried to scry Cala Palace. But the distance was too extreme, nor was he able to make any sense of the wind-shout itself. Nevertheless, he had no doubt that it was a reaction to the attack by Kilian's agents.

Had they successfully made off with Darasilo's Trove? There was no way for him to find out without bespeaking them, and no way to do that without knowing their individual signatures and the password that Kilian had refused to entrust to him.

Curse the bloody secretive alchymist! Beynor decided to re-invade his dreams and demand the information yet again. Both of them needed to know what was happening.

He concentrated in the usual way, calling Kilian's name over and over, but there was no answer. The bastard was probably awake.

Beynor attempted to envision Zeth Abbey with his windsight and was rewarded with a ghostly mental picture of the fortresslike structure. Built of pure white limestone, it was perched high among the crags of the southern Sinistral Mountains. There were certainly loud strands of windspeech being exchanged between its inhabitants and persons in Cala Palace. Beynor could not understand the messages, but it seemed likely that the Brothers in Cala were bespeaking tidings of the disaster to their fellows at the abbey.

Someone was bound to tell Kilian what had happened. But he, Beynor, would be kept in suspense for hours, until the next time the alchymist went to sleep! He ground his teeth in frustration.

Just then, a disquieting thought sprang into his mind, and with great care he sent another probe winging in a new direction, towards the kingdom of Moss, Fenguard Castle, and the chambers of his sister Ullanoth. Was it possible that she'd also perceived the wind-scream from Cala? Might she be observing the scene with her Subtle Loophole?

The refurbished old stronghold was much closer than Zeth Abbey and clearly visible to his scrying, but Ulla's private rooms were not. Even though she no longer owned a Fortress sigil, a heavy spell of couverture shielded her quarters from his mind's eye. The good news was that no betraying trace of the Great Stone's sorcery shone out through the concealing opacity. Ulla was not using Loophole to oversee Cala Palace or anything else. It was quite likely that she had failed to hear the outcry.

He maintained his watch on Fenguard for another hour or so without detecting any unusual arcane activity. The wind-senses of the Glaumerie Guild members were not as keen as his own, and they remained oblivious. None of them seemed interested in observing Cala, and none of Conrig's windvoices attempted to communicate with the Conjure-Queen. Thus far, the thieves fleeing with the trove would seem to be safe from Loophole's invincible oversight. And if Kilian was right about Conrig's distrust of Ulla, they'd stay that way.

At this minute, the precious books and the sigils were probably being spirited out of the ruins of the palace's cloister wing by the agents. Before long, the trove would be on its way north. By day's end, the well-disguised thieves might be almost halfway to the designated rendezvous in the north country, taking advantage of the initial confusion as Kilian had planned. Beynor himself would be within easy wind-searching range of the fleeing agents before another day went by – not that such a search was practical. Without knowledge of their signatures, or at least their names and physical appearance, he had little chance of scrying them out.

Names and physical appearance . . .

A half-formed idea crept into his mind, and he drew in his breath sharply, hardly able to acknowledge that such a thing might be possible. It seemed almost too fortuitous, too perfect.

If Conrig's officials were efficient in organizing pursuit of the agents, they might unwittingly give Beynor his chance to secure the trove for himself before the thieves could hand it over to Kilian. The alchymist had rightly feared that Beynor might try to waylay his men and seize the sigils and books; but the revised plan that now suggested itself to the deposed young king was far more ingenious than a simple ambush.

All I need do, Beynor thought, is find them with my mind's eye. There was no need to confront the men physically or even have a wind-conversation with them. If they simply listened to a certain irresistible temptation insinuated anonymously into their dreams, and succumbed to it, the trove would be his!

And the temptation *would* be irresistible.

The site of the allurement would have to be chosen with care. It must be a lonely spot, where no one was likely to stumble upon the abandoned books and sigils before he retrieved them.

Kilian was no problem. Even if his windpowers were somehow restored, he'd be unable to scry out the unscriable. No adept could oversee magical moonstones. They were secure from the windsight of every sorcerer save Ullanoth and her Subtle Loophole, and she had no reason to go looking for them because she didn't know they existed.

Such a simple plan . . . He wondered why it hadn't occurred to him before. He'd wait a few hours, until Conrig's officials recovered from the initial shock of the conflagration and organized the pursuit of the fire-raisers. Images of the suspects with their names would surely be transmitted by palace alchymists to every reliable wind adept and wizard in the southern part of the Sovereignty. The magickers would be commanded to draw up reward notices carrying the pictures and post them in all the principal towns of Cathra and Didion.

What Beynor had to do was scry one of those notices – trickier than it might seem – or find some person willing to do the job for him. Unfortunately, he had few loyal friends left, and most of them lived in Moss, too far away to be of use.

It came to him.

There *was* someone he could bespeak, someone who would – by the end of the day, if not before – have obtained a full description of the awful events that had taken place down in Cala. One who would probably also know whether those responsible for the conflagration had been identified, and how the hunt for them was progressing. The man he was minded to bespeak was by no means completely trustworthy, but neither was he a friend to the Sovereign of Blenholme. He'd probably tell the truth, as he knew it, especially if Beynor passed on useful information of his own in exchange.

All I need do is wait, he thought, until matters in the south have stabilized a bit, and Queen Risalla's wizards have transmitted details of the disaster to their colleagues in Holt Mallburn.

The choppy waves had subsided a little, and Beynor finally dozed off in spite of himself. His dream was a familiar one – frightening to begin with, as the small boy found himself trapped on the broad flats of the Darkling River with the oncoming tide racing toward him. The dream turned even more terrifying when the red-eyed monsters appeared, surging up out of a deep-water channel to seize him while he screamed.

Then the dream became amazing and joyous as he realized that the fearsome creatures were *rescuing* him! The reclusive Salka of the Little Fen had for some reason taken pity on the doomed small human. In time they would befriend him, teach him their language, and open his mind to the world of the wind and the potential of the magical moonstones –

Beynor woke with a cry of pain. The speeding boat crashed and smacked over the waves with stunning violence, hurling

him against the gunwale and dousing him with icy sea water.
The pleasant dream was extinguished, leaving reality.

He began screaming furious curses at the amphibious brutes
in the tow-harnesses, not stopping until Ugusawnn, the
Supreme Warrior, compelled his companions to slow down.

The two brown-robed Brother Caretakers who brought
breakfast to the prisoners could hardly stop talking about the
disaster, even though they seemed to know few details aside
from the obvious: the entire cloister wing of Cala Palace was
burning fiercely, and the Royal Alchymist, Lord Stergos, had
been so badly hurt that physicians feared for his life.

'But how could a fire take hold and spread in a place housing
so many wind adepts?' Kilian asked. 'Surely their combined
powers would have stopped the flames in their tracks.'

'It's said the incendiary agent was tarnblaze.' The older of
the caretakers spoke in a tone freighted with dread. 'That
stuff can't be quenched by talent, and it gives off great heat.
I didn't talk to anyone at the palace myself, of course. My
powers are too puny. But the Brother Cellarer was in the
kitchen when we fetched your food, and he had windspeech
with his opposite number down there, who said there were
two great explosions inside the Alchymical Library. It had to
be tarnblaze. And not simple firepots, either: steel bombshells!'

'How dreadful,' Kilian said. 'I shall pray for Lord Stergos,
of course, but the loss of all those precious books is also
devastating.'

'Books!' the second caretaker piped up. 'Nearly forgot,
what with all the excitement.' He opened a lidded basket
smaller than the ones that had held the food, took out several
volumes and some candles, and began passing them through
the door-hoppers to the prisoners. Whcn he came to Kilian's
cell he said, 'Prior Waringlow selected this book for you
special, my lord. He hopes it'll help you pass the time. Just

poke the candlewick through the wire mesh on this peep-slot and I'll get it burning for you.' Using a bit of straw, he transferred flame from the wall-lantern to Kilian's candle.

'Please tell Father Prior that I'm grateful for his kindness,' Kilian said. His cronies also murmured thanks as the other caretaker lit their candles.

'Is there aught else you need, my lord?' The older Brother added sheepishly, 'Save liberty, o'course.'

'We have no view of the outer world.' Kilian gave a sad sigh. 'Tell me – is this Solstice Day sunny and bright?'

'A bit overcast. What we countryfolk call buttermilk sky. There might be rain before the midnight chime.'

'Ah. Thank you, Brother.'

'We'll see you again at suppertime. Should be a fine meal. We're roasting six pigs and four fatted calves in honor of the holiday.' He and his companion gathered up the empty baskets and left the dungeon.

'Rain!' Cleaton exclaimed. 'Our prayers are answered.'

'So it would seem,' said Kilian. 'But no more talk. Let's eat our food before it gets any colder.'

The meal was an excellent one – breadrolls with a crock of honey-butter, boiled eggs, a cheese ramekin, and a squat jug of brown ale. But instead of following his own order, Kilian opened the book he had received and leafed through the pages. Almost immediately he found just what he expected.

Drawing the candle closer, he began to read the note from Prior Waringlow. When he finished he burned the bit of parchment, then ate with a hearty appetite.

The next time Beynor woke the sky was grey and the sea undulated with great slow rollers. He crawled out from under the dodger and saw the dark hunched forms of the Salka surging through the water. Eight of them were linked to his boat and ten more functioned as outriders, leading the way toward a distant black peninsula with a tip like a gnarled finger pointing south. Beynor recognized the distinctive silhouette of Gribble Head. Beyond it was the entrance to Didion Bay, and at the bay's end was the mouth of the River Malle, and King Honigalus's capital city of Holt Mallburn.

His animal-skin garments were sodden and slimy, so he took time to shed them and don dry things from one of the sacks. Then he took the makings of a meal from another. Just as he'd been forced to improvise clothing during his stay with the monsters, he had also developed his own food supply. The Salka had plenty of seafood, but they invariably ate it raw. By trial and error, Beynor learned to cook and smoke fish and other marine edibles. He eked out his diet with the starchy tubers of the reedmace, boiled or baked, and small quantities of berries he could glean from the tundra surrounding the citadel. For seasoning he had sea-salt and an onionlike arctic plant with red flowers that the Salka called *cheev*. His only beverages were water and various herbal teas. Beynor's talent now heated up a flask of willow-wintergreen tisane, which not only alleviated his chill but also took away the worst of his aches and pains. He ate a slab of smoked salmon and some of the bland roots. Then he settled himself comfortably and prepared to bespeak Fring Bulegosset, the Archwizard of Didion.

First Beynor scried him – a hunched, fleshy man with pallid features, whose dark-lashed blue eyes had a frankly sensuous gleam. He wore an elegant robe of black brocade and a matching skullcap. As Beynor watched he moved about a small alchymical laboratory gathering stoppered phials and small boxes, which he then packed carefully into a compartmented leather traveling bag. No doubt he was getting ready to accompany the royal family on its progress upriver tomorrow.

Fring was Didion's most powerful wind-talent – which wasn't saying much. That barbarian nation's finest adepts were half-baked dabblers compared to the top conjurers of Moss or Tarn. Even Cathra's Brothers of Zeth possessed more innate magical talent. But Fring was reasonably competent, and if rumors from Beynor's confidants in Moss could be believed, the Archwizard was also a political malcontent who secretly favored Somarus, the rebel brother of the Didionite king.

It was high time Beynor and Fring became reacquainted.

'Archwizard! Respond to one who knew you some years ago, and now wishes to share certain valuable information.'

Who's that? Good God – it's the failed boy-king, Beynor of Moss!

'To be sure – but now I'm a man of one-and-twenty, and preparing to mend my somewhat battered fortunes. Do you recall the last time we were in contact? You and Honigalus were aboard the flagship of Didion's warfleet, sailing south to attack Cathra while Conrig crept in through your back door and sacked Holt Mallburn.'

Of course I remember. You were Didion's staunch ally then. Honigalus bade you use your Weathermaker sigil to speed our vessels along to Cala Bay, while delaying the Tarnian mercenaries who were coming to the aid of Cathra. As I recall, you did a fine job of it. So fine that the huge storm you created sank the navies of Cathra and Didion without discrimination – to say nothing of the luckless Tarnians and a flock of Continental corsairs.

'It was my sister Ullanoth who unwittingly caused the storm, not I! And by good fortune, you survived. Less happily, so did Conrig . . . and Honigalus. If either man had perished, both our nations would have been spared vassalage.'

I am the loyal servant of the King of Didion. And of his liege lord, Conrig Wincantor

'Of course you are. But how much happier we both would be if a stouter-hearted monarch ruled in Holt Mallburn. One who would never have signed the damned Edict of Sovereignty. You know who I mean! The information I wish to share with you concerns him. But if you aren't interested –'

I'm very interested in anything that might pertain to a certain brave prince, who is always in my prayers.

'I thought as much. I've learned something that may redound greatly to his advantage. And that of his good friends! But before I speak of it –

You want something in return.

'A mere trifle. As it happens, I'm curious about the conflagration that took place earlier today at Cala Palace. My windsight is insufficiently powerful to oversee it directly, just as your own is, but I hoped that wizards in Queen Risalla's entourage would have bespoken you concerning what happened. Were many people killed or injured?'

Why do you wish to know?

'I'll be frank with you, Fring. I hate Conrig Wincantor with every fiber of my being. He conspired with my sister to rob me of my throne. If he's suffered a great setback as a result of this disaster, I'll rejoice. What damage was done? Is it known who was responsible?'

Rejoice then. My sister's boy, who is an adept in service to Queen Risalla, told me that the library and the entire cloister wing of the palace were destroyed. The king's brother Stergos and some two dozen Zeth Brethren were injured. Six people were killed – including one man who may have helped start the fire.

'Who was he? Did he act alone?'

He was a Brother of Zeth, one Vitubio Bentland. It seems he and two other alchymical scholars came to the palace together, from Zeth Abbey, some months earlier. No one seems to know much about them yet. The two survivors have disappeared. There's a royal warrant for their arrest and a great hue and cry throughout Cathra and Didion, with a sizable reward for their capture. And here's a fascinating detail: the three used tarnblaze to blast open a secret crypt in the Royal Alchymist's bedroom. By now, half the palace has seen the hole with their own eyes. It's said that some treasure was stolen from there. No one in authority will admit that, but it would explain why the attack occurred in the first place. If someone merely wanted to kill Stergos, they could have found an easier way.

'And no one knows which way the surviving thieves went?'

If they were wise, they hopped on a fast boat and sailed away. Pictures of the pair are being circulated in all parts of Cathra. The roads leading from the capital are blocked, and every traveler is being questioned.

'I don't suppose your informant transmitted images of the fugitives?'

Hah! Now we come to it. He did indeed, and I etched them on vellum with my talent . . . for reasons of my own. If you wish to oversee the portraits, produce the valuable information you said you would share with me.

'Very well: under no circumstances should you accompany Honigalus and his family on the royal barge upriver. Become diplomatically ill. Say you will travel overland to catch them up when you feel better. See that you *don't* feel better until they approach Boarsden Castle, in six days.'

. . . What's going to happen?

'Nothing you would enjoy participating in.'

But – but I should give warning! The royal children –

'The one you should alert is Prince Somarus. Roust him out of his lair in the Elderwold wilderness. Tell him to trim his beard, pare his fingernails, and clean up himself and his drabble-tailed band of followers, so he appears approximately regal when he's unexpectly summoned by Duke Boarsden and the other high lords of Didion to take up the crown.'

Almighty God! How can you know –

'I do know. Now show me the picture of the two thieves, and give me their names.'

Kilian heard the approaching footsteps long after the midnight bell. His three companions had long since surrendered to exhaustion and filled the dungeon with their snores, but he lay sleepless, turning over details of the plan endlessly in his mind, trying to anticipate potential obstacles and working out methods to overcome them.

The dim lantern-shine in the corridor outside his cell brightened. Rising, he waited at the iron door of his cell until a key grated in the lock and it swung wide open. Standing there was the tall figure of Vra-Waringlow, wearing the usual red robes of the Order. But the gammadion pendant hanging at his neck was not gold inlaid with onyx, as befitted the abbey's second-ranking official. It was finely wrought platinum.

'So all went as we hoped!' Kilian said by way of greeting.

Waringlow's impassive face showed the barest flicker of a smile. 'Noachil was a tenacious old man, in spite of his many painful ailments. He entered into eternal peace shortly after a noon collation of shirred eggs with anchovies, one of his favorite dishes. It was an easy death. God grant such to all afflicted souls.'

Kilian nodded piously. 'May I offer my felicitations upon your elevation, Father Abbas?'

'Thank you, my son. And I, in turn, must express my profound gratitude for your having taught me the subtle coercive spell that swayed the vote of the governing council in my favor. I thought it best to use the magic before your departure – not that I doubted the spell's efficacy for a moment.'

'Vra-Garon has returned with the horses?'

'He awaits you in the ravine just outside the postern gate.' The new leader of the Mystic Order of Zeth lifted a tiny key. 'Please turn around.'

Hands manipulated the lowered hood of Kilian's robe. He heard a sharp click and his onerous neck-chain, together with the iron gammadion it held, fell to the floor. He felt his heart leap with a sudden influx of arcane power. Now he was no longer dependent upon the chancy goodwill of

Beynor, who had claimed – perhaps falsely – to know a spell that would free him of the talent-quenching iron.

'It may take a few days for you to regain the fullness of your natural abilities,' the abbas said, 'especially the ability to windspeak and scry over distance. I'll do my utmost to confuse any pursuers until you are once again able to weave a spell of couverture.'

'You've been a staunch and loyal friend, Waringlow. In time, when the tyrant Conrig is overthrown and my own power is consolidated, be assured that I'll reward you further.'

'No further recompense is necessary. Thanks to you, I have what I've always wanted.' He picked up the iron gammadion and handed it to Kilian. 'You'd better dispose of this. It's a pity that the totality of your magical endowment as an ordained Brother of Zeth cannot be restored to you. But as you know, new golden gammadions for you and your companions would render you perceptible to ordained wind-searchers. Still, I have no doubt that you'll find other ways to augment your sorcery.'

If you only knew! Kilian thought. But he simply inclined his head.

Waringlow continued. 'You should know that our Brother, Vitubio Bentland, perished in the Cala disaster. Felmar and Scarth are suspected of starting the fire. Interestingly enough, they are reported to have stolen certain items belonging to the Royal Alchymist, but no description of the things has been circulated. As yet, the authorities seem to have no notion as to the whereabouts of the fugitives. They are presumed to have discarded their own golden gammadions early on.'

After Waringlow opened the other three cells. Kilian roused his associates with sharp commands, then stood by while their iron pendants were also removed. He ordered them to sink the things in the deepest part of Elk Lake when they embarked the next day.

'Vra-Garon will be blamed for engineering your escape,' Waringlow observed. 'If I were you, I wouldn't trust that young fellow overmuch in a tight situation. Loyalty is hardly his strongest virtue.'

Kilian nodded. 'I know the strengths and weaknesses of all my men well enough.'

'It's time to go. Link arms and come up behind me very closely, two by two.'

They did as he bade them. The abbas lifted his hand and pronounced an incantation, and the former prisoners vanished from sight.

'Now follow me as silently as you can, and you'll soon be free. The night's a rather nasty one, I fear, with both wind and heavy rain.'

'Good,' said one of the invisible men.

The new Father Abbas lifted his lantern and headed for the flight of stairs, chuckling.

EIGHT

Ullanoth, Conjure-Queen of Moss, slept for nearly thirty-six hours, paying her enormous pain-debt during slumber, as it had to be paid. When she could endure it no more she broke away and awoke on the morning of the day after Solstice. It was only with difficulty that she forced herself to leave her bed. The latest act of Sending had left her with almost no physical energy.

I should have told Conrig to wait, she thought. There was no good reason why he needed to know the truth about Queen Risalla's unborn babe immediately. He was driven only by impatience and his desire to remain in control of every situation that concerned his Sovereignty.

But he had begged so urgently for her help . . .

She summoned servants to help her dress. An attendant held a mirror up after her pale hair had been combed, and she sighed as she saw her face. She was only twenty-three years of age, but the reflection now seemed to be that of a woman almost ten years older, gaunt and ravaged, with circles like bruises about her abnormally sunken eyes and deep lines furrowing her brow.

She had still been beautiful when she last Sent herself to Conrig; she was beautiful no longer.

The Lights had not done this to her. She had done it to herself, freely, in exchange for the sorcery of her Great Stones – Sender and Weathermaker, and above all Subtle Loophole. A lesser proportion of her debt had accumulated through helping her own people: she had used Weathermaker to generate storms to beat back the clumsy incursions of the Salka, and studied her evil younger brother through Loophole to make certain that Beynor remained securely exiled during the uneasy first years of her reign. But by far the greater component of her devastation was due to her inability to deny Conrig Wincantor when he sought her assistance.

I'm a fool, she told herself, gesturing for the mirror to be taken away. How often has he given himself to me or my Sending since assuming his throne? Less than two dozen times in four years! And each time we bedded, my desire for him strengthened, while he remained the same – professing love, taking me with a fierce passion, yet never opening his soul to warmth, never cherishing my self but only the hurtful magical power that comes through me.

And my people: do *they* love me? Moon Mother have mercy, but I think not . . .

Servants had been bustling about the royal apartment while she was being dressed, but when she dismissed the tirewomen and forced herself to leave her bedchamber she found no food set out for her in the adjacent sitting room, as was usual.

A little old man wearing a green satin tabard emblazoned with the golden swan of the royal arms bowed and smiled.

'Majesty, your breakfast table is laid on the balcony, since the rain has gone away and the day is gloriously clear and mild. But if this is not to your pleasure –'

His name was Wix, and he had been her personal slave

from the time of her girlhood. When she became queen she freed him and created him her Lord of Chamber. He was elderly but strong of body, and he had dedicated his life to her service. No woman had ever been Ullanoth's confidante, but she trusted Wix without reservation, and on occasion shared with him her innermost thoughts.

'I'd enjoy eating outdoors,' she said, returning his smile. 'Thank you for thinking of it. And please have a second chair brought to the table, for I wish to speak with you.'

The other servitors saw them seated, and poured mead before withdrawing and closing the balcony doors.

Ullanoth was silent for some time, sipping her drink, gazing over the broad estuary of the Darkling River, and thinking on the notable achievements of her reign. Wix sat comfortably and nibbled on a bread roll. Across the river, the expansive flats of the Little Fen were brilliantly green with summer growth, their ponds sparkling like mirrors amidst silvery skeins of the narrow waterways. The peat-brown Darkling itself was alive with boats heading to and from the settlements surrounding Moss Lake, west of Fenguard. The docks below the castle bristled with the masts of merchant ships and fishing vessels.

No longer was Moss the poorest nation of High Blenholme, as it had been in her father's day and during the abortive reign of Beynor the Patricide, as she had officially styled her deposed brother. She had made her country prosperous, using Conrig's generous annual guerdon to finance the revival of the amber mines and the seal-fur industry, rebuild neglected by-roads, and promote commerce on the great river and along the seacoast. Through cajolery and magical coercion, she had compelled Moss's self-centered conjure-lords to stop squandering lives and treasure on ancient feuds and let their peasantry live in peace, growing crops and livestock to the advantage of the entire realm. She had founded a brand-new industry by encouraging the marshfolk to gather herbs and simples that were prized by physicians and cooks of the south. She brought in military consultants from Cathra to create a small standing army that now patrolled the Rainy Highroad, Moss's only land-link to the other island nations, and put down the gangs of human bandits that had long infested it and rendered it useless to traders and travelers. From Didion she acquired six fighting frigates and contracted for ten more, so that in future Moss need never again suffer the depredations of the Dawntide Salka. The monsters dwelling in the Great Fen were still unremittingly hostile; but that part of the country had few human inhabitants and little in the way of resources.

'It's hard to believe that only four years have passed,' she said to Wix at last, 'so greatly has our kingdom been transformed. I've worked without stint to improve the lot of our people. And yet I fear that their hearts are not fully with me. Do you agree?'

He nodded slowly but refrained from speech. The sad acknowledgment was sufficient.

She said, 'So many of our leaders and learned ones continue to mistrust my motives. It saddens me that they still believe me to be a tool of Conrig Wincantor rather than a loving monarch who puts the needs of her own folk above all other considerations. The people loved my ancestor Rothbannon, for all his sternness, but I sense that they do not love me. Why is this, my friend? You must speak honestly, even if the truth be hard for me to accept.'

Wix said, 'I'll tell you, Majesty, if you promise to eat. Your body will not recover its strength without food, and if the body is weak, the spirit lacks that resolve necessary to bring about change.'

She sighed, but lifted the silver dish covers and took portions of coddled duck eggs, poached cod, and rush-pollen fritters.

'First,' Wix said, after a hearty pull of mead, 'let's compare the first years of your reign with those of Rothbannon. He was a hard man but highly revered, as you say, even though the foundation of his kingdom came through Coldlight sorcery. He obtained his Seven Stones a century ago by outwitting the Salka of the Dawntide Isles, and in time managed to turn the monsters' own ancient magic against them, to the benefit of his people. He was able to do this because he took the time to study the sigils, and because he only used the Great Stones rarely and for the furtherance of his new realm. Indeed, he never used the Unknown Potency at all, believing it would undermine the magic of the other sigils.'

'I know this.' She spoke petulantly, through a mouthful of fish. 'It's always been my intention to study Rothbannon's writings about the stones when I have sufficient time.'

'But you haven't found the time,' Wix pointed out. 'Neither have you used your stones as the first Conjure-King did – with careful circumspection and only for the good of your nation.'

She did not look up from her plate. 'You're right. Far too often, I used the magic of the sigils for Conrig, whom I love.'

'And who is hated by our proud people, for daring to make Moss his vassal.'

'Most of our progress in the past four years came about because of Conrig's gold! Don't the people understand that? Would they rather live independently and be destitute?'

'They would rather you had not helped Conrig to establish his Sovereignty in the first place. They would rather you had not spent your physical strength so profligately through use of Sender and Loophole – only because this foreign overlord asked it of you, and you were too spineless to refuse him. Majesty, they believe that you love Conrig more than you love them.'

She started up from her seat, letting her napkin slide to the balcony floor. 'They're wrong! They don't understand modern politics. Being a part of the Sovereignty has made Moss stronger and safer – and God knows we're richer than we've ever been before.'

'You have done your queenly duty well, Majesty. The people know that and are thankful. But you asked me for the truth – why they don't love you. And the only answer to that is your determination to love another – to serve another – ahead of them. And this person is clearly unworthy of your devotion. Conrig Wincantor is ruthlessly ambitious and arrogant. True, he's been generous to Moss – but his treatment of Tarn and Didion has been very harsh. Furthermore, he cast aside his first wife for expediency's sake and entered into a loveless match with the Princess of Didion. He has no true devotion to you, either, my lady, and in your heart I think you know it.'

She slid slowly back into her seat, her face drawn with anguish. 'I once thought to use him as a stepping stone to domination of this island. But I've ended up being used by him. I never intended to love him, either! Yet I can't help it, even though I know what manner of man he is. He may not love me . . . but he needs me.'

'We need you more.'

They sat together quietly. He finished his cup of mead and his bread and sat with folded hands, waiting to be dismissed. It was plain that he had no more to say.

'Thank you for your candor, Wix,' she said finally. 'I'll think about all of this. You may go now. Please tell Grand Master Ridcanndal that I'll attend today's meeting of the Glaumerie Guild. I require the guild's advice on a thaumaturgical matter.'

'Very good, Majesty.' He bowed and withdrew from the balcony.

She could not stomach the greasy fritters, but she forced herself to eat most of the eggs, some fish, and a single roll with butter, thinking furiously all the while.

There was one way sure way to escape Conrig's thrall. It had come to her as the good old man spoke: a solution both drastic and permanent, but one that could only come about if she no longer owned that which the Sovereign needed . . .

Do I dare give them up? Can Moss survive if I render them lifeless and destroy them? Can Conrig?

His downfall was not the only thing she had to fear. Shortly after she assumed her throne, a flash of unwelcome insight had come to her. Was it possible that her own collection of moonstones, which she had found hidden in the fens, was not the gift of her dead mother after all? What if the dream of Queen Taspiroth had been a cruel deception of the Coldlight Army, and the gift of sigils intended to further some scheme of theirs?

Why the Lights might do such a thing was incomprehensible to her. But *someone* had led her to the moonstone cache, presumably for a good reason. She was no longer so naive as to believe in benevolent ghosts – especially the ghost of poor Taspiroth, who had suffered an atrocious death after misusing one of Rothbannon's Great Stones. No mother would risk exposing her daughter to a like fate – a fate that now seemed all too probable if she continued using the sigils . . .

Conjure-Queen Ullanoth. Do you hear? Vra-Sulkorig Casswell bespeaks you on behalf of High King Conrig.

Moon Mother mine! Could *that* be the answer to the why of it? But if she were actually destined to advise and safeguard Conrig, then who besides the Lights could have led her to the gift?

Do you hear me, Conjure-Queen?

'I hear you,' she replied. The matter would have to be

thought through later. 'Why is it that you bespeak me,
Sulkorig, rather than the king's brother Stergos?'

*So the news hasn't reached you, Majesty? Alas! There's been a
terrible fire at Cala Palace, and Lord Stergos was gravely injured.*

'I am grieved to hear it. What is the outlook for his recovery?'

*The alchymists have high hopes, but he may be much scarred by
burns.*

'Perhaps my Royal Physician can provide valuable consul-
tation. There is a certain rare plant growing in our fens that
Moss's healers have long used to prevent disfigurement by
burning. I will have Master Akossanor bespeak you about it
immediately. The medicine can be put aboard one of our
fastest schooners and will reach Cala in a few days.'

*Gracious queen, I'll tell King Conrig of this welcome offer. There
is another matter, also concerning the Royal Alchymist, that the High
King commands me to put to you. The two malefactors responsible
for the attempted murder of Lord Stergos are called Scarth Saltbeck
and Felmar Nightcott. They are renegade Brothers of Zeth, who may
be expected to use powerful magic to foil those who pursue them.
Here are images of their faces . . . His Grace beseeches your help in
tracking them down.*

'My help?' She felt a mortal chill stab her vitals.

*The High King requests that you use your Subtle Loophole to
find the pair, so that they may be brought swiftly to justice. He real-
izes all too well that using the Great Stone will wreak a lamentable
toll of pain upon you in your already weakened state, but he begs
that you will agree to the search for the sake of the great love he
bears you.*

There was silence on the wind.

*Your Majesty? What answer shall I give King Conrig? He is here
at my side, praying you will help him and his suffering brother.*

'Tell – tell the king that I will try. As the compassionate
Moon Mother knows, I can only try. But since the effort will
endanger my life, I request of my liege lord a twofold promise.'

The High King asks what it might be.

'If my land of Moss should ever be threatened by an enemy either natural or supernatural, he must promise to come to its aid with all the forces at his command. And if I am disabled or expire through performing this service for my liege, he must continue paying Moss its annual guerdon so long as the Sovereignty endures.'

Conrig Wincantor, Sovereign of Blenholme, swears on his Iron Crown that he will fulfill both promises without reservation.

'Thank him for me, Vra-Sulkorig. If I find the fire-raisers, information about them will be spoken to you on the wind by one of my people. I myself will probably be indisposed. Farewell.'

Ridcanndal, Grand Master of the Glaumerie Guild, hovered over her couch, his face grey with apprehension. The Royal Physician and the High Thaumaturge, Lady Zimroth, stood by him.

'For the last time, Majesty, I implore you to reconsider this rash action,' Ridcanndal said. 'Your physical condition is too delicate to endure further pain-debt. And finding those who set the fire in Cala Palace is hardly crucial to the recovery of Lord Stergos.'

Akossanor, the physician, added, 'I've consulted with the doctors who care for him and sent them the proper physick. His life is not in danger – but yours may well be if you undertake this search.'

'Conrig only wants revenge,' said Lady Zimroth. 'Either that, or he hasn't told you the full truth about the conflagration. I've heard a rumor on the wind that the arsonists are also thieves, who stole some important magical items from Stergos. Whatever these things may be, they can hardly be worth jeopardizing your life.'

Thieves? Ullanoth felt her breath catch in her throat.

There was indeed something the fire-raisers might have stolen that was beyond price. She'd known about Darasilo's Trove for four years, yet had never tried to find it with loophole. Whenever the notion occured to her, it always seemed imperative that she must set it aside until later. And so she had.

Why?

'Please don't do this, Majesty. Think of the needs of your kingdom. Of your duty!'

The aged High Thaumaturge had been one of Beynor's closest friends. Lady Zimroth had never fully reconciled herself to his dethronement and exile, even though the Beaconfolk, and not Ullanoth herself, had ultimately brought it about. Nevertheless her probity and loyalty to the throne were beyond reproach.

'I do think of my duty to Moss,' Ullanoth said. 'But this one last time I must help Conrig.'

'Last time?' Zimroth's eyes widened. 'You'd deny him sigil magic in future?'

'I had meant to discuss the matter, together with a certain course of action I'm considering, with the entire Guild today. As it happens, the discussion is now unnecessary, since I've extracted certain promises from Conrig that ensure the survival of our beloved realm, even if this use of Loophole should disable me . . . Ridcanndal, give me the box. I must do this before I lose my courage.'

The Grand Master picked up a small casket of platinum from a table beside the Conjure-Queen's couch. 'But Majesty, what are these promises?'

She shook her head. 'Attend me closely. This effort will require all of my remaining stamina. If I do locate the fugitives, I'll not be able to speak. You will have to extract the result directly from my mind. Later, when you bespeak the Cathran alchymist Vra-Sulkorig with the search results, he will tell you about Conrig's promises. Now open the box for me.'

The head of the Glaumerie Guild bowed his head and obeyed. The velvet-lined box contained her six remaining sigils: Beastbidder, Interpenetrator, Concealer, Weathermaker, Sender, and Subtle Loophole. The latter was a small open triangle with a handle attached, exquisitely carved from translucent moonstone and glowing with arcane energy. Looking through it, one obtained a vision of anything that was requested. But unlike the silent and often murky oversight vouchsafed by windsight, Loophole showed its objective clearly, with all sounds attending.

Lying in her private sanctum, with the most powerful sorcerers in her realm kneeling at her side, Ullanoth took the sigil and lifted it to her eye.

By noon on the day after Solstice, the Salka had towed Beynor's boat to the entrance to Didion Bay. He directed them to continue on a course well to the north of the main shipping lanes so that his singular method of propulsion would not be detected, and continually scanned the sea for stray fishing smacks and coasters. All went well and no one noticed them.

Round about the ninth hour he ordered the great creatures to pull into a deserted marshy inlet about twenty leagues north-east of Holt Mallburn. They came to a halt in a salt-pond, well hidden among the tall grasses and shrubs, and Beynor summoned the Supreme Warrior for a conference.

Ugusawnn's hideous face rose slowly above the gunwale and his great red eyes blinked in the low sunlight. 'Well?' he inquired with an ill-natured sneer.

Beynor responded mildly. 'We'll stop here for the night. It's time for me to step the boat's mast, rig her, and switch to sail. From here on, we must travel more slowly, and any towing by you Salka will have to be done very cautiously, with only a few knots' advantage over the local small craft, so I won't look conspicuous.'

'Knot? What kind of a knot?' The Supreme Warrior's brow wrinkled in a fierce scowl.

'It's a unit of velocity. A way humans have of saying how fast a boat moves over the water . . . Oh, never mind. If your haulers just follow my bespoken instructions, I'll keep us moving along properly. You Salka will have to swim deep as we enter Mallburn Harbor. The sea there will be cloudy from river-mud after the rain, but even so, we don't want to risk some crow's-nest loafer catching a glimpse of you.'

'Mmm.' The monster was thinking. 'It is necessary that I stay close enough to the surface to keep you in sight at all times. And I – not you – will give directions to the Salka haulers.'

Beynor tipped him an ironic salute. 'It's your decision, Eminent Ugu. But once we get into crowded waters, you'll have to look sharp to avoid dangerous mistakes. If I ram another vessel because your warriors ignore my orders, the Harbor Patrol will be on us like stink on a swamp-fitch. They'll arrest me and confiscate the boat to pay for the damage. Do you understand what I'm saying? Once we start up the river, it would be best if you let me sail completely unencumbered –'

Ugusawnn gave a furious growl. 'I think you hope to trick me, human excrement! It will not work. Abandon any thought of escaping my vigilance.'

Beynor gave a shrug. 'I want this scheme to succeed. So should you. I've sailed through busy harbors and up crowded rivers before. I know the kind of problems that can arise.'

An awful smile spread across the countenance of the amphibian. His teeth gleamed like crystal marlinspikes. 'I have a solution. We will disconnect all but one harness. I myself will wear it – pulling you as it becomes necessary, and also keeping you secure.'

'Suit yourself.' While the Salka milled about in the marsh, reorganizing themselves and catching fish for a meal, he set about preparing the boat. It took the better part of two hours, and while he worked he sent his windsight in search of the royal barge.

It had left the capital early and made its first overnight stop at the large town of Twicken, where the king and his family received the homage of prosperous local landowners and merchants at a dinner party held aboard. Beynor found the barge tied up at a riverside jetty splendidly decorated for the occasion. It was a handsome craft with a snow-white hull and abundant gilt trim, adorned with banners, bunting, and swags of flowers, designed to be propelled by forty sweeps that could be augmented by sails if the wind was favorable. Its figure-head was a gigantic black bear, emblem of the barbarian nation.

Honigalus Mallburn and his family were plainly visible to Beynor's windsight, resplendent in full regalia and gathered with their guests at a long table under a white-and-gold striped awning on the poopdeck. The king was a stocky man of medium stature and plain features. His wife Bryse Vandragora, daughter of the greatest of Didion's timberlords, resembled him so closely that they might have been brother and sister. They were a couple devoted to one another and to their three young children. Crown Prince Onestus, who was seven years of age, and his brother Bartus, who was five, perched solemnly on highchairs at the feasting board with their parents and the guests from the town. Their little sister Casabarela, who had celebrated her first birthday only two months earlier, lay asleep in the arms of her nurse, who sat behind the queen.

Beynor could hear nothing on the wind, of course, but the occasion was plainly more sedate than jovial, with the worthies of Twicken showing no particular enthusiasm for the royal visitation.

Good to know the king's still unpopular among the

commons, Beynor thought in satisfaction. Four years was a long time, and he had not entirely trusted the dream-reports periodically given to him by Somarus. It seemed as though the seditious prince had gauged the temperament of the middle class accurately enough, but the nobility might be another kettle of fish. The only important peer who was openly sympathetic to Somarus was Duke Lynus Garal, whose rich tin mines were heavily taxed by King Honigalus. Lynus was a cousin of Somarus's wife Thylla. He had kept her and her two young children under his protection during the years that Somarus ranged about the wilderness with his rebel army, stirring up trouble.

Over time, Beynor had managed to invade the sleep of Lynus Garal, as well as that of most of Didion's other landed peers and timberlords; but lacking their explicit cooperation in the intrusion, he had been able to sift only fragmented information from their minds. It would probably be a good idea to bespeak Fring and attempt to clarify the situation. There was no sign of the archwizard at the royal dinner party, and Beynor presumed he had stayed behind in Holt Mallburn . . .

The musclepower of the Salka helped Beynor to erect the small boat's mast. After he had fastened the shrouds and stays that kept it upright, he rested and called out soundlessly on the wind.

'Fring Bulegosset! Respond to a good friend who wishes you well.'

So it's you. You're a lot closer to the capital than you were yesterday.

'I'm moored in a marsh twenty leagues away from Mallmouth Quay, getting my vessel all shipshape before starting up the river. Are you still at home in Holt Mallburn?'

Yes. I'm supposed to be suffering a severe case of griping bowels after dining on suspect shellfish.

'Regrettable.'

Is it still going to happen?

'Of course. Would you like to watch?'

I believe I would.

'There's a stream called Boar Creek that flows into the Malle just below Boarsden Castle. Be there in late afternoon on the day of the king's scheduled arrival. It would be useful if any number of impartial observers from the castle accompanied you. Perhaps you and the duke and duchess and some others could ride out to watch the royal barge negotiate the rapids and the deep eddy in that section of the river. Always an exciting spectacle – and apt to be especially memorable this year.'

Ah. Yes, of course.

'Were you able to bespeak one of the wizards in Somarus's company and pass on my advice?'

I did so. The prince will be within a day's ride of Boarsden on the day in question . . . in case he should be needed.

'He will be. You have my solemn word on it. Tell me now the mood of Didion's nobility. If Somarus assumed the throne and declared war on the Sovereignty, how would they react?'

War?!

'My dear Fring – do you know so little of your prince's temperament? Of course there'll be war! Which peers will support a call to arms?'

The barons of the outlands will certainly follow Somarus, since they never approved the capitulation of Honigalus to the Sovereignty. Duke Lynus Garal is no friend of the present monarch, as you already know; he might well favor a war of independence. The Duke of Karum on the west coast rules his fief like an independent principality. He'd favor any king who turned a blind eye to the marauding forays his cronies mount against shipping in the Western Ocean. If a war enhanced his opportunities for piracy, he'd rally round. Duke Boarsden was a first cousin to the late Queen Siry, Somarus's mother. He might declare for the new king or he might not. His fief is close to the Cathran border and would be a prime target for attack by the Sovereignty.

'Which lords might balk at accepting Somarus?'

The lords of Riptides and Highcliffe are solidly for Honigalus. The Sovereignty has brought tremendous prosperity to their traders and shipbuilders, even with the higher taxes imposed by Conrig. They'd resist going to war. So also, I think, would Duke Kefalus Vandragora, the most powerful peer in our nation, whose wealth derives from timber sales. With Conrig continuing to augment Cathra's navy and trade fleet, Duke Kefalus can only grow richer. War would be disastrous to his fortunes.

'Unless the war were won quickly – by Didion!'

And how might this miracle take place?

'In the same manner that Conrig Wincantor obtained his victory over your nation: through high sorcery.'

I – I am at a loss for words, Beynor. Am I to understand that you yourself intend to give some sort of magical aid to Didion?

'Yes.'

Forgive me for pointing out the obvious: in the late conflict, your efforts proved wretchedly inadequate. And thanks to your sister Ullanoth, all Blenholme knows that you have been cursed by the Great Lights and denied use of their sigils. So from what will this new font of high sorcery derive?

'I had intended to impart this news to you later, after Somarus was crowned. But perhaps it's for the best that I reveal it now. I have gained access to an entirely new collection of moonstone sigils. Their usefulness no longer depends upon the vagaries of the Beaconfolk, nor do the stones exact a toll of crippling pain as the price of their magic.'

Astounding! If true . . . May I ask how these sigils came into your possession? Did you obtain them from the Dawntide Salka?

'Where they came from is irrelevant. Neither am I prepared to use them until the appropriate time. I told you about the new sigils so that you might help bolster the confidence of Somarus . . . and convince him that I'm a worthy friend to him and Didion. You and the prince may well ask what I require in return for my magical assistance. The answer is simple. Help me destroy the Sovereignty and bring down the two people who deprived me of my own kingdom of Moss: Conrig Wincantor and my sister Ullanoth. All I want is to rule my native land, free of vassalage. I presume Somarus and the Sealords of Tarn have the same ambition.'

Tarn? Oh, I see . . . I see!

'Keep this knowledge secret until the day Somarus becomes king. Then share it with him. Use it, both of you, to convince the lords of Didion to throw off Conrig's yoke. I myself will convince Tarn to join us.'

You'll demonstrate this magical power, I presume.

'When the time is ripe, and only then. I've spent four years planning the downfall of Conrig and my sister, and I won't have my hand forced. Somarus will have to trust me. I'll give him ample reason to do so – in just a few days. And now farewell. I'll be preoccupied with other matters until the royal barge approaches Boarsden, so don't attempt to bespeak me.'

Very well. May all transpire as we would wish!

Beynor took more smoked salmon and reedmace root from the victual sack and went to the boat's cockpit for a brief meal. The pond was almost mirror-calm in the bright evening. Ugusawnn was nowhere in sight, probably lurking underwater, but the other Salka had hauled out on a mudbank to rest after feeding. A casual observer might have mistaken them for giant sea-lions, save for the green-black color of their bodies and the occasional languid movement of a tentacle.

The deposed young king watched the monstrous creatures without emotion. They'd brought him safely to Blenholme, and he had no doubt that they'd follow his orders from here on, albeit grudgingly. No Salka had ventured up the River Malle for nearly a millennium. In such unfamiliar circumstances, surrounded by humanity and its swarming watercraft, even their brutish self-confidence would falter. They'd be unlikely to countermand his decisions or quarrel with him out of sheer bloody-mindedness.

Beynor gave a great sigh and allowed himself to relax for the first time in many days. He'd travel in more comfort once they reached the river. It would be a huge relief to have some personal control of the boat at last, rather than jouncing about like a bale of inanimate cargo. He'd still have to rely on Salkan motive power when the wind was insufficient . . . until the time came when he was ready to escape.

Going into exile, he'd taken a well-filled purse to the Dawntides, not realizing there'd be no way to spend the money. He'd spend it now, no matter how much the Salka might object – not only on decent clothing, but also on food. A loaf of real bread! A spicy meat pie! A beaker of ale! Fresh strawberries . . . Beynor choked back a moan of longing and tore off another leather-tough mouthful of salmon. Soon, he told himself. Soon!

NINE

Snudge and his companions reached the town of Teme very late on the day following the Solstice. Vra-Mattis had bespoken ahead to the mayor's windvoice, informing him of the royal warrant they carried, which obliged all subjects humble or exalted to extend the king's men every possible comfort and assistance.

It had been a hard day's ride from Cala. The armigers and the novice were taken at once to the kitchen of the mansion for a late supper, while the two young knights dined more formally at a table in the breezy parlor, reluctantly vacated on the warm evening by the lady mayoress and her women.

'I wished us to eat alone for a reason,' Snudge said to his friend, while chewing on a roasted pheasant leg. 'I have a confidence to impart and something to show you. I request that you keep these things secret unless grave circumstances dictate otherwise.'

'Say on!' Gavlok heaped a piece of soft manchet bread with thin slices of beef, slathered on mustard, and took a huge bite.

'You would have known about this years ago, had Mero

Elwick not taken your place on the expedition to Mallmouth Bridge, during our invasion of Didion.'

'I remember. The bastard convinced Lord Feribor to remove me from the mission at the last minute.' He rolled his eyes. 'Of course, if I'd gone along, I'd be dead in battle – like Mero and the other two luckless sods who accompanied you. All heroes, to be sure, but I'd as lief be unheroic and abide among the living.'

'The armigers Saundar and Belamil were not killed in battle, as was said at the time. Mero slew them foully after we secured the bridge for Conrig's army.'

'No!' Gavlok lowered the bread and meat from his mouth and quenched the fire of the mustard with a gulp of beer.

'Yes. He committed murder because he coveted this.' Snudge wiped his greasy hands on the tablecloth and opened the front of his shirt, extracting a small square carving of milky stone hung on a golden chain. In the shadowed room, it shone with a greenish inner radiance. 'Do you remember this amulet of mine?'

Gavlok nodded. 'The lucky charm you wore when first you joined the Heart Companion company of armigers. I remember Mero teasing you about it. I don't remember it glowing, though.'

'It wasn't alive then. Now it is – and it's not a lucky charm. It's a powerful magical tool, a moonstone sigil named Concealer, able to render a man invisible. I took it from the body of Beynor's agent Iscannon, the one I killed in Castle Vanguard.'

'Bloody hell! How does it work?'

'All I do is command it. The sigil obeys only me because I'm its rightful owner. I can also use it to hide other persons who stick close to me, and even conceal things such as the horse I'm riding or a small boat that I sit in, if they're within about four ells of me and the stone. On the Mallmouth mission, I made all four of us armigers invisible. This is how we gained access to the drawbridge tower and opened the way for our army.'

'Futter me blind! And you say Mero wanted to steal this sigil from you?'

'Yes, and when it seemed he would fail in the attempt, he tried to smash it with his broadsword, not knowing that a sigil can defend itself from one who would separate it from its bonded owner. My Concealer burnt Mero to ashes and was unharmed by his blow. I told King Conrig that the moonstone was lost during our fight to secure the bridge. I've maintained this fiction ever since – although His Grace suspects the lie.'

'But why deny the sigil's existence? The ability to go invisible would be a priceless asset for . . . one who is a king's man.'

'You mean a spy,' Snudge said without rancor. 'I declined to use Concealer anymore because it draws its power from the Beaconfolk, those terrible entities who masquerade as the Northern Lights.'

Gavlok looked at him askance and quaffed more beer. 'I – I thought they were only a tale told to frighten naughty children.'

'Here in Cathra, where the Brothers of Zeth practice an orderly and scientific form of magic and influence the beliefs of the people, the true nature of the Beaconfolk has been nearly forgotten. But the people of Didion, Tarn, and Moss know full well that the ones they call the Great Lights or the Coldlight Army are very real. The Beaconfolk had a shadowy relationship with the Salka, the spunkies, and other inhuman beings who inhabited this island long before Bazekoy's conquest. Through moonstone sigils like this Concealer, the Lights are capable of exerting a malignant influence on humankind as well.'

Gavlok eyed the thing with apprehension. 'But only if you use its magic, right?'

'Yes. The Great Lights share their power with sigil owners, and extract a price in return. Each time one uses a sigil, one suffers subsequent pain during sleep until the debt is repaid. The suffering is proportional to the type of sorcery produced by the stone.'

'But . . . why should this be so?'

'The Beaconfolk have still another name: they're the Pain-Eaters. Ages ago, they encouraged the Salka and some other inhuman creatures living on our island to make sigils so they could satisfy their diabolical hunger. Much later, a few human beings also used the stones. I was told by Lord Stergos that the Beaconfolk are both irascible and capricious. If they become angered – or sometimes for no good reason that people can fathom – they may abruptly condemn a sigil user to death, or even damn his soul to the Hell of Ice, where he lives and suffers forever.'

'Blessed Zeth, what a horror! I marvel that you're willing to dare such peril by using that thing.'

Snudge replaced the moonstone inside his shirt. 'Concealer is deemed a very minor sigil, and the pain it gives is not so severe, nor is there much danger of insulting the Beaconfolk through its use. But there exist so-called Great Stones, such as those owned by the Conjure-Queen, that inflict a prolonged and debilitating agony upon the owner, and place the person using them in a more precarious position. One sort of Great Stone is called Weathermaker. Both Ullanoth and her brother Beynor used Weathermakers during the war with Didion to create strong winds and storms. Even worse is a sigil called Subtle Loophole, also owned by the Conjure-Queen. This kind of stone is capable of scrying anyone or anything in the world, given proper instruction. Ullanoth has used her Great Stones overmuch in the service of our High

King, out of besotted love for him, and greatly injured her health. I think the woman must be daft . . . but then, I've never been in love myself.'

'So it's true,' Gavlok whispered. 'Conrig gained his Sovereignty through high sorcery, even though he publicly denies it.'

'I believe that our king's own bravery and intelligence played a greater role in his triumph. This is why I remain his faithful servant. But the magic of the Beaconfolk also aided his cause, and so my conscience has been torn between loyalty to my liege lord and certain knowledge that sigils are evil and can't help but ruin the souls of those who use them. Queen Ullanoth may do as she pleases with her own awful stones. But I faced a moral dilemma with my lesser one. I still don't know if I've made the proper choice – but after thinking the matter over, I decided I would use Concealer again if it became absolutely necessary. I do this only because I've judged King Conrig's cause to be worthy.'

'I understand.'

'On the Mallmouth Bridge mission, I didn't tell my companions the true nature of Concealer: its link to the Beaconfolk. They knew only that it was a magical thing I'd taken from a Mosslander wizard. They were unaware that it could kill. They were also unaware that if I had died, its bond to me would have been severed – whereupon some foolish or wicked person might seize the inactive sigil with impunity and perhaps bring it to life again. There is a particular danger of this happening in Tarn, where we're headed, because the shamans of that nation are both powerful and resentful of the Sovreignty. To prevent my sigil from falling into the wrong hands, I ask a boon of you. If I should perish on this mission, take Concealer from my body and smash it to dust. You'll know it's harmless if the pale inner glow disappears. But if I only seem to be dead, or am separated somehow from the sigil and it still glows, then beware. The thing will harm you or even kill you if you touch it. Scoop it up instead with a metal implement and bury it deep where no man will ever find it. Will you do this for me, Gavlok?'

'I will.'

'My friend, I thank you.'

Snudge frowned as an unpleasant notion came to mind. There was small chance that their party would stumble upon the two thieves carrying the Trove of Darasilo. He'd wind-searched for them on the journey from Cala to Teme as the king had commanded him, finding nothing. He thought it probable that the pair were well hidden by some sort of strong magic and traveling nowhere near the Great North Road, which was alive with royal troops and reeves' deputies who stopped and questioned anyone fitting the fugitives' description. Nevertheless, Snudge decided Gavlok had to be warned, in case the unlikely should happen.

'There's something else I must tell you. Concealer isn't the only moonstone sigil in existence. Will you swear to simi-larly dispose of any others you may happen to find – whether they be alive or dead?'

'Of course I'll swear, Deveron, if you really believe it's necessary.'

'The notion of acquiring the powers of high sorcery doesn't tempt you, then?'

'Great God, no!' The young knight was aghast. 'It scares me stiff.'

Snudge released a long breath and slumped back in his chair. 'You're a fortunate man. Pronounce the solemn oath.'

After Gavlok did so, the two of them ate ravenously. They were finishing jam tarts and the last of the beer when there came a scratching at the chamber door.

'Enter!' said Gavlok.

The apprentice windvoice Vra-Mattis poked his tousled

head in. His face glowed with excitement. 'Sir Deveron, I've been bespoken by Vra-Sulkorig. It's an important message for you from the High King.'

Snudge felt the food in his belly congeal into an indigestible lump. In his fatigue, and his anxiety at confiding in Gavlok, he'd forgotten that Conrig had promised to transmit his decision about seeking help from the Conjure-Queen and her Loophole.

Gavlok climbed to his feet. 'I must visit the jakes anyhow. I hope the news is good.' He pushed past the little Brother and disappeared.

Snudge said, 'Come in, Mat, and close the door. The beer's gone, or I'd offer you some. Have a tart, if you wish. I hope you and the others ate well.'

Mattis shrugged off the irrelevancy. 'The High King wishes to inform you that there is fresh word of Princess Maudrayne.'

'What!'

'A witch of Donorvale in Tarn bespoke a blanket windcall to the Brethren at Cala Palace. This person, whose name is Yavenis, is an unsavory character who peddles nostrums and spells to the lower orders in the Tarnian capital. Nevertheless, she claimed to have important information about the princess, which she said she'd reveal in exchange for a large reward. The king authorized payment through the Sovereignty's ambassador in Donorvale, and Yavenis related the following tale, which she supposedly received from an outlaw shaman of Northkeep called Blind Bozuk.'

He recited an abbreviated version of Maudrayne's escape from the sea-hag, her arrival at Northkeep Castle with her maid 'and the maid's small son,' and her subsequent abduction by Ansel Pikan.

'But this Blind Bozuk has no notion of where Ansel may have taken the princess and the others?' Snudge asked.

'Yavenis says he told her that he didn't know. He may have lied. Bozuk is apparently a talented spell-weaver who cannot be controlled by Ansel, hence his designation as an outlaw. His windsearching ability is exceptionally keen even if his eyesight is not. He was obliged to use Yavenis to bespeak his message to Cala Palace, since he lacks the ability to converse across great distances. Thus the two magickers will split the reward. Yavenis suspects that Bozuk will hold back any further information he may have about the princess until he can be sure of receiving a larger reward that he can keep all for himself.'

'Hmph.' Snudge nodded with grudging respect. It was the sensible thing for the rogue to do.

'Yavenis threw in another piece of intelligence for free. High Sealord Sernin set sail from Donorvale in the wee hours of this morning, accompanied by a fleet of fifteen swift warships. He was said to be en route to Northkeep, which is ruled by Maudrayne's brother. All of the windvoices in the vicinity of that castle save Bozuk have been bound to silence by Ansel Pikan. It's possible that the Lord of Northkeep intends to meet Sernin at sea and discuss his sister's visit with him. Vra-Sulkorig said you would understand the potentially flammable political repercussions of this.'

Snudge groaned. 'God's Blood! If only we had set out to Tarn by ship! It'll be more than ten days before we can reach the Tarnian coast traveling overland. Vra-Sulkorig gave no order for us to turn back?'

'Nay. As a matter of fact, we are instructed to ride north with all speed this very night.'

'What's that?' Snudge leaped to his feet, his face suffused with incredulous anger. 'You silly knave! Why didn't you tell me this before?'

Mattis was unruffled. 'Because I was ordered to relate the other information first. Sulkorig said you must assimilate the news of Princess Maudrayne calmly, before being informed about Queen Ullanoth . . . and Lord Kilian.'

'Kilian?' Snudge was dumfounded. 'What of *him?*'

'I'm ordered to tell you of the Conjure-Queen's doings first. At the king's request, she has used her sorcery to locate the fleeing fire-raisers, Scarth and Felmar. The two Brothers are traveling up the eastern shore of Elk Lake, probably having ridden north from Cala through Heathley and the Beech River valley with many changes of horse. The queen oversaw them in early evening, approaching a village called Pikeport. They were then disguised as royal dispatch riders and were screened by a spell of couverture such as the Conjure-Queen had never encountered before. Both the reeve of the lakeshore and Viscount Olvan Elktor sent out large search parties, but they found nothing. However, if the villains realized that pursuit was closing in, they'd likely change their appearance and go to ground.'

'But why hasn't Queen Ullanoth kept them in sight, guiding the chase?' Snudge demanded.

'Because she is at the point of death. Whatever magic she used to find the miscreant pair took a frightful toll of her strength. Indeed, the doctors at Royal Fenguard are fighting to save her life.'

So Ullanoth had peeped through Subtle Loophole once too often! 'But surely the Brethren at Zeth Abbey would also have been enlisted into the search.'

'Vra-Sulkorig said they've had no success using windtalent. He suspects that the fugitives are shielded by an entirely new type of cover-spell that defeats scrying. If this is true, and they have also discarded the golden gammadions of their Order, it would explain why they've eluded all wind-searchers save the Conjure-Queen up until now. The High King says the matter now rests in *your* hands, Sir Deveron.'

The apprentice eyed Snudge with a mixture of puzzlement

and speculation. 'Vra-Sulkorig had no notion what those curious words might mean, nor would King Conrig explain further.'

Snudge did not enlighten him, but instead rose from the table and gazed out of the solar window. It was nearly midnight and the sky had a carmine sunset glow that would linger for hours without fading. There was plenty of owl-light to enable them to press on, much as he shrank at the prospect. He was less sanguine than Conrig, however, about his own ability to windsearch the thieves. He'd exerted his talent heavily on the journey from Cala to Teme, and he was flagging like a foundering horse. And if the fugitives were indeed hiding under an impervious spell of couverture –

He said to Mat, 'Tell me about Kilian Blackhorse.'

'He escaped from Zeth Abbey, either late last night or early in the morning, taking three fellow-traitors and a young alchymist named Vra-Garon Curtling along with him. The Brethren of the abbey have windsearched for them without success. The High King believes that Kilian intends to meet the two fire-raisers for some nefarious purpose.'

Nefarious indeed, Snudge thought. Especially if Kilian had already learned how to activate the Trove of Darasilo.

But if that calamity hadn't happened, Snudge realized there was a small chance that he might yet outwit the bastards, given the fact that they would be unable to wind-watch *him* as he pursued them! He had a few other tricks up his sleeve as well, as Conrig was well aware – although he'd hardly be able to utilize them while dead tired.

And then there was Concealer . . .

Aloud, Snudge said, 'We must do our utmost to forestall a meeting between the thieves and Kilian. Fortunately, he and his fellow-traitors were completely stripped of all talent by the iron gammadion, so we need not fear them using sorcery against us. The thieves and this Vra-Garon are perhaps another matter. What was it you said earlier about discarding golden gammadions to foil windsearchers?'

Mattis held up the silver pendant that hung about his neck. 'I'm only a novice, and my own gammadion is a mere symbol without magical power. But an ordained Brother of Zeth who wears the sacred pendant of gold gains significant arcane abilities in addition to whatever natural talent he was born with. Also, the gold makes him subject to the commands of his superiors in the Mystical Order. Among other things, this means that the superiors can easily scry Brothers who wear gold gammadions. Felmar, Scarth, and this fellow Garon would certainly have got rid of theirs. Keeping them – even for the powerful defensive magic the pendants confer – would have been much too dangerous.'

'So all we have to contend with are the natural talents of those three, plus whatever cover-spell Felmar and Scarth have conjured.'

The novice hesitated. 'I wouldn't want you to think natural talents are negligible, sir. My own are rather meager, except for my ability to windspeak. Yet I'm able to hide myself from ordinary folk without much difficulty. I simply compel them not to notice me! The deception doesn't always succeed – particularly in bright daylight, or when more than two or three people are looking.'

'Hmm.' Snudge pretended to think this over. He himself possessed the selfsame natural ability; but as Mattis had noted, it was a chancy thing – not to be compared to Concealer's powerful and versatile spell of invisibility. 'Well, there are six of us hunters, so we may hope that the quarry won't escape us . . . Now go along and tell the others to prepare to ride out.'

'I've already taken the liberty of doing so, sir. The mayor's lackeys are readying fresh horses.'

'Good. We'll head for Northway Castle and change mounts

again there before cutting west to the lake. Bespeak the local lord's windvoice and tell him we'll need the strongest coursers he has, as well as a remount for each of us. It may be impossible to obtain sufficient numbers of good replacement animals in the villages along the lakeshore.'

'I'll see to it, sir.' The apprentice withdrew and closed the door.

Snudge paced before the parlor window, striving to make sense of the tangled situation. If Kilian had already discovered a way to activate the sigils of the trove, and if Felmar and Scarth managed to reach him and hand over the moonstones, then the peace of the Sovereignty of Blenholme (and perhaps the rest of the known world) would come to an end in a burst of cataclysmic sorcery.

But if Kilian still lacked a vital part of the puzzle – if he and Beynor were still allied, with each one of them perhaps possessed of some essential element the other lacked – then hope remained, at least until the two conspirators linked up with one another.

Where might such a meeting take place? There was no sure way to tell, but it seemed unlikely to occur in the civilized regions of Cathra, where the Sovereignty was strongest and both Kilian and his thieving agents were marked men. The rugged mountains between Cathra and Didion were a far more attractive option – or even the barbarian northern nation itself, where vast tracts of land were little more than a howling wilderness.

Snudge called to mind a map of the Elk Lake area. If he were in the thieves' place, reasonably safe from oversight but actively endangered by pursuers on land who might recognize him with ordinary vision, he'd take to the water. The big lake provided a perfect way to avoid roadblocks and close scrutiny by the law. In addition to the inland manors, which had vast flocks of sheep, there were many small villages along its eastern side, whose people earned a living selling freshwater fish and mussels, livestock, fruits, and vegetables to the large cities of Elktor and Beorbrook to the north. All of those little places were bound to have trade-boats willing to carry passengers. There might even be regular longshore ferry services between the towns, since roads in the area were rather poor. The western side of the lake was more sparsely inhabited, being almost wholly pastoral, but Kilian's party might well have embarked from a village called Elkhaven, which was only thirty leagues from Zeth Abbey.

Was it possible that the two groups of villains planned to meet somewhere at the head of the lake? Elktor was situated up there; but why risk using the city as a rendezvous when there were uninhabited mountains a dozen or so leagues further north, where the Elk River carved a great gorge before spilling into the lake?

Roaring Gorge, famed in Cathran legends as a haunt of demons . . .

Might there be a way over the mountains somewhere in there? Snudge had never heard of such a thing, but that meant nothing. The precipitous range that virtually bisected High Blenholme Island was so hostile and impenetrable that only three widely separated passes were used by ordinary travelers. The fugitives would be obliged to avoid the nearest and most heavily used, Great Pass, at all costs because it was so closely guarded. If they were bound for Didion, they'd have to find another route, one not too far from the lake-head, but so obscure it was unlikely to be on any map. The gorge seemed as likely a prospect as any.

And if the renegade Brothers were heading that way, where ordinary search-parties would be reluctant to follow, then the Royal Intelligencer might well be the only one with a chance of finding them. King Conrig's enigmatic message showed that he realized it, too.

Snudge was too muddle-headed from fatigue and beer to attempt using his wild talent tonight. He'd try tomorrow, when he and the others reached the shore road and they were presumably closer to the fugitives. It seemed strange that Kilian and his talent-stripped cronies had evaded wind-searchers from Zeth Abbey, but perhaps the young alchymist Vra-Garon had learned how to weave the novel cover-spell, just as the thieves had done.

Did Snudge and his men on horseback have any chance of reaching the gorge before boats did? He had no idea, but he had to give it a try. If the weather stayed fair and there were no serious delays, they might get to Elktor in less than two days, with minimal time lost in sleeping. Beyond there, the mountain track would be so bad that horses would do well just to maintain a fast walk. Still, the quarry would probably be riding no faster; they might even be going afoot.

If fortune smiles, Snudge thought, we might bag one lot or the other – Kilian or the thieves. It was a plan with long odds against its success, but all he could think of in his present weary state.

Sheer luck, having nothing to do with magic, was all that saved Felmar Nightcott and Scarth Saltbeck after they were found by Ullanoth's Subtle Loophole.

Their dispatch-rider masquerade had enabled the pair to travel much faster than their pursuers expected, attesting to the excellence of Kilian's advance planning. They comman-deered new horses every forty leagues or so with a flourish of their counterfeit royal warrant, and by the eve of the day after Solstice they had reached a sizable village on Elk Lake called Pikeport, situated on a bay above the outflow of the Beech River. There they stopped at an inn to switch mounts once again and have supper.

Fortune favored them in that the local windvoice was a

wretched draftsman, and the posters he drew carrying their alleged likenesses might have depicted half the men in town.

Their royal livery made the clientele at the White Waterlily stand-offish, so they dined alone at a small table in a shadowy corner, while locals sat at the long trestle-board and ate family-style from a kettle of fish stew, bowls of new peas, and plates of salad greens with radishes, vinegar, and bacon grease. More men, and a handful of women, were there to drink, whooping and laughing as the potboy kept stoups of ale and beer coming.

Then a trumpet sounded outside.

Nearly a score of the male patrons groaned and uttered obscenities. One of them said, 'A whole day's work draggin' for mussels, and now the fockity reeve musters us to posse afore we've even et!'

He and the other complainers gobbled what food they could and guzzled the last drops from their beakers before scrambling out the front door. Those left behind were either elderly, less than able-bodied, or not subject to posse-duty that year.

The host emerged hastily from the kitchen, cursing up a storm as he ran after the ones who had decamped. 'Think ye can run off without payin' just 'cause the bugle sounds? I know who ye are!'

One of the remaining diners remarked, 'Poor sods. Wonder what the deputy wants with 'em so late in the day? Any of you lot heard of a kiddie gone missing or other trouble?'

The remaining men gave negative responses. A skinny shabbaroon reached for one of the unfinished bowls of food that had been abandoned and began tucking in.

Felmar caught his companion's eye. 'Outside, if you value your life.'

'You think the alarum's raised for us?' Scarth murmured.

'We knew it'd happen sooner or later. For the love of Zeth, don't look like you're in a hurry.'

They retrieved two leather fardels embossed with the royal
arms from under the table and ambled to the stableyard,
where the new horses that the landlord was compelled to
provide for the royal messengers awaited them. Felmar gave
the old ostler a halfpenny tip, then the two thieves swung
into the saddle without haste and rode slowly back the way
they'd come, activating the magical spell taught them by
Kilian that would make them all but unnoticeable to passers-
by and secure from ordinary windsight. The distant trumpet
was still sounding Assembly. More freemen trudged along
the road toward the center of town, carrying rusty swords,
billhooks, fishgaffs, and staves.

'The hunt for us is well and truly on,' Scarth remarked.
'I wonder how they pinpointed our position?'

'Who knows? Turn off here.' Felmar guided his horse
into a crooked path that led down an embankment toward
the shore. At the bottom of the slope the track turned soggy
and clouds of biting midges rose up to torment them. Like
most arcane practitioners, the runagate Brothers were incapable of performing more than one magical action at a time.
They opted to deactivate the cover-spell and use their talent
to shoo away the bugs. They were now well hidden from
people on the road, and there wasn't much chance of
anyone windwatching them amidst the thick brush. They
picked their way along the strand until they came to a
tumbledown boatshed with a rotting dinghy lying near it
in the mud.

'Perfect,' Felmar said. 'Unsaddle your beast and bring your
things inside. We have a little while before anyone thinks to
look here.'

From the beginning, they'd been prepared to take on new
identities if conditions warranted it. They carried beggar's
rags and peasant clothing, among other things; but the
magnitude of the search presently being organized suggested

that only the most ingenious disguise was going to get them safely out of Pikeport.

Hence Pregnant Goodwife and Worried Woodsman Husband.

Scarth, who was tall and brawny and lantern-jawed, portrayed the male member of the duo. Felmar, being small of stature and fine-featured, was to be the woman. He needed his companion's help to get the bodice laced over his hugely augmented chest and stomach. Then he shaved so closely that his face was nearly scraped raw and arranged his wig and linen cap. All the time this was going on, Scarth suppressed snorts of laughter.

'You'll laugh out of the other side of your face,' Felmar snarled, 'if there's a more competent resident wizard in the next town, and he puts up decent pictures of us.'

'Don't bother your pretty head, Felmie dear,' Scarth chortled. 'No one will recognize us in this get-up.' He began converting his own neat beard into a scruffy stubble, adding smears of grime to his features.

'They damned well better not,' muttered Felmar. If the pair came under the close personal scrutiny of law officers they were bound to be recognized. The cover-spell's eye-clouding aspect was only effective beyond a distance of five feet.

Kilian had given instructions to divide the trove into two portions in case they became separated, so each Brother had carried a fardel holding a single ancient book and a leather pouch with fifty-odd inactive moonstones. Now that they were obliged to go on foot, this arrangement was no longer practical. They wrapped the loot in a few pieces of spare clothing and shoved the bundle inside the foldable wicker cage that swelled Felmar's front. Scarth sorted out food and other supplies and put them into a saddlecloth that he gathered into a pack. This he tied to a thick cudgel that could be carried over his shoulder. In his woodsman disguise, he wore a cased hatchet at his belt, along with a large hunting knife;

but their suspiciously fine swords had to be concealed beneath Felmar's voluminous skirts, where the scabbards knocked against his legs with every step.

After they had weighted the saddles and the rest of the discarded baggage with stones and sunk them in the lake, the two fugitives led their mounts along the shore until they came to another path that was at least half a league distant from the shed. There they stripped off the horses' bridles and turned them loose. The animals began to graze unconcernedly on the lush grass.

'Up to the high road now,' Felmar said, 'and back to the Pikeport jetty, bold as brass. That's the safest course. This village is one of the stops for the ferry that serves shore towns between Beech River and Elktor. The boat'll be here early in the morning. We're lowly folk now, you and me, not high-flown royal dispatch riders, so we don't want to waste silver taking a room for the night. The weather's fine after the early rain. What we do is find a place to snooze at the ferry dock, as is perfectly natural, and stay there till the boat for Elktor comes by tomorrow.'

'Wouldn't it be safer to buy passage on some other vessel with fewer passengers?' Scarth said.

Felmar shook his bewigged head. 'No. The more folk around us, the better. Your name's Hoddo and mine's Juby. Anybody questions us, I'll snivel and bewail my lot like preggie women do. You act short-tempered and distraught, and scold me for wanting to go to my mother at Elktor instead of having the babe in our hut down in the Beech Swamp. Trust me: none of the other ferry riders will want to have anything to do with us. Once we reach the city, we'll buy horses and new clothes and head for Roaring Gorge. If all goes well, we should reach the rendezvous with Lord Kilian in a couple of days.'

*   *   *

The wind on the lake was light and variable after the early morning rainstorm passed, less than ideal for the livestock boat Vra-Garon had hired to take Kilian and his party to the head of the lake. They had left Elkport at dawn, but after several hours under sail, the boat had traveled less than five leagues. The surly crew were disinclined to man the sweeps until Kilian promised to pay an extra fee, but even then the craft made a slow go of it, creeping northward along the rugged western shore of the lake at a relative snail's pace throughout the first part of the day.

Kilian spent most of his time in the cockpit, pumping the skipper for local information. His natural talent had recuperated to the extent that he was capable of distorting his facial features. That and the lay garb he now wore would make him unrecognizable to casual windwatchers. He still lacked the ability to screen the other four members of his party, however, so they were forced to stay inside the boat's deckhouse where they were less likely to be noticed. The cabin was cramped and odorous, even with its door and two tiny portlights open, because the doorway faced astern and the feeble breeze came from the starboard quarter. The only furniture consisted of bench-lockers with torn leather padding that doubled as bunks, a cold cookstove sitting in a tray of sand, a woodrack, and a splintery table.

'It wouldn't be so bad,' Raldo fretted, 'if the boat weren't utterly filthy! The deck outside is so crusted with manure that I can't bear the thought of setting foot on it.'

Garon, a handsome young man with chestnut curls and a cleft chin, whose fondness for female company had undermined his acceptance of a celibate lifestyle, only laughed. 'It's a cattle-transport, Brother Butterball. What d'you expect? Drifts of rose petals?'

'I don't see why we couldn't leave our horses behind and secure new ones at the head of the lake,' the fat man grumbled. 'Then we might have hired a faster and more comfortable boat.'

Cleaton had been sitting in gloomy silence, mending a split seam in his new riding gauntlet. He lifted his saturnine face and gave Raldo a sour look. 'If you'd taken the trouble to study the terrain as the rest of us have done, you'd know that there's no settlement at the place where we intend to disembark – and certainly no seller of decent horseflesh.'

'According to the maps I saw at the abbey, there's *nothing* at the mouth of the gorge,' Niavar said. 'Nothing inside it either, except a skimpy path above the river that seems to peter out well before it reaches the border divide. But it's still the safest route out of Cathra for the likes of us. Right, Garon?'

'Oh, yes,' the young Brother agreed. 'There's a game-trail that goes over the top into Didion. I herded the family sheep up Roaring Gorge in summertime when I was a boy and explored all its nooks and crannies. We may have a few sticky moments in places where we have to ford torrents or cut around landslides or washouts, but at least we don't have to worry that Count Elktor will lead his troops very far in there after us.' He laughed. 'Like most folk of the region, Lord Olvan has a superstitious dread of the deep interior of the gorge. Thinks it's crawling with demons, the simpleton! What a disappointment he must be to his father, Duke Parlian. Members of the Beorbrook family have been Earl Marshals of the Realm forever, but Parlian knows his lummox son lacks the stones to inherit the office. When the old man can no longer serve, the Sovereign is sure to bypass Ollie Elktor and install another clan in Beorbrook Hold.'

'Look!' said Cleaton, who had ignored the dynastic discourse. 'The boat crew have pulled in their oars. I think there's a fair breeze filling the sail again.'

'Well, thanks be to Zeth,' muttered Niavar. 'Maybe we'll reach the lakehead later tonight after all.'

'The very idea of sleeping aboard this floating dungheap turns my stomach,' said Raldo.

A coarse joke at the stout Brother's expense occurred to Garon, but before he could get it out of his mouth, the tall form of Kilian appeared at the deckhouse door.

'Good news, comrades,' he said. 'A breeze is rising now that the sun is lowering behind the mountains. We'll move along a little faster from here on, and enjoy more fresh air as well.'

The others murmured gratefully.

Kilian said, 'I've been exploring the wind-world very cautiously, trying to sharpen my disused talent, and I discovered some interesting things. There's a great to-do going on, with windspeech threads filling the air like spider gossamer. Searchers from Zeth Abbey are raking both shores of the lake.'

'Looking for us?' Niavar inquired grimly.

'It's possible, although Abbas Waringlow promised to deflect the hunt away from vessels on the lake. I rather suspect the surge of magical activity involves Brothers Felmar and Scarth – the two coming up from Cala to meet us.'

'With the treasure?' Raldo blurted.

Kilian stared at him wordlessly for a long minute. 'They carry an important collection of arcana, which I was forced to leave behind in the palace when I was sent to the abbey. It's hardly a treasure, since it has no value to anyone but me. Still, if my property is safely returned, all of us will be immeasurably better off in our new lives at the Didionite court.'

'Ah!' said Garon, his eyes narrowing with interest. 'Will you tell us more about this arcana collection, my lord?'

'Not until it's safely in my hands.'

'Have you bespoken these other Brothers to see how they fare?' Garon persisted.

'That would be the height of foolishness, since my windspeech thread might be backtracked to me by an expert practitioner, revealing my own location.'

'Oh.' Garon was abashed. 'I didn't think of that.'

'A person who was rash enough to attempt to contact those men before we've reached the safety of the mountains – or windsearch for them – would jeopardize all that we've accomplished so far. Is this clearly understood?'

They murmured in unison, 'Yes, Lord Kilian.'

'Good.' He went to the table and unrolled a small map. 'Come close and study this. It was procured for me by my sister, Queen Mother Cataldis, and shows the region between Roaring Gorge and the Lady Lakes of Didion, according to the best of current knowledge. Of course, much of the high-mountain area is still *terra incognita*, but we must trust that our Brother Garon will be able to guide us through it safely.'

'Absolutely, my lord!' Garon bent over the sheet. 'Well, just look here: The good queen's mapmaker is evidently unaware of the cave where we're to rendezvous with our two other companions. That's fortunate. I haven't been there for nearly ten years, and I feared the hole might have been discovered by others. It'd be a nasty surprise, wouldn't it, if we got there and found someone else besides our friends waiting for us.'

The others looked at him, appalled.

'Don't worry, I'll go on ahead and scout it out,' Garon reassured them. 'And Lord Kilian can give the cave a good scry before we venture inside. We wouldn't want to meet a bear!'

'A bear?' Raldo wailed.

'Some Tarnian shamans can windsearch through solid rock,' the alchymist said in a distant voice. 'And certain conjurers of Moss are also said to have that ability. But I do not. So you see, Vra-Garon, our security will rest entirely in your hands.'

'You can depend on me.' The young Brother gave him a confident smile. 'Don't worry about bears. They leave signs of their presence and they're afraid of fire, like all animals. If I find that one is living in our cave, I'll roust him out. We may end up having him for dinner!'

'Zeth forfend,' Kilian snapped. 'Garon, I want you to explain the details of the gorge travel route to our comrades while I go back to the captain. I've decided that it's most important that I understand how this boat is steered.' He set a tall glass bottle that he had been carrying onto the cabin table. 'Here's a treat for all of you to share later – a magnum of vintage Stippenese Moen Valley wine, courtesy of my sister's friend, Lady Sovanna, whose hospitality we enjoyed last night in Elkhaven. I've already given the crew members and the captain a taste, and they were very appreciative of its quality. You may finish it off with your supper before settling down to sleep.'

Warm cries of gratitude.

Raldo asked timidly, 'Master, is there no hope that we might reach our destination tonight?'

'Small chance of that, I fear, even with the lug-sail up. And these gathering clouds are a sure harbinger of more rain. Nevertheless, I suggest you all bed down atop the deck-house, amongst our baggage and horse tack. It's certainly the cleanest place aboard, and you can cover yourselves with squares of canvas from our camping supplies. I doubt you'd enjoy sleeping in this cabin with the crew members not on watch. They're even more aromatic than the boat, and I flicked a flea off myself not long ago. Just take care not to roll off the roof and fall into the lake. Some of the black eels living in these waters weigh more than twelve stone. They don't hesitate to attack full-grown elk wading in the shallows, and you can imagine what they might do to a floundering man.'

He left the deckhouse, laughing softly.

Not long afterward, the Brothers unpacked food for a cold

supper and the wine began its first round. Garon held the bottle out to Raldo. 'You look a bit pale, Brother. A good swig of this will perk you up.'

'No, thank you,' the fat man whispered. 'I'm not feeling at all well, and red wines give me a headache. I think I'll light a fire in the stove and brew up a pot of mint tea instead.'

'All the more for the rest of us,' Niavar said, seizing the bottle. 'Cheers!'

'Source! Respond to Ansel.'

I'm here, dear soul.

'How is she – our poor Dobnelu? Is her physical body still viable?'

It may take more time for me to ascertain that, but I have high hopes. The fragile bones and gristle of her throat were not crushed as she was throttled, nor were the great bloodvessels in her neck irreparably damaged. She died gently – not that this is a good thing, for it means that she teetered on the brink even before the boy Vorgo touched her. It may be possible to coax lifeforce back into this material shell, but whether her soul can safely lodge there is quite another matter.

'I see . . . Perhaps you already know that I've recovered Maudrayne and her son, along with the maidservant.'

Yes, I oversaw her for a short time. Did the princess confide her secrets to anyone at Northkeep?

'I'm not sure. She and the others remain in an enchanted sleep in the back of my wagon. I may have to keep them unconscious for some days, at least until we cross Gold River and reach the land between the volcanos, and there's no chance of their trying to escape. Liscanor put out to sea in his frigate and is heading south. It's possible Maude told her brother everything, but I think it more likely that she didn't.'

Soul, this hope may be a vain one.

'I scried the people in Northkeep Castle and read their lips.

Liscanor's wife and her servants believe that young Dyfrig is the maidservant's child. That's one secret safe – and Maude would hardly reveal Conrig's talent without also revealing his son and heir. I think all we need worry about at the moment is keeping Maude's location unverified. Thanks to my threats to the windvoices in the area, what news there is won't spread from Northkeep for at least ten days. Liscanor himself is another matter. Once he reaches the Tarnian capital, he'll tell the council of sealords that his sister is alive. Whether they believe him is problematical. I'll try to sow doubts in their minds.'

Can you reach a suitable hiding place before too long?

'I'm considering three possibilities. Which one I choose depends upon factors still beyond my control. But be easy, Source. No one save Conjure-Queen Ullanoth has the power to scry me on this journey, and she is mortally ill and unable to use her Great Stone. Even if it becomes generally known that Maude lives, the fact matters little if no one can find her.'

TEN

Waterfowl filled the saltmarsh with their cries, and Beynor found himself unable to sleep, so he spent much of the undark night windsearching. He had no luck finding Kilian, which made him wonder whether the alchymist's lost talent might somehow have been restored. After a few hours he abandoned that effort and turned his attention to the two thieves, methodically scrying the villages along the eastern shore of Elk Lake, since only fools or lunatics would have risked travel on the Great North Road, and Kilian's agents presumably were neither.

In time, he noticed the hue and cry going on in the vicinity of Pikeport and gave the place special scrutiny. Even so, he almost missed his quarry, who were dossed down on the village ferry dock together with a number of other sleeping travelers too frugal to take rooms for the night.

Something about the snoring knot of people seemed odd, yet Beynor felt disinclined to study them more closely – a fact that finally rang alarm bells in his head. He forced himself to intensify his oversight and finally detected the unusual spell of couverture. After some hard work, he unraveled it to his satisfaction.

There they lay, Scarth and Felmar, dressed as a countryman

and his pregnant wife, sleeping like well-fed babes with their heads pillowed on a pack that might hold Darasilo's Trove. Felmar looked rather peculiar because his linen coif was twisted awry – and so was the wig beneath it.

Beynor had to admit that the magic obscuring the scapegrace Brethren had been most cleverly wrought. There was none of the fuzziness that often betrayed the presence of cover-spells, only a subtle hint of distortion that was easy to miss. It had to be Kilian's work. None of the other Zeth Abbey alchymists possessed such expertise, which would have done credit to a member of Moss's Glaumerie Guild. Cathran adepts were rather good windspeakers; but most of them were mediocre at best in the arcane arts of visualization and couverture, except for Kilian.

And one other . . .

Beynor very nearly cursed aloud as a long-forgotten name flashed into his memory: Deveron Austrey! *He* might be able to locate this well-concealed pair of thieves, just as he'd managed to track down and slay Beynor's wizard-spy Iscannon a few years earlier. In addition, King Conrig's wild-talented intelligencer was as unscriable as the moonstone sigils themselves. His total spectrum of arcane abilities was a mystery – apparently even to himself. One might almost suspect him of having Tarnian blood.

Beynor wondered why Austrey should pop suddenly into his mind unbidden. Was it a forewarning that the wretch was about to meddle in his affairs again?

Deveron Austrey had dared to steal Beynor's own Concealer sigil from Iscannon. He had somehow penetrated Kilian's inner sanctum while he was still Royal Alchymist of Cathra and had taken one of the three ancient books with moonstone disks fixed to their covers. He'd resisted Beynor's dream-threats and refused to turn over Concealer and the book to Salka couriers sent to retrieve them. The book had been taken away by Ansel Piken to some unknown place, but not before the shaman had helped Deveron Austrey use its medallion to empower Concealer – with consequences that had proved disastrous to Beynor's former allies in Didion.

It seemed certain to Beynor that King Conrig would send his intelligencer after the men who had stolen Darasilo's Trove. Deveron could be closing in on Felmar and Scarth even as Beynor oversaw them. Was there some way to alert the pair, to get them out of harm's way?

Reluctantly, Beynor decided that there was nothing useful he could do. Knowing their names and faces, he was now in a position to invade the thieves' dreams, even if he couldn't windspeak them directly without the necessary password. But if he suggested that they alter their chosen route to avoid Deveron Austrey, the Brothers would suspect a trick. Kilian had seen to that.

No, Felmar and Scarth's best chance to evade capture was to get aboard a boat – as they obviously intended to do – and flee over the Sinistral Range into Didion. The mountainous country at the head of Elk Lake was the worst sort of terrain for scrying, which tended to be inhibited by massive barriers of rock. He'd have to keep a close watch on the pair from now on. Once they were well into the highlands, they'd be almost impossible for any windsearcher to find – including Beynor himself.

On the other hand, his plan for injecting a fatal temptation into their sleeping minds remained perfectly feasible. They must already be extremely curious about the nature of their arcane booty, since Kilian would never have dared tell them the truth about the things they'd stolen. They were thus predisposed to yield to his urging. It would be best if he began planting the impulse immediately, making it more imperative each time the fugitives closed their eyes. He'd compel them to *do it* just as soon as they reached a resting place that was suitably remote.

With luck, both of the thieves would succumb to his inducement and perish without a trace, leaving Darasilo's Trove for him to retrieve at his leisure.

Raldo dozed uneasily on the deckhouse roof. His corpulent body was unable to find a comfortable recumbent position on the planks, so he slept sitting up, propped against a heap of saddlebags, a piece of tent-canvas fending off most of the warm drizzle. Kilian's half-jocular warning about rolling off was unnecessary, since the roof had a low railing around it. All the same, Raldo chose a sleeping spot well away from the edge.

So when the first noisy splash woke him, he didn't immediately realize what had happened.

The twilit sky of early morning was covered by low rainclouds that had swallowed the jagged tops of the mountains. Their looming expanse was black and featureless, seeming to close ominously around the lake like a great wall now that the boat approached the narrowing northern end. Overhead, the much-patched sail was filled by a moderate breeze. Raldo looked about with his befogged vision but saw only the shapes of his companions scattered among the baggage. They were all sleeping deeply, not even snoring.

A soft sound of footsteps came from the main deck below. Horses snorted, whiffled, and stamped their hooves uneasily. Then there was a second splash.

Raldo lifted the canvas away and looked astern, squinting in the half-light. He saw the boat's wake, partially obscured by the bellying sail. In the midst of the foam was a dark object resembling a piece of driftwood with twigs at one end. The object moved, extending itself up from the water before slowly sinking from sight.

Not driftwood. An arm, with fingers.

Another splash, this time on the opposite side of the boat. Raldo waited, and another black shape bobbed in the wake until it was lost to sight.

The fat man felt his skin crawl. His Brethren slept on. He wormed his way further aft so that he could peer down onto the deck where the horses were tied. The cockpit in the stern was empty and the tiller lashed tight with a length of rope to keep the rudder steady.

A noise, directly below him. Someone was emerging from the deckhouse. Raldo held his breath as the indistinct form of a naked man appeared. He was obscured by what was evidently a weak cover-spell, dragging an inert body that had dark-stained clothing. The man heaved his burden over the side, then returned to the deckhouse. Moments later, he reappeared with another limp form and disposed of it, leaving obvious bloodstains on the rail.

God save me, Raldo prayed, he's murdered the crew! There must have been something in the bottle of wine that rendered them senseless. By chance, Raldo was the only one who hadn't drunk any.

What will I do if he comes up here on the deckhouse roof?

Raldo saw the blurry naked man go to the boat's water-butt and pour several full dippers over his besmeared body. After washing himself thoroughly, he used a bucket to slosh more water over certain areas of the deck and the rail. Murky liquid disappeared into the scuppers. Then the man sluiced out the deckhouse as well. When he finished he went to the stern, dried himself with a rag, and donned clothing that lay neatly folded on the stern thwart. Bending over the tiller, he removed the line that had secured it and settled down to correct the boat's course. His identity was still hidden by magic.

But Raldo knew that only one person among them was capable of weaving a cover-spell. Kilian's natural talents had yet to regain their full strength, but they were adequate to cloud his bodily form while he went about his pernicious work.

The fat man shrank back from the edge of the deckhouse roof, too petrified to move further. It seemed that he and the other Brothers were going to live – at least for a while longer – and he thought he knew why. If their pursuers caught up with them during the flight over the mountains, Kilian would require the combined magical abilities of all his companions to defend himself. Later, when the alchymist joined Prince Somarus and his band of warriors in Didion, the Brothers' pitiful portions of talent would no longer be needed . . .

Raldo lay with his face pressed against the wet boards, tasting bile in his throat and feeling tears mingle with the soft rain trickling down his cheeks. His iron gammadion and its chain, which he'd hidden in his jerkin pocket and forgotten to toss overboard, pressed uncomfortably against his hip.

What am I going to do? he asked himself. But he could think of nothing except the giant black eels of Elk Lake, and what they were feeding upon this early morning.

Snudge and his men reached Pikeport at about the seventh hour after midnight, after riding all night. They stopped at the White Waterlily, the only tavern in town, where their perfectly genuine royal warrant and demand for free horse fodder, a meal, and a quiet place to catch a few hours' sleep aroused the suspicions of the short-tempered landlord.

Inexplicably, he decided that the mud-splashed, well-armed strangers purporting to be king's men had to be in league with the masquerading firebugs who had stopped at his establishment on the previous evening, victimized him with a fake warrant, and got him in trouble with the law. A wild commotion ensued, in which breakfasting tavern patrons happily took the aggrieved landlord's part. Snudge's party were forced to draw their swords and make a stand.

Order was restored by the deputy reeve and the town watch only after the local windvoice bespoke Lord Northway's castle and confirmed the legitimacy of those purporting to be the king's men.

While the still-simmering landlord had his people lay out food and see to the needs of the horses, Snudge learned from the deputy that the ferry plying between Beech River and Elktor had called at Pikeport and left over an hour earlier. More than a dozen other commercial sailboats had also embarked round about the same time, fishermen and transports of every sort, heading in all directions for various purposes. No persons bearing the slightest resemblance to Brothers Felmar and Scarth had been discovered yestereen in the vicinity of the village quay or anywhere in the surrounding countryside. The posse was preparing to set out again, but it seemed that the false dispatch riders had vanished without a trace, leaving only their abandoned mounts behind.

Without much hope, Snudge left his men eating a meal of scorched porridge, hard cheese, and flat beer and retired to the grain store behind the stables. This was the only place the disgruntled landlord would let them use as sleeping quarters, but it was at least fairly quiet, while the inn itself was not.

Snudge composed himself and began to windsearch, trying to ignore his throbbing head as he closely scrutinized more than two score small boats sailing, rowing, or drifting about the southern half of Elk Lake. In the end, his debilitated talent was unable to detect anything at all, so he gratefully surrendered to sleep.

Somarus Mallburn, Prince of Didion and one-time general of its armies, soaked in a steaming hot spring in a bosky dell of the Elderwold while birds sang their morning songs, squirrels romped on the moss-hung branches of the venerable trees, and his shieldbearer Kaligaskus knelt by the pool and combed his master's newly trimmed hair with a fine-toothed comb to banish lice and nits.

'Almost done, Highness,' the lad said cheerily. 'Might be a good idea to give it a rinse of turpentine, though, to make sure none of the wee devils slipped past me.'

'No turpentine!' the prince barked. 'You can rub in a dose of delphinium tincture if you think it necessary. At least it doesn't stink so badly.'

'Yes, Highness.' The boy climbed to his feet and trotted back to camp to fetch a phial of the stuff from Tesk the wizard.

Somarus slowly submerged, closing his eyes against the slight sting of minerals in the water, and stayed under until his breath was gone. Then he rose up, inflated his lungs with sweet-smelling forest air, and let himself float. The water was less than three feet deep, but it was marvelous to lie there, warm and supported, gazing up at the leaf-framed sky, thinking about the wonderful things that might – just might – take place within the next few days.

Fring had warned him not to get his hopes too high. Both of them knew that Beynor of Moss was a vainglorious young blowhard, treacherous as a weasel and even more wily. But if there was any chance at all that the deposed Conjure-King could pull off the assassination of Honigalus and his heirs, Somarus would embrace him as his newfound brother – Beaconfolk curse and all.

For as long as it was expedient to do so.

Through Fring, Beynor had suggested that Somarus hold himself in readiness a day's ride from Boarsden Castle. But why not move in closer and actually witness the fateful deed himself? Fring had known none of the details, only that the killing was supposed to take place at the Big Bend of the Malle three days from now, late in the afternoon.

He could ride out with a small party from the Lady Lakes camp, using only the simplest form of disguise, reach

Castlemont Fortress in a couple of days and enjoy the hospitality of his friend Lord Shogadus, complete the journey easily
by traveling the Boar Highroad –

And stand on the south dike of the river, watching the
yellow-bellied traitor die!

True, Somarus wouldn't fulfill his greatest dream. He'd
never know the satisfaction of sinking his blade into the heart
of the half-brother who'd cravenly yielded Didion to Conrig
Wincantor because he'd lacked the courage to die in battle.
But what the hell! All that mattered was that the throne
might come to him at last.

It was another cherished dream of his, one that seemed
even more impossible than the first because Honigalus had
begotten two sons and a daughter, who stood ahead of him
in the line of succession, along with their mother, Bryse
Vandragora, who might only inherit under special and
unlikely circumstances. But if Beynor actually did manage
to wipe out the entire viper's nest, then he, Somarus, would
become King of Didion.

And at that same hour, he vowed, though I must keep it
secret in my heart until the time ripens, will I declare war
on Conrig Wincantor's Sovereignty, and dedicate my life to
its destruction . . .

'Highness?'

He opened his eyes, let his body sink to the bottom of the
pool, and knelt upright in the water. The wizard Tesk stood
there in a dusty black robe, nervously licking his too-red lips
and blinking short-sighted eyes that always watered in
summer. He held out a little corked bottle.

'I brought the tincture myself, Highness, because I've just
received a message on the wind for you, from High Queen
Risalla.'

Yesterday, after first hearing of Beynor's amazing intention, the prince had sent a carefully worded inquiry to his

younger sister in Cala Palace, hoping that she would find a way to side with him if he rebelled against the Sovereignty. The two of them had always been devoted to one another, being the offspring of the valiant Queen Siry Boarsden, second wife of the late King Achardus. Both royal parents had died fighting Conrig in the Battle of Holt Mallburn.

'Tell me quickly what Risalla said!' Somarus demanded.

'Highness, she asked that her response be quoted verbatim: "Dearest Brother, my heart and soul will always be with you in every worthy undertaking. But my duty now lies with my husband and children. For the sake of my conscience, tell me nothing of your plans. Only know that I will always love you."'

'Damn!' said Somarus. 'She was ever a mild-tempered but stubborn lass, even as a girl. Having pledged her loyalty to Conrig at her marriage, she'll remain steadfast to him. Duty is everything to her. Do you recall how she came boldly before Conrig on the day he conquered Holt Mallburn, demanding the bodies of the king and queen for proper burial? Conrig could not withstand her. I suppose I knew how she would reply to my request, even before you gave me her message. But it's a bitter draft to swallow.'

'I believe that those striving for high goals must be prepared to drain such cups rather often,' the wizard said sadly. 'Shall I apply the delphinium tincture now, Highness? You might wish to return quickly to camp. The sentries have captured a Green Man.'

'What?! Great Starry Bear – is the whole world turning upside down? How did the slippery thing let himself be taken alive by a human?'

'Perhaps I should have said Green *Woman*, Highness. As to your question, I suggest you put it to the creature yourself. She's asked to speak to you. Or to be more exact, she asked for an audience with King Somarus of Didion.'

'Well, well! Flattering – if a bit premature. Never mind the tincture, man. Fetch me my clothes.'

A light tunic and trews of fine linen had been laid out for him as undergarments, along with woolen stockings and new boots. The garb he intended to wear on the trip to civilization was still in a coffer in his pavilion. He dried his body with a homespun cloth, then dressed without assistance. Somarus was a man far more impressively built than his older brother the king, lean and hard-muscled as a result of years living in the open since his withdrawal from the court. His beard and brows were red and his long hair was a few shades lighter, like the dark gold of cloudberries. His face was weathered and high-colored, with eyes like blue flint, webbed with fine lines at the corners. He was one-and-thirty years of age.

The camp had been set up in a large forest clearing divided by a brook. The smallest of the three Lady Lakes was partially visible beyond a stand of trees downstream, sparkling in the sun. To the south, the steep rampart of the Sinistral Mountains rose with daunting abruptness from behind wooded hills, the loftiest peaks piercing a cap of white clouds. Northward lay the Elderwold, over five thousand square leagues of desolate heath, boglands, and dense primeval forest, where the ancient and beleaguered race of Green Men had retreated in a final stand against humanity.

The warrior band of Somarus, which was often augmented by men loyal to the outland robber-barons, ventured into the Elderwold only rarely. Most of their raids and skirmishes took place much further to the north-west, where they preyed on caravans of Tarnian and Cathran merchants traveling the Wold Road during the warm months of the year. During winter, they holed up in the castles of the prince's secret sympathizers. Somarus had only lately brought his core group of men into the Lady Lakes country, after one of

Beynor's dream-visitations promised that a climactic event of surpassing importance would likely take place round about the Summer Solstice. The prince had told no one about Fring's hint of the proposed assassination, and so the captive Green Woman's styling of him as 'king' both puzzled and intrigued him.

The force in the camp was small but well-equipped, and included not quite three score mounted warriors, eleven landless knights, four barons who had been outlawed and stripped of their fiefs by King Honigalus for crimes against the Crown, and a flock of servants, shieldbearers, and itinerant wizards. All save the knights and nobles were accommodated in twenty tents, set up in two lines and separated by a wide aisle of trampled ground. The larger pavilions of the prince and his officers had been erected across the brook in an area of scattered trees, while the horses were picketed downstream where abundant grass grew. This early in the morning, a multitude of cook-fires sent up plumes of smoke as breakfast was prepared.

Preceded by Tesk, Prince Somarus went to the pavilion of Baron Cuva, the highest-ranking of his followers, where a murmuring crowd had gathered in a rough circle. At the wizard's cry of 'Make way!' the throng parted, and the prince passed through to find Cuva seated on a folding stool, a quizzical expression on his hawkish face. Three glowering wizards and two huge warriors with drawn swords stood in front of the baron, guarding a small figure.

Cuva rose as Somarus approached, offering his own seat to the prince with a gracious gesture. 'Highness, a most unusual capt – uh – *visitor* has asked to see you. I'm not sure I got her name right. Was it Sithalooy Cray?'

'Call me Cray,' the Green Woman said.

The voice was surprisingly low and resonant for one who stood less than five feet tall. Her aspect was completely human, save for the vivid emerald hue of her somewhat over-large eyes. It was impossible to tell her age. Her unlined face was deeply sun-tanned, and her neatly plaited hair was dull silver, streaked with primrose-yellow. She wore a calf-length moss-green gown with a divided skirt. Her boots were deerskin, and her hooded cloak of mingled shades of grey, brown, and black almost perfectly mimicked treebark. A bulging purse embroidered with colored thread hung from her belt, along with a little gold-hilted dagger in a skin sheath.

As Somarus sat down on the stool and regarded her with what he hoped was appropriate aloofness, she stepped forward a few paces. One of the warriors guarding her lifted a restraining hand, but she gave a negligent wave and the gigantic man froze like a statue. Cries of consternation came from the gathering.

'Let her be,' Somarus said. 'You may come closer, Cray.'

'Are you King Somarus of Didion?'

He said, 'Not yet.'

The little woman gave him a casual bob of her head and smiled. 'You will be king . . . after the drownings.'

More astonished exclamations from the crowd.

'Be silent!' the prince said. Then to Cray: 'Did you come here to tell me that?'

'No. I was sent by the Source, commanded by him to accompany you on your journey to the wide river.'

'Is that so! Well, I've never heard of this Source, so why should I do as he says?'

'Because you want very much to be king.'

'And your Source would forestall me if I declined to obey? Or *you* would?' The questions were asked without heat.

'We have no wish to do so. Only take me with you and all will go well. I'll be no trouble. I eat very little and I can ride pillion behind one of your men if you can't spare me a palfrey. If need be, I'll protect you from your foes' – she shot a sly glance at the still-motionless warrior – 'more adroitly than your pack of hedge-wizards.'

The affronted magickers fixed her with venomous glares.

Somarus threw back his head and roared with laughter. 'I believe you could! What else do you want of me, Mistress Cray?'

'A cup of ale would be lovely,' she said. 'I've come a long way. There was wildfire in the wold and I had to go around it.'

Somarus rose to his feet, still grinning. 'Come and have breakfast. I'd like to talk more with you. Like most human beings, I've never seen one of your race before. I was told you had green skin and pointed ears and leaves instead of hair, and that your women – uh – bewitched luckless fellows who lost their way in the Elderwold.'

'We used to do that in days gone by,' she said demurely, 'but not so much of late. Tastes change.'

Someone sniggered nervously.

Somarus swept his gaze around the hovering group of nobles, warriors, and wizards. 'All of you, get back to your duties! Baron Cuva, I'll ride out this morning for Castlemont with you and a party of ten knights. Light armor and weaponry, surcoats and banners with the Boarsden blazon for disguise, everyone looking spruce and stalwart. Find a suitable mount for Mistress Cray.' He looked down at her. 'Shall we go to my pavilion?'

'In a moment.' She went to the paralyzed man and spoke a word softly. The warrior straightened, sheathed his sword, and walked off dazedly after the others. 'I hope his friends don't tease him too badly,' Cray said.

'He's big enough to take care of himself. Come along now. I'm famished.'

She stood before the prince, staring at his right shoulder with a little frown. 'Oh, my. You missed one.' She reached up and touched a damp lock of his curling hair. There was a sizzling snap and Somarus smelled a whiff of smoke. 'That's taken care of the creeping little whoreson! Now you look much more like a king.'

The ferry put into eleven lakeside towns and villages before reaching the end of the line at the city of Elktor, and at each stop people got off and on, while crewmen unloaded and loaded cargo at tedious length. The clouds had lowered steadily throughout the day; and by late afternoon, when the knoll crowned by Elktor Castle finally came into view of the passengers, rain was falling steadily and the dramatic mountains above the walled lakeside city were wreathed in eerie swags of mist.

Felmar and Scarth had secured inside seats on the boat early on, so they had a fairly comfortable trip, even though the benches were hard and the cabin atmosphere fuggy with the odor of unwashed humanity. Their quarrel-and-snivel act, performed regularly, kept most of the other passengers at bay, although one garrulous old biddy insisted on sharing memories of her own catastrophic pregnancies with the fake mother-to-be.

Most of the time the two fugitives slept. So when they finally disembarked at Elktor Quay they were ready to set out for Roaring Gorge as soon as they could purchase suitable clothing and equipment and secure horses. It was only the fifth hour after noon, but their hopes of a speedy getaway were deflated almost at once when a one-eyed dockside loafer informed them that most of the shops and market stalls had shut down early because of inclement weather and a dearth of customers.

'As for horses,' the fellow continued with lugubrious relish, 'ye won't have an easy time gettin' anything first-rate. Town's all skimble-skamble, with a grand hunt on for a pair of scoundrelly Zeth Brothers who set Cala Palace on fire and like to killed the High King's brother. Word came to Count Ollie late yesterday to beat the bushes for 'em hereabouts, and his captains have commandeered damn near every sound nag in the city to mount search parties. Maybe ye could hire a wagon –'

Felmar uttered a falsetto squall. 'No, no, the track to Mother's croft is too steep for wheels. We need horses to get there. Hoddo, *do* something! We can't keep standing here in the rain!'

Scarth patted his mate's hand and said, 'Now, now, Juby. Calm down, lambykin, or you'll drop that babe of your'n afore its time.'

The idler screwed up his face in an orgy of concentration. 'Lemme think now. There might be one place still with a mount or two left to sell. If I could just recall . . .'

Scarth gave a grunt of disgust and pulled a silver penny from his belt wallet. 'Does this jog your memory?'

The one-eyed man smirked. 'No – but add another and the name's bound to come to mind.'

Without a word, Scarth pressed two coins into the dirty outstretched palm.

'Bo Hern's stable. Follow the Quay Road a quarter-league to the north edge of town, nigh unto the Mountain Gate. Old Bo sells donkeys and mules. Good for ridin' in rough country. And he has saddles and tack, too.' The rascal tugged his forelock. 'Luck to ye, master and mistress.'

'Is there an inn or cookshop near the stable where we might get something to eat?' Scarth asked.

'Bo's wife can fix you up. Otherwise there's the Rusty Gudgeon tavern acrost the way – but some say they use catmeat in their pasties.' The one-eyed man ambled off, ignoring the rain.

'I vote for Bo's place,' Felmar said. 'We can't hang about here any longer.'

Scarth hoisted the bundle to his shoulder and they set off

along the waterfront. 'Mules aren't a bad idea, Fel. They're not fast, but a good one is more reliable on a bad track than a horse. Our map shows that it's fifteen leagues or so to the gorge mouth, and most of the way is twistier than earthworm guts. Then almost an equal distance to the cave, over a miserable sheep-trail. We're in for a rotten time of it if we press on. Maybe we should stop at the stable for the night and start out early tomorrow.'

'No,' said Felmar emphatically. 'We're well-rested. All we need is a meal and some food and drink to take with us. And I've got to shed this wicker birdcage tied to my belly! I'll keep the rest of the woman's garb till we're well away from the city, but there's no way I can ride wearing this futterin' thing.'

'It's raining harder,' Scarth said. 'We could at least wait a few hours to see if it stops.'

'We've got to move on. I don't like the feel of this town. There are alchymists up in Elktor Castle and other windvoices prowling about with the searchers. I can sense them! Thus far, our spell of couverture is holding firm, but something's not right. I almost feel as though we've been overseen. Right through the bloody cover.'

'I won't say you're imagining things,' said Scarth, 'since you've got more talent than I do. But if the Brethren did have a windeye on us, Lord Elktor's guardsmen would have met us at the ferry dock and clapped us in irons.'

'The windwatching – if that's what it was – wasn't done Zeth-style.' Felmar was silent for a few minutes. They splashed on through spreading puddles, paying no attention to the occasional beggar who whined from a doorway. Most of those walking along the quay were seamen, some with giggling doxies on their arms. Half a block ahead, a hanging sign with a lion's head designated a good-sized inn. Unattached sailors were heading toward it like iron filings to a magnet, but the two disguised Brothers tramped on past, steeling themselves against the scent of brown ale and roasting mutton. It was not a place where poor countryfolk, such as they were supposed to be, would be welcomed.

'There's another strange thing,' Felmar said, after a time.

'What?'

'While I was sleeping off and on in the ferry, I had the most unsettling dreams. About the things we took from the Royal Alchymist's crypt. Noises would wake me up, but when I slept again the same dream always returned. This happened three, maybe four times.'

Scarth stopped short with his mouth open in dismay. A single drop of rain hung at the tip of his long nose. 'You know what? I had strange dreams, too. I'd forgotten. I only remember bits and pieces, but I think I dreamt of Lord Kilian. Something about him frightened me, but I can't for the life of me think what.'

Felmar tugged his friend's arm. 'Keep walking . . . I dreamt that when we finally brought these moonstones and books to him, he laughed like a fiend and called us idiots for never suspecting how valuable the things are, for not realizing that we could have used them to become the most powerful sorcerers in the world!'

'I don't remember anything like that. But I think I do recall Lord Kilian laughing at me.'

'Think about it, Scarth. We agreed to risk our lives stealing this mysterious collection of arcana for him. He told us the sigils pre-dated Bazekoy's invasion, that they were ancient magical tools able to conjure the power of the Beaconfolk, and only Beynor of Moss could bring them to life. He said that Beynor had sworn an unbreakable oath, promising to share the activated stones with him and us. Kilian claimed he had a foolproof way to prevent Beynor from playing us false. But what if his talk of the Mossland conjurer was only a red herring, intended to distract us from the truth?'

'What truth?'

'It stands to reason that Kilian *didn't* know how to conjure these moonstones while he lived in Cala Palace and kept them hidden. But what if he's since learned how to do so, perhaps by studying some long-forgotten materials in the abbey? He's had access to the great library throughout his four-year confinement. What if the method for activating the sigils is contained in the two books that were in the cabinet with them? They're written in a strange language, you know.'

'Do you mean that Kilian might have been unable to read the books before – but now he can?'

Felmar shook his head uncertainly. 'My dream seemed to hint at something else. I can't remember what. All I'm really sure of is that we've both been deceived. I'm starting to suspect that if we give these things meekly over to Kilian, he won't bother sharing them with us. In fact, we may be lucky to escape with our lives!'

Scarth's heavy jaw hardened in growing anger. 'Brother, if I hadn't had my own dreams about Kilian, I'd deny your conclusion with my dying breath. He had me completely persuaded. But now . . . I think you may be right about the danger. I feel like a fool.'

'I was taken in, too,' Felmar muttered, 'as well as poor dead Vitubio. Even wearing the iron gammadion, Kilian Blackhorse is a consummate wizard. He converted Prior Waringlow, the greatest intellect in the abbey, to his cause. It's no wonder we were taken in.'

They walked in silence for some time. There were fewer people on the streets as the rain intensified and the air grew more chilly. The small shops, brothels and drinking establishments were thinning out as they neared the great wall at the northern end of the city, giving way to shuttered wool warehouses, empty and deserted at this time of year. When a sheltered alcove presented itself, Felmar discarded his artificial pregnancy, wrapping the arcana that had been concealed inside the basketry in his apron and tucking the bundle securely under his arm.

While the smaller man was rearranging his cloak, Scarth said, 'Have you any notion what we should do now? I'm damned if I'll simply keep heading for that cave in the gorge where Kilian's waiting.'

They began to walk again. Felmar said, 'I'm trying to think. We've got to get up into the mountains quickly, that's for certain. The masses of rock will help foil windsearchers – whoever they may be. North of the city, the road forks. To the left is the steep shepherd's path that we were supposed to follow to Roaring Gorge. To the right is a better track that leads eastward to Beorbrook Hold and the Great North Road. It winds through desolate moors and foothills, but avoids the most rugged part of the mountains.'

'You think we ought go that way?' Scarth was dubious.

'Only for a short distance, until we find a suitable place to go to ground. You and I must do some heavy thinking about our future.'

'Look there.' Scarth pointed ahead. 'It's the wall and the northern city gate. We're almost to Bo Hern's stable. I hope to God the goodwife's willing to feed us. All this scary talk's made me peckish.'

Felmar chuckled. 'If we're going to die tonight, let's hope we can at least do it with full stomachs.'

'You don't think we've much of a chance then?'

'I'm not so sure about that. You know, Scarth, we were so busy fleeing King Conrig's men that we never had a chance to look closely at the things we stole. I think it's high time we did, don't you?'

ELEVEN

The abrupt blast of powerful wind came out of nowhere, just as Kilian was congratulating himself on having successfully guided the cattleboat single-handedly to the mouth of Roaring Gorge. Earlier, the unsuspecting skipper had told him about the tricky route through the gravel-bars at the lakehead, and how important it was to stay in the middle of the channel.

In a light, fair breeze, Kilian had navigated well enough. But the sudden freakish blast turned the boat toward the shallows. The keel grated alarmingly on loose stones, and the five horses began to squeal with fright and pull against their ties.

He tried to correct the course with a quick thrust of the rudder and a tug on the lugsail brace, but he'd misjudged the potential contrariness of the clumsy boat in a strong wind. It yawed, charged toward the opposite side of the channel, struck a submerged rock, and slewed about wildly. The sail flapped like thunder, the deck tilted, and two of the horses were thrown down.

'Futterin' hell!' the alchymist cursed. The damned wind might capsize them unless –

He seized a small axe from a bracket on the side of the cockpit, clambered onto the angled deck, clawed his way toward the mast, and severed the halyard ropes. The lugsail, yard and rigging tumbled down, causing further panic among the horses, but at least the wind no long threatened to push them over and the deck came level again. Avoiding flying hoofs, he made his way to the bow and heaved out both anchors. One of the chains went taut and the boat swung about. With a piercing squawk, the hull came free of the rock and scraped along more gently into gravelly shoals before grounding in about three feet of water. As suddenly as it had risen, the gale fell off.

The horses calmed, and so did the alchymist. Amazingly, none of the animals had been injured by the falling yard. The ones that had lost their footing rose amidst the tangle of canvas and rope and stood trembling and blowing. Several pieces of baggage had tumbled from the cabin roof onto the deck, but the four Brothers sleeping up there appeared to be safe. With groans and a few muttered oaths, they threw off the pieces of tarred cloth that had sheltered them from the elements and stared wide-eyed at Kilian.

'Stop gawking,' he ordered. 'Pull yourselves together, get down here on deck, and give me a hand with this mess. We've arrived.'

'What happened?' Raldo mumbled in bewilderment. The impact had rolled him like a human ball, crushing him against the row of saddles.

'Why are we still so far out in the water?' Niavar wanted to know. 'I thought the skipper was going to bring the boat close to shore.'

'Where *is* the skipper?' Cleaton asked. 'And the rest of the crew?'

Young Garon surveyed the bleak panorama of encompassing cliffs, the whitewater of the Elk River rushing from the gorge mouth, the stony beach, and the weeping grey sky. He knew very well that their vessel had gone aground and

was unlikely to move again, and even entertained suspicions
about the missing boatmen. Shaking his head, he silently
started down the ladder. After a few minutes, the others
followed. Raldo came last, after pulling his jerkin closed and
buttoning it. He never noticed that the iron gammadion and
chain had fallen from his pocket and draped itself inconspicuously around one of the roof stanchions.

'I regret to tell you that our crew deserted us during the
night,' Kilian said.

Three of the Brothers reacted with astonishment. 'But why
would they do that?' Niavar asked.

Kilian said, 'Late yesterday, the captain attempted to back
out of our agreement to land in the vicinity of Roaring Gorge.
He claimed it was too hazardous and told me he intended to
put in at Elktor Quay instead. Its lights were visible in the
mist by then, over on the eastern shore. Naturally I told him
it was out of the question. He demanded a huge sum of money
to fulfill his part of the bargain. I realize now that he was all
but asking me to purchase his boat outright. When he
remained adamant, I finally agreed and turned over to him
almost all of the gold I received from Queen Cataldis. Then
I settled down in the cockpit with him to make certain that
he kept his promise. Unfortunately, I fell asleep. When I woke,
I discovered that the tiller was lashed and the captain and his
men were missing. They seem to have gone away in those
two coracles that were fastened on either side of the deckhouse. We were only a league or two away from land.'

Garon regarded the alchymist with frank incredulity. 'And
so you just carried on through the night, sailing the boat
slick as a whistle all by yourself?'

'No.' Kilian's patrician face was like granite. He stepped
close to the young Brother so that their eyes locked, and
forced him against the rail. 'I muddled through with considerable incompetence, if you must know. Even though I'd

done my best to learn how the boat was driven, I ultimately made a hash of matters and piled us up on a gravel bar. But we're alive, our horses have survived, the boat doesn't seem to be sinking, and all of our equipment is safe. We'll have to wade ashore, but at least we're on the proper side of the Elk River. Your sheep path should be somewhere up that steep slope to the right.'

He stepped back, to Garon's evident relief. 'Yes, I suppose it is. We'll find a way to it somehow. Maybe by backtracking down the shore.'

The alchymist nodded, satisfied that he was once again in control. 'I don't know the hour, but it can't be too late in the day. It looks like the rain will continue, so we may not reach the cave before owl-light. But let's give it our best try. Before we disembark, we'll feed the horses and ourselves. Raldo, will you please build a fire in the deckhouse stove?'

'Certainly, Lord Kilian,' said the fat man. In a half-daze, he shuffled into the cabin, wondering whether the horrifying events he had witnessed earlier might have been some sort of nightmare.

Then he saw rusty spots still staining the damp floor around the wood-rack.

He stood immobile, feeling the pulse pound in his temples, unable to breathe, unable to take his eyes from the telltale stains. They were more brownish than scarlet, and might have been caused by anything. Very probably the other Brothers would never even notice them. If he pointed them out, who would believe his explanation?

Repressing a shudder, he stacked a few bits of kindling in the stove's firebox, struck a light with his talent, and watched while the little flames reluctantly took hold.

Sir Gavlok Whitfell was a man of unusually sensitive temperament, and he was becoming deeply concerned about

Deveron Austrey. The party had just ridden out of the lake-side village of Badgerhead, about fifty leagues south of Elktor, where the road made a wide detour inland in order to avoid a great swamp. All of the members of the group were still tired, having eked out only four hours' sleep; but Deveron seemed hovering on the brink of collapse.

The second time that his friend nearly fell out of the saddle, Gavlok took hold of his bridle and slowed both horses, telling the others to ride on ahead. When they were beyond hearing, he said, 'Deveron, I know that something's very wrong with you. You're in much worse shape than the rest of us, for no reason that I can fathom. Have you taken sick? If so, we'll turn back and find you a bed in the last village –'

Snudge took a deep breath. He could no longer avoid the issue. If the two of them were to ride in close company for weeks, on a quest involving heavy use of his talent, Gavlok would have to be informed of the toll that even ordinary magic could take upon the human mind and body.

'All right, I'll confess. Vra-Mattis will have to know, too, I suppose. I was foolish to think I could keep it hidden.'

'For the love of God, man – what is it?' The young knight's lean features were drawn with anxiety.

Snudge spoke in a low, hurried monotone. 'The moonstone named Concealer isn't my only dangerous secret. I have another, known only to the High King, Lord Stergos, the earl marshal, and a handful of other people. I'm a wild talent, Gavlok. A secret magicker. This is what makes me so valuable to King Conrig as an intelligencer. My faculties are strong, and they're also largely imperceptible to other adepts such as the Zeth Brethren. This is why they never found me out and forced me to join their Order. I can perform any number of useful tricks, but the most important are super-sensitive windspeech and the ability to scry intently over extreme distances. Also, I myself am immune from being scried by other adepts. Only Ullanoth's Subtle Loophole sigil can oversee me.'

Overwhelmed, Gavlok rode in silence, staring at the pommel of his saddle.

Snudge continued. 'The reason I'm so bloody beat is that I've been cudgeling my brains windsearching for Brothers Felmar and Scarth since we left Pikeport. When I'm not scrying about for them, I have a go at Kilian Blackhorse and his henchmen, who escaped from Zeth Abbey and are likely on their way to a meeting with the two thieves. So far, I haven't been able to spot any of them. Finding these men is the most important thing King Conrig has ever asked of me – although he may not realize what a great threat they are to him.'

'But why should this be? Kilian is a vile traitor, and the fire-raisers are guilty of murder and mayhem. But how are they a danger to the High King?'

'When I told you that more moonstone sigils taking magical power from the Beaconfolk exist, I wasn't referring to the ones owned by Ullanoth or Beynor or the Salka monsters. There's another collection of sigils – over a hundred of the damned things, all of them inactive. They were hidden in Cala Palace, and the thieves stole them under cover of the fire. I must try to get them back before they're handed over to Kilian. King Conrig wants the moonstones returned to him, but I intend to do my best to destroy them. No man living should own such terrible weapons – even if they're inactive.'

'It's strange that I've never heard of them before,' Gavlok said. 'When I was Lord Stergos's armiger, I often delved into his books of sorcery. But there was no mention of moonstone sigils and their link to the Beaconfolk.'

'Even most of the Zeth Brethren know nothing of them. The stones were found centuries ago by an early Royal

Alchymist of Cathra named Darasilo. He secretly passed them on to his successor, and so they were handed down for centuries until they came to Kilian. None of the alchymists before him tried to bring the sigils to life – maybe because they were too afraid of the Beaconfolk. Kilian had other ideas. The trove also includes some ancient books written in the Salkan language that probably describe how to activate the sigils. No modern-day Cathran is able to read those books – but the Royal Family of Moss can.'

'Beynor,' Gavlok said in a flat voice.

Snudge inclined his head in weary assent. 'It's obvious that he and Kilian made a devil's pact to share the stones and the knowledge. They bided their time after the alchymist was convicted of treason. Then Kilian sent his agents to steal the trove from its hiding place. What I'm not sure of is whether or not he might have learned the Salkan language while imprisoned in the abbey. There are thousands of old tomes in that place, some dating nearly to the time of Bazekoy.'

'God's Toenails! Then Kilian might not need Beynor –'

'I don't know where that Mossbelly whoreson is or what he's up to.' Snudge gave a great yawn and rubbed his reddened eyes. 'He was supposed to have been cursed by the Great Lights and exiled to the Dawntide Isles, forced to live with the Salka. This is where Ullanoth thinks he still abides . . . By the way, she apparently knows nothing of Darasilo's Trove. Conrig kept its existence secret from her. He was afraid she'd come after it herself. Ordinarily, moonstones can't be scried. But Ulla's Loophole sigil . . . can oversee them if given a direct command to do so . . . We don't . . . think that's happened . . . yet.'

As he spoke, Snudge's eyes slowly closed and his head drooped lower and lower onto his breast. He caught himself with a start and an oath. 'Gavlok – can you lash me to the saddle again, as you did on Solstice Eve when I was dead drunk? If you lead my horse I can sleep until we reach Elktor. Maybe . . . be of some damned use when we get close to the mountains and start the *real* search.'

'Of course. Pull up and I'll see to it. If the armigers ask, I'll say you have a slight fever.'

'Good. Tell Vra-Mattis all of this . . . *Don't* tell squires, 'specially Wil Baysdale.'

'What about young Wil?'

But Snudge only whispered, 'Don't trust him.'

Gavlok had climbed down from his horse and was removing the long belt that symbolized his knighthood. After detaching his sword, dagger, and purse, he used the stout strap to tie his friend firmly to the saddle. Even before he finished, Deveron Austrey was lost in oblivion.

Using his own limited-range windsight, Garon finally found the shepherd's path – but only after a tedious search. It was much higher above the river than he remembered, nearly two hundred ells. Getting to it from the lakeside, up a treacherous talus slope in pouring rain, was a daunting ordeal. The horses had to be led, and their hooves dislodged loose stones at almost every step. More than once, an animal faltered and crashed to its knees, barely avoiding a fatal fall back down the trackless incline. Kilian and the Brothers were forced to zigzag back and forth to ease the steep angle of the gradient, more than doubling the distance traveled. And all this before they made a single step in the direction of the cave . . .

On Garon's instructions, each of them – even the alchymist – used his recovering talent to calm the increasingly agitated minds of the horses. By the time they attained their goal, an exiguous ledge along a cliff-face, Raldo was sobbing with fatigue and urging his animal to pull him up. Mercifully, the horse obeyed. The two of them were the last to arrive at the path.

The fugitives sat hunched under their capes without moving for some time, regaining their strength, while their mounts licked trickles of rainwater from the streaming rock wall.

Saying nothing to his companions, Kilian experimented with his formidable new spell of couverture. If he could summon the strength to erect it, it would shield them all. But he was not yet fully recovered and had no success. For the time being, he contented himself with an easier kind of magic that altered his overseen appearance, while his aspect remained unchanged in the eyes of his companions.

Finally, he gave the command to mount and move on, watching in silence as the sweating, crimson-faced fat man, too drained to climb into the saddle on his own, was boosted up by the others. They set off in single file, moving at a slow walk. The track was extremely narrow, with a sheer drop to the river on the left. It climbed higher and higher, but the horses seemed willing to negotiate it without complaint. For over three hours, they traveled without incident. Then they became aware of a deep rumbling sound, which grew louder as they continued on, rising eventually to a tumultuous roar.

'Waterfall,' Garon shouted in explanation.

The source of the noise remained unseen until they came around a sharp corner into an area where the path widened, forming a natural terrace at the opening of a deep vertical cleft carved by a tributary stream. The upper section of the waterfall was deep within this cleft, pouring down from a height hidden within low-hanging grey clouds. Billows of vapor surged around the foot of the falls, where a plunge-pool had been gouged from a relatively flat rock shelf that was a continuation of the terrace where they had halted. This was littered with jagged chunks of stone fallen from above, some of them as large as cottages. Water flowed from the pool across the shelf in a wide, shallow stream until it reached the edge, where it dropped off in a second cascade to the floor of the gorge.

Beyond the submerged rock shelf, the path resumed.

'Merciful God,' Raldo exclaimed. 'How can we possibly get past here?'

Garon gave him a superior smile. 'Now you know why I brought rope from the cattleboat.'

'It looks hopeless to me,' Niavar said. His face had gone white and his vagrant eye had nearly retreated behind his nose. 'The passable section near the lip of the lower cascade is only a few feet wide, and it's at least a dozen ells long.'

'It can be crossed,' Garon insisted. 'I've herded sheep across here – although I must admit I never tried it when the water volume was so great. There must have been heavy snows last winter.'

'Explain what we must do,' Kilian said.

'We blindfold the horses and go one at a time. I'll be first, carrying the rope and paying it out behind me. When I get to the other side, I'll fasten the line to that knobby formation under the overhang. One of you will tie the other end here, to this rock, after pulling it tight. As you ride over the shelf, guide your mount only with your knees. Keep one hand on the reins and the other on the rope. If your beast stumbles and starts to go over the edge, let him fall and hang onto the rope.'

'Bazekoy's Blazing Bunions!' Cleaton groaned. 'I'll need a blindfold myself to get across.'

The alchymist was calm. 'Why don't I go next? When I reach the other side, I'll use all my talent to compel your horses to set their feet safely among the stones and running water.'

They tied rags over the eyes of the mounts. Garon handed Kilian the rope coil, took the free end, and rode his raw-boned, powerful chestnut across the streaming shelf as though it

were Cala High Street. When both ends of the rope were
fixed in place, Kilian followed suit on his tall sorrel mare,
moving much more slowly. He, too, reached the other side
with apparent ease.

'I'll go next,' Raldo declared, striving to keep a tremor out
of his voice. 'I can't bear the suspense of waiting.'

The fat man's huge bay gelding lost its footing after going
only a few ells and gave a heart-stopping lurch; but it recovered its equilibrium and went on successfully to the other
side, whereupon Raldo burst into tears of relief.

Cleaton set out with lips clamped tight and his eyes
narrowed to slits. In the middle of the shelf, his rather nervous
red roan suddenly stopped dead and refused to move. He
thumped its sides with his heels, uttered lurid curses, and
exerted all of his talent. The animal resumed its hesitant pace
and joined the other three on the opposite side. The men
there had dismounted, leaving blindfolds on the horses, and
stood in the partial shelter of the overhanging cliff.

'Last but not least! I'll be right along, boys!' Niavar called,
urging his mount into the shank-deep water. The small black
cob squealed at the unexpected sharp cold and tossed its
head violently. The knot of the blindfold slipped and an
instant later the cloth fell away. Stricken with terror at the
sight of the dropoff and the pressure of the flowing stream
against its short legs, the beast shied. One of its forefeet came
down atop a precariously balanced rock and it collapsed, legs
flailing. There was a sickening crack as a bone snapped. The
cob screamed, rolled to the lip of the shelf, and fell to its
death in the misty depths of the gorge.

Kneeling in rushing water up to his crotch, wiry little
Niavar clung to the sagging rope with both hands. He was
unable to stand, so he used his arms to haul himself the
remaining three ells across. The others grabbed hold of him
and pulled him safely up.

'Am I going to have to walk to the bloody cave, then?' he grumbled.

'You can ride pillion with me,' Garon said. 'My chestnut is strong and neither of us is heavy.'

The Brothers took Niavar close to the cliff and began to strip off his soaked clothes. Kilian opened one of his saddle-bags and took out a long shirt, wool stockings, and spare boots; Garon contributed homespun trews that fit well enough when rolled up seven inches and cinched with a piece of rope; Cleaton found a short waxed-leather cape with a hood.

As he dressed, Niavar thanked them all.

Raldo said sheepishly, 'I'm sorry I didn't have anything that would fit.'

'Just be thankful it wasn't *your* horse that fell,' Kilian said to him.

They resumed their journey, with the fat man bringing up the rear and mumbling prayers under his breath, trying vainly to forget the frightful image that Kilian's words had evoked, and the pitiless tone of the voice that had spoken them.

Beynor's voyage up the Malle was not as carefree as he'd hoped, but at least the Salka swimming around him remained unnoticed, and no one in authority challenged him as they passed the teeming wharves and docks of Holt Mallburn. The strong seabreeze that blew during the hours of hot sunlight kept his dinghy's sail well-filled throughout the first day on the river. Assisted by his unseen Eminent hauler, he forged nimbly upstream past less fortunate boats and reached Twicken by the time the sun dipped low and the breeze slackened off.

'There are food-stalls and small shops on the waterfront of this town,' he bespoke Ugusawnn. 'I'm going to put in, tie up, and buy something to eat. Don't worry, I won't try to leave the boat. Just see that you stay out of sight.'

The only response was a surly growl on the wind.

He lowered the sail and rowed to the public landing-stage, where he tied up, paid the toll, and then began restowing the various bundles in the boat. After a few minutes a stout, pink-cheeked matron in a clean gown came along, carrying a wide basket covered with a cloth. She stopped at each vessel with people aboard, offering cold meat pies, but sold only a few.

'A fine evening, goodwife,' Beynor said, when his turn came. He proffered a silver quarter-mark coin. 'I'll gladly take two of your pies.'

'I don't have the change for this,' she admitted. 'Business has been slow this evening. The big crowd came to the river-side this morn to see off the royal barge – but I couldn't get my baking done in time for selling to them. My old dad came over poorly, and I've had to nurse him most of the day. If you care to trust me, I'll step over to yonder inn and get the change there.'

'You look like an honest woman,' Beynor said. Her easy friendliness might have its uses. He gave a winning smile and opened his purse. 'I'm very sorry for your hard luck. I've had a bit of that myself today, out on the water. Gave my ankle a bad knock, and now I can barely walk. I don't want to go tramping about ashore if I can help it, but I've not much food left in the boat, and no drink at all. If I gave you more money, could you also fetch me some some loaves of good wheat bread from the inn, and maybe some butter and jam, and some boiled eggs in their shells if the kitchen has such things? And ask the potboy to roll over a firkin of ale for me. I'll gladly pay you for your trouble.'

'Oh, you poor lad! Of course I will. Just guard my pies whilst I'm gone. Is there anything else you're needing?'

'Fresh strawberries?' Beynor ventured, 'I live on a island

far up the coast, and earn a good living from sealing. But I haven't had such luscious things for four years, since last I came to visit my people up in Mallthorpe Greenwater.'

'If anyone on the Twicken waterfront has any, I'll bring them to you,' the woman said. 'Imagine! Four whole years without strawberries!'

'I'd also be most grateful if you could send my way any old-clothes vendor who might be out and about this evening. As you can see, my garb is unsuitable for the warm weather you enjoy here, although it served me well in the chill at sea. I'd buy more comfortable things if I could.'

The women was thinking. 'You're a tall, thin one, just like my old father. And he, poor soul, spends much of his time abed these days and has small need of street clothes. After I see to your provisions, I'll slip away home and look in his coffer. There might be something you can use.'

'I'll pay whatever you think is fair,' Beynor said. He gave her another quarter-mark and she bustled off.

After a minute or two, Ugusawnn spoke truculently on the wind.

What did you say to her, groundling?

'I only asked her to fetch more food and some clothes for me. She had some interesting news to report. The royal barge left here this morning. It'll be upriver at Tallhedge by now, and tomorrow it goes to Mallthorpe Castle and stays for two days before going on to Boarsden. We'll have to get ahead of it to set up the ambush. The distance from here to the Big Bend is nearly ninety leagues. You may have to do some night hauling to get us there in time.'

I will do what is necessary.

'Good. You and your warriors can give the barge a good look-see while it's tied up at Mallthorpe, so you'll be clear about what I expect you to do later.'

Ugusawnn gave an ill-tempered grumble.

'The matter has to be handled just right. You must follow my orders exactly, or –'

Or WHAT, you insolent heap of whale-puke?!

'Eminence, I'm not trying to insult your intelligence, or that of your warriors. I'm only anxious that we succeed. Be easy in your mind! When the present King of Didion and his family are dead, we'll have taken the first step in destroying Conrig Wincantor's Sovereignty – and giving the Salka back their ancestral home.'

So you've said . . .

'Believe it,' Beynor assured him, with all the coercive power his great talent could summon. 'Believe it!'

Snudge and his men reached the south gate of Elktor at about the tenth hour after noon. It had been locked for the night an hour earlier; but Vra-Mattis had previously bespoken the Brothers resident at the castle warning of their coming, so they were admitted with alacrity. They paused in the shelter of the guardhouse, and Snudge showed the royal writ to the sergeant of the guard. By then the rain was coming down steadily, but the intelligencer had managed to sleep in the saddle in spite of it and felt much refreshed.

'Sir Deveron,' said the sergeant, handing back the parchment with a salute, 'one of my men will lead you to the castle if this is your wish. Count Olvan is in residence. He'll be eager to tell you of the search for the fire-raisers being conducted in this region, as well as offering his hospitality.'

Snudge thanked him. 'We'll tarry here a moment while my windvoice announces our arrival, then welcome an escort.'

While the novice attended to this, Snudge beckoned the other riders to come close to him. 'If it's true, as I believe, that the fugitives have gone into the mountains at some point above this city, then they must necessarily travel much slower than heretofore. Mat and I will confer with the

Brethren at the castle and make contact with Zeth Abbey as well. We'll ask that all windsearching now be concentrated in the area of Roaring Gorge.'

'Will we go after the villains at once if they're overseen, sir?' asked the armiger Valdos.

'All of you are in need of sleep,' Snudge said. 'We'll likely wait until morning. Vra-Mattis and I will confer with the resident wind adepts to see if there are new developments. But it's likely the fugitives have also stopped to rest – especially if they're mounted. We'll ride out with a force of Lord Olvan's rangers tomorrow.'

Vra-Mattis pushed the hood of his cloak back from his face and announced, 'They're awaiting us at the castle.'

One of the guards joined them, having fetched a horse. 'Mortal steep road up the castle knoll,' he said with a grin. 'Those poor beasts of yours look about done in, so I'll take it nice and easy.'

He set off. Snudge motioned for Mat and the armigers to follow, while he and Gavlok brought up the rear.

'Do you really think someone will be able to scry out our quarry?' the lanky knight murmured doubtfully. 'Surely these local magickers have already combed the area to the best of their ability.'

'My hope is that I myself might catch an oversight of the thieves from the high vantage point of the castle, now that I've recovered my strength somewhat. We can always pretend that Mattis found them, and he can direct the searchers with my prompting.'

'Ah.' Gavlok smiled. 'The lad nearly popped the eyeballs from his skull when I revealed your wild talents to him earlier. He was very impressed with my tales of your prowess – defeating Iscannon, taking Redfern Castle, and opening the Mallmouth Bridge. I had to caution him not to make his hero-worship of you too obvious.'

Snudge gave a brief bark of mirthless laughter. 'Me, a
hero? I think Vra-Mattis – and the High King – will find
another name to call me if I have no luck finding those two
wretches and the stolen trove!'

TWELVE

Riding on muleback, Felmar and Scarth traveled eastward for about nine leagues along the Beorbrook track from Elktor. They were still without a firm plan of action, and tonight their only wish was to get as far away from Kilian as possible. The rain increased to a near-blinding downpour. Soon it became obvious that they could go no further. Even the sure-footed mules were starting to balk as they sank into deepening mud.

Dropping the cover-spell briefly, both Brothers cast about with their talent for a likely place to take shelter. They had purchased a piece of stout canvas that could be used as a tent in a pinch; but the deserted croft, when they scried it, was a much more attractive option, even though it looked more like an animal lair than human habitation. The hut was situated in a sheltered moorland hollow where stunted junipers grew, backed and hemmed about by outcroppings of bedrock. It was well out of sight of the track and looked reasonably secure from windwatchers as well. A rill of clear water ran nearby and there was even a patch of rain-flattened grass for the mules.

The entrance was an inverted V formed by two slabs of

rotting wood. There were no windows and the interior was dark. Felmar struck a flame at the tip of his finger with his talent and peered inside, alert for wildlife, but the place was empty except for some ancient sheep droppings. The field-stone walls and the turf roof were still sound and the dirt floor almost dry, except in the corner where a smokehole above a simple hearth let rain drip in.

'This is as good as we'll find tonight,' Felmar decided. 'Let's hobble the mules and get our things inside.'

A little later, after Scarth had chopped up dead branches from the small trees with his woodsman's axe and got a fire going, they were reasonably comfortable. The canvas covered most of the dirt floor, and saddles and pads made acceptable beds. Felmar was finally able to remove his hated female disguise. The two of them shared some of the harsh brandywine that Bo Hern's goodwife had sold them at exorbitant cost, and ate some of her excellent honey-raisin oatcakes.

Then they decided it was time to examine the Trove of Darasilo.

For the next two hours, they pored over the books and the two bags of moonstones they had taken from the crypt in Cala Palace. The fragile volumes contained pictures of countless sigils, along with blocks of indecipherable text. The trove included one hundred and twelve milky translucent carvings of varying shapes, most rather small and some duplicates. Many stones were strung on golden chains or decaying leather cords, and all of them were minutely incised with arcane symbols or exquisite tiny pictures that gave tantalizing hints of their function.

'This book shows fewer stones,' Felmar noted as he turned crumbling pages, 'but the illustrations are larger and more elaborate than those in the other one, and the descriptions are much longer. I suspect that my book describes the more-important sigils. Let's see how many of those we can find in the collection.'

To their vast disappointment, only four of the carvings matched the criterion: a moonstone finger-ring; an oblong sigil that looked just like a tiny door, complete with simulated latch; a thing about the size of a man's little finger that was shaped like a carrot or an icicle; and a short rod or wand with a drilled perforation at one end, incised with the phases of the moon.

'Well,' Felmar said with an ironic smile, 'at least there are two for you and two for me. Shall we draw straws for first pick?'

Scarth gave him a startled look. 'Are you suggesting that we somehow keep back these – these *important* sigils for ourselves?'

Felmar set the stones aside, put more wood on the fire, and sighed. 'I'm only joking.'

He unsheathed his knife, picked up a stick, and began to trim off splinters. 'Here's something we have to consider, Brother. Lord Kilian promised to bespeak us when he was well into the mountains and there was only a small chance of the thread of his windspeech being traced back to him. Very soon – perhaps tomorrow or the next day – we're bound to hear his call. If his talent has sufficiently recovered from the strictures of the iron gammadion, I wouldn't be surprised if he tried to scry us as well.'

'We won't answer him! And if we keep the cover-spell in place, he won't be able to find us.'

Felmar gave an exasperated grunt. 'Kilian devised the spell of couverture we're using. You can be sure he knows how to puncture it – or even turn it off completely. We can only hope that his powers remain weak for a while longer, giving us a chance to put more distance between us. The mountains will help block his windsight if he does obliterate the cover-spell.'

'But eventually, he'll be able to find us, Fel! And if he thinks we're running away from him with the trove, he'll come after us and kill us.'

'True. That's why we can't simply ignore his call on the wind. When it does come, we must answer him, so his suspicions aren't immediately aroused. But what we ought to say . . . as yet, I don't know.'

'What would he do,' Scarth said carefully, 'if we didn't take the trove with us when we fled? What if we hid it in some safe place and told him where to find it?'

Felmar paused in his whittling. His eyes glittered in the firelight. 'Brother, you may have hit on the solution! He'd certainly be furious at us for abandoning the trove – but not to the point of chasing us down. He's a fugitive, too, and his life depends upon getting over the border into Didion as fast as possible.'

'He'd know he could retrieve the things sooner or later,' Scarth said. 'He could even scry them in their hiding place and know we were telling the truth.'

'Yes. Good point! If we spin a plausible yarn, I think Kilian would be satisfied to let us go our own way. When he bespeaks us, why don't we say that we were unable to follow the path to Roaring Gorge. We only escaped a search-party by the skin of our teeth. They're hot on our heels and we don't want the trove to fall into their hands. Our only chance now is to travel cross-country – north into the trackless mountains.'

'That's no lie, either.' Scarth's long face was somber. 'The story sounds good to me. We could leave the trove right here – maybe hide it up in the roof of this hovel.'

Felmar resheathed his knife. He had made four tiny wooden sticks of differing lengths. 'Ready for the magical moonstone drawing?'

Scarth frowned. 'I thought you were just fooling.'

'Come on! Just for the fun of it.' Felmar put his hands behind his back, fumbled, then held out a fist with the stick-ends peeping out. 'Take any two. Longest chooses his important sigil first, then we take turns, on down to the shortest. Each man says what his sigils are capable of. Then we decide who's the greater sorcerer.'

'Oh, hell. Why not?'

Scarth won the first and third choices. He picked the ring and the icicle. Felmar got the miniature doorway and the wand.

'A pity we *can't* take these with us,' Scarth mused. 'I suspect this ring might be a Weathermaker, like the one Conjure-Queen Ullanoth owns. And maybe the moonstone icicle can freeze a person in his tracks! Can you better that?'

Felmar rubbed his fingers over his own treasures. 'This thing of mine looks like a door. It must *be* a door! Conjure it and it opens into a better world – one full of sunlight and good food and friendly, carefree folk who don't have to work for a living.'

'Take me with you when you step through,' Scarth said wistfully, 'and I'll concede you the sorcery contest hands down . . . What do you think that other thing of yours does?'

But Felmar was tiring of the game. 'Who cares? Probably nothing that would be of any help to us. We'd better turn in so we can make an early start tomorrow. Help me get these regular sigils back into their sacks. Let's wrap the four important ones in the linen hood from my goodwife disguise before we tuck them in with the others.'

'You're still thinking about keeping them when we run?'

Felmar shrugged. 'Only thinking. We could probably sell them for a pretty penny to a magicker up in Didion – or better yet, in Moss. Would Kilian even know they were missing when he scried the two bags of sigils? Seems to me it'd be nigh impossible to count the things, all bunched together like that. And he might not be able to fetch them for years.'

They discussed this interesting topic at some length, passing the brandy flask back and forth, speculating on what the four stones might be worth. Why, they might even offer them to the Conjure-Queen herself! She'd know their true value.

'She c'd perteck us from Kilian's revenge, too.' Scarth gave a tipsy giggle. 'Maybe help us join the Glaum'rie Guild! I w-wouldn't mind takin' a job at the Mossback court.'

'Better'n holin' up in the Diddly morass f'rest of our lives.'

Neither of the Brothers had tasted hard liquor since entering the Order, where it was forbidden because of its deleterious effect on talent. But when Bo Hern's wife offered plum brandy in addition to the other provisions, they'd hesitated only a moment. Hard times lay ahead of them. Ardent spirits were medicinal. They banished aches and pains and helped a man sleep when his mind was plagued by fear and worry.

Scarth and Felmar hadn't planned to empty the flask that first night, but somehow it happened anyway. With all their troubles forgotten, they settled into inebriated slumber.

At first, Felmar's dream was much as it had been before. He was a young boy again, no more than ten or eleven years old, sitting under a flowering apple tree in the garden of the family manor house. His kindly grandsire was there beside him, warning him to beware of great danger from the wicked Kilian Blackhorse.

Now Felmar was able to tell Grandad about the newly hatched plan to outwit the alchymist. He described it eagerly, in much detail. But the old man shook his head in disagreement.

No, my lad. There's a much easier way to get the better of Kilian. One of those moonstones you stole can provide a foolproof means of escape for both you and Scarth. I can show you how. You very nearly guessed the secret when you were playing your game.

'What do you mean?'

The sigil resembling a tiny carved door is called Subtle Gateway. It won't take you to paradise, but it can transport you and your friend anywhere in the world in the blink of an eye.

'But the stone is inactive, Grandad! I can't read the conjuring instructions.'

That's not necessary, Felmar. There's a simpler method of bringing sigils to life. Of course, only a very brave man can make use of it! But you're no coward. I'm confident you can do it. Darasilo, the silly fool who first found the stones, never knew anything about this. Neither did his successors – including Kilian Blackhorse. All one need do to activate the sigil is hold it firmly, then touch it to one of the moonstone medallions affixed to the book covers.

'That's . . . all?'

If this is done, the supernatural Guardian of the Moonstones will pronounce a strange phrase three times. A great sense of fear will come over you. There'll be a good deal of pain, too. But if you keep up your courage until the phrase is said for the fourth time, the sigil will come to magical life, glowing with a green inner light. Hang it about your neck. Then all you need do is take hold of your friend's hand – or anything else you want to transport along with you – and speak your destination in a loud voice. Instantly, you'll be there!

'It seems too wonderful to be true.'

Try it! What have you got to lose?

'What about the other stones in the trove? Can they all be activated in the same way?'

Of course.

'I could . . . take all of them for myself?'

If you wanted to.

'Thank you for telling me, Grandad.'

Felmar forced his eyes open and struggled into a sitting position with his back against the saddle. His head spun from the brandy he'd consumed, even though Scarth had taken

the lion's share. The dim interior of the croft seemed to ripple
like a disturbed reflection in water. He smelled acrid woodsmoke and wet leather, heard the other man's slow snores
and the rustle of gentle rain. The fire was still burning wanly.

The dream.

Could it be true?

He pushed aside the blanket covering him and crawled to
where the bags of sigils and the books lay. Through bleared
eyes he saw milky mineral disks in narrow gold frames
fastened to each cover. Mere ornaments, surely.

Or were they?

Try it, a remembered voice inside his head seemed to urge.
What do you have to lose?

He emptied both bags of moonstones onto the canvas that
covered the floor, pawing and scattering the sigils in a frenzy
of impatience until he found the tight wad of cloth that held
the four important ones. He shook it open, dumped the
stones, and selected – what had Grandad called the thing?
– Subtle Gateway! The magical door leading to safety and to
power. More power than he'd ever imagined.

Felmar grasped the little oblong carving and pressed it
against a book disk, then gave a low cry of astonishment.

Both the sigil and the medallion began to shine with a
gentle greenish light. He thought he saw a movement within
the croft out of the corner of his eye, but before he could
turn to look at it a deep voice that had nothing human about
it spoke a question inside his head.

CADAY AN RUDAY?

Terror, deeper and more paralyzing than he'd ever known
before, seized him like some ravening beast. There was pain
as well, as though an ice-cold lance were being driven into
his breast.

CADAY AN RUDAY?!

The awful voice was bespeaking him on the wind, more

loudly this time and with angry impatience. The Guardian of the Moonstones, Grandad had said. The swelling pain was atrocious. His ribs were being torn apart and his heart crushed by frigid pincers. If he let go of the sigil, let it fall away from his flesh, the suffering would end. But then he would lose all chance of bringing the Gateway sigil to life –

CADAY AN RUDAY?!!!

He was deafened by the monstrous voice, blinded by hurt, shrieking voicelessly into the wind as the nerves of his body burned in icy flames. But he was brave. He would persevere, hold fast until the fourth time that the Guardian asked his question. He would remain courageous until the end.

The end came, engulfing him in an agony of silent Light.

Beynor withdrew his bedazzled windsight, shaken to the core in spite of himself, and lay trembling in the bottom of the dinghy.

He rested for a long time, then sent his sight soaring once again to the interior of the faraway hut. Felmar Nightcott was gone, his flesh, blood, and bone reduced to a heap of gritty cinders. Although Beynor was unable to scry them, he presumed that the ancient books and the sigils were unharmed. From the conversation of the thieves, he had managed to identify three of the four Great Stones in the trove. The fourth was still a tantalizing enigma.

Perhaps when he entered the dream of the second man, he could coerce him into describing it.

But Beynor discovered very quickly that Scarth Saltbeck lay in a drunken stupor so profound that his mind was inaccessible to any invader. The jug-bitten wretch was incapable of dreaming! His natural talent was also totally incapacitated, and the protective spell of couverture had dissolved even before he and his companion had fallen asleep.

Beynor gave up trying to penetrate Scarth's sodden brain

after numerous failed attempts. His own head ached abom-
inably from the effort and he cursed his bad luck. There was
no helping it: he'd have to wait until later, when the liquor's
poisonous effects had worn off a little. Meanwhile, he'd keep
windwatch on the surviving thief as best he could, hoping
no one else would scry out the unshielded lummox and come
after him.

He relaxed on the pallet he'd made up in the bottom of
the boat and stared up at the crimson night sky. With sail
furled, oars stowed aboard, and no one at the tiller, the
dinghy glided arrow-straight up the wide River Malle. Only
a handful of people near the docks at Tallhedge noticed its
uncanny passing, and they turned away from the sight in
superstitious fear and told no one.

On Snudge's orders, the guards at Elktor's Mountain Gate
had been questioned about strangers leaving the city late in
the day. The officer who had been on duty clearly recalled
a quarreling married couple mounted on mules – the man
tall and robust, the wife petite and bristly about the chin.
They had passed through shortly before the gate was locked
for the night, even though the guards had urged them to
wait until morning.

Heartened by this first solid evidence that the fugitives were
in the area, Snudge told Count Olvan Elktor that he would
use a map to guide his windvoice, Vra-Mattis, in a fresh search.
The two of them ascended to the top of the castle's lofty north
tower, and from that vantage point Snudge himself had
labored for over three hours, nearly exhausting his limited
store of energy in a futile scan of the land route to Roaring
Gorge. Meanwhile, Mattis dozed peacefully at his master's
feet, wrapped in a frieze cloak against the persistent drizzle.

To Snudge, the shepherd's path leading to Roaring Gorge
had seemed the most logical way for the thieves to go. But

the precipitous rock formations in the area proved a near-insurmountable barrier to his talent. The only living things he scried among the misty crags and ridges were animals.

Finding the boat was an unexpected piece of luck.

He had all but decided not to extend his search all the way to the gorge mouth, since it lay twelve leagues from Elktor, and there had hardly been time for the thieves to travel so far on such a difficult path. But wishing to complete the job he'd begun, he continued scrying the portions of the path most readily visible to his mind's eye, and at length came to the broad stony beach at the outflow of the river. The abandoned livestock boat out in the shallows caught his attention almost at once, and his heart leapt with hope. The presence of horse droppings on the deck at least made it feasible that the vessel had transported Kilian and his party.

Intent on finding something to confirm his judgment, he focused more closely on the craft, even exerting himself to scry through the wooden bulkheads. He saw an empty wine bottle fallen into the scuppers. Its label revealed that it had held a fine Stippenese vintage – a beverage far too dear for the purses of lowly watermen.

A promising sign, but it wasn't proof positive.

He inspected the cockpit, the deck where the horses had been penned, and the interior of the little cabin, finding nothing of interest. A ladder had been positioned so that the roof of the deckhouse could be accessed, and something seemed to be caught on one of the rail stanchions up there, dangling down the opposite side. Again he strained to scry through the wood, and realized he was looking at an iron gammadion on its chain . . .

Snudge withdrew his sight and slumped down onto the parapet, drained by his efforts. Mattis was still asleep. The efficient castle steward had provided them with a covered basket containing a stoppered flask of spiced cider, bread rolls, and smoked goat-cheese. Snudge drank from the bottle and forced himself to chew several mouthfuls of bread. After a few minutes he felt himself recovering from the ordeal.

He now had a solid clue to the whereabouts of Kilian; but if the alchymist and his companions had gone into Roaring Gorge, there was probably no chance he'd be able to oversee them from here. They would have to be hunted by a ground party – and most probably not one including him and his people, unless King Conrig himself gave the order.

He reached out a hand to awaken Vra-Mattis and have him bespeak Cala Palace, then hesitated. A wild notion had popped into his mind. Rising to his feet, he walked across the flat roof of the tower to the opposite side. On his left soared the dark rampart of the Sinistral Range. Rolling moorlands lay at the foot of the mountains and extended eastward, interspersed with isolated masses of upthrust rock similar to the tor on which the castle stood. There was a track down there that wound over the heath toward Beorbrook Hold.

What if the thieves had gone that way? What if something had prevented them from taking the fork in the track that led to the gorge, giving them no choice but to turn in the other direction?

Shutting his eyes and summoning his last reserve of talent, he focused his windsight once again.

Conrig Wincantor brought his fist down with a bang on the table of the Council Chamber, causing Vra-Sulkorig, who was seated on his right, to blink in unspoken disapproval. The other chairs were empty and the table was littered with abandoned sheets of parchment, rolled charts, waxed tablets, and styluses. The candles in their gilt stands burned low.

'What do I care if he's busy helping Vra-Mattis windsearch?' the king bellowed. 'He can take a few minutes off to talk to his liege lord! He should have given me a progress report yesterday. We wouldn't even know that he'd reached Elktor if Ollie's windvoice hadn't had the sense to notify you.'

'Let me bespeak Vra-Alamor again, Your Grace. I'll insist that he interrupt Sir Deveron.' The Keeper of Arcana drew his hood over his face and bowed his head.

Conrig sat back in his chair, fuming. It was well after midnight and he'd dismissed all the Privy Council members except Sulkorig, who was serving as deputy to Stergos, after a long but none too productive conference about the situation in Tarn. The king had felt it necessary to inform his advisors about Maudrayne's possible survival after another windspoken message was relayed to the palace from the outlaw shaman, Blind Bozuk – this time through a different, and presumably less expensive, intermediary.

Bozuk claimed to know where Ansel was taking the princess. He was willing to part with the information in exchange for five thousand gold marks, which the shrewd magicker demanded be kept in escrow for him until Maudrayne's capture. The Sovereignty's Ambassador to Tarn, Lord Grendos Wedmorril, had no such enormous sum at his disposal. It would have to be borrowed – either from bankers in Donorvale, who would demand punitive interest, or from the Tarnian Lord Treasurer, who would hem and haw and perhaps even insist on tax concessions. News of the extraordinary transaction was bound to spread quickly to Cathra via the financial grapevine, and the Lords of the Southern Shore would ask embarrassing public questions of the Crown.

Conrig had put the matter up to his Council: should he respond to Bozuk's offer and obtain the money, or put the shaman off – at least for the time being – until the Royal Intelligencer was on the scene and in possession of all the facts?

The Council had waffled. In the end, Conrig decided to wait. But he was not willing to wait for a report from Snudge.

How dare the intelligencer remain incommunicado? He was
supposed to report to the palace every evening, even if there
were no new developments –

Sulkorig straightened and pushed back his hood. 'Your
Grace, I've bespoken Vra-Mattis. He says that Sir Deveron
has scried out the hiding place of one of the fire-raising
thieves, Scarth Saltbeck. He has also located an abandoned
boat at the head of Elk Lake, which was very likely used in
the escape of Kilian Blackhorse from Zeth Abbey.'

'Thank God!' cried the king, starting up from his chair at
the head of the table. 'Tell me more!'

'The man Saltbeck is hiding in a hut on the moors some
eight leagues east of Elktor. A party of warriors, led by
Deveron, will set out shortly to arrest him. When this is
accomplished, Deveron will bespeak me personally with all
details of the venture.'

'I trust that the miscreant has Darasilo's Trove with him.'

'There would be no way to determine that, sire, until the
thief is taken. Sigils cannot be scried. Neither, I presume, can
the two magical books, since they have moonstones on their
covers.'

Scowling, Conrig expelled a noisy breath. 'I'd forgotten.
God grant that the entire trove be there in the hut, and the
intelligencer is able to take it safely in hand! What's this
about a boat?'

'Sir Deveron is convinced, from various clues he oversaw
on the empty vessel, that it transported Kilian, his fellow-
traitors, and their horses to Roaring Gorge at the head of Elk
Lake. It's possible that the chasm would provide an escape-
route into Didion for the whole gang of conspirators, provided
they had an expert guide. When Kilian and his three friends
fled the abbey, they took with them a young Brother named
Garon Curtling. He belongs to a mountain clan and would
likely know the gorge area well. A force led by Lord Olvan

Elktor will pursue Kilian and his companions – although the troops will have a hard time of it because of dangerous terrain and unfavorable weather.'

'I don't give a damn whether Kilian escapes into Didion, so long as he doesn't carry the Trove of Darasilo with him.' Conrig pulled a wry face. 'I won't sleep this night until I know whether Deveron's pursuit is successful. Will you keep watch with me?'

Sulkorig rose. 'Why don't we go to Lord Stergos's chambers, sire? We can wait comfortably in his sitting room without being disturbed. If we receive good news, we can inform the Royal Alchymist at once. Lord Stergos would be greatly comforted. Perhaps he can also advise Sir Deveron how best to ensure the security of the recovered trove – no small matter, you'll agree.'

'No,' Conrig agreed. 'It's not. I'll have to give it careful thought myself.'

They thundered down the steep road from Elktor Castle and galloped apace for the Shore Road and the Mountain Gate: six of the count's most intrepid household knights and four times that number of men-at-arms, heedless of the misty drizzle that enveloped the countryside, intent upon apprehending at least one of the Sovereignty's most wanted criminals. Snudge led the troop, with Vra-Mattis riding at his side. He had deemed the other members of his party too inexperienced to accompany him, and had left them behind in the castle, sound asleep and heedless of the climactic events now unfolding.

Persuading his eager host, Lord Olvan, to lead the hunt for Kilian rather than the more exciting apprehension of Scarth Saltbeck had been a touchy matter. Although the young nobleman was brave, generous, and of a cheerful disposition, Ollie Elktor's character disastrously combined rash impetuosity with a truly monumental fat-headedness. His people loved him in spite of his flaws and were inclined to overlook his errors of judgement; and happily, these had become less egregious since the viscount's redoubtable father, Earl Marshal Parlian Beorbrook, had installed a handpicked steward to manage the castle household and an iron-willed constable to maintain discipline among its knights and warriors.

Lord Olvan yearned with all his heart to go after the notorious villain who had fired Cala Palace; but in the end, even a valiant dullard such as he understood the reasons why Sir Devron Austrey sent him in the opposite direction. Chasing a fugitive over the eastern moorlands presented no special tactical difficulties to a newcomer to the region, provided he had local men riding with him. Roaring Gorge, on the other hand, was hazardous territory where specialized knowledge was vital to survival. Lord Olvan had actually ventured into the dreadful, haunted place a few times, if only for short distances. Sir Deveron knew nothing about the gorge, and confessed to being inexperienced in mountain travel to boot.

So Ollie manfully conceded the point. While Deveron and his men raced off on their lightning foray, the viscount assembled a larger force that was equipped for a long haul, and rode out at a more prudent pace an hour later. By then, Snudge was more than halfway to the croft where Scarth Saltbeck lay in a state of sodden insensibility.

The truth was that the intelligencer had a stronger reason for not wanting Olvan – much less any of his sharper-minded lieutenants – witnessing the arrest of Scarth. He intended that none of the Elktor people should ever know about the Trove of Darasilo, much less what he planned to do with the trove if he found it.

Before leaving the castle, he had begged its master mason to lend him a certain tool, saying vaguely that the thing might help in extracting the criminal from his hiding place.

But if the opportunity arose, Snudge planned an entirely different use for the sledgehammer wrapped in sacking, which was now lashed to the back of his saddle.

Being only human, Beynor dozed off.

His more vigilant inner self – or something – caused him to wake with a cry of dismay and a great start that set the briskly moving dinghy to wallowing.

What is wrong with you, groundling? the Supreme Warrior inquired in a peevish tone, from somewhere under the river. *Did your execrably unappetizing meal disagree with you and bring on an evil dream?*

'Something like that,' Beynor muttered. The monsters had no notion what he'd been up to. His ability to invade dreams was a secret he didn't intend to share.

How long had he been asleep? Long enough for Scarth's binge to have worn off a little? He sent the thread of his over-sight aloft on the wind, ranging west-south-west to the desolate highland region between Elktor and the Great North Road, to the tiny hut crouching in its rocky hollow, well out of sight of the only track. The mules stood their patient vigil amidst dripping junipers. Inside the croft, the surviving renegade Brother had shifted his position slightly and started to snore. Behind their closed lids, his eyes were moving just a bit. The spell of couverture was still extinct, but that was to be expected.

Before attempting another dream-invasion, Beynor decided to cast about with his windsight to determine if any search-parties were abroad. It was unlikely. The local lord, famed as he was for happy-go-lucky stupidity, would hardly send his men out scouring the moors in the middle of a rainy night . . .

Beynor bit back a disbelieving curse when he saw the double line of torches moving eastward along the rough track. It couldn't be happening! The heavily armed knights and the

warriors wearing Elktor livery had to be riding out for some
entirely different reason; perhaps they'd been summoned to
reinforce the troops at Beorbrook Hold.

He focused closely on the men at the head of the column.
How strange! The apparent leader was a slight figure dressed
in a rain-cloak, beneath which were the robes of a Zeth
Brother. He rode beside a saddled horse that lacked a rider,
and yet the adept turned his head now and again toward
the empty saddle, as though someone invisible were there.

Someone who could not be scried . . . such as Deveron
Austrey.

In a panic, Beynor wasted no time surveying the troop
further. He screamed into Scarth's unconscious mind with
all the power he could muster.

He'd only just begun to dream the new dream.

He was in the opulent throne room of the Conjure-Queen,
approaching her with a confident stride. He wore the black
garb of a high-ranking Didionite wizard, flowing robes of rich
silken brocade trimmed with sable, and a matching skullcap.
The queen's counselors, clustered about her dais, whispered
to each other behind their hands, wondering who this
magnificent stranger might be, not knowing he was there by
royal invitation!

Warlock-knights of the Royal Guard presented their flaming
swords in salute as he went down on one knee before Ullanoth
of Moss. Smiling, he lifted the lid of the simple little honey-
wood box he carried. 'I've brought the stones, Great Queen,'
he said, going straight to the point, 'just as I said I would.'

The courtiers murmured at his temerity, but Queen
Ullanoth rose to her feet, her lovely narrow face alight with
avid anticipation and her eyes like green stars. She beckoned
for him to approach. He did, holding out the open box so
she could see its contents for herself.

The young queen reached out a slender hand. On one finger was a moonstone ring, identical to the one he had brought to her except for the glow of power that suffused it. Hanging on thin chains about her neck were two more living sigils – one small and drop-shaped, the other an open triangle an inch or so wide, with a short handle.

'May I examine these stones of yours, wizard?' she asked him with regal courtesy.

'Certainly, Your Majesty.'

She took the icicle-shaped stone from his box, regarded it in silence for a moment, lifted her head to meet his gaze –

And screamed at him: *Scarth! Scarth Saltbeck! Wake up, you fool! They're coming for you – the king's men! You have less than half an hour before they find you.*

He staggered back, dropping the box. 'What are you saying?' he gasped.

Gather up the sigils and the books. Put on your cloak and boots. Hurry! Don't bother with anything else except your sword. Saddle the strongest mule. Go north across open country, to the mountains. And if you value your life, put up the cover-spell before you ride out! . . .

She vanished, along with all of her court.

Scarth was back in the rude moorland hut, lying on the floor, half-covered by a rough blanket. A faint red glow came from the embers of the dying fire, but he could see nothing clearly. His head throbbed with agony and the Conjure-Queen's warning seemed to echo inside his skull like the clanging of Zeth Abbey's gigantic bronze bell.

A dream. It had been another intensely vivid dream.

'Felmar?' he called out, in a voice roughened by phlegm. 'Felmar?'

When there was no answer he crawled to the hearth, tossed on a few sticks, and puffed at the coals until the wood caught and there was enough light to see by. He sat up and called his companion's name again, turning about and squinting into the shadows. But he was alone in the hut. Felmar's saddle, his improvised pallet, and all of his things lay as Scarth remembered them. Moonstone sigils, for some odd reason, were scattered everywhere, and the leather sacks that had held them were tossed aside. Even stranger was the abundant sandlike material strewn over the canvas floor-covering. The two old books were nearly buried in it, as was the cloth packet that had held the four important sigils. What did it mean?

Moving with trancelike slowness, he crept toward the door. Maybe Felmar had gone outside to answer a call of nature and got lost. Stupid idiot. But what did it matter, when he himself felt so tired and ill? The mystery of his companion's disappearance seemed unimportant, as did the curious mess on the floor. To hell with Felmar. Sleep was all that mattered. Sleep, and his dream of the lovely Queen of Moss –

Scarth! Scarth Saltbeck! Wake up, you fool! They're coming for you – the king's men! You have less than half an hour before they find you.

Shocked into wakefulness again, he found himself on his hands and knees before the croft's open doorway, straining to see what might be outside.

'Felmar!' he yelled. 'Where are you?' The only reply was a soft grumble from one of the mules. He turned about, picked up a pinch of the stuff on the floor and rubbed it between his fingers. Ashes. They felt nothing like the residue of burnt wood but were grainy and foul-smelling, like sea-coal cinders. Mixed with the ash were sharper fragments that almost resembled charred bone . . .

Terror smote him like a blow to the gut. Somehow, he knew what had happened – if not why. Vomit rose in his gullet and he was barely able to crawl out the door into the grey drizzle before he spewed the contents of his stomach.

He moaned his friend's name one last time, knowing that there would be no answer. Then he wiped his mouth on his sleeve, staggered to his feet, and re-entered the croft to gather the things Queen Ullanoth had commanded him to take. His hands trembled violently, his vision was still impaired, and he was half-crazed with fear. The need to flee this awful place without delay overwhelmed every other thought in his pain-wracked brain.

All those sigils scattered about . . .

Let them be! Take only the four important ones!

Where were they? He found the ring, the rod, the stone icicle – but the tiny stone carving of a door wasn't there. He scooped up the three and put them in his jerkin pocket.

Why take both books? Only one is needed. Hurry!

He stuffed the tome pertaining to the Great Stones inside his shirt and next to his skin, where it would stay dry, then buckled on his sword with fumbling fingers and fastened his cloak.

Hurry!

The rain had almost stopped by the time he clumsily saddled the mule, and the sky was brighter in the east. He put a foot into the stirrup, swung up after three ineffectual tries, then drew a deep breath and pronounced the incantation for the spell of couverture. To his surprise, it worked.

Hurry, damn you! To the mountains!

'To the mountains,' he mumbled. They weren't far away, and there were other large rock formations even closer, where he might be able to find a good hiding place.

He turned the mule's head, kicked its ribs, and set off.

THIRTEEN

Snudge had been windwatching the sleeping thief inter-
mittently since he and the warriors rode out from the castle,
even though his talent was greatly fatigued. The empty
brandy flask lying on the floor of the hut showed plainly
enough why the heretofore impenetrable cover-spell had
failed in its protection. But the two empty wash-leather
bags on the floor – plus the even more ominous presence
of the missing Brother's gear and mule – filled him with
foreboding.

Then Scarth awoke. The man's inexplicable terror, nausea,
and frantic preparations to ride out caused Snudge to bark
out an oath of vexation.

'What's wrong, sir?' Mattis shouted over the noise of
pounding hoofbeats.

'Use windspeech,' Snudge bespoke him. 'Our thief is
preparing to flee. Scry him out yourself, if you can. He's
frightened out of his mind for some reason, but not saying
much, so I can't read his lips and find out what's going on
. . . Damn it to hell! He's put up the cover-spell again.'

'I don't see him, sir,' Mattis admitted. 'There's only the
stone hut and a mule.'

'There were two mules a moment ago,' Snudge said tightly. 'Look carefully at the ground around the place. Let's see if either of us can scry a trail of hoof-marks in the mud.'

Close scrutiny was all but impossible while jouncing along on horseback. As the troop came closer to the croft, Snudge was finally able to determine that there were no fresh prints ahead of them, on the track to Beorbrook. So their prey had taken off cross-country, probably in the direction of the mountains.

'We won't be able to track him over the open moors until we reach the hut,' Snudge said. 'The ground's too stony and cluttered with heather and brush for close scrying. On the other hand, he's not going to be able to go very fast. Do exactly as I say when we arrive at the hut. Don't forget that *you* are the only windvoice in our company.'

'I understand, sir.'

They reached the faint side-path leading to the croft in another quarter-hour. Snudge held his hand high as a signal for the troop to stop, then pointed out the new direction. The men followed single-file over the rougher ground, at a cautious walk. When they rode into the hollow and caught sight of the tiny dwelling in the murk, Snudge once again called for a halt and motioned for the six knights to come close for a conference.

'Gentlemen, my windvoice and I are going to ride forward and call on Scarth Saltbeck to surrender. Fan out your warriors and follow us. Keep back about ten ells and be alert if he tries to run. Remember: we want this man alive.'

One of the knights said, 'Is he likely to attack us with sorcery?'

'It's not likely. Mattis is very weary from having performed an arduous windsearch earlier, and he's temporarily unable to scry through the stone wall of the hut. But when he oversaw our villain half an hour ago, he was lying dead drunk inside. Inebriation quenches talent completely. Ready? Here we go . . .'

They closed in on the empty hovel. Snudge dismounted, drew his sword, and made the surrender demand. When there was no response, he ducked inside the croft, swiftly surveyed the interior, and gave a sigh of relief as he saw the sigils strewn on the floor and one of the books partially buried in some kind of sand or ash.

He emerged, looking crestfallen, and called out, 'Bad news, lads! Our bird has flown.'

There were disappointed groans and curses from the entire troop.

'All right, here's what we do. I'm going to search this hut. He's left a lot of stuff behind that might provide valuable clues. Meanwhile, Vra-Mattis will scry the ground round about here until he finds the bastard's tracks. He'll lead the new pursuit. Follow him and keep your eyes well peeled. I have to warn you that our villain may be hiding beneath a cover-spell. This kind of magic doesn't really make a person invisible to the naked eye – but it *does* try to fool you into not noticing the one who's covered. If you think you might've glimpsed a man on a mule and your mind tells you it was only fancy, don't believe it! Point him out to your mates and ride straight at him. If you can get within five feet, he'll become clearly visible.'

'Swive me,' one of the men-at-arms muttered. 'Tricky business, running down magickers. Gimme plain old sheep-stealers and bandits any day.'

Mattis had been sitting his saddle with eyes squeezed shut while Snudge addressed the troop, casting about with his windsight. 'Here they are!' the novice cried. 'Tracks made by the fugitive!' He urged his horse up the far side of the hollow and the rest of the warriors streamed after, shouting eagerly.

Snudge waited until the last one had disappeared before

sheathing his sword and tying his horse to a juniper branch. He retrieved the sledgehammer and searched until he found a flattish rock the size of a cottage loaf. Leaving them just outside the croft, he entered the low door. Two men had certainly been here. One had ridden away while the other had disappeared, leaving all his gear, his saddle, a fine sword, and his mount behind. Carefully, he shook out the blankets and other equipment and piled them in a far corner, away from the canvas groundcloth where the sigils and ashes were scattered. The two wash-leather bags had obviously held the moonstones. He squatted and began collecting them, shaking off the clinging grit as best he could.

What *was* that filthy stuff? It had a faint noisome odor that was somehow familiar. He filled both bags with sigils, dusted off the book, and sat back on his heels, pondering. He'd seen ash like this before.

It came to him. The dank lower chamber of Mallmouth Bridge's bascule machinery. The treacherous armiger Mero Elwick in a rage of frustration, knowing he could never use Concealer himself and vowing that Snudge wouldn't have it, either. A tremendous blow with a broadsword that left the sigil unharmed, while Mero himself was incinerated in a flash of defensive sorcery.

Something like that had happened to the missing thief.

'Yes,' said a low-pitched voice from the hut's doorway.

'Who's there?' Snudge cried. Drawing his sword, he crouched back against the opposite wall. A small cloaked person was standing there, visible only in silhouette.

'Come out, sir knight,' he said, 'and bring the sigils and the book with you.'

'Aroint thee, whoreson!' Snudge cried, reaching with his left hand to touch Concealer and turn himself invisible –

He froze stock still, paralyzed in every muscle save those of his face. He spat out a curse.

'Be silent, Deveron Austrey. Or may I call you Snudge?'
The figure stepped back and became discernible in the
dawnlight, a little man whose head would have come barely
to Snudge's shoulder, dressed in a suit of well-cured skin
and wearing a cloak of mingled dark colors in a pattern
that mimicked tree-bark. His skin was sun-browned and his
large eyes were a startling green. 'Be calm. I mean no harm
– not to you, especially, since you're of the blood. I
command you to put away your sword and come out. Bring
the Trove of Darasilo.'

Compelled to obey, Snudge emerged in furious silence,
placed the bags and the book on the ground, and glared at
the stranger.

'My name is Odall,' he said, 'and I've been sent by the
Source. Do you remember Red Ansel's Source? The one he
spoke of when you and he sat in a small boat on Cala Bay,
and you summoned the Light and quickened the Concealer
sigil you wear next to your heart?'

Snudge felt his scalp prickle and his throat grow tight.

'Do you remember?'

'Yes,' Snudge whispered. He began to inch toward Odall.

'The Source has decided that you're needed in the New
Conflict. Ansel himself doesn't know, and we Green Men aren't
allowed to tell him about you for a while yet. Don't *you*
mention this meeting of ours to him or anyone else, either.'

'You're . . . a Green Man?'

'Yes. There's more of us about than you'd think. In the
Elderwold, we sometimes rob caravans! But mostly we stick
to the wild places where humans seldom go. If we're taken
unawares by one of you giants, we haven't much of a chance.'

Snudge tried to keep his voice steady. 'What do you want
with me?'

'I came to stop you from smashing the sigils in the trove.'

'The things are evil! They destroy people's souls and bodies.

I know that for a fact.' He continued to edge almost imperceptibly toward the little man.

Odall grinned. 'Nevertheless, you're willing to use your Concealer sigil in what you think is a good cause. You'd use it to help your master, Conrig Wincantor – and oddly enough, that's as it should be. Conrig will never know it, but he's been enlisted to help in the New Conflict, too.'

'I don't know what you're talking about,' Snudge said sullenly.

'It's not necessary that you should.' The cheerful demeanor of the Green Man vanished like a snuffed candleflame, and Snudge realized that he was once again quite incapable of movement. 'Do you recall the words you used to bring Concealer to life?'

'Yes,' Snudge said through his teeth. 'Why do you ask?'

Odall didn't answer. He went into the croft, and after a few minutes came out with the saddle and harness that had belonged to the missing thief. The things should have been too heavy for one of his slight build to carry, but he flung pad and saddle onto the back of the mule as though they were weightless, expertly tightened the cinch, and shortened the stirrup leathers. 'How splendid that I can go home in style! I've had a long foot-slog.'

When the mount was ready he picked up the ancient book, and as Snudge watched in fascinated horror, he tore off the cover with its moonstone disk and set it carefully on the rock Snudge had selected earlier as an anvil for his hammer. Then he opened one of the sigil sacks and took out a small oblong moonstone.

'See this? It's name is Subtle Gateway, and it's one of the Great Stones. Hold it tight, close your eyes, and say EMCHAY MO. Then tell it where you want to go. It will carry you anywhere in the world. If you should desire to take up to ten other persons with you, or three horses, or a boat up to four ells long, or a heap of goods equivalent to the weight of three horses, say EMCHAY ASINN. Clear enough?'

'No, it's not, damn your eyes!' Snudge strove without success to overcome the paralysis. His feet seemed rooted to the ground. 'I don't want to use a Great Stone that'll put me in deep thrall to the Lights!'

'Well, that's as may be, and you do have a point. But the Source thinks you'll need Subtle Gateway in order to carry out your bounden duty, so you're obliged to take it. With luck, you may only have to use it a few times and the pain-debt will be not too onerous. When your duty's fulfilled, we'll show you how to drain the stone's life, then get rid of it for you.'

'It should be destroyed now, and so should the rest of Darasilo's Trove! For God's sake, Odall, why are you preventing me from ridding the world of these terrible things?'

'Easy, lad. Have no fear. These bags of sigils and the cover-less book I'm taking will be destroyed, all right. But not just smashed to bits, as you planned to do. They'll be disposed of in a manner that serves the Source and hastens the downfall of the Evil Lights.'

Odall placed the sigil named Subtle Gateway on the book cover and vaulted onto the back of the mule. 'Don't forget now: EMCHAY MO and EMCHAY ASINN are the words that conjure its power. The words of activation are the same as those you used for Concealer. And be very sure to name yourself Snudge to the Light, rather than Deveron Austrey, just as you did before. As Ansel told you, Snudge is your name, and yet it's not. And so you're not as beholden to the Lights when using their sigils as are certain other persons I could mention.'

'But you haven't explained –'

The Green Man flicked the reins and turned the mule in the direction that Mattis and the warrior troop had taken.

Speaking over his shoulder, he said, 'See that you move along to Tarn as soon as possible. Your duty lies there.' Odall and the mule vanished into thin air, and Snudge's body came back under his control.

'Wait! Who is this Source? What's he up to? How did he know how to find the sigils? They can't be scried!'

True. But since sigils are a channel to the power of the Great Lights, the Lights may decide who shall oversee them. These were known about from long ages past, but were inaccessible until the two thieves removed them from Cala Palace. And of course we had to keep them safe from the Conjure-Queen as well.

The soft voice seemed to emanate from no particular direction, and was weighted with a profound sadness.

Snudge eyed Subtle Gateway and the torn book cover with loathing. 'Curse you, Odall!' he shouted at the unseen speaker. 'I'll be no one's cat's-paw!'

Someone laughed, a melancholy sound. *If you believe that, then see that you fulfill your duty to King Conrig – not blindly and without question, but only as best you can.*

'I wasn't talking about the king.' Snudge looked about in bewilderment.

When you've finished activating the Gateway, crush the moonstone medallion and the book cover. Tell Lord Stergos – no one else – what happened here today. He, not you, is the proper one to pass on news of the trove's destruction to his brother Conrig.

Snudge felt his anger fade, leaving a mounting fear. 'You're not the Green Man. Who are you?'

I am the One Denied the Sky, the lowliest of the Likeminded, but despite that, designated to lead the New Conflict. Someday I hope I may tell you my tale. But that cannot happen until there is an ending.

'An . . . ending?'

Bespeak your young friend, Vra-Mattis. Have him inform the warriors that he has lost the trail of Scarth Saltbeck. They must all return to Elktor with you now.

'Do you intend to let Scarth escape? What happened to the other thief, Felmar, and the second book?'

Both wretched men had roles in the New Conflict. Felmar is dead and Scarth will not live much longer. You may also tell this to Lord Stergos. The second book need not concern you. Eventually, it will also be destroyed.

'What about Kilian Blackhorse? Is he also a participant in your Conflict?'

Yes. And so is Beynor ash Linndal of Moss, who has returned to this island to commit heinous sins. But ask me no more questions. Do the things I've requested of you, Snudge. You must, if it's all to come right in the end. Otherwise the Pain-Eaters will triumph. Farewell.

He took off his gauntlet and pressed the carving of the tiny door to the disk with his bare hand. As before, the irascible inhuman voice boomed on the wind, asking what he wanted.

CADAY AN RUDAY?

'GO TUGA LUVKRO AN AY COMASH DOM.' May the Cold Light grant me power.

The pain was tentative as the terrible being asked who he was. *KO AN SO?*

He told the truth that was not the truth, praying that Ansel and the Source were right. 'SNUDGE.'

An icy spear plunged into his breast, but stopped short of his heart. He endured, suffered, waited while the Great Light pondered his request to share power and pay the price. They were fickle beings, fond of deadly jests, as likely to slay a supplicant as to bestow their awful gifts. But once again, Snudge was one of the fortunate.

THASHIN AH GAV. We accept.

'MO TENGALAH SHERUV.' Thank you.

He was struck down then, as before, only to come to his senses later with the memory of horror causing hot tears to pour from his eyes. The agony had been much more severe than that he experienced during the activation of Concealer. Giving thanks for his survival, he lay there until his face dried and the sound of hoofbeats vibrating in the ground under his ear warned him that the others were returning.

He sat up. It was bright dawn, with the dark clouds all fled to the east. The small oblong carving glowed faintly green when he opened his clenched fist. The sigil was perforated, like Concealer, and fit easily on the same golden neck chain. He tucked the two stones away, feeling them warm and alive against the flesh of his chest. Then he got to his feet, took up the sledgehammer, and smote the book cover and its moonstone disk again and again, until they were so pulverized that no man could ever tell what they had been.

When Garon deemed the evening light too faint for safe travel, he called for the men behind him to halt. It was perhaps two hours until midnight. The clouds, tinctured faintly with crimson and violet, had lifted and the rain was over.

Kilian's party had attained a flattish triangle of land covered with grass and alpine herbs, several acres in extent, that jutted out over the depths of the gorge like the prow of a rockbound ship. On two sides the drop-off was almost sheer; the third abutted the shoulder of a hulking mountain. Shrubs and a few gnarled pine trees had taken root among the large rocks closest to the path, and a ring of fire-blackened stones revealed that someone had previously used the place as a campsite.

'We'll stop here,' the young Brother told the alchymist, after he and his pillion-rider, Niavar, had dismounted. 'Later on, it may get windier than we'd like, but now that the rain has let up it shouldn't be too uncomfortable. I grazed sheep in this little meadow betimes. With my dog keeping guard, I never lost one over the precipice, but it won't be safe for the horses to graze free. We'll tie them up by the trees and cut grass for them.'

Raldo, who had suffered some bad bumps earlier when his mount wrong-footed and he tumbled off, was appointed cook so he would not have to move about too much. Cleaton took charge of the horses, and Niavar was sent to a nearby cascade with a canvas bucket and leathern bottles for water. Garon and Kilian prowled the flower-dotted open area, cutting grass with their keen-bladed hunting knives and gathering whatever dead plant material might be coaxed into burning.

'If you look beyond this south-facing cliff,' Garon remarked to the alchymist, 'you can see part of the way we've come. The lake is at the horizon. Double Waterfall is visible if you follow the course of the river back to the great rock-cleft. The eroded section of trail where Raldo fell lies beyond that ridge of very dark rock.'

Kilian approached the edge of the precipice and scanned the striking panorama. 'We've climbed very high today, but not traveled as far from the lake as I hoped. What do you estimate – seven or eight leagues?'

Garon shrugged. 'Closer to five as the raven flies, I fear. The two near-disasters slowed us considerably. It's a miracle that Raldo's bay didn't slide down into the ravine when he mis-stepped. We'll have to poultice the beast's right front fetlock, but he'll be fine. I wish I could say the same about Brother Butterball. The man must be a mass of bruises. By tomorrow, he'll hardly be able to move.'

'It could be a problem,' Kilian said.

'We won't have an easy time of it crossing into Didion. In some spots, we'll have to climb on hands and knees, hoping the horses can follow along after us. A disabled man will find the going hard. If the track turns truly foul, we may have to leave our mounts behind altogether.'

'Mmm. Will we be able to find food?'

'I have a shortbow and arrows to take hares and marmot-squirrels. There are also plenty of snowcocks, although their flesh is sometimes unpalatable. Beyond the divide, where the climate is wetter and there are alpine bogs, there'll be elk and red deer. We won't starve.'

'What about creatures who would eat *us?*' The chiseled features of the alchymist wore an expression of academic curiosity.

'The great brown bear is all we have to fear, my lord. Tundra-lions don't live in the eastern Sinistrals, and the lynxes and wildcats are too shy to bother humans.' Garon paused, smiling dismissively. 'Some say that small enclaves of Green Men make their homes in the mountains further to the west, and they may be the demons who give Roaring Gorge its fearful reputation. But I've never seen a trace of the little devils myself, nor has any member of my clan.'

'Well, I'll give our route a careful scry as we proceed. And since we have attained an admirable vantage here, I believe I'll attempt a cautious windsearch right now, seeing what lies ahead of us – and behind as well. The two Brothers coming from Cala to join us may already have set out along the gorge path.'

'I'll take the grass you've cut to the horses,' Garon said. 'It'll be a while before Raldo gets supper ready. After I've gathered fuel for the fire, I'll give him a hand.' He added Kilian's sheaf to his own and meandered back to the camp.

The alchymist seated himself among a heap of lichen-scabbed rocks at the cliff-edge, pulled the hood of his cloak over his head, and sent out the slenderest possible thread of wind-sight. It swept those portions of the gorge path ahead that were not obstructed by thick rock. The track continued to climb toward the jagged northern skyline. About two leagues beyond the camp was a vast tumble of slabs that they would have to negotiate in the morning. In one part of the rockfall, the way seemed totally impassable, but that might have been an illusion of perspective. Kilian devoutly hoped so.

When he could no longer scry the forward route, he turned his attention to the way they'd come. The sections visible to his mind's eye were empty of both human and inhuman beings. Finally, he scrutinized the portion of the shepherd's track they had not traversed, which skirted the lakehead and led to the Mountain Gate of Elktor.

Rain still fell on the city and the region east of it. No search parties were abroad outside the walls, and there was no unusual activity apparent within. The cottages and huts scattered among the nearby hills were shuttered and locked against the short summer night, their domestic animals safe in folds or byres.

Kilian extended his windsight further to the east, along a moorland track where mist obscured the countryside, and in time discovered a dilapidated hovel with a tiny plume of smoke coming from its roof-opening. Two sleek mules were tethered outside of it. The stone walls made scrying the interior difficult, but he was able to discern two covered human forms lying asleep on the floor.

He frowned. They had to be benighted travelers, taking refuge from the rain. It was impossible for him to see their faces, but one of the bodies was much larger than the other . . . Surely they weren't Felmar and Scarth! Why would they have taken the track leading away from the gorge? No, the sleepers had to be other men. Still, it might be wise to scry them out more closely early tomorrow morning and make sure.

Kilian rose and stretched his aching muscles. It had been several years since he'd ridden, and his legs would have to readjust to the saddle. A pity the waterborne part of their journey to Didion had been so brief! Idly, he scried the grounded cattle-transport. It was as they had left it, bound to be discovered sooner or later, but with nothing left aboard that could point conclusively to them. By the time that the boatmen were missed and their connection to the abandoned vessel established, he and his men would be so deep in the mountains that pursuit was impossible.

Tomorrow, he'd try to bespeak Felmar and Scarth. He'd have to make a stab at contacting Beynor, too, unless the young Mosslander invaded his dreams tonight. The ambush of Honigalus was scheduled to take place only a few days hence, and Kilian was keen to know how matters were progressing with his co-conspirator and the Salka.

Interesting times lay ahead.

'Supper!' Raldo croaked. The tantalizing scent of grilled sausages wafted through the dusk. Kilian smiled and trudged over the meadow to where the others were gathered around the fire.

He slept well that night, even though the ground was hard and rocky, and his dreams were inconsequential rehashings of his days as a Privy Council member under King Olmigon, uninterrupted by Beynor. When he awoke, he sat up with a start of alarm, not remembering where he was, thinking he'd heard Zeth Abbey's rising bell. But the only sounds were the snores and wheezes of his companions, quiet movement among the horses, a distant rushing noise from the torrent in the gorge below, and the thin sweet song of some alpine bird. Pink and gold beams of dawnlight glorified the east where clouds still lingered. The sky above Roaring Gorge was almost clear and duck-egg green. The crisp, chilly air would likely warm quickly once the sun came up.

Kilian threw off his blanket and rose. Like the others, he'd slept fully dressed. Thinking to perform another windsearch,

he crossed the dew-spangled meadow to the southern edge
of the projecting precipice. Before attempting the more difficult task of scrying the path, he let his sight range to the
moor beyond Elktor. The travelers who'd sheltered in
the stone hut had roused his curiosity. The distance between
Elktor and Beorbrook Hold over that track was only thirty
leagues – less than a day's journey on horseback. So why
had the men spent the night in an abandoned croft, rather
than organizing their trip more prudently? Could they be
brigands?

To his surprise, he found no mules tethered there. A well-
caparisoned knight's courser had inexplicably taken their
place, and stood munching the trampled grass. The hut itself
was empty except for a few odds and ends of equipment.
Outside its front door, a sledgehammer lay beside a medium-
sized rock.

The track was empty for leagues in both directions, so
Kilian turned his talent to the area between the dwelling
and the mountains. Immediately, he scried a troop of more
than two score mounted men, milling about a small hooded
rider who sat a horse much too large for him. They were
knights and men-at-arms, and the central figure wore the
robes of a Brother of Zeth. As Kilian watched in consternation, the adept gave a hand signal and the entire troop set
out at a fast trot in the direction of the hut.

Great God! Who had they been pursuing over the open
moors?

He searched further, among the great rock formations that
reared up from the heath closer to the looming bulk of the
mountains, but found no one. No one who could be perceived
by scrying . . .

Kilian cut the thread of windsight and stood irresolute at
the edge of the cliff. If Felmar and Scarth had been in that
hut, and if they'd fled pursuit under the spell of couverture

he'd taught them, the hoof-prints of their mounts might have been followed by the troop of warriors. And now the hunters had given up the chase, perhaps because they'd lost the trail in increasingly rocky ground.

I could extinguish the Brothers' cover-spell now without putting them in danger, Kilian thought, and confirm that they've gone wildly astray, carrying the Trove of Darasilo with them.

But that was a drastic step and one he was loath to perform. He'd have to use a generalized incantation that would lift the spell *wherever Felmar and Scarth might be.* What if they weren't on the moorland after all, and stood in a vulnerable position elsewhere? Once he broke the spell, he could not re-establish it; that would have to be done by the two agents themselves. But would they realize what had happened? From within, a cover-spell was manifested to its wearer only by the most subtle alteration of one's surroundings. The Brothers might not realize they'd been exposed until it was too late to save themselves from capture. No, Kilian decided. It wasn't worth the risk.

If the moorland commotion did indeed have nothing to do with Felmar and Scarth, the two men might be on their way up the gorge path at this very minute. It was preferable to let things be so long as there was a chance they might still be heading for the cave.

He settled himself again, pulled down his hood, and began windsearching for them along the gorge route, beginning at the fork in the track outside the city wall. He didn't find them – but in time he did discover the mounted force of Count Olvan Elktor, halted in a rough bivouac on the near side of Double Waterfall. It was obvious that they had set out from the city during the murky night hours. They'd made the dangerous crossing and then paused to rest, but they were certain to move on before long.

Grimly, he counted at least forty men wearing the livery of the castle garrison, a dozen household knights in bright-colored surcoats, three Brothers of Zeth, and numbers of servants on ponies leading sumpter mules loaded with supplies. The presence of such a large force could only mean that the authorities were fairly certain that either Felmar and Scarth or Kilian and his party had come into the gorge.

White-faced, the alchymist withdrew his sight and hurried to waken his companions. Garon, Niavar, and Cleaton heard him out in bleak silence, while Raldo made incoherent sounds of distress, too stiff and aching even to rise from his pallet.

'It took us three hours to get here from the waterfall,' Garon said, rolling up his blankets with swift economy. His brow was creased by concern. 'We were tired and didn't travel very fast. The pursuers will come on much faster.'

'But can we outrun them?' asked Kilian. 'Or perhaps go another way?'

'There is no other way. As to outrunning them – it would be better to prevent pursuit altogether. By blocking the track.'

Niavar and Cleaton brightened at this and began to ask eager questions. Raldo stood by, apparently apathetic, but his eyes were alert. Garon bade all keep silent and continued addressing Kilian. 'My lord, when we planned this journey, you spoke of combining our talents to produce defensive magic. Is it not possible for the same type of joint effort to block a section of the trail behind us, so that no one would be able to follow? Perhaps we could amplify the landslide where Raldo took his fall.'

The alchymist said, 'To make an effective blockade, we'd need to find a spot where rocks above the path were already unstable and a modest bolt of magic might bring them down. The place where Raldo's horse slipped is hazardous with loose surface stones, but not susceptible to rockfalls. The mountainside itself is virtually solid there. Without golden gammadions, our group lacks the strength to burst apart living rock.'

Garon nodded in understanding. 'I think I know the perfect spot for our purposes. A short distance beyond this camp, we come to a hanging valley between two tall peaks. A side-path leads to extensive grassy pockets, dead ends all, where I used to pasture my sheep for weeks at a time. I never took the flock beyond there because forage becomes scanty at higher altitudes, but I did explore the ongoing route for my own amusement. If one continues along the gorge track for another hour or so, one arrives at a broad slope composed of great cracked slabs, where some cataclysm caused half the mountainside to break away and fall into the chasm.'

'I know about this area,' Kilian put in. 'I scried it last night and thought it looked uncommonly perilous.'

'Normally, the slabs can be crossed with care by a man on foot,' Garon said. 'I believe our horses could negotiate them if they were led. Having overseen the place, my lord, do you think we'd be able to bring down more rock and render it totally impassable?'

Kilian said, 'Wait,' and left them, going out into the meadow where the scrying angle was better. After a few minutes he returned with a wolfish smile on his face. 'We may not be able to render the slope impassable. But if the column of pursuers were strung out all across it and we *then* caused a rockfall . . .'

Garon, Niavar, and Cleaton stared at him in comprehension. Raldo only hung his head.

'Let us move on as quickly as we can, then,' said the alchymist. 'We'll have to break our fast as we ride.'

Garon, Niavar, and Cleaton packed their gear with alacrity, while Raldo hobbled about, tumbling the unwashed cups and bowls and spoons from last night's supper into a sack, scraping bits of cold porridge from the pot with a spoon, and wiping the greasy wire grill with a handful of grass. His sunken eyes, pursed lips, and trembling hands betrayed his misery.

'How do you fare?' Kilian asked blandly.

'I'm doing the best I can, my lord. I'll scour the cooking things well at the end of the day.'

The alchymist grunted and said to Garon, 'Saddle his horse, lash his bags in place, and help him to mount.'

They set out at a quick pace, most of them feeling more confident riding the narrow path than they had been on the previous day. The sun shone brilliantly and the air was crystalline, with every detail of the landscape sharply visible. The hanging valley, when they reached it, was a concave emerald corridor between peaks layered with brick-red, ochre, and black rock strata, sublimely beautiful against an azure sky. But by that time none of them was in a mood to appreciate it – especially Raldo.

He sat in his saddle as inert as a sack of grain, his head lolling and his hands hardly keeping hold of the reins. One foot had slipped from its stirrup. His big bay was an intelligent beast, and it sensed that its rider sat unsteadily. Rather than take advantage of the situation and toss Raldo off, as the animal had done yesterday, it moved more and more slowly and delicately, almost as though it felt compassion for the wretched man on its back. Raldo brought up the rear of the group, and lagged ever farther behind the others.

Finally he seemed to rouse from his stupor and shouted in desperation, 'Wait! Please wait for me!'

Kilian pulled up and said to Garon, 'Go back and see if anything can be done for him.'

The young Brother dismounted and picked his way through the others along the narrow path, then continued to the place where Raldo had stopped. The two men spoke for some minutes. Garon replaced the fat man's foot in its stirrup and wrapped the reins about one hand before returning to Kilian, shaking his head.

'I'm at a loss, my lord. Brother Raldo insists he can ride on. But he seems very ill. I wonder if he might have suffered some internal hurt in the fall? At any rate there seems little we can do, save hope he will regain his energy. I think it would be unwise to attempt to lead his horse. The animal is enormous, and if it should fall it would pull down the horse and rider leading it as well.'

The small Brother with the squint said, 'Old Butterball's a goner, then? We just leave him?'

'He said he intends to press on,' Garon said. 'He may be lucky enough to reach the slide before the troops are upon him.'

'We must continue,' said Kilian, 'as fast as is safe.' He clicked his tongue and urged his mount forward. After a moment, the others followed suit, not looking back.

Raldo cried, 'I'll follow! I'm coming!' But his horse stood still, receiving no signal to move from its rider. After a time, the others were lost to his sight around a bend in the trail.

Raldo shut his eyes and exerted his negligible windsight. They weren't scrying him – at least they hadn't lowered their hoods. To be safe, he waited a while longer, then dismounted with more agility than might have been expected. He led the big bay horse to a place where there was shade and a trickle of water. His bruises ached and he was unable to walk without a limp. But there was a small smile on his face as he took bread and smoked meat from his saddlcbag, lowered his ample fundament to a flat rock, and began to eat his delayed breakfast.

Around noon, Kilian and his three remaining companions came to the slide. It was a formidable thing, in places resembling a giant staircase with tilted treads, nearly a hundred ells

wide and frightfully steep and rugged. The way across that
Garon remembered from his youth was now obstructed by
slabs and boulders that had shifted position during the intervening years, so he spent another hour scouting a new path,
after which they all made their way slowly to the other side.

They tethered their mounts further on, well out of sight
of those who were coming after them, and concealed themselves among rocks where they would not be easily scried or
endangered by falling rock. Kilian led them in thaumaturgical exercises to refresh their minds in the technique of
melding talent. Then they essayed a practice bolt, aiming at
a small slab balanced far up the opposite side of the slope. A
flash jolted the target, and an instant later there came a loud
crack and a rumble as the rock bounced a few ells downhill.

'Not very impressive,' Kilian admitted, and the others gave
nervous laughs. 'But then, we didn't put our hearts into it.'

Garon eyed him askance. 'Do you think we have a chance
of pulling this off, master? I've never been one for overt
magic myself.'

'Needs must when the devil drives,' muttered Niavar. 'If
you can save your skin no other way, you'll find your overt
talent sharpening along with your resolve.'

'Can you scry them coming, Lord Kilian?' Cleaton asked.

The alchymist pulled his hood down and concentrated. 'It
won't be long.'

They waited. The air was still and hot. They loosened their
jerkins and eventually shed them, drinking ale from the
leather bottles they'd tied to their belts. They'd left their
swords hanging on their saddles. Physical weapons would do
them no good.

'How far is the cave?' Niavar asked, breaking a long silence.

'Another two hours' slow ride,' Garon said. It's off to the
side and up a ravine, not on the main path.'

Somewhere, a raven gave a raucous bark.

Cleaton said, 'My lord, what of Brothers Felmar and Scarth?'

'And the treasure?' Garon appended softly.

'I tried windsearching for them back at the campsite yesterday,' Kilian admitted, 'and made another attempt while were were riding here. They don't appear to be anywhere on the gorge trail as yet, but if they're using the spell of couverture I wouldn't be able to scry them unless I obliterated it – and that's too dangerous. I've held off attempting to bespeak them because puncturing a heavy cover-spell requires a very 'loud' windvoice. As I said before, I don't want to risk some adept tracking the thread back to me. But perhaps that doesn't matter any more. The hunters seem to know we're here.'

'Then why not give the two lads a shout?' Niavar suggested. 'It'd ease my mind, for one, to know that Felmar was in good fettle. We were mates back in the abbey. Runts sticking together.'

'We'll wait,' Kilian said, 'until this situation is resolved. 'Here comes the vanguard of the troops, rounding that tall crag.'

They exerted their windsight for a closer view. 'Codders!' Garon said. 'It's Ollie Elktor himself leading the pack. Who'd have thought it?'

The count and his knights spurred their horses to the edge of the rockfall but made no attempt to enter it. 'They'll send scouts ahead to find the route,' Garon murmured, 'just as I did for us.'

But nothing of the sort happened. Lord Elktor and his knights dismounted and so did the warriors. For the next half hour they waited. At last a man-at-arms rode up through the stationary column from the rear, leading a huge bay horse carrying a bulky figure directly to the viscount's side. The two men spoke. The fat man pointed to the upper section of the rockslide and made a sweeping gesture.

'Raldo!' Cleaton exclaimed.

'He's told them of our plan,' Kilian said in a voice gone flat. 'They're not going to cross en masse. We've lost our chance to panic them.'

The others groaned. Niavar said, 'Damn that Butterball! He must have been gulling us, acting more sick than he really was.'

'He was in very bad shape,' Garon protested. 'I examined him before we slept. He had bruises and scrapes almost from head to toe. He kept me awake with his groans of pain.'

'I think our Brother despaired of being able to make this difficult journey,' Kilian murmured, 'and conceived of a plan to ingratiate himself with our pursuers and thus gain lenient treatment when he surrendered.'

'Let's smite him with a bolt!' Cleaton's swarthy face was merciless. 'That'll show the lard-arse weasel!'

'No,' the alchymist decided. 'We won't waste our talent in petty revenge. We'll need every bit of it in making our escape.'

'But it's a stalemate, master,' Niavar said. 'They won't cross while we're waiting to bring the rocks down. But if we run, they'll be after us like wolves. You can be sure those local Brothers riding with them are adept at scrying. They've probably got a mind's eye on us right this minute.'

Kilian said, 'They won't scry us if we're under a cover-spell.'

'You said you couldn't cover us all!' Garon said.

'I propose weaving a new kind of spell, incorporating all our talents. I'm stronger now, and we're no longer encumbered with Raldo. I'm afraid we must leave our horses behind, but that would strengthen the illusion that we were still lurking here. All we need is an hour or so head start. A man can move nearly as fast as a horse on this wretched track. And even though Lord Elktor has a reputation for rashness, I think we can trust him to wait at least that long before daring the rockslide.'

'Will we be safe once we're inside the cave?' Niavar asked.

Kilian glanced at Garon. 'You said its entrance was hard to see from the path. I'll be able to disguise it with my talent as well.'

'And so we *walk* to Didion?' Garon said.

'Would that be impossible?'

'No, but –'

'Other opportunities will present themselves,' the alchymist said with serene confidence. 'No doubt we'll have to stay in the cave for a few days until the searchers lose heart and return to Elktor, but that will give Felmar and Scarth time to catch us up.'

He retrieved his jerkin and gestured for the others to do the same. 'No time to waste. Come close to me, one behind the other with a hand on the shoulder of the man ahead.' He described to them how they should blend their talent with his to reinforce the extended blanket of couverture. 'There's still a long chance we might be spotted by the naked eye. We'll duck-walk to the horses to lessen the possibility. Ready?'

They murmured assent. He took a few moments weaving the spell, than laid it over the four of them. The bright sunlight turned fractionally dimmer. The others augmented the enchantment as they'd been told to.

'Now,' Kilian said. They crouched and moved off to safety while the Brothers who accompanied Lord Elktor exerted their windsearching faculties in vain.

FOURTEEN

It was not until late morning that Beynor was able to finish dealing with Scarth.

Much earlier, an hour or so after the small troop of knights and warriors from Elktor had abandoned their pursuit of the fleeing thief, Beynor had tracked him into a region of broken cliffs at the southern edge of the mountains. There the density of the rock formations, combined with the cover-spell, defeated even his powerful windsight. From Scarth's ravaged appearance, it seemed likely that he would soon need to rest. Once he was asleep and susceptible to dream-invasion, his fate would be sealed.

With the advent of strong daylight, Beynor had been obliged to hoist the dinghy's sail and be content with slower progress upriver. The assistance of the submerged Salka Eminence was now all but imperceptible to human observers. Beynor spent the boring hours on the Malle scrying the barge of the royal family, watching Prince Somarus's party as it emerged from the wilderness and set out along the road to Castlemont, and scrutinizing events taking place at Elktor, where Sir Gavlok, the youthful windvoice called Mattis, who had led the chase after Scarth, three other squires, and presumably the unscriable Deveron Austrey, seemed to be making preparations to leave the castle. The large force that had gone after Kilian was only sporadically viewable as it continued to search high in the mountains near the head of the gorge. Of the alchymist himself there was no sign.

A bell in a village on shore tolled the eleventh hour of morning, and Beynor decided to try Scarth again. His wind-search once more proved fruitless, so he attempted a dream-invasion. He found the thief not only asleep, but also suffering a horrendous nightmare – the best possible framework for mental manipulation. Beynor waited while the awful scenario played out in the dreamer's mind, so that he himself might fully understand its portent and make use of it. Then he artfully banished all remnants of Scarth's fear, leaving the man's unconscious open to coercion.

Nothing was moving inside the dark fissure in the cliff-face. It was probably sleeping off its meal, the lucky brute, while *he* felt his empty belly knocking against his backbone, tormenting him with spasms of hunger.

Scarth was well concealed behind a large rock, not badly wounded after all, carving collops of meat from one of the haunches of the mule's partially devoured body and stringing them on a stick for roasting over the little fire he'd started with his talent.

A noise! Someone was coming up the slope. The sound of footsteps crunching over broken rock was steady and undoubtedly human, perhaps a local hunter or trapper who could render aid. He decided to risk a cautious hail.

'Psst! Over here! And for God's sake, if you value your life, tread softly and keep your voice down.'

A familiar small figure came into view. It was Felmar! Scarth almost whooped for joy, but restrained himself as his friend crept to his side and clasped him in an enthusiastic embrace.

Scarth, Scarth, I thought I'd never catch up with you. But look at you, Brother, all banged and bloody! And what in hell's happened to your poor mule?

'I thought you were dead, Fel. Thought the moonstones had burnt you to ashes.'

No, but it was a narrow squeak. Did you get away with the book and the sigils?

Scarth slapped the pouch hanging at his belt. 'Three of the important stones are safe. The fourth was lost in the confusion of my escape. I've still got the book stuffed in my shirt. But tell me how you found me here!'

No, you go first. My escape was pretty ordinary, but I can see you've had a rare old time of it.

'Well, yes. I was chased across the moors by troops from Elktor, but I gave 'em the slip under my cover-spell . . . But how were you able to find me? I've still got the spell in place.'

This is a dream, friend. Everything's possible in a dream! What happened next, after you evaded pursuit?

'Things went well enough until I reached this place and started looking about for a path into the mountains, or at least a place to rest where scryers wouldn't spot my mule when I dismounted. There's a deep cleft yonder where the rock-face rises up. It looked ideal, so I lit a faggot and started inside to look it over. Then I caught a whiff of this vile stench, and saw the bones. But by then it was after me, roaring and slavering. Whether it smelled me or just saw through the spell, I don't know. I thought I was a dead man for sure, but it stopped to savage the mule I'd left hobbled. I got away down the slope, slipping and sliding and blubbering like a baby. I fell and smashed my head and bled from the scalp like a stuck pig, but the wounds aren't serious. I hid for a while, then came out to take a bit of meat from the mule's carcass. By then I was starving.'

Booger me! What a tale. You've had rotten luck, Brother. But thanks be to God and Saint Zeth you're all right . . . Which sigils did you take with you from the hut?

'Three of the four important ones we played the game with. They were all I had time to gather up. The doorway sigil must have been buried by the strange ash that lay all over the floor.'

Felmar smote his own forehead, and his face was twisted in an expression of frustration. *You know, I can't remember what the other three stones look like! My mind's gone blank from all the travails I've suffered. Will you just describe the things?*

Scarth fumbled with his belt wallet. 'I'll show you –'

No, don't go to the bother. Just tell me what they look like.

Scarth frowned. 'Well, there's the ring I thought might be a Weathermaker, and the icicle or carrot or whatever it is.'

Yes, its name is Ice-Master. And the third?

'A little wand with phases of the moon carved on it.'

Felmar's eyes went wide with shock and he gave a loud gasp. *Just a simple rod, with a hole at one end? And phases of the moon, you say?*

'Yes . . . Look, let me take them out. You can see for yourself.' He opened his pouch and proffered the sigils in the palm of his hand.

But Felmar had closed his eyes, as if in ecstatic contemplation.

A Destroyer! That's what it is. One of the greatest of the Great Stones. The Lights slew my poor mother for using it contrary to their wishes. But if it were neutralized by the Potency, there'd be no danger at all to the user.

'Fel, I don't know what you're saying. What's a Destroyer?'

We'll have to keep the sigils safe until I can come for them. I don't suppose the book matters anymore, since I don't need it for the activation, but we might as well include that, too. Take one of the empty saddlebags from the dead mule, old friend. Put the book and the stones inside, strap it up tightly, and follow me.

It was only a dream, so Scarth obeyed without argument.
He was curious to see what would happen next. Felmar beckoned him to follow, circled around the little fire and the dead
animal, then set out uphill, straight for the tall opening in
the rock. He peered into the fissure, then put a finger to his
lips.

*Come on. But be very, very quiet! There's a nice dry ledge, head-
high on the right and only a couple of ells from the entrance. Put
the saddlebag there.*

Scarth held back. 'Be careful! What if it wakes up and
smells us? It's a monstrous thing! Nearly six feet tall at the
shoulder!'

*Listen. I've found a fine place for us to hide out. Good food and
drink, comfortable beds for as long as we want them, and no one
can scry us there. You'll love it. But we don't dare bring the sigils
and book. We've got to put them in a safe place and pick them up
later, when the hue and cry has died down. Understand?*

'All right.'

Scarth could smell decaying flesh inside the den even
before he entered. The bones underfoot and the rough rocky
floor had smears of fresh blood. Alert for the slightest sound
from the inky depths, he pushed past Felmar and set the
leather bag on the high ledge. Felmar was right: this was a
perfect place to hide it. No one who looked casually inside
the hole would catch sight of the bag, and it was surely safe
from scrying.

'That's that.' He turned about, ready to leave – and saw that
Felmar was gone. Quickly, he strode toward the fissure's mouth
and looked outside, but there was no trace of his friend.

Wake up. Both of you.

'Fel?' He opened his eyes, felt his knees buckling, caught
his breath in stark terror at the strange hooting snuffle that
came from the darkness behind him. Something stepped on
a dry bone and crushed it. He heard a low growl, risked a

fearful glance, and saw beady black eyes and lips drawn back in a snarl from enormous ivory teeth.

'It's a dream!' Scarth Saltbeck screamed at the top of his lungs. But he had been sleepwalking . . .

He stumbled down the slope, but the giant brown bear caught him easily before he reached the shelter of the tall rocks, and dragged him back to its den.

The exhausted men-at-arms, the knights, the windvoices, and their dauntless leader Lord Olvan straggled back down the mountain path even before daylight had begun to fade, intending to make a safe camp on the far side of the great rockfall, where they'd left their mounts and supplies before pursuing their quarry on foot.

Kilian and his companions watched the retreat through the spell of couverture disguising the entrance to their cave. When the last of the hunters had disappeared, he extinguished the magic.

'They'll be back tomorrow,' Garon said. 'There are game trails up there going in different directions. The wind-searchers can't have explored them all. Do you want to move on? The weather's fine, there'll be a nearly full moon tonight, and we've had a good rest. We might almost reach the divide by dawn tomorrow. I don't think they'd dare follow us much further than that. These are castle garrison troops, not crack mountaineers like the ones on duty at Beorbrook Hold. A lot of them are looking over their shoulders, afraid that demons might be stalking them.'

Kilian thought about it. 'I must try to windspeak Felmar and Scarth again. There's a useful high point on the ridge above the cave. I can reach it if I go up this ravine. Let me try to scry our friends from there. Should I fail in that, I'll extinguish their cover-spell and bespeak them. If I still have no luck, we'll move on without them.'

Garon inclined his head. 'As you wish, my lord. However, for your own safety, I insist on accompanying you on the climb up to the ridge.'

'Very well.'

The two of them left the cave together. Niavar and Cleaton came out to stretch their legs and relieve themselves.

'Wicked hike it was, getting here,' Niavar observed. 'Maybe not so tiring for you, with your long legs, but I'm not keen to press on, I can tell you.'

'We'll make young Garon carry you pickaback,' Cleaton said with an evil grin. 'Give him less breath to talk down to us, the conceited gowk. Just because he's highland-born, he thinks the sun shines from his bum.'

Niavar shrugged. 'The lad knows we'd be helpless up here without him – and he's right. Possess your soul in patience, Clete. When we've safely reached Somarus's camp, it'll be different. Lord Kilian won't let a jumped-up highlander lord it over two experienced administrators like you and me.'

They sat without speaking for a time. Then Cleaton said, 'I think we made a great mistake not blasting Butterball to smuts back at the rockslide.'

'How so?'

'He won't be content telling the king's men about our failed ambush. Mark my words, Var, he'll spill his guts of everything he knows. Felmar and Scarth and the treasure. Waringlow's complicity. Even Kilian's intention to ally with Beynor and Somarus.'

'Well, how bad can that be for us? Who cares if the new Father Abbas gets the chop? And the sigils and books were only a kind of bribe for Beynor, weren't they? I mean, it'd be a fine thing for Kilian and the Mosslander to have a few active moonstone sigils at their command – but if the things are lost, our master won't give up on his great scheme. He'll change tactics, that's all. He implied that Beynor has a plan to put Somarus on the throne of Didion sooner rather than later. All kinds of interesting opportunities might present themselves to clever magickers if a hothead king reigns in the barbarous northland.'

Cleaton gave a gloomy grunt. '*Interesting.* A nice word. I suppose we're talking war with the Sovereignty.'

'Wars provide interesting opportunities, too,' said Niavar.

They fell silent again, then by mutual consent unrolled the blankets of their bedrolls, intending to catch a few winks of sleep before Kilian and Garon returned.

'So you think both Felmar and Scarth are dead, my lord?' Garon asked. 'And the treasure's gone?'

Kilian wiped perspiration from his brow. He sat on the summit of a crag, waiting for his heart to slow after the strenuous effort needed for the generalized call on the wind. His windsearch of the desolate border region where the moor met the mountains had eventually revealed the mutilated body of a mule and a bloody trail leading to an animal den. A man's boot and a dead campfire with uncooked pieces of meat on a stick were the only other clues.

There had been no need for him to obliterate the coverspell shielding Felmar and Scarth. It no longer existed anywhere within the range of his windtalent. His attempt to bespeak the Brothers using their private password had failed. So had the only remaining option, an open windcall that might have been perceived by anyone. All he had done was call the men's names. The timbre of his windspeech was sufficient to convey the urgency of his cry.

But there had been no answer.

'Yes, I believe they are dead,' Kilian replied. 'And what you have so blithely referred to as "the treasure" is lost to us. It's a severe disappointment. but by no means an insurmountable disaster. Other magical resources are available to me – and to those who are loyal to me – in Didion.'

'I'm happy to hear it, my lord. Shall we go back to the others? If we're to set out again tonight, we won't want to waste time.'

Going down the steep ridge was harder than the ascent. But even as Kilian concentrated on placing his hands and feet as Garon directed, a part of his mind was occupied by more urgent thoughts. He'd spoken confidently to the young Brother, minimizing the effect of the trove's loss on their future. But the reality of the situation was more ominous – especially as it pertained to Kilian's alliance with Beynor. The Mossland sorcerer cared only about the Trove of Darasilo. Once he learned that the large cache of moonstones had been lost, he was bound to view Kilian as an ally of questionable value.

It was even possible that Beynor already knew about the fate of Felmar, Scarth, and the trove. Why else would he have held off bespeaking Kilian in his dreams? Beynor's tremendous natural talent might have been able to pierce the new cover-spell, in which case he had probably wind-watched the lot of them ever since he arrived on High Blenholme Island.

I may be in serious trouble, the alchymist thought. However, there was a small ray of hope . . . or perhaps even two rays!

Firstly, Beynor still lay under the Lights' curse, which prevented him from utilizing sigil magic. Nevertheless he coveted his sister's stones and might also have designs on stones possessed by the Salka. Perhaps he might be foolish enough to think he could use Kilian as a sigil-wielding deputy, as he had once used the wizard-assassin Iscannon.

The second hopeful possibility lay in the other principal player in their Didionite adventure. Prince Somarus Mallburn was a mature warrior who was justifiably wary of Beynor.

He had been present at the young Conjure-King's unforgettably calamitous coronation, where Ullanoth had made her brother the laughing-stock of the entire island. The prince would also remember Beynor's magical failures that had culminated in Conrig's victory over Didion at sea. So wouldn't the new King of Didion welcome an advisor who was intimately acquainted with the minds of both Beynor and Conrig? The gold intended as a bribe for Somarus was gone, alas, left behind with his horse – except for the small amount Kilian had been able to secrete about his person. But he still had his wits and his talent. They'd have to serve.

I must get to Somarus before Beynor does! Kilian said to himself. He wondered where the prince was, right at this very minute. Beynor must have told him to be ready to come out of hiding immediately upon the assassination of his brother. Would Somarus be rash enough to lurk about the vicinity of Boarsden, hoping to observe the deed? And if he were hiding there with an entourage, might not one of his men be a windvoice who'd respond to a general hail?

'Watch your foot, my lord!' Garon exclaimed. 'That rock's unstable. Use the one to the right instead. Please pay closer attention to my instructions. A fall from here could result in serious injury.'

Kilian hastened to obey. 'I'm sorry, my boy. My mind was wandering. I won't let it happen again.'

When the discouraging news came from Lord Elktor's adepts that evening, and it seemed likely that Kilian had made good his escape into the high country, Snudge knew he could no longer postpone his long-delayed personal report to the king. He bespoke Vra-Sulkorig, asking if Lord Stergos was strong enough to receive and transmit wind-messages.

The Keeper of Arcana replied with understandable coolness.

The Royal Alchymist may be able to hear you, Sir Deveron, but it would still tax him to bespeak you over such a long distance. I fear you'll have to make do with my own humble talents.

'Oh, come off it, man.' Snudge was too downhearted to be bothered with hurt feelings. 'I need his advice on a personal matter, that's all. It can wait . . . Is His Grace there with you?'

Yes. We've been waiting to hear from you for a night and a day, here in the sitting room of the Royal Alchymist's new apartment. The High King believed you would wish to consult immediately with Lord Stergos concerning the safeguarding of the recovered trove, so he wished to stay close to his brother. He's been conducting all his business from here. Please wait while he finishes issuing instructions to the Lord Treasurer.

'Feribor Blackhorse?' Snudge was taken aback. 'Well, well! Nothing to do with my mission, I trust.'

His Grace will discuss the matter with you if he sees fit. Please wait.

Snudge relaxed in the padded chair that sat before the cold fireplace in the chamber he shared with Gavlok. The other knight was elsewhere in Elktor Castle, making arrangements for their departure on the morrow, should the High King approve it. Gavlok had forgiven Snudge for not taking him on the hunt for Scarth, but the squires Valdos and Wiltorig were still nursing their wounded pride.

Sir Deveron? If you please, I shall now relay the High King's words to you. His first remarks are full of colorful language expressing his resentment at your lack of courtesy. I leave them to your imagination. From here on, I give you his words verbatim: Have you recovered the Trove of Darasilo?

'Tell His Grace that its fate is still uncertain. However, both of the thieves are dead. Of this I am sure. Within another day or two, I hope to learn more about the trove. It certainly has not fallen into the hands of Kilian Blackhorse or any other evil person.'

The king is gratified to learn that, but justifiably impatient to know where the trove is, and why you're unable to get your hands on it. He regrets that the thieves were not taken alive so that they could be questioned and then given their just desserts. How fares the hunt for Kilian?'

'Ollie Elktor's forces chased him far up Roaring Gorge. They narrowly avoided a deadly trap the alchymist had planned. Their escape was due to the fortuitous capture of one of Kilian's henchmen, a certain Raldo – the former Palace Novicemaster who was called Butterball by some of the Brethren. This man was injured and his companions rather foolishly left him behind . . . and alive. He traded some very useful intelligence in return for clemency, which Count Elktor was glad to grant.'

His Grace says that Ollie has a futtering great nerve pardoning an enemy of the Crown, but under the circumstances he'll not object. What did the fellow have to say?

'First, Kilian and his cohorts escaped Zeth Abbey through the good offices of Abbas Waringlow. This worthy hastened the demise of his predecessor so that he could coordinate the abbey's windsearch efforts, and ensure that Kilian and the two thieves were not found by any of the resident Brethren.'

The king's reply is lamentably obscene. What was Waringlow's motive for committing treason?

'The oldest in the world: power. Kilian taught his friend a spell that subtly coerced the ruling council of the abbey so that they'd elect Waringlow as successor to old Noachil.'

His Grace notes that the new abbas will have a brief tenure. What other information did this Raldo convey?

'Kilian and Beynor of Moss are in league with Prince Somarus of Didion. Beynor is on High Blenholme, but I'm not certain where. He and Kilian are plotting to assassinate Honigalus and put Somarus on the throne in his place. Unfortunately, Kilian didn't disclose details of the scheme to underlings such as Raldo. It may be proper to warn King Honigalus of the danger.'

The High King will take that under advisement. Anything further?

'Kilian and his cronies had their iron gammadions removed by Waringlow. I myself saw one of the discarded pendants on the boat they used in their escape. I'll leave it to you to explain the ramifications of this to His Grace. The most crucial thing is, Kilian now has the potential ability to activate moonstone sigils and use them – while Beynor, who is under a curse, cannot.'

His Grace asks your opinion about the odds of capturing Kilian.

'I don't think Ollie has a hoot in hell of pulling it off. I might be able to track Kilian myself if I go into the mountains. But that could take weeks, and he has an excellent guide – a young Brother from the abbey who knows the country. Tell His Grace in the strongest terms that I would prefer to carry on with my mission to Tarn. Leave the search for Kilian in the hands of Lord Olvan.'

. . . After consideration, King Conrig agrees. He commands you to proceed to Beorbrook Hold early on the morrow. There you will be joined by two highly experienced Mountain Swordsmen, members of Earl Marshal Parlian's elite force, who will assist your incursion into Tarn. You will not spend the night at Beorbrook, but instead go on directly to the principal fort at Great Pass. After resting there, continue along the Wold Road with all speed. Enter Tarn by whatever route you think best.

'I understand. Is there further news of Princess Maudrayne? It's very important that I know which area of Tarn to concentrate my search upon.'

A renegade local shaman claims to know where the princess is being hidden. He may be lying. We're looking into the situation. If his information is plausible, we'll inform you without delay. Do you have more to say to his Grace?

'Not at this time. Apologize for my tardy report. So much

was happening, and I wished to convey as complete a picture of events here as possible.'

The king graciously forgives you, and bids you rest well.

'Tell him the same from me, Sulkorig. But for God's sake let me know immediately when Lord Stergos is able to speak on the wind.'

I will. Good luck to you, Sir Deveron.

'Thanks,' Snudge replied tersely. He cut the wind-thread and sat back in his chair to recuperate. 'Rest well,' he muttered. 'Not bloody likely.'

Then he bespoke the head windvoice at Beorbrook Hold, and told him to collect the men who had been assigned to help him. They would have to confer on the wind at some length, organizing the mission to Tarn.

Conrig took his wife Risalla to his bed that night, and after they had enjoyed the consolation of their bodies, he did not sleep but instead rose up, put on a light robe, and invited her to join him on the balcony.

'It would be my pleasure, husband,' she said.

Barefoot and wearing only a shift of delicate lawn, she took two goblets and a ewer of mead, then came out and sat with him at the wicker table where they sometimes ate breakfast in high summer. The night was clear and warm, with a great silver moon. Mercifully, a breeze from the west spared them the lingering odor of the burnt cloister wing.

Conrig sipped mead for a few minutes before speaking. 'I had communication with my intelligencer, Sir Deveron, earlier this evening. The pursuit of the fire-raisers has ended with their deaths. He was able to question neither man, but we've learned that they're connected to a conspiracy headed by my former Royal Alchymist, Kilian Blackhorse. He was confined to Zeth Abbey but has recently escaped. He's presumed to be fleeing into Didion.'

'Ah.' The queen waited for him to continue.

'I've not spoken to you about this man before, Risalla, but I suppose you've learned something of Kilian's unsavory history from the court ladies. He and the former Conjure-King of Moss, Beynor, were closely linked in a plot to kill me.'

'I had heard,' she said evenly, 'that they also tried without success to thwart your invasion of Didion. And Beynor, at least, attempted to assist the fleet of Honigalus when he fought against your Cathran navy.'

'True,' he admitted, not meeting her gaze. He drank deeply from the cup and poured more mead. 'You have been a loyal and dutiful wife and a loving mother to our children. But you're not a woman made of stone. I know that deep sorrow and resentment must remain in your heart because of my own role in the death of your mother and father, as well as Didion's submission to the Sovereignty.'

'I pray for King Achardus and Queen Siry each night. But nothing can bring my parents back to life. I take what consolation I can from the knowledge that they died with honor, fighting for our country. My older brother Honigalus surrendered to the Sovereignty and accepted you as his liege lord. So did I, because he asked it of me. I have pledged you not only my bodily fidelity but also my political allegiance. Never would I do anything to harm you or the union of nations you have forged. And may God strike me dead if I lie.'

She put down her goblet and extended both her hands to him. He clasped them, and she could see his dark eyes glint in the moonlight.

'I believe you,' he said. 'And I trust you. So you must know what else I learned from Sir Deveron tonight. An informant he believes to be truthful claims that your brother Somarus has conspired with Kilian and Beynor to assassinate Honigalus, with a view to putting Somarus on the throne.'

She cried out, drawing away from him. 'I don't believe it!

I know Somarus is bitter about our brother's surrender, for if Hon had died in battle, our nation would still be free. Or thus Somarus believes, as do many others who sympathize with him. He foments rebellion against your overlordship and attacks Cathran caravans traveling to Tarn, but he's not a fool. If he was known to have engineered the death of Honigalus, all Didion would turn against him in revulsion. Our people are fierce and contentious, but they're also unshakably devoted to tradition. A regicide can never occupy our throne. The great dukes and barons will not allow it.'

'But if murder could not be proven?'

'Didion and Cathra are no longer at war. In wartime, the succession devolves to the claimant most likely to lead the nation to victory. But in peacetime, the dead king's progeny succeed him – male and female without discrimination. If Honigalus were to die, his oldest son Onestus would inherit the crown and Queen Bryse would be named regent until his majority. Next in line are Prince Bartus and his sister Casabarela. Furthermore, if it were approved by the great lords, Queen Bryse herself might be named queen regnant. She would then have the option of marrying and declaring her husband co-monarch. This is the ancient law of our country.'

'What if not only Honigalus, but also his wife and three children were to be slain? And Somarus was left the only surviving heir?'

'Impossible!' Risalla exclaimed. 'My brother would never sanction such an infamous crime.'

'Are you certain? I think no crime is too heinous for Kilian and Beynor to perpetrate if it would serve their own ends. And I wonder if Somarus might not give tacit consent to the deeds of villains, if those deeds opened to him a clear path to Didion's throne.'

'I know Somarus,' she insisted. 'He would never stoop to such dishonor.'

Conrig sighed and rose to his feet, the moonlight giving luster to his fair hair and beard. 'Wife, your sisterly loyalty does you credit. Nevertheless, I beg you to have your wizards bespeak Honigalus as soon as possible, warning him of the potential danger to him and his family. And if you have any influence over Somarus, beseech him to abandon this horrendous scheme forthwith and sever any alliance he might have made with Kilian and Beynor.'

She looked away. 'I – I had intimations that Somarus would soon rebel against the Sovereignty and Honigalus in some manner. He sounded me out, sent a message asking if I would side with him secretly. I refused. I told him I'd always love him, but said I would never go back on my pledge of fealty to you. I also ordered him not to tell me anything more of his plans. So – so that my conscience would not compel me to reveal them to you.'

'I wish you had told me of his message,' Conrig said evenly. 'But I understand why you did not, and I can't hold it against you. Love will not be gainsaid.'

'If I'd known he was contemplating murder . . .' She trailed off, her voice full of woe. 'But perhaps he isn't, after all. Kilian and Beynor may have kept him in the dark, and I pray this is so. Still, I don't doubt he'd take advantage of the death of the royal family without a second thought. Somarus is a firebrand, Conrig – once set burning, he must flame on until his consummation. Whatever that may be.'

'Will you at least warn him that Kilian and Beynor don't have Didion's best interests at heart? Somarus means nothing to them, except as a potential weapon to use against me. Both of them are sorcerers who wouldn't hesitate to ally themselves with the Beaconfolk. Beynor is half mad, like his father before him. He seeks revenge against his sister Ullanoth and is convinced that she cost him his throne. The truth is, he affronted the Beaconfolk and they laid a curse on him.'

Risalla's face went blank, as though her flesh suddenly shuttered her soul. She whispered, 'There are those who say that *you* are in league with the Great Lights.'

'I know about the rumors. But they lie. I formed a pact with Ullanoth, that's true enough. She promised to use her magic to assist the cause of the Sovereignty. But never was any unholy bargain made with the Beaconfolk to assure my success.'

'Other rumors say she is your lover, who can deny you nothing – not even at the cost of her own life! Oh – don't look on me that way. I'm not jealous. You said it yourself: love will not be gainsaid! But I do pity her, poor soul, since it seems that her great sacrifice on your behalf was all in vain. Is it not true that she's dying after exerting her sorcery overmuch hunting for the fire-raisers?'

He turned away from her, arms crossed, and stared over the balcony rail at the moonlit palace gardens. 'So her close advisors say. If it gives you satisfaction, know that I never had a heartfelt love for her. I was infatuated for a time, but that passed away, leaving only – only respect and appreciation for all she had vouchsafed to me. You're right to pity her, Risalla . . . And any other woman who loves without being loved in return.'

Risalla rose on tiptoe and kissed his unyielding lips. 'I'll go back to my own chambers now. Good night, my lord husband. It may give *you* satisfaction to know that some women are content with other things besides love.'

He said nothing, but only stood looking down at the silvered trees and flowerbeds until a deep-throated double hoot rang over the palace grounds. The huge winged form of an eagle-owl glided above the curtainwall like a wraith and disappeared behind a clump of weeping willows in the garden. Something screamed. The giant bird lofted up again, carrying its prey, and flew off toward the parklands along the River Blen.

Snudge! the king thought. His self-chosen heraldic device was an owl, the stealthy hunter.

'Hunt her down, lad,' he whispered. 'For Maude will never be content as needy Ullanoth and wise Risalla are. Lacking my love, *her* only satisfaction will be in my destruction.'

FIFTEEN

'Induna!' the old man cried testily. 'Are you wasting time picking wild strawberries again, you idle chit? Attend me at once!'

When there was no response he repeated his demand on the wind, and this time the saucy young minx condescended to reply. *It won't do you any good to yell and call me names. I'm coming as fast as I can. And if you don't treat me with the respect I deserve, I'll just go back to Barking Sands — see if I don't! — and you can bully someone else into doing your longspeaking and scut-work.*

He ground his few remaining teeth in fury, but held back the stinging rebuke she deserved. She was only seventeen, and the young boys and girls out berry-picking along the river were better company than a cranky old blind man on a fine sunny day. She'd make a good shaman in time, once she got the girlish giddiness out of her system. He should have thought of her before, rather than using that greedy old witch, Yavenis, to relay his overtures to the Cathran king. And now his need for a trustworthy confederate had become even more crucial.

He picked up his staff and moved painfully to the door of

his cottage. His oversight picked her out, coming up the path with a basket in one hand, a wee slip of a thing in a blue kirtle, with hair as brightly golden-red as rowan fruit. When she came to the stout gate in the fieldstone wall surrounding his steading she flicked open the latch with her talent and walked through the herb gardens without haste, humming a tune.

'Hurry!' he growled. 'I need you to bespeak Cala Palace for me immediately.'

'Then I suppose you've no time to share my strawberries,' she said with a sly smile. 'I picked enough for two, Eldpapa, but if you're going to be grumpy and hateful . . . well, never mind.'

The notion that she'd do him that small kindness shamed him out of his ill humor. 'I'm sorry, Induna. I'm impatient. And I'm worried that King Conrig thinks I'm only a charlatan trying to dupe him out of a bucket of gold. He should have replied to my proposal by now, even if the answer was No.'

'You asked for too much,' the girl said. 'If he wants to bargain, don't slam the door in his face.' She took two bowls from the cupboard of the neat, well-appointed kitchen, then sat down at the table and began to hull the tiny sweet berries.

'It's what I need to retire to Andradh in style,' he mumbled resentfully. 'Young people don't understand these things. If you settle in a foreign land, they only respect you if you've got money.'

'You already have a nice cottage, with Tigluk and Wollu to take care of you. I don't know why you want to go to Andradh. They're all wicked pirates.'

He started for his sanctum. 'It's none of your business why I want to go there. Come along with me. Let those berries be till after we bespeak the Cathran king, and I'll have Wollu bring clotted cream from the ice-house for us to eat with them.'

The girl sighed. 'Oh, very well, Eldpapa.' She wiped her reddened fingers on her apron and followed.

Blind Bozuk's sanctum was in the loft of the cottage. There were dormer windows of real glass in gablets on all four sides so he could scry in any direction without material hindrance. The walls were lined with shelves full of jars, crocks, and boxes containing the magical ingredients that he used to concoct his wonderful spells and potions. None of the containers had labels; he knew where every item was. Cobwebs dripped from the rafters, and all the surfaces were filthy with dust because he never allowed the housekeeper upstairs to clean. Induna planned to do something about that before too much longer. She had good eyes, even if her grand-father didn't, and she wasn't going to work and study in a pigsty. If he wanted to be her teacher, he'd have to change his slovenly ways. Otherwise she'd go back to her own home at Barking Sands and carry on as Mother's apprentice.

'Sit down, girl,' Bozuk growled. He plumped himself into a heavy old armchair with tattered cushions.

She wiped off a stool with her apron. 'I'm ready, Eldpapa. Shall I bespeak the Cathran wizard Vra-Sulkorig, as before?'

'Yes. Tell him I have important new information for King Conrig, which I'll pass on to him gratis. It concerns a rendezvous between Tarnian ships that took place early today off Kolm Head. The High Sealord, Sernin Donorvale, met and conferred with Liscanor Northkeep, the brother of Princess Maudrayne. I read their lips. They talked about a boy who should by rights be sitting on the throne of Cathra. They said that the boy's father is ineligible to reign, because he secretly possesses arcane talent. Ask if King Conrig would like to have the conversation between Sernin and Liscanor repeated to him, word-for-word. At no charge, of course.'

Induna sat with her head bowed for some minutes. Then she opened her eyes and grinned.

The blind old man snapped, 'Well? Well? What does the Cathran king say?'

'He's very eager to hear what the two sealords said, Eldpapa. And he says it gives him great pleasure to agree to your fee of five thousand gold marks for information on the whereabouts of Princess Maudrayne and her son.'

The old man let out a gusty sigh of relief. He recited the conversation between Liscanor and Sernin, and prompted Induna as she relayed it to Conrig. When the girl finally cut the thread of windspeech and would have left the sanctum, he held up a hand and said to her, 'Wait. There's more.'

'Another message to be sent?'

He shook his head, 'No, Granddaughter, a more difficult thing by far. Please be seated again while I tell you.'

Rolling her eyes impatiently, she resumed her place on the stool.

'Ansel Pikan has taken Princess Maudrayne and her son into the far east, beyond the volcanos. At such a distance, with such massive rock bastions hindering even my mind's eye, it becomes increasingly difficult to track him and his captives. Thus far, Ansel has used a cover-spell that has proved no hindrance to my oversight. I am fairly certain of his ultimate destination, and when the Cathran king's messenger arrives with the gold I shall know where to direct his men in their preliminary search.'

Her shrewd little face had tightened with premonition. 'Eldpapa, what has all this to do with me?'

'Be patient! When the Cathran manhunters set out after Maudrayne, Ansel will know it. He'll shift her to another hiding place. And this time, he'll erect a more formidable magical cover – one that I'll be hard put to pierce because of the great distance that now separates us from the fugitive princess and her son. And so, my dear, I desire that you should leave here at once, and travel to the region where the precious pair are secreted, and be my agent on the spot to direct Conrig's hunters. I'm not so foolish as to believe you to be too frail and vulnerable to undertake such a mission. You're tough as a sealhide boot – and a formidable magicker already, in spite of your tender years. There will be perils on the journey, Induna, but none, I think, that would overwhelm you. You need not endanger yourself by approaching the princess's hiding place. You need only oversee her from a safe distance and report to me if Ansel Pikan attempts to spirit her away elsewhere.'

'Where am I to go, then,' she asked in a level voice. 'If I accept this charge? And what will be my payment?'

He burst into delighted laughter. 'A wench after my own heart! Your fee, little love, will be one-third of what I wring from Conrig. And the place you must go is the uttermost eastern coast of Tarn, north of that Fort Ramis which is held by a kinsman of Ansel. Of course I shall find stout companions to accompany you –'

'No,' she said.

'No?' The blind eyes widened in dismay. 'But all could be lost to me otherwise, for Conrig will never pay what he owes until he has the woman and her son in hand!'

'Silly Eldpapa! I didn't mean that I would not go, only that I wish no clumsy guardians hindering my freedom.' She rose from her stool and took his bony hands in hers. 'I rejoice at the opportunity to have a real adventure. Have no fear that I might behave rashly: I value my own skin too much to risk it as a foolhardy boy might do. Even less would I risk losing such a fine reward for my services.' She unhanded him and stepped back. 'We must plan everything with care. Come back downstairs, and we'll do it while we eat the sweet berries.'

They were two hours out of Elktor, riding at a fast pace over the moorlands toward Beorbrook, when Sulkorig sent out the brief hail.

Snudge let his mount fall behind the others, after making

the excuse of an urgent call of nature, then halted beside a peat-stained stream where graylings leapt from the water in pursuit of clouds of gauze-winged insects. The place was also alive with voracious midges, but at least Snudge was able to sit on firm ground while windspeaking.

'I'm ready. You said there was both good news and bad.'

The good is that the Tarnian shaman Blind Bozuk has agreed to tell us where Ansel has taken Maude. For reasons of state, the High King has decided to send the shaman's considerable payment to him by ship, guarded by the Lord Treasurer, and so we will not have Bozuk's information immediately.

'Feribor Blackhorse! I wish to God it were anyone but him going to Tarn. He might insert himself into this affair whether King Conrig wills it or not, and the results could be disastrous. The man's a villain, Vra-Sulkorig, but the king will hear no bad word spoken against him.'

He's embarking around noon on the high tide, taking the fastest naval frigate available. With luck, he may reach Northkeep, where this rascal Bozuk resides, in five days. The agreement is, we hand over half of the sum, and he tells us Maudrayne's hiding place. It's somewhere in the deep interior of Tarn. Lord Feribor wanted to set out after the princess himself with an armed company, but the king has strictly forbidden it and commanded him to wait in Northkeep with the balance of the payment. His Grace has no mistrust of the Lord Treasurer, but rather fears that Ansel Piken would easily discover what Feribor was about and move the princess elsewhere. The king believes you will have better luck outwitting the High Shaman and capturing her than any military force, since you come from an unexpected direction and have unexpected tactical advantages.

'Well, at least I'll have a solid lead to follow by the time I reach Tarn myself. Now tell me the bad news.'

The princess seems to have told her brother all of her secrets. And Liscanor has spilled the beans to the High Sealord. They met earlier this morning at sea and are returning to Donorvale, where Lord Sernin plans to call a secret meeting of his high council.

'My God! All of Maude's secrets? Not just the fact of her son being Conrig's legitimate heir? Do you mean she actually told her brother of the High King's . . . personal problem?'

Yes. You needn't dissemble. I'm aware now that His Grace possesses a small portion of talent – although Zeth knows I would rather be in ignorance. The princess feared that something might happen to her and the boy, Dyfrig, before she could confide in Sernin Donorvale. She was determined that Conrig's secret should be revealed to the world. Or at least to the sealords of her homeland, so they might use it and Prince Dyfrig as a lever to free themselves from the yoke of the Sovereignty.

'How has His Grace reacted? Is he there with you'

He has closeted himself in his private apartments to consider his options. The salient fact, of course, is that the Tarnians will have to present incontrovertible proof of both their allegations. This is not as easy as it may seem, especially since they don't have custody of the princess and her son, so they probably won't act in haste.

'Are there any new instructions for me from His Grace?'

No. Nor are there likely to be, until the Sealords make their first move.

'Then I request that any new messages to me be relayed via Vra-Mattis. Our armigers still remain ignorant of my talent, and I hope also to keep the knowledge from the two Mountain Swordsmen who will join our party later today.'

Very well.

'The only exception will be news of Lord Stergos. It's crucial that I bespeak him as soon as possible – but on no account should you say anything of this to the king. There are uncanny forces actively at work on our island, Sulkorig, and not all of them are human. Beynor could not have left the Dawntide Isles without the consent and active assistance of the Salka. I fear that he may intend to use the monsters in an attack against Moss and Queen Ullanoth, now that she is unable to defend herself. And the Salka may not be the only inhuman beings involved in Beynor's mischief-making.

Surely you don't refer to the Beaconfolk!

'Tell Lord Stergos what I've said. Beseech him to windspeak me soon. The fate of all High Blenholme may depend on it.'

Ullanoth's torment was oceanic, ebbing and flowing, sometimes a wild tempest of agony and at other times a flat melancholy devoid of all hope and ambition. She would plunge into the abyss, believing that the end was sure, only to be buoyed up through sweet transparency where the pain was absent. But the sure knowledge that suffering would soon return haunted her like the mocking laughter of a torturer. During the brief respites she was aware of her surroundings, although incapable of movement or speech, and remembered why she had come to this terrible pass.

For his sake. Because he had seemed in desperate need of her help.

In hindsight, she realized that his request that she use Loophole must have been motivated by something more than vengeance upon the two fugitive villains. He had certainly been robbed of Darasilo's Trove. But his desperation had been real. He had been convinced that she was the only one who could find the pair, and she could not help but respond.

And now she would die and spend eternity in the Hell of Ice because of her foolish, unrequited love.

'O Mother,' she prayed, 'why was I compelled to do as Conrig asked? Knowing!'

It is one of love's mysteries.

'And your leading me to find those terrible stones – was that, too, a perverse act of love?'

No, dear soul. It was an act of necessity.

Suspended in the clear void, resigned to the renewal of pain, she did not realize at first that the voice had a Source other than her fevered imagination.

'Mother? Queen Taspiroth? Is it you?'

I am not your mother. But I am the one who took on her form and bespoke you in a dream long years ago. I led you to the hidden cache in the fens so that you would not be crushed by the power of your brother Beynor. So that you would become Conjure-Queen, and bend the destiny of Conrig Wincantor. Both of you are part of the New Conflict that pits the Pain-Eaters against their enemies.

'Pain-Eaters?' Her mind was fogged and weary unto death, but the words cut to her mind's core and kindled a blaze of understanding. 'The Great Lights feed on my pain, and the pain of all who use their sorcery. This came about . . . how?'

Through the Old Conflict, when the Lights were first divided. One who was very wise and very foolish played a game – as his kind have done from time immemorial – thinking it would bring no great harm to the slow-witted game-pieces. But the game's awful potential was seized upon by others. The Source of the game lost control of it, sought help from Likeminded ones who tried to stem the burgeoning calamity, and failed. Vanquished, the Source was degraded and enchained, while the Pain-Eaters ate their fill.

'You are the one called the Source. Someone spoke of you to me once, long ago. Was it my mother?'

Queen Taspiroth was a brilliant sorceress who delved, perhaps too eagerly, into many mysteries. But she was consumed before we could enlist her in our just cause.

'You speak of a just cause . . . but you still play your game!'

War is a game. A contest between two sides. We Likeminded are vastly outnumbered, but we still must fight. I created the channel between the Sky and the Ground through which the pain flows. I am the One Denied the Sky and only I can lead the Likeminded to close off the channel. You will help me either willingly or not, as others of your race have done, beginning with Emperor Bazekoy.

'I have no choice?'

I offer you respite from agony. A temporary oblivion in which you live but have no sentience. Others who have helped us, but come perilously close to the Hell of Ice in the end as you have done, we have snatched to safety in the same manner. You will not die, but your new existence is not true life. Your consolation – and you will remain aware of it, comforted by it – is that the hoped-for victory will restore you again to the world you renounced. And that world will no longer be subject to the thrall of the evil Lights.

'Why me? You let my poor mother fall into hell.'

She clung to the power! You took the first steps in renouncing it. And sadly, her life did not have the potential to bring about change, as yours does.

'I don't understand . . . and I feel them returning to feed.'

Yes. I must tell you that there is a small chance you may survive their present devouring. You might recover your physical strength, as you did many times before, and re-enter the world of groundlings. So the choice you must make now is a real one. Will you join in the New Conflict, or trust that the capricious Great Lights will preserve your life once again rather than destroy you?

'If I let you take me, what will become of my people?'

Some will die, but not in the appalling manner that the Lights kill. War is coming, dear soul, which you cannot prevent. It will be fought in the Sky and on the Ground. If you come to me, the Conflict may be shortened and a good outcome is more likely.

'But not certain?'

No.

'When I put myself in peril at my lover's behest, I extracted a promise from him: that if anything happened to me, he'd defend Moss. I think he's able to do this more effectively than I, since I'm so weakened. Therefore, I agree to join your side of the Conflict . . . What must I do?'

Look upon me.

'Oh, Moon Mother! You're a Salka!'

No. I'm the One Denied the Sky. One of those you call the Great Lights. But since my essence is incorporeal, it cannot suffer. After the Old Conflict was lost, the victorious Pain-Eaters would have destroyed all the Likeminded if I had not agreed to this base transformation. It's right that I suffer in a Salka body, since in my heedless pride I used them, more than all the other entities, as pieces in my game.

'Source, I begin to understand. But don't tell me any more. I can't bear it. Just take me.'

It seemed to swim through the lucent transparency toward her, an apparition as dark as the spaces between the stars, lacking eyes and mouth, both of its coiling limbs cuffed and chained in dull-glowing sapphire links. She extended her hand and touched it.

Immediately she was gone, and the tiny green sphere began to fall. It splashed into the ocean of pain and drifted down toward the abyss of ice, until a black tentacle caught it up and bore it to safety.

Maudrayne came to her senses after Rusgann and Dyfrig woke, so her first awareness was of familiar voices, the boy asking bewildered questions and the serving woman doing her best to reassure him. She opened her eyes and saw a canvas roof overhead, held up by a curved framework. Heard clopping hooves. Smelled straw and equine sweat and musty wool. Felt movement.

Rusgann was saying, 'We're riding in a covered cart all laced up tight so we can't peek outside. But there's nothing to be afraid of, Dyfi. Your mother and I won't let anything happen to you.'

'The bumps make my stomach feel queer,' the boy fretted. 'I need to pee, too.'

A man's deep voice said, 'We'll stop in a few minutes.'

'Who's that?' the child said. His eyes were wide with fear.

'I think it's our old friend, Red Ansel,' Rusgann said drily.

She raised her voice. 'Master shaman! Did you hear what the lad said? Stop this wagon at once!'

Maudrayne pulled herself up to a sitting position, but almost at once was knocked down again as the wagon gave a sudden lurch and began to bounce more violently. She groaned, and Dyfrig cried out, 'You're hurting my mama!'

'Hang on,' Ansel called out. 'We're almost to a smoother place.'

They jounced along for a few more minutes, then came to a stop. Those inside the covered wagon heard high-pitched whinnying and the stamping of hooves. Crunching footsteps came around to the rear of the wagon and someone began to undo the fastenings. A moment later, the canvas flaps were pulled aside and Ansel's ruddy face greeted them with its usual broad smile. He held out a hand to Dyfrig.

'You'd better come first, lad, and we'll see to your needs. Put your shoes on. The ground has sharp bits of glassy stuff here and there. Ladies, take your time alighting.'

The boy clambered out and he and the shaman promptly disappeared from sight, leaving the princess and her maid crouching amidst a tangled nest of blankets and bundles, staring in astonishment at the strange landscape. Most of the surface of the ground was tumbled, pitted rock – cindery scoria and solidified dark lava. The irregular areas were interspersed with broad drifts of windblown, glittering black sand, unmarked save for the fresh ruts of their wagon wheels and the dimpled impressions of small hooves. Here and there, pockets of lighter-colored soil supported wiry shrubs and wild-flowers. Two enormous volcanos dominated the far horizon behind the wagon, emitting thin white plumes of vapor.

Maudrayne murmured, 'Mornash and Mount Donor? Great God of the Heights and Depths! Could we have come so far east? How long have we slept?' She climbed out of the wagon-bed, followed by Rusgann.

'Madam, have you any idea where we are?' the maid whispered. An uncanny silence surrounded them.

Maudrayne turned slowly about. The wagon, which she had remembered being drawn by two mules at the Northkeep waterfront, was now hitched to a team of four rough-coated ponies that drooped in their traces. A league or so onward the black wasteland came to an abrupt end in a row of hills, their lower slopes clothed in green and their summits nearly bare. The tallest, toward which the wagon seemed to be heading, was a nearly perfect dome of pale grey rock.

'I've never been here,' Maudrayne said, 'but I believe we've nearly crossed Tarn from west to east. Behind us are the volcanos and goldfields of my nation's interior. This black desert is part of the Lavalands, a desolate wilderness where nothing human can survive. Beyond those strange-looking hills lies the sea, the Icebear Channel that separates High Blenholme from the Barren Lands.'

Rusgann was shading her eyes from the hazy sun, studying the hills. 'There's something man-made on that highest baldtop. Like a little castle.'

Ansel's voice said, 'It's Skullbone Peel, our destination. It takes its name from the rounded shape of the hill.'

The two women turned about to find him and Dyfrig returning to the wagon from behind an upthrust monolith of reddish rock. 'Why?' the princess asked in a harsh tone. 'Why in God's name have you brought us here, to one of the most isolated and untenanted parts of Tarn?'

'For your safe keeping,' the shaman said to her. He lifted the little prince into the wagon, saying, 'Wait inside for a few minutes, and then I'll show you something interesting.'

'But I'm hungry!' Dyfrig protested, thrusting his head from between the canvas curtains. He would have climbed out again, but Ansel laid his hand atop his tawny curls.

'Rest, child, until I summon you.' The boy's eyes went blank and he withdrew without another sound.

Maudrayne addressed the shaman in a low, furious voice. 'And will you force Rusgann and me to rest again as well? Why not keep all of us sunk permanently in magical sleep? It would be so much more convenient for your purposes.'

'But not good for your health,' he said without heat. 'Your well-being is very important to me, dear Maudie.'

'Drop your pretense of solicitude for our welfare, Ansel Pikan! That was never your true motive for hiding my son and me. For if that were so, you would have no good reason to prevent us from taking refuge with my brother Liscanor or with my dear uncle, the High Sealord Sernin.'

Ansel said, 'If Conrig found you and Dyfrig, he would have you killed. And that is the truth.'

'But not the entire truth!' she raged. 'My son overheard you and the sea-hag talking one day, and even though he was unable to understand, he remembered your words well enough to repeat them to me: "We must make certain he remains king. He's the only one strong enough to hold them back. Without him, we have no hope of liberating the Source."'

'I'm sorry you learned of this. The matter is complicated and –'

'And you believe me too simple-minded to understand? I think not! You've kept me and my son prisoners for Conrig's sake, not ours. You seek to protect *him* from *me*!'

'My love for you dictated my actions. I would not have the king harm you, but I couldn't allow you to endanger his Sovereignty, either.'

'Your precious Source – whoever or whatever it is – commands your first loyalty. Protecting this Source is your paramount concern. You believe that Conrig Ironcrown is the only one strong enough to defeat the Source's enemies in battle, so you shield him from my righteous retribution. Admit it!'

He inclined his head without a word.

'Who is the Source?' she demanded.

'A force for good. That's all I may tell you now.'

'Who are its enemies?'

'There are two, who threaten both my master and all of humankind who dwell upon this island. Neither enemy is human. The one is incorporeal and can only be influenced indirectly by the might of High King Conrig. The second enemy is all too material, and Conrig is the only sure bulwark against it. I speak of the Salka.'

Maudrayne was incredulous. 'Those miserable amphibian monsters? They were vanquished and decimated by Emperor Bazekoy over a thousand years ago! The few that survive hide in the fens of Moss and in distant islands of the eastern sea. They are no threat –'

'They *were* not, so long as they remained disspirited and bereft of hope. But their mental outlook has changed. Someone has offered them a powerful new weapon that bids fair to restore their ascendance. And their numbers are not few. Over the centuries their population has grown until once again they represent a formidable menace. As yet, only the Salka of the Dawntide Isles have been roused from their ancient lethargy. But if their more numerous Moss-dwelling kin were inspired by the battle-success of the Dawntiders . . .'

Rusgann had been listening intently, and now with her usual forthrightness she did not hesitate to interrupt the shaman. 'You talked about two inhuman forces. Who's the second?'

'You call them the Beaconfolk,' Ansel replied. 'And because you are a native of Cathra, you've long since forgotten their power and their malignant nature, relegating them to legend. But the Great Lights are real, and their evil threatens all parts of the world where the aurora shines regularly in the sky.'

Rusgann gave a guffaw of disbelief, but the princess silenced her and addressed the shaman. 'I am no Cathran. I'm a daughter of Tarn, and perhaps willing to concede that you may be telling the truth. I say *perhaps*, because your word on this weighty matter is no longer enough to sway my conscience. I was greatly wronged by Conrig Wincantor. My son's injury is greater, since he is being denied his royal birthright. If I'm to postpone my demand for justice, you must convince me that there is good reason.'

'I can but try. There are other calls on my time, but from time to time I can visit you in your new residence –'

'Prison!'

'– in your new place of confinement and explain this very complex matter at greater length. I was probably remiss not to have explained it to you earlier. My excuse is that the Source has not fully confided in me, either, and the threat to humanity from the Salka hordes became obvious only a few months ago.' He came closer to her and laid a hand on her shoulder. 'Maudie, you are as dear to me as a daughter. To cage you and your little son tears the heart from my body, and I would that it were possible to set you free. But at present, I cannot. Not while you still threaten Conrig . . . and he threatens you. But the situation is not without hope. The Source has assured me of that.'

She pulled herself away in a sharp motion and stepped back, eyes flashing. 'How gratifying for both of you! Meanwhile, Dyfrig and I must languish in a wilderness, deprived of human companionship and all the things that make living worth while.'

'This place where I'm taking you is far more agreeable than Dobnelu's steading.' The shaman almost seemed to be pleading with her. 'You won't be so closely guarded. You can ride and hunt and fish, and even take short voyages on a

small sailboat. You'll have more congenial people around you
– even young playmates for Dyfrig. I've provided an extensive library for your pleasure. There are musical instruments
and art supplies for your use and for the education of your
son. If you have need of anything, your custodians will do
their utmost to supply it.'

'Really?' Almost as quickly as it had flared, the fire went
out of her and she seemed diminished and subdued. The
high color faded from her face and even her vivid auburn
hair seemed to dull. The sunlight was waning as the overcast thickened. To the west, the tall volcanos on the horizon
were turning to opaque grey shadows.

He drew a silver tube from inside his tunic and held it out
to her. 'It was to be a gift for young Dyfrig – the "something
interesting" I promised to show him. Spy through it at the
summit of the tallest hill, and you'll see where we're bound:
Skullbone Peel, the fortified summer residence of Ontel
Pikan, my cousin, and his family.'

With reluctance, she lifted the cylinder to her eye. It was
far from being a conventional spyglass, and she saw the
distant structure enormously magnified, a small but massive
square keep, built of shining white stone and topped by
battlements. A gable-roofed wing extended from its south
side, at the end of which rose a narrow round turret topped
with an odd construct that looked like a windmill.

She lowered the glass. 'It looks impregnable.'

'No one will harm you while you dwell there. The view
from the watertower is said to be stupendous. On a clear
day you can see for sixty leagues in all directions. There are
broad steps hewn from the living rock descending the
seaward side, and at their base is a sheltered cove where
whalers and other boats that ply the Desolation Coast may
put in during storms. Skullbone Peel is an outpost of Fort
Ramis, which lies forty leagues to the south. The fort is also

held by my cousin Ontel, who is a skilled shaman famed for accurate predictions of the weather. He is much respected by the seamen of the area.'

'A weather-wizard.' She sighed. 'I hope he's better company than the crabby old sea-hag.'

'We'd better be moving on,' Ansel said. 'It'll be two more hours before we reach the hill. Please take your ease while I check the team. There's food and drink in a basket inside the wagon. Dyfrig will wake if you touch his forehead.' He went to examine the ponies' harness.

Silently, Maudrayne handed the spyglass to Rusgann, who peered eagerly at their new home. 'I see someone on the battlements. A woman!'

'My cousin's wife, Tallu,' Ansel said. 'She's a remarkable person, Maudie. You may get on well with her.'

'Another magicker?' the princess asked, turning away with a conspicuous lack of interest.

'Oh, no,' said the shaman. 'Tallu is a noted sea-warrior of the Desolation Coast. She'll take very good care of all of you.'

The conferring of honors and the great feast were finally over. Duke Berkus Mallthorpe was resting his gouty foot and listening to a string quartet. Duchess Kenna had taken Queen Bryse to her private quarters for quiet conversation, and nursemaids were putting the royal children to bed in the guest chambers. Left to his own devices – a rare enough thing on the closely orchestrated royal progress – King Honigalus strolled the parapet atop the wall of Mallthorpe Castle with Galbus Peel, Fleet Captain of the Realm, who was also his closest friend and most trusted adviser.

The King of Didion was a stocky man whose thoughtful features were almost homely, and not even the most sumptuous attire was capable of making him an imposing figure. Once he had joked to Peel that the royal regalia made him

look like an honest packhorse tricked out in the gaudy caparison
of a tournament destrier. He was happiest at sea, and before
the death of his father Achardus, he had commanded the Fleet
with reasonable efficiency, acknowledging his continuing debt
to the naval prowess of Galbus Peel.

On the throne he had been less of a success. He came to
the kingship bearing the onus of defeat. But even if he had
not surrendered to Conrig, he was perhaps too civilized to
reign over a land barely lifted from barbarism. He utterly
lacked the fighting panache and animal vitality that had made
his hulking father respected even by the marcher lords who
regularly rebelled against him. Honigalus Mallburn had
accomplished near-miracles restoring his vanquished,
starving nation to prosperity, but many of the great merchants
and lords seemed unwilling to grant him credit for his efforts,
while the common people had never forgiven his capitulation to the Sovereignty.

Honigalus knew all this, and accepted it stolidly. What
happiness he gleaned from life came from Queen Bryse's
unconditional devotion, the gratification of having sired three
handsome, intelligent children who loved him with all their
hearts, and the support of a handful of staunch friends such
as Galbus Peel, who were not afraid to speak to him as though
he were a man, rather than a monarch.

'Look at that moon,' the Fleet Captain murmured. 'Red
as blood! They say forest fires are burning in the Elderwold.
The smoke in the air no doubt causes the baleful color.'

'It may be a portent as well, Galbus,' the king said quietly.
He rested his elbows on the hewn stone of the battlement
and stared at the carmine orb rising downriver.

Peel shot him a look of concern. 'Of what, sire – if I may
ask?'

'Before we sat down to feast, my wizard was bespoken by
a high-ranking Brother who is a senior servant to King Conrig.

It seems that the Cathrans have uncovered a far-ranging conspiracy. The conflagration at Cala Palace was a sort of opening salvo in a series of other inauspicious events designed to undermine our Sovereign's rule. The good Brother was careful not to go into specifics – which leads me to suspect that the happenstances must be very dire indeed. Conrig warns me that there might also be dirty work afoot in Didion.'

'What kind of dirty work?'

'Conrig's people have heard rumors that Somarus may be plotting against my life.'

'Anything specific that we can look into?' Peel was pragmatic.

'Not much. My sister Risa had a message from Somarus, asking if she'd support him if he challenged the Sovereignty. She refused, God love her.'

'Prince Somar's been trumpeting insurrection for years, sire, and doing precious little else but spouting hot air. What reason have we for taking him seriously now?'

'The tip about an assassination scheme came from an unusual source,' the king said. 'Old King Olmigon had a Royal Alchymist who exerted an unhealthy influence in the Cathran Privy Council. The man's name is Kilian, and he and Conrig were at daggers drawn from the time the Prince Heritor earned his belt and began to take an active role in affairs of state. Kilian was convicted of high treason and imprisoned. He recently escaped, and seems to have instigated the big fire in Cala Palace – among other high crimes. One of Kilian's cronies turned his coat and exposed details of a grand conspiracy the alchymist had hatched. Part of it involves killing me and all my family so that Somarus can assume the throne.'

'Great Starry Dragon! I've heard of this Kilian, sire. He was supposed to be working with Beynor of Moss at one point.'

Honigalus nodded. 'And may still be, according to Conrig's

windspeaker. Kilian has lost a lot of his magical power, but he's still a force to reckon with. What's more, he's apparently making his way into Didion – presumably to link up with Somar in the Elderwold.'

Galbus Peel blew out a relieved breath. 'Well, then! If the bastard is nowhere near here, we need have no immediate fears for your safety. We can obtain a sketch and a description of him and spread the alarum throughout the kingdom. Archwizard Fring can cope with sorcerous threats.'

'Fring!' The king's fingers drummed on the stone and he frowned. 'He still hasn't joined the progress. Let's make certain he does so before we leave Boarsden. He's the best windsearcher we have. We can put him to work ferreting out this traitorous Cathran magicker.'

'Sire, you may have to look closer into your brother's activities as well. I know you've been loath to take him seriously, but that may have been unwise. He needs to be put under constant wind surveillance, if our bumbling wizards can manage it. And we should try again to insert normal-minded secret agents into his mob of followers – naval types rather than adepts beholden to Fring. I'm not sure how trustworthy the Archwizard is.'

The king sighed. 'How I wish we could stay here in Mallthorpe another day! Duke Berkus is a kindly old stick without a conspiratorial bone in his body, and my wife adores the duchess. Things are likely to be much less pleasant at Boarsden Castle tomorrow. My late stepmother's people are obliged to extend their hospitality, but I'll likely have to turn a blind eye to all manner of petty affronts.'

'If that's all that disquiets your visit, sire, you may count yourself lucky. I wouldn't put it past Prince Somarus to pop in on his uncle and auntie just to pay his respects.'

'He wouldn't dare!' Honigalus exclaimed. 'He's banished from court.'

'Duke Ranwing is a quirky sod. It might just tickle his fancy to encourage a surprise encounter between you and Somarus.'

'I'll have Ran's guts for garters if he does,' the king growled. But both of them knew the sad truth: Lord Boarsden was too important a peer to antagonize. If Somarus turned up, Honigalus would have to grin and bear it.

The king and his friend stood side by side for a few minutes more, watching the moonrise, then decided to go to bed early. The royal party was scheduled to embark before dawn because the voyage between Mallthorpe and Boarsden was a long one. The rapids in that section of the river and the eddy off Boar Creek would test the mettle of the oarsmen and the nerves of the barge's more timid passengers.

'It'll be a lively ride tomorrow,' the king observed. 'Gorgeous scenery, and the thrill of breasting the whitewater. Queen Bryse and the older children always enjoy the excitement. And knowing what I might have to face later on in Boarsden, I'm looking forward to a little fun myself.'

SIXTEEN

Royal Fenguard Castle was thrown into an uproar when Ullanoth vanished from her bed of pain, for her counselors knew she was too weak to walk, and no servant would admit to having assisted her in leaving her private apartment.

Wix, the queen's elderly Lord of Chamber, the only one she had entrusted with keys to every room in her tower, was the one who finally found her. Reluctantly, he dared to enter her inner sanctum, where she had been accustomed to perform her most delicate magical operations. He burst into tears when he saw her, cold and unbreathing and without a heartbeat, lying on the peculiar tilting couch that she sometimes used while Sending. Still weeping, he summoned Grand Master Ridcanndal, the High Thaumaturge Zimroth, and Akossanor the Royal Physician. They were the ones whose official duty it was to confirm that the Conjure-Queen was dead.

The doctor studied her ruined young face, all bony angles and transparent, tight-stretched skin. He lifted one of her eyelids. The pupil was wide and black, indicative of lifelessness. A mirror held to her nostrils remained unclouded. She had no pulse, and her lips were tinged with blue. Rigor seemed to have passed already from her body, but it was cold as ice and nearly as unyielding to the touch.

'Our poor queen is gone from this world,' Akossanor announced in a somber voice. 'Summon her tirewomen. Let her corpse be washed and dressed in full royal regalia, so that she may sit upon her throne according to our custom and receive the homage of the people one final time.'

'Wait,' Lady Zimroth said. 'Stand aside, physician.' The elderly Thaumaturge, dressed all in grey samite, lifted Ullanoth's right hand, which had been partially covered by her gown. The moonstone ring on the queen's index finger glowed faintly green. 'Look there. That stone is alive!' Cautiously, Zimroth pulled up two thin chains that hung about the queen's neck and drew from the bosom of her night-shift two more Great Stones. Subtle Loophole and Sender also retained their inner luminosity. 'Her lesser sigils! Fetch the container, Wix!'

The loyal old man's grief had vanished in an instant. Eagerly, he took a key from the ring at his belt and unlocked the cabinet where the sigils were kept when not in use. He removed a platinum casket and lifted its lid. 'They're glowing!' he cried. 'Beastbidder, Concealer, and Interpenetrator are alive!'

'And therefore Queen Ullanoth also lives,' Zimroth declared, 'but not, I think, within this poor physical shell.'

'Where is she then?' Wix implored her.

Zimroth and the Grand Master of the Glaumerie Guild exchanged glances. He shook his head and said, 'Only the sorcery of the Great Lights could have done this to her. I know not how it was done, or to what purpose. The matter will have to be studied.'

'But is she still suffering?' Wix asked anxiously. 'Oh, tell me that her soul is safe somewhere and not in pain!'

'I have no answers,' Ridcanndal said. 'Never have I heard

of such a thing as this happening before. She certainly has not been cast into the Hell of Ice as her mother was, since her flesh is unfrozen and her features tranquil for all their ravaged appearance.'

'I believe Ullanoth may be in a kind of limbo state,' Zimroth said. 'Neither alive nor dead. We must take special care of these remains. There must be no evisceration, no packing with spices, no enshrouding, no interment in an airless crypt. Her body must be kept ready to receive her soul if it should suddenly return from its uncanny exile.' She looked away, thinking. 'We require a room, totally secure, where no enemy may intrude. Let her be dressed well, and her hair arranged. Lay her out on a couch as a woman sleeping. Every day, someone must look upon her in case there is a change . . . for better or worse.'

'So you think she may yet die?' Akossanor asked quietly.

'If the body falls into corruption, it cannot be reanimated and we shall have to consign it to the usual funeral pyre. But I believe it will not decay so long as she remains in this peculiar state, and the possibility remains that she may return.'

Wix drew himself up with pride. 'I take it upon myself to prepare a suitable place of repose for my beloved mistress. With your permission, I'll put her in the uppermost chamber of this tower, where tall crystal windows give a broad view of our land of Moss. There I will guard her until she wakes – or until my own death supervenes.' He looked uncertainly at Zimroth and Ridcanndal. 'Will she keep her sigils with her?'

'I think not. Even though they are still active and bonded to her, there are certain complex spells written down in the Book of Rothbannon able to annul the bonding and transfer ownership of the stones to someone else. We must not let this happen.'

Zimroth went to a nearby workbench and took up a pair of golden tongs. Using these, she teased the Weathermaker

ring from Ullanoth's skeletal finger. Cutting pliers severed
the delicate neck chains and let the two pendants fall free.
With the tongs, the Thaumaturgist placed the three Great
Stones in their velvet nests within the platinum box. This
she handed to the Grand Master. 'The stones must be secured
in the traditional place for ownerless sigils – Rothbannon's
tomb, where his ashes lie along with his most arcane writings. See to it, Ridcanndal.' She turned to Wix and the physician. 'You two must take care of her body. And I . . .' She
grimaced. 'I shall announce to our people that Conjure-
Queen Ullanoth lies enchanted, and until she is restored, the
government of the kingdom devolves upon the Glaumerie
Guild's officers. After that, I intend to bespeak Conrig
Wincantor's windvoice with this melancholy news. I will ask
the Sovereign how he intends to fulfill the solemn promise
he made to our queen, before she agreed to perform what
was to be her final service for him.'

PRINCE, RESPOND!

The generalized hail on the wind contained but two words.
It was launched from the crest of the Sinistral Mountains,
as Kilian and his weary party paused to rest at the top of
the secret pass before beginning their descent from the divide.
The alchymist hoped to minimize the possibility of being
overheard – although he knew there was scant hope of shutting out Beynor if he was minded to eavesdrop – so he
projected the call northward, in the direction of the Lady
Lakes, where he believed the intended recipient of his
message to be. In that he was mistaken; and he received no
reply. His next attempt was even more powerful, directed
more to the east.

This time, Tesk the wizard and the Green Woman Cray,
riding along the Boar Highroad behind Prince Somarus, heard
Kilian's hail clearly. So did another adept, who was surprised

to recognize a once-familiar signature unheard on the wind for many years. This listener found the subsequent exchange both revealing and worrisome.

PRINCE, RESPOND!

Tesk was red-eyed and runny-nosed from summer rheum, so shocked by the vehemence of the mental shout that he reacted with a great sneeze that nearly flung him from the saddle of his stocky cob. Cray, who sat astride a dapple-grey pony next to the wizard, merely cocked her head and said quietly, 'Did you hear it, too?'

'Aye. But which prince is its intended recipient?'

'Foolish man! A very powerful adept uttered that hail. Do you really imagine he wants to speak to King Honigalus's infant sons?'

Somarus looked over his shoulder, frowning. 'What's all this, wizard?' The prince, like the others of his cavalcade save Tesk, was disguised as a simple household knight of Duke Ranwing Boarsden.

'I believe I heard windspeech intended for you, Highness. It would be best if we drew aside and stopped for a few minutes.' He shot a glance at Cray. 'The Green Woman heard it, too.'

Somarus spoke a word to Baron Cuva, riding beside him, who in turn commanded the ten knights of the prince's escort to pull up. They had spent the previous night under the friendly roof of Castlemont Fortress and set out very early so as to reach Boarsden and the River Malle by afternoon. It was now about the third hour and the air was hot and muggy, with a faint scent of smoke. This section of the Boar Road crossed a treeless marshland, and the company was sweaty, midge-bitten, and short-tempered, the knights not hesitating to express their unhappiness at being made to pause where there was no shade.

Somarus, Tesk, and Cray drew apart from the others but remained mounted.

Cray said, 'King-in-Waiting, will you be guided by me in responding to this call? I sense overtones of peril on the wind. Answer this person only in general terms and with great circumspection.'

'Indeed! Perhaps I shouldn't answer at all.' Somarus scowled. 'But what if it's Beynor of Moss, wanting to tell us that something's gone awry with his scheme? We'd better know what's happening.'

Cray said to Tesk, 'Did you determine the direction of the hail?'

'Hard to tell with a blanket shout, but I believe it emanated from the mountains, to the south-west.'

'Not Beynor, then,' Cray said to Somarus.

'My curiosity's roused,' the prince said. 'Give an answer, Tesk. Find out what he wants, but don't name me to him.' The wizard covered his eyes with his hand, since it was too hot to wear a hooded cloak. 'An adept servant of a certain nobleman responds to you,' he spoke on the wind. 'My name is Tesk. Identify yourself and state your business.'

Kilian Blackhorse here! My felicitations to His Lordship and to you, Master Tesk. I am the former Royal Alchymist of Cathra and a one-time member of King Olmigon's Privy Council. I now have the honor to be a mortal enemy of the Sovereign of Blenholme, and recently escaped from the dungeon at Zeth Abbey after instigating a notable conflagration at Cala Palace. It's my intention to offer my services as sorcerer and political adviser to the new King of Didion. I believe I can be of good use, assisting his nation to throw off Conrig Wincantor's detestable yoke.

Tesk repeated the communication word for word.

'Well, well,' said Somarus. 'Not Beynor, but rather his shadowy crony! Ask Kilian why he speaks of a "new King of Didion" when everyone knows that Honigalus sits the throne.'

Tesk transmitted the terse message and gave its reply.

After today, there will be a new king. I've been assured of this by one who is not quite a friend, but not yet an enemy . . . to both His Lordship and myself.

'Mysteriously spoken.' Somarus said with a cynical smile. 'Tell Kilian I'd already intended to keep a sharp eye on this not-quite-friend. I don't need sly warnings popping out of thin air. I probably don't need Kilian! Let him prove he can be of value to me – and do it at once. Otherwise this exchange of ambiguities is over.'

Poor Tesk was a simple man, but he did his best to translate the message diplomatically.

As a sample of my usefulness, suppose I reveal to His Lordship how the transfer of royal power is to be accomplished without casting suspicion upon the obvious person?

Somarus nodded. 'All right. I wondered about that myself.'

Of course you did. Even those who might otherwise welcome a new monarch would reject him if he took the throne through foul and dastardly means. After much thought, I found a sure way to preserve the royal person's integrity. I myself conceived this plan, not the one who has doubtless taken credit for it! That one – that not-quite-friend – had neither the wit nor the subtlety to consider all aspects of this pivotal situation. I did.

'Tell me how it's going to be done, then,' Somarus demanded. 'Prove you're as clever as you say you are. All I've heard of the affair from my own informant is a hint about a calamity on the water. I assumed some hired villains were planning a surprise attack – although I must say the idea doesn't seem especially practicable. The – er – objects of the action are very well guarded. And how could the attackers be certain of getting clean away? If even one of them were taken and tortured into confessing, the scheme would unravel. To my detriment!'

The ambush on the water will be perpetrated by Salka.

'The hell you say!' exclaimed the prince. Tesk passed along the essence of the ejaculation.

Unimpeachable eye-witnesses on shore will see the deed done by the monsters. No human guards could possibly capture such enormous creatures, and if any are killed, it matters little. Who would ever believe that the King-in-Waiting could have coerced Salka into acting to his advantage? No, he will be held blameless, accepted as legitimate by Didion . . . and by Tarn as well.

'How did you talk the slimy brutes into cooperating?'

I didn't. This, I freely concede, was done by our friend, who has a certain influence over them because of his nationality.

'I only have your word that you're the great scheme's author.'

I have other proposals for the new king's advancement, equally valuable. Perhaps we might discuss them face to face.

'Or perhaps all three of us can talk things over! You, me, and our not-quite-friend. Then I can pick and choose.'

As you wish. But he may balk at a personal meeting. He much prefers dream-invasion.

'So you know about that, do you?'

He's done it to me, as well as you. But since I know how dangerous the invasion can be to the dreamer, I always take special precautions. Otherwise, the invader may plant evil seeds in the mind of the sleeping person, compelling him to act against his will or reveal secrets. I earnestly hope you have been spared such outrages, Your Lordship.

'Great God of the Starry Roads! I never realized . . . These precautions: can you teach them to me?'

I spent a good part of my earlier life as teacher to a king. Until His Grace's son, out of jealousy and spite, named me a traitor and cast me down. This is why I now seek a new position with a more congenial liege lord, whom I will gladly instruct as he bids me.

'How soon can you reach Boarsden Castle?'

It may take as long as four days. I travel afoot through rugged mountains, with a few trusted companions. But our not-quite-friend is capable of reaching you much sooner. He may already be in the vicinity of the castle, waiting upon developments.

'Then I'll keep him waiting a little longer! Come and talk to me, Kilian Blackhorse, and we'll see whether congeniality prevails. Now, I bid you farewell.'

Tesk lifted his head and opened his eyes. 'The alchymist responds: *Until our meeting.*'

'What did you think of him?' the prince asked. 'Well-spoken sort of fellow, wasn't he?'

'I'm sure he could serve you better than I,' the little wizard said humbly. 'If he really was Royal Alchymist to the Cathran king, he must be a very powerful sorcerer indeed.'

Somarus grinned and clapped Tesk on the shoulder. 'But is he trustworthy? That's the real question. I know I can trust you, old friend.'

'Thank you, Your Highness.'

Somarus turned to the Green Woman, who had been listening with a grave expression on her face. 'Mistress Cray, will you tell me what you thought of this Kilian's proposal – and the man himself?'

'Why should my opinion matter to you?'

The prince persisted. His tone was light and bantering, but nonetheless fraught with intensity. 'You've insisted on attaching yourself to my entourage. Only God knows why – or maybe your Source! You warned me to be cautious while bespeaking this man, and you seem like a person of great good sense. Please do me this small courtesy. Tell me what you think of Kilian Blackhorse.'

'He will never be any man's friend,' she said, not meeting the prince's eye. 'There is no true loyalty in him, only expediency. He would serve you well in time of war, but not in peace. More I cannot tell you.'

'So Kilian would serve me well in time of war, eh?' The prince urged his horse forward with a body movement. 'That sounds good enough . . . Baron Cuva! We'll ride on now.'

*   *   *

Well-concealed in a green cave of dense, overhanging branches at the river's edge, Beynor crouched in his boat and called down silent imprecations on his wily confederate. So Kilian had regained his talent! He'd managed to rid himself of the iron gammadion without the help Beynor had promised him. And now the perfidious alchymist made bold to foment doubt in the mind of Somarus concerning Beynor's integrity, apparently unconcerned about his windspeech being overheard.

That Kilian would act against him so blatantly – and so soon! – was ominously significant. It seemed plain that the alchymist felt himself in real danger of being denied a position of power in Somarus's new regime, and knew he had to act swiftly. He was attempting to bolster his prospects at Beynor's expense because he had precious little else to bargain with.

No trove.

Beynor realized that Kilian must have found out that most of the sigils and both magical books had been unaccountably lost by Felmar and Scarth. He'd know that both thieves were dead, because they would have failed to respond to his windspeech. But had he been able to oversee Scarth on his final journey? Did he know that the lesser sigils and one of the books had vanished into thin air, but that three Great Stones and the other magical book were hidden in a bear's cave on the wrong side of the mountains?

Neither Kilian nor Beynor would be able to go after the things now. The alchymist would not dare to re-enter Cathra while he was being actively hunted, even if he had some notion of the place Scarth had hidden them. It was imperative that Kilian respond immediately to Somarus's rather half-hearted invitation if he hoped to obtain a place in the new king's court. He'd worm himself into a position of influence, too; Beynor had no doubt of that.

As for me, the young sorcerer thought, I have more urgent

business to look after! Earlier, Lady Zimroth had bespoken him the welcome news of Ullanoth's enchantment and the secreting of the queen's own collection of active sigils in Rothbannon's tomb. Beynor had been hard-put to damp the elation in his windspeech as he responded to the news. It could not have fallen out more perfectly, had he planned it so! Moss was left vulnerable to a massive invasion by the Salka, and his sister's stones lay in a place that he alone might easily access.

The remnant of Darasilo's Trove was still vitally important to him because it contained the Destroyer sigil, the key to ultimate power. But one step at a time – the Great Stone would keep. All he need do was make certain that Kilian never tried to approach it . . .

He spent some time observing the slow progress of the royal barge up the river. Its enormous square sail was furled because there was little wind; the boat's motive power through the strengthening current was supplied by the forty laboring oarsmen.

He called out quietly on the wind. 'Eminence, are your warriors arrayed in position yet?'

The reply came from under his boat. *My people are in readiness. Are you aware that a party of well-dressed groundlings has ridden out from the castle and now travels slowly eastward along the dike path?*

He wasn't. He'd been absorbed in thought and had noticed nothing. Without acknowledging the fact to Ugusawnn, he scried across the water. On the southern shore, a league or so upstream, Boarsden Castle's gilded gatehouse ornamentation, window frames, and tower finials gleamed in the afternoon sunlight. It was an impressive pile, more lavishly furbished than any other Didionite ducal fortress to reflect the wealth and political importance of its lord. In honor of the royal visit, its battlements and the balustrade rail along the riverbank

esplanade were decorated with colorful banners and swags of
bunting. Boarsden's urban precincts lay further upriver, where
the Malle made its Big Bend to the north. Behind and below
the castle, an extensive marshy area threaded by Boar Creek
provided a natural water defense. The Boar Highroad from
Castlemont crossed the morass on a broad causeway before
coming to a Y junction. The left branch went north to Boarsden
Town. The right, now called Malle Highroad, continued east
to the Firedrake Bridge and the large valley towns before
ending at Holt Mallburn.

The party coming out from the castle did not take the high
road, but instead followed a lesser track along an earthen dike
much closer to the river. As Beynor scrutinized the nearly
two dozen richly dressed riders and their entourage, he was
gratified to discover that they included Duke Ranwing,
Duchess Piery, and the Archwizard of Didion himself, Fring
Bulegosset, seeming to be completely recovered from his
diplomatic illness. Trailing the nobles was a gaggle of liveried
servants on mules, bearing hampers of food and drink, folding
stools and tables, and poles and bundles of gaily painted canvas
that would soon be converted into awnings sheltering the
privileged picknickers from the glaring sun. The destination
of the procession was obvious: a few hundred ells above a
stout timber bridge at Boar Creek, where the river rapids were
at their most dramatic and a great eddy added to the navigation challenge, the dike widened and formed a perfect
observation platform where those on shore could view boats
struggling upstream through the surging whitewater.

The witnesses were gathering.

At the age of seven summers, Crown Prince Onestus of Didion
was still too young to appreciate the richness of the countryside through which the royal barge now traveled, nor could
he understand how such wealth made the great landholders

prickly and independent-minded in their relations toward the Crown. In this region west of Mallthorpe were ripening fields of barley and oats, orchards that would produce pears, plums, and apples, and lush meadows where large herds of shaggy long-horned cattle grazed and fattened. As the barge passed each prosperous shore village, the prince and his royal father and mother stood together on the boat's ornate sterncastle, beneath a suncover brave with colored pennants, and waved to the yeomen and villeins who had gathered to watch their passage. Some of the villagers cheered and called out blessings, as the citizens of the large cities had done earlier in the progress; but most were silent, only holding high the white banners with Didion's heraldic Black Bear as they had been commanded to do by the overlords of their districts.

The single exception to the tepid welcome vouchsafed the royals by the countryfolk of the upper Malle came late in the afternoon, as the barge passed beneath the high-arched Firedrake Bridge that lay about ten leagues downstream from Boarsden. Several hundred spectators crowded the decorated span, waving banners of the timberlords of the north and shouting, 'Long live Queen Bryse Vandragora!' Bouquets of roses were tossed down onto the maindeck, and Onestus was kept busy retrieving the flowers and heaping them into the arms of his mother. Each time she inclined her head in a gesture of thanks to those on the bridge, they responded with a roar of applause.

The prince said in a low voice to his parents, 'I wish people at the other places had been so friendly.'

'These are free northern folk loyal to my family,' the queen told him, 'who have come a long way of their own will to show their love – unlike the others, who were compelled to show homage.'

'I see,' the boy said somberly.

'Take the roses down to the cabin and ask the ladies to

put them in water,' the king said. 'Soon we'll come to the lively section of the river. Your little brother is already on the foredeck where the view is best. Why not join him? I'll be there shortly myself.'

The boy bowed. 'Yes, sire.'

When he was gone, Honigalus and Bryse watched the crew raise the great sail again. The oarsmen would need all the help they could get as they strove against the force of the swift-flowing water.

The queen said, 'Nesti is beginning to understand the reality of our situation, poor lad, for he's wise beyond his years. Yet how I wish his childhood could be as carefree as mine was – and yours.'

Honigalus sighed. 'It was a simpler age. All we can do is pray that by the time he wears the crown, the old enmities will be forgotten and he will have won the love of his subjects.'

'You have long years ahead of you to accomplish the same thing,' Bryse said gently. 'Your reign has only just begun.'

In spite of the day's warmth, the king felt a sudden chill, but shrugged away the portent with a defiant smile and rose to his feet. 'Ah! Look down there on deck – Captain Peel has come to supervise the helm as we breast the rapids. I think I'll have a word with him. Shall I summon a few of your ladies to keep you company here?'

'Nay,' said the queen. 'I'll join them and our daughter in the grand saloon. My presence will have a calming effect on the fainter of heart. It would be a pity if dear little Casya should be frightened by the hysterics of a few silly women. She's a brave girl, but some of my younger ladies are as timid as sheep – and you know how infectious fear can be – even when there's no good reason for it.'

Prince Bartus knew enough to stay out of the way of the boatmen while they attended to their duties, so he had climbed into the pulpit just behind the bowsprit, where he amused himself by tossing leftover bits of bread roll into the water, pretending they were men overboard and seeing how long it took them to drown or be devoured by some hungry fish.

Then the big thing had come swimming along and finished off the last victim, and he'd pointed it out excitedly to the men and asked what it might be.

'A water-kelpie, I reckon,' said the sailor named Zedvinus, winking at his mate, while the two of them checked the headstay. 'My great-great-grandad got dragged off the deck of his lugger by one when he was fishing by Tallhedge. Terrible monsters, they be – ain't that right, Dagio? Bite a man clean in half.'

'Oh, aye,' muttered the other man, not bothering to glance over the side. 'Fearsome critters, water-kelpies. You want to be careful when they're about, Prince Bart.'

'Really?' The five-year-old prince's eyes were wide with interest, but the sailors had failed in their attempt to frighten him.

'All deckhands to the mainsheet!' cried an authoritative voice. 'Double-man the sweeps! Coxswain, beat to cadence! Secure the waist-ports and stow all loose gear!'

The two sailors started aft. As Zedvinus passed the Crown Prince, who was just coming onto the foredeck, he said, 'Keep a weather eye on your little brother as we go into the whitewater, Prince Nesti. Best if you crowd into the pulpit with him and lash the pair of you to the rail so you don't bounce around.'

The prince said, 'Thank you for your advice.' The small enclosed platform would provide cramped accommodation for two full-grown men, but there was room to spare for a couple of small boys.

'I don't want to be tied in like a baby,' Bartus growled, as his brother joined him. 'I'm not afraid. And I'll hang on tight.' He brightened. 'I saw a water-kelpie out there in the water. It's been swimming right beside the barge ever since we went under the big bridge.'

'Kelpies are fairy tale creatures,' Onestus scoffed.

'Zedvinus and Dagio say they're real,' the little boy insisted. 'And I saw it myself. It was huge.'

'It's probably just an old tiger salmon,' Prince Onestus said. 'They can weigh seven stone.'

Bartus pointed. 'Here it comes again. Look!'

At first the older boy saw nothing because of the reflection of light on the river's surface. Then, to his surprise, he caught sight of a great dark shadow, only a couple of ells away from the barge's cutwater and swimming a parallel course. The thing was shaped something like a bull sea-lion, but appeared to be nearly three times the size of the marine mammals common in Didion Bay. Its head was broader and more rounded, too, and while the body was indistinct, Onestus thought he saw some sort of paddle-like appendages or elongated flukes at its hind end that propelled it along at a smart pace.

'Codders!' the Crown Prince breathed, awestruck. 'I see it, too! But that's no kelpie. Maybe it's a young whale. Sometimes they come up rivers by mistake. The fresh water's bad for them and they can't find the right food, so they get sick and die.'

'That one doesn't look sick,' Bartus said. 'And it doesn't look like a whale. I think it wants to race.'

'No, he's gone under the barge.' Onestus was disappointed. 'Crumbs! I wish I could've got a better look at him.'

'Look at what?' asked an interested male voice behind the boys.

They turned and saw their father the king standing on the foredeck. 'Papa!' Bartus exclaimed. 'A water-kelpie was right beside us!'

'Probably a whale, sire,' Onestus said loftily. 'Something large.'

Honigalus glanced over the side. 'Nothing there now. Was it white or grey? Did it have a long horn at its snout like a sea-unicorn?'

'It was greeny-black,' Onestus said. 'More than three ells long. Almost like a monster sea-lion, but without the pointed nose.'

The king's brow furrowed in puzzlement. 'Whales and sea-lions aren't green. Very few large sea-creatures are.' Except one, he thought. But that was impossible. None of them had been seen in the rivers of Didion since the country was first settled, some nine hundred years ago . . . 'It was probably a whale, just as you thought. And the greenish color was just a trick of the light, reflecting off weeds in the water.'

Onestus was gazing at the shore. 'The other boats going upriver are tying up at the jetties. We must be getting close to the rapids.'

'Will we tie up, too, Papa?' Bartus asked.

'No,' the king said. 'Ordinarily, only a few boats are allowed to breast the rapids at a time. For safety's sake, they take turns. But our royal barge has precedence. That means we can go on without waiting.'

Honigalus climbed into the pulpit with his sons. Since it was Bartus's first time up, after having spent the previous voyages in the cabin with the women, the king planted himself firmly behind the little boy, leaving Onestus well-braced at his side with one arm locked nonchalantly about a stanchion.

'I see Boarsden Castle on its hill,' the Crown Prince said. 'And here come the rapids!'

One of the royal trumpeters sounded three long warning notes. The coxswain began to beat his drum, so that the sweep of the oars might be perfectly coordinated, and the lookouts assumed their positions fore and aft.

'Whitewater ho!' cried the first mate, and a moment later the barge carrying the royal family of Didion began its cautious ascent of the foaming, rock-choked waters.

Cray the Green Woman showed Somarus the near-invisible path that led from the high road, along the reedy eastern bank of Boar Creek, to the dike track.

'But there's a better place to watch boats in the rapids further upstream,' Somarus protested. 'We used to go there often as children, when my mother visited her relatives at the castle.'

'Other persons have got there ahead of you,' Cray said. 'And the backcurrents in that place don't suit my purposes.'

'Your purposes?' The prince reined up and turned to regard her. 'The time has come to tell me just what those purposes are.'

'No,' she said simply.

'Damn you!' roared the prince. 'I'll know sooner or later.'

'Let it be later,' the small woman said. 'And I advise you to ride on without delay, lest both of us come too late to view the dire event we've traveled so far to see.'

So they continued as swiftly as they could, and now and then a horse bogged down and had to be pulled to firm ground, but none came to serious harm. By now, all of the prince's party had a good idea what was about to happen. The knights murmured among themselves and made coarse jokes to cover their nervousness and rising excitement, while Somarus and Baron Cuva rode on in preoccupied silence. A dirty brownish haze thickened in the western sky, turning the sun orange and casting odd-colored shadows over the stands of reedmace, bulrush, and spikegrass that lined the creek. Some small birds began to sing, as though dusk were falling or a storm were on the way. Far away, three horn notes sounded.

'The barge enters the rapids,' Cray said to Tesk, speaking so low that none other could hear. 'It has begun.'

The wizard bobbed his head, licked his overlarge lips, wiped his leaking eyes on his sleeve, and said. 'Strange-looking sky.'

'There are wildfires in the Elderwold, below the Lake of Shadows,' Cray said. 'They were not extensive when I came to your camp, but they'll spread until a hard rain beats them out.'

'So you came from Lake of Shadows?' Tesk asked her. 'Do your people dwell there? Oh, I hope they're not imperiled by the flames!'

'Thank you for your concern,' she said, smiling, 'but my home lies elsewhere, and glad I'll be to return to it. I'm not a body who travels gladly. As the saying goes, "East, west, home's best."'

Her eyes were like emeralds, Tesk realized, and her hair gleamed like white gold. No wonder her kind had bewitched men in days gone by! 'When will you able to go back?'

Cray looked straight ahead. 'Soon, when I have that which I came for.'

'Mistress Cray,' the wizard said eagerly, 'if there is aught I can do to help you, please ask.'

She tilted her head and pursed her lips, but her frown was not unkind. 'And why should a human – and a magicker attending a future king at that – wish to assist one such as I?'

The plain-faced little wizard flushed. 'I – I admire your courage, coming so far to fulfill a duty laid upon you by another. And you are very beautiful.'

She gave a soft peal of laughter, reached out, and touched his sleeve. 'Beware, Tesk! Many a human male has fallen into the thrall of Green Women, to his doom.'

'You make fun of me. Yet some eldsire of mine must have indeed loved one of you, to have engendered a wizard like me. I ask nothing of you, mistress. But if your appointed task is hard, I stand ready to give you aid.'

'Can you swim?' she asked him, bringing her mount closer. 'Running water is inimical to my people. Indeed, some of us are loath even to cross a stream on a bridge, although I am not quite so constrained. This thing I must do could take me into the river, and I confess to dreading it. If a friend were to stand by me –'

'I will,' he declared. 'And I swim like a fish.'

'Then stay close, for in a little while I'll disappear from the sight of this company, and if you would help me, you must vanish as well.'

'Ahead of us!' Baron Cuva called out. 'The dike – and the bridge across Boar Creek.' He urged his mount forward, with the prince following, and the knights who rode behind Cray and Tesk were so eager to stay with their masters that they splashed into the creek shallows so they could pass by the Green Woman and the wizard.

The two of them straggled up to the dike track at last, where the others were already dismounted and scanning the turbulent river downstream in search of the approaching barge, the knights shouting to one another in order to be heard above the loud noise of the water. The Malle was almost a quarter of a league wide in this place, and made a slight bend below the creek, where willow and alder thickets obscured the view. Finally a tall red-and-gold striped sail hove into sight from behind the trees. Then they saw the royal barge with its flashing oars, fighting against the current, constantly altering course to avoid the perilous places where great dark rocks thrust up from the white pother.

Prince Somarus had pulled a little spyglass from his belt pouch and used it to search the boat and the waters surrounding it. 'By the Great Starry Goblet – Honigalus and his two sons are perched right above the boat's prow!' He thrust the slender brass tube at the baron. 'Have a look, Cuva.'

'I see them,' the dour nobleman said. 'Nothing unusual out on the water yet. But perhaps the ambushers will wait to spring the trap until the barge is above the eddy. If I were running the show, that's what I'd do.' He lowered the instrument and handed it back to Somarus. 'Do the most damage with the least effort expended. Classic tactics.'

Somarus lifted the glass again. 'Then we've got a bit longer to wait. The eddy's rather hard to see from here. It lies a bit to our left, just upstream from the worst of the rocks. The river deepens suddenly at that point, and it's skipper beware! Just when you think you're free and clear of the rapids, the whorl takes hold and flings you about like a berry-basket in a riptide. Of course, experienced river-pilots skirt the thing easily enough. It mostly takes small craft coming downstream who happen on it unexpectedly.'

He swung the glass away from the boat and searched the river's opposite shore.

'What are you looking for, Highness?' Cuva asked.

'A certain sorcerer,' the prince replied grimly, 'on whom all my hopes ride. I'm certain he's out there somewhere, but I don't think I'll find him.'

SEVENTEEN

As the three notes of the trumpet sounded the alert for approaching whitewater, Queen Bryse took the drowsy baby girl from her breast and handed her over to the nursemaid. 'Casya should be quiet enough now. Go sit with her in the forward part of the saloon, where you can get fair warning of bumps and bounces. And hold her in your arms as we go through the rapids, rather than putting her in her cradle. I want her to feel comforting arms about her in case my ladies become affrighted and start a commotion.'

'Yes, Your Majesty.' The maid Dala wore a superior smile. She herself was afraid of very few things now that horrible old King Achardus was dead, and no longer able to threaten her with skinning alive and boiling in oil if she should shirk her duties toward the royal offspring. She took Princess Casabarela from the queen, wiped the baby's tiny mouth, and patted her back to raise a bit of wind. 'That's a good little madam! Now let's find a cozy place up front.'

The saloon was a very large cabin, gorgeously appointed with gilded woodwork, damask draperies, and the finest Incayo carpets, raised above the maindeck and situated just behind the stout mast of the barge. Used variously as a sitting, dining, and presence chamber during the progress, it had glazed casement windows all around to provide the best possible view of the passing scene. These were now firmly shut in anticipation of water being shipped aboard, and the external galleries on either side, which allowed the passengers to stand in the fresh air and watch the laboring oarsmen below, were deserted.

Most of the queen's high-born attendants had gathered in the stern of the saloon, where heavy curtains had been drawn to shield delicate eyes from the sight of the tempestuous river. Shrill exclamations and giggles attested to the ladies' strained nerves, and pages were kept busy passing out scented pomanders, handkerchiefs, and flagons of witch-hazel rosewater to those who already felt faint. A few of the women sipped wine or spirits from lidded drinking vessels. A stack of silver basins stood ready in a corner to accommodate the queasy.

Dala settled herself and baby Casya in a big cushioned chair facing forward, where she could see not only the expanse of rapids but also King Honigalus and his two sons, perched bravely above the bowsprit in their small railed platform. Behind her, the court musicians begin to play, but after a few minutes the soothing melody was almost drowned out by the growing roar and hiss of the water. To relieve the tension, Queen Bryse commanded all the ladies to sing with her, leading them in a clear soprano through the many long verses of *The Blossom Moon Song*.

> *Rosebud, spring rosebud, tight and green,*
> *No soft, fragrant rose petals e'er to be seen;*
>   *When will you open wide to me?*
>   *When shall I my true love see?*
> *In Blossom Moon, in Blossom Moon, it will surely be.*

Dala hummed along, rocking Casya gently, and the baby slept even as the barge began to rear and plunge like a rampaging living thing. The noise of rushing water swelled to thunder. Some of the women's voices faltered, but none of them dared to wail or weep so long as the queen kept singing; and this she did, keeping her back turned resolutely away from the tumult outside. The barge surged on, expertly steered by its skipper and powered by the muscles of the valiant oarsmen, evading boulders and monstrous standing waves, skirting each rocky patch and climbing the foaming chutes like a huge homing salmon.

As the last verse of the song began, with only Queen Bryse and two of the bravest ladies still singing, a faint huzza came from the men on deck outside. Dala saw that the whitewater was ending. Only the eddy, a broad, swift-spinning gyre of foam and floating debris some twenty ells in diameter, now blocked their way. The skipper steered far toward the heavily wooded right bank to take them safely around it, then guided the barge proudly up the deceptively glassy looking center of the Malle, where the current ran swift and the waters were dark and deep.

The queen's song ended and the relieved women clapped and cried out for joy. The cheering of the deckhands intensified and was augmented by glad shouts from male courtiers swarming out of the sterncastle and racing forward to call out congratulations to King Honigalus and the two princes for having held steadfast throughout the passage.

'Well,' said Duke Ranwing Boarsden to the Archwizard Fring, 'that was mildly exhilarating to watch, but hardly the momentous spectacle you hinted at when you convinced us to ride out here. Just what did you think was going to happen, wizard?'

Fring's brow was spangled with sweat and his jaws

clenched tightly together. His gaze was fixed not on the barge but on the smooth expanse of river just ahead of it, where his talent perceived something moving just beneath the water. In the bow pulpit, little Prince Bartus seemed to see something as well. He pointed at it and gave a high-pitched scream as loud and penetrating as the cry of an eagle.

Fring said quietly, 'There. Half a dozen ells in front of the boat. They look something like smooth rocks just breaking the surface of the water. But they're not rocks.'

'Nothing!' Prince Somarus raged. 'Nothing at all happened to Honigalus and his barge! Where are the damned Salka hiding? What are they waiting for? Tesk! Tesk! Curse that sneaky wee magicker – where's he got to, now that I really need him to scry out what's going on?'

Baron Cuva cast a swift glance around the shore near the Boar Creek bridge where the prince's party stood watching the river, but the little black-robed adept was nowhere to be seen. 'Not a sign of him, Highness. And the Green Woman's gone missing as well. I wonder –'

'Shite!' whispered Somarus. His sturdy form went rigid as he stared out onto the river, aghast. 'Father Sun and Mother Moon – will you look at that?'

The barge's skipper set the helm over, steering toward the left bank, and signaled for a last great pull of the sweeps to bring the barge out of the mainstream current and into the backwaters above the landing stage at Boarsden Castle.

The dark heads of the Salka rose from the water.

Carbuncle-red eyes blazing, spiky crests uplifted, maws agape, and crystal teeth flashing in the low sun, the monsters came rocketing downstream toward the barge in a broad inverted-V formation before a single person aboard could give warning. The creatures on the flanks closed in on the sweeps. Their powerful tentacles ripped the oars from their housings with sharp cracks, rending the stout timbers of the hull. Some of the Salka began to pluck howling rowers from their benches, flinging them overboard to other monsters who waited with open jaws. The barge slewed violently as its motive power was lost, and began to drift downstream toward the eddy. Some of the shore observers gave cries of horror as they discerned huge shapes massed at the sides and stern of the vessel, beginning to clamber aboard. A explosive noise signaled that the rudder had been ripped away by main force. A few valiant souls on the boat, having armed themselves with swords and pikes, tried to beat off the inhuman attackers, but the Salka on deck hurled screaming boatmen and courtiers aside as though they were dolls. Black tentacles tipped with clawed digits lashed the air like flexible tree-trunks, making a shambles of the standing rigging and toppling the mast with its square sail.

Then the broken barge reached the rim of the eddy and slowly began its death spin. Terrified men jumped from the fast-settling stern, which the Salka had abandoned in favor of a concerted attack on the glass windows of the saloon cabin. The openings were too small to admit the enormous bodies of the amphibians, so they groped inside with their tentacles in search of prey. Those on shore gasped at the sight of King Honigalus, menaced by three bellowing monsters on the foredeck, taking a small son under each arm and leaping off the bow pulpit into the whirling water. The barge circled faster and faster until it was sucked beneath the surface of the water and disappeared from view.

'Futter me!' Somarus exclaimed. His ruddy features had turned the color of chalk. 'That was grim. At the end, the great brutes were going after the women. I could hear them screaming.'

Baron Cuva only shook his head, speechless. The knights stood in small groups, cursing or dazedly silent, staring upstream at the place where the great boat had vanished.

Then one man pointed to the rapids below the eddy. 'I see floating wreckage coming down toward us. The whirlpool has spat it out! Could it be that some have survived the disaster?'

'You think so?' another said somberly. 'Look – the cursèd fiends are cavorting out there among the rocks, tossing things to one another in some hideous game! Those who drown will be the fortunate ones.'

The others uttered cries of abhorrence and pity.

'It happened as Beynor promised,' Somarus whispered, his eyes glittering. 'As the renegade Royal Alchymist Kilian planned it, so that no man could lay the deed at my doorstep.'

'No, Highness.' Baron Cuva's voice was steady. 'The tragedy cannot be ascribed to you. But the former Conjure-King and Kilian Blackhorse are perhaps not so easily exonerated. It would be wise to keep that fact in mind.'

Somarus was silent.

'What will you have us do now?' the baron asked, after some minutes had passed.

'It'll be awhile before those at Castle Boarsden dare to send search parties out on the water,' the prince decided, 'although land patrols may begin combing the banks for survivors rather sooner. It won't do for anyone to discover us loitering here. We'll have to return to the highway as quickly as we can, then ride back the way we came to the road leading to Boarsden Town. It should be safe to wait there in some handy alehouse until word of the disaster is cried about the city streets.'

'You might be recognized,' Cuva warned.

'What does it matter? This is my tale: I came out of the Elderwold intending to present my respects to King Honigalus as he held court at Boarsden Castle. If I had actually conceived such a saucy notion, dear Cousin Ranwing would not have turned me away, loving a good row as he does . . . So I'm properly appalled at the awful news, and I vow vengeance against the devils responsible, and wait with the duke and his people to see whether any of the royal family has survived.'

'What if one or more of them did?' Cuva asked softly.

'Then Beynor and Kilian Blackhorse will have their work cut out for them. But I don't think we need worry over-much. I'll deplore this lamentable tragedy, while at the same time *you* will make a great show of thanking Providence that the Crown of Didion passes not to a weakling child, as it would have done if Honigalus alone had perished, but rather to a mature warrior ready and able to lead our nation in these difficult times.'

Cuva inclined his head. 'Highness.' His smile was sardonic. 'You must forgive me if I postpone styling you Majesty until the time is ripe. I'm not as audacious as the Green Woman Cray in such matters.'

Somarus scowled and began looking about again, muttering low-voiced oaths. 'Where is she? And that rascal Tesk?'

One of the younger knights smirked. 'Earlier, I saw the wizard making sheep's eyes at the Green Woman. Unlikely as it might seem for two such creatures to be smitten by love's thunderbolt here in a muddy morass, we can't discount the notion.'

'Then let them swive amongst the frogs and midges and be damned,' Somarus said, 'for I won't wait another minute for them.' He turned about, squelched up the creekside path to where they had left the horses, and swung into the saddle.

The nursemaid Dala got up from her chair, holding drowsy little Princess Casabarela tightly against her breast, and watched in frozen disbelief from one of the saloon windows as the nightmarish dark creatures rose from the river. *What were they?* Not seals, not giant squid or octopods, not any kind of animal she had ever seen before. They roared with demonic jubilation as they attacked, and she knew that the frightful things were worse than dumb beasts: they were thinking beings bent on slaughter. The royal barge was their target, and the people aboard were their intended prey.

She was . . . and the baby girl entrusted to her.

Sleek and greenish-black, red saucer-eyes glowing and enormous mouths wide open, the monsters snatched the sweeps away from the oarsmen and began pulling the helpless men overboard to their doom. The barge lost momentum and began to swing broadside to the current. Dala saw King Honigalus and his sons clinging to the rails of the bow pulpit. She felt the vessel shudder, then lurch. A terrible rending sound filled the air, as though the stout wooden frame of the great barge were being torn apart.

She lost her balance and crumpled to the carpeted deck with the baby still in her arms. Unhurt but frightened by the fall and the jolt, the year-old girl began to cry. Without thinking, Dala snatched up a long knitted shawl that had earlier served to cover the baby and swathed the small body completely, head and all, in soft wool. Then she crammed herself and her precious burden into the small space between the heavy padded chair and the bulkhead and began to pray.

At the other end of the long cabin, the court ladies were screaming at the top of their lungs. Someone shouted, 'We're sinking! God have mercy, we're sinking!'

Because of the drawn draperies at the windows round about them, few of those in the stern of the saloon had any real idea of what was happening on the deck outside, nor did the queen seem to understand the atrocious nature of the peril that threatened them. She shouted vainly for all to remain calm, while the boat wallowed and heaved and furniture tumbled and women ensnared in long skirts fell about weeping and moaning.

'Dala!' Bryse shouted desperately. 'Is my little Casya safe?'

'I have her with me, Majesty,' the maid called out from her hiding place, which was nearly ten ells away from the queen, and out of her eyeshot. 'I can swim. I'll do my best to save her.'

'Bless you –' Bryse began to say.

Her words were lost in a great crash as several of the casement windows shattered simultaneously. Boneless dark limbs, dripping blood and water, thrust through the billowing drapes and began ripping the thick fabric away with sharp talons. In moments all those within the saloon knew what was outside, trying to get in.

Dala, at least, had seen them from a distance. Most of the women caught unawares by the sight of the invading Salka fainted dead away from the shock. A few braver souls, including Queen Bryse, tried to escape by opening the doors leading onto the external gallery; but by then the barge was foundering, and a great gout of discolored, debris-laden river water flooded into the saloon, washing them back inside.

A rumbling noise now swelled amidst the human cries and the almost continuous roaring of the triumphant Salka. The barge vibrated like the sounding box of a titanic lute as the eddy currents strummed and whirled it in a narrowing spiral. Then came a crackling fusillade deep within the hull, loud as tarnblaze explosions, as the unbearable pressure of the water began to snap the dying vessel's beams and planking.

Dala was too terrified to move, cringing away from the tangle of writhing tentacles flailing about in search of victims. A glistening black arm encircled the waist of Queen Bryse Vandragora and dragged her out through a broken window frame. With dreadful precision, the monstrous questing limbs sought out and found the noblewomen, the pages, the musicians, and the servants, those who lay senseless and those who frantically tried to escape, and hauled them all away.

The nursemaid no longer heard the human screams or the booming Salka howls. She was conscious only of the rising water now, and the fact that the barge was being engulfed stern-first as it sank into the maelstrom. The forward section of the saloon where she and the baby hid still had most of its windows intact. Equally important, the massive chair had become wedged in a clutter of other furniture. It continued to shelter her, but no longer slid toward the sumberged area where the Salka and the last of the victims continued their struggles. Even when the rising waters finally forced her to stand, Dala was able to conceal herself and the baby behind the sodden folds of the undrawn draperies near her. The child's muffled wails could hardly be heard above the tumultuous racket made by the breaking hull.

Finally, the obscene snarl of probing tentacles withdrew from the saloon. She risked looking out through the window. The landscape spun like a demented carousel, shore and water combined in a dizzying blur. On the tilted foredeck above her, Dala saw King Honigalus leap from the bow pulpit with his sons in his arms. A pack of Salka dived after him. Only three monsters still clung to the hulk of the barge, and as she watched they rolled easily into the water and were gone.

Working quickly, Dala unwound the long shawl from around the baby and used it to bind the small body tightly to her chest, making sure that the child's head was above her shoulder. She studied the latch of the nearest casement. It was a simple thing, and when she turned it the window easily opened inward, letting water pour in. She waited, crooning *The Blossom Moon Song* to the baby. The water rose swiftly and she climbed onto the chair seat and then onto the back, clutching at the drapes, keeping their heads in the air until the last possible moment.

Then she took a deep breath, ducked under, and pushed out through the open casement.

Almost immediately, a powerful current took hold of her. She could see nothing, for the waters of the eddy were not only murky with sediment but also streaked and splotched by bizarre areas of moving light. She kicked and pumped her arms to no effect: swimming was impossible. She would have to let the river take her where it would.

But it was taking her down, down, tumbling her head over heels. The light was dimming and her lungs burned and dearest God what must be happening to the poor baby . . . ?

She struck something, felt a sharp pain in her upper leg, another as her elbow smashed into an unyielding surface. Rocks! The whirlpool was floored with rocks. Panic dug its claws into her pounding heart and she folded her arms protectively about Casya's fragile head.

Then her own skull was struck a glancing blow. White light flared in her brain. The hoarded air burst from her lungs and she sucked in water almost with a sense of relief.

I tried, she thought, drifting into quiet darkness, feeling the motionless tiny body still bound tightly to her. I tried.

The cry of a whooping swan, far away, and the rustle of wind in the reeds. A magenta sky. Softness beneath her aching head. More pain in legs and arms and a lingering rawness in her throat and chest. She was covered to the chin by a blanket.

'She's awake,' a soft voice said. Two faces appeared, smiling down at her: a handsome little blonde woman with brilliant green eyes, and a very ordinary-looking man who sniffled a little and wiped his nose on his sleeve.

'Baby,' she managed to whisper. 'Baby!' Her voice broke and she began to cough.

'Right here beside you,' the man said, 'lying in a nest of dry grass and wrapped in her fine shawl, sleeping soundly.'

'Drink this,' said the green-eyed woman, lifting her head and holding a cup to her lips. She sipped a few drops of warm herb tea, sweetened with honey, then drank deeply and eagerly until the woman said, 'Enough for now,' and let her lie down again.

'Little Casabarela is quite well,' the woman said, 'sleeping off her ordeal as you were. I fed her a bit of mushy bread and cheese curd. But she'll wake betimes and need milk, so we'll have to move along and find a farmstead with a cow or goat. Parties from the castle will be searching the river-bank for survivors, too. And even though they won't be able to see us, we don't want to leave too many traces of our presence to arouse suspicion.'

They were in a dense grove of small trees. River waters gleamed through the leaves and the pungent smell of marsh-land mingled with woodsmoke in the air. Two small horses grazed nearby. A campfire burned briskly in a ring of stones. Hung up to dry beside it on an improvised frame of sticks was a black robe and a set of raggedy trews, evidently the outer clothing of the man, who was clad only in a long undershirt. A second drying-frame held pieces of female clothing: her own! She realized that she was naked beneath the blanket.

'You saved our lives,' she said to the man, overcome with amazement and gratitude. 'You pulled us from the water even though it was alive with ravening monsters!'

He ducked his head modestly. 'You drifted quite a way downstream from the rapids before the counter-currents brought you close to the bank and I was able to swim out and grab hold of you. The monsters are still lurking in the waters near Boarsden Castle. I was never in any danger from them.'

'All the same, I owe you profound thanks – most especially for saving the dear child I had sworn to protect with my own life. May I know your name, messire?'

'I'm Tesk, an itinerant wizard by profession, and this is my friend Cray, who is also adept in magic.'

'I'm Dalaryse Plover, called Dala. I am – I was – the chief nursemaid to the Royal Family of Didion.' She was suddenly stricken at the thought of them. 'But you don't know, do you? Something terrible has happened to the king and queen, and the two little princes!'

'We know,' Cray said. 'The barge was sunk by the Salka monsters, and all aboard save you and Princess Casabarela have died abominable deaths.'

'All?' Dala wailed.

'Every one. And I admit that I never expected to find that you had survived along with the baby.'

'You expected –' Dala felt her senses begin to reel. 'You're a magicker? You knew this terrible thing was going to happen and gave no warning?'

'Yes,' Cray admitted freely. 'It was not my duty to issue warnings, nor would anyone have taken me seriously if I'd tried. I was sent here from a faraway place by another who is wiser than I, expressly to rescue Casabarela Mallburn.'

'If the others of the royal family have perished,' Dala said slowly, 'then the poor orphaned babe is the Queen of Didion.'

'Some day she will be,' Cray said. 'But not now. There are dire things happening in your country and in other parts of High Blenholme Island. If it became known that little Casya were alive, scheming men would try to murder her. The monsters did not attack the royal barge by chance. They were incited by sorcerers who intend for Prince Somarus to take up Didion's crown.'

Dala's eyes widened. 'But how –'

'We'll explain it to you later,' Cray said. 'You have a right to know everything, since it seems obvious that you were fated to be saved along with your tiny mistress – although the Source neglected to mention the fact to me. And glad I am that you're here, Dala! For I know much of magic but very little of child-rearing, and I admit my heart sank to my boots when the Source laid this strange charge upon me. But, there – it'll work out splendidly now, with you and dear Tesk to share the burden.'

The man nodded and smiled and went to the fire to feel the cloth of his robe. 'Just about dry. I'll leave you ladies for a few minutes so Dala can get dressed. Then we must be off. We've a long way to travel.' He took his garments and disappeared into the bushes.

'Where are we going?' Dala asked. 'Can any place in Didion be safe from men so evil that they would kill an entire royal family, innocent children and all, in order to steal a throne?'

'No one will follow us into the Elderwold wilderness,' Cray said. 'That's where we'll go.'

The nursemaid's face crumpled with dismay. 'But the terrible Green Men live there! Have Casya and I escaped one set of inhuman monsters, only to fall into the hands of others?'

'We'll risk it,' Cray said rather tartly. 'Sit up now, and I'll help you get your clothes on.'

EIGHTEEN

As soon as the Salka began their attack, Beynor put his own escape plan into action.

He crouched low in the dismasted sailboat and sent his windsight underwater to find the Supreme Warrior. Ugusawnn was still harnessed to the boat; but he was well out from the riverbank, at least five ells away and slightly downstream, resting on the mud bottom. His great body was poised in a tense attitude that seemed to indicate he was in mental contact with his company of warriors, directing them in their initial sprint toward the unsuspecting people on the royal barge.

Beynor's great Sword of State, which he had brought with him from the Dawntide Citadel, had a double edge keener than the sharpest razor. He removed it now from the oilskin bag where he'd kept it out of sight, buckled on the ornate scabbard, and drew the blade. Then he cut the boat's stern line, which had been tied to one of the trees.

He held his breath, his heart thudding in his breast. The Eminent monster was so absorbed in the events taking place out on the water that he had paid no attention to what Beynor was doing.

Moving cautiously, with the sword still in hand, he went to the bow and checked to make sure that the little craft had not drifted into an unfavorable position within the over-hanging brush and small trees that screened it. All was well. The boat's anchor was not out. Instead, a bow-line tied to a branch kept its stem pointed upstream.

Beynor waited until the Salka warriors attacked the barge's oarsmen, and death-screams began to punctuate the wind. Then he leaned over the side and sliced through the mooring line and the leather harness traces attached to the gunwales, setting the sailboat free. Sheathing the blade, he scrambled to the stern, heedless of the noise he made, seized the tiller, and exerted all of his magical strength to propel the small boat out of its hiding place and into the open river. It was a simple trick, known to almost every talented child in Moss but rarely employed by mature sorcerers, and he counted on it now to save his life.

He gave a mighty shout on the wind: 'Ugusawnn, take care! Press the attack! Fighting men are coming at us from the castle in boats and I must intercept them. Stay here and don't try to follow me. I'll beat them back!'

What?! The distracted Salka still didn't realize that the traces had been cut. *What are you saying?*

With the centerboard up and the small craft drawing less than a foot of water, Beynor raced away upstream through the shallows along the northern shore, praying that Ugusawnn would fall for the ruse and remain with his warriors.

A bellow of rage split the air behind him. *Stop! Where are you going?*

'Do your job!' Beynor retorted on the wind, 'Make certain that no human escapes the ambush alive – else you and your people will never regain this island home that was stolen from you!'

The humans on the barge will be slaughtered and eaten – and

*so will you, when I catch you! Scheming traitor! No one is coming
at us from the castle. You're trying to escape.*

Beynor made the boat go faster, zigzagging and swerving
among the rocks with no thought of the danger. He dared
not pause to scry out possible pursuit, but no monstrous tenta-
cled limb had yet laid hold of his boat, and he was already
opposite Boarsden Castle, where the banners and decorations
still hung out to welcome a king who would never arrive.

Stop! Come back!

'Sink the barge! Kill the people! Do what you came to do
and I'll carry out my own part of the bargain!'

The ground along the right bank was rising now, changing
rapidly from fertile pasture and field into upthrust bedrock
dotted by thin stands of pine. A few minutes later the boat
turned right and charged along the base of the towering
palisade that forced the Malle into its Big Bend. Across the
broad elbow of water lay Boarsden Town with its crowded
jetties and docks and the warehouses of the wool-merchants
and northern timberlords. Clogging the shallowing river
nearly to midstream were anchored rafts of logs sent down
from the forests of interior Didion, waiting for the rains of
autumn to raise the water and give them swift passage to
the mills and shipyards of Holt Mallburn.

Beynor steered for the opposite shore and the town,
crossing the open channel and darting in among the rafts,
agile as a minnow fleeing from a pike. The log platforms
were anchored with multiple iron chains. Swimming underwater among them at speed would be a perilous business,
even for a Salka. If Ugusawnn was still in pursuit, he would
have to move more slowly, perhaps even put his head into
the air to see which way the boat was going. But no tentacles took hold of the brash young sorcerer, nor did the
Supreme Warrior bespeak him with fresh threats. Had the
crafty monster swum on ahead? Was he waiting for his prey

to arrive at the dock before putting a heartbreaking end to the escape attempt?

The wind-world had become a howling chaos of dying minds that Beynor paid no more heed to, feeling no compassion or other emotion at the loss of so many lives, but only a sense of stark and necessary fulfillment. The first difficult step in his rebirth to glory had been taken. If he could only evade Ugusawnn's wrath for a few more minutes, the next step would follow quickly – and be so much easier.

His boat skimmed the water like a leaf blown before a gale, drawing the attention of river boatmen who called out to him with indignant shouts. He ignored them, continuing on his wildly erratic course through larger vessels moored offshore, heading toward the public landing stage. The racing boat's wake made the small craft tied up at the slips wallow and scrape their fenders. Sailors and dockside hangers-on cursed and yelled at him as he reined in his talent, then forced his boat to halt abruptly in a welter of foam just as it was about to crash into the quayside.

He'd arrived.

'A madman!' somebody yelled. Another cried, 'A wizard!'

'Stand clear!' Beynor shouted at the gathering crowd. 'I'm coming ashore.'

He seized the oilskin bag holding his money and personal effects, crouched, and made a great talent-assisted bound high into the air. He flew over the heads of the people on the dock's edge like an acrobat and landed on his feet six ells away from the water. No enraged Salka monster surged up after him. He was safe. He'd won the gamble.

'Here now!' cried the dockmaster, a stout, red-faced functionary who came rushing up with a pair of armed toll-collectors. 'Here now! You can't come roaring in here like this, sirrah! Who do you think –'

Beynor opened his purse and sent a gold mark coin spinning

straight into the master's admonishing hand. The man stopped dead in his tracks, eyes bulging, and finished his sentence lamely.

'– you are?'

The tall, pale-haired young man with the darkly compelling eyes drew himself up proudly. He wore modest garments and had a seaman's duffel slung over one shoulder, but girded about his loins was a sword and scabbard more magnificent than any Didionite prince could hope to wear.

'I am a visiting wizard,' Beynor said politely. 'My name is Lund.'

The angry murmurs of the crowd were stilled and the people shuffled their feet and looked uneasy. It didn't do to offend a wizard, even one who had no notion of how to behave on the water.

Beynor produced another gold coin and proffered it to the incredulous dockmaster. 'If I have trespassed upon your laws or customs by my informal arrival, I beg your pardon. I trust that the gratuity I've vouchsafed to you will be adequate to ensure my temporary welcome here.'

The dockmaster was all smiles now. 'Certainly, my lord! How may we assist you? Do you require accommodation for the night?' The common people began to drift away, along with the two sullen-faced toll-collectors, who were well aware that there'd be no chance of extorting special fees from this well-feathered bird of passage while the lucky dockmaster had him in tow.

'Much as I would like to enjoy the hospitality of Boarsden Town,' Beynor said, 'I regret that urgent business summons me elsewhere. I wish to purchase two blood horses, a fine saddle and harness, and a few other pieces of travelling gear. Perhaps you can direct me to a suitable stable.'

'I myself will take you to the best purveyor of horseflesh in all of central Didion! But what of your small boat?'

'I leave it in your good hands, since I have no further need of it. Just give me a moment to collect my thoughts, and then we'll be off.'

'Certainly, my lord.'

Beynor turned away, sending his windsight soaring downstream, and drew in a sharp breath as he saw the royal barge being sucked down into the eddy. There was no time to waste. He must be well away from here before the magnitude of the disaster became generally known. He cut off the dreadful oversight and bespoke Ugusawnn silently.

'Eminent One, it seems you and your warriors have done the job. I congratulate you. May I also commend your good sense in not pursuing me.'

I was sorely tempted to seize you and rip you limb from limb for daring to escape me. But I thought the better of it.

'And well you did. If you'd followed your instincts, you'd have to explain to the other three Eminences why the Known Potency would never be activated. The fact is, I'm still quite willing to bring the sigil to life for you, and lead you to my sister's collection of stones. But I intend to do it in my own way and under my own terms. I'm tired of your bullying and your stupid threats.'

Stupid? You dare to call me stupid?

Resentment and frustration flared in Beynor like a tarnstick igniting waxed tinder, but the tone of his mental speech was glacial. 'Ugusawnn, I've no doubt that you're a brave battle-leader. But when it comes to matters of high policy you're naught but a blubber-brained fool. You have no notion of how to accomplish important deeds save by brute force – no way of seeking other beings' cooperation save through violent coercion. Back in the Dawntides, I tried to deal with you like a civilized being while making my proposal. Your three colleagues treated me with respect – but not you, Supreme Warrior! All you've done from the start is bluster and try to intimidate me. Well, Eminent Ugu, that's all over now.'

What do you mean, groundling?

'You won't carry me back to the Dawntides as your prisoner, nor will I immediately bring the Known Potency to life for you.

You promised –

'I don't trust you to fulfill your part of the bargain. I believe you've intended from the beginning to kill me just as soon as I activated the Potency. If you deny it, you lie. Therefore, the rules of our agreement have changed.'

How?

'I intended to travel directly to Moss by land. You and your warriors go down the River Malle as quickly as you can. Return to the Dawntide Isles. Assemble your invading army, proceed to the Darkling River below Royal Fenguard, and meet me there in six days. You can do it easily. Bring the Known Potency with you.'

And then?

'Help me kill my sister Ullanoth. When she's well and truly dead – and only then – I'll bring the Potency to life, in a manner that doesn't endanger me. You can use it to activate the Conjure-Queen's remaining sigils without the usual pain. In a short time, with the help of the stones, the entire nation of Moss will belong to you and your people. If you use Moss as a base of operations, you can conquer all of High Blenholme.'

How do I know you're telling the truth?

'Bespeak your colleagues,' Beynor said wearily. 'Ask their advice, and for God's sake follow it, for they are far wiser than you. I'll be at Royal Fenguard myself within six days. Either join me there, or forget that you ever knew me. And throw the Known Potency into the depths of the Boreal Sea, for it will never be more to you than a useless bit of rock.'

*   *   *

It was late afternoon when the remount Sir Gavlok Whitfell had acquired at the Great Pass garrison pulled up lame. By that time, Snudge's party had almost reached the Didionite fortress of Castlemont. Ordinarily, even though the barbarian nation was now a loyal vassal of the Sovereignty, the king's men would have passed the place by and continued on twenty leagues further up the Wold Road to the walled way station of Rockyford, long operated by Cathra for the benefit of royal dispatch riders and important commercial travelers. Gavlok was all for pressing on, insisting he'd be content to ride pillion with one of the two burly Mountain Swordsmen who had joined them at Beorbrook Hold. But Snudge had doubts.

'There's a brown haze spreading over the sky from the west,' he pointed out, 'and a smell of smoke. I'm not one to believe in omens, but I do know that beyond Castlemont we ride into lonely country where outlaws loyal to Prince Somarus prey on caravans and well-found travelers with hardly a blink of disapproval from the local lords. What if villains have fired the Elderwold in places, so as to slow down those on the road and have easy pickings? If there's trouble brewing, it would be folly for us to head straight into it with one of our party lacking a sound mount.'

'There was no hint of bandit activity in the area reported at Great Pass, Sir Deveron,' rumbled one of the Mountain Swordsmen, who was named Radd Falcontop. 'Still, I confess to feeling a prickling of my own thumbs. Have you noted how few people we've met riding south today?'

'It might only be the lull in traffic normal around Solstice time,' said the second Swordsman, Hulo Roundbank. 'But what if it isn't? I believe you're right to stop at Castlemont, messire. We can rest, feed ourselves and our beasts, and pay the castle stable's outrageous price for a fresh horse for Sir Gavlok. Meanwhile, Radd and I can try to pick up some useful gossip. After so many years in the earl marshal's service, we've managed to make a few friends in this part of Didion.'

Falcontop and Roundbank were men of Beorbrook Hold, veterans of border skirmishes and fights along the Wold Road, the only reliable land route connecting Cathra and Tarn. They were of an age with Earl Marshal Parlian, having served him since he was newly knighted six-and-thirty years earlier. The two Swordsmen were long widowed and had only grown children, but although they bore the scars of many battles they were still hardy as badgers. They had volunteered for this strange mission knowing that it involved high sorcery and dangerous state secrets; and if they were surprised at the youthfulness of the expedition's leader, they'd concealed their thoughts well.

Falcontop was the shorter of the pair, stocky, with broad shoulders and arms so powerful they could wrestle down and foot-lash a stag. His hair, thinning on top but ample below and worn in leather-bound plaits, had once been brick-red; but it and his bushy beard and brows were now so diluted with white as to be nearly pink. His dark eyes were hooded and his habitual expression was one of calm forbearance. He had killed twenty-two men in battle.

Hulo Roundbank was two heads taller than his fellow-warrior, not nearly as massive, but giving an impression of indefatigable strength and endurance. His long face was split by a thrusting beak of a nose topped by a single long brow of tangled silver. The rest of his skull was shaven to stubble, save for the area just before his ears, where he had spared two dangling white tresses threaded with bright blue beads that had plainly been chosen to match his eyes.

Both men wore chausses and vests of well-tanned deer-skin, stained blackish brown by long usage, lightweight linen shirts of the same anonymous hue, heavy boots, and oddly folded caps with projecting bills in front. Their impressive array of personal weaponry left no doubt as to their occupation, but for this mission they wore no man's badge.

With Gavlok up behind Hulo and his limping horse on a lead-rein, they traveled the last few leagues to Castlemont. The fortress crowned a rugged crag and guarded the important intersection of the Great North Road, the Wold Road, and Boar Road. At the foot of Castlemont Crag was a high-walled enclosure built of rock, where carts or pack animals carrying valuable cargo could be secured for the night. It had a tall guardtower, a bare-bones inn that offered shelter from the elements and little else, rows of hitching posts, a well, and a store of fodder supervised by a sleepy-looking ostler. The place was empty except for a Didionite mule-train carrying slabs of choice wood, being off-loaded so that the animals might rest well before making the steep ascent to Great Pass and the Cathran border on the morrow.

'No stable down here, no horses for sale or hire,' Gavlok noted. 'We'd best take ourselves up to the fort.'

To reach the stronghold, it was necessary to climb a track with many switchbacks, reminiscent of the approach to Elktor Castle. The gate to the track was barred. At the guardpost, Snudge presented a document identifying him as the son of a Cathran merchant-peer, traveling to Tarn on family business.

The watch-captain's eyes gleamed as he studied the parchment, then let his gaze wander over the collection of dusty but well-dressed young men and the two hardbitten warriors who shepherded them.

'Not a wise thing these days, traveling by land to Tarn,' the officer observed, re-rolling the parchment and giving it back to Snudge. 'Our local breed of lawless men well know what to do with a letter of credit – should you just happen to be carrying one of those! They roast the bearer's feet till he signs it over. My lord, take my advice and hire more

guards when you reach Rockyford Station.' He nodded at
Vra-Mattis. 'Your good Brother there can bespeak the old
windvoice who lives at the place and arrange it all for you
in advance. But first, enjoy the good cheer of Castlemont
Fortress. We're always happy to welcome guests who know
the value of top-notch service.'

'Stay and spend money,' muttered Gavlok's saucy highland squire, Hanan, as they started up the hill.

'Odds on, Sir Deveron, that captain thinks you're going to
Tarn to purchase gold for your daddy.' Radd Falcontop
grinned. 'He's got you pegged: a young spark and his good
mate and your squires and bodyguards, off to do a little business and have a fine adventure in the wild north country.
Then you'll sail comfortably home from Donorvale City, and
brag to your friends back in Cala Blenholme that you dared
the big, bad Wold Road.'

Hulo chuckled. 'The captain might not bother to sell us
out to the nearest robber-band if we tip him well on the way
out of here.'

'We could stay the night,' Gavlok suggested. 'It's the last
civilized place we'll find short of Castle Direwold near the
Tarnian frontier. We'll live rough from here on.'

'I'll consider it,' Snudge said. 'Let's see which way the
wind blows after we've taken our ease and bought you a
new horse.'

The wind blew from Cala Palace, and the voice precariously
riding on it was that of Lord Stergos, the convalescent Royal
Alchymist.

His words came only to Snudge's brain, and were perceived
there very faintly, as he and his companions ate an early
supper together at a trestle table in an open porch near the
fort's kitchen, accompanied by a few other wayfarers. In the
outposts of Didion, there was little regard for the niceties

due to rank; if a noble was too fastidious to sup at the common board, he was invited to take his meal in one of the tiny sleeping cubicles in the dormitorium provided for paying guests.

The intelligencer gave no sign that he'd heard words on the wind, only silently bespoke the novice, Vra-Mattis, who sat on the opposite side of the table. 'Give a low cry – then tell me quietly that you have a wind-message for me.'

The apprentice played his rôle to perfection, so none of the outsiders at the table heard what he said to his master. Gavlok and the armigers exchanged knowing smiles and Radd and Hulo pretended indifference.

Snudge rose. 'Sir Gavlok, explain to our new companions why we must suffer arcane interruptions in our mundane activities from time to time.'

He and Mat strode off to the curtainwall, and after receiving permission from the sergeant of the watch, climbed to the southern parapet with the excuse of viewing the mountain panorama, but in actuality wishing to ease Lord Stergos's bespeaking over distance. None of the fort's men-at-arms approached or questioned them after Vra-Mattis cast a light spell to discourage curiosity. They settled into a broad embrasure between the merlons of the battlement, and then Snudge covered his eyes and responded to Stergos.

'I'm here, my lord, Deveron Austrey in Castlemont Fortress in Didion. I'm in a secure place. There are no expert wind-talents round about here able to eavesdrop upon us, only Vra-Mattis, who cannot overhear unless I permit it – which I won't. Are you in better health?'

I'm mending, thanks to a potion that came some days ago from the Conjure-Queen, sent before she sank into a profound trance.

'Sulkorig told me of her strange fate. What's become of her sigils?'

For safekeeping, they're being stored in the traditional place –

*the tomb of the first Conjure-King, Rothbannon – where they will
remain inaccessible to anyone save members of the reigning family
of Moss: Ullanoth herself, of course, should she be restored to her
body, and Beynor also. When I remonstrated with Lady Zimroth
and warned her of the potential danger from him, she remained
unmoved. Mossland tradition, it seems, may not be flouted! And
Beynor is accursed, so even if the stones were inactive he could not
touch them without perishing. At least this is what she and the rest
of the Glaumerie Guild believe . . . And now please tell me why you
are so eager to bespeak me, Deveron, rather than relay messages
through Vra-Sulkorig. The effort to speak on the wind is very taxing.*

'Lord Stergos, bear with me. Since you were so badly
injured, much has happened to me – and some of it may
pertain to the situation in Moss. I have secrets to impart.
Some must be withheld from His Grace the High King, while
others he must hear only from your own lips. This is why I
needed to bespeak you so urgently.'

Tell me.

Haltingly at first, then in a torrent of detailed windspeech,
Snudge described his meeting with the Green Man Odall at
the croft east of Castle Elktor. He said nothing of the unwelcome gift of the sigil Subtle Gateway, but he did tell of
his amazing encounter with the One Denied the Sky.

*The Source – Ansel's mysterious Source – you say HE is this
One Denied the Sky? And you believe him to be one of the
Beaconfolk?*

'I do, my lord. He said little but implied much during our
strange conversation. We of Cathra have long believed that
all of the Great Lights are evil. But the Source's talk of a
New Conflict betokens that an Old Conflict once took place
– and that it must have involved a dispute between good
and evil entities of the sky realm over the morality of moonstone magic and pain-eating.'

And the evil Lights won this ancient battle?

'Almost certainly, for the sigils still belong to them. As I understand it, the New Conflict has the aim of severing this pernicious linkage between sky and ground beings. The Source spoke of how I had been *enlisted* in this New Conflict. And I wasn't the only one: the Source spoke of King Conrig, the thieving Brothers, and even Beynor of Moss in this way. Some of the enlistees, like me, were given free choice to join the Conflict or refuse. Others, like His Grace, seem to serve the purposes of this Source all unawares. In my opinion, Queen Ullanoth has also been drawn into the Conflict – or perhaps taken out of it until the Source reinstates her. Even Princess Maudrayne and her little son appear to be part of this supernatural war, since the Source ordered me to continue on to Tarn without delay and fulfill my duty there.'

This is incredible! Do you mean to tell me that the entity called the Source uses human beings as agents or weapons in this battle between factions of Lights?

'So it would seem, my lord.'

Deveron, I – I am at a loss. I know not what to say to you. What you've told me has a terrible plausibility, and yet my soul shrinks from the idea that a merciful God might permit his human creatures to be manipulated in such a cavalier manner by supernatural beings!

'I'm no great thinker, my lord. But even I know that the lesser people of our world are routinely used by the greater for their own purposes. Children are ruled by parents; wives are ruled by husbands; men are ruled by overlords . . . It's the way things are. At least the Source seems to be motivated solely by good intentions.'

My royal brother would find this notion of being used by the Lights to be insupportable. His pride would never accept it as truth, and so I will not tell him about it, lest he doubt the rest of your explanation for failing to retrieve the Trove of Darasilo.

'I agree that would be the wisest course, my lord.'

I myself, on the other hand, am inclined to believe in this One Denied the Sky and his laudable goal. If the opportunity arises, tell him I would cooperate willingly in the New Conflict.

'I'll gladly tell him, my lord, if I can.'

Now I must pass on other important information to you that's only recently come to us at the palace. The shaman Blind Bozuk has told us that Maudrayne and her son are no longer sequestered on Tarn's west coast, but have been carried off by Ansel Pikan to a place far to the north-east, beyond the great volcanos. The region is nearly inaccessible to foreigners, and she's supposedly guarded now by magic more powerful than before. I fear that this will make your own mission impossible to accomplish.

'Not at all, my lord. There's still hope.'

Then tell me of it, for I'm very close to despondency. My poor brain is on fire with pain from the effort of bespeaking you and from my own fruitless efforts to unravel this wretched knot of plots and counterplots. And we still don't know what manner of evil scheme Beynor of Moss and Kilian are cooking up! But to hell with them and their devilry. If you have any consolation for me, lad, be quick to offer it. I won't be able to bespeak you much longer.

'Listen, my lord, and take heart! The Source himself gave me a . . . clue as to the whereabouts of Princess Maudrayne. And after my talk with him, I conceived an idea that may enable us to neutralize the threat she poses to King Conrig – and do it without any dishonorable actions. As yet, my idea is a seed lacking soil to sprout in or water and sunlight to help it grow. But it could work, and it has the potential to save the Sovereignty. I envision a certain compromise, whereby His Grace and the Princess Maude each gain while yielding in part to the other, with the result that the most dangerous of His Grace's secrets will remain hidden, and the consequences of the other secret will be postponed for many long years. With two such prideful and stubborn royal persons involved, getting them to agree to the compromise will not be easy. But there are other things besides sweet persuasion that might compel their acceptance.'

Tell me more.

'Soon, my lord, when I have it straight in my own mind. The Source would of necessity be a party to it.'

Bazekoy's Bones! You'd think of pressuring such a being? Deveron, are you mad?

'No, my lord, I'm a snudge: a sneaking, devious, crafty spy. You'd think the Source would have better sense than to enlist me in his unearthly Conflict! Since he didn't, let's hope he's not surprised at the consequences. He said that he needed me. Well, I also need him, and he'll help whether he wants to or not.'

I can't bear to hear any more. Bespeak Sulkorig when you can tell me your plan in full, and I'll listen. Farewell, Deveron. May you succeed – or at least do more good than harm.

Snudge opened his eyes slowly and found himself lying flat on the fortress parapet, with a throbbing skull and every other bone aching as if from a fierce beating. Ofttimes strenuous bouts of windspeech still afflicted him sorely, although he suffered less than he had when he was younger.

He groaned, rolled over, and pulled himself up on his elbows. And gave a cry of dismay as he saw Vra-Mattis.

The apprentice windvoice was sitting with his back against the battlement, clutching his knees with white-knuckled hands. Tears ran down his face, soaking the front of his robe, and his mouth was an open square of misery, although he uttered not a single sound.

'Good God, Mat! What's wrong?'

The young man's voice was scarcely audible. 'Listen, master! Listen to the wind. So many souls, dying so horribly! I tried to scry out the cause, but the flood of pain and desolation overwhelmed my talent.' He lifted a trembling hand

and pointed eastward. 'In that direction, toward Boarsden.'

Snudge overheard it himself now. But it was many minutes before he recovered his strength enough to survey the scene on the River Malle with his oversight. He saw the Salka sporting in the water, but did not fully understand what had happened until he read the lips of Duke Ranwing Boarsden, the Archwizard Fring, and the other noble witnesses who stood transfixed at the riverside, watching the monsters feast.

NINETEEN

Grand Master Ridcanndal, head of Moss's Glaumerie Guild, finished drafting the appeal to High King Conrig, sanded the ink, and perused what he had written, wondering whether his language had conveyed the urgency of the situation:

. . . The terrible tragedy that took place this day in Didion serves to confirm what we have long suspected: that the Salka monsters have for some reason shaken off their age-old torpor and reclusiveness. Emboldened and aggressive, they once again threaten the safety of all human life on High Blenholme. And with Conjure-Queen Ullanoth sunk in a helpless trance, the kingdom of Moss, your loyal vassal, now lies particularly vulnerable to their attacks.

While it is true that scriers of our Glaumerie Guild have not been able to detect any evidence of overt hostile activity among the monsters of the Dawntide Isles, it seems reasonable to believe that they were responsible for the heinous attack on Didion's Royal family, which would have required careful planning and a level of leadership lacking in other populations of these ferocious creatures.

However, the normally shy Salka resident in the Little Fen

*have lately been seen in broad daylight, cruising boldly about the
environs of Fenguard Castle and the Royal Naval Yards. Rumors
also have it that the Great Fen Salka are migrating southward
toward parts of Moss occupied by humanity, an unprecedented
event that the Guild and our Grand Council of Lords view with
grave concern.*

*In light of these ominous circumstances, the Guild and Council
members, acting with full royal authority while our queen is incapacitated, respectfully request that the Sovereign fulfill his solemn
commitment to defend Moss from enemies human and inhuman.
We ask that a squadron of Sovereignty warships be dispatched at
once, to patrol the waters between the Darkling Channel and the
Dawntide Isles in a show of strength and solidarity . . .*

Ridcanndal nibbled on the feather tip of his pen, wondering
whether he should have written *demand* instead of *request*.
Ullanoth, in her mortal illness, had not hesitated to speak
bluntly to the Sovereign, forcing him to reiterate his obligation to defend the smallest and least prosperous nation of his
Sovereignty before she would agree to help him. But with
her voice now silenced, and the Salka menace apparently
turned toward the much more important nation of Didion –

Someone knocked sharply at the outer door of the Grand
Master's tower chambers, breaking his thread of thought. He
rose from his desk in the great sanctum, grumbling, and shuffled
out into the sitting room. It was early evening, but the sky
outside had gone dark as a storm rolled down from the north.
Rain pelted the windows and the fire was burning low. He
felt a chill rake the flesh between his shoulder-blades. The
knocking came again, louder than before.

'I'm coming!' He flung open the door and cried out in
astonishment, 'You!'

'None other.'

The tall woman of ample figure was dressed in robes of

dark-blue silk, with a silver girdle and silver bands about the sleeves and neckline. Her hair was also silver, worn in a coronet of braids, and her face was amiable and serene, except for a certain sadness clouding her jade-green eyes. On either side of her stood warlock-knights of the Royal Guard, impassive as marble images in their handsome gilt armor and swan-blazoned surcoats, She lifted her hand in a dismissive gesture. 'You men may leave us now.'

'Yes, my lady.' They turned on their heels and marched away.

'Will you invite me in, Ridcanndal?' Thalassa Dru inquired in a gentle voice. 'Or would you prefer that I state my business here in the corridor?'

He backed away from her, bowing slightly. 'Please enter, Conjure-Princess. Forgive my surprise and confusion. It's been – how long?'

'Four-and-twenty years since my late brother Linndal banished me for opposing his marriage to Taspiroth sha Elial. But the Conjure-King and I were reconciled in his final year of life, as you doubtless know, and so I come here to my birthplace a member in good standing of the royal family of Moss, for the purpose of averting a terrible catastrophe.'

Ridcanndal felt the muscles of his upper body stiffen with dread at the formality of her pronouncement. Surely she would not dare –

'Take me to Rothbannon's tomb,' she continued. 'Immediately.'

'Lady, what do you intend to do?' He had to force the words from his lips. 'You are a royal princess of Moss and have the right to enter the tomb, but I cannot believe that you would meddle with the sigils that are the bonded possessions of our stricken queen. Not while our nation stands in such peril, and may have need of them!'

Thalassa Dru came close to him, lifting her plump warm

hands to his jowly cheeks as though she were comforting a terrified child. 'Why are you so worried about what I might do with the sigils? Ullanoth is incapable of using them, or even giving permission for their abolition and re-bonding. Such permission can only be granted by another member of the royal family. Since you did not welcome me and urge me to perform this important service for Moss, I must assume you are expecting another to do so. Are you waiting for Beynor? Tell me the truth.'

He gave a guilty start and withdrew from her touch, knowing that his colleague Zimroth, the Royal Thaumaturge, who loved the deposed young king as a son, entertained just such an intention and had already proposed it to the Guild and the Grand Council.

'I pray with all my heart and soul that Queen Ullanoth will recover and reclaim her sigils,' he said. 'Yet it seemed prudent to some senior royal advisers to consider what might happen if she should never awaken. Prince Beynor is her only suitable successor. In these dire times, the crown of Moss cannot possibly be offered to the boy Habenor, who was placed in the line of succession by our late monarch Linndal. Even though Beynor is debarred from using the stones himself, he can legally give permission for a surrogate to pronounce the spells separating them from our helpless queen and binding them to another person who nevertheless remains subject to the crown's authority. Thus we would retain the magical defensive properties of the sigils, while having a suitable ruler for our country.'

'The scheme might have worked,' Thalassa Dru said, 'if Beynor had not already made a pact with the Salka, agreeing to assist them in an invasion and takeover of Moss.'

'No! He would never do such a thing – any more than he would have slain his royal father.'

'Ullanoth named him patricide and regicide.'

'In this belief, the Conjure-Queen was mistaken!'

'She spoke the simple truth, Ridcanndal – and so do I. Beynor's heart is so warped by bitterness and hatred that he has vowed to admit the monsters to this very castle. While Salka destroy the body of his sister, he intends seize her sigils for his own perverted uses. I have been commanded to prevent the last two calamities.'

'Who commanded you?'

'The Source of the Old Conflict gave the order – he who is called the One Denied the Sky.'

'He's . . . only a myth.' But a spark of doubt flickered in the old sorcerer's eyes.

'No more so than the Great Lights themselves, as the oldest of our histories affirm. The Source is alive and determined to repair the damage he inadvertently caused. I am only one of his servants. Queen Ullanoth, in her last minutes of conscious volition, became another.'

'Unbelievable . . .'

'The New Conflict is upon us, Grand Master, and you'd better think long and hard about which side you choose to support. Beynor is too self-centered to serve the evil Lights of his own free will, but I believe that they have nevertheless made him their puppet. As you are well aware, it's difficult for them to interact directly with our material world, except through the subtle fluxes of power and pain. They need groundling agents – just as my benevolent Source does – and Beynor is their perfect choice. Have you forgotten that he carried away the Unknown Potency when he sought refuge in the Dawntide Isles? All of his other sigils were taken from him – save that one, which the Lights unaccountably permitted him to keep.'

'Thalassa Dru, what are you saying?' Ridcanndal looked at her askance. 'Has Beynor activated the Potency to use against us?'

'It's quite possible that he has – perhaps with the connivance

of the Lights themselves, if they see him as a useful adjunct
to their capricious schemes. Now take me to the tomb!'

It was impossible to deny her. The right of access was hers
by law. But what did she intend to do? Ridcanndal sighed,
took up a tall oil lamp, and ignited a flame that burned within
its crystal chimney. 'Has the Source also sent you to stave
off the incursion of Salka into our lands? Will you take up
the Crown of Moss yourself?'

'Alas, I have no such mandate. Conrig Wincantor is the
only one who can defend you from invading monsters.'

'I was finishing the draft of an appeal to him when you
came to my door. The Conjure-Queen assured us that the
Sovereign of Blenholme would come to our aid if we were
attacked. But what if his help comes too late? In the Salka's
last assault upon us, it was only the queen's use of her Great
Stone Weathermaker that beat the brutes away from our
shores. The warships sent by Conrig served only to harry
and punish them once they had already withdrawn.'

'Thanks to Ullanoth, Moss now has its own small navy
and a force of trained fighting warriors. Use them. But make
plans also against the blackest contingency. This is the only
advice I can give you. Now take me to the tomb with no
further ado.'

He could only obey, knowing that no magic of his could
stop her. He led her from his tower into the main keep of
the castle, and from there down seemingly endless winding
staircases of black, dripping rock into a labyrinth of tunnels
and disused chambers, where walled-off sections masked
ancient secrets or led to places long forgotten.

The tomb of the first Conjure-King was less than a century
old, although Fenguard Castle itself predated Rothbannon by
nearly five hundred years, having long been the home of
renegade Didionite wizards. Some legends hinted that the
deepest shafts and burrows were the work of the Salka, and

humankind had raised the castle on foundations built in primordial times by the amphibian monsters.

'My brother Linndal, when he was a reckless young boy, explored these ancient subterranean portions of Fenguard,' Thalassa Dru remarked as they traveled the maze of dark corridors. 'I'd not be surprised if Beynor did also. Have you considered that some of these passages might lead outside the castle walls, below the Darkling River and into the waters of the Little Fen itself? They might provide a way for Salka to penetrate the defenses of Fenguard Castle – provided they had a guide.'

'I never thought of such a thing,' Ridcanndal admitted. 'We'll take what precautions we can against such an intrusion.' He was becoming increasingly rattled – not only by the way this woman had compelled him to obey her, but also by the confident portentousness of her remarks. How in the world was he going to explain all this to Zimroth and the Glaumerie Guild? At the very least, he should have found a way to alert them to the arrival of the late king's mysterious sister. But bewilderment and chagrin (or was it her sorcery?) had distracted him, and now it was too late.

They had come at last to the sealed entrance to Rothbannon's tomb, which lay at the end of a dry tunnel that looked almost freshly hewn. 'Unbind the defensive spells blocking the door,' Thalassa Dru told him.

Meekly, Ridcanndal pronounced the lengthy incantation that protected the tomb against ordinary intruders. Then the sorceress laid her own hand upon the solid stone door-panel. It was incised with the swan insignia and an inscription:

ROTHBANNON ASH BAJOR
C.Y. 911–1052
FIRST CONJURE-KING OF MOSS AND LIBERATOR OF THE
SEVEN STONES
'PUISSANCE AND PRUDENCE'

'What a pity,' she murmured, 'that he was the only one of his blood to follow that wise motto! Recite the rest of the spell, Grand Master.'

He hesitated only for a moment, then spoke the words, concluding in a loud voice, 'Open to a true descendant of Rothbannon!'

With a harsh grating rumble, the stone door rolled away. She admonished Ridcanndal to wait outside and entered. The sepulchre itself was a polished black marble cube that measured less than an ell on each side, containing the cremated remains of the great sorcerer. Resting on its lid in a carved depression that fitted it perfectly was the small casket of solid platinum that had been made to hold the original Seven Stones Rothbannon had taken from the Salka.

Thalassa Dru lifted the lid, saw the gleam of the six living sigils and the empty place where the Conjure-Queen's lost Fortress stone had once rested. Reverently, she closed the container and carried it out of the tomb.

Ridcanndal stared at her apprehensively, still having no idea what she intended to do. 'And now, my lady?'

'Lead me to the room where my niece's body lies. And then I pray you to secure for me a small drum.'

Dear soul, you've been successful!

The subtle form of Thalassa Dru opened the golden box and emptied the sigils onto the frost-encrusted floor of the Source's prison. Her aura was a triumphant blaze of rainbow colors. 'As you see, my master. The cursèd things are still alive and bonded to her, but that should make their abolition all the more precious to our cause.'

The dead-black shape shackled in sapphire uttered a deep sigh of satisfaction. One of the gemlike manacles confining him now glowed so faintly that it was nearly as transparent as the iceflows streaking the cavern walls. *Shield your eyes,*

*then, while I unite with the Likeminded to deal with these abomi-
nations. I think – I hope – But let's see what happens this time,
now that the obliteration of Darasilo's Trove has already brought
me so much closer to atonement.*

The flash of dissolution was more intense than she had
ever experienced before. When Thalassa Dru opened her
eyes, long moments passed before she could focus her vision.
Then she saw what had happened, and tears of joy sprang
to her dazzled eyes.

'One of your arms is free!' she breathed. The pale manacle
and its chain lay on the cavern floor, shattered like glass.

*I am still held fast by the other limb. But we progress, Thalassa
Dru. We progress.*

He reached out with the unshackled tentacle and gently
pressed one talon into the wall of ice, extracting a small
object which he held out to the sorceress. It was a sphere
no larger than a pea that shone like an emerald star.

*Here is her essence, liberated from their evil thrall and from all
pain. You and Dobnelu know how to reunite it to her body. But she
must remain with you in your mountain sanctuary until the last
remnants of power-hunger are cleansed from her soul. You two will
be her guides and teachers. Ansel Piken, unfortunately, can no longer
be trusted to act without prejudice.*

She tucked the green gem into her bodice. 'What are we
to do about him, master? It seems plain that his sentimental
attachment to Maudrayne Northkeep has clouded his judgment and perhaps even diminished his commitment to the
Conflict. Without consulting us, he's hidden the woman
and her son in a place where Conrig Wincantor's men are
unlikely to find them. I think he still hopes to solve the
problem of the princess and her son peacefully.'

*As I would also hope to do! I've put into play certain factors that
may yet bring about such a fortunate resolution. But ultimately,
Maudrayne's fate rests in her own hands. The doleful truth is that*

Conrig's Sovereignty cannot be allowed to fall because of her thirst for revenge. Ansel must be made to understand this. If he balks, then we must remedy the situation as best we can. I'll bespeak you if the necessity for action arises. And now farewell, dear soul.

Thalassa Dru awoke in the castle chamber where Ullanoth's body had lain in state. Two candles burned low on either side of the Conjure-Queen's bier. The samite-draped platform was empty. She uttered a deep sigh.

'My lady?' A tentative voice came from behind the cushioned chair where the sorceress had sat while performing the drum ritual. Wix, the little old man who was Ullanoth's most devoted friend, came to stand in front of her with both hands clasped humbly over his heart. 'Did it go well? Oh, please tell me that my dear queen will live again!'

'What did you see when the drumming stopped?' she asked him.

'You went into a trance. The platinum casket in your lap melted away like smoke, and then so did her poor lifeless husk – only before it vanished utterly it seemed transformed, so that she was once again as young and beautiful as she had been before the terrible stones consumed her with pain . . .'

'Ah.' Thalassa Dru smiled, then took the spherical emerald from the bodice of her gown and showed it to him. 'Her body has been transported through subtle means to my own dwelling place far away in the mountains of Tarn. But her living essence resides here. The unnatural link between her and the Coldlight Army has been severed. I shall carry this soul receptacle safely home with me now, and after a time Ullanoth sha Linndal will indeed live again.'

Wix bent closer to look at the shining gem, his face suffused with wonder. 'I've served the dear lass for all her natural life. Will you allow me to continue? Will you take me with you?'

'The journey will be long and we'll sometimes travel in strange ways, but if you wish, you may come along.'

'I'm ready now,' he said simply.

Thalassa Dru restored the emerald to its hiding place, went to the chamber door, and opened it. In the corridor outside were Ridcanndal, Lady Zimroth, and a group of other Glaumerie Guild members, looking both fearful and angry. She swung the door wide, and with a wordless gesture invited them to enter.

'Gone!' Ridcanndal exclaimed. 'The sigils are gone – and you've taken our queen away as well!'

'She was already far from here.' The sorceress's gentle face grew stern. 'And while she reigned, you withheld your love and trust from her. So now prepare to receive a different sort of ruler.'

'Who?' Lady Zimroth demanded. 'Who will take Ullanoth's place? Will it be Beynor?'

But Thalassa Dru walked past her without another word, followed by Wix. The Guild members would have come after them and remonstrated further, but they were overcome by a strange lethargy that slowed their steps, and by the time they recovered, both the sorceress and the old man had vanished.

Snudge bespoke news of the royal assassinations to Vra-Sulkorig at Cala Palace, making it plain to the Keeper of Arcana that he, not Snudge himself, was the appropriate one to gather further information from official Didionite sources before informing the High King.

'And if His Grace shows signs of wanting to send *me* to Boarsden Castle,' Snudge added, 'you must do your utmost to dissuade him. The place is in a wild state of uproar, Brother Keeper. I read a few lips as I briefly scried it and learned that Prince Somarus has sprung up out of nowhere. He's expected

to arrive at the castle within the hour, to supervise the search
for survivors of the disaster – not that there are any! – and
give notice to the world that he's the new King of Didion.
You know what Somarus thinks of the Sovereignty. He'll
declare war on it as soon as he thinks he has a chance of
winning. And he'd probably throw the lot of us into a
dungeon if he caught us snooping around. The lads and I
intend to hotfoot it out of Didion as soon as we can. Our
job is to find Princess Maudrayne, and I'm confident that we
can do it. Tell Lord Stergos I might have important news for
him soon.'

*Bespeak me each day without fail, Sir Deveron. The High King
insists that you keep him informed of your whereabouts.*

'I'll do my best. Farewell, Brother Keeper.'

Snudge cut the wind-thread and sat quietly on the floor
of the parapet for a few minutes to recover his strength.
Overcome by shock, Vra-Mattis hadn't budged from the place
where Snudge had left him, while spending some two hours
overseeing the River Malle and Boarsden Castle. The young
Brother's tears had dried, but his eyes were flat and staring
and he seemed only half-conscious.

Snudge gently shook his shoulder. 'Mat. Time to go back
to the others. Up you get.'

'They were eaten,' he said in a listless voice. 'Eaten.'

Snudge pulled the unresisting novice to his feet. 'It was a
terrible thing, I agree. Perhaps you can say prayers for the
victims later, when you're feeling better.'

The two of them negotiated the curtainwall stairway with
some difficulty, then returned to the trestle table outside the
castle kitchen. The other guests had retired to their rooms,
leaving only Snudge's men dawdling over mugs of ale in the
thickening twilight. The sky had become overcast. Torches
flickered in a rising wind and a sound of clanking pots, sloshing
water, and vulgar banter came from the adjacent scullery.

'We thought you'd fallen asleep somewhere, Deveron,' Sir Gavlok joked. Then he noticed his friend's grim face. 'What is it, man? You look like death.'

'Death's what we have to deal with,' Snudge said. He beckoned to his younger armiger, Wil Baysdale. 'Vra-Mattis has been overcome by exhaustion after a difficult windspeaking session. See him off to bed and sit with him for an hour or so, to be sure he rests comfortably.'

Will sprang up, a solicitous expression on his face, and led the faltering novice away.

When the two were gone, and Snudge had been served with ale by Valdos, his other squire, Gavlok said, 'What's this about death?'

'Salka monsters have attacked the barge carrying the royal family of Didion on its progress along the Malle River. The king and queen and their children have perished, along with all of their retainers and servants. So far, no one has any explanation why the monsters should have done such an incredible thing. They haven't penetrated into Didion for nine hundred years. Prince Somarus is on his way to Boarsden Castle, which is a stronghold of his mother's people, to seize the advantage. He'll proclaim himself king, and I wouldn't put it past him to do something rash – if not immediately, then perhaps within the next few days. All hell's broken loose in Tarn as well. Princess Maudrayne has told her brother Liscanor that she's the mother of King Conrig's eldest son and heir. Liscanor has passed the information on to the High Sealord Sernin. Unless I'm much mistaken, it won't be long before he and Somarus begin exchanging seditious messages on the wind.'

While Gavlok and the squires sat in silence, stupefied by the enormity of the disaster, the Mountain Swordsman Radd Falcontop spoke up. 'Sir Deveron, I must make bold to give you some advice. With conditions now so unsettled, and likely to get worse, it will be highly dangerous for a small party such as ours to continue along the Wold Road and into Tarn. The situation was dicey enough before – but the lawless partisans of Somarus will run rampant now that they need not fear retribution from King Honigalus. No travelers from Cathra will be safe. If you are determined to go on, I beg you to bespeak Earl Marshal Parlian and request that a heavily armed company of troops be sent from Great Pass garrison to escort us.'

'I agree with Radd,' Hulo Roundbank said.

'But then we must forgo our disguise as simple young merchant-lords,' Gavlok protested. 'Our entire mission was predicated upon going stealthily, but it will be obvious that we're on the king's business if we travel with a mob of warriors.'

'We risk being killed from ambush if we continue in our present state.' Hulo said. 'At best, we'd be taken prisoner and held for ransom by one of the robber-barons. All of western Didion favors Somarus for having denounced his late brother's submission to the Sovereignty.'

Gavlok made a helpless gesture. 'Perhaps we can adopt a different disguise. Or retrace our steps, go over to the Westley coast, and take ship from one of the ports there –'

Snudge said, 'All of you be silent. There is another course of action open to us – one that I had fervently hoped to postpone until we were inside Tarn and close to the hiding place of the princess.'

They stared at him. His face was pale as he opened his shirt and drew out the golden chain with its two glowing moonstones. Gavlok uttered a gasp of astonishment at the sight, for he had no idea that his friend had acquired a second sigil. The others were only puzzled.

'My friends,' Snudge said, 'all of you were told when you agreed to accompany me that this adventure had much to do with sorcery. Princess Maude and her son are guarded by the High Shaman of Tarn, one of the great magickers of the

northland. Earlier, although you were not told of this, the
two fire-raising villains were also involved in a matter of
high sorcery. They used the fire to cover their theft of a valuable collection of magical amulets from the Royal Alchymist
. . . amulets such as these.'

He lifted the stones for their inspection. When Radd
reached out a curious hand and would have taken hold of
them, Snudge exclaimed, 'Beware! Anyone who touches
these things without first gaining the permission of the owner
risks being severely burnt or even killed. They are called sigils
and are tools of the Beaconfolk, capable of formidable magic.
I must also tell you that this magic exacts a price from the
one who wields it, according to the difficulty of the action
performed. A price of pain.'

'Then you are a sorcerer?' Hulo seemed dumfounded.

'No, only the Royal Intelligencer – King Conrig's trusted
snudge. I use the magic of the Beaconfolk only rarely and
with great reluctance, and only in the service of the King's
Grace. How I obtained these stones is a story I may not share
with you. I will only say that I wish I had never laid eyes on
the damned things, for they put my very soul in peril . . .
Nevertheless, since I *do* have them, I will use them as I must.'

'How do they work?' Radd asked. His face wore no expression of awe, as did those of his companion Swordsman and
the two squires. His was a coldly practical interest.

'This sigil is called Concealer. Using it, I can go invisible.
And not only I myself, but also a few companions who stay
close to me. You may have heard of the way the Mallmouth
Bridge was opened to our invading army. Four fellow-
armigers and I used Concealer to do the trick.'

'Could we use it to travel unseen to Tarn?' Radd asked
eagerly.

'Alas, I fear not. It hides those within four arm's-lengths
of me only. All of us and our mounts would not fit within

its compass, and we could not go on foot.' He sighed and took up the second moonstone. 'This other sigil, which I acquired only very recently, is the one that will, I think, enable us to fulfill our mission despite the difficulties facing us. Its name is Subtle Gateway. It is capable of transporting me to the destination of my choice, instantly. It will also carry the lot of you along with me, if I ask it to.'

'Great God, Deveron!' Gavlok exclaimed. 'Where did you find such a treasure?'

'I didn't,' Snudge said bleakly. 'The Subtle Gateway sigil was given to me, although I tried to refuse it, because a certain person wishes me to find Princess Maude and her son.'

'Who?' Gavlok demanded. 'The Conjure-Queen? Lord Stergos?'

Snudge gave a hollow laugh, but only shook his head. 'You must not ask me about him. All you need know is that using this magical transport is not a trivial matter. It will cause me to suffer agony while the magic is accomplished and afterward as well, while I sleep. I suspect that the greater the distance traveled, the greater the pain must be, and the longer I must endure it.'

They stared at him, horrified. The squire Valdos said softly, 'So that's why you hoped to hold off using it until we were closer to the hiding place of Princess Maudrayne.'

Snudge inclined his head in agreement. 'If I ask Gateway to transport us for hundreds of leagues, the consequences will likely incapacitate me for several days. You, of course, would feel nothing.'

Someone gave an exhalation of relief.

'Practically speaking,' Snudge continued, 'we'll have to go to ground and hide out in some secure bolt-hole until I recover. Then I'll use the other sigil, Concealer, to get the princess and her son away from her captors –'

'Wouldn't Concealer's magic afflict you sorely all over again?' Radd asked.

'No. Concealer is a so-called minor sigil. Its pain-debt is rather small, so long as one doesn't go invisible for a considerable time. But Subtle Gateway is one of those deemed a Great Stone. If you use it, you pay a great price.'

'Oh.' The rugged old warrior was nonplussed, as though realizing for the first time the terrible import of what Snudge had been saying.

'What happens when we have Princess Maude?' Gavlok asked. 'Do we take her and the boy back to His Grace in Cala?'

Snudge lowered his eyes. 'That part of it remains to be seen. I have a certain proposal to put to the lady. Lord Stergos and I both pray she will accept it, since it would solve His Grace's dilemma concerning her and the lad.'

The lanky knight's gaze flickered and he said no more, not wanting to talk of what might happen if Maudrayne refused.

The two Mountain Swordsmen also exchanged knowing glances. Hulo gave a tiny shrug, then said, 'Sir Deveron, when would you undertake this magical journey?'

'Tomorrow will be soon enough. We need time to prepare. We'll ride out of here at dawn, then disappear on a lonely section of the Wold Road, leaving our horses behind. It would be useful if you'd think about the supplies and equipment we'll require for a mission that might take as long as a sennight. Princess Maudrayne is being kept in a wild and remote part of Tarn. All that we need, we'll have to carry with us on our backs. I'll leave you for a time now, since I must bespeak . . . someone and obtain his approval and certain important information.'

The others nodded and murmured, thinking he meant to use Vra-Mattis to consult the High King on the wind. Radd and Hulo began to put forth useful suggestions concerning food and weaponry.

'One further thing I must tell you.' Snudge spoke in a low voice. 'We'll not be taking my armiger Wil Baysdale along with us. I have good reason to believe he's not reliable, which is why I sent him off to care for Mattis before telling you about all of this.'

The other armigers were thunderstruck, but Gavlok merely said, 'A good idea. We should have done something about him before this. I had meant to speak of something odd that happened last night at Great Pass garrison, but the day's excitement drove it out of my mind.'

'What is it?' Snudge said grimly.

'I saw Wil and Vra-Mattis whispering together before we retired. Wil was speaking with great urgency, as though pleading for some favor. Finally the windvoice drew his hood over his head for a few brief minutes, then uncovered. Young Wil then seemed relieved in his mind and went off.'

Snudge muttered a curse. 'I wish you'd told me earlier. But no harm done. I'll deal with this later.'

He tucked the glowing sigils back into his shirt, rose from the table, and walked off toward the guesthouse. But he turned aside once he was out of the others' sight, touched Concealer and murmured the words that made him invisible, then returned to the curtainwall parapet to bespeak the Source.

Wiltorig Baysdale, cousin to Duke Feribor Blackhorse, was well aware that he'd been excluded from the group conference because Sir Deveron didn't trust him. The Royal Intelligencer had never accused him of disloyalty: he was too clever for that. But all too often he'd found errands for Wil to perform, sending him out of hearing while certain others were taken into his confidence – with the result that Wil had not yet been able to pass on a single bit of really useful information to the duke.

Tonight, the squire vowed, that wouldn't happen. Something vitally important was about to be discussed, and he didn't intend to miss out on it.

When Duke Feribor had first insinuated his clever young relative into the service of the Royal Intelligencer, there was no hint of the grave matter that would eventually cause the king to order a clandestine expedition into the north country. The newly dubbed young knight commander required two armigers, so Feribor put forth his cousin as a suitable candidate – simply because he enjoyed the irony of having a spy of his own to spy on the wretch who'd come so close to disclosing Feribor's rôle in the irregular handling of the Royal Treasury funds.

Later, when Deveron was sent off on his supposedly secret mission, having Wil Baysdale available to keep tabs on the search for Princess Maudrayne was a fortuitous stroke of luck for Feribor. He'd heard the same rumors of her survival that had worried Earl Marshal Parlian, but hadn't known what to make of them. Why would Conrig be so desperate to track down his former wife? Why should the High King care if Maudrayne Northkeep was alive and hiding in Tarn? At first, the questions seemed unanswerable.

Until Feribor deduced the obvious solution, and an elegant scheme was born in his mind. Then later, the extrordinary demands of the venal wizard Bozuk played perfectly into Feribor's hands, almost as though fate had decreed it . . .

Wil Baysdale led Vra-Mattis to his pallet in the fortress dormitorium. But instead of caring for the ailing novice's needs, he merely tossed a blanket over him, then crept away through a back passageway to the kitchenhouse. Two silver pennies handed over to the crew of sniggering scullion-lads convinced them to let him eavesdrop on Deveron and the others from behind the partly open door of the scullery.

With mounting excitement and apprehension, he overheard

information more crucial than he might have hoped for in his wildest dreams.

Wil knew that Feribor had taken ship to Tarn with the shaman's bribe. Not appreciating the depths of Feribor's villainy, the squire also believed that the duke meant to go off after Princess Maudrayne himself, after Bozuk revealed her hiding place, simply in order to ingratiate himself with the king.

But if Deveron found the princess first –

The treacherous armiger had nipped off back to the guest-house and Vra-Mattis the moment Snudge mentioned the necessity of bespeaking someone. Being absent when Gavlok voiced his grave suspicions of him, Wil still had expectations of continuing his spying after they all made their magical leap to Tarn.

He began hauling off the novice's boots and clothing, services he'd earlier neglected, intending to look innocent when Sir Deveron arrived. Vra-Mattis was already half-asleep and hardly noticed what was being done for him, muttering vague words of thanks as Wil tucked a pillow beneath his head and offered him water.

Nervously, Wil waited for his master to appear; but no one came. After nearly ten minutes had passed, he went outside to see what had happened. The others were still sitting at the trestle table with their heads together, probably planning the new expedition. But there was no sign of Sir Deveron anywhere in the inner ward.

Where had he gone? Wil was certain he'd heard Deveron say he was going off to bespeak someone about an important matter. But he hadn't approached Mattis, and surely he wouldn't seek out some Didionite wizard to send his wind-message –

Then Wil froze, remembering what Cousin Feribor had said during their final hurried conversation in Cala Palace:

'*Be very careful not to underestimate Deveron Austrey. My disgraced uncle, Kilian Blackhorse, once told me that the bastard is a wild talent – a secret magicker. And after what he did at Redfern Castle and Mallmouth Bridge, I'm inclined to believe it.*'

What if Sir Deveron was away somewhere doing the bespeaking *himself*?

Will had entertained small hope of getting off his own wind-message until the middle of the night or even tomorrow morning, since Mattis seemed so weak and sick – but perhaps he wasn't as bad as he seemed.

'Mat! Wake up! I need your help.' Wil slapped the youth's face and shook him by the shoulders.

Mattis opened his eyes and moaned, 'What? What's wrong?'

Wil knelt next to the pallet, pulled the windvoice upright, and spoke with every evidence of concerned dismay. 'Oh, Mat – I don't know how to tell you. Sir Deveron is so worried about your fragile state of mind that he's decided to send you back to Beorbrook Hold with one of the Swordsmen. The rest of us are going to continue on to Tarn after picking up another windvoice at Rockyford Way Station.'

Tears sprang into Mat's eyes. 'I'm – I'm not surprised. What a disappointment I must be to the master, falling to pieces like some cringing little wench.'

'It's not your fault that your talent makes you overly sensitive to terrible events,' Wil averred. 'We're all made differently. You're a good friend. I'll always be grateful that you were willing to bespeak my family's windvoice back in Blackhorse Duchy, letting me converse with my poor sick mother. I've been so worried about her, Mat! And now I'll have no more word of her at all. I'd never dare ask this other Brother who's joining us for such favors as you were kind enough to grant me.'

'I'm sorry, Wil. I wish there was something I could do.'

'Well . . . there is, only I hesitated to ask. But if you could send Mother one last message – if you feel strong enough—'

Mat ventured a tremulous smile. 'I'll try. Just give me a minute.' Lying back on the pillow, he covered his eyes with his hands. His lips moved without making a sound. Then he spoke aloud. 'Your family windvoice hears me, Wil. What would you like to tell your mother?'

'Say I'm about to ride into great danger, but all will be well because Sir Deveron has just been given two magical amulets to protect us. One is named Concealer, and it can make all of us invisible. The second is called Subtle Gateway, and it will transport us directly to the place where Princess Maudrayne is hidden. Tell Mother not to worry, even if I can't have you bespeak my messages anymore. We'll all be home safe in Cala in less than a tennight. Sir Deveron has promised it.'

Vra-Mattis opened his eyes wide. 'Wil! Is it true?'

The armiger's gaze shifted to the door. 'Yes, of course it is. I wasn't supposed to tell you about that – but what difference can it make? Mother will be so glad to hear we'll all be home soon, with our mission successfully accomplished. Bespeak the message, Mat. Please!'

The novice smiled feebly and closed his eyes once more. 'Of course I will. What wonderful news!' He began to windspeak soundlessly at some length. Wil rose to his feet and darted to the doorway. No one was coming. There'd be time to do what had now become necessary.

'Wil?' The young Brother's voice was very weak. 'I – I've done it. It took all my strength, but I've done it.'

'Thank you!' Wil Baysdale's gratitude was sincere, overflowing with relief. He crouched beside the exhausted windvoice. 'You'll never know how much this means to me. Now rest well. Let me just fluff up your pillow for you.'

He lifted Vra-Mattis's head, drew out the cushion, and pressed it with all his strength over the novice's face. His struggles did not last long. When they ended Wil replaced the pillow, closed the dead eyes, and smoothed the features into a semblance of peaceful sleep.

Then he went off to tell the others the dreadful thing that had happened.

TWENTY

Late in the evening, Maudrayne climbed the spiral staircase of the tall turret that bore the peel's windmill and freshwater reservoir. The rain had stopped for the moment, but the wind keened like a lost child and a muffled boom of heavy surf came from the little cove far below. She'd invited Dyfrig to accompany her on her first exploration of the odd structure, but the boy had refused in favor of a game of chess with Rusgann in front of the parlor fire.

The two days of steady downpour that had kept him indoors since their arrival had turned Dyfrig apathetic and withdrawn. He was also disappointed that the sons of Shaman Ontel and Sealady Tallu were taciturn lads of nine and eleven – much too old to be willing playmates to a four-year-old, even one who was bright and mature for his age. After a few initial hours of kindly attention to their young guest, the Tarnian boys had abandoned him to follow their usual pursuits, while Dyfrig was left with only Rusgann and his mother to entertain him. There were no domestic chores for him to perform here, as he'd done so eagerly at Dobnelu's steading; silent, glum-faced servants took care of everything. Lessons would not begin until

Ontel's family and the prisoners moved to the winter residence at Fort Ramis, at the start of Harvest Moon. Soon,
Maudrayne knew, the boy would grow bored and fretful.

And so would she, for Skullbone Peel was hardly living
up to Ansel's glowing description.

The keep was much larger and more elaborately
appointed than the sea-hag's farmhouse, but it was also
charmless – especially on overcast days of summer rain.
The floors and walls were of stone, only sparsely softened
by rugs and hangings, and the rooms were chill and only
dimly lit by narrow windows having panes of yellowish
translucent seal-bladder. There was a library, as promised,
but aside from a small shelf of crudely inscribed storybooks
that had probably been copied out by the boys as school-
room exercises, the volumes were mostly ponderous tomes
without pictures that dealt with Tarnian history and
shamanistic practices – no doubt fascinating to Master
Ontel, but of no interest to a young child.

Ansel himself was still in residence, although he had
informed her at their noontide dinner that he would soon
be departing. Maudrayne's sharp temper had been provoked
by disappointment in the new place of confinement, and she
had rebuffed all of his attempts at friendly conversation.
Eventually he gave up trying to cheer her and went off to
confer with his cousin Ontel, probably organizing her secure
detention.

She was in a foul mood as she reached the top of the
turret, and her heart sank even lower as she surveyed the
domain where she and her son were to be imprisoned. It
was a part of Tarn that she had never visited, proverbial
among the livelier folk of the west for its bleak solitude and
comparative poverty.

The windows up here were thick glass, probably because
the turret also served as a watchtower – although heaven

only knew what kind of sea-raiders would be foolish enough to attack the tiny local settlements. Visibility was fairly good after the rain, revealing a vista of savage ruggedness. Skullbone Peel lay at the northern end of Tarn's Plateau of Desolation, a nearly roadless expanse of tundra and bog that was almost completely uninhabited. The Desolation Coast, pummeled throughout much of the year by arctic winds and ferocious seas, comprised two hundred and sixty leagues of eroded limestone and basalt cliffs, reefs and stacks, and a myriad of rocky islets softened by sparse vegetation where only seals, birds, foxes, and lemmings lived. To the north lay a sterile black-rock peninsula called the Lavalands. Born of extinct volcanos and ridden with shoalwater, it was a menacing barrier to coastal shipping even in summer, when the pack-ice receded. South of the peel were whaling stations and fishing hamlets, and a single isolated castle, Fort Ramis, around which huddled the only town of any size in all of northeastern Tarn. The family of Shaman Ontel and Sealady Tallu dwelt there during the long arctic winter, and so, Maudrayne had been told, would she and Dyfrig and Rusgann.

We'll never escape from here, she said to herself. They'd capture us easily if we tried to flee inland over that black desert, and to get away by water is virtually impossible. Small wonder Ansel had said she'd be allowed to use a sailboat! There was nowhere to go. After consulting a chart in the library, she'd discovered that the only sizable ports she could hope to reach, where sealords dwelt who might sympathize with her plight and defend her from pursuers, were Ice Haven on Havoc Bay or Cold Harbor up north on the Icebear Channel. Both places were over three hundred and fifty leagues away, and neither had road access to the rest of the country.

So we're trapped here, she thought, at least for now. But

it can't last forever, not if my brother Liscanor has done what he should . . .

The windmill on top of the small tower must have been well-greased, for the only sound it made as it spun in the gale was a lugubrious low-pitched moan, like some enormous animal softly humming. The noise was insufficient to mask the approaching footsteps of someone climbing the turret stairs. Maudrayne seated herself on the circular bench that surrounded the shaft housing of the windmill and waited for her visitor to arrive.

Ansel Pikan's fiery red hair and beard popped up through the opening in the floor. His face was grave rather than friendly. 'May I join you?'

'As you wish.' She gazed out over the grey sea, white-scalloped with lines of advancing surf.

'I've been bespoken by one of my principal colleagues in the capital. He had some unsettling news. High Sealord Sernin has called for an emergency meeting of the Company of Equals in Donorvale six days from now. Lady Tallu and I will be leaving immediately to attend.'

A small smile curled the ends of Maudrayne's lips. She said nothing.

'Oh, Maudie! What have you done?' Ansel's voice was full of reproach. 'How much did you tell your brother Liscanor?'

'Ask him, when you get to Donorvale,' she retorted.

'If it was only the truth about Dyfrig, then there's a chance Conrig's Sovereignty may survive. But if you revealed the High King's secret talent, then all of Blenholme might be in deadly danger. Do you know that the Salka have attacked Didion for the first time in almost a millennium? It happened late yesterday.'

She shrugged in disdain. 'What is that to me? Let Honigalus and Conrig send their navies after the brutes. Let the Conjure-Queen thrash them with her Weathermaker. The monsters will flee, as they did when they raided Moss a while ago, and that'll be an end to it.'

'The Salka swam up the River Malle and slaughtered Honigalus and all of his family. Somarus is now King of Didion, and there are ugly rumors abroad in Cathra that he might have conspired with Beynor of Moss to bring on the attack. If this is true, then the monsters are his allies. He won't go to war against them.'

Maudrayne was shocked in spite of herself. 'Well, then, it falls to Ullanoth and Conrig to –'

'Ullanoth is dead . . . or as close to it as a human being may be. She fell into a mortal trance as a result of sorcery gone awry. Her magical moonstones can be used by no other person. And the wizards of Royal Fenguard are in a panic, fearing that Beynor will urge the Salka to attack Moss next.'

She flashed him a look of poisoned triumph. 'And so Conrig Wincantor is the one great champion left to defend our island against these inhuman brutes? And *I* am obliged to withdraw my accusations against him and deny my son's birthright in order to preserve his Sovereignty? *Never!* He's an unworthy king – an illegitimate king, by the law of his own land.'

'The Salka will attack Moss in force,' Ansel said. 'My Source has solemnly assured me of this. And they won't stop there. Neither Beynor nor Somarus will be able to control them.'

'And Conrig is the only one who can stop their advance? Nonsense! The Salka have no ships, no weapons except a few puny moonstones. They're stupid, clumsy on land, and there aren't enough of them to be a serious threat to humanity.'

'Uncounted thousands of them dwell in the Dawntide Isles. Even more have lived quietly in the fens of Moss up until now. But the fenland Salka are suddenly on the move, approaching areas inhabited by humans. Some of them are slow-witted, but by no means all. The Dawntide Salka are the elite members of their race, the ones who retained their ancient culture and magical science. The Source believes that they were the ones who attacked Didion's royal family. And thanks to Beynor, who is either criminally insane or else acting as a tool of the Beaconfolk, the Salka leaders will soon obtain new moonstone sigils – powerful weapons of sorcery that haven't been seen since Emperor Bazekoy's day.'

'You're lying,' she said in a voice of ice. 'You and your Source would say anything to protect Conrig. God only knows why! But you don't frighten me with your tales of invading monsters, and you won't shut my mouth. Once the Company of Equals hears all that Liscanor has to say, they'll compel you to deliver me and Dyfrig and Rusgann over to them so we can bear witness to the truth of my accusations. You won't dare defy them.'

He stared at her, unspeaking.

And her eyes widened in speculation. 'Or would you? There's one sure way to make certain that I never endanger Conrig. Are you ready to undertake it?'

When he was well away from Boarsden Castle, after taking supper at a little village below Firedrake Water, Beynor bespoke the Conservator of Wisdom in the Dawntide Citadel, requesting a conference with him, the First Judge, the Master Shaman, and the Supreme Warrior. There was a brief delay while the three Eminences summoned Ugusawnn on the wind, since he was at that time leading his warriors down the River Malle at speed, but soon all was in readiness.

We Four are now prepared to hear you, Beynor, the Conservator said. *But before you speak, know that all of us are mightily displeased with your behavior. The Supreme Warrior has told us how you fled from him.*

'It was Ugusawnn's fault,' Beynor snapped. 'He treated me as a despised servant, not an honored ally, during our journey into Didion. However, in spite of his rude behavior and blatant expressions of mistrust, I still intend to fulfill my promises to the Salka. The King of Didion and all of his family were slain, just as I requested, so I'll activate the Known Potency for you, and I'll also give you the sigils of my sister, Conjure-Queen Ullanoth . . . provided that you first repair the insult to my esteem by vouchsafing another favor.'

You want us to kill the Conjure-Queen, the Master Shaman said. *Ugusawnn has already informed us of this demand. But are you not aware that she lies in an enchanted sleep? She is totally helpless. You can easily destroy her yourself.*

'No! You Salka must be seen to do it, just as you were seen to be responsible for the deaths of Didion's royal family. I'm already unjustly accused of killing my father Linndal. This is a vicious lie – but it would be given credence if people learned that I personally slew Ullanoth. As I told you, I wish to make a new life for myself on the Continent. In order to do this with my honor intact, there must be no proof that I colluded in your conquest of Moss, or had anything to do with the death of the Conjure-Queen.'

I see no reason to deny him, said the First Judge.

He's not to be trusted! the Supreme Warrior roared. *Once the queen is dead, there's nothing to prevent him from rallying the Mosslanders against us and posing as a hero to his former subjects. He could refuse to empower the Potency and deny us Ullanoth's sigils! They lie in Rothbannon's tomb, where only a descendant of his can reach them. Let me remind the other Eminences of another fact: once the queen is dead, her moonstones are dead as well. Beynor could easily instruct a loyal confederate how to re-activate the sigils. Even though he is unable to make use of the six stones himself, his crony could use them against us at his bidding.*

The difficulty can be circumvented, said Kalawnn, the Master Shaman. *Let Beynor come to Dawntide Citadel! After our forces kill the queen, Beynor will activate the Potency, bonding it to me, rather than to the Supreme Warrior. Then Beynor can go in peace, while we open Rothbannon's tomb by means of the Potency.*

Would that work? the First Judge wondered.

In my opinion, Kalawnn replied, *the Greatest Stone should be able to transcend all lesser forms of sorcery.*

'With respect!' Beynor exclaimed, feeling the situation showed signs of getting out of hand. 'This alternative isn't acceptable to me. I won't be satisfied unless I *see* Ullanoth's body destroyed. Not by means of scrying, for clever magic is able to deceive windsight, but rather see the remains with my own two eyes. Only then will I activate the Potency and bond it to one of you. I also refuse to return to the citadel. Within its walls, I am reduced to my former powerless state, dependent not only upon the goodwill of you three Eminences who now reside there, but also upon that of Ugusawnn, the Supreme Warrior, who has forfeited my trust.'

We seem to have come to an impasse, the First Judge said, sighing.

The problem was caused by Ugusawnn, said the Conservator. *He is the bravest and strongest of us all, but nevertheless he has antagonized our would-be benefactor and otherwise shown a lack of wisdom. I must suggest that we reconsider bonding the Potency to him. This problem can be readily solved if our esteemed Master Shaman, Kalawnn, agrees to be bonded to the Potency in Ugusawnn's stead. He can carry the Greatest Stone to Moss, in the company of our army and the Supreme Warrior. Once there, he will stand aside from the fighting, well guarded, so there will be no danger to him or the sigil. Beynor must agree to join him. When the queen is dead, and Beynor confirms this with his own eyes, then let him activate the Potency and bond it to Kalawnn.*

What do you say to that, Supreme Warrior? the First Judge demanded.

I . . . submit to the will of my Eminent colleagues. Under protest!

The judge said, *And you, Beynor of Moss?*

'Let my dear old friend Master Kalawnn carry the Potency to the vicinity of the Darkling River. Let him and his protectors stand safely aside with me while the valiant Ugusawnn takes the castle and destroys my sister. Then I solemnly swear by my human God that I will bring the Known Potency to life and open Rothbannon's tomb.'

Then we are finally agreed? said the Conservator of Wisdom. His ancient mental voice betrayed a profound fatigue.

YES.

All of them voiced affirmation – Beynor declaring it with a fervency greater than that of the Salka, for he had held back from them the vital fact that the Potency bonded to no single person, but might be utilized by anyone once it was conjured alive. And while he was not absolutely certain that the sigil would neutralize the curse of the Beaconfolk, he was willing to wager his life on it. He would find a way to snatch the Potency away from Kalawnn just as soon as it was activated, then escape from the monsters. With both Potency and Ullanoth's sigils in hand, he would turn his attention to securing the Destroyer sigil; and when he owned that last necessary stone, he'd be ready to found his empire . . .

There is one final thing, the Master Shaman said. *A last precaution against misadventure which I would like you all to witness. Beynor, Ugusawnn – please transfer your talent to oversight mode so you may scry what I am about to do. I intend to guard this treasured sigil in the best way I know.*

Puzzled, Beynor complied. He saw Kalawnn slither from his kelp-padded couch in the dank audience chamber of the citadel, take the small carving from its golden tripod, and hold it up delicately between his taloned fingers for all to see.

Then Kalawnn opened his enormous, hideously fanged mouth, put the moonstone on his purple tongue, and swallowed – sending the Known Potency into the secure coffer of his gizzard.

Snudge stood again on the fortress parapet, wondering if he was doing the right thing. Earlier, Lord Stergos had been aghast at the notion of his trying to pressure the Source. But what other course was open to him? Even with a general knowledge of where Princess Maudrayne was confined, he had no way of getting to her. There was only the Gateway. And to use it, he needed to state a specific destination . . . didn't he? And only the Source could tell him exactly where to go.

Or would the Great Stone transport him and his men if he simply commanded it to put them down in a safe place half a league away from Maudrayne's prison?

No. That wouldn't work. Such an irregular request might even antagonize the Lights and have disastrous results.

'Source! You can read my thoughts?' Snudge was horrified at the notion.

Only when you unconsciously aim them at me, dear soul. Have no fear. The contents of your mind are your sole possession. No one can violate them.

'Do you already know the question I planned to ask you?'

I know the impudent plan you confessed to Stergos. But there's no need to threaten me or demand tit for tat. I'll willingly tell you: Maudrayne is in a place called Skullbone Peel, a small keep on the north-eastern Tarnian coast. Command the sigil to carry you and your people to a ravine two thousand paces south of it. There you'll find a sheltered spot beneath an overhanging ledge – not quite a cave, but deep enough to keep you out of the elements while you recover from the pain-price, and shield you from casual oversight.

Snudge hesitated. 'Was – was I correct in thinking that my suffering will be more severe, the farther I travel?'

Unfortunately, yes. And the number of people carried with you also affects your debt. Keep this in mind as you make further excursions.

'Further? I don't understand. What am I to do after I make my proposal of compromise to the princess? Surely you're not suggesting that I use Gateway to carry her and the child back to His Grace at Cala Palace!'

You must do as you think best – for her and her child, for Conrig, and for the Final Conflict in which all of you participate.

'What *I* think best? Damn you, Source, I'm only a poor devil of a spy! How can I make such fateful decisions by myself? What if I make a stupid mistake and get nabbed by the guards at the Tarnian keep? What if the princess won't agree to my compromise – or His Grace declines it? What if Ansel Piken finds out what I'm up to and uses his sorcery to – to stop me?'

Ansel won't stop you. I've already seen to that. As to the other matters, I can't say. Now go and do what you must do.

'You're not being fair, Source! You've got to give me more explicit instructions. I'll abandon the whole thing if you don't! Source? Answer me! Source . . .'

He howled the Light's name on the wind, furious and frightened, but there was no response. Finally he severed the thread of speech, waited until he stopped shivering in the tepid evening air, and asked himself whether he'd really give up the mission now that it seemed so close to being accomplished.

He answered his own question, then sat in numb misery on the parapet floor wondering whether to bespeak Stergos and ask *him* for advice.

'Futter that!' he growled, on due consideration. 'I'll do it my way, just as the Source told me to.'

Feeling dead tired, but at the same time strangely exhilarated, he climbed to his feet and descended to the ward to see what progress his men had made on the preparations for the trip.

They showed Snudge the body of Vra-Mattis Temebrook, which lay as if peacefully sleeping. No one had touched him except Radd Falcontop, who had pronounced him dead. Not a one among the party seemed to have any doubt that the sensitive novice had died of a brainstorm, brought about by his visualization of the unspeakable atrocities committed by the Salka.

'This is still another crime to be laid at the monsters' door,' Sir Gavlok said, knuckling away unashamed tears. 'Poor Mat is their victim as much as the luckless Didionites. I only pray that some day we may be able to avenge him.'

The three squires murmured agreement. Radd and Hulo were silent, their weathered features immobile.

'What will you have us do now, Deveron?' Gavlok asked.

'Without our windvoice, sir, do we dare proceed?' Wil asked ingenuously.

'Oh, yes, we'll go on as planned. That is – all except you, young Wil.' Snudge showed the dismayed squire a sad smile. 'It falls to you, as my junior armiger, to convey the body of our fallen comrade back to Cala Palace. Go at once and find the headman of the mule train that's spending the night here. Arrange to accompany it over Great Pass in safety tomorrow. Proceed directly to Beorbrook Hold with the body, where the resident Brothers of Zeth will perform the necessary mortuary offices for poor Mattis and provide a lead-lined coffin for your journey south. The captain of the Hold garrison will assign you an escort.'

Wil Baysdale hung his head, cursing inwardly. 'Yes, messire.' Surely Sir Deveron could not suspect what he'd done! But Wil nevertheless was well aware that he'd do no more spying for Duke Feribor on this mission.

He consoled himself with the thought that there would surely be others.

Rain began during the small hours, and continued persistently as the king's men quit Castlemont and started north on the Wold Road at the sixth hour of morning. The pack train had departed earlier, but not before Snudge had a quiet word with the grizzled leader of the muleteers. After learning the man's name and his home village, Snudge took his hand and pressed a gold mark into it.

'Swive me!' the fellow muttered, at the sight of the extravagant boon. 'Not that I ain't grateful, my lord, but —'

'I thank you for allowing my squire and his somber burden to go along with you into Cathra,' Snudge said. 'However, my young friend is a headstrong boy, and was keenly disappointed not to continue on with us. There's a chance he may approach you and request that you convey the corpse to Beorbrook, while he himself turns back and foolishly attempts to rejoin our group. I ask that you prevent him from doing so — by force, if nothing else suffices. I won't suffer disobedience or a frivolous disregard for the dead.'

The muleteer's shaggy brows knit as he digested the import of Snudge's words. 'How much force?' he asked quietly.

'Don't damage him any more than necessary. But see that he stays with you for at least half the day. After that, he'll know it's too late to follow us.'

Now, as he and Gavlok rode out side by side, bringing up the rear of their small cavalcade, Snudge told his friend what he'd done. The other knight nodded in approval and said, 'I lay awake all last night in the little guesthouse cubicle we shared, with my sword unsheathed at my side, just in case Wil Baysdale decided to pay us a visit.'

'You think he might actually have done us violence?' Snudge said.

'Not only that. I believe he murdered Vra-Mattis.'

'Good God! Have you any evidence to support your accusation?'

'Just before I retired – you were already asleep – I went to Mat's cubicle to collect his writing materials from his scrip, thinking we might have need of them. I glanced at his face and saw that one of his eyes had come open, as sometimes happens. In the end, I had to put a farthing on the lid to keep it decently shut. But before that . . . I've had little experience with dead bodies, but my grandsire was a great storyteller who oft entertained us children with tales of murder and mayhem. One curious fact he told us is that the whites of a smothered man's eyes will sometimes show small specks of blood. Mat's open eye did indeed have such a sign.'

'Codders! Then the whoreson slew him!' Snudge frowned fiercely in thought. 'Wil must have listened in on our talk of the sigils. As Duke Feribor's creature, he would have thought it imperative to send a message to his master about the magical moonstones. He'd use Mat's windvoice, as he must have already done on other occasions. I don't believe Mat realized who the earlier messages were intended for. They could have contained nothing important, anyway. But this final one, with its news of me having the ability to use high sorcery, might have troubled him when he recovered his wits. Mat might have confessed to me what he'd done, and Wil Baysdale couldn't allow that to happen. Now Feribor knows we have the means to go invisible, as well as a quick way of reaching Maudrayne.'

'We'll surely get to the princess before he does,' Gavlok said. 'How long has he been at sea? Three days? I've lost count.'

'Perhaps a little less than that. But with fair winds, a fast frigate could easily get him to Northkeep and the shaman Bozuk late tomorrow. Feribor is under orders not to search for Maudrayne, but I'm certain he'll disregard them. The temptation would be irresistible. He might offer the shaman an additional bribe to serve as his guide to her hiding place. The old magicker is blind, but there's nothing wrong with his scrying ability. He could do the job.'

'But you said we'll shortly be on her doorstep! I realize we can't do anything until you're fit again, but surely you'll have recovered long before Feribor can get to her.' He broke off, staring at his friend with sudden concern. 'Won't you? I mean, you said you'd just be unwell for a few days.'

'The fact is,' Snudge said, 'I don't know how long I'll be afflicted. Perhaps, since this will be my first use of the Great Stone, the consequences won't be too severe.'

But even as he spoke, he didn't believe it.

After a brisk two-hour ride, during which they encountered no other travelers, the king's men came to a section of the Wold Road that traversed a stretch of open ground. Beyond it on their left rose thickly wooded low mountains and a rough little track that led toward the Lady Lakes. It was possible to see for nearly a league in all directions, and the soggy landscape was empty of other human beings.

'This place will do as well as any for our embarcation,' Snudge said, reining in. 'Valdos, Hanan – gallop your horses up and down that side track a ways, then churn up the mud around here. We want to make it look as though we were set upon by a gang of kidnappers. Word of our supposed abduction will reach Rockyford soon enough.'

And from there, the news would fly on the wind to Cala. Snudge had debated with himself whether to tell Lord Stergos the details of his plan. But in the end he'd held off, fearing that the Royal Alchymist would consider himself duty-bound to inform the High King about Concealer and Subtle Gateway. Every instinct warned him not to risk letting this happen. Let Conrig think what he would of their abrupt disappearance. With luck, Stergos would counsel his brother to have patience.

Snudge dismounted and began to unstrap his pack. Gavlok, Radd, and Hulo followed suit. The two Mountain Swordsmen tied big bundles to each other's backs. They carried most of their food. The pair had also acquired a pair of stout staves back at the fortress, and extra arrows for their shortbows.

'I wish we could take the horses with us.' Gavlok looked at his fine tall chestnut with regret. The mounts would be abandoned here, with all of their tack.

'They'll do us no good where we're going.' Snudge was curt. 'We can only hope that local villains will come across them soon and take them off into the wilderness.'

Finally the excited squires finished their trampling and the mounts were shooed away down the Lady Lakes track, although they did not go far. All members of the party had shouldered their burdens save Snudge, who would simply rest his pack between his feet so as to keep his body unencumbered. He called everyone to draw close to him. His face had gone very pale.

'Friends, let me be frank. I know not what will happen when I make use of this Beaconfolk sorcery. The creatures that some call Great Lights and others deem the Coldlight Army are obscure and terrible. Even the Mosslanders, who are most familiar with them, know little of their true nature. The Lights savor pain. They torture with whimsical cruelty, as wicked boys sometimes torment hapless bugs or animals for the fun of it. If they fancy themselves offended, they may cast the person who insulted them into the Hell of Ice for all eternity, as we would consign a worn boot or a broken pot to a midden-heap. I myself am willing to risk such a fate out of duty. But here and now I give each of you the opportunity to withdraw from this mission – to decline to accompany me, with no stigma attaching to the act. To any man who would leave, I will give a signed note of quittance, and never think less of his courage.'

They stared at him in silence, while the rain streamed over their leather cloaks. Finally, Gavlok's squire Hanan Caprock spoke up with cheeky bravado. 'The horses are gone, and it'd be a devil of a job catching them. So I figure we're all bound to go with you, Sir Deveron, even though we're scared stiff. Let's just get on with it! Maybe it won't be so futterin' wet on the other side of your magic Gateway.'

When the explosion of laughter faded, Snudge said, 'When we arrive, I'll probably be prostrate and useless. Gavlok is your new commander until I recover, but I appoint Hulo and Radd to organize the camp in the ravine as they think best for the security and comfort of the group. You squires are forbidden to wander off on your own. All of you, remember there are magickers inside Skullbone Peel. To avoid being overseen by them, be as silent and wary as an animal. Use rocks and vegetation to screen your movements so no lookout spots you with his ordinary vision. Windwatchers ordinarily don't keep constant vigil; it's too taxing. But they'll be on you like hounds if they suspect intruders are prowling about – and the highly talented ones can scry you in darkness as well as in daylight.'

He drew from his shirt the chain with the sigils and grasped the door-shaped moonstone carving tightly. 'Well, it's time to go. Crowd close to me now. Make no noise, no matter what happens, and don't move a muscle until we arrive and are safe.'

Their damp bodies pressed against him, and he heard only the sounds of their breathing, the creak of their harness and packs, and the anonymous rumble of someone's stomach. Gavlok said, 'Shhh!'

Snudge closed his eyes and intoned 'EMCHAY ASINN,' and told the sigil where to take them.

He was alone, seeming to drift in a cold night sky with no land or sea perceptible beneath him. The uncountable stars were hard and brilliant as gems, at first unwinking against a background of utter blackness, then growing dim as other Lights, many-colored and strangely shaped, began to burgeon and overwhelm them with swelling radiance.

None of the Lights resembled the familiar auroral formations of the Boreal winter sky; there were no flickering beacons or curtains moved by cosmic winds or luminous arcs or glowing clouds. These shining insubstantialities writhed and danced with hectic, intelligent purpose. Some of them showed eyes or evanescent limbs. All of them had what appeared to be mouths that seemed to form words of the Salka language. They asked questions, and he replied.

CADAY AN RUDAY? . . . What do you want?

EMCHAY ASINN . . . Transport all of us.

KO AN SO? . . . Who are you?

SNUDGE.

He braced for the onslaught of pain but it held off. Instead, a wild cacophony of hisses, crackles, and shrill whistles assailed his ears, almost as though millions of small birds were trapped in a confined space, clamoring in fury. The throng of Lights whirled about him at vertiginous speed and their noise resolved into the speech of many individuals, fully understandable for all that the words were churned together.

His name his name we need his name! Snudge? SNUDGE?!
  It is. It's not. It's a trick!
  Snudge? A snudge is a JOB not a name.
His name his name we need his name we must have it to bind him!
  We need his name to own him. This one is trying to cheat us.
  But he is Snudge! He was accepted twice over by us!
  He was given power and gave pain. As Snudge.
For a Great Stone for the Great Link it's not enough.
  His name his name we need his own true name!
  He is Snudge. We accepted it and him. Snudge.
He cheats he holds back he slips away!
  He pays the price whatever his name. Let be.
  Rage rage against the rule-twister!
Hurt him kill him damn him to the Hell of Ice!
  His name is Snudge but it is not. Let be.
  Indifference. Eat his pain. He wins.
Laughter. The jest is on us. FOR NOW.

The chaos of colored Light flared in blinding brilliance as the laughter became thunder.

Then they were gone, leaving him wrapped wholly in pain.

He moaned aloud, felt himself lose balance and start to fall. Down through the jet-black starless void he plunged, down and down and down.

Strong arms took hold of him. 'Easy, sir,' Hulo Roundbank's voice said. There was firm earth beneath his feet, a smell of wet leaves and the sea.

He forced open his eyes and gave a gasp of agony. Daylight made the suffering all the worse. But he had to know whether the Gateway had opened to the right place, whether all of them had passed through safely.

He saw the eroded stone walls of a steep ravine, an over-hanging ledge, thick brush growing round about that gleamed wetly with leftover rain. Gavlok and Hulo were on either side of him, holding him up. Hanan was on his knees a few ells away, shorn of all his cocky courage, losing his breakfast while Valdos patiently held his head. Only Radd Falcontop seemed to be missing.

But then the stocky Mountain Swordsman stepped out from the tangled vegetation as silently as a ghost.

'I climbed to the rim of the ravine, Sir Deveron. Saw a little keep on a baldtop hill maybe half a league away. It's Skullbone Peel, sure as dammit. Don't worry. No one saw me. There's plenty of cover up there, and naught about but a few birds.'

Snudge gave vent to a great sigh, unclenched his fist, and let Subtle Gateway drop away on its chain. 'We've done it,' he said aloud.

His eyes closed, and he fell into a dark pit of fire, surrendering completely to the pain.

TWENTY-ONE

Duke Feribor Blackhorse, Lord Treasurer of the Realm, had been confident he could bamboozle the Tarnian magicker and compel him to cooperate. Blind Bozuk wanted money – enormous amounts of it. By agreeing to pay the shaman's original outrageous fee without dickering, King Conrig had undoubtedly suggested to the old rascal that even more gold might be forthcoming, given a bit of crafty maneuvering. Feribor intended to beat him at his own game.

But not for the Sovereign's benefit . . .

The shaman and the duke were now face to face across a table covered with a fine red damask cloth, in the commodore's cabin of the crack frigate *Peregrine Royal*, the swiftest warship in the Cathran Navy, presently docked at the deepwater quay of Northkeep Castle. The duke had politely declined the hospitality of its chatelaine, Lady Freda – Sealord Liscanor was regrettably away from home – and arranged to receive Bozuk on shipboard. After regaling the ancient shaman with a splendid meal and ample amounts of fine wine, Feribor got down to business. He dismissed the ship's officers, had the table cleared – except for the wine ewer and goblets – and commanded the first of the money-chests to be brought in and opened.

Then he and the blind man were left alone, and the game commenced.

The evening was now well advanced. Rain beat dismally against the stern windows and it was quite dark outside. The luxurious cabin was lit with gilded lanterns, and their mellow light glittered on the gold coins that Bozuk had piled in neat stacks. His eyes were shuttered pits but his manner was that of a sighted man, and Feribor was quite convinced that his guest scried everything.

'Two thousand and five hundred gold marks,' Bozuk said, fingering the last of the coins. 'Half of the amount pledged. I suppose you intend to hold back the rest until you get your hands on Maudrayne and the child.'

'This is what my Sovereign has commanded. You are to tell me where the Princess Dowager resides. My windvoice, Brother Colan, will bespeak the information to Cala Palace, and from there it will fly on the wind to the Royal Intelligencer, one Deveren Austrey, who is already on his way to your country. Austrey will conduct the apprehension. When the High King is satisfied that Maudrayne and the child are alive and in custody, I shall pay you the remaining half of the reward.'

The shaman tilted his nearly hairless head and offered a gap-toothed grin. 'And meanwhile, you cool your heels here in Northkeep, keeping me and my money hostage on your great ship.'

Feribor was suave. 'You will be entertained in the most lavish style for the length of your visit.'

'And yet, I have a feeling that you hold something back, lord duke! I sense another proposition lurking in your clever mind, one you would have got 'round to after plying me with more drink. Well, I shan't refuse another beaker of your wine. But why don't we cut right to the chase? You'd prefer to nab the woman yourself, rather than waiting upon this Austrey fellow. And once you had her, you'd use her to bring down Conrig Wincantor and claim the throne of Cathra and the Sovereignty of Blenholme for yourself.'

Feribor threw back his head and roared with laughter. 'You sly old rapscallion! And to think I once thought I'd find myself dealing with no more than a greedy bumpkin!'

'I am both,' said Bozuk with cool offhandedness, 'and much more. Have I fathomed your scheme correctly, then?'

'You've hit on it, I don't deny. The lady and the boy are the keys to Conrig Wincantor's ruin, and there will be many other great lords in Cathra besides myself who'll rejoice to see him cast down. The Sovereignty is a political millstone about Cathra's neck, as is Conrig himself, with his insane ambition to emulate Bazekoy the Great. My plan was to force him to recognize Maudrayne's son as his legal heir. In time – perhaps a very short time, now that Somarus sits on the throne of Didion – Conrig would perish in some ill-advised battle. Without him, Blenholme would soon become as it was before – four states who trade and squabble as the spirit moves them. While I –'

'While you,' Bozuk said softly, 'dispose of the boy-king and his half-brothers and take the throne to which you have a legitimate claim, through your mother Jalmaire, who was old King Olmigon's only surviving sibling.'

'You've studied up on Cathran genealogy.'

Bozuk cackled with laughter. 'But there's something I know and you don't know, that would make a second deplorable massacre of royal children unnecessary. And give you the throne even before Conrig was dead.'

'What?' Feribor inquired with arch skepticism.

'First,' the old man said blithely, 'the other half of the money. Now! And then the other five thousand marks in gold . . . with which you intended to bribe me to guide you to Maudrayne.'

Feribor went white. 'You can't have known about that! *How did you know?*'

'You and I are fox-kits of the same dam, Feribor, brothers beneath the skin, guileful and wicked and having goals we would kill for, if need be! I want a secure old age in a warm country. You want a throne. Bring in the money and we'll both win this game of wits.'

Without another word, Feribor strode to the cabin door and barked out an order. Then he returned to his seat at the table and sat in stony silence, flexing and unflexing his strong hands into fists, as though crushing something invisible.

Bozuk sipped wine while his sightless eyes seemed focused on the columns of golden disks lined up before him. After a while, the ship's captain ushered in the bo'sun and his mate, carrying naked swords, and a file of seamen bearing money-chests.

'Is there anything else, my lord duke?' the captain inquired, when the open boxes rested upon the table and the men had withdrawn to the corridor.

'There is,' Blind Bozuk declared in a firm voice. 'Outside on the quay, near the foot of your gangplank, you will find my servant Tigluk. He is a man of middle age, strongly built and having a notable black beard. Tell him this: "The master orders you to bring the banker Pakkor Kyle, a dozen of his well-armed lackeys, and the armored cart to this ship."'

The captain looked to Feribor for confirmation. 'My lord?'

'It must happen this way,' Bozuk addressed the duke without heat. 'Either we do this thing together, forced to trust one another by circumstances, or we will not do it at all. You cannot coerce or harm me.' Again he smiled – mostly toothless, cheeks furrowed and white-bristled, balding head dotted with age-spots like the egg of some enormous bird. Bozuk looked incapable of swatting a fly, but behind that unprepossessing, empty-eyed face Feribor Blackhorse somehow saw the shadow of a snarling wolf's-head.

'Do as he says,' the duke told the captain, who saluted and left the cabin.

'And now you wish to know the other secret.' Bozuk opened one of the three newly arrived chests and again began to stack coins. 'It's one that Maudrayne Northkeep has already shared with her brother Liscanor, when she also told him about her son. Liscanor, in turn, informed High Sealord Sernin of it, and before long all of the other sealords of the Company of Equals will know it, too.' He paused. 'They'll know it, but be unable to prove it. Yet.'

Feribor scowled. 'Bazekoy's Ballocks! Get on with it, old man!'

Unfazed, the shaman continued in a leisurely fashion. 'When I learned of the secret myself, lip-reading as I scried the Tarnian leaders discussing it, I freely gave the information to King Conrig, since he hesitated to pay my reward and I feared he'd slough me off as a backcountry crank. But he sooned learned better. Oh, how distressed – how stricken with fear! – Conrig must have been to hear his windvoice repeat my dire words. But he agreed at once to pay all that I asked.'

'Tell me the secret, damn you!'

'Oh, very well. The second secret is this: Conrig Wincantor possesses a small portion of talent.'

'What! That's ridiculous.'

'His arcane abilities are imperceptible to members of the Zeth Brotherhood, but Princess Maudrayne learned of them through the Conjure-Queen of Moss. The king's brother Stergos also knows, but is sworn to secrecy. However, if the king were to be accused before a Royal Tribunal, and Stergos made to testify under oath, he would not perjure himself or dishonor his vows to Saint Zeth. He would affirm the truth.'

'Great God,' Feribor breathed. 'And you say that some of the Tarnian leadership knows of this already?'

Bozuk nodded. 'There is no way Conrig can stop them from accusing him and demanding an official inquiry. It would be up to your cronies, the Lords of the Southern Shore, to make sure that the inquiry proceeds.' He continued making neat piles of gold. 'It would also suit your purposes, while the king's brother Stergos is under oath, to ask him whether Conrig's two younger sons by Risalla Mallburn carry the same taint as their father. It may be that they do not. I think it likely that they do possess talent, as does their older brother! Whatever the case, Stergos would feel obligated to tell the truth.'

Feribor sat back in his chair, his face aglow with ferocious triumph. 'If all this is as you say, then my enemy is delivered into my hands.'

'Maudrayne would willingly act as principal witness to the king's talent, especially if she thinks her son will inherit the throne. But later, if you should challenge the boy's birthright – who can prove for certain who his father is? Your Cathran laws declare that one such as he may inherit the throne *only* if there is no reasonable doubt that the divorced queen never lay with another man while married to the king.'

'Witnesses will surely attest to her fidelity,' the duke said, 'but it would hardly be difficult to ensure that opposing witnesses also came forth.'

Bozuk nodded. 'As I understand it, Conrig was often away from Maudrayne, and she reproached him openly for his neglect.'

The duke was staring at the rows and rows of gold coins. Ten thousand marks, a prince's ransom, half of it the fruit of his own raid on the royal revenues. So, in delicious irony, Conrig would pay entirely for the loss of his crown.

'I agree to pay what you ask!' Feribor said suddenly. He jumped to his feet. Going to a set of cabinets, he opened them and pulled out a rolled parchment. 'Where is the Princess Dowager? Show me her precise location on this map,

and instruct me on the difficulties that we might encounter
gaining access to her. You will be my guide, of course, as
you anticipated. You must also agree to hold me and my
men unharmed by the sorcery of the Grand Shaman Ansel
Pikan, who is Maude's guardian.'

Bozuk repressed a sudden pang of doubt. Would he be
able to do that, even with the wench Induna to help him?
But he spoke with full confidence, continuing to count the
money. 'Unroll your map and find a place called Fort Ramis
on Tarn's eastern coast. The woman is imprisoned near there.
In a moment, when I finish here, I will use my windsight
to confirm absolutely that she and the boy are still in the
place where Ansel Pikan put them.'

Feribor uttered an impatient growl, but contented himself
with studying the region in question. It was dismayingly
remote, with very few settlements, and would be a formidable ride overland from Northkeep. A single track led from
Fort Ramis to a mining center called Gold Creek, that marked
the head of navigation on the Upper Donor River. To Feribor's
surprise, Donorvale City was only 130 leagues downriver
from Gold Creek. But of course the Tarnians would have
made certain that their greatest national asset might be easily
transported to the capital . . .

'There!' Bozuk heaved a sigh of contentment. 'Ten thousand, as you said, and every coin true gold. Now do me the
favor of leaving me alone for a time while I perform the
scrying. It's a ticklish business, because of the bulky volcanos
lying between here and our goal, so I require perfect silence
while I concentrate. Return to me when the banker arrives.'
Again, the snaggly grin. 'And you might have your own
windvoice bespeak King Conrig, and inform him that Princess
Maudrayne and her son are to be found in the stronghold
of Cold Harbor, on Tarn's northern coast. That should put
his Royal Intelligencer nicely off on a false scent.'

'Well thought,' Feribor conceded grudgingly. 'Do what you must do. But remember that you will travel with me every step of the way, and woe betide you if you think to trick me!'

'Don't talk like an idiot,' the old shaman snapped. 'Either trust me, or take back your damned gold. But I will not stand for insults.'

Feribor stared at the old man with clenched teeth, a muscle in his jaw working. Then he bowed. 'I apologize. And I'll return soon.' He left the cabin and closed the door.

When Bozuk's oversight perceived the duke take up a rain-cloak and head for the main deck, he bespoke his grand-daughter Induna. It was a few minutes before she responded.

I was being shown to my bedroom in the cottage loft by my hostess, she said. *I arrived on the Desolation Coast only today, and have found lodging in a whaling station called Lucky Cove. My hosts think I'm a western herbalist in search of rare plants – which, of course, I am! I've already found some interesting things around here – although a more wretched spot than this never existed on God's green earth. The oil-rendering works is only a few hundred ells downshore from this cottage, and the stink from the blubber-trying pots fair turns my stomach. I'm going to have little but whale-meat to eat here, as well. I've a mind to demand an extra share of your loot, Eldpapa.*

'Never mind that, you silly chit! When I die, everything I own will be yours. Now tell me: where's the princess? Did Ansel lock her up in Fort Ramis, as I thought he'd do?'

No. She's in a small square keep called Skullbone Peel, on the coast five or six leagues north of this hamlet. It's the summer residence of the Shaman-Lord Ontel and his family, who have their principal residence in Fort Ramis. I scried Maudrayne and her son very clearly. There's a rough path that goes along the cliffs from here to there, but nothing my horse can travel. This part of the coast is all cut up with ravines. But I can probably get to the peel's vicinity on foot if need be.

'You're not sure? Why aren't you sure?'

Eldpapa, I only just got here! Don't be so difficult and crabby. I scried the path hindered by intervening rocks, just as I scried the prisoners – and them right through solid stone walls, if you please! Which explains why I couldn't find them earlier. Princess Maudrayne and her son Dyfrig and maid Rusgann are held by Ansel Pikan's cousin. This Ontel isn't much of a wizard himself – except for being a good predictor of weather.

'I know of him.'

But he does have three retainers who are fairly decent windtalents, and a pack of armed guards. His wife, Sealady Tallu, is a famed Wave-Harrier who'd fight tooth and nail to protect the prisoners, but she went away yesterday to a meeting of her peers in Donorvale. And she took Ansel Pikan with her! As the Grand Shaman of Tarn, he's obliged to attend the meeting of the Company of Equals, along with all the Sealords and Sealadies. She and Ansel went off over the cinder desert to Mornash Town, intending to ride south from there and pick up a riverboat at Gold Creek.

'Oh, bless you, Granddaughter! That's such wonderful news. I was so afraid you and I would have to trade thunderbolts with Ansel!'

You . . . and I? Eldpapa, what are you up to?

'King Conrig's emissary is here in Northkeep. A thoroughgoing rogue named Duke Feribor, who has some distant claim to the crown of Cathra. He wants to seize Princess Maudrayne for reasons of his own, and he insists that I guide him to her hiding place. I agreed. For full payment of the reward, delivered immediately – and an extra five thousand gold marks on top of that! Banker Pakkor is on his way to pick up the coin right this very minute. Once it's in his vaults, not even the High Sealord will be able to winkle it out.'

Ohhh. Eldpapa, you fool! Even if this scoundrel pays you, how can you hope to ride all this way? It's a horrible journey, even for an able-bodied young person. I daresay this Feribor won't want to

be encumbered with anything so slow as a wagon – but it'll kill
you to ride horseback so far, at the pace the duke will likely set.

'Don't fuss. We won't be riding.'

What then?

'Duke Feribor came in a fine tall ship, the swiftest in
Cathra. If I lend magical winds of my own to its great spread
of sail, two or three days is all it will take to reach Skullbone
Peel by way of Icebear Channel. And the ship is armed with
tarnblaze cannons, my dear! That chymical is immune from
magical defenses, as you well know. If Duke Feribor threatens
to blast the peel to gravel, don't you think Ontel Pikan will
be happy to be rid of Princess Maude and her brat?'

Brilliant, Eldpapa. Quite brilliant. Your plan will certainly work.

'Well, I had some doubts. If Red Ansel were there, along
with Sealady Tallu, he'd probably find a way to stop us. Take
the prisoners somewhere else, out of reach of the ship's guns.
But I know Ontel Pikan's manner of thinking. He's slow and
steady, not given to quick action. By the time he decides
what to do, the duke and I and the royal prisoners will
already be well on our way to Lucky Cove, to pick you up
and sail home to Northkeep.'

'Deveron Austrey is *what?*'

Conrig shouted so loudly that his spirited white stallion
shied, and it was necessary for the king to hold off questioning Vra-Sulkorig more closely until the beast was brought
back under control.

On this beautiful summer morning, with so much bad
news already sticking in his craw, Conrig had decided to
escape the palace and ride out boar-hunting in the great oak
forest preserve across the River Brent. He took with him
certain old friends and several members of his Privy Council,
as well as the Keeper of Arcana, who still served as Acting
Royal Alchymist and was a keen huntsman. Indeed, it had

been Vra-Sulkorig who scried out the first boar, rightly
assigning the quarry to High King Conrig because it was such
a huge animal, almost of trophy size. But the ground where
the creature stood at bay was boggy, and the king's horse
misstepped in the muck, so that his lance failed to pass
between the boar's ribs but struck a bone and glanced off.
The great beast crashed away bleeding into an adjacent marsh
where the hunters could not follow.

Conrig seemed to shrug off the loss, but in his heart he
blamed Sulkorig for not having chivvied the boar toward
firmer ground before announcing its presence. Such use of
overt talent would have been deemed unsportsmanlike, had
there been proof of it. But with no other Zeth Brethren on
the hunt, who would have known? Unfortunately, Sulkorig,
like Conrig's brother Stergos, was a model of righteousness.

And therein lay the difficulty.

Ever since the shaman Bozuk had bespoken them the news
of Maude's sensational revelations to her brother, Conrig had
been afire with anxiety. Not so much because the Sealords
of Tarn had been told that he was talented (lacking proof,
they'd debate the matter long and hard before bringing it
into the open), but because there was now one more person
in a position to take the perilous allegation seriously, whether
he had proof or not.

Before now there had been only five who knew for certain:
Snudge, Ullanoth, Stergos, Ansel, and Maude, with only the
latter posing a danger to Conrig's crown. Now Bozuk also
knew, and the Tarnians, but they were not the ones who
most worried Conrig.

The problem was Vra-Sulkorig Casswell, the austere former
soldier whose own strong talent had only tardily manifested
itself, making him all the more zealous to defend the Zeth
Codex.

After relaying Bozuk's message to the king, the Keeper of

Arcana had seemed to accept Conrig's assertion that Maude
had been lying. But a few days earlier, the king had learned
from Stergos that Sulkorig was in an agony of conscience
over the matter. The Keeper had asked Stergos's advice,
wondering whether he was obliged to report the allegation
to the Council of Brethren or the Lords Judicial of the Royal
Tribunal. Stergos had counseled silence, since Maude's statement was plainly inspired by spite and revenge and was
apparently backed by no proof. The Royal Alchymist assured
his brother the king that Sulkorig would obey. There was no
need to worry.

But Conrig worried.

The Sovereignty that had seemed so secure at the start of
Blossom Moon now was under assault from every direction,
as was he himself; and Sulkorig's qualms were the last thing
Conrig needed to top his other troubles. Thanks to Maude,
the bloody-minded Tarnians must now think they possessed
leverage to defy his edicts. The advisers of poor entranced
Ullanoth ranted hysterically of an impending Salka invasion
and demanded that he defend them with his navy. Honigalus
of Didion and his family were slain, astoundingly enough,
by the same monsters, leaving the hellraising Somarus as
unchallenged ruler of that unstable nation. Cathra's ambassador to Didion had reported that none other than Kilian
Blackhorse had been welcomed at the new king's court and
now had the royal ear. According to Earl Marshal Parlian,
war-clouds were gathering. It was only a matter of time.

And Snudge, in whom Conrig had placed such high hopes,
Snudge –

What was the Keeper of Arcana trying to tell him about
Deveron Austrey? . . .

'Your Grace,' Vra-Sulkorig said in a low voice, as the king
finally calmed his fractious steed and the two of them drew
apart from the other hunters, 'I beg you to keep your voice

down. A terrible message has just come to me on the wind, concerning the Royal Intelligencer. He and all of his party have vanished near Castlemont Fortress in Didion. They are believed to be either kidnapped or killed.'

'Who says so?' Conrig hissed.

'Several well-harnessed mounts were found running loose along the Wold Road, south of our own Rockyford Way Station. A caravan of honest merchants came upon the animals and brought them to the station garrison. The saddle of one horse bore the owl blazon of Sir Deveron. Another saddle had Sir Gavlok Whitfell's pierced cinquefoil insignia. The station captain directed his windvoice to consult with Beorbrook Hold, and it was from there that he learned the identity of the horses' probable owners – and the fact that they were king's men traveling on the king's business. The mounts were found near the junction of the Wold Road and a track leading to the Lady Lakes, the notorious haunt of Somarus's band of erstwhile outlaws.'

Conrig groaned. 'And to think I cursed Snudge last night when he failed to bespeak me as ordered!'

'The windvoice at Rockyford informs us that a troop of Mountain Swordsmen from Beorbrook will begin searching at once, as will men from the station itself.'

'Commend them,' Conrig said in a dull tone. 'Order the windvoice to keep Cala Palace informed of any progress.'

Vra-Sulkorig drew the hood of his capuchon over his face and spoke on the wind. When he had finished, he said, 'Shall we rejoin the others, Your Grace? There may be another boar less than a league away, near Cadlow Brook. I had just scried it out as the wind-message came.'

'Stay with me a moment, Brother Keeper. There's an important thing I would ask you.'

'Certainly, sire.' The sturdy Brother in the well-cut hunting habit spurred his mount closer.

'Vra-Sulkorig,' said the king, 'let me ask you one question, which I adjure you to answer in all honesty: Is your conscience troubled by the assertion of the Princess Dowager that I possess secret talent?'

Sulkorig reacted to the query almost with relief. 'So it is, Zeth help me! The notion bedevils me to the point where I can scarce think of anything else. Why should it not, since if it were true, then you must forfeit your crown, and our kingdom and the Sovereignty must be turned over to an infant. And with so many perils assailing us! But right is right in so grave a matter, as I told your lord brother.'

'And he told you to keep silence, and gave good reason for it.'

Sulkorig inclined his head. 'And so I will.' But his voice was unsteady.

Conrig smiled. 'Don't be troubled. All will go well. Come – let's rejoin the others. You must tell them of the new boar.'

Later, a second enormous animal was found and chased and dispatched with wild panache by the Lord Constable of the Realm, Tinnis Catclaw, who had proved his courage during the Battle of Holt Mallburn. Conrig lavished praise on the youngest member of his Privy Council, then took him aside for a quiet word while the other nobles shared wine, and the retainers prepared the dead boar for conveyance to the palace.

Tinnis Catclaw had been a minor baron of the Dextral Mountain country when he first served as an officer in Conrig's victorious small army. He was famed for his fighting prowess, however, and for his unfashionably long golden hair, in which he took a naive pride. When other nobles teased him for keeping it shining clean and dressed with perfumed unguents, he shrugged and pointed out that, when braided, the stuff made perfect helmet padding. After Didion's surrender, Tinnis became one of several redoubtable warriors invited to Cala Palace to help reform Cathra's standing army, which had fallen into a sad state during the reign of Conrig's late father, Olmigon. There the baron showed such outstanding organizational ability that the king eventually named him Lord Constable, in spite of the fact that he was not yet forty years of age. Together with Earl Marshal Parlian Beorbrook, he supervised the land forces of the Sovereignty.

But Lord Catclaw's prowess as a general was not what Conrig needed at the present time.

'Tinnis,' the king said, 'do you love me enough to follow any command of mine without question?'

'Sire, you know I do,' the Lord Constable replied. 'There is no man in the Sovereignty more loyal. I would lay down my life for you.'

'I require that you take life.'

'Even so, I'd fight for your cause to the last drop of my blood.'

Conrig turned his head away, looking at the torn and gory forest undergrowth where the constable had slain the boar. 'There are two persons who pose mortal threats to my life and crown. One is very far from here, in the Tarnian stronghold of Cold Harbor, on its arctic coast. Earlier, I hoped that another agent of mine would be able to deal with this enemy, but now that's become impossible. So I'd send you – alone, save for a troop of trusted retainers of your choice – if you would consent to it. A fast ship will carry you north this very day, and every resource will be placed at your disposal.'

'Sire, I'll rid you of this Tarnian foe gladly. Only give me particulars on where he's to be found, and I'll be off –'

Conrig lifted a gloved hand. 'Wait. There's a second villain, whose perfidy only came to light recently. He's here in Cathra . . . in this very woodland clearing not six ells away from us. He must be killed so artfully that it appears an accident. I care not how you arrange it, so long as the deed is done by yourself alone, before you leave the kingdom.'

Tinnis Catclaw's pale blue eyes glittered. 'Name the whoreson!'

'Vra-Sulkorig Casswell.'

'Futter me blind!' the constable whispered. 'A Zeth Brother?'

'And the one you must kill in Tarn is my former wife, Maudrayne Northkeep, who is alive and conspiring with her countrymen to ruin me and break up the Sovereignty. Tell me plain, Tinnis, whether you're prepared to ease both of these persons from this life, only because I ask it.'

The Lord Constable of the Realm pressed his right fist against his heart. 'My liege, I will.'

No, Ansel. You may not return to the peel and Maudrayne, nor may you bespeak your cousin Ontel and warn him of the danger from Duke Feribor. My foresight counsels against it, although I don't understand why.

'Feribor will take them, Source! He'll use Maude and Dyfrig against Conrig! What will become of our plan to have the king defend High Blenholme against the Salka hordes?'

We can only hope that our plan will succeed, as Feribor fails in his evil purpose.

'Why can't we make sure that he fails? Let me return to the peel and carry Maudie and Dyfrig to a safer place! Or at least let me defend them with my sorcery.'

No. She is shortly to have an important meeting there. With someone else. You would interfere. You may not go to her.

'So. A meeting, is it? With the Royal Intelligencer, I presume! I know he's on his way to Tarn, and I also know that Conrig all but commanded the spy to kill Maude and the child if there's no other way to save his damned crown.

Are you still prepared to sacrifice Maude and the boy for the sake of Blenholme's Sovereign?'

Dyfrig will certainly live. He's to be enlisted in the Conflict – as you knew full well when you rescued his suicidal mother from the sea. Maudrayne's fate is up to her. She will choose life or death by her own response to a proposal that will shortly be made to her.

'What proposal? Do you mean to say that a compromise might still be arranged between her and Conrig?'

Yes.

'When will you put the proposal to her?'

I will not. I cannot. Another will do that, provided he survives his incautious use of Subtle Gateway.

'Source! Did you give that Great Stone to Deveron Austrey? Is he already in Tarn, near Maude's hiding place?'

The Green Man Odall gave him the sigil, at my direction, during an encounter that I engineered with marvelous precision. But the young spy was rash in using the stone. I never expected him to carry numbers of his companions with him through the Gateway to Skullbone Peel. He should have gone alone to lighten the pain-debt. Poor fool! Now he lies senseless at his destination, his flagging body enduring an extremity of torture for the past two days. He may survive. You must pray that he does, and so will I, for the proposal he'll make to Maudrayne may yet solve our problem.

'Prayers?! You might have warned Deveron of the danger!'

I thought I had. He must have misunderstood. I can't think of everything. I've been so long Denied the Sky that both wisdom and resolve begin to crumble. And I also suffer, you know.

'Great God, and now you whine! I wish I'd never known you.'

Go to Donorvale, dear soul. Force the Company of Equals to wait until Maudrayne's choice is made before revealing her secrets to the world. Will you do that for me, at least?

. . .

Ansel Pikan, will you do that?
. . .

The hunt supper was winding down, having been served in the palace rose gardens between two fountains that filled the perfumed air with cooling spray. King Conrig and most of the others at the high table settled back to drink and listen to ballads sung by a remarkable Forailean bard, brought to court especially for the midsummer festivities.

The Lord Constable excused himself to the king, left his seat, and went to speak to Vra-Sulkorig, who sat near the other end of the board. Tinnis Catclaw's handsome features bore an expression of diffident concern. 'Brother Keeper, it was made plain to me during today's sport that you are one wise in the ways of horses, as well as in arcane matters. You may have noticed my own fine stallion, Windhover, a beast of high spirits that I love like a child. Of late he has puzzled me with a strange and annoying mannerism that neither the stablemaster nor the horse-leech can explain. I wonder if you would be so kind as to stroll with me to the royal stables now, while all is quiet there, and perhaps advise me on what might ail him? The odd quirk is not easily described, but I'm sure we can provoke the animal into demonstrating it to us.'

Sulkorig smiled. 'Why not? Puzzles amuse me, and one involving a horse might prove more diverting than most.' He addressed the king. 'With Your Grace's permission, I'll withdraw with Lord Tinnis.'

'Go, by all means,' Conrig said, catching the eye of the constable for the briefest instant.

As they left the gardens and circled round to the rear of the palace, Tinnis Catclaw questioned the Brother casually about how talented persons made use of the so-called 'wind' to scry and to bespeak one another. Sulkorig did his best to simplify the arcane technicalities for this interested layman, making what he thought was a good job of it by the time they reached the stableyard. Only a few grooms were still about the building where Windhover was stalled, the animals having been settled for the night some time ago.

'That was a most fascinating explanation, Brother!' Tinnis said, as he unlatched the stall door. The powerful sorrel, who stood at least eighteen hands high, whiffled and snorted as his master caressed his cheek. 'Now let's hope your talent – or perhaps your horse-sense – is able to penetrate the brain of this recalcitrant beast and fathom the motive behind his peculiar behavior. Be pleased to enter the stall with me.'

The enclosure was good-sized, as befit such a large animal. Windhover stood placidly enough as Tinnis fed him a carrot from his large belt-wallet.

'Now be so good as to stand at his left shoulder, facing his rear and resting your own left hand on his withers . . . Excellent. Is he shuddering faintly at your touch?'

'I feel nothing unusual,' Vra-Sulkorig said.

'Soon you will. Tap him a little with your fingers.'

The constable stepped behind the other man, pulled a horseshoe from his wallet, and smote Sulkorig a mighty blow on the right temple with the iron. With a groan, the Brother fell into the straw. Windhover shied away, rolling his eyes. Tinnis knelt, then took from his wallet a harness-maker's awl, thin-shafted as a quill and sharply pointed. This he drove with great force into Sulkorig's right ear. The Brother's body gave a single convulsive jerk, then went limp, its sphincters relaxing in death.

Windhover let out a shrill scream and retreated stamping to the far side of the stall, frightened by the smell of the fast-pooling blood and effluvia. Tinnis wrapped the tools of murder in a piece of wash-leather and replaced them in his wallet.

Then he took hold of Sulkorig's robe and began hauling him
out of the stall, shouting for help at the top of his lungs.

'So he is dead, with his poor skull cracked by a startled horse!'
Tears spilled from Stergos's eyes as the king told him of the
dreadful accident. They were together in the bedchamber of
the Royal Alchymist, who had not yet retired, seated in a
large window-seat that overlooked the now-deserted
gardens. 'And he loved the animals so.'

'Vra-Sulkorig was attempting to advise the Lord Constable
on some crochet of his stallion's behavior when the beast
lashed out with his forefeet for no good reason. The Brother
died instantly. There was nothing the alchymists and physicians could do. Tinnis is devastated by sorrow, but there's no
question of his remaining in Cala for the funeral. He must
take ship for Tarn on the morrow. I need him to talk some
sense into the sealords in Donorvale before going in search
of Maude and the boy.'

'Help me into bed, Con,' Stergos said. 'This death on top
of the ominous disappearance of Deveron has drained me
sorely. Aside from losing a dear friend and colleague in
Sulkorig, we are now deprived of our confidential windvoice.
I shall have to shoulder that task again myself, I suppose –
at least when we deal with the miserable shaman Bozuk. Do
you think he told us the truth about Maudrayne's place of
captivity? When Duke Feribor's windvoice Vra-Colan
bespoke Sulkorig with the tidings, there seemed to be a tinge
of reservation in his windspeech. Sulkorig spoke to me about
it and was anxious. If only he were still alive, Con! We could
have analyzed his memory of the message's nuances. Perhaps
compelled Colan to repeat it –'

The king drew fine net midge-curtains around the bedstead
after Stergos was composed for sleep. 'We can talk of that
later, Gossy. For now, you must rest. The Lord Constable will

sort matters out when he reaches Tarn in a few days.'

'Yes. I'm sure he'll do his best – for one not possessed of talent.' Stergos lay back on his pillows. His next words were weighted with grief. 'Sulkorig might have discovered the truth much quicker. He was an extraordinary adept and a *good* man, steadfast and loyal for all that he was deeply troubled by the secret knowledge that he learned so inadvertently.'

'You think he would have kept silent about my talent, as you advised him?'

'I explained to him at length the dire political ramifications of revealing it, and also the strong moral arguments in favor of keeping the secret. He seemed fully convinced.'

The king went to the chamber windows and drew the drapes to shut out the twilit sky. 'Well, the question is now moot. The only ones who can still attest to the truth are Maude, Ansel Pikan, Ullanoth . . . and you, Gossy. My former wife can accuse me, but has no sure proof. Ansel's testimony may impress the sealords, but it would never sway a Cathran tribunal. Ullanoth, even if she lives, would never betray me – and neither would you.'

His brother said nothing.

'Gossy?' Conrig felt ice stir in his vitals and hastened to return to the bedside. 'Would you, Gossy?'

But the Royal Alchymist was already asleep.

TWENTY-TWO

The heavy rain returned, and all that the king's men could do was huddle beneath the rock ledge, share tales of their exploits, sing bawdy songs very softly, and consume endless cups of tea improved by their fast-dwindling supply of spirits. It was early in the morning. Their leader had been unconscious for two days now. Radd Falcontop, who had the most experience with ailments and was the closest they had to a physician, was growing apprehensive.

'The chills and sweats are worse,' Radd confided to Sir Gavlok. They were in the deepest part of the overhang, where the ground was driest and Snudge lay beside a tiny fire. 'That's not all. He almost never moves. I can't rouse him enough to get water down his throat, and he gags at swallowing mush. His piss is scanty and orange in color. If this was anything but a sickness brought on by sorcery, I'd fear he was dying of poison.'

'He warned me that doing the magic would provoke awful pain, but said nothing at all about these other things. Perhaps he didn't know.' Gavlok bent over the figure shrouded entirely in blankets, uncovered his friend's face, and laid a hand on his forehead. 'Shite! His brow's like ice. And if he won't drink, he's surely in a bad way. Have you tried plying him with a bit of liquor?'

The Swordsman shook his head. 'It'd do harm to one in his state, that I'm sure of. Sweet warm tea and broth are the best drinks for Sir Deveron – if we could only get him to swallow. But what our commander really needs is a doctor and some stronger remedies. The map shows a wee village not far south of here. It might have a resident herb-wife, if nothing else.'

Gavlok winced at the thought. 'Do we dare risk it? They'll be wary of strangers. They're bound to report us to their overlord in Skullbone Peel. We'll be captured, perhaps killed if they suspect we're after Princess Maude. At the least, our mission might fail.'

'As it will in certainty if Sir Deveron never awakens,' Radd said starkly. 'None of us can use these magic amulets to rescue the lady and her son. You must make the decision. But if we're to try the village, it's best we do so at once, before Sir Deveron gets any worse. We'd have to bring the healer here. Gold would provide incentive enough in a poor region like this. Maybe gold would stop the healer's gob, too – at least for a little while! We could say our boat's pulled up in the ravine cove for repair of a sprung garboard strake. We were taking on water so fast we couldn't make it to the village harbor. Our sick shipmate that we were hoping to bring to the shamans at Fort Ramis took a turn for the worse.'

Gavlok bowed his head, either in thought or prayer. After a long moment he looked up and held Radd's eye. 'It'd have to be you and me who go. We can't leave the armigers alone. They might betray themselves to the enemy with some incautious action. Hulo must stay with them.'

Radd climbed to his feet. 'We're off, then, right now! You find some money and put on clothes that aren't so grand.

I'll talk to Hulo about how to care for Sir Deveron, and fetch the things we'll need.'

Induna was vexed with her grandfather.

After two days aboard Duke Feribor's speeding frigate, Bozuk was in misery from seasickness and the strain of generating favorable winds. The ship had made a splendid rate of knots until reaching the area of the Icebear Channel off the upper Lavalands Peninsula. There the natural wind fell off and thick fog closed in. More ominous, there were many icebergs. The captain had immediately demanded that the shaman either push away the bergs and melt the fog with sorcery, or else use his scrying ability to guide them through the treacherous waters. All this while keeping the ship's sails filled.

Bozuk had already worn himself out generating the wind. Moving drifting mountains of ice was impossible, and as fast as he dissipated the fog, more rolled in from the Barren Lands to the north. So he was obliged to search out their route, which meant huddling on the cold, damp quarterdeck for hours on end, giving orders to the steersman. Unlike weaker magickers such as the Zeth Brethren and the Glaumerie Guild wizards of Moss, a top-notch shaman such as he had no difficulty performing two acts of sorcery at once – provided neither was too strenuous. So he kept a breeze blowing in near dead-calm conditions as he oversaw the ship's course, shivering in a cocoon of woolen shawls and calling down curses on Duke Feribor or anyone else who had the temerity to interrupt his work.

Including Induna.

You've got to bespeak me, Eldpapa. It's important. I won't wait until later. Listen to me!

Damn the wicked jade! Why wouldn't she let him be, stop breaking his concentration? It was too hard to hear her from so far away whilst scrying and wind-whistling together. Let

her wait until the ship rounded the tip of Lavalands and
escaped the cursèd fog and ice.

*Eldpapa! Someone else is here. Five men – maybe six. They're
hiding near the peel. I think they might try to rescue the princess
and her son.*

He gave it up. 'Lower sail,' he commanded the first mate,
who stood on the other side of the helmsman. 'Drag an
anchor – or however you slow the bloody ship down. Have
your own men watch out for ice. I must cease this work for
a time and go to my cabin.'

The mate began to protest. 'But my lord duke has given
orders –'

'Futter Feribor and his orders!' Bozuk shrieked. He threw
off the wrappings and tottered to the companionway. Before
he entered his little cabin, he told an amazed seaman: 'If any
man dares to disturb me, I'll turn him into a toad! Give
warning – and be sure you tell the damned duke!'

He slammed the door, shed his damp robe, and flopped
onto his bunk, rolling himself in the feather-tick he'd insisted
on bringing and making sad moan until he finally felt warm
and dry and fit to bespeak Induna.

'Granddaughter, respond to me at once! Tell me everything you know about the men you've found. Everything –
or it'll be the worse for you.'

More nasty threats, Eldpapa? Will you never learn?

'You young ingrate! Why can't you show respect? I've a
good mind not to share the second part of the bounty with
you. Why should I? Our agreement was for you to get a
third of the five thousand. It's quite enough. What does a
young wench like you need with more? You'd only squander
it on baubles and gowns –'

*Stop it. You'll waste what little strength you have left. Now listen!
I only just located these interlopers, and I don't think the talented
ones at the peel have taken note of them yet. They're encamped in*

a seaside ravine about half a league from the peel. Five of them are hale and sturdy and well armed. The sixth man – if he is indeed a person and not merely a heap of blankets and gear, lies unmoving and may be sick. It's impossible for me to scry him clearly, covered up and hidden beneath a rock ledge as he is. The style of the men's garb is Cathran, and I believe they've surely come for the princess and her son.

'Did they arrive by sea? On horseback? How could they have eluded the oversight of Lord Ontel as well as your own?'

I know not. There's nary a trace of boat or mounts. As to why they weren't scried, I can't say, except that I never thought to look for such persons earlier, as I rode toward the whaling village from the Mornash track. Perhaps Lord Ontel didn't think anyone would come looking for his prisoners so soon. The men are very craftily concealed from oversight down in the ravine. The true mystery is why Red Ansel never spotted them. What do you want me to do?

'Slay them!' Bozuk cried in a frenzy.

Eldpapa, be sensible. I'm a healer! I don't use my talent to harm people. Only in self-defense would I even consider smiting another with my sorcery.

'We're stuck in the damned fog up here,' the old man raged. 'We won't sail out of it until tomorrow, at least, and then it's another eighty leagues to the cove below Skullbone. Our arrival might be delayed until day after tomorrow. These mysterious fellows must not be allowed to leave their hiding place. If Lord Ontel is alarmed, he may remove the prisoners to another place. Then my plan to coerce him with the ship's guns and tarnblaze will be ruined – and God knows what Duke Feribor would do! The man's temper smolders like a volcano, Induna. He ordered a seaman flogged to death for a petty bit of insolence this morning. The day before, he smote a clumsy steward senseless for spilling the soup. The poor knave's jaw was broken! What if Feribor turns against me?'

Freeze him solid. Fling a ball of lightning at him. Send him mad with frightful visions . . . Why do you ask me what to do, you silly thing? Aren't you Blind Bozuk, the mightiest renegade shaman in all of Tarn?

'Feribor could attack me before I realized the danger. And I'm so weary, Induna! Too old and decrepit to perform the magical feats that have been demanded of me. I thought I'd only have to create a little wind. The God of the Heights and Depths knows that this ship of the duke's is a marvel of speed even without my pushing its sails. But in a dead calm, such as we have in this miserable fog . . . is there much wind where you are?'

There was yesterday. Today the sea is flat and it rains straight down.

Bozuk gave a croak of despair. 'Do what you can to keep the strangers away from Skullbone Peel. Will you promise me that, lass?'

Certainly. I'll think of something. Take care of yourself, Eldpapa. Farewell.

The old man groaned again. And then there came a strong rapping at his cabin door. 'Master Bozuk! It's Feribor. Open to me! What's this nonsense about toads?'

'Coming, my lord,' the shaman said. Slowly, he unrolled himself from the feather-tick and shuffled to the door.

Induna sighed as she cut the wind-thread. Rain tapped on the slate roof of the cottage, but her little loft chamber was cosy enough. It was almost time for the mid-day meal: whale stew. She shuddered.

Well, perhaps she ought to scry out the lurking men again and give serious effort to reading their lips. They might furnish useful information.

She sat on a stool and covered her eyes.

Five minutes later, with her face gone very pale, she pulled on a pair of stout boots, grabbed up her cloak and a leather sack of herbal medicines, and was off into the pouring rain before the affronted goodwife of the cottage could object.

Radd Falcontop beckoned Gavlok to join him. Both lay prone amidst a dripping patch of willowherb and dwarf birch on a seacliff overlooking Lucky Cove. Rain beat down on them, and on the anchored boats and bleak little houses and factory buildings of the whaling station. Smoke from the chimneys hung low, and an odd, pervasive stench filled the air. There was not a flower or a patch of greenery to be seen anywhere within the muddy precincts of the hamlet. Three men in oilskins worked on the hull of a careened sailboat, hauled up on a shingle slope just below the cliff. Aside from them, not another soul was to be seen.

'What a hellhole,' Gavlok murmured. 'And this is high summer! Imagine what it must be like in wintertime, when the sun peeps over the horizon for scarcely two hours a day and the arctic tempests roar.'

'Folk live where they can find work,' Radd said mildly. 'We are not all belted knights attending upon a king and dwelling in a palace.'

'I didn't mean –'

'Hush!' The veteran Swordsman had wrenched his body about about and stared in narrow-eyed alarm at the rolling plateau behind them. He muttered a curse. 'I hear someone coming up the path from the village. Crouch down in the weeds and don't move.'

Gavlok obeyed. After a few moments, he heard the foot-steps, too, splashing and crunching and now and then dislodging a loose stone, becoming ever louder. But no one came into sight.

'Where is he?' Gavlok whispered frantically. 'God knows, he makes enough noise – but I see no one.'

A female voice said, 'Because I don't wish to be seen.'

Both men gave great starts. Still acrouch, Radd drew his long dagger and assumed a fighting stance. Gavlok was too bemused to do anything save sit on the wet ground and stare wildly about.

'Who are you?' the voice said. It was high and clear. 'What do you want?'

Radd said, 'We're Cathran mariners in trouble, beached a few leagues to the north. One of our number is taken ill. We hoped to find a healer in yonder village, but we hesitated to approach, not knowing how we'd be received. Some folk hereabouts don't welcome strangers.'

'Put up your blade. As it happens, you're in luck.'

Wondering, Radd sheathed his dagger. He and Gavlok were now on their feet, looking this way and that for the unseen speaker.

She appeared, and even as they exclaimed in surprise, they realized that she'd been there all the time – but somehow their minds had refused to admit the fact. Small of stature, she was nevertheless a woman full-grown, sixteen or seventeen years of age, with a round pretty face and steady dark eyes. Strands of curly red-gold hair stole from beneath the hood of her raincloak, and she carried a bulging leather scrip and a walking staff.

'I am Gavlok Whitfell and this is Radd Falcontop.' The tall knight bowed politely and touched his brow in salute. 'Madam, are you a sorceress?'

'I'm an apprentice shaman and a healer,' she said. 'My name is Induna of Barking Sands.'

Gavlok cried out eagerly, 'Will you come and look to our sick friend, Mistress Induna? We fear he may be dying. We'll gladly pay for your services –'

'I'll come, and no payment will be necessary.'

Radd's eyes went slitty as he studied her with a slow smile. 'We're indeed lucky to have met you, all dressed for travel and willing to accompany us with no ado. It's almost as though you were expecting us! Do you carry medicines in your bag?'

'Yes.' She was unperturbed. 'And I can but hope they will be the proper ones to give succor to your friend. Perhaps you had better describe his ailment in detail as we walk along. As I said, I am yet an apprentice, but my studies are far advanced. Perhaps I can help.'

They started along the clifftop path. Gavlok gave a halting description of Snudge's symptoms without saying how the illness came upon him. When she inquired whether the sick man might have eaten tainted food or some poisonous plant, or if he had suffered a blow to the head, Gavlok denied it.

'So your friend Deveron is the only one among you who is ill,' she summarized, 'and all of you ate the same meals, and he did not sample any strange mushrooms or berries, nor suffer an injury to the skull. And he is a man of twenty years who has always enjoyed excellent health.'

'Aye, mistress.' Gavlok's reply was uneasy.

'Such persons may be suddenly laid low in the way you describe, without obvious cause,' she said. 'But this happens only rarely, perhaps due to the abrupt failure of some vital body part that was overfragile from birth with no one the wiser. If this is the case with your friend, I regret to say that his outlook is very grave indeed, and I probably can do nothing to cure him . . . But there is one other thing that might be wrong, and for this I might have remedy.'

'What?' Radd asked.

She paused on the path, her calm gaze sweeping over them. 'You must be honest. Is it possible that your friend Deveron is bewitched?'

Gavlok's face had gone ashen, but he pressed his lips together and shook his head, intending to keep the secret of the sigils as he had solemnly promised. But Radd had no such scruples when his leader's life was at stake, and the success of his mission as well.

'Mistress, you may have hit on it,' the Swordsman said. 'Deveron is a petty trickster, able to perform only a few simple conjurations. He attempted a more serious piece of magic, and it was after this that he fell into the mortal swoon.'

'Ah,' said Induna. 'I would not be surprised to hear that a hedge-wizard of Didion was so afflicted. But I had thought that all Cathrans possessed of talent were forced to join the Mystic Order of Zeth.'

'In most cases, they are,' Gavlok admitted. 'But Deveron's magical abilities are so very slight that no one in authority took note of them. He reveals them only to his closest friends. We refrain from exposing him, since a free spirit such as he would pine away in a life that was both regimented and celibate, such as the Zeth Brothers must embrace.'

'I can only be thankful that Tarnian shamans are not treated that way,' Induna murmured. 'This Deveron sounds like an interesting young man. With all my heart, I pray that I can restore his health.'

Three hours later, she and her companions arrived at the ravine. She said not a word about the nonexistent 'boat' the men were supposed to have arrived in, nor did she comment on the unusual quality of their weapons and equipment. After a brief examination of the sick man's face, without removing his body coverings, she asked for as many candles as they possessed, and had them lit and placed round about Snudge's pallet. Then she commanded the five to leave her alone with the patient. When they had withdrawn as far away as possible, while keeping to the shelter of the ledge, she turned down the blankets and opened Snudge's shirt.

'By the Icebound Sisters!' she gasped, lifting the golden chain with its softly glowing amulets away from his bare flesh. 'So that's it!' She eased the chain over his head, being careful not to touch the stones herself, and laid them aside on the dry dust of the shelter floor. For an instant, the internal light of the one shaped like a tiny door flashed a brighter, baleful green. Then it was as dim as before.

Induna sat back on her heels, thinking furiously. She knew what the amulets were: moonstone sigils of the Coldlight Army. She'd even seen one once, years ago, a quaintly carved translucent octagon that her mother Maris, who was also a healer shaman, had found washed up on the Barking Sands after a tremendous winter storm. That sigil possessed no glowing heart; it was not alive, as were the stones of her patient. Mother was deeply afraid of the moonstone she had found, and when Induna timidly suggested that they give it to Eldpapa, Maris had slapped her shocked little daughter and screamed that she must never, never tell Bozuk of the thing's existence.

Later, Mother had gone off secretly in a small boat to visit the terrible sea-hag Dobnelu, and had given the sigil to her. When Maris returned, she explained to Induna that the moonstone was a thing accursed and supremely perilous – not only to humankind, but also to Green Men and Salka and Morass Worms and Small Lights. Only the sea-hag and a few other great shamans such as Ansel Pikan had the power to dispose of them safely. As for using their sorcery –

Maris told her daughter the story of Rothbannon of Moss, and how he tricked the Salka monsters into giving up the legendary Seven Stones, and how he alone had managed to use them without harming himself or losing his soul. Then Maris related the histories of Rothbannon's royal successors, who were not quite so lucky, ending with the gruesome fate of Queen Taspiroth, who had managed to offend the Great Lights and was cast into the Hell of Ice. Young Induna had suffered nightmares from those tales until her mother laid on her an ameliorating spell.

As a young woman and an apprentice shaman herself, Induna learned about the fate of Taspiroth's insane husband Linndal and the rivalry between their son Beynor and daughter Ullanoth. But like the other low-status wonder-workers of Tarn, she had believed the Mosslanders were the only humans to use sigil magic.

So what was this young Cathran adventurer doing with two of them?

Did he intend using them to take Princess Maudrayne and her son away from Ansel Pikan, the almighty Grand Shaman, who evidently didn't even know that Deveron and the others were here?

Induna came close to the unconscious man and studied his countenance. He was good-looking in an unexceptional way, pallid and blue-lipped and with dark circles about his eyes from the arcane illness. It was not a face belonging to a person who had surrendered his soul to evil – nor even come danger-ously close to doing it, as Eldpapa had. She touched his clammy brow and he stiffened. His eyes flew open. They were black, the pupils so distended that the color of the irises could not be perceived. After a moment, he relaxed again and his eyes closed. He let out a long, sighing breath. His heartbeat, which had been irregular, overslow, and weak, quickened minutely as he partook of a small portion of her vitality.

'Tell me who you are, Deveron. Tell me what you are!'

Her insight, which was one of the keenest aspects of her talent, now informed her that he was one who sought the good and tried to shun wickedness, but was sometimes torn between duty and conscience. He was, her perception assured her, a ranking agent of the Sovereign of Blenholme, Conrig Wincantor. But he also served another, much greater cause.

What cause might that be?

But there was no answer to that, save the one that might come from his own lips, were he to be healed.

'Shall I cure you, then, Deveron?' she whispered. 'Shall I share with you my own most treasured gift, of which I possess only a limited amount, in order to learn your story? Is it possible, after all, that you've sought out this beleaguered princess and her child without evil intent, even though you possess two moonstones that take power from the Great Lights?'

The thought came to her unbidden: Was he a rescuer rather than an abductor?

Induna had been deeply confused by the implications of Bozuk's messages, those she had relayed over the wind to the Sovereign. She was unable to decide whether Maudrayne was victim or villainess or political pawn. Conrig Wincantor, on the other hand, was beyond doubt a ruthless man with a heart of stone. All of Tarn knew he'd cruelly cast this once-cherished wife of his aside because she seemed unable to have children. He'd deceived his people about his secret talent. But he'd also unified the four nations of the island and saved them from being invaded by Continental opportunists eager to take advantage of the late Wolf's Breath disaster.

Induna felt she had two clear choices. She could obey Eldpapa and keep these men away from the mother and child until Duke Feribor seized them, or she could try to get to the bottom of this strange situation and do what was right and just.

Once again, she placed her hand on the unconscious young man's forehead. 'Will you tell me the whole truth of it if I remove your pain and heal your tortured body?'

She waited, and after a long time, the answer came.

Yes.

He knew that the price exacted by Gateway would be terrible, but never expected that it would overwhelm him so completely. For one thing, the agony was part of his sleep, a condition so contrary to the natural order of things – when unconsciousness always brought relief from suffering – that his mind screamed at the injustice of it.

The Lights laughed at his resentment, and fed.

In all his short life he'd had little experience of excruciating pain. The debt owed for his few uses of the minor Concealer sigil had been insignificant. He'd suffered far worse while enduring toothache and a broken arm when he was a child. The more eldritch tortures of Iscannon and his master, Beynor, had introduced him briefly to the horrors of the icy sky-world inhabited by the Lights; and the price he recently paid in order to activate Gateway had been severe but easily forgotten – as though the Lights didn't want to frighten off a fresh victim with juicy potential.

This pain was very different, being both physical and mental, combining bodily hurt with the wrenching terror of nightmares. It was relentless and all-consuming, and Snudge was certain it was going to be the death of him.

He accepted this for a fact; and the fury and despair he felt, knowing that his loyal companions would soon find themselves abandoned in the shambles of his failed mission, gave a fresh dimension to his misery. His only prayer was that he would die soon. He saw the way to eternal peace, strove with all his willpower to follow it, but was denied.

Live on! the Lights said, laughing, *for as long as we choose. And suffer.*

Then he saw her, coming toward him in the bright abyss of woe: a young woman with curling red-gold hair, slender and spare of stature, with a round face that shone confident and serene. Was she only a fever-dream, a device to magnify his torture? She asked him many questions, but he hung mute in hideous Light, unable to reply.

Finally, she said, *Will you tell me the truth of it if I remove your pain and heal your tortured body?*

He forced the word from his numbed mind: *YES!*

The Lights howled their frustration, drawing away from him as the woman approached. He saw her reach into her own heart and take out a pearl-colored thing like a girl-doll or a tiny statue, no larger than a finger-joint. As she did this, her own body shimmered like an image reflected in water and was diminished in some subtle manner. She reached out to him, smiling, and pressed the pearly homunculus into his own breast. He saw its minute arms and head move before it disappeared, and knew that the thing was alive. She had taken part of her own soul's substance and donated it freely to him.

The pain vanished. The wrathful Lights vanished. His ordeal ended.

The Source said, *Now let me tell you the rest of it, so you know what is at stake when you put your proposal to Maudrayne, and so that she knows it, too.*

He listened. And then he opened his eyes.

Induna's transfer of vital energy effected a perfect cure. Snudge was instantly restored to consciousness and his damaged body was rendered whole again. For all that, he was like a fine clock or other delicate mechanism new-made, which must not be allowed to work at full capacity until its parts are tuned and lubricated.

He would have risen at once from his pallet, but she forbade it, as she also forbade him to speak. First he must drink little but often from a decoction of warm water infused with centaury, melissa, rosehip, and honey. Then, every hour, all throughout the rest of that day and all night long, he must sup a few spoonfuls of thin oatmeal gruel. The next morn, she allowed his squire Valdos to wash his body and dress him in fresh clothes. After dismissing the squire, she herself anointed his limbs and back with a mild monkshood liniment to invigorate the muscles, then felt for the pulse in his neck.

'It's good and strong,' she pronounced, 'but to be safe, we'll physick you with a modicum of foxglove.' She let fall two drops of liquid from a glass phial into a cup of water and had him drink it down. 'Now, Sir Deveron Austrey, Knight Banneret and Royal Intelligencer, you may sit up at last and speak if you wish, for you are very nearly as whole as you were before undertaking your rash experiment with sigil sorcery.'

Snudge's voice was at first hoarse and weak, but he grinned at her as he said, 'You're a benevolent tyrant, Induna of Barking Sands, but I thank you heartily for healing me. May I ask you some questions?'

She nodded. 'And I'll answer – provided you also respond to mine.'

Gavlok and the armiger Valdos, their faces shining with relief, had been helping as they could during the final hour of Snudge's treatment and still hovered near. Induna now turned to them with kindly firmness. 'Please allow Sir Deveron and me to speak privately.'

Gavlok blushed, for he, like both squires, was already half in love with the winsome shaman. 'Certainly, mistress. If you need us, only call.' They went to join Hanan, who was watching the Swordsmen play a game of draughts using stones and squares scratched into the earth.

When they were out of hearing, Deveron's smile faded. 'What have you done with my sigils, Induna?'

'They are safely buried somewhere in this shelter. An important part of your cure involved removing the stones from contact with your bare flesh. However, I'll be frank: I came here not only to heal you, but also under orders from my grandsire, the shaman Blind Bozuk. He has commanded me to prevent you from apprehending and harming Princess

Maudrayne and her son Dyfrig. Duke Feribor Blackhorse has delivered your king's gold to Bozuk. But the duke has also offered my grandsire an equal additional sum to guide *him* to Maudrayne.'

'What?' Snudge gaped at her.

'I won't let you have your sigils back, or allow you or your men to leave this place, until the princess and her child are safe in the hands of the duke. At this moment, he is approaching Skullbone Peel in a great ship. It will arrive before this day ends.'

Snudge was aghast. 'Induna, you don't understand why I've come here! I hope to help Maudrayne and the little boy – not harm them. They'll hardly be safe in the hands of Feribor. Just the opposite!'

She inclined her head, as if this was the response she'd expected. 'If that's true, you must explain everything to me. Everything! For I confess that I'm both perplexed and worried by my grandsire's actions. I came here from Northkeep thinking only to help him obtain the rich reward that would ensure his comfortable retirement. He's a rascal, but he loves me in his own way. However, since my arrival here, the situation has changed drastically. I'm troubled by his new alliance with Duke Feribor, who appears to be a blackguard. Eldpapa may have been too clever by half, agreeing to assist this man. He's frightened.'

'And well he might be, mistress. Feribor's only purpose in rescuing Maude and her child is to use them against High King Conrig.'

She gave him a level look. 'Who is himself no paragon of virtue – and no good friend to the lady.'

Snudge groaned and lay back against the pack that served as a pillow. 'Shall I tell you the whole tale, as I understand it?'

She sat beside him, poured more warm herb tea into his

cup, and proffered it. 'Please do. Drink this as you speak. It will help your voice. And as you relate the story, be sure to include mention of the great secret cause that you serve, which commands more of your loyalty than does your liege lord Conrig.'

He froze with the cup halfway to his lips. 'How do you know of that? I've told no one of it!'

She tapped her temple. 'One of my talents is that of insight. It's not mind-reading, but it does reveal to me the bent of a person's temperament, and suggests what things are most dear to him in life.'

'Good God.' Snudge looked at her more intently. 'What manner of archwizards does Tarn breed? And you're so young!'

'And so are you,' she retorted, 'to use the sorcery of the Coldlight Army when you are but a wild talent and a spy. Tell me all.'

So he did, not knowing why he felt impelled to trust her. It had nothing to do with her empty threats. He knew instinctively that if he called out to his stolen sigils they would respond to him, and he'd find them easily enough. Once they were in hand, this girl's magical restraints would be impotent against him. His urge to confide in her was motivated by something else, which he did not understand.

He poured it all out: his early years, his unwitting use of his wild talents, his recognition of Conrig's magical taint and the uneasy relationship they had shared ever since. He told Induna of his fear that the king intended him to kill Maude to eliminate her threat to the Sovereignty, and his knowledge of Feribor's numerous criminal actions and his craving for a crown. Then he told her about the Source and the New Conflict and his own voluntary enlistment in a battle between inhuman forces.

Last of all, he explained the compromise proposal he intended to put to Maudrayne and to Conrig, in hopes of resolving their antagonism without bloodshed, and how the Source had encouraged him to deal with the princess as best he could.

'And now I must go to her at once,' he concluded, rising up again from his pallet and reaching for his boots. 'If, as you say, Feribor is shortly to arrive on the scene, there's no time to waste. Will you try to prevent me, Induna?'

She slowly shook her head. 'Nay. For as you told me all of this, my insight sifted through it and concluded that you mean well. Your proposal is a wise one that might succeed . . . if this lady's bitterness and ill will are not so strong as to override her good sense.' She paused, then continued almost shyly. 'If you think I could help – either by bolstering your shaky strength with my magic or by lending my own support to your words as you beseech the princess – then let me come with you.'

He considered it. 'I'll have to use my sigils again. The one called Concealer, which is a minor stone not demanding much pain from me in its use, will allow me and my men to creep close to the peel unseen, enter through some subterfuge, and slay the guards. You might easily be included within the sigil's shield of invisibility, which extends for about four ells in each direction as I command. There is no pain inflicted upon my companions, of course. But Concealer's magic does derive from the Great Lights. Are you willing to compromise your integrity by making use of it, as I do?'

She shrugged. 'If necessary. However, I myself am able to move about without being seen through use of my own sorcery. Furthermore, I can easily bewitch the guards at the small fort to open the sallyport, then forget what they've done. They need not be slain, and my integrity thus remains intact.'

He chuckled, climbing to his feet and offering a hand to assist her rising. 'Mistress Induna, I'm glad we've decided to be friends, rather than foes.'

She waved that off, deep in thought. 'Had you anticipated any magical assaults inside the peel? Shaman-Lord Ontel's sorcery isn't very strong, but he has three other magickers attending him who could prove difficult if they scry us. Your Concealer sigil will give protection as we all make our way to the princess's chambers. But you can hardly put your proposal to her while invisible. And someone might chance to scry you as you converse with her.'

Snudge said, 'No one can scry me. This is *my* unique talent! And so while the rest of you stay safely hidden, I'll emerge and present myself to her. If it seems safe, you might also appear.'

'And if she agrees to your proposal?'

Snudge told her what he intended to do then.

'Oh, no!' she cried. 'It would be too perilous! There must be another way. Let's discuss –'

'There is no other way,' he said flatly. 'I've considered the options long and hard. Maude must survive if God wills and she herself does also. Her son *will* survive, for I have the Source's own word on it. But equally important is that no harm come to Conrig Wincantor and his Sovereignty – either through the vengeful princess, through her Tarnian friends, or through the perfidious Feribor. We will do it my way.'

She lay a hand on his upper arm and studied his face with a whimsical frown. 'Are you always so stubborn?'

'Others have asked the same question,' Snudge said, 'and one of them a king.'

TWENTY-THREE

'Are you ready?' Snudge asked his men. They were all armed, but the rest of their equipment was to be left behind. Whatever transpired at Skullbone Peel, they would not be returning to the ravine shelter.

'Ready,' they replied, but their doubt and hesitancy were still evident. Lengths of thin leather strapping fastened to their belts linked them together and to their leader like some bizarre Tarnian dog-team hitched to a sled: but the sled – which was Snudge – would draw the team along after him. Two men were to follow on his left and two on his right, the pairs keeping close, while a longer center strap allowed the sixth man to bring up the rear. They had been warned that when Concealer's spell enveloped them, no man would be able to see the other, nor would he easily know how far distant he was from the boundary of the shielding bubble emanating from their leader's sigil.

'At first,' Snudge said, 'we must move along very slowly until you become accustomed to being invisible. It'll be difficult. We'll have bumps and tangles. If one of you somehow becomes separated from the rest and pops into clear view, stand utterly still and give a soft whistle. I'll bring you back under cover as quickly as I can.'

Hulo Roundbank, the tailman, fingered the strap that attached him to Snudge. 'This is a bloody awkward way to travel. And how can we fight, lashed together like this?'

'You won't,' Snudge told him. 'When and if our situation demands violent action, you men must forgo the safety of invisibility. By then, we should be inside the peel and carrying out our plan of attack.' He turned to Induna. 'And you, mistress, being the only one of us unencumbered, will scout out the path for us and otherwise serve as advance guard until we reach the gates of the fort.'

She nodded, her lips twitching from a suppressed grin. 'I will. And I give fervent thanks that I need not creep through rocks and brush on a leash like you poor lads.' She folded her hands, closed her eyes, and disappeared from their sight. 'And now, Sir Deveron, show me how your Concealer works.'

He pulled it from his shirt and gripped it, then spoke the Salkan words. 'BI DO FYSINEK. FASH AH.'

Curses and gasps came from unseen mouths. Somebody said, 'Swive me! I'm gone!'

'Up the side of the ravine,' Snudge commanded, and they were on their way.

They approached the peel with irritating slowness, hindered by the inadequacy of the exiguous little path, which was severed completely at one point by the collapse of an undercut part of the cliff. The result was a sheer drop-off to the heaving sea, and no easy way to proceed across the gap because of the nature of the shore rocks. They were thus forced to detour inland, picking their way cautiously for two hours through trackless brush, before they were able to turn back in the direction of the shore. They made better time then, hiking down a watercourse that skirted the peel's partially wooded hill.

The sky was still overcast, but the hard rain had ceased, leaving the air humid and abuzz with hungry midges who were undeterred by invisibility. The men were out of temper and simmering from their constraint, having to halt frequently to restore their disrupted marching order when one or another came to grief. Induna, who ranged ahead more freely, was the one who first reached the beach that rimmed Skullbone Cove. She surveyed the little harbor, where only a few small boats were tied up at the docks, and was relieved to see no one about. The long flight of steps leading to the block-shaped peel was still wet, another welcome development. No one inside the fort would see their footprints as they ascended.

Then she thought to scan the hazy northern horizon with her talent, and scried the approaching ship.

Quickly, she dashed back up the stream to the invisible men, who were perceptible from the weird depressions their boots created in the shallow waters. 'Stop!' she hissed.

There were splashes and profanities as several of them came up short and collided with one another. Radd Falcontop's voice grumbled, 'I hate this.' Someone else said, 'Mind your damned sword, whoever you are.'

'Silence!' Snudge commanded. 'What is it, Induna?'

'Feribor's ship is coming. It might be nine or ten leagues distant. We have a little over an hour to act, if my estimate of its speed is correct. Even though the air is still, my grandsire Bozuk is creating wind to propel the vessel.'

Radd asked, 'What manner of ship, mistress?'

'It's plainly Cathran by its rigging, although it shows no flag. It has three masts and is of a goodly size.'

'And is probably armed with goodly guns,' the Swordsman muttered.

'Let's get down to the water,' Snudge said. 'I need to scry into the fort more closely and see what kind of opposition we might expect.'

They moved on as fast as they could. Snudge paused to fill a spare sock with sand from the beach, then ordered the group to continue to the small quay at the foot of a long flight of stone steps. There he had the other men sit or crouch near him, while he concentrated on looking through the stone walls and ironbound oaken doors of the peel that loomed on the knoll above them.

'Can you count the guards, Induna?' he asked softly.

'Oh, yes.' Her tone was tart. 'I also can scry through stone, sir knight.'

They took note of four warriors at the main gate and fifteen others posted in other parts of the peel or at work in the armory. Ontel, his three associate magickers, and a man who might have been the captain of the guard were huddled together on the ramparts, staring anxiously out to sea. They'd spotted the ship, too.

'Can we find a way to keep them up there?' Induna wondered. 'I see two trapdoors giving access to the roof.'

Snudge said, 'Open wooden steps lead from the armory in the south-western corner of the upper level, and from the adjacent guards' dormitory in the north-western corner. The other rooms on that floor, a library and two smaller chambers that may be laboratories used by the resident shamans, give only onto the corridor and main staircase. It may be possible to trap the men on the roof if we act quickly.'

The peel was simply constructed, having three levels and a cellar. On the lowest floor were the gate vestibule and guardroom, the great hall, the kitchen, washrooms, cramped dormitories for the housecarls and maids, and some small offices. The middle floor had a solar, the master sleeping chamber, three other fine bedrooms, and sleeping cubbies for the lord and lady's bodyservants.

'I see ten or a dozen servitors here and there,' Snudge said, 'and two well-dressed older boys in a chamber near the kitchen working at some manner of woodcarving. Perhaps they are part of the shaman's family. And up in the library is a much younger lad who must be Prince Dyfrig. But the woman with him is not Maudrayne. She has the look of a servant. Where can the princess be?'

'Look to that low annex building at the right of the main keep,' Induna said. 'The lady is in the uppermost part of the windmill turret, also watching the ship. But she uses a spyglass, not talent. How beautiful she is! One would know she was once a queen, even though her dress is plain.'

Snudge oversaw the tall, proud figure crowned with unbound fiery hair. Her gown was unadorned light-green linen, but she wore a magnificent necklace of opals mounted in gold. After a moment she set the long brass instrument aside and seated herself. Her lovely face was unreadable, but she would surely know that the ship was Cathran. Did she speculate that rescuers might be aboard – or would she make a more realistic judgment and think that Conrig's agents had found her at last, and she and her son had not long to live?

'Comrades,' Snudge said, 'the presence of the ship, and the fact that the princess and her son are so widely separated, complicates our mission. The little prince is in a room close to the armory, where at least eight guards are at work, and Ontel and his shamans are also very near to the boy. I had hoped to avoid fighting, but now it may be inevitable. This is what we're going to do.'

Once Induna's compulsion had forced the four guards at the gate to open the sallyport, Snudge and his men, come out from Concealer's spell and freed of their hated straps, made short work of the ensorcelled defenders. The four stood silent and as docile as lambs while being bound, gagged, and stripped of their livery and armor. The captives were then consigned to a dark nook in the guardroom while Gavlok, Hanan, Radd, and Hulo assumed their identities.

Valdos had to wait briefly while invisible Induna sought out and bewitched a household lackey of appropriate build, then conducted him to the guardhouse. This fellow's garb provided a suitable disguise for the task assigned to Snudge's squire.

While his men were changing their clothes, Snudge took Induna aside. 'I'd be more easy in my mind if you'd accompany me to Princess Maude's turret, rather than sharing the more perilous work.'

'I might be sorely needed,' she said, 'if Ontel or one of his magickers comes down from the roof before the steps can be destroyed, or if a mêlée ensues. And I can protect little Prince Dyfrig better than your men can.'

Snudge scowled. 'Very well. You've persuaded me. But take care. You must all be with me and the princess inside the turret before the ship comes within cannon range of the peel. Feribor will surely threaten to bombard it as a ploy to obtain the prisoners. He may even lob a shell or two for emphasis – and only heaven knows how Ontel will respond. He's probably thinking of using one of those catapults from the armory. I scried some guardsmen tinkering with them. It'll be devil catch the hindmost if Ontel tosses a bombshell at the ship, and it fires back. The peel will have the worst of it. I doubt a backwoods Tarnian castellan like Ontel has any notion of the power and range of a modern frigate's guns.'

'We're ready, Deveron,' Gavlok said. He and the others who had put on the guards' helmets, mail shirts, and surcoats formed up and smote their breasts in mock salute. Valdos hung behind them, smirking. He'd been forced to give up his sword but had hidden two daggers under his servant's smock.

Induna said, 'I'm going with you soldier boys. But don't give me a second thought. I can take care of myself – and I may even be able to make myself useful in a pinch.' She vanished.

'God go with you all,' Snudge said, and took up Concealer.

There was a single workman in the annex, making some repair to the water-pump machinery at the base of the turret. The rest of the stone building comprised a stable, a byre for two milch cows, a fowl-coop, and a warren of miscellaneous storerooms.

Snudge crept up on the kneeling engineer while invisible and hit him a tap just above the ear with the sock he'd filled with beach sand. The man fell over, moaning, and was quickly trussed and put out of the way. Then Snudge mounted the turret's spiral iron stairway, moving slowly. The initial pangs resulting from his use of Concealer had sapped some of his strength, but the worst of it would come the next time he slept, and would no doubt be submerged in the greater pain-price he anticipated paying later . . .

When he reached the top of the tower, making no sound, the princess was looking through the spyglass again, standing with her back to him. He cleared his throat and spoke low.

'Lady Maudrayne, please refrain from turning around.'

She could not help flinching at the unexpected voice, but displayed no fear. 'Why should I not?' she asked sharply, and lowered the spyglass and began to turn anyway. 'Who are you? How dare you accost me here? Lord Ontel gave me this place for a private sanctum. Where are you hiding, you impudent knave?'

'Lady, the shamans may be scrying you as you speak. I beseech you to compose yourself! You must not rouse their suspicions. Go back to the window and resume your study of the sea or else sit quietly on the bench. Please show no excitement, and cover your mouth with your hand if you must speak. I'll explain myself. I've come to free you and your son.'

She plopped down on the circular seat surrounding the

shaft housing, eyes wide and lips parted in astonishment as she realized she was being addressed by one who was invisible. An instant later she lowered her head and allowed her thick auburn tresses to veil her face. 'Are you a wizard, then? Perhaps come here from yon ship?'

Snudge intoned, 'BI FYSINEK.' He appeared, sitting beside her.

Her blue eyes blazed behind the gleaming curtain of hair. 'You,' she whispered. 'Deveron Austrey, my husband's strangely talented spy! I think you've come not to liberate us, but to put an end to us.'

'Not so, my lady. These days, I serve not only the High King, but also another master – whose commands supersede those of Conrig, and who wishes no harm to befall you.'

'So you say,' she jeered. 'Aren't you afraid the shamans will scry you talking to me?'

'You called me talented, and so I am, and *very* strangely. No one can scry me. But we must not bandy words, for there's little time. The ship you observed approaching the peel carries Duke Feribor Blackhorse. He intends to steal away you and your son and force you to serve his own purposes before disposing of you both.'

'No!' she cried.

'It's true. Whereas I hope to transport you to the safe custody of your uncle, High Sealord Sernin, after making to you a proposal that may insure your future safety – and give to your son some of his birthright.'

'What are you saying?' she breathed, leaning closer to him. 'What sort of a proposal? Who is your master, if not the man who is my greatest foe?'

'Lady, there's no time to speak of this now. He is a person of great power, that is all I can tell you about him. He knows how you were taken away and safeguarded by Ansel Pikan, but also knows that Ansel is no longer able to protect you from those who would deny your destiny. He's the one who permitted me to come to you, when Ansel would have tried to prevent it. Most important . . . he is one who knows that only Conrig Wincantor can save our world from the terrible catastrophe that threatens it. Only the Sovereign will be able to defend our beloved island from an impending invasion by Salka monsters.'

'Salka?' She was skeptical. 'But they hide in Moss's fens.'

'No more! These inhuman fiends have already murdered the entire royal family of Didion. They are poised to take over the kingdom of Moss, now that Queen Ullanoth is gone. After that, they'll attack Cathra and Tarn, using the same moonstone sorcery of the Beaconfolk that confronted Emperor Bazekoy when he conquered Blenholme on behalf of humanity. No other ruler living has the military prowess of Conrig. He is a flawed man: in many ways, a wicked man. But he is the only one who can save our island. And for this reason you will not be permitted to destroy him.'

'I . . . will not be *permitted* . . .' Outrage robbed her of speech.

'Lady, you have been cruelly wronged. You thought yourself justified in avenging yourself and your son by revealing Conrig's two great secrets to your brother and to the other sealords. Perhaps you believe that the king's fate is already sealed. It's not. He won't be deposed because of what you've done. He will not lose his Iron Crown. But he *will* be distracted, and his energies will be diverted from more important matters as he defends himself against you. His human enemies will also assail him if he seems vulnerable. Thus he may be prevented from defeating the monsters . . . if you do not recant your accusation.'

'Never!' She was ashen with reined-in fury. 'Never never never will I take back my words, because I have spoken only the truth!'

'Let me tell you what you would receive in exchange,' Snudge said. 'First of all, your son Dyfrig would be given special status by the king. Since you cannot prove absolutely who his father might be –'

She drew a breath to scream an imprecation, but Snudge covered her mouth with a firm hand and said urgently, 'Listen! Listen, for the love of God. We have no time for your temper!'

She slumped forward as though he'd struck her. He felt hot tears on his hand and she shuddered, shaking her head.

He released her. 'There is no proof that Dyfrig is Conrig's first-born, but neither is there proof that he is not. And so by royal decree he can be placed third in the line of succession, behind the king's young twin sons by Queen Risalla, Orrion and Corodon. Dyfrig will be adopted by the Earl Marshal of the Realm, Parlian Beorbrook, a nobleman of impeccable character. He will be styled Prince. If Dyfrig shows competence, he will eventually inherit Lord Parlian's familial office and the great Duchy of Beorbrook. The marshal's only surviving son, Count Elktor, cannot in justice fill his father's boots, and he already has lands of his own. Should Parlian die untimely, the office of earl marshal will remain vacant and its perquisites held in abeyance until Dyfrig is of a suitable age to take them up. If for some reason he cannot do this, he will still be provided for as a prince royal.'

'Third in the succession?' Maudrayne said tremulously. 'Adopted by dear old Parli?'

'This is my proposal. As for yourself, you will live in Tarn under the protection of your uncle, who will be responsible for your good conduct. You'll have no physical contact with your son until he has reached his majority. He will know you are his mother, however, and you will be permitted to write to him – although not secretly.'

'And to attain all this, I must say I lied when I revealed Conrig's secret talent.'

'You must *convince* the sealords of it,' Snudge corrected her gently. 'There can be no half-heartedness, no sly winks, no mental reservations or future denials or treasonous schemings. Or else Dyfrig will suffer the ultimate penalty, while *you* will live on.'

She wiped away her tears. 'This is hard. Harder than you know. Conrig betrayed me with Ullanoth –'

'He never will again. She is as good as dead.' Snudge waited, but Maudrayne only raised her head and stared out to sea. The ship was perceptibly closer. 'Well, my lady?'

She sighed. 'I agree to all of it . . . But how will we now escape from here? You said you would carry us safely to Donorvale, but that seems hardly possible.'

'It is possible, and it will be done. But first I must put the proposal to the High King and obtain *his* agreement.'

'What! He doesn't know?'

Snudge's expression was rueful. 'I could say nothing to him until I successfully reached your side, and heard from your own lips that you would agree. I am a wild-talented windvoice. With your permission, I'll now bespeak Lord Stergos in Cala Palace, and he'll put the matter to His Grace.'

She was trembling with shock and anger, and for a moment it seemed her fierce pride would overturn everything. But then she threw back her head and laughed. 'Go ahead. But oh – how I wish I could see Con's face when he's told!'

'I've sent for him,' Stergos told Snudge on the wind. 'He's at a meeting of the Privy Council and the Lords of the Southern Shore, attempting to quash the rumors that already filter out of Tarn. But I've informed him that the message is crucial – and that you're alive.'

But not that I'm with Princess Maudrayne, I hope!

The recuperating Royal Alchymist lay in a long chair on a shaded balcony of the palace. He had dismissed the Brother Secretary who was assisting him with his papers as soon as Snudge bespoke him, and now carried on their wind-conversation with one hand shading his eyes. 'No, no, I've said nothing to the king about Maude – but I couldn't contain my happiness and my relief at your survival. How in Zeth's name did you ever get to Tarn?'

Through sigil magic. I was given a Great Stone called Subtle Gateway by the Source, who also told me where Maudrayne and the boy were being held. Gateway is able to carry me and my companions anywhere, at a price. We're in a small place on the eastern coast of Tarn, near Fort Ramis.

'But the shaman Bozuk told Duke Feribor she was imprisoned at Cold Harbor, far to the north! The Lord Constable was sent in search of her when it seemed you might be dead.'

Bozuk lied, my lord. And Duke Feribor has played our king false. He bribed Bozuk to take him to Maude, thinking to use her in support of his own claim to Cathra's throne. At this minute, Feribor's ship is only a few leagues distant from us. The situation is tricky, but I believe we'll surely be able to escape before he arrives.

Stergos groaned. 'My royal brother would never believe ill of the duke, no matter how we two sought to persuade him. Perhaps now he'll listen.'

Your windvoice falters, my lord. Are you strong enough to continue? Perhaps Vra-Sulkorig should relay my message to the king while you stand by.

'Oh, Deveron! Of course you don't know. Poor Sulkorig is dead by misadventure, his head broken by the hoof of the Lord Constable's horse. The beast took fright for some reason while the two men were examining it in its stall.'

I regret to hear it. Sulkorig was an able man, and an honest one.

'Although he did give me much cause for concern,' Stergos

admitted in all innocence. 'His conscience was troubled by his inadvertent discovery of the king's talent, but I convinced him that he had no moral obligation to report it to the Royal Tribunal.'

And His Grace knew of this?

'Well . . . yes. But you can't think that –'

'Gossy! What is it?' Conrig strode out onto the balcony, his face shining with excitement. 'Is it really Snudge bespeaking you?'

The Royal Alchymist's hand flew away from his eyes and he stared at his brother with a mixture of consternation and fear. 'Con! Oh, how you startled me!'

'Are you well?' the king asked in concern. He lowered himself to a padded stool.

'Yes, yes.' Stergos forced a smile. 'I'm well, and Deveron is *very* well. Con, he's found Maudrayne and the boy! And he says he's managed to convince her to recant her accusation concerning your talent. There are some concessions required, but I do believe we've found the solution to your terrible dilemma.'

'Great God,' Conrig murmured. 'Snudge talked Maude around?' He scowled. 'What concessions?'

'Just a moment, while I let Deveron know you're here. Then he can tell you everything himself.' He spoke on the wind, then pulled himself to a sitting position. At length, he presented to the king a verbatim account of Snudge's proposal and Maudrayne's acceptance.

Conrig listened, thunderstruck. When Stergos finished, the king said, 'But how will Snudge get Maude and the boy to Donorvale? For that matter, how in hell did Snudge get to Tarn?'

'He has a new sigil named Gateway,' Stergos admitted with reluctance. 'Acquired from some . . . some wizard he met along the way. I still have to get the straights of it myself.

The thing is able to transport a number of persons from one place to another through sorcery.'

'God's Teeth! Our Snudge is a veritable wellspring of surprises. The proposal is ingenious. I quite like the notion of having Parli Beorbrook adopt the lad. But can we trust Maude's word? I must think hard about this.'

'Deveron says there can be no delay. Your friend Feribor has deceived you and is about to attack the place where Maude is being held. If you accept Snudge's proposal, he'll carry the princess and the boy Dyfrig to Donorvale, using the Gateway sigil. The sealords can witness her recanting and her acceptance of the agreement. If you decline or withhold a decision, Deveron says he'll take Maude and Dyfrig else-where and – er – find them a new home.'

'Damn him for a treasonous whoreson!' Conrig bellowed. 'He dares to bargain with me?'

Stergos stiffened. 'His proposal is a good one, Con. Without Maude's accusing testimony, there is no cause for any tribunal, here in Cathra or in Tarn, to look into the matter of your talent.'

The king gave him a mutinous glare. 'It's lèse-majesté! I'm the Sovereign!'

'For now you are,' his brother said sadly. 'Con, agree to it. You gain much and lose nothing but Maude's bitter enmity and the threat to your throne. I implore you! So much lies in the balance.' More than you know, the Royal Alchymist thought, but I can say nothing to you about the Source and the New Conflict, for you would never believe me!

Conrig said, 'Very well.'

'What?' Stergos leapt like a trout, recalled from his abstraction.

'I'll do it. Our Tarnian ambassador can be one official witness and the Lord Constable the second. I draw the line at facing that hellcat myself. Let it be part of our agreement that I never see Maude again. Tell Snudge to get her and the boy to Donorvale without delay.'

'I will!' Stergos covered his eyes and sent the message on the wind, weeping for joy all the while.

Conrig Wincantor, the Sovereign of Blenholme, turned away from his brother and helped himself to the wine that was on a small refreshment table near the balcony railing. Then he looked out over the expanse of Cala Blenholme Harbor, sipping from his crystal cup and smiling. Tinnis Catclaw's ship was speeding to Tarn. He was already commanded to stop at Donorvale to confer with the sealords, and now there was no need for him to proceed further. He would witness the agreement.

And then, if Conrig thought it was for the best, he might fulfill his original task.

No one in the peel challenged the squad of bogus guardsmen as they marched up the grand staircase from the gate vestibule to the third level, trailed by a youthful servant. Many of the residents had already learned that a strange warship had hove into view, causing the shaman-lord much anxiety. A timid-looking housemaid clutching a feather-duster even ventured to ask the passing king's men if Skullbone Peel was in danger.

'Nothing to concern you, wench!' Gavlok told her sternly. 'Back to work.'

At the armory door, the armiger Valdos whispered to the others, 'Can you give me a minute or two to get the child out of the library before you raise a ruckus in there?'

'Only that,' came the voice of unseen Induna. 'Take the prince to the turret as fast as you can.'

Valdos trotted to the library at the far end of the corridor and pulled open the door. The four-year-old boy sat at a long table amidst the shelves, reading very slowly from a book while pointing out the words with his finger. A homely, big-boned woman, evidently his nursemaid, sat across from him mending a shirt.

'Prince Dyfrig!' Valdos called out. 'Your lady mother has urgent need of you. You must come with me to the turret at once, where she awaits.'

Dyfrig said, 'After I finish this sentence. Is there such a word as ee-num-russ?'

'You must come now!' Valdos crossed to the table.

The maid scowled at him. 'Is something wrong?'

'No. Yes!' Valdos spluttered. He held out his arms to the boy. 'Here, I'll carry you.'

Dyfrig was patient. 'Rusgann can't read. Can you? Look – what's this word? Ee-num-rus? I never heard of it.'

Outside, there were shouts and a sudden metallic clash. The maid surged to her feet with a squawk of alarm and dashed to the open door.

'Don't go out there!' Valdos cried. 'Laddie, come to me!'

'The word,' came the implacable demand.

Frantic, Valdos peered at the place indicated by the small finger. *'Enormous!'* he shouted, and scooped Dyfrig up.

'Thank you,' said the little prince.

Induna appeared, pushing Rusgann back into the room and slamming the door behind her. 'It's going wrong, Val. Come close to me and we'll make a run for it. I can probably shield you and the boy with my magic while still going unseen –'

'What's happening?' Rusgann demanded.

'We're rescuing the boy and the princess,' Induna snapped. 'Stand aside, woman. There's fighting in the corridor.'

'I won't go without Rusgann!' Dyfrig shrieked. 'I won't!' And he began to squirm and flail his limbs like a mad thing, so that Valdos nearly dropped him.

'Stop it!' the armiger pleaded. 'We'll take her, we'll take her!'

Dyfrig was instantly still in his arms. 'Good.'

Induna cracked the heavy door open, then closed it again, cutting off the sound of a loud affray. Her expression was bleak. 'There's a shaman out there. He didn't see me. He must have come down the stairs in the guards' dormitory just across the hall. He's creeping toward the armory, prob- ably sent by those on the roof to investigate the fighting. A scrier wouldn't make any sense of it – guard fighting guard. We've got to take down the magicker, Val. Give the boy to the maid and grab that big book. I'll go invisible and trip him up, and you swat him with the book when he's down.'

'Swat him? I'll carve out his lights!' the squire blustered, fumbling for his dagger.

She slapped him roundly. 'Do as I say,' she hissed.

Valdos took up the huge tome from its stand, muttering. A moment later he and Induna were out the door.

'Are we really being rescued, Rusgann?' Dyfrig was safe in her strong arms, an expression of keen interest on his face.

'God only knows. Hold onto my neck, Dyfi.'

The sound of a tremendous explosion rocked the room. Induna flung the door open. 'Come with me! Go carefully and don't trip over anything.'

The corridor was filling with smoke that poured from the armory. Shadowy figures moved about in it, yelling and cursing. Swords clanged. On the floor lay a man in a shabby brown gown, his head hidden beneath a book. Radd Falcontop, with a sinister black iron sphere in one hand and a sword in the other, came running toward them. He cleared the fallen shaman with a single leap and darted into the dormitory, shouting at Rusgann. 'Get the hell out of here, wench – down the stairs!'

'This way!' said Induna's voice. The strapping maid felt an invisible person tugging at her apron, drawing her into the smoke. She clung tight to Dyfrig, was momentarily blinded by the swirling fumes, heard coughs and screams, stumbled over a guard's bleeding body. Then she saw the small woman beckoning to her, pointing out the way of escape.

'Over here! The stairs. Go down. Go to the windmill turret. Take the boy to his mother!' The witch vanished again.

Another explosion shook the peel, coming from the dormitory. A thunderous voice called out in the murk, 'It's done! Both sets of steps to the roof gone. All you king's men – fall back. Fall back and run!'

Rusgann said, 'Hang on, Dyfi,' and plunged down the stairs.

'We're within range of Skullbone Peel, my lord duke,' the captain said to Feribor. 'You, wizard! Keep light airs blowing so we can maneuver. Quartermaster! Raise the colors of the Sovereignty and the duke's pennon.'

Feribor used a spyglass to survey the peel from the quarterdeck of the frigate, which lay broadside to the shore. 'They've finally got the catapult set up on the fort roof, and it's loaded with a sizable tarnblaze shell. The silly damned fools! That engine couldn't fling a bomb more than a hundred ells . . . I wonder what the two columns of smoke are all about? Think it might be a signal of some sort?'

The captain shrugged. 'I can't say, my lord. Shall we fire a dummy charge to attract their attention?'

'Not yet. But see that the guns are readied.'

'It's already done.'

Feribor turned to his windvoice, a slope-shouldered older man with a long, sardonic face. 'Vra-Colan, bespeak Shaman-Lord Ontel. Tell him who we are and present my personal compliments.'

The Brother pulled up his hood so that his face was shadowed, except for the mouth. After a few minutes had passed, he reported, 'Ontel also conveys the usual sentiments of greeting to you, my lord. He asks what brings you to the Desolation Shore.'

'Say we have come to take away Princess Maudrayne Northkeep and her son, who are his unwilling guests. Have him be so good as to send them out to our ship in a small boat. He has exactly one half-hour to comply.'

Vra-Colan spoke on the wind, paused, then gave the reply. 'Ontel asks what you will do if he declines.'

'Tell him that my ship's guns will pound his wretched little fort to rubble. And assure him that I care not whether the lady perishes along with him and his people, since she is already under sentence of death for having threatened grave harm to the Sovereign of Blenholme.'

The message was sent, and Feribor waited impatiently for the reply. When the minutes continued to drag by in silence, he finally barked, 'Colan! Demand that they answer!'

Blind Bozuk sat slumped in a chair a few paces away from the duke, the windvoice, and the captain, close beside the helmsman at the wheel. He called out feebly. 'They're preparing their answer! One of them is lighting the fuse of the great bombshell in the catapult.'

The captain burst into derisive laughter. 'Tarnian lunacy!'

'Let's hope so,' Bozuk wheezed.

An instant later the arm of the engine threw the missile high into the air. As it soared to the top of its trajectory, Feribor sneered, 'Far short! Even I can see that it – God's Bones! Look! It can't be!'

The shell was not falling, as all logic said it must, but instead continued on toward the ship as though it were an airborne balloon rather than a heavy ball of steel loaded with explosive chymicals.

'The three shamans.' Bozuk's tone was oddly apologetic. 'They're pushing it with their overt talent. Quite an impressive meld of magical power. Who knew they had it in them?'

The captain shouted, 'Helm, hard aport! Wizard, all the wind you can muster!'

'I have no strength left in me,' Bozuk admitted, 'not even enough to lift a feather. Nor am I able to divert the projectile from its path. It may yet fall short or miss us.'

'She don't answer the helm, cap'n!' cried the man at the wheel. 'We're flat becalmed.' His eyes were wide with terror, fixed on the rushing sphere that trailed sparks and a thin plume of smoke. It came at them a few ells above mast-height, giving hope that it might indeed pass over the ship. But the magic of the shamans halted it in midair, where it paused and plummeted straight down.

The helmsman screeched, 'Cap'n, it's coming right at us! Cap'n!'

But that officer was already dragging Feribor forward toward the quarterdeck stairs. Both men tumbled down them as the hissing, smoking ball struck the ship's wheel, causing it to disintegrate into a hail of lethal fragments that shredded the flesh of the helmsman and the ancient shaman cowering in his chair, killing both of them instantly. Vra-Colan was left moaning in a small pool of his blood, only slightly injured. The missile penetrated deck after deck as it fell, demolishing the ship's steering mechanism and finally ending in the bilges of the aft hold with all of its momentum spent.

There it exploded.

Bruised and battered, Duke Feribor felt the tremendous jolt and heard the smothered roar of the detonation as he lay on the upper deck beside the captain. A few seamen had fallen but most were on their feet, dashing about in response to orders screamed by the mates and petty officers. The guns of the starboard battery crashed out a single broadside. The captain stirred, groaning, and clutched at his left arm.

'Broken, curse it! Lord duke, can you haul me up?'

But Feribor was still too shocked to move, and it was the quartermaster, leaking blood from a gash in his scalp, who

pulled the captain to his feet and helped sling his broken
arm inside his jerkin.

'Arlow! Belay firing the guns and get the pumps going,'
he said. 'Bendanan, find Chips and survey the damage to
the hull.'

Other officers were crowding around the captain as he
issued further orders. A seaman helped Feribor to arise, and
at his request led him to the starboard rail where he might
survey Skullbone Peel. The blocky white fort was undamaged, although two black columns of smoke still issued
from its roof, where tiny figures seemed to be dancing on the
battlements. Only a single cannonshell had found its mark:
the windmill turret was a ragged stub, its top half missing
save for twisted fragments of its spiral iron stairway.

'Well, that's small loss,' Feribor said. He stumbled back
to the captain. 'Get me a small boat and a squad of marine
warriors! I've got to go ashore and hunt out Princess
Maudrayne.'

'You may eventually hunt your pathetic quarry, my lord,'
the captain snarled, 'but not until I've secured my ship from
sinking – if that's possible. Go to your cabin. Now! And don't
set foot outside it until you're sent for.'

'My lord?' a weak voice inquired.

Crimson with rage, Feribor whirled to find Vra-Colan
standing there, his robes ripped to shreds and his face a mass
of small cuts. A youthful sailor supported the windvoice, who
said, 'I think she was in there. Princess Maudrayne, in the
room atop the blasted turret. I oversaw her only briefly and
then she eluded my windsight – a woman very beautiful,
with auburn hair, amidst a group of other people. I said
nothing to you at the time because I was unsure of her identity, and you were engrossed with your spyglass.'

Feribor clutched the windvoice's upper arm, causing him to
flinch in pain. 'Scry the place now! See if you can find her!'

'Do it from the duke's cabin,' ordered the captain tersely.

None of Feribor's protests or threats availed, and so he and Colan went below. For hours the debilitated Brother did his utmost to see through the stone walls of the peel, hindered by smoke. He reported small fires and damage to two chambers on the upper level, and wounded men being cared for, and even numbers of dead bodies. Toward the end of his long surveillance, the persons trapped on the roof were finally rescued with ladders. But nowhere in any part of the fort was there a tall woman with auburn hair, or a very small boy.

Finally Feribor permitted the exhausted Brother to abandon the windsearch and sleep. He sat brooding in a chair until well after midnight, when the captain came at last and told him that an improvised patch on the hull was holding, and they were not in immediate danger of sinking.

'But we're a long way from home, my lord duke, in hostile waters, with our steering shot to hell. So if you know any good prayers, start saying them.'

Rusgann ran like a deer with Dyfrig in her arms when she finally reached the ground floor of the peel – through the kitchen and the scullery, along a covered passage to the annex building, past the half-enclosed animal shelters and the store-rooms, and into the pumproom below the turret. No one pursued them, nor did the young witch or her servant-lad confederate or any other person follow after.

'Let me catch my breath,' the maid gasped, setting Dyfrig down at the foot of the iron stairs leading up into the tower. 'I've got a fierce stitch in my side.'

A woman's voice called faintly from above. 'Rusgann? Dyfi? Are you there?'

The boy squealed, 'Mama!' And before Rusgann could stop him he was up the stairs and out of sight, and she heard people approaching through the barn rooms, their low conversation punctuated with coughs and an occasional moan. Hastily, she ducked out of sight behind a huge piece of wooden machinery, all cogs and shafts and lever-arms shining with grease, but unmoving because a piece of it had been detached and lay on the floor along with scattered tools.

Three men dressed in the uniforms of peel guardsmen, with helmets and mail shirts missing, entered the pump-room. All were filthy with soot and blood. A stocky youth and a tall skinny fellow half-carried a much older man whose head lolled on his breast. Rusgann recognized him as the fighter who'd run at her carrying a tarnblaze grenade and sword, who had warned her to flee.

At the foot of the iron stairs, the skinny man yelled, 'Deveron? Are you up there?'

'Gavlok!' The reply echoed off the turret walls. 'Thank God. I tried to scry you but the smoke got too thick. The princess and her son are here, safe! And she's agreed to the proposal.'

'Hanan and I have Radd with us,' the one named Gavlok called. 'He's badly bashed up but we're fine. Poor old Hulo's dead. We had a nasty fracas in the armory. I don't know what's become of Val . . . or Induna.' Laboriously, the unin-jured pair began to pull their comrade up the narrow steps.

Rusgann waited until they reached the top, then climbed up herself. The small tower room seemed crowded wall to wall with people. Through the window on the seaward side she saw a three-masted man o'war lying not far offshore.

'My lady!' she cried, pushing past the youth called Hanan, who was tending to the wounded man. 'Have these knaves harmed you?'

'They're friends. It's all right.' Maudrayne held Dyfrig in her arms. Both of them had wet cheeks, but they were smiling. 'Come sit beside us on the bench and I'll explain.'

Snudge stood with Gavlok, staring at the frigate. 'There's

some kind of a parley going on between the shamans on the peel roof and the warship. I can't decipher it but the direction of the bespoken wind-threads is plain.'

'The castle people had the catapult up at the battlements before we arrived at the armory,' Gavlok said. 'We demolished both sets of stairs with small bombshells. It'll be a while before Ontel and his wizards get down. We're safe here for awhile.'

Snudge turned his attention to the roof of the keep. 'What the devil do they think they're doing over there? Look – the pan of the catapult is loaded and they're cranking down the arm. The ship's far out of range.'

'Its starboard gunports are open,' Gavlok pointed out. 'If the cannons let loose, we're finished. But Feribor wouldn't really dare endanger Maudrayne and the boy, would he? I mean, it has to be a bluff.'

'Does it?' Snudge gave an edgy little laugh. 'Cathran naval gunners are well-trained. They could pepper Skullbone with shells, putting the pressure on. Unfortunately, this windmill turret is a perfect target for a demonstration of marksmanship. We've got to get out of here soon, Gav. Let me try to scry Induna and Val again.'

He covered his eyes. After a few minutes, he gave a cry of distress. 'I see them, just entering the kitchen. Val's hurt. Looks like he's senseless. Induna's holding him up with her arms and her talent and moving him along, but the squire's heavy and she's tired.' He opened his eyes and flashed a look of desperation at his friend. His next words were delivered in a whisper. 'I don't dare leave here. If things fall apart, I'll have to use the Gateway sigil to take these people away at once. Maude and her son *must* reach Donorvale safely, and the others deserve to go as well.'

'So many?' Gavlok was incredulous. 'Has that been your plan from the beginning? You'll kill yourself! Look what happened to you the last time! And with me and two others as well –'

'But no heavy equipment. Donorvale's only a hundred and fifty leagues away – a third of the distance we traveled before. I ought to be able to do it, even carrying seven adults and a child. But I'll probably have only one go at it. The sigil will strike me down and I won't be able to come back. So . . . will you try to fetch Induna and Val? I'll wait for you until the last minute.'

'Oh, shite,' said the lanky knight. 'Of course I'll go.' He spun about and vanished into the stairwell.

With a sinking heart, Snudge focused his windsight on the quarterdeck of the ship. Bozuk looked a complete wreck, the evil old bastard. It was his fault that Feribor had come here. The sight of the duke, so debonair and merciless, almost choked Snudge with rage. Of all the people King Conrig might have sent to Tarn . . . He seemed to be waiting now, glaring at his hooded windvoice and tapping his foot on the deck. Waiting –

Bozuk was pointing at something, speaking. His withered lips were hard to read. *Answer . . . lighting fuse . . . catapult . . .*

Snudge caught his breath. From the roof of the peel soared a missile that was surely fated to fall into the sea. Uncannily, it did not. At the top of its arc it seemed to hesitate, then continued onward in an unnaturally straight path toward the warship, moving much more slowly than before, gradually losing altitude as though it were rolling down a smooth incline.

The mad Tarnian buggers were pushing the thing along with sorcery.

'Look!' Rusgann cried. She'd seen the smoking shell – and an instant later most of the others did, too. All save prostrate Radd Falcontop rushed to the eastern side of the tower to watch, exclaiming in wonderment and morbid speculation.

When the shell made its dramatic halt above the ship and began to fall, Maude screamed, seized Dyfrig, and turned away with the boy howling his disappointment in her arms. The others cried out in horror at what happened next, so that Snudge almost missed hearing the sound of voices rising from the base of the tower.

He shouted down the stairs. 'Gavlok? Induna? Hurry, for the love of God!'

Can I use my talent to help them up? he asked himself. It was not a type of magic he was good at, but the situation was desperate. He sent out a shout on the wind: *Source, help me if you can!*

He reached out to the slow-moving climbers, took hold, and pulled with all the soul-strength he could command.

The tall knight and the tiny woman and the collapsed squire shot upward and knocked Snudge over. They all skidded into Radd's body, and he uttered a great groan. 'All of you!' Snudge cried from the squirming heap. 'Come quickly to me. Come close.' He pulled Subtle Gateway from his shirt and gripped it in his fist. Gavlok got to his knees and dragged Maudrayne and Dyfrig to him.

'Oh, look!' Rusgann said. 'The ship's cannons are firing back.'

'Right at us,' Hanan said. He and the nursemaid stood frozen at the window.

Were the two close enough to be carried? Snudge cried out, 'EMCHAY ASINN – to the High Sealord's palace in Donorvale!'

The white flash of the sigil's sorcery and the golden blast of the tarnblaze cannonshell coincided.

TWENTY-FOUR

He was adrift in darkness again, only this time there were no stars. Neither were there any malignant auroral luminosities taunting him. He was sure that the Lights were there; but they were in eclipse, almost but not quite ignoring his presence, as though he were a distraction from more important business. They spoke to one another in their unique and peculiar manner, and he listened.

Calamity may happen. What was postponed in the Old Conflict.
  The abomination made by the One Denied . . .
    When debased, he made it.
An abomination then called Unknown Potency, lost then stolen.
  And now in a stupid brute's gizzard, renamed! So what?
    He is not stupid. And he goes to Rothbannon's castle.
The wise thief! He wrote down the means of activation in a book.
  But never dared to bring the Potency to life.
    It may yet live. Calamity may happen, and a New Conflict.
Look: the one we cursed goes to meet the brute.
  Cursing a mistake. He now may be our one hope!
    Shall we not convert the Wrong-Named, then?
Snudge? He is not ripe and may never be. Rethink the one cursed.

The One Denied the Sky is half-free. Think of that!
    Better to think of the brutes. And the Moon Crags.
BEST to think of feeding! Amusement! Irony! Paradox!
    Best for now.
There's time. A lot of it.

He heard them laughing, laughing. The pain and fear took hold of him and he fell –

But not far. He forced his eyes open and saw the bodies.

Rusgann and Hanan standing upright, looking about them in stunned disbelief. Gavlok and Induna crouching protectively over Valdos and Radd, who still lay unconscious. Maudrayne on her knees, cradling Dyfrig, whose eyes were still squeezed tightly shut. All eight of them surrounding him as he sprawled on the flagstones of the forecourt of Sealord Sernin Donorvale's riverside palace. A squad of household guards were running toward them, shouting.

Snudge chuckled weakly and murmured, 'All of us here. That wasn't so bad, was it?' He felt the pain blossom hideously, saw Induna crawling toward him with her face intent. 'The bad stuff starts now, I guess,' he told her. His eyes, black and deep as wells, began to close again as he surrendered.

'No, you don't!' cried Induna of the Barking Sands. She ripped the chain holding the two sigils from his neck and flung it aside, warning the others, 'Don't touch those stones. They'll burn you.' Then she plucked forth a pearly little female image from her breast, and for the second time gave away a part of her soul. '*Now* you may sleep. For as long as you like.'

His eyes opened again, and she saw that this time they were a vibrant, glinting blue, full of unasked questions. But before he could speak, he succumbed to the warm, quiet dark.

*   *   *

Beynor watched them come with his windsight, wave after wave surging up the Darkling River estuary, over ten thousand monsters, armed with the most effective minor sigils still in the race's possession. They had already laid waste to Moss's second-largest city, Sandport, and crushed the sealing town of Balook. They sank the six frigates and twelve fighting sloops of Moss's Navy. They overwhelmed Salkbane Fortress and slaughtered its conjure-lord and defending wizards, and then the victorious army of amphibians closed in on Royal Fenguard itself. They expected to find Beynor waiting for them there, expected their human ally to lead them through subterranean passageways into the bowels of Rothbannon's castle, straight to the tomb that secured Ullanoth's sigils. There Beynor would activate the Known Potency for the Salka, initiating the reconquest of their ancestral home. That's the way it was supposed to happen – but would not.

He sat on a tall black horse, cloaked head to toe from the rain and unrecognizable to the monsters' relatively puny windsight, amidst rocks on a lofty hill above Fenguard Castle. From that vantage point, Moss's one-time Conjure-King oversaw the teeming invaders, led by their Supreme Warrior, Ugusawnn. He also saw Moss's uprisen population of native Salka converging on the capital from the Little Fen and the Great Fen, making casual slaughter of humans as they rejoiced that a new era had begun.

Beynor saw it all taking place. As he saw his own cleverly crafted scheme in ruins.

It was not until he had nearly reached Fenguard, and his long journey's end, that he had finally been able to scry through the castle's thick granite walls and bedrock-shrouded cellars to perceive the debacle: Beynor discovered that Rothbannon's tomb held only Rothbannon's ashes. The platinum casket that should have secured his sister's living sigils was gone, as was her enchanted body.

He had planned to destroy that body (as he once planned to kill the living woman by stealth), and by doing so render her truly dead, and her sigils dead as well. Then, when the Salka arrived, met him, and followed him to the tomb, they would believe that the box still contained moonstones that were alive, deadly, and useless to them – until touched by the activated Potency. It was impossible for the Salka to scry out the truth about Ulla's stones: sigils could not be seen through talent. And no one save a descendant of Rothbannon could enter his tomb.

Beynor would have declared himself ready to fulfill his part of the bargain. He would have asked his mentor Kalawnn to disgorge the Potency and hold it up, then he would have coached the Master Shaman in conjuring the spell that activated the Stone of Stones.

Kalawnn would never have suspected that his human protégé contemplated a magical coup. (Although Ugusawnn might have!) The Master Shaman, like the other Eminences, believed that Beynor could not touch or use the activated Potency. He thought, erroneously, that the sigil would bond to the person who activated it, as others of its ilk did, and burn or kill anyone who tried to steal it. But Beynor had discovered that the Potency bonded to no one; and he had hoped and prayed that its sorcery transcended the Lights' curse as well. ·

Beynor had planned to invite Kalawnn alone to enter the opened tomb with him. After all, there was hardly room inside for more than one of the huge amphibians! He had been confident that he could snatch the Potency from the clumsy Salka shaman, open the platinum box, and activate Ullanoth's Concealer and Interpenetrator sigils within a split second.

He'd planned to vanish with the box of moonstones, scathelessly penetrate the Salka mob in the passage, then activate Subtle Loophole to spy out the best escape route.

And all of it would have been accomplished without a debt of pain . . .

But now it would never happen. The best he could hope for was to retrace his path before the monsters overran all of Moss, make his way into northern Cathra, and retrieve the last remnant of Darasilo's Trove that luckless Brother Scarth had concealed in the bear's den: another Weather-maker, an Ice-Master, and a Destroyer. Three inactive Great Stones that would become, when activated by the incantations contained in the book hidden with them, superlative and hazardous weapons . . . but not for him.

It was enough to make the most stalwart sorcerer weep! On the hill in the rain, windwatching the monster horde encircle doomed Fenguard Castle, Beynor ground his teeth together and cursed the God of the Heights and Depths and the most peculiar of the deity's creatures, the Coldlight Army.

Beynor! Beynor, where are you? Respond to Master Kalawnn!

No, he wouldn't respond – just in case there was a chance, sometime in the dubious future, of getting the Known Potency back. It would be good if Kalawnn thought he'd been prevented from making the rendezvous through some misfortune.

Beynor of Moss, you groundling conniver, respond to Ugusawnn the Supreme Warrior! Respond – or suffer the dire consequences!

He whooped with caustic laughter, startling his horse, which gave a nervous whicker and stamped its hooves. The dire consequences were already at hand! Since the Lights' curse prevented him from using those three hidden Great Stones, he'd have to give them up to someone else. With luck, he'd find a way to retain some vestige of control over the surrogate wielder.

That person would *not* be Kilian Blackhorse.

The traitorous alchymist was already secure in King

Somarus's new court, along with his cronies, stirring up trouble for Conrig Wincantor. No, Beynor would need to find one who was both loyal and none too clever. It was a problem that would keep until later.

Beynor! Respond to Kalawnn: We have begun our assault on the castle. Come and join me without fear, young human. The Supreme Warrior shall neither insult nor abuse you, for I am the designated Master of the Potency, not he. Beynor! . . .

He could hear human screams and death-cries on the wind now, and the triumphant roars of the monsters. With a shudder he sent his thread of oversight winging far away to the southwest, beyond the Dismal Heights and the Dextral Range to the upland moors of Cathra where the bear's den was. The remains of Scarth and his mule had long since been scattered by scavengers, and the great brown predator himself was not at home. But the leather saddlebag was still on the rock shelf, besmirched a little now by bat droppings and mold, but safe for all that.

Beynor banished the vision. Once again he erected the ingenious spell of couverture he'd learned from Kilian. Then he backed his horse out of the rocks and set off down the hill toward the Moss Lake road.

Stergos heard of the Salka invasion from the High Thaumaturge Zimroth, as she and most of the other members of the Glaumerie Guild barricaded themselves in a castle tower in a last stand against the attackers. Even as she related the frightful events then transpiring, her windvoice was abruptly stilled. No other Mossland magicker bespoke Stergos after that, nor was he able to scry so distant a scene himself. In haste, he bespoke the new head of Zeth Abbey, Abbas Bikoron, and begged him to learn what he could of the disaster.

It was very late. Stergos had been reading in bed when

he was bespoken, and most of Cala Palace had retired for the night. It would not be appropriate to summon the High King to him, and yet Stergos felt he could trust no one to pass on such politically sensitive tidings. So he rose from his bed, took a walking stick, and limped to the royal suite, brushing aside the Knights of the Household standing guard and pounding on the door with the silver knob of his stick.

'My liege! Sire, open to me, your own brother!'

After a few minutes the sitting-room door flew wide. Conrig yanked the Royal Alchymist inside and shot the bolt. 'What the devil d'you mean by this, Gossy? Risalla and I were fast asleep.'

Stergos tottered to a chair and dropped into it. 'Moss has fallen to a huge army of invading Salka. I had the news from Lady Zimroth, trapped with other ranking conjurers in a Fenguard tower. I believe she perished even as she bespoke me.'

'Bazekoy's Blood! So the rumors were true after all.' The king perched on the edge of another chair. He'd thrown on a light robe but wore nothing else. 'Lord Admiral Skellhaven heard from fishermen that a vast pod of the brutes had been sighted on the high seas off the Dawntides, but I'd hoped it was some mistake.'

'Master Ridcanndal besought the aid of our navy,' Stergos said, staring at the floor. 'He feared this was coming.'

'And I could not send the navy!' Conrig said. 'My promise was made to Ullanoth, and she's dead – if not before this, then surely now, after the Salka have despoiled her unbreathing body. Our navy, and our armies as well, must stand ready to quell a rebellion in Didion. That bastard Somarus has "postponed" coming to Cala Blenholme in order to tender his oath of fealty. He'll come in two weeks, he says! The uproar in Moss will now give him an excuse to put the thing off indefinitely. Our fleet will take to sea, Gossy, but it will sail to Didion Bay, not Moss, to remind that saucy kinglet whose vassal he is.'

'What will you do about Moss?' Stergos asked, without much hope.

'The only thing possible for now: contain the monsters there. The fens are ideal places for them to dwell, and they may not wish to move into drier lands. But we must learn what set them off. And if it seems that they show signs of expanding beyond the miserable corner of Blenholme they now occupy, we must look more closely into the weaponry at their disposal.'

'Zimroth said the assault forces used minor sigils. It was long thought that the Salka had only a few of the things, but perhaps the supposition was wrong.'

'Beynor was exiled to the Dawntide Isles,' Conrig recalled. 'He could be the instigator. Zeth knows he wanted revenge against his sister and the others who would not support his pilfered kingship. Ulla believed him to be as mad as their slain father Linndal.'

'The earl marshal warned of warclouds building in the north, Con, but I doubt he foresaw anything like this. Do you really think Somarus will disavow fealty and challenge you?'

'Oh, yes,' the king said wearily 'Once I would have thought he'd come charging headlong over Great Pass with no more thought than a stampede of wild oxen. But now that Kilian has become his adviser, Somarus may learn more of generalship than any of his barbarian ancestors. If so, he may become a formidable adversary.'

'And large numbers of his people love him,' Stergos said, 'as they did not love Honigalus.'

'A more serious worry of mine, now that we know the Salka threat is real, concerns a possible alliance between them and Didion. *Why* did the creatures kill Honigalus and his family? No one professes to have a clue. My Privy Council dismisses the notion of a human-nonhuman alliance as unthinkable. But is it?'

'We'll have to find out the truth, Con.'

The king rose, stretched, and yawned. 'And so much more! Is our Lord Treasurer a villain? Will the Lords of the Southern Shore oppose my naming Dyfrig third in the succession and hold out in favor of Feribor? Will the Sealords of Tarn remain loyal to the Sovereignty with Maude in their midst to remind them of how close they came to casting off vassalage?'

'The Princess Dowager has meekly recanted and signed the document,' Stergos reminded him. 'We can hope this will defuse the situation in Donorvale. Arrangements are already made for Dyfrig to go to Beorbrook, and the earl marshal has pledged to welcome him. And yet . . . I'm loath to admit it, Con, but I can't help but wonder whether long years of separation from her son might eventually harden Maude's heart. She's a woman of strong Tarnian passions, as we both know.'

'She'll not break her word.'

'Can you be sure?' Stergos asked.

'Oh, yes,' the Sovereign said. 'I'm very sure.' He took his brother's arm, helped him up, and led him to the door. 'One of the knights will see you safely to your chambers. Try to put all troublesome thoughts from your mind now and sleep well. That's what I intend to do.'

It was always this way at the end of a complicated mission: Snudge felt let down, at a loose end, restless and moody. In a few days, he and his men would sail back to Cala Blenholme in the Lord Constable's fast frigate *Cormorant*. Until then, he diverted himself in the High Sealord's palace doing what he did best: spying. Rendering himself unnoticeable in the usual way, with his talent, he prowled about eavesdropping and snooping in a desultory fashion, at first learning nothing much.

His men spent their time eating, drinking, hashing over the great adventure, or indulging in pure relaxation. Their hero-worship of him was intensely embarrassing.

Princess Maude was understandably morose and subdued in temper, since Dyfrig would also be departing in the ship of Lord Tinnis Catclaw. The mother and son were constantly together, and she had engaged a local artist to paint a portrait of the boy and also of herself, so that each could have a lasting memento of the other.

Rusgann attended her mistress in glum silence and seemed to harbor formless apprehensions; she'd boldly asked Snudge whether he felt uneasy, too, and he'd been unable to deny it.

The Lord Constable, whom Snudge had had little to do with before, proved jovial, friendly, and eager to please. He ordered a special refit of *Cormorant* to accommodate the crowd of civilian passengers in comfort, and provisioned the ship with the best of food and drink for the voyage home.

Induna stayed on in the palace as an honored guest of the High Sealord, who had conferred upon her the largely symbolic title of Sealady of Barking Sands in recognition of her efforts. She intended to return to her home in the northland after the others had sailed away, having been thoroughly bemused by two messages sent her on the wind within a day of her abrupt arrival in Donorvale. The first, from Shaman-Lord Ontel Pikan, informed her that Bozuk, her grandsire, was indeed dead, buried at sea with a length of anchor-chain weighting his corpse. The second message, from the Northkeep banker Pakkor Kyle, requested instructions for the investment of her new inheritance – ten thousand gold marks. She had no notion what to tell him, but Sealord Sernin was giving her sound advice.

Snudge had almost taken Induna's sacrifice for granted, not really understanding what she'd done for him until one of the palace's resident shamans explained it. Then he was abashed and a little angry, as the recipients of some great benevolence often are. *Why* would she do such a thing for a stranger? What did she expect in return? But he found himself strangely unwilling to ask the questions of her, nor had he any wish to spy on her. After congratulating her on her marvelous legacy, Snudge avoided her company, although he saw her each day at dinner in Sernin's great hall and made polite conversation as a courteous knight should. Yet his thoughts returned to her at odd moments, and this both puzzled and disturbed him.

Snudge's fit of somber self-absorption came to an abrupt end when he found the three forged suicide notes.

He'd come again to the guestroom of the Lord Constable, wondering why it was always kept locked, intending to examine his portfolio of official papers more thoroughly for clues to the man's character. (Locks had never deterred Snudge's investigations.) The forged notes, together with an undeniably genuine short letter of Maudrayne's, were stuffed in Lord Tinnis's briefcase any old way, as though he'd been interrupted while perusing them . . . or more likely, penning them. Each suicide note was the same, and each mimicked the handwriting of the princess with more accuracy.

> *My dearest Uncle Sernin: Without my beloved son, life is no longer worth living. The potion I have taken will lead me to the peace I can find in no other way. Forgive me for causing you sorrow. Tell Dyfrig I will always watch over him.*

Snudge felt his heart turn over in his breast, then a tidal

wave of fury and grief smote him with such force that he almost cried out aloud.

Conrig was responsible for this. What Snudge had balked at, Tinnis Catclaw was all too willing to do. The High King, believing his intelligencer dead, had beyond doubt dispatched the Lord Constable to Tarn to apprehend Maudrayne and Dyfrig and slay them. Later, with the circumstances altered, the death-sentence of the little boy was rescinded – but Maude's was not. Conrig was not ready to risk that she might someday withdraw her recanting.

With shaking hands, Snudge replaced the parchment sheets as he'd found them and slipped out of the room. His first thought was to track down Lord Tinnis on the Donorvale docks and slip a dagger between his ribs – but Conrig would only send another assassin. His second thought was to warn Maudrayne and Sealord Sernin that she was about to be poisoned – but this might provoke the very calamity the Source had been trying to prevent. The princess could not be allowed to testify to the High King's talent. Conrig Wincantor must keep his Iron Crown.

Distraught to the point of incoherence, Snudge stumbled to his own small guestroom and locked himself inside. Then he cried out on the wind for the Source.

'Why did you forbid Deveron to do anything at all?' Red Ansel asked.

He was in the eerie place of icy imprisonment on other business, consulting with the One Denied the Sky about the fall of Moss, and the near-certainty that Master Shaman Kalawnn would soon find in Rothbannon's library the book containing the incantation that would activate the Known Potency.

Because Maudrayne must make her own choice in the matter.

'I see no choice! There's only death awaiting poor Maudie!'

The Source was calm. *You don't foresee far enough, dear soul. She will still choose freely, and so will Deveron. As for Kalawnn, his discovery was inevitable. Rothbannon always possessed the means to activate the Potency. He was only afraid to do it – as his successors were – because he knew not the purpose of the enigmatic stone.*

Ansel sighed. 'So this, too, is part of the New Conflict: an empowered Potency in the possession of the Salka.'

Yes.

'The monsters will go after the two Crags, you know. They'll hunt them down one way or another and manufacture new moonstone sigils.'

Perhaps. I can't tell. The Potency can either activate such stones or abolish them – remember that! We must ask ourselves how the Lights will react to the presence of sigils that draw power from them, while vouchsafing no satisfaction of their hunger. The Likeminded and I are still mulling over the matter, and its possible effect upon the New Conflict.

Ansel Pikan gave a tired little laugh. 'Mull away! I must leave you to it and go to Thalassa Dru. But be sure that I'll be windwatching my dear princess all the while. And doing some mulling of my own – over my personal role in your great game.'

When he failed to come to the farewell feast held for the departing voyagers, Induna went looking for him, thinking he might have suffered a delayed reaction to his healing, which had been unexpectedly rapid. She found him in the palace stables, strapping saddlebags onto a powerful blue-roan stallion. He was dressed in traveling garb.

'Sir Deveron! What are you doing here?'

'Do you like my new steed?' he inquired archly. 'His name is Stormy, and he's supposed to be a holy terror. But we'll get along. I've a talent for dealing with horses.'

Induna glanced swiftly around the stableyard. None of the grooms were near. She spoke softly. 'Aren't you leaving for Cala tomorrow with the others, sir knight?'

Snudge fastened a buckle, then began to lash on a bedroll wrapped in waterproofed leather. 'No. I intend to stay and seek my fortune in Tarn . . . and I'm no longer a knight, although my royal master hasn't heard the bad news yet. I've given up being the Royal Intelligencer of Conrig Wincantor. My heart tells me that I can never again serve him in good conscience, since he has ordered a shameful act to be committed. The king will probably be livid when he finds out I'm gone for good, and he may put out a death warrant on me. But I'm unscryable, and Tarn is a large and lonely place.'

Induna watched him work. 'There is a long, somewhat perilous track I know, that leads to Northkeep and then to a tiny place called Barking Sands.'

He froze, catching her gaze. 'What are you saying?'

'Only that I admire and respect you, sir,' she said in a low voice, 'and even more so now, after you've confided your crisis of conscience to me. I'd welcome your enduring friendship. I would also welcome you to my home' – she smiled slyly at him – 'which, as you know, will soon be much more commodious than before. My mother is a superior healer-shaman, and she'd welcome you, too. The lot of Tarnian magickers is an interesting one, with many challenges. Do your talents include healing?'

'I don't know. I'm self-taught. There may be things within me that I never suspected.'

'Yes, as one matures, they sometimes manifest – not always as one might wish. Perhaps Mother and I together can work with you. To help you control and enhance your talent, if you should wish it.'

He cocked his head to one side and lifted one eyebrow.

'And will you also show me how sands can bark, if we ride up there together?'

'Oh, yes!' Her face shone with eagerness.

'Mind you,' he added more soberly, 'I intend to be away within the hour, before a certain Cathran lord notices I'm missing. But if you're serious, I'll secure a horse and tack for you while you fetch what you intend to bring.'

'I agree.' She nodded judiciously. 'Give me half an hour, sir.'

'You must now call me Deveron, for that is my name.'

'Very well – Deveron. I'm glad we are to be friends.' She turned and ran off lightly, her red-gold hair gleaming in the lowering sun.

He'd acted impulsively, perhaps foolishly. But the feeling of oppression that had earlier haunted him and the later pangs of anger, hatred, and sorrow were no longer so intense.

Induna! His previous experiences with women had been brief and casual and few. Perhaps this would be different.

The evening was still very warm. Feeling a sudden thirst, he strolled to the well that supplied both the stable and the laundry. As he bent over the stone rim to note its depth, he felt the two sigils slip out of his open shirt and dangle at the end of their chain.

The waters below gleamed darkly and deep.

He took hold of the glowing things, slipped the chain over his head, and let the moonstones dangle in space. Perhaps it was time, now that he was ready to begin a new life . . .

Not yet.

The voice was regretful, sad, and utterly compelling.

He sighed, hung the chain around his neck again, and went off to find the stablemaster. He had quite forgotten to take a drink of water.

Maudrayne was gowned in her favorite emerald green, wearing her opals and a little matching tiara that Sernin had given her as a homecoming gift. When the Lord Constable invited her to walk with him on the shining black marble esplanade beside the river, she readily agreed. It had been overwarm inside the great hall. Most of the visiting sealords and other highborn palace denizens were still in there with Sernin and his lady, drinking vast quantities of mead and spirits, not quite celebrating and not quite mourning her recantation and her agreement to what they thought was Conrig's proposal.

'It's blessedly cool out here, isn't it?' Tinnis said to her. 'And quiet as well, with no one about. Would you like to take a short stroll to the docks and cast an eye over my ship? It would please me to show you the fine accommodation the carpenters have wrought for Prince Dyfrig.'

'I don't fancy a tuppence tour given by groveling officers,' she said shortly.

He only laughed. 'They're all ashore, as are most of the rest of the crew. Come, a little air will lift your spirits.'

So she took his arm and they walked to the palace landing stage where the tall ship was berthed. The two guards at the gangplank's foot saluted them but made no comment as they went aboard. Maudrayne dutifully admired the small luxurious cabin, and was particularly appreciative of the nautical books that had been collected for Dyfrig's pleasure, and the colored charts pinned to the bulkhead that showed both the sea route to Cala Blenholme and the land route from there to Beorbrook.

'Dyfi will enjoy these greatly.' Maudrayne was sincere. 'I thank you for your consideration, my lord. He's a clever lad, but so very young – and he'll be afraid.'

Tinnis Catclaw chuckled. 'That one? Not for long! He'll be up in the rigging before we're out of Gayle Firth and bedevilling the officer on watch wanting a chance to steer.'

'Shall we return to the palace?' she said. 'I feel a small headache coming on.'

'Ah! I have the very thing in my own cabin. It's just next door.'

He ushered her to it, found a crystal decanter and two silver cups, and went to rummage in a hanging locker above the washstand.

'Here it is, my mother's own remedy for all manner of megrims. I never travel by sea without it.' He lifted a small glass phial that gleamed ruby-red, removed its stopper, and put four drops into a cup. Then he filled both cups with wine and handed her the one with the physick. 'Drink up, my lady, and by the time we're back at the palace, I guarantee that all your suffering will be gone.'

'Truly?' She met his eyes. 'And tell me, Lord Tinnis: will it even banish my anguish at losing Dyfrig?'

'It will,' he said very quietly. 'In a short hour.'

She looked into the cup, her lips tight. 'Has my former husband, the King's Grace, ever made use of this medicine?'

'No . . . but I've heard him recommend it most highly for distress such as yours.'

She said, 'I know he sent you north to search me out, when Deveron Austrey was thought lost.'

'Yes.' He lifted one hand and gently touched the long tress of fiery auburn hair that spilled over her shoulder. 'I came eagerly, as was my duty. But I would have come even more swiftly, had I recalled how beautiful you were. I saw you only three times when you dwelt in Cala Palace, for I was then a callow young mountain baron with small reason to visit the capital.'

'Ah.' With delicacy, she turned and stepped back, so that his hand must fall away. 'Yet now I must drink.'

She lifted the cup, but before it could touch her lips he took hold of her wrist, staying it. 'We – we could talk. I may have another remedy that would better suit you.'

'Even though I'm prepared to take this one? Lord Tinnis,

you perplex me. I'm weary and bereft and in need of peace.'

'My dear lady – Princess Maudrayne! It could be done. Not easily – but if you choose, it could be done.'

They stared each one at the other for a long moment, and then she told him her choice.